Alexander Dundas Ogilvy Wedderburn

The Wedderburn book

A history of the Wedderburns in the counties of Berwick and Forfar 1296 - 1896

Alexander Dundas Ogilvy Wedderburn

The Wedderburn book
A history of the Wedderburns in the counties of Berwick and Forfar 1296 - 1896

ISBN/EAN: 9783741190865

Manufactured in Europe, USA, Canada, Australia, Japa

Cover: Foto ©Andreas Hilbeck / pixelio.de

Manufactured and distributed by brebook publishing software
(www.brebook.com)

Alexander Dundas Ogilvy Wedderburn

The Wedderburn book

THE WEDDERBURN BOOK.

VOLUME II.

THE

WEDDERBURN BOOK,

A HISTORY OF THE WEDDERBURNS

IN THE COUNTIES OF

BERWICK AND FORFAR,

DESIGNED OF

WEDDERBURN, KINGENNIE, EASTER POWRIE, BLACKNESS, BALINDEAN
AND GOSFORD;

AND THEIR YOUNGER BRANCHES; TOGETHER WITH SOME
ACCOUNT OF OTHER FAMILIES OF THE NAME.

1296–1896.

BY

ALEXANDER WEDDERBURN.

VOL. II. THE EVIDENCE.

PRINTED
FOR PRIVATE CIRCULATION.
1898.

CONTENTS OF VOLUME II.

LIST OF FAC-SIMILES.

Additions,
etc.

p. 5, S.W. 13. At end of note *add* " See post, D.P.B. 260."
p. 14, S.W. 106, *for* " 1593 Feb. 18," *read* " 1596 Feb. 18. See G.S.R. 56."
    „   „   S.W. 107, *for* " 1595," *read* " 1593."
p. 21, S.W. 176, line 3, *insert* " of " *before* " Dundee."
p. 29, S.W. 236, *for* " curator," *read* " curators."
p. 30, S.W. 238, line 6, *for* " Scrymgeour." *read* " Scrymgeour."
p. 38, S.W. 296, *for* " their mother," *read* " mother of the said Margaret."
p. 40, S.W. 313. The date " 1654 " here given must, I think, be wrong (though I cannot now refer to
    the original), as Easter Powrie was not purchased by Alexander Wedderburn till some years later,
    so that he could not be designed of it in 1654.
p. 49, S.W. 394. Here again I cannot now refer to the original, but doubt the *Sir* George Mackenzie,
    as he was not knighted till 1674.
    „   „   S.W. 400, *for* " I., ii., 101," *read* " 1., i—ii., 101."
p. 65, S.W. 533. Here " May 12," *should be* " March 12." See post, G.S.R. 135, note.
p. 80, S.W. 682, *for* " March 20," *read* " March 19-24."
    „   „   S.W. 685. Earl of Rosslyn, *i.e*, afterwards Earl of Rosslyn, as he was not so created till 1803.
p. 81, S.W. 699, *for* " (4) Sir John," etc., *read* " (4) the late Sir John," etc., as he died in 1803.
p. 93, Bl. 9, line 14, *for* " Aug't," *read* " Ap'."
p. 95, Bl. 11, line 10, *for* " March," *read* " ffebruary."
p. 105, Bl. 45, *for* " March," *read* " May."
p. 110, Bl. 81, lines 13-16. These *should be* dated " 1659," *not* " 1689," and inserted in order of date
    in the list.
    „   „   Bl. 81, line 19, *for* " April," *read* "Sept."
    „   „   Bl. 83 (4), *for* " Mary," *read* " Margaret."
    „   „   Bl. 88, *for* " Mary," *read* " Maria."
p. 116, M.P. 6, *for* " Krap," *read* (I think) " Knap," as there were Moncurs of Knap.
p. 119, n. This note should be at the foot of p. 118.
p. 125, line 15 from foot, *for* " tutor," *read* " tutors."
p. 144, J.W. 39, line 7, *for* " 18 May," *read* " 18 Aug."; and line 12, *for* " Ellen," *read* " Eden."
p. 146, J.W. 62. This letter, though accurately given from the original, is full of errors.
    „   „   J.W. 66, line 4 from foot, *for* " 1769," *read* " 1771."
p. 149, J.W. 80, last line but one, *dele* " Sir " *before* " Alexander."
p. 157, J.W. 107, *for* " perspicacissimus," *read* " perspicacisimus."
    „   „   J.W. 112. *for* " Municipal," *read* " Burgh."
p. 160, S.A.R., note, *for* " Alexander Pittormie," *read* " Alexander of Pittormie."
p. 161, S.A.R. 32. This individual is more probably the son of Sir Peter Wedderburn, Lord Gosford,
    and not the person suggested in the note.
    „   „   S.A.R. 37. Here again the person matriculating may be the natural son of John Wedderburn
    of Gosford, of whom an account is given in vol. i. (p. 373).
p. 165, line 21 from foot, *for* " Symsome," *read* "Symsone."
    „   „   line 11 from foot, *for* " lite," *read* " litel."
p. 181, line 12 from foot, *for* " great great," *read* " great."
p. 191, last line, *for* " modern," *read* " earlier."
p. 200, D.L.B. 13. I have now, but not certainly, identified this William Wedderburn. See vol. i.,
    p. 97.
p. 201. D.L.B. 15. This note is in error. The James Wedderburn there referred to died before 1547,
    and I have great difficulty in identifying the James Wedderburn named in this entry.
    „   „   D.L.B. 16, *for* " s.v.," *read* " D.B.R. 53."
    „   „   D.L.B. 22, *for* " The elder," *read* " One," as it is not known which was elder, and, indeed, they
    may have been twins.
p. 202, D.L.B. 32 n. This note is, I think, in error, as from D.C.B. 14 the reference would appear to be
    not to the merchant but to his namesake, the notary.
p. 207, line 12, *for* " 1617," *read* " 1609."
p. 209, D.P.B. 13, *for* " Argylgate," *read* " Argylegate."
p. 219, D.P.B. 160, *after* " Edward Wedderburn," *insert* " lawful son of the said James."
p. 221, D.P.B. 179. *Add* after " Welgait," " James Wedderburn, younger, witness."
    „   „   D.P.B. 180, *for* " the tenement," *read* " his interest in the tenement."

Additions,
etc.

p. **229**, D.P.B. 275, *for* "wife," *read* "sister german."
p. **231**, D.P.B. 290, *for* "(190)," *read* "(90)."
p. **232**, D.P.B. 302 (*b*), *for* "Argylgate," *read* "Argylegate."
p. **239**, D.P.B. 388 n, *for* "23," *read* "4."
p. **247**, D.P.B. 471. *Dele* "Sir" *before* "Alexander," as, though the reference is to Sir Alexander of Blackness. he was not knighted at this date. See vol. i., p. 204, n. 4.
p. **251**, D.P.B. 521, *for* "dispone," *read* "dispones."
p. **253**, D.P.B. 551, *for* "Sir Peter," *read* "the late Sir Peter," as he was, of course, dead at this date.
p. **254**, D.P.B. 562, *for* "wife," *read* more accurately "relict," although the original protocol has "wife."
p. **256**, D.P.B. 581. *for* "£62,905. 15. 2.," *read* "£62.985. 15. 2.," and see D.D. 104. The note also is not clear. The date of the decreet was 18 Feb. 1719 (D.D. 104 ; R.A.D. 154) : that of the sasine does not appear ; while the date 1734 June 12 is that of the record or registration.
„   „   D.P.B. 583, *for* "grandfather," *read* "great grandfather."
p. **257**, D.P.B. 591, *for* "1752. June 14," *read* "1753. Jan. 14."
p. **266**, D.B.R. 83, *for* "considerit to," *read* "considerit to be."
p. **286**, D.B.R. 351, *for* "objection," *read* "obligation."
p. **290**, D.B.R. 389, *after* "(c)," *insert* "Dec. 11."
p. **301**, D.C.B. 3, *after* "piermasters," *insert* "(78)."
„   „   D.C.B. 8, *for* "(10)," *read* "(107)."
p. **303**, D.C.B. 36, *dele* "Mr.," *before* "Alexander Wedderburn, merchant."
„   „   D.C.B. 37, *for* "Dundee," *read* "Dunbar."
p. **309**, D.C.B. 104, *for* "1562," *read* "1652."
„   „   D.C.B. 109. *for* "surrender." *read* "render."
p. **321**, D.D. 21. With regard to this note, see now vol. i., p. 47, u. 1.
p. **323**, D.D. 45, *for* "John." *read* "Alexander."
p. **324**, D.D. line 15, below Vol. 10, *insert* "1700-3."
p. **326**, D.D. 77, *for* "June 11," *read* "June 24."
p. **327**, D.D. 82. *for* "1117," *read* "1711."
p. **339**, D.Dec. 44, *after* "various sums," *insert* "to Alexander Wedderburn, clerk of Dundee, both."
p. **354**, D.M.D. 28. The note is in error. Rachael Dunmure died before 1695. See S.W. 502. I am unable to identify the person referred to.
p. **355**, D.M.D. 41, 46. in each case *for* "G." *read* "S."
p. **356**, D.M.D. 68. See now vol. i, p. 383, note 3.
p. **361**, No. X., *for* "Wigtoun," *read* "Wigtown."
p. **369**, G.S.R. 108-12. See now for these entries the volume of the Great Seal Register, 1634-51 (published in 1897), §§ 412, 480, 1178, 1783 aud 1927.
p. **374**, line 12, *for* "Alexander," *read* "Andrew."
p. **379**, G.S.R. 144. line 13, *insert* "Alexander," *before* "Scrymgeour."
p. **386**, R.P.C. 55, line 3, *for* "defender," *read* "defenders."
„   „   R.P.C. 60. The following reference to David Wedderburn in the *Particular Register of Sasines for Aberdeenshire* has been lately sent me :—

> 1626.   June 6.—Sasine on Charter of Alienation by John Hay of Cremoudmogat, to Mr. David Wedderburn, master of the Grammar School of Aberdeen, and Bethia Mowat, his spouse, and the survivor of them in conjunct fee, and the heirs lawfully procreated between them, which falling to the heirs and assignees of the said Mr. David whatsoever, heritably, of an @-rent of 210 merks. to be uplifted forth of the lands of Tillicorthie, lying in the parish of Uduie, under reversion for 2,100 merks due by the said John Hay to the said Mr. David and his spouse : At Aberdeen 18 May 1626.   Rodger Mowat, advocate, and James Mowat of Ardo are witnesses : Sasine on 19 May 1626 (Aberdeen Sasiues, vol. v., fol. 279).

p. **390**.   *Add* the following note at foot :—

> Since this page was printed two more volumes (xvi. and xvii.) of the Exchequer Rolls have been published, and contain the following material entries :—
> "1532.   July 20. } James Wedderburn, one of the bailies of Dundee, renders account at
> "1533.   „   „ } Edinburgh for the bailies of Dundee (xvi., 235).
> "1543.   April 2—Aug. 8.—Sir Thomas Wedderburn renders account as customar of Dundee (xvii., 52).
> "1551.—David Wedderburn in Welgait is named as owning land in Dundee, bounded by those once belonging to James Wedderburn, junior (xvii., 514).
> "1553-54.—Patrick Lyon, customar of Dundee, and Elizabeth Wedderburn his wife, are named (xvii., 196. 222, 256)."

p. **399**, R.P.S. 6, line 2, *for* "Laswon." *read* "Lawson."
p. **406**, G.R.S. 19, "Johne" in the title of the sasine is an error in the record for "James."   See G.R.S. 25.
p. **407**, G.R.S. 35, *for* "Dunmur," *read* "Dunmuir" *or* "Dunmure."
p. **408**, G.R.S. 43, line 14, *dele* "Sir," *before* "John."
p. **409**, G.R.S. 54 n, *for* "£560," *read* "£550, aud cp. R.D. 311."
p. **417**, F.S. 56, *for* "Kingenny, provost," *read* "Kingenny, provost)."
p. **418**, F.S. 66. The note is in error. The reference is to Patrick Wedderburn and his son, Alexander. See vol. i., pp. 77-79, and as to the use of Peter and Patrick as the same name *ib.*, p. 78, n. 7.
„   „   F.S. 70, *for* "possession by James," *read* "provision by David."
p. **420**, F.S. 93. line 6, *for* "confirm." *read* "conform."
p. **423**, F.S. 129, line 14, *for* "Wedderbun," *read* "Wedderburn."
p. **430**, R.D. 74, *for* "1610." *read* "1620."
p. **432**, R.D. 105, line 3, *dele* "(*sic.*)."

p. 437, R.D. 162, *for* " Lowman," *read* " Lownan."

p. 438, R.D. 181, *for* " Mr.," *read* " Sir."

p. 441, R.D. 213, line 1. The year "1688" must be an error, but I have no time to refer to the record.

p. 445, R.D. 261, line 2, *for* " said," *read* " late."

p. 452, R.D. 349, line 4, *for* " disposition thereof by the said minister to," *read* " and assignation thereof (2 Feb. 1714) by the deceased Alexander Rait, eldest lawful son and heir retoured to the said minister, to . . ."

p. 455, R.D. 378, *for* " home," *read* " house."

p. 461, R.D. 445, last line but one of note, *dele* " probably."

p. 463, R.D. 459. *for* " griev," *read* " grieve."

pp. 465, 468-470. The following additional extracts from the Register of Acts and Decreets have reached me quite recently, and should be inserted in order of date :—

1542. June 13. Obligation by Patrick, Lord Gray, baron of Fowlis, to David Wedderburne, burgess of Dundee, and Helen Lawson, his spouse, anent half of the Mains of Huntlie (vol. i., fol. 119).

1543. June 13.—Contract between Patrick, Lord Gray and David Wedderburn, burgess of Dundee, and Helen Lawson, his sponse, anent the third part of the Mains of Huntlie (vol. vi., fol. 397).

1542. June 13, Aug. 23.—Charter by Patrick, Lord Gray, baron of Fowlis, to the said David Wedderburne and Helen Lawson, his spouse, of half of the Mains of Huntlie. Dated 13 June 1542. Precept of Sasine thereon of same date. Instrument of Sasine thereon 23rd August 1542 (*ib.*, fol. 553).

1552. July 28.—Obligation by Patrick, Lord Gray, to David Wedderburne and Helen Lawson, his spouse, anent one-third of Hilton of Wester Cragy, sold to them (*ib.*, fol. 556).

1552. —— Reversion by David Wedderburne and Helen Lawson, his spouse, to Patrick, Lord Gray, over the lands of Hilton of Cragy.

1552-53. March 18.—Gilbert Wadderburne, John Wadderburne, in Leith, and many others, give cautioun to the provost, bailies and Council of Edinburgh, to obey a decreet of the lords (vol. viii., fol. 129).

1553. Dec. 18.—Contract between David Wedderburne, burgess of Dundee, on one part, and Robert, James, and George Rollok, brothers, burgesses thereof (and William Carmychall, burgess thereof, cautioner), ou the other part, whereby the third part of Wester Crage is transferred to the brothers by the said David Wedderburne and his spouse (vol. viii., fol. 359).

1552. Nov. 9.—Obligation by John, abbot of Lundors (Lindores), to the provost, bailies and council of Dundee to £500 for repair of the kirk thereof. The cautioners are George Rollok, elder, and David Wedderburne, elder, burgesses of Dundee (*ib.*, fol. 31).

1611. Feb. 6.—Action at the instance of Alexander Cowtie, merchant burgess of Dundee, v. Jonet Wedderburne, relict and executrix to the late William Donaldson (*sic*, for Davidson), younger, merchant burgess of Dundee. and James Cochran, her servitor, touching payment to the pursuer of £180 resting by the said Jonet Wedderburne and James Cochran for certain plaidding furnished by the pursuer to the late William Donaldson (*sic*), who died in May 1610 and certain silver lent by the pursuer to him. The pursuer referring the matter to the defenders' oaths of verity, they, are ordained to appear personally for that purpose (258, 13).

1611. Feb. 21.—The Lords continue till 15 May next an action by Donald Thornetoun, merchant in Edinburgh, v. the said Jonet Wedderburne anent payment-making to him of 8 barrels salmon and 4 barrels grissellis, 100 goat skins, etc., sold to the said pursuer and to the late William Davidson, spouse to the said Jonet Wedderburne by Andro Munro, tutor of Foulis (258, 168).

1611. March 16.—The Lords assign the 15 May next to Alexander Cowtie, merchant in Dundee, for summoning Jonet Wedderburne, relict and executrix of umquhile William Davidson and James Cochraue, her servitor, to give their oaths in the action foresaid (258, 194).

1611. March 6.—The Lords assign the 20 May next in the action by Alexander Cowtie, merchant burgess of Dundee, v. Alexander Bultie and others, cautioners, and Jonet Wedderburne, relict of William Davidson, merchant burgess of Dundee, and Richard, Elspet, Jonet, and Margaret Davidson, bairns of the said William Davidson, and William Davidson, his son and heir, touching an obligation for £1,000 granted by the said umquhile William to see the same registered in the Books of Council and Session (262, 57).

1611. May 31.—Action at the instance of Alexander Bultie, William, Richard, Elspet, Jonet, and Margaret Davidson v. Alexander Cowtie continued till June 10 next (262, 130).

1611. June 19.—Compeared Mr. John Russell, advocate, as procurator for Richard, Jonet, and Elspeth Davidson, bairns and executors confirmed to umquhile — Davidson, burgess of Dundee, and Jonet Wedderburne, their mother, tutrix testamentar to them, and produced a copy of our sovereign Lord's letters of date 12 March last, whereby they were summoned at the instance of Thomas (*sic* for William) Davidson, merchant, touching the production of claim pursued by the said bairns and their said mother before the provost and bailies of Dundee v. the said William Davidson (262, 177).

1613. Dec. 8.—Summons raised at the instance of Agnes Wedderburne, oy and heir lawfully retoured and sensed to the late Gilbert Wedderburne in Leith, her goodsire, and Abacuth Bisset, writer, her spouse, against Isobel Ferguson, relict of John Brown, skipper iu Leith, John Ochiltrie, maltman there, and others ; making mention that the said pursuers obtained a decreet of removal against the foresaid persons upon the 6th Nov. 1612, charging them to flit from their lands and houses, lying iu Leith, on the south side of the water thereof, in the

Additions, etc.

barony of Restalrig and shire of Edinburgh, in the west end of the wynd called the Rottinraw, betwixt the land of umquhile Andro Mowbray on the south and east, and the said common vennel of Rottinraw on the north and the "common gait" on the west, appertaining to the said pursuer in heritage, as the infeftments of her umquhile goodsire, her own infeftment and retour proport : Yet they refuse to remove from the said pursuer's lands and houses, especially the back part of the same ; and have built a brew-house and stable in the back part of said lands. The Lords of Council assoilzie the Defenders; Because it was shown that the said Agnes' sasine was only "under and above," and not "back and fore" ; Also, because the late Andrew Mowbray, to whom the said John Brown was successor by progress, was infeft in a tenement in Leith, within which the said back land lies, on a disposition of Patrick Gray, and confirmed by the Master and Preceptor of Bethleme in the month of April 1469 : Like as William Brown, one of the defenders, was infeft in the last-mentioned tenement by the Colledge of Aberdeen ; as his "predecessors were infeft be the said Colledge of Aberdeen by the Preceptouris of Bethleme and Sanctgermains in the samyn Tenement" (287, 70).

68 *a.*   1617. July 25.—Action at the instance of George, Elspet, and Janet Crails (or Trailles), lawful children and executors testamentary to the late Robert Craile, merchant burgess of Dundee, against debtors, including Sir John Ogilvy of Innerquharity, David Wedderburn, etc. (312, 225).

68 *b.*   1618. July 22.—George, Elspet, and Jonet Trailles (or Crailles), children and executors of the late Robert T., merchant burgess of Dundee, and the said George as heir to his father, and Andro Traill, chirurgeon, burgess of Dundee, tutor of the said children, sue Mr. John Leslie of Newton, David Durie of Scottiscraig, and many others, including Mr. James Wedderburn in Dundee, Helen Lovell and Peter Wedderburn, now her spouse, as debtors to their father, for payment of the debts (318, 290).

68 *c.*   1618. July 4.—Action by James, Lord Stewart of Ochiltree, Harie Stewart, his brother german, and Peter Balmanno, now of Torlonzie, against Mr. Alexander Wedderburne, common clerk of Dundee, for production of certain writs in his custody, etc. (319, s.d.).

68 *d.*   1620. Jan. 20.—Action by James Arnot, merchant of Edinburgh, *v.* Mr. David Wedderburne, burgess of Burntisland, and Alesone Watson, his spouse, for a debt of £302. 13. 4. as the price of wines bought by them from the pursuer, continued (333, 217).

68 *e.*   1620. Jan. 29.—Action by Mr. James Wedderburne, lawful son of Mr. Alexander Wedderburne of Kingennie, clerk of Dundee, and Margaret Goldman, his spouse, *v.* Charles Goldman, merchant burgess of Dundee, for payment of 500 merks contained in the first testament of the late Margaret Jak, relict of James Goldman, merchant burgess of Dundee, and of 500 merks "with ane furnist fedder bed, best goun bodie and skirt, best clokis, and best hewit plaid" contained in her second testament, continued (333, 243).

68 *f.*   1620. March 16.—Mr. Patrick Wardlaw of Torrie sues Mr. Alexander Wedderburn, clerk of Dundee, for production of a contract between the pursuer and Robert Arbuthnot of Findownie (333, 353).

68 *g.*   1620. March 29.—Action by David Wedderburn, burgess of Dundee, *v.* James Strachan, elder, notary there, Mr. James Strachan, his son, Charles Goldman, and others, for payment of annual-rent of 20/- due to the pursuer from a tenement in the Argyll's gate, not paid for the last twenty-one years (333, 377).

68 *h.*   1620. March 29.—Action by the said David Wedderburn *v.* David Robertson, maltman, burgess of Dundee, to make payment to the pursuer, as chaplain of the chaplainry of Mekle Sanct James in the parish kirk of Dundee, of an annual-rent of 10/- from a tenement in Sanct Salvator's close, continued (ib.).

68 *i.*   1620. June 14.—Suit by George, Elspeth, and Janet Traills, children and executors of the late Robert Traile, merchant burgess of Dundee, and Andro Traill, surgeon, their tutor, against their father's debtors, including Mr. James Wedderburne in Dundee, Helen Lovell, and Peter Wedderburne, now her spouse (343, 16).

68 *j.*   1620. Dec. 9.—Sir John Scrymgeour of Dudop, Knt., *v.* his debtors, including David Wedderburn, burgess of Dundee (344, 133).

68 *k.*   1620. Dec. 15.—John Norie, citizen of Brechin, *v.* Marjorie Dunbar, wife of Robert Dunbar, younger of Moynes, Thomas and Bessie Low, brother and sister of the late Mr. Thomas Low and Patrick Wedderburne, husband of the said Bessie, anent the escheat goods of the said Mr. Thomas Low, of which the pursuer had a gift under the privy seal (347, 361).

68 *l.*   1621. July 22. John, Lord Balmerinoch, *v.* Mr. James Wedderburn, son lawful of the late Mr. Alexander Wedderburn, common clerk of Dundee, having in his hands and keeping the prothogall books of umquhile Robert Wedderburn, notary, and James Lovell, son and heir of umquhile William Lovell, fear of Ballumbie, for his interest ; and mentioning sasine, of date 15 July 1579, granted by John Lovell of Ballumbie to his son William, of the lands of Morroös, and other writs, written by the said Mr. Robert Wedderburn, notary, in his protocol books, now in the custody of the said Mr. James Wedderburn. The pursuer produced a sasine of his infeftment in the said lands, dated 13 February 1614, under the sign and subscription of Mr. Edward (*sic* for Robert) Wedderburn, notary ; Mr. James Wedderburn, defender, produced the protocols and verified the handwriting of the late Robert Wedderburn, notary (348, 32).

In this entry Edward is clearly an error for Robert.

68 *m.*   1622. March 9.—Catherine Wallace, relict or John Watson, skipper burgess of Bruntisland, and John Matheson, elder, now indweller in Leith, her spouse, *v.* Allieson Watson, indweller in Bruntisland, and Mr. David Wedderburn, now her spouse, for a debt of £350 of arrears of rent of a tenement of land due since 1617. Continued to March 20 (363, 20).

68 *n.*   1623. Feb. 3.—John Wedderburn, notary, burgess of Dundee, *v.* David Coustoun, brother of the late Thomas Coustoun, burgess of Dundee, etc. (363, 255).

68 *o*. 1623. March 28.—Decree on summons at the instance of John Wedderburn, merchant
burgess of Dundee, *v.* David Coustoun, brother of umquhile Thomas Coustoun, burgess thereof,
for payment to the pursuer of £40 scots, together with "ane servit covering of ane bed and
thrie scoir elnis of plaiding, left in legacy to the pursuer by the said T.C. in his will dated
— day of — 16 (372, 200).

68 *p*. 1623. July 26.—Summons raised by Mr. John Sydserf, servitor to David, Lord Carnegie of
Kynnaird, assignee of Mr. Thomas Spittell, minister at Airtlie, *v.* Mr. Adam Wedderburne,
minister, for his interest, and John, Archbishop of S. Andrew's, for 1,000 merks arrested in the
hands of the said archbishop at the instance of the pursuer and addebted, as to at least
500 merks thereof, by him to the said Mr. Adam W. who was ordained to make payment
thereof to Margaret (?) Scrymgeour, cedent to the said Mr. Thomas Spittell, forthcoming to the
said Mr. John Sydserf. The defenders not compearing are ordained to compear (374, 94).

68 *q*. 1623. Nov. 15.—Summons at the instance of Patrick Gray of Innergowrie, son and heir of
the late Sir Patrick Gray thereof. *v.* Mr. Alexander Wedderburue, clerk of Dundee, Mr. James
Wedderburn his son, John Gray portioner of the Mylntoune of Craigie, William Gray, sheriff
clerk of Forfar, and others, touching the productiou of an obligation libelled to be delivered to
the complainer. Action continued (374, 129).

68 *r*. 1623. Dec. 23.—Summons at the instance of Mr. Thomas Charters, merchant burgess of
Edinburgh, *v.* Mr. David Wedderburn, burgess of Burntisland, to see him decerned to pay to
the complainer £15 balance of £—, the price of a tun of French wine bought and received by
him in March last : and also £373. 6. 8d. the price of a tun of Spanish wine seck. Action
continued (374, 181).

68 *s*. 1626. March 31.—Decreet for the pursuer in action by Euphame Wedderburn, relict and
executrix of Archibald Blythe, skipper in Dundee, *v.* Thomas Mortimer of Flemington, Patrick,
bishop of Ross, Alexander Lyndsay of Pittarlie, Thomas Gray of Worlend, Doctor James
Eliott, minister of Forfar, Robert Rollok of Kirktoun of Aberlemmo, Mr. George Fletcher, and
David Lyndsay of Balgayis, for payment to her of the debts incurred by them to her late
husband (396, 177).

68 *t*. 1626. June 3.—Mr. David Wedderburne, burgess of Dundee, *v.* Andro Wedderburn, his
son, Doctor James Wedderburn, and John Wedderburn, merchant burgess of Dundee, nearest
of kin to the said Andro on the father's side, Andro Watsone in Bruntisland, and William
Watson in Leith, nearest of kin on the mother's side, narrating that on 1st October 1621 the
complainer with his own hand resigned, infeft, and seized the said Andro, his son, in that
tenement of land back and fore, with yaird, wall, closs," etc., in Dundee, on the south side of
the Flowkergait, betwixt the lands sometyme of John Baxter, one of the heirs of the late
George Rollok, on the east, the lands of Robert Gairdin, and of the late Commendator of
Balmerinoche on the west, the flood mark on the south and the said gate on the north, under
reversion for 40s., to be redeemed by the complainer at any time of his life, or by his heirs ;
which he was now of intention to do : but the said Andro being yet minor, and having no
tutors or curators, and the complainer being his tutor at law, it was necessary that the said
Andrew be provided with curators ; the parties compearing, the pursuer chose the said John
Wedderburn and William Watson as curators *ad litem* to the said Andro : which choice the
Lords confirmed (396, 194).

68 *u*. 1626. July 28.—In the action pursued at the instance of Mr. David Wedderburne. burgess
of Dundee, against Androw Wedderburne, his lawful son, pretended heritable fiar of the
tenement of land, yard, wall, and close thereof undermentioned, John Wedderburne, merchant
burgess of the said burgh, and William Watson in Leith, curators to the said Androw Wedderburue, for refusing to resign in favour of the said Mr. David Wedderburne, his father, all
and whole that tenement of land lying within the said burgh of Dundee, on the south side of
the Flukergnit, between the lands sometime of John Baxter and of the heirs of umquhile
George Rollok on the east, the lands of Robert Gardyne, sometime pertaining to the commendator of Balmerinoche on the west, and the flood mark of the sea on the south, wherein the
said Androw Wedderburne was infeft on 1st October 1621, on resignation by his said father ;
under reversion mentioned in the said infeftment containing the sum of 40s. scots to be paid or
consigned by the said Mr. David at any time during his own lifetime to the said Androw on
premonition of 10 days ; the Lords of Council find and declare that the said tenement of land
is lawfully redeemed, in respect that Alex. Wedderburne elder, merchant burgess of Dundee,
as procurator for the said Mr. David Wedderburne, on the 22 June 1626, compeared in the
west kirk of Dundee and offered the said sum, but neither the said Andro Wedderburne nor his
curators appeared to receive the same : Therefore the said Alex. Wedderburn elder consigned
the said sum in the hands of Mr. Alex. Wedderburne, one of the bailies of the said burgh of
Dundee.

68 *v*. 1627. Jan. 26.—William in Hundwod for Sir Patrick Home of Aytoun, co. Berwick, *v.*
William Wedderburne and others for the rents of the lands occupied by them as tenants to Sir
Patrick (397, 234).

68 *w*. 1627. July 7.—Janet Kynimmonth, life-renter, and John Lyndsay, her spouse, *v.* David
Wedderburn, burgess of Dundee, anent an annual-rent furth of a tenement in Dundee claimed
by the pursuer (continued) (397, 453).

68 *x*. 1627. March 16.—Robert Winrahame, Albany herald, *v.* Bessie Wedderburn, relict of
Mr. Harie Danskine, schoolmaster at S. Andrew's, for a debt owing by her late husband
(398, 216).

p. 478, R.A.D. 154 (*b*), *for* " Feb.," *read* "July."
p. 483, Ed.T. 7-8. This note is not quite accurate, as there is one Wedderburn will, which my searcher
had overlooked, in 1665. See p. 518 of the Additions in vol. i, s. page 48, line 32.

Additions,
etc.

p. 492, D.M. 29. In this entry Elizabeth is an error for Isobell. The two names were sometimes used interchangeably, but can hardly have been so in the Pearsie family at this time, as Isobell Wedderburn, who married James Stormonth, had an eldest sister Elizabeth, who married James Graham of Meathie.

p. 498, D.B. 58, *for* "godfathers," *read* "godmothers."

p. 500, note 3. The theory of this note will not hold good, as Alexander Wedderburn died in 1730, and the Wedderburn Laurie of this entry would thus, in 1798, be nearly seventy years of age.

p. 502, Ed.B. 27. This entry (1701) is in error in describing Wedderburn of Blackness as Sir John, his baronetcy dating from 1704.

p. 511, P.B., note 22, *for* "1639," *read* "1629."

p. 519, L.W. 17, line 5, *dele* "the late."

p. 520, L.W. 38, *for* "1887," *read* "1878." .

p. 525, (ii.) *for* "James," *read* "John."

NOTE.

At the close of my work on this book, a fresh batch of old papers has been unexpectedly found at Birkhill. It includes a considerable number relating to the Wedderburns. Many of these are of minor interest, and very few, it is satisfactory to find, involve any addition to or alteration in the history given in the first volume. The few which do, are as follows :—

1. The marriage contract of Helen Wedderburn and Barton Belsone, dated 15 Aug. 1657. (Vol. i., p. 114.)

2. A discharge (9 June 1606) for 2,500 merks, part of 5,000 merks tocher made by George Campbell of Crunane to Alexander Wedderburn of Kingennie. This refers to the marriage contract of Colin Campbell and Elizabeth Wedderburn as of date 20 March 1606. (Vol. i., p. 138.)

3. A discharge (4 Oct. 1637) granted by John Wedderburn, "mariner, sone naturall of umqle Alexander Wedderburn of Kingennie to Alexander Wedderburn now of Kingennie." The account of John Wedderburn at p. 146 of vol. i. must thus be corrected, both as regards the position of this individual and as regards his suggested death in 1635. The pedigree at p. 131 must also be corrected. (Vol. i., p. 146.)

4. A discharge (23 Jan. 1687) by the minister and kirk-session of Murroes to Alexander Wedderburn, fourth of Kingennie, for 200 merks left to the poor of the parish by his late father.

5. Various letters and papers relating to Marion Scrymgeour and her affairs (vol. i., p. 174). From these it appears that she married George Hewett in 1722 and had issue, of whom in 1745 only two survived, viz., Alexander, who, in 1746, was in business at Chester-le-Street, and Jean or Jane. The Fleming, Scrymgeour, and Mary Hewett named in the text are, thus, not the children of Marion Scrymgeour, but, I think, of her son ; and the Mrs. Hewett mentioned in 1773 is more probably his wife and not his mother, who was, however, certainly alive in 1757. From these documents it also appears that Jean Scrymgeour, who married Alexander Watson, died before 1745. Her husband was the son of Thomas Watson of Grange and Grissell Wedderburn. See vol. i, p. 251 n, where I have omitted to identify her. Her two daughters, Margaret and Janet, of whom the latter must have been born after 1740, lived in Newcastle with their aunt, Mrs. Hewett, who at one time (1745) proposed that Janet should go and live with her maternal (great) uncle, Dr. Wedderburn, in Dundee.

6. Papers relating to David Scrymgeour. Among these is a letter giving the date of his death as 13 Dec. 1779, although from another it appears to have been reported at the India House as 26 Nov. 1779. The date in the text—Sept. 1780—given on the authority of J.W., is inaccurate. (Vol. i., pp. 175-76).

7. The marriage contract of Matilda Wedderburn and James Brisbane (15 Aug. 1676). This refers to her as the daughter of the late Sir Alexander Wedderburn of Blackness, so that the view given in the text that he died in 1675 (not 1676) is established as correct. (Vol. i., p. 210).

8. A discharge (1 March, 1673) by Helen Wedderburn, relict of David Dickson of Hartrie, shews that her first husband was then dead. (Vol. i., p. 214.)

9. The testament dative of James Brisbane (granted 3 Oct. 1693) recites that he died in 168—. He died, therefore, before 1690. (Vol. i., p. 215.)

10. A discharge of 1674, describing Peter Wedderburn, son of Sir Alexander Wedderburn of Blackness, as merchant burgess of Edinburgh. At one time, therefore, he traded there as well as in Dundee. (Vol. i., p. 221.)

PRIVATE RECORDS.

THE SCRYMGEOUR-WEDDERBURN CHARTER CHEST.

THE BLACKNESS PAPERS.

THE WEDDERBURN PAPERS AT MOUNIE.

PAPERS COLLECTED BY JOHN WEDDERBURN, 1819-39.

REGISTER OF St. ANDREW'S UNIVERSITY.

ADMISSIONS OF ADVOCATES TO THE SCOTCH BAR.

DAVID WEDDERBURN'S MS.

THE SCRYMGEOUR-WEDDERBURN CHARTER CHEST.

The following inventory of documents now in the possession of Mr. Henry Scrymgeour-Wedderburn includes both all those which are, strictly speaking, Wedderburn papers,[1] and also almost all in which any mention of members of the family is incidentally made.[2] Nothing could exceed the facilities kindly given me for the examination of these papers. Not only were those in the possession of his lawyers in Edinburgh placed at my service, but a thorough search was made through various likely repositories at Birkhill. In the result there was found a great mass of papers each one of which has been carefully examined, although, as the different bundles came to my hands at different times, they have not been classified as well as might be wished, documents relating to the same matters being placed in different bundles.

Scrymgeour-Wedderburn Papers.

The papers are here numbered in order of date for the purpose of this work, while the figures added at the end in each case give the number attached to the document in the charter chest, thus ix., xvi. 1, signifies Box ix., Bundle xvi., Document I. This might imply that there are nine boxes of documents, which is not the case, all the papers having now been collected into two large chests. When, however, I began my examination of the documents I found that they had formerly been placed in several small boxes, and that an inventory of the papers in two of those boxes (numbered II. & III.) had been made by Mr. John Riddell, the eminent Peerage lawyer, who had examined some of them in 1846 with a view to elucidating the Scrymgeour pedigree, and showing the Kirkton family to be entitled to the Scrymgeour Peerages of Dudhope and Dundee. He seems never to have completed his search, but, as I found his inventory still extant, I adopted the word "box," using it in the sense of "division." I have not re-examined the papers inventoried by him, but have accepted his inventory as accurate : it contains but few Wedderburn papers. All the other papers I have myself examined with the help of the Rev. Walter Macleod, the well known expert in old records.

I now proceed to give—

    I. An inventory of the Wedderburn papers contained in the two chests.

    II. A brief catalogue of their entire contents.

I.—INVENTORY OF DOCUMENTS RELATING TO WEDDERBURNS.

1. **1464.** April 16.—Retour of inquest held at Kyrymoir in the sheriffdom of Forfar, finding Marjorie de Strazawquhyn heir to the late Elizabeth de S. her sister in the lands of Kyngenny and Carntonn, in the barony of Athebetonn and regality of Kyrymoir, which lands are now worth yearly ten pounds and in time of peace ten merks, and are held of the Earl of Angus as lord superior. On the inquest are thirteen persons, among whom are Walter Ogilvy of Innerquharity, David Rossie of that ilk, John Wischard of Logy, David Wischard and David Wedderburn. I, i-ii, 1.

    (Latin, small parchment, in fair condition.[2] Three seals remain attached, viz. : those of Wischard, David Rossy (?) and David Wedderburn. This last is a good deal broken, but the bearings, a chevron between three cinque-foils, are quite clear. See the chapter on the arms of the family.)

2. **1484.** April 27.—Sasine on precept by Archibald Earl of Angus, in favour of Robert Graham of Fintre, of an annual rent of 10 merks out of the lands of Kirktoun of Earls Stradichty. Done on the ground of the said lands. Witnesses James Matland of Quenysberry, David Wedderburn and others. (Latin, paper.) v, v, 4.

---

[1] I use the word "papers" in a wide sense, to include all documents whether on paper or parchment.

[2] A good many which relate to a long law suit by Margaret Scrymgeour, daughter of Major William Scrymgeour, brother to John Scrymgeour of Kirkton, against her tutor Alexander Wedderburn, third of Kingennie, are, however, almost all omitted, as not adding anything to the history of the family. See Box IV., Bundle iv., and Box VI., Bundle iv.

[2] In some cases I have, through inadvertence, omitted to note the condition of the document and the material on which it is written.

3. **1506**. Sept. 28.—Instrument narrating that there compeared an honourable man James Scrymgeour elder, burgess of Dundee, as procurator for William Quhit, son and heir of John Quhit burgess of the said burgh, and resigned a S. Marketgate tenement belonging to the said William, into the hands of James Wedderburn, bailie for a noble man James Scrimgeour, constable of Dundee, with full consent of Mr. John Scrimgeour of Glasre, tutor of the said constable ; on the which the said bailie gives susine thereof to William Quhyt, elder, burgess of the said burgh.   Witnesses, Robert Wedderburn, John Scrimgeour and others. (Latin, parchment.) VIII, i, 2.

4. **1509**. Feb 8.—Sasine on resignation by a prudent man Robert Wedderburne, burgess of Dundee, into the hands of the bailie, of a N. Moraygate land, bounded W. by that of John Lawsone and E. by that of the heirs of the late James Rogh, on which the bailie gives susine to the said Robert Wedderburn, resigner, and Jonet Froster his spouse, in conjunct fee, and to the survivor of them. (Latin, parchment)   VIII, i, 3.

5. **1515**. Aug. 7.—Sasine on a breve of Chancery for infefting William Newman of Dundee in a N. Ratonraw land, bounded E. by that of the heirs of the late Andrew Wedderburn. (Latin, parchment.)   VIII, i, 4.

6. **1518**. Jan. 31.—Notarial instrument appointing William Arnot and others, as procurators for Mr. George Ferne, to go to David, Earl of Craufurd, and there resign all his lands lying in the territory of Aberbothry, in the barony of Alith and sheriffdom of Perth, into the hands of the said Earl, in favour of Janet Froster, daughter of David Froster in Methven.   i, i ii, 2.
(Latin, small parchment. See below, Nos. 2 and 8.   Two Janet Frosters, daughters respectively of David F. in Methven and David F. in Nevay, married the one Robert Wedderburn, and the other James Wedderburn, junior. See Vol. i)

7. **1522**. Feb. 14.—Sasine to Agnes Quhit, daughter and only heir of the late William Quhit and spouse of George Kermychall, of a S. Marketgate land in Dundee, given "by delivering into her hands the hammer of the door."   James Wedderburn, bailie of the constable, is a witness.   v, v, 5.
(Latin, parchment.   See below, No. 10.   Agnes Quhit or White married firstly Thomas Anderson and by him had a daughter Isobella who married Alexander Wedderburn the elder, of whom an account is given in Vol. i.)

8. **1530**. Oct. 8.—Notarial instrument narrating that there compeared personally before the notary and witnesses a worthy woman Janet Froster relict of umquhile Robert Wedderburn, burgess of Dundee, and resigned into the hands of the bailie the N. Moraygate land of her said spouse and her conjunct interest therein, in favour of a prudent man James Wedderburn her son, and heir of the said umquhile Robert, and of a worthy young man Robert Wedderburn her grandson, and apparent heir of the said James, to whom state and possession are given by the bailie accordingly.   David Wedderburn, Alexander Wedderburn, coulburgesses of Dundee, and Master Robert Wedderburn, notary public, are among the witnesses.   i, i-ii, 3.
(Latin, small parchment in good condition.)

9. **1531**. July 8.—Notarial instrument narrating that there compeared a worthy woman Elizabeth Olifer, spouse of an honourable man Robert Mylne, burgess of Dundee, in a Court held by David Rollok, one of the bailies of the said burgh, and there gave her bodily oath in the absence of her husband, that she was not forced to the resignation in favour of William Mylne her son of an annual rent of 8 merks furth of the land of David Wedderburn, in N. Moraygate.   The said David W. is a witness.   VIII, xiv, 1[b].

10. **1533**. Aug. 16.—Charter by Agnes Quhit, relict of George Kermichael, burgess of Dundee, in favour of her daughter Isobella Anderson (by her umquhile spouse Thomas Anderson) of the S. Marketgate land, mentioned ante No. 7. James Wedderburn, burgess of Dundee, is a witness. (Small parchment, in good condition.)   IV, ii, 1.

11. **1540** (?)—Charter by James Wedderburn, son and heir of the late Robert Wedderburn, burgess of Dundee, whereby he sells to his dearest brother Robert Wedderburn,

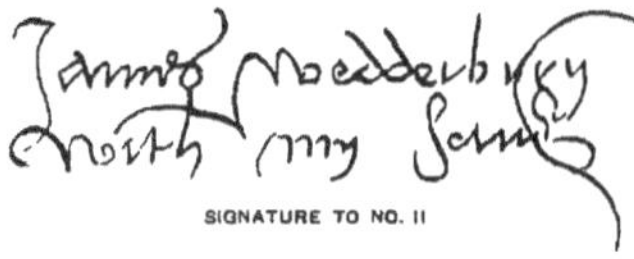

SIGNATURE TO NO. 11

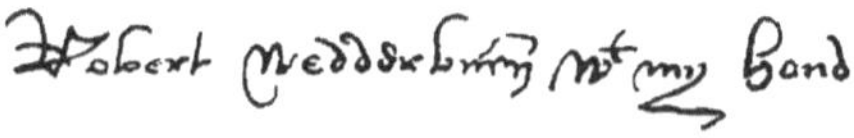

SIGNATURE TO NO. 12

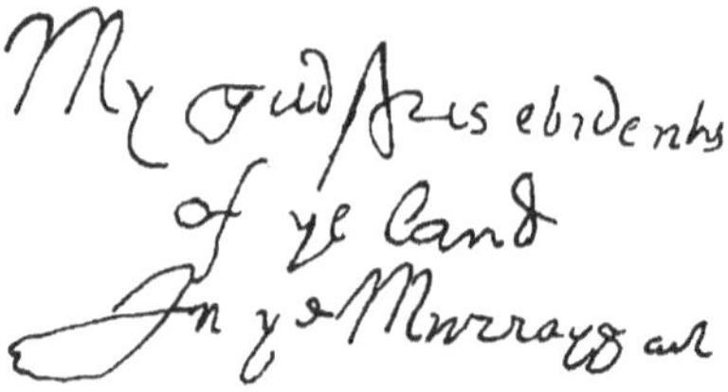

SECOND ENDORSEMENT TO NO. 12.

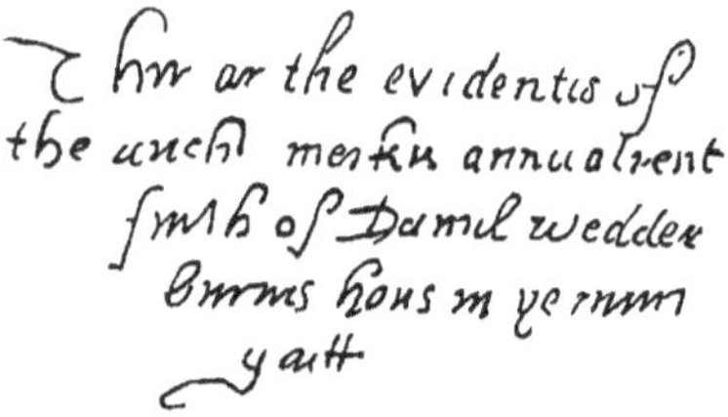

SECOND ENDORSEMENT TO NO. 19.

NOTARIAL SYMBOL OF ALEXANDER WEDDERBURN, NO. 30.

SIGNATURE OF ALEXANDER WEDDERBURN, NO. 27.

burgess of the said burgh, his land or tenement in N. Rattonraw, for a certain
sum of money paid to him in his urgent need. Signed by the granter, whose
seal is attached. VIII, i, 5.

Scrymgeour-
Wedderburn
Papers.

(Latin parchment. No date is given, but it is clearly before 1547 ; see next charter, at the date
of which James Wedderburn was dead. The seal remains entire and shows a chevron between three
roses, rather than cinquefoils, each having a distinct centre. For the signature see opposite.)

12. **1547.** April 1.—Charter by Robert Wedderburn, son and heir of the late James
Wedderburn, burgess of Dundee, to his beloved Robert Wedderburne, senior,
burgess of Dundee, and Jonet Kyd his spouse, jointly, and to the survivor of them,
and their heirs, of the granter's land in N. Moravie Street bounded E. by the land
of James Routh and W. by that of Henry Riehardsone, for a sum of money paid him
by the said Robert and Jonet in his great and urgent necessity. Signed by the
granter "Robert Wedderburn w[t] my hand " before various witnesses. The seal
of the granter is attached. I, i-ii, 5.

(Latin, small parchment, in good state. Endorsed in old hand, " Charter of Robert Wedderburn
of a tenement of land in Moravie street 1 April 1547 " and also in the hand of Alexander Wedderburn, first of Kingennie, " My gud syris evidentis of ye land In ye Murraygait." The seal is entire
and fairly perfect. It was very nearly detached from the deed, the band having worn, and was
then removed altogether in order that it might be engraved for this work. after which it was
re-attached to the charter. See the chapter on the arms of the family for an engraving of the seal,
and on the plate opposite for facsimiles of the signature and second endorsement.)

13. **1551.** April 4.--Charter of Sale by William Mylne, burgess of Dundee, to James
Mylne, son and heir of the late James Mylne, the granter's brother, and to Robert
Mylne, the granter's elder brother, tutor of the said James, of an annual rent of
8 merks, furth of the S. Murraygate land of David Wedderburne. I, i-ii, 6.

(Latin, small parchment in good condition, with a perfect Mylne seal attached. There are two
endorsements. Of these, the first is in the hand of Alexander Wedderburn, the old clerk (d. 1585,)
who writes : " The charter of viii merkis annuall off David Wedderburnis land in the Murragait
maid be my broder William Mylne to the barin Jamis Mylne son and air to umquhill my broder
Jamis Mylne &c." The second (see opposite) is in the hand of his son. Alexander of Kingennie :
" Thir ar the evidentis of the aucht merkis annual rent furth of David Wedderburnis hous in ye
Murraygait." By " broder " in the former endorsement is meant brother-in-law, the writer having
married Janet Mylne.)

14. **1556.** Feb. 26.--Instrument on the resignation by John Browne, son and heir of
the late George Browne, burgess of Dundee, of a land in N. Marketgate, bounded E.
by that of Robert Wedderburn, in favour of his mother Margaret Lowsone. VIII, xiv, 5[a].

15. **1557.** Feb. 13.—Instrument on resignation by Margaret Lowsone, relict of George
Brown, burgess of Dundee, of the said land (ante No. 14) bounded E. by that of Robert
Wedderburn. The notary is Harbert Gledstanys. (Latin, parchment.) I, i-ii, 6[a].

16. **1563.** Sept. 28.—Instrument of cognition by Andrew Annand, bailie of Dundee, of
Alexander Kyd, son of the late Alexander Kyd, burgess of Dundee, in a certain
S. Seagate land. Witnesses, Robert Kyd, George Kyd, &c. Notary, Alexander
Wedderburn, clerk of Dundee. VIII, xiv, 6.

17. **1563.** Sept. 28.—Another instrument of sasine in favour of the said Alexander Kyd,
in a N. Seagate land. Same witnesses and notary. VIII, xiv. 7.

18. **1563-64.** March 20.—Charter by John Scrymgeour of Dudop, constable of Dundee,
to William Man, burgess of Dundee, and Janet Wedderburn his spouse, and to
Robert Man their son and his heirs &c. heritably, of two roods of land on the road
from Dundee to Forfar, bounded W. by the granter's lands of Dudop, now occupied
by John Wedderburn. Witnessed by the granter's brother-german, James Scrymgeour
of Henderstoun and others. (Latin, parchment.) VIII, i, 6.

19. **1565-66.** Feb. 22.—Instrument on resignation to the bailie by John Doge, son and
heir apparent of David Doge, burgess of Dundee, of an annual rent of 40/ furth of
two tenements of land lying on S. Seagate, for sasine to Alexander Wedderburn,
younger, and Janet Myln his spouse, in conjunct fee. VIII, xiv, 8.

20. **1571.** March 22.—Cognition of John Fotheringham, shipmaster, as son and heir of
the late James F. in an annual rent. Witnessed by Alexander Scrymgeour, dean of
gild of Dundee, James Scrymgeour of Henderstoun, Robert Wedderburn, younger,
and others. Alexander Wedderburn, common clerk of Dundee, is notary, and adds
his symbol, with the motto " Deum Time." (Latin, parchment, in good condition.) VIII, i, 7.

21. **1571.** April 1.—Instrument on the renunciation of Alexander Cockburn to Sir David
Grahame of Fentrie of the lands of Barriemuir. Alexander Wedderburn, clerk of
Dundee, is notary, and David Wedderburn and others are witnesses.   VIII, xiv, 11.

22. **1573.** May 7.—Instrument on the resignation by John Brown and Agnes Brown his
spouse, into the hands of Alexander Scrymgeour, bailie of Dundee, of a N. Argylegate
land, bounded E. by that of Robert Wedderburn, &c. John Wedderburn is a witness,
and Alexander Wedderburn, clerk of Dundee, is notary.   VIII, xiv, 12.

23. **1573.** May 30.—Reversion by Eufame Bell, relict of Thomas Young, to John
Brown, burgess of Dundee, and his wife, of a N. Argylegate foreland, bounded
E. by the lands of Robert Wedderburn. Witnessed by Alexander Wedderburn,
notary, and others.   I, i-ii, 8.
(English, small parchment, in good order. On the back is a sasine to Thomas Young as heir to
Eufame Bell of the said foreland, and resignation thereof by him to John Traill 13 Dec. 1600.
Witnessed by David Wedderburn &c. Mr. Alexander Wedderburn, clerk of Dundee, is notary.)

24. **1573-74**—Resignation by the said John Brown and his wife to Alexander Traill of
the said N. Argylegate land, bounded E. by that of Robert Wedderburn, elder.
Alexander Wedderburn, clerk of Dundee, is notary. (Latin, parchment.)   I, i-ii, 10.

25. **1573.** July 22.—Sasine in favour of Richard Wedderburn, burgess of Elsinore in
Denmark, son and heir apparent to the resigners, of a S. Marketgate tenement in
Dundee, bounded E. by the lands of Patrick Wedderburn, &c., on resignation in his
favour by his father and mother, Alexander Wedderburn, senior, burgess of Dundee,
and Isobella Anderson his wife, but reserving to them their frank tenement and life
rent of the said premises. Robert Scrymgeour is witness, and Alexander Wedderburn, the clerk, is notary, and adds his symbol as in No. 20. II, viii, 10 ; VIII, i, 8.
(Latin, parchment, in good condition.)

26. **1574.** April 16.—Resignation by James Scrymgeour, elder, *alias* " Frensche James,"
and Alexander Scrymgeour, in favour of James Ker, of a Spalding's Wynd tenement,
to which Alexander Wedderburn, clerk of Dundee, is notary.   VIII, xiv, 13.

27. **1574.** May 29.—Renunciation by Alexander Quhytlaw of New Grange and Gelis
Gray his spouse, in favour of Walter Myln and Isobell Gray his spouse, and
Eufame Watson, relict of John Myln, portioner of Wester Gourdy, of an annual
rent of 16 bolls vietual furth of the lands of Wester Gourdy, now redeemed for 300
merks paid by James Carmichael of Ethybetoun in name and on behalf of the said
persons. Dated at Dundee. Alexander Wedderburn, notary, subscribes the writ and
adds his symbol. (English, small parchment, in good condition. See opp. p. 5.)   I, i-ii, 9.

28. **1575.** March 5.—Charter by Robert Rollok in favour of Alexander Mathow, burgess
of Dundee, and David his son, of a certain feu ferme rent. Witnessed at Dundee
by John Wedderburne, and Alexander Wedderburne, notary, and others. I, i-ii, 11.
(Latin, parchment, in good state.)

29. **1575.** May 16.—Contract between James Carmichael, portioner of Ethybetoun, and
Robert Carmichael in Ethybetoun, brother to David Carmichael of Balmedie, his
cautioner, on the one part, and " Alexander Wedderburne, common clerk of
Dundee, Jonnett Mylne his spous, and Alexander Wedderburne, younger, thair
sone and appeirand air" on the other part, whereby for the sum of 600 merks "all
in guid silver usuall money of the realme of Scotland" paid by the said Alexander
W. to the said James Carmichael, the latter is bound to infeft the said Alexander
and his wife in life-rent, and their son and his heirs in fee, in an annual rent of 27

SIGNATURES TO NO. 32.

SIGNATURES TO NO. 37.

("Alex^r Wedderburne scriba civitatis burgi de Dundie
premissa vera esse assevero.
Peter Wedderburn witnes.
David Wedderburne witness.")

NOTARIAL SUBSCRIPTION OF ROBERT WEDDERBURN, NO. 61.

("Robertus Wedderburn, notarius ac scriba curiæ deidonanæ pro tempore,
scribit teste hoc eius signo et syngrapho.")

SIGNATURES OF ROBERT WEDDERBURN, MERCHANT, AND ROBERT WEDDERBURN, NOTARY,
NO. 68 (b)

bolls victuall, half oatmeal and half beir, out of the sunny half of the lands of Scrymgeour-Wester Gourdie, with the teind sheaves thereof, &c., and the said Alexander Wedderburn and his wife engage to give a letter of reversion to the said James. Dated at Papers. Dundee. (English, paper, in good state.) I, i-ii, 12.

30. **1575.** Oct. 14.—Instrument following on the said charter by Robert Rollok (ante No. 28). Alexander Wedderburne, clerk of Dundee, is notary, and adds his signature and symbol. See opposite p. 5. (Latin, small parchment, in good state.) I, i-ii, 13.

31. **1576.** April 21.—Instrument on resignation of Robert Rollok in favour of Alexander Mathow, to which Alexander Wedderburn, clerk of Dundee, is notary. VIII, xiv, 14.

32. **1576.** July 14.—Disposition by "Alexander Wedderburn, elder, bourges off the bourght off Dundee in Scotland," by which he ratifies, approves and acknowledges his eldest son "Rechardus Wedderburn, bourges off Elsingneur in the realme of Denmark . . . to be his verray lauchfull heritier air and onlie assignay" after his deceis and the deceis of Isobell Anderson his spouse in and to all his lands &c. and specially to that tenement "back and foir" lying in S. Marketgate, Dundee, and bounded E. by the lands of Peter Wedderburne, and S. by Skirling's Wynd, &c. and also to three acres which pertained to Effem Fowler and now to the granter and his spouse, lying in the barony of Dudop; also to that S Cowgate yard with the pertinents which belonged before to unquhile James Wedderburn his (the granter's) brother, and now to him and his spouse by reason of the alienation thereof by Robert Wedderburn nearest and lauchfull oy and air to the said unquhill James Wedderburn, reserving to the granter and his wife their life rent in the said subjects. At the end of the document the granter adds "and I am content and consentis that the auld evidentis presentlie in my possession, to the number of twente thre peces, all in parchment, sall incontinent efter our deceiss be truely delyverit to the said Rechardus, butt ony fraude gyle or impediment." Subscribed at Elsingneur ; witnessed by "Peter Wedderburn my sone, Robert Wedderburn and David Wedderburn." I, i-ii, 14.
(English, small parchment, in good state. Signed "Alex. Wedderburn, elder (the granter), Peter Wedderburn with myn hand ass witness, David Wedderburn." See facsimile opposite.)

33. **1576.** Nov. 7.—Notarial renunciation by James Scrymgeour, alias "Frensche James," of an annual rent of 5 merks out of the mill of Powry Ogilvy. Extracted from the book of late Alexander Wedderburn, clerk of Dundee, by David Wedderburn, notary public, his son. (Small piece of paper, in fair state) IV, ii, 2.

34. **1577.** Nov. 8.—Sasine of two roods in Dundee in favour of Thomas Davidson. Alexander Wedderburn is notary, and appends his notarial symbol with the motto "Deum Time." (Latin, small parchment, in good state.) I, i-ii, 15.

35. **1577.** Dec. 30.—Notarial instrument narrating that Robert Wedderburn lawful son of Alexander Wedderburn, clerk of Dundee, with consent of his said father as tutor to him, resigned into the hands of the bailie the back land, waste and ruinous, of the late Robert W. elder, burgess of Dundee, in N. Argylegait, upon which the bailie at the mandate of the resigner, gave sasine thereof to a respectable young man, Alexander W., eldest son and apparent heir of the said Alexander and brother german of the said Robert ; whereupon the said Alexander Wedderburn, younger, with consent of his said father as tutor, resigns certain other premises to the said Robert by way of exchange ; reserving always to the said Alexander W. the father and to Jauet Myln his spouse their life rent in all the premises. Among the witnesses is Peter Wedderburn. (Latin, parchment, in good state.) I, i-ii, 16.

36. **1577.** Dec. 30.—Duplicate of No. 35. I, i-ii, 17.

37. **1577.** Dec. 30.—Charter on resignation by Robert Wedderburn to his brother Alexander, of the back land, &c., following on No 35. Signed by Alexander Wedderburne, clerk of Dundee, Peter Wedderburne and David Wedderburne witnesses (see opposite). (Latin, parchment, in good condition.) I, i-ii, 18.

Scrymgeour-
Wedderburn
Papers.

38. **1579.** Sept. 18.—Instrument of resignation and sasine following thereon of a tenement in Dundee to Marion Rolland and William Lyell her spouse. Alexander Wedderburne, clerk of Dundee, is notary and appends his symbol.   I, i-ii, 19.
(Latin, small parchment ; ink much faded.)

39. **1580.** Aug. 25.—Charter by Ninian Guthrie of Kingennie in favour of William Guthrie his grandson ; witnessed by Mr. Alexander Wedderburn, and Alexander and Robert W. notaries. (Parchment.)   VIII, iv, 12.

39ᴬ. **1580.** Aug. 25.—Similar charter by Ninian and William Guthrie to Elizabeth Fethie, future spouse of the said William, of the life rent of half of Kingennie, with the same witnesses as No. 39. (Parchment.)   VIII, iv, 13.

40. **1580.** Aug. 25.—Sasine following on No. 39. Witnessed by Mr. Alexander Wedderburn. (Parchment.)   VIII, iv, 14.

41. **1581.** Aug. 28 —Procuratory of resignation by Alexander Auchinlek son and heir apparent of John Auchinlek of Woodhill and Agnes Beaton his spouse, with consent of James Auchinlek, burgess of Dundee, his brother, for resigning the sunny half of Woodhill into the hands of Henry, Commendator of Balmerinoch.   Witnesses, David Wedderburn, and Robert and Alexander Wedderburn notaries. VIII, xiv, 15.

41ᴬ. **1581.** Aug. 28.—Charter by the said Commendator in favour of the said Alexander Auchinlek and his wife of the said lands. Similarly witnessed.   VIII, xiv, 16.

42. **1581.** Aug. 28-31.—Sasine on charter in favour of Alexander, son and heir of John Auchinlek of Woodhill, witnessed at Balmerinoch by Alexander Wedderburn, clerk of Dundee, David W., and Robert W., notary. (Latin, very thin parchment.) VIII, i, 9.

43. **1582.** Sept. 20.—Minute of the bailie Court of Dundee held in the Tolbooth thereof, before which compeared Alexander Wedderburn, common clerk of the burgh, and "resignit and demittit" his office of clerkship with all fees &c. pertaining thereto, into the hands of the bailies, in favour of Master Alexander Wedderburn his eldest lawful son ; whereupon the court, according to the tenor of a letter subscribed by the provost, bailies, council &c. of the burgh, anent the disposition of the said office to the said Mr. Alexander, did now elect and create him their common clerk, with all privileges &c, and the said Mr. Alexander then gave his oath for faithfully using the said office, and, with consent of the said Mr. Alexander, did also make and constitute the said Alexander Wedderburn, elder, substitute in the said office during his lifetime. The extract is subscribed by Thomas Ireland and Hercules Rollok notaries. (English, small parchment, in good state)   I, i-ii, 20.

44. **1582.** Nov. 7.—Charter by the town council of Dundee to James Goldman and Margaret Jak his spouse of a S. Argylegate land. Alexander Wedderburn, clerk, is witness. (Latin, parchment)   VIII, i, 10.

45. **1582.** Dec. 15.—Notarial Instrument narrating the resignation by Alexander Wedderburn, clerk of Dundee, and Mr. Alexander W. his son of a N. Argylegait tenement, bounded S. by the fore tenement of Robert Wedderburn &c., and narrating that sasine thereof was given to Helen Ramsay, affianced spouse of the said Mr. Alexander W. in terms of their marriage contract dated 21 Nov. 1582, which sasine the bride's father, consenting. David Wedderburn writes the deed and is a witness to it, while the notary is Robert W. who appends his symbol and motto "patior ut potiar." I, i-ii, 21.
(Latin, small parchment in good state, with seal attached, but worn almost smooth.)

46. **1583.** Mar. (?).—Sasine on resignation of William Forbes of Dronlaw in favour of Robert Kyd and Isobell Forbes his wife, daughter of the said William, of a rood of land in the Rattouraw, bounded N. by that of Robert Wedderburn. The notary is Robert Wedderburn.   VIII, xiv, 17.

47. **1583.** Aug. 3.—Sasine in favour of Janet Rollok, wife of David Gairdin, sailor, to which Robert Wedderburn is notary.   VIII, xiv. 17ᴬ.

48. **1583.** Nov. 24.—Charter by James Scrymgeour, constable of Dundee, to Adam **Scrymgeour-**
     Smyth of two roods of land in Dundee. Witnessed by David Wedderburn, Robert **Wedderburn**
     W. notary, &c. (Latin, parchment)   viii, i, 11. **Papers.**

49. **1584.** June 6.—Charter by James Jack to David Fleming. Alexander Wedderburn
     signs for the granter.   viii, xiv, 18.

50. **1585-86.** Jan. 23.—Sasine on resignation by Alexander Scrymgeour to Herbert
     Stewart, his brother uterine. Robert Wedderburn, burgess of Dundee, is witness
     and Mr. Alexander Wedderburn is notary.   viii, xiv, 19.

51. **1586.** March 19.—Charter by William Guthrie of Kingennic to Elizabeth Fethie
     his wife, &c. Written and witnessed by Mr. Alexander Wedderburn. viii, iv, 16.

52. **1586.** Nov. 12.—Discharge by David Mathow, burgess of Dundee, to Mr. Alexander W.
     clerk of Dundee, and Helen Ramsay, his spouse, for £100. (One sheet of paper.) viii, ii, 1.

53. **1586.** Nov. 12.—Charter by James Scrymgeour of Dudop, provost and constable of
     Dundee, in favour of " Master Alexander Wedderburn, clerk of Dundee, and Helen
     Ramsay his spous" and their heirs, of au £8 feu ferme out of the N. Mornygate lands
     of James Ferriar &c., on resignation by David Mathow. Witnessed by Robert W.
     notary and others. (Latin, small parchment, in perfect state)   i, i-ii, 22.

54. **1586.** Nov. 14.—Precept of sasine by James Scrymgeour of Dudope, provost and
     constable of Dundee, for infefting Master Alexander Wedderburn, clerk of the court
     of Dundee, and Helen Ramsay his spouse and the survivor of them, in the said
     feu ferme of £8.   viii, xiv, 20.

55. **1586.** Nov. 19.—Sasine following on No. 54. Robert Wedderburn is notary and
     appends his symbol and motto. "The evidentis of the feu maill of aucht pundis furth of
     Kingennic. "The evidentis of the feu maill of aucht pundis furth of James ferriaris
     Land on ye north syid of ye Murraygait coft by Maister Alexander Wedderburn."
     (Latin, small parchment, in good state.)   i, i-ii, 23.

56. **1587.** Feb. 3, 4.—Precept and sasine thereon by James Scrymgeour of Dudop, in
     favour of Elizabeth Carnegie. Robert Wedderburn, notary, is witness to the precept,
     and notary to the sasine. He adds his sign with the mottoes " Bona fide " and " Nihil
     tam occulte q. non revelabitur." (Very thin parchment, in bad state.)   iv, ii, 3.

57. **1587** June 29.—Obligation or bond by Peter Imry, burgess of Dundee, to Mr.
     Alexander Wedderburn, clerk thereof, for 200 merks. Signed at Dundee " Peitter
     Imry " and witnessed by Robert Wedderburn, father's brother to Mr. Alexander, and
     John Auchinlek his servant. (One small piece of paper, in good state.)   viii, ii, 1*.

58. **1587-88.** March 9.—Sasine on resignation by Cristina, daughter and heir of John
     Ferriar, to which Mr. Alexander Wedderburn, clerk of Dundee, is notary. viii, xiv, 20*.

59. **1588.** May 25.—Sasine on resignation by John Wobster, burgess of Dundee, to Mr.
     Alexander Wedderburn, clerk of the burgh, and Helen Ramsay his wife, of a N. Argyle-
     gate yard, bounded W. by the lands of Mr. Alexander Wedderburn. David W. brother
     of the said Mr. Alexander is a witness. (Latin, parchment, in good state.) viii, i, 12.

60. **1538.** Oct. 16.—Notarial instrument narrating that there compeared before the
     bailies of Dundee " Robert Wedderburne younger, lawful sone to umquhile Alexander
     Wedderburne, commone clerk of the said burgh, and by thir presents, he being now
     of perfytt eage and past twentie ane yeiris of aige compleit," ratifies the infeftment
     made by him in favour of his brother Alexander 30 Dec. 1577 (see Nos. 35-37) of
     the N. Argylegait tenement now occupied by him. Robert Wedderburn (elder) is
     notary, and adds his symbol. (Latin, parchment, in good condition.)   i, i ii, 24.

61. **1588.** Oct. 16.—Duplicate of No. 60. See facsimile of docket opposite p. 7. I, i-ii, 25.

62. **1589.** Jan. 20.—Precept of clare constat by James Scrymgeour of Dudop for infefting the daughters of the late David Gardin heirs to their father in a rood of land in Dundee. Robert Wedderburn is a witness. (Latin, parchment.) v, v, 15.

63. **1589.** May 23.—Sasine on resignation by Henry Blair, shipmaster, burgess of Dundee, in favour of Thomas Blair his son, of three annual rents out of tenements in Dundee. Robert Wedderburn, merchant, David Wedderburn, and others, are witnesses. Mr. Alexander W. clerk is notary, and adds his symbol and docket. IV, ii, 4.
(Small parchment, in good condition, but the ink faint.)

64. **1590.** April 7.—Notarial instrument on agreement by Mr. George Spens, burgess of Dundee, with Mr. Alexander Wedderburn clerk thereof (and his wife Helen Ramsay), and Mr. George Halyburton (and his wife Susanna Ramsay), who acknowledge the receipt from G. Spens of their respective tochers with their wives, his "oyes." It recites an agreement by them as to the marriage of Marjorie Ramsay, also "oye" to Spens, with their advice and consent, and an obligation by Spens to bequeath to the said Mr. A. W. and Mr. G. H. an equal share of his estate with his children "oyes" and friends. Done about 3 p.m. in the yard of the said Mr. A. W. VIII, ii, 2.
(One sheet of paper, fair state.)

65. **1590.** July 22.—Sasine on resignation by James Goldman, merchant, burgess of Dundee, of a N. Argylegate tenement to his son Robert G. Mr. Alexander Wedderburn, clerk of Dundee, is notary. VIII, xiv, 21.

66. **1590.** July 28.—Charter by Richard Wedderburn burgess of Elsingoir in Denmark, son and heir of the late Alexander Wedderburn, elder, burgess of Dundee, whereby to his evident advantage he sells to his beloved Patrick Wedderburn, merchant, burgess of the said burgh, his brother german, and Elizabeth Low his spouse in conjunct fee, and to their heirs, whom failing to the heirs whomsoever of the said Patrick, all that tenement of burghal land, with a foreland newly built, and backlands occupied by Isobella Anderson, the granter's mother, and her servants lying in S. Marketgate, and bounded as therein mentioned (see No. 25) ; also three acres in the Eastfield of Dudop bounded on the north by those of the late Robert Wedderburn (see No. 32) ; reserving to the said Isobella Anderson her life rent in the said tenement and acres. Dated at Dundee 28 July, 1590. Witnesses Mr. Alexander Wedderburn, clerk of Dundee, &c.
(Latin, parchment.) VIII, i, 13.

67. **1590.** July 31.—Confirmation by Sir James Scrymgeour of Dudop Knt., of the foregoing charter (No. 66). Dated at Dudop. Mr. Alexander W. clerk, is among the witnesses to the confirmation. (Latin, parchment, in good state.) I, i-ii, 26.

68. (a) **1590.** Aug. 27 —Charter by Rannald Brown in Wester Gourdie and Barbara Rollok his spouse, to Robert Wedderburn son and heir of the late Mr. Robert Wedderburn, of the lands called Kilmanyis taek, lying on the N. of the muir of Wester Gourdie in the shire of Forfar ; also of 2½ acres of arable land in the Cottertoun of Wester Gourdie, and that for the sum of 250 merks, in the terms of a contract therein referred to ; to be holden in fee and heritage and blench ferme. Dated at Gourdie 27 Aug., 1590. Witnesses John Wedderburn, Robert W. notary, &c. (Latin, parchment.) VIII, i, 14.

The above is cancelled and on the back of it is written another document, viz. :

(b) **1591.** Nov. 9.—Renunciation by the said Rannald Brown and Robert Wedderburn, merchant of Dundee, to James Carmichael, bailie of Dundee, and Mr. Alexander Wedderburn, common clerk of Dundee, of the lands aforesaid, for 250 merks received from them. Dated at Dundee. Witnesses David Wedderburn, burgess of Dundee, Robert Wedderburn, &c.

A duplicate of this renunciation is among the papers (I, i-ii, 29) and has on the back of it a cancelled wadset dated 16 Oct., 1589, by James Carmichael to R. Brown of the acres called Kilmanyis taek. Witnessed by Robert Wedderburn, and Robert Wedderburn, notary. See facsimile opposite p. 7. I, i-ii, 29.

69. **1591.** Jan. 28.—Renunciation by Robert Carmichael sometime in Ethiebetoun, burgess of Dundee, in favour of Mr. Alexander Wedderburn, common clerk thereof, of an annual rent of 20 merks furth of the sunny half of Wester Gourdie. II, iv, 20. Scrymgeour-Wedderburn Papers.

70. **1591.** Feb. (?).—Contract between Mr. Alexander Wedderburn, common clerk of Dundee, on the one part, and David Dunmuir, portioner of Wester Gourdie, and Marion Turnbull his spouse, on the other part, by which the said D. D. sells and dispones to the said Mr. Alexander, his heirs and assignees, all and haill the shadow half of the town and lands of Wester Gourdie, sometime possessed by umquhile Isobell Brown, mother to the said David, together with the teind sheaves of the said half lands, lying in the lordship of Scone and sheriffdom of Forfar. II, ii, 2.

71. **1591.** April 28.—Charter by John Cokburne in Burnsyd of Barrie, and his wife, to John Clark of Revinsbie and his wife &c., of the lands of Arnotts, alias Burnsyd of Barrie. Robert Wedderburn, notary, &c. witnesses. (Latin parchment.) VIII, i, 15.

72. **1591.** June 6.—Contract between James Carmichael, burgess of Dundee, and Elizabeth Lovel his spouse, on the one part, and Alexander Wedderburn, common clerk of the said burgh, and Helen Ramsay his spouse, on the other part, by which in consideration of 4000 merks paid by Mr. Alexander, the said James &c. bind themselves to infeft him and his heirs heritably and without reversion in all and haill the sunny half of the town and lands of Wester Gourdie with the teind sheaves thereof &c. II, iv, 13.

73. **1591.** June 6.—Charter by James Carmichael, portioner of Ethiebetoun, burgess of Dundee, with consent of Elizabeth Lovel his spouse (in implement of No. 72) in favour of Mr. Alexander Wedderburn, common clerk of Dundee, and Helen Ramsay his spouse and their heirs, of all and haill their half of the town and lands of Wester Gourdie, called the sunny half, with the teind sheaves thereof. II, iv, 14.

74. **1591.** June 6.—Duplicate of No. 73, containing precept of sasine. II, ii, 3.

75. **1591.** June 14.—Charter by John Wedderburn, portioner of Hiltoun of Cragie, and Margaret Strathauchin his spouse, whereby in implement of a contract made between them and the vendees, they sell to Mr. Alexander Wedderburn, clerk of Dundee, and Helen Ramsay his spouse, in conjunct fee, and their heirs, an annual rent of £10 furth of the lands of Hiltoun of Craigie in the regality of Lindores, and sheriffdom of Forfar. Precept of sasine is added, dated at Dundee 14 June, 1591 and signed "John Wedderburn with my hand." (See opposite p. 13.) James Wedderburn is a witness, and Robert Wedderburn and James Gleg, notaries, sign for Margaret Strathauchin. I, i-ii, 30. (Latin, small parchment in good condition, but cut through and with both seals gone.)

76. **1591.** July 24.—Discharge by James Carmichael, burgess of Dundee, to Mr. Alexander Wedderburn, clerk thereof, for 700 merks scots, in part payment of 4000 promised to be paid by the said Mr. Alexander, for the heritable alienation to be made by the said James of his half lands of Wester Gourdie with the pertinents. Dated at Dundee. II, iv, 16.

77. **1591.** Oct. 7.—Sasine, following on charter of 6 June, 1591 (No. 73 ante.) II, iv, 17.

78. „ Oct. 7.—Duplicate of No. 77. II, iv, 18.

79. „ Nov. 9.—Renunciation by Barbara Rollok, relict of Henry Abercrombie, in Wester Gourdie, and Rannald Brown now her spouse, for his interest and as tutor to — Abercrombie, son and heir of the said Henry A., in favour of James Carmichael, bailie, and Mr. Alexander Wedderburn, clerk of Dundee, of an annual rent of £20 scots alienate to them by the said James furth of the lands of Gourdie. II, iv, 19.

80. **1591.** Ncv. 18.—Assignation by Mr. Alexander Wedderburn, clerk of Dundee, to his
cousin Robert Wedderburn, elder, merchant burgess of Dundee, and Euffame Coustoun
his spouse, of an annual rent of 50 merks from the lands of Craigie Hiltoun, redeemable by Richard Blyth, the owner of the lands, for 500 merks. Signed by the granter
and grantee and by Robert Wedderburn, notary, as witness.   VIII, ii, 3.

81. **1591.** Nov. 26.—Discharge by James Carmichael, bailie of Dundee, to Mr. Alexander
Wedderburn, clerk thereof, for 1000 merks, as promised for the heritable alienation
of the sunny half of Wester Gourdie, with the teind sheaves thereof, in the regality
of Scone. (English, very small parchment, in good state.)   I, i-ii, 31.

82. **1592.** Feb. 1.—Contract between David Dunmure, portioner of Wester Gourdie, and
Marjorie Turnbull his spouse, with consent of Robert Turnbull of Bogmill, to whom
the said David is interdicted, on one part, and Mr. Alexander Wedderburne, common
clerk of Dundee, on the other, whereby the former engage to iufeft the said Mr. A. W.
in the shadow half of Wester Gourdie ; for which the said Mr. A. W. agrees to pay
2700 merks, and also to give the said D. D. and M. T. a tack of the said lands for
their lifetimes at the yearly rent of 40 pennies. Subscribed by the parties at
Dundee. ·(English, paper, in good state.)   I, i-ii, 28.

83. **1592.** (date blank.)—Discharge by the said D. D. and M. T. his spouse, to Mr. Alexander W., clerk of Dundee, for 3500 merks scots in complete payment made to them
of their shadow half of Wester Gourdie with the teind sheaves of the same alienated
by contract dated Feb., 1591.   II, ii, 4.

84. **1592.** May 6.—Renunciation by Andro Gourlay in Dargo and Matilda Abercrombie
his spouse, in favour of Mr. Alex. W., clerk of Dundee, assignee of David Denmuir,
sometime portioner of Wester Gourdie, of an annual rent of 16 bolls vietual furth of
the shadow half of the lands of Wester Gourdie.   II, iv, 21.

85. **1592.** May 8.—Charter by David Denmuir, portioner of Wester Gourdie, with
consent of Marjory Turnbull his spouse, and Robert Turnbull of Bogmyln, in
implement of a contract made between them and Mr. Alex. W., clerk of Dundee, in
favour of the said Mr. Alex., of all and haill the shadow half of Wester Gourdie, &c.
Dated at Dundee.   II, ii, 5.

86. **1592.** May 8.—Duplicate of the above charter.   II, iv, 23.

87. ,, May 9.— Renunciation by Patrick Mortimer in Dryburgh, in favour of Mr.
Alexander Wedderburn, clerk of Dundee, assignee of David Denmuir, sometime
portioner of Wester Gourdie, of an annual rent of 32 merks furth of the shadow half
of W. Gourdie.   II, iv, 22.

88. **1592.** May 12.—Sasine on the above charter (ante No. 85).   II, iv, 24.

89. **1592.** May (?)—Charter by David Denmuir portioner of Wester Gourdie &c. in
favour of Mr. Alexander Wedderburn, of the shadow half of Wester Gourdie &c. to be
held of the Commendator and Monastery of Scone.   II, iv, 25.

90. **1592.** May (?)—Charter same to same of the said shadow half of Wester Gourdie, to
be held of the Earl of Gowrie.   II, iv, 26.

91. **1592.** May 12.—Sasine following on preceding charter (No. 90).   II, iv, 27.

92. **1592.** May 15.—Discharge by David Denmure in Wester Gourdie in favour of Mr.
Alex. W. clerk of Dundee, for 570 merks " in haill and compleit payment of the sum
of fyve thousand merkis money of Scotland " promised him by the said Mr. A. W. for the
heritable alienation of the shadow half of Wester Gourdie &c. Dated at Dundee.
The granter's signature is by the notary Robert Wedderburn, because he could not
write. (English, paper, in fair condition.)   I, i-ii, 35.

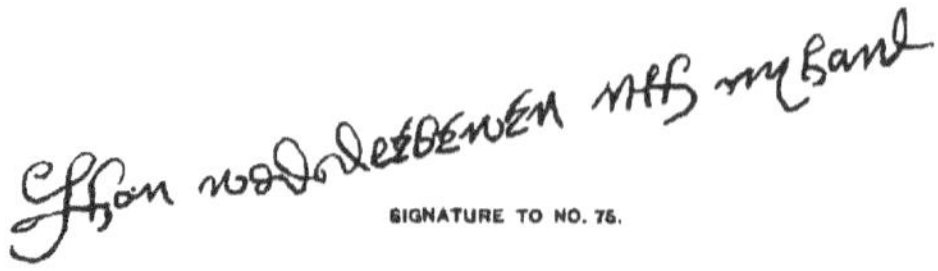

SIGNATURE TO NO. 75.

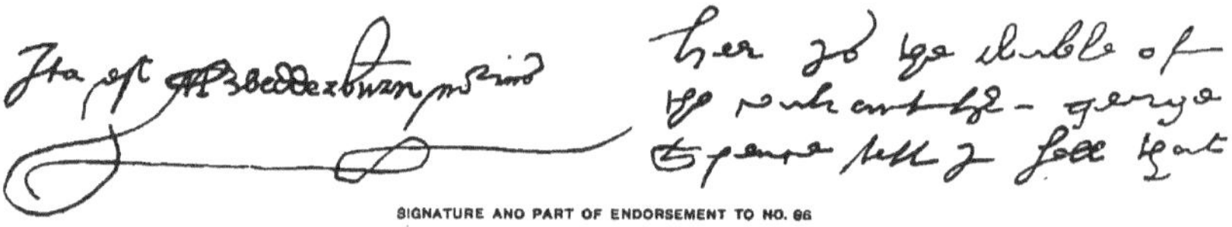

SIGNATURE AND PART OF ENDORSEMENT TO NO. 86

SIGNATURE TO NO 105.

ONE OF THE SIGNATURES TO NO. 104

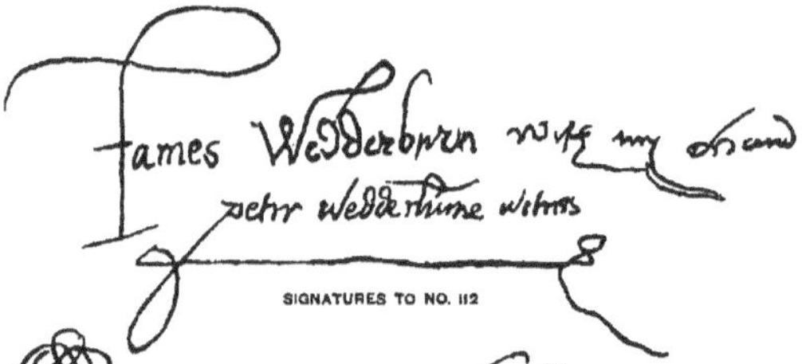

SIGNATURES TO NO. 112

NOTARIAL SYMBOL TO NO. 164

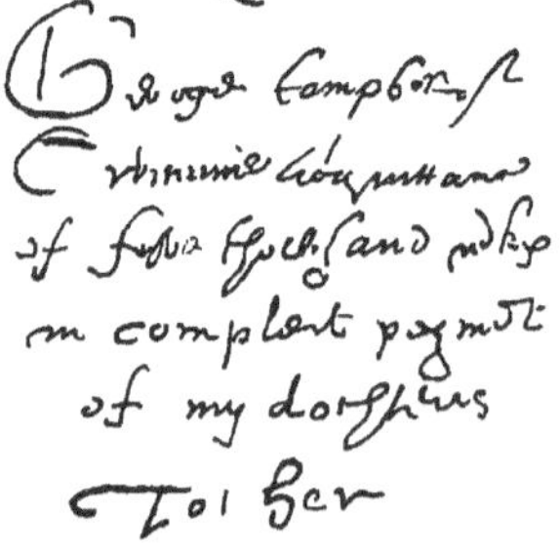

ENDORSEMENT TO NO. 162

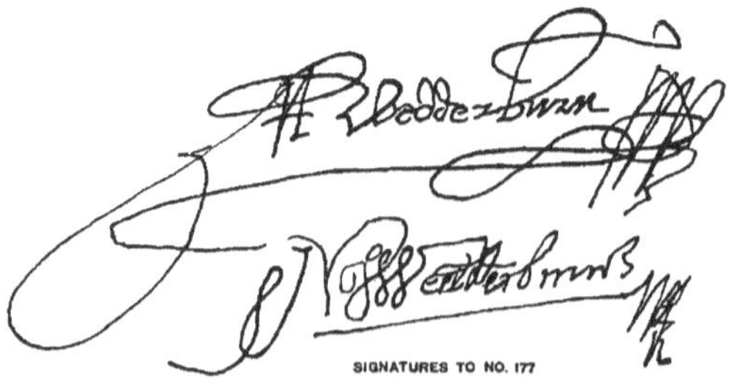

SIGNATURES TO NO. 177

93. **1592.** July 29.—Tack by Alexander Wedderburn (with consent of Helen Ramsay his spouse) to David Denmuir and Marjory Turnbull, his spouse, of all and haill the backseats of his lands of Wester Gourdie &c. ii, iv, 28. Scrymgeour-Wedderburn Papers.

94. **1592.** July 29.—Tack same to same of the whole shadow half of the said lands of Wester Gourdie &c. for two years. Dated at Dundee. ii, iv, 29.

95. **1592.** July 29.—Duplicate of No. 94. ii, iv, 30.

96. ,, Dec. 4.—Copy contract between George Spens, burgess of Dundee, and John Moffit, burgess thereof ; dated at Dundee, and witnessed and signed by Mr. Alexander W. clerk thereof. (English, paper, in good state.) i, i-ii, 31ᵃ.

On the back is written in the hand of Sir Alexander Wedderburn, Knt., of Blackness :—"Heer is the double of the contract quhair George Spens sett in feu that hous quhich Johne Maill had : It is attested and subscrybed be my grandfather ; their is on provision in this feu that without any declaration, if the feu deutie were thre termes unpayed, this should be void : and be vertue hereof John Maill being four or five yeers re-taud, I possessed the same and hes disposed the same to my some George Wedderburne." For a facsimile of part of this endorsement, see opposite.

97. **1592.** Dec. 25 and 31.—Renunciation by Walter Hay, merchant burgess of Dundee, and Barbara Watt his spouse, and Patrick Hay in Erroll, his brother german, in favour of Mr. Alex. W. clerk of Dundee, now heritable proprietor of the shadow half of the lands of Wester Gourdie, of two annual rents furth of the said lands alienate to them by David Denmuir &c. Dated at Dundee and Kirkton of Erroll. ii, iv, 31.

98. **1593.** Jan. 9.—Notarial instrument by which Rannald Brown, sometime in Wester Gourdie, ratifies the renunciation made by him in favour of Mr. Alexander Wedderburn of the sunny half of Wester Gourdie, and grants him to have renounced all possession which he had or could pretend to the teind sheaves thereof. ii, iv, 33.

99. **1593.** March 5.—Transumpt from the protocol books of the late Alexander Wedderburn, clerk, of a protocol dated 15 July, 1579, on resignation by Robert Barry to George Mathow. The transumpt is subscribed by Mr. Alexander Wedderburn. viii, xiv, 22.

100. **1593.** May 4.—Contract of marriage between John Scrymgeour of Kirktoun, and Marion Fotheringhame, daughter of Mr. James Fotheringhame (brother german of Thomas Fotheringhame of Powrie) and his wife Margaret Lindsay. Dated at Dundee. Mr. Alexander Wedderburn. clerk of Dundee, is a witness but does not sign. iv, iv, 1.
(Two pieces of paper, originally joined together, in fair state)

101. **1593.** May 17.—Confirmation by John Earl of Gowrie of three charters relating to Wester Gourdie, viz. :—(1), 1574, June 10, by Euphamia Watson to James Carmichael ; witnessed by Alexander Wedderburn, notary. (2), No. 54 ante. (3), No. 71 ante. This confirmation is dated at Edinburgh. i, i-ii, 33.
(Latin, large parchment, in good state. Seal gone.)

102. **1593.** June 1.—Charter by William Fairnie of that ilk to Peter Rolland of Dundee, of two parts of Grange of Barrie, eo. Forfar. Witnessed by John Wedderburn, son to Alexander W. burgess of Cupar, and others. Dated at Cupar. (Latin, parchment.) viii, i, 16.

103. **1593.** Aug 3.—Discharge and renunciation by Robert Wedderburn, elder, brother of the late Alexander Wedderburn, clerk of Dundee, for the sum of six score pounds payed to him by Robert Wedderburn, lawful son of the said umquhile Alexander, and heritable proprietor of the land hereby renounced, namely "that foir land up and down . . . pertaining to the said Robert in heritage, by and upon the North syid of the Ergylisgait." Signed "R Wedderburn wᵗ my hand," and witnessed by Patrick Wedderburn and others, all of whom sign. i, i-ii, 36.
(English, small parchment, in good condition, but the seal gone. See facsimile opposite.)

104. **1593.** Aug. 23.—Renunciation of an annual rent furth of a Dundee tenement by John Ratray of Dundee to George Mathew, burgess there. Witnessed by Mr. Alexander W. clerk of Dundee. (English, small parchment, in good state. See opposite.) i, i-ii, 34.

Scrymgeour-
Wedderburn
Papers.

105. **1593**. (date blank.)—Renunciation by Andrew Henrisoun, lawful son of James H. in Seone, in favour of Mr. Alexander Wedderburn, of an annual rent of 22 bolls victual furth of the half of Wester Gourdie, once pertaining to David Denmuir and alienated by him to the said Mr. Alexander.   II, iv, 33.

106. **1593**. Feb. 18.—Confirmation under the Great Seal, dated at Edinburgh, of two charters, viz. : (1) Charter 1 June, 1593, by William Fairnie of that ilk to Peter Rolland, burgess of Dundee, of two parts of the lands of Grange of Barrie, dated at Cupar, and witnessed by (among others) John Wedderburn, lawful son of Alexander Wedderburn, burgess of Cupar. (2) Charter 13 March, 1593-4, by John Auchinlek son and heir of the late George Auchinlek, portioner of Grange of Barrie, with consent of Grissell Lindsay, his mother, to the said Peter Rolland of a third part of the said lands. (Parchment, great seal entirely gone.)   VIII, xiv, 22^b.

107. **1595**. Nov. 9.—Sasine on precept from chancery in favour of John Auchinlek as heir to his father the late George A., portioner of Grange of Barrie, in a third part thereof. Mr. Alex. W. of Wester Gourdie is a witness, but does not sign. VIII, i, 17.

108. **1595**. June 9.—Grant by Peter Hay to his weil belovit Mr. Alexander Wedderburn, clerk of Dundee, of certain wheat, &c., yearly, furth of the granter's lands during the granter's life. David Wedderburn is a witness. Dated at Dundee.   I, i-ii, 36^a.

109. **1595**. Nov. 15.—Renunciation of David Denmuir, burgess of Dundee, sometime portioner of Wester Gourdie, in favour of Mr. Alexander Wedderburn, now heritable proprietor thereof, of the life rent tack let to the said David and his late wife (ante No. 93).   II, iv, 34.

110. **1596**. May 22-23.—Charter by William Guthrie of Kingany to John Traill of Dundee of the lands called the " Crymbillis " or " Trumbillis " of Kingany with teinds, &c. Witnessed by Mr. Alexander Wedderburn, town clerk of Dundee. VIII, iv, 21, VIII, xiv, 23.

111. **1596**. May 24.—Reversion by John Traill to William Guthrie of the said lands, &c. Witnessed by the said Mr. Alexander W. (Parchment.)   VIII, iv, 22.

112. **1596**. May 29.—Charter by James Wedderburne, lawful son of the late Mr. Alexander Wedderburne, clerk of Dundee, in favour of Mr. Alexander Wedderburne, now clerk of Dundee, the granter's brother german, of his feu ferme of 10 merks, 6/8, furth of a tenement in Dundee, for £120 paid to the granter by Mr Alexander, to hold of the King in burgage. Dated at Dundee. Witnesses Peter Wedderburn, the granter's brother german, and others. Signed by the granter and Peter W., his brother, as witness. See opposite p. 13. (Latin, parchment.)   VIII, i, 18.

113. **1596**. June 4.—Sasine on resignation by John Mure and Agnes Gray his spouse to Andrew Panter, of the East half of a S. Flukergate land, bounded S. partly by the lands of Peter Wedderburne and William Lochmalony. Mr. Alexander Wedderburn clerk of Dundee is notary.   VIII, xiv, 24.

114. **1596**. June 7.—Charter following on No. 113. Witnessed by Mr. Alexander Wedderburn. (Latin, parchment.)   VIII, i, 19.

115. **1596**. Sept. 6.—Procuratory of resignation for resigning the west half of the said tenement. Mr. Alexander Wedderburn is notary.   VIII, xiv, 25.

116. **1596**. Sept. 14.—Sasine following on above resignation. Mr. Alexander Wedderburn is notary.   VIII, xiv, 25^a.

117. **1598**. Oct. 14.—Sasine on resignation by Thomas Blair, shipmaster, burgess of Dundee, to Robert Goldman of a N. Argylegate land. James Wedderburn is witness and Mr. Alexander W. clerk of Dundee notary.   VIII, xiv, 26.

118. **1600.** Feb. 17.—Disposition by Mr. David Carnegy of Kynnard, in favour of Mr. Scrymgeour-Alex. Wedderburn, common clerk of Dundee, "for thankfull service done and to be Wedderburn done" to him by the said Mr. Alexander, of a yearly pension for life of 8 bolls heir Papers. furth of the lands of Panbryde in the sherifdom of Forfar. Dated at Kynnard. Witnesses, David Ramsay, apparent of Bawmayne, and Mr. John Ramsay, parson of Teilling. Signed by the disponer and witnesses. (English, on paper, much decayed.) I, i-ii, 37.

119. **1600** Mar. 29. – Charter by the said John Mure (ante Nos. 113-14) and his wife to Androw Panter, of a S. Flukergate tenement. Mr. Alexander Wedderburn notary signs for the wife. VIII, xiv, 26ª.

120. **1600.** April 12.—Sasine in favour of William Small of Dundee, of a tenement in Dundee, to which Mr. Alexander Wedderburn, clerk of Dundee, is notary and adds his symbol and docket. (Latin, on parchment, in good state.) I, i-ii, 38.

121. **1600.** April 21.—Contract between William Guthre of Kingennie and Elizabeth Fethie his spouse, with consent of Henri Maull and Andrew Maull of Gouldie on one part, and John Traill, bailie of Dundee, on the other part (narrating two earlier contracts) by which the former parties agree to infeft Traill in the Maynis of Kingennie, &c. in few ferme, for 24 bolls victual yearly. Dated at Dundee. (Three sheets in good state.) VIII, ii, 4.

122. **1600.** (date wanting.)—Renunciation by John Traill, burgess of Dundee, to Mr. Alex. Wedderburn, common clerk of Dundee, of an annual rent of 8 bolls victual furth of the Maynis of Kingennie, which the granter had from William Guthre of Kingennie, under reversion for 460 merks, now redeemed by the said Mr. A. W. (Conclusion and date wanting, one sheet, in fair state.) VIII, ii, 5.

123. **1600.** Sept. 6 —Contract between Wm. Guthre of Kingany, Elizabeth Fethie his spouse, and Marion Mauld his mother, on the one part, and Mr. Alexander Wedderburn Clerk of Dundee, on the other part, for the sale of the lands of Kingany to the latter for the sum of 10,800 merks. Signed at Dundee by the parties and witnesses. (Scroll of two sheets, in fair state.) VIII, ii, 6.

124. **1600.** Sept. 17 —Obligation by William Guthre of Kingany not to sell any of his lands nor to dispose of the money received from Mr. Alexander Wedderburn as the price of Kingany, without the advice and consent of Henry Fethie of Ballilish, Henry Maull, portioner of Skryne, Andrew Maull of Gouldie, William Maull burgess of Edinburgh, Henry Ramsay of Ardowny, and the said Mr. Alexander Wedderburn. Signed at Monyfuith by all the parties. (One leaf, fair.) VIII, ii, 7.

125. **1600.** Oct. 20.—Renunciation by Henrie Maull, now of Skryne, and Isobell Mauld his daughter to whom he was tutor, in favour of Mr. Alex. Wedderburne common clerk of Dundee and "now heritable proprietor" of the lands of Kingennie, of an annual rent of 20 merks, furth of the said lands, which the said Mr. A. W. as assignee to William Guthre of Kingennie had redeemed for 200 merks. At the Skryne. Signed by Henry Maull. (English, parchment.) VIII, iii, 2.

126. **1600.** Nov. 1.—Discharge by Walter Graham of Balgray to Mr. Alexander Wedderburn, clerk of Dundee, in name of William Guthrie of Kingany of £40 in payment of arrears of annual rent furth of the lands of Kingany. Dated at Dundee. VIII, xi, 11.

127. **1600.** Nov. 1.—Contract between William Guthrie of Kingany, Elizabeth Fethie his spouse, Marion Mauld his mother, &c. on the one part, and Mr. Alexander Wedderburn, clerk of Dundee, and Helen Ramsay his spouse, on the other, for the sale to the latter of the lands and mayns of Kingany, for which the said Mr. Alexander becomes bound to pay 11,200 merks, which with 4,800 paid for clearing off reversions, makes 16,000 merks in all. Signed at Dundee. David Wedderburn is a witness. (Scroll of three sheets, in fair state.) VIII, ii, 8.

Scrymgeour-
Wedderburn
Papers.

128. **1600.** Nov. 1.—Renunciation by William Guthre of Kingany, with consent of Elizabeth Fethie his spouse, Marion Mauld, and Henrie Fethie of Ballisak, in favour of Mr. Alexander Wedderburn, common clerk of Dundee, and Helen Ramsay his spouse, of the feu maill which they had bound themselves to pay for the lands of Kingany, with manor place, orchyards, mill, mill lands and pendicle, before called Carneton, now Crymbills of Kingany, all of which were sold to the said Mr. Alexander and his spouse heritably, without redemption. Dated at Dundee. (English, parchment.) VIII, iii, 3.

129. **1600.** Nov. 1.—Judicial ratification by the said Elizabeth Fethie of the said contract of sale of the lands of Kingany (see No. 123), done in the chamber of the said Mr. Alexander Wedderburn. (English, parchment.) VIII, iii, 4.

130. **1600.** Nov. 1.—Procuratory of resignation by William Guthre of Kingany, with consent (as in No. 128), &c. in favour of the said Mr. Alex. W. and Helen Ramsay his spouse, in conjunct fee, and their heirs, of the lands of Kingany by delivery of stuff and baton in the hands of William, Earl of Angus. Dated at Dundee. Seal of William Guthre attached. (English, parchment.) VIII, iii, 5.

131. **1600.** Nov. 1.—Charter by the said William Guthre, with consent of his said wife and mother and others in favour of the said Mr. Alexander Wedderburn and his wife in conjunct fee and the heirs procreate between them, whom failing, the heirs of the said Mr. Alexander whatsoever, of the lands of Kingany, &c. for certain great sums of money, to hold of the granter in feu-ferme (*the duty is not stated*). Contains precept of sasine and is dated at Dundee. (Latin, parchment; seal gone.) VIII, iii, 6.

132. **1600.** Nov. 1.—Charter in similar terms to hold *a me* of the Earl of Angus. (Latin, parchment. Seal of Wm. Guthrie.) VIII, iii, 7.

133. **1600.** Nov. 4.—Renunciation by John Fethie lawful son of David F., brother german of the late Henry Fethie of Ballisak, to Wm. Guthrie of Kingany, of an annual rent of 40 merks furth of the lands, &c., of Kingany, now redeemed by payment of 400 merks. Dated at Dundee. David Wedderburn, burgess of Dundee, and Mr. Alexander Wedderburn, clerk thereof, are witnesses. VIII, iv, 29.

134. **1600.** Nov. 25.—Gift by William, Earl of Angus, to Mr. Alexander Wedderburn, clerk of Dundee, of the noncutry maills and duties of the lands of Kingany, since the decease of the late Wm. Guthrie of Kingany, grandschir to William Guthrie, now of Kingany. Dated at Canongate. Witnessed by James Johnstoun of Westraw, James Fethie of Gwynde, &c. (Seal gone. English, parchment.) VIII, iii, 8.

135. **1600.** Dec. 3.—Discharge by William Guthrie of Kingany and Elizabeth Fethie his spouse to Mr. Alexander Wedderburn, clerk of Dundee, for 11,200 merks in complete payment of 16,000 merks promised by the said Mr. Alexander W. as the price of the lands of Kingany. Dated at Dundee. (English, parchment.) VIII, iii, 9.

136. **1600.** Dec. 5.—Receipt by James Fethie to Mr. Alexander Wedderburn, common clerk of Dundee, on behalf of Mr. William Guthrie of Kingany, for 5000 merks. Written by David Wedderburn, who signs as a witness, together with Mr. William Graham of Claverhous. (One leaf, fair.) VIII, ii, 9.

137. **1600.** Dec. 5.—Notarial instrument on the consent of William Guthrie sometime of Kingany, John Traill, burgess of Dundee, and others, to remove from the lands of Kingany, in favour of Mr. Alexander Wedderburn, now heritable proprietor thereof. Robert Wedderburn is co-notary and David Wedderburn, burgess of Dundee, witness. (One sheet, fair state.) VIII, ii 10.

138. **1600.** Dec. 10.—Portion of a tack or assedation by Mr. Alexander Wedderburn to John Traill, of the mains of Kingany, with condition as to holding the said lands, and removing therefrom, and ratifying the infeftments formerly granted by Wm. Guthrie of Kingany to the said J. Traill of the said mains as principal, and the mill, mill lands, &c., in warrandice, reserving the right of redemption by the said Mr. Alex. W. Subscribed at Dundee by both the parties and by various witnesses. I, i.ii, 39, (The last sheet of this deed is all that remains; it is in English, and on paper, much decayed.)

139. **1600.** Dec. 10.—Contract whereby John Traill, burgess of Dundee, sells for 1,200 **Scrymgeour-** merks to Mr. Alexander Wedderburn, common clerk of Dundee, that land and **Wedderburn** tenement lying on the north side of Argyle's gate, between the lands of the said Mr. **Papers.** Alexander, and the foreland of the heirs of the late Robert Wedderburn his brother on the east, the lands of Thomas Traill and John Goldman on the west, the common burial ground on the north, and the said Argyle's gate on the south ; to hold of the King in free burgage, for payment yearly to the Kirkmaister of Dundee of 8 lib. of wax or 40/- instead thereof ; also to the chaplain of . . . . 40/- ; and to the hospital master of Dundee 13/4. Dated at Dundee. Witnesses George Hay of Ross, Mr. John Lovell, Alexander Ramsay, burgess. (English, paper, in good state.)   I, i-ii, 40.

140. **1600.** Dec. 13.—Charter by the same to the same, in similar terms. Witnessed and signed by William Duncan, bailie, Thomas Traill, and David Wedderburn, burgesses. (Latin, parchment, in good state ; seal gone.)   I, i-ii, 41.

141. **1600.** Dec. 13.—Instrument of sasine in favour of John Traill, burgess of Dundee, son and heir of the deceased Alexander Traill, of a tenement of land formerly belonging to the said A. T. lying on the north side of the Argylegate between the lands of Mr. Alexander Wedderburn, and the heirs of Robert W., his brother.   II, viii, 11.

142. **1600.** Dec. 13.—Contract between John Traill, burgess of Dundee, and Mr. Alexander Wedderburn, clerk thereof, for the redemption by the latter of an annual rent of 8 bolls victual out of the mains of Kingany, &c. Signed at Dundee. (Scroll of two sheets, fair state.)   VIII, ii, 11.

143. **1600.** Dec. 13.—Contract between Mr. Alexander Wedderburn, clerk of Dundee, and John Traill, burgess thereof, whereby the latter acknowledges the receipt from the former of 400 merks, due to him by William Guthrie of Kingany, and renounces an annual rent of 8 bolls victual from the lands of Kingany, and agrees to conditions anent the redemption of the said lands for 4,000 merks. At Dundee. David Wedderburn burgess is a witness.   VIII, ii, 17. (One sheet and a half, in fair state. A note in the hand of Mr. Alexander records Traill's subsequent renunciation of the lands on 13 Aug, 1601. See post No. 148.)

144. **1600.** Dec. 13.—Renewal of a Reversion by John Traill, bailie of Dundee, in favour of William Guthrie of Kingany and Elizabeth Fethie his spouse, over the mains of Kingany for 4000 merks, payable within four days of any Whitsunday "besyd the pulpit within the Lyttil East Kirk of Dundee," and dated 6 Oct., 1600, (viii, iii, 1) made in favour of Mr. Alexander Wedderburn, now heritable proprietor of the lands of Kingany. Dated at Dundee. (English, parchment.)   VIII, iii, 10.

144ᵃ. **1600.** Dec. 15.—Sasine following on the charter (ante No. 131) and attested by Robert Wedderburn, notary, and John Pattou, notary ; dated at Dundee. (Latin, parchment.)   VIII, iii, 11.

145. **1600.** Dec. 15.—Sasine in same terms following on the charter (ante No. 132) and attested as in No. 144ᵃ. (Latin, parchment.)   VIII, iii, 12.

146. **1600.** Dec. 15.—Sasine following on precept of clare constat by William, Earl of Angus, for infefting William Guthrie of Kingany in the lands of Kingany, Carneton, &c. as heir to the late William Guthrie of Kingany, his great-grandfather. The precept (viii, iv, 30) is dated at Canongate 25 Nov., 1600, and has the seal of the Earl entire ; the sasine is dated 15 Dec. at Dundee, and is witnessed by David and Robert Wedderburn ; the notary also being Robert Wedderburn, who appends his docket. (Parchment.)   VIII, iv, 31.

147. **1601.** Feb. 13.—Inhibition by Mr. Alex. Wedderburn, clerk of Dundee, v. William Guthrie that he should not sell his lands in default of the complainer. Dated at Edinburgh. (One sheet, fair condition.)   VIII, ii, 12.

D

Scrymgeour-
Wedderburn
Papers.

148. **1601.** June 11.—Extract registered discharge (20 May, 1600) by Peter Rolland of Dundee, to William Hunter, of Dundee, his wife and son, for 3320 merks, in complete payment of 6320 merks for the alienation of the Grange of Barrie. Witnessed by Mr. Alexander Wedderburn of Kingennie, clerk of Dundee. Registered at Edinburgh 11 June, 1601.   VIII, x , 13.

149. **1601.** Aug. 13.—Renunciation by John Traill, burgess of Dundee, in favour of Mr. Alexander Wedderburn, of the reversion over the mains of Kingany (see No. 144), now redeemed for 4000 merks. Dated at Dundee. Robert Wedderburn, notary, is a witness. (English, parchment.)   VIII, iii, 13.

150. **1601.** Aug. 13.—Renunciation by the said John Traill of the said reversion (No. 144 supra). (Extract. English, parchment.)   VIII, iii, 14.

151. **1602.** Jan. 27.—Receipt by Mr. John Traill to Mr. Alexander W., clerk of Dundee, for £155. 9. 4. as the price of 72 sheep. Dated at Dundee. (One leaf, fair stae)   VIII, ii, 13.

152. **1602.** May (?) —Discharge same to same for 4000 merks for the granter's right to Kingany. Dated at Dundee, written by the grantee. (One sheet, fair.)   VIII, ii, 13ª.

153. **1602.** May 21.—Discharge by James Crichton, assignee of Sir James Scrymgeour of Dudop, Knt., with consent of David Wedderburn, chaplain to the said Sir James, to Alex. Littlejohn of Dundee for 20/- rent of N. Seagate lands occupied by the said Littlejohn and belonging to the goodman of Kirktoun. Dated at Dundee.   VIII, xi, 16.

154. **1603.** May 4.—Discharge by John Yeaman of Dundee to Gilbert Scrymgeour, brother german of John S. of Kirktoun. Witnessed by Mr. Alexander Wedderburn, common clerk of Dundee.   VIII, ix, 11.

155. **1603.** July 10.—License by David, Earl of Crawford to Mr. Alexander Wedderburn of Kingenny, whereby the Earl "for services, &c., done to us by Mr. A W. of Kingenny, common clerk of Dundee, grants and gives license, tolerance and liberty to the said Mr. Alexander his heirs and their tenants and occupiers of the lands of Kingenny to pasture or caus to pasture their goods and bestial within all the bounds of our muirs, firths, and myres of our baronie of Downy, lying within the sheriffdom of Forfar, and that yearly and ilk year hereafter following, and sicklike to caus win and lead away furth of our mosses and muirs of the said barony, turfs and peats to their own proper use and furniture only, when they think expedient, Discharging therefore all our bailies, grieves, and officers of all troubling, molesting or making impediment to the said Mr. Alexander and his forsaids in the using of the said liberty, privilege and tolerance." Dated at Dundee ; signed by the Earl before Mr. George Halyburton of Kelour, David Lindsay of Corrat hill, Mr. James Elliot, minister at Fynneltone, and David Wedderburn, burgess of Dundee. At the foot is written "The wretter was the clerk him selff." (One sheet of paper, in good condition.)   VIII, ii, 14.

156. **1603.** July 10.—Modern transcript of No. 155.   VIII, ii, 14ª.

157. **1604.** Feb. 2.—Discharge by David, James, Peter, Margaret, and Catherine Wedderburne, brothers and sisters of the late William Wedderburne, burgess of Dundee, narrating that Mr. Alexander Wedderburn, common clerk of Dundee, had paid to the said William "in his awin tyme" the sum of 300 merks "quhich fell to the said umquhile William as bairnis pairt of geir threw deceiss of his father and mother, and lykwayis the soume of 200 merkis . . . for redemptione frome him his airis and assignayis of ane annual rent of sevine bollis victuall quhairin the said umquhile William was alledgeit to be infeft be umquhile Alexander Wedderburn, common clerk of the said burgh, his father," furth of the half lands of Balruthrie, sometime pertaining to David Lessellis, lying in the shire of Perth ; whereupon the said William gave a discharge containing renuneiation to the said Mr. Alexander, of date 13 August, 1602. The granters now ratify the said discharge which is also specially ratified by the said James Wedderburne because it was granted at his desire. Signed by David and James Wedderburne, witnessed by James Durham of Pitkerro, &c.   I, i ii, 42.
(English, on paper, in good condition.)

158. **1604.** Mar. 29.—Letter from King James VI. to the Commissioners of Burghs **Scrymgeour-** anent the nomination of Alexander, eldest son of Alexander Wedderburn of Kingennie, **Wedderburn** as clerk of Dundee in event of his father's death. This letter is set out in the account **Papers.** of Alexander, second of Kingennie, in Vol. 1. (On paper, in perfect state.) I, i-ii, 43.

159. **1606.** Jan. 4.—Charter by Sir James Scrymgeour of Dudop to James Fethie, burgess of Dundee, of a shop or booth in Dundee. Signed by the granter, whose seal, in good condition, showing the Scrymgeour crest (a hand grasping a scimitar), is still attached to the charter, and entire. Witnessed and signed by David Wedderburn and Robert Wedderburn, merchant. (Small document on vellum, ink very faded.) IV, ii, 5.

160. **1606.** June 18.—Discharge by Barbara Wedderburn, relict of the late Peter Imbrie, burgess of Dundee, to Mr. Alexander Wedderburn, clerk of Dundee, on payment by him to her of 350 merks in full satisfaction of everything due from him to her or Peter Imbrie, her son. Signed by her "with her hand at the pen led by Robert Wedderburn, notary." (One piece of paper, somewhat torn.) VIII, ii, 15.

161. **1606.** Sept. 15.—Discharge by Robert Wedderburn, burgess, merchant in Dundee, to Alexander Wedderburn clerk for certain sums of money. Signed "Robert Wedderburn with my hand." (One small piece of paper.) VIII, ii, 16.

162. **1607.** May 24.—Discharge by George Campbell of Crunane, to Mr. Alexander Wedderburn, common clerk of Dundee for 2500 merks scots, in complete payment of the sum of 5000 merks promised by the said Mr. Alexander to the granter in name of tocher with Elizabeth Wedderburn his lawful daughter, now spouse to Colin Campbell, the granter's eldest son, procreate betwixt him and Elizabeth Beatoun his spouse, and that in virtue of marriage contract between the parties, dated . . . . 16 . . The granter also becomes bound to cause the said Colin and Elizabeth his spouse to renounce in favour of Mr. Alexander and his heirs, all lands and annual rents wherein the said Elizabeth was infeft by her said father before her marriage ; and all legacies left to her by the deceased George Spens, her great grandsire (see ante No. 64). Dated at Dundee. Witnessed by Sir William Graham of Claverhouse, Knight, Alexander Bishop of Brechin, Archibald Campbell of Persie, Patrick Wedderburne, burgess of Dundee, and Thomas Wichtane, servitor to the said Mr. Alexander. Signed by the granter, Sir William Graham, &c. Endorsed by Kingennie, "George Campbell of Crunane's acquitance of fyve thousand merks in compleit payment of my dochters Tocher." See facsimile opposite p. 13. I, i-ii, 44. (English, paper, in perfect state.

163. **1607.** April 29.—Charter by Sir James Scrymgeour of Dudop, Knight, provost of Dundee, in favour of Robert Guthrie, miller, burgess there, and Christina Cockburn his spouse, of a tenement in the said burgh. Dated at Dudop 29 April 1607. Signed by the granter, and witnessed (but not signed) by David, James, and Peter Wedderburn, burgesses of Dundee. (Small vellum ink faded.) IV, ii, 6.

164. **1607.** Sept. 14.—Sasine in favour of John Traill, smith, burgess of Dundee, of a tenement resigned by James Fermorer, burgess there, and — Nairne his spouse, lying on the N. side of the Flukergait, at the N. end of the vennel called Seres Wynd between the lands of Oliver Powrie on the West, and the said vennel on the East. Done at the said tenement 14 Sept. 1607. David Wedderburn, Alexander Nairne, &c., are witnesses, and Mr. Alexander Wedderburn, clerk of the Court, is notary, and adds his docket and symbol. See facsimile opposite p. 13. I, i-ii, 45. (Latin, small parchment, in good state.)

165. **1608.** May 9.—Discharge by Mr. Alexander Wedderburn, common clerk of Dundee, to Mr. John Seharp of Houstoun, advocate, for £1000 scots received by Mr. Alexander Wedderburn on behalf of Elizabeth Wedderburn, lawfull daughter to the late John Wedderburn, portioner in Cragie Hiltou, and Margaret Strathauchin his wife, in respect of a contract between the said John Seharp and John Wedderburn of date

12 Nov. 1594. The discharge is dated 14 May 1602, and signed by Mr. A. Wedderburn. There is a footnote of approval by Elizabeth Wedderburn and James Kynnaird her spouse, dated March 1608, and two endorsements signed by them and John Kinnaird of that ilk, and both dated 9 May 1608. (Paper, good state.)　I, i-ii, 45ᵃ.

166. **1608.** May 22.—Discharge by Henry Ramsay of Ardownie, as factor to James, Lord Balmerino, in favour of Mr. Alexander Wedderburn, clerk of Dundee, for £80 scots price of the teind sheaves of Kingennie. (One piece of paper.)　VIII, ii, 18.

167. **1610.** (date blank).—An inventory of the writs and evidents delivered by Mr. Alexander Wedderburn, clerk of Dundee, of the lands of Kingennie, to be produced in the action by the Earl of Angus v. certain of his tenants. There are nine documents named beginning with a charter of Kingennie granted (1 Dec. 1511) by Archibald, Earl of Angus, to William Guthre and Janet Arbuthnot his wife, and including a sasine (1600) under the hand of Robert Wedderburn, notary, and a charter by William Guthre to Alexander Wedderburn and Helen Ramsay his wife, and other titles of Kingennie down to 1610. (One short of paper.)　VIII, ii, 20.

168. **1610.** May 10.—Tack of the teinds of Kingennie granted by James, Lord Balmerino, to Mr. Alexander Wedderburn of Kingennie. Signed by the granter.　VIII, ii, 19. (One sheet of paper.)

169. **1610.** May 12.— Sasine given to Christina Mathew, daughter of George Mathew, burgess of Dundee, of a tenement belonging to the latter. Mr. Alexander Wedderburn, clerk of the Court of Dundee, is notary and appends his docket and symbol. (Latin, small parchment, in fair state.)　I, i-ii, 46.

170. **1610.** July 27.—Confirmation by Mr. William Oliphant of Newtoun, advocate to our sovereign lord the King, and commissioner for William, Earl of Angus, of the charter (No. 132 ante). Dated at Edinburgh. Mr. Alexander Wedderburn, lawful son of Mr. Alexander Wedderburn the granter, is a witness. The seal of the Earl is attached and remains entire but worn. (Latin, parchment.)　VIII, iii, 15.

171. **1610.** Sasine following on the charter (No. 132 ante). Mr. James Wedderburn, son of Mr. Alexander Wedderburn, clerk of Dundee, is attorney for his father. David Guthrie in Kingany is a witness. (Latin, parchment.)　VIII, iii, 16.

171ᵃ. **1610.** Oct. 22.—Sasine on cognition of Elizabeth Duncan as lawful daughter and heir of the late John Duncan, burgess of Dundee, in an E. Wellgate tenement of her said father. David Wedderburn, burgess of Dundee, is witness, and Mr. James Wedderburn is notary. (Parchment.)　VIII, xiv, 26².

172. **1610.** Nov. 6.—Charter by Mr. Alexander Wedderburn of Kingany, clerk of Dundee, in favour of Mr. Alexander Wedderburn, his eldest son, his heirs and assignees, of all and haill the lands of Kingany and Cairuton of Kingany otherwise called Crymbills, with the manor place, mill, &c., reserving to the granter and to Helen Ramsay his spouse, their frank tenement or life rent of the same, to hold from William, Earl of Angus, in fee and heritage, paying therefor yearly at the feast of the Assumption of the Virgin one sparrow hawk, if asked, with other services due and wont. Contains a precept of sasine and is dated at Dundee 6 Nov. 1610. Witnesses, George Campbell of Crumane, George his son, Mr. David Lindsay, minister of Dundee, Mr. James Robertsone, also minister there, &c. (Seal gone; Latin, parchment.)　VIII, iii, 17.

173. **1610.** Nov. 17.—Confirmation by Mr. William Oliphant of Newtoun, King's advocate, and commissioner for the Earl of Angus, of the foregoing charter. Dated at Edinburgh. (Latin, parchment; seal of the Earl appended.)　VIII, iii, 18.

174. **1610.** Nov. 26.—Sasine following on No. 172. (Latin, parchment.)　VIII, iii, 19.

175. **1612** April 15.—Instrument on the cognition by James Boytar, bailic of Dundee, Scrymgeour-of Alexander Clayhills, as son and heir of the late Peter Clayhills, merchant burgess **Wedderburn** of Dundee, in several annual rents, including one furth of the N. Argylegait land of **Papers.** John Isak, deceased (bounded N. by that of the late James Goldman and Patrick Wedderburn), whereupon the said A. C., in implement of an obligation granted by him to Mr. Alexander Wedderburn, clerk of Dundee, for £500 paid to him by the said Mr. A. W., resigns the said subject in favour of the said Mr. A. W., reserving the life rent of Margaret Wedderburn, mother of the resigner. VIII, xiv, 26ᵇ.

176. **1612** May 16.—Instrument on the resignation by Peter Man, merchant, burgess of Dundee, of a certain annual rent in favour of James Wedderburn, merchant, burgess Dundee, and David Wedderburn, burgess there, as attorney for Cristina Lovell, spouse of the said James W., in conjunct fee, &c. Mr. Alexander Wedderburn, clerk of Dundee, is notary. VIII, xiv, 27.

177. **1612** May 18.—Charter by Mr. Alexander Wedderburn of Kingany, clerk of the court of Dundee and Mr. Alexander Wedderburn, his son and apparent heir, in implement of a contract of marriage (dated at Dundee 3 April 1612) between Mr. James Fotheringham, rector of Balumbic, John Scrymgeour of Kirkton his son-in-law, Gilbert Scrymgeour, brother german, and Magdalen Scrymgeour, daughter of the said John, with advice and consent of the said Mr. J. F. her grandfather, and the said J. S. her father, on the one part, and the granters with the consent of Helen Ramsay, wife of the said Mr. Alexander elder, on the other part, whereby they grant to the said Helen Ramsay in liferent, the lands of Wester Gourdie, with the backseatts and teind sheaves thereof, lying in the lordship of Scone, and within the sheriffdom of Forfar, and that in satisfaction to the said Helen of her liferent or conjunct fee of the lands of Kingany, with the mills, &c., in the said sheriffdom, which she in virtue of the said contract renounced in favour of the said Mr. Alexander, younger, her son, and the said Magdalen Scrymgeour his future spouse, to be holden of the granters as in liferent and free blench ferme for payment of one penny yearly. Dated at Dundee and contains precept of sasine. Witnesses David Wedderburn, James Boyak, maltman, &c. Signed by them and by both granters. See facsimile opposite p. 13. (Latin, parchment, in perfect state.) I, i-ii, 47.

178. **1612** May 18.—Charter by Alexander Wedderburn of Kingany, town clerk of Dundee, in favour of Mr. Alexander Wedderburn his son and heir, of all and haill his lands of Wester Gourdie, with the pertinents together with the teind sheaves of the same, lying in the lordship of Scone and sheriffdom of Forfar, Reserving the liferent of the said lands to himself and Helen Ramsay his spouse, and that in implement of contract of marriage entered into between Mr. James Fotheringham, rector of Ballumbie, John Scrymgeour of Kirktoun, his son-in-law, Gilbert Scrymgeour brother, and Magdalen Scrymgeour, daughter of the said John, with consent of the said James Fotheringham, grandfather of the said Magdalen, and John Scrymgeour of Kirktoun, her father, on the one part, and the said Alexander Wedderburn of Kingany, Helen Ramsay, and Mr. Alexander Wedderburn, son and heir of the granter, on the other part, &c., containing precept of sasine. Dated at Dundee. David Wedderburn is a witness. On the back is written "XIX May, 1612. Witnesses W. Gray, notar, David Smyth, skipper in Dundie, David Myln thair, and Wm. Philp in Gourdie. John Liddell in Gourdie, baillie, gaif heritable stait and seasing of ye landis respective within wrettine, to Mr. Alexander Wedderburn younger present, according to the tenour of ye chartour and precept within contenit." II, ii, 6.

179. **1612** June 2.—Part of a tack by William Blair of Balgillo to Mr. James Fotheringham of the teind sheaves of the half lands of Glenboyc, Dated at Dundee. Written by James Scrymgeour, lawful son to Mr. Alexander W., clerk of Dundee. (One leaf, fair state ; the first part of the tack is missing.) VI, xi, 12.

180. **1613** May (?).—Discharge by Mr. William Wedderburn, minister at Dundee, to Alexander Wedderburn, clerk thereof, his father-in-law, on payment to him by the said A. W. of the tocher of 3000 merks due to the said Mr. William W. by virtue of

Scrymgeour-
Wedderburn
Papers.

his marriage contract dated 1 June 1611, and made between the said Mr. Alexander W. and his daughter Magdalen of the one part, and the said Mr. William W. and his father Alexander W, burgess in Cupar, on the other part. Dated at Dundee, and signed by the said spouses William and Magdalen, and by witnesses, including David Lindsay, minister at Dundee, and Mr. James Wedderburn, lawful son to the said Mr. Alexander W. the clerk. See facsimile opposite p. 24.   I, i-ii, 48ᴬ.
(Paper, in good state.)

181.   **1613.** July 23.—Discharge by Mr. Alexander Wedderburn, clerk of Dundee, to Mr. James Fotheringhame, persone of Ballumbie, for 5500 merks of tocher promised in the marriage contract (dated at Dundee 3 April, 1612), made between the said Mr. J. F. and John Scrymgeour of Kirkton on behalf of Magdalen S. "oye" to the said Mr. James F. and daughter to the said J. S. on the one part, and the granter, Helen Ramsay, his spouse, and Mr. Alexander W., their son and apparent heir, on the other part (ante Nos. 177-78). Dated at Dundee. Signed by the granter and by his said son as witness. (English, on paper, in good state.   I, i-ii, 48.

182.   **1614.** Jan. 13.—Sasine on precept by the provost, bailies, &c. of Dundee to John Schairp of Ballindoch, son and heir of the late Mr. Alexander Schairp, brother german of the late Sir William Schairp of Ballindoch, of the lands of Hiltoun of Craigie conquest by the said Sir John from James Scrymgeour of Glaswell, &c. The deed is written by Mr. James Wedderburn notary, son of Mr. Alexander Wedderburn clerk of Dundee, who with Mr. Alexander W., councillor, witnesses it.   VIII, viv, 27ᴬ.

183.   **1614.** Jan 31.—Bond by William Durham of Umaquhie to Mr. Alexander Wedderburn of Kingennie. Witnessed by (among others) "Pd (Peter) Wedderburn, lawful son of the said Mr. Alexander" but not signed by him. (One sheet of paper.) VIII, ii, 21.

184.   **1614.** June 16-18.—Confirmation by Mr. Peter Hay of Nauchtane, of a charter of this date by John Hay of Sandfurd and Mr. James Hay his son and heir, with consent of Agnes Barclay, spouse to the said Mr. Peter Hay, in favour of William Goldman, merchant in Dundee, and Marion Maisterton his spouse in conjunct fee, &c. of the lands of Nether Sandfurd, &c. Written by Mr. James Wedderburn, lawful son to Mr. Alexander W., clerk of Dundee, and witnessed by him and his father. Dated at Dundee, Langraw, Kynneir and Sandfurd. The confirmation is dated at Nauchtane 4 Oct., 1638. (Vellum, in good state.)   IV, ii, 7.

185.   **1614.** June 24.—Tack by John, Lord of Balmerino, heritable proprietor of the Kirk of Monyfuith, and of all the lands lying in the parish thereof, with consent of Sir Alexander Drummond of Medhop, Knight, one of the senators of the College of Justice, to Mr. Alexander Wedderburn of Kingany, clerk of Dundee, of the teind sheaves of his said lands of Kingany, &c., in the parish of Monyfuith and shire of Forfar, during his lifetime, paying yearly therefor £20. At Edinburgh and Carse 24 June and 9 Sept. 1614.   VIII, xi, 18.

186.   **1615.** May 18.—Discharge by Alexander Wedderburn, son and heir of the deceased Robert Wedderburn younger, merchant burgess of Dundee, as having right from Peter Imbrie, son and heir of Peter Imbrie, merchant burgess of Dundee, to all that the said Peter could claim of his said father's, or of Barbara Wedderburn his mother's geir, for £80 received from Mr. Alexander Wedderburn, clerk of Dundee, in full of the said geir received by the said Mr. Alexander W. after decease of the said Barbara, from——Annand of Persie. This discharge is warranted by James Thomson, litster, burgess of Dundee, as father-in-law to the granter. Dated at Dundee. Witnessed by David Wedderburn burgess, Peter W., son of the said Mr. Alexander W. &c. VIII, ii, 22.
(One sheet, fair. The term father-in-law here signifies not wife's father, but stepfather, or rather stepmother's husband, J. Thomson having married Elizabeth Hering, third wife and relict of Alexander's father, Robert W.)

187.   **1615.** Dec. 2.—Contract of marriage between Thomas Halyburton (eldest son of Thomas Halyburton, dean of gild of Dundee) and Margaret, daughter of Mr. Alexander Wedderburn, clerk of Dundee. Her tocher is 4000 merks. Signed by Mr.

Alexander Wedderburn, Thomas Halyburton, father and son, and, as witnesses, by James Wedderburn, brother of Mr. Alexander, and James W., son to Mr. Alexander. Mr. William Wedderburn, minister at Dundee, is also a witness but does not sign.

VIII, ii, 23.

(One sheet of paper, somewhat torn. This contract seems never to have been acted on, as some fifteen months later a fresh contract of marriage was made between the same parties. See post Nos. 192-93.)

188. **1616.** March 22.—Charter by Patrick Wedderburn, merchant burgess of Dundee, and Alexander Wedderburne his son and heir apparent, with consent of Elizabeth Low, wife of the said Patrick, and of Barbara Auchinlek, wife of the said Alexander, in favour of Mr. Alexander Wedderburn, clerk of Dundee, his heirs and assignees, heritably, of a foreland in Dundee on the S. side of the Marketgate between the lands sometime of Alexander Gray on the east, the lands formerly of Thomas Chyhills on the south, the cemetery of the church of Saint Clements, and the passage which leads from the east side of the Tolbooth to the part of the said burgh on the west, and the said Marketgate on the north, to be holden from the granters, of John Scrymgeour of Dudop, in fee heritage and free burgage : rendering therefor to the Constable of Dundee, the service of burgh due and wont ; also to the chaplain of St. Serf, seven merks and 20 pennies yearly. Contains precept of sasine. Dated at Dundee. Witnesses John Scrymgeour of Dudop, Mr. George Halyburton of Keillour, Thomas Wiehtan, notary, &c. Signed by the granters and their wives, and by the above and other witnesses. I, i-ii, 49.
(Latin, parchment, in good condition, but all the seals, originally three or four, gone.)

189. **1616.** May 17.—Disposition by Patrik Wedderburne, merchant burgess of Dundee, and Alexander Wedderburn his son, with consent of Elizabeth Low, spouse of the said Patrik, and of Barbara Auchinlek, spouse of the said Alexander, in favour of Mr. Alexander Wedderburne, common clerk of Dundee, for the sum of 2000 merks paid by him, of that "great foir land and tenement up and down, bak and foir," lying on the south side of the Marketgate, between the lands of Thomas Gray on the east, the common passage that leads from the Marketgate to St. Clement's Kirkyard on the west, the backland of the heirs of Robert Fairwedder on the south, and the Marketgate on the north : to be holden of John Scrymgeour of Dudop, on payment of seven merks to the chaplain of St. Serf's chaplainry. Dated at Dundee. Witnessed by Mr. William Fergussone, bailie of Dundee, Mr. John Ramsay, persone of Tealling, William Fergussone, son to the said Mr. W. F., Mr. John Dynmuir, notary and Thomas Fyiff. Signed by the granters and their wives, and by all the witnesses. See facsimile opposite p. 24. (English, on paper, in perfect state.) I, i-ii, 50.

190. **1616.** May 28.—Discharge by Margaret Guthrie, daughter of the late David Guthrie, burgess of Dundee, and the late Barbara Wedderburn his wife, with consent of Thomas Wal'ace her spouse, and also by John and Isobell Walkee, their eldest son and daughter, to Mr. Alexander Wedderburn, clerk of Dundee, for payment of various sums of money. (One sheet of paper.) VIII, ii, 24.

191. **1616.** December 21.—Discharge by William Tyrie of Drumkilbo, to Mr. Alexander Wedderburn, clerk of Dundee, and the late Mr. William Wedderburn, sometime minister of Dundee. It refers to Mr. William as alive in 1615, and is witnessed by Gilbert Scrymgeour, brother german to John Scrymgeour of Kirkton and others. (One sheet of paper.) VIII, ii, 25.

192. **1617.** Feb. 25.—Contract of marriage between Thomas Halyburton, bailie of Dundee, and Thomas H. his eldest son on the one part, and Mr. Alexander Wedderburn, clerk of Dundee, and Margaret W. his lawful daughter on the other part, for the marriage of the said Thomas Halyburton, younger, and the said Margaret ; in contemplation of which the said Thomas Halyburton elder becomes bound to infeft his son and the said Margaret in her virginity and the survivor of them and the heirs to be gotten between them in that great tenement with yard &c., lying on the South side of Our Ladygate (and bounded as in the contract specified), and also in another tenement on the N. side of the said gate, reserving to the said T. H. elder and Agnes

Guthrie, his spouse, their liferent in the said first-named tenement. Also the said
T. H. becomes bound to provide and employ by the advice of the said Mr. Alexander
W. the sum of 8000 merks for the behoof of the said pair, and to "wair" and bestow
on lands the sum of 12,000 merks for the said purpose, and to give instantly to his
said son Thomas 1000 merks "to be imployed by him in his tred and handling." The
said Mr. Alexander W. becomes bound to pay 4000 merks of tocher with his said
daughter Margaret. Dated at Dundee 25 Feb. 1617. Witnesses Andrew Kynnaird,
Mr. Alexander Wedderburn, younger, Mr. James Wedderburn, lawful son of the said
Mr. Alexander, James Wedderburn, merchant burgess of Dundee, &c. Signed by
Thomas H., elder and younger, Mr. Alexander W., elder and younger, Mr. James W.
and others. See faesimile opposite.   i, i-ii, 51.
    (English, on paper, in fair state, but a little torn and mended ; two sheets originally joined, but
now separate. See ante No. 187.)

193. **1617.** Feb. 25.—Instrument of sasine following on the above contract of marriage,
whereby sasine of the said premises is given to the said Thomas Halyburton younger,
and to the said Margaret W., his affianced spouse, now in her pure virginity, in
conjunct fee, and to the heirs to be begotten between them. Mr. James W , son of
the said Mr. Alexander, acts on behalf of the said Margaret his sister. Done on the
said lands about the fifth hour after noon on the above date. Witnesses the said Mr.
Alexander, Andrew Kynnaird, &c.   Mr. John Dynmuir is notary.   i, i-ii, 52.
    (Latin, small parchment, in good state)

194. **1617.** Sept. 18.—Obligation by Mr. William Fergusson, dean of gild of Dundee,
with consent of William Fergusson, his eldest son and apparent heir, whereby, upon
consideration of the benefits which the said Mr. William received by his marriage
with Catherine Wedderburne now his spouse, and for the love which he bears to
Magdalen Fergusson, lawful daughter procreated betwixt him and the said Catharine,
he becomes bound to infeft the said Magdalen and the heirs of her body, which
failing the heirs of the said William to be procreated betwixt him and Helen Dunean
his future spouse, in an annual rent of 400 merks furth of the lands of Balbeuchlie
and temple lands thereof, with teinds, &c. in the barony of Dunkeld and shire of
Forfar : reserving the granter's life rent and that of his said spouse. Dated at
Dundee.   Witnesses, Robert Murray, one of his Majesty's guard, William Halyburtone, A. Wedderburn, Peter Wedderburne, burgess, and Mr. James Wedderburn,
lawful son of Mr. Alexander W., clerk of Dundee. There are four Wedderburn
signatures, viz. : that of A. Wedderburn younger, who signs the docket of registration, and those of the clerk and his two younger sons, James, and Peter.
See facsimile opposite.   i, i-ii, 53.
    (English, on two sheets of paper, originally joined together, in bad condition. That the Peter W.
named as witness is son to Mr. Alexander, the clerk, is proved by the signature being the same as that
to the next document, where he is expressly so designed.)

195. **1617.** Dec. 20.—Discharge by Mr. Alexander Ramsay, son and heir of the late
George Ramsay of Kirkton of Balmerinoeh, burgess of Dundee, to Mr. Alexander
Wedderburn, clerk of Dundee, for the haill writs and evidents received and intromitted
with by him at any time bygone, and made to the said umquhile George and his
authors and predecessors concerning the security of the lands of Kirktoun of Balmerinoeh lying in the Sheriffdom of Fife : also the granter is content that the
said Mr. Alexander W. deliver to Mr. James Wedderburn, his son, all the writs
and evidents now in his hands concerning the security of the granter's burghal lands,
lying on the south side of Our Ladygate of Dundee, providing that the said Mr.
Alexander W. take a discharge to the granter from the said Mr. James on the
receipt thereof, conform to the contract between the granter and the said Mr. James
anent the disposition of his principal inner lodgings. Dated at Edinburgh. Witnessed
and signed by John Dickson, merchant burgess of Edinburgh, and Peter Wedderburn,
son of the said Mr. Alexander   See facsimile opp. p. 32.   i, i-ii, 54.
    (English, on paper, in perfect state.)

196. **1618.** May 22.—Sasine on resignation by James Brown of Dundee and
Jonet Strathauchin his spouse, in favour of James Walker of Dundee and Helen
Symson, his spouse, of a S. Murraygate tenement. The bailie is "an honourable man,

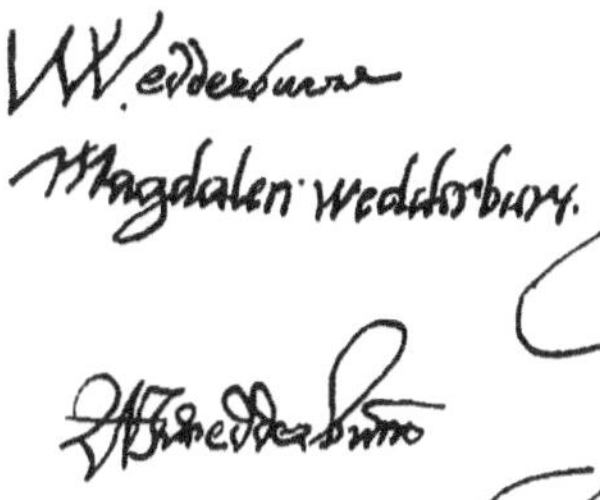

SIGNATURES TO NO. 180

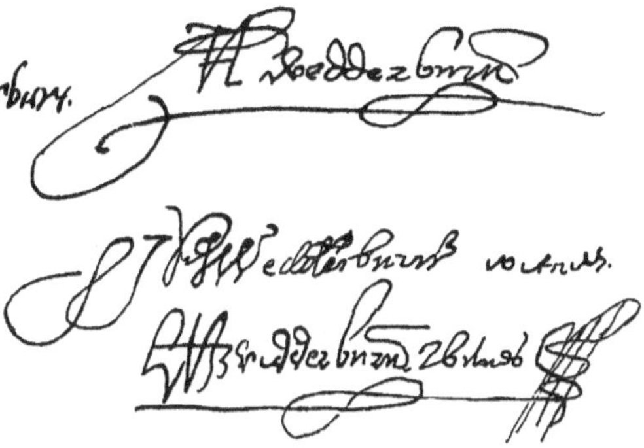

THREE OF THE SIGNATURES TO NO. 192

FOUR OF THE SIGNATURES TO NO. 184

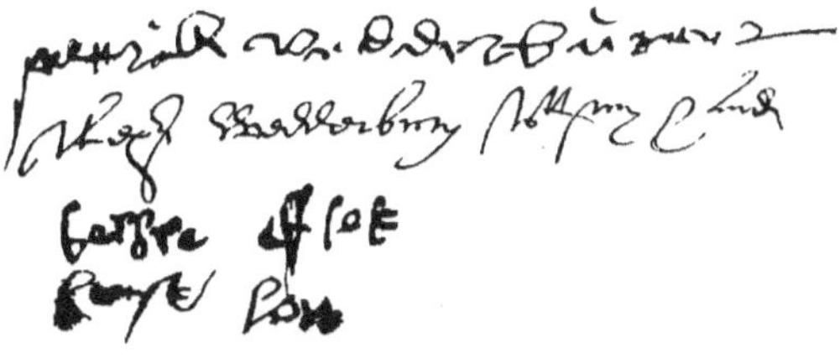

SIGNATURES TO NO. 189

Mr. Alexander Wedderburne younger, one of the bailies of Dundee," Mr. Alexander Wedderburne, clerk, being notary, David Wedderburne, burgess, attorney for Helen Synuson, and Alexander Wedderburne, merchant, witness (Latin, parchment.) VIII, i, 20.

Scrymgeour-Wedderburn Papers.

197. **1618.** July 9.—Contract between John, Lord Balmerinoch, heritable proprietor of the Kirk of parish of Monyfuith on the one part, and Mr. Alexander Wedderburn of Kingany, clerk of the burgh of Dundee, on the other part, whereby for the sum of £1000 paid by the latter, the said lord dispones to him heritably, without redemption, reversion, or regress, all and sundry the teind sheaves of the lands of Kingany, with the mill lands thereof, and that pendicle thereof called the Crimblis, to be holden by two manners of infeftment, namely, one of the said lord in free blench, the said Mr. Alexander and his foresaids furnishing yearly and proportionately the bread and wine for the Communion celebrated in the Kirk of Monyfuith, and relieving the said lord of all the King's taxations to be imposed on the said teind sheaves, and also of "beitting and repairing of the fabrike of the said Kirk" proportionately; and the other to be holden of the King for the yearly payment of the blench duty; and the said lord becomes bound to warrant and defend the said subjects to the said Mr. Alexander and his foresaids, from his lordship's own facts and deeds, and also from the facts and deeds of Sir Alexander Drummond of Medop, Knight, one of the senators of the College of Justice, and whereas by contract of alienation dated 3rd and registered in the Books of Council 5th February 1614, James, Marquis of Hamilton disponed to the said Sir Alexander Drummond the teind sheaves and vicarage teinds of the said Kirk and parish, which right was transferred by the said Sir Alexander to the said lord, he, the said lord, hereby transfers the same with all other securities to the said Mr. Alexander Wedderburn. Witnesses Mr. James Durham apparent of Pitkerro, &c. Signed by Lord Balmerino and Mr. Alexander Wedderburn. (English, on paper, in fair condition.) I, i-ii, 55.

198. **1618.** July 9.—Tack of the teinds of Kingennie by John, Lord Balmerino, to Mr. Alexander Wedderburn of Kingennie, clerk of Dundee, for 101 years. VIII, ii, 27. (One sheet of paper.)

199. **1618.** July 9.—Charter by John Lord Balmerinoch to Mr. Alexander Wedderburne, of Kingany, clerk of Dundee (following on the above contract), of the teind sheaves of the lands of Kingennie, Crymbles, &c., to hold of the Crown in fee and heritage and free blench for the yearly payment of two shillings, &c. Contains precept of sasine and is dated at Edinburgh. Mr. James Durham, apparent of Pitkerro is a witness. (Seal gone. Latin parchment.) VIII, iii, 20.

200. **1618.** July 9.—Duplicate of above charter. I, i-ii, 56.

201. **1618.** Sept. 8.—Instrument of sasine following on the above charter (Nos. 199, 200). Done on the ground of the lands on 1st, and recorded in the particular register of Sasines at Dundee, 8 Sept. 1618. (Latin, parchment ; ink faded.) I, i-ii, 57.

202. **1618.** July 22.—Discharge by Peter Wedderburn, lawful son of Mr. Alexander Wedderburn, clerk of Dundee, to Helen Ramsay, spouse of the said Mr. Alexander, and mother of the said Peter, for 800 merks scots, whereof 300 merks were delivered to him by his said parents of their own goodwill and benevolence and the remaining 500 merks were promised to him in manner and for the causes contained in the contract of marriage made betwixt the said Mr. Alexander, taking burden on himself for the said Peter on the one part, and Helen Lovell, daughter of the late John Lovell, bailie of Dundee, with consent of her curators and friends of the other part, of date —— 16—. Dated at Dundee. Witnesses, James Wedderburn, merchant, burgess of Dundee, and Thomas Wichtan, notary. I, i ii, 58.

(English, on paper, in perfect state. Peter Wedderburn's signature is the same as that to Nos. 194 and 195 ante. See facsimile opp. p. 32.)

203. **1618.** Aug. 13.—Discharge by Sir John Scrymgeour of Dudope, Knight, in name of Andrew S. his lawful son, to John Scrymgeour of Kirktoun, in respect of the estate of the deceased Gilbert Scrymgeour, brother to Kirkton. Witnessed by Thomas Fyiff, servitor to Mr. Alexander Wedderburne, clerk of Dundee. Dated at Dudope.

(English paper, fair state.) VI, iii, 5.

E

204. **1620**. Jan. 19.—Agreement between Thomas Halyburton elder, merchant burgess of Dundee, on the one part, and Thomas H. younger, his eldest son, merchant burgess of Dundee, with consent of Mr. Alexander Wedderburne, clerk of Dundee, on the other part, anent the investment of 12,000 merks by the said Thomas H. elder, with advice of the said Mr. A. W., in terms of the marriage contract (see ante No. 192) between the parties. (One sheet.)   VIII, ii, 26.

205. **1620**, Feb. 2.—Discharge by James Peter, burgess of Dundee, to John Scrimgeour of Kirktoun, as executor to the late Gilbert S. his brother, for 200 merks legacy left him by the said Gilbert. Dated at Dundee. James Wedderburne, merchant burgess of Dundee, is a witness and signs. (On paper, in fair state.)   IV, ii, 8.

206. **1620**. May 16.—Discharge by Agnes Rankene, relict of Thomas Burntfield, burgess of Dundee, William Halyburton, brother german of umquhile James Halyburton of Pitcur, Knt., and Mr. Alexander Wedderburn, clerk of Dundee, tutors testamentar to the children of the said T. B., to John Scrymgeour of Kirkton, brother german and heir of the late Gilbert Scrymgeour, for certain bonds and writs therein specified. Dated at Dundee. Witnesses, Mr. Alexander Wedderburn, bailie in Dundee, David W. burgess thereof, who both subscribe, as does Mr. A. W. the clerk.   IV, ii, 9.
(On paper, in good state. See facsimile of signatures opp. p. 32. The witness A. W., bailie, is the eldest son of Mr. A. W. the clerk.)

207. **1620**. July 13.—Sasine on resignation by George Ogilvy of Dundee to Thomas Bowak and Agnes Fethie his wife, of a N. Marketgate tenement. David Wedderburne, burgess, is witness, and Mr. Alexander W., clerk of Dundee, is notary. VIII, i, 21.
(Latin, parchment.)

208. **1620**. Oct. 26.—Summons at the instance of David Wedderburn, burgess of Dundee, in the complaint by him against William, Grissell, Margaret, and Katharine Davidson, children of the deceased William Davidson, burgess of Dundee, and Barbara Jak his relict, for non-payment by the said deceased William to the complainer as chaplain of St. James chaplainry, of the dues payable from five acres of arable land lying in the West field of Dundee, holding of the said chaplainry, to which acres the said William Davidson, deceased, had right by letter of gift of nonentry granted by the pursuer and superior. Dated at Edinburgh 28 March and signetted 2 July, 1620. Endorsed by David Wedderburn is a discharge in favour of the "relict, bairnes, and executors of William Davidson," in respect of the said claim. Signed by D. W. and dated at Dundee 26 Oct., 1620. (English, one sheet of paper in good state.) I, i-ii, 59.

209. **1621**. May 11.—Discharge by Mr. David Kinneir, minister at the kirk of Seres, to Mr. Alexander Wedderburn, clerk of Dundee, for 140 merks. (One sheet of paper.) VIII, ii, 28.

210. **1621**. July 12.—Grant by Colin Campbell of Lundie to Mr. Alexander Wedderburn, clerk of Dundee, of a pension of wheat, &c. (Paper, good state.)   I, i-ii, 59ᴬ.

211. **1621**. Nov. 17.—Charter by Thomas Ogilvy of that ilk to Sir William Graham of Claverhouse of the fourth part of the lands of Balkello. in the barony of Tealing and shire of Forfar. Dated at Dundee. Witnessed by Mr. Alexander Wedderburn, clerk of Dundee. who signs, and written by his servitor, Thomas Fyiff.   IV, iii, 1.
(Vellum, in good state, but the ink faded. See facsimile opp. p. 32.)

212. **1623**. June 30.— Sasine on charter of Colin Campbell of Lundie, with consent of Dame Jean Sterling his spouse in favour of Sir William Grahame of Claverhouse and Mr. George Grahame, his lawful son and heir apparent, of the fourth part of Balkello. Mr. Alexander W. (son of the clerk, and afterwards second of Kingennie) writes and signs the registration docket on 22 August, 1623. IV, iii, 2.
(Vellum, fair condition, but ink faded.)

218. **1624.** March 6.—Obligation by John Sturrock, mariner in Dundee, acknowledging Scrymgeour-
receipt of a certain sum of money from James Wedderburne, merchant, burgess of Wedderburn
Dundee, for which he becomes bound to infeft him in the west part of a fore tenement, Papers.
sometime belonging to the late George Robertson, on the south side of the Seagate,
and in a lodging adjacent thereto. (One leaf, somewhat wormeaten.)   VIII, ii, 32.

214. **1624.** July 15.—Sasine on precept by John Lord Balmerino in favour of
Patrick Kyd of Grange of Barrie and Isobella Durham his spouse, in con-
junct fee, of the lands of Nether Barrymure; and in favour of the said Patrick Kyd
in liferent and James Kyd, his son, in fee, of the lands of Over Barrymure, &c.
Certified and registered in the Register of sasines for Forfar by "Mr. Alexander
Wedderburn, younger, clerk and keeper of the said register."   VIII, xiv, 28.

215. **1625** Jan. 13.—Assignation by Mr. Alexander Wedderburne, clerk of Dundee,
narrating contract between William Tyrie of Drumkilbo, and Elizabeth Hering his
spouse, on the one part, and the late Mr. William Wedderburn minister at Dundee,
and Magdalene Wedderburn his spouse, on the other part, whereby for 5500 merks
the former were bound to infeft the latter in the half of Logie-Megill and Drumkilbo,
in the shire of Perth, under reversion for the said sum; in security of which the said
Mr. Alexander assigns to the said Magdalene W. relict of the said Mr. William W.,
certain sums due to him and to Mr. Alexander his eldest son, amounting in all to 5500
merks. Sir William Graham of Claverhouse is a witness. (One sheet, fair.) VIII, ii, 33.

216. **1625.** March 5.—Contract of marriage between Mr. George Halyburton of
Fotheranee, advocate before the Lords, and Magdalen Wedderburn, relict of the late
Mr. William Wedderburn, sometime minister of Dundee, with consent of Mr.
Alexander Wedderburn, clerk of Dundee, her father. By this contract Mr. G. H. is
to pay 2500 merks to Margaret and Cristeane Wedderburn, children of the said Mr.
William W. deceased, and Magdalene W. Signed by the spouses, the bride's father,
and various witnesses including James W, bailie of Dundee, Robert Carnegy of
Leuchland and others.   One long sheet of paper.)   VIII, ii, 34.

217. **1625.** June 7.—Discharge by Robert Carnegy of Leuchland and Marjory Wedderburn his spouse to Mr. Alexander Wedderburn, clerk of Dundee, for 2000 merks,
part of 8000 merks, tocher of the said Marjorie. Signed by the spouses. See
post No. 220. (One piece of paper.)   VIII, ii, 31.

218. **1625.** June 8.—Charter of confirmation by King Charles I. confirming three
Graham of Claverhouse charters dated (a), 12 Oct 1619; (b), 10 Aug. 1620; and (c),
17 Nov. 1621. Of these (b) is witnessed by Mr. Alexander Wedderburn, clerk of
Dundee, and Mr. James W. his son, and (c) is that noted above No. 211. IV, iii, 3.
(Large parchment, in good condition, with a considerable part of the great seal appended.)

219. **1625.** Aug. 25.—Receipt by Agnes Rankene, relict of Thomas Bruntfield, burgess
of Dundee, and Nicolas B. their daughter, to Mr. Alexander Wedderburne, clerk of
Dundee, for 50 merks paid in the name of Thomas Lyell of Murthell as annual rent
of 1000 merks due by him. (One leaf, fair.)   VIII, ii, 29.

220. **1625.** Nov. 12 (and 1626, Feb. 25).—Discharge by Robert Carnegy of Leuchland,
and Marjory Wedderburne his spouse to Mr. Alexander Wedderburn elder, clerk of
Dundee, and father of the said Marjory, for the sum of 8000 merks tocher due by
virtue of their marriage contract dated 7 Jan. 1625, and received in satisfaction of a
legacy of 2000 merks left to the said Marjorie by the late Eufame Ramsay, Lady of
Keillour, and another legacy of 500 merks left her by the late Mr. George Halyburton
of Keillour, and also of all the said Marjory might claim by the decease of the late
Helen Ramsay, her mother. Signed by the said Robert Carnegy and 'Marcore'
Wedderburn, his wife, before, among other witnesses, David Wedderburne, burgess of
Dundee. (One sheet of paper.)   VIII, ii, 30.

221.　1626 Jan. 27.—Contract of marriage between Thomas Boyter, son of James Boyter elder, bailie of Dundee, and Jean Wedderburn daughter of Mr. Alexander W., clerk of Dundee, whereby the said James B. engages to infeft the said Thomas and Jean in conjunct fee and their heirs heritably in his 8th part of the lands of Blackness and certain other lands in security, and the said Mr. Alexander Wedderburn engages to pay 4000 merks tocher with his said daughter, and the said Thomas B. obliges himself to provide himself and the said Jean and their heirs in the lands of Pilmure, called the Kirklands of Forgrund in Cowrie, &c.　viii, ii, 35.
(Incomplete, four sheets of paper, originally joined in a scroll.)

222.　1626. May 23.—Precept of Clare constat of David, Viscount Stormont, for infefting Alexander Wedderburn, now of Kingennie, as heir to the deceased Alexander Wedderburn of Kingennie, formerly town clerk of Dundee, his father, in all and haill the sunny half of all and haill the town and lands of Wester Gourdie, with the pertinents, together with the teind sheaves of the said lands, &c. Dated at Scone.　ii, ii, 7.

223.　1626. May 23.—Discharge by Elizabeth, alias Bessie Wedderburn, eldest lawful daughter of umquhile Mr. Alexander Wedderburne, elder of Kingennie, sometime clerk of Dundee, procreated between him and Helen Ramsay his spouse, with consent of Dr. Peter Bruce, principal of St. Leonard's College, St. Andrews, now her spouse, to James Gray of Ballegernoch, for himself, and in name and behalf of Mr. Alexander Wedderburn now of Kingennie, one of the bailies of Dundee, eldest son and heir of the said umquhile Mr. Alexander and only executor nominated to him in his latter will, for 1050 merks, promised and resting to the said umquhile Mr. Alexander by James Gray of Ballegernoch as principal and Alexander Gray, maltman, burgess of Dundee, as cautioner, by their bond of date at Dundee 6 Jany., 1624, which sum of 1050 merks, the said Mr. Alexander Wedderburn assigned to the said Elizabeth, his daughter, by his assignation dated 28 September, 1625, which assignation was ratified by the said Mr. Alexander W., now of Kingennie, and that in satisfaction of all goods and gear which the said Elizabeth could ask as her portion natural or bairn's part. Dated at Dundee and —— 11th and —— days of May and —— 1626. Witnesses, Mr. John Wedderburn, one of the regents of St. Leonard's College, St. Andrews, and Thomas Wichtane, notary.　i, i-ii, 64.
(English, on paper, in perfect condition. The first witness became Sir John Wedderburn of Gosford, the eminent physician See the account of him in Vol. I, and two facsimiles of his signature opp. p. 32 of this volume.)

224.　1626. July 3.—Instrument on the cognition and sasine in favour of Cristina Mathew, relict of David Blyth, mariner, burgess of Dundee, as heir of the late George Mathew her father, and also of Henry Mathew her brother german, in a tenement in Dundee, and in an annual rent of 50 merks therefrom. James Wedderburn, bailie of Dundee, officiates, and the notary is Mr. Alexander W., clerk of the burgh, who appends his symbol. (Latin, small parchment, in good condition, but the ink faded.) i, i-ii, 60.

225.　1626. Nov. 11.—Discharge by Mr. John Duncansone, minister at Dundee, to Mr. Alexander Wedderburn of Kingennie, executor to Mr. Alex. W., clerk of Dundee, for 100 merks legacy left him by the said clerk. John Scrimgeour, servant to the legatee, is witness.　(One piece of paper.)　viii, ii, 36.

226.　1626. Nov. 25.—Discharge by Mr. George Halyburtoun of Fotherance and Magdalen Wedderburn, his spouse, to Mr. Alexander W., dean of gild of Dundee, eldest son and heir and only executor to umquhile Mr. Alexander Wedderburn, common clerk of Dundee, for 2500 merks promised to the granter in name of tocher with the said Magdalen, his spouse, by virtue of their marriage contract dated 5th March, 1625, and in full satisfaction to the said Magdalen of her "bairn's pairt of geir, portion natural" and movables Signed by the granter and Mr. Andrew H. his brother.
(English, on paper, in good state.)　i, i-ii, 65.

227.　1627. May 18.—Sasine following on the precept of clare constat (ante No. 222). Registered 14 July, 1627.　ii, ii, 8.

228. **1627.** May 31.—Discharge by Mr. George Halyburton, advocate, to Mr. Alexander **Scrymgeour-** Wedderburn of Kingennic, for 2000 merks due to him by Mr. A. W.'s bond. Signed **Wedderburn** by the granter and by Alexander Wedderburn, merchant, burgess of Dundee, and **Papers.** David Yeaman, notary there, as witnesses. (One piece of paper.)   VIII, ii, 37.

229. **1627.** July 3.—Sasine on resignation by John Goldman, eldest son and heir of the late Thomas Goldman, merchant burgess of Dundee, into the hands of an honourable man James Wedderburn, one of the bailies of the said burgh, of an annual rent of 12 merks out of that tenement of land of the late John Mathow on the west of the Windmill of the said burgh. Alexander Wedderburne, elder, merchant, is witness, and Mr. Alexander Wedderburne, clerk of Dundee, is notary, and adds his symbol. VIII, i, 22.
   (Parchment. The Mr. A. W. is Alexander Wedderburn, second of Kingennie, who was clerk of Dundee from the death of his brother James in 1627 till the succession to the office of James' son Alexander, afterwards Sir Alexander Wedderburn of Blackness.)

230. **1627.** July 3.—Sasine in favour of John Goldman as heir of the late James Goldman, merchant, burgess of Dundee, of a tenement in S. Argylegate which the said J. G. thereupon resigns in favour of Alexander Wedderburn, merchant, burgess of Dundee. James W., bailie of Dundee, officiates, and Mr. Alexander W., clerk of Dundee, is notary, and adds his symbol. See facsimile opp. p. 32. I, i-ii, 61.
   (Latin, small parchment, in good condition.)

231. **1627.** July 3.—Duplicate of No. 230.   I, i.ii, 61ᵃ.
   (Latin, very small parchment, in fair condition.)

232. **1627.** Nov. 8.—Discharge by William Wedderburn, lawful son to the late Mr. Alexander Wedderburn of Kingennic, sometime clerk of Dundee, and procreate betwixt him and Helen Ramsay his wife, to Mr. Alexander W., now of Kingennie, his son and heir and only executor, for various sums. Marjorie W., daughter to the said late Mr. A. W. is named. Dated at Dundee. Signed by William W.   I, i ii, 61ᵇ.
   (Paper, in good state. See facsimile opp. p. 32.)

233. **1628.** Jan. 14.—Discharge by James, Earl of Murray, to Mr. Alexander Wedderburn, clerk of Dundee, for a bond for 4000 merks due by the Earl to Mr. Patrick Guthrie, minister at Kimbethok, and Jean Blak his spouse, which had been assigned to the said Mr. Alexander on the refusal of the lenders to accept payment from the Earl, who consigned the money into the clerk's hand.   VIII, ii, 38.

234. **1628.** April 9.—Precept of clare constat by John Scrymgeour of Dudop, Knt, constable of Dundee, for infefting Mr. Alexander Wedderburne, now of Kingennie, as heir to the deceased Mr. Alexander W., elder of Kingennie, his father, in all and whole a feu ferme of £8 yearly furth of that land or tenement of the late James Ferriar, burgess of Dundee, lying on the north side of the Moraygate, between the lands of the heirs of the late Robert and Thomas Jack on the east, the lands of the heirs of the late Thomas Gairdin on the west, the common meadow on the north, and the lands of the heirs of the late James Lovell on the south. Dated at Dundee. Witnesses, Andrew Pitcairn, servitor to the granter, John Falconar, son of Mr Alexander Falconar of Halkerstown, Knt., and Thomas Wichtan, notary. Signed by them and the said John Scrymgeour. (Latin, on parchment, in good condition.) 4, i-ii, 62.

235. **1628.** June 7.—Charter by Robert Clayhills of Baldovie, to Sir William Grahame of Claverhouse in liferent and Mr. George Grahame, his eldest son, in fee, of the lands of Hiltoun of Craigie. Dated at Dundee. Mr. Alex. Wedderburne of Kingennie is witness. (Vellum, in good condition. See facsimile opp. p. 32.)   IV, iii, 4.

236. **1628.** Oct. 25.—Discharge by Mr. Alexander Wedderburne, eldest son and heir of umquhile Mr. James Wedderburne, sometime common clerk of Dundee, with consent of his curator, to Mr. Alexander Wedderburn of Kingany, and James Wedderburne, burgesses of the said burgh, tutors testamentary to William and Peter Wedderburne, lawful sons and executors testamentary to the said umquhile Mr. James, the granter's father, and that in name and on behalf of the said executors, for 1000 merks disponed

Scrymgeour-
Wedderburn
Papers.

to the granter by his said father and contained in his testament ; and also in name of
the said executors for all and whole the heirship, goods, and gear falling to the
granter as heir to his father. Dated at Dundee. Signed by the granter. (See
facsimile opp. p. 32.) The curators who sign are T. Halyburtone and Sir Wm. Grahame
of Claverhouse, and the witnesses are T. Halyburtone, younger, bailie of Dundee, and
John Henrysone, notary.   (English, on paper, in good condition.)   I, i-ii, 66.

237. **1628.** Nov. 13.—Discharge by Peter Wedderburne, lawful son to umquhile Mr.
Alexander Wedderburn, elder of Kingennie, sometime clerk of Dundee, procreate
betwixt him and umquhile Helen Ramsay his spouse, to Sir Peter Ogilvy of
Inschmartine, Knt., and Patrick Kynnaird of Inchesture, for themselves, and in name
and on behalf of Mr. Alexander Wedderburn, now of Kingennie, one of the bailies of
Dundee, eldest son and heir of the said umquhile Mr. Alexander, and only executor
testamentar to him, for £1000, and for the sum of £1050 promised and due to the
said umquhile Mr. Alexander by the said Sir Patrick Ogilvy and Patrick Kynnaird, by
their bond of date 7 June, 1623, which sums were assigned by the said umquhile Mr.
Alexander to the granter by assignation dated 5 Nov. 1623, which assignation is
confirmed by the said Mr. Alexander Wedderburne, now of Kingennie.   Dated at
Dundee.   Witnesses Andro Halyburton, mariner, burgess of Dundee, and Thomas
Wichtane, notary, and William Hill his servitor.   I, i-ii, 67.
(English, on paper, in good state. Peter Wedderburne's signature is the same as that to Nos.
194, 195, and 202.)

238. **1629.** Feb. 3.—Discharge by Mr. Alexander Wedderburne, now of Kingennie,
narrating that umquhile James Fotheringhame, persone of Balumbie, and John
Scrymgeour elder of Kirktoun, his son-in-law, did in the life time of the late Mr.
Alexander Wedderburn, elder of Kingennie, the granter's father, pay to the latter
5,500 merks of tocher, with umquhile Magdalen Scrymgeour, spouse to the granter,
eldest daughter of the said John Scrymgeour, in terms of their marriage contract
dated at Dundee 2 April 1612 ; also that umquhile Gilbert Scrymgeour brother
german of the said John did pay to the granter 600 merks as promised by him, of
which sums the granter now discharges the said John Scrymgeour.   Dated at
Dundee.   Signed by the granter, Alexander Wedderburne, now of Kingennie.
(English, on paper, in good condition.)   I, i-ii, 68

239. **1629.** Sept. 23 and 30.—Charter by Mr. Alexander Wedderburn of Kingennie, son
and heir of the late Mr. Alexander Wedderburn, to William Wedderburn his brother
and Jean Peirsoun (daughter) of . . . . . Peirsoun, burgess of Aberdeen, his spouse,
in conjunct fee, &c., of a foreland bounded as therein described (see post No.
249), in implement of an obligation therein mentioned. Dated at Dundee and
Dudop.   VIII, i, 23.
(Latin, parchment, but a large portion of it is cut away, and much of what remains is blotted out.
The year is marked on the back in a later hand.)

240. **1630.** (date wanting).—"An inventare of the Chartouris of the Landis of
Kingenny." This is a list of six charters of Kingennie :—

   (a) Charter of alienation by Andrew Parker of Kingennie to William Strachan of Dundee, 20
        Sept., 1443.
   (b) Confirmation thereof by James, Earl of Angus, 7 Jan., 1443-44.
   (c) Charter by George, Earl of Angus, to Elizabeth Inglis, spouse of William Strachan. Dated at
        Edinburgh, 21 Sept. 1458.
   (d) Charter by Archibald, Earl of Angus, to William Guthrie, son and heir apparent of Malcolme
        Guthrie of Dundie, and Marion Strachan. Dated at Edinburgh, 5 March 1478.
   (e) Charter by Archibald, Earl of Angus to William Guthrie and Janet Arbuthnot his wife, &c.
        Dated at Edinburgh, 5 Dec. 1511.
   (f) Charter of confirmatione by William, Earl of Angus, whereby he confirms a charter granted
        by Mr. Alexander Wedderburn to his son Alexander Wedderburn. Dated at Edinburgh,
        12 June, 1630. See post Nos. 244-45.

(On paper, in good condition.)   I, i-ii, 63.

241. **1630.** (date wanting.)—Discharge by Andrew Mortoun, son and heir of the late Mr.
Andrew Mortoun, minister at the Kirk of Lundie, and his curators, to Mr. Alexander
Wedderburne, fiar of Kingennie, sometime dean of gild of Dundie, for 700 merks,

which had been consigned in his hands on 4 June, 1625 by Sir Colin Campbell of Scrymgeour-Lundie, son and heir of the late Colin Cambell of Lundie, for redemption from Wedderburn Margaret Blackhall, relict of the said Mr. Andrew Mortoun, of the third part of the Papers. lands of Argaith, in the barony of Lundie, which had been wadset by the said late Colin Campbell. Dated at Dundee. (English, on paper, in good condition.) I, i-ii, 69.

242. **1630.** May 15.—Receipt by Robert Gray of Drummellie to Mr. Alexander Wedderburne for 70 merks, balance of a bond for 770 merks, so that the debtor has still to pay at Martinmas next 700 merks with the annual rent, namely 35 merks. Dated at Dundee. I, i-ii, 153.

243. **1630.** May, 3, 7, 27.—Two charters by Sir Colin Campbell of Lundie, Baronet, with consent of Lady Jean Stirling, his spouse, to Sir William Grahame of Claverhouse in liferent, and Mr. George Grahame (his eldest son) heritably, (1) of the lands of Polkello, Polealk, Tealing, &c (2) of the barony of Lundie, in warrandice. Dated at Canongate. John Wedderburne, merchant, burgess of Dundee, is a witness and subscribes. (Vellum, in good state. See facsimile opp. p. 32.) IV, iii, 5 ; VII, i, 4.

244. **1630.** June 8.—Charter by Mr. Alexander Wedderburne of Kingany, clerk of Dundee, to Alexander Wedderburne, his eldest son, his heirs and assignees, of all and whole the lands of Kingany, &c. holding of William, Earl of Angus, in fee and heritage, reserving the granter's liferent. Contains precept of sasine addressed to Alexander Wedderburn, elder, merchant in Dundee, and is dated at Dundee, 1630. Witnesses, James Kyd, surgeon, &c. (Latin, parchment.) VIII, iii, 21.

245. **1630.** June 12.—Confirmation by William, Earl of Angus, of the foregoing charter. Dated at Edinburgh. (Latin, parchment, seal broken.) VIII, iii, 23.

246. **1630.** June 21.—Sasine following on Nos. 244-45. Alexander Wedderburn, elder, merchant, burgess of Dundee, is bailie in the sasine, and Alexander W., younger, mariner, burgess of Dundee, is a witness. (Latin, parchment.) VIII, iii, 22.

247. **1630.** Oct 6.—Receipt by George, Viscount Dupline, Lord Hay of Kinfauns, Lord Chancellor, to Mr. Alexander Wedderburne, for a discharge granted by Wm. Tyrie of Drumkilbo to the late Lawrence, Lord Oliphant, for 12,500 merks for redemption of an annual rent of 1250 merks out of Oliphant's lands ; also for another discharge between the same parties for 4,600 merks the redemption price of an annual rent of 460 merks. VIII, ii, 39.

248. **1631.** April 14.—Sasine in favour of Isabella Bowar as heir of the late Roger B. of Dundee, of certain tenements in Dundee. Alexander Wedderburn, elder, merchant, is witness, and Mr. Alexander W., clerk, is notary. (Parchment.) VIII, i, 24.

249. **1631.** May 8, &c.—Charter by Mr. John Wedderburne, lawful son of the late Mr. Alexander Wedderburne, elder, of Kingennie, sometime clerk of Dundee, and brother german and heir of the late William Wedderburne, merchant, burgess of Dundee, in favour of Mr. Alexander Wedderburne, now of Kingennie, also his brother german, heritably, of that foreland formerly belonging to the late Patrik and Alexander Wedderburne, burgesses, lying on the S. of the Marketgate, between the lands now of Thomas Gray on the east, the lands of Thomas Clayhills on the south, the cemetery of S. Clement, and the passage leading from the Tolbooth to the gate of the said burgh, on the west, and the said Marketgate on the north, to hold from the granter, of Sir John Scrymgeour of Dudop, Knight, constable of Dundee, in fee and heritage and free burgage. Dated at Dundee and Dudop 8th May, and 28th July respectively, 1631. (Latin, parchment. See note to No. 233, and facsimile opp. p. 32.) VIII, i, 25.

250. **1631.** July 28.—Sasine following on the said charter. (Latin, parchment.) VIII, i, 26.

251. **1631.** Sept. 5.—Obligation by Patrick Quhytheid sometime in Kingennie, now in Ffficbeatoun, to Mr. Alexander Wedderburne of Kingennie, for the amount of 42 bolls

of oat meal, and 30 bolls beir "guid and sufficient heilsome stuff of the met and measour of Dundie," and that for his occupation of the lands of Kingennie belonging to the said Mr. Alexander for the crop and year 1631 ; also for the amount of 10 bolls of the quality following "Tua bollis muked land aitis, tua bollis effe muked land, tua bollis ley, tua bollis award, and tua bollis thrid crop aitis, and that for the mylne multour dentie " owing to the said Mr. Alexander, of his mill of Kingennie of the crops and years 1631, 1632 ; and also five dozen of poultry. Robert Durhame in Craigie is cautioner.   Dated at Dundee.   (English paper, somewhat mended.)   I, i-ii, 71.

252.   **1632** Feb. 4.—Disposition by James Durham of Pitkerro to James Durham his oye (whom failing to other heirs in succession) of the lands of Easter Powrie, erected into one free barony of Powrie.   David Wedderburn, burgess of Dundee, is a witness.
(Paper.)   VIII, v, 8.

253.   **1632.** Feb. 4.—Charter in terms of the foregoing disposition ; David Wedderburn, burgess of Dundee, is a witness.   (Seal entire.)   VIII, v, 9.

254.   **1632.** Jan. 22.—Letters of inhibition at the instance of Thomas Halyburtoun, merchant, burgess of Dundee, against Thomas Halyburtoun younger his son, "and Margaret Wedderburne his spouse, and Mr. Alexander Wedderburne, sone and air of umquhile Mr. Alexander Wedderburne, commone clerke " of Dundee, that they should not sell their lands to the hurt of the complainer and loss of the sum of 8000 merks paid by him to his said son and uplifted from the lands of Inchesture, in terms of the marriage contract dated 25 Feb. 1617 (ante No. 192.)   I, i-ii, 70.
(English, paper, somewhat worn and mended.)

255.   **1632.** July 7.—Discharge by Marion Fotheringhame, relict of John Scrymgeour of Kirktoun, to John Scrymgeour, now of Kirktoun, her son, for the mails, &c. of part of Kirktoun.   A. Wedderburn (second of Kingennie) is a witness and signs.   VIII, ix, 43.

256.   **163—.** Sept. 29.--Sasine upon resignation by Marion Mudie in favour of Thomas Mudie, her younger son, of the tenement and annual rent mentioned ante No. 224. Alexander Wedderburn, older, merchant, is attorney for the said Thomas M. and Mr. Alexander Wedderburn, clerk of Dundee, is notary.   I, i-ii, 74.
(Latin, parchment, in bad condition.   The notarial symbol is that of Alexander Wedderburn, second of Kingennie.)

257.   **1632.** Dec. 11.--Extract decreet in action by Sir Andrew Fletcher of Innerpeffer, Knt., and Patrick Maule of Panmure v. George Erskine of Carnbuddo, Alexander Wedderburn of Kingennie, and others for molesting the pursuers and their tenants in possession of their lands in the barony of Downy.   Alexander Wedderburn and a tenant of his alone compear for the defence, and the said Alexander produces a tolerance (ante No. 155) granted by David, Earl of Crawfurd, to his father Mr. Alexander Wedderburn.   The Lords continue the case.   VIII, ii, 40.

258.   **1633.** Feb. 2.—Extract decreet of the Lords of Council in the said action by which it appears that on consideration of the said tolerance dated 10 July 1603, the Lords assoilzie the said Mr. Alexander Wedderburn of Kingany, son of the aforesaid Mr. Alexander W., from the points of the summons.   VIII, ii, 41.

258ᵃ.   **1633.** Feb. 2.—Copy of No. 258 in the hand of Alexander Scrymgeour Wedderburn of Wedderburn (circa 1800).   VIII, ii, 14ᵇ.

259.   **1633.** May 16.—Sasine on apprising by Archibald Kyd, burgess of Dundee, to Patrick Jak., his heirs and assignees, of a S. Seagate land and other subjects. Mr. Alexander Wedderburn is notary.   VIII, xx, 20.

260.   **1633.** List of Wadsetters in the shire of Aberdeen, 1683 onwards. This is much torn.   On page 8 " Mr. William Wedderburne, minister at Balhelvie " is named.
(Paper, nine folio pages, besides two blank and three of index.   English.)   VII, iii, 11.

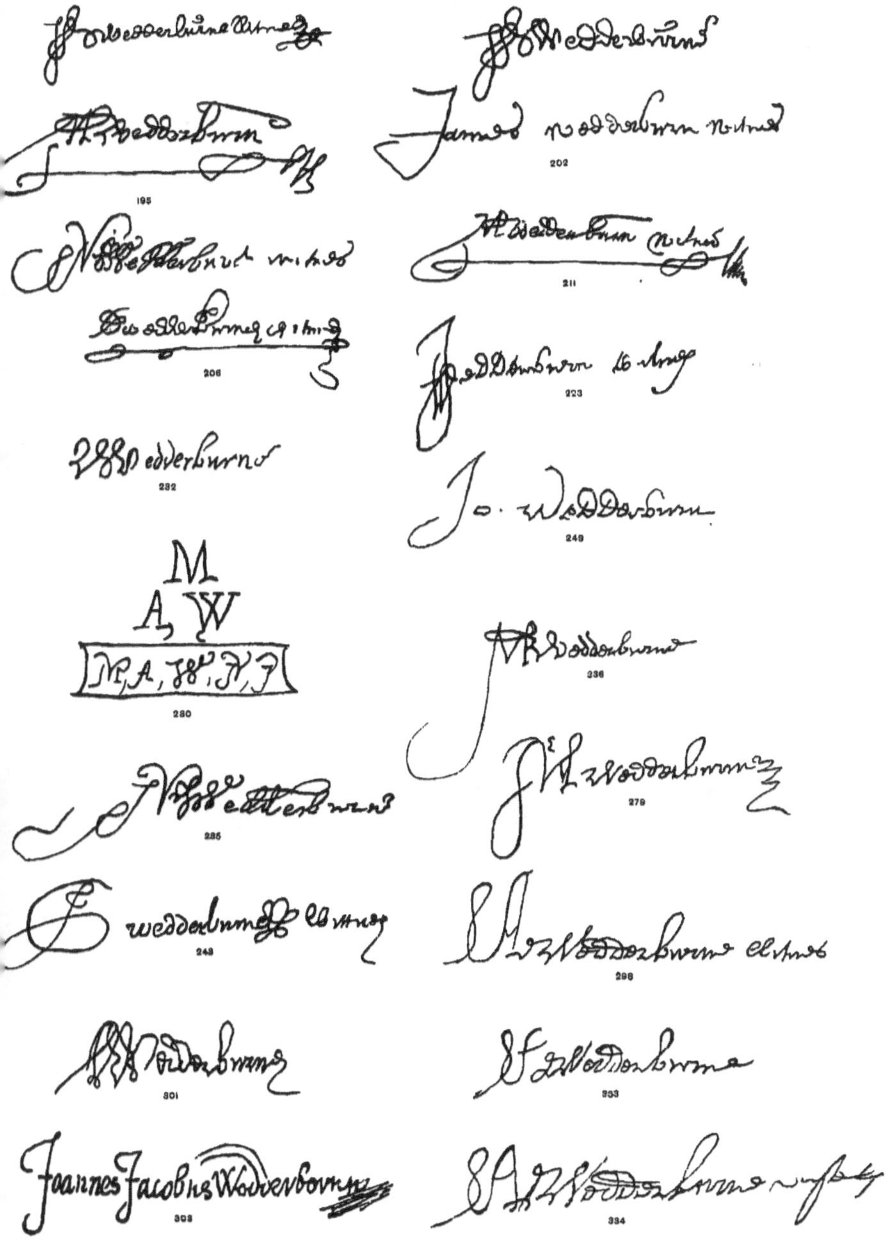
195
202
205
206
211
223
232
236
243
249
279
280
285
298
301
303
333
334

261. **1633.** June 11.—Obligation by Thomas Anderson to Mr. Alexander Wedderburn **Scrymgeour-** of Kingennie, written by David Carnegie, servitor to Mr. Alexander Wedderburn, **Wedderburn** common clerk of Dundee, and witnessed by Alexander Wedderburn, elder, merchant **Papers.** burgess of Dundee. (Paper, good state.) I, i-ii, 71ᴬ.

262. **1633.** Aug. 10.—Tack by Mr Alexander Wedderburn of Kingennie, to John Beaton of Oehlair, late tenant of the lands of Kingennie, of the mill of Kingennie with multures, &c , and of the lands adjacent thereto, called the Crynibles, with the teind sheaves, for three years, for the yearly duty of 10 bolls bear and 17 bolls of meal. Dated "at Kynganie." James and John, sons of the said John Beaton, are witnesses. (One sheet, fair condition.) VIII, ii, 42.

263. **1634.** Jan. 24.—Decreet for surrenders and teinds made in favour of the pursuer by the Lords Commissioners of Parliament in the action by Mr. Alexander Wedderburne of Kingennie, common clerk of Dundee, against Mungo, Viscount of Stormonth, for not denuding himself of his right to the teinds of the lands of Wester Gourdie in the parish of Liff, and ordaining him to dispone them to the pursuer for payment of the amount fixed by the valuation of the said Commissioners. Dated at Edinburgh. (English, on paper, in good condition. Endorsed "Teinds of Wester Gourdie.") I, i-ii, 72.

264. **1634.** May 27-28.—Contract between Mungo, Viscount of Stormonth, heritable proprietor of the teinds of the united parishes of Liff, Logy, and Innergowrie, of the one part, and Mr. Alexander Wedderburn of Kingany, clerk of Dundee, heritable proprietor of the lands of Wester Gourdie, of the other part, by which the said Viscount sells, alienates, and dispones to the said Mr. Alexander, his heirs and assignees whatsoever, heritably and irredeemably, all and sundry the teind sheaves or parsonage teinds of all and haill the said Mr. Alexander's town and lands of Wester Gourdie. Contains obligation to infeft the said Mr. Alexander in the said lands, &c. Dated at Dundee and Perth. II, iv, 35.

265. **1634.** May 28.—Tack by Mungo, Viscount of Stormonth, lord of Seone, in favour of Mr. Alexander Wedderburne of Kingany, common clerk of Dundee, of the teind sheaves or personage teinds of the lands of Wester Gourdie belonging to the said Mr. Alexander lying in the united parishes of Liff, Logy, and Innergowrie in the shire of Forfar, and that for the space of the said Mr. Alexander's lifetime, and the lifetimes of five heirs in succession, and for five successive periods each of nineteen years thereafter, paying therefor yearly the sum of two shillings at Lammas, if asked, together with two bolls two pecks meal, to the minister of the said united parishes and for the remaining teinds the duty owing to the King. Dated at Perth. Witnesses Sir John Moncrieff of that ilk, Knt. ; James Peirsonn, of Easter Liff, &c. (English, two pieces of paper, joined together, in perfect state.) I, i-ii, 73.

266. **1634.** May 28.--Duplicate of foregoing tack. II, iv, 38.

267. **1634.** May 28.—Charter by Mungo, Viscount of Stormouth, to Mr. Alexander Wedderburn of Kingennie, of the teinds of his lands of Wester Gourdie, containing precept of sasine, &c. II, iv, 36.

268. **1634.** June 23.—Sasine following on No. 267. Registered 12 Aug. 1634. II, iv, 37.

269. **1634.** Sept. 8.—Extract minute of the bailie Court of Dundee, held in the writing chamber of Mr. Alexander Wedderburn, clerk of the court of the burgh, by Thomas Halyburtone, bailie, whereat compeared James Kyde, merchant, burgess of Dundee, and Margaret Duncan his spouse, and produced an obligation by them to infeft Patrick Kyde of Grange of Barric in the said James' S. Seagate tenement ; to which, being read over, the said Margaret gives her consent. Signed by Mr. Alexander W., the clerk, (afterwards Sir Alexander of Blackness). (One piece of paper.) VII, ii, 43.

270. **1636.** May 31.—Bond by Robert Rollok of Muretoun to sign and consent to the disposition to be made by him and Isobell Lyon, in Dundee, of an E. Wellgate

tenement to whoever shall buy the same at the sight of and for such price as may be fixed by Mr. Alexander Wedderburn of Kingennie, and Patrick Murray, servitor to the Earl of Kinghorne. (One leaf, fair.)   VIII, ii, 44.

271. **1637.** Dec. 15.—Special retour of Alexander Wedderburn of Kingany as heir to the deceased Alexander Wedderburn of Kingany his father in all and haill the half of the town and lands of Wester Gourdie, called the sunny half, with the pertinents and teind sheaves thereof. John Scrymgeour of Kirkton and Mr. Alexander Wedderburn, clerk of Dundee, are on the inquest.   II, ii, 9.

271ᵃ. **1637.** Dec. 18.—Sasine on resignation by James Kyd, merchant burgess of Dundee, and Margaret Duncan, his spouse, to Patrick Kyd of Grange of Barrie and William Kyd, son to the said Patrick by Isobell Durham his spouse, of a S. Seagate land. James Wedderburn, merchant burgess of Dundee, is procurator for James Kyd.
VIII, xxi, 6.

272. **1638.** Feb. 6.—Precept from Chancery following on the above retour (No. 271) for infefting Alexander Wedderburn in the said lands.   II, ii, 10.

273. **1638.** March 23.—Sasine on resignation ·by Alexander Wedderburn, merchant, burgess of Dundee, as procurator for Alexander, Thomas, and Patrick Jack, and for Alexander Kyd, of a tenement therein named, in favour of Mr. James Kyd, portioner of Craigie. Mr. Alexander Wedderburn is notary and adds his symbol, and John Wedderburn, merchant, is witness but does not sign. (Latin, parchment.) VIII, i, 27.

274. **1638.** March 27.—Extract instrument of sasine in favour of Alexander Wedderburn following on the precept of 6 Feb. 1638 (ante No. 272). Registered 2 April 1638.
II, ii, 11.

275. **1638.** Oct. 13.—Tack by Alexander Wedderburn of Kingany to Gilbert Thayne in Wester Gourdie, of all and haill that half of the town and lands of Wester Gourdie with the pertinents, presently occupied by the said Gilbert, lying within the parish of Liff and lordship of Scone, together with the teind sheaves of the said lands, and that for the space of five years.   II, ii, 12.

276. **1639.** Jan. 26.—Discharge of Mr. Archibald Pearsone, sheriff depute of Forfar, in name of David Grahame of Fentrie, sheriff principal, to Alexander Wedderburne of Kingennie for £27 16. 8. for his "entrie silver" as heir to the late Mr. Alexander Wedderburn of Kingany, his father, in Wester Gourdie.   VIII, ii, 45.

277. **1639.** May 24.—Instrument of sasine on precept of clare constat granted by James Scrymgeour apparent of Dudop, as commissioner for Sir John S. of Dudop, Knt., constable of Dundee, his father, for infefting Alexander Wedderburn now of Kingany as heir of the late Mr. Alexander W. of Kingany, clerk of Dundee, his father in (1) a tenement of land of old belonging to Peter and Alexander Wedderburn, burgesses of Dundee, on the S. side of the Marketgate between the lands of Thomas Gray (E), Thomas Clayhills (S), St. Clement's Cemetery, &c. (W), and the said Marketgate (N).—(2) a feu ferme of £8 yearly furth of a tenement of land of the late James Ferriar, burgess of Dundee, lying on the N. side of the Murraygate, between the lands of the heirs and successors of the late Robert and Thomas Jack (W), the lands of the heirs of the late Thomas Gairdyne (E), the common meadow (N) and the lands of the heirs of the late James Lovell (S). Sasine having been given to Alexander Wedderburn elder, merchant burgess of Dundee, as attorney for the said Alexander W. of Kingany, the bailie in obedience to the precept gave sasine of the same subjects in liferent to Elspet Ramsay, spouse of the said Alexander Wedderburn of Kingany and daughter of John Ramsay, bailie of Dundee, who acted as attorney for her. (Latin parchment,)   VIII, iii, 24.

278 **1640.** Nov. 21.—Testament dative and inventory of the goods &c. of the late Mr. Alexander Wedderburne of Kingennie, who died within the burgh of Dundee, in September 1637, given up by Alexander Wedderburne of Kingennie, his only lawful

son and executor dative, by decreet of the commissaries of Brechin. The inventory Scrymgeour-
amounts to £100. John Ramsay, bailie of Dundee, is cautioner. Confirmed at Wedderburn
Brechin, 21 November 1640. Signed by George Steill, clerk of court. I, i-ii, 75. Papers.
(English, on paper, in perfect state.)

279. **1640.** April 15.—Instrument on transumpt by the provost &c, of Dundee, of a
sasine contained in the protocol book of the late Mr. Alexander Wedderburn of
Kingany, town clerk of Dundee, dated 25 April 1632, made on cognoscing Margaret,
Euphamia, and Sara, daughters and heirs of the late Charles Goldman, and entering
them in a W. Marketgate tenement, which they resign in favour of John Ramsay,
bailie of Dundee. For proof of the protocol are cited, at the instance of John
Ramsay and Barbara Jack his spouse, certain faithful witnesses, including Alexander
Wedderburn, elder, who having been sworn with uplifted hand, and appealing to
God, declared the said protocol to be subscribed by the hand of the said umquhile
Mr. Alexander Wedderburn and that he was held to have been a faithful and legal
notary. Dated at Dundee. Subscribed by Mr. A. Wedderburn (*afterwards Sir
Alexander of Blackness*) and sealed with the great seal of the burgh. I, i-ii, 76.
(Latin, parchment, in fair state. See facsimile opp. p. 32.)

280. **1641.** Feb. 8.—Instrument of sasine in favour of Henry Fethie, minister at Maynes
of Fintrie, of a tenement in the Seagate of Dundee, resigned by his brother Robert F.,
merchant burgess of Dundee. Sasine is given by Alexander Wedderburn of Kingennie,
bailie of Dundee. (Latin, parchment, in good condition.) I, i-ii, 77.

281. **1642.** Jan. 5.—Sasine on resignation by Mr. Henry Fethie minister at Maynes
in favour of Robert F., his brother german, of a S. Seagate tenement. Mr. Alexander
Wedderburne, clerk of Dundee, is notary, and adds his docket and symbol, with the
motto " Deum time." (Latin parchment, in fair condition.) I, i-ii, 78.

282. **1642.** Jan. 22.—Disposition by Mr. Alexander Wedderburne, common clerk of
Dundee, in favour of Alexander Wedderburne, skipper, burgess of Dundee, heritably,
of " that foirland of that great tenement of land sumtyme perteining to umquhill
maister James Wedderburne my father, lyand within the said burgh of Dundie upon
the north syde of Ergyllis gait thairof . . . as also in all and haill those two inner
ludgings sumtyme occupiet be James Lundie and Robert Broune, also perteining to
the said umquhill Mr. James my father, lyand upon the west syde of the cloise of
the said great tenement of land and contigue to the said foirland betwix the malthous
set . . . be my said umquhill father to Alexander Nicoll and now disponed be me
at the north, and the said foirland at the south pairtis; And siclyk in all and haill
that tenement of land with the wall and cloise of the same sumtyme perteining to
umquhill Peter Wedderburne younger, merchand, burges of the said burgh of Dundee,
immediat younger brother to the said umquhill Mr. James my father, lyand within
the said burgh of Dundie upon the eist syde of the said cloise betwix the landis of
Alexander Symmer, merchand, burgess of the said burgh, at the north, the landis of
the said Alexander Wedderburne at the south, the landis of William Davidsone at
the eist, and the said cloise at the west pairtis." Dated at Dundee. James Wedderburne, one of the bailies of Dundee, is a witness and subscribes, as does Mr.
Alexander Wedderburn, the granter. (English, paper, somewhat decayed.) I, i-ii, 79.

283. **1642.** March 7.—Extract retour of the general service of Elspet Ramsay as heir to
the late John Ramsay, merchant, burgess of Dundee, her father, expede in the Tolbooth of Dundee on March 5, 1642, before honourable men, James Wedderburne and
others, bailies, by an inquest of faithful and worthy burgesses of the said burgh.
Extracted by Sir John Scott of Scottistarvett, Knt., one of the Lords of Council and
Session and director of His Majesty's Exchequer. I, i-ii, 80.
(Latin, small parchment, in perfect state.)

284. **1642.** July 9.—Bond by Barbara Jak, relict of John Ramsay, merchant, burgess of
Dundee, to Alexander Wedderburne of Kingennie, and Elspet Ramsay his spouse,

only lawful daughter, heir, and executrix dative of the said deceased John Ramsay, to pay to them £320, promised to the granter by James Jacksone of Wattriebutts in name of duty for the lands of Grange and Wattriebutts.   VIII, ii, 46.

285. **1642.** Nov. 17.—Sasine on resignation by David Mason, burgess of Dundee, into the hands of Alexander Wedderburne of Kingennie, bailie of Dundee, of a tenement of land outside the Flukergate port, in favour of Thomas Brown and Elizabeth Smyth his spouse, &c. Alexander Wedderburn, shipmaster, is a witness, and Mr. Alexander Wedderburne, clerk of Dundee, is notary. (Latin, parchment.)   VIII, 1, 29.

286. **1643.** April 5.—Testament dative and inventar of the goods, &c., of the late John Ramsay, bailie of Dundee, in common betwixt him and Barbara Jack his wife, at the date of his death in or about January 1642, given up by Alexander Wedderburne, of Kingennie, his son-in-law, in names of Alexander, John, and Magdalene Wedderburne his oyes and executors dative. (One piece of paper.)   VIII, ii, 59.

287. **1643.** Oct. 18.—Sasine of a tenement in Dundee (same as that dealt with ante No. 256) given by Thomas Abercrombie, merchant burgess of Dundee, to Margaret Wemyss his spouse, reserving to Marion Mudie, mother of the said Thomas, her liferent. Mr. Alexander Wedderburne, clerk of Dundee, is notary, and adds his symbol and docket, as in No. 281 ante.   I, i ii. 82.
      (Latin, parchment, in good condition, but the ink faded.)

288. **1643.** Nov. 21.—Letters of horning, at the instance of Alexander, John, and Magdalene Wedderburne, grandchildren and heirs of the late John Ramsay, bailie, and Alexander Wedderburne of Kingennie, as their father and tutor, v. Gilbert Monorgund in Bothill for a debt of £33. 12., due by obligation   VIII, ii, 47.
      (One sheet, in fair condition.)

289. **1643.** Dec. 29.—Contract of marriage betwixt Alexander Wedderburne of Kingany, bailie of Dundee, on the one part, and Margaret, eldest lawful daughter of Mr. John Fotheringhame, brother german of umquhile Thomas Fotheringhame of Pourie, that last deceased, with consent of her father, on the other part, for the marriage of the said Alexander and Margaret, in contemplation whereof the said Mr. John Fotheringhame becomes bound to pay 5,000 merks in name of tocher with his said daughter betwixt now and Martinmas 1644, and the said Alexander Wedderburne becomes bound to lay out the said sum at the sight and by the advice of Thomas Fotheringhame of Pourie, Mr. David Kinloch of Aberbothrie, John Scrimgeour of Kirktoun, and Mr. Alexander Wedderburne of Blacknes, with other 5,000 merks of his own, making 10,000 merks in all, upon some lands or annual rents within the sheriffdom of Forfar, to the profit of himself and his said future spouse in conjunct fee, and the heirs to be gotten betwixt them, which failing, his own heirs whatsoever, and also to provide the said Margaret in liferent, to his great lodging and tenement "up and down with the well clois, office hous, yeard, and pertinents presentlie occupied by himself " in the said burgh of Dundee, on the north side of Argyll's gate, or to pay her an annuitie of £80 instead thereof, and that in full satisfaction of all terce or conjunct fee of his other lands, annual rents, and heritages, which may belong to him at the time of his death. He also becomes bound to provide the children of the marriage to all lands, sums, and other means and estate wherewith God may bless and increase him, during his lifetime with her the said Margaret his future spouse, to be a further provision and patrimony to the said children : and further to pay to one heir male of the marriage, if there be no other issue alive, the sum of 7,000 merks ; but if no heir male, and only two female children, then he binds himself and the heirs of his former marriage to pay to the said heirs female 5,000 merks, and if there be three of them 7,000 merks, to be divided amongst them at the pleasure of the granter : all of which sums are to be out of his further means and estate, and payable to the said heirs at the age of fourteen years. He also becomes bound to give "sufficient interteinment, maintenance and liberall education " to the said heir male. Dated at Dundee.· Witnessed by Mr. John Duncanson, minister at Dundee, and others ; written by Mr. John Dunmuir.· Signed by the spouses, Mr. John Fotheringhame and others. (English, on paper, in perfect condition.) ·   I, i-ii, 83.

290.   **1644.** March 11.—Transumpt at the instance of Alexander Wedderburne of Scrymgeour-Kingany, burgess of Dundee, of an instrument of sasine (dated 19 June 1629) of the **Wedderburn Papers.** late Mr. Alexander Wedderburne of Kingany, burgess of Dundee, of three tenements of which one (1) belonged to the late Robert Wedderburne, brother of the late Mr. Alexander Wedderburne of Kingany, clerk of Dundee ; another (2) to the late John Wobster and the third (3) to Thomas Traill, now all united into one great tenement of land or lodging, lying contiguously on the N. side of the Argyllgate between the lands of the late Robert Kendow and Patrick Yeaman on the west, the lands of the heirs of Patrick Wedderburne, John Yeaman and David Hunter on the east, the common burying ground on the north, and the lands of Alexander Wedderburne, shipmaster, and William Mirriman on the south ; wherein the said Mr. Alexander Wedderburne of Kingany, clerk of Dundee, was then cognosced as eldest son and heir of the said Mr. Alexander Wedderburne, as also in an annual rent of 10 merks furth of a tenement, some time of the late John Robson in S. Flukergate, near the meal market, between the lands of the heirs of William Spens on the west, the lands sometime of Andrew Fyffe, now of John Alysone, on the east, and the said gate on the north ; and in various other similar annual rents out of lands in Dundee therein described. The said transumpt was made before the provost and bailies of Dundee from the protocol book of the late Thomas Fyffe, notary, in the tolbooth of Dundee. The secret seal of the burgh is appended. (Latin parchment.)   VIII, iii, 25.

291.   **1644.** July 30.—Letter from Alexander Halyburton at Stockholm to his uncle Dr. John Wedderburne of Moravia. (See the account of Dr. John W. in vol. I.)   I, i-ii, 86ᵃ.

292.   **1644.** Nov. 4.—Extract registered (post-nuptial) contract of marriage between John, Viscount of Dudop and Lady Anna Ramsay, eldest daughter of William, Earl of Dalhousie. The first witness is Mr. Alexander Wedderburn, clerk of Dundee.
        (English, paper, in bad condition.)   IV, iv, 3.

293.   **1646.** Aug 10.—Extract minute of the Kirk session of Dundee, before which "compeired Alexander Wedderburn, elder, merchant burgess of Dundie, air and executor to umquhile James Wedderburn, suuntyme baillie of the burgh, and gave in to the session ane silver bason weyand thrie pundis and ten unce weight, dedicat be the said James the tym of his decease to the use and behailf of the sacrament of baptisme of the said Kirk in all tyme cuning, as a monument of his affection in decoring Godis house, and desyred that the same suld be insert in ther Session Booke ther to remane ad futuram rei memoriam, and the extract to be given to him. Dated 10 Aug. 1646 ; extracted by Robert Stibbillis, clerk to the session, on 18 Jan. 1647.
        (English, small parchment, the ink faded. See post s. Brechin Wills, 1 June 1643.)   I, i-ii, 85.

294.   **1646.** Nov. 26—Bond of provision by Thomas Boyter of Pilmore in favour of Anna, his daughter, of 4000 merks to be payed to her after her marriage, in satisfaction of her portion natural, because the provisions made in the marriage contract between the granter and his first spouse Jean Wedderburne should fall after his decease to James Boytter his eldest son and heir, and no portion had thereby been provided to the said Annas or to Helen her sister. (One sheet, fair; see ante No. 221.)   VIII, ii, 48.

295.   **1646.** Nov. 27.—Extract Retour of the general service of Alexander Wedderburne, shipmaster, burgess of Dundee, as heir of the late James Wedderburne, merchant burgess there, his paternal uncle. The service is subscribed by Sir Alexander Wedderburne of Blacknes, Knt., clerk of Dundee. Dated at Dundee. (Latin, parchment.)   VIII, i, 30.

296.   **1646.** Dec. 31.—Bond by Margaret Wedderburn "onlie bairn now on life, and heir of umquhile Mr. William Wedderburn, suuntyme minister of Dundie " and Doctor Andrew Bruce, principal of St. Leonard's College, St. Andrews, her spouse, of one mind and consent, to warrant and relieve "Alexander Wedderburn, now of Kingany, his airis, &c., and all uthairs the airis and executouris and successouris of umquhile Mr. Alexander Wedderburn of Kingany, his father, and umquhile Mr. Alexander Wedderburn, elder of Kingany. common clerk of Dundie, his guidschir" of all action expense, &c. which he or they might incur "for and anent the making and granting in

name of the airis of the said umquhile Mr. William Wedderburn, in the moneth . . . jm{vjc} saxtene yeiris or thairby, to umquhile William Tyrie of Drumkilbo of ane renunciation of his soucy half landis of Logy Megill over and nethir " lying in the parish of Megill and sherifidou of Perth, as principal, and, in special warrandice thereof, of the sunny half lands of Drumkilbo, in the same parish, which were sold to the said Mr. William Wedderburn and Magdalen Wedderburn, his spouse, in conjunct fee, and to their heirs, by contract of sale at Dundee and Little Blair, 31 May and 14 June, 1615, under reversion for 5000 merks : which sum being now secured to the granters by decease of the said Magdalen their mother, they grant this bond of relief, and become bound to grant a renunciation of the said lands to the heirs of the said William Tyrie. Dated at Dundee. Witnessed and subscribed by Sir George Haliburton of Fothrauis, Knt., Sir Alexander Wedderburn of Blacknes, Knt., &c.

(English, ou paper, in good condition. See facsimile opp. p. 32.)   I, i-ii, 81.

297. **1649.** May 15.—Discharge by Thomas Scot, merchant burgess of Dundee, to Alexander Wedderburne of Kingany, for certain writs therein described, relating to lands in Dundee, amongst which are (1) an instrument under the subscription of umquhile Alexander Wedderburn notary, sometime clerk of Dundee, dated 29 April 1569 (2) other writs signed by him, and his son and grandson, Alexander Wedderburn, first and second of Kingennie, in 1572, 1612-18, and 1632. (3) a procuratory by Mr. Hercules Rollok to Patrick Wedderburn 13 Nov. 1593 and (4) a procuratory by the late Elspet Ramsay, only daughter and heir of the late John Ramsay with consent of Alexander Wedderburne of Kingennie her spouse, dated 22 June 1642.

(English, two pieces of paper joined together, in good condition.)   I, i-ii, 86.

298. **1650.** Aug. 1.—Testament of Major William Serymgcour, indweller in Dundee, whereby he nominates Sir John Carnegy of Craig, Knt., Mr. John Fotheringham, and Mr. Alexander Wedderburn of Kingennie, tutors testamentar to Margaret and Janet Serymgeours his children, and to the child to be born. He leaves ·the said Alexander W. 5,000 merks. Dated at Dundee.   VIII, ix, 54.

299. **1650.** Aug. 1.—Duplicate of the foregoing will.   VI, iv, 1.

300. **1650.** Aug. 5.—Testament testamentary of the late Major William Scrymgeour, brother german of John Serymgeour of Kirktoun, who died in September 1650. The inventory is given up by Alexander Wedderburne of Kingennie, one of the tutors testamentar to Margaret Serymgeour, only daughter and executor to the said major. (The daughter Janet, named along with Margaret in the will, thus died before the date of its confirmation.) The provision for Janet Guthrie, the testator's widow, is the interest of 12,000 merks during her widowhood. Dated at Dundee, 5 Aug. 1650 and there confirmed 23 Dec. 1653. (English, paper, wasted in several parts.)   VI, iii, 22.

300ᵃ. **1650.** Aug. 5.—Duplicate confirmation of the said will.   IV, iv, 7.

301. **1650.** Nov. 27.—Inventory of writs belonging to the deceased Major William Serymgeour, signed by A. Wedderburn of Kingennie. It includes the contract of marriage between Major W. S. and Janet Guthrie, dated at Dundee, Aug. 1643, and a bond for 300 merks in favour of Kingennie.   IV, ii, 10.

(English, on paper, in good state. See facsimile opp. p. 32.)

302. **1651.** Inventory of the Papers of Wester Gourdie :—
      1558. March 6.—Confirmation of the charter made be Walter Milne of half the said lands.
      1561. Aug. 6.—Sasine of John Milne aud Eufame Watsou, his spouse, in half of Gourdie.
      1568. Sept 22.—Sasine of Walter Milne in the half lands of Wester Gourdie.
      1574. May 29 —Renunciation of Wester Gourdie by James Carmichael and Alexander Whytelaw. (Ante No. 27.)
      1574. June 10.—Charter by Eufame Watson, relict of John Milne, and Walter Milne their son, with consent of Isobell Grey his wife, to James Carmichael, portioner of Ethiebeatonu, and his airs, of the sunnie half of Wester Gourdie.
      1574. June 10.—Charter by Walter Milne to James Carmichael of the half of Wester Gourdie.
      1574. June 11.—Sasine to James Carmichael of the sunnie half of Wester Gourdie.
      1589. March 17.—Discharge of ane ground aunnall of 20 lib for payment of 300 merks out of Gourdie, granted to James Carmichael be Rannald Brown, Barbara Rollok, and others.

Scrymgeour-Wedderburn Papers.

1589. June 3.—Renunciatione by John and Andro Smith of Wester Gourtlie.
1591. Jan. (?).—Iustrument v. Rannald Brown for his removing from the lands of Wester Gourdie in favour of Mr. Alexander Wedderburne.
1591. Jan. 28.—Renunciation by Robert Carmichael of ane annual rent out of Wester Gourdie. (Ante No. 69.)
1591. June 6.—Contract betwixt James Carmichael and Mr. Alexander Wedderburne for Wester Gourdie. (Ante No 72.)
1591. Oct. 7.—Sasine of Mr. Alexander Wedderburne and his spouse. (Aute No. 77.)
1591. Nov. 9 —Renunciation by Brown and his spouse. (Ante No. 79.)
1591. Nov. 9.—Renunciation Robert Wedderburn and Rannald Browne. (Ante No. 68.)
1591. Nov. 26.—Discharge by James Carmichael, bailzie in Dundie, to Mr. Alex Wedderburne, clerk, for 8000 merks as the price of the sunnie syde of Gourdie. (Aute No. 81.)
1612. May 18.—Charter by Mr. Alexander Wedderburu for infefting Helen Ramsay in liferent in Wester Gourdie. (Ante No. 177.)
163(7.) Dec. 15.—Retour of Alexander Wedderburn of Kingennie as air to his father in the lauds of Wester Gourdie. (Ante No. 271.)
1638. Feb 5.—Brief for serving Alexander Wedderburue, air to his father Mr. Alexauder W., in the half of Gourdie. (Ante No. 272.)
1651. June 6.—Charter of Mr. Alexander Wedderburn in one half of Wester Gourdie.
1651. June 6.— Charter of the same iu the other half of the said lands.
(Euglish, paper, in fair condition.)   I, i-ii, 32.

303. **1651.** July 14.—Letter from John James Wedderburn (son of Dr. John Wedderburn) to Alexander Wedderburn of Kingennic. Dated at Brünn in Moravia. Sealed with the Wedderburn arms.   I, i-ii, 86b.
(See the account of Dr. J. Wedderburn in vol. i. and the facsimile of the writer's signature to this letter opp. p. 32 of this volume.)

304. **1652.** July 5.—Draft Latin reply by Kingennie to the above. Dated at Kingennie.
(See vol. i. ibid.)   VIII, ii, 49.

305. **1652.** July 4.—Letter from John James Wedderburn in reply to No. 304. VIII, ii, 50.
(One piece of paper, torn. See the account of J. J. Wedderburn in vol. i.)

306. **1653.** July 2.—Letter from Alexander Wedderburne of Kingennie to Janet Guthrie as follows :—

Kinganie, ii July, 1653.

"Mistres,
    I reaseaiwid youris togeather with the copie of the comprysiug but I admir werie much that ye cannot fiud the Iuhibitione for I am confident ther is on, but in respect I have not the Iuventar besydis me, I cannot tell whether the Iuhibitione be on the comprysing or ment the sowiue thousant mark bant, but if it be concerning that land I iutreat let me have (it) with all deligence and I shall be as deligent in that bussenes as possiblie I cane not farther remembring my be ... wishes to yourself and dochter I rest

                                        Your loving cousine
For his worthy and much respectit   To be commaudit,
ant Janet Guthrie   A. WEDDERBURNE.
        Thes.

    Sealed with a small seal of red wax, shewing the writer's arms, a chevron charged with a fleur-de-lys between three cinquefoils, surmounted by the letters A.W. It will be noticed that the writer addresses Janet Guthrie both as cousin and as aunt. The former word may be used in the sense of kinswoman (consanguineus) only, although the Guthries were in fact directly related to Kingennie the mother of his great-grandmother, Jauet Myln, having been Elizabeth Guthrie. (See also post Duudee Protocol Books vol. 251, fol. 137). As to the word " aunt," Kingennie's mother was Magdalen Scrymgeour, sister to John Scryuugeour of Kirktoun, one of whose younger brothers, Major William Scryuugeour, married Janet Guthrie, who was thus aunt by marriage to Kiugennie. She married secoudly Dougal McPhersoun, who sold his lands of Easter Powrie to Alexander Wedderburne, and thereafter seems to have beeu involved in various litigation with him, and to have encouraged his step-daughter Margaret Scrymgeour in a suit against Wedderburue, who was her tutor. See post No. 399a, where Wedderburn charges that in his ward's action against him she is " led on by Dougal McPhersone, her father-in-law (i.e., stepfather) out of a private splean." I, i-ii, 87a.

307. **1653.** Oct. 14.—Contract of marriage, dated at Dundee, between James Thomsone, indweller in Barrie, with consent of Hendric Thomisone, his father, and Marioric Wedderburn, naturall sister to Alexander Wedderburn of Kingennie. Signed by the parties and by (among other witnesses) John Wedderburn, naturall sone to the said Kingennie. (One sheet of paper.)   VIII, ii, 51.

308. **1653.** Nov. 22.—Gift under the Privy Seal by the Keepers of the liberties of England by authoritie of Parliament to Alexander Wedderburn of Kingennie of the

escheat of the goods of the late Patrick Guthrie of Auchmuthie, who was put to
the horn 8 May 1650, at the instance of the late Major William Scrymgeour, for not
removing from his lands of Auchmuthie and Bruntoun.　　　　　　IV, ii, 12.
(English, on paper, somewhat worn.)

309.　**1654.** Jan. 11.—Letters of apprising at the instance of Alexander Wedderburn of
Kingennie as donator to the escheat aforesaid *v*. Janet Read, relict of the said Patrick
Guthrie, and her daughters Isabel and Margaret.　Dated at Dundee.　　IV, ii, 13.
(English, one sheet of paper, mended, but in fair state.)

310.　**1654.** Jan. 25.—Execution by David Doig, messenger, of a precept of arrestment
at the instance of Alexander Wedderburne of all debts &c. owing by John, Earl of
Eathie, to Janet Read, and Isabel and Margaret Guthrie; particularly the sum of
£10,000.　Done at Eathie.　　　　　　　　　　　　　　I, i-ii, 154.

311.　**1654.** Jan. 26.—Inventory of the production made by the Earl of Lauderdale in
the action by the Lord Dundee's creditors against him, containing (*inter alia*) :—
　　13.　Item ane extract of ane instrument of sasine in favour of Sir Alexander Wedderburne of
　　　　an annual rent of £584 furth of the lands of Dudope, redeemable for 14,600 merks.
　　　　Dated 25 Jan. and registered at Dundee 26 Jan. 1654.
　　(English, four sides of foolscap closely written, in good state.　The inventory itself is of later date
than 1654, the Dundee peerage of the Scrymgeours dating from 1661.)　　　IV, ii, 15.

312.　**1654.** March 27.—Extract registered bond of John, Viscount of Dudope, to John
and Grissell, children of the late James Dunean, skipper, burgess of Dundee, for
£1,000.　Dated at Dundee.　Witnessed by Sir Alexander Wedderburn of Blackness,
Knt, and others.　Registered in the books of Council and Session 6 October 1663.
(Two sheets of paper, somewhat torn and decayed.)　　　　　　　IV, ii, 14.

313.　**1654.** May 31.—Compt of the bands and soumes assignit be Alexander Wedderburne of Easter Pourie to Mr. William Durham of Omachie for payment of a pairt
of the debt due by Major William Scrymgeour to him, and whairupon he has procured a discharge from Omachie dated as above.　David Campbell younger of
Kethick and James Ogilvy of Shanally, are named.　(One piece of paper.)　VIII, ii, 52.

314.　**1655.** June 12.—Discharge by Alexander Goldman to Alexander Wedderburn of
Kingennie for £250 merks.　(One piece of paper, a good deal decayed.)　VIII, ii, 53.

315.　**1656.** Inventory of writs produced by William Luke writer in Forfar before the
Lairds of Inverearity and Monorgund, commissioners for administering the oath to
the said William.　Various mentions of Alexander Wedderburn, third of Kingennie,
occur in this paper, but none are important.　(Small piece of paper.)　IV, ii, 11.

316.　**1656.** May 26.—Sasine by Walter Rankyne of Dundee to Patrick Betoune and
Helen Nicoll his spouse of certain N Murraygate property.　Sir Alexander Wedderburn, clerk of Dundee, is notary.　　　　　　　　　　　　VIII, xiv, 30.

317.　**1656.** May 29.—Sasine in favour of Mr. David Ferguson, as heir to his guidsif·
Mr. William F., sometime bailie of Dundee, in a 5 merks annual rent furth of a
tenement in Dundee.　The notary is Sir Alexander Wedderburne, who appends his
symbol and docket with his motto "fear God" in English, instead of in Latin as in
No. 281.　(English parchment, in good condition.)　　　　　　I, i-ii, 87.

318.　**1656.** July 8.—Extract decreet in action by Margaret Scrymgeour, daughter and
executrix of the late Major William S., *v.* the daughters and heirs portioners of the
late Patrick Guthrie of Auchmuthie.　Mr. Peter Wedderburn is a procurator for the
pursuer.　　　　　　　　　　　　　　　　　　　　VIII, x, 8.

319.　**1657.** April 1.—Copy summonds of suspension raised by John, Viscount of Dudop *v.*
Margaret Scrymgeour and Alexander Wedderburne to compear and produce all bonds
and other grounds of debt due by the said Viscount.　　　　　　IV, iv, 8.
　　(A small piece of paper in good state, endorsed " Charge given be My Lord Dudope to Margaret
Scrymsor and Kingenzie her tutor.")

320. **1657.** April 1.—Execution of summons by John, Viscount of Dudop *v.* Margaret Serymgeour and Alexander Wedderburne of Kingennie, her tutor, to produce writs. Dated at Edinburgh. vi, iii, 26.

Scrymgeour-
Wedderburn
Papers.

321. **1657.** July 9.—Disposition by Mr. David Ferguson, son of the deceased William F. merchant burgess of Dundee, in favour of Sir Alexander Wedderburne of Blackness, of the said 5 merks annual rent (see ante No. 317), for a sum of money paid to the granter by the grantee. Dated at Dundee. i, i-ii, 88.
(English, two pieces of paper joined, in good state, but much faded.)

322. **1658.** . . . . "Compt Kingenzie to Mr. Peter Wedderburne debursed in the action of reduction against Margaret Serymgeour." Dated on the back. i, i-ii, 89.
(English, a scrap of paper in good state.)

323. **1658.** July 15.—Paper endorsed "Instrument anent the moor of Kingennie." Alexander Wedderburne, younger of Kingennie, appears as the procurator to his father Alexander Wedderburne, elder of Kingennie, and in the presence of witnesses, including John, son to the said Alexander W. elder, requires certain tenants of William Durham of Omachie to desist from "casting up the heretage" of his said father, Alexander W. elder, in the moor of Kingennie. (One piece of paper.) viii, ii, 54.

324. **1658.** Aug. 2.—Registered obligation by Alexander Wedderburn of Kingennie to Patrick Drummond of Gairdrum for £40. (One piece of paper.) viii, ii, 55.

325. **1658.** Sept. 21.—Extract of the teinds of the lands of Kingennie and Wester Gourdie. (One sheet of paper.) viii, ii, 56.

326. **1658.** Oct. 13.—Instrument of sasine upon cognition by Alexander Halyburtoun baillie of Dundee of "Alexander Wedderburne of Kingenny, air by progress to Robert Mylne, burges of Dundie, that was father to Janet Mylne, granddame to the said Alexander Wedderburne of Kingenny on his father's side," in an annual rent of 8 merks "furth of that tenement of land which pertainit of old to David Wedderburne burgess of Dundie and sensyne to Jhone Lowsone, baxter burgess thairoff" and now to James Lowsone his son, lying on the S. side of the Murraygate, bounded by the lands of the chaplain of Saint Paul on the west &c. (See ante No. 13.) Sir Alexander Wedderburne, of Blackness, clerk of Dundee, is notary and adds his symbol and docket. i, i-ii, 90.
(English, parchment, in good state. Janet Mylne, however, was paternal *great* grand dame to Kingennie, and her father's name was James, not Robert.)

327. **1659.** Feb. 4.—Extract registered disposition by John, Earl of Loudoun, to Alexander Wedderburn of Kingennie of the annuities of the teinds of Kingennie and Wester Gourdie. Dated at Edinburgh. Registered in the Books of the Exchequer, 11 Feb. 1659. (English, parchment.) viii, iii, 26.

328. **1659.** March 22.—Disposition by Mr. James Durhame of Powrie, one of the ministers of Glasgow, and taking burden on him for Margaret Muir his spouse, and with consent as therein mentioned, to Dougall McPhersone of Bellachroan, of the lands of Easter Powrie, with mill, &c., lying in the barony of Powrie, &c., as principal, and the barony of Ogilvy in warrandice. Dated at Edinburgh, Glasgow and Dundee, 15 Dec. 1655, 2 Jan. 1656, and 22 March 1659. Sir Alexander Wedderburne of Blackness, Knight, is a witness. (Paper.) vii, v, 24.

329. **1659.** March 22.—Charter of the same dates and signed at the same places following on the above disposition. Sir Alexander W. is again a witness. At the foot is a note of sasine being given 17 Jan. 1656. viii. v, 25.

330. **1659.** July 4.—Contract of marriage between John Serymgeour of Kirktoun, eldest son and heir male of the deceased John Serymgeour of Kirktoun, with consent of Jean McGill his mother, and Maidelene Wedderburn, eldest lawful daughter to Alexander Wedderburn of Kinganie, with consent of her father, by which the said

John becomes bound to infeft the heirs male to be gotten of the marriage (whom failing there is a reversion to the said John, his nearest and lawful heirs male and of taillie whatsoever) in the lands of Kirktoun. (English, in good condition.)   VI, ii, 9.

331. **1659.** July 11.—Disposition of John Scrymgeour, eldest son and heir of the late John S. of Kirktoun, in favour of Maidlane Wedderburne, eldest daughter of Alexander Wedderburne of Kingany, and future spouse to the granter, in her pure virginity, of the lands of Kirktoun of Erlistradichtie with the dovecots, manor place &c. in the regality of Kirriemuir, to be holden by the said Maidlane in liferent, and by the heirs male of the marriage, &c, for the yearly payment of one penny of blenche ferme. Contains precept of sasine. Dated at Kirktoun. Witnessed by Mr. Harry Auchinleck, minister of the Maines, James Scrymgeour, brother of the granter, &c. (English, parchment, in good condition, but the seal removed.)   I, i-ii, 91.

332. **1660.** July 11.—Instrument of Sasine proceeding on the said disposition, and recorded in the particular register of sasines for Forfar on Aug. 1 thereafter. (English, parchment, in good state The Forfar Register for this date is not extant.) I, i-ii, 92.

333. **1659.** (date wanting)—Contract of sale between John, Viscount of Dudope, (with consent of Dame Anna Ramsay, his spouse,) and Sir Alexander Wedderburne of Blackness, Knt., whereby for the sums of money therein specified, borrowed from the latter by the former, viz. : 14,600 merks by bond dated 15 June, 1650 and registered in the court books of justice on 14 April 1654, for which the said Viscount became bound to infeft Sir Alexander in an annual rent of £484, furth of the lands of Dudope ; and £13,804 13, 9 advanced by the said Sir Alexander at Whitsunday, 1658, for defraying of the said noble viscount his weightie affaires, the said viscount "for frething and liberating" himself of the annual rent of £6,632, 16, 3 as part of the greater sum above mentioned, and in discharge of the balance amounting to £7,171, 17, 6, sells to the said Sir Alexander heritably, the sheds of land called the Brieve bauck, Nether Howlands, and others, to be holden of the granter in feu ferme and heritage, for the yearly payment of £4, 4, 0.   IV, iv, 4.
(See facsimile of Sir A. W.'s signature opp. p. 32. The date is missing through part of the paper being torn away at the end, otherwise it is a scroll of four sheets joined together, in fair condition.)

334. **1659.** Sept. 23.—Contract of sale between John Viscount of Dudope. Lord Scrymgeour, with consent of Dame Anna Ramsay, his spouse, and others, including Sir A. Wedderburne of Blackness, who signs, though he is not named in the deed itself, and John Fotheringhame of Denoone, whereby for the sums therein mentioned the said Viscount sells to the said J. F. the lands of Langlands and others in the barony of Dundee. Dated at Dundee.   IV, iv, 5.
(Scroll of four sheets of paper, joined, also in good order, except the top of the first sheet. See opp. p. 32 for facsimile of signature "A. Wedlerburne consents.")

335. **1659.** Sept. 29.—Sasine in favour of Dame Anna Ramsay, Viscountess of Dudope. spouse of John, now Viscount of Dudope, on bond of provision of same date, made in her favour by the said Viscount, of an annual rent of ten chalders victual furth of the dominical lands and mains of Dudope, as the same are divided from the remanent lands thereof, sold and disponed by the said Viscount to Sir Alexander Wedderburn of Blackness, and others, his creditors, &c. Registered 13 Oct., 1659.   II, vii, 2.

336. **1660.** Jan. 25.—Instrument of Sasine proceeding on marriage contract made between Barten Bilsone. Englishman, merchant in Dundee, and Helen Wedderburne. relict of William Goskine, Englishman, of date 15 Aug. 1657, in favour of the said Barten Bilsone and the heirs to be gotten between him and the said Helen, which failing, to the survivor of them two and their heirs, of the half of a fore tenement sometime pertaining to Sir Alexander Wedderburne of Blackness, Knt., and disponed by him to the deceased Alexander Wedderburne, father of the said Helen, lying on the N. side of the Argylegate ; also the half of those two tenements or dwelling houses, sometime belonging to the said Sir Alexander, lying on the W. side of the close of the aforesaid tenement ; also the half of that tenement sometime pertaining to the said Sir Alexander lying on the E. side of the said close ; also the half of that

tenement on the N. side of the Argylegate, between the lands of the heirs of John Scrymgeour Cowen, merchant, on the west, the lands of the heirs of Donald Dunbar on the east, the lands of Alexander Wedderburne on the north, and the said gate on the south ; the half of an annual rent of 24 merks furth of the tenement of old belonging to Archibald Kid, on the south side of the Seagate ; also the half of an annual rent of 8 merks out of a tenement sometime belonging to John and William Walker, on the N. side of the Murraygate ; the half of an annual rent of £3 furth of the tenement sometime belonging to the heirs of Thomas Logie on the N. side of the Murraygate, all which the said Helen Wedderburne resigned in favour as aforesaid. Done on the grounds of the lands on 25 Jan. 1660. The notary is Sir Alexander Wedderburne of Blackness, clerk of Dundee. (English, parchment, in good condition.) I, i-ii, 93.

337. **1660.** April 19.—Discharge by James Thomson, indweller in Kingany, to Alexander Wedderburn of Kingany for £100 part of a larger sum due to the said James Thomson by the said Alexander Wedderburn under the contract of marriage dated 14 Oct. 1653. See ante No. 307. (One small piece of paper.) VIII, ii, 57.

338. **1660.** May 4.—At Blackness. Obligation and disposition of a foreland in N. Argylegate, made by Barton Belsone, Englishman, merchant in Dundee, to Alexander Wedderburn of Kingany to take effect in event of Belsone having no children who reach "perfyte age," and conditional on a payment to be made by Alexander W. to the heirs of Bessie Wedderburn. Signed by B. Belsone and three witnesses. (One piece of paper.) VIII, ii, 58.

339. **1660.** May 19.—Contract of marriage between Alexander Wedderburn of Kingennie and Margaret Milne, relict of Major Robert Lindsay, whereby for 3000 merks belonging to the said Margaret, and for the liferent right and benefit of such sums as she is provided to by her late husband, to which the said A. W. will have right *jure mariti*, during the marriage, he becomes bound to provide of his own means the sum of 6000 merks and to join it with the aforesaid 3000, and to lay the whole out on land or annual rent to themselves in conjunct fee and liferent, and to the heirs of the marriage &c. Dated at Dundee. Witnessed and subscribed by the parties and by John Graham of Fentrie, Sir Alexander Wedderburn of Blackness &c. I, i-ii, 94.
(English, two pieces of paper joined together, a little torn. See facsimile of signatures opp. p. 56.)

340. **1660.** May 19.—Duplicate of the said contract. (One piece of paper.) VIII, ii, 60.

341. **1660.** June 8.—Bond by Alexander Wedderburne of Kingany, to the effect that forasmuch as Margaret Mylne, relict of Major Robert Lindsay, and affianced spouse to the grantee, has in her possession and custody the following goods and plenishing, namely :—

"ane large double hall table of wenschoat ; ane like chamber table of wenschoat ; two like chamber tables of fir ; six cheares covered with reid russie leather ; six wenschoat chaires covered with cloath, whereof thrie green and thrie blew, and whereof thar is ane of each color large and armed ; thrie oakin cheares armed and uncovered ; thrie conicue cheares of ashe : ane large wenschoat bed of old worke ; tua large frinch standing beds of fir, one whereof culored grein and another blew ; sex good feather beds ; sex good feather bolsters ; twell pillowes ; fifteen pair of linnen sheets ; sex pair of round sheets ; tua dussone of coadwaires ; ten pair of small new bed phaids ; ten pair of rounder bed plaids ; ane bed covering ; ane pand and courtines for surrounding ane bed, with ane tuffell cloath, all of green clonth, having ane green silk frenge about all of them ; ane bed covering, pand, curtines, and taffill cloath all of green chamlet having upon the pand ane worset frenge of grecu and gold culor, and ane silk lace sutable thereto upon the said pand, courtines, covering, and taffill cloath ; ane bed pand and courtines for facing of tua beds of green dyced chamlets, having on the said pand ane worset frenze of red and yellow, and ane silk lace suitable thereto therupon, and upon the said courtines ; ane yellow sewed covering ; ane sute of blew courtines, pand, and taffill cloath of linnen, and wooll cloath, having ane blew and whyte lace on ilk ane of them, and ane sutable frenze about the pand ; irone rods for ilk ane of the said beds and courtines ; three woven coverings for servants beds ; ane large green hall table cloath whereupon is sewed M. R. L. and M. M.[1] with ther arms, with yellow worset ; ane linnen board cloath, taffill cloath and twenty servites, all of dornyk work ; tua small and three rounder board cloaths of linnen with four dussone of servits sutable ; seven lesser round board cloaths of lynnen ; three dussone and ane halfe dussone of servits, and sex hand towells sutable thereto ; tua long small linnen hand towells ; fyve small drinking cloathes and fyve pair of small linen head sheets ; ane large holland kist of oack ; tua smaller kists quharof ane of wenschoat

---

[1] These initials stand, of course, for Major Robert Lindsay and Margaret Milne.

and the other of fir ; ane long candle kist of fir, and tua truukes, quherof ane is bandit with oak and the other with iron, and both large ; .... ane stand of stowpes comprehending ane quart pynt, chopin, and mutskin stoups ; fourtine plaitis, sex trunsheuris and foure little saucers, all pewter and hollauds wark ; ane staud of service stoupes, comprehending ane pyut, ane three mutskin, ane chappin mutskin and halfe mutskin stoupes ; fyve chandlers of yellow brasse, quherof three old fashioned and tua with ane plate about the midle, and ane pair of candle sheires ; tua saltfats, ane of tun and another of caine; aught silver spooues, quherof sex markit with M. R. L. and and M. M. and tua markit with A. M. and E. FF.[1] ; ane silver driuking pot markit with M. R. L. and M. M. ; ane large hall iron chimney gallowes, raxes, tua crewkes, and ane speel ; tua chamber iron chimneys ; tua pair of tongs ; ane purring iron, ane pot irou, and ane iron bak ; three brasse pans, ane large, another midling and three lesser ; ane roast pau of copper and ane frying pau, aud ane brasse mortar and pestle ; four punsheones for meall ; tua beeffe tubs ; tua aik barrells of three gallones, and tua of ane gallon the peece ; ...... tua lint wheels ; aue wool wheell ; ane check wheell ; ane pair of gairn waird bleads ; and aue large baick bread."

and although by matrimonial contract of date the ... of May last between the granter and the said Margaret Mylne, she has accepted the sum of 9000 merks in full satisfaction of all lands, annual rent, goods, gear, &c , which she might ask or crave through the decease of the granter, in case she survive him, yet nevertheless for the love which he bears towards her, he binds himself and his heirs that the aforesaid articles of plenishing shall be delivered up to her immediately after his decease, to be kept and used by her during her lifetime, and after her decease to be made forth-coming to the granter's heirs, executors or assignees, excepting such movable heirship goods as shall be drawn out of the said plenishings, which he binds himself and his heirs to make forthcoming to the heirs of the said deceased Major Robert Lindsay. Dated at Dundee, 8 June, 1660. Signed by A. Wedderburne (see opp. p. 56.) Witnesses, Mr. Alexander Milne, minister at Longforgund, and Robert Lauder, clerk depute of Dundee. (English, oue sheet of paper, in good state.) I, i-ii, 95.

342. **1660.** June 8.—Duplicate of the above bond. (English, one piece of paper.) VIII, ii, 61.

343. **1660.** July 4.—Discharge by John Scrymgeour of Kirktoun to Alexander Wedderburne of Kingauy for 7000 merks by way of tocher with Magdalen Wedderburne, daughter of the said A. W. and now spouse to the said J. S., according to contract of marriage dated July, 1659. (See ante Nos. 330, 331.) Dated at Dundee. Signed by the granter. (On paper, in perfect state.) IV, iv, 6.

344. **166—.** June 29.—Disposition by John and Grissel Duncan, children of the deceased John Duncan, son of the deceased James Duncan, burgess of Dundee, to John Scrymgeour of Kirktoun, of an annual rent therein specified. Dated at Dundee. Witnesses, Alexander Wedderburne, younger of Kingennie .... Wedderburne, younger...... IV, ii, 18.
(Four sheets of paper, originally joined together, all much decayed and in bad state. The second Wedderburu wituess is, no doubt, John Wedderburu, younger of Blackness.)

345. **1660.** (date wanting).—Rental of the lands belonging to the Lord Dudope, including " the feu duty of the acres sometime pertaining to David Wedderburn. now to James Simpson, £26. 13. 4." Undated, but about 1660. IV, ii, 17.
(One sheet, in good state.)

346. **1660.** Sept. 22.—Extract burgess ticket admitting William Kyd, son of Mr. James Kyd of Craigie, as burgess of Dundee. Signed by Sir Alexander Wedderburn. VIII, xiv, 31ᵃ.

347. **1661.** Jan. 15.—Sasine in favour of Mr. Charles Smith, advocate, of a feu duty furth of certain tenements in Dundee. The notary is Sir Alexander Wedderburn, of Blackness, clerk of Dundee. III, iii, 13.

348. **1661.** June 17.—Bond by Andrew Watt, flesher, burgess of Dundee, to Sir Alexander Wedderburn of Blackness for £406 scots. Dated at Dundee. III, vi, 1.

---

[1] The initials of Margaret Milne's parents, Alexander Milne and Elizabeth Fletcher.

349. **1661.** Aug. 15.—Back bond by Thomas Bower merchant burgess of Dundee to **Scrymgeour** Alexander Wedderburn of Kingany, as to his use of the excise of salt imported **Wedderburn** within Tay and the duties to be levied thereon from strangers and native merchants **Papers.** respectively. (One small piece of paper.) VIII, ii, 62.

350. **1662.** Sept. 10.—Discharge by Henry Gib, indweller in the Canongate of Edinburgh, to Alexander Wedderburne of Kingennie, provost of Dundee, for certain victual. (One small piece of paper.) VIII, ii, 63.

351. **1662.** Sept. 12.—Extract registered (28 May 1663) disposition by Dougal McPhersone of Easter Powrie for himself and for Janet Guthrie his spouse and John their son, for 38,000 merks advanced by Alexander Wedderburne, elder of Kingenny, provost of Dundee, made in favour of the said Alexander W., heritably and irredeemably, of the lands of Easter Powrie with the mill &c. as therein described, all erected into the free barony of Powrie in the shire of Forfar, as for the principal, and the lands and barony of Ogilvie, called the Glen of Ogilvie, in warrandice ; with the teinds of the said lands, and containing procuratory of resignation and precept of sasine. Dated at Edinburgh. Sir Alexander Wedderburn of Blackness, Knt, clerk of Dundee, and Colonel James Menzies of Culterallers, are among the witnesses. (Scroll of eight sheets.) VIII, ii, 66.

352. **1662.** Sept. 12.—Copy registered obligation by Alexander Wedderburn of Kingennie, provost of Dundee, to Dougal McPhersone of Easter Powrie for himself and in name of Janet Guthrie his spouse, whereby for the sum of 8000 merks, borrowed by him from them, the said Alexander binds himself to infeft the said Dougal and his spouse in conjunct fee and liferent, and the heirs procreated between them, which failing John McPherson his eldest son by the late Jean Lyell his first spouse, and the heirs male of his body, which failing Archibald McPherson his only son by the late Grissell Campbell his second spouse &c., in an annual rent of £320 furth of the lands of Easter Powrie. Dated at Edinburgh. Sir Alex. Wedderburn of Blackness, Knt., clerk of Dundee is a witness. Registered in the Books of Council and Session 23 June 1665. (See post s. Register of Deeds, Dalrymple Office.) VIII, vii, 1.

353. **1662.** Sept. 13.—Sasine on resignation by Dougall McPhersone of Easter Powrie, and John McPhersone, his eldest son, of all and haill the lands of Easter Powrie, erected into a free barony of Powrie, in favour of Alexander Wedderburn elder of Kingennie, provost of Dundee. The sasine is given before the Commissioners of her Majesty's Exchequer. VIII, vi, 1.
(English, one piece of parchment, in good condition, endorsed "Instrument of sasine in favors off Alex. Wedderburne off Kinganie.")

354. **1662-63.**—Compt of the payment of the price of the lands of Easter Powrie amounting to £25,333. 6. 8. (One piece of paper.) VIII, ii, 65.

355. **1663.** Jan. 19.—Great Seal Charter of the barony of Powrie (with the barony of Ogilvie in warrandice) erected of new into a free barony of Easter Powrie, in favour of Alexander Wedderburn elder of Kingennie, provost of Dundee. his heirs and assigns. Dated at Edinburgh. VIII, vi, 2.
(Latin, large parchment in good condition, with fine impression of the Great Seal attached.)

356. **1663.** Jan. 19.—Extract of the foregoing charter. VIII, vi, 3.
(Latin, parchment, in good condition, no seal.)

357. **1663.** Feb. 12.—Act or license of the Privy Council in favour of Alexander Wedderburn, provost of Dundee, granting for one year his petition to be allowed to eat flesh in time of Lent and upon the three weekly fish days mentioned in the late proclamation. The license includes "those at his table." Dated at Edinburgh. Signed Rt. Murray, and "Pet. Wedderburne," clerk to the Council. I, i-ii, 97.
(English, small piece of paper, somewhat torn.)

358.　**1663**. April 28.—Sasine of the lands and barony of Easter Powrie, &c., in favour of Alexander Wedderburn, elder of Kinganie, pursuant to the said charter of 19 Jan. (ante No. 355). Alexander Wedderburn, younger of Kinganie, is a witness. In the fold is endorsed "At Dundee the second of May, 1662, the instrument of sasine within wrettin, produced be Robert Lauder, nottar in Dundie, is signed in the first volume of the publict register of sasines, &c., for Forfar, fol. 255-57." viii, vi, 4.
(Latin, parchment, in good condition, no seal. See post s. Forfar Sasines 2 May, 1663.)

359.　**1663**. April 28.—Sasine on precept (April 8) of clare constat by Alexander Wedderburn of Kingany, provost of Dundee, as superior, for infefting Mr. Francis Durhame, eldest son and heir of the late Mr. James Durhame, minister of the Word of God at Glasgow, in an annual rent of £200 out of the barony of Powrie. Alexander Wedderburn, elder son and apparent heir of the granter, is a witness. viii, xiv, 32.

360.　**1663**. May 26.—Letters of Lawburrows at the instance of the said Alexander Wedderburn, against Dougal McPherson in Powrie and John his son for troubling and molesting the complainer. Dated at Edinburgh. viii, vii, 2.

361.　**1663**. June 8.—Notarial instrument of protest by John Haistie, indweller in Dundee, as procurator for Alexander Wedderburn of Kingennie, provost of Dundee, against Dougal McPherson of Easter Powrie, for not fulfilling of his obligation to the said Alexander Wedderburn of date 12 Sept. 1662 whereby he bound himself to give the said A. W. inspection of the whole fixed work that was within the manor place of Easter Powrie that he might inventory the same. Dated at the said manor place. viii, vii, 3.

362.　**1663**. June 22, July 6.—Renunciation by Mr. Francis Durham to Alexander Wedderburn of Kingany of an annual rent of £200 out of Easter Powrie, which the granter had from Dougal McPherson of Balmacron, now redeemed by Kingany for 5000 merks. (One piece of paper.) viii, ii, 64.

363.　**1663**. July 7.—Procuratory by Alexander Wedderburn of Kingennie &c., to James Carnegie, writer in Edinburgh, to pass to the presence of Dougal McPherson, sometime of Bellachroane, and to make an offer to him. Dated at Edinburgh. viii, vii, 4.

364.　**1663**. July 7.—Notarial instrument of protest by James Carnegy, writer in Edinburgh, as procurator for the said Alexander Wedderburn, against Dougal McPherson, late of Easter Powrie, being in Edinburgh for the time, for his refusing to accept of the offer then made to him of the bond granted by the said D. M. to the late Mr. James Durham, minister of Glasgow, dated 27 Dec., 19 Jan., 27 Feb. 1656 for 5000 merks, and to return the bond granted by the said Alexander Wedderburn to him to retire the aforesaid bond. Done in the burgh of Edinburgh, over against the head of the Kirk heuch on 7th July 1663. viii, vii, 5.

365.　**1663**. Oct. 27.—Execution of Lawburrows at the instance of Alexander Wedderburn of Kingennie, provost of Dundee, against Dougal McPherson in Powrie, and John McPherson his son, charging them to find caution that the said complainer, his wife, and children, shall be harmless and skaithless of them. (See ante No. 360.) viii, vii, 6.

366.　**1663**. Summons in process of suspension at the instance of Alexander Wedderburn of Kingennie, provost of Dundee, v. the said Dougal McPherson and his son to produce the bonds specified (ante No 364) and letters of horning raised thereon, that they may be suspended. Dated at Edinburgh. viii, vii, 7.

367.　**1663**. Nov. 7.—Summons at the instance of the said Alexander Wedderburn v. the said Dougal McPherson and John his son, for suspension of letters of lawburrows (No. 365) raised by them v. the pursuer. Dated at Edinburgh. viii, vii, 8.

368.　**1663**. (date wanting)—Disposition by John Mathew of Dundee, only son of David M. deceased, and grandson and heir of John Mathew, to Thomas Lyn of a tenement in Dundee, bounded partly by that of umquhill Peter Wedderburn and William Kinloch. ix, ii, 2.

369. **1664.** Feb. 2.—Instrument of sasine on precept by Mr. James Grahame of Monor- Scrymgeour-gund to James Kinloch, second son of Mr. David K. of Bandoeh, of a tenement in Dundee. Sir Alexander Wedderburn, clerk of Dundee, is notary. VIII, xiv, 33. **Papers.**

370. **1664.** Feb. 18.—Extract decreet in action of reduction by Margaret, daughter of the late Major William Serymgeour and her curators v. Alexander Wedderburn of Kingannie, provost of Dundee. He is assoilized. (Two sheets of paper, joined.) IV, iv, 9.

371. **1664.** June 3.—Notarial instrument by Alexander Wedderburn of Kingennie v. Harry Guthrie, writer in Dundee, as procurator for and in name of Dougal McPherson, sometime of Easter Powrie, for his detaining from him the keys of a thrashing barn, and other houses therein mentioned. Dated at the Barns of Easter Powrie. VIII, vii, 9.

372. **1664.** Aug. 12.—Discharge by Dougal McPherson to Alexander Wedderburn of Kingennie, provost of Dundee, of a bond granted by the latter, to relieve the said Dougal of the sum of 4,500 merks as balance of debt due by him to the late Mr. James Durhame of Easter Powrie. (One Sheet.) VIII, ii, 67.

373. **1664.** Nov. 5, 25.—Extract Act of the Lords in Council and Session appointing David Fotheringhame of Powrie, commissioner to take the depositions of parties in a complaint by Rachel Lindsay, relict of Captain Patrick Lindsay, and James Lindsay their son, as donators to the escheat of Alexander Lindsay of Pittallic, against Alexander Wedderburne, provost of Dundee, and the other magistrates thereof, for a certain debt. John Wedderburne, advocate, is procurator for the defenders.
(English, on paper, in bad condition.) I, i-ii, 98.

373ᵃ. Duplicate of No. 373. (One leaf, fair.) VII, iii, 21.

374. **1664.** Dec. 29.—Depositions of the magistrates of Dundee anent the said complaint. Signed by A. Wedderburne of Kingennie and others. (English, paper, fair state.) I, i-ii, 99.

375. **1665.** May 18.—Sasine to Dougal McPhersone, &c., of an annual rent of £320 out of Easter Powrie, pursuant to the obligation of 12 Sept. 1662. (Ante No. 352.)
(English, parchment, in good state.) VIII, vi, 5.

376. **1665.** Oct. 17.—Execution by David Doge, messsenger, of charge v. John (sic) Wedderburn of Kingennie, for payment of 30/- for each pound land of his £5 land of Easter Powrie for six terms of certain taxation. Dated at Edinburgh. V, i, 2ᴬ.
(English, paper, in bad condition. The name " John " is an error for Alexander.)

377. **1665.** Dec. 18.—Contract of marriage betwixt Alexander Wedderburne, only lawful son of Alexander Wedderburne of Kingennie, present provost of Dundee, procreat betwixt him and umquhile Elizabeth Ramsay his first spouse, and Grissell Wedderburne, fourth lawful daughter of Sir Alexander Wedderburne of Blackness, Knight. Signed at the foot by the said spouses and their respective fathers, and as witnesses by John Serymgeour of Kirktoun, George Fletcher, merchant burgess and bailie, Mr. Alexander Milne minister at Dundee, Mr. Thomas Gleg, doctor there, Johne Wedderburne, eldest lawful sone to the said Sir Alexander, William Wedderburne, brother german to the said Sir Alexander and others. I, i-ii, 99ᵃ.
(English, scroll of seven sheets of paper, in good condition. For fac-similes of the Wedderburn signatures see opp. p. 56.)

378. **1665.** Dec. 18.—Duplicate of the above contract. I, i-ii, 99ᵇ.

379. **1665.** Dec. 18.—Charter dated at Dundee in implement of the said marriage contract, entailing the lands and barony of Powrie on the said spouses and the heirs of their bodies. Witnessed and signed by Sir Alex W. of Blackness, John Serymgeour of Kirktoun, Patrick Kyd of Craigie, and others. VIII, vi, 6.
(Latin, parchment, in good condition.)

380. **1665**. Dec. 23.—Sasine following on the foregoing charter, dated at the manor place of Powrie. (Latin, parchment, in good condition.) VIII, vi, 7.

381. **1665**. Dec. 14,—Execution of Inhibition at the instance of Robert Campbell of Glenlyon *v.* Alexander Wedderburn of Kingennie, provost of Dundee, inhibiting him from selling or wadsetting his lands in defraud of the pursuer. (One small leaf.) VIII, ii, 68.

382. **1666**. Feb. 1.—Letters of loosing and arrestment raised at the instance of Alexander Wedderburn of Kingany *v.* Robert Campbell of Glenlyon, Margaret Scrymgeour, only lawful daughter of the deceased Major William Scrymgeour, Dougal McPherson of Powrie, Janet Guthrie his spouse, and John and Archibald his sons, over the fermes, maills, &c., of the lands of Kingany for the years 1664 and 1665. At Edinburgh 9 Jan. 1666. Endorsed with two executions 22 Jan. and 21 Feb. 1666. VIII, vii, 10.

383. **1666**. July 18.—Extract decreet of the Lords of Council and Session at the instance of Alexander Wedderburne of Kingennie, provost of Dundee, *v.* Margaret, daughter and only executrix of the late Major Scrymgeour, brother german of John Scrymgeour of Kirktoun, anent a legacy of 5000 merks due to the pursuer out of the estate of the said Major S. (Case continued.) Signed A. Primrose, Clk. Reg. (Two sheets of paper joined together, in good condition.) IV, iv, 10.

384. **1666**. (date blank).—Condescendance of Margaret Scrymgeour craving reduction of her obligations anent the legacy claimed by Alexander Wedderburn of Kingennie. (One foolscap sheet, in good state.) IV, iv, 11.

385. **1667**. March 28.—Petition by Alexander Wedderburne of Kingennie to the Commissary of Brechin for license to pursue before the Judge ordinary for such debts as were omitted furth of the confirmed testament of the late John Ramsay, bailie of Dundee, to whom the petitioner is executor confirmed on 5 April 1643 (ante No. 286). The license, dated 28 March 1667, is endorsed on the petition. I.i-ii, 100.

386. **1667**. June 22.—Execution of summons at the instance of Alexander Wedderburn of Powrie *v.* the curators of Margaret, only daughter and heir of the late Major William Scrymgeour, to compear before the Lords of the Council to exonerate the said A. W. of his executory as tutor to the said Margaret. v, iii, 9.

387. **1667**. Oct. 29.—Ratification by Janet Guthrie, wife of Dougal McPhersone of Powrie, in favour of Alexander Wedderburn of Kingennie of the disposition, ante No. 351. (One sheet.) VIII, ii, 70.

388. **1667**. Nov. 1.—Procuratory by Dougal McPhersone, lately of Easter Powrie, to Archibald McPherson to pass to the presence of Alexander Wedderburne, elder of Kingennie, late provost of Dundee, and there to make lawful requisition to him six days before Martinmas next for payment of 8000 merks &c. contained in an heritable bond (ante No. 352) granted by the said Alexander to the said Dougal and Janet Guthrie his spouse, of date 12 Sept. 1662. Dated at Dundee. VIII, vii, 11.

389. **1667**. Nov. 2.—Recognition by Dougal McPherson to Alexander Wedderburne for payment of 8000 merks due by the latter under bond dated 12 Sept. 1662, (ante No. 352) with protestation that, if he failed to pay, he should be liable in £1000 penalty. Instruments are taken thereon by Archibald McPhersone, son of the said Dougal, on his father's behalf. Done on the manor place of Easter Powrie on the date aforesaid. Francis Guthrie is notary. (One sheet.) VIII, ii, 69.

390. **1667**. Nov. 12.—Ratification by Janet Guthrie, spouse of Dougal McPherson of the disposition (ante No. 351) granted to Alexander Wedderburn, elder of Kingennie, of the lands of Easter Powrie. (One sheet.) VIII, ii, 72.

391. **1667.** Nov. 12.—Notarial instrument by Alexander Farquharson of Carnbirns as Scrymgeour-procurator for Dougal McPherson, late of Powrie, against Alexander Wedderburne Wedderburn '. älder of Kingennie, for not accepting certain discharges exhibited and offered to him Papers. for loosing arrestments. Dated at Dundee.　　　　　　　　　　　　　　viii, vii, 12.

392. **1667.** Nov. 19, 22.—Letters of horning at the instance of Dougal McPherson, sometime of Powrie, and Janet Guthrie his spouse v. Alexander Wedderburn of Kingany for not paying 8000 merks due by bond dated 12 Sept. 1662. Dated, Edinburgh 19 Nov. 1667, with execution attached dated 22 Nov.　　　　　viii, vii, 13.

393. **1667.** Nov. 21.—Discharge by Dougal McPhersone, Janet Guthrie his wife, and John McPhersone, his eldest son, to Alexander Wedderburne of Kingennie, of the summons raised by them against him for redemption of their disposition to him dated 12 Sept. 1662. See ante No. 351. (One sheet.)　　　　　　　viii, ii, 71.

394. **1668.** Jan 14.—Decreet in process of suspension at the instance of Alex. Wedderburn of Kingany against Dougal McPherson sometime of Powrie, and Janet Guthrie, who had raised letters of horning v. the pursuer, upon the said bond of 12 Sept. 1662 (ante Nos. 352 and 392), which horning is hereby suspended. Sir George McKenzie, Mr. David Dunmuir, and Mr John Wedderburn, advocates, are procurators for the said Alexander. Dated at Edinburgh.　　　　viii, vii, 14.

395. **1668.** Feb. 15.—Agreement between Alexander Wedderburne, younger of Kingany, and John Rany, weaver in Cottown of Murrosse, for setting in tack to the latter of the mill and mill lands of Kingany for 5 years, for which the said J. R. agrees to pay to the said A. W. yearly 15 bolls of oatmeal, one dozen of capons and one dozen of hens, and the said A. W. is to uphold the mill " in hir lyeing geir," and the said J. R. to uphold " hir goeing geir." (One sheet.)　　　　　　viii, ii, 73.

396. **1669.** May 18.—Discharge by William Gray of Haystoun, factor for William Duke of Hamilton, collector-general of the rents of the taxation granted in 1633, to Alexander Wedderburn of Kingany, for £9 as for the last three terms payment of the said taxation. Dated at Forfar. See ante No. 376. (English, paper, frail) v, i, 2.

397. **1669.** June 8.—Execution of letters raised at the instance of Alexander Wedderburn v. Dougal McPherson and Janet Guthrie his spouse.　　　　viii, vii, 15.

398. **1670.** (date wanting).—Note of sums contained in the production made by the Earl of Lauderdale in the action against him by the creditors of Lord Dundee, including " Item Sir Alexander Wedderburne £9733. 6. 8., annual rent £484. 0. 0." Undated, but about 1670. (One sheet in fair state.)　　　　　　　　iv, ii, 19.

399. **1670.** Feb. 4.—Act of the Lords of Council and Session nominating and appointing Sir James Dalrymple of Stair, Knt., and Sir Peter Wedderburne of Gosfuird, Knt., two of their number, to be auditors jointly in the process between Margaret Scrymgeour and Alexander Wedderburne of Kingennie, her tutor. Dated at Edinburgh.　　　　　　　　　　　　　　　　　　　vi, iv, 5.

399ᵃ. **1670.** (date wanting).—Petition for Alexander Wedderburn of Powrie to the Lords of Session to grant warrant to the clerk of Court for extracting their lordships' Interloquitur on a query reported to the Court by the Lords auditors aforesaid (No. 399), alleging that he knew the pursuer to be led on in their suit " by Dougal McPhersone her father-in-law out of a private splean he beares to the petitioner."　　　　　　　　　　　　　　　　　　　　　　　vi, iv, 6.

400. **1670.** March 2.—Protest and disclaimer by Alexander Chaplane, writer in Edinburgh, on behalf of Sir Alexander Wedderburne of Blackness and Alexander Wedderburne of Kingany, as curators to Mr. Alexander Milne, in regard to a certain assignation. Dated at Edinburgh, and made in the house of Sir George Mackenzie, advocate, before him, James Carnegie, writer to H.M. signet, and Robert Kinloch, merchant in Dundee. William Whyte is notary to the protest.　　i, ii, 101. (English, on paper, in good condition.)

H

401. **1670.** June 9.—Summons at the instance of James Horne v. John (*sic* for Alexander) Wedderburn of Kingennie of a bond granted to the pursuer by the late Mr. William Durham of Omachie.   I, i-ii,102.
(English, on paper, in fair condition. The word " John " is added in a different hand to that in which the body of the document is written.)

402. **1670.** July 1.—Letters of charge in the said cause.   I, i-ii, 103.

403. **1670.** July 1 —Warrant of Court for the said letters.   I, i-ii, 104.

404. **1670.** July 7.—Disposition to John Scrymgeour of Kirktoun, by Anna, Countess of Dundee, narrating bond of provision by the late John, Earl of Dundee, her husband, of date 29 Sept. 1659, whereby, in consideration of her renouncing her life-rent in certain lands, he became bound to infeft her in an annual rent furth of the mains of Dudope, as divided from the remaining lands thereof disponed by the said Earl to Sir Alexander Wedderburne of Blackness and others, his creditors, &c. (See ante No. 335). Dated at Edinburgh. (English, paper, frail.)   V, v, 16.

405. **1671.** Jan. 27.—Sasine on resignation by James Kinloch to Robert Waules of Dundee of a S. Nethergate land. James Wedderburn, writer in Dundee, is attorney for the resigner.   VIII, xxii, 4.

406. **1671.** June 17.—Petition for Alexander Wedderburn of Easter Powrie, referring to the aforesaid process between himself and Margaret Scrymgeour, and its long continuance, and explaining that he " hes beine much damnefied thorrow his constant attendance ilk session at Edinburgh " occasioned by the pursuer not insisting in the case except in his absence, and averring that though he had already obtained a decreet of exoneration, he was still ready to "compt and racken with the pursuer." The Lords ordain this declarator to come in before the auditors.   VI, iv, 15.

407. **1671.** June 17.—Petition for Margaret Scrymgeour that in respect she was to adduce "Lord Gosford and brother and remanent relations of the said tutor" as witnesses to prove his acting as tutor before accepting the office, Lord Colinton or Lord Castlehill be adjoined with Lord Newbyth as auditors, especially as Lord Gosford was willing. The Lords remit the compt and reckoning &c. to Lord Newbyth alone, with power to advise with Lord Gosford who was acquainted with the matter from the beginning.   VI, iv, 16.

408. **1671.** July 22.—Bond of relief by Alexander Wedderburne of Kingennie, narrating bond by John Scrymgeour of Kirktoun as principal, and David Fotheringham of Powrie as cautioner, for 8000 merks to Sir John Gibson of Adestone and "at the earnest desire of the said John S." relieving the said D. F. of his obligation as cautioner, and for his security, obliging A.W. to infeft the said D. F. in an annual rent of £320 out of Kingennie. (One sheet.)   VIII, ii, 74.

409. **1671.** Sept. 26.—Summons at the instance of Charles Maitland of Hatton v. the ladies Jean and Mary Scrymgeour, sisters of the late John, Earl of Dundee, and others, including Sir Alexander Wedderburn of Blackness, to have it declared that the late Viscount of Dudope, father of the said Earl, was vassal of the crown and died in 1644 leaving the said John his heir a minor and unmarried &c. &c.   V, iv, 6.

410. **1671.** Nov. 8.—Petition by Sir Alexander Wedderburne of Blackness, and James Wedderburne, town clerk of Dundee, his second son, anent the summons served on them at the instance of Dougal McPherson, sometime of Easter Powrie, to compear before the Lords of this date to swear as witnesses in the action raised by the said Dougal against Alexander Wedderburn now of Easter Powrie "anent matters of fact" done in the year 1651 or thereabouts ; alleging the said summons to be given out of malice and " meir splean and invy " to bring them into trouble, he "knowing very weill that I the said Sir Alexander (am) ane old and infirme man, not able to travel in the winter seasone for fear of incressing seikness and bringing infirmenes upon my bodie, not haveing stirred abroad from chamber this six or seven weekes

past, and not intending thorrow infirmenes to goe abroad this winter." The said **Scrymgeour-** James W. declares that he was not above 5 or 6 years of age when the facts in question **Wedderburn** happened. The petition craves therefore that a commission might be granted to **Papers.** take their oaths at Dundee. The Lords grant a commission to Provost George Brown or bailie George Forester in Dundee. vi, iv, 26.

411. **1671.** Nov. 8.—Extract of above commission, for report on Feb. 6. vi, iv, 27.

412. **1672.** Feb. 6.—Report of the said commission with depositions of the said Sir Alexander, aged 6 2, and of James W., aged 22. vi, iv, 28.

413. **1672.** June 24.—Discharge by Robert Lindsay (eldest son of the late Major Robert Lindsay and Margaret Milne), now long after his majority, to Alexander Wedderburn of Easter Powrie, now husband to the said M. Milne, for 1000 m. contained in a bond of provision granted by the deceased Janet Milne, sister of the said Margaret, and daughter of the late Alexander Milne, merchant in Dundee. (One sheet.) viii, ii, 75.

414. **1672.** June (?).—Roll of defenders in the action of declaration of recognition by Charles Maitland of Hatton, donator to the barony of Dundee, v. John Scrymgeour of Kirktoun, Sir Alexander Wedderburn of Blackness, and others. iii, v, 8.

415. **1672.** July (?).—Minutes of proceedings of the above action. iii, v, 9.

416. **1672.** July (?).—Executions (eight in number) of principal summonses to the defenders in the above action. iii, v, 10.

417. **1672.** Sept. 7.—Back-bond by Alexander Wedderburn, younger of Kingany, narrating bond by John Scrymgeour of Kirktoun to him, of the same date, by which the said John engaged to infeft the said A. W. in an annual rent of 480 merks furth of his lands of Kirktoun, under reversion for 8000 merks, which bond was merely for the relief of the said Alexander of another bond granted by him in 166- to David Fotheringham of Powrie, whereby the granter became bound to relieve the said D. F. of his cautionery for the said J. S. to Sir John Gibson of Aldinston for a similar amount (ante No. 408) and now for the security of the said J.S., the granter's brother-in-law, he becomes bound to grant a renunciation of the said annual rent as soon as the bond to Gibson is discharged. Dated at Dundee. J. Wedderburn, fiar of Blackness, is a witness. (English, paper, fair condition.) v, iii, 11.

418. **1672-73.** Jan. 9.—Summons of Recognition at the instance of Charles Maitland of Hatton, donator to the Lands and Barony of Dundee, &c., v. various persons, including Sir Alexander Wedderburn of Blackness. iii, x, 3.

419. **1673.** (about).—Copy of the family register of Sir Alexander Wedderburn of Blackness, Knt., in the hand of Alexander Scrymgeour-Wedderburn of Wedderburn. Made by him from the original in 1799. See Blackness papers No. 9. i, i-ii, 155.

420 **1673.** July 5.—Decreet in action at the instance of Charles Maitland of Hatton v. George, only son of George Dunbar of Aslisk and the late Margaret Carnegie, and others, including David, Earl of Northesk, and Sir Alexander Wedderburn of Blackness, as tenants and possessors of the lands and baronies of Rossie and of Dundee, for decerning the said lands and baronies as now in the King's hands by recognition. The Lords find that Northesk and Wedderburn are exempt from the action because they were infeft in their parts of the lands of Dudhope long prior to the pursuer's right. Dated at Edinburgh. iv, iv, 15. (Scroll of twelve sheets, a good deal torn and injured at either end.)

421. **1673.** July 29.—Inventory of the writs not produced by Kingennie which it is yet craved he may be ordained to exhibit to Margaret Scrymgeour his pupil. i, i-ii, 105. (English, paper, in good condition. Various members of the Scrymgeour family are named.)

422. **1673.** Oct. 21.—Discharge by Robert Lindsay, eldest son now on life of the late Major Robert Lindsay, residenter in Dundee, by his wife Margaret Milne, now spouse to Alexander Wedderburne of Easter Powrie, acknowledging receipt from his mother and her said present spouse of all the heirship goods due to him by his father's decease. (One sheet.)   VIII, ii, 76.

423. **1673.** Nov. 27.—Scroll of depositions in the action by Viscount Dudope *v.* Kingennie and others, including *inter alia* :—"Item, as to the 21st article anent the inventar, the samen being referred to Kingennie's, the defender's, oath anent the having of the samen, depones negative as he shall answer to God. A. Wedderburn." (signed). Dated at Edinburgh. (Paper, in good state.)   IV, ii, 16.

424. **1674.** June 26.—Assignation by Sir Alexander Wedderburne of Blackness to John Wedderburne fiar thereof, his eldest son, of the sum of £406. 3. 4. scots, with expenses, contained in a bond, dated 17 June 1661, and granted to the said Sir Alexander by Andrew Watt, flesher, burgess of Dundee. (See ante No. 348.) III, vi, 3.

425. **1674.** Sept 15.—General charge at the instance of John Wedderburn *v.* (John) Watt, son and apparent heir to the deceased Andrew Watt, flesher, burgess of Dundee, to enter heir to the said Andrew his father for implement of divers contracts and other securities &c. Indorsed "6 of October, chargit John Watt his tutors or curators for their entres."   III, vi, 4.

426. **1675.** March 12.—Summons at the instance of John Wedderburn, fiar of Blackness, against John Watt as heir to his father, for payment of the abovementioned bond (ante No. 424), granted to Sir Alexander Wedderburn and assigned to the said John Wedderburn.   III, vi, 5.

427. **1675.** Aug. 14.—Decreet of poynding; Alexander Wedderburne of Kingany *v.* John Scrymgeour, heritor of the Kirktoun of Strickmartine, &c. and others, his tenants, for non payment of an annual rent of 480 merks upon the principal sum of 8000 m., in which the pursuer was infeft on 29 July, 1673, to be levied from the defenders' lands of Kirktoun of Erlistradichtie, lands of Balgovan, &c., &c , all erected into one free barony called the Tenandrey of the Banke. (Scroll of three sheets.) VIII, ii, 77.

427ª. **1676.** July 26.—Objections by Margaret Scrymgeour against the scroll of the Interloquitor in the action pursued by her *v.* Kingennie her tutor. I, i-ii, 105ª. (English, paper, in good condition.)

428. **1676.** Aug. 24.—Summons at the instance of Alexander Wedderburne of Kingany *v.* John Scrimgeour of Kirktoun, now furth of the realme, for poinding his goods in satisfaction of an annual rent of £320 scots. (English, on paper, in fair state.) V, iii, 12.

429. **1676.** Feb. 22.—Discharge by David Lindsay, merchant in Edinburgh, son of the said Major Robert Lindsay of Dundee, in favour of Margaret Milne, relict of the said Major R. L., and execentrix of the late Janet Milne her sister, and Alexander Wedderburne of Easter Powrie her husband, for £1000 left him by the said Janet. Dated at Dundee. (One sheet of paper.)   VIII, ii, 78.

430. **1677.** April 16.—Extract act of apprising by the bailies of Dundee of certain tenements therein, the owners of which had not paid their ground annuals. Dated April 16 and 21, and May 14, 1677. Signed by James Wedderburne. It names Alexander Wedderburn of Easter Powrie and John Wedderburn of Blackness. (Parchment.)   VIII, I 31.

431. **1677.** May 26. Assignation by Walter Graham of Duntrune to Elizabeth Guthrie his wife, and Alexander Graham, their son, of a bond granted to him by Alexander Wedderburn elder of Kingennie, provost of Dundee, with Alexander Wedderburn younger of Kingennie, his eldest son, as cautioner, for 800 m. VIII, ii, 79. (One piece of paper.)

432. **1677.** Dec. 22.—Discharge by Wm. Carnegie in Edinburgh to Alexander Wedderburn of Kingennie. Witnessed by Peter Wedderburn, merchant in Dundee, and Peter Wedderburne, son to Lord Gosford. (Paper, in good state. See facsimile opp. p. 56.) I, i-ii, 105[b]. *Scrymgeour-Wedderburn Papers.*

433. **1678.** June 18.—Extract retour of special service of John Graham of Claverhouse, as heir to the late Sir William Graham of Claverhouse, his great grandfather, in the lands of Gotterstoun, &c. Alexander Wedderburne of Kingennie is on the inquest. Expede in the Court-house of the burgh of Forfar.   IV, iii, 6.
(The heir retoured became the great Viscount Dundee, who died at Killiecrankie in June, 1689.)

433[a]. **1678.** June 18.—Similar retour of the same as heir to the late William Graham his father in the barony of Ogilvie. Kingennie is again on the inquest. Expede the same as No. 433.   IV, iii, 7.

434. **1678.** July 18.—Extract decreet at the instance of Alexander Wedderburne, younger of Kingany, v. Sir George Kinnaird of Rossie, Knight, John Bruce, merchant burgess of Dundee, and others, for implement of a bond granted by Robert Lindsay, merchant burgess of Dundee, dated 5 June 1677, for 800 merks due to the pursuer, the said amount having been arrested in the hands of the said Sir George and other defenders. Case continued till Nov. 1. Dated at Edinburgh.   I, i-ii, 106.
(English, on paper, torn and much soiled.)

435. **1678.** Nov. 15.—Obligation by Alexander Wedderburn, younger of Kingennie, to James Graham, chamberlain to the Laird of Claverhous, for 200 merks, signed by him at Dundee before David Grahame of Duntroon and Thomas Steell. Endorsed with a discharge thereof to the said Alexander W. "now of Easter Pourie," dated 22 Jan., 1686, by David Grahame of Duntroon, George Grahame, minister at Innerearitie, and Mr. Alexander Grahame at Claverhous, tutors dative to Walter, James, Euphame, and Christian Grahame, children of the late James Grahame, grantee of the bond.
(One sheet of paper.)   VIII, ii, 98.

436. **1678.** Dec. 17.—Discharge by Alexander and Margaret Ogilvie, indwellers in Dundee, to Alexander Wedderburn of Easter Powrie, provost of Dundee. VIII, ii, 80.
(One piece of paper.)

437. **1679.** Feb. 21.—Instrument in favour of James Lyon of certain tenements in Dundee resigned by Isabella, daughter and heir of William Brugh, merchant there. James Wedderburne, clerk of Dundee, is notary.   VIII, xiv, 34.

438. **1679.** June 7.—Petition by Christiane Scrymgeour, one of the three daughters and heirs portioners of umquhile Hugh Scrymgeour of Ballraymons, with deliverance of the Lords, signed for them by Pet. Wedderburne (Lord Gosford).   III, vi, 7.

439. **1679.** Aug. 1.—Copy of Lord Maitland's confirmation from the Crown of the lands and parish of Benvie and Balruthrie, mains and manor place of Dudop, &c., lands vulgarly called Aikerdale or Blackness Acres, lately belonging to Sir Alexander Wedderburn of Blackness, consisting of 38 acres or thereby, which are parts of the barony of Dundee and in the parish of thereof, &c. (One long sheet, fair.)   VI, iii, 90.

440. **1679.** Dec. 29.—Discharge by David Grahame of Duntroon to Alexander Wedderburn of Easter Powrie, provost of Dundee, for £24 interest for 3/4 of a year on 800 merks due by the granter to Alexander Graham, brother of the granter, in fee, and to his mother in liferent, and granted by him as executor of his late father Walter Graham of Duntroon. (One small piece of paper.)   VIII, ii, 81.

441. **1680.** July 12.—Decreet of poynding by John Scott and John Mair, bailies of Dundee, at the instance of Robert Cristan, deacon of the wrights, for an annual rent of £12 due to the incorporation of the wrights from a S. Flukergate tenement. Extracted by James Wedderburne and signed by him. See opp. p. 56. I, i-ii, 107.
(English, parchment, in good state.)

Scrymgeour-
Wedderburn
Papers.

442. **1680.** July 17.—Disposition by Alexander Wedderburn, youngest lawful son to the
deceast Sir Alexander Wedderburn of Blackness, Knight, in favour of Alexander
Wedderburn of Easter Powrie, of certain land on the N. of the Argylegait, once
disponed by Barten Bilsone to the said Sir Alexander on 4 May 1660 (ante No. 338).
Signed by the granter, and as witness by his brother german George Wedderburn,
merchant in Edinburgh.   (Paper, in good state.)   I, i-ii, 107ᴬᴬ.

443. **1680.** July 22, &c.—Contract between the said granter and grantee, reciting the
said disposition (ante No. 442), and agreeing that, as there may be some persons
pretending right to the said subjects, the granter shall, if the grantee be evicted therefrom, return him the price thereof. Dated at Edinburgh 22 July and at Dundee 22 Sept.
Signed by the parties and witnessed by George Wedderburn as in No. 442.
(English, paper. See facsimile of signatures of granter and witness opp. p. 56.)   I, i-ii, 107ᵃ.

444. **1680.** Sept. 14.—Contract between David Lindsay and George Wedderburne,
merchants burgesses of Edinburgh, on one part, and James Angus, skipper, burgess
of Bruntisland "maister (under God) of the good ship Blissing of Bruntisland " on
the other part, whereby the latter engages to ship certain goods for the former, at the
port of Penleiff in the river Hautize in France, and for that purpose, to have his ship
well equipped and manned : for which the former parties engage to pay him or his
heirs £96 sterling. Dated at Dundee. Signed by the parties.   I, i-ii, 107ᵇ.
(English, on paper, in good condition.)

445. **1680.** Oct. 19.—Discharge to Alexander Wedderburn of Easter Powrie granted by
Elizabeth Guthrie, relict of Walter Graham of Duntroon, for £32, a year's interest
on 800 m. (see ante No. 440.) Dated at Claverhouse.   VIII, ii, 82.
(One small piece of paper.)

446. **1680.** Nov. 1.—Discharge by David Fotheringhame, laird of Powrie, to Alexander
Wedderburn of Kingennie of the bond (ante No. 408) dated 22 July 1671, for
8000 m. (One sheet of paper.)   VIII, ii, 83.

447. **1680.** Nov. 4.—Sasine on resignation by George Rattray, writer in Dundee, as
procurator for and in name of Alexander Wedderburn, younger son of the late Sir
Alexander Wedderburn, of various subjects, into the hands of John Serimgeour,
one of the bailies of Dundee, as into the hands of the King, immediate superior
thereof, in favour of and for new infeftment to Alexander Wedderburn of Easter
Powrie his heirs and assignees, to whom sasine was given accordingly by the said
bailie. The notary is James Wedderburne. (Latin, parchment.)   VIII, i, 32.

   The subjects resigned are eleven in number :—

(1) Half that fore tenement of land sometime pertaining to the said Sir Alexander and by him dis-
    poned to the said Alexander his son, lying on the N. of the Argyllgate, between the lands of
    David Ramsay baker on the E., the lands of Robert Symsone on the W. .... on the N.
    and the said gate on the South.
(2) Half of those two houses or interior tenements of land, sometime pertaining to the said Sir
    Alexander and disponed as aforesaid lying on N. Argyllgate and on the W. side of the said
    fore tenement and adjacent thereto, between the malthouse now pertaining to .... on
    the North, and the said fore tenement on the S.
(3) Half of that tenement sometime pertaining to the said Sir Alexander on N. Argyllgate on the
    E. side of the said close, between the lands of the heirs and successors of the late Alexander
    Symer on the North, the lands of the heirs of William Davidson on the East, the said close
    on the West and the said gate on the South.
(4) Half of an annual rent of 24 merks furth of that tenement sometime belonging to the late
    Archibald Kid, afterwards to the heirs of James Kid his grandson (nepos) lying on the S.
    side of the Seagate, between the lands sometime of the late James Fethie and now of
    .... on the East, the lands of Patrick Burgh, skinner, on the West, the tide mark on the
    South, and the said Seagate on the North.
(5) The half of an annual rent of 8 m. furth of that tenement of land sometime belonging to the
    late James Mackie and now to the heirs of Hendrie Davidson, baker, on the South side of
    the Moraygate, between the lands sometime of Andrew Robertson, now of the heirs of
    David Gourlay on the East, the lands of the heirs of James Anderson on the West, the lands
    of William Man on the South, and the said gate on the North.
(6) Half of an annual rent of 30s furth of that tenement sometime of John and William Walker
    successively and now ... ... lying on N. Moraygate between the lands of the late John

Barrie and now of the heirs of John Spalding on the East, the close and back tenement of that tenement sometime of James Roch now of .... on the West, the lands of the heirs of Alexander .... on the North, and the said gate on the South.

(7) Half of an annual rent of £3 furth of that tenement formerly of Thomas Logie and now of the heirs of William Fitulloch on the N. of the Moraygate, between the lands sometime of James Baxter and now of the heirs of Patrich Ruthven merchant on the west, the lands of the heirs of Andrew Watsone and James Thomsone on the East, the lands of .... on the North, and the said gate on the South.

(8) Half of an annual rent of 10 merks, furth of that tenement sometime of the late Duncan Udnie, and now of the heirs of the late William Lyne, dyer, on N. Moraygate, between the lands of Andrew Guthrie on the East, the lands sometime of Robert Barrie on the West, the lands of the late William Lyne on the North, and the said gate on the South.

(9) Half of an annual rent of 5 merks furth of that tenement of land sometime of .... and now of the heirs of Andrew Paull, maltman, on W. Wellgate, between the lands of .... on the N , the lands of .... on the S, the acres of Dudhope on the West, and the said gate on the East.

(10) Half of an annual rent of 10 merks out of that tenement of the heirs of .... and now of the heirs of William Petrie, maltman, lying on the head of the shore of the said burgh between the lands of .... on the West ; the lands of .... on the East, the lands of .... on the North, and the shore on the South.

(11) An annual rent of 10 merks out of that tenement of land sometime belonging to .. .. and now to the heirs of Gilbert Guthrie younger, lying on the said shore between the lands of .... on the East, of .... on the West, the said shore on the South, and .... on the North.

448. **1680.** Nov. 4.—Instrument of sasine proceeding on disposition by an honourable man, Alexander Wedderburn of Easter Powrie, provost of Dundee, in favour of Patrick Wedderburne, his only lawful son by his wife Margaret Mylne, of the just and equal half of 10 various subjects. The notary is James Wedderburne, who adds his signature and motto " Dum spiro, spero." The subjects are, with the exception of No. 3, those contained in the preceeding instrument (No. 447.)   I, i-ii, 108.

(Latin, on parchment in good condition, but the ink much faded. In this sasine the first subject is wrongly described as once that " of Sir Alexander Wedderburn, and by him disponed to *the late* Alexander Wedderburn, merchant, instead of to " his son Alexander Wedderburn " as in No. 447.)

449. **1680.** Nov. 29-30.—Obligation by Robert Hunter of Baldovic to James Grahame of Monorgan and Alexander Wedderburne of Easter Powrie, his tutors and curators, that in view of their faithful management of his affairs he will never question the same.

(One sheet of paper.)   VIII, ii, 85.

450. **1680.** Dec. 9.—Extract decreet of the Lords of Council and Session at the instance of George, Earl of Panmure, v. Alexander Wedderburn, present provost of Dundee, and other magistrates of the burgh, for allowing Alexander Lamb, younger, in Carsbank, who was imprisoned for debt to the pursuer, to escape out of the Tolbooth of Dundee. The defenders plead non-liability, and the Lords sustain their defence.

(English, two pieces of paper joined together, in good condition.)   I, i-ii, 109.

451. **1680.** Dec. 27.—Tack by Alexander Wedderburn of Kingennie to Thomas Smyth of the lands of Burnsyde in the barony of Easter Powrie. The tack duty is 15 bolls bear and 15 bolls oat meal. Signed by the granter and witnessed by Peter Wedderburn, merchant in Dundee.   VIII, ii, 84.

(One sheet of paper. The granter is Alexander W. fourth of Kingenuie, and second of Easter Powrie.)

452. **1681.** May 18.—Assignation by Alexander Wedderburne, merchant, burgess of Dundee, master of the good ship called " Johne of Leith," in favour of George Wedderburn, merchant, burgess of Edinburgh, of two bonds therein specified, one of which was granted by James Wedderburne, clerk of Dundee, " therein designed brother german " of the said Alexander, and was dated 25 April last past, for £416. 13. 4. Dated at Edinburgh. Signed by the granter.   I, i,ii, 110.

(English, two pieces of paper joined together, in good condition. The signature is the same as that to No. 443. See opposite p. 56.)

453. **1681.** July 27.—Bond of provision by Alexander Wedderburne of Easter Powrie to Elizabeth Wedderburne, his only daughter now on life by Margaret Milne his wife. The sum provided is 3000 merks. The granter's signature is torn out.   VIII, ii, 87.

(One sheet of paper).

454. 1681. Aug. 10.—Discharge by Elizabeth Guthrie, relict of Walter Graham of Duntroon, to Alexander Wedderburn of Easter Powrie for £32 interest due Whitsunday 1680-81. Signed by Eliz. Guthrie. See ante Nos. 432, 445.   VIII, ii, 86.
(One small piece of paper.)

455. 1681. Aug. 20, 24.—Bond by Alexander Wedderburne, younger of Kingennie, as principal, and by his father Alexander W. of Easter Powrie, provost of Dundee, as cautioner, to John Wedderburne of Gosford for 5000 merks. Signed by the said principal and cautioner before John Wedderburn of Blackness and other witnesses.
(One piece of paper, somewhat torn.)   VIII, ii, 92.

456. 1682. March 7.—Decreet in the process raised by David Lindsay of Edzell *v.* Margaret Milne and Alexander Wedderburne of Powrie, her spouse, for suspension of letters of horning at their instance against him for non-payment of the annual rent on 3000 merks due since Whitsunday 1676 conform to bond granted by said David to Robert Lindsay, merchant burgess of Dundee, dated 2 June, 1675, and assigned by the said Robert to the defenders. The Lords decern for the said Margaret Milne and her spouse, with deduction of sums due by the said Robert Lindsay to the pursuer,
(Six sheets of paper, formerly joined together.)   VIII, ii, 88.

457. 1682. July 22.—Letter signed "Yoʳ loving cousin and servant" from Alexander Wedderburne of Kingennie to George Wedderburne, merchant, Edinburgh, dated from Dundee, referring to their troublesome correspondence, and the difficulty of settling differences in that way. It adds :—"Sir, I hope when yowe consider that all the rights in the person of Alexander Wedderburne or James Wedderburne to the twa ground annuell ar wanting except the sasine, yeat I hope there is no great hazard becaus of possession. I hope ye will not be stickling to requyr bond of warrandice of your brother's disposition, for that bond yowe alreadie grantit," &c. The reference is clearly to the contract (ante No. 443) of 22 July 1680.   I, i-ii, 111.
(One sheet, in very bad state. The signet seal of the writer is still on the paper, and shows a chevron between three roses, and part of the motto "Non Degener." There is no fleur de lys on the chevron.)

458. 1682. Sept. 15-16.—Disposition by Isobell Stewart, relict of John Haisils, in favour of her son John of an East Wellgait tenement in Dundee. Witnessed by James Wedderburn, clerk of Dundee.   VIII, xii, 28.

459. 16—. (undated.)—Memorandum for Alexander Wedderburn of Easter Powrie, relative to the disposition by him to Peter Wedderburn his son, of the lands of Wester Gourdie "which are provided to him and the heirs of his body, quhilks failzeing to his heirs male, reserving Powrie's life-rent and his wife Margaret Milne her life-rent in so far as may effeir to the annual rent of nine thousand merkes provided to hir be hir contract of marriage."   II, ii, 16.
(Undated, but of course before the death of Easter Powrie 9 April 1683.)

460. 1683. Nov. 22.—Discharge by William Whyte, factor to John Wedderburne of Gosfoord (conform to letters of factorie, dated 13 Feb. 1640, registered in the books of Council and Session 17 Feb. 1680), in favour of Alexander Wedderburne of Easter Powrie for £200 scots, a year's annual rent on the sum of 5000 merks due to the said John Wedderburne by the said A. W. and the late Alexander Wedderburne conform to a bond dated 20 Aug. 1681. See ante No. 455.   (One piece of paper.)   VIII, ii, 89.

461. 1683. Dec. 20.—Great Seal charter confirming the lands and barony of Powrie to Alexander Wedderburne, now of Powrie, son to the late Alexander Wedderburne of Powrie.   (Latin, parchment, part of the great seal attached.)   VIII, vi, 7ᵃ.

462. 1684. Jan. 7.—Act of conversion in favour of Alexander W. of Easter Powrie, relative to the S. Murraygait land once belonging to David Wedderburne, burgess of Dundee, and then to the Lowsones. Extracted and signed by James Wedderburne.
(English, parchment, in good state. See ante Nos. 13 and 326.)   VIII, vi, 8.

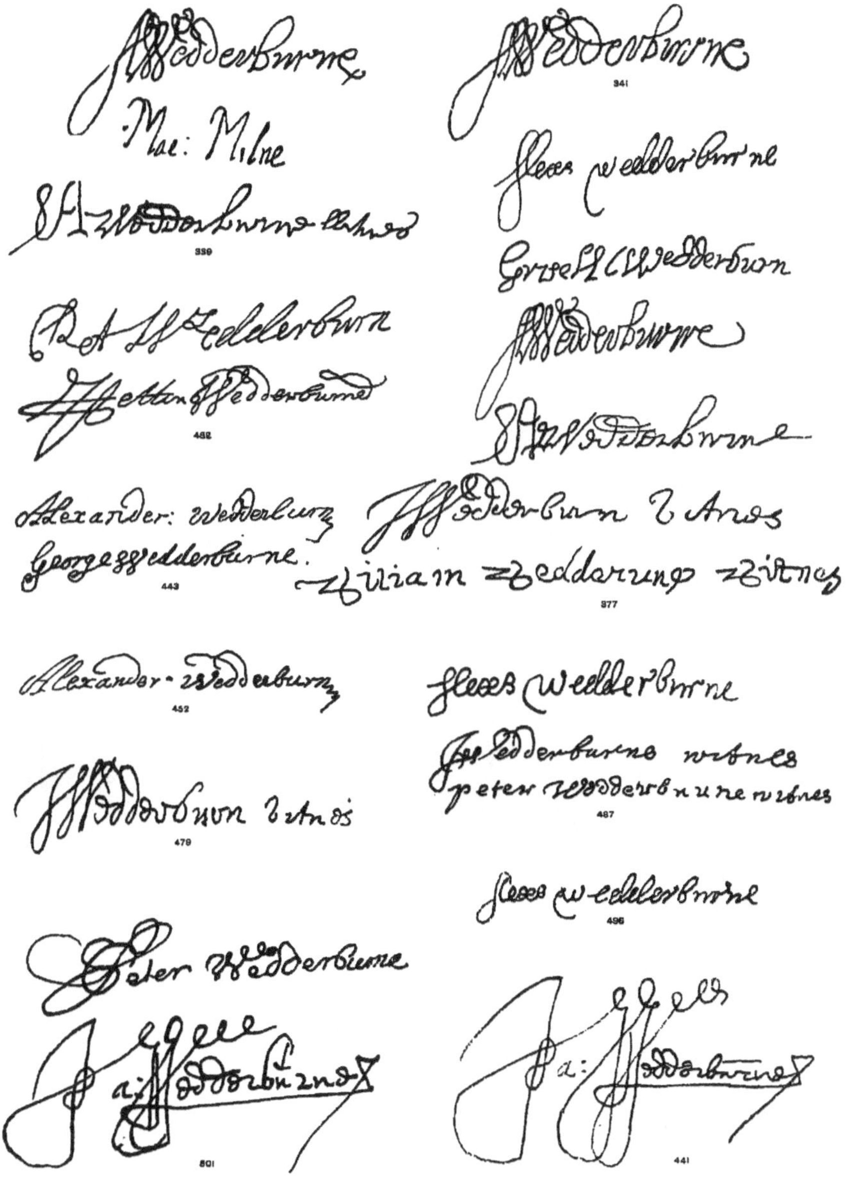
339
341
482
443
377
452
479
487
496
501
441

463. **1684.** (date wanting).—Information for Sir William Nicolson and Sir William Murray of Newtoun, in the action raised *v.* them by John Wedderburn of Gosford, as heir to the late Sir Peter W his father, for payment of the tack duty of the coal of Innerwick. (English, on paper, in good state.) I, i-ii, 112.

Scrymgeour-Wedderburn Papers.

464. **1684.** (date wanting).—Information for John Wedderburn of Gosford in the same matter. (English, on paper, in good state.) I, i ii, 113.

465. **1684.** (date wanting).—Interrogatione for Colonel John Grahame of Claverhouse *v.* the Earl Lauderdale, inquiring thirdly "How much land is within the park that belonged to umquhile Sir Alexander Wedderburne of Blackness or John Wedderburne now of Blackness, and was excambed by the Earl of Lauderdale with them, and if the lands disponed by Lauderdale to Blackness in excambion did belong to the Earl of Dundee, and were accompted a part of the old rental and what rent the said lands so disponed to Blackness payed yearly. Signed Jo. Ouchterlony " I, i-ii, 114.
(English, a small piece of paper, somewhat worn.)

466. **1684.** Feb 15.—Report of commission in the case between these parties and depositions of witnesses. (English, two pieces of paper joined together, in good state.) I, i-ii, 115.

467. **1684.** June 14.—Discharge by Elizabeth Wedderburne, "onlie lawful daughter of the late Alexander Wedderburne of Easter Powrie, sometime provost of Dundee," to Alexander W. now of Easter Powrie, for £120 scots, being one year's annual rent on 3000 merks due to her under a bond of provision made to her by her late father of date 27 July 1681 (ante No. 453). Signed, Eli : Wedderburne. VIII, ii, 90.
(One small piece of paper.)

468. **1684.** July 16.—Extract retour of the general service of Alexander Wedderburne of Easter Powrie as heir to the deceased Alexander Wedderburne his father. Expede at Dundee. (Latin, parchment, fair.) V, i, 4.

469. **1684.** July 16.—Inquest and retour of the said Alexander W. as heir to the late A. W. his father. (Latin, two pieces of parchment, in good condition.) VIII, vi, 9.

470. **1684.** July 18.—Charter by James, Marquis of Douglas, confirming the lands of Kingennie to Alexander Wedderburn of Kingennie and Grisild Wedderburn his wife and their heirs. (Latin, parchment, in good state, part of the seal still attached.) VIII, vi, 10.

471. **1684.** Dec. 19.—Discharge by John Wedderburne of Gosford to Alexander Wedderburn of Easter Powrie for £200 scots, one year's interest &c. (as in No. 460). Signed at Edinburgh by the said John W. before William Whyte and Archibald Law, his servants. (One piece of paper.) VIII, ii, 91.

472. **1685.** Dec. 19.—Extract judicial ratification by Marjorie Butchart, wife of Thomas Scott of Dundee, of a disposition made by them. Extracted and subscribed by James Wedderburne, "nottar publiet and towne clerk of the said burgh." VII, xiv, 35.

473. **1685.** Dec. 19.—Sasine thereon. Witnessed by the said James W. VIII, xiv, 36.

474. **1686.** Discharge by Mr. Robert Edward, minister of Murroes, and by the Kirk session thereof, to Mr. Alexander Wedderburn of Easter Powrie, for various payments. Signed by the granter. (One sheet of paper.) VIII, ii, 93.

475. **1686.** March 16.—Special retour of Alexander Wedderburn of Easter Powrie as heir to the deceased Alexander Wedderburn of Easter Powrie, his father, in all and whole the sunny half of the lands of Wester Gourdie with the teind sheaves thereof. II, ii, 13.

476. **1686.** May 12.—Precept from chancery following on the above retour in favour of the said A. W. · · II, ii, 14.

I

477. **1686.** May 20.—Instrument of sasine in favour of the said A. W., following on the above precept. Registered 5 July.   II, ii, 15.

478. **1686.** May 1.—Contract of marriage, dated at Dundee, between George Jack, maltman in Dundee, and Magdalen, daughter of James Thomsone, with consent and advyce of Alexander Wedderburn of Easter Powrie, who pays the said spouses 200 merks and some other small sums by way of tocher and in discharge of all the said Magdalene can claim through the decease of her mother . . . Wedderburne or under the will of the late Alexander Wedderburne of Easter Powrie. Alexander W. signs the contract. (Two sheets of paper joined together.)   VIII, ii, 94.

479. **1687.** Oct. 7.—Bond of provision by Alexander Wedderburne of Easter Powrie as principal, and John W. his eldest son and apparent heir as cautioner, in favour of Peter Wedderburne, second son of the said Alexander, " for his better helpe to ane honest lyviehood and sustentatioue in this world," providing him to the sum of 6000 merks, payable at the first term of Whitsunday or Martinmas after the death of the granter, and, in the event of the said Peter departing this life before attaining the age of 21 years, the sum aforesaid is to be divided in favour of his brothers and sisters thus : to the said John W. 4300 merks, and 500 m. each to Alexander, Margaret, and Rachel Wedderburnes. Dated at Easter Powrie. John W. of Blackness signs as a witness. (English, on paper, in good state, but one corner torn off. See opp. p. 56.)   I, i-ii, 116.

480. **1687.** Jan. 18.—Discharge by John Wedderburn of Gosford to Alexander Wedderburn of Easter Powrie for £200 scots, a year's interest on the sum of 5000 merks. (See ante Nos. 455, 460.) Signed by John Wedderburn before Alexander Dunbar and William Whyte as witnesses. (One sheet of paper.)   VIII, ii, 95.

481. **1687.** May 20.—Instrument of sasine, proceeding on disposition by James Kyd of Craigie in favour of Helen Fotheringhame his spouse, of 15 chalders of victual, of wheat, barley and meal proportionately, furth of the lands and barony of Craigie, in life-rent, without prejudice to the liferent right of Margaret Wedderburn, relict of Patrick Kyd of Craigie, in terms of her jointure. The disposition is dated at Dundee 20 May, and Mr. James Brisbane, advocate, is a witness. Sasine is given on May 24, and Mr. George Fotheringhame of Bandean is a witness. Registered in the particular Register of Sasines for Forfar, 8 May, 1687.   I, i-ii, 117. (English, parchment, in good condition.)

482. **1687.** Nov. 30.—Similar discharge to No. 480, for the said £200 annual rent. Signed by John Wedderburn before the same witnesses. (One piece of paper.)   VIII, ii, 96.

483. **1688.** (date wanting).—Petition by John Wedderburn of Blaknes, clerk to the bills, Mr. David Scrymgeour of Carpmore and others, as creditors of George Wedderburne, asking the Lords of Session to ordain one of the clerks of Session to inventory and take into his custody all the papers of the said George W. " he having turned back on his affairs and departed out of these kingdomes," and the said papers " being lying within ane closet in the house of James Sutherland."   I, i-ii, 119. (English, on paper, in good condition.)

484. **1688.** June 13.—Bond for 5000 merks by Alexander Wedderburn of Easter Powrie to James Wedderburn, clerk of Dundee, signed by the said A. W. before " John Wedderburne my eldest laufull sone " (who also signs) and other witnesses. VIII, ii, 97. (One sheet of paper.)

485. **1688.** (undated).—Roll of the creditors of Foodie, in Fife, among whom is "Beatrix Wedderburne, widdow in Couper." See No. 486.   I, i-ii, 120. (English, on paper, in bad condition.)

486. **1688.** July 18.—Summons at the instance of certain tenants of Foodie, for suspension of letters raised against them by .... Scrymgeour, baillie in Dundee, Margaret Turnbull, widow in Cowpar, Beatrix Wedderburne, widow in Cowpar, and others, for payment of their mailis. (English, on paper, a good deal torn.)   I. i-ii, 121.

487. **1688**. Dec. 4, 5.—Contract of marriage between William Wallace, son of Patrick Scrymgeour-Wedderburn Papers. Wallace, in the ground of Megganes, on one part, and Elspeth Thomsone, youngest daughter of James Thomsone and umquhile Marjory Wedderburne, natural daughter of umquhile Mr. Alexander Wedderburne of Kingennie, town clerk of Dundee, goodsire to Alexander Wedderburne now of Easter Powrie, with advice and consent of him and her father, on the other part, for the marriage of the said William and Elspeth, in contemplation of which the said Patrick Wallace dispones to the said William his son and his said apparent spouse and the survivor of them, and to the bairns of the marriage, all his movable goods and gear, including money and securities, together with his right to possession of Megganes, on condition that the grantees do maintain and entertain the said Patrick " in familie with themselves according to his rank and degrie," and also reserving power to provide his eldest son Thomas Wallace to the sum of 100 merks. The said Alexander Wedderburn of Easter Powrie, with consent of the said James Thomsone, becomes bound to pay 200 merks in name of tocher with the said Elspeth. Dated at Dundee and Woodhill. Signed by the said A. W., and as witnesses by John Wedderburn, younger of Easter Powrie, Peter Wedderburn his brother, and others.   i, i-ii, 118.
   (English, paper, in good condition. See facsimile of signatures opp. p. 56.)

488. **1689** Oct 25.—Discharge of James Kinnaird in the hillok of Ethiehetoune to Alexander Wedderburne of Easter Powrie for the annual rent of 600 merks.
   (One small piece of paper.)   VIII, ii, 99.

489. **1690**. July 22.—Discharge by David Hunter of Burnsyde to Alexander Wedderburn of Easter Powrie for the annual rent of 800 merks. Signed D. Hunter.
   (One small piece of paper.)   •   VIII, ii, 102.

490. **1690**. Oct. 13.—Discharge by James Wedderburne, clerk of Dundee, to Alexander Wedderburne of Easter Powrie for the annual rent of 5000 merks. Signed by James W. before Peter Wedderburne, merchant in Dundee, and James Ramsay, clerk depute of Dundee, witnesses. (One piece of paper.)   VIII, ii, 103.

491. **1690**. Nov. 26.—Contract of marriage between John Pearson, baxter, burgess of Dundee, on one part, and Margaret Wedderburne, daughter of the deceased John Wedderburne, baxter in the said burgh, with the special advice and consent of Alexander Wedderburne of Easter Powrie, on the other part, in contemplation whereof the said John Pearson engages to provide 600 merks of his own means and money, and to add thereto 400 merks of " tocher good " belonging to the said Margaret, making together 1000 merks, to be bestowed on land for annual rent or other security, in favour of himself and the said Margaret in conjunct fee, and to his own heirs, and if children be born of the marriage to provide them to the fee of 800 merks; and the said money is to be laid out at the sight and by advice of the said Alexander Wedderburne, or, failing him, of Peter Wedderburne his brother, the said Alexander W. becoming bound to pay the aforesaid " tocher good " which the said Margaret engages to accept in satisfaction of any legacy left to her by " umquhile Alexander Wedderburn of Easter Powrie." Dated at Dundee. Mr. James Wedderburne, clerk of Dundee, and James Ramsay, notary, subscribe for the said Margaret who asserted that she could not write. A. W. of Easter Powrie also signs.   i, i-ii, 122.
   (English, one sheet of paper, in fair condition.)

492. **1691**. June 1.—Discharge by James Wedderburne, clerk of Dundee, to Alexander Wedderburn of Easter Powrie for the annual rent of 5000 merks. Signed by the said J. W. before two witnesses. (One piece of paper.)   VIII, ii, 100.

493. **1691**. June 14.—Discharge by James Kyd of Craigie to Alexander Wedderburn of Easter Powrie for the annual rent of 1000 merks. Signed at Craigie by the said J. Kyd. (One small piece of paper.)   VIII, ii, 101.

494. **1691**. July 28.—Discharge by William Wallace, tenant to Adam Drummond of Meggineh, to Alexander Wedderburn of Easter Powrie for the annual rent of 200 merks. See ante No. 487. (One piece of paper.)   VIII, ii, 104.

Scrymgeour-
Wedderburn
Papers.

495. **1691.** Oct. 10.—Sasine in favour of John Drummond of an annual rent out of a tenement in Dundee. James Wedderburne is notary. VIII, xiv, 36ª.

496. **1691.** Oct. 22.—Will of Alexander Wedderburne of Easter Powrie :—

"I, Alexander Wedderburne of Easter Powrie, being sick in body but perfyt in memory and judgment praised be God, considering ther is nothing mor certaine nor death nor mor uncertaine than the tyme and maner theruf Doe therfor mak my latter will and testament as followes, That is to say, I recommend my soul to God Almightie my Creator thorrow the merits and mediatione of Jesus Chryst his only sou and my alone Saviour and ordaines my body to be honestly buryed in the ordinar buriall place of Dundie besyd my neirest freinds and relationes upon the proper charges and expeuss of my executer ; afterward and as twitcheing my worldly affaires and bussienes I hereby nominat and appoint Alexander Wedderburne my only lawful sone to be my sol and only executer, universall legatour and intromittour with my whole movabill goods, gear, debts, soumes of money, cornes, cattell, horse, neat, sheep, iusight plenishing, and others quhatsomevir perteining and belougeing to me the tyme of my decease, and failieing of him be decease before he be major or maryed or thir presents put in executione I heirby nominat, mak, substitut and appoint Peter Wedderburne my brother to be my sol executour, universal legatour and intromittour with my goods, gear, and others above specifiet And I heirby leave and in legacie dispones to the said Alexander Wedderburne my sone and executour forsaid the debts, soumes of mouey, goods, gear, iusight and outsight plenishing, and others quhatsomevir falleing under the compass of executorie with and under the burden and payment of my just and lawful debts resting be me to quhatsomevir persone or persones and particularly but prejudice of the generalitie forsaid of the soume of seven thousand merkes with annual rents and expenses conteined in a bond of provisioui made be me to Margaret Wedderburne, my eldest daughter, of the date heirof ; And of the soume of sex thousand merkes with annual rents and expenses conteined in aue other bond granted be me to Rachell Wedderburne, my second daughter, also of the date of thir presents, and quhich two soumes I heirby (in fortificatione and corroboratione of the said two bonds and without innovatione thereof, hurt or derogatione therto, in any sort) leave and in legacie dispone to my saids daughters in manner above devyfled ; and of the soume of twentie pounds yeirly to Alexander Kinmonth, and the lyk soume to William Crawford, both my servauts, yeirly and ilk yeir so loug as they remaine servants of the said Alexander Wedderburne my son, and that by and attour ther fies; and of the soume of aue hundreth merkes to Thomas Miller my servant, payable at the first term after his marriage and alsoe of the soume of fyftie merkes to Jean Duncau my servatrix at the first term after marriage and both the saids last soumes to be by and attour quhat fies I shall be resting the said Thomas Miller and Jeane Duncane the tyme of my decease. And I heirby nominat and appoint John Wedderburne of Blacknes, the said Peter Wedderburne my brother, Thomas Mylne of Mylnefield, Robert Huuter of Baldovie, John Duncan, ane of the late bailies in Dundie, James Wedderburne, towne clerk thereof, and Alexander Wedderburne, skipper there, to be tutors to the said Alexander Wedderburne my sone during his pupilaritie, for ruleing and guidiug him, his meanes and estat, and auy four of them to be aue quorum, the said John Wedderburne and Peter Wedderburne-being alwayes two of them and sine quo nou, and in absence of Blacknes at auy tyme the said James Wedderburne to be in his roume and stead, and in case of the said Peter Wedderburne his absence the said John Duncau to be in his roume. And I heirby earnestly intreat my good friends above named to accept of the said office in and upon them lykas I heirby will and desyr the said Alexander Wedderburne my sone after expyreing of his pupilaritie to elect and choise the forsaid persones to be his curatours, and four of them to be a quorum, the said John and Peter Wedderburnes being always two of them and sine quo nou, and faileiug of them, the said James Wedderburne and John Duncan And failleing of my said sone befor he be major or maryed or thir presents execute I heirby leave and in legacie dispone to the said Peter my brother and substitut executor all falleing under the compass of executorie with the burden and payment of all just and lawful debts resting be me to quhatsomevir persone or persones and particularly but prejudice of the generalitie forsaid of the soumes contained in the bonds above writtiue granted be me to the said Margaret and Rachell Wedderburnes my daughters thereby obleigit to be payed to them be him in maner therin specifeit and of the said twentie pound yeirly to ilk ane of the saids Alexander Kinmouth and William Crawford during all the dayes of their lyfetymes and of the said Thomas Millar and Jean Duncan their legacies above writtine at the terme above specifiet and that notwithstanding my sone and brother are named my universall legatours, as said is, with full power to the said Alexander Wedderburne my soue with consent of auy two of his tutors abovenamed, ... (sic) being alwayes one of them, to give up inventar of my whole goods, gear, and debts, quhich shall be als sufficient as if I hade don the same iuyself and to obtaine the same duely and lawfully confirmed and to pay the dues of confirmatione, with power also to my saids respective executours to uedle with my wholl movabill goods and gear, debts and soumes of money, and if need be to persue therfor as accords of the law, give acquitances and discharges therof, and to pay all my just and lawfull debts and legacies aud generally all other things any other executor testamentar hes don or may doe be the law And this my latter will and testament I notifie and mak knowen to all quhom it effeirs annulling and dischargeing all former testaments if any be made be me. In witness quhairof ... (writtine be James Ramsay, clerk depute of Dundie) I have subscrivit these presents at Dundie the tweutie two day of Octr. jmvjc, fourscor ellevin years before these witnesses George Grieve appothecarie in Dundie and the said James Ramsay. Alex. Wedderburne.

(On paper, in perfect condition. See opp. p. 56.) Geo. Grieve, witnes, Ja. Ramsay, witnes.

497. **1692.** March 4.—Extract retour of the general service of Alexander Wedderburne, Scrymgeour- now of Easter Powrie, as nearest heir of the deceased Alexander Wedderburne of Wedderburn Easter Powrie, his father. Expede in the tolbooth of the burgh of Forfar. I, i-ii, 125. Papers. (Latin, small parchment, in perfect condition.)

498. **1692.** March 24, April 25.—Inquest and special retour of Alexander Wedderburne of Easter Powrie as heir to his father the late Alexander Wedderburne of Easter Powrie. Dated at Forfar. (Latin, two large parchments, in good condition.) VIII, vi, 11, 12.

499. **1692.** May 6.—Sasine of the barony of Powrie in favour of Alexander Wedder- burn of Easter Powrie. Done at the tower, fortalice, and manor place of Powrie. James Wedderburne, clerk of Dundee, is a witness. VIII, vi, 13. (Latin, large parchment, in good condition.)

500. **1692.** June 27.—Inventory of the estate of the deceased Alexander Wedderburne of Easter Powrie :—

The rental of the mains of Kingennie, Easter Powrie, &c. amounts to 6 bolls of wheat, 118 bolls bear, 150 bolls meal, £533, 3, 4 of silver duty, 5 dozen capons, 7 dozen and six hens, 19 dozen poultry, 2 dozen cocks, 5 dozen and six chickens, 6 heaps of yarn.

Among the debtors are John Wedderburn of Blackness, £1000 by bond ; Alexander Wedderburne, skipper £780 as price of the 16th part of the 'James of Dundee,' belonging to the deceased ; James Wedderburne, clerk, £50 per " ticket."

The list of stock and other property includes " ane greatt tenement, or Ludgeing, lying in the Overgait of Dundie lyfrented by Margaret Milne, relict of the old laird of Easter Powrie " and several ground annuals in which the deceased was never infeft.

Inventory containing *inter alia* " ane purse sett with pearles, quhairin is ane reigne with uyne diamond sparks ; Item one other reigne with fyve diamond sparks¹ ; ane other with one spark ; ane plane woop ; ane breast tablet of gold with ane greatt bleu ston and eight litle ones ; ane gold bracelet ; ane silver box, and ane silver chaiue ; ane large peice of gold weighting more then a doucat doune ; two meddells of King Charles the first his portrait, of money ; Item ane sword with ane silver handle ; Item aue silver tumler ; aue silver saltfoot gilt with gold." In the house of Easter Powrie (*inter alia*) " aue candle chist quheriu are some books. The chist is scalled with Peiter Wedderburnes seall " ... "Item black murning cloaths for two horses." ... " The map of Angus, and the descriptioue therof and the map of Africk." In the Dundee house " aue baggag chist ... four muskets, three firelocks guns. Item ane sadle with holsters and pistolls, strib irons and girds conform. two sadles with strib irons and girds, another sadle without strib irons, two pair of hulster cairds with aue paire ot pistolls. two gallon bitts with reignes, ane caribine belt, &c.

The document concludes " In witness quherof the tutors abovenamed have subscribed these presents with two other doubles thereof, at the sight of the nearest friends to the minor on the father and mother syde. att Dundie the twenty sevent aud ...... days of Junij ... jmvje nyuty two years. Signed by Tho. Milne, Peter Wedderburne, Ja. Wedderburne, Rot. Hunter, Jo. Duncan.

(Three pieces of paper, apparently not complete.) VIII, ii, 105.

501. **1692.** June 27.—Duplicate of the last two sheets of the above inventory. (Two sheets joined together, much worn at the edges. See facsimile opp. p. 56) I, i-ii, 124.

502. **1695.** Jan. 29.—Summons at the instance of Alexander Wedderburne, eldest son of John Wedderburne of Blackness, clerk of the Bills, procreate betwixt him and the now deceased Rachel Dunmuir, eldest daughter of the late Mr. David Dunmuir, advocate, and so one of the apparent heirs portioners to the said Mr. David, his grandfather, for exhibition of the writs and evidents which belonged to the latter,' and were now in the keeping of Mr. John Kinloch, writer in Edinburgh, and others. (English, paper, in bad state, with two smaller papers relating thereto attached.) I, i-ii, 128.

503. **1695.** Feb. 5.—Signed account of the charge and discharge of Wedderburn's estate, for the year 1691-92. It contains (*inter alia*) :—

" Item delivered to Mrs. Margaret and Rachel Wedderburnes, the deceast Easter Powrie's daughters, the tyme they stayed in familie in their father's lodgeing at Dundie from his death to Whitsunday thereafter, 1692, &c. £4.

Giveu to Mrs. Margaret Wedderburne by Peter Wedderburne, her uncle, after her father's death, £28.

Item expens for serving Easter Powrie heir to his father at ffarfar £37, 12, 0.

Item payed for aue yeall to Erroll for carrieing up of Alex. Wedderburne and his governour's chists when they were at Erroll £1. 4. 0.

¹ This is probably the ring, still in the possession of the family, given by King James VI. to Alexander Wedderburn, first of Kingennie. See the description of it in the account of him in vol. I.

Scrymgeour-
Wedderburn
Papers.

Item payed Mrs. Margaret Wedderburne, the deceast Easter Powrie's daughter, £140.
Item payed Mrs. Rachel Wedderburne, &c. £120.
(Ten leaves of foolscap sewn in a cover, Signed with the same signatures as the following
account. See facsimile of three of them opp. p. 72.)   I, i-ii, 127.

504. **1695.** Feb. 5.—Similar account of Wedderburn's estate 1692-94. Signed at
Dundie Feb 5, 1695 by Alex Wedderburne, Tho Mylne, Ja : Wedderburne, Ro^t
Hunter, Peter Wedderburne, Jo : Duncan. It includes :—

CHARGE.

Item with thirttien bolls oats cropt forsaid sold at £4 per boll wherof 10 b. to the Lady Easter
Powrie and 3 b. to James Wedderburne, clerk £52, 0, 0

DISCHARGE.

Imprinis payed to the school master and doctor in Dundie 3 quarters payment for Easter Powrie, preceding Hallowmas, 1694, at 1 rex dollar the quarter to each is 6 rex dollars, iude ...	£17 8	0
Item to the janitor for said 3 quarters at 10 shilliugs per quarter	1 10	0
Item to the schoolmaster and doctor at handsell Moouday, 1694	2 18	0
Item to the janitor	10	0
Item to Easter Powrie to give George Crockat's servants of handsell	14	0
Item to Easter Powrie himselfe	14	0
Item to him at the fairs ... '	1 8	0
Item payed for aue pair of bleu stockings to Easter Powrie	2 8	0
Item for one pair of shoes to him	1 16	0
Item payed for 3 actorneys out of the Chancellerie for Easter Powrie, one for the Shirefe court of florfar, one for Kirrimuir, and another for Scoon	2 2	0
Item postage to and from Ediuburgh auent the said actorneys	6	0
Item sent with the actorneyes to the three severall procurators, one at each of the said courts, for answering at the head courts ; to each a 40 shilliug piece and for postage 10 shilliugs is in all	6 10	0
Item to William Crawfurd for drink to his meall for the 12 weeks discharged for him by the discharge of meall at 4 shillings per week is	2 8	0
Item to the servants for salt to their meall from 12th January to 2 October 1693 at 1 lippie per boll is	11	0
Item for building nyutien score and 10 rood of fold dycks 1692 at 1 shilling per rood	19 10	0
Item disbursed for Mistres Margaret Wedderburn's funeralls conforme to an accompt hierwith giveu in	79 13	4
Item payed to James Smyth for Mistris Margaret Wedderburu's coffin conform to his recept dated 23 Dec. 1693	24 0	0
Item payed to George Crockat, merchant in Dundie, two hundred and fourtie pounds scots for Easter Powrie and his Governour's boord from Mertimes 1692 to Candlemas 1694 conforme to his recept Feb. 1694 is	240 0	0
Item payed to Doctor Arbuthnot by orders of the tutors for his atteudance ou Mistress Margaret Wedderburu, Easter Powrie's sister, twelfe rex dollers couforme to his recept dated 14 Junij. 1694 is	34 16	0
Item payed to Mistres Rachell Wedderburne to accompt of her annual rents conforme to her recept dated 27 Septr 1694..	429 13	4
Item payed to Mr. John Hill for two new books to Easter Powrie conforme to his recept dated 27 Sept^r, 1694	2 8	0
Item payed to Patrick Kyde, merchaut, for cloath for aue coat aud justi-coat to Easter Powrie conforme to his accompt, the tutors precept, aud his recept end thereof dated 6th October 1694	32 0	0
Item payed to the Lady Easter Powrie sextie pounds scots as aue year aud aue halfes annuitie payable to her at Whitsunday 1694 conforme to her discharge dated 16 October 1694 is	60 0	0
Item half ane years boord of the Laird and his Governour is	10J 0	0

Memorandum : mynd to detaine in the factor's hauds Mistres Rachell's proportion of
Mistres Margaret's funerall charges and the halfe of the accompt payed to Robert
Rankene out of the first eud of her annual reuts.
(Six leaves of foolscap paper, in a cover, in good condition.)   I, i-ii, 126.

505. **1695.** Aug. 6, 14.—Discharge by Jean Lowsone, wife of Gilbert Blair, minister at
Blair, and only sister of the late John Lowsone, minister at Alyth, aud by Jean
Gray, relict of the late James Lowsone of Dundee, of a bond for 800 merks granted
by Alexander Wedderburn of Kingennie and the late Alexander W. of Easter
Powrie his father to Andrew Gray in Logie, now deceased. The discharge is granted
to Alexander W. of Easter Powrie (on payment by Thomas Milne of Milnefield his
curator) son of the said Alexander W. of Kingennie. (One sheet of paper.) VIII, ii, 106.

506. **1696.** March 3.—Cognition of Andrew Gib, son of Andrew Gib of Dundee, as heir
to Elizabeth Bowman his maternal great grand aunt, in a S. Murraygate tenement.
Alexander Wedderburne, clerk of Dundee, is notary.   VIII, xiv, 37,

507. **1696.** Sept. 11.—Letter from Rachel Wedderburn, daughter of the late Alex. Wedderburn of Easter Powrie, to Thomas Milne of Milnfield as follows :—

Scrymgeour-Wedderburn Papers.

Edb., ii September, 1696.

Sir,
Haveing stayed two yeares hear with my uncle Blacknes preceadihg the fourth day of Agust last by-past I find I am resting him for bed boord and money he has given me for clothes and other uecessars the soumme of five hundred fortic thrie pounds eight shillings four penis scots; therfor I desyre you will pay it to hem out of the first end of what annuelrents my brother is restiug me, And this without any recept from him shal oblige me to allow it accordingly and if you can without straitening my brother's affairs let me have the rest of what @-rents will be resting me at mertimis nixt a little efter the same it will be a singular favour to Your Jouiug Coosin
and seruant,

I, John Wedderburn, above desigued, one of her Curators,   Rachell Wedderburn.
consents. J. Wedderburn. Peter Wedderburne consents.
Addressed on the back " for the Lord of Milfield." (Paper, in good condition. See facsimile opp. p. 72.)   I, i-ii, 128ᵃ.

508. **1697.** Feb. 6.—Receipt as follows :—

"Receaued then from Thomas Myln of Mylnfield in name and behalf of Alexander Wedderburn of Easter Powrie my brother the soume of ane huudreth pounds scots money in peirt of payment of @-rents dew by my said brother to me which soume of ane hundreth pounds money forsaid I oblidge my self by ther presents to Discharge my said Brother therof. As witnes my hand at Edᵣ. this sixth day of february in this present year jamvᶦᵉ and nyntie seventh.   Rachell Wedderburn.
Endorsed, " Receit Rachell Wedderburn To the Laird of Mylnfield for an 100 lib. Scots, 1697."
(Paper, in good state.)   I, i-ii, 128ᵇ.

509. **1696.** Dec. 29.—Discharge by Alexander Wedderburne, clerk of Dundee, to Thomas Milne of Milnefield, as faetor for the curators of Alexander Wedderburne of Easter Powrie, for 275 merks, being the annual rent (1695-96) on a bond for 5000 merks dated 13 June 1688 (ante No. 484) and granted by the late Alexander Wedderburne of Easter Powrie to the late James Wedderburne, clerk of Dundee, father of the said Alexander W., now clerk, who signs the discharge.   VIII, ii, 107.
(One piece of paper.)

509ᵃ. **1696.** Dec. 29.—Discharge by Margaret Wedderburne, relict and executrix of the deceast John Pearsone, baxter in Dundee, to Thomas Milne of Milnefield as faetor etc. (as in No. 509) for the annual rent due on a sum of 400 merks, owing by the late Alex. W. of Easter Powrie under the contract of marriage (ante No. 491) made with consent of the said A. W. between the said granter and John Pearsone. Signed by Alexander Wedderburne, clerk of Dundee, notary for the said Margaret. VIII, ii, 108.
(One piece of paper.)

510. **1697.** Jan. 9.—Discharge by Alexander Edward, minister of Kembak, to Thomas Milne of Milnefield, tutor to Alexander Wedderburn of Easter Powrie, for part of the stipend of Murroes assigned to Jean Johnstone, reliet of the Rev. Robert Edward, minister there. (One small piece of paper.)   VIII, ii, 109.

511. **1697.** Jan. 27.—Discharge by Peter Wedderburne, merchant in Dundee, only son to the late Margaret Milne, last spouse to the late Alexander Wedderburne of Easter Powrie, to Thomas Miln of Milnefield, tutor to Alexander W. now of Easter Powrie, for the annual rent of 1000 merks bond granted by the said first-named A. W. to the said Margaret Milne. Signed by Peter Wedderburne. (One piece of paper.) VIII, ii, 110.

512. **1697.** Feb. 9.—Queries for Alexander Wedderburne of Easter Powrie and his tutors. This is a case for counsel's opinion as to the holding of the lands by Easter Powrie of the Marquis of Douglas, and the desirability of agreeing with the latter for changing the holding from ward to blench &c. The procurator is Sir Patrick Horne. (English, on paper, in perfect state.)   I, i-ii, 129.

513. **1697.** May 22.—Precept of clare constat by James, Marquis of Douglas, in favour of Alexander Wedderburne of Kingennie eldest son and heir of the late Alexander Wedderburne of Kingennie. (Latin, small parchment, in fair state.)   VIII, vi, 14.

514. **1697.** June 11.—Sasine in favour of Alexander Wedderburne of Easter Powrie, of the lands of Kingennie. (Latin, parchment, in good condition)   VIII, vi, 15.

515. **1697.** June 14, 15, 30.—Procuratory of resignation of the lands of Kingany into
the hands of James, Marquis of Douglas, superior thereof, by Alexander Wedderburn
of Powrie, proprietor thereof, for a charter of novo damus to be granted to himself.
It is made with consent of John Wedderburne of Blackness, Thomas Milu of Milnfield, John Duncan, late bailie of Dundee, and Peter Wedderburne, merchant there,
"my curators" (all of whom sign) and recites an agreement with the Marquis to
change the holding of the said lauds from ward either to a few holding or taxt ward.
Alexander Wedderburn signs.   (One sheet of paper.)   VIII, ii, 111.

516. **1697.** July 12.—Instrument of resignation by Alexander Wedderburne of the
lands of Kingennie into the hands of James, Marquis of Douglas, for new infeftment
to him &c. as in 515.   (One sheet of paper.)   VIII, ii, 112.

517. **1697.** July 12.—Charter of resignation of the lands of Kingennie by James,
Marquis of Douglas, in favour of Alexander Wedderburn of Easter Powrie his heirs
and assigns.   (Latin, parchment, in good condition, with fine seal attached.)   VIII, vi, 16.

518. **1697.** July 30.—Sasine in favour of the said Alexander Wedderburn of Easter
Powrie of the lands of Kingennie, following on the above charter.   VIII, vi, 17.
(Latin, parchment, in good condition.)

519. **1697.** Aug. 16.—Instrument of sasine in favour of James Fletcher of various
tenements in Dundee, including one in S. Murraygate, bounded west and south by
the lands of the heirs of James Wedderburne. Alexander Wedderburne, clerk of
Dundee, is notary.   (Parchment.)   VIII, xiv, 38.

520. **1698.** (date wanting).—Inventory of writs produced for Alexander Wedderburn,
clerk of Dundee, in the process at the instance of Mary Dick v. Little Gill. I, i-ii, 130.
(English, on paper, in good state.)

521. **1698.** April 5.—Sasine on resignation by Andrew Morisone, merchant, burgess of
Dundee, in favour of Alexander Wedderburne, common clerk of Dundee, of an annual
rent of £20 furth of a tenement of land lying on the south side of the Nether or
Flukergait, between the lands of Thomas Read on the E., Patrick Yeaman on the S,
the vennel called Cauties Wynd on the W., and the said gate on the N., and
redeemable for 500 merks.   (Latin, parchment.)   VIII, i, 33.

522. **1698.** June 27.—Disposition by James Scrymgeour, eldest lawful son of John
Scrymgeour, late of Kirktoun, to Mr. Alexander Scrymgeour, professor of philosophy
in the old College of St. Andrews, his brother german, of the whole sums of money
&c., contained in the contract of marriage between the said John Scrymgeour their
father, and Magdalene Wedderburn their mother, of date ... day of ...... 16.. (ante No.
330.) Dated at Edinburgh. Henry Scrymgeour in Edinburgh is a witness. VIII, ix, 64.

523. **1699.** Jan. 31.—Scroll summons at the instance of Peter Wedderburne, merchant
in Dundee, and John Young, skipper there, v. George Small, merchant there. The
cause is not stated in the summons, but the execution (dated 3 Feb.) which is
enclosed with it, mentions the arrestment, in virtue of the summons, of the third part
of the ship "The Providence of Dundee."   I, i-ii, 131.
(English, one piece of paper in bad state, with two smaller pieces attached to it.)

524. **1699.** March 10.—Extract decreet by the Lords of the Admiralty, at the instance
of John Morice of Cleppington v. John Young, master of the vessel called the
"Providence of Dundee," in which also compear John Scrymgeour, eldest son of John
Scrymgeour of Kirktoun, and Peter Wedderburne, merchant in Dundee, there being
produced for the latter a libelled precept at his instance v. the said John Young.
(A long roll of nine sheets joined together, in fair state.)   IV, ii, 20.

525. **1699.** May 15.—Discharge by Alexander Wedderburn, town clerk of Dundee,
eldest son and heir served and retoured to the deceast James W., town clerk of
Dundee, with consent of Elizabeth Davidson, relict of the said James, and mother of

the said Alexander, to Alexander Wedderburn of Easter Powrie for the sum of 5000
merks due by virtue of a bond (ante Nos. 484, 509), granted by the late Alexander
Wedderburn of Easter Powrie. Signed at Dundee by the said Alexander Wedderburn, clerk, Elizabeth Davidsone his mother, and John W. his brother. VIII, ii, 113.
(One sheet of paper.)

526. **1701.** June 5.—Scroll summons in action at the instance of John Young, skipper
in Dundee, Patrick Wedderburn, merchant there, John Scrymgeour of Kirktoun, and
Robert Young, writer in Edinburgh, for a reduction of a decreet obtained by John
Moris of Clepington, preferring him to the pursuer before the high Court of Admiralty.
(English, on paper, in good condition.) I, i-ii, 133.

527. **1701.** Sept. 20.—Execution of the said summons by George Clunnes, messenger.
(English, small piece of paper, in good condition.) I, i-ii, 132.

528. **1702.** Dec. 31.—Contract of marriage, dated at Midletowne of Gardyne, between
Alexander Wedderburne of Easter Powrie, and Grissell, youngest daughter of Robert
Gardyne, younger of Latoun. The bridegroom charges his estates with an annuity of
1000 merks in favour of the bride, whose tocher is 7000 merks. Signed by the
spouses, the said Robert Gardyne, and by Peter Wedderburne, merchant in Dundee,
and others, as witnesses. (Scroll of four sheets of paper, joined together.) VIII, ii, 114.

529. **1705.** April 12.—Summons at the instance of Margaret Wedderburne, relict of
Mr. Andrew Balfour, writer to the signet, and now sponse to Dr. William Eccles,
physician in Edinburgh ; Margaret Balfour, only surviving child of the said deceased
Mr. Andrew Balfour ; and Sir John Wedderburne of Blackness, elder, Alexander
Wedderburne thereof, younger, and Mr. John Dallas of Prestoun, her tutors
testamentary, v. Sir John Swinton of that ilk, for implement of a bond granted by him,
of date 9 March 1694, to John Watson, merchant burgess of Edinburgh, for £20,000
(scots) secured over the lands and lordship of Swinton, and barony of Cranshaws in
the shire of Berwick, which bond was transferred by the said John Watson to the said
Mr. Andrew Balfour and his heirs to the extent of £18,000. I, i-ii, 134.
(English, seven pieces of paper, some in bad state.)

530. **1706.** June 1.—Charter by the provost and bailies of Dundee in favour of Thomas
Abererombie, merchant there, of a property in the hilltown of Dundee. Signed by
(among others of the council) A. Wedderburne, shearmaster, and witnessed by
(among others) A. Wedderburne, clerk. IX, xvi, 1.

531. **1706.** June 10.—Charter of alienation to the society of mariners of Dundee of lands
in the Hilltown of Dundee. Signed and witnessed as in No. 530. IX, xvi, 3.

532. **1707.** Nov. 28.—Bond by William Graham of Duntroon to Alexander Wedderburn of
that ilk for 500 merks scots. Dated at Dundee. (Paper, in good state.) I, i-ii, 134ᵃ.

533. **1708.** May 12.—Great Seal Charter by Queen Anne, granting and confirming to
Alexander Wedderburn of Easter Powrie and the heirs male of his body, whom
failing to the heirs female of his body, whom failing to his heirs and assigns whomsoever, all the lands of Easter Powrie, with the lands and barony of Ogilvie in
warrandice, created anew into a barony to be called the barony of Wedderburn, and
also confirming the marriage contract of Alexander Wedderburn and Grissell
Gardyne his wife, dated 31 Dec. 1702 (ante No. 528). Sealed and written to
the Great Seal 25 May 1708. VIII, viii, 1.
(Latin parchment, twelve pages including the cover, folded bookwise, in good condition, with the
great seal attached.)

534. **1708.** Sept. 14.—Sasine following on the above charter in favour of the said
Alexander Wedderburn of that ilk (de eodem). Endorsed as registered at Edin-
burgh 11 Nov. 1708 in the new register of Sasines, Book v, fol. 179-88. VIII, viii, 2.
(Latin, parchment, in good condition.)

K

535. **1709.** (date wanting)—Wedderburne of that ilk *v.* the minister and elders of Liff. Objections against a disposition produced by Wedderburne, with his answers thereto. (One sheet of foolscap, closely written.)   VIII, ii, 115.

536. **1710.** July 24.—Bill for £78 scots drawn by Alexander Wedderburn of that ilk and accepted by William Grahame, laird of Duntroon. Dated at Wedderburn. (Paper, in good state.)   I, i-ii, 134[b].

537. **1710.** Dec. 13.—Summons at the instance of Margaret and Janet, daughters of the late David Hunter of Burnside, and others, *v.* Alexander Wedderburn, town clerk of Dundee, and another, for arresting in their hands the sum of £100 each, &c., &c.
VII, iii, 59.

538. **1711.** July 27.—Contract of marriage, dated at Wedderburne, between Mr. Gilbert Stewart, merchant in Edinburgh, and Mistress Rachel Wedderburne, daughter of the late Alexander Wedderburne of Easter Powrie. The bride's tocher is 10,000 merks, and Gilbert Stewart settles 26,000 merks. Signed by the spouses before various witnesses, including Alexander Wedderburne of that ilk, Peter W. merchant in Dundee, Alexander W. clerk of Dundee, David Brisbane, and John Stewart of Stenton.   VIII, ii, 116.

539. **1711.** Nov. 26.—Tack by Alexander Wedderburne of that ilk to Andrew Rob in Whitelawstoun of all and whole the lands of Wester Gourdic, lying in the parish of Liff, as the same were possessed by David Keill last tenant thereof, for the space of nine years from his entry thereto. Dated at Dundee.   II, ii, 17.

540. **1712.** April 19.—Extract registered assignation by Alexander Kirkwood in favour of his children, registered in the Edinburgh burgh court books 21 Jan. 1715. It refers to a bond for 1000 merks, granted by the late Sir Alexander Wedderburne of Blackness and Major David Wedderburne in General Macartney's regiment, and dated 16 Feb. 1708.   (English, on paper, in good state.)   I, i-ii, 135.

541. **1713.** Nov. 4.—"Double testament of the Laird of Wedderburne in favour of Peter Wedderburne, his son, 1713" (so endorsed) :

> The testator " being tender and sickly in body but sound in mind " appoints "Peter Wedderburne, my eldest lawful son, my sole executor and universall legatee and intromittor " and ordains him to pay to " Grizell, David and Gilbert, my three younger children," the sums named in their bonds of provision, and to deliver to " my well beloved spouse, Grizell Gairdyne, her share of household furniture, provided to her by our contract matrimoniall." He nominates as tutors to his four children " Peter Wedderburne, merchant in Dundee, my uncle, Gilbert Stewart, merchant in Edinr., Mr. Alexander Scrymsour, professor of divinity in S[t] Andrews, Mr. Alexander Wedderburne, shiriff clerk of Forfar, Dr. John Wedderburne, doctor of medicine in Dundee, the said Grizell Gardyne (during her widowity), Robert Gardyne of Latoun, David Gardyne, fiar thereof, and Peter Barclay of Johnston, merchant in Montrose." Dated at Dundee. Dr. John Wedderburne is a witness. Registered in the sheriff court books at Forfar 12 Dec., 1713. (See opposite p. 72.)   I, i-ii, 135[a].

542. **1713-31.** Minute book (cover wanting) of 23 foolscap leaves relating to the affairs of the children of the deceased Alexander Wedderburne of that ilk and Grissell Gardyne.   On the outside sheet (unpaged) is pasted a label inscribed " Minute Book of the Curators of the children of Alexander Wedderburn of Wedderburn, beginning in 1713."   I, i-ii, 136.

The following extracts from it are of interest :

> "13 Xber 1713. Sederunt of the Persones following, tutors to the children of the deceast Alexander Wedderburne of that ilk, conforme to his latter will and testament dated the 4th day of Nov. 1713." Then follow the names of all the tutors, except that of Peter Wedderburne, who declines to act (p. 1.) David Brisbane is appointed factor by the tutors, and an annuity of 1000 merks, settled on the defunct's ladie by her marriage contract, is to be paid (p. 2.) "The said tutors considering that the old manner place of Wedderburne has not been habitable for some years past and now is in a ruinous condition, and least the timber and other materialls yrof perish Doe appoynt the factor to take ont the timber and all the other usefull materialls of the said old manner Louse And to secure the same in the East jamm of the said old house (which is not to be taken down). . . . The pupill is to be served heir to his father before the Shiriff of Forfar at once " (pp. 3-4).
> 1713 Dec. 14. Dundie. The tutors order a sale of the household plenishing except (*inter alia*) the new house Bible, the marable table, and pictures " (p. 5).

1714 Oct. 21. The factor is "to pay Margaret Wedderburne[1] 100 merks in part payment of her principall together with the bygone annual rents," and is "to take out brieves for serving of David heir to his brother before the Shiriff of Forfar . . . after the same manner that his brother was served." "Taken out of the Charter chist and delivered to Mr. Stewart the defunct's latter will and testament with the bonds of provision to David, Gilbert and Grissell Wedderburne, And the tutors recommends to the said Mr. Stewart to consult lawiers how farr Grissell Wedderburne has interest in the moveable estate of her father and her brother Peter" (p. 7).

1715 Aug. 3. "The speciall retour and sasine in favour of the deceast Peter Wedderburn with the speciall retour, precept, and sasine in favour of David Wedderburn, now of that ilk, was delivered by the factor and putt in the Charter chist As also delivered in to the Charter chist by the factor the three Bonds of provision and the defunct's testament which was given out to Gilbert Stewart" (p. 10).

1716 Aug. 9. The factor to pay Margaret Wedderburne her principall sum (p. 12). . . . "The tutors considering that David their pupill is not infeft in the lands of Kingennie holding of the Duke of Douglas, therefor recommends to Gilbert Stewart to whom the last entrie is delivered, viz: a charter of resignation in favour of the late . . . Wedderburn and sasine following thereon, to make out a composition for our pupille's eutrie and obtain a precept of clare constat yrnpon . . ."

"The ffactor to confirme Grissell exerix to her father as coming in the place of Peter who was exor. nominate by the father . . . as also to confirme the said Grissell exerix to her grandfather" (p 13).

1717 May 14. "Gilbert Stewart has returned the last charter and sasine yron in favour of the late Wedderburn for the lands of Kingany with a precept of clare constat in favour of the Pupill of the saids lands and a sasine thereon, which are putt in the Charter Chist " (p. 15).

1718 May 1. "The tutors considering that it's high time some effectuall course be taken for their pupill's education and that his health may readily not allow him to goe class to a publick schoole think it most expedient that he should have a governour who may carry on his education whether at schoole or not and doe agree that an offer of this trust be made to the Reverend James Goldman ..." (p. 16). This is the last minute signed by Grissell Gardyne. She had married agair. 5 March, 1718 (to David Graham of Duntroon) and her tutorship had therefore really ceased even at this date.

1719 Sept. 9. It appears that a Mr. Lyon had been engaged as "governour to the pupill," but the tutors now propose to dismiss him, and put "the pupill under Dr. Scrymsour at S. Andrews" (p. 20).

1720 Aug. 2. The factor is "to make up a separate account of Grissell Wedderburn's executorie by the death of her father and brothers" (p. 21).

1721 Aug. 3. It is stated that last Whitsun was the first term after Grissell attained to the age of 16. The factor is "to gett a transmission from Grissell in favour of David, her brother, of all the debts in her persone as exerix confirmed to her father and grandfather" (p. 24).

1724 May 6. The minutes are for the first time signed by David Wedderburn himself, who, having been born 21 April, 1710, had now turned 14. The terms "minor" and "curators" now take the place of "pupill" and "tutors" (p. 32).

1725 May 12. The minor not agreeing with his governour, the latter is to leave. The curators propose that the minor have "a discreet young man as governour" or "goe to the Humanitie class at S. Andrews," but the minor "declaires his resolution to stay at the schooll of Dundie " (p. 34).

1725 Aug. 24. "The question being proposed what was fitt for the minor to do at the first of Nov. when he is to leave the schooll of Dundie, he, being desired to tell his own inclination, declair'd that he inclin'd to S. Andrews to the Colledge to eat at the Colledge Table and have Mr. Mudie for his governour, And to this the majority of his curators present agreed. And furder, seeing he is not sufficiently perfect of the Latine, they agreed he should be for one year in the humanity class in the old colledge and as to Mr. Mudie's yearly pension agreed yt it shall be one hundred pounds scotts." (pp. 37-38).

1727 July 20, Aug. 12. The minor and curators buy the lands of Baldovan for 46,000 merks scots (p. 40).

1731 May 15. Wedderburn (now of age) discharges his curators and the executors of two of them (Robert Gardyne and Peter Barclay) who have died, and also his factor David Brisbane (p. 43). See facsimile of signatures opp. p. 72.

543. **1714**. Feb. 25.--Inquisition held at the Tolbooth, Forfar, by, among others, Dr. John Wedderburn, for the retour of Peter Wedderburn of that ilk as heir in the barony of Wedderburn, lands of Wester Gourdie &c., to his father the late Alexander W. of that ilk. VIII, viii, 3.
(Latin, twelve pages of parchment, including cover, folded bookwise, in perfect state.)

544. **1714**. April 21.--Precept from chancery for infefting Peter Wedderburn, now of that ilk, as heir to his father the deceased Alexander W. of that ilk, in the lands of Easter Powrie &c. as principal (with the lands and barony of Ogilvy in warrandice), created into one whole free barony of Wedderburn conform to Crown Charter dated 12 March 1708, and also in the lands of Wester Gourdie. VIII, vi, 18.

545. **1714**. April 29.--Sasine at the Tower, fortalice and manor place of Wedderburn, following on the said retour and precept. Endorsed as registered in the Forfar Sasines Register, xii, 408-13. (Latin, parchment, in good state.) VIII, viii, 4.

[1] See ante No. 491. She was daughter to John Wedderburn, natural son to Alexander Wedderburn, the provost, third of Kingennie, and first of Easter Powrie. See the account of him in vol. I.

546. **1715.** Feb. 14.—At Forfar. Inquisition for the retour of David Wedderburn of that ilk in the barony of Wedderburn, lands of Wester Gourdie, &c.   viii, viii, 5.
(Latin, parchment, twelve pages, including cover, folded bookwise, in good condition).

547. **1715.** March 24.—Similar retour, dated at Edinburgh.   viii, viii, 5ᵃ.
(Latin, one piece of parchment, in good condition.)

548. **1715.** April 7.— Sasine following on the above retour in favour of the said David, of the said barony and lands. Endorsed as registered in the Forfar Sasines Register, xii, 486-91. (Latin, parchment, in good condition.)   viii, viii, 6.

549. **1715.** May 15.—Discharge, renunciation, and grant of redemption by Alexander Wedderburne, clerk of Dundee, to Henry Crawfurd, elder and younger, lairds of Monorgan, for £612. Signed by A.Wedderburne. (One sheet of foolscap.) viii, ii, 118.

550. **1716.** Aug. 22.—Confirmed testament dative of the late Alexander Wedderburn of that ilk, who d. in Dec. 1713, given up by the tutors of Grizell W. lawful daughter and executrix dative decerned to her father by the commissary of Brechin 22 Aug. 1716.   i, i-ii, 135ᵇ.

551. **1716.** Nov. 28.—Letter from Gilbert Stewart dated "Edinburgh 28 Nov. 1716" to Mr. David Brisbain, as follows :—

Sir, I wrote you last week by...... (illegible) aquainting you that I did receive yours by the carrier with Mrs. Brisbain's six pounds ..... (illegible). Above you have a copy of what John Gordon of Rotterdam writes me anent Sir John Wedderburn ...... and I desire you may aquaint the Clerk and the Dr. with it. You have inclosed Sir John's bill upon you for £28. 11. 11 stg. which you will accept and returne me. I see his friends will not find they (?) account in keeping him at Scool for I cannot see he will live under eighty pound a year considering cloaths and other necessaries and I find my friend wold gladly be freed of the truble of him. I salute all friends and I am, Sir, your most humble servant, Gilbert Stewart.
Let me know if the Lady Wedderburn (i.e., Grissell Gardyne, widow of Alexander Wedderburn of that ilk) be cum into the towne.

This is written below the foregoing :

Rotterdam, 24 Novemr., 1716.
Copie ; Mr. Gilbert Stewart,
Sir, I refer to my last of 6 currant. Herewith I remitt you for your proper accompt £28. 11. 11. in Mr. Wedderburn's bill at 14d/ sight on Mr. David Brisbaine being of valow of £298. 8. exchange at 28, which put to my credit. If the drawer's friends grudge his spending so much money (it) is what I cannot help, have paid 80 guilders 18 Stuivers therof to ye french master for his board, paper, pen and ink and pocket money £42. 0, for 6 shirts and 6 cravats, £64 to Peter Stevens for his passage over and money he depursed for him in Scotland. If you please, shall send you the particulars of all the rest. I've been at gt. pains to pay out for his stockens, shoes, &c. as spareing as possibly I could and now I am importuned by him for a sute of winter cloaths which I endeavour to putt off till he have orders from his curators. Believe me Sir there's many governours have a £100 a year that have not such a troublesome pouple yet if he Improve his time well I shall continew with the more pleasure to undergoe the trouble on your account." (One page, closely written.) viii, ii, 117.

552. **1717.** Feb. 20.—Precept of clare constat by the commissioners of the Duke of Douglas in favour of David Wedderburn of Kingennie, as heir to his father, the late Alexander Wedderburne of Easter Powrie, in the lands of Kingennie.   viii, viii, 7.
(Latin, thin parchment, in fair condition, seal gone.)

553. **1717.** May 4.—Sasine following on the above precept in favour of David Wedderburn of that ilk. Endorsed as registered in the Forfar Sasines, xiii, 46-49.   viii, viii, 8.
(Latin, parchment, in good state.)

554. **1718.** Jan. 1.—Abbreviat declaration and adjudication at the instance of Grissell Wedderburne and her tutors v. William Graham of Duntroon and the officers of state. Recorded 25 Feb., 1718. This is a decree in her favour, some difficulty having arisen to the Wedderburn estate thro' the attainder (for his share in the '15) of William Graham of Duntroon. John Scrimsour of Tealing, provost of Dundee, and John S. his son are named.   i, i-ii, 135ᶜ.

555. **1718.** Jan. 1.—Decreet of declarator and adjudication as above.   i, i-ii, 135ᵈ.

556. **1718.** April 11.—Discharge by Alexander Wedderburne, sheriff clerk of Forfar, in favour of Sir John Wedderburn, apparent (the word "apparent" is, of course, mere surplusage, Sir Alexander having died in 1710) heir of the deceased Sir Alexander Wedderburn of Blackness, his father, of various debts contained in bonds therein specified, and to which the granter has right by assignation, amounting in all to the sum of £50,741, 5, 0, in consideration of which the said Sir John with consent of his curators sold to the said Alexander W. the lands and barony of Blackness and the lands of Logie, &c. The curators are James Haliburtoun of Pitcur, James Kyd of Craigie, Mr. George Seton, advocate, David Campbell, younger of Kethick, and John Wedderburne, doctor of medicine in Dundee. Dated at Dundee.

Among the bonds specified are :—

Bond by Sir John Wedderburn of Blackness (now deceased) as principal, and the said deceased Sir Alexander, his son, as cautioner, to Margaret Wedderburn, daughter of the deceased James Wedderburn, clerk of Dundee, for 1800 merks, dated 8 and 14 July 1704, which bond the said Margaret with consent of Mr. John Paterson of Craigie her husband, assigned to Sir David Threepland of Fingask &c.

Bond by the said deceased Sir John Wedderburn of Blackness to John Wedderburn, son of the late Peter W. merchant in Dundee, for 500 merks, dated 17 June 1686, to which the granter has right by assignation, dated 6 November 1717, granted by Alexander Wedderburn, shipmaster in Dundee, as factor for the said John W.

Bond by the deceased Sir Alexander Wedderburn to Peter Wedderburn, merchant in Dundee, for 500 merks, dated 28 Jan. 1709.

Bond by the said deceased Sir Alexander Wedderburn to Robert Wedderburn, mariner in Dundee, for 1000 merks, dated 26 June 1707.

Bond by the said late Sir John Wedderburn of Blackness, to the now deceased Mr. Andrew Balfour, writer to the signet, and Margaret Wedderburn then his spouse, in liferent, and to their daughters Rachel, Margaret, and Elizabeth for 708 merks, dated 19 Nov. 1697.

Bond by the said deceased Sir John Wedderburn of Blackness and Alexander Wedderburn younger thereof, to the late Margaret Wedderburn, then spouse to Mr. William Eccles M.D., for 2000 merks, dated 7 Dec. 1704.

(English, on 22 foolscap pages, in good condition. Each page is signed at the foot "Al: Wedderburne.") I, i-ii, 138.

557. **1719-20.** Rentall of the lands and Baronies of Wedderburn, Wester Gourdie, and Kingennie, for cropts 1719-20. (One sheet of paper.) VIII, ii, 119.

558. **1720-21.** Petition of Alexander Wedderburne, sheriff clerk of Forfar, to the Lords of Council and Session for his expenses in an action of ranking and sale v. Harry Crawfurd of Halkerston. (English, on paper, in good condition.) I, i-ii, 139.

559. **1724.** June 30.—Sasine of the lands of Bullion in favour of David Brisbane. Sir Alexander Wedderburn of Blackness, baronet, is bailie. Reg. at Edinburgh 6 July. Gen. Reg. Sas. Book 123, fol. 206-8. IX, xv, 12.

560. **1724.** Dec. 6.—Memorandum and queries for Wedderburn of that ilk and his tutors. This is a case for counsel's opinion and states that Wedderburn of that ilk died in December, 1713, leaving four children, viz. : Peter, eldest son and heir, and so served ; David, now of that ilk ; Grissell, still living, and Gilbert, who died before his brother Peter. The point for opinion is the right division of certain property between David and Grissell having regard to their father's will, dated 4 Nov. 1713. (One sheet of paper.) VIII, ii, 120.

561. **1725.** (date torn off).—Submission by John, Lord Gray, and John Thomson, feuar in Liff, anent the price of two ploughs of land in Liff, to be purchased of them, to the arbitration of Patrick Ogilvy of Inchmartin, Sir Alexander Wedderburn of Blackness, and James Johnston and David Brisbane, writers in Dundee. Undated, but in the decreet arbitral endorsed on it the year 1725 is mentioned, as if then current. (English, on paper, fair, but imperfect.) V, vi, 2.

562. **1726.** Feb. 5.—Letter, dated from Dundee, by David Wedderburn of Wedderburn to Dr. Alexander Scrymgeour desiring him to approve of Robert Mudie as his "governour," some of David's curators having objected to him; with draft of Dr. Scrymgeour's reply, declining to act in opposition to the other curators. VI, v, 4.

563. **1727.** Inventar cf writs belonging to Mrs. Grissell Wedderburn and produced in the process of ranking of the creditors of Duntroon. This merely gives ante Nos. 532, 536, 550, 554 and 555.   I, i-ii, 140a.

564. **1727-31.** A foolscap book of 52 pages in a marbled cover, labelled " Wedderburn his book, 1727-31 " and containing the rent-roll of his estates for those years.   I, i-ii, 137.

565. **1731.** May 15.—Registered Discharge by David Wedderburn of that ilk to his tutors and curators, registered in the sheriff court books of Forfar. It begins thus :—
    " Be it known ...... me David Wedderburn of Wedderburn, eldest lawful son now on life of the deceast Alexander W. of W. and also heir served and retoured to the deceast Peter W. my brother german who was heir served and retoured to the said deceast Alexander W. my father, Forasmuch as the said deceast A. W. by a nomination in his latter will dated 4 Nov. 1713 did nominate the deceast Peter W. merchant in Dundee, Doctor Alexander Scrymgeour, Mr. Alexander Wedderburn, sheriff clerk of Forfar (now Sir Alexander W. of Blackness), Doctor John W. doctor of medicine in Dundee, Grissell Gardyne my mother, and others, tutors and curators to his children &c., &c." It then recites that the said Peter W. brother to David died in May 1714 and that David is now aged 21, and ends with his discharge to his tutors and curators. Signed by David W. before David Scrymgeour, son to the said Dr. Alexander S., and others, as witnesses."
    (One sheet of paper.)   VIII, ii, 121.

566. **1735.** Submission and decreet arbitral between the heritors of Liff (including Sir Alexander Wedderburn of Blackness, David Wedderburn of Wedderburn, Alexander Read of Turfbeg and others) and Thomas Donaldson, their minister.   IX, ii, 35.

567. **1736-79.** Bundle of 83 old accounts, &c. of David and Grizel Wedderburn of that ilk. They include :—
    4. Bond by David Wedderburn of W. to Dr. John Wedderburn, physician in Dundee, 30 Nov. 1742, for 3800 merks, discharged by Thomas Kyd as factor for John Wedderburn, eldest lawful son to the deceased Sir John W. and now surgeon in Jamaica, assignee of the said Dr. John W. of Idvies, 15 May 1752.
    5. Obligation by David Wedderburn of W. to his sister german Grizel W. to pay her half a sum of 10,000 merks in which Gilbert Stewart, merchant in Edinburgh, has bound himself to David. 5 March 1742.
    13. Discharged account of David W. of W, debtor to Ann Bruce, wife of Peter Lobry, periwig maker in St. Petersburg. 1751. (See post No, 570).
    71. Account for the service of Grizel W. as heiress to Alexander Wedderburn of Cangenny (sic) her great grandfather. 1769. (See post No, 635).   VI, vii, 4, 5, 13, 71.

568. **1739.** Aug. 11.—Contract of marriage between David Scrymgeour of Birkhill, advocate, and Mistress Katharin Wedderburn, lawful daughter of Sir Alexander Wedderburn, baronet, with advice and consent of her said father and of John Wedderburn, younger, of Blackness, her brother german. Dated at Dundee, John Wedderburn of Idvies, physician in Dundee, Alexander Read of Turfbeg, Alexander Watson, surgeon in Dundee, Peter Kinnimond, writer there, and Robert Wedderburn, sheriff clerk of Forfar and writer of the contract, are witnesses. Signed by the spouses, the bride's father, &c. (English, paper, in good condition. See opp. p. 72.)   v, i, 6.

569. **1739.** Oct. 8.—Sasine in favour of Katharin Wedderburn, Lady Birkhill, of an annuity of £55, furth of the lands of Newgrange. David Scrymgeour subscribes. The notary is Robert Wedderburn (of Pearsie) who adds his motto " Libertas optima rerum."   VIII, xii, 5.

570. **1740.** July 16.—Letter dated "St. Petersburg, July 16, 1740 " from Anna Lobry to " Mrs. Gressel Wedderburn in Dundie " as follows :—
    "Madam, I am now to return you thanks for all your favors when in Scotland last and I have herewith sent you a present of a vere courios pees which my husband recved from her Imperial Majesty's sister ; it is the figeur of the feier workes that was let of in mosko at the corenation of thir present Empres. I have taken cear to have it translated into English that you may the better understand it, only tack cear as you unfould it that you misples not the derectons. I sent the last year to the cear of my ounkell Francis as much furr as meak your mother a clook for the winter but I have not heard if she his recved it ; there is hear inclosed a small meddell of the peas for your brother to whom with Mr. and Mrs. Graham, your sisters and all other friends pray meake my serves exceptabile and believe me to be, Madam, thers and your most humble servant, Anna Lobry."
    (The writer of this letter appears to have been a family servant, who married a periwig maker in St. Petersburg. See ante No. 567 (13). The sisters named in the letter were half-sisters of Grisell Wedderburn, whose mother had married secondly, in 1718, David Graham of Duntroon.)
                                                                    I, i-ii, 140.

571. **1730.** Copy of the family register of Sir Alexander Wedderburn, fourth baronet of Blackness, made from the original by Alexander Scrymgeour-Wedderburn in 1799. See Blackness Papers, No. 11. It is endorsed by A.S.W. thus, "Taken from a holograph list left in Sir Alex. Wedderburn's handwriting, in the custody of his grandson, Sir John, March 1799." **Scrymgeour-Wedderburn Papers.** I, i-ii, 156.

572. **1742.** Sept. 8.—Promissory note of John Wedderburn (afterwards 5th baronet of Blackness). Dated at Dundee. VI, vi, 1.

573. **1744.** Aug. 10.—Bond by David Wedderburn of Wedderburn to Dr. John Wedderburn *re* a trust of £300 for Sir Alexander Wedderburn, late of Blackness, and Katharin Scott his wife, for liferent, and, on the death of both of them, equally for John, James, Peter, Alexander, David, Margaret, Katharin, Susan, and Agatha Wedderburn, children of John Wedderburn, late of Blackness, younger. VI, vi, 2.

574. **1744.** Aug. 10 —Copy of the foregoing in the hand of Alexander Scrymgeour (afterwards Wedderburn) and signed by him, with a note of its having been recorded "feb. 13, 1771. D. R." (*i.e.*, Dalrymple or Durie Register.) VI, vi, 3.

575. **1744.** Sept. 22.—Letter from John Wedderburn (afterwards 5th baronet of Blackness) addressed "To Mr. David Scrimgeour of Birkhill, Advocat, att Birkhill," (his brother-in-law)—

Dr Sir,

As the Do^r and I had caused write Mr. Alison at the Board that the money should be payed on Munday have therefore sent the Express your way and the Do^r and I agree that you shoud be payed out of the first and readiest that shall be levied (?) My father is now confined to his Bed, has a touch of a fever, and it's scarce expected he'l put of next week.

I am,

Dear Sir,

Your aff; brother and most humble servant,

JOHN WEDDERBURN.

Dundee 22 Sept. 1744.

(See opp. p. 72.) VI, vi, 4.

576. **1744.** Sept. 24.—Bond by Thomas Wedderburn, collector of excise in Inverness, as principal, Sir John Wedderburn, baronet, Robert Wedderburn of Pearsie, sheriff clerk of Forfar, and Alexander Read of Turfbeg, as cautioners, to Dr. John Wedderburn and Mr. David Scrymgeour. It recites that Sir John Wedderburn, Dr. John Wedderburn in Dundee, and David Scrymgeour of Birkhill, advocate, have on 24 Sept. 1744, at the request of Thomas Wedderburn, advanced to the commissioners of excise £136 and that it was desired to secure Dr. John W. and Mr. David S. Signed by Sir John W. and Robert W. and Alexander Read, at Dundee 28 Sept. 1744 and by Thomas Wedderburn at Inverness 25 May 1748. VI, vi, 5.

577. **1745.** June 15.—Claim by William Smith and others *v.* Dr. John Wedderburn, physician in Dundee, 15 June 1745. VI, vi, 6.

578. **1747.** March 2.—Discharge James Smyth, W. S., to the Honble Mrs. Jean Fullerton, relict of the late Sir John Wedderburn, for £50. VI, vi, 7.

579. **1747.** June 13.—Discharge by Dr. John Wedderburn to David Wedderburn of Wedderburn for half a year's interest, from Whitmonday to Martinmas 1746, on £300 held on trust for the children of the late Sir John Wedderburn in fee and for their grandmother in liferent. Signed by John Wedderburn at Dundee. VI, vi, 8.

580. **1747.** Nov. 24.—Receipt by Patrick Crichton, clerk to the creditors of the late Sir Alexander and John Wedderburn of Blackness, to Alexander Hunter of Balskellie for £220. Dated at Dundee. VI, vi, 9.

581. **1749.** March 13.—Receipt by the said P. Crichton to Balskellie as purchaser of Blackness. VI, vi, 10.

582. **1749.** June 8.—Bond by Mr. David Græme, advocate, and David Wedderburn of Wedderburn to Mr. Charles Cunningham, minister at Tranent, for £50 stg. Dated at Edinburgh. V, vi, 3.

583. **1749.** June 25.—Short letter by David W. of W., to the said David Græme, dated at Edinburgh. I, i-ii, 141.

584. **1750.** (undated.)—Scheme of David Brisbane for settling his affairs, by which he proposes to leave Bullion and a house in Dundee to his sister for life, and to David Wedderburn of Wedderburn in fee, and small legacies of £50 stg to David Wedderburn, son of the late Sir John Wedderburn, and David Read, son of the late Alexander Read of Turfbeg. (Undated, but about 1750.) VI, ix, 14.

585. **1752.** Feb. 12.—Cognition in favour of Margaret Brisbane as heir to David Brisbane, her brother, in a tenement in Dundee, once that of the late James Pearson, sometime provost of Dundee, then of Mr. James Brisbane advocate, then of Matilda Wedderburn, his relict, on the S. of the Flukergate, now called the Nethergate.
(English, parchment, in perfect state.) I, i-ii, 142.

586. **1752.** Aug. 7.—Receipted account of Robert Wedderburn, sheriff clerk of Forfar, to David Wedderburn of Wedderburn. Signed by Robert W. VI, vi, 11.

587. **1753.** Nov. 19.—General disposition and nomination of tutors and curators to his children, Alexander, John and David, by Mr. David Scrimgeour of Birkhill, advocate. Dated at Edinburgh. The curators are David Wedderburn of Wedderburn, Mr. David Falconer, advocate, Henry Scrimgeour, W. S., Robert Wedderburn of Pearsie, James Paterson of Carpow, "Katharine Wedderburn, my beloved spouse," &c. VI, v, 13.

588. **1753.** Feb. 5.—Missive letter by David Græme to David Wedderburn of Wedderburn, relieving him of any obligation in reference to the bonds therein specified viz. :
1. Bond for £100 stg. to the late Margaret Gilchrist, wife of William Millar, merchant in Edinburgh, dated 9 March 1747.
2. Bond (ante No. 582) dated 8 June 1749.
At the end of the page is a note dated Edin. 17 Dec. 1779, signed by A. Scrymgeour-Wedderburn, to the effect that he had received back the first bond with a discharge thereof by George Millar, son to Margaret, dated 6 Jan. 1763. V, vi, 4.

589. **1754.** July 15.—Discharge by Dame Katherine Scott, widow of Sir Alexander Wedderburn, baronet, to David Wedderburn of W. for £7. 10. 0. half a year's @-rent on £300 due to her in liferent and to the children of the late Sir John Wedderburn in fee. Witnessed by Rot. Wedderburn of Pearsie and David Webster. Signed "Kathrine Scot." (One small piece of paper.) VIII, ii, 123.

590. **1754.** Aug. 30.—Discharge by Jean Fullarton, Lady Wedderburn, on behalf of David Wedderburn, her youngest son, for £5, being two years, 1752-54, @-rent on a legacy of £50 left to him by David Brisbane of Bullion; granted in favour of Mrs. Margaret Brisbane, the testator's sister, and David Wedderburn of Wedderburn. Signed at Dundee "Jean Wedderburn." VIII, ii, 128.

591. **1754.** Sept. 19.—Discharge by David Read, son of the late Alexander Read of Turfbeg, although a minor, to Mrs. Margaret Brisbane, sister of the late David Brisbane of Bullion, and David Wedderburn of that ilk, for a legacy of £50 left him by the said David Brisbane. Signed by David Read before Robert Wedderburn of Pearsie and other witnesses. His brother, Alexander Read of Logie, is surety for his executing the discharge when of age, and a letter from him, 12 Sept., 1754, is annexed. Ratified by David Read 24 Nov., 1778. VIII, ii, 122.
(One sheet of paper, with the above letter annexed.)

592. **1754.** Dec. 9.—Discharge by Katharine Scot, similar to that of 15 July, 1754 (ante No. 589). VIII, ii, 124.

593. **1755.** July 30.—Similar discharge by Katharine Scot. VIII, ii, 125.

THREE SIGNATURES TO NO. 503

SIGNATURES TO NO. 507.

SIGNATURE TO NO. 541.

SIGNATURES TO NO. 569.

SIGNATURE TO NO. 575.

SIGNATURES TO NO. 542.

SIGNATURES TO NO. 618.

SIGNATURE OF ALEXANDER SCRYMGEOUR-WEDDERBURN
OF WEDDERBURN.

SIGNATURES TO NOS. 854 AND 665.

SIGNATURE OF CHARLES WEDDERBURN OF PEARSIE
(SEE NO. 673)
AND HIS BROTHER, DAVID WEDDERBURN WEBSTER.

TWO SIGNATURES OF HENRY SCRYMGEOUR-WEDDERBURN
OF WEDDERBURN.

594. **1756.** April 26.—Discharge by Robert Wedderburn of Pearsie in favour of David Scrymgeour-Wedderburn of W. for £55 stg. "for what I am to get Lady Wedderburn's discharge for the said £50, and five pounds as bygone interest, legate her son David by the deceast David Brisbane of Bullion." Signed "Rot. Wedderburn." VIII, ii, 127. *Scrymgeour-Wedderburn Papers.*

595. **1756.** May 14.—Letter by Jean Fullarton, Lady Wedderburn, to David Wedderburn of Wedderburn, as follows :—

"Sir, As you have now paid the sum of fifty pounds sterling bequeathed by David Brisbane of Bullion, writer in Dundee, to David Wedderburn my son and as he is not yet of age nor has any curators nominated and therefore (is) not capable of granting a further discharge and it being reasonable that you should in the mean time be indemnifyed, therefore I hereby promise to procure you a proper discharge from my son as soon as he shall be of age, and in case of his death before he is not, to indemnify you at all hands either as Mr. Brisbane's heir, or exōr. or otherways.

And as this letter is not formall therefore I hereby promise (when required) to grant you what other reasonable security you shall think proper. I am, Sir, your most obedient humble servant,
Dundee, 14th May, 1756. JEAN WEDDERBURN.
To David Wedderburn of Wedderburn, Esquire.
(One piece of paper. Only the signature is in the hand of Lady Wedderburn.) VIII, ii, 129.

596. **1758.** Dec.—Memorial for Robert Wedderburn of Pearsie, Esq., on behalf of Charles and John Findlays, lawfull sons of the deceast James Findlay of Easter Lithnot. An old case for opinion, laid before David Scrymgeour of Birkhill, advocate ; it refers to James Findlay, elder brother of Charles and John. VI, vi, 12.

597. **1759.** July 10.—Obligation by David Wedderburn of Wedderburn to Walter Tullideph of Balgay, referring to a minute of sale between them, of the same date, of the lands of Baldovan, &c. V, vi, 5.

598. **1759.** Nov. 14.—Bill of exchange drawn by David Scrymgeour and accepted by Thomas Wedderburn (of Cantra). VI, vi, 13.

599. **1759.** Nov. 24.—Obligation by David Wedderburn of Wedderburn, to Walter Tullideph of Balgay, in regard to the writs of the lands of Baldovan, sold by Wedderburn to Tullideph. Dated at Edinburgh. V, vi, 6.

600. **1759.** Dec. 24.—Inventory of the progress of writs of the lands of Baldovan, &c., referred to in the disposition thereof granted by David Wedderburn of Wedderburn, to Walter Tullideph of Balgay. It enumerates 39 writs, including :—

2. Sasine in favour of Sir John Scrymgeour of Dudope, signed by Alexander Wedderburn, notary. 3 April 1605.
18. Bond by John Scrymgeour of Kirktoun in favour of Alexander Wedderburn, younger of Kingennie, for 8,000 merks. 7 Sept. 1672. (See ante No. 417.)
21. Decreet in action of multiple poynding by the tenants of the said lands v. John Scrymgeour, Alexander W. of Kingennie &c. 19 January 1676.
22. Disposition by assignation of the said bond by said A. W. 3 June 1680. - V, i, 7.

601. **1759-71.** (date wanting).—Bundle of 24 papers relating to matters between David and Grizell Wedderburn of Wedderburn and Thomas Milne of Milnefield. One of these is inventoried below (No. 603), the rest are of no importance. VI, viii, 1-24.

602. **1760.** (date wanting).—Answers for Robert Wedderburn of Pearsie to the representatives of James Gardyne and David Moodie, merchants in Arbroath. Relates to the estate of one John Gardner. I, i-ii, 147.

603. **1760.** Registered submission and decreet arbitral between David Wedderburn of Wedderburn and Thomas Miln of Milnfield as to Bullion, and D. W.'s proposal to build his residence there. VI, viii, 3.

604. **1761.** Feb. 3.—Extract registered submission and decreet arbitral between David Wedderburn of Wedderburn and Mrs. Marion Clayhills of Innergourie, with consent of Dr. George Murray, her husband, for adjusting the marches between the lands of Bullion and Innergourie. Registered at Edinburgh 8 March, 1762. (Mackenzie's Office, vol. 191, pt. 1.) V, vi, 7.

L

605. **1761.** Feb. 3.—Duplicate of the foregoing.   v, vi, 8.

606. **1761.** July 6.—Receipt by Margaret Brisbane of Bullion to Mrs. Grisel Wedderburne for £16. 13. 4 as the price of 30 bolls meal; £16. 10. 0 for 30 bolls bear, with £1. 7. 6 of kain,[1] in full discharge of the rents of the lands of Bullion for the year 1760; and for 200 merks as interest on a bond for 4000 merks granted to her by the late David Wedderburne. Dated at Dundee.   i, i-ii, 143.

607. **1762.** Jan. 21.—Extract retour of the special service of Grizel Wedderburn of that ilk, as heir to her brother german, the late David Wedderburn of that ilk, in the lands of Easter Powrie, as for the principal, and the lands and barony of Ogilvie, in special warrandice thereof; which lands and others were erected into one whole and free barony to be called in all time coming the Barony of Wedderburn, by charter granted by the late Queen Anne, of date 12 March, 1708, in favour of the late Alexander Wedderburn, father of the said Grizel: also in the half of the lands of Wester Gourdie, &c. Expede in the Tolbooth of the burgh of Forfar, 21 Jan., 1762, before George Campbell, sheriff substitute of Forfar. Robert Wedderburn of Pearsie is on the inquest   In the writ (page 2) Alexander Wedderburn, grandfather of the said Grizel, is mentioned in connection with the warrandice lands.   i, i-ii, 144.
(Latin, parchment, eight pages, bookwise, in good state.)

608. **1762.** April 8.—Precept from Chancery for infefting the said Grizel in the lands specified in the service. (Latin, parchment, in good state.)   i, i-ii, 145.

609. **1762.** May 12.—Instrument of sasine following on the said precept. Registered at Dundee 26 May. (Latin, on parchment, in good condition.)   i, i-ii, 146.

610. **1762.** May 12.—Extract of the foregoing instrument.   i, i-ii, 146a.
(Latin, ten pages of foolscap, in good condition.)

611. **1762.** Nov. 4.—Decreet of the sheriff substitute of Forfar in an action by Dr. John Willison, physician in Dundee, v. Grissell Wedderburn of Wedderburn as executrix to her late brother, David Wedderburn of W., for fees due to the pursuer's father (now deceased), and for money due to the pursuer himself for attending the said David W. on his journey from Scotland to Bath, not long before his death.
   The contentions on either side are stated and restated with great elaboration, but the decreet is against the defender.   viii, ii, 130.
(Twenty-eight closely written pages of foolscap.)

612. **1763.** Feb. 24.—Confirmed testament dative and inventory, &c., of umquhill David Wedderburn of Wedderburn, Esq., given up by Mistress Grizell W. of W., sister german and executrix qua nearest of kin decerned to the said defunct. Confirmed at Brechin. David Campbell elder, and younger, of Kethick, are named as indebted to the deceased.   viii, ii, 131.

613. **1763.** April 20.—Bond of provision by Mr. David Scrymgeour, advocate, of Birkhill to his younger children and sister. The former are "my younger sons John, David, and Henry, and my daughter Janet;" the latter "Marion Scrymgeour, my sister, spouse to George Hewett of Newmilns." Dated at Birkhill.   vi, v, 19.

614. **1763.** April 30.—Power of attorney by James Wedderburn, practitioner in physick and chirurgery, Peter Wedderburn, millwright, both of the parish of Westmoreland, co. Cornwall, Jamaica, and Alexander Wedderburn of the parish of Hanover there, appointing their loveing brother John Wedderburn of Westmoreland aforesaid, practitioner in physick and chirurgery, intending to go from off the Island to Great Britain, their lawful attorney. Signed by the said James, Peter, and Alexander W.
(Three sheets of paper.)   vi, vi, **14.**

[1] Kain, i.e., payable in kind (poultry &c.) to the value of £1. 7. 6.

615. **1763.** May 26.—Discharge by Robert Wedderburn of Pearsie to Grissell Wedderburn for £15 one year's annuity of the sum of £300 due to the deceast Dame Katharine Scott, widow of Sir Alex. Wedderburn, baronet, in life rent, and to the children of the also deceast Sir John Wedderburn in fee. Dated at Pearsie and signed by Robert W. (One small piece of paper.) Scrymgeour-Wedderburn Papers. VIII, ii, 126.

616. **1763.** Aug. 19.—Discharge by John Wedderburn for himself and as attorney for James, Peter and Alexander, his brothers german, now on life and in Jamaica, and also for Margaret Wedderburn, wife of Richard Dundas of Blair, as also by Katharine, Susanna, and Agatha Wedderburn, to Mrs. Grizel Wedderburn and all the heirs of the late David Wedderburn of Wedderburn for the sum of £300 and all interest due thereon. Colonel William Fullarton (son of Wm. F. of that ilk) is a witness. VI, vi, 15.

617. **1763.** Aug. 19.—Copy of foregoing in the hand of Alexander Scrymgeour-Wedderburn, made about 1800. VI, vi, 16.

618. **1763.** Aug. 19.—Bond by Mrs. Grizel Wedderburn to Dame Jean Wedderburn *alias* Fullarton, widow of the late Sir John Wedderburn of Blackness for £300 to be paid to her for life and then to Katharine, Susannah, and Agatha her daughters. Endorsed with discharge dated at Dundee 12 Nov., 1768, and signed by Jean Wedderburn and her daughters Katharine and Susannah. (See facsimile opp. p. 72.) VI, vi, 17.

619. **1765.** Feb. 15.—Precept of clare constat by Allan Whiteford, as commissioner for Archibald Douglas, Esq., in favour of Grizel Wedderburn of that ilk, as heir to her brother, David W. of that ilk, in the lands of Kingennie. VIII, viii, 9.
(English, parchment, in good state.)

620. **1765.** April 13.—Disposition by John, Lord Gray, in favour of Mrs. Grizel Wedderburn of Wedderburn, of the lands of Wester Gourdie and other subjects therein described. (English, six pages of foolscap, each signed at the foot "Gray;" in good state.) I, i-ii, 148.

621. **1765.** May 23.—Sasine following on above precept. Endorsed as registered in the General Reg. Sasines, Book 263, fol. 244-47. VIII, viii, 10.
(English, parchment, in good state.)

622. **1766.** May 26.—Discharge by Jean Wedderburn *alias* Fullarton, widow of Sir John Wedderburn of Blackness, to Grizel Wedderburn of Wedderburn for the interest on the said £300 (ante No. 618). Dated at Dundee. Signed by Jean Wedderburn. VI, vi, 18.

623. **1766.** June 25.—Instrument of sasine following on the above disposition (No. 620). Registered at Dundee 28 June. I, i-ii, 149.
(English, on parchment, in perfect state.)

624. **1766.** June 25.—Extract of the said sasine. I, i-ii, 150.
(English, five pages of foolscap, in good condition.)

625. **1766.** July 31.—Extract registered settlement by Grizell Wedderburn of Wedderburn, of her moveable estate, to her heirs of taillie as in bond of taillie of the same date. Dated at Edinburgh. Recorded in the Books of Council and Session 19 Aug. 1766. (English, paper, in fair state.) V, i, 9.

626. **1766.** July 31, Aug. 6.—Registered bond of taillie by Mrs. Grizel Wedderburn of Wedderburn entailing the lands of Easter Powrie erected into the barony of Wedderburn, and also the lands of Wester Gourdie, the lands of Kingennie, and the lands of Bullion upon the heirs of her body, whom failing on various substitutes of entail in order, as in the Great Seal Charter of 7 Aug., 1769. See post No. 637. VIII, ii, 132.
(Nineteen pages of foolscap, the last much torn.)

627. **1766.** July 31, Aug. 6—Copy of the foregoing deed of taillie. VIII, xi, 20.

628. **1767,** Sept. 23.—Modern inventory of twenty papers relating to the lands of
Bullion, including the following :—
19. Extract Retour of Grizel Wedderburn as heir to David W. of W. her brother, 23 Sept., 1767.
20. Sasine in her favour, 2 Jan., 1768.   Recorded at Ediuburgh, 25 Feb., 1768. (Post No. 630.)
VI, ix, 35.

629. **1767.** Oct. 14.—Extract disposition of Bullion by David Brisbane to Margaret
Brisbane and David Wedderburn, 13 Jan., 1752 (see ante No. 584).   Registered at
Edinburgh 14 May, 1767 (Mack. Reg. Deeds, vol. 201, pt. 2), with endorsement,
14 Oct., 1767, of Grizel Wedderburn of Wedderburn's infeftment in Bullion. VI, ix, 22.

630. **1768.** Jan. 2.—Sasine in favour of Grizel Wedderburn of that ilk, of the lands of
Bullion, eo. Forfar, following on a disposition of such lands by David Brisbane,
deceased, in favour of Margaret Brisbane, his sister (now also deceased), in liferent,
and then to David Wedderburn of that ilk (now also deceased), heritably, and
following also on a general retour of the said Grizel, as heir to the said David
Wedderburn, her only brother german, of date 25 Sept. 1767.   Endorsed as registered 25 Feb. 1768, in the General Register of Sasines, Book 268, fol. 197-201.
(English, parchment, in good state.)   VIII, viii, 11.

631. **1768.** April 16.—Paper in action by Mrs. Grizel Wedderburn of Wedderburn to
check encroachments on the lands of Cangenny (Kingennie).   VIII, ii, 134.
(One sheet of paper.)

632. **1768.** June 3.—Similar discharge to No. 622, dated at Dundee the "threed day
of June 1768."   VI, vi, 19.

633. **1769.** (date wanting)—Inventory of writs by which the charter of the Barony of
Wedderburn in favour of Mrs. Grizel Wedderburn of Wedderburn, is to be revised.
It enumerates ten writs, including (1) the retour of Grizel W., as heir to her brother
David in Wedderburn and Wester Gourdie. Forfar, 21 Jan. 1766. (3) Bond of
Taillie by Grizell W., 6 Aug. 1766. (See ante, No. 626.)   VIII, ii, 135.

634. **1769.** (date wanting)—Duplicate of foregoing inventory.   VIII, ii, 136.

635. **1769.** April 13.—Extract retour of the general service of Mrs. Grizell Wedderburn
of Wedderburn, as heir to her great grandfather, Alexander Wedderburn of
Cangennie, (sic) clerk of Dundee.   Expede in the Court of Dundee.   v, i, 10.
(Latin, parchment, in fair condition.)

636. **1769.** May 30.—Discharge signed at Dundee by Margaret Brisbane, daughter to
the deceased Mr. James Brisbane, in favour of Mrs. Grizel Wedderburn of Wedderburn.   (One piece of paper.)   VIII, ii, 133.
This discharge presents great difficulty as regards the date of Margaret Brisbane's death. It is
signed by her in an evidently feeble hand, and she was eighty-four at its date But in No. 630,
dated 2 Jan. 1768, she is described as already deceased. There is clearly some error in one of
the documents, both of which I have carefully examined, and correctly abstracted in the text. See
also below, No. 646.

637. **1769.** Aug. 7.—Great Seal Charter of the lands and barony of Wedderburn in
favour of Grizel Wedderburn of that ilk and the heirs of her body, whom failing in
favour of the following substitutes and the heirs of their bodies in order (1) David
Serimgeour of Birkhill, advocate, (2) Alexander Serimgeour, eldest son of the said
David and his wife Catharine Wedderburn, (3) John Serimgeour, their second son,
(4) David Serimgeour, their third son, (5) Henry Serimgeour, their fourth son,
(6) Janet Serimgeour, their eldest daughter, (7) Marion Serimgeour, eldest daughter
of the late Dr. Alexander Serimgeour, (8) the heirs of the late Jean Serimgeour, his
second daughter, (9) John Wedderburn of Idvies, eldest son of the late Sir John
Wedderburn of Blackness, (10) his brothers and sisters, James, Peter, Margaret (wife
of Richard Dundas of Blair), Catharine, Susanna, Agatha (wife of John Smyth),
(11) the heirs whomsoever of the said Grizel. Written to the Great Seal and
registered 9 Sept. ; sealed 11 Sept., 1769.   VIII, viii, 12.
(Latin, parchment, eighteen pages bookwise, including cover, in good condition.)

638. **1769.** Oct. 2.—Sasine in favour of Grizel Wedderburn of that ilk following on the Great Seal Charter of 7 Aug., 1769 (No. 637). Endorsed as registered, 13 Nov. 1769, in the General Register of Sasines, Bk. 275, fol. 102-118. VIII, viii, 13.

(Latin, parchment, sixteen pages including cover, in good state.)

639. **1769.** Oct. 2.—Draft of the above sasine. (Latin, parchment, in good state.) VIII, viii, 14.

640. **1770.** May 3.—Letter to Lady Pitfour, Edinburgh, from (Sir) John Wedderburn of Balindean. Dated from Dundee. VI, vi, 20.

641. **1770.** Nov. (?)—Similar letter, same to same. Dated from Balindean. VI, vi, 21.

642. **1771.** Jan. 24.—Letter to "Alexander Scrymgeour, Esq., Advocat, Edinburgh," from Mrs. "Grissall Wedderburn." Dated from Dundee. VI, vi, 22.

643. **1771.** Feb. 13.—Opinion of David Rae, advocate, on the bond of 10 Aug., 1744 (ante No. 573) as to the proper division of the £300 therein mentioned. There is a footnote by Richard Dundas stating that the share of his wife (Margaret Wedderburn) "amounts to £54. 7. 6 for principal and interest from Martinmas, 1762 to Martinmas, 1771, the term immediately subsequent to Lady Blackness's death." The opinion expressly refers to the death of one of the nine children named in the bond as having occurred in the lifetime of Lady Blackness. VI, vi, 23.

644. **1771.** Feb. 20.—Contract between Mr. David Scrymgeour, elder of Birkhill, advocate, and Mr. Alexander Scrymgeour, younger, of Birkhill, advocate, whereby in view of the marriage of the latter with Mrs. Elizabeth Ferguson, second daughter of the Hon. James Ferguson of Pitfour, Senator of the College of Justice, the said David makes a general conveyance in his favour of his estate both heritable and moveable, and the said Mr. Alexander Scrymgeour becomes bound to pay to his said father and to Mrs. Katharine Wedderburn, his mother, in event of her surviving his father, certain annuities therein specified. Dated at Birkhill. V, i, 11.

645. **1771.** Feb. 20.—Contract of marriage between the said Mr. Alexander Scrymgeour, advocate, and Mrs. Elizabeth Ferguson. Dated at Edinburgh and Birkhill, 20 Feb. 1771. V, i, 12.

646. **1771.** April 17.—Registered settlement by Margaret Brisbane, daughter of the late Mr. James Brisbane, advocate, in favour of Helen Davidson, daughter of the late Robert Davidson of Balgay, and Grizell Wedderburn of Wedderburn. Registered in the Books of Council at Dundee. (See ante, note to No. 636.) VIII, ii, 137.

647. **1771.** Oct. 5.—Discharge of Richard Dundas of Blair and his wife, Margaret Wedderburn, to Mrs. Grizel Wedderburn for one-eighth part of the £300 named in the said bond. VI, vi, 24.

648. **1773.** Jan. 6.—Letter, dated from Dundee, addressed by Sir John Wedderburn (of Balindean) to William Hay, clerk to the signet, Edinburgh, relating to the affairs of Doctor Graham and Mrs. Helen Crawford. VI, vi, 25.

649. **1773.** Oct. 15.—Letter dated from Balindean, addressed by Sir John Wedderburn of Balindean, to Alexander Scrimgeour, Esq, advocate, Old Assembly Close, Edinburgh. It alludes to the departure of Henry Scrimgeour (afterwards Wedderburn of Wedderburn) for Jamaica, and to David Scrimgeour (another brother of Alexander) being at Balindean. In the fold is a note from Lady Margaret Wedderburn to Mrs. Scrimgeour. VI, vi, 26.

650. **1773-74.** (date wanting)—Address of a letter from Henry Scrymgeour to his brother Alexander Scrymgeour, Esq., of Birkhill, care of Messrs. Webster, druggists, 35, Leadenhall Street, London. VI, vi, 27.

651. **1776.** May 18.—Marriage settlement of Janet Scrymgeour, only daughter now on
life of Mr. David Serymgeour of Birkhill, advocate, deceased, and John Gillespie,
only son of Dr. John Gillespie of Kirktoun.   Dated at Edinburgh.   IV, iv, 18.
(Eleven pages of foolscap, in perfect condition.)

652. **1776.** July 23.—Letter in very broken hand from David Falconer, advocate, to
—— giving instructions for his will. It refers to the recent death of "my sister"
and to the state of his own health as reasons for the settlement. Mr. Alexander
Serymgeour, advocate, of Birkhill is universal legatee and executor. John, Henry
and David Serymgeour, brothers to the said Alexander, are left legacies. £200 is
also left to "Janet Hewet, my cousin, daughter to the reverend Mr. George Hewet and
Marion Serymgeour, aunt to the said Alexander" and £300 "to my cousins Janet
and Margaret Watsons, daughters to (Alexander) Watson, surgeon, and Jean Serymgeour, also aunt to the said Alexander Scrymgeour.   VI, v, 40.

653. **1778-79** (date wanting)—Memorial or case for opinion on behalf of Alexander
Serymgeour-Wedderburn as to his succession to Mrs. Grizel Wedderburn. It states
that he in fact succeeds by virtue of her entail, but that "if there had been no
settlement he would have succeeded in right of his great grandmother who was sister
to the tailzier's grandfather." It relates to his right under the said entail to quarter
the Scrymgeour with the Wedderburn arms.   VI, vi, 33.

654. **1779.** June 26.—Letter from "Al : Wedderburn" (afterwards Lord Loughborough,
and Earl of Rosslyn) to Alexander Scrymgeour-Wedderburn anent the Fife elections.
(See facsimile opp. p. 72.)   VI, vi, 28.

655. **1779.** Aug. 9.—Letter from Sir John Wedderburn of Ballindean to Alexander
Scrymgeour-Wedderburn.   VI, vi, 31.

656. **1779.** Oct. 2.—Letter from John Ure of Forfar to S. Mitchelson of Edinburgh
W.S., anent the service of Alexander Scrymgeour-Wedderburn as heir general and
special to Mrs. Grizel Wedderburn of Wedderburn.   VI, vi, 29.

657. **1779.** Nov. 16.—Inquisition at Forfar for the retour of Alexander Scrymgeour-
Wedderburn of Wedderburn, as heir of taillie and provision under deed of taillie
dated 31 July 1766 (ante No. 626) to Mrs. Grizel Wedderburn of Wedderburn, in
the barony of Wedderburn.   Endorsed 1780.   VIII, viii, 15.
(Latin, parchment, sixteen pages bookwise, in good condition.)

658. **1780.** Nov. 16.—Retour following thereou. Endorsed 1780.   VIII, viii, 16.
(Latin, parchment, in good condition.)

659. **1780.** Jan. 4.—Letter by S. Mitchelson to John Ure, anent the said service and as
to the rents of Wedderburn, Bullion, &c.   VI, vi, 30.

660. **1780.** March 30.—Letter from Alexander Serymgeour-Wedderburn to Samuel
Mitchelson giving the date of Mrs. Grizel Wedderburn's death, 7 Nov., 1778. VI, vi. 32.

661. **1780.** April 21.—Charter in favour of Alexander Scrymgeour, now Wedderburn,
as heir to the late Mrs. Grizel Wedderburn of that ilk, of the barony of Wedderburn.
(Latin, parchment, twelve sheets bookwise, in good state.)   VIII, viii, 17.

662. **1780.** May 4.—Sasine following on the said charter. Endorsed as registered in
the Forfar Sasines, vol. xxviii, fol. 41-51.   VIII, viii, 18.
(Latin, parchment, twelve pages bookwise, including covers, in good state.)

663. **1780.** May 4.—Duplicate of the said sasine.   VIII, viii, 19.

664. **1781.** June 20.—Memorial and queries for Alexander Scrymgeour-Wedderburn,
Esq., of Wedderburn, anent the entail of the estate of Wedderburn, executed by
Mrs. Grizel Wedderburn, with Mr. Hay Campbell's opinion thereon.   VIII, ix, 94.

665. **1782.** Aug. 24.—Letter from Alexander Wedderburn (Lord Loughborough) to
Alexander Scrymgeour-Wedderburn, as follows :— vi, vi, 34. Scrymgeour-
Wedderburn
Papers.

Buxton, 24th August 1782.

My dear Sir,

    An application has been made to me by the compiler of an additional volume of the Peerage, for
an account of my family ; it would be sufficient for me to state, that my Grandfather was descended
of the Family you represent, and the article so far as it immediately concerns me, would be very
concise ; but I thought it too favourable an opportunity of expressing my respect for the Family to
which I belong—not to mention it to you. If you choose to have the article extended, and will
supply me with the Materials for an accurate account of our family—I will take care to have them
properly arranged. Douglas's account is very imperfect, and I imagine, not very correct, but as the
copying his account will answer the purpose of swelling the volume intended to be published, I have
no doubt, unless I can send a better account, that the Publisher will adopt his. It would be usefull
(if it is not attended with much inconvenience to you) to mention the Documents by which the
several descents are proved, as I am persuaded you would incline as little as myself, that anything
should be published concerning the Family, that could not be well supported.

    I shall not return to London for some weeks, but, after I leave this place, I shall go into Yorkshire,
and any Letter directed for me, to the care of Mrs. Barnward at Leeds, will find its way to me. I
have the honor, to be, My Dear Sir, Yours very Sincerely, (Signed) LOUGHBOROUGH.

666. **1782.** Sept. 24.—Draft reply of A. Scrymgeour-Wedderburn to the foregoing
letter :— i, i-ii, 151.

Birkhill 24 Sept. 1782.

My Lord,

    I had the honour of receiving your Lop's letter from Buxton and immediately set about an
accurate inspection of my papers ; having not met with anything, I thought I might be more
successful in Edr. There I was happy to find Cummyng in the Lyon office, whom I meant to engage
in the pursuit already begun and had made some progress ; he has promised to send me the statement when finished and to come over here if I am so fortunate as find anything to the purpose ; in
the meantime I am going on with my search. There is one thing I beg leave to suggest to your
Lop. I have always heard that our family came over from the Merse or Berwickshire but have not
been able to find any evidence of it, although I see Mr. Cummyng has mentioned it in the Memorial
he is writing. If you could obtain the evidence of that from Mr. Hume of Wedderburn or liberty to
examine his papers I submit if it would not tend to better the account. I have heard he is not fond
of granting this liberty but I think he will hardly refuse your Lop. I am much flattered by the
very handsome manner (in which) you have given me a share in this investigation. I shall spare no
pains in obtaining information and will be happy if in this or anything else I can in the least contribute to what is agreeable to you. I have the honour to be &c.

667. **1782.** Dec. 16.—Draft letter same to same on the same subject, mentioning the
marriage of Elspeth, daughter of Alexander Wedderburn, first of Kingennie, to
Alexander Fotheringhame, brother of Powrie vi, vi, 35.

668. **1783.** Jan. 4.—Draft letter same to same. vi, vi, 36.

669. **1783.** (date wanting).—List in the hand of A. Scrymgeour-Wedderburn of documents in his possession, relating the family of Wedderburn, and probably made in
connection with the search above referred to. It refers to some 25 documents only, all
of which are entered in this present inventory, except the following :— i, i-ii, 157.

    1502.   Vide.   ⎫   These are so marked in the list, but no particulars of them are given, and
    1526.   N. B. Vide. ⎭   the originals are not now forthcoming.
    1528.   Sasine in favour of James Wedderburn, son and heir of Robert W.
    1546.   Sasine in favour of Rot. W. son and heir of James W.
    1584.   Sasine in favour of Alex. W. and Janet Mylne his spouse.
    1634.   Elspeth W. spouse to Mr. Alexander Fotheringhame, brother to the Laird of Powrie,
             discharges her brother of her tocher, &c.
    1661.   Town Clerk of Dundee, designed Sir Alex. W. of Blackness.
    1662.   July 10.   A. W. of Kingany designed Provost of Dundee.

670. **1784?**—Memorial for A. Scrymgeour-Wedderburn of Wedderburn, as to his
obtaining a charter of the lands of Kingennie from Mr. Douglas of Douglas. vi, vi, 37.

671. **1785.** May 6.—Charter of resignation of the lands of Kingennie, made by Archibald Douglas of Douglas, in favour of Alexander Scrymgeour-Wedderburn of
Wedderburn and his issue, whom failing to John Scrymgeour, his second brother,
and his issue, whom failing to Henry Scrymgeour, his fourth brother, and his issue,

whom failing to the issue of his sister, whom failing to that of his aunts in order, whom failing to John Wedderburn of Idvies, &c., &c., as in the entail of 1766, ante Nos. 625-26. VIII, xii, 14.

(Parchment. David Scrymgeour, the third brother, is not named here, as he had died unmarried in 1780.)

672. **1787-92.** Six receipts or discharges by Katherine Scrymgeour (formerly Wedderburn) to her son Alexander Scrymgeour-Wedderburn in respect of her annuity. Dated 29 May 1787 ; 31 May 1788 ; Mountwhany Aug. 1789 ; 30 May 1791 and Mountwhany 11 April 1792. VI, v, 46.

673. **1787.** April 23.—Letter dated from Dundee addressed by Charles Wedderburn of Pearsie to A. Scrymgeour-Wedderburn about the affairs of the writer. VI, vi, 38.

(A facsimile of a signature of Charles Wedderburn of Pearsie and one of that of his brother David Wedderburn Webster are given at the bottom of the sheet facing p. 72.)

674. **1787.** Sept. 21.—Letter dated from Pitfirrane addressed by Sir John Wedderburn Halkett to A. Scrymgeour-Wedderburn anent the enrolment of "my two sons" as burgesses of Cupar. VI, vi, 39.

675. **1787.** Oct. 27.—Letter same to same on the same matter and as to the education of John Halkett. VI, vi, 40.

676. **1792.** June 10.—Letter by Thomas Davidson of Dundee to A. Scrymgeour-Wedderburn as to the late David Brisbane, &c. VI, vi, 41.

677. **1793.** Feb. 4.—Memorandum as to the teinds of Kingennie and other lands belonging to Mr. A. Scrymgeour-Wedderburn. VIII, ii, 138.

678. **1793.** March 11.—Letter from Sir John Wedderburn of Balindean to Henry Scrymgeour (afterwards Wedderburn) on his engagement to Miss Maitland. In it Sir John writes : "Be sure you do your part and make a good husband, for our family was always remarkable in that, so says my sister Mrs. Dundas." VI, vi, 42.

679. **1794.** Aug. 22.—Letter from James Graham of Meathie to A. Scrymgeour-Wedderburn, announcing his start in business. VI, vi, 43.

680. **1795.** Aug. 1.—Letter from Lord Loughborough to Alexander Scrymgeour-Wedderburn anent the Fife elections. VI, vi, 44.

681. **1796.** March 10.—Letter from Sir John Wedderburn at Balindean to A. Scrymgeour-Wedderburn. In it he says : VI, vi, 45.

"This day completes David's 21st year ; his birthday I have never yet taken notice of, it only brings back the memory of a melancholy scene which is as fresh to me as when it happened. Old age is not desirable ; it has many things to bide."

682. **1796.** March 20.—Envelope containing (a) Formal letter in the hand of A. Scrymgeour-Wedderburn of Wedderburn, announcing the death of his mother Mrs. Scrymgeour, widow of the late Mr. David Scrymgeour of Birkhill, at 3 p.m., 19 March 1796, and inviting to her funeral at Balmerino on the 23rd ; (b) List of persons so invited in the same hand ; (c) Copy of the *Edinburgh Evening Courant*, 24 March 1796, containing notice of her death. IV, iv, 20.

683. **1797.** Oct. 6.—Copy of the will and codicils of James Wedderburn (son of Thomas Wedderburn), of Westmoreland, Jamaica. VI, vi, 46.

(See post s. Public Records, London Wills).

684. **1800-2.**—Copy nomination by Sir John Wedderburn of Balindean of Curators to his children. (See post s. Blackness Papers, No. 82.) VI, vi, 49.

685. **1802.** Feb. 12.—Letter dated from Bath, addressed by Alexander Wedderburn, Earl of Rosslyn to A. Scrymgeour-Wedderburn, anent the Fife and Forfar elections. I, i-ii, 152.

686. **1803.** Feb. 24.—Letter from Sir John Wedderburn of Balindean to Mrs. A. Serymgeour-Wedderburn announcing the engagement of his daughter Margaret to Philip Dundas.
vi, vi, 47.

687. **1803.** June 25.—Inventory of papers found on opening the repositories of the late Sir John Wedderburn of Balindean. (See post κ. Blackness Papers, No. 83.) vi, vi, 48.

688. **1803.** Nov. 5.—Letter, dated from London, addressed by Sir David Wedderburn to A. Serymgeour-Wedderburn on the affairs of the writer's brothers and sisters.
vi, vi, 50.

689. **1804.** Jan. 23.—Further letter same to same. vi, vi, 51.

690. **1804.** March 7.—Printed petition of A. Scrymgeour-Wedderburn for warrant to record his deed of entail (dated 3 May 1803) of his estates of Wedderburn, Birkhill, &c., in the register of tailzies. vi, vi, 52.

691. **1805-6.**—Fifteen letters dated between Oct. 1805 and Feb. 1806 on Sir David Wedderburn's successful candidature as M.P. for the Perth Burghs. vi, vi, 53.

692. **1806.** March 24.—Letter dated from Edinburgh addressed by Charles Wedderburn of Pearsie to A. Scrymgeour-Wedderburn. It names "young James Wedderburn" and speaks of "the death of John Wedderburn's youngest daughter Thomasina, ill of a three week's fever." vi, vi, 54.

693. **1806.** Sept. 3.—Sasine of the lands of Kingennie, in favour of Alexander Serymgeour-Wedderburn of Wedderburn, following on the charter of 6 May 1785 (ante No. 671).
viii, xi, 15.

694. **1807.** April 23.—Letter from Sir David Wedderburn to A. Serymgeour-Wedderburn referring to the "loss of my sister." vi, vi, 55.

695. **1808.** Oct. 27.—Letter from Alicia Wedderburn (second wife of Sir John W. of Balindean) to A. Serymgeour-Wedderburn. vi, vi, 56.

696. **1809.** March 13.—Letter from Sir David Wedderburn to A. Serymgeour-Wedderburn mentioning "my brother James' unfortunate career in Jamaica" so that "he is unexpectedly thrown on my hands." vi, vi, 57.

697. **1811.** June 9.—Letter from Charles Wedderburn of Pearsie to A. Serymgeour-Wedderburn, mentioning "leaving my country to go to London in 1770."
vi, vi, 58.

698. **1811.** July 4.—Sheet with four papers attached, all in the hand of Henry Serymgeour-Wedderburn. (a) Memorandum of the last illness and death, 4 July 1811, at Edinburgh, of his brother Alexander Scrymgeour-Wedderburn ; (b and c) note of his own birth 3 Nov. 1755, and that of his wife 24 Oct. 1768 ; (d) note of the death of Capt. Hon. F. L. Maitland, R.N., 16 Dec. 1786, and of Captain Maitland's wife's grandmother a month later, 13 Jan. 1787, in reference to the estate of Rankeillor.
vi, v, 55.

699. **1812.** Jan. 15.—Charter of the resignation of the lands of Kingennie by Charles Douglas in favour of Henry Serymgeour-Wedderburn of Wedderburn and his issue, whom failing to the following persons :—(1) Janet Scrymgeour, relict of John Gillespie ; (2) Marion Serymgeour, deceased ; (3) Jean Serymgeour, deceased ; (4) Sir John Wedderburn of Balindean ; (5) James Wedderburn his brother ; (6) Margaret Wedderburn, wife of Richard Dundas of Blair, and sister of Sir John ; (7) Charles Wedderburn of Pearsie ; (8) John Wedderburn, son of the late Thomas Wedderburn ; and the heirs of their bodies in order. (Parchment.) viii, xi, 16.

700. **1812.** April 17.—Sasine following on above charter in favour of Henry Serymgeour-Wedderburn. (Parchment.) viii, xi, 17.

M

701. **1813.** July 3.—Memorial and additional memorial for Henry Scrymgeour-Wedderburn anent the entail of Mrs. Grizel Wedderburn.   VIII, ix, 95-6.

702. **1814.** Dec. 6.—Letter dated from London addressed by John Wedderburn (of
Spring Garden) to Henry Scrymgeour-Wedderburn upon the marriage of the latter's
daughter, Catharine, to Robert Catheart of Pitcairlie, eo. Fife.   VI, vi, 59.

703. **1817.** March 16.—Letter from Charles Wedderburn of Pearsie to H. Scrymgeour-
Wedderburn.   VI, vi, 60.

704. **1818.** Feb. 8.—Letter from James Wedderburn, Solicitor General for Scotland, to
H. S. W. with a note on Mr. David Scrymgeour, keeper of His Majesty's signet,
whom the writer wrongly supposed to be the grandfather of H. S. W.   VI, v, 56.

705. **1819.** Feb. 9.—Long letter, dated from Devonshire Street, Portland Place, addressed
by John Wedderburn (afterwards of Auchterhouse) to Henry Scrymgeour-Wedderburn,
asking for various information as to the descendants of David Scrymgeour of Birkhill
and Katherine Wedderburn.   VI, v, 57.

706. **1819.** Feb. (?)—Draft answer to the foregoing in the hand of Mrs. Henry
Scrymgeour-Wedderburn with notes in that of H. S. Wedderburn, thus forming
with No. 705 a family register. (See post s. J.W.'s Collection, No. 12.)   VI, v, 58.

707. **1819.** May 15.—Letter Charles Wedderburn of Pearsie to Henry Scrymgeour-
Wedderburn. It mentions the death of Lord Ogilvy and that his son hopes to obtain
his title, &c. "James Wedderburn and family (it adds) are on the way home
from Nice. .... Old Mr. Wedderburn is about to occupy his new purchase at
Chigwell."   VI, vi, 61.

708. **1820.** Feb. 13.—Letter same to same on the death (of fever at Edinburgh) of the
latter's eldest son Alexander.   VI, vi, 62.

709. **1820.** Feb. 17.—Letter from John Wedderburn (afterwards of Auchterhouse) to
H. S. Wedderburn on the same subject, with H. S. W.'s draft reply dated 1 March.
                                                                             VI, v, 62-63.

710. **1820.** Feb. 17.—List of persons to be informed of above death, with note at head
"he died 7 Feb. 1820." It includes Charles Wedderburn of Pearsie ; Peter
Wedderburn, Islabank, Meigle ; Mrs. Wedderburn Colvile, Torryburn ; the Solicitor
General (James Wedderburn), George Street, Edinburgh ; Miss Wedderburn, 3, James
Street, Edinburgh ; John Wedderburn, 35, Leadenhall St., London ; Andrew Colvile,
35, Leadenhall St. ; Lady Wedderburn, George's Sq., Edinburgh ; Sir David Wedderburn, Luffness, East Lothian ; James Wedderburn Webster, Piccadilly, London.
                                                                             VI, v, 64.

711. **1823.** April 17.—Letter by Charles Wedderburn of Pearsie to Henry Scrymgeour-
Wedderburn. He adds a postscript :—"My nephew, cornet Charles Webster-Wedderburn writes from Castle Mahon, eo. Cork, that he is to be in Scotland next month
and will introduce his young wife to us."   VI, vi, 63.

712. **1824.** March 6.—Letter, addressed from "Lincroft Lodge, near York" by Sir James
Webster-Wedderburn to Henry Scrymgeour-Wedderburn, asking the latter to become
one of the trustees of Sir James' marriage settlement. He writes :—

"With a view to children's protection I am naturally desirous that some of my own family should
be in the trust ...... I am here on a visit to my brother Charles, who you may know lately married a
sister of Sir James Chatterton's of Castle Mahon, co. Cork, ... I expect to be in Scotland next
month ...... my visit must be still attended with the circumspection that my circumstances require."
                                                                             VI, vi, 64.

713. **1824.** March 10 —Reply from H. Scrymgeour-Wedderburn, declining the trustee-
ship.   VI, vi, 65.

714. **1824.** April 16.—Letter from Charles Wedderburn of Pearsie to H. Scrymgeour-Wedderburn. vi, vi, 66.

715. **1824.** Sept. 6.—Letter same to same. vi, vi, 67.

716. **1826.** July 19.—Letter to H. Scrymgeour-Wedderburn from John Wedderburn (afterwards of Auchterhouse) at Beddington, co. Surrey, announcing the birth of a son "yesterday." vi, vi, 68.

717. **1829.** Dec. 16.—Letter from Sir James Webster-Wedderburn to H. Scrymgeour-Wedderburn, dated from 115, Park Street, Grosvenor Square. In it he writes :—

> "As I fear that the unparalleled injustice of my late uncle's settlements does not afford me an early prospect of visiting my native country and having the pleasure of seeing you, I must be excused for troubling you on this occasion and begging you the favour of your friendly services, I am about to undergo in Edinburgh what I believe is termed *general service* as heir of line to my great-grandfather (? *sic*), Robert Wedderburn of Pearsie. As we merely want evidence or proof of the births, or register thereof, it would, as I am informed, very much facilitate matters :—any parole testimony of repute, such as the representative of a family or other member of consequence.
>
> Now when my jury is convened, should you happen to be then in Edinburgh, perhaps you would not object to do me the kindness merely to appear and state what you know either from documents or general repute, viz :—that old Pearsie was a son of Sir Alexander, and that David Webster, my father, was Robert Wedderburn's son, &c.
>
> Will you at all events oblige me with a few lines in reply as soon as convenient ? Lady Frances & my daughter, who are still in town, unite in my best regards to Mrs. Wedderburn & my cousins."
>
> (Sir James seems to have been under the impression that owing to the conviction of Sir John Wedderburn in 1746 on the charge of high treason, all his descendants were to be regarded as dead in law, and that his baronetcy, therefore, could be properly assumed by himself as the heir male of Sir John's next brother Robert Wedderburn of Pearsie. (See post, No. 720.) The mention of Robert Wedderburn in the first sentence of the letter is of course an error for " Sir Alexander Wedderburn of Blackness.") vi, vi, 69.

718. **1830.** March 11.—Letter from John Wedderburn of Auchterhouse to Henry Scrymgeour-Wedderburn announcing the birth of a daughter "yesterday morning." vi, vi, 70.

719. **1834.** March 22.—Letter from Sir James Webster-Wedderburn to H. Scrymgeour-Wedderburn, dated from 5, Baker Street, Portman Square, asking for information to aid him in his suit *v.* Wedderburn, Colvile & Co., with draft answer in full (dated 29 March 1834), in which H. S. W. says that he is unable to give the requested information. vi, vi, 71.

720. **1834.** Nov. 13.—Letter from Sir James W. W. to H. S.W., dated from 15, Hertford Street, Mayfair, in which he says :—

> "Having been in Germany all summer and only lately sufficiently recover'd from ye dreadful illness with which it pleased God to afflict me last year, I am only now enabled to reply to your extraordinary letter of the 29th March. As to its being "out of your power" to give me the information I require as to the sale of an estate by which you rec^d £5000 or more, I think I have some right to request an explanation of that. If you refuse me this, I shall give my Counsel your letter, & have it read in Court when the Wedderburn suit is heard which will be very shortly, & the world will recognize in it a part of the friendly and honourable conduct which my father's family have met with from his relatives and friends in business.
>
> I don't know that any information you can give me will be of any great import to the suit. But I feel I have a right to the information which I again request you to send me, or a good reason for y^r refusal to do so.
>
> Tho' it is a matter of perfect indifference to me how you address me, I think it proper to inform you that I have assumed the Baronetcy of Nova Scotia, since the death of Mr. Charles Wedd^n of Pearsie, as the heir of my great grandfather Sir Alexander ; that our King always receives me as such, ministers, &c , and that in consequence (now I think I am able to make it out) I shall have printed a case of all the law opinions which for years past I have taken upon my claim, proving it to be as good as that of any man to his lands which he now occupies. My duty to my son has imposed this upon me, tho' no one can suppose me weak enough in such times to care about the rank, &c., &c.
>
> vi, vi, 72.

721. **1835.** Feb. 17.—Letter from John Wedderburn of Auchterhouse to **H. S. W.** on the Wedderburn monuments in the Howff of Dundee and proposing to **H. S. W.** to have them put in order, and the following inscription added :—

HENRICUS WEDDERBURN

DE EODEM

HEREDITARIUS REGIUS VEXILLARIUS

SCOTLÆ,

HOC MARMOREM POSUIT

OSSA ET RELIQUIAS FAMILLE SUÆ PROTIGERE,

1835.

II.—CATALOGUE OF THE CONTENTS OF THE SCRYMGEOUR-WEDDERBURN
CHARTER CHEST.

NOTE.—In this catalogue the reference numbers of the documents contained in the foregoing inventory are added after the account given of each bundle. Where, however, a number is placed within brackets [sic], it is that of the document in the box of the charter chest, and not in the inventory.

CHEST I.

Box I. Two bundles containing 186 documents, 1464-1802, of which all relate to the Wedderburns, except Nos. 4, 7, 27, 81, 96. Some are on parchment (bundle i.), and the rest on paper (bundle ii.) They are all, the above four excluded, given in the foregoing inventory.

(See Nos. 1, 6, 8. [4], 12, 13, 15, [7], 23, 27, 24, 28, 29, 30, 32, 34, 35, 36, 37, 38, 43, 45, 53, 55, 60, 61, 67, [27], 82, 68, 75, 81, 96, 302, 101, 104, 92, 103, 108, 118, 120, 138, 139, 140, 157, 158, 162, 164, 165, 169, 177, 181, 180, 188, 189, 192, 193, 194, 195, 197, 200, 201, 202, 208, 210, 224, 230, 231, 232, 234, 240, 223, 226, 236, 237, 238, 241, 254, 251, 261, 263, 265. 256, 278, 279-83, [81], 287, 289, 296, 295, 297, 291, 303, 317, 306, 321, 322, 326, 331, 332, 326, 339, 341, [96], 357, 373, 374, 377, 378, 385, 400, 401, 402, 408, 421, 427-1, 432, 434, 441-44, 448, 450, 452, 457, 463-66, 479, 481, 487, 483, 485-86, 491, 496, 501, 497, 504, 506, 502, 507, 508, 512, 520, 523, 527, 526, 529, 532, 536, 540-41, 550, 554, 555, 542, 564, 556, 558, 570, 563, 583, 585, 606-10, 602, 620, 623-24, 666, 685, 242, 310, 419, 571, 669.)

Box II. Bundle i.—Contains 37 documents (1575—1778) relating to the "lands and town" of Cultray, co. Fife, acquired by Dr. Alexander Scrymgeour in 1728. There is no mention of Wedderburns, but among the families named in this set of papers are Forester, Balfour of Mountquhany, Wood of Largo and Lumlathane, Bayne of Pitmossie, Halkerstone of Rathillet, Kirk, Ball, and Gregory.

Bundle ii.—Contains 19 documents (1585-1711) relating to the lauds of Wester Gourdie, co. Forfar, acquired in 1591 by Alexander Wedderburn, first of Kingennie, from David Dunmuir (son of Richard D. and Isobell Brown) and his wife Marion Turnbull. Nos. 2-17 (except 4¹) refer to the succession of Wedderburns in these lands, and are given above. (See Nos. 11, 70. 74, 88, 85, [4¹], 178. 222, 227, 271, 272, 274, 275, 475-77. 459, 539, [18].)

Bundle iii.—Contains 42 documents (1552—1788) relating to the "lands and town" of Newgrange, co. Fife, acquired by Dr. Alexander Scrymgeour in 1723 for 22,000 merks. There is no mention of Wedderburns, but among the families named are Oliphant, Balfour of Balbuthie, Kinneir, Watson, Auchinowtie, Balfour of Mountquhannie and Grange, Balfour of Forret, Balfour of Raderry, Melvill, and Halkerston. None of these papers are inventoried above.

Bundle iv.—Contains 38 documents (1564—1634) relating to part of Wester Gourdie purchased from James Carmichael by Alexander Wedderburn (first of Kingenuie) in 1591. All but 1-12 and 15 refer to Wedderburns, and are inventoried above. (See Nos. [1-12], 72. 73, [15], 76, 77, 78, 79, 69, 84, 87, 86, 88, 89, 90, 91. 93, 94, 95, 97, 105, 98, 109, 264, 267, 268, 266.)

Bundle v.—Contains 24 documents (1260—1852) relating to the lauds of Wester Little Kinueir, co. Fife, once those of Andrew Kinloch, the Patersons of Overdunmure, Mr. James Halkerston of Cleish, and the Falconer family, and ultimately, through his wife Janet Falconer, of Dr. Alexander Scrymgeour, grandfather of Alexander and Henry Scrymgeour-Wedderburn of Wedderburn. None of these are inventoried above.

Bundle vi.—Contains 25 documents (1200?—1681) relating to the Baronies of Ogilvie and Easter Powrie, co. Forfar. These documents contain no mention of Wedderburns, but relate to the Ogilvies and Grahams of Claverhouse, proprietors of the Barony of Ogilvie, held by the Wedderburns in warrandice for that of Easter Powrie, acquired by them in 1660. None of these are given in the above inventory.

Bundle vii.—Contains 14 documents (1644—1687) relating to the Scrymgeours. Of these only one (No. 2) mentions Wedderburns, and this is inventoried above (No. 335).

Bundle viii.—Contains 12 documents (1441-1603) relating to the Scrymgeours. Of these only two (Nos. 10 and 11) are material, and these are inventoried above (Nos. 25 and 141).

Box. III. Bundle i.—Contains 23 documents (1498-1686) relating to Scrymgeours. Nothing material.   **Scrymgeour-Wedderburn Papers.**

Bundle ii.—Coutains 20 documents (1537-1661) relating to Scrymgeours. Nothing material.

Bundle iii.—Contains 13 documents (1503-1661) relating to Scrymgeours. Only one (No. 13) is material, and this is inventoried above (No. 347).

Bundle iv.—Contains 6 documents (1509-1543) relating to the Scrymgeours of Myres. Nothing material.

Bundle v.—Contains 35 documeuts (1659—1686) relating to the Scrymgeours of Dudhope, &c. Of these, three (Nos. 8, 9, 10) refer to Sir Alexander Wedderburu of Blackness (1672), and are inventoried above (Nos. **414, 415, 416**).

Bundle vi.— Contains 19 documeuts (1661—1704) relating to Scrymgeours and Wedderburns. Of these, those relating to Wedderburns (Nos. 1, 3, 4, 5, and 7) are inventoried above (Nos. **343, 424, 425, 426, 438**).

Bundle vii.—Contains 11 documents (1661—1696) relating to Scrymgeours. Nothing material.

Bundle viii.—Contains 11 documents (1671—1673) relatiug to Scrymgeours. Nothing material.

Bundle ix.—Contains 7 documeuts (1705—1765) relating to Scrymgeours. Nothing material.

Bundle x.—Contains 15 documeuts (1671—1674) relating to Scrymgeours. Of these, one (No. 3) mentioning Sir Alexander Wedderburn of Blackness (1672) is inventoried above (No. **418**).

Box IV. Bundle i.—Coutains 16 documents (1523—1793) relating to Abercrombies, Barries, Guthries, Duncans, Davisons, Edwards, &c. Nothing uaterial to Wedderburns or Scrymgeours.

Bundle ii.—Coutaius 20 documents (1533—1699) all naming Wedderburns, and all inventoried above. (See Nos 10, 33, 56, 63, 159, 163, 184, 205, 206, 301, 315, 308, 309, 312, 311, 423, 345, 344, 398, 424).

Bundle iii.—Contains 7 documents (1621—1678) relating to the Grahams of Claverhouse, and lands of Balkello and Gotterstown, &c. All of these name Wedderburns, and are inventoried above. (See Nos. 211, 212, 218, 235, 243, 433, 433ᵃ.)

Bundle iv.—Contains 20 documents (1593—1796) relating the Scrymgeours. Of these all except seven—Nos. 2, 16, 17 and 19, which are uot material, and 12, 13 aud 14, which relate only to the suit of Margaret Scrymgeour aud her trustee, Alexander Wedderburu, third of Kingeunie—name Wedderburns and are inventoried above. See Nos. 100, (2), 292, 333, 334, 343, 300s, 319, 370, 383, 384, (12, 13, 14), 420, (16, 17). 651, (19), 682.

Bundle v.—Contains 45 documents (1583—1786) relatiug to the Falconers and Brydies, &c. (See the account of Dr. Alexander Scrymgeour iu vol. i.) Nothing material.

Box V. Bundle i.—Contains 23 documeuts, 1562-1842. Of these, Nos. 2, 2a, 4, 6, 7, 9, 10, 11 aud 12, are inventoried above (Nos. 396, 376, 468, 568, 600, 625, 635, 644 and 645). Nos. 3 and 5 relate to Scrymgeours, and Nos. 16, 17, 22, and some others to the affairs of Henry Scrymgeour-Wedderburu (1805-42).

Bundle ii.—Contains 13 documeuts (1634—1729) relatiug to the Leslies of Newton, Dicks, and Alisons, once proprietors of the lands aud barony of Birkhill. Nothing material.

Bundle iii.—Contains 14 documents (1595—1698) of which some name Scrymgeours, and three (Nos. 9, 11, 12) mention Wedderburns are inventoried above (Nos. 386, 417, 428).

Bundle iv.—Contains 33 documents (1644—1673) mostly relating to Scrymgeours. No. 6 names Sir Alexander Wedderburn of Blackuess (1671), and is inventoried above (No. 409).

Bundle v.—Contains 30 documents (1260—1738) relating to the lands of Wester Little Kinneir, the Scrymgeours, Kirks, &c. Of these (Nos. 4, 5, 15 and 16), name Wedderburns, and are inventoried above (Nos. 2, 7, 62 aud 404).

Bundle vi —Coutains 16 papers (1659—1803). Of these, Nos. 2—8 refer to David Wedderburu of that ilk, and are inventoried above (Nos 561, 582, 588, 597, 599, 604 and 605).

Box VI. Bundle i.—Contains 45 documents (1467—1667, 1713) relating to the Scrymgeours. None of them uame Wedderburns.

Bundle ii.—Coutaius 50 documeuts (1459—1697) relating to the Scrymgeours. Of these, one (No. 9), the marriage coutract of John Scrymgeour and Magdalen Wedderburu, 1659, is inventoried above (No. 330).

Bundle iii.—Contains 170 documents (1533—1716) mostly relatiug to Scrymgeours. Of these Nos. 5, 11, 22, 26 aud 90 name Wedderburns, and are inventoried above (Nos. 203, 260, 300, 320, aud 439). Nos. 24, 42, 88, 149-50 also name Wedderburns, but are of no importauce aud are not inveutoried.

Bundle iv.—Contains 64 papers (1663-74) relatiug to the suit of Margaret, daughter of Major William Scrymgeour, v. her tutor, Alexander Wedderburn, third of Kingeunie. Of these, Nos. 1, 5, 6, 15, 16, 26, 27 aud 28 are inventoried above (Nos. 299, 399, 399ᵃ, 406, 407, 410, 411, aud 412); the rest being omitted as material only to the history of the suit.

Bundle v.—Contains 64 Scrymgeour and Scrymgeour-Wedderburn papers (1701—1820). Of these Nos. 4, 13, 19, 40. 46, 55-58, 62-4, are inventoried above. (Nos. 582, 587, 613, 652, 672. 698, 704, 705, 706, 709 and 710).

Bundle vi.—Contains a bound volume of 73 Wedderburn papers (1742—1835), all of which are inventoried above. (See Nos. 572-81, 586, 596, 598. 614, 616-18, 622, 632, 640-43, 647-50, 654, 656, 659, 655, 660, 663, 665, 667, 668, 670, 673-76, 678-81, 683, 686-87, 684, 688-92, 694-97, 702, 703, 707, 708, 711-21).

Bundle vii.—Contains 83 papers (1736-79), being mainly old accounts, &c , relating to the affairs of David and Grizel Wedderburn of that ilk. Of these, Nos. 4, 5, 13, and 71 only are of any interest, and are inventoried above. (See No. 567).

Bundle viii.—Contains 24 Wedderburn of Wedderburn papers (1759-71) of no importance. Of these, only one (No. 3), is inventoried above (No. 603).

Bundle ix.—Contains 35 papers relating to the estate of Bulzeon (1648—1813). Of these only three (Nos. 14. 22 and 35) are inventoried above (Nos. 584, 629 and 628).

Bundle x.—Contains 6 papers (1774—1804) relating to excambions between Alexander Scrymgeour-Wedderburn and Lord Dundas, Lord Duncan, &c. Of these none are inventoried above.

Bundle xi.—Contains 21 papers relating to the lands of Glenboy (1568—1659). Of these, only one (No. 12) names a Wedderburn, and this is inventoried above (No. 179).

Bundle xii.—Bound volume of 152 papers (copies of documents, memorials, notes, &c.) relating to the claim of Alexander Scrymgeour-Wedderburn, and his successors, to the peerages of Dundee and Dudhope, and to the office of Hereditary Standard Bearer of Scotland (1780—1811). Not material to the Wedderburn family and not, therefore, inventoried above.

Box VII.   Bundle i.—Contains 30 Graham of Claverhouse writs (1552—1716). Of this one (No. 4) names a Wedderburn and is inventoried above (No. 243).

Bundle ii.—Contains (a) 6 Read of Turfbeg papers (1778—1804), Elizabeth, daughter of Sir Alexander Wedderburn, fourth baronet of Blackness, having married Alex. Read of Turfbeg. (b) Five Maitland-Makgill papers (1803-27). None of these are inventoried above.

Bundle iii.—Contains 65 miscellaneous papers (1543—1720) with occasional references to Scrymgeours, and two to Wedderburns. The latter (Nos. 21 and 59) are inventoried above (Nos. 373 and 537).

Bundle iv.—Contains 30 old law papers (1699—1805) not connected with either Scrymgeours or Wedderburns. None of these are inventoried above.

Bundle v.—Contains 62 papers (1712—52) relating to the Jacks and Kirks in Cultray, and to the Alisons of Birkhill. Not inventoried above.

CHEST II.

Box VIII.   Bundle i.—Contains 33 parchments (1488—1698), of which all but two (Nos. 1 and 28) relate to Wedderburns and are inventoried above. (See Nos. [1], 3, 4, 5, 11, 18, 20, 25, 42, 44, 48, 59, 66, 63, 71, 102, 107, 112, 114, 196, 207, 229, 239, 248, 249, 250, 273, [28], 285, 295, 430, 447, 521).

Bundle ii.—Contains 143 Wedderburn papers (1586—1793). All inventoried above.
(See Nos. 52, 57, 64, 80, 121, 122, 123, 124, 127, 136, 137, 142, 147, 151, 152, 155, 156, 258ª, 160, 161, 143, 166, 168, 167, 183, 186, 187, 190, 191, 204, 198, 209, 219, 220, 217, 213, 215, 216, 221, 225, 228, 233, 247, 257, 258, 262, 269, 270, 276, 284, 288, 294, 304, 305, 307, 313, 314, 323, 324, 325, 337, 338, 386, 340, 342, 349, 350, 362, 364, 351, 372, 381, 339, 387, 393, 390, 395, 408, 413, 422, 427, 429, 431, 436, 440, 445, 446, 451, 449, 454, 453, 456, 460, 467, 471, 455, 474, 478, 490, 492, 484, 435, 498, 489, 492, 493, 494, 500, 505, 509, 509ª, 510, 511, 515, 516, 525, 528, 535, 536, 541, 549, 557, 560, 565, 591, 589, 592, 593, 615, 694, 590, 596, 611, 612, 626, 636, 631, 633, 634, 646, 677).

Bundle iii.—Contains 26 parchments (1600—1659) relating to Kingennie. Of these all except one (No. 1) relate to Wedderburns and are inventoried above. See Nos. [1], 125, 128, 129, 130, 131, 132, 134, 135, 144, 144ª, 145, 148, 150, 170, 171, 172, 173, 174, 199, 244, 246, 245, 277, 290, 327.

Bundle iv.—Contains 31 parchments (1443—1600) relating to the owners of Kingennie up to 1600. Of these eight (Nos. 12, 13, 14, 16, 21, 22, 29 and 31) refer to Wedderburns and are inventoried above (Nos. 39, 40, 39ª, 51, 110, 111, 133, 146).

Bundle v.—Contains 25 writs of Easter Powrie (1631-1659). These relate to the Ogilvies of Ogilvie, Durhams of Pitkerro, and Dougal McPhersone, predecessors in title of Alexander Wedderburn in these lands. Of these four (Nos. 8, 9, 24, 25) mention Wedderburns and are inventoried above (Nos. 252, 253, 328, 329).

Bundle vi.—Contains 19 writs of Easter Powrie (1662—1714). All of these relate to Wedderburns, and are inventoried above. (See Nos. 353, 355, 358, 375, 379, 380, 461, 462, 469, 470, 498, 499, 513, 514, 517, 518, 544).

Bundle vii.—Contains 15 writs of Easter Powrie (1662—1660). All of these also relate to Wedderburn, and are inventoried above. (See Nos. 352, 360, 361, 363, 364, 365, 366, 367, 371, 382, 388, 391, 392, 394, 397.)

Bundle viii.—Contains 20 Wedderburn parchments (1708—1780), all inventoried above. (See Scrymgeour-Nos. **533, 534,** 543, 545, 546, 547, **548,** 552, 553, 619, 621, **630,** 637, **638, 639,** 657, **658,** Wedderburn **661, 662, 663**). Papers.

Bundle ix.—Contains 99 Scrymgeour papers (1582-1813). Of these, seven (Nos. 11, 43, 54, 64, 93, 94, 95) are inventoried above (Nos. 154, **255, 268, 522, 664,** 701).

Bundle x.—Contains 21 papers (1643-1675) relating to the affairs of Major William Scrymgeour and the suit of his daughter Margaret v. Alexander Wedderburn of Easter Powrie, her tutor. (See above, Box VI. Bundle iv.) Nothing material, except No. 8, which is inventoried above (No. 318).

Bundle xi.—Contains 28 miscellaneous papers (1567—1682) relating mostly to the Guthries of Kingennie, Hunters of Balgay, &c., and 11 papers (1601—1714) relating to the Kyds of Grange of Barrie. Of the former, five (Nos. 11, 13, 16, 18, and 28) are inventoried above; of the latter none are material (Nos. **126.** 149, **153, 185, 458**).

Bundle xii.—Contains 28 parchments (1729-1832) relating to the affairs of Dr. Alexander Scrymgeour, David Scrymgeour of Birkhill, his son, and his descendants. Of these, six (Nos. 5, 14-17, and 20) are inventoried above (Nos. **569, 671, 693, 699, 700,** and 627).

Bundle xiii.—Contains 14 writs (1516-1685) relating to the lands of Newgrange, Balmerino. (See ante Box II, Bundle iii) Nothing material.

Bundle xiv.—Contains 53 parchments (1509—1697), almost all of them naming either Scrymgeours or Wedderburns, or both. Of these all, except 1, 1ᵃ, 2, 3, 3ᵃ, 4, 5, 9, 10, 22ᵃ, 29, and 31, are inventoried above. (See Nos. 9, 14, 16, 17, 19, 21, 22, 26, 31, 41ᵃ, 41, 46, 47, 49, 50, 54, 58, 65, 99, 106, 110, 113, 115, 116, 117, 119, 175, 171ᵃ, 176, 152, 214, 316, 346, 359, 369, 437, 472, 473, 495, 506, 519)

NOTE.—The documents contained in the following bundles in this Box relate to various properties in which the Scrymgeours or Wedderburns or their predecessors have had an interest : e.g., Kingennie, Powrie, Newgrange, Wormit, Birkhill, and different small holdings in Dundee and S. Andrews. Of these documents only four (xvi, 9 ; xx, 13 ; xxi, 11 ; and xxiv, 3) refer to Scrymgeours, and three (xx, 20 ; xxi. 6 ; xxii, 4) to Wedderburns. These last are included in the foregoing inventory (see 259, 271ᵃ, 405.)

Bundle xv.—Contains 15 parchments (1468—1539) relating to Guthries, Fernies, Kyds, &c.

Bundle xvi.—Contains 16 parchments (1540-1567) relating to the families of Lovell, Gilgour, Barry, Brog, Rait, Feltric, Cockburn, &c.

Bundle xvii.—Contains 21 parchments (1568—1585) relating to the families of Yeoman, Rait, Brydie, Kynneir, Corstophine, Fotheringham, Beaton, Brog, Wellwood, Bruce, &c.

Bundle xviii, Contains 16 parchments (1586-1599) naming Welwood, Lentrone, Beaton, Kynneir, Crichton, Fethie, Brydie, Guthrie, Yeaman, Rolland, Hunter, &c.

Bundle xix.—Contains 15 parchments (1601—1615) naming Rolland, Hunter, Boytar, Balfour, Bruce, Sandilands, Carncross, Rollok, &c.

Bundle xx.—Contains 20 parchments (1616—33) naming Forester, Boytar, Brog, Davidson, Carstairs, Yeaman, Finlayson, Dalgleish, Young, Kyd, Carncross, Kinloch, Moffat, Martine, &c.

Bundle xxi.—Contains 16 parchments (1635—58) naming Arnott, Kynneir. Carstairs, Kyd, Welwood, Lentrone, Dudingstone, Bower, Quhyt, Kinloch, Durhame, McPhersone, &c.

Bundle xxii.—Contains 15 parchments (1662—78) naming Kynnaird, Kyd, Carstairs, Campbell, Wane, Guthrie, Welwood, Panter, Maitland. &c.

Bundle xxiii.—Contains 12 parchments (1680—1697) naming Walker, Watson, Welwood, Leslie Ayton, Barclay, &c.

Bundle xxiv.—Contains 12 parchments (1692—1705) naming Constable, Lauder, Milne, Watts, Watson, Oliphant, Gray, Douglas, Nairn, Rodger, Maxwell, Gardyne, Lyon, Mungo Carnegie, &c.

Box IX.

Bundle i.—Contains 9 bundles of, in all 299 papers (1650—1745) relating to the Leslies of Newton, Dicks, Mungo Carnegie and Alexander Alison, predecessors in title to Birkhill of David Scrymgeour, purchaser thereof in 1733. (See ante, Box v. Bundle ii.) Nothing material.

Bundle ii.—Contains 39 miscellaneous papers (1660—1774), of which two (Nos. 2 and 35) relate to Wedderburns, and are inventoried above (Nos. 368, and 566).

Bundle iii.—Contains 20 papers relating to the Crawfords of Monorgan (1710—1731). Of these a few name Alexander Wedderburn, clerk of Dundee (afterwards fourth baronet of Blackness) as witness or notary, but none are material.

Bundle iv.—Contains 16 papers (1669—1785) relating to the Glens, Jacks, &c., in Cultray. (See ante, Box VII. Bundle v.) Nothing material.

Bundle v.—Contains 14 papers (1632—1688) relating to the Lentrones, Welwoods, Brydies and Falconers. (See ante, Box IV. Bundle v.) Nothing material.

Bundle vi.—Contains 27 dispositions by the creditors of Alexander Alison of Birkhill in favour of David Scrymgeour, purchaser thereof (1746-56). Nothing material.

Bundle vii.—Small bundle of letters relating to the affairs of Alexander Scrymgeour-Wedderburn of Wedderburn (1778—1811). Not material.

Bundle viii.—Various papers of no interest, relating to the affairs of David and Grizel Wedderburn of Wedderburn (1750—1778). Not material.

Bundle ix.—Seventeen long scrolls (1630—1744) of which some relate to the lands of Easter Powrie before its acquisition by the Wedderburns; others to the Alisons of Birkhill. Not material.

Bundle x.—Two rent-books of the Wedderburn estates (1755—73). Not material.

Bundle xi.—Various papers relating to the Moor of Liff road, and to excambions between Alexander Scrymgeour-Wedderburn and Lord Dundas (1779—97). Not material.

Bundle xii.—Inventory of the writs of the lands in co. Argyle of Col. Patrick McKellar of Drumfie. Probably obtained on the chance of its containing Scrymgeour information. Not material.

Bundle xiii.—Contains 9 papers (1650—1735) relating to the Dicks and Alisons of Birkhill. Not material.

Bundle xiv.—Contains 6 burgess-tickets of David Scrymgeour of Birkhill (1736—43), viz:— Aberbrothock (1736), Dundee (1738), Pittenweem (1742), Ayr (1742), Stirling (1742), and Elgin (1743).

Bundle xv.—Contains 14 miscellaneous parchments (1703—1786), some relating to Cultray, and one (No. 12) to Bullion (1724, June 30), which is inventoried above (No. 559).

Bundle xvi.—Seven miscellaneous parchments (1706—25) relating to the Abercrombies, Gardynes of Latouu, John Ogilvy of Newhall, &c. Nos. 1 and 3 name Wedderburns, and are inventoried above (Nos. 530 and 531).

THE BLACKNESS PAPERS.

These papers are in the possession of Sir William Wedderburn, Bart., to whom my best thanks are due for the free access he has given me to them. Their existence was for a long time quite unknown to him. They were placed many years ago by his father, Sir John, in the secret compartments of an old cabinet, where they remained till 1893, when Sir William, in moving the cabinet from Inveresk to Meredith, looked to see what hidden spaces it contained, and in one of them found these documents. At his request I arranged them and had them bound (together with a few more modern ones, which he desired to include) in a handsome volume, of which the following inventory gives the contents.

In addition to this volume, Sir William has in his possession an old pocket-book which belonged to his great-grandfather Sir John, and which contains a family register from his time down to the present. A copy of this register, which is all there is in the book, is given below, No. 93.

As, naturally, these papers relate chiefly to the Blackness and Ballindean branches of the Family, I have entitled the collection the " Blackness Papers."

SUMMARY OF THE BLACKNESS PAPERS.

FRONTISPIECE. Arms of Sir Alexander Wedderburn, Bart., 1707.
1. Copy of Patent of Baronetcy, 1704.
2-3. Two old Notarial Instruments, 1537, 1583.
4-8. Royal letters : two originals, three copies, 1586-1664.
9-11. Family Registers, 1610-1730.
12-22. Marriage Contracts, &c., chiefly of the heads of the Blackness line, 1608-1801.
23-33. Marriage Contracts of minor importance, 1611-1766.
34-35. Dispositions : Jean Fullarton, Lady Wedderburn, to her daughters, 1761-1769.
36-41. Letters to Sir Alexander Wedderburn of Blackness, Knight, 1639-1661.
42. Letter : Doctor John Wedderburn (of Moravia), brother of James, Bishop of Dunblane, to Alexander Wedderburn of Kingennie. 1617.
43. Agreement between Sir Peter Wedderburn, Lord Gosford, and John Wedderburn of Blackness, 1676.
44-59. Letters relating to the trial and execution of Sir John Wedderburn, 1745-47.
60-61. Letters relating to Lady Margaret Ogilvy, first wife of Sir John Wedderburn of Ballindean, 1774-75.
62. Bond to Sir John Wedderburn of Ballindean, 1791.
63. Letter from Sir John Wedderburn of Ballindean, 1795.
64-65. Letters as to the Ballindean Patent, 1803.
66-76. Modern papers relating to the family of Ballindean, 1803-1837.
77. Note of Parchments in the possession of Sir William Wedderburn, 1894.
78-81. Draft Genealogies of the family.
82-92. Appendix—Some papers of minor importance and modern date, 1800-81.
93. Pocket Book containing family register, 1724-1883.

INVENTORY OF THE BLACKNESS PAPERS.

FRONTISPIECE.—Engraving of the Arms of Sir Alexander Wedderburn, second baronet, of Blackness.

This is from a plate about 9½ x 6¼ in. and gives the following bearings :—On a shield argent, three roses gules ; below the shield the motto " Consilio et Cura ;" above the shield a baronet's helmet surmounted by an eagle or griffin's head, the ears of the animal being erect, and the head very like that of the supporters of the shield, which are two griffins. Above the crest is the motto " Spernit pericula virtus." In chief, on the sinister side, is a square argent, charged with St. Andrew's cross azure, on which is placed, on a shield of pretence, the arms of Scotland surmounted by the Royal crown.

At the foot of the engraving, which is very elaborate, especially in the mantling, is a label, on which is printed " Atchivment of Sir Alexr Wedderburn of Blackness." In the corner of the plate are the words " Rob Wood, Sculp."

It is noteworthy that the shield has no chevron between the roses ; perhaps the impression is a proof of an unfinished plate.

N

1. **1704.** Aug. 9.—English translation of Queen Anne's original patent of a baronetcy
    to John Wedderburn of Blackness, and his heirs male for ever. Given at Windsor.
    See below No. 77 (3) for copy of the original.

    2—3, Two Old Notarial Instruments, 1537—1583.

2. **1537.** Oct. 11.—Notarial instrument narrating that in presence of the notaries and
    witnesses, a worthy woman, Isobella Andersone, the affianced of an honourable man
    Alexander Vodderburne, burgess of the burgh of Dundee, compeared outwith the
    presence of the said Alexander her spouse, in a full court, held by an honourable
    man James Serimgeour, constable of the said burgh, and Lord superior of the Castle
    Hill, and gave her great bodily oath that she was not compelled by her said spouse
    to resign and surrender all and whole her land and tenement burghal, both outer
    and inner, lying on the south side of the Market gate of the aforesaid burgh, between
    the land of the heirs of the late David Oliver, and the vennel commonly called
    Skirling's Wynd to the eastward, the cemetery of the church of St. Clement's to the
    westward, the land of Andrew Barry, younger, to the southward, and the said market
    gate to the northward, in the hands of the said lord superior of the same, in favour
    of and for new infeftment to be made to the said Isobella and the said Alexander
    her spouse, and swore that she should never come in the contrary thereof in judge-
    ment or without ; which things being done, and lawfully deduced, the said Isobella
    freely resigned the said tenement in the hands of her said lord superior, who there-
    upon gave sasine, heritable state, and real, actual and bodily possession of the said
    land and tenement to the said Isobella Andersone and Alexander Vodderburne her
    spouse, and the survivor of them in conjunct fee, and to the heirs procreated or to
    be procreated between them, which failing, to the heirs whatsoever of the said
    Alexander, according to the tenor of a charter of new infeftment to be made there-
    upon, and of her old infeftment which she had thereof ; reserving, however, the
    freehold of her land or fore tenement, and of one cellar, namely, the nether cellar of
    the Inner land, to a worthy woman, Agnes Quhit, mother of the said Isobella, for
    the lifetime of the said Agnes only ; and for the yearly payment and satisfaction of
    the annual rents and burdens arising from the land and tenement aforesaid, the said
    Agnes Quhit straitly bound herself, and hypothecated the aforesaid fore land and
    cellar above written, during her life only, whereupon the said Isobella and Alexander
    craved instruments one or more, to be made to them by the notary. These things
    were done within the close of George Rolland, upon the ground of the said land and
    tenement, about the eleventh hour before noon, on the 11th October 1537, the
    witnesses present being the honourable men, James Vodderburn, Henry Haye, David
    Vodderburn, John Fleschar, George Rolland, James Carnege, James Durvard, officer,
    Robert Seres and Mr. David Robertson, co-notaries, the latter signing himself "David
    Luyde N.P." and presbyter of the diocese of Brechin, of which diocese also Robert
    Seres is a clerk.

    (Latin, parchment, in good condition, no seal. It is variously endorsed. the only note of interest
    being in the hand of Alex. Wedderburn, first of Kingennie, "Concerning Patrik Wedderburnis land
    besyd the ...... (word illegible). The other endorsements are quite modern, and add nothing to the
    contents of the deed. The James and David Wedderburn named in the document as witnesses are
    no doubt James Wedderburn, junior, and David Wedderburn in Murraygait.

3. **1583.** Nov. 28.—Notarial instrument narrating that an honourable man, William
    Duncan, one of the bailies of the burgh of Dundee, personally went to that tenement
    of land of Margaret Myln, lawful daughter of Robert Myln, burgess of the said burgh,
    lying in the same burgh, on the south side of the Argyle Gate of the same, between
    the lands of the late David Watsone, vestment maker, now of Edward Chalmer, on
    the east, the lands of David Tendell on the west, the cemetery of the parish church
    of the said burgh on the south, and the said Gate on the north ; and there the said
    Margaret Myln, with express consent and assent of Robert Wedderburn, her husband,
    resigned all and whole her said tenement in the hands of the said bailie, as in the
    hands of our sovereign lord and King, superior thereof : whereupon the said bailie,
    by virtue of his office, and on the special mandate of the resigner, gave heritable
    sasine and actual bodily possession of all and whole the aforesaid tenement, by delivery
    of earth and stone thereof to the aforesaid Robert Wedderburn and to Margaret
    Myln his wife, and the survivor of them in conjunct fee; and to the heirs lawfully

gotten or to be gotten between them, which failing, to the heirs and assignees what-soever of the said Robert. Moreover, the said Margaret Myln, in the absence of her husband, compeared in an open and full court, held by the said bailie upon the ground of the said tenement, and asserted that she was not forced, but of her own proper will did all and sundry the premises, and gave her bodily oath that she would not deny the same in future. Upon all which the said Robert craved instruments. Done upon the ground of the said tenement about the tenth hour before noon of the 28th day of November, 1583. Witnesses, David Hay, Anthony Layng, David Wedderburn and Mr. Hercules Rollok, co-notary. Mr. Alexander Wedderburne, scribe of the community of Dundee, is notary in chief to the instrument, and he and Mr. Hercules Rollok add their signs and signatures.

(Latin, parchment, the ink somewhat faded and the seal gone, but otherwise in fair condition. The sign of Alexander Wedderburn is his usual one, with the motto " Deum Time.")

4—8, *Five Royal Letters*, 1585—1664.

4. **1585**. June 23.—Letter from James V. to the Town Council of Dundee. Signed by the King.

Richt traist freindis, We greit you weill. Be ressoun of the present infectioun of the pestilence in our burgh of Edinburgh, and for the furthering of our commoditie upon the speciall trast quhilk we have in zou, We have commandit our cunzeous to be transportit thair And hes send our generall and Maister cunzeour to conferre with zou thairupoun desiring zou effectuualie as ze respect the avancement of our seruice and commoditie That with all diligence efter the ressait of this our lettre, ze caus sic a hous be preparit and deliuerit vnto thame as they sall find maist apt and con-venient for this vse, And that ze have the credit of that house and wark in speciall recommendatioun, sen ze have best habilillitie And that we doubt nothing in your guidwill, prouiding specialie that the officiaris and seruandis of our said cunzehous be thankfullie ressauit and weill interteynt, fre from all exactioun watcheing warding, and to have and vse like priuilege and fredome within zour burgh during thair remaning thair as thay enjoyit in Edinburgh or other thair places of residence of befoir, Quhairin ze sall do ws speciall gude seruice and acceptable plesour, And sa remitting the mair speciall declaratioun of our mynd to the messengeris committis zou to the protectioun of God At Dumferunling the xxiii of Junii 1585.

JAMES R.

(Addressed) To our richt traist freindis the prouest ballies and counsell of Dundie.
(A single sheet of paper in good condition. The royal seal, however, is worn away, and the paper a good deal stained.)

5. **1592**. April 16.—Letter from James V. to the Town Council of Dundee. Signed by the King.

Traist freindis we greit zou hartlie wele Vpoun sum vrgent occasiouns fallin out sen our cuming heir We have heirby taken occasioun to requeist zou verray ernistlie to send heir toward ws ane hundreth of your best equippyt and experimentit hagbuttaris the morne anis in the day, or aganis Tyisday hefor none at the fardest, to attend vpoun ws, as thai salbe desyrit, As ze will report our verray speciall and hartlie thankis and do ws acceptable plesour and seruice, Swa having appointit the berar our seruand (quhom ze sall credeit) to Impairt our mynd mair amplie to zou heirauent We commit zou to God from Perth the xvi of Apryle 1592.

JAMES R.

(Addressed) To our traist freindis the Prouest bailleis and counsele of our burgh of Dundie. (Similar to No. 4, and in like condition).

6. **1649**. July 6.—Copy of a letter addressed by Charles II. to Mr. Alexander Wedder-burn, town clerk of Dundee, and dated at Brussels.

This copy is signed "A true copy taken by me, Chas. Wedderburn " (of Pearsie). It is given in full in the account of Sir Alexander Wedderburn of Blackness in vol. I.

The originals of this and the next letter were in the charter chest of Henry Scrymgeour Wedderburn of Wedderburn and Birkhill, but were presented by him to the Town Council of Dundee, and are now in their Charter Room (Charters, &c., Box I, Nos. 158, 159). See "Charters and Docu-ments relating to the Burgh of Dundee " by Wm. Hay, 1880.

7. **1651**. Jan. 17.—Copy in the same hand of another letter from Charles II. to the Provost bailies and council of Dundee, dated at Perth. Printed at length in the account of Sir Alexander Wedderburn of Blackness in Vol. i.

8. **1664**. Feb. 12.—Copy of a letter, superscribed Charles R. and subscribed " Rothes thes'" (treasurer), " Lauderdaill " and others, being the gift by Charles II. to Sir Alexander Wedderburn of Blackness of a pension of £100. Dated at Whitehall. Printed at length in the account of Sir Alexander in vol. I.

Blackness Papers.

This paper is apparently also in the hand of Charles Wedderburn of Pearsie. It is endorsed by him "Signature of Sir Alexander Wedderburn" (*i.e.*, signature of the king in his favour) and then below, in the hand of Sir John Wedderburn of Ballindean, is written "The copies of these papers, also a grant of a pension by Charles Ist to Sir Alexʳ Wedderburn on the wine duties of Dundee were delivered by Rᵗ Wedderburn of Pearsie to Sʳ Robᵗ Douglas and never returned. J.W." Whether this charge is correct may be doubted, for though it does not appear where the original now is, it would seem to have been at Pearsie in October 1836, as J.W. in his MS. account of the family gives a copy of it and attempted facsimiles of the signatures made "from the original at Pearsie" at that date. It was no doubt at one time lent to Sir Robert Douglas, who quotes it in his Baronage (p. 281).

9—11, *Family Registers*, 1610—1730.

9.   **1610-1673.**—Family Register in the hand of Sir Alexander Wedderburn of Blackness, Knt. giving the birth dates of all his children and other details of his family.

(One sheet of paper, the ink much faded. A facsimile of this document is given opposite, but for the sake of distinctness does not show the faded colour of the ink). The register is as follows :—

REGISTER OF SIR ALEXANDER WEDDERBURN, OF BLACKNESS, KNT.

" Heer followes the dait of my aige, bedfellowes and childrens.

I was borne in March 1610 upon the 2ᵈ day yrof, my bedfellow in March 1620.

1.
Margaret.
Upon the 22 of March 1638 my eldest daughter Margaret was borne. Witnesse to her baptisme, William Auchinlek, lait provest, James fletcher, present provest, my father in law.

2.
Alexander.
Upon the 26 of Octʳ 1639 my eldest sone Alexʳ was borne. Witnesse to his baptisme, Alexʳ Campbell of Balgershoe, Alexʳ Wedderburne of Kingennie, Alexʳ Mylne, and Alexʳ Simmer, baillies.

3.
Johne.
Upon the 12 of febʳ 1641 my second sone Johne was borne. Witnesse to his baptisme Mʳ Joⁿ Wedderburne my uncle, Mr Joⁿ fotheringhame, tutor of powrie, Mr Joⁿ Duncansone, minister, Mr Joⁿ Robertsone, minister, and Joⁿ Goldman.

4.
James.
Upon the 3ᵈ day of Maij 1642 my third sone James was borne. Witnesse to his baptisme, James fletcher, provest, James Wedderburne, James peirsone, James Symsone, baillies, and James Hodge.

5.
Alexander.
Upon the ii day of May 1643 my fourt sone Alexander was borne. Witnesse to his baptisme Alexander Wedderburne of Kingennie, Alexander Halyburton, baillie, and Alexʳ Wedderburne, pier master.

6.
Jeane.
Upon the 15 of Janʳ 1645 my second daughter Jeane was borne. Witnesse to her baptisme Mr John fotheringhame, tutor, Mr Patrick Yeaman of dryburgh, Robert fletcher, merchant, Mr Alexʳ Mylne, and Alexʳ Jack of Woolhill.

7.
Helen.
Upon the 2ᵈ of March 1646 my thrid daughter helene was borne. Witnesse to her baptisme Sir George halyburtone of fodrines, on of the lords of sessione, thomas halyburtone and Robert Davidsone baillie and Mr George halyburtone.

8.
Grissell.
Upon the 8ᵗʰ of febʳ 1647 my fourt daughter Grissell was borne. Witnesse to her baptisme Major Generall Middletone of fettercairne, Alexʳ Wedderburne of Kingennie, thomas Mudie and Robert Davidsone, baillies.

9.
Alexander.
Upon the 4ᵗʰ of April 1648 my fyft sone Alexander was borne. Witnesse to his baptisme, Sir Alexander Gibson of Durie, lord register: Alexʳ Wedderburne of Kingennie: Mr Alexʳ Mylne, parsone of forgone, Alexander fletcher and Alexʳ Goldman.

10.
James.
Upon the 8 of Novʳ 1649 my sext sone James was borne. Witnesse to his baptisme Mr James Kyd of Craigie, Mr James Gleg, Doctor James betton, James brisbane, James Ramsay.

11.
Cecilia.
Upon the 27 of Jaʳʸ 1651 my fyft daughter Cecilia was borne. Witnesse to her baptisme, Sir George preston of Craigmillar, Mr Joⁿ Gilmor and Mr Joⁿ Wishart, advocates, and Mr John fletcher advocat and Arᵈ Sydserff, baillie of Edʳ.

12.
Peter.
Upon the 18 of Sepʳ 1652 my sevinth sone peter was borne. Witnesse to his baptisme Mr Peter and Kingennie.

13.
George.
Upon the 13 of Sepʳ 1654 my eight sone George was borne. Witnesse to his baptisme George Kinnaird of Rossie, George fletcher my brother, George browne and George fairmone.

14.
Matilda.
Upon the 15 of Augᵗ 1656 my sext daughter Matilda was borne. Witnesse Dʳ Thomas Gleg, Thomas bultie, Roᵗ Stratton.

History of the
Children of Alex.ʳ after
Sr Alex. Wedderburn,
first of Blackness.
first Date 1610⁴
last Date: 1673

Margaret

2

3

4

5

6

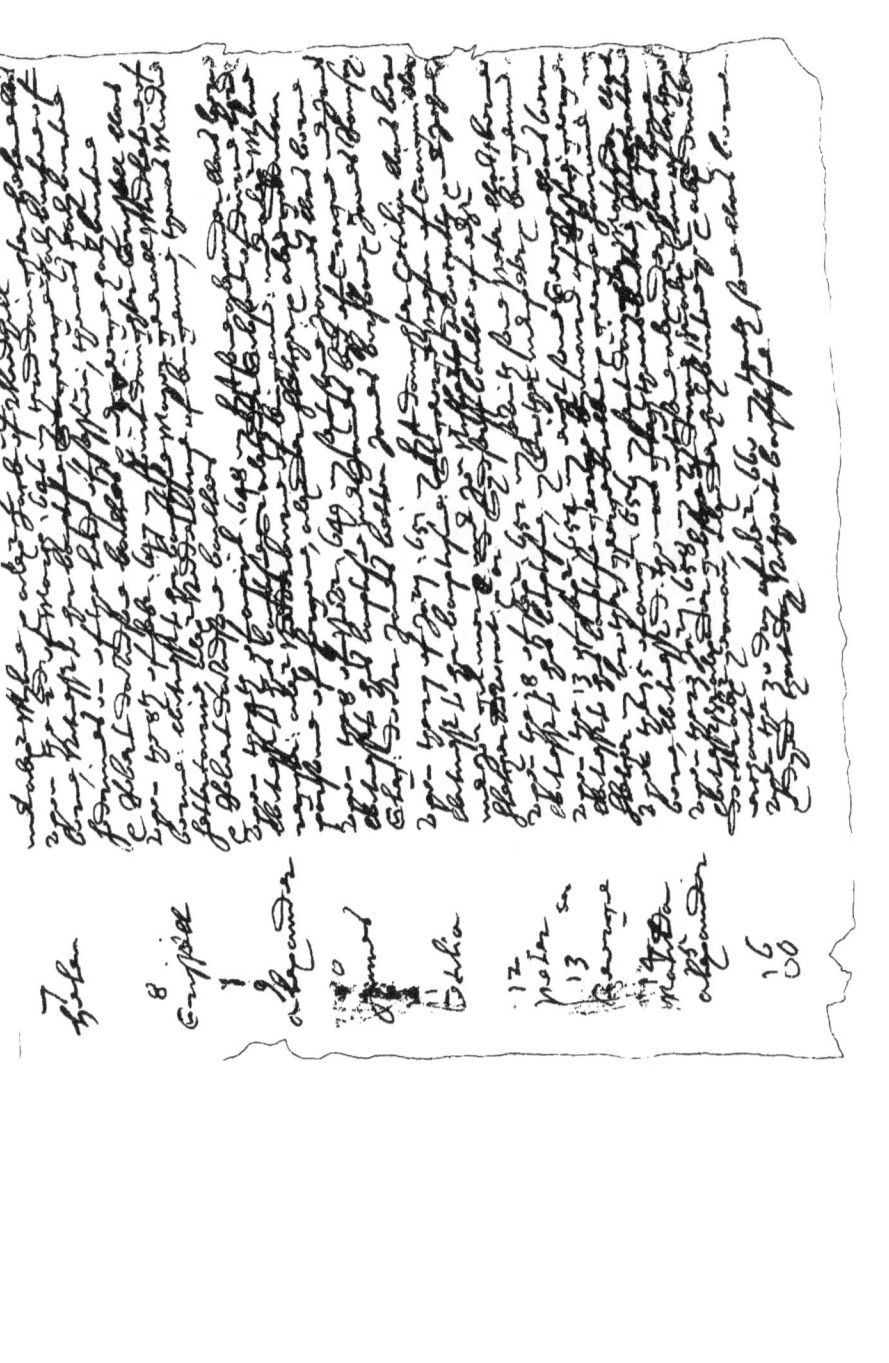

15.
Alexander.

Upon the 23 Jaᵗʸ 16ᶾ8 my nynt sone Alexander was borne. Witnesse Sʳ Alex- **Blackness** ander Gibsone of durie, Sʳ Alexʳ blair of Bathayok, Doctor Alexʳ Yeaman, Alexander **Papers.** halyburtone yᵗ, and Alexʳ duncan, merchant.

16.

Upon the 30 day of deʳ 1660 my tenth sone was borne and dyed that day without baptisme.

Bairnes'
Marriadges
Margaret.

In August 1655 my daughter Margaret was mareed with patrik Kyd of Cragie upon the 28 day of the said month.

Jean.

In Novʳ 1664 my second daughter Jean was mareed to William Kyd brother to Cragie upon the   day of the said month.

Helen.

In Junij 1665 my thrid daughter helen was mareed to david dicksone of hartree peeblesshyre upon the 28 day of the said month.

Grissell.

Upon the 20 of december 1665 my fourt daughter Grissell was mareed to Alexander Wedderburne of Kingennie.

Joʰ

Upon the 9ᵗʰ of Augᵗ 1667 my eldest sone Johne was mareed at Edʳ with Rachel Dynmuire daughter to Mʳ David dynmuir, advocat.

Upon the 27 of apryle 1673 my second sone James was mareed to elᵗ davidsone daughter to Roᵗ davidsone of balgay."

(Endorsed in the hand (I think) of Sir John Wedderburn of Ballindean " History of the children of Alexʳ, after Sʳ Alexʳ, Wedderburn, first of Blackness ; first date 1610, last date 1673 ")

9ᵃ. **1610-1673.**—Modern copy of No. 9 with one or two marginal notes of no value.

10. **1668-1693.**--Family Register in the hand of Sir John Wedderburn, first baronet of Blackness, giving the birth dates of all his children, &c., and, on the same sheet,

1694-1703.—Family Register in the hand of Sir Alexander Wedderburn, second baronet of Blackness, giving the birth dates of his children up to 1703. Another child, Alexander, was born later, 1705.

(One sheet of paper, the first register on the first two pages, the second on the bottom half of the third page, the top half of which is cut off ; the ink is much faded in parts, but its condition makes it clear that the document was written up from time to time.) These registers are as follows :—

I. FAMILY REGISTER OF SIR JOHN WEDDERBURN,
FIRST BARONET OF BLACKNESS.

1.
Matilda.

" Upon the 4 August 1668 my daughter Matilda vas born   Vitnesses to her baptisme Sʳ Alexʳ Wedderburn of Blacknes, Mʳ David Dunmuir, advocat, Alexander Wedderburn of Kinganie elder and younger, Patrick Kyd of Craige, and William Kyd his brother.

2.
Margaret.

Upon the 4 Decemb : 1670 my second daughter Margaret vas born.   Vitnesses to her baptisme Alexʳ Wedderburn of Kingenie elder and younger, Pat : Kyde of Craigie, William Kyde his brother german and John Kinloch baillie in Dundee.

3.
Alexander.

Upon the 7 Aprile 1672 my son Alexander vas born.   Vitnesses to his baptisme Alexʳ Wedderburn of Easter Powrie, Alexʳ Vatsone provest of Dundee, Alex : Wedderburn of Kinganie, Alex : Duncane late baillie ; Sʳ David Nevoy of that ilk, one of the Senators of the Colledge of Justice ; Pat : Kyde of Craigie and William Kyde of Woodhill.

4.
David.

Upon the first day of Januar. 1674 my second son David vas born.   Vitnesses to his baptisme Alexander Wedderburn of Easter Powrie, George Brown provest of Dundie, Pat : Kyd of Craigie, Alexʳ Wedderburn of Kinganie, Doctor Gleg, Will : Kyd of Woodhill, George fforrester baillie, Tho. Vatsone, dean of Gild, Henry Crawfurd, Mʳ Da. ffergusone minister at Strickmartine, David Carnegie and David fforester, and Mr David Dynmuir advocat (altho absent) prinell godfather.

5.
Peter.

Upon the twentie fyft day of Ag. 1675 my third son Peter vas born.   Vitnesses to his baptisme Sʳ David Nevoy of that ilk, one of the senators of the Colledge of Justice, Sʳ Alexander Wedderburn of Blacknes, Alexʳ Wedderburn of Easterpowrie, Pat : Kyd of Craigie, Alexʳ Wedderburn of Kinganie, Will : Kyd of Woodhill, Roᵗ Davidson of Balgay, Henry Crawfurd of Seaton, Jeames Wedderburn, and Sir Peter Wedderburn of Gosfoord, one of the Senators of the Colledge of Justice, and my brother Peter (though absent) vas sole godfather.

Upon the 31 day of March 1677 my third daughter Matilda vas born. Vitnesses to her baptisme Alex : Wedderburn of Easter Pourie, provest of Dundee, Patrick Kyd of Craigie, Alex : Wedderburn of Kinganie, Robert Davidson of Balgay, Henry Crawfurd of Seaton, Jeames Wedderburn, clerk of Dundie, Mr Jea. Brisbane advocat ...... Wedderburn merchant. John Maitland, collector of the customs in Dundie.

Upon the 2 day of Januarie 1679 my fourt son Jeames vas born. Vitnesses to his baptisme, Alex^r Wedderburn of Easterpowrie, provest of Dundie, Patrick Kyd of Craigie, Alex^r Wedderburn of Kinganie, Jeames Wedderburn, clerk of Dundie (ppall godfather) Jeames fletcher, Peter Wedderburn, Jeames Man, and Alex : Patullo, merchants in Dundie.

Upon the 26 day of March 1681 my fyft son George was born and becaus of my indispositione he was presented to be baptised by my brother the clerk, And was so named after my brother George Wedderburn merchand in Edin^r.

Upon the 10 day of October 1682 my sixt son John was born. Vitnesses to his baptisme Alexander Wedderburn of Kinganie, Thomas Mill of Moortown, my brother the clerk and Will : Carnegie vreater in Edin : my Coosin Gosfoord and my self godfathers.

Upon the 16 day of februarie 1685 my fourt daughter Jean was born And becaus of my being at Edin : she was presented to be baptised be Alex : Wedderburn of Easter pourie : she is named Jean efter my deceast sister the Lady Woodhill.

Upon the 16 day of Aprile 1689 my sevent son was born at Edin : and named Thomas after Mr Thomas Nicolsone of Coberspath and Sr Thomas Nicolsone his maj : advocat, my wife's uncle. Vitnesses to his baptisme Mr David Dunmuire advocat my father-in-law and George Wedderburne merchand in Edin: my brother.

Upon the first day of June 1693 my eldest son Alexander was maried at Edin : with Elizabeth Seaton eldest daughter to Sr Alexander Seaton of Pitmedden Knight and Baronet "

II. FAMILY REGISTER OF SIR ALEXANDER WEDDERBURN,
SECOND BARONET OF BLACKNESS.

" Upon the 24 daij of March 1694 mij son John was born att Ed^r And so named after my father.

Upon the last daij of March 1696 mij daughter was born att Ed^r and named Margaret after Dame Margaret Lauder my mother-in-Law.

Upon the ninth daij of September 1698 my second daughter was born att Blackness and named Rachell after Rachell Dunmure my deceist mother.

Upon the second of December 1700 my second son John was born att Blackness.

Upon the second of ffebruarij 1702 my third daughter was born att Edinburgh and named Elizabeth after my wiffe and her grandmother Elizabeth Johnston, Countess of Hartfield [1]

Upon the eight of Julij 1703 my fourth daughter was born at Blackness and named Matilda after Dame Matilda fletcher my grandmother."

10^a. **1668-1703** —Modern copy of No. 10 with some notes, which are, however, of no value.

11. **1675-1730.**—Family Register of Sir Alexander Wedderburn, fourth baronet of Blackness, giving the birth dates of all his children, &c.

(One sheet in good state. See facsimile opposite.) This register is as follows :—

FAMILY REGISTER OF SIR ALEXANDER WEDDERBURN,
FOURTH BARONET OF BLACKNESS.

"Accompt of my Children's ages, and also of my son's John's Children" (so endorsed).

"Alex^r Wedderburne eldest law^{ll} sone to James Wedderburne, Clerk of Dundie, Borne on the 4th day of November 1675 : was upon the 27 day of October 1697

---

[1] Elizabeth Seton's paternal grandparents were John Seton of Pitmedden and Elizabeth Johnston (daughter to Sir Samuel Johnston of Elphingston), who on the death of John Seton m. (as second wife) James, Earl of Hartfield or Hartfiell. She must have died before 1647 as in that year the Earl married thirdly, Margaret, d. to Thomas, first Earl of Haddington. The title of Hartfield merged in the dormant title of Annandale. (See Douglas' "Baronage," s. Seton of Pitmedden, and G.E.C.'s "Complete Peerage," s. Hartfield)

Accompt of my
Children Lacey
and also of my
Jung John's Children

1. Abr: McDorbians & Book line & Sons of James McDorbians
Clerk of Smiths Briag on the 1st day of November 1675
Was upon the 27 day of October 1697 Marid to Katherine
Scott Younges daughter to John Scott smith and Isabel:
Smith of Smith who was born on the 16th day of of first
1680 yeare Provost Bethnell us the ch—th of James Bar

I cunay McDorbians who was born on the 25 day of July
1690 & baptist on the —

2. Abr above was born on the 25th day of October
1699 and baptist on the 30th day of october 1699

3. Christian was born on the 14th day of November 1700 1707
and baptist on the 19th day of october very year 1700

4. John was born on the 27th day of february 1702 years
and Baptist on the 3 day of March 1702 years

5. Alexander was born on the 22 day of Aprile 1703 years
and baptist on the 26th day of mind of aprile 1763 years

6. John in al Born upon the of august of August 07 years
Baptist upon the 8th day of the said month of august 1707 years

7 Gilbert ... was Born upon ... 20 ...

Baptised upon ye 30 of ... day ...

8 Robert ... Born upon ye 13 of ... 1708 ...
Baptised upon ye 16 day of ... 1708 ...

9 Alexander was Born upon ye 22 of ... 1709 ...
Baptised upon ye 29 of ... in ye month ...

10 Thomas was Born upon ye 2 of ... Apryll 1710
... Baptised upon ye 5 ... of ye said month

11 Katherin was Born upon ye 25 ... November 1711
... Baptised upon ye 29 ... of ... Mary ...

12 Margaret was Born ye 13 of May 1713 and Baptised
ye 17 day of ... 1713 ...

13 Katherin ... my ... daughter was Born upon ye 19 ...
... 1715 & Baptised ... 22 May ...

14 Mary my ... daughter was Born upon ye 26 ... of
August 1716 & Baptised ye 30 ... 1716 ...

15 Alexander my Eight son was Born upon ... ye 9
1710 and Baptised ye 14 day of ... 1718 ...

Mr ... [illegible] ... John ... Margaret ... Mullendon
... Daughter of John Mullendon ... the
22 Octor 1724

Margaret was Born y 30th of September 1725
William was Born y 12 ... December 1726

Alexander was Born the 2 ... of November 1727 ...
John was Born ... 21 the ... February 1729
James Born the 20th August 1730

maried w⁺ Kathrine Scott, youngest lawˡˡ daughter to John Scott mer⁺ and late baillie of Dundie, who was borne on the 16ᵗʰ day of Septem⁺ 1680 years. Proercat betwixt us the children after named, viz :

   1.ₚ James Wedderburne who was borne on the 25 day of July 1698 and baptised on the   Dead.

   2. Elizabeth was borne on the 25ᵗʰ day of October 1699 and baptised on the 30ᵗʰ day of October 1699.

   3. Christian was borne on the 14ᵗʰ day of Decem⁺ 1700 years and baptised on the 19ᵗʰ day of Decem⁺ 1700 years. Dead.

   4. John was born on the 27ᵗʰ day of March 1702 years and Baptised on the 3ᵈ day of March 1702 years. Dead.

   5. Alexander was born on the 22ᵈ day of Aprile 1703 years and baptised on the 26ᵗʰ day of yᵉ sᵈ month of Aprile 1703 years. Dead.

   6. John was Born upon the 4ᵗʰ day of August 1704 years Baptised upon the 8ᵗʰ day of the said month of August 1704 years.

   7. Grissell was Born upon the 26 day of July 1706 years And Baptised upon the 30ᵗʰ day of the sᵈ month of July 1706 years.

   8. Robert was Born upon the 13 day of ffeb⁺ʸ 1708 and Baptised upon the 16 day of the said month of ffeb⁺ʸ 1708 years.

   9. Alexander was Born upon the 22ᵈ of ffeb⁺ʸ 1709 and Baptised upon the 29 day of the said month. Dead.

   10. Thomas was Born upon the 2ᵈ day of Apryle 1710 and Baptised upon the 5ᵗʰ day of the said month.

   11. Kathrin was Born upon the 25ᵗʰ day of November 1711 and Baptised upon the 29ᵗʰ day of the said month. Dead.

   12. Margaret was Born upon the 13ᵗʰ day of May 1713 and Baptised the 17ᵗʰ day of the said month. Dead.

   13. Kathrin my Sexth daughter was Born upon the 19ᵗʰ day of January 1715 and Baptised on yᵉ 22ᵈ day of yᵉ sᵈ month.

   14. Mary my seventh daughter was Born on the 26ᵗʰ day of August 1716 and Baptised the 30ᵗʰ day of the sᵈ moneth. Dead.

   15. Alexander my Eight Sone was Born upon the threteen day of Septem⁺ 1718 and Baptised the 19ᵗʰ day of the said month.

My Eldest son John was married w⁺ Jean Fullarton, eldest daughter of John Fullarton of y⁺ ilk upon the 22 Oct⁺ 1724.

Margaret was Born yᵉ 30ᵗʰ day of August 1725.
Katharine was Born yᵉ 12ᵗʰ November 1726.
Alexander was Born the 24ᵗʰ Novem⁺ 1727.
John was Born the 21ˢᵗ ffebruary 1729.
James Born the 28ᵗʰ August 1730.

12—22, *Marriage Contracts, &c., chiefly of the heads of the Blackness line*, 1608-1801.

12. **1608**—Contract of Marriage between Margaret Jak, relict of James Goldman, merchant, burgess of Dundee, William Goldman, bailie of said burgh, and Robert Goldman, his brother german, for themselves, and taking burden on them for Margaret Goldman, daughter of the said Margaret Jak, and sister german of the said William and Robert, and the said Margaret Goldman for herself with their consent, on the one part, and Mr. Alexander Wedderburn, common clerk of Dundee, and Helen Ramsay his spouse, and Mr. James Wedderburn their second son, on the other part. Dated at Dundee ..... 1608. The witnesses are Mr. David Lyndsay, minister of Dundee, and Mr. Alexander Wedderburn, eldest son of the said Mr. Alexander. Signed by the said Margaret Jak, Wm. Goldman, Alexander Wedderburn, and Mr. James Wedderburn (see facsimile opp. p. 97), and also by the witnesses. Margaret Goldman does not sign. The day and month are left blank.

By this contract the said Mr. James promises to take to wife the said Margaret Goldman, and to solemnize "the band of matrimonie with hir in face of Christis Kirk with all gudelie diligence," in contemplation of which the said Alexander Wedderburn, with consent of his sponse, becomes bound to infeft the said Mr. James his son, and Margaret Goldman in her pure virginity, and the survivor of them in conjunct fee, and the heirs lawfully to be gotten betwixt them, which failing, the said Mr. James's heirs and assignees, heritably, in that land and tenement lately "coft" by him (Mr. Alexander

W.) from Peter Imbrie, burgess of Dundee, lying on the north side of the kirkwynd of the said burgh between the lands of George Lindesay on the west and the lands sometime of Alexander Carnegy and William Drummond on the east, and also in that croft of land called Monorgonud's Croft, together with that piece of land adjacent thereto called the Grene, or Yard, on the north side of the yard of Argyle's Gate, betwixt the lands of the heirs of Patrick Andersone on the west, the lands of Dudhop on the north, and the friars' lands now occupied by David Aberdene on the east ; and also in the foreland of his great tenement called the grene land, lying on the north side of Argyle's Gate, between the lands sometime of David Ramsay, baxter, on the east, and the lands sometime of Robert Smyth on the west ; and likewise in two "Inner ludgeingis" presently occupied by James Laudie and Robert Broun, lying on the west side of the Close of the said great tenement next adjacent to the said foreland, having the malthous set in few ferme to Alexander Nicoll, on the north ; and also in a few maill of twenty merks yearly furth of the said malthous, kiln, and coble thereof, with reservation to the said Mr. Alexander and his spouse, of their liferents of the subjects, except of that principal lodging "coft" from the said Peter Imbrie, now occupied by Mr. John Duncan. Reserving also and excepting the tenement aforesaid on the north side of the kirk wynd wherein William Wedderburn, son of the said Mr. Alexander, was infeft on his father's resignation, but under reversion, and redeemable by the said Mr. James for 1000 merks, which redemption the latter becomes bound to accomplish immediately after his father's decease, but in the meantime the said Mr. James and his promised sponse shall enjoy the said tenement in manner above provided, freely, and without payment of any duty for the same to his father. And the said Margaret Jak and her sons above named become bound, conjunctly and severally, "to wair and bestow" by the advice of the said Mr. Alexander Wedderburn, before the term of Martinmas ensueing, the sum of 5000 merks, upon "sure lands or annuel rents," and to infeft the said Mr. James Wedderburn and Margaret Goldman therein, in conjunct fee and said liferent, and their heirs aforesaid, which failing, the heirs of the said Mr. James heritably, and under reversion for the said sum ; and further, they shall resign in favour of the said Mr. James and Margaret that tenement belonging to the said Margaret Jak, lying on the north side of Argyle's Gate between the lands of David Carmannow on the west, and the lands of Thomas Lundy on the east, and the said Mr. James and Margaret shall accept thereof in satisfaction of all sums of money, goods or gear left to the said Margaret by her father, or that may fall to her by decease of her mother when it shall happen ; reserving the latter's own good will to leave or dispone any of her goods to the said Mr. James and Margaret, or their bairns, during her lifetime, providing also that the goods or gear that may fall to the said Margaret Goldman, by the decease of the late Patrick G. her brother, shall in no wise be comprehended in the sums before mentioned ; and the said Margaret Jak becomes bound to keep the said William and Robert, her sons, skaithless of the whole premises, and the said Mr. Alexander Wedderburn undertakes to repair and uphold the fore land of the said tenement called the Grene land during his lifetime.

(Two pieces of paper, joined together in one long strip, in good condition.)

13. **1608.**—Contemporary copy of No. 12, in which the place of the contract is filled in as "Dundie." (One sheet of paper, written on three sides ; in fair condition.)

14. **1638.** Jan. 5.— Contract of Marriage between Mr. Alexander Wedderburn, common clerk of Dundee, on one part, and James Fletcher, provost of the said burgh, and Matild Fletcher his daughter on the other part, dated at Dundee. Witnesses, Alexander Wedderburn of Kinganie, James Hodge, etc. Signed by Mr. Alexander Wedderburn. (See facsimile opp. p 97.) Matild Fletcher signs "wᵗ my hand at ye pen led by ye notarie at my comand because I can not write."

By this contract the said Mr. Alexander and Matild become bound " to accomplish and solemnizat the holy bond of marriage with utheris in face of chrystis congregationne " ; in contemplation of which the said James Fletcher becomes bound to pay to the said Mr Alexander the sum of 5000 merks, in name of tocher ; and the said Mr. Alexander "to eik and adjoyne" 3000 merks to the said sum, making 8000 merks in all, and to lay out the same on land or annual rent "whair best commoditie may be had within the schirefdome of Forfar or Perth", by advice of Alexander Wedderburn of Kinganie, and Mr. John Wedderburn his uncle, as friends for his part, and by the advice of Sir Andrew Fletcher of Innerpeffer, knight, one of the Lords of Session, and Mr. John Fletcher, advocate, as friends for the said Matild, and therein to infeft himself and his future spouse in conjunct fee, and the heirs of the marriage heritably.

(One sheet of paper, in good condition.)

15. **1665.** Nov. 18.—Discharge by David Dicksone of Heartrie, with consent of his curators, to Sir Alexander Wedderburne of Blackness, his father in law, for 2000 merks, in part payment of 9000 merks, of "tocher good" contained in the marriage contract made between the granter and Helen Wedderburn daughter of the said Sir Alexander, of date (13 May) 166(5). This discharge is dated at Edinburgh, the witnesses being James Dicksone, merchant burgess of Edinburgh, and others. The curators subscribe, viz., Peter Wedderburne, Geo. Mackenzie, John Rollo.

(One sheet of foolscap, in good condition.)

16. **1663.** Oct. 28.—Contract of marriage between William Kid, second son of the late Mr. James Kid of Craigie, with advice of his curators, on the one part, and Jean

BLACKNESS PAPERS.
Nos. 12, 14, 16A, 16, 18, 42.

NO. 12.

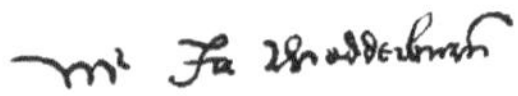

SIGNATURE OF JAMES WEDDERBURN (D. 1627)
TO HIS MARRIAGE-CONTRACT, 1608.

NO. 14.

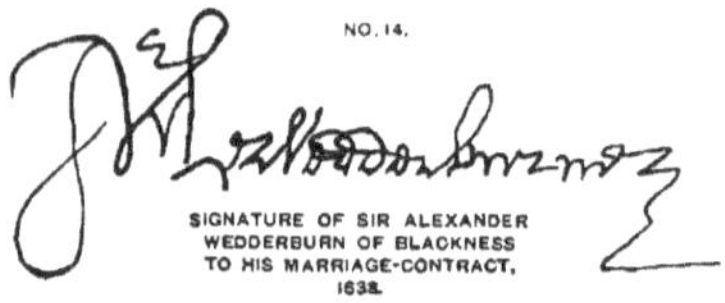

SIGNATURE OF SIR ALEXANDER
WEDDERBURN OF BLACKNESS
TO HIS MARRIAGE-CONTRACT,
1632.

NO. 16A.

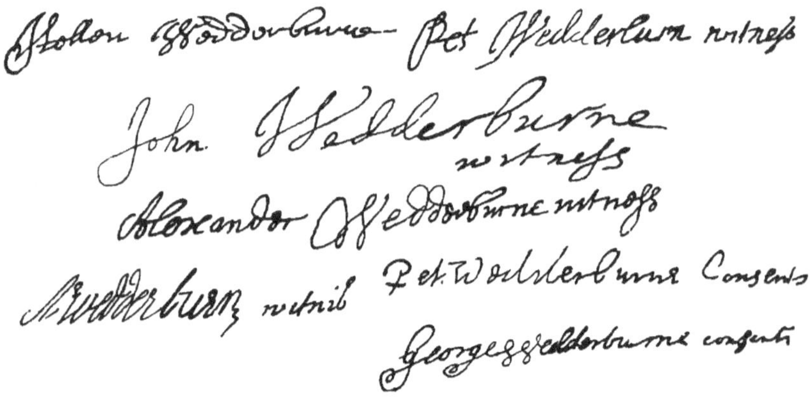

SIGNATURES TO THE MARRIAGE-CONTRACT OF
HELEN WEDDERBURN AND THOMAS MILN,
1679.

NO. 16.

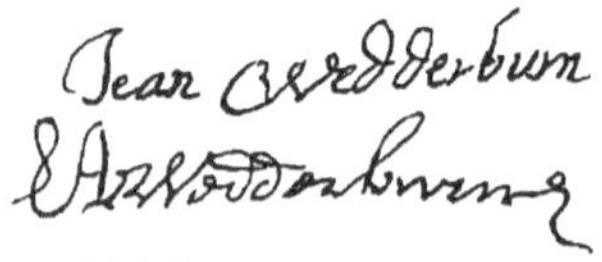

SIGNATURES OF JEAN WEDDERBURN AND
HER FATHER TO HER MARRIAGE-CONTRACT
1663.

NO. 18.

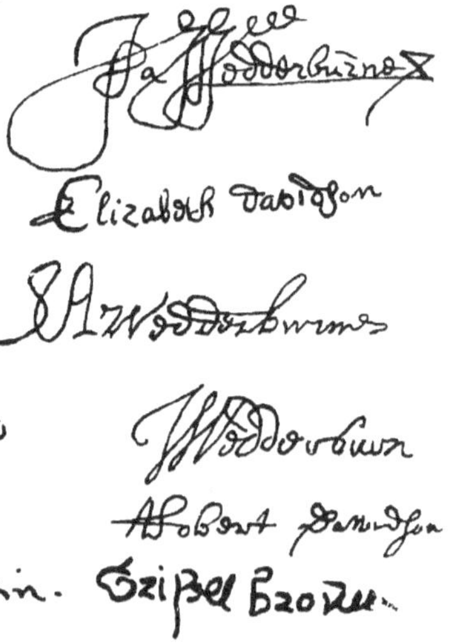

NO. 42.

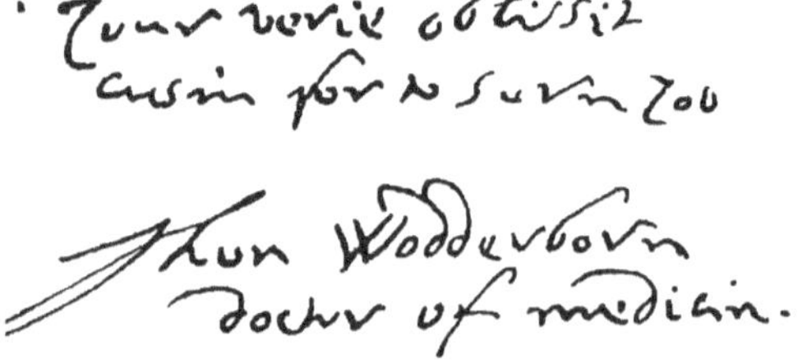

SIGNATURE OF DR. JOHN WEDDERBURN
OF BRINTHE, MORAVIA, 1647.

SIGNATURES TO THE MARRIAGE-CONTRACT OF
JAMES WEDDERBURN AND ELIZABETH DAVIDSON,
1675.

Wedderburn, second daughter of Sir Alexander Wedderburn of Blackness, knight, **Blackness** with his advice and consent, on the other part. Dated at Dundee 28 October 1663. **Papers.** Signed by W. Kyd, Jean Wedderburn, Sir A. Wedderburn of Blackness, and by various witnesses, including John Wedderburne, eldest son of the said Sir Alexander, William Wedderburne, brother german of Sir Alexander, and Alex. W. of Kingennie.

"By this contract the said William and Jean ' bind and obleidge them to accept and take other of of them utheris as lawfull spouses in the honourabill bond of matrimony,' and to solemnize the same ' by all ceremonies and solemnities requisite '; in contemplation of which the said Sir Alexander Wedderburn becomes bound to pay to the said William Kid 'in name of dote and tocher guid with his said daughter,' the sum of 8000 merks ; and the said William Kid becomes bound to provide his said future spouse, in liferent, and the children of the marriage, in an annualrent of 1000 merks, furth of ' the first and reddiest of such sums as belong to him," or such lands and heritages as he may happen ' to conqueish and acquire, be the speciall advyce and consent of Alexander Wedderburn of Kinganie and George Fletcher ' one of the bailies of Dundee, for the said Jean, and of Mr. Thomas Gleg, Doctor of Medicine, and John Fothringhame of Denune, for the said William, or any three of them, or their heirs ; and also to obtain the said Jean his promised sponse in liferent, and the heirs of the marriage in fee, heritably infeft and seized in his tenement of land, with the well close yard, and privileges thereof, lying within the burgh of Dundee, on the south side of the Seagate, and that upon his own resignation, for which he grants a procuratory ; and the curators become bound for his performance of the premises 'at his majority and perfyte age of twenty-one years compleit.'"

(One piece of paper, in good state. See facsimile of the signatures of the bride and her father opposite..)

16ª. **1679.** Feb. 20.—Contract of marriage between Thomas Milu of Muirtowne and Helen Wedderburn, Lady Heartrie, made with the consent of Sir Peter Wedderburne of Gosford, and George Wedderburne, merchant, in Edinburgh, her brother. Signed by the contracting and consenting parties, and witnessed by John, Peter and Alexander Wedderburn (three sons of Sir Peter), and A. Wedderburn.

(See facsimile opposite. The last-named witness, A. Wedderburn, is, no doubt, the bride's nephew, Alexander Wedderburn, afterwards second baronet of Blackness. The contract also names Agnes Fletcher, mother to Thomas Milu, and refers to the former contract of marriage, 13 May 1665, made between Helen W., with consent of Sir Alex. W. of Blackness, her father, and David Dickson of Heartrie, second son of the deceast John D. of H.)

17. **1685.** April 8.—Contract of marriage between Alexander Wedderburn, merchant in Dundee, son of the deceased Sir Alexander Wedderburne of Blackness, knight, on one part, and Christian Kinloch, daughter of the deceased James Kinloch, merchant burgess there, with advice and consent of Issobell Stirling, her mother. Dated at Dundee. Witnesses, Mr. James Brisbane, advocate, Thomas Mudie, late bailie of Dundee, the said Patrick Kinloch, &c.

By this contract the said Alexander and Christian " mutuallie faithfullie promitts to marie and take in marriage ilk ane other for lawfull husband and wyff respective, and solemnizat the bond of mariage according to and so soon as the order and discipline of the Church of Scotland will or doeth allow and admitt " ; in contemplation of which the said Christian Kinloch assigns to her said promised husband the sum of £1000, as her portion of 6000 merks due by the Laird of Claverhouse by his bond to the said deceased James Kinloch and the said Christian, Robert, Patrick, James, John and David Kinloch his children ; and also a further sum of 500 merks due by the same laird of Claverhonae to the said James and his children, which Patrick Kinloch, brother of said Christian assigned to her ; and further the said Issobell Stirling becomes bound to pay to the said Alexander Wedderburn, his heirs etc. the sum of 500 merks, as in full satisfaction of all the said Christian could claim through the decease of her said father ; And the said Alexander becomes bound to lay out the sum of 5000 merks on good security, for himself and his said promised spouse in conjunct fee, and the children of the marriage, besides what further estate he may acquire during the existence of the marriage. (Two pieces of paper joined in one strip, in perfect state.)

18. **1673.** Jan. 8.—Contract of marriage between James Wedderburne, common clerk of the burgh of Dundee, with consent of Sir Alexander Wedderburne of Blackness, his father, and of John Wedderburne, ficar of Blackness, his brother german, on the one part, and Elizabeth Davidsone, daughter of the late Robert Davidsone of Balgay, merchant and late bailic in Dundee, with consent of Robert Davidsone, now of Balgay, her brother german, and of Grissill Broune her mother, on the other part, for the marriage of the said James and Elizabeth. Dated at Dundee. Witnesses the said Alexander Wedderburne, Patrick Kyd, William Kyd, George Broune, William Watson, William Rait, Alexander Wedderburne of Kingany, George Davidson, brother german to the said Robert, &c. (See facsimile of six signatures opposite.)

By this contract the said James becomes bound to provide and secure himself and his said future spouse in conjunct fee and liferent, and the children of the marriage, in the principal sum of 14,000 merks, during the lifetime of the said Grissill Broune, and after her decease, in the principal sum

O

of 16,000 merks, counting the aforesaid 14000 m. "in the first end thereof," and to lay out the same on land or annualrent, by advice of Alexander Wedderburn of Easter Powrie, the said John Wedderburn, Patrick Kyd of Craigie and William Kyd of Woodhill "freindis nominat be the said James Wedderburne for his part," and of George Broune of Weathorne, the said Robert Davidsone, William Watson and William Rait, late bailies of Dundee, "freindis nominat " by the said Elizabeth for her part. For which cause the said Sir Alexander and John Wedderburn become bound to pay to the said James the sum of 8000 merks, and that "by and attoure the ludging or great tenement of land " lying on the south side of the Nethergate of Dundee, presently possessed by the said Sir Alexander, wherein he has already provided and infeft the said James his son in fee ; which 8000 merks and tenement shall be to him in full satisfaction of all he might claim through the decease of the said Sir Alexander his father or of Dame Matilda Fletcher his mother, or of either of them. And the said Robert Davidsone becomes bound to pay to the said James Wedderburn in name of "dote and tocher good," with the said Elizabeth his sister, the sum of 7500 merks ; and also to infeft the said James and Elizabeth in conjunct fee and the heirs of the marriage heritably, in "that malthous, kill, coble and pertinents " sometime belonging to Janet Howatt, and disponed by her to the said deceased Robert Davidsone of Balgay, lying in Dundee, on the north side of the Seagate ; which sum of 7500 merks, and malthouse etc. the said Elizabeth accepts in full satisfaction of all that might accrue to her by the decease of her said father or of her mother.

(Three pieces of paper joined together to form one long strip, the last piece a good deal torn.)

19. **1725.** April 22.—Contract of marriage of Sir John Wedderburn, fifth baronet of Blackness, and Jean Fullarton.

This document is signed by John Wedderburn, Jean Fullarton, Sir Alexander Wedderburne, John Fullarton, and by the following witnesses, Alex. Read of Turfbeg, William Fullarton, eldest lawful son to the said John Fullarton, James Johnston, writer in Dundie, and Patrick Johnston, his second lawfull son.

The document is endorsed "Contract of marriage betuixt John Wedderburn and Mrs. Jean ffullarton 1725," and below this is a second endorsement "Blackness &c. 27th June 1737, betuixt 4 and 5 afternoon Pat. Scott, shipmaster in Dundee, Baillie, gave sasine to Wm. Fullarton of that ilk, as acturney for Mr. Wedderburn and his lady, of the within annuities &c. Witnesses Wm. Scott, merchant in Dundee, and Wm. Winter, residenter there, P.O. N.P." The contract begins thus :—

"At ffullarton the 22 day of Aprille 1725, betuixt John Wedderburn eldest lawfull son to Sir Alexander Wedderburn of Blackness with the speciale advice and consent of his said father, and the said Sir Alexander for himself on the one part And Mistress Jean ffullerton eldest lawfull Daur to John ffullerton of that ilk now spouse to the said John Wedderburn with the speciall advice and consent of the said John ffullerton her fayr." It recites that though the spouses are already married there is hitherto no contract betwixt them securing a jointure for the wife or provision for the children, nor security given to the husband for the tocher of his wife, and that therefore now Sir Alexander charges his land and barony of Blackness etc. in favour of the said wife with an annuity of "twelve hundred merks Scots" during the lifetime of Dame Catherine Scott his spouse and after her death with an annuity of £1000. He also binds himself to infeft and sease the said spouses in his lifetime in an annuity of £1000 charged on Blackness and he settles on the heirs male of his said son John, by this or any other marriage, whom failing, on the heirs female of the said John by this or any other marriage "the eldest alwise succeeding without division and marrieing a gentleman of the name of Wedderburn or such as shall assume the name and use and bear the arms of Wedderburn of Blackness", whom failing, on his own heirs or assigns,—(a) The lands and barony of Blackness as comprehended in a charter under the Great Seal in favour of Alexander Wedderburn grandfather of the said Sir Alexander and dated 4 July 1666. (b) The lands and barony of Pitarrow in warrandice of the said lands of Blackness. (c) certain lands in the Westfield of Dundee purchased by his said deceased grandfather, and now belonging to Sir Alexander upon a charter of resignation under the Great Seal made by Sir John W. of Blackness and dated 26 July 1722. The tocher of Jean Fullarton is 8000 merks.

(Twelve pages of foolscap, originally sewn bookwise. At the foot of each page are the signatures of the spouses and their respective fathers.)

20. **1780.** Dec. 22.—Extract from the sheriff court books of Perth of the registered (2 Sept. 1794) contract of marriage (dated at Edinburgh 22 Dec. 1780) betwixt Sir John Wedderburn of Ballindean, baronet, and Miss Alicia Dundas, second lawfull daughter of the deceased James Dundas of Dundas.

It charges the lands of Ballindean and Balledgarno (now called the half lands of Ballindean) with an annuity in favour of the wife. Sir John's contract of marriage made on his first marriage is referred to, but no details of it are recited.

(Sixteen pages of foolscap.)

21. **1800.** Oct. 10.—Bond of annuity (additional to that contained in the said contract No. 20) by Sir John Wedderburn, Bart., in favour of Alicia Dundas his wife. Dated at Dundee. (One sheet of foolscap.)

22. **1801.** April 8.—Disposition and settlement by Sir John Wedderburn, Baronet, of
Ballindean, dated at Edinburgh.

It dispones to the following substitutes, David Wedderburn, merchant in Loudon, his eldest son and the heirs of his body, James W., John W., Alexander W., his second, third, and youngest sons and the heirs of their bodies respectively, Margaret W., his eldest, and Jean W. his second daughter, Maria, Susan, Louisa and Ann, his third, fourth, fifth and youngest daughters, and the heirs of their bodies respectively, all his lands in Great Britain and Jamaica and especially the lands of Ballindean, bought by him from the late Thomas Carnegy of Craigo, the lands of Balledgarno, bought by him from William and John Gray of Balledgarno, and from Charles Lord Kinnaird, and his joint interest in the estates of Blue Castle and Glenisia, Jamaica, &c., &c. upon trust to pay his debts and make certain provisions for his wife and children.

23—33, Marriage Contracts of minor importance, 1611-1766.

23. **1611.** June 1.—Contract of Marriage between Alexander Wedderburn of Pittormie, burgess of Dundee, and Mr. William Wedderburne, minister at Pittinweme, his son, on the one part, and Mr. Alexander Wedderburn common clerk of the said burgh, and Magdalene, his daughter, on the other part. Dated at Dundee. Signed by Alex. W. of Kingennie, and William W., the witnesses being Mr. David Lyndesay, minister of Dundee, Mr. John Dynmuir, notary; and Sir William Grahame of Claverhous. Endorsed by Kingennie "my daughter Magdalene's Contract of Marriage."

By this contract the said Mr William promises "to tak to his lawfull wyiff the said Magdalene" and she also "faithfullie promittis to tak the said Mr William to hir lawfull husband" and both of them "to solemnize the bond of matrimonie with utheris in face of Christ's Kirk, with all gudelie diligence": In contemplation whereof the said Alexander becomes bound to infeft the said Mr William, and Magdalen his affianced spouse in her virginity, and the survivor of them, in conjunct fee, and the heirs to be procreated between them, which failing, the heirs of the said Mr William whatsoever, in that part and pendicle of the lands of Wester Fairnie called the Bruntoun, occupied by Elizabeth Ramsay, with the teind sheaves and pertinents thereof in the sheriffdom of Fife: also to infeft the said Mr William his heirs and assignees heritably, in that part of the lands of Monquhany, occupied by James Kirkcaldie, lying at the east end of the Mains of Monquhany, extending to eight oxengate of land or thereby, bounded between the remainder of the said Mains at the west, the lands of Monquhany at the north and west, the mill burn at the east, and the meadow of Rathill and the medow of Monquhany at the south : reserving to the said Alexander and Christian Fairny his spouse their liferents respectively of the said portion of Monquhany : reserving also the Reversion granted to him by Robert Arnot of Fairny upon the redemption of the said lands of Bruntoun for 3300 merks : and also that reversion of the said portion of Monquhany granted .... for 2000 merks : and on the redemption of the said lands the said Alexander shall, by the advice of the said Mr Alexander "wair and bestow" the sums mentioned upon sure lands or annual rents, with infeftment of the parties therein : For which causes the said Mr Alexander Wedderburn becomes bound to pay to the said Mr William the sum of 3000 merks of tocher, "to be wairit and bestowit" by advice of the said Alexander and Mr Alexander upon sure lands or annualrents etc.

(Two pieces of paper joined together in one strip, in perfect condition.)

24. **1612.** Aug. 17.—Contract of marriage between Mr. Peter Bruce, principal of St. Leonard's College in the city of St. Andrew's, on the one part, and Elizabeth Wedderburn, relict of Colin Campbell of Balgirsho, with consent and advice of Mr. Alexander Wedderburn of Kingennie, common clerk of Dundee, her father, on the other part. Dated at Dundee. Signed by Peter Bruce, Kingennie, and Elizabeth Wedderburn ; the witnesses being Mr. George Haliburtoun of Keloure, Mr. David Lindsay, Mr. James Robertson, Mr. William Wedderburne, Minister of Dundee, Mr. William Fergussone, bailie thereof, James Wedderburne and Mr. James Dunmuir, burgesses.

By this contract the said Mr. Peter and Elizabeth promise in the usual manner to solemnize the bond of marriage with each other ; and the former, in consideration of the benefit he shall receive by the conjunct fee to which the said Elizabeth was provided by the said Colin her former husband and by the late George Campbell of Crunan his father, and by the money and goods presently belonging to the said Elizabeth, becomes bound "to wair and bestow" by the advice of the said Mr. Alexander Wedderburn, the sum of 7000 merks upon sure lands or annual rents, with infeftment to himself and her in conjunct fee, and the children to be gotten between them heritably, and that to be in satisfaction to her of all terce she might claim of the remanent lands or annualrents which may belong to the said Mr. Peter at the time of his decease. And in case the said Elizabeth should depart this life without children of the marriage, within the space of four years after the date hereof, the said Mr. Peter becomes bound to pay to her executors the sum of £1000 at the term following her decease ; and in case of her death without children at any time later than the said space of four years, he shall pay to her executors the sum of 2000 merks, and that in satisfaction of all that they can claim of him " saifand and exceptand the said Elizabeth her jeuallis and abuilziamentis of hir bodye," etc.

(One piece of paper, in good condition. The witness James Wedderburn is her uncle, the merchant, and not her brother, afterwards clerk of Dundee).

25. **1647.** Nov. 26 —Contract of marriage between Rootmaister Robert Lindsay on the one part, and Margaret Mylne, daughter of Alexander Mylne, one of the bailies of Dundee, with advice and consent of her said father, on the other part. Dated at Dundee, the witnesses being Frederick Lyoune of Brigtoun, Peter Young of Easter Seatoun, Sir Alexander Wedderburn of Blackness, Knight, Doctor Patrick Blair, and Thomas Mudye, dean of Guild of Dundee.

By this contract the said Robert and Margaret engage to solemnize the bond of marriage with each other ; in contemplation of which the said Robert becomes bound at Whitsunday, 1648, to lay out on land or annualrent, at the sight and advice of Lyon of Brigtoun, and Peter Young of Easter Seatoun, as friends for his part, and of Mr. John Fletcher, advocate, and Mr. Alexander Mylne, minister at Forgoun, as friends for the said Margaret, the sum of 16,000 merks, with infeftment to him and her in conjunct fee, and the children of the marriage heritably ; and the said Alexander Mylne becomes bound to pay to the said Robert the sum of 8000 merks of tocher with the said Margaret.

(One piece of paper in good condition.)

26. **1657.** Aug. 15 —Contract of marriage between Barten Bellson, Englishman, merchant, indweller in Dundee, on one part, and Helen Wedderburne, relict of William Goskine, Englishman, some time indweller in Dundee, on the other part. Dated at Dundee.

By this contract the parties agree to "solemnizeat the holie bond of matrimonie, in face of Chrystis holie congregation" before the 26th day of August next, and the said Helen Wedderburn becomes bound to infeft the said Barten with herself in conjunct fee, and the children of the marriage, in her half of a fore tenement of land, sometime belonging to Sir Alexander Wedderburne of Blackness, Knight, and disponed by him to the late Alexander Wedderburne, father of the said Helen, lying in the said burgh, on the north side of Argyle's Gate, bounded by the lands sometime pertaining to David Ramsay, baker, on the east, the lands of Robert Sympsone on the west, and the said gate on the north ; also in her half of those two dwelling houses or iuner tenements of land, sometime belonging to the said Alexander Wedderburne, lying on the west side of the close of the said tenement of land and adjacent thereto ; also in her half of that other tenement of land some time pertaining to the said Sir Alexander, on the east side of the said close ; also in the half of that other tenement lying on the north side of Argyle's Gate, between the lands of the heirs of John Colliue, merchant, on the west, lands of the heirs of Donald Dunbar on the east, lands of Alexander Wedderburne of Kiugenny on the north, and the said gate on the south ; also in the half of that tenement sometime pertaining to the late Archibald Kyd, and now to the heirs of the late James Kyd, merchant, his "oye," lying on the south side of the Seagate of Dundee, between the lands of the late James Fythie on the east, lands of Patrick Brugh on the west, the flood mark on the south, and the said gate on the north ; also in her just half of that other tenement sometime pertaining to the late James Mackay, now to the heirs of Henry Davidsone, baker, lying on the south side of the Murray Gate, between the lands of the late Andrew Robertsone, now of David Gourlay, on the east, lands of the heirs of James Andersone on the west, lands of the late William Man on the south, and the said gate on the north ; also in her half of that other tenement, sometime belonging to John and William Walkers, successively, lying on the north side of the Murray Gate, between the lands of the late John Bursey and the heirs of John Spalding on the east, the close of the tenement sometime of James Roch on the west, lands of the heirs of Alexander Elmsby on the north, and the said gate on the south ; and in her half of that tenement sometime of the heirs of Thomas Logy, now of the heirs of William Patilloch, lying on the north side of the Murray Gate, between the lands sometime of James Boyter, now of Patrick Ruthven, merchant, on the west, lands of the late Andrew Robertsone and James Thomsone on the east, and the said gate on the south ; for which causes the said Barten Bellson becomes bound to lay out on lands or annualrent within the shires of Perth or Forfar, the various sums of money due to him by the persons therein named, with infeftment therein to himself and the said Helen Wedderburn, and the children of the marriage, &c.

(Three pieces of paper, joined into one long strip, in good condition.)

27. **1701.** April 15. —Contract of marriage betwixt Peter Wedderburne and Helen Lyon.

This contract is dated "at Dundie" and made betwixt Peter Wedderburne merchant burgess of Dundie and Mrs. Helen Lyon, second lawfull daughter to the deceist Mr. Patrick Lyon of Carnoustie advocat, with advice and consent of Jean Alexander, his relict and her mother. The husband settles 9000 merks and the wife's tocher is 1000 merks. It is signed by the spouses, and the bride's mother, and by the following witnesses, George Gollan, writer in Edinburgh, Alexander Watson, his servitor, Alexander Wedderburn of Easter Powrie, Mr. William Lyon, brother german to the Laird of Carse, Mr. Patrick Nevoy, tutor of Nevoy, Captain William Cramond of Moortoun and James Tailzeor, writer in Dundee. (One sheet of paper in good condition.)

28. **1705.** Aug. 25.—Contract of marriage betwixt Peter Wedderburne and Barbara Auchinlek.

This is also dated "at Dundie" and made betwixt Peter Wedderburne, merchant in Dundie, and Barbara Auchinlek, lawfull daughter to the deceast Mr. John Auchinlek, minister of Largo. The bride assigns to her husband her portion of 3000 merks left to her by her father, of which 2000 is owing to her by James Kyd of Craigie, and 1000 by Sir Archibald Hope of Rankeillour, senatour of the coleadge of justice, and William Ayton of that ilk. The husband settles 9000 merks, and declares Blackness the value of his stock to be 17600 merks. The document is signed by the spouses and witnessed by Papers. Mr. Thomas Auchiulek, minister in Anstruther Wester, by Mr. James Auchiulek, merchant in Dundie, and John Dick, writer there.

(Two pieces of paper joined together to form one strip. The signature shows that this Peter Wedderburne is the same as the one who m. Helen Lyon. He was half brother of Alexauder Wedderburu, fourth of Kingennie.)

29. **1723.** Dec. 1.—Extract of the registration of the above contract of marriage between Peter Wedderburne and Barbara Auchinlek. Registered in the books of the Council and Session at Edinburgh. (Mack: Deeds, vol. 134, pt. ii.)

(According to this document it would seem as if both spouses were then alive aud appeared by their counsel, but this cannot be, as she died 1721-22. See the account of her husband given in vol. i.)

30. **1690.** June 20.—Contract of marriage betwixt Mr. Andrew Balfour and Mrs. Margaret Wedderburn.

Dated at Ediuburgh aud made between Mr. Andrew Balfour writer to the signet and Margaret Wedderburne, eldest lawfull daughter to John Wedderburne of Blackuess, clerk of the hills, with the advice and consent of her said father. The husband settles 25,000 merks, and the bride's tocher is 5000 merks. Signed by the spouses and the bride's father, and witnessed by Thomas Dunbar of Grange, Mr. David Dunmure, Mr. Coliu McKenzie, Mr. William Baillie, advocates, George Dallas of St. Martines, and Jobu Davidsou and John Richardson, servitors to Mr. Andrew Baifour, the husbaud. It is also endorsed " On the back of this is a discharge of the tocher be Mr. Audrew Balfour to Blackuess." The discharge is dated at Edinburgh 31 July 1691, and witnessed by the said John Richardsou and by David Wedderburu. (Three pieces of paper joined together in oue long strip.)

31. **1720.** Feb. 19.—Contract of marriage, Doctor Wedderburn with Margaret Balfour.

Dated at Dundie aud made between " Doctor John Wedderburn, phisiciau in Dundie, and Margaret Balfour, relict of the deceast Henry Eccles, merchant in Ediuhurgh." It recites that the parties married in January 1716 but without auy contract, and that Margaret Balfour having assigned to Dr. Wedderburn 10,000 merks, he for his part adds another 10,000 to it, and thus settles the sum of 20,000 merks. It refers to the contract of marriage between Margaret Balfour and ber first husband Henry Eccles, dated 13 January 1713, and to Doctor William Eccles, physician in Edinburgh, the father of the said Henry Eccles, and Dr. James Eccles, also physician in Ediuburgh, brother german aud heir retoured to the said Henry Eccles. Execution is to pass on this contract against the husband at the iustance of James Haliburton of Pitcurr aud David Campbell of Kethick. The document is sigued at the end and at the foot of each page by the sponses, aud wituessed at the end by Alexander Wedderburu, sheriff clerk of Forfar, and David Brisbane.

(Sixteen pages of foolscap, sewu bookwise, of which the first two and last four, but for the endorse- ment, are blauk.)

32. **1715.** Aug. 20.—Contract of marriage betwixt Alexauder Read and Elizabeth Wedderburn.

Dated at Dundie 20 August 1715, and made between Alexauder Read of Turfbeg aud Elizabeth Wedderburn, eldest lawfull daughter to Alexander Wedderburn, clerk of Dundie, with the advice aud consent of her said father. The husband settles on the wife au annuity of 800 merks to be increased to 900 merks after the death of his mother Margaret Thomson, charged on his lauds of Turfbeg lyiug in the parochine and sheriffdome of Forfar. The bride's tocher is 4,000 merks. Written by David Brisbane writer in Dundie, aud sigued at the foot of each page and at the end by the spouses and the bride's father. It is witnessed at the end by Thomas Scott, merchant and late bailie of Dundie, Dr. John Wedderburu, Patrick Balneaves, Thomas Read, merchaut in Dundie, Thomas Read, brother german to the said Alexander Read, James Tailzeour, writer iu Dundie, aud the said David Brisbane.

(Sixteen pages of foolscap, sewn bookwise. The four pages forming the cover and the last page are blank, but for the endorsement.)

33. **1766.** June 2.—Articles of marriage betwixt John Smyth and Miss Agatha Wedder- burn. Signed at Perth, 2 June 1766, by the said John Smyth and James S., his father, James Carnegie, and Richard Dundas, before John Drummond of Logic-almond, James Paterson of Carpow, and Patrick Duncan, junior, writer of the contract, and at Dundie, 4 June 1766, by Agatha Wedderburn and Dame Jean Fullarton, her mother, before Robert Wedderburn of Pearsie, and Charles Wedderburn, his son. James and John Smyth, James Carnegy, Richard Dundas, and Agatha Wedderburn also sign at the foot of each page.

Made between John Smith, writer iu Edinburgh, only son aud child as yet procreate of the marriage between James Smyth, younger, of Balharry, parish of Alyth, co. Perth, and Mrs. Cicilia Kinloch his wife, and Miss Agatha Wedderburn, youngest daughter of the deceast Sir John Wedder- buru, Barouet of Blackness, procreate between him and Dame Jean Fullarton his wife, now his widow, with advice and conseut of James Carnegie of Bosack, aud Richard Dundas, Esq. of Blair, com- missioners for John Wedderburn, Esq. of the island of Jamaica, her eldest brother. The husband aud his father charge the lands of Balharry, Wester Liffie, Powder-wells, and St. Ninians, all in the

said parish of Alyth, in favour of the bride, and the father also agrees to retire from his business and settle his son therein and in his house in Geddes' Close, Edinburgh. The bride assigns to her husband all her possessions, especially £400 sterling promised to her on her marriage by her brother and taken by her in satisfaction of £100 left her by Dr. John Wedderburn, her grand-uncle.
(Eight pages of foolscap, the last blank but for the endorsement.)

> 34—35, *Two Dispositions by Jean Fullarton, Lady Wedderburn, to her daughters,* 1761-69.

34. **1761.** May 15.—Testamentary disposition and assignation, Mrs. Jean Fullarton to Catharine, Susan and Agatha Wedderburn her children. Dated at Dundee.
She decribes herself as " Mrs Jean Fullarton, relict of the deceased Sir John Wedderburn of Blackness," and leaves all her property, household plenishing etc. equally betweeu her said three daughters, who are appointed her sole executrices. It is signed by her at the foot of the first page and at the end, and is witnessed by James Carnegy of Boysack, Pat: Crichton, writer in Dundee, and James Jamieson, his clerk. (Four pages of foolscap, written on the first two and endorsed on the fourth.)

35. **1769.** Jan. 4.—Extract Registrat Disposition, Lady Wedderburn to her daughters.
This is the Registration in the Court Books of Dundee (18 Dec. 1769), of a later disposition by Jean Fullarton, dated at Dundee, 4 Jan. 1769, and made iu favour of her unmarried daughters, Kathrine and Susauna, only, as her sole executors, legatees. and iutromitters, debarring thereby all her other children. The witnessss are James Smyth, younger of Balharry, WS., and James Ballingall, writer of the document.

> 36—41, *Letters from various persons to Sir Alexander Wedderburn of Blackness, Knt.,* 1639-61.

36. **1639.** July 3.—Letter from Sir J. Dalzell to ——. Dated at Carnwathc.
Richt honrable,
Aud my varre noble lord I reavit your lordships letter the last of June and acknaulage my self your lordships servand for your lordships kynd advays bot I am sorrie that your lordships sould hauf beine pout to the panes to hauf writtine souche ane letter to your lordships houmble servand oupon the report of thos that cau uot make one word guid aganst me that they hauf informit your lordship of, bot I knau thair gratest ambitioue is to speik eveil of tham that dois tham na wrong aud be al apeirance I may say desayres ua peas in the lund, for if your lordship hard the reports that hes bene spokine heer I protest to God fleshe aud bloud could not indur it and as for actiones I ned not speek of tham bot tym til tray al and quhair thay iuformit your lordship that I repyne at the presbytre apoyntng ane man to preche in the kirk of Carnewathe Your lordship sal find it fals for I soud be glad of ane guid man iu it and hoipes ve sal get him and for this I sal other cleer my self to your lorlship or els al sal be treuthe thay hauf said of me and quhair thay hauf informit your lordship that I hauf spokine many grit wordes aud hes maid grit thratning of men sence my home coming I hoip your lordship knaues that am not al togither ane foull for I hoip God has giuen me that knauleg to knau soum thing quhat I am doing bot I knau if I tiar ane sant it is thar delyt to spek eveil of me bot do thair uorst and quheu ever thar actiones and myue sal com to licht and thar cairng towardes me I hoip your lordship sal think that I haif nather done nor spokine bot thay haif deseurfit moir at my hand and quhair thay say to your lordship that I haif takiue of my aune guid rondle agaue I til assour your lordship of the coutrar I hauf takiue na thiug agane from na mau bot from theifes that steilit my geir quha had ua warrand from ua bodie that had pouer and I hoip your lordship til uot think that ane falt I am sorrie to trouble your lordship with al thar prosedinges agaust me with out caus til I hauf the happiness to sie your lordship and til that tym I intend to obey your lordships commandments and sal ever acknauleg myself to be your lordships faithefoull and bonorable servand to my pouer.
Carnewathe the third of Julie 1639.   Sir J. Dalzell.
the barer wil informe your lordship soum quhat of the bysines and of my carring."
(Endorsed on back " Sir J. Dalzell, Letter 3 Julie 1639 " in contemporary hand ; and also in more modern one " About Covenauters settling kirks, To Sʳ Alex. Wedderburn," but there is nothing in letter itself to show to whom it is addressed. The date is apparently 1639, tho' it *may* be 1659. If it is the former it can hardly be addressed to Sir Alexander, who was not yet prominent in affairs ; if the latter, it may be to him, tho' the expression " my varre noble lord " looks as if the writer was addressing one of higher rank.)

37. **1655.** Jan. 22.--Letter addressed to Sir Alexander Wedderburn of Blackness, Knt., by Dr. Thomas Gleg.
                                                              Dundy, 22 Jan. 1655.
Right Honorable
Their is nothing can be mor acceptable to me then to heare of the continuance of your health, for which we your freinds her ar Labouriug the best way we cau at such a distance to be instrumentall, in our earnest desyrs, aud the outward testimony of them in a cup of Liquor which now and then we wald gladly exchange for your Canary. I thank God I need non of Robins Advysings for the present, he himself hath taken a little dint of his last years disease, but all to no purpose " cum semina mandet areuis," you wald doe well to give him your best counsell least you want a faith-

full servant and I a reall freind, I may study my brains out befor I light on any expressione which **Blackness** shall com up the height of the sense I have of your undeserved favour and therefor shall end with **Papers.** the ordinary close in wryting myself, Sir, Your Ho⁵ humble servant,

Thomas Gleg.

Addressed on the back " For the right Honorable Sir Alexand' Wedderburn.

Thes."

Endorsed later (a) " Docter Gleg to Sir A. W. when in England with his uncle the Docter " ; and still later (b) " Letter. Doctor Gleg to S' Alexander Wedderburn when in England with his uncle. 22 Jan. 1655."

(Both these endorsements are of considerable age. One small piece of paper closely written. The Latin quotation is from Ovid [Her. v., 115]. " Semina mandare anenis "—to " scatter seed on the sands," or, as we should say, " to the winds," was a common proverb.)

---

38. **1660.** May 11.—Letter addressed to Sir Alexander Wedderburn of Blackness Knt. by the Earl of Rothes.

Honored S' Maj 11th, 1660.

Being extraordinarily stiaitued wᵗ tyme I Cannot at present say Much, But the Effects of this Meeteinge is just nothinge receaved only that steall report of Mr. Morayes, thoᵗ it was thoᵗ that bussines at this tyme would be at a great hight, as it is, and as ye knew Longe befor this time. I have receaved Ane Advice And Command ffrom London to depart this Countrie, and goe to the Kinge, which I am Accordingly to doe the morrow, havinge good hoopes to gett A ship and iff disapointed I purpose to goe post the Morow to London and ffrom that over to the kinge, iff I heare not of his Beeinge on his way ; what soever services you have to Command me wᵗ ther ye may Confidently persuade your Self that whatsoever station I shall be in I shall aprove my Self most Asidiously.

Your humble servantt

Rothes.

I hoop ye know Durie is gone over from London but I affraid ther will be a speet against him, as to that plan yee and I could wish him in.

Addressed " ffor The Much Honored S' Alex' Wedderburne of Blackness

Thes."

(One sheet of foolscap, written on the first and addressed on the fourth page.)

---

39. **1660.** June 10.—Letter addressed to Sir Alexander Wedderburn of Blackness by Viscount Dudop.

London, 10 June,

honored Sir 1660.

Conforme to your Leter I have receaved fiftie fayñe pund sterling from mestᵣ cheuk which I most intreat ye will returne upon the sight of his order to any that he will apoynt he did answer yuor Leter with Such spied and sevilletie that both you and I ar most obledged to him and I mor then obledged to your self but if ther be any thing that I can serve you in her lay your comands on him wha shall ever be redy to witnes himself

Your most affectionat frend and servant

Dudop.

as for news the King canot imagin that which the parliament dons not, I pray God ours may don the layk which is to be shortlie and in the interim the comite of atetes.

Addressed on back " for The much honored Sir Alexander Wedderburn."

(One piece of foolscap paper.)

---

40. **1661.** Sept. 27.—Letter addressed to Sir Alexander Wedderburn of Blackness by James Sharpe, afterwards Archbishop of St. Andrews.

Craill, Sept. 27, 1661.

Ryᵗᵗ worshipfull

I receaved yours of the 17 when I was at Edinburgh from whence I came yesterday and doe acknowledge this testimony also of your continued favoure and kyndness. had I known of your beeing in Fife, as I told Sᵣ Peter, I would have endeavoured to have mett you at Lesly or at any oyᵣᵉ place of conveniency to you. the king having takin the resolution which appeareth to be just and as advantageous to the peace and interest of this poor church as to his own, he will have it prosecuted as speedily as may be, and in order thereunto hath commandit three ministers M. And. Fairfull, M. Ja. Hamiltonn and myself to repair to London this next month. I must give obedience from Fife this next week ; if you have any comands for me let me have notice ; I have laitly spoke again to my Lᵈ Chancelor and president of Mr. Al Milar ; my respects to him and knowledge of his worth are such as doe ingage me to use my endeavours yᵗ he may bear a part of the Government of the Church for which I hope ther shall not be wanting men of abilities and reputation ; the king I know does expect yᵗ all who are faythfull to his service will co'operat in ther sphear for this settlement of the Church and when I come to London I shall doe you the right as to make known your affection and serviceableness thereunto of which I hope you shall not have cause to repent. they who will in sobriety review former carriages and consider ye present condition of this distracted tossed church, will see that the king could take no other way. I receaved since my returne one letter from my Lᵈ Lauderdaill

in which he promises to wreat to his friends, but since he has wreat to nobody I failed not why I
was there to be a remembrancer to his Lo^p in that particular. as to Dr. Gleg his busines I hear it
lyes in dependance befor the session ; for my part I did not press to his condescendance, I shall be
ready to doe any act of friendship to him in my power and in whatsoever station the Lord shall putt
me to carrye, as Sir, your very affectionate friend and servant,

(Signed) Ja. Sharp.

Addressed on back :

"for The Ry^t worshipfull Sir Alex^r Wedderburn of Blackness."

Endorsed in old hand "Letter from James Sharp, afterwards Archbishope of St. Andrews, to
Sr Alex^r Wedderburn bearing an account of the intended alteration or reformation of the church.
This contradicts a part of the history of this man given by the Covenanters who say he went to
London, employed by them : the contorar is here evident."

(One piece of foolscap folded in two, written on the first and addressed on the fourth page.)

41.   **166--.** March 20.—Letter to Sir Alexander Wedderburn of Blackness, Knt., from
       the Earl of Lauderdale.

Sir,

From many of my friends, and particularly from the E. of Rothes and Sr Wm Thomson I have
heard how heartie you have been on all occasions to express yor kindenes and respects to me Give me
Leave therfore to returne my heartie thankes And to beg this further favor That the Royall burroughs
may not misunderstand the ante I have made to them not to impose on me the caracter of their Agent
which is not at all usefull for them nor fitt for me. I have returned my most heartie thankes for
their confidence they repose in me, and have assured them of my reale indeavour to deserv it as his
maj^tie servant, but I beg they wold not Laye any other charge on me seing in this I can and shall
indeavour to serv them as well. My ante then to you is That you wold use yor interest that I be not
misunderstood in this. And that you wold beleev that wherein I can serv you none shal be willinger
then   Sir, Yo^r affectionat servant

Whitehall 20 of March 166   Lauderdaile.

Addressed on back :

For my much respected freind Sr Alex^r Wedderburn.

(One piece of foolscap folded in two, written on the first and addressed on the fourth page.)

42, *Letter Dr. Wedderburn at Brinthe to Alexander Wedderburn of Kingennie,* 1647.

42.   **1647.** July 29.—Letter addressed to Alexander Wedderburn of Kingennie, by
       Doctor John Wedderburn of Moravia, brother of James, Bishop of Dunblane.
       Dated at Brinthe. See facsimile of signature opp. p. 97.

(This letter is printed in extenso in vol. I. in the account given there of its writer.)

43, *Agreement Sir Peter Wedderburn and John Wedderburn, of Blackness,* 1676.

43.   **1676.** Nov. 21.—Agreement betwixt Sir Peter Wedderburn (Lord Gosford) and
       John Wedderburn of Blackness, anent settling of differences. It is as follows :—

At Edinburgh the twenty one day of November jajvi^c and seventy-six years it is agreed betwixt
Sir Peter Wedderburne of Gosford, one of the senators of the Colledge of Justice, and John Wedderburne of Blackness ffor takeing away all differences or grounds of debate or pley that might arise
betwixt them or their representatives upon any subscryved agreement or wrytting Betwixt Sir
Alexander Wedderburne of Blackness and the said Sir Peter relateing to the estate of Sir John
Wedderburne their uncle when he was then living in England that the same shall be voyd and null
and cancelled As Lykwise being both resolved thankfully to acquiesce in the goodwill and favor
showeu to us by the said Sir John farre above our deserving Therefore we declare that we nor our
heirs shall never question the same any manner of way And to the effect that what he hath been
pleased to bestow upon the said John may be secured to him, the said Sir Peter, as having right by
assignation to a bond granted by the said Sir Alexander in anno jajvi^c and fiftie two to the said Sir
John for the principall soume of twenty five thousand five hundred and threttie three merks or
thereabout with the yearly @-rents thereof since that tyme which soume the s^d Sir John hath bestowed
upon Blackness And hath made the fors^d assignation that he and his successors may be relieved in the
termes fors^d and secured from all payment the said Sir Peter Wedderburne to make the same
effectuall hath instantly at the said Sir John's desyre delyvered up the s^d band And farder forasmuch
as the said Sir Alexander by his band of borrowed money was debitor to the said Sir Peter in the
soume of sixe thousand nyne hundred and fourtie eight merks bearing @-rent from mertimes jajvi^c
nud sixtie two by the said presents the said Sir Peter to testifie his goodwill and affection discharges
the said John as representing his father from all payment thereof And hath also cancelled the same
for his securities Lykas the s^d Sir Peter Wedderburne obliges him and his forsds to free and relieve
the said John as representing his father of all bands subscryved by him conjunctly with the said Sir
Peter at Sir John's direction to the daughters of Leuchland or Parkgate the a^d Sir John's nieces
And the said John Wedderburne for the causes forsds bindes and obliges him and his forsds never
to question or quarrell any deed done or to be done by the said Sir John Wedderburne in favor of ye
said Sir Peter Wedderburne or his representatives upon any ground or title whatsoever And both

parties to secure this present settlement and agreement bindes and oblidges them their heirs and Blackness successors never to resile therefrom bott to warrant the same ...... In witness whereof both parties Papers. hath subscryved these presents written by William Whyte servitor to the said Sir Peter Wedderburne place day moneth and year of God above written Before these witnesses Alex* Chaplane wrytter to the signett and the said William Whyte.

R. Chaplane witnes   Pet. Wedderburne.
W. Whyte witnes.   J. Wedderburn.

(One sheet of foolscap, written on the first, endorsed on the fourth page.)

44—59, *Letters relating to Sir John Wedderburn*, 1745—47.

44-59. 1746-47.—Letters relating to the trial and execution of Sir John Wedderburn. All these are printed *in extenso* in the account of Sir John's share in the '45 given in the first volume of this work.

44.—Letter from Sir John Wedderburn, 5th Baronet of Blackness, after he was taken prisoner at Culloden, addressed to Mr Thomas Kyd, merchant in Leith. Dated Inverness, 27 April 1746.

45.—Letter from John Wedderburn (son of Sir John) written under the assumed name of John Thomson, after his escape to Edinburgh. Dated Edinburgh 8 March 1746. Endorsed by Sir John Wedderburn of Ballindean "John Thomson (apparently my father's assumed name) to his mother."

46.—Letter, Sir John Wedderburn to his wife. Dated London, Southwark New Jaille, 24 June 1746.

47.—Letter, Same to Mr Thomas Kyd in Leith. Dated at the same place, 5 July 1746.

48.—Letter, Same to his wife. Dated at same place, 15 July 1746.

49.—Letter, Same to Lady .... Dated at the same place, 30 Aug. 1746.

50.—Letter, Same to his wife. Dated 4 Nov. 1746.

51.—Letter, Same to his wife the night before his execution. Dated Southwark Gaoll, 27 Nov. 1746

52.—Letter, Same to Doctor John Wedderburn of Idvies, physician in Dundee. 27 Nov. 1746.

53.—Copy of a Letter, same to Mr Paterson of Carpow. 27 Nov. 1746.

54.—Copy of a Letter, same to his son John. 27 Nov. 1746.

55.—Copy of a Letter, same to H.R.H. Prince Charles Stuart. 27 Nov. 1746.

56.—Copy of a Letter from Miss Grizel Paterson (daughter of Mr Paterson of Carpow) to Margaret, daughter of Sir John Wedderburn. Dated Dundee Dec. 6, 1746.

57.—Copy of a Letter, James Wedderburn, second son of Sir John, to his sister Margaret, dated Feb. 2, 1747.

58.—Copy of a Letter from John Wedderburn, eldest son of Sir John, to his sister Margaret, dated Westmorland, Jamaica, 24 May 1747.

59.—Copy of another Letter, same to same. Dated from same place, 17 Nov. 1747.

60—61, *Letters, &c., relating to Lady Margaret Ogilvy*, 1774—75.

60. 1774. Nov. 26.—Letter endorsed "David Ogilvy's last letter to his sister." It is dated London, and signed David Ogilvy, and was written to Lady Margaret Wedderburn, first wife of Sir John Wedderburn of Ballindean.

61. 1775. March 23.—Letters addressed to Sir John Wedderburn of Ballindean, on the death of his first wife, Lady Margaret Ogilvy.

1.—Letter, David Fyffe to Sir John Wedderburn of Ballindean on the death of his first wife Lady Margaret Ogilvy. Dated London March 23, 1775.

2.—Letter, Lord Airly (Lady Margaret's father) to the same on the same subject. 26 March 1775.

3.—Letter, Walter Ogilvy to the same on the same subject. Dated Balnaboth 26 March 1775.

4.—Letter from Walter Johnstone to the same on the same subject. Dated Dumfries 31st March 1775.

5.—Letter, Sir James Johnstone of Westerhall to the same on the same subject, dated Belmount, 4 April 1775, with an undated draft of Sir John Wedderburn's reply (Sir James was Lady Margaret's mother's brother).

6.—Letter, Lord Airly to the same on the same and another subject. 10 April 1775.

7.—Letter, Alexander Wedderburn of St. Germains to the same on the same subject. Dated St. Germains 20 April 1775. The writer speaks of "Susan, whose good offices you so naturally meditate for your children."

8.—Letter, Lord Elibank to the same on the same subject. Dated 3 Aug. 1775.

9.—Design for the monument erected by Sir John to Lady Margaret in the Howff of Dundee. (This does not show the bas-relief.)

P

62—76, Papers relating to Sir John Wedderburn of Ballindean, 1791-1837.

62. **1791.** Feb. 1.—Boud by David Webster (formerly Wedderburn, third son of Robert Wedderburn of Pearsie) and John Wedderburn (son of Thomas Wedderburn of Cantra) of Leadenhall Street, London, merchants and co-partners to (their first cousin) Sir John Wedderburn of Ballindean, James Wedderburn of Inveresk (his brother), and William Read of Dundee, in £2,000. Signed by David Webster and John Wedderburn.

63. **1795.** Sept. 1.—Letter from Sir John Wedderburn of Ballindean to Mrs. Dundas of Dundas. Dated at Queensferry.

64. **1803.** Aug. 17.—Letter from Alexander Wedderburn, Earl of Rosslyn, to Sir David Wedderburn, Bart., of Ballindean, as follows:—

St James Square, 17th Augt 1803.

Dear Sir,

Tho' I have no doubt that Mrs Wedderburn will give you a better account than I shall of your Business, yet I cannot deny myself the Pleasure of writing to you, as I find I shall not be too late for the Post. I met Mr Addington this morning at the King's Levee who informed me that His Majesty had received the application very graciously and that It should have appeared in the last Gazette. He would have the goodness to add to It the remr to the Heirs male of Sir Alexander Wedderburn to which he assented very frankly and desired me to give Him a note of it in writing which I did upon the spot. Sir Wm Pulteney was a Party to the conversation and we neither of us have any doubt that the First or second Gazette will notify the King's Pleasure. I shall give a note of the limitations of the title to Vernon who will take care that they are properly inserted in the Gazette and that the Patent is duly forwarded. This is a business in which he is very conversant and remembering your kindness to his Brother I am sure He will execute it for you, with great zeal. I am sorry to be obliged to leave Town again before your return is expected But Mrs Wedderburn flatters me with the Hope that you may bring her to Baylias before our fine Weather is gone, which I can venture to say will be an equal satisfaction to Ly Rosslyn and my nieces as to myself. I beg you would make my best Compliments to Genl Hope and present my Respects to your sister.

I am, Dear Sir, Yr faithfull and obedient servant,

Rosslyn.

65. **1803.** Oct. 8.—Letter by James Wedderburn Colvile of Inveresk, to Sir David Wedderburn as follows:—

Inveresk, 8th Oct. 1803.

Dear Sir,

Mr. Cork writes me he has sent a certified copy of the Patent from the office some days ago. The original Patent must be amougst your own papers. Our grandfather was undoubted heir male to the Patentee, succeeded to the estate and got all the papers of the Blackness family now in your possession. A certain portion of envy is natural to God's human creatures which passion they often indulge. The Fullartons and Pitfirrau family have always whispered our grandfather had improperly assumed the title knowing he was not descended from the Patentee and not allowing the force of the destination in the Patent. Our grandfather was remarkably correct in all his actions and in business. No doubt this observation would be pressed upon Lord Rosslyn. The Pitfirran family have been very busy to lessen our respect and Interest there, being jenlous of our getting favour and of a partiality to us which his father and mother always shewed to us since 1745. The historys in Douglas Baronage are made out correctly by Balberry from your father's papers and Mrs. Grizel's the heiress of Wedderburn. The Pitfirrans wished to discredit it. When Lord Rosalyn had his history drawn I saw to it myself with the Clerk of the Heralds' Office from all the Gosford papers, yours and Scrymgeours. This history confirmed the former in Douglas' Baronage, and the Gosford was proved to be only the second and younger branch of the Blackness family to Lord Rosslyn's surprise. Vanity is satisfied with light food ; those historys are only read by old women in the country ; they will not go to market. Lord Rosslyn despises all titles below peerage. He is the youngest branch of all the clan. But younger Brothers are always most pushing, goaded by family pride and necessity. The eldest son generally sits still and improves neither in knowledge nor fortune. Our chief was a blockhead and remained so 4 generations till extinct. His two brothers Blackness and Gosford were clever and active. May you become active as a younger Brother.

I am, Dr David, Yrs ever

J. W. Colvile.

Addressed to

Sir David Wedderburn, No. 35 Leadenhall Street, and Hanover Square, London.

(With regard to this letter, it may be observed that the writer is wrong in stating that the history of the family in Douglas' Baronage is correct. Its early part is, on the contrary, full of errors. His strictures on the Kingennie line are also undeserved, and based on a confusion of facts. Alexander Wedderburn, second of Kingennie, was not brother, but uncle, to Blackness and Gosford. Nor was he a blockhead, but a competent clerk of Dundee, and keeper of the Forfar Register. His son was beyond doubt a man of energy and public spirit. He added largely to his estate, and was active in the affairs of Dundee, of which he was twice provost, and which he repeatedly represented in the Scottish Parliament. The three next owners of Kingennie seem, however, to have been less prominent in affairs.)

66. **1808.** March 8.—Letter by Sir John Wedderburn of Ballindean to his daughter Louisa, lately married to General Hope (afterwards Lord Hopetoun). Dated at Ballindean.

67. **1807.** Sept. 12.—Letter by Alicia Dundas, Lady Wedderburn, to her stepson Sir David Wedderburn. Dated at Ballindean. It relates to her son Alexander Wedderburn's choice of the army as a profession.

68. **1807.** Sept. 14.—Letter by same to her son, Alexander Wedderburn, on his said choice. Dated at Ballindean.

69. **1812.** July 22.—Copy of the will of James Wedderburn (half brother of Sir David). His executors are his mother and Sir David, and he leaves legacies to his sisters Maria and Susan, and his brothers John (at Bombay) and Alexander. Signed at Weymouth, with a codicil dated 26 June, 1814.

70. **1814.** June 29.—Copy of a letter, dated London, written by the said James Wedderburn, on his leaving England for the continent. Addressed to Messrs. Wedderburn and Co., 35, Leadenhall Street.

71. **1815.** May 30.—Copy memorandum by the said James Wedderburn confirming his said will and and adding a codicil thereto, dated at Toulouse in France.

72. **1818.** Jan. 4.—Letter by Alicia Dundas, Lady Wedderburn, dated George's Square, Edinburgh, to her two daughters, Mary and Susan, in case of her death.

73. **1824.** March 30.—Similar letter, same to same, dated at same place.

74. **1820.** May 30.—Copy of Letter by Mr. Seton to Sir D. Wedderburn containing an account of the sums left secured on the estate of Ballindean at its sale in 1820. Dated London. The sums are as follows :—

	£
Mrs. Oliphant ...	4,000
James Wedderburn's estate	2,000
Miss Maria Wedderburn	1,000
Miss Susan Wedderburn	1,000
Lady Wedderburn (for jointure)	8,000
Lady Wedderburn (junior)	4,000
For small annuities	1,000
John Wedderburn	1,000
Alexander Wedderburn	1,000
Estate of P. Dundas	3,000
	£27,000

75. **1831.** Sept. 2.—Will of Mrs. Barbara Ogilvie, formerly Dundas, widow of the deceased George Ogilvie of Langley Park and sister to Alicia Dundas, Lady Wedderburn. Her executrix is her sister Elizabeth Dundas. She died soon after, before 12 Jan., 1832.

76. **1837.** May 29.—Will of the said Elizabeth Dundas. Dated at Edinburgh, with a codicil dated 1 Jan., 1838. She died before May in that year.

77, (1-10), *Matriculations of arms, Patent of Blackness Baronetcy, &c.,* 1673-91.

77. **1673-1791.** Note of parchments in the possession of Sir William Wedderburn (1894) and kept by him separate from the bound volume.

1. 1673. Matriculation of the Arms of Sir Alexander Wedderburn, Bart., of Blackness.
To All and Sundrie whom it effeers *I Sir Charles Araskine* of Cambo Knight baronet *Lyon King of Armes Considering* that be the Twentie one act of the third Session of the second parliament of our dread Soveraigne Lord *Charles the Second* Be the Grace of God *King* of Scotland, England, France, and Ireland, defender of the Faith, I am Impowered to visit the whole armes of Noblemen Prelats Barons and Gentlemen within this Kingdome And to distinguish them with congruent differences And to matriculate the same in my books and registers, And to give armes to vertuous and weal

deserving persones Aud Extracts of all armes expressing the Blazoning of the armes under my hand and seall of office Which register is therby Ordained to be respected as the true and unrepealable rule of all armes Expressing the Blazonry of the armes under my hand and seall of office Which Register is therby ordained to be respected as the true and unrepealable rule of all arms and bearings in Scotland to remaine with the Lyons Office as a publick register of the kingdome *Therefore* conforme to the teuor of the said Act of Parliament I testifie and make knowen that the Coat armour appertaining and Belonging to the Right Worshipfull *Sir Alexander Wedderburne of Blackness* Knight And approven of and Confirmed be me to him Is matriculat in my said publick register upon the day and dait of thir preseuts And is thus blazoned *Viz.* The Right Worshipfull *Sir Alexander Wedderburn of Blackness* for his atchievement and ensigne armoriall *Bears* Argent on a Cheverone, Betuixt three roses Gules Barbed Vert, A crescent of the first. Above the Sheild and helmet befitting his degree marked Gules doubled Argent Next is placed on ane Torse for his Crest Ane Eagles head Erased proper And for his motto in aue escroll above the Crest *Aquila non Captat Muscas* Which Coat above blazoned I declare to be the right Worshipfull *Sir Alexander Wedderburn of Blackness* his true and unrepealable Coat and bearing for ever. In testimonie wherof I have subscryved this Extract with my hand aud have Caused append my seale of office Thereto. Given at Edinburgh The Twentie fyft day of June And of our said Soveraigne Lords raigne The Twentie fylt year. 1673.

Ch. Araskiue, Lyon.
(Parchment, the Lyon seal much broken, attached.)

2. 1673. The above armour and crest blazoned in colour, but the crescent not shown on the chevron ; perhaps it has woru off. Signed
Ch. Araskine, Lyon.
(Parchment. The Lyon Seal [1673] attached.)

3. 1704. Patent of Baronetcy to heirs male general, 1704. This is as follows :—"Anna Dei gratia Magnae Britannicae Franciae et Hiberniae Regina fideique Defensor Omnibus probis hominibus ad quos praesentes Literae nostrae pervenerint Salutem. Noveritis nos dedisse concessisse et contulisse sicuti nos tenore praeseutium ex potestate nostra regia et prerogativa regali pro nobis nostrisque successoribus Damus concedimus et couferrimus in fidelem et dilectum Joannem Wedderburne de Blackness ob intaminatam ejus fidelitatem et integritatem et haeredes ejus masculos iu perpetuum, titulum honorem ordinem gradum et dignitatem militis Baronetti Perque presentes facimus creamus coustituimus praedictum Joannem Wedderburne ejusque haeredes masculos antedictos in perpetuum milites Baronettos Atque eusque eorumque uxores et liberos rexive eodem titulo cum loco et praecedentia tam publice quam privatim post datam praesentium frui et gaudere poterint cumque generalitate praesentium omnibusque aliis formalitatibus et solemnitatibus quibuscumque similibus occasiouibus perprius usitatis dispensamus Leoni porro Armorum Regi fratribusque ejus faccialibus talia insignia armorea seu praesentibus insignijs additamenta quae huic occasioni congrua et idonea videbuutur praefato Joanni Wedderburne dare et prescribere imperamus Iu cujus rei testimonium praeseutibus magnum sigillum nostrum appendi mandavimus Apud aulam uostram de Wiudsor Castle nono die mensis Augusti Anno Domini millesimo septingentesimo quarto et auno regui nostri tertio. Per signaturam manu S.D.N. Reginae suprascriptam.

It is endorsed
(1.) Diploma Joannis Wedderburne de Blackuess, de titulis et diguitate militia baronetti. 1704. Regrat 1704.
(2.) Written to the Great Seal and regrat the 4th day of October, 1704. Charles Kerr.
(3.) Sealed at Ediuburgh the fourth day of October one thousand seveu hundred and four years. In Absence of Sir Alex* Stewart of fforglen. Jo. Stewart, Dep*.
The Seal which is partly broken shows a shield with a St. Andrew's cross in chief, and iu base the figure of a man holding a thistle in one hand and a small shield in the other.

4. 1705. Extract of the matriculation of arms of the Right Worshipfull Sir John Wedderburn of Blackness, Bart., as follows :—" Argent a cheveron betuixt thrie Roses gules and iu chief two branches of Laurel disposed in Saltyre proper with the badge of Nova Scotia as Barouet, above the shield ane helmet befitting his degree mautled gules, doubled argent : next is placed on ane torse for his Crest ane Eagles head erased proper and for his motto in ane Escroll above the Crest 'Speruit pericula Virtus.'" Dated 18 April 1705. Signed Alex* Araskine, Lyen.
(Parchment. The Lyon seal is goue. The formal parts of the document are like those of the above 1673 extract.)

5. Burgess admission of Sir Alexander Wedderburn of Blackness to the freedom of the city of Perth. Dated 23 May 1709.
(Parchment, Latin, slightly illumiuated. Seal attached, unbroken, but the impression worn.)

6. Diploma of Sir John Wedderburu of Idvies, baronet, as a burgess of Montrose. Dated 3 Oct. 1769. (Parchment, Latin, seal attached, unbroken but worn.)

7. Diploma of Sir John Wedderburn of Ballindean, baronet, as a burgess of Aberdeen. Dated 20 Feb. 1770. (Parchment, Latin, perfect seal attached.)

8. Burgess ticket of Sir John Wedderburn of Ballindean, baronet, as burgess of Glasgow. Dated 14 Jan. 1774.

9. Burgess Act in favour of Sir John Wedderburn of Ballindean, baronet, as burgess of Banff. Dated 30 June 1775. (Parchment, English, seal attached unbroken.)

10. Admission of David Wedderburn, Esquire, as burgess of St. Andrews. Dated 19 April 1791. (Parchment, Latin, wafer seal attached.)

78—81, *Inscription in Canterbury Cathedral.*

78. **1764.** Feb. 20.—Memorandum of the inscription on the tomb in Canterbury Cathedral of James Wedderburn, Bishop of Dunblane.

79—81, *MS. Genealogies of the Family,* 1798.

79. **1798.** Draft of the latter part of the account of Wedderburn of Blackness, printed in Douglas' Baronage.

80. **1798.** Draft of the account of the Wedderburns of Ballindean, printed in the Supplement to Douglas' Baronage, with some notes in the hand of Sir John Wedderburn of Ballindean. This account is full of errors.

81. **1798.** Genealogical account of the descent of the Rt. Honble. Alexander Wedderburn, Lord Loughborough.

The early history of the family as given in this account is of no value, being very full of errors, which may be best summarized by a tabular statement of its imaginary pedigree.

James Wedderburn, co. Forfar, descended in male
line of the Barons of Wedderburn, co. Berwick.
|

David, named in the Great Seal Register.   James.=Janet Forrester, d. David F. of Nevay.

John, of Tofts, Tullochhill, co. Forfar, only son.   Named
in Great Seal Register 20 June 1527, 31 Aug. 1533.

David, of Tofts, Craigie and Huntly Mains.=Helen Lawson.   John, Vicar of Dundee, named in
Great Seal Reg. 8 Oct. 1552.   Pitscottie's History of Scotland.

Alexander, First of Kingennie.   James, Bishop of Dunblane.

The later account from the time of Sir John Gosford and his nephew Sir Peter, is, however, of value, as the compiler had access to the Pitfirrane repositories, from which he quotes various documents. By permission of Sir Arthur Halkett of Pitfirrane, these have all been embodied or referred to in vol. I of this work. They are as follows :—

1648. Jan. 10. Privy Seal Warrant of Pension of 2000 merks to Sir John Wedderburn of Gosford.
1649. June 9. Letter from Sir Peter Wedderburn at Edinburgh to Sir John, in London.
1660. Aug. 28. Great Seal appointment of Sir Peter, as clerk to the Privy Council in Scotland and Keeper of the Signet for life.
1661. May 11. Letter from the Marquis of Argyle to Sir John Wedderburn.
   „   June 28. Privy Seal writ confirming the pension (of 1648), to Sir John Wedderburn.
[?] July 17. Letter from the Earl of Southesk to Sir John Wedderburn.
1661. Aug. 1. Disposition to Sir Peter by Walter, Lord Torphichen, of the lands of Lochill, East Lothian.
1662. Feb. 19. Letter from the Duke of Lauderdale to Sir Peter. Dated from Whitehall.
   „   „   22. Letter from the Duke of Lauderdale to Sir Peter. Dated from Whitehall.
   „   Dec. 2. Disposition to Sir Peter by Sir Thomas Hamilton, of the lands of Standelane, East Lothian.
   „   „   4. Letter from the Earl of Rothes to Sir Peter.
1663. June 4. Great Seal Charter in favour of Sir Peter, creating Lochill into a barony.
   „   July 29. Disposition to Sir Peter by Patrick, Lord Elibank (then a minor), of the West Mains of Ballincrieff, East Lothian.
   „   Sept. 7. Great Seal Charter of Standelane, in favour of Sir Peter.
   „   Nov. 3. Instrument of Sasine following on the said charter.
1667. July 30. Disposition to Sir Peter by John Ellies of Ellies town of the lands of Myrtoun.
   „   Aug. 2. Great Seal Charter thereof.
   „   „   2. Instrument of Sasine following thereon.
   „   „   2. Great Seal Charter to Sir Peter of the lands of Redspittal, &c.
1670. July 11. Great Seal Charter in favour of Sir Peter of the Barony of Thorntoun.
1671. Jan. 13. Great Seal Charter in favour of Sir Peter of the Barony of Innerwick.
   „   Oct. 31. Bond of annuity from Sir Peter to Sir John Wedderburn.
   „   Nov. 24. Instrument of Sasine of Respittal in favour of Sir Peter.
1672. June 3. Ratification of Ballincrieff by Patrick, Lord Elibank, on attaining his majority.
1673. Sept. 9. Letter from the Marquis of Montrose to Sir Peter.
[Undated]. Letter from James, third Earl of Salisbury, to the same.
1675. April 5. Letter from John, first Marquis of Tweedale to the same.
   „   May 28. Letter from the Duke of Roxburghe to the same.
1678. Sept. 7. Discharge of the Minister and Elders of Aberlady to Sir Peter Wedderburn.

1679. Feb. 26. Letter from the authorities of St. Leonard's College, S. Andrews, to the same.
    [Undated]. Letter from Sir George Mackenzie of Rosehaugh to the same.
1680. April 8. Return of John Wedderburn of Gosford as heir to his father Sir Peter.
    „ May 20. Instrument of Sasine in his favour.
    [Undated]. Agreement by him to furnish the King of Denmark with a regiment.
1686. Mar. 26. Commission of Peter Wedderburn as 2d Lieutenant in Captain Ogilvie's company in
        the Earl of Dunbarton's regiment.
1688. Feb. 14. Will of John Wedderburn of Gosford.
    „ May 26. Copy of a funeral sermon by the minister of Aberlady upon his death.
    „   „ 26. Copy of Inscription on Monument to John Wedderburn of Gosford.
    „ Sept. 20. Commission of Peter Wedderburn as Captain of Grenadiers.
    „ Oct. 11. Return of Peter Wedderburn as heir to his brother John Wedderburn of Gosford.
1689. Jan. 3. Disposition of Gosford by Sir Alexander Auchmnctie to Sir Peter Wedderburn.
    „ „ 28. Resignation thereof by Sir Peter to Richard, Lord Protector.
    „ March 2. Great Seal Charter thereof by Richard, Lord Protector, to Sir Peter.
    „ „ 14. Instrument of Sasine following on the said charter.
1697. Dec. 30. Patent of Baronetcy to Peter Wedderburn of Gosford and heirs of his Body.
1706. Mar. 14. Disposition by him to the parish of Aberlady.
    „ April 9. Entail by him of his estate of Gosford.

82—92. *Appendix*, 1800—1881.

82. **1800**. June 10.—Nomination by Sir John Wedderburn, Baronet, of tutors and curators to his children. This document begins thus :—

"I, Sir John Wedderburn of Balindean, Baronet, being at present in perfect health of Body and sound Judgment, yet considering the uncertainty of Life, and being persuaded that I can make a better choice of Tutors and Curators for my Children than they could do for themselves Therefore and in virtue of the act of Parliament Sixteen hundred and Ninety six I hereby Nominate and Appoint Dame Alicia Dundas, my present Wife, David Wedderburn, Esquire, my eldest son, John Wedderburn, Esquire, of London, Andrew Wedderburn, Esquire, my Nephew (son of James Wedderburn, Esquire, my Brother Germau), and Alexander Wedderburn, Esquire, of Wedderburn, To be Tutors and Curators to James, Maria, Susau, Louisa, Dorothea, Ann, John, and Alexander Wedderburn, Children procreated of the marriage between me and the said Alicia Dundas, my present Wife, and to any other Child or Children to be procreated of my present marriage, And that during the whole years and space of the respective Pupillarities and Minorities of my said Children."

It is written by David Livingstone, Clerk to William Chalmers, Town Clerk of Dundee, and is signed by Sir John at Dundee, 10 June 1800, before the said William Chalmers and David Livingstone as witnesses.

There are two additions to the nomination both dated at Balindean—(a) 9 Feb. 1801, when Sir John appoints his brother James Wedderburn a Guardian to his Children, stating that when he made out the above appointment he put in his son Andrew in his place, "as he is near my own Age, I thought his Life not much better than my own, but I have found myself failing fast this winter :" (b) 23 Sept. 1802, appointing Sir John's second son James Wedderburn a Guardian to his younger Children.

83. **1803**. June 23.—Note of the opening of the repositories of Sir John Wedderburn, Bart. Signed by Sir David Wedderburn, Robert Dundas, Charles Wedderburn of Pearsie, and Alexander Scrymgeour-Wedderburn of Wedderburn. This is as follows :—

Balindean, 25th June 1803.   Present—David Wedderburn, Esqr, Thos. Dundas, Esqr, of Blair, Charles Wedderburn, Esqr, of Pearsie, and Alexr Wedderburn of Wedderburn.

On opening the repositories of the late Sir John Wedderburn, which had been sealed up at his death, there were found—

1. Disposition and settlement by Sir John Wedderburn, Bart. Dated 20th May 1800.
2. Nomination of Tutors and Curators Sir John Wedderburn to his children, dated 10th June
    1800, with two Codicils dated 9th Jany 1800 and 23rd Sept. 1802.
3. Disposition and settlement by Sir John Wedderburn dated 8th April 1801. This was pro-
    duced by the above David Wedderburn, to whom it had been entrusted by the late Sir
    John soon after it was executed.
4. Bond of Provision Sir J. Wedderburn to Mary and Jean Wedderburn, dated 13th August
    1796.
5. Bond of Provision Sir John Wedderburn to his children within named, dated 13th August
    1796.
6. Bond of Provision Sir John Wedderburn to his Children within named, dated 5th July 1798.
7. Bond of Annuity, Sir J. Wedderburn to Mrs. Alicia Dundas his spouse, dated 10th Oct. 1800.
8. Additional Bond of Provision to James Wed- ⎫
    derburu   ⎪
9. Do. Bond of Provision to John Wedderburn ⎬ All these Bonds are dated 19th Dec. 1801.
10. Do. Bond of Provision to Alexr Wedderburn ⎭
11. Extract Bond of Provision by the Earl of Airly to his Grandchildren, dated 26th June 1761.
12. Bond to Jean Wedderburn £1,500, dated 15th May 1797.

13. Extract Bond of Provision, David Ogilvy Esqr of Airly to David &c. Wedderburn, his Grandchildren, dated 4th May 1784.
14. Extract Bond of Provision, David Ogilvy of Airly to David &c. Wedderburn, his Grandchildren, dated 19th April 1785.
15. Extract Reg^d Contract of Marriage betwixt Sir J. Wedderburn and Miss Alicia Dundas, dated 22nd Decr 1780.
16. Certificate of £1,000 Stock in the hands of the above David Wedderburn Esqr.

In witness whereof we have subscribed the above Inventory,

David Wedderburn.
Rob. Dundas.
Charles Wedderburn.
A. S. Wedderburn.

84. **1819.** Dec. 5.—Letter from William Milburn to his daughter Henrietta, afterwards wife of Sir John Wedderburn, son to the foregoing Sir John.

85. **1823.** Feb. 18.—Letter from Alicia Dundas (Lady Wedderburn) to Henrietta Milburn, then Mrs Wedderburn.

86. **1823.** Sept. 22.—Copy of a letter from Louisa Wedderburn (Countess of Hopetoun) to Lady Melville.

87. **1823.** Nov. 22.—Copy of another letter from Louisa Wedderburn (Countess of Hopetoun) to Lady Melville.

88. **1834.** April 3.—Letter from Louisa Wedderburn (Countess of Hopetoun) to Mary Wedderburn, on the death (2 April 1834) of the Hon. Jane Hope.

89. **1826.** April 28.—Letters from Alicia Dundas (Lady Wedderburn) to Henrietta Milburn (Mrs. Wedderburn).

90. **1827.** Oct 27.—Another letter, same to same.

91. **1837.** Jan. 13.—Address to John Wedderburn (afterwards Sir John) on his leaving Bombay.

92. **1881.** Jan. 1.—Address to Sir David Wedderburn, Bart., M.P. for the Haddington Burghs, from South African Colonists.

93. *Family Registers,* 1724-1883.

93. **1724-1883.** Copy of Family registers contained in an old pocket book, formerly belonging to Sir John Wedderburn, fifth baronet of Blackness, and now to his great grandson, Sir William.

REGISTER IN THE HAND OF SIR JOHN WEDDERBURN, B. 1704, D. 1746.

John Wedderburn and Jean ffullarton were married upon the 22^d of Octr 1724.

Margaret Wedderburn was born the 30th day of August 1725 at 4 of the Clock afternoon being Munday, Doctor Wedderburn, Godfather.

Kathrine Wedderburn was born on Saturday the twelth day of Novr 1726 betwixt 8 and 9 in ye morning. James Graham of Meathie Godfayr L. Blackness and Craeope, G-Moyrs.[1]

Alexander Wedderburn was Born on friday the 24th Day of Novr 1727 betwixt 3 and 4 in the morning John ffullarton of that Ilk and Sr Alexander Wedderburn of Blackness, Godfathers, and Margaret Balfour, Dr John Wedderburn's Lady, Godmoyr.

John was born on friday betwixt 6 and 7 in the morning being the 21 day of february 1729 John ffullarton of that Ilk and Dr John Wedderburn Godfathers, and my mother Godmother.

[1] L. Blackness, i.e., Lady Blackness. wife of Sir Alexander Wedderburne, and grandmother of the infant. G-Moyrs, i.e., Godmothers.

James was Born on ffriday the 28 Aug. 1730 betwixt six and seven of the Clock in the morning. Godfathers John ffullarton of that Ilk and James Graham of Meathe, L. Blackness Godmother.

William ffullarton[1] was Born on tuesday the 21 of March 1732 betwixt 8 and 9 in the morning. Godfathers John ffullarton of that Ilk and myself—Lady Clunie, Godmother.

Charles Wedderburn after the master of Aberdour, was Born on Thursday betwixt 4 and 5 in the morning being the fourth day of May 1732. John fullarton of y[t] Ilk and D[or] John Wedderburn, Godfathers, and D[or] Wedderburn's Lady, Godmother.

1733 March 25 Dyed my son Charles. 1733 March 27 Dyed my son Alexander.

1734. Wednesday 9 January at 4 afternoon my Daur Susanna was born. Sir Alex[r] Wedderburn, Godfather. D[or] Wedderburn's Lady and Ann ffullarton, God-mothers. Called after W[m] ffullarton's wife.

2 January 1736 friday betwixt twelve and one afternoon Peter was born and called after Peter Wedderburn, secretary to the Commissioners of excise, godfathers W[m] ffullarton of that Ilk and Doctor John Wedderburn, and my moyr Godmoyr.

1737. [Blank in orig.]

REGISTER IN THE HAND OF SIR JOHN WEDDERBURN, B. 1729. D. 1803.

23[d] June 1748, new stile. Lady Margaret Ogilvy was born at Boulogne in France. Godfather, Theodore Hay, Godmother, Eliza[b] Trotter. 23 June, new stile, 1748. Christened by Father Graham, a Capuchin Friar.[2]

26 Nov. 1769. Sir John Wedderburn and Lady Margaret Wedderburn were married at Cortachy.

My son John, named after my father, was born on Tuesday the 27th of february 1771 between 8 and nine in the morning and christened next Tuesday, myself and Robert Wedderburn of Persie, Godfathers—Miss Betty Johnstone, Godmother.

My daughter Margaret was Born on Munday between 7 and 8 in the evening on the 1st of June 1772 and Christened next Munday. William Fullarton, Godfather, and M[rs] Walter Ogilvy and M[n] Alexander Scrymgeour, godmothers—named after my Wife's mother.

My daughter Jean was born 31st July 1773 being Munday between one and two in the morning and christened next Thursday. James Paterson elder of Carpow, God-father, Katharine and Susan Wedderburn, Godmothers; she was named after my mother.

My son David was born 10th March 1775 being friday at 7 in the evening and christened the same night. Doctor Alex[r] Douglas and myself, Godfathers, my sister Katharine, Godmother; he was named after his grandfather Lord Airly.

On Thursday evening 23 March 1775 Died my spouse Lady Marg[t] Wedderburn of a consumption got by a sudden cold 5 months before, and with her ended all my happy prospects; in five years we never differed in word or Deed, every year if possible added to our mutual affection and firm Freindship, the merit was on her side not mine, perhaps so compleat a character scarce ever existed. Her great Wisdom, Forti-tude, and piety supported her amidst the Afflictions of her Father's family, a most Benevolent and generous heart, conducted with the œconomy her circumstances

---

[1] This is no doubt a nephew of his wife's.

[2] The following document is pasted into the pocket book :—
"Extrait du Registre des batêmes de L'Eglise paroissialle de St Nicolas basse ville de Boulogne sur mer pour l'année mil sept cens quarante huit.
Margueritte fille Legitime de milord David Ogilvie et de dame Margueritte johnston est née Le vingt trois juin sur Les trois heures du matin, a eté baptisée Le vingt quatre. Le parain a eté monsieur Theodore haij, La maraine damoiselle Elizabeth Trotter qui ont signé : Theod. haij. E. Trotter. f. archange d'Ecosse.
Lequel extrait je charles Antoine Baudelicque alias pat. qvone, Cap. j.v.d. .... Pretre curé doien de La dite Eglise paroissialle certifie avoir tiré mot a mot d'un Registre de cette paroisse. fait a Boulogne ce vingt quatrieme jour du mois de Septembre. L'an mil sept cens soixante onze, en foi de qui j'ai sigué, Baudelicque Curé doien.

[Stamp.] C. D'Amiens .... Sol.
      J[C] (fleur de lys.)

Blackness Papers.

required ; so free of guile or Hypocrisy, she never said what she did not think, nor did I ever hear her speak a single word I could have wished unsaid, her Affection for her Husband and[1] children was unbounded.

Her person was above the middle size being 5 feet 10 inches and a quarter, an open expressive Countenance, where every Virtue of her mind shone forth with uncommon Dignity, tempered with infinite sweetness nor did ever Passion deform her lovely face.

Her innate modesty and reserve made so parade of so many Virtues and extraordinary Qualities, therefor the extent of them were best known to her Intimate friends, such excellence was too much for this world.   John Wedderburn.

My Son John Died 22d June 1783 at Mr Webster's at Clapham near London of an Inflamory fever, aged 12, remarkably handsome in his Person and more forward in his Education than common, a severe and unexpected misfortune to his Father.

(The rest of this page is left blank ; then follows on the next page :—)

Sir John Wedderburn was married to his 2d Wife Alicia Dundas aged 26, 2d daughter of James Dundas of Dundas at Edinsh 27 December 1780.

1.   James his son was born Janry 16th 1782, called after his Maternal Grand Father, his Godfathers William Fullarton and Charles Hunter of Burnside, Lady Airly his Godmother.

2.   Maria Wedderburn my Daughter born 18 Septr 1783 called after her Grandmother, her Godfather George Paterson of Castle Huntly, her Godmothers Miss Barbara Dundas and my Daughter Margaret Wedderburn.

3.   Susan Wedderburn my Daughter was born 18th Janry 1785 and was named after Lady Fullarton and my Sister Susan. Godfather Mr David Fyffe, Godmothers Lady Burnside and Miss Mary Stewart.

4.   Louisa Dorothea my Daugr was born 8 June 1786 and the name was given by her Aunt Mrs Brown. Godfather James Webster, Godmothers Mrs Allen and my Daughter Margt Wedderburn.

5.   Anne my Daughter was born on Thursday at 1 of the morning 14th Febry 1788 called after Lady Airly. Godfather Robert Dundas, Godmother Lady Airly.

6.   John my Son was born on friday 1st May 1789, called after my father. Godfathers George Ogilvy of Langley and Charles Wedderburn of Persie, but, he not being able to attend, Mr Alexr Anderson stood for him, and Mrs Anderson Godmother.

7.   Alexander my son was born on Saturday 18th June 1791 and Christened on Tuesday the 28th June, called after my Grandfather and Brother. Godfathers Charles Wedderburn of Pearsie and James Yeaman of Murie. Mrs Ogilvie of Langley Park, Godmother.

David Wedderburn, now my eldest son, was married 2d Septr 1800 to Margt Brown 2d Daughter of George Brown, Commissioner of Excise at Comrie, both in their 26th year. Their first child named John James was born the 16th October 1802 in Hanover Square London.

My Daughter Louisa Dorothea was married 9th Feby 1803 at Balindean to the Honle Major General John Hope of Craigy Hall ; she is between 16 and 17 years old.

My Daughter Margaret was married 5th May 1803 at Balindean to Philip Dundas, M. Parliament, and youngest Brother of Robert Dundas of Arniston, Chief Baron of the Exchequer.

REGISTER IN HAND OF LADY HOPE (ALICIA HENRIETTA WEDDERBURN), ELDEST
    DAUGHTER OF SIR JOHN WEDDERBURN, SECOND BARONET OF BALINDEAN.

Jean was married in 1807 to John Hope Oliphant, and had one daughter Jane (married to Sir James Ramsay Bart of Banff and died 1843).[2]

Sir David Wedderburn's eldest son, John James, died 1810, aged 8 years. His second son, George, died 1822, aged 18.

(Seven pages are then left blank, after which Lady Hope gives a record of her father and his family.)

John Wedderburn and Henrietta Louisa Millburn were married at Bombay, September 7th 1822.

---

[1] These words " husband and " are interlineated.   [2] Quære, 1842 ?

Q

Children.

Alicia Henrietta (Alice) born at Woodgreen, Bombay, August 20th 1828. God-father, Sir Charles Colvile. Godmothers, Lady Wedderburn and Honble Mrs Buchanan.
John born at Woodgreen, Bombay, May 9th 1825. Godfathers, Mr Farish, Col. Alex : Wedderburn. Godmother, ——
Elizabeth Born at Woodgreen, Bombay, Feb^ry 7th 1827. Godfather, Mr Bruce. Godmothers, Susan Wedderburn ......
Margaret Born at Woodgreen, Bombay, May 10th 1828. Godfather, Mr Ritchie. Godmothers, Mrs Dick and Mrs Telfair.
William, Born at Woodgreen, Bombay, May 19th 1830. Died May 24th.
Mary Anne, Born Neelgherry Hills, Novr 26th 1832. Died August 1833.
David, Born at Woodgreen, Bombay, December 20th 1835. Godfathers, Sir Robert Arbuthnot and Mr Greenhill. Godmother, Lady Hope of Pinkie.
William, Born Atholl Crescent, Edinburgh, March 25th 1838. Godfathers, Honble Charles Hope, Mr Johnstone. Alva. Godmother, his sister Alice.
Louisa Jane, Born at Keith House, Haddingtonshire, September 16th 1842. God-father, Sir John McNeill G.C.B. Godmothers, her sister Elizabeth, Mrs Tyrrhitt Drake.

John Wedderburn (eldest son of John Wedderburn and Henrietta L. Milburn) and Alice Bell were married in Edinburgh Jan^ry 29th 1856.
Their son John James born 15th November, 1856. Godfathers, Hon. Adrian Hope and David Wedderburn. Godmother, Mary Jane Bell.
John and Alice Wedderburn and their only child, John James, fell during the Indian rebellion at Hissar, North West Provinces 29th May 1857.

Alicia Henrietta Wedderburn (eldest daughter of John Wedderburn and Hen^ta L. Wedderburn) was married at Keith House, Haddingtonshire, to Lt-Col. William Hope, C.B., 71st Highland Light Infantry, son of Sir John and Lady Hope, Jan^ry 22^d 1862.

REGISTER IN THE HAND OF SIR WILLIAM WEDDERBURN, BART.

William Wedderburn was married on the 12th of September, 1878 to Mary Blanche only daughter of Henry W. Hoskyns of North Perrott Manor, Somerset.
Dorothy Hope, my daughter, was born on the 24th of June, 1879 at Poona in India, Godfather, H. W. Paget Hoskyns. Godmothers, Mrs. W. Hope, Mrs. Arthur Hoskyns.

William Wedderburn, 26th Septemb^r '83.

WEDDERBURN PAPERS AT MOUNIE.

These papers are preserved at Mounie Castle, co. Aberdeen, and are now in the possession of its owner, Major Alexander Seton, by whose permission I am enabled to give an account of them here. When Sir Alexander Wedderburn, second baronet of Blackness, died in 1710, he left his children, all of whom were then under age, in charge of curators, of whom the two principal ones were their maternal uncle, Mr. George Seton, of Mounie, an advocate in Edinburgh, and their father's first cousin, Alexander Wedderburn, clerk of Dundee. The affairs of Sir Alexander seem to have been much involved, and the curators found the management of them fruitful in difficulties. Various papers in connection with them, and with the affairs of his nephews and nieces, naturally came into the hands of George Seton, and a considerable number of letters on the subject of their curatorship passed between him and the clerk during the years 1710-20. None of those addressed by George Seton to the clerk remain, but those received by him were docketed and preserved, and, although many of them are now decayed or mildewed, they are still extant at Mounie. In 1825 Mr. Alexander Seton gave one or two of the papers to my grandfather, John Wedderburn, and also allowed him full access to the remainder. Of this he freely availed himself, and a catalogue of the papers, with full extracts from them, is among his papers. (See post. page 141.) In 1891 I wrote to the late Mr. David Seton and in reply he sent me an elaborate catalogue which he had made of them in common with other family papers in his possession. From his catalogue and that of my grandfather I have edited the following inventory.

Mounie Papers.

INVENTORY OF WEDDERBURN PAPERS AT MOUNIE.

1. **1698.** March 10.—Discharge by Sir Alexander Anstruther of Newark to John Wedderburn of Blackness, as follows :—

    "I, Sir Alex. Anstruther of Newark, hereby grants me after compt and Reckoning had with John Wedderburne of Blackness anent the profits of the Bill Chamber to have received compleat payment and satisfactione of my share of the emoluments of the said office for all tyme preceeding the first day of February last, and I hereby Discharge him and all concerned of all bygones relating thereto, preceeding the said day exclusive ; dispensing with the grallity hereof, as if every particular were here insert. In witness whereof (writen by Philip Davidsone my servitor) I have subscribed thesɜ presents att Edinburgh, the tenth of March, saxteen hundred nyntie eight yeares.—AL. Anstruther."
    (Only a copy of this is among the papers now at Mounie the original having been, no doubt, given in 1825 by Alexander Seton of Mounie to J.W. among whose papers it now is. See post p. 141, No. 3(b)).

2. **1709.** April 8.—Discharge by Alexander Ogston, in the name of Mrs. Ogston, bookseller, in Edinburgh, for £452. 3. 0., due to her for books supplied to Sir Alexander Wedderburn of Blackness, from 23 Feb. 1708 on. Dated at Edinburgh.
    (Three pages of foolscap.)

3. **1709.** Nov.—"Accompt of Mōc (money) received by Sʳ Alexʳ Wedderburne of Blackness att Dundee and Edʳ."
    This is a small piece of paper containing four entries, amounting to £9,905. 10. 0. and signed "Jo. Pilmor." It is headed as above and is endorsed "George Seton, Double of Pilmer's ..... "
    (docket partly torn off.)

4. **1709.** "Note of Bonds granted by Blackness at Mart 1709."
    This paper is so endorsed. It is apparently a list of the bonds as they stood at Martinmas 1709 with interest counted to about Whitsunday 1711.

5. **1710.** An account of annual rent 1673-1711 on a principal sum, calculated from year to year.
    This paper has no docket and there is nothing to show to what transaction it relates.

6.   **1710.** Jan 19.—Letter from Alexander Wedderburn to George Seton as follows[1] :—

Dundie 19th Januar 1710.

Sir,
I hope this will find you and company safe at home. Since your parture from this I'm told y^t probably Collector Beathune will take the house and yeards of Blackness. And since he's now at Ed^r I intreat you'l take the opportunity of speaking to him or some body else who has influence w^t him. I'm of ye opinion he may give fyfteen lib sterling for ye house, gardyne, tree yeard, and grass in ye avenue and among ye planting, but doe in it as you can, only I wish you could bring him ye lenth of taking a tack and then (I need not tell you) to cautione ye preserving ye planting, Allowing ye pictur to stay at Blackness and upholding ye glass windows but verbum sapienti sat est. I now tell you y^t y^r is a debt of 50 lib St. which was due y^t Lady Krap payed. I offer my service to yourself and Lady and family which I'm now more particularly concerned in, And I am,

Sir,
Your most humble ser^t
Al Wedderburne.

(Addressed on the back)
   To Mr George Seton, Advocat, at Ed^r.

(This letter is in good condition and is sealed, as are most of the clerk's letters, with a small seal bearing the Wedderburn arms, charged with a crescent for cadency. In this instance the wax used is black, but generally it is red. A similar address is on almost all the letters. A facsimile of this one is given opposite.)

7.   **1710.** Feb. 14.—Letter from same to same.
In this letter the writer says, " I forgott to tell you at last painting that it was Mr James Martine's opinion and myne that the day of the auction of Blackness' Books and the roup of his household furniture and plenishing should be published by the *Currant* ; as also that you will be at the trouble to call at Robert Crammond for Blackness Books, and send them with Crockat. · I wish your father may consider well of his action for the children's acc^t ; for my own pairt I am readie to answer his demands, but his proving the tenor till once the exhibition be done is what I will not agree to for reasons known to yourself for I am als much for the youngest as for the Eldest .... I have also sent the belt and buckle which are charged at one pound fifteen shillings Sterling, and the sword at four pound ten shillings." Various other details are alluded to, amongst them a wish that " something be done immediately against John Pilmor " (ante No. 3 and post Nos. 10 and 19).

(This letter is signed by the clerk, but is not written, except as to one small part, by him.)

8.   **1710.** Feb. 22.—Letter same to same, dated from " Brichen."
In this the clerk acknowledges receiving, while taking journey on his collection for excise, a letter from George Seton, and proceeds to give his view as to realizing various parts of the late Sir Alexander's estate, including his "part of Mr. Jaffray's ship." He objects strongly to a proposed change of day for the roup, as he has " told severals of it who designe to be at Dundie for the purpose and the Inventars (catalogues) are very much longed for by severals." He suggests that Seton be " trying for a merchant (*i.e.*, purchaser) for the chair," and is " clear that the diamond cross should be sold. Perhaps Pitcur might be inclined for it, and in the meantime you may try the value of it at such as have skill. This with my service to your Lady and children is from, Sir, your most humble serv^t, Al. Wedderburne."

9.   **1710.** Feb. 22.—Letter same to same, dated from Brechin.
This is by way of postscript to the foregoing letter. In it the clerk " thinks it " absolutely necessary that the lands of Omachie and the lodging in Dundie be disposed of and suggests " that it can be done without convening the creditors." He says he has " told you that the miln is renounced already and we be obliged to keep it in our hand or give something down of(f) the Rentall. The Judiciall Inventar will be ready to goe w^t Crockat on Monday seven night." (See post No. 12.)

10.   **1710.** March 6.—Letter same to same.
After mentioning the sale of part of the ship (see ante No. 8), he says " I'm well pleased that the Diamond Cross be sold and the chair with the satine in Blackness' Chamber. ...... As for the silk stockings you mention, they look as if they had been used ...... I am surprised at Mrs. Ogston's acc^t for Books, and if way be given to all these accounts I think £1000 sterling will not pay them, which will alter all our measures ...... I desire to know what your father is designed to doe anent the children, and I wish it were resolved to pursue John Pilmor and Mrs. Patillo for Blackness's linnens, for it's unaccountable they should slip. The reasone I mentione Mrs. Patillo is because she was contemporary servant w^t John Pilmer, and probably might be judged the keeper of them."
The letter also refers to two mares which the clerk had sent to Mr. Lassaget and Deacon Kerr, apparently in part payment of their accounts, but about which difficulties seem to have arisen. He also wishes that the inventar of the Books had been printed, and hopes G. Seton will be present at the roup of the furniture which is to begin on the 20th inst., and which is calculated to last eight days. He encloses £52 scots for paying the demands at the Bill Chamber, and wants an account made of what was due to Sir Alexander at his death.

(This letter is whole, but much mildewed. It has the usual seal of arms in black wax).

---

[1] This and the following letters are docketed with the date only. They are numbered 2 or 4 on the back, these numbers being evidently the post mark. Except where otherwise noted, they are dated from " Dundie," begin " Sir," and end " Your most humble servant," &c.

Sir

                     I hope this will find you & your
Company safe at home. Since your departure from
this I'm told yt probably Collector Beatson
will take the house & yards of Blacknesse And
since he's now at Edgr I intreat you'll take the
opportunity of speaking to him or some body else
who has influence w't him. In my opinion he
may give twenty fifteen lib Sterling for yt house &
half yr 200 yeard of grass in yt about & manage
yr planting. but doe it as you can only I wish
you could bring him yt length of taking yt back &
then (I need not tell you) he considers yt preserving
yr planting. Allowance for jnctures both of Blacknes
& upholding yr Glass windows And within Sepairs
Is lost. I now tell you yt yr is a debt of gold
It which way doe yr Lady thinks payed. I offer my
service to your self & Lady & shall be happy which it
now more particularly concern'd in. And I am

Dundie 19 Janry 1710

               Sir
           your most humble servt
           Al Wedderburne

11. **1710.** (date wanting)—" List of debts due by Sr Alexander Wedderburn of Blackness Mounie at Candlemas 1710."   Papers.

This is a list of the names of creditors with the amount of their debts set opposite each. Their total is £65,764. 17. 0. (Scots). It is apparently in the handwriting of George Seton and is a good deal torn and decayed. The date of Candlemas is Feb. 2.

12. **1710.** March 15-20.—Judiciall Inventory of the means and estate of Sir John Wedderburne of Blackness. To the friends on the mother's syde. (So endorsed).

This is a full inventory of everything of which Sir Alexander died possessed and covers nine sheets of paper, originally joined together into one long scroll. It is in fairly good preservation. It is as follows :—

" Inventar of the Lands and other Heretage and Moveables belonging to Sir John Wedderburne of Blackness ffaithfully given Up by James Hallyburton of Pitcurr Mr James Martine of Grainge Mr George Seton advocat Peter Wedderburne Merchant in Dundie and Alexander Wedderburne Town Clerk of the said burgh, Tutors to the said Sir John Wedderburne With Consent of Robert and John Wedderburne Latill Children to the deceast James Wedderburne town Clerk of the said burgh of Dundie two of the nearest of kin to the minor on the ffather side And Mr William Setton younger of Pitmedden and James Setton his brother two of the Nearest of Kin to the Minor on ye ffather¹ side.

ffollows The Inventar of the Lands

Impr^s All and Haill the Lands and Barronie of Blackness Comprehending the Teinds thereof and oyrs nnderwritten Viz^t All and Haill the village and Lands of Blackness and windmill thereof with the manner place houses biggings yeards orchards aunexis connexes parts pendicles and pertinents of the same q'soever And all the teinds parsonage and vicarage of the sds Lands with the fruits rents profits and emoluments thereof lying in the Lordship of Scone and sherreffdome of fforfar now erected in une Barronie called the Barronie of Blackness and that as prinll and All & Haill the Lands of Pitarro in warrandice yrof As also those eighteen aickers and ffour butts of arable land with the parts pendicles & pertinents of ye same lying in the west feild of Dundie in the Barronie of the same and sheriffdome of fforfar and all and Haill the Lands and oyrs underwritten : Viz^t All and Haill the Lands of Logie with the mannor place houses biggings yeards orchyeards parts pendicles and pertinents yrof bounded in manner specified in his Charter and All & Haill that part and portion of the Lands of Balgay called the Long fore bank of Balgay consisting of sixteen aikers or yrby w^t that piece of land commonly called the latche with the Teind Sheaves parsonage and vicarage of the sds Lands and fruits profits and emoluments yrof : Itt. All and Haill those two aikers of land Comonly called the haulk hill purchast from Robert Christie & William Alisone : Itt. All & Haill those four aikers of land and barnes At Dundie purchast from Baillie James Man & James Man : Itt. aue Lodging lying w^tin the Nethergate of Dundie lately purchast from Robert Carnegy of Newgate.²

Follows the Bonds Tickets and Bills due to the defunct : Impr^s Ane obligatione be James Gordon Senior to deliver to the defunct or order ane hogshead good and sufficient claret upon demand dated the eighteen day of Nover Jaj^{vij} and eight .... 1708. Itt. obligations and assignatie by James Brown, sone to Hugh Brown, Chirurgeon Apothecary in Edinburgh, to the defunct, bearing the receipt of nyntie five pound six shillings Sterling, and one Assignatie to the equall half of one sixteen part of the Union Galley and her cargo, whereof William Jaffery, Master, dated the tenth of December, 1708. Itt. Receipt of Dr William Eccles to the defunct for nyntie pound Scots, oblidging himself to allow to the defunct the said sum at comptiug, dated the fifth of Aprile, 1706. Itt. Bill of Patrick Kyd on the defunct payable to James Gordou Senior, for one hundred seventie fyve pound five shilling, four pennies, Scots, discharged by the said James Gordon on the eight of Aprile, 1707, which Patrick Kyd desires by the said Bill to be placed to his account. Itt. Bond of Relief by James Halliburton of Pitcur to the defunct, for relieving him of the soume of 1000 Merks principall, contained in ane Bond granted by them to Mr Alexander Hay, Advocat, dated the nynth of May, 1705. Itt. Obligement by Doctor William Eccles to the defunct for nyne hundredth nyntie pound, sax shilling eight pennies, which was owing by Mr George McKenzie of Inchcoulter, to Margaret Balfour daughter to Mr Andrew Balfour, writter to the signet, and qch was received by the said Sir Alexander as her Tutor, from the said George McKenzie, and qch soume the said Dr Eccles oblidges him to len out ageu for the use of Margaret Wedderburne, his Spouse, in liferent, and the said Margaret Balfour in fee, or to redeliver the money to the said Sir Alex^r or the said Margaret Balfour her tutors, which obligatione is dated the nynteenth of February, Jaj^{vij} and eight. Itt. Ticket by Patrick Ogilvy of Templehall to the deceast Sir John Wedderburne of Blackness, for fourty pound, which is daited the twelth of December, jaj^{vic}, eighty five, 1685 which ticket is desperat. Itt. Ticket by Rachell Wedderburne to the defunct, for fiftie merks Scots, daited the fourth of June, 1706. Itt. Bond, John Stewart of Grantullie to the defunct for three hundred and sixtie pound, one shilling, two pennies principall, payable at the first terme of Whitsunday or Martimas after the decease of Mrs Jean Fotheringham, Ladie Bainamoou, dated fourth of December, 1708. Itt. Haretable Bond be James Earle of Senthesque, with consent of his Curators, to the said Sir Alexander Wedderburne, for 12,600 Merks principall, with interest from Candlemas, 1708, dated 3 Aprile 1708, with ane Sasine following thereupon under the signe and subscription of James Striven Nottar Public, dated 4 May, 1708, aud regrat att Dundie on the eight day of the said moneth. Itt. Bond of Relief, Mr James Martin of Grainge to the defunct, for relieving him of three several saumnes amounting in haill to 12,600 Merks. contained in three several Bonds, dated 7 February, 1708 ; and

---

¹ A clerical error for " Mother."
² The Lands of Omachie are omitted from the above inventory, and are added at the very end of the document thus :—" Itt. the Lands of Omachie and milne yrof and haill pertinents of the same."

118   THE WEDDERBURN BOOK.

Mounie Papers. which soume of 12,600 Merks the said Mr James Martin affirms to be in lieu and place of the fore-said heretable Bond for 12,600 Merks. Itt. obligation Margaret Oven spouse to Alexander Hay vintner in Edinburgh, to the defunct for ane hogshead of Claret wine of the Bourdaux kind, comonly called the prise wine, daited 24 November, 1708. Itt. Bill accepted by Mr George Settou, Advocat, indorsed to the defunct, for £40 sterling, dated 9 May, 1707, which the said Mr George affirmes to be paid by discharge readie to be producit. Itt. Bill and assignañe, Mr. Charles Kinnaird, uncle to Patrick Lord Kinnaird, to the defunct, for 1000 Merks principall, dated 7 June, 1709, bearing interest from the date, and payable on 2 January 1710, bearing ane assignañe to certain victual and other moveables on the lands of Drimmie, disponed by the said Lord Kinnaird to the said Mr Charles, by his disposition of the dait 24 Aprile 1709. Itt. Discharge by Sir Alexander Wedderburne to Mr James Martin for 3000 Merks principall, contained in ane bond granted by the said Mr James to the defunct, and bearing an obligation to deliver the Bond to Mr James, in respect the same was not in his custodie the tyme of granting the discharge, which is daited 2 July, 1709, and quhilk Bond of 3000 Merks is delivered to the said Mr James, and his receipt taken for it, on the end of the Dis-charge, on 16 January, 1710. Itt. Bill of Alexander Bruce, vintner in Dundie, on the defunct, for £50, Scots, payable to and discharged by James Gordon, Senior, which soume the said Alexander Bruce is to hold compt for to the defunct. which bill is daited 8 July, 1702, Itt. Bond of Relief by Thomas Lundie of Glasswell, to the defunct, for releiving him of ane coûrie (sic) in lowsing of ane arreastment at the instance of Margaret Lundie, relict of Alexander Lesslie, writter in Edinburgh, dated 25 February, 1708. Itt. Bond of relief by Mr William Setton of Pitmedden younger, to the defunct, for relieving him of ane Bond of Cautionrie granted by the said Sir Alexander and oyrs, for the said Mr William his collecting and accounting for the Bishop's rents, dated 4 December, 1705.[1]

Itt. Bond, the toune of Dundie to the defunct for 3000 Merks principall, and interest, and expences, dated 5 February, 1704, regrat att Edinburgh 20 September, 1704, for which Bond the said Alexander Wedderburne affirms he has ane back bond from the said Sir Alexander. declaring the same to be on trust. Itt. Bond of Relief, Major David Wedderburne in Brigadier McKertney's regiment, to the defunct, for relieving him of 3000 Merks contained in ane bond granted to John Scott of Milleny for the soume of 4000 Merks, dated 19 February 1708. Itt. obligement by William Alison, Merchant in Dundie, to the said Sir Alexander to warrand and keep him from all diligence raised at the instance of Robert Christie, Cordiner in Dundie, his creditors, which may anie ways affect two sikers of land purchast from the said William, dated 20 September, 1708. Itt. Bond by Jean Settou, daughter of Sir Alexander Setton of Pitmedden, to the said Sir Alexander, for the soume of £10 Sterling, dated 7 February 1709. Itt. obligement, David Rattrey to pay four dollars to the defunct, dated 3 January, 1702. Itt Catalogue of Books contained in eight pages and a half, given to Mr David Freebairn, Minister, containing his receipt, and obligement to compt for the said books, dated 7 August, 1699. Itt. obligement granted be Mr James Martin to the defunct to pay on demand 30 Guineas at 21/6^d Sterling per piece, and two pistols at 17/6 per piece, dated 19 August, 1708. Itt. venditione be Robert Raitt, Skipper in Dundie, of ane eight pairt of the ship called the Alexander of Dundie, dated 6 sept^r 1709. Itt. ane other venditione granted be the said Robert Raitt of a sixteen pairt of the said ship, dated 6 September 1709, also in favor of the defunct. Itt. five receipts be George McKenzie to the defunct, for 10/- sterling each, advanced as the half of the price of the second volum of the lives and characters of the Scotts writters. Itt. Receipt of John Vallange, bookseller to the defunct, for £3 Scots as the half of the subscription for Spotswood's Praticks. Itt. Receipt of Patrick Aber-crombie to the defunct for 10/- as the first subscription to the Martiall Achivements of the Scots Nation. Itt. Receipt of Mr Andrew Simson and Robert Grahams to the defunct, for 5/- Sterling, as the first payment of the subscription for Gavin Douglasse's Virgill. Itt. Receipt of Mr George Cramond, vintuer, to James Thomson, tenuant of Blackness, for ten bolls beer cropt 1708. Itt. dispohie and assignahe to Sir Alexander Wedderburne of Blackness to John Wedderburne, his sone, of all and sundrie goods, gear, &c., dated 3 January, 1710. Itt. Letter Will, and Testament of the said Sir Alexander Wedderburne nominating the said John Wedderburne his said sone, his exor, sole legator, and universall intromitter with his haill goods, gear, and effects, of the dait of the said dispositione. Itt. letter be James Setton in Dantzick to the said Sir Alexander with ane Currant Account enclosed, bearing the ballauce of 84 Gilders, 27 Gross, to be payed to Mr Wedderburne, who is supposed to be Robert Wedderburne, Mariner.[2]

ffollows the houshold plenishing And other furnitur belonging to the Defunct. In the high South roume of the Lodging in Dundie Imprimis ane bed stead with Courtens head and foot pands sued green upon white lyned with white liunen Itt ane feather bed with ane bolster and three pillows Itt ane chalmer box and pan of pewther Itt ane litle round table oak Itt ane Scruittore with two mirrors Itt in cash lying by the defunct the time of his death fiftie two guineas gold qrôf two suspected to be badd. Itt Seventeen pounds eighteen Shillings and Six pence Sterling money Itt two peices of Gold, like Ducats Itt ane two crowne peice of Scots coyn Itt aue locket of Gold in the shape of ane hart marked on the stone R D s[1] Itt Inclosed in ane paper sealed direct on the back for Matilda Wedderburn, the defunct's daughter, ane pearle necklace and three peices of Gold weying (blank) ...... Itt ane other paper sealed and Direct on the back for Rachell Wedderburne, his

---

[1] William Seton, younger, of Pitmedden had a Commission to collect the Bishop's Rents in Scotland for the Crown, Bishoprics having been abolished in Scotland. He appointed his brother, George, as his Deputy, to collect the Rents of those Bishoprics which were situated north of the Forth. The accounts aud discharges of these transactions, in so far as George Seton was concerned, are preserved at Mounie.

[2] This long list of bonds is probably due to the fact that the Scotch currency at this date was altogether inadequate to meet the necessities of commerce, and it thus became common practice to give bonds or I.O.U's for quite small amounts in place of cash payments. The same scarcity of current coin of the realm, accounts for the use in Scotland, at this date and ever since the time of James VI., of all sorts of foreign coin, ducats, dollars, pistoles, guilders, &c.

daughter, two breclets of Gold weying .... (blank) .... and ane two guinea peice. Itt ane curell Mounie neckless Itt ane litle box of Shagrine and within the same ane Diamond ring with seven atons and Papers. twelve little stons round the same Itt ane ring sett with ane Amarold Itt anoyr Diamond ring with ane large stone and eight lesser ones round the said large Stone Itt thirteen Dollars of Scots coyn Itt eight half Dollars Ditto coyn Itt Sixteen ffourteen shilling peices of Ditto coyn Itt two Scots crown peices of the latest coyn Itt ffive old Scots crowns and two half ones Itt ane Scots crown of the coyn of King Charles the first Itt seven ffourty shilling peices of Scots coyn Itt ten ten shilling peices of Ditto coyn Itt ffive Seven shilling peices of Ditto coyn Itt two ffive shilling peices of Ditto coyn Itt ffour three pence half pennies of Ditto coyn Itt two peices of Silver of old coyn one qröf of the bigness of ane Dollar and the other of ane lesser syse Itt the ffourth part of ane Scots crown Itt two peices of Silver of the bigness of half a crown each Itt ffive pieces of Silver of the bigness of ane shilling each Itt ten peices of ane lesser Syse of Silver of old coyn Itt eight peices of Silver, ane lesser syse, old coyne Itt two litle peices of Silver old coyn Itt ane large Crucifix of Silver double gilded Itt ane litle Crucifix of Silver Itt ane large Silver box with ane Aggat Stone Sett in the top of it Itt ane litle Silver box Itt ane Shagrine pocket book mounted wᵗ Silver glasps and pen Itt twentie two litle brass medalls of litle value Itt the hangings of the high south bed chamer being linnen and woolne stript Itt ane chimney wᵗ tongs shuffell & poeing iron Itt ten China Trinchers, six course china trinchers of blew and white Itt ane fine Teapott of china Itt two ten potts of a course sort Itt eight litle china plates Itt ffour litle china dishes Itt two litle china plates wᵗ ane china Server Itt ffour litle china plates Itt a china candle-stick, two large china cups, eight china cups of different sorts Itt two China Sugar boxes, Six conceits of china for ane Chimney Itt four large china plaits qrof one broke in the lip Itt ane basket twilted, Itt ane oyr china dish."

Follows the Inventar of Silver Work, &c.

Imprimis, ane large silver mouteth with ane timber caice, two large salvers, and two lesser salvers. Itt. ane pair candlesticks. Itt. ane pair braw candlesticks. Itt. two pair snuffers with snuff dishes. Itt. ane duzon knives with silver handles. Itt. ane duzon forks. Itt. thirteen silver spoones with ane litle spoone for a child. Itt. two salts. Itt. ane pair of Cruits. Itt. ane silver dish. Itt. ane big silver spone. Itt. ane silver tanker. Itt. ane litle silver dish guilded within. Itt. seven tart pans of coper. Itt. ane duzon pewther plaites on trinchers, new. Itt. four earthen potts with honye, two courten roads. Itt. two fixed beds, ane fether bed, and two bolsters. Itt. in the outer roume thre writt broads, ane quhereof contaiuing the ten comandements, the other a list of the Nobilitie of Scotland, and the third a letter of Publicus Lentulus concerning Jesus Christ. Itt. ane painted broad. In the high northe roume, Ane standing bed with courtens, head and foot pands, of linen and woolen, and bolster piece tufted with silk. Itt. ane fether bed and bolster with four pillows, ane chimney with tongs, and ane shuffell, fourteen chairs and two elbow chairs, all covered with Rushia lether. Itt. ane table covered green with ane glass and two hanging standards. Itt. aue chamer box and pan, twelve knives and forks with menell handles and silver firles. Itt. twelve pewther spoones, two bigg broath dishes. Itt. three lesser broath dishes. Itt. three large dishes, new. Itt. three other large dishes, five dishes of lesser syse. Itt. four dishes of lesser size, and two ashets. Itt. three standards of pewther. Itt. two basons for washing, eight candlesticks and three pair snuffers, and socketts, twentie five trinchers, more, fourtie trinchers. Itt. three glass botles. Itt. ane double glass cave. Itt. twa chapeu quaichs and ane mutchkin.

Follows the account of furniture, &c., in little dyuing roume, the roume of the dyning roume, &c., naperie in chists, fire arms, swords, pistols, &c.

In the Dyning roume eighteen cain chairs of one sort, quhereof three elbow chairs. Itt. twelve cain chairs of another sort, quhereof one elboued Itt. a cloak and caice. Itt. a litle old cave with two glasses. Itt. a waxed candlestick of brass. Itt. a brass hand for botles. Itt. ane pair bolster tops, ane iron chimney with tongs and shuffell. Itt. six flower potts of different shapes. Itt. other four flowr potts, quhereof two wanting the bottoms. Itt. ane lime crame dish. Itt. two marble statutes with four pedestals of marable. Itt. ane scrine. Itt. ane large ovall table of winescott. Itt. ane mirror with japaned frame and gilded top. Itt. ane fyne japaned table, and two standards suitable. Itt. ane old litle square oak table. Itt. ane pair old brass shells. Itt. six peices of paper hangings stamped. Itt. ane tea table and coffie mill. Itt. four white iron boxes, and a tin flaggan, wanting the head, ane brass snuffer broke in one of the skeers. Itt. ane large telescop. Itt. two litle earthen Jars.

Inventar of picture brought from Blackness, vizt from the outter roume ffour pictura qrof three in colours and one in stamped leather Itt. ffive landskips Itt. The pictur of lott and his daughters, a nuditie Itt. A Roman in prison and his dochter giving him suck Itt. King Charles the first and his Queen in two picturs with gilded mullers Itt. ane fancie in ane ovall muller gilded Itt King James the Sixth, King Charles the first, King Charles the Second, King James ye Seventh, Arch-Bishop Spotswood, Arch-Bishop Sharp. Itt. Two oyr litle picturs in square mullers gilded Itt Picturs in Talidence ; King William, Prince George, Queen Marie, Queen Ann, A Cupid and Venus a nuditie—Andromida, a nuditie—A Magdalen—King Charles the first—Archibald (sic) Laud and Strafoord (sic) in one pictur represented in different lights Itt. Mr. Alexᵗ Hendersone in ane ovall frame Itt. John Calvin Itt. Hugo Grotius Itt. John Knox Itt. George Buchanan Itt. Martin Luther Itt. Luther and Calvin in square frame Gilded, ye Reformers in Talidence square framed Itt. Picturs in Black and White Vizᵗ the viscount of Duudie, Arch-Bishop Sharp, Mr Saige, The Laird of Grantullie Itt. Neper of Merchiston Itt. ane old man in water colours in ane ovall frame.

ffollows the account of glasses Ane Glass cooler ffour decanters a great Bowle glass with a Stalk " .... " Two incorporating glasses " .... " Itt. Six Sylebob glasses" .. .. (a long list) ....

¹ ₑ ᴰ ₛ = Dame Elizabeth Setou.

Follows the account of confections, wearing apparel, toilette articles, &c. "Itt. ane new hunting Stock Itt. ane Tea Ketle and lamp of Copper Itt. two charter chists one of iron and anoyr of oak ... ... Itt. ane large Cabinet with shutties ... ... Itt. ane strong box covered with brass Itt. two boxes with a selcha skin being a piriweig box and a litle coffer Itt. A fyne writing table Itt. ... ... Itt. a brass penner with ink glass ... ... Itt. ane leather caise wᵗ ane Jocktaleg and fork Itt. ane oyr leather caise wᵗ two jocktalegs. Itt. a penkniff Jocktalege ... ... Itt. a bagiuet and belt mounted with brass ... ... Itt. a hunting whip Itt. ane pair pistolls Itt. a fine cain wᵗ ane ambur head ... ...

In the roume of the dyning roum ane pair (pinuts) one pair virginalls wᵗ yʳ staudards ... ... Itt. five peice of fine arras hangings Itt. ... ... Itt. Seventeen amonition guns five beginets and a broil sword Itt. a reifled gun Itt. a fine caraben and cover ... ... Itt. a fire shuffel and poeing iron ... ... Itt. a large Clock bag ... ... (a number of blankets of different sorts specified) "Itt. a Duzon dornick naperie and Table cloth— marked H.I., ane other Dozen marked B. anoyr Dozou marked E.S.¹ anoyr duzon cours without mark Itt. anoyr Duzon fine merked E.S. anoyr duzou fine marked E.S. anyor duzon marked G.ff. Itt. anoyr Duzon fine marked E.S. anoyr duzon fine marked I.M. anoyr duzou ffine E.S. anoyr duzon fine S. ff. (or S. St ?) another duzon G.ff. anoyr duzon G.S. Itt. six plain servitors Itt. ane oyr duzon naprie not marked Itt. auoyr Ditto uumarked Itt. anoyr duzon fine dornick E.S. Itt. anoyr duzon G.ff. Itt. a fine teick to a bed Itt. anoyr duzou naprie uumarked Itt. ane old fashion'd cover for a bed of Holland Itt. aue old dornick table cloth Itt. anoyr ditto table cloth Itt. two dornick Tuills, Sixteen codwares Itt. ane peice fyne twidlen " ... ... (A number of pairs of Sheets but it is not stated that they are marked) ... ...

"In the brewhouse ... ... (tubs barrels bottles &c. &c) ... ... In the sellar one ale barrel ... ... (tubs, nails &c) ... ... "The Pictur of Beheading of John the Baptist " ... ... "In the baike house of Blackness " " ane baiking table fixed " ... ... "weights of stone for weying servants meall standing in Blackness Itt. ane great meall Chist " ... ... Itt. ane old Jack and two wand ruskes ... ... Itt. a pilgit ... ... Itt. in the nurserie of Blackuess ... ... Aue fixed table, ane salt backet ... ... ane bucket " ... ... (some common furniture and cooking utensils) ... ." In the Kitchen of Blackness ... ... Itt. ane ambrie ... ... In the room above the Kitchen of Blackness " (some furniture, apparently common) "Itt. aue glass amrie Itt. ane side saidle covered with red velvet ... ... In the kitchen in the Lodging of Duudie " (Kitchen furniture & cooking utensils ; but not very much) ... ...

"Inventar of the Horses, Cattle, and other plenishing on the lands of Blackness " (It enumerates thirteen horses of which no doubt most, but not all, were kept for working the farm.)

"Inventar of the horses, catle, and other plenishing on the Lands of Logie.

Imprs. two staks of peise Three staks of bear Three staks of Oats ane stak half oats half peise In the barne two bolls of bear Three bulls of peise Itt. a stak in the barne consisting of twelve bolls three firlots Itt. six bolls of oats of ye remaius of twentie seven bolls oats as the product of anoyr stak " ... ... (agricultural implements, harness &c) ... ... "Three fforks, eight horses, eight bridles, twentie oxen, ten soams, and ten yoaks, three pleughs and " ... ... &c ... ... "Itt. a parcel of Choice Books conform to Three Catalogues Signed of the date of these pnts, Itt. a parcel of Coalls lying at the lodging in Dundie a parcell of coalls lyiug at Blackness Itt. The Lands of Omachie and milne yrof and haill pertinents of the same."

Imprs ane brown horse, ane black horse Edward, ane brown mair boughte from Craigie, aue horse bought from Thomas Brain, ane other horse bought from Craigie, called the Oled, ane horse called the Staige, ane horse called ffotheringham, ane black mair bought from Mr. McLachlan, ane dip mair bought from him, ane stone cairt horse, ane coach mair, ane horse called Laurenkirk, a muck horse called Dogie, two kyne, three staiges, ane blew staig, twelve pair tbeats, three pleughs with their graith, four curne cairts, two ston cairts, two muck cairts, four pair heims, and four staid saidles— two pair muck creels, a gray mair, a mouse coloured mair, (various farm implements, stacks &c) "two stacks and aue staithle of bear, ane stack of oats, and ffour staithles, ffour staks and ffive stakheads of peise ... ... a gray mair, a moua colered mair Itt four bee scaips & a bee house ... ... Itt. seventeen duzon of bottles counted twice.

The above Inventar of the Lands and oyr heritage and moveables, belonging to Sʳ Jobu Wedderburn of Blackness, is signed by Williaᶻ Seton younger of Pitmedden, and James Seton his brother, as nearest of kin to the said Sir John on the Mother's side, and by Mr. George Seton, Advocat, on of his tutors, att Ediuburgh, the fifteen day of March, 1710, before witnesses John Low and Thomas Lyon, both servitors to the said Pitmedden ; And by Robert and John Wedderburnes, lawful children to the deceaste James Wedderburne Clerk of Dundie, two of the nearest of kine to the Minor on the Father side, and by the other tutors after named, att Dundee, the twentie day of March, 1710, befor those witnesses, Thomas Hendersone and David Brisbane, both servitors to the said Alexander Wedderburne, Clerk of Dundie.

Alexʳ Ballingall.	W. Seton.	Peter Wedderburne.
Ja. Ramsay.	James Seton.	John Wedderburn.
Jno Low, witness.	Geo. Seton.	Robert Wedderburne.
Thomas Lyon, witnes.	Ja. Martine.	A. Wedderburne.
Da. Brisbane, witnes.		James Hallyburton.
Tho. Hendersone, witnes.		

(The above inventory is endorsed as having been examined and confirmed, "att Dundie," 22 April 1710, by Alexander Ballingall, baillie, and James Ramsay, clerk depute of Dundee, whose signatures testify this. The endorsement also states that three copies of the inventory, and of the Catalogue of Books (No. 13), were produced, one for Alexander Wedderburne, another for Robert Wedderburne, and a third, that now extant at Mounie, for William Seton. The document is a long roll of sheets joined together, and signed at each junction by all or some of the tutors. It is in fairly good condition.)

¹ E.S. of course stands for "Elizabeth Seton." It does not appear for whom the other initials stand.

13. **1710.** March 20.—Catalogue of the Library at Blackness, similarly attested to Mounie Papers.
No. 12 :—

This is the printed catalogue just referred to in the note to No. 12. It is a pamphlet about 7½ in. square, and consists of a title page with a blank reverse, and thirty-five pages of print, with the last page blank. The title page is as follows :—

CATALOGUE

OF

BOOKS

To be Sold by Way of Auction

At *Dundee*, the 20th of *March*, 1710.

EDINBURGH :

Printed in the year 1710.

On the reverse side of this is a written note of a few books, which had by oversight been omitted from the printed catalogue. Then follows the printed list of books, beginning with " Books in Folio," and going on to " Books in Quarto," " Books in Octavo," " Books in Duodecimo and Infra." At the end of the Quartos and Octavos are lists of a few " Books stitched in Marable Paper." The name of the purchaser of each book is written in on the inner margin of each page, while on the other margin the price paid for each book is recorded. The total amount fetched by the books on each page is added up at the foot, and these amounts are carried out and added up at the end of the catalogue after the word " FINIS " on the last page. The total sum realized by the whole of the books was £3,533. 6. 4 (scots).

This catalogue is probably of bibliographical interest, as some of the books in it are now no doubt rare, and it also provides an interesting record of the value of books in Scotland at the time. I should like to have printed it *in extenso*, but am precluded from doing so by the space it would occupy, and must content myself with a full account of it.

There are 170 folios, 148 quartos, 555 octavos, and 86 smaller books. Many of these are in several volumes, so that the total number of volumes would appear to be over 1,100. The books are of all sorts, Historical, Philosophical, Greek and Latin classics, a few books on law, a great many on theology, and a small number of " belles lettres." The oldest books in the catalogues are :—

Among the Folios :—

					£	s.	d·
Mr. Greig	Joannis Duns Scoti Quæstiones		Vcue.	1506	1	13	0
Mr. Charles Kinnaird	Polidori Virglii Adagia de Inveut. rerum Hist. Anglic.		Basil	1521	6	12	0
Mr. Charles Kinnaird	Quiutiliani Institutiones Oratoriæ		Basil	1529	3	12	0
Mr. Charles Kinnaird	Biblia Sacra vet : and uov: testa: juxta vulg: edit.		Paris	1548	6	18	0
Mr. Thos. Wilson	Budæi Lexicon Græc: Lat.			1554	8	2	0
Tho. Rattray	Euclidis Elementa Græca.		Basil	1553	1	15	0
pitcurr	Hector Boethii Hist : Scotica.		Paris	1574	13	10	0
Baldovan	Buchanani Hist : Scotica		Edinb.	1582	10	12	0
Dr. ffotheringham	Julii Cæsaris Commentaria		Lug.	1574	4	10	0
Dr. ffotheringham	Calepini Dictionarium decem linguarum		Lond.	1588	2	5	0
Mr. Rot. Whyte	Terentii Comædiæ cum commentariis Donati and Calphurini		Paris	1559		13	0
Mr. Tho. Wilson	Rerum Anglicarum Scriptores		Lond.	1566	1	17	0
poncrie	Sigonius de Jure Romauorum, Republica Atheuiensium and Lacedæmouiorum		Paris	1576	1	1	0
Mr. Ja. Paton	Flores Historiarum per Matheuu West-monasteriensem		Lond.	1570		17	0
Mr. Thos. Rattray	Iustitutiones juris civilis, Græce		Lovaniæ	1536		8	0

Among the Quartos :—

					£	s.	d·
Mr. Whyte	Clavii noni Calendarii Romani Apologia		Romæ	1588		19	0
Mr. James Greig	Joa: Majoris de festis Scotorum	Apud Ascensi:		1521	6	14	0
Mr. Wm. Lyon	Couper's Chronicle			1555		12	0
Mr. Wm. Lyon	Ben Syræ Sententiæ morales & Tobias. Heb : and Lat.		Isræ	1532	(not priced)		
Mr. Tho. Cartaris	Stukius de Angelis angelicoque hominum perfidio		Figuri	1595		13	0
Mr. Greig	Petri Lombardi Senteutiæ		Lovanii	1557·	1	1	0
fullertoun	Platonis Timæus and Aristotelis Phisica		Paris	1542		6	6

And among the Octavos :—

					£	s.	d·
Innerichtie	Artemidorus de Somniorum Iuterpretatione		Basil	1546		18	0
poncrie	Psalterium Davidis, Versibus elegiacis redditum a Paulo Dolscio Græce		Basil	1555		11	0
Horn	Ant : Cucelii Institutiones Juris Canonici		Coloniæ	1564		6	6
Mr. Jo. Hill	Ful : Ursini Virgilius collatus cum Græcis Scriptoribus		Antwerp	1567		9	0
Mr. Ja. Greig	Quiutiliani Iustitutiones Oratoriæ		Basil	1555		14	0
Mr. Greig	Status Religionis Reipublicæ ...... sub. Hen : 2do., Franc : 2do. & Carolo nono			1572		10	0
Mr. Menzies	Commeutaria de Magistratibus Romani		Lausannæ	1578		6	0

R

Mounie Papers.

The Greek classics include the works of Anacreou (Cant. 1705) ; Aristotle (Paris : fol : 1654) ; Aristophanes (Lond. 1605) ; Euripides (Cantab. 1694) ; Thucydides (Oxon 1696), with Hobbs' translation (Lond. 1676) ; Plato's Timæus and Aristotle's Phisica, apparently in one volume (Paris 1542) ; Aristotle's Ethics (Hanover 1640) ; Aeschluus in Ctesiphontem and Demosthenes de Corona (Oxf. 1693) ; Demosthenes, in English (Lond. 1702) ; Theocritus (Oxf.) with an English translation (Oxf. 1684) ; Xenophon (Oxf. 1703) ; Herodotus, Englished by Littlebury (Lond. 1709) ; and a Greek Grammar (Lond. 1700).

In Latin there are Cæsar (Lug. 1574), with an English translation (Savoy 1695), Tacitus, two editions (Ant. 1627), (Lond. 1698) ; Cicero (Lug: Bat: 1692), and an English rendering of the " De Finibus " (Lond. 1702), Horace (Delph. ed. 2 vols., Paris 1691) and another edition (Ant. 1685), also Creell's translation (1684) ; Juvenal (Lug. Bat. 1695) ; Juvenal and Persius (Paris 1684), and Dryden's translation (Lond. 1667) ; Lucretius (Delph. ed. Paris 1691) and another edition (Lug. Bat. 1695), two copies of Virgil (Delph. ed. Amst. 1701), (Ultrajecti 1704), and two translations, Dryden's (Lond. 1709) and Lord Lauderdale's ; three copies of Terence (Paris 1559), (Delph. ed. Paris 1675), (Amst. 1688) ; Ovid's Metamorphoses, translation (Lond. 1587) ; Cornelius Nepos (Aust. 1705) ; Sallust, Row's ed. (Lond. 1709) ; Quintilian, three editions (Basil 1529), another (ed. 1555), and yet another (Oxf. 1693) ; Plutarch (Paris 1624) and, in English (Lond. 1703) ; Lucian (Elzevir, 8vo ed. Amst. 1688), Phædrus (Amst. 1698 and 1701) ; Claudian (Delph. ed. Paris 1671) ; and Seneca (Antwerp 1615). There is a " Petwinu's (? Petronius) Arbiter " among the books omitted from the printed catalogue and written in on the back of the title page, and a " Petronius Arbiter, uncle English by Mr. Barnabie (Lond. 1694)," appears among the octavos. There is also Littleton s Latin and English Dictionary (London 1703) which was bought in " to the pupill."

Of historical books there are Clarendon's History (Oxf. 1706), the History of Philip de Comines (Lond. 1674), Hector Boethius (1574), Camden's History of Queen Elizabeth, the History of Catherine de Medici (1693), the History of Gustavus Adolphus (1689), Josephus' Historie of the Jews, Bentivoglio's History of flanders, "Nalson's true copy of the Journal of the High Court of Justice for King Charles I.'s Trial " (London 1684), and a good many political pamphlets. In Philosophy, Confucius (1687), Spinosa (1677), Bacon's Advancement of Learning (1674), Locke on the Human Understanding (1706), Hobb's Leviathan (1651 and 1670), &c. The Law Books include Durie's Decisions (1690), Nisbet's Decisions (1698), Mackenzie's Precedents (1680), Spotswood's Praticks (1706), Durham on Scandal (1680), and the Acts of the Scottish Parliament (1681). In Theology, we have Hooker's Ecclesiastical Polity (1676), Jeremy Taylor's, Stillingfleet's, and Tillotson's works, two editions of Thomas a Kempis (1700 and 1707), the Liturgy of the Church of England (Lond. 1631), the Liturgy of the Church of Scotland (Edin. 1637) ; a folio Hebrew Bible in two volumes (Basil 1620) ; various other Bibles, and a great many such works as " A dialogue betwixt Timothy and Philanethus ag^t ye Rights of ye Christian Church," and Wilkins' " Gift of Prayer and Preaching." For the rest there are two editions of Milton (1698 and 1705) but no Shakspeare ; Butler's Hudibras (1704) ; the works of Machiavelli (Lond. 1675) ; Evelyn's Silva (1706) ; Swift's " Tale of a Tub " (1704) ; the Characters of De La Bruyère (1698) ; Sir W. Temple's works (1701) ; and a miscellaneous collection of other books, " Nostradamus' Prophecies " (1685), " Webster's Witchcraft " (1677), " King James VI.'s Works " (1616). There are two or three books in French, e.g., Recuile de quelques discources politiques " (A. Gervais 1633), and a few volumes of light literature such as " The Gentleman's Recreation " (1686), " The Spanish Libertines " (1702), " Letters of a Turkish Spy " (1702), " The Works of a London Spye " (1706), " The Secret History of the Calv's Head Club " (1709), Mr. de Bellgrade, his Ridicule and Letters (2 vols), &c., &c.

The largest prices fetched were £60. 1. 0. for Bayle's Historical and Critical Dictionary (London 1710) quite a new book at the date of the sale, and no doubt one of Sir Alexander's latest purchases from Mrs. Ogston in Edinburgh (ante No. 2), £57 for Kircher's Works in six volumes (1660-78) and £49. 10. 0 for a two-volume Plutarch (1624).

The sale would seem to have been well attended, as there were over eighty different purchasers, vizt :—Lord Pitmedden, Sir James Dunbar, Sir David Thriepland, Sir James Kinloch ; the lairds of Ardownie, Auchterhouse, Auldbar, Baldovan, Balharrie, Balnamoon, Craigie, Denhead, Drunkelboc, Dunsinnen, Fullertoun, Horn, lunerichtie, Lundie, Milnehill, Monorgan, Nevoy, Pitcurr, Powrie (elder and younger), Ogile, and Wormistoun ; the Ministers of Leuchars (Mr. Robertsone) and Kellins ; Doctors Blair, Fotheringham, Watson and Wedderburn ; Bailies Henry Guthrie, Murray, Oliphant, and Preston ; Mr. James Martine (a large purchaser), Mr. Martine of Clermount, Mr. Charles Kinnaird, Mr. James Goldman, Mr. John Brown, Mr. Greenhill, Mr. Patrick Greenhill, Mr. Robert Whyte, Mr. Thomas Rattray, Mr. Pat. Crichton, Mr. William Anderson, Mr. Thomas Carstaire, Mr. Hamiltoun, Mr. Jo. Crie, Mr. James Paton. Mr. Thos. Wilson, Mr. Vallenge, Mr. Rob Fotheringham, Mr. William Drummond, Mr. Wm. Lyon, Mr. Rankine, Mr. Norrie, Mr. Ross, Mr. Greig, Mr. James Greig, Mr. McLauchlan, Mr. Whyte, Mr. James Cambell (sic), Mr. Jo. Hill, Mr. Henry Guthrie, Mr. McFarlane, Mr. George Maule, Mr. Menzies, Mr. Alexander Wedderburn, the clerk, and his brother, Robert Wedderburn, Captain Cramond, Patrick Ogilvie (" son to Balfour "), Thomas Hannan, Robert Norris, Alex^r Alison, Samuel Stewart, Henry Smith, Frederick Corsor, John Dick, Robt Pringle, James Fairweather, Alexander Achterlony.

The Lairds of Powrie, elder and younger, in the above list, are the Fotheringhams of Powrie, and not the Wedderburns of Easter Powrie and Wedderburn, whose younger laird at that time was a mere child. The Laird of Wedderburn does not seem to have attended the sale or, if he did, made no purchases. Alexander Wedderburn, the clerk, bought three books : " Ainsworth on the five Books of Moses, Psalms, and Song of Solomon " (fol. Lond 1627) at £4. 16. 0 ; Mr. F. Manning's " Life of the Emperor Theodosius " (8vo, Lond. 1693) at £1. 1. 0 ; and " A Lady's Letters of Travels into Spain " (8vo, Lond. 1697) at £1 12. 0 ; while his brother, Robert Wedderburn, bought one book " Choice Collection of Scots Poems by several Hands " (8vo, Edin. 1706) at 17s.

The only Member of Sir Alexander's family who bought to any extent was the clerk's other **Mounie**
brother, Dr. John Wedderburn, who purchased the following :— **Papers.**

	£ s. d.
Grotius of the Rights of War and Peace, Englished by Evats (fol, Lond. 1682)	8 14 0
Sam Puffendorseus de jure naturæ et gentium (dor : deaur :[1] 4to, Amst. 1688)	6 0 0
Joannes Leskeus de titulo & jure quo Maria Scotorum Regina Regni Angliæ successionem sibi juste vindicat (dor: deaur: 4to, Rhemis 1580)	3 2 0
Rich. Simonis Historia Critica veteris testamenti latiue reddita (dor: deaur: 4to, Paris 1681)	2 15· 0
Alexandri ab Alexandro Geniales Dies cum uotis variorum (dor: deanr: 2 vols, 8vo, Lug: Bat: 1683)	6 0 0
Xenophontis opera omnia cum versione Latina, una cum Chronologia Dodwelli & tabulis Geographicis in 5 vol (8vo, Oxf. 1703)	15 0 0
Testamentum Novum Græcum cum variis lectionibus (8vo, Oxf. 1675)	3 8 0
L. C. Lactantii opera (8vo, Cantab. 1685)	1 17 0
Drelingcourt's Defence against the Fears of Death, Englished by M. Deasigny (8vo, Lond. 1701)	2 0 0
William Beveridge, Bishop of S. Asaph's thoughts upon Religion, &c. (8vo, Lond. 1709)	1 17 0
Dr. Tillotson's sermons in 9 vol. (8vo, Lond. 1694)	19 13 0
Lord Verulam's Essays with the Character of Queen Elizabeth (dors: deaur: 8vo, Lond. 1696)	1 11 0
Sutherland's Hortus Medicus Edinburgensis (8vo, Edin. 1683)	1 0 0
Dr. Gastrell's Certainty and Necessity of Religion in eight sermons at Dr. Boyle's lecture, anno 1697 (8vo, Lond. 1703)	2 8 0
A bundle of 18 pamphlets	1 12 0
Sallustius cum variis, etc. (12mo, Oxf. 1701)	1 8 0
Rattræi prognosis medica (12mo, Glasg. 1666)	5 0

This list of books, bought by Dr. Wedderburn, is fairly typical of the rest of the catalogue,
from which, however, a few more books may be selected at random :—

FOLIOS.

				£ s. d.
Sir Jas. Kinloch	D. Gregorii Astronomiæ Elementa		Oxon. 1702	12 2 0
Mr. Ja. Goldman	Bibliotheca Patrum, 8 vol.		Paris 1624	28 4 0
Mr. Ch. Kinnaird	Vaillant Numismata Ænea		Paris 1698	13 10 0
Mr. Hamilton	The Jesuits' Morals by a Doctor of the Sorbon		Lond. 1670	3 0 0
Mr. Jo. Crie	Echard's Ecclesiastical History		Lond. 1702	3 12 0
Mr. Robert Whyte	Jamblichus Chalcedonensis de misteriis, liber ex editione Thomæ Gale Græc : Lab :		Oxon. 1678	4 16 0

QUARTOS.

Mr. Ja. Martine	Selden's Mare Clausum		Lond. 1689	1 17 0
Mr. Martine	1 : Bodin Angevin de la Demonomanie des Sorciers dor: deaur:		A. Paris 1582	1 12 0
Innerichtie	Blunt's Remarks upon Poetry		Loudon 1604	1 17 0
Dr. Watson	Il Seminario de governi di State & di Guerra		Geneva 1645	2 3 0
pat. Crichtoun	Tractatus de præcadamitis		1655	2 8 0
Mr. Rob. Whyte	Wil Molyneux dioptica nova		Lond. 1709	6 0 0
Mr. Tho. Wilson	Horæ Beatæ Virginis secundum usum Sacrum			1 1 0
Mr. Th. Wilson	The Form of Ordaining Ministers and Consecrating Bishops in the Church of Scotland		Edinb. 1620	1 4 0
Mr. Th. Wilson	Geo. Sinclair's Ars nova and magna		Roter : 1669	1 11 0
fullertoun	Prose de Mousignor Giovanni Crampoli		Rome 1649	4 4
Rob. Pringle	Collection of Plays by Dryden and others		Lond. 1676	2 9 0
Mr. Martine	A short view of the Affairs in Scotland the first six years after the Revolution ; (Manuscript)			2 4 0
Innerichtie	Jo. Wierus de præstigiis demonum ●		Basil 1577	17 0

OCTAVOS.

fullertoun	Forbes on Tyths		Edinb. 1705	1 18 0
fullertoun	Knox's Liturgy with Psalms in Metre and Prose		Aberd. 1663	1 10 0
powrie	Mons. Rapin's Critical Works in 2 vol., Englished by several hands		Lond. 1706	6 0 0
Mr. Martine	The Phrenia, or a Revival of Valuable Pieces in 2 vol.		Lond. 1707	6 0 0
Auldbar	Don Quixot's History of the Renowned, 4 vol.		Lond. 1706	9 12 0
Mr. John Hill	Dr. Duncan's Advice, against the Abuse of Hot Liquors, done from the French		Lond. 1766	2 0 0
Mr. Martine	Montaing's Essays, made English by C. Cotton in 3 vol.		Lond. 1693	6 11 0
Drumkelboe	Beaumont's Treatise of Spirits, Apparitions, &c.		Lond. 1705	3 12 0
Horn	Juan Hewart's Tryal of Witts, Euglished by Master Bedlam		Lond. 1678	3 0 0
	Etc., etc., etc.			

[1] Dorsum Deanratum—Gilt-backed.

Mounie
Papers. 14.   **1710.** April 1.—Letter, Alexander Wedderburn to George Seton as follows :—

Sir,

I have been so hurried with Blackness' Auctione and Roup yt I may say I was never engaged in ye like. Our Books are now almost sold, and I believe generally to good purpose. Wee think to end them on Monday w^tout a returne of any unsold. I Bought the pistolls at 14lib. 14s. Scots ; if you incline for them, they shall be sent you, oyrways acquaint me for sealls (severalls) are seeking them. I shall doe my best to answer your demands in Blackness' affairs, next week ; in the mean time I give you thanks for the care of my horning and desire you'l let me know its charges y^t I may order it. This w^t my service to your self and Lady w^t our tw.) pupills is from

Sir, your most humble serv^t,
Al. Wedderburne.

(In good condition, with the usual seal of arms, much broken.)

15.   **1710.** April 15.—Letter, same to same.

" I send you enclosed Mr. Brown's discharge which you are to subscribe yourself, in regaird the ship was not publickly rouped, so every tutor must bear a pairt.

Mr Lyon was at the rouping and can best answer you anent the commissione for the Books, for his own name was insert in all he bought. When I cleared with Mr Martine anent his part of the rouping—the sum of which is about 12,000 merks, furniture and books—he desired that Dr Eccles should be paid his £150 sterling which I agreed to. I also agreed that 2,000 merks should be paid at Whitsunday, of the 4,000 which he engaged for to Bailie Ballingall, which he thinks to get done besides Mr. Dick's 5,000 merks." .... He proposes that " the whole amount of the Roup and auctione be applied for payment of principal sums, and that the estate answer the @-rents." .... " Wedderburne bought the tanker, Mr. Martine the snuff box, and Nevoy the Kane." .. .. I am in a straight to answer you about Deacon Kerr, for you may remember when all the tutors were together it was agreed that no acc^t above ten pounds Scots should be paid without Decreet. I am very clear that the Lodging in Duudie should be sold with the Lands of Omachie .... This with my service to yourself and Ladye, and wishing to hear she is safely brought to bed is from, Sir, your most humble servant, A. Wedderburne.

(Signed by the clerk, but written by another in a very small, close, neat hand.)

16.   A Schem of the Probation of the Rentall and value of the Lands of Blackness, &c., upon a Sale at the Tuters instance for a power to sell the Land of Omachie and House in the town of Dundee. The Lords found the Lybel Relevant and granted Commission to prove the Rentall, the value of the Lands, deductions and Holding and also for Recovering (?) the grounds of debts, &c., and the same as proven in manner underwritten.

		Meal & Bear	Money.
Proven by Henry Watson & Ja. Greme 1 & 2 Wit. as Set A in the Report.	Imprimis the Rentall of the Lands of } Blackues J^a	472. 3. 2. 2.	109. 6. 8.
Proven by Ja. Miln & Tho. Thomson 8 & 9 Wit.	It. the Rent of the Lauds of Logie is	332. 0. 0. 0.	366. 13. 4
Proven by Ja Anderson & Tho. Wilson 3 & 5 wit.	It. the rent of the Lands of Omachie possest by James } B Anderson viz the mains & &c	86. 0. 0. 0.	
Proven by Rod. Anderson & Thos. Wilson 4 & 5 Wit.	It. The rent of Land possest be Rod Anderson anoyr Tennant y^r for the Milne &c	36. 0. 0. 0.	120. 0. 0. 0. — 66. 13. 4.
	Deductions Victual Money.	724. 3. 2. 2.	342. 13. 4.
Proven by discharge marked on back A payable }	To the minister of Liff 8.0.0. 15. 9.0.		
p. discharge marked B payable {	To the minister of } Dundee 12. 0. 0. 111. 0. 0.		
p. discharge marked C payable	To feud Duty 00. 0. 0. 25. 15. 6.	20. 0. 0. 0.	151. 15. 6.
	20. 0. 0. 151. 15. 6.		
	Rests	704. 3. 2. 2.	190. 17. 10.

The foresaid Lands hold of the Crown as is proven p^r Charter produced. Carnegie of p.bineven depones that the ordinary value of Lands holden of the Crown is 2000 M^{ks} the Chaldor of Victual and 100 lib for each M^k of money Rent & peter Durham of Omachie depones that the value of Lands in the Shire qr the Lands Lybelled Lie is commonly estimate at 100 M^{ks} pr chald, bear & meal, & if holden of ye crown will give 20 years purchas.

Which 704 Bols 3ff 2p 21 being converted into Chald. Is 44 Chald. 3ff 2p 21 which at 2000 p. chalder is proven by the forsds 2 definitions to be...				58742.	2.	6.
and which 190£ 17ss 10d of money Rent computed at 100£ sterl. for each 100 Mks extends to				3436.	1.	0.

And for the proving the yearly Rent of the Lodging iu Dundie David Nevay of that ilk & Alex^r Blair, provost of Duudie, 6 & 10 witnesses in the Report depones that same payed yearly 11 Lib St, fude   132. 0. 0.
Which yearly rent being computed at 12 years purchas extends to   ...   ...   1584. 00. 0.

                                                                         63762. 3. 6.

Aud for proving the necessity of selling by the extent of the debts there is .... & produced a great many bonds conform to an acc^t & Inventar qrof, the priucipall sommes qrof exteud to   ..   ..   42763. 3. 4.

                                                                         20999. 0. 2

      (This is now among the papers collected by J. W., to whom it was given by Mr. Seton of Mounie, in 1825.) See post p. 141, No. 3 (c).

17.   **1710.** (date wanting).—" State of the Process of Aliment : Alexander, Margaret, Rachell and Matilda Wedderburns, younger children to ye deceast Sr Alex^r Wedderburn of Blackness Agt Sr John Wedderburn now of Blackness, their elder brother."
      This is a rough draft. It appears that immediately on the death of Sir Alexander the tutors instituted the above proces in which it was "lybelled" or alleged by the pursuers "that the defeuder has an opulent fortuun be ye father and y^t he ought to pay to each of them 300 merks yeirly of aliment" during their minorities. The course of the proceedings is traced in this paper, it being stated that "the Lords found the lybell relevant & assigned to the pursuer's procurator a day for proving the value & rentill of the defunct's estate, & the same day to the defender's procurators to prove the debts aud burthens affecting the said estate." It does not appear how the process ended, but the ages of the pursuers are stated to have beeu "proven by a declaration uuder the said Tuttors y^r hands, viz., y^t the said Rachel was borne in September 1698, Matilda in July 1703 and Alexander was borne in July 1705. (Margaret having died pending the process, her age is not given.) There is another similar rough draft with this paper, and also a paper endorsed "Scheme of the probatiou aud rentall of Blackness for the process of aliament 1711," which gives "The Rentall as proven p^r ye teuneuts' depositions each on y^r own rentall w^t a sub^r rentall given iu be ye tuttors agreeable and concurring togidder as follows.—Bears (so much) Meales (so much) and Money (so much)." Theu follow the figures. There is also a note to the effect that "there is avisandum made with the foresd probatiou and wrytes produced ou 15 Dec. 1710.

18.   **1710.** May 29.—Letter, Alexander Wedderburn to George Seton.
      He returns some document relating to the sale "executed as you desire," and speaks of summoning creditors to the amount of £40,000. He then proceeds, "I thiuk 300 merks is reasonable for the two children with you (i.e., Peggie and Rachell) when they are 14 years of age, but its too much for them under it. I am sorrie to hear of Peggie's tenderuess ; it's storied here she has lost the watch and chain and rings, which, if true, is probablie the occasioue of her distemper. I thiuk of seeing you the leugth of Juue or thereby ......"
      (In good condition, but the ink faint.)

19.   **1710.** Juue 10.—Summonds and execution in a process by Wedderburn Ag^t John Pilmour, Wrytter iu Dundie, and Raehael Pitillo.
      This is a summons by Sir Johu Wedderburn the minor and his curators against the two defeudants charging them with having takeu advantage of their positious as clerk and housekeeper to the late Sir Alexander Wedderburn to plunder his estate and make off with the property.
      The summons, which begins "Auu by the Grace of God, Queen of Great Britaiu, ffrance and Ireland, &c." uames as the pursuer "Sir Johu Wedderburn of Blackness with consent of James Halyburton of Pitcur, Mr. James Martine of Grange, Mr. George Seton, advocat, Peter Wedderburn, merchant in Dundie, and Alexander Wedderburue, town clerk of Dundie, his tutor, for their interest," and recites that "John Pilmor wreater in Dundie late Servitor to Sir Alex^r Wedderburue of Blacknes Did intromett and receave of the said Sir Alex^r Wedderburue his master mouey conform to accompt (herew^t given out & holden as repeited brevitatis causa) the soume of nyne thousand nyne hundred and five pound ten shilling Scots money as also the said Johu Piluor did at his master's death take at his owne haud Two dozen of fine hollan shirts two dozen musline gravats a fine sword a suit of cloaths aud a piece of musliue The value of which goods amounts to five hundred pound Scots moe And also Rachaell Patillock late servitrix to the s^d Sir Alex^r Wedderburne (now spouse to Daniell Sharp vintner in fferrie Port on Craiges) did at her s^d master's death intromett with and carrie off a peice of holland and two pair fine sheets one Dozen doruick napkines of a stern kuot and a table Cloath of the same Three doruick table cloaths two holland shirts & a bedding of cloatha The value of qch goods amounts to ffour hundred pound Scots, as also ye sd Rachell Pittillo did dispone and Imbasle ye provisions of ye Deceast Sir Alex^r Wedderburu her master such as beef muttou Meale butter & cheese & such like to ye value of two hundred pounds mouey fors^d ; Aud albeit it be of verity That the s^d pursuer & his saids tutors hath oft & diverse tymes desyred & required the sds Johu Pilmour

& Rachell Pitillo and the sd Danielle sharpe her husband for his interest To make pay^t and delivery to the sd purss^r of the sounes of money goods and gear uplifted by them and each of them for y^r own parts in manner as lybelled or of the availls and pryces of the saids goods sua intrometted with by them in manner forsaid yet nevertheless they wrougously refuse postpone & deferr to do the same as is alleg^d."

It then proceeds thus :—" Our will therefore is and wee charge you strictly and command that Incontiueut thir our letters seen ye pass and in our name and authority laufully summond warn and charge the saids John Pillmor and Rachaell Pattillock and Daniell Sharpe her husband for his interest personally or at their duelling places if they be withiu this place of our realm called Scotland upon Twenty oue Aud six dayes waruing And if furth thereof be open proclamation at the mercat Cross of Edinburgh aud pear shoar of Leith upon sixty and flyfteen Dayes waruiug for flirst aud second Dyets and their Tutores & Curators if they any have for their Iutcreets be open proclamation at the mercat cross of ......(blauk)... .. And at other places needfull To Compear before the Lords of our Councill and Session at Edinburgh, &c., &c. Given under our Signet at Edinb^r the Tenth Day of June, and of our reign the nynth year 1710."

This summonds has various eurlorsemeuts on it, (1) " Summonds Wedderhurue &c. ag^t ...(blauk)." (2) " June 1711, Tablatiug p^d, Edward Callendar, Ed^r 22 June 1711. Given out to Mr. Jo : Elphinstone advocat to see this Summonds aud execut^ne sub^t acco^td by me, G, Seton." (3) " 30 June 1711 seen and retureued by me, Jo Elphinstoue." (4) " Enrolled 24th Nov. 1711."—Inside on the margin at the top is written " Call per Seton, Sir John Wedderhurue of Blackness and his tutors ag^t John Pilmour, Wryter in Dundie for himself, Rachaell Pittillo lau^{ll} daughter to ye deceist Alex^r Pittillo soue tyme mer^t in Duudie, now spouse to Daniel Sharpe, vintner in ferrie port ou Craig, and the s^d Daniell for his iuterest, &c." (somewhat illegible). Attached to the summons is a note of its execu- tion or service on the defenders ou 24th and 27th June 1710.

20.　**1710.** June 17.—Letter, Alexander Wedderburn to George Seton.

" I was surprised to see your niece Margaret at this place. She is very ill and Dr Watsoue does not think she'l recover. She is very impatient for some things she left behind her. Please send them by this carrier direct to herself.

When your conveniance allows advise me how you have cleared with Dr Brown and how matters staud betwixt us. I shall obey your desire anent your father and sister's debts. I think it proper y^r be a compeirance for John wheu ye alimeut is pursued and I expect you'l let me kuow when it comes iu."

21.　**1710.** July 6.—Letter same to same.

" Sir,—Peggie is now dying very fast and is somewhat (troubled ?) aud wonders you have uot sent over her cloaths, &c. She gave me an Iuventar of which a double is adjoined, which you may compare with the particulars, and I thiuk she should be satisfied since they will be secure for the other children at her death. I shall eudeavour to send the seasines (?) and reutall with Crockat the begiuning of next week. I wish the aliment were settled before Peggie died, that I may be warranted for what is dispensed. This with uiy service is from, Sir, Your most humble servant, Alex^r Wedderburne "

INVENTAR.—Impr. Aue luit string hood and scarfe ; Itt. a creep hood and scarfe ; Itt. a gais scarfe ; Itt. a blew silk damasc gouu aud petticoat ; Itt. a cotton satine gouu, with a green shag lyuiug and a black luitstriug petticoat ; Itt. a mascurad gouu and coat ; Itt. seven holland shirts ; Itt. a plaiu musliue head suit with edgiug ; Itt. a striped musliue head suit, with rufles, with edging uumade ; a suit critt works wanting musliue ; a white petticoat half shewed ; a breed of silk ; Itt. a suit of green aud white ribbons ; Itt. a suit of yellow aud white ribbons ; Itt a suit of blew ribbons ; Itt. a sult of cherry aud scarlet ribbons ; Itt. a pair of plain louslin rufles ; four faus ; a scarlet gaze whyte flowered uapkaiu ; Itt. aue buckle sett iu silver, with aue gold bolt ; a big volume of the Whole Duty of Man ; Itt. a booke call'd the guide to Eternity ; Itt. the English Paraphrase bound ; Itt. a white peeced necklace ; Itt. a black necklace and eare riugs ; Itt. a pair of black shambo gloves ; Itt. two pair of silk stockings ; Itt. aue pair uf luggs ; Itt. aue large trunk ; aue clock bag ; Itt. aue blew gallie mauky pettiecoat.

22.　**1710.** July 15.—Letter same to same.

" I have beeu obliged to be in ye country ever since my last, and since my arrivall I gott a letter from Mr. Wedderburne for Dr. Brown's annal rent which I desire you'l pay him, since I'm of opinion you'l have also as much on your hauds as will doe it, if not I desire to be advised and acc^t seut me that it and oy^r @-rents may be ordered.

Peggie is very uneasie that you have uot sent her watch and oy^r things as she desired.

23.　**1710.** July 18.—Double Letter will and testament of Mrs. Margaret Wedderburne (so docketed.) This is as follows :—

I Mrs Margaret Wedderburne lawful daughter procreat betwixt the deceast Sir Alex^r Wedderburne of Blackuess and Dame Elizabeth Setou his Spouse, knowing the frailtie of this life aud the uncer- taintie of the time of my death, am therefor resolved so to order my affairs iu my own time, that all differences that may fall out thereanent after my death may be obviated and prevented ; therefor I make my letter will and testament, as followes—In the first, I recommend my Soul to God my Creator, hoping to be saved by the merits of Jesus Christ my ouly Lord and Redeemer ; aud I desire my friends when it pleases to God to call me to cause deceutly to iuterr my body in my Father's buriall place in the church of Duudie ; aud as to the wordlie estate, I with cousent of Mr James Martiue of Grange, Peter Wedderburne, Merchant in Dundie, and Alexander Wedderburne, Clerk of the said Burgh, my Curators, nominate Sir John Wedderburne of Blackness, my brother german, his heirs and assigneys qtsoever, to be my only exŏr and universall legator and intrŏr with my haill goods gear, debts, soumes of money, and moveables of qtsoever nature pertaining, or that shall happen to pertaine and be resting to me the time of my decease and falling under testament, to whom I leave and bequeath the samen : With the burthen allwise, of the delivery of ane diamond ring to Rachell Wedderburne, my sister german, legat be the said Dame Elizabeth Seton my mother to me, together with my mother's wearing cloaths and abulziements, and my own wearing cloaths and abulziements of my body. As also, with the burthen of the delivery of ane whoip with ane agit handle and silver foirles to Mathilda Wedderburne, my sister german ; And sicklike with the burthen of the delivery of ane gold wuip and ane silver meddail to Alexander Wedderburne, my brother german ; And likewise with the burthen of payment to Barbara Brisbane, eldest lawful daughter to the deceast Mr James Brisbane, Advocat, of the soume of thirty pound Scots due to me by Mr George Seton, Advocat, my Uncle ; And also, with the burthen of the delivery of the Whole duty of Man, in folio, to the said Mr James Martine, formerly gifted be him to my mŏyr ; As also, wt the burthen of the deliverie to him, of the English liturgy with Cutts ; And all the said par'lars legat to the said Rachell, Mathilda, and Alexander Wedderburnes, to be keeped by the said Alexander Wedderburne, Clerk, ay and while they be major, or married, the wearing cloaths exeepted, which is also to be distribute by him, as they shall have occasion for them. In witnes qrof (written be David Brisbane sert to the said Alexander Wedderburne, Clerk) Wee have subd these Nts Att Dundie the Eighteen day of July Jajvijc & ten years Befor these witnesses Thomas Hendersone also sert to the said Alexr Wedderburne & the sd David Brisbane—Sic subtr Margaret Wedderburne. Ja. Martine consents, Peter Wedderburne consents, Al: Wedderburne consents ; Tho. Hendersone witnes, Da. Brisbane witness."

24. **1710. Aug. 30.**—Letter, Alexander Wedderburn to George Seton, dated from "Blackness."

A short letter referring to a thousand pounds of consigned money which he hopes to be able to pay in early October, "and I know that's better payment than Sir Alexr Anstruther used to make." It refers to the sale of the chair, and to the then pending process of sale and aliment, and to the harvest " which is great but good, and if prices be good, I hope will do us good service. Peggie is named as having taken a change for the worse " which I think will carry her off."

25. **1710. Sept. 15.**—Letter same to same.

This letter deals solely with money matters and encloses " a short acct of that money I gave you," including " diamond cross £240; Mr. Brown's ship £150," &c. It adds " mind the chair," which seemingly was not yet sold.

26. **1710. Oct. 24.**—Letter same to same.

" I expected that 1000 lib. due by consignatione before this time, and now I'm put off till Mertimes. Rachell wants a gown and coat and has writt me for it, I suppose not wtout your advice which might have been spared, for if you will not take the freedome to order a gown and coat for her, which I reckon will not be of great value, I know not how to act ; for that which is called management, and means the intromitting, for the weans, I am wearied of it, especially with so much labouring. .... Let me know how our process of sale and aliment stands, and what's proper to be done the first of the Session. For, if it be not done quickly, there must be ways and means fallen upon to preserve our pupill's credit."

27. **1710. Nov. 4.**—Letter same to same.

A short letter to the effect that now the Session has begun he wishes something effectual were done about getting their decreet of sale and aliment, " for nothing shall stand at my door. If there be a commission to ania bodie here to take up the Reutall, it's time it were extracted and sent, and it shall not want dispatch, though I wish we were not brought to that trouble."

28. **1710. Nov. 9.**—Letter same to same.

Again a short letter. " I return you (he writes) the Act and Commissione and Dilligence in regard Glasawell hes this day gone to Edinr, and James Guthrie, baillie, died before granting it out, but if you will make James, Henry Guthrie, it will doe weell. for I suppose you have mistaken the name." In a posterript he says, " It's proper the debts due in Edt be summoned before ye Lords, primo loco, and yt it be a part of yo Quota to be condescended upon, viz., 60,000 merks."

29. **1710. Dec. 10.**—A very small piece of paper written closely on both sides, and headed " mony given out on Blackness' acct."

This is an account kept by George Seton, and in his own hand-writing, of various sums of money expended on account of the affairs of Blackness, chiefly in court frees, law business, advertisements, gratuities to clerks, and so forth, but there are no charges on his own account for business done. It is not signed but is closed at the bottom thus : " This acct is stated and Closed betwixt the Clerk of Dundee and me. 10th Decr 1710."

Mounie Papers.

29ᵃ. 1710. Dec. 10.—An account between George Seton, and Sir John, from which it appears that Rachell Wedderburne had boarded with George Seton from 19 January 1710, to 19 January 1711 ; and Peggie from 24 November 1709, to 1 May 1710. The Diamond Cross, mentioned under date of the Clerk's letter, 6 March 1710, was sold for £240 scots. (See ante No. 25.) This account was settled on Sir John's behalf by his cousin and factor, the Clerk, 10 Dec. 1710.

30. 1710. Dec. 18.—Letter, Alexander Wedderburn to George Seton, signed by A. W. but written by a clerk.

"Being now to clear my accounts of my bygone Intromissions for Blackness I send you inclosed the papers following" (a great many papers about receipt and payments are here inventoried) ......
"I find a receipt of your sister, Mrs. Jean's, for £5 stg. which bears to be received from Robert Cramond for Blackness' use, which I'm apt to think has been Imployed for yᵉ conjunct process against your flather, therfor before clearance with her I think it's not amiss wee have the agent's accoᵗˢ (who it was I know not) that at least what may be due yᵗ be payed. I doubt not but you recᵈ your seall from Mr. Duncan. I intreat you'l not forget one process of seall and aliment and particularly that process against John Pilmor and Rachell Patilock." (See ante No. 19.)

31. 1710. Dec. 23.—Letter, same to same.
This letter again mentions the sale, and begs Seton to get up the shop-rents and the money for the chair, which had thus been sold. It ends "Alexᵣ is distressed wᵗ yᵉ small pocks, and this is the eight day. Mathild recovers very slowly."

32. 1711. Jan. 4.—Letter same to same.
After acknowledging the receipt of the Act and Dilligence, &c., as he was taking horse for his rout of excise, and after dealing with other business, he says, "The picture case I left wᵗ Doctor Eccles' Lady who will part wᵗ it, for she was very indifferent of it. I shall (send ?) what @-rent is resting by Henderson. Pray get part of the 100 lib for yᵉ chair ; send over the Hunens wᵗ yᵉ Cloath(s) for yᵉ merᵗ lives here and promises to take it at yᵉ price. I wrote Mʳ Martine anent Deacon Kerr."

33. 1711. Jan. 19.—Letter same to same.
"Sir, I designe to see you tuesday next and then shall ansᵣ yᵉ demands of all your formers. Please acquaint Mʳ Henry Scrymseour to tell yᵉ Lady Singletone yᵗ I'll ansᵣ her demands when I come over. Being in heast, I am, Sir, Yoᵣ most humble Serᵗ, A. Wedderburne. Doe me yᵉ favour of acquainting Dʳ Eccles of my coming over."

34. 1711. Feb. 9.—Letter same to same. Signed by Alexander Wedderburn, but written in another hand.
A short letter of no importance.

35. 1711. Feb. 22.—Letter from Katharine Scott (wife of Alexander Wedderburn) to George Seton.
"Sir, I broke open your letter in the Clerk's absence And found that it was about business relating to Blackness' children. I thought it fitt to give you account that the Clerk is from home, and does (sic) not expect him before the third of March. But I've forwarded your letter to him, Sʳ John was extremely ill yesternight with his rupture but is a little better today. I offer my humble Service to your lady and Self and am, Sir, Your most humble servᵗ, Katharin Scott.
Dundie, 22 ffebry 1711.
This letter was originally among the Mounie papers, but is now among J.W.'s (see post p. 141, No. 3 (d)) having been given to him by Mounie in 1825. It is signed, according to the custom of the time in Scotland, with the writer's maiden name.

36. 1711. March.—Document endorsed "Declaration Mr. John Cunningham to the Clerk of Dundee."
It appears from this document that Sir Alexander Wedderburn owned a shop in Edinburgh which was possessed (occupied) by Martha Weir, relict of John Glendoning, merchant in Edinburgh. This document relates to the rent, and contains four receipted bills, for repairs done in 1707-1708. In one of these the shop is described as "the Shop at the head of the Bank closs." Mr. John Cunninghame describes himself as "writter to the Signet." The tradesmen who did the repairs are Andrew Wardrop, glasier ; John Pratt, smith ; William Smellie, mason ; and John Wardrop, wright. The attesting clause runs thus, "In witness whereof I have subᵗ thir pᵗts (wrytt be James Schaw my Servant) Att Edinᵣ the Twenty seventh day of March jᵐvijᶜ Eleven years before thir witnesses, Hugh Cunningham also my servant and also be the sd James Schaw."

37. 1711. March 10.—Letter from Alexander Wedderburn to George Seton.
"Sir, Ever since yours came here I have been on my survey of yᵉ Lights, and not being perfected shall at this time only send you the inclosed Discharge and Assignatione to Mr. Cunninghame for 100 lib. ...... Being in heast I only add that I am, Sir, yours, &c."

Mounte
Papers.

38. **1711. June 2.**—Letter, same to same.

"I have been so throng of business and yet not quite free y⁴ I could not aus⁴ yours ... ... You've sent over a very willfull self-conceited Gentlewoman y⁴ I doe not (know?) how to manage her, she pretends she is perfect of every thing and understands but very little ...... I find there is no money to be had from the Bank on heretable security ...... I make no doubt but you'l take care of any process our pupill is concerned in."

39. **1711. June 9.**—Letter, same to same.

This letter is about borrowing money on the security of the tutors, for the purposes of the tutory and estate, and also refers to a process brought against young Sir John by one Alexander Alison, although "Blackness was never his debtor." (See post No. 45.)

40. **1711. June 20.**—Letter from Thomas Hendersone to Mr. George Seton.

The writer was clerk or servitor to Alexander Wedderburn, and he encloses by his master's order a bond by Blackness to Hunter.

41. **1711. June 28.**—Letter, same to same, enclosing another bond "in my master's absence."

42. **1711. July 26.**—Letter from Alexander Wedderburn to George Seton.

This refers to a loan from the bank for the use of the pupil, and asks Seton to "get Mr. Wedderburne's report from the Bank."

43. **1711. Aug. 4.**—Letter, same to same.

This is addressed "To Mʳ George Seton, Advocat, at his Lodgings in Gray's Close, Northside of the street, Edgᵇ." It is a short letter, the writer being "straitened wᵗ time," and refers to the loan on account of the pupil and other money matters.

44. **1711. Aug. 10.**—Letter, same to same.

This letter refers to Mʳˢ Ogstou's claim (see ante, No. 2). It adds a postscript, "I'll be from home till yᵉ 24th of this month and if business (requires?) direct to me at Montrose.

45. **1711. Sept. 1.**—Letter, same to same, dated at Dundie.

Refers to Ogston's account and various other claims against the estate, including a decree which Alexander Alison had obtained for £84 principal with @-rent from Apryle 1708." (Ante, No. 39.) It proceeds, "I have drawn a bill on you for 50 merks scots, to repay which doe me the favour to deliver the income to my Cousine Mˢⁱˢ Stewart out of your own hand a part and she will give you the 50 merks which she was owing Blackness by accᵗ book and its all yᵉ debt she owes." (Mrs. Stewart is no doubt Rachel Wedderburn, sister to Alexander Wedderburn of Wedderburu, and wife of Mr. Gilbert Stewart, merchant, in Edinburgh.)

46. **1711. Sept. 1.**—A draught on Mr. George Seton, Advocat at Edin., for a small sum, payable on sight to Alex. Alisone, writer to the signet, or order, signed "Al : Wedderburne." Dated at Dundie.

47. **1711. Nov. 19.**—Letter, Alexander Wedderburn to George Seton.

This refers to various claims and encloses a bond to Peter Wedderburne. Proposes to be at Edinburgh about the first of next month.

48. **1711. Dec. 6.**—Letter, same to same, dated at Leith.

In it he says that having been "so straiteued with time that I could not wait on you," he now writes to "put you in mind of sending the linnens and chest from Dʳ Eccles with the cloaths." He mentions some payments he has made, and others he has not been able to make, and a claim for £100 stg. by Sir David Thriepland "as assiguey to Craigie." He begs Seton to press Lady Baugour for payment and to get payment of the shop rents due last term from Mr. fiifo. "I entreat (he adds) you'l push the sale for if it be not ended this session it will be a great loss to our pupill, for the half of Omachie will be cast ou our hauds. I'm just going ou Board the boat, yᵗ allows me only to add that I am, Sir, &c." (P.S.) "Let me have your opinion about Peggie's board, and if yʳ be anything to be made of her testament."

49. **1711. December 29.**—Letter same to same, dated at Dundie.

This acknowledges the receipt of a letter from Seton asking some question "but you know what confusione Blackness' papers were in, yᵗ it's impossible for me iu a short time to give a positive ansʳ about it." ....

"In my last I desired to know if you could help me iu paying some @-rents at Edgᵇ particularly Mʳ Brown because I was exhausted in paying Peter Blair 185 lib. of @-rents, aud at this time you may easily guess I cannot be in cash when servᵗˢ and harvest fies and cess is payed out of the grains of oats and pease, yᵉ boar term being past, and if you give me not some comfort of yᵉ docᵗ of sale's being past or very near it I doe not know what to doe in our pupill's affairs for our prices for this cropt will be small. .... My aunt Mʳˢ Brisbane is not yet payed of Margaret's board from the time she came from you till her death. I will not determine it without order from the tutors because she is my relatione. I'm told by second hand she'l writt and therefor by this I take occasione to tell you that for her board and trouble I could be satisffed she had 50 lib scots though at the same time I

8

think the legacies should not all be payed. ...... Make your own use of this. I wrote you likewise by my last to send the linnens and to take the trouble to cause a servant call at Dr Eccles for the chist and cloaths, for I am at a vast charge for the bairns for want of them.

Hasten y^r dec^t of sale at any rate as you tender yⁿ wellfare of your pupill and it will also oblige, Sir, &c.

50. **1712. Jan. 29.**—Letter, same to same.

Again urges that the process of sale should be pressed forward. "If you doe not finish the warrand for sale of our lands this sessione, it will doe us more harm than we are aware of ; I hope you'l doe your utmost to get it effectual." .... "Three of our pupils to witt, Mathild, and ye two lads are ill and confined to the house, but I hope (it will) not prove dangerous."

51. **1712. Jan. 30.**—Letter, same to same.

A short letter about various claims and payments, "Mrs Stewart my cousine" is again named. Unlike almost all the others this letter ends "I am, yours, Al. Wedderburne."

52. **1711. Feb. 13.**—Letter, same to same.

Asks if the decreet for sale is yet past, and encloses an account from Robert Crystie.

53. **1712. Feb. 22.**—Letter from Mathilda Wedderburn (Mrs. Brisbane) to George Seton. This letter, though signed by Mrs. Brisbane, in her maiden name (see ante No. 35), is not written in her hand, but in a small neat hand, possibly that of Dr. John Wedderburn, afterwards of Idvies. It is as follows :—

"Sir, I doubt not but you know that Margaret Wedderburne, Blackness' daughter, stayed with me from the time of her last coming from Ede^h until her death and that she was long confined to her bed, whereby she not only required the closer attendance, but every object of necessity behoved to be according to her mind. I think my attendance weel bestowed for her affection she carried to me and my daughter in her latter will which I expect Blackness' tutors will consider when thronger matters or such of greater consequence are by hand : but I doubt'd not but her board and charges of attending would have been payed 'ere now. My nephew, the Clerk of Dundie, declines to pay me without ane order from the tutors. I have delayed these sixteen months past, and have now presumed to trouble you with this, and to desire your assistance and advice to the Clerk to pay what you think proper for her board and attendance about her Sickness. This with my service is from, Sir,

Your most humble Ser^t,

I shall expect your answer with conveuience.   Mathilda Wedderburne.

54. **1712. March 5.**—Letter from Alexander Wedderburn to George Seton.

"I am glad we have got the dec^t of sale ...... Advise me of the nature of the dec^t ; if the lands can be sold without a ronp or not, and what method shall be takeu in it ; it's fit it be done before White^sy, for half of Omachie is on our hands at White^sy."

55. **1712. March 6.**—Discharge by David Fyffe to Sir John Wedderburn of Blackness, and his tutors.

This is a discharge by David Fyffe, Chyrurgion in Edinburgh, to Sir John Wedderburn of Black-ness, from all liability to refund a sum of £531. 9. 10 Scots, overpaid to the latter, from his own, his father's, and his grandfather's intromissions with a tenement on the Bank close head in Edin-burgh, conveyed to the said Grandfather by George Wedderburne, merchant in Edinburgh, and creditor of the deceast Patrick Fyfe merchant there, and father to David, and obtained by George from Patrick for a limited time, in payment of an accumulated debt therein specified, which debt had been in time overpaid in the above amount. The discharge is granted on the surrender of the tenement to David, by Sir John, the minor, through the medium of his Tutors ; it is dated at Ediuburgh and signed by David Fyffe ; Rob. Innes, Thos Aitken. witnesses.

56. **1712. March 25.**—Letter, Alexander Wedderburn to George Seton. It is signed by A. W., but written in another hand.

It refers to extracting the decreet of sale and to selling the lands. "If you think fitt, lett the ronp be on the 29th day of Aprile next in the house of Patrick Kyd viutner here." It proposes the insertion of advertisements in the *Edinburgh Courant and Gazette*, describing the lands thus :—

(*a*) The lands of Omachie, milne, milne lands, mauner place and houses thereto belonging, con-sisting of 34 bolls bear, 36 bolls meall, 350 merks scots in money, and 11 duzone of Poultrie according to the judicial rentall of the present possessors taken upon the eight of November 1709 which is never yet antired. The Laud holds of the Duke of Douglas few for pay^t of ffourty shilling yearly.

(*b*) A lodging lying in the Nethergate of Dundie on the South syde of the Church cousisting of Kitchiug, brewhouse, seven fire rooms, and two closets, all weel lighted to every airth with sellars and one yard lying conveniently by its side with ane large close and well.

57. **1712. April 16.**—Letter same to same.

A short note in regard to certain debts, and the sale of Omachie, &c. In it he says, "Our pupill Alex^r is very ill of a fever and been so some dayes past."

58. **1712. April 22.**—Letter same to same.

Again about debts, payments, &c. It adds, "Our pupill Alex^r is still very ill and my brother thinks he cannot recover. Our pupill John doeth not learn and his Master says he will not be a scholar so that I'll waut your advice to lay before our meeting on Tuesday next, which I intreat you'l send by the first post."

59. **1712.** May 3.—Letter same to same, signed by A. Wedderburn but written in another hand.
This letter informs Seton of the result of the sale, by which Omachie fetched 19,900 merks, and the lodging 2,800 merks. It consults Seton as to the necessity of getting Sir John specially served heir in these properties in order to make up the titles, and incloses £12 stg. in bank bills to pay various charges, including the decreet of sale.

60. **1712.** May 15.—Letter same to same.
A very short note, with a postcript " Our pupill Alex' is still dying."

61. **1712.** May 26.—Letter same to same, signed by A. Wedderburn but written in another hand.
It deals with the application of the purchase money received for Omachie and the lodging in Dundee.

62. **1712.** June 19.—Letter same to same.
A short note explaining that Crockat, the carrier, did not go this last week, whence delay in sending money for payments.

63. **1712.** Aug. 22.—Letter, same to same.
" When Mrs. Eccles was here she proposed the sending your nephew John, to Mr. Laing in y° Cannongate, by whom she thinks he will be carefully taught and cheaper—the latter I doubt not wranglie ; he'll want his servant and the odds there will be unfavourable. But he has been informed that there is ane Mr. Forrest at Leith who teaches better, has boarders in excellent order and a doctor to wait on them wherever they goe, and at the same charge as Mr. Laing. This I think better and I entreat you'l enquire about him and his method and the whole charge, that if you think it convenient John may be transported before Winter."

64. **1712.** Oct. 1.—Letter, same to same.
This letter deals with various money matters and apologizes that " being now entering on my tour of excise " he cannot answer every point in Seton's last two letters.
" As to our pupil since you do not write if a Doctor waites solely on the boarders, and of the charges thereof otherwise, I'm of opinion (with submission to better judgment) to try him this winter quarter, and if wee can think of a governour to give it him then because of ane infirmitie, I judge occasioned by his rupture, that it's better to be among friends than strangers " ... .

65. **1712.** Nov 14.—Letter, same to same.
States that the price of Omachie will not all be paid at this time, and that the writer has been indisposed for some time and is yet confined to the house.

66. **1712.** Several pieces of paper which seem to have been mere memoranda kept in the rough, of outlays and disbursements, which were settled from time to time, apparently in 1710, 1711, 1712, docketed—
" Accompt of mony Laid out by Mr. Geo. Seton for Blackness." " Double of the stated acct betwixt the Clerk of Dundee & me." " Accompt of particulars laid out for Blackness."
The one which appears to be the last concludes thus :—" The within & above accompts of Charge & Discharge are cleared & the whole Instructions yrof delivered to Mr Alex' Wedderburn, Clerke of Dundie. In witnes qrof I have writt & subscrived these presents at Ed' the twentie ninth day of Jully Jajvij° & twelve years. Geo. Seton."

67. **1712.** Inventar of papers delivered by Mr. George Seton, Advocat to Alexander Wedderburne, Clerk of Dundie, and by him delivered to the persones following, to whom the samen are granted, viz. :—
Impr. ane Extract of ane Bond granted be the deceast S' Alexander Wedderburne of Blackness to George Dempster merchant in Dundie for the princ' soume of ffour thousand merks
Itt. anoyr Extract of a Bond granted be D° to the said George Dempster for 2000 Ms.
Itt. ane Extract of a Bond granted be D° to William Miller, Chirurgion in Dundie, for the soume of 3000 Ms.
Itt. Extract of another Bond granted be D° to M' William Mitchell, one of the ministers of Dundie for £666.13.4.
Itt. Extract of another Bond granted be D° to David Hunter, merch' in Dundie, for the soume of £2000.
Itt. Extract of another Bond granted be D° to the s'd David Hunter for the soume of 3500 Ms.
Itt. Extract of anoyr Bond granted be D° to John Dick, writer in Dundie, for the sum of 5000 Ms.
Itt. Extract of another Bond granted be D° to Grissell Brown, relict of John Scott yo', mer' in Dundie, and his children yrin named, for the soume of £1333.6.8.
Itt. Extract of another Bond granted be D° to John Scott, mer' and late bailie of Dundie, for the soume of £430.10.0.

Itt. Extract of anoyr Bond Granted be Dᵒ to Alexander Wedderburne, Shipmaster in Dundie, for the soume of £666 13.4.

Itt. Extract of anoyr Bond granted be Dᵉ to Robert Wedderburne, mariner in Dundie, for the soume of £666 13.4.

Itt. Extract of anoyr Bond granted be Dᵒ to David Fletcher, shipmaster in Dundie, for the soume of £1333.6.8.

Itt. Extract of another Bond granted be Dᵉ to Alexander Ballingall, Chirurgion in Dundie, for ye soume of £2666.13.4.

Itt. Extract of anoyr Bond granted be Dᵒ to Mr John Brown, minister of the Gospel, for ye soume of £2200.0.0.

Extract of anoyr Bond granted be the deceast Sir John Wedderburne of Blackness to John Wedderburne, lawᵈˡ sone of wmq ᵉ Peter Wedderburne, for the soume of £333.6.8.

Itt. Extract of anoyr Bond granted the said Deceast Sʳ Alexʳ Wedderburne to Peter Wedderburne, merᵗ in Dundie, for the soume of £333.6.8.

Itt. Extract of anoyr Bond granted be Dᵒ to Elizabeth Goldman for the soume of £133.6.8.

Itt. Discharge of ane Bond of Relief granted be Dᵒ to me the said Alexander Wedderburne for ye soume of 3000 mks.

Itt. Discharge of Lord John Gray to the said Alexander Wedderburne for £50.13.0.

Itt. Discharge Mʳ Samuell Johnstone to the said Alexʳ Wedderburne for £111.0.0.

Itt. Discharge Mʳ Alexander Scott, minister of Liff, to the xᵈ Alex. Wedderburne for £15.9.0.

The above writts recᵈ & delyᵗ as above By these (phts) sntᵈˡ by me att Dundie the nynteen day of Apᵣyle 1712.

Al. Wedderburne.

Endorsed on back, "Inventar of Papers delivered by Mr George Seton to Alexander Wedderburne. 1712."

This is now among J. W's papers. See post p. 141, No. 3 (c).

68. **1713.** March 19.—Letter, same to same. Signed by A. Wedderburn, but written in another hand.

This is almost entirely about the accounts, &c. It mentions Lady Bangour's bond and Lord Polton's @-rent.

69. **1713.** Letter, same to same, signed by A. Wedderburne, but written in another hand. It is as follows :—

Sir, I was from home when Crockat went last from this, else my acctˢ for the first two years had been sent you. I have sent by this bearer Nynteen pound six shilling for satisfying the Consigned money you writt was demanded. I also send ffour pound four shilling as the odds betwixt the ballance in your hands for Margaret's accoᵗ which was twenty eight pound one shilling and the addition of Therty two pound five shilling to the Law accᵒᵗ my Cousine David Brisbane sent you, seventy three pound six shilling eight pence for satisfieing the four years rent due to Turnbull, for which please return a Discharge. Peggie's cloaths came safe to hand according to your list sent.

I desire you'l send me receipt for 33. 6. 8. placed in last accoᵗ for Rachell's intertainment from 19th of January to 19th may 1711 As also of 22. 3. 10. for postage of letters and other incident charges from Blackness death to the 30th of July last, which is the date of the discharge of your last accoᵗ, in the charge of which accoᵗ I observe there is received 53. 17. 4. from James Brown for Blackness share of the Cargoe of the Union Galley whereas by his letter to me which I send inclosed there is due our pupil 105. 1. 0. for which I think he should give receipt till accoᵗ of @-rents.

I send you two Coppies of accoᵗˢ by your sister agsᵗ your father. Lett me know how I am to Discharge the remainder of your fathers accoᵗ of books amounting to 16 lib and odd moᵉ of which you have only received 8. 14. 0.

Ther's a peice of barren ground at the east syde of the house of Logie which was commonly eat by the Cottars Cows, it marches wᵗ the estate of Dudhop ; I have inclosed all parts of it save that next Dudhop, And our march stones appears to make it very clear but the tennent will not allow me to make the Dyke straight, though he acknowledges it's not worth the quarrelling nor does he think the Earle of murray would. The scheme of the march is on the other syde. Please take the trouble to speak to his Lordship and get his consent that the dyke may be finished after the bear is sowen for I have made Cottars build the dyke for their most and I only desigue to sow (ro)wan trees in it. . .

I am, Sir,

Your most humble servant,

Dundie 27th Aprile 1713.

Al. Wedderburne.

I have also sent my acctˢ for the first two years. I shall not promise much on the exactness of the last but shall wait your opinion befor I book them in my princⁱˡ ...... (?) book. You'l get the accoᵗˢ of third year, when I come home, which will be a litel after the terme.

[Below in the clerk's own hand is a note and a sort of plan, thus] :—

The laboured ground goes according to the llues of each extreme.	March ☐ Stone	Logie Laboured ground Grass Dudhop	☐ March. Stone

70. **1713.** June 13.—Letter same to same. This is written in a high, slanting hand, perhaps a clerk's, but badly written. It bears the usual seal in red wax, tolerably well preserved.

Not of much interest. It refers to Lord Pitoun wanting his @-rent so long "but it is not my fault for our Brewers are so much failed that I know not what to say of them."

71. **1713.** Oct. 24.—Letter same to same. Written in the same small distinct hand as No. 53.

It refers to the difficulty of getting money to meet certain claims. "I know not how wee shall dispose of our fermes this year. I wish you would write me how prices rules with you upon every occasion you write me for I cannot think but the bear will give a good price this year if it be with you as with us."

"I would fain think of selling the lands of Logie by roup, if you'l agree to it. I have all my accot⁸ ready and desire to know if I can be discharged of them by the Tutors now living or if I most wait till our pupill choise his Curators which I designe how soon he attains the age of fourteen."

"I have by advice of friends here bespoke a Pedagogue to wait on our pupill at One hundreth pound per annum which I could not gett for less."

There is a postcript as follows :—"Dr. Eccles was desiring his Ladie's age which I find by a note wrote by her father that she was born on the 4th Dec' 1670." Margaret Eccles was a sister of Sir Alexander, and the "note" mentioned is no doubt her father's family register. (See note Blackness Papers, No. 10.)

72. **1713.**—"Abreviat of the Accompts & Intromissions of Alex' Wedderburne wᵗ the Estate of Blackness Reall & personall."

The above is written in one line along the top of the paper. A half sheet of pot or small foolscap. It is in the handwriting of Alex' Wedderburn (the Clerk) and is for Cropts, 1709, 1710, 1711, 1712, 1713. This accompt (which is a sort of summary) includes under Cropt 1711, the price received for the Lands of Omachie, and the house in Dundee, which were sold. (Ante No. 59.)

73. **1714.** March 3.—Letter, Alexander Wedderburn to George Seton. This letter is among the papers of John Wedderburn of Auchterhouse, having been given to him by Mr. Alex. Seton of Mounie. See post. p. 141, No. 3 (f).

Sir, I have yours of the 1ˢᵗ instant. The want of money is the only reasone I want yᵉ papers of yᵘ house which I shall call for next week if I should borrow it, for not one farthing I can make of our pupill's estate at present and the people here are crying alse much out for yᵗ @-rents as wᵗ you. I intreat yon'l get payᵗ of yᵉ bond of Pauraland (?) and let it be applyed for @-rents.

I think it very hard wee should be compelled to pay yᵗ Consignatioue so long agoe and being marked taken up—however I shall heare further about it.

Nobody has yet taken our Lauds of Logie ye Displenishing wherof was to be applyed for paying M' Weems and you, which straitens me so yᵗ I know not what to doe and only wish it could be delayed till our pupill choose curators which should be done before January next, he being 14 yᵉ last of December next.

You'll hardly believe how I have been tossed wᵗ our bear, our brewers having combined together and forced the gentlemen, by whom our price is cominouly ruled, to sell their bear to mertᵗ for export at eight merks yᵉ boll: however, I have delivered most part of bear and will I think get six pound half a merk which is reckoned a great price wᵗ us and none will exceed it if they but (?) ....

I did not expect you would have despised my advice in extracting the decreet or any such thing where your pupill is concerned, the sooner it's done and diligence employed on it the better (for I hope the books is liquid). Gordon and Hay being in yᵉ town proves it were proper for our exoneration that their absolvitor were in yᵉ decᵗ. Let me know what's due to ye prior and your paius shall, as very reasonable it should, be payed. It would be a mighty compliment if you would get Mr. Weyms to delay his pnutˢ till Whits. 1715, and peremptorily his and yours shall be paid then for I make little doubt of getting Logie sett ere that time and yᶜ is the only fond you know wee have for paying pnutˢ, for if curators were chosen, which shall be as you think fitt there might be oyᵗ methods taken for making us easie. Our pupill is mightilly reformed since he gott his governour who is very carefull and knowing in his trade. I'le borrow money on my Credit to clear Mr. Weyms' @-rent if he'll comply wᵗ my desire. This, with my service to your Self and Lady, is from

Dundie, 3ᵈ March, 1714.

Sir, your very humble Serᵗ,
A. Wedderburne.

Endorsed on back in Mounie's writing "3ᵈ March, 1714, Blakness' age and about payᵐᵗ of the mony due to me."

74. **1714.** July 24.—Letter, same to same.

"Altho' returned from my Circuit a good time ago, yet could not answer yours of 18th Ultᵒ nor can well do it yet.

As for that Consignatione of Blair's, which Mr. ffogo of St. Andrews had some Commission about, am inclined to think it was payed, but must have time to search Blackness Papers..... If our pupill should be obliged to produce his book ...... believes he would get justice of Sir Alex' Anstruther whose ballance though small would doe much to clear matters.

As to my inhumane views about Blackness, I don't care though I were to clear myself before the Lords, and if you had been kind you might have come this way and seen your Nephew and Nieces, and then I would also have endeavoured to satisfie you of the great charge of Lands, hushulde plenishing, and books being trully accounted for. Aud if you will in your journey Northward (which I judge may be in the vaccauce) give yourself the trouble of coming this way, I shall show you my accounts of intromissioue to the day you come here, for that's my method that if anie I am concerned with will allow me as much time as transcribe my accounts, I'm clear in a moment. And I'm sure I'm able to satisfie any man y¹ I am not gainer by Blackness' flactorie, nor have the use of his money.

I return you thanks for your concern in me for the security to our pupill, aud shall do him justice and secure all the tutors which you may depend upon from

Sir, Your most humble serv¹, &c."

75. **1715.** Jan. 1.—Letter same to same, as follows :—

"Sir, I have yours of ye 6ᵗʰ ulto. If Mr. Pringle and Mr. Stewart are not satisfied w'out my letters to delay yʳ pay¹ till Whitsunday next I cannot help it for it's not to be expected I'll give such to Blackness' Cʳᵉʳˢ. You write me you had obliged Helen McGilla to take a day to prove y¹ our pupill is Debitor to Mr. Wilsone, but I understand ye debt is against me nomination which I did not expect for you may know y¹ I'm alwayes at freedome to depone y¹ I am not Debitor to our pupill, and except at sale of the Lands, and for a very little time after, I never was debitor, but always in advance, besides Mr. Wilsone is only liferenter in ye ˢᵈ soume, and whether there be als much due of @-rent or not I doe not know, but ye summe being, as I am told, small, the hazard is not great.

Aud now y¹ our pupill is 14 years of age I desire you'l raise letters in Supliment of ye Magistrat's pretext here for charging his curators and execute the same ag¹ your Brother and your self to ye 15ᵗʰ instant which is the day appointed by Pitcurr and Mr. Campbell who are very willing to accept as curators y¹ day and thereafter goe in w¹ you such way as shall be necessar to prosecute our pupills estate by giving ye credit w'out which it will not doe, and I believe you'r convinced yʳ will be no hazard so that I beg you'l come here and accept as one and stay als short time as you please for I designe yᵉ beginning of yᵉ next week to send you doubles of my acc¹ˢ y¹ you may not be detained and if you do not think it convenient to stay such time as you'l judge necessar for examining and discharging my acc¹ˢ, only stay and suggest (?) measures at the best ? (least ?) for the future management and disposall of our pupill ; these things are so very essentiall y¹ I must intreat you'll make no excuse and it being on a Saturday you may come off upon ffryday and so it shall be in your own power to lose one or two sessione dayes at most.

Pitcurr proposes my Brother yᵉ Doctor to be joined with him, Mr. Campbell, Peter Wedderburne, your self and me, but whether he'l accept or not I know not, and I think it's proper ye Major part accepting be a quorum for him against a sine quo non. If you can remember ye acc¹ due by your father for books was not payed ; he sayd yʳ was something due for Margaret but I never gott receipt for it.

As for Mr. Gibson's acc¹ its very proper ye Dec¹ˢ obtained be extracted I mean yʳ Condemnatione, for its not worth our while to extract yʳ Absolviturs and what is due to your self preceeding this including yʳ Suppliment pbtly desired and executiug yʳof trnnsmitt yᵉ same w¹ yᵉ Minister of Scoones discharged and it shall be payed, though I'm already near 2000 mks in advance not to be repayed till ye last is due. To be free w¹ you I always found you ouly friend John had by his mother and uo excuse will be taken for your not cuming yᵉ time above appointed. Excuse the freedome of   Sir, Your very affectionat and most humble Servant

Dundie 1ˢᵗ Janʸ 1715.   A. Wedderburne.

I offer my service to your self and Lady and wish you both a good new year and many returns of it.
(Addressed) Mr. George Seton. Advocat at Edgʳ.

76. **1715.** Jan. 17.—Letter hastily written by Alexander Wedderburn and signed by him and three others to George Seton. It is endorsed, " Letter from Pitcur and oyʳˢ desiring me to accept to be on of of (*sic*) Blackness Curators."

"Sir, This day Blackness has made choice of us, with you and Doctor Wedderburne to be his Curators ; and wee have with that view, and promise by yours to the Clerk to accept, accopted to be Curators. Wee have been talking about our pupill's settlement and whither to educat him as a Writter or Merchant, wee have not determiued w'out your advice ; if the former, where and to whom ; if the lattor be agreed to, wea are also in a strait how it will suit with our pupill's circumstances, quhilk the Clerk says are ill beyond our expectatione. We will depend on your advice in the above, and not in the least doubt of your acceptauce, and assistance in the management. Direct your answer to Craigy or the Clerk.

(Signed) And wee are, Sir, your most humble serv¹ˢ, James Hallyburton, David Campbell, J. Kydd, A. Wedderburne.

Dundie 17 January 1715.

(Addressed) To Mʳ George Seton, Advocat at Edgʳ

77. **1715.** Sept. 1.—Letter from Alexander Wedderburn to George Seton. It is endorsed, "1 Sept. 1715 The Clerk is willing to Loose Blackness from his Indentures." It has a seal in red wax, which is broken, but shows a head, with round it the words, D.G., King of Han(r ?).

" So the carriage of our pupill makes my heart cold in doing him any farther service, aud even to regret what I have done, for neither good words nor stroaks will prevail with him ; and now he's possitive to goe to the sea. This I have communicat to the rest of his curators, and they are extremely incensed at him for such resolutione, and know not what to doe. I have proposed to the other gentlemen that he get a trying voyage with such as would strip him, and after that probably he may take up himself. I also offer to free him from the Indentures, or let them stand and dispense Mounie for that time. I intreat you'll seriously consider this, and let me know if I shall send him to you, Papers. for without your special approved I will not yield to anything, seeing he has no other on his Mother's side to give advice about him." The letter also mentions "my daughter's marriage."

78. A list of debts, well preserved, but only a fragment without a docket. It is in another hand, and more recent—perhaps of 1716 or 1718.

Mistress Lander in Dundie	..	...	...	...	861	0	0
Robert Wedderburn, Shipmaster	...	...	...	...	666	13	4
Mr. John Paterson of Craigie	...	..	...	...	666	13	4
The Laird of Pitcur	...	...	...	...	1333	6	8
Mr. Alexᵣ Keith in Dundie his heirs ..	...	..	...		371	16	8
David Hunter merᵗ in Dundie for one bond	...	..	2336	6	8			
Do. Hunter per another Boud	...	...	2000	0	0			
Do. Hunter per another Bond	..	...	1200	0	0			
Do. Hunter as assignee to Andrew Hunter of Dod	...	666	13	4			
					6200	0	0
Doctor Wedderburn, assignee to William Robsoue	..	...	1333	6	8
Alexander Kirkwood's heirs	...	...	...	1333	6	8
Mr. Henry Scrymsonr, writer to the Signet	...	...	666	13	4
Margaret Balfour, daŭr to Mr And. Balfour, and her husband	...	4068	6	8
Alexᵣ Wedderburn, Clerk, assigney to Mr Thomas Weems	...	..	1333	6	8
Mr George Maule assigney to David Fletcher	...	...	...	1333	6	8
Mr John Brown in Dundie	..	...	...	2200	0	0
The Laird of Glaswell's heirs	...	...	...	2538	6	8
George Dempster, merchant in Daudie	...	...	...	4000	0	0
Jnᵒ Scott elder merᵗ there his heirs ..	...	...	...	430	10	0
John Dick writer there ...	..	...	...	3333	6	8
David Bisset, tennent in Monorgou ...	...	...	...	333	6	8
William Millar, Surgeon in Dundie ...	...	...	...	2000	0	0
Elizabeth Durham and her sister, daŭrs to Omachie	...	...	1600	0	0
Mr Thomas Wilson, sometime vintner in Dundie	...	...	2333	6	8
Patrick Murray, soue to Auchtertyre	...	...	...	3333	6	8
William Wilson	...	...	...	...	666	13	4
John Scott merᵗ in Dundie his relict and childreu	..	..	1333	6	8
Mr James Goldman, minister, his assigney	...	...	...	136	0	0
Alexᵣ Wedderburn, Shipmaster	...	...	...	666	13	4
Alexᵣ Wedderburn, Clerk, assigney to Mr William Law	...	..	1937	4	0
Peter Wedderburn, mert in Dundie ...	...	...	..	333	6	8
Agnes Henderson and her husband Turnbull	...	...	..	333	6	8
My Lord Polton, assigney to Mollenie	...	...	...	2666	13	4
Mr Wm Mitchell, minister of Dundie, his heirs	...	...	666	13	4
Margaret Wilson and her husband James Chisholm	...	...	500	0	0
Mr George Seton, Advocat	...	...	...	666	13	4
Mr Henry Guthrie, late Provost of Dundie	...	...	...	233	6	8
Doᵣ Wedderburn, assigney to Doᵣ Brown	...	...	...	666	13	4
James Brown in Edinᵣ ...	...	...	..	...	1200	0	0
					54271	10	8
Alexᵣ Wedderburn, Clerk, per Bond of the pupill and Curators			1333	6	8
Total	...		55604	17	4

79. 1716. Sir John Wedderburn of Blackness.

Dᵣ yearly to his Creditors for @-rent &c.

Imprimis: the @-rent of £55604. 17. 4. at 5 per cent. is 2780 4 10
Itt. to the Parson of Dundie yearly . 111 0 0
Itt. to the Minister of Liff yearly ... 15 9 0

This besides the children's maintainance.

There is two years @-rent of the above totall debt resting at Martimas 1716.

Per Contra Cr.

The yearly rent of the Estate for bear (the other grains, such as oats wheat & peise, will not produce so much as defray the expenses of the labourings, paying servants, & shearers fies & their maintainance) will be 460 bolls accoᵏing the same at 5. 13. 9. per boll 26064 13 4
By mouey rent of the Lands of Blackness & Logie yearly ... 92 3 4
Common charge¹ of wooll yearly ... 24 0 0
Common charge of old sheep sold yearly 30 0 0
Common charge for straw sold is ... 600 0 0

(This account is in the same hand as the preceding list of creditors. As it is not balanced it is of little value, although the first entry on the Per Contra side is of interest as shewing the relative value of corn, &c., at the time, and also that rent was then calculated on the grain, more than on money.)

¹ i.e., Average.

80. **1716.** Feb. 20.—Alexander Wedderburn to George Seton as follows :—

Sir, I have yours of the 17th with relatione to our pupill, whom I wish I had never known, for besides the loss I'm in hazard of, his actiones whyle here, though a child, are like to prove hurtful to me. I shall be mighty glad of a disapointmente about him, and comport with my loss, if he answer your expectatione, and intreat you'll give me favourable accot of him two months hence. You know David Brisbane is ffactor for the Estate, whom I shall order to transmitt what money he has or can gett, to ansr your demnuds. I have ordered him to make his accounts for the bygone year, which shall be transmitted you when ready. I imagine you are not thinking I have money of Blackness's in my hands, for since my accounts were cleared I never had, nor shall have any somme of his money. Some time ago, I gott two or three letters from our pupill's Creditors, desiring payment of their principalls; I wish you would satisfie them, for att last Whitsunday my brother and I transacted 6000 merks, besides what is owing to myself. What necessarys (?) our pupill has here shall be sent with our Carrier tomorrow. I hope this answers your letter in every particular, for I shall give you no umbrage for misunderstanding, and be glad to keep a good correspondence. .... I know our pupill had knowledge iu arithmetick and you'll find that, with the rest, is labour in vain, though I shall not disagree with any proposall his friends make for his educatione, for it shall be seen by the worlde I never had a desigue of making money to myself. I wish you take notice of what companie he keeps, for I know whyle in your presense he'll give you ground for speaking favourably of him. I am, Sir,

Your most humble Servant,

Al : Wedderburne.

81. **1716.** July 17.—Letter from Sir John Wedderburn, Baronet, of Blackness to George Seton, as follows :—

" D. Uncle,

" This day there being such a great rain, it's impossible for me to come up to the town to-day, so I hope you'll be so kind as to procure me a Pass so yt I may proceed in my voyage, if I get no my Pass very quickly this day I will miss the occasion. I am very sorry that I have disobliged you and I beg your pardon, and wt the assistance of God, I shall never commit such extravagancies again. I expect my answer very soon for there is nothing hinders me but it. This wt my service to my Grandfather, Grandmother, and to my uncles and aunts is all from

Your affectionat nephew and most humble servant,

Leith, 17 July 1716.   Jn Wedderburn."

(The relatives to whom the writer sends "his service" are, of course, on his mother's side, viz., Sir Alexander Seton, Lord Pitmedden, and his wife, and their family.
This letter is iu very bad couditiou from damp and mildew.)

82. **1717.** August 2.—Letter from Alexander Wedderburn to George Seton :

" I received yours of the 29th which your Nephew has seen, and expects to serve in Shannon's Regiment in ye statione of ane Eusigne, but where the money is to be gott I know not unless some part of ye Lands were sold, and Logie is yt which will soonest sell. Mr. Stewart was long time asking about it for James Clark, Graver in ye Mint. I entreat you would speak to him about it. The character you give of our pupill's Estate is very true, but yt which diminishes it very much is its being in ill tennendrie and a considerable part in our own hand yt never produces the rent which certainly if in another hand would force a conversioue of hear to oyr Grains. I have been conversing wt Craigie about ye value and he's of opinion it may yield 2,500 Ms for the Chalder Victuall, but cannot say any thing about the house and planting unless a mer were offering.

I intreat you'd answer by the first post as to our pupill .. ... I shall acquaint the ffactor to take course wt ye @ -rents."

83. **1718.** Jan. 8.—Letter from Dr. John Wedderburn, of Idvies, with a short postscript written by James Hallyburton of Pitcurr, to George Seton.

Sir, When my brother made the proposal of purchassing our pupill's estate, to Pitcur, Craigie, and me, we all thought him a very frank marchant, nay, Piteur and I used arguments to diswade him from the bargain, and indeed in my thought he could not lay out his money with a less view of profite in all this countrie : but the thoughts of his grandfather's having possest that estate overcomes all difficulties.

Upon receipt of yours I conversed with severals aunent the value of the lands particularly My Lord Gray and the Master ; both of them allow me to assure you that they would not come to my brother's length ; they are just now wanting land here, in place of their interest at Aberdeen which is upon the sale, if not sold. Miln of Milnfield, a very intelligent man, tells me he would concurr to accept the price for Blackness & the aikers and think he did his pupil good service : Keithick Campbell too told me some time agoe that he thought the price offered was a good one : in short, all the objections I meet with are only against the manner of the sale. Thus you have my thoughts and Pitcur will add his on the other side. But I wish you would stand upon your own legs in this matter, you have a rental, please consider it with others, as I have done : you know that the whole estate (except Logie) is measur'd and ferm'd by the akre, and pays all bear, it has no grass, only a barren piece upon the river which is burdened with a servitude to the town of Dundie of playing at goutf & exercising their men, and a small piece upon the North side that is wett, and does not exceed an akre : all the tennauts reside in Dundie, so that they must drive dung near a mile to their farthest ground & must bring their corus as far, or be at a too great a distance in looking after the threshing of them : you know also that about 100 acres in Blackness have been labour'd by our pupil for some years to a great disadvantage as the factor assures me, and is yet upon our hand : these circumstances I am perswaded will iu some measure justifie what I have advanced above.

You'l observe by the reutal that my brother pays 2508 mks for the haru aud yard at the port, it is an old house built with mortar & roofed with thatch aud has no loft : I am perswaded he has committed au error in this, there is also twentie shilling of bleuch dutie to the crown not charged, it is due pretty farr back, as is half a merk to the Bishop of S¹ Audrews for Logie ; the poultrie too are rentald, there are but few of them. You know the state of the house and Garden as well as I do. As for Logie some thiuk it worth more mouey thau what it has past for at the three last sales viz : 17500 Mks, it pays a mixt ferm and has outfield ground ; the last tack I can learn of it payed 5 chalders of bear and 3 of meal, the reutal shows you what is pay'd out of it. I once thought of delaying to write you untill we should kuow what was done aunent the iuterest of money ; if its alter'd a new scheme must be made. I am,

Sir, Your most humble ser¹

Dundie Jan. 8th 1718   John Wedderburn

Logie pays to the parson of Duudie 12 bolls bear and to the Miñr of Liff 8 bolls meall, 16s/8d money, besides 8 lib or so of vickerage aud 60/8d to the Bishop of St. Andrews.

(Postscript by James Hallyburton.)

The above is so full that I shall only signe myself

Sir Your most humble servant

James Hallyburton

As to the last pairt of Doctor Wedderburn's letter I shall ouly observe that as this Cession of Parliament has brought down the Interest of monie, another my (*sic*) very soon raise it again so I cannot satisfie myself how we can aske or expect the Clerk to offer for ane uncertintie.

(This letter is in bad couditiou from damp and mildew.)

84. **1718.** Jan. 9.—Letter, Alexander Wedderburu to George Seton, signed by A. W., but written by another hand, as follows :—

Sir, My ffrieud Balgleasie, Bearer hereof, is to deliver you a Letter from Pitcurr and My Brother showing (as I suppose) their cousent to my purchase of Blackness. Whatever may be the objectiones made by some, I am sure I give a good price for it. I have also sent by this Bearer the scroll of a Dispositioue which I designe should be immediatly extended, seeing I'm in a conditione presently to pay the greatest part of the price as the bearer can informe you. I intreat you'l be at the trouble seriously to peruse the scroll of the Disposition und amend what you find amiss, return the same to the bearer with your answer to Pitcurr's Letter and my Brother's so as I may gett the Dispositione subscryved by Blackness and them before our pupill's Commission come here because probably he may be very soon after removed with the Regiment.

I intreat also you'l let me know how the Two Daughters shall be provided by their Brother. That is, what may be the proper onerous cause of the Bond to be gruuted them. I shall be glad to hear of your firm health which with my service to your self and Lady is from,

Sir,

your most humble serv¹,

Dundie 9th January 1718.   (Sigued) Al: Wedderburne.

(The estate of Balglessie, or Balglassie, at this date belonged to Dr. Thomas Arbuthnott of Montrose. The " two daughters " are of course Rachel and Matilda Wedderburn, sisters to Sir Johu. This letter is not in very good condition.)

85. **1718.** Jan. 17.—Letter, Alexander Wedderburn to George Seton, dated at " Forfar," as follows :—

Sir, I have received yours of the 13th and likewise seen your answer to my brother ; as to the difficultie proposed about the Dispositioue with respect to my obligatioue, your deyre shall be complyed with. I think to be iu a conditione to discharge more than 86,000 merks of the debt againe I gett the Dispositione in readieness. You shall have a double of yᵉ list of Debts, and (I) am satisfied ......

As to yours to my brother with respect to the price of yᵉ Lands, if the Rentall were good and oÿr circumstances about it helped, certainly you are right ; but as it stands I'm convinced none would give more, yea, I believe, hardly so much as I have offered and I suppose my Brother wrote so to you.

There is nothing .... from a legall sale than the want of yᵉ papers aud yᵗ uunecessary charge it brings to our pupill, for I do uot know what may be the consequence of blazing yᵗ particular abroad. If you think a warrand may be procured from the Lords to the Curators to sell, upon a representatioue made of yᵉ Debt and productione of the rights and yᵗ yᵉ rentall formerly made at purchasing a warrand to sell Omachie may be sustained. And .... (illegible) .... that the curators would incline to sell wᵗout making it publict I should in the state thiuk all well and contribute for payiug the charge and .... any other footing I presume to think it .... (illegible) I have proposed this .... they were of opinion that the loss of public sale and .... was a great obstacle to .... Direct your answer for me at Dundie, or if you please send it by Balgiessic.

Sir, Your most humble servant,

Addressed   A. Wedderburne.

To Mr. George Seton, Advocat at Edgr.

(Very much damaged and staiued by damp.)

85ᵃ. **1718.** Feb. 1.—Letter, same to same.

" I have yours of the 24th, I think I told you several times that all remains of the Rights of Blackness is the Charter in favours of Sir John, which is in your custody, and this is the reasone I was so much against a public roup, especiallie since ane adjudicatione, as you say, will be als good

T

security and that my getting a voluntar right, which in itself is imperfect as being revocable, may
only serve to show that I give ane adequate price, which is truly and fairly paid by the transactions
of the debts" (several lines erased) "I'm satisfied to go into anie measures that may satisfie the
Curators and convince the world (which I think I'm little concerned with) that all justice is done by
me. And upon the whole I desire something may be done for my security in the debts I have
transacted, so long as Blackness is here. Wherefor I intreat your final answer, whether it's absolutely
necessar, and for the Minor's profit, to have a warrand to roup legally or sell voluntarly, or if a
voluntar Dispositione without either is to be granted me; for in all I'll be directed by you."
       (Very much decayed and stained by damp.)

86. **1718. Feb. 17.—Letter, same to same.**
       "As I told you our pupill would of necessity see your brother and seeing he still urges the
settling of his affairs, by knowing the balance of his estate, I have, in order to that, sent with him the
two Dispositiones of the Lands, the one for the Lands of Blackness and Logie, and the other for the
Barnes and aikres held by Burgage, wherein he is not infeft. I hope the Draughts of the Dispositiones will please, and if you think fitt, they and the three inventars of the Debts may be subscryved
by our Pupill, yourself, and Pitcurr, who I suppose may be at Edinburgh." .... "This I give
as a compliment to our pupill, besides 96,000 Merks, the price of the Lands, which, with the necessary
charges I'll inevitably be put to, will make the price of the Lands very near 100,000 Merks; which
is a price so sufficient as I think may stop the mouth of any officious persone who does not know
particulars, nor is concerned in the affair."—(the rest is illegible, or immaterial).
       On the back is a memorandum in George Seton's handwriting, viz.: "The within Allexr Wedder-
burn, is to give obligatione to the within Sir John Wedderburn, to satisfie at Whit: 1718, the
following debts viz.: £861 to Sir Al: Seton, 2000 Merks to Al: Kirkwood's children, 1000 Merks
to Mr William Mitchell's representatives, 3500 Merks to Mr Tho: Wilson at Dundie, at least as much
thereof as will extend to 5630lb, which, with the debts contained in the Inventar, to quhilk he has
right, compleats 96,000 Merks as the price of the Lands of Blackness."
       (Almost fallen to pieces with mildew.)

86ª. **1718.** Inventar of debts due by Sir John Wedderburn of Blackness, for himself, and
       as representing the deceast Sr Alexander Wedderburn of Blackness, his father, and
       Sr John Wedderburn of Blackness, his grand ffather, to Alexander Wedderburn,
       Sheriff Clerk of fforfar, for himself and as having a right from the persons afternamed.
       (This document is a single large sheet, attested at the foot.)

Whose Bonds.	Creditor's Names, etc.	To whom assigned, etc.	Principall Soumes Sunday 1718.		Ann. Int. at Whit-Sunday 1718.			Totall Soummes Whit-Sunday 1718.		
Sir John, the Minor,	with consent of Curators	Alexander Wedderburn	1333	6 8	216	13	4	1550	0	0
Sir Alexr to	Wm. Law, Professor of Phily at Edgh	Do.	1937	5 0	290	11	9	2227	16	9
Do. to	Thos Weems, Advocat ...	Do.	1333	6 8	200	0	0	1533	6	8
Do. to	Jno Brown, son to Hugh Brown, Surgeon in Edgh ...	Do.	1200	0 0	60	0	0	1260	0	0
Do. to	Jas Guldman, Minister	Doctor Wedderburn	133	6 8	34	6	8	167	13	4
Do. two to	Geo : Dempster, Mercht in Dundie ...	Do.	4000	0 0	500	0	0	4500	0	0
Sir Jno & SirAlexr to	Margt Wedderburn, conveyed by Dr. Hunter in Dundie to	Alexander Wedderburn	1200	0 0	120	0	0	1320	0	0
Sir Alexr to	David Hunter, Merchant in Dundie	Do.	2333	6 8	233	6	8	2566	13	4
Do. to	Alexr Rankin in Dundie, trans-ferred to	Do.	666	13 4	100	0	0	766	13	4
Do. to	David Hunter	Doctor Wedderburn	2000	0 0	250	0	0	2250	0	0
Do. to	David Bissett in Monorgan ...	Alexander Wedderburn	333	6 8	41	13	4	375	0	0
Do. to	William Miller, Surgeon in Dundie ...	Do.	2000	0 0	250	0	0	2250	0	0
Do. to	Henry Guthrie, Merchant in Dundie	Do.	233	6 8	35	0	0	268	6	8
Do. to	John Brown Minister ...	Do.	2200	0 0	302	10	0	2502	10	0
Do. two to	Thomas Lunday of Glasswall ...	Do.	2533	6 8	443	6	8	2976	13	4
Do. to	John Dick, Writer in Dundie ...	Do.	3333	6 8	416	13	4	3750	0	0
Do. two to	Patk Murray, son to the Laird of Oughtertyre ...	Do.	3333	6 8	416	13	4	3750	0	0
Sir John to	John Wedderburn, son to Peter Wedderburn	Do.	333	6 8	113	6	8	446	13	4
Sir Alexr to	James Kelso, by Dr. Alexr Brown's Assignee	Do.	666	13 4	33	6	8	700	0	0

Whose Bonds.	Creditor's Names, etc.	To whom assigned, etc.	Principall Sommes Sunday 1718.			Ann. Int. at Whit-Sunday 1718.			Totall Sommes Whit-Sunday 1718.			Mounie Papers.
Sir Alex^r	to William Robertson, one of the under Clerks of Session	Alexander Wedderburn	1333	6	8	66	13	4	1400	0	0	
Do.	to Baillie Wedderburn in Dundee	Do.	666	13	4	116	13	4	783	6	8	
Do.	to David Fletcher, Shipmaster in Dundee	Do.	1333	6	8	200	0	0	1533	6	8	
Do.	to John Scott of Mollenie ...	Do.	2666	13	4	433	6	8	3100	0	0	
Do.	to Margaret Wilson	Do.	500	0	0	115	0	0	615	0	0	
Do.	to James Hamilton of Pitkatland	Do.	666	13	4	125	16	8	792	10	0	
Do.	to Robert Dallas, writter in Edinburgh	Do.	333	6	8	90	8	4	423	15	0	
Do.	to James Seton, Advocat	Do.	666	13	4	100	0	0	766	13	4	
Do.	to Dame Janet Wallace, Lady Singletoun	Do.	666	13	4	135	0	0	801	13	4	
Do.	to Peter Wedderburn, Merchant in Dundie ...	Do.	333	6	8	38	15	0	372	1	8	
Do.	to James Haliburton of Pitcur	Do.	1333	6	8	270	0	0	1604	6	8	
Do.	to The Children of the deceast Baillie Jn⁰ Scott, Jr in Dundie	Do.	1333	6	8	233	6	8	1566	13	4	
Do.	to Robert Wedderburn, Mariner in Dundie ...	Do.	666	13	4	66	13	4	733	6	8	
Do.	to Alex Keith, Precentor in Dundie and his children	Do.	371	16	8	51	2	6	422	19	2	
Do.	to Baillie Jn⁰ Scott Senr in Dundie ..	Do.	430	10	0	53	16	3	484	6	3	
Do.	to Eliz : Jean : Helen & Annie Durhams, Dafrs of Omachie ...	Do.	1600	0	0	240	0	0	1840	0	0	
Do.	to John Paterson of Craigie	Do.	666	13	4	33	6	8	700	0	0	
Sir Jn⁰ & Sir Alex^r five	And : Balfour, Writter in Edinburgh, by Dr. Eccles	Do.	4068	6	8	1271	6	8	5339	13	4	
		£50741	5	0	7648	13	10	58389	18	10		

The above Inventar is a just double of the debts discharged by Alexander Wedderburne, Sherriff Clerk of Forfar, to the above designed Sir John Wedderburne, relative to two Dispositions of his estate subscryved by him and his Curators of the date hereof, to the said Alexander Wedderburne. In witness whereof thir presents are subsᵈ by the said Sr John Wedderburne his Curators, and the said Alexander Wedderburne as follows : Vizᵗ by the said Sr John Wedderburne, Mr George Seton, Advocat, and James Hallyburtone of Pitcurr, two of his Curators, Att Edsh 28th February Jajvᵈ and Eighteen years (1718), befor these Witnesses, Charles Menzies Writter to the Siguet, and Alexander Seton, lawll son to Sir Alexander Seton of Pitmelden ; And by Doctor John Wedderburn, Doctor of of Medicine at Dundie, another of his Curators, and the said Alexander Wedderburne, Att Dundie, 29th Apryle, and year foresaid, before these Witnesses, David Brisbane, and Thomas Traill, Writter in Dundie.

Da. Brisbane witness.   J. Wedderburn.   Al: Wedderburne.
Tho. Traill witnes.   Geo Seton consents.
Chas Menzies witnes.   James Hallyburton
Alexr Seton witness.   John Wedderburn consents.

87.   1718. May 28.—Letter, Alexander Wedderburne to George Seton, as follows :—

Sir, I receaved yours of yᵉ 20ᵗʰ instant. Your money was sent to Edgr and returned, which I have now ordered Mr. Hamiltone, Collr of Excise, to pay you on demand to whom deliver my Bill. I am sory you have not got it sooner, but it seems your blame is more peremptor than is wᵗ us. I did not expect you would have been so uukind as not calling for me when at Dundie, and I cannot but blame the Landlord whom I ordered on your arrivall to acquaint me. Had you but sent to my Brother he could have satisfied you that I have performed everything required of me wᵗ respect to your Nevoy's affair. There was a claime duely given in for yᵗ debt of yᵉ Earl of Southesk's. This and my service is from   Sir, your most humble servant,
Blackness, 23 May 1718.   A. Wedderburne.
(Addressed)
Mr George Seton, Advocat at Aberdeen.

88.   1720. Aug. 24.—Letter, from Sir John Wedderburn, Baronet, to George Seton of Mounie.

D. Sir,—Upon advice from Scotland of the high price of Lands, I arrived here last night, and in order to know what benefit I can make of this opportunity, a full and true information of our transaction with the Clerk will be absolutely necessar, which I earnestly pray you may send me, with your advice upon the whole by first post. In particular, I beg you'll favour me with ane exact reutall of my estate with all the Casualties as my Curators made up at their admission whereof you no doubt have a copie, and knows also what altertions happened during their administration. In the next place you'll know I'll want the extent of the debts paid or brought in by the Clerk ; and if you have ane exact inventer of them, it will as I'm informed be of great use to enable us to make aue estimet of the purchase according to the present rates ; you'l please to be speciall as to the nature of the debts, if they are old apprysinings or expyred adjudicationes against my Father, or if they are only of his contracting, and no legall diligence done upon them befor his death for evicting the property of the estate.   You know we will also want principalle and copie of the Disposition to the Clerk, and if the debts be ingrossed as I think they are, it will give us that most certain and full view of the matter.   It will also be of use to know how ye lands hold, what the publick burthens are, stipends and few duties I mean, and all other circumstances of the estate which behoved to pass my Curators' review during their administration.   These and all other things that come to your knowledge of my affairs, I must certainly beg you'l give me information of, with your best advice what method I should now take to bring the estate to the present mercat ; as I am very sensible you never Consented to the former sale, but att the full price any land gave att the time, so now yon'l be so good to give me all assistance to bring me in my old place again, so as to doe justice to the Clerk, that he lose nothing of the monie he really payd my father's creditors,   If I have the good fortune to get a share of high prices now a going, I am resolved to give a handsome provision to my sister.   I know I need use no arguments to induce you to this good office, your own incliuations, your near relation to me, and late concern in my affairs, are all such powerfull motives as secure me of your friendship, and assistance, which will put an infinit obligation upon

D. Uncle,

Yonr aff: Nevoy and most Humble Servant,

Pray give my humble duty to my Aunt.   J. Wedderburn.

In middling good preservation. It is in a large regular hand (like the other from Sir John, No. 81), and is addressed

3   To
Mr. George Seton of
Munie
to the care of the post
master of Aberbeen.

From the style of the letter, there can be little doubt that it was dictated to or drafted for Sir John by some professional adviser.

This collection consists of the documents, correspondence, &c., collected by my grandfather, John Wedderburn, when engaged on the history of the family printed by him in 1824, and later, when writing his more elaborate MS. account, often referred to in vol. I. of this work. His genealogical MSS. now consist of three divisions, viz.,

    i. The MS. account of the family, written 1824-39, two quarto volumes now in possession of the Rev. John Walter Wedderburn of Stornoway. A manuscript copy of it is in mine.

    ii. A folio volume in my possession containing (1) the MS. of his printed account ; (2) some notes on and copies of various documents, &c., relating to the family ; and (3) extracts from the Wedderburn papers at Mounie made by him in 1825. These were bound up by me in one volume in 1892.

    iii. A quarto volume in my possession containing various papers and letters received by J. W. during the preparation of his printed history and MS. These were formerly lying loose in a box, but were arranged by me and bound in one volume in 1892. The following is an inventory of the papers in this volume.

INVENTORY.

1—2, MEMORANDA.

1. Memorandum of documents at Birkhill. This is a copy of No. 669 in the Scrymgeour Wedderburn chest. Some rough notes are added on the back.

2. Note of Great Seal charters in favour of Wedderburns 1426, 1527-1722. (See below s. Public Records.)

3, SIX ORIGINAL DOCUMENTS.

3. Six Original Documents :—
    (a) Burgess ticket admitting Thomas Mudy, burgess of Dundee. Signed by Sir Alexander Wedderburn of Blackness, 23 Sept., 1672.
    (b) Discharge by Sir Alexander Anstruther of Newark to John (afterwards Sir John) Wedderburn of Blackness. Dated at Edinburgh 10 March 1698. Originally among the Mounie papers and given to J. W. by Seton of Mounie in 1825. See ante. s. Mounie Papers, No. 1.
    (c) A Schem of the probation of the Rentall and value of the Lands of Blaknes, &c. Originally among the Mounie papers, &c. See ante, ibid No. 16.
    (d) Letter from Katharin Scott to George Seton, 22 Feb. 1712. See ante, ibid No. 35.
    (e) Inventory of papers delivered by Mr. George Seton to Alexander Wedderburne 1712. Originally among the Mounie papers, &c. See ante, ibid No. 67.
    (f) Letter, 3 March 1714, from Alexander Wedderburn to George Seton. Originally among the Mounie papers, &c. See ante, ibid No. 73.

4—9, LETTERS RELATING TO THE WEDDERBURN MONUMENTS IN THE HOWFF OF DUNDEE.
(See the account of the Howff in vol. I.)

4. Letter from James Thomson (the historian of Dundee) to John Wedderburn, dated Small's Wynd, Dundee, 23 Dec. 1836, giving copies of the Wedderburn inscriptions in the Howff of Dundee.
    (a) Tomb of Grissell Wedderburn & James Anderson.
    (b) Tomb of Alexander Wedderburn of Easter Powrie, Provost of Dundee.
    (c) Tomb of Dr John Wedderburn of Idvies.
    (d) Tomb of Lady Margaret Ogilvy, wife of Sir John Wedderburn.
    (f) Tomb of the Wedderburns of Blackness.
    (g) Tomb of Margaret Wedderburn wife of Peter Clayhills (fragmentary).
    (h) Tomb of Sir Alexander Wedderburn of Blackness, Knt.
    Of these the first five were then legible, the sixth partly so, while the seventh was copied " from an old book in the library of Blackness." They are all given *in extenso* in the chapter on the Howff in this book.

142 THE WEDDERBURN BOOK.

Papers Col-
lected by
John Wedder
burn 1819-39.

5. Letter from the Hospital Master in Dundee to John Wedderburn, dated 29 Jan. 1835, anent a proposed alteration of the position of the Wedderburn monuments in the Howff.

6. Letter same to same, dated 3 Feb. 1835, on the same subject, &c., anent a proposal to rail in the monuments.

7. Letter from James Thomson to John Wedderburn, dated 3 Feb. 1835, giving some further inscriptions.
   (a) Tomb inscribed " Insignium virorum tumulus terra universa, A.W."
   (b) Tomb on which P.W. and C.M. is still legible.
   (c) Tomb of David Brisbane.
   (d) Tomb of Elizabeth Wedderburn, wife of James Graham of Meathie.

8. Letter same to same, dated 11 April 1835.

9. Letter same to same, dated 22 March 1835, giving two further inscriptions :
   (a) Tomb of Elizabeth Wedderburn, wife of Alexander Blyth.
   (b) Tomb of Catherine Wedderburn, wife of William Duncan.

10. Letter same to same, dated 28 March 1835.

11—23, SCRYMGEOUR-WEDDERBURN PAPERS.

11. Letter from Henry Scrymgeour-Wedderburn to John Wedderburn (of Spring Garden), dated 16 Feb. 1806, announcing the death of his son Alexander that day.

12. Letter same to same, dated 18 Feb. 1819, returning a paper of queries sent him by J. W., and giving in answer an account of the descendants of David Scrymgeour and Katherine Wedderburn.   (See ante s. Scrymgeour-Wedderburn Papers, No. 705-6.)
   This gives the death of Katharine Wedderburn, 19 March 1796, and her burial at Balmerinoch: with a list of her children :—
   1. Alexander Scrymgeour-Wedderburn, admitted advocate 1766 ; m. 2 March 1771, Elizabeth second d. to James Ferguson of Pitfour. She d. 13 Oct. 1810. He d. 4 July 1811.
   2. John Scrymgeour, captain H.E.I.C.S. ; d. s.p. at Bangalore, March 1791.
   3. David Scrymgeour, H.E.I.C. civil service, d. s.p. in India, Sept. 1780.
   4. Henry Scrymgeour-Wedderburn ; m. 5 April 1793 Mary Turner Maitland, with a list of their children ; and
   1. Catharine d. æt. 3.
   2. Janet m. John Gillespie 20 May 1776 ; d. 18 March 1811.
   3. Grizel d. young.
   4. Elizabeth d. young.
   5. Marion d. young.

13. Letter same to same, dated 26 April 1819, enclosing copies of some documents in his possession.   (See ante s. Scrymgeour-Wedderburn Papers, Nos. 571 and 665.)

14. Notice of the death of Alexander, eldest son of H. S. Wedderburn, at Edinburgh, 8 Feb. 1820.

15. Letter from H. S. Wedderburn to J. W., dated 23 Oct. 1820, as to his claim to appear at the Coronation of George IV. as hereditary standard bearer of Scotland.

16. Letter same to same, dated 28 July 1824.

17. Letter same to same, dated 7 March 1825, acknowledging receipt of J. W.'s printed history of the family.

18. Letter same to same, dated 16 March 1825, giving his own birth date, 3 Nov. 1755.

19. Notice of the death of Capt. Cathcart of Carbieston, at Pitcairly, Nov. 1833.

20. Notice of the death of Isabella, d. to H. Scrymgeour-Wedderburn, at Edinburgh, 19 April 1826.

21. Letter from Thomas Gardyne of Midletoun, dated 13 Jan. 1826, 'to William Stirling-Graham of Duntroon, in which he speaks of his great aunt Grissell Gardyne having married first Wedderburn of Wedderburn and secondly "your maternal great grand-father." *Papers Collected by John Wedderburn 1819-39.*

22. Memorandum of the cntail of Grizell Wedderburn of Wedderburn, dated 31 July, and recorded 6 Aug. 1766. (See ante s. Scrymgeour-Wedderburn Papers, No. 626.)

23. Draft Pedigree of Alexander Scrymgeour-Wedderburn of Wedderburn showing him to be heir male of the Earl of Dundee 1789.

24—35, DOCUMENTS RELATING TO THE FAMILY OF BALINDEAN IN THE HAND OF COLONEL ALEXANDER WEDDERBURN, YOUNGEST SON OF SIR JOHN WEDDERBURN OF BALINDEAN AND ALICIA DUNDAS.

24. Note of his own birth and military career, and also of the birth and career of his brother, John, dated 22 Dec. 1819.

"Born at Balindean, 18th June 1791, Ensign, 17 Sept. 1807 ; Aide-de-Camp to L.-Gen. Sir John Hope iu the Walcharen Expedition ; embarked 27th July and returned 2nd Septr 1809. Embarked for Lisbon. 13 Sept. 1809 and returned Feby. 1812 ; A.D.C. to Sir J. Hope, when Commander iu chief iu Ireland, from Feby 1812 to Oct. 1813. Embarked with him for Passages in Spain, Octr 1813, and returned from Bayonne, June 1814. Lieut. and Capt. in Guards, 19th Novr 1811 ; Brevet Major, 22nd Jany 1819 ; Adjutaut, 8th Jany 1818. Army of occupation from June 1817 to Nov. 1818.

"John Wedderburn, born at Balindean, 1st May 1789, embarked for India, June 1808. Civil and Military Paymaster, Accountant General and Civil Auditor."

25. Letter from him to John Wedderburn, dated 31 July 1825, as to the ring bearing P. W. 1571, the Wedderburn arms, found in Ireland, (see the chapter on the family arms).

26. Letter same to same as to the advisability of applying to parliament for the restoration of the Blackness baronetcy. Dated 21 April 1826.

27. Letter from John Wedderburn to Col. A. W., dated 25 April 1826, as to the probable cost of so doing.

28. Letter same to same, dated 16 June 1830, on the same subject.

29. Letter Col. A. W. to J. W., dated 20 April 1835, as to the family monuments in the Howff of Dundee, which J. W. proposed to put in order.

30. Letter same to same, dated 2 May 1835, on the same subject and giving the birth dates of his brother John's children, as follows :—

"Alicia Heurietta, 20 Aug., 1823 : John, 9 May 1825 : Elizabeth, 7 Feb., 1827 ; Margaret, 10 May, 1828." He adds, "There were also two infauts who died in India, named William and Mary Anne, but I cannot give you the dates of either births or deaths."

31. Letter same to same, dated 15 May 1835.

32. Letter same to same, dated 11 Feb 1835, as to placing a stone to his father, Sir John, in the Howff of Dundee. This was subsequently done.

33. Letter same to same, dated 24 March 1835, on the death of J. W.'s mother.

34. Notice of the death of Alicia Dundas, Lady Wedderburn, at 32, George's Square, Edinburgh, 24-25 June 1831.

35. Notice of the death of Louisa Dorothea Wedderburn, Countess of Hopetoun, at Leamington, 16th July 1836.

Papers Collected by John Wedderburn 1819-39.

36—41, DOCUMENTS RELATING TO THE WEDDERBURN-COLVILES OF OCHILTREE.

36. Copy of the order in Council, 22 Jan. 1814, entitling Andrew Wedderburn to take the name and arms of Colvile.

37. Copy license pursuant to above order, dated 22 June 1814.

38. Copy of record of above and grant of arms thereon by the Heralds' College, London.

39. Queries addressed, 21 Dec. 1819, by John Wedderburn to Andrew Colvile, as to his family, with the answers of the latter noted thereon as follows :—

He says that he believes his father James Wedderburn went to Jamaica about 1749-50 and returned thence about 1773 ; that his marriage contract is dated 7 March 1774, and that he died 14 Dec. 1807 and was buried at Inveresk. He adds that he himself was born at Inveresk, 6 Nov. 1779, came to London in 1796, settled there 1799, and sold Inveresk (to the sisters of Sir David Wedderburn) in 1808. He gives the birth of of his brother John at Inveresk 18 May 1776, and his death in Jamaica 19 May 1799 ; also the birth of his sister Jean (Lady Selkirk) at Inveresk 3 May 1786, and her marriage in Nov. 1807. He then gives a list of his own children, thus :—
"Eleanor b. 23 Sept. 1808 ; James William, b. 12 Jan. 1810 ; John, b. 16 Jan. 1811 ; Isabella, b. 24 April 1812 ; George, b. 23 Oct. 1813 and died 27 June 1814 ; Louisa, b. 21 Oct. 1815 ; Emily, b. 24 June 1817 ; and Ellen, 12 Feb. 1819. (All at Beckenham, except James William, b. in London.)

40. Notice of the death of Mrs. Wedderburn-Colvile, at Craigflower, 14 Jan. 1821.

41. Letter from Andrew Colvile to John Wedderburn, announcing the death that day (at Langley Farm, Beckenham) of his daughter Eleanor. Dated 30 Nov. 1824.

42—43, DOCUMENTS RELATING TO THE WEDDERBURN-OGILVYS OF RUTHVEN.

42. Letter from Peter Wedderburn-Ogilvy of Ruthven to John Wedderburn dated "Islabank, Meigle, July 3, 1819." In it he says :—

"I was born on the 23rd September 1781 at Inveresk .... Entered the East India Company's sea service 1797, made six voyages, the two last as commander, and left the service on my marriage August 1810. Married 30th April 1811 Anne, only child of James Ogilvy of Islabank co. Forfar, born 6 April 1778 at Islabank. My eldest son James James was born on Feb. 4th 1812 at Edinburgh ; 2. Jane, a daughter, born at Islabank on 24th May 1813 ; 3. Thomas, a son, at Islabank Sept. 8th 1814 ; 4. Peter, a son, at Islabank Nov. 15th 1815 ; 5. Isabella, a daughter, at Islabank 8th January 1817 ; 6. John Andrew, born at Islabank 2nd July 1818." (Attached to this letter are slips recording the subsequent births of two other children, James, 4 Aug. 1820 and Anna, 8 Sept. 1822.)

43. Notice of the death at Islabank, 13 Sept. 1819, of James James Wedderburn, eldest son of Peter Wedderburn-Ogilvy.

44—45, DOCUMENTS RELATING TO THE FAMILY OF JAMES WEDDERBURN, SOLICITOR-GENERAL FOR SCOTLAND.

44. Letter from James Wedderburn to John Wedderburn, dated 6 June 1819, giving the following account :—

"Isabella Clerk was born on the 10th April 1789 in the city of Edinburgh. Her father was James Clerk, a younger son of Sir George Clerk Maxwell, Bart., of Penicuik, co. Edinburgh, and Middlebie, co. Dumfries. Her mother was Janet Irving, eldest daughter of George Irving, Esq. of Newton, co. Lanark. We were married on the 28th October, 1813, and have now four children : 1, James, born 23 Sept. 1814 ; 2, Janet Isabella, born 2 Oct. 1815 ; 3, George, born 25 March, 1817 ; 4, Jean, born 7 August, 1818. They were all born in the city of Edinburgh, and are alive.
I was born in the parish of Inveresk in the co. of Edinburgh on the 12th Nov., 1782 ; became a member of the Faculty of Advocates on the 17th Dec., 1803 ; was elected one of the collectors of decisions by the Faculty of Advocates on the 11th July, 1807, which I resigned on the 10th July, 1811 ; was appointed by the Lord Advocate to the situation of one of the deputy advocates on the 12th Aug., 1810, which I held till the 9th March, 1811 ; was appointed Sheriff depute of the co. of Peebles on 9th March, 1811, which I resigned in July, 1816 ; was appointed Solicitor General of Scotland on the 10th July, 1816."
To this J. W. has subsequently attached three slips in the hand of Isabella Clark, giving the birth dates of three younger children, John, b. 5 July, 1820 ; Andrew, b. 16th Dec., 1821 ; and Jamima, b. 1st May, 1823.

45. Letter from Isabella Clerk (Mrs. Wedderburn) to John Wedderburn, dated 8 Sept. 1825.

46—60, Documents Relating to the Wedderburns of Pearsie.

Papers Collected by John Wedderburn 1819-39.

46. Note as follows (? in whose hand):—

"Robert m. Isobel Edward of Pearsie 1 Feb., 1738, who was born 12 Nov., 1718. They had childn as follows :—John, b. at Pearsie July 28, 1744 ; Eliz., b. at Dundee June 1, 1746 ; Charles, b. at Pearsie Aug. 1, 1748 ; Kath., b. at Pearsie June 6, 1750 ; Isobel, b. at Pearsie Oct. 9, 1753 ; David, b. at Pearsie Aug. 15, 1757."

47. Letter to John Wedderburn from Elizabeth Read, relict of David Wedderburn (or Webster, third son of Robert Wedderburn of Pearsie) and then wife to Robert Douglas of Brigton, dated Brigton, 30 July 1819. She writes :—

"To the best of my knowledge and memory the following is correct. David Wedderburn was born at Dundee 15 Aug., 1756 ; married there the 28th December, 1785, to Elizabeth Read, who was born at Logie. eo. Angus, the 13th of Oct., 1770 (daughter of Alexander Read of Logie and Ann Fletcher). He died at Bath 21 March, 1804 .....

My son James was born 30th May, I think the year 1788, but he is just two days older than your brother James. ... his marriage I am rather in doubt about, but think it took place in January, 1811, to Lady Frances Caroline Annesley ; they have had issue, a daughter Lucy and son Charles Byron, the latter died at Nantz in 1817. My eldest daughter Anne was born at Clapham 2nd March, 1791 and married Aug., 1814, to Captain Archibald Douglas, of the 52nd Foot, has issue Elizabeth, William, and Mary. My 2nd daughter Mary was born at Clapham 15 Sept., 1793, and married 22nd March, 1814, to George Hawkins of Harnish House, Wilts. They have no issue. My son Charles Wedderburn was born in London 10th Sept., 1799. My son David was born in London 10 August, 1801, and died at Brigton 14 May, 1816, and was buried there.

48. Letter same to same, dated 2 Aug. 1819.

49. Letter same to same, dated 20 Sept. 1819.

50. Letter from Charles Wedderburn of Pearsie to John Wedderburn, dated " Pearsie, by Kirriemuir, May 21st 1824." He writes in answer to J. W.'s queries :—

"Robert Wedderburn of Pearsie died in February, 1786. John, his eldest son, born at Pearsie, July 28th, 1744, died in India, held the rank of Lt.-Col. ; was not in possession of Pearsie before his father's death. Charles Wedderburn, second son, was born at Pearsie, August 1, 1748, held the rank of Captain of Infantry, returned from Bengal in August 1785. Date of his first marriage August, 1787. Date of present marriage is December 5, 1797.

Captain Henry Wedderburn of Gosford held the rank of Master Attendant in the H E.I.C.'s Marine, a very lucrative office given in reward for his services ..... He was married to Miss Belshes of Invermay, who died at Calcutta in 1771 or 1772, being his second marriage. Lady Cumming, his daughter, by his first marriage. I do not recollect the mother's name. Captain Wedderburn married third time Miss Tetley, by whom he left issue a daughter ; if I am not mistaken, Mrs. Murray, who possessed the old family ring ; but I am not certain whether there was any child by Miss Belshes ; I think not : she died in child bed.

Charles Wedderburn Webster (my nephew) married Miss Chatterton, daughter of Sir William Chatterton of Castle Mahon, Ireland. He has just announced the birth of a son at Lincroft Lodge, near York ....

Alexander Wedderburn, youngest son of Sir Alex. Wedderburn of Blackness, died in Dundee ......

51. Letter same to same, dated Pearsie, 7 Jan. 1829.

52. Notice of the death of Mrs. Wedderburn, second wife of Charles Wedderburn, of Pearsie, at Daventry, 25 Feb. 1823.

53. Notice of the death of (Elizabeth Wedderburn) Mrs Graham of Balmuir, 13 Sept. 1825.

54. Letter from her son David Graham (afterward Wedderburn of Pearsie) to John Wedderburn on this occasion. 16 Sept. 1825.

55. Notice of the death at Pearsie of Charles Wedderburn of Pearsie, 15 Feb. 1829.

56. Letter David Graham-Wedderburn of Pearsie (son of Elizabeth Wedderburn and James Graham) to John Wedderburn, dated at Pearsie, 11 Feb. 1830.

57. Notice of the death at Balmuir of Miss (Isabella) Graham of Balmuir (d. of Elizabeth Wedderburn and James Graham) 21 Aug. 1830.

U

58. Invitation to the funeral of Miss Graham.

59. Notice of the death of Robert Douglas of Brigton (second husband to Elizabeth Read, widow of David Wedderburn-Webster) at Brigton, 2 Aug. 1835.

60. Letter from Miss Catherine Graham to John Wedderburn enclosing an account by her brother of the Grahams of Duntroon and Balmuir, showing her brother James Graham Webster to be heir male of John Graham of Claverhouse, Viscount Dundee.

61--65, LETTERS, &c., RELATING TO THE WEBSTER-WEDDERBURNS.

61. Letter from Sir James Webster Wedderburn to John Wedderburn, dated Oct. 1821, as to his use of the names Webster and Wedderburn.

62. Letter same to same, Dec. 28 1821, enclosing (1) a copy of the case submitted to counsel (Mr. Horne) and counsel's opinion on it with regard to his use of the above names, dated 30 Oct. 1819 ; (2) an extract thereanent from James Webster's will ; and (3) the following family register :—

> David Wedderburn of Shenley Hill Co. of Herts, Esq. born in 1759, the 3rd son of Robert Wedderburn of Pearsie in Angus, Esq. married in 1787 Miss Eliza Read, daur of Alex. Read of Logie Esq. & Miss Fletcher, daur of Robert Fletcher of Ballhshoe Esq. & Brother to Colonel Sir Robert Fletcher, Commander in chief at Madras.
>
> In 1790 David pursuant to the will of his great uncle James Webster of Clapham, Esq. & by royal license, assumed the name & arms of Webster for himself & his heirs in lieu of that of Wedderburn. He was for many years partner in the house of Wedderburn, Webster & Co. By & under the will of his uncle aforesaid he acquired a considerable property & died, aged 42, at Bath, of a decline in 1801. leaving issue of his marriage. three sons and two daughters, James Webster, born in May 1789, Charles born in 1799. a cornet in H.M. 8th dragoon Guards, David born in 1801, died at Brigton aged 14 yrs. Anne born in 1790, Mary do. in 1788.
>
> The eldest son. James Webster Wedderburn of Clapham aforesaid, for some years a lieut in H.M. 10th and 11th Reg^t of Lt Dragoons married in Oct 1810 R^t Hon. Lady Frances Caroline Annesley, 2d dau. of Arthur late Earl of Mt Morres by the Hon. Sarah Cavendish his second countess & has issue 2 sons & a daur. Lucy Sarah Anne, born 2nd March 1812. Charles Byron Wedderburn, born Sept. 1815, & died & is buried at Nantes in Oct. 1817, Charles Francis Webster born in Piccadilly 1st July 1820.
>
> Of David Webster's daughters Annie, the elder, married in 1815 Captain Archibald Murray Douglas of H.M. 82nd Reg^t & has issue. Mary m. at Brussels in 1816 George Hawkins of Harnish House, co. Wilts, Esq. second son of the late Sir Jno. Cæsar Hawkins of Kelstone House, Somerset, & as yet have no issue.
>
> Mrs Eliza Webster the widow of David aforesaid, remarried in 1803, Robert Douglas of Brigton in Angus, Brother of the late Colonel Sir Wm. Douglas C.B. of H.M. 91 Reg^t & next heir in remainder to the Baronetcy of Glenbervie after his cousin, the Hon. Sylvester Douglas, Lord Glenbervie, who has no issue. Of this marriage there is issue one son—William, younger of Brigton.
>
> November 10th 1821.
J.W. Wedderburn.

63. Letter same to same, dated Brigton 11 Nov. 1828, giving particulars of the arms and supporters of Sir Alexander Wedderburn, second baronet of Blackness, and his mottoes "Spernit pericula virtus" and "Consilio et cura," found by him in an old Latin history of Scotland in the library of Mr. Hunter of Blackness.

64. Printed leaflet of a song by Sir James W. Wedderburn, entitled "Farewell to thee, Scotland," Jan. 1825.

65. Two newspaper cuttings :—

> (a) Report of an action brought by one Richards, a printer, v. Sir James W. Wedderburn, in respect to the cost of printing the latter's pamphlet "Upon the Policy of England."
>
> (b) Letter, 2 May, 1838, from Sir James to the Courier in regard to an action by one Thomas against him. In each of these actions he is designed "Baronet."

66—74, DOCUMENTS RELATING TO THOMAS WEDDERBURN OF CANTRA AND HIS FAMILY.

66. Family register in the hand of Katherine Dunbar, wife of Thomas Wedderburn.

> This measures about 8 x 12½ inches, and is written in a large round hand. A reduced facsimile of it is given opposite. The date given for the death of her husband (1766) is an error for 1769. On the back of the sheet to which it is pasted are some notes by J. W. giving the date of the deaths of his aunts. Mary at Quebec in 1771, Elizabeth at Moutrose 8 Feb., 1819, and of his grandmother, K. Dunbar 13 Feb., 1818.

In the hand writing of Katharine Dunbar, wife to Thomas Wedderburn at [illegible]

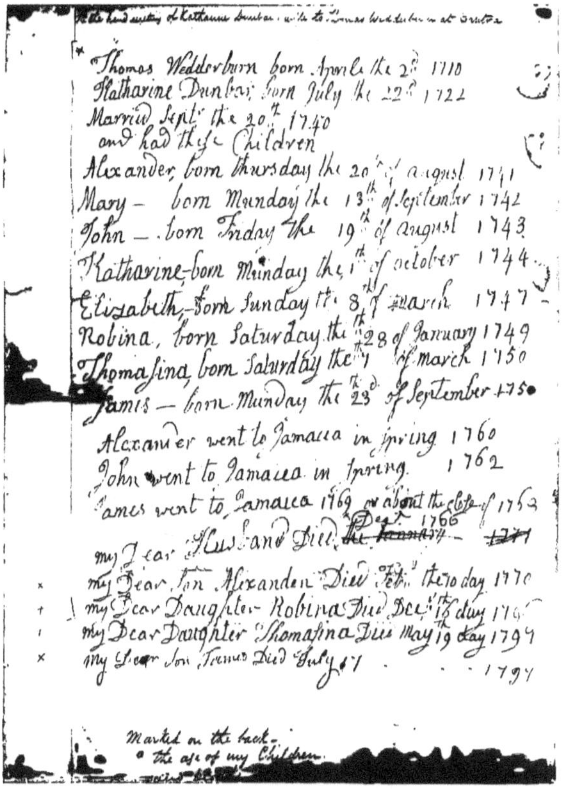

Thomas Wedderburn born Aprile the 2d 1710
Katharine Dunbar born July the 22d 1722
Married Sept. the 20th 1740
and had these Children
Alexander, born thursday the 20th of august 1741
Mary — born Munday the 13th of September 1742
John — born Friday the 19th of august 1743
Katharine — born Munday the 1st of october 1744
Elizabeth — born Sunday the 8th of march 1747
Robina, born Saturday the 28th of January 1749
Thomasina, born Saturday the 1st of march 1750
James — born Munday the 23d of September 175[illegible]

Alexander went to Jamaica in spring 1760
John went to Jamaica in spring 1762
James went to Jamaica 1769 or about the close of 1768
my Dear Husband Died ~~the January~~ Dec. 1766 ~~1771~~
× my Dear Son Alexander Died Feb. the 10 day 1770
† my Dear Daughter Robina Died Dec. 17th day 176[illegible]
my Dear Daughter Thomasina Died May 19th day 1794
× My Dear Son James Died July 17 1797

Marked on the back —
the age of my Children

FAMILY REGISTER

OF

KATHARINE DUNBAR

(*wife of Thomas Wedderburn*).

67. Five memoranda in the hand of Katherine Dunbar.

Papers Collected by John Wedderburn 1819-39.

(a) Copy of the inscription " Hold fast the profession of your faith " on her husband's tomb, with his birth date 2 April, 1701 (sic for 1710), and death date Dec. 1766, and a note " I came to Edinr June the 20, 1793."

(b) Family register of her son John's family :—" My dear son John was marryed the 27 May, 1782. His eldest daughter born Janry 7, 1784 ; his second daughter Mary born August 2d 1786 ; James born 2d June, 1788 ; Katharine in spring, 1791 ; Thomasina in harvest, 1793 ; John born Janry 1798. In summer, '90 my dear son came to Nairn."

(c) Memorandum of the places of her children's births, in the hand of Katherine Dunbar. " Alexander, born at Grangehill, parish of Dyke : Mary, born at Forress, parish of Forress ; John, born at parish of Forress ; Katharine, born at Fortross, parish of Rosemarkie ; Elizabeth, born at Fortross, parish of Rosemarkie ; Robine, born at Fortross, parish of Rosemarkie ; Thomasina, born at Fortross, parish of Rosemarkie ; James, born at Merkuish, parish of Inverness.

(d), (e) Memoranda as to her wishes in regard to her own burial, &c.

68. Note of inscription proposed to be put on the grave of Robina Wedderburn, d. 16 Dec. 1796, and Thomasina Wedderburn, d. 19 May 1797. With some verses from Young's " Night Thoughts," added below.

69. Letter from Katherine Dunbar to her brother-in-law, Robert Wedderburn of Pearsie, thanking him for kindness to her eldest son Alexander, when on his way to Jamaica. Signed Katharine Wedderburn. Dated " Katharine Dunbar, March 20th 1760."

70. Letter from Thomas Wedderburn to his wife, at Grangehill, dated " Invs (Inverness) 11 April 1746. This is printed at length and a facsimile of it given in vol. I.

71. Copy of the inscription on the tomb of Thomas Wedderburn in the churchyard at Cray, eo. Nairn, as follows :—

Thomas Wedderburn Esqre
Born April 1710, Died Decr 1769.
Hold fast the profession of your faith, etc.

72. Letter from Alexander Dunbar to John Wedderburn, dated "Serabster, by Thurso, Caithness, Jan. 12 1832," enclosing an account of the Dunbar family.

73. Copy of the inscription on the tomb of Catherine Dunbar and her daughters in the graveyard of the Buccleuch chapel at Edinburgh, as follows :—

In This Place are Interred the Remains
of
Mrs Catherine Dunbar
Relict of the late Thomas Wedderburn Esquire
Collector of the Customs at Inverness.
She was born on the 22nd April 1722
And died on the 12th February 1818
And of
Their Daughter Robina
Who was Born on the 28th January 1749
And Died on the 16th December 1796
And Thomasina who was Born on the 7th March 1750
And Died on the 19th May 1797.

(The date of Catherine Dunbar's birth should be 1720. This inscription is now quite illegible, the stone, though set in the wall above the grave, having worn almost smooth.)

74. Register (? in whose hand) of the family of John Wedderburn of Spring Garden and Mary Bedward, on three pieces of paper, of which the first and third are in the same, but the second in a different hand.

1. " George Bedward of Spring Garden, Jamaica, married Susannah, daughter and heiress of Robert and Elizabeth Rutherford of .... (sic) in 1761 and (had) issue : George James, born 2 Oct. 1762, Mary Wisdom, born 1 June 1716 and married John Wedderburn eldest son of Thomas Wedderburn of Blackness¹ and had issue as follows :—Elizabeth Susannah, born 1 June 1784 ; Mary, born 2d August 1786 ; James, born 2d June 1788 ; Catharine Georgina, born 1st Feb. 1791 ; Thomasina, born 19th September 1793 ; John, born 8th Jan. 1798—the three elder children born in Jamaica, the three younger in England.

2. Elizabeth Susannah married her cousin Andrew Wedderburn, the 27th of December 1802, and died without issue the 22d December 1803. Thomasina died 21st March 1808.

3. Catherine Georgina married to Patrick Stirling eldest son of John Stirling of Kippendavie, Perthshire N.B., 13th Feb. 1810. Issue as follows :—1st. John, born 19th August 1811. 2nd. Patrick, born 19th August 1813. 3rd. Mary Wedderburn, born 19 November 1814."

¹ This word is added in another hand and is not correct ; his father was of Blackness.

Papers Col-
lected by
John Wedder-
burn 1819-89.

75. Commission of John Wedderburn to be an ensign in Colonel Hine's regiment of foot raised or to be raised in the parish of Hanover, Jamaica. Dated 28 March 1765, and signed by Wm. Hy. Lyttleton, Captain General and Governor of Jamaica.

76. Commission of John Wedderburn to be a lieutenant in Col. Myric's Westmoreland regiment of foot, Jamaica. Dated 27 August 1776. Signed by Sir Basil Keith, Knt., Captain General and Governor of Jamaica.

77. Commission of John Wedderburn as *aide-de-camp* (with the rank of Lieut.-Colonel) to John Dalling, Governor of Jamaica. Dated 20 Nov. 1778. Signed by the Governor.

78. Burgess ticket of James Wedderburn of London (eldest son of John Wedderburn of Spring Garden) as burgess of Forfar, 30 May 1807.

79—84, DOCUMENTS RELATING TO THE WEDDERBURNS OF GOSFORD, AFTERWARDS HALKETTS OF PITFIRRANE.

79. Letter from Sir Peter Wedderburn of Gosford to Lord ——. Dated 20 Feb. 1666.
This is printed at length, and a facsimile of it given in the account of Sir Peter in vol. I.

80. Four printed law papers in a suit by Sir Peter Halkett of Pitfirrane and his curators *ad litem v.* John Wedderburn of Gosford, Captain Henry Wedderburn and others, defenders, in regard to the succession to Pitfirrane and Gosford, under the deed of tailzie of 1706, and in the circumstances of the lunacy of Sir Peter. These papers are as follows :—

(a) "Nov. 6, 1761. Information for Sir Peter Halket of Pitfirren, Baronet, and his curators ad litem, pursuers, against Captain John Wedderburn, Captain Henry Wedderburn, and others, defenders."

The following are extracts from this information :—

"The deceased Sir Peter Wedderburn of Gosford, and Dame Janet Halket of Pitfirren, his wife, did, in the year 1706, Sept. 9, execute two entails of their respective estates, of the same date, and, in effect, of the same tenor, *mutatis mutandis*.

By the tailzie of Pitfirren ...... Dame Janet Halket, grants the estate of Pitfirren in favour of themselves, and the longest liver, in liferent ; and to Peter Wedderburn, their eldest son, in fee, and the heirs-male of his body ; whom failing, to the daughters or heirs-female of his body, without division ; whom failing, to Charles Wedderburn, their second son, and the heirs-male of his body ; and thereafter to a series of other substitutes.

The tailzie contains an obligation upon the heirs to take the name and arms of the family, under an irritancy ; and recites the tailzie made by Sir Peter of his lands of Gosford to Charles Wedderburn, his second son, and the heirs male and female of his body, and other substitutes ; and that it was their joint intention, that the two estates should be kept separate. And therefore it is provided, that in case the estates shall happen to coincide, and be united in the person of Charles Wedderburn his second son, through the decease of his elder brother Peter without issue, then it should be in the option of Charles, either to retain the estate of Gosford ; in which case he shall be obliged to denude himself of the estate of Pitfirren, in favour of James, his immediate younger brother, and the other heirs substitute or otherwise ; or it should be lawful to Charles to enter to the right and possession of the estate of Pitfirren ; in which case he shall be obliged to denude himself of the estate of Gosford in favour of the said James, and the other heirs..........

Of the same date with the above tailzie of the lands of Pitfirren, Sir Peter Halket executed a tailzie of his estate of Gosford, in favour of himself in liferent, and Charles Wedderburn, his second son, in fee, and, the heirs-male of his body ; whom failing, to the daughters or heirs female of his body *successure*, without division ; whom failing, to James Wedderburn, his third lawful son, and the heirs-male of his body ; and failing them, to the other substitutes therein mentioned. And this tailzie contains clauses of the same tenor as above recited, from the tailzie of Pitfirren, to provide for the separation of the two estates, in case they should be united in the person of Charles Wedderburn, or of any of Sir Peter's children or grandchildren, or other heirs of tailzie. ....

The said Peter Halket afterwards intermarried with Lady Æmilia Stewart ; and, by contract of marriage of this date, Feb. 15, 1738, he became bound, with his father's consent, to resign the estate of Pitfirren in favour of the heirs-male of that marriage, and the heirs of their bodies, and the other heirs-substitutes of the tailzie 1706, under the provisions, conditions, limitations and restrictions therein contained.

Of this marriage three sons were procreate, Peter, Francis, and James ; and though Sir Peter was bound by the tailzie 1706, as well as by his own contract of marriage 1738, not to do any fact or deed whatsoever, directly or indirectly, to alter or innovate that tailzie in the order of succession ; yet he thought fit, in the year 1751, (Oct. 14), to make a new settlement of the estate, in which he granted the same "in favour of himself ; and failing him by decease, to Francis Halket, his second son, and the heirs whatsoever of his body without division ; whom failing, to James Halket, his 3rd son and the heirs whatsoever of his body without division ; whom failing to any other sons or heirs-male to be procreate betwixt him and Lady Æmilia Halket, and the heirs of their bodies without division &c. ; whom all failing, to the other heirs of tailzie, &c. destinate and appointed to succeed by the deed of tailzie, dated 9th September 1706." ....

Of the same date, Sir Peter Halket executed a bond of annuity, for the sum of £100 sterling yearly, payable to Lady Æmilia Halket, his wife, and after her death, to certain other trustees, for the use and behoof of his eldest son Peter Halket, now pursuer, during all the days of his life, upon a narrative, That his eldest son did, from his infancy, discover many symptoms of weakness of mind and genius ; and now that he is arrived at the full age and stature of a man, he continued still to betray that weakness of mind and judgment, and such an obvious defect of intellectual faculties and understanding, that he may be deemed in the sense of law a fatuous person, and no wise fit or capable either to manage an estate or marry.

Some years after, Sir Peter Halket went over to America, and was killed at the head of his regiment, in a battle with the French, in the year 1755 ; by which the succession of the estate of Pitfirren opened to his eldest son Sir Peter in terms of the entail 1706. But Major Francis Halket, his second son, was served heir of provision in general to his father, June 20, 1759, in terms of the above settlement 1751, ...

Major Halket died at Naples on the 11th November last (1760) ; and his younger brother James had died two years before ; both of them without issue.

The said Sir Peter Halket having thereafter, Feb. 20, 1761, been found fatuous, by an inquest, a commission was issued under the Great Seal, to Captain John Wedderburn of Gosford, the eldest son of his uncle Charles Wedderburn, to be his curator, and administrator of all his lands, heritages, possessions, and goods, moveable and immoveable, donec Deus, clementia sua, sibi morte vel convalescentia providebit.

Sir Peter Halket and his curator being advised that the deceased Sir Peter had no power to alter or innovate the tailzie made by his father and mother in the year 1706, have raised a process of reduction of the settlement 1751, &c. in which they have called in the whole heirs that are substitute either in the tailzie 1706 or 1751. The cause came before the court, in the course of the ordinary action roll, the last summer session ; and after counsel were heard, the Lords were pleased to appoint information to be given in. This is humbly offered in behalf of the pursuer."

(Here follows legal argument, but no further facts.)

(b) "Nov. 11, 1761. Information for Alexander Wedderburn of St. Germains, Esq. and others, Defenders v. Sir Peter Halket, &c." This adds no facts to the above except that it (p. 5) describes the marriage contract of Sir Peter Halkett and Lady Emilia Stewart (15, 17 Feb., 1738) as postnuptial and speaks of Alexander Wedderburn as "the only surviving younger brother of the late Sir Peter Halkett."

(c) "Dec. 11, 1761. Petition by Alexander Wedderburn of St. Germains, Esq. and others, Defenders." This again adds nothing to the facts of the foregoing information (a).

(d) " Jan. 15, 1762. Answers for Sir Peter Halket, &c. to the petitions of Sir Alexander Wedderburn of St. Germains, &c."

81. Letter from John Halkett to John Wedderburn, dated Seymour Place (London), March 6, 1819, in answer to various queries by J. W. In this he says :—

(a) Robert Wedderburn of Dunfermline (his great uncle) had issue two daughters, 1, Rachel, d. unm. ; 2, Janet, m. George Bruce of Langlees, near Melrose, and had two sons, "parents and issue all now alive."

(b) Mary Wedderburn, eldest daughter of (his uncle) Henry Wedderburn of Gosford "sold Gosford to pay her father's debts ......," married Sir John Cumming, an officer in the E. I. Company's service. Issue, three sons, all in the army, Henry (m. Miss La Tour and had issue) ; Alexander, and John. both d. unm ; and three daughters.

(c) James Wedderburn "died (unm.) in the Black Hole in Calcutta in 1756. See Annual Register for that year."

82. Letter from Sir James Webster Wedderburn to J. W. relating to the Marquis de Lally Tollendal who m. Elizabeth, only child of Sir John Wedderburn-Halket by his first wife, Elizabeth Fletcher.

83. Copy memorial for Captain Henry Wedderburn (of Gosford) to the Court of Directors of the East India Company, 1767, as follows :—

MEMORIAL FOR CAPTN HENRY WEDDERBURN,

To the Court of Directors of the East India Company,

Humbly sheweth that your Memorialist having been bred up to the Sea, went out to the East Indies in the Year 1740—a free Mariner, to settle in Bengal & Contd to follow that profession till the Commencement of the War with Suraja Dowlah, when he was appointed Captn Lieut in the Grenadier Company of Militia.

We beg leave to inform the Honble Court, that soon after the loss of Calcutta, the post of Master Attendant became vacant & was Immediately given to him as a Reward for his services.

In that Office he served the Compy for Eighteen Months with Diligence & Attention, when by an Order by the Honble Court of Directors it was conferred on Captn Jas Barton which put your Memorialist again under the Necessity of going to sea.

The Rupture with the Dutch soon following he again Offerd his services, as a Volunteer, which were accepted of by Colonel Ford, who on the Army's Marching to Chandernagore, Left your Memorialist with the Command of Janna & Tobehannaoch Forts, in Order to prevent the Dutch ships from proceeding up the River.

The five Boats were likewise put under his Command & when the Dutch Engaged the Company's ships, your Memorialist with a party of the Corps of Volunteers, went on board Captⁿ Wilson's & the other ships.

Upon taking the Dutch ships your Memorᵃˡᵗ's service in the River became no longer Necessary, he therefore the same Night, joined the Army then lying at Chandernagore, but a Cessation of Hostilities taking place, the Army did not proceed further, & he again entered into the sea service, having obtained the Command of a ship in Mʳ Vansitart's employ.

Soon after this, Advice arrived from England that a Squadron was to be sent under the Command of Mʳ Kepple, to make an attack on the Islands of Mauritius and Bourbon. Your Memorialist was immediately Ordered on that Service, with provisions &c, for the use of the Ships on that Expedition, but as that scheme was after given up, his Voyage thither served no other good purpose but that of looking into the Harbour of Mauritius & bringing an exact account of the situation of the French in those parts, in Respect to their force both by Sea and Land.

Your Memorialist on his arrival at Bombay finding it unsafe to proceed to Sea again on Account of his Ships being Leaky, He immediately transmitted the information he had procured to Admiral Cornish to whom it was very acceptable as he was just at that time preparing for the Expedition to Manilla. Your Memorialist likewise sent as much of the Provisions as he Could possibly spare, for the use of the Squadron at Madras, to whom it proved a very seasonable supply, & having repaired his Ships he set sail for Madras with Two Thousand Barrels of Powder & two Companies of the King's Troops to reinforce that Garrison.

In his passage he fell in with a French Frigate of 20 Guns, much superior to his Ship, which being Dutch built was more adapted for carrying Goods than that of either Engaging, or Escaping from an Enemy.

In this situation as part of the Powder lay above the Water's edge the only means that occurred to him of securing his Ship from being taken or blown up, was to attempt to Board the Frigate, He therefore bore down upon her, & the stratagem succeeded; they immediately made all the sail they could from him, while he continued in Chace for some hours, & afterwards anchored in Telly-chery Road where he was inform'd by Mʳ Hornby chief at that place that there was a French Squadron on the coast of Malabar in consequence of which & by an Order from that Gentleman, your Memorialist the day after his arrival, landed the Troops & proceeded to Bengal when upon his arrival after an unsuccessful Voyage of 8 Months he found the situation of affairs did not permit him to remain long Inactive, as the Governor & Council were alarmed with the accounts of a French Squadron being in Ballasore Roads & blocking up the River.

As there were then several Company's Ships preparing to sail & others daily expected to arrive, your Memorialist proposed to Mʳ Amyatt, acting Governor, in the absence of Mʳ Vansitart then at Mongheir, to fit out an armed Vessel, to observe the Motions of the French Ships, & at same time to give advice to the expected Ships to prevent their falling into the hands of the Enemy then lying in the Mouth of the River, & on this occasion your Memorialist offered his Service which was readily accepted of & he had the satisfaction of bringing in safe the Company's Ship Boscawen, Captⁿ Braund, & several Country Ships in the face of the enemy which so much baffled their expectations that they left their Cruise, & returned to the Islands. The River being then open, your Memorialist reassumed his former employment in which he continued till the commencement of the late War with Cossim Ally Cawn.

The situation of the Company's affairs at that time calling for the warmest exertion, of every one who felt for the unhappy state of their countrymen animated your Memorialist to offer his Services to the Governor and Council by raising a Company of Voluuteers, to be composed of Seamen, Commanders, & Officers of Ships.

This being the only offer of the kind made to the Governor & Council, it was recᵈ with Uncommon approbation, & your Memorialist immediately raised his Company & in the Space of eight days proceeded to join the Army then Marching to Woodanulla under the command of Major Adams.

As that Campaign lasted no longer than the taking of Patna & driving Cossim Ally out of his Country, He was ordered to return to Calcutta, but a Mutiny among the Troops soon following, the Army was obliged to retreat from the banks of Cariemnassie down to Patna, whereby the communication from Calcutta to that place being entirely cut off by the enemy, your Memorialist was again ordered from Calcutta to join the Army then lying at Patna, which he soon affected & continued to act with the Army till the Peace with Sujah Ulla Dowla was concluded by Lord Clive.

And further your Memorialist humbly setts forth that in all these different employments, he has had the satisfaction to meet with the approbation & thanks of the Gentlemen who were Entrusted with the Company's affairs abroad.

Copies of five letters to Captain Henry Wedderburn which are refered to in his letter of 14th Oct. 1767, to the Court of Directors of the East India Company.

(1)   Fort William 2ⁿᵈ Febʸ 1763.
Sir,

I have received your favour of the 31ˢᵗ with the news of the Boscawens safe arrival at Ingeelee, I think the Company are much obliged to you for your services on this Occasion, & I assure you I have a proper sense of them

Signed, Henry Vansitart.

(2)   Fort William 18ᵗʰ Octʳ 1763.
Sir,

I am much obliged to you, [for the services you] have performed since you joined the Army, & think you have the best right to be first considered for any employment that may offer. For my own part I shall hardly have an opportunity of shewing you the regard I could wish as I intend to leave Bengal about the 1ˢᵗ Janʸ but if anything offer before I go, you may depend on my remembering you.

Signed, Henry Vansitart.

(3)   Benares 26ᵗʰ Decʳ 1764.   **Papers Collected by**

Sir,   **John Wedderburn 1819-89.**

Yours of the 10ᵗʰ Ultᵒ came safe to hand & by to-morrow, Cassetts shall send you the letter you desire to Mʳ Spencer. I make not the least doubt but that you will easily obtain whatever you have in view, the material services you have given to our operations, I am sure deserves every thing they can do for you. I have recommended you to the board in the strongest manner & told them in plain terms that if you had not been with us, the operations of the Campaign could not have been carried on. I hope on these considerations the Gentlemen will reward you, at least recommend you in such a manner to the Court of Directors, that they will take Notice of your merit, when you arrive in England & should you be inclined to return to India, I am persuaded, they will not only concur, but give you every Indulgence your Services deserve at the hands of the Company.

Signed, Hector Munro.

(4)   On the Banks of the Gumly opposite to Sultanpour April 13ᵗʰ 1765.

Sir,

I was never consulted upon, or any ways interposed in the appointment of a Commissary, but had I had the least intimation of your being desirous of that Post, I would have exerted whatever Interest I might have to procure it for you, from a conviction, that you deserve that and much more, in return for the many Material Services you have rendered to the Company. The admission of Captⁿ Mᶜpherson has put our Captⁿˢ so much out of humour, that there could not have happened a worse time to introduce the proposal you signified to me, yet your case is so very different & there seems to be a general sense of your Merit throughout the Army, that I am inclined to think were you to write to some of the Captⁿˢ who would be affected thereby that their consents might be obtained, this would bring in others, & perhaps a Majority, & I could then with a good grace help forward your Business by my recommendations, which be assured I am heartily disposed to do. I wish you a speedy recovery being very desirous to have you again with us.

Signed, John Carnac.

(5)   Benares 2nd August 1765.

Sir,

As the Campaign is now over, I think it necessary to inform you, that the Company have no further occasion for the service of your Corps: you will be pleased therefore to give them orders to return to Calcutta acquainting them that their Battⁿ will be continued till the expiration of this month. Your own good behaviour in particular, as also that of the Officers & men under your command, have been reported to me, in the strongest terms, by General Carnac, who joins with me desiring that you and your Officers will accept our thanks for the assistance so cheerfully given to our military operations in these parts.

Signed, Clive.

84   Notes as to the career of Captain Henry Wedderburn of Gosford in the hand of J. W.

LETTERS RELATING TO THE WEDDERBURNS IN AMERICA.

85—95.   Eleven letters from William Wedderburn in Alexandria to J. W., 1823-1837. The material parts of these are quoted in the account given of him and his family in vol. I.

96—102. VARIOUS LETTERS RELATING TO DAVID WEDDERBURN, THE POET, AND MASTER OF THE GRAMMAR SCHOOL, ABERDEEN, AND HIS FAMILY; WILLIAM WEDDERBURN OF BETHELNAY, AND ALEXANDER WEDDERBURN, MINISTER OF FORGAN AND KILMARNOCK.

96.   Letter, 16 July 1837, from Hercules Scott to J. W., promising to look into the records of King's College, Aberdeen, and referring to Kennedy's *Annals of Aberdeen*, vol. I. 136, 471; II. 125.

97.   Letter same to same, 14 Sept. 1837, enclosing the following account of David Wedderburn, written by Mr. A. Taylor, librarian to King's College.

Notice of David Wedderburn, Rector of the Grammar School Aberdeen.

From an inspection of the Registers preserved in the town House of Aberdeen.

The father and mother of David Wedderburn were William Wedderburn and Margery Annand. They were married on the 6th Feb. 1575. They had a son (the eldest, so far as appears) baptized, called David, on the 2nd June 1580; a son Alexander, on the 3rd Sept. 1581; a daughter, Isabel, on the 25th Aug. 1583; a son, George, on the 28th Nov. 1585; a daughter, Bessie, on the 6th Augᵗ 1588; a daughter, Marjory, on the 5th Nov. 1590.

Mr David Wedderburn was married to Janet Johnston on the 30th April 1611. They had a son baptized (name omitted) on 25th March 1612. Janet Johnston (sponse of Mr. David Wedderburn) was buried on the 23d October 1613.

Papers Collected by
John Wedderburn 1819-39.

Mr David Wedderburn was again married, to Bathia Mowat, on the 25th October 1614. They had a daughter baptized, by name Bathia, on the 31st Jan. 1616 ; a son, William, on the 25th Jan. 1617 ; a son, David, on the 28th Oct. 1619 ; a daughter, Janet. on the 19th March 1622 ; a daughter, Jean, on the 16th Feb. 1629 ; a daughter, Bathia, on the 12th June 1630. Of these children the interments of two, William and Margaret, took place on the 16th June and 8th Nov. 1620.

William Wedderburn (the father of David) was buried on the 15th June 1620 and his mother Marjory Annand on the 25th March 1635.

Marjory Wedderburn (David's youngest sister) was married to Matthew Robertson on the 17th Feb. 1614. They had a son, William, baptized on the 11th March 1618 ; a son, James, on the 26th July 1619 ; a daughter, Marjorie on the 23d July 1621 ; a son, Walter, on the 6th November 1623 ; a daughter, Bessie, on the 9th August 1628. Marjory Wedderburn was buried on the 17th Feb. 1630.

The only other person of the name of Wedderburn mentioned in these Registers from 1570-1670 is a Mr William Wedderburn who is a witness, two or three times, of the baptisms of David and Marjory Wedderburn's children and whose wife was buried on the 27th July 1657.

He was probably a younger son of William Wedderburn and Margery Annand, born after 1590, as there is a blank in the registers for some years about that period. If so, being the brother of David and Margery, he would be a very likely guest at the baptisms of their children. From the prefix "Mr." by which he is always distinguished we may also infer that he belonged to one of the learned professions.

David Wedderburn was no doubt educated under Thomas Cargill, master of the Aberdeen Grammar school from 1580 to 1602, who was also the preceptor of Dempster, by whom he is termed " vir literatissimus " and " præcipuus grammaticus " Wedderburn introduces him in his Apotheosis of Duncan Liddel along with Carmichael and Arbuthnot, those " vates, nati melioribus annis," whose songs resound through the happy grove, and when they go to welcome the newly arrived spirit of Liddel, it is Cargill "huic facundia semper prosiguis" who addresses him " venisti tandem Liddele ?" It was no doubt under Cargill that Wedderburn became to Dempster " pueritiæ meæ collega."

It is generally said that both Wedderburn and his bosom friend, Arthur Johnston, were alumni of Marischal college, but no decisive authority has been hitherto alleged. On the contrary, Lauder in the Life of Johnston, prefixed to his "Musæ Sacræ" expressly affirms that Johnston was an alumnus of King's college, " in collegio Regio Aberdonensi diligenter institutus." Wedderburn, likewise, in his " Suspiria " on the death of Johnston, published in 1641, states that their friendship had lasted for 50 years. This would make it commence in 1591, as it could hardly have commenced till they met at College, since Johnston was born at Keith hall, and learned Latin at Kintore. But the deed of foundation of Marischal college is dated only in 1593, and there is no proof of any class being opened before 1595. It would therefore appear that the probabilities are almost all in favour of King's College.

In 1602 Wedderburn was appointed along with Thomas Reid, afterwards Latin Secretary to K. James VI. " coæqual and conjunct master of the Grammar school of Aberdeen."

In 1603 he resigned the school with the view of taking on him the functions of the ministry, but soon resumed his duties.

In 1612 his scholars rebelled and took possession of the song school, which they held for two days, but the ringleaders were imprisoned and 21 of them banished from the schools of the town.

In 1613 he published a Latin poem on the death of Prince Henry. In 1614 he was appointed to teach the high class of Marischal College. In 1619 he published two Latin poems on the occasion of King James' visit to Scotland, the one entitled " Syncophanteriou in reditu Regis in Scotiam " and the other " Propempticou caritatum Aberdonensium." In 1619 he was appointed to teach a lesson in Humanity once a week to the students of Marischal College. In 1620 he was named Grammarian (professor of Humanity) in King's College by the visitation of Bishop Patrick Forbes, but having little or no salary he probably did not resign the Grammar School. In 1625 he published a poem on on the death of James VI, entitled "Abredonia Atrata sub obitum Jacobi VI" (4o Aberd. pp. 12). In 1630 he wrote a new Grammar and went to Edinburgh and other places to get the authority of the Privy Council and Clergy for printing and introducing it. In 1631 the Town Council of Aberdeen allowed him 100 merks to defray his charges in Edinburgh, St. Andrews, and Glasgow when employed in this business. In 1632 he published a " Short Introduction to Grammar " (8o Aberdeen). In 1633 an act of Parliament passed in favour of his grammar. In 1634 he published " Institutiones Grammaticæ " (Aberdeen 8o). Another grammatical work of his, frequently subjoined to Simson's Rudiments. was "Vocabula cum aliis Latiuæ linguæ subsidiis." Among Johnston's poems in the " Delitiæ Poet. Scot " 1637, is one entitled "Despanterius Davidis Vedderburni Reformatus." In 1635 he contributed a poem to the memory of Bishop Forbes, printed in the " Funerals " (Aberd. 4o). In 1640 on account of his bodily infirmity he resigned the Rectorship of the Grammar School at the age of 60, subscribing the minute " M. David Wedderburne, sexagenarius et ultra," and in consideration of his long and faithful services. as well as " by reason he had the burden of a wife and children," he was allowed a pension of 200 merks per annum.

In 1641 he published his " Suspiria " on the death of his fifty years' friend, Arthur Johnston. In 1643 he published his " Meditationum Campestrium seu Epigrammatum moralium centuriæ duæ." In 1644 appeared a " Centuria Tertia," and, the same year, an elegy on the death of the painter Jameson. In 1646 Wedderburne died and was buried "gratis" in the Kirk of St. Nicholas on the 13th Feb. In 1651 a medical treatise of Duncan Liddel's, edited by Dr. Pat. Dun, was published at Aberdeen to which some verses of Wedderburn's are prefixed.

In 1664 his brother Alexander published at Amsterdam an edition of Persius, with David's notes and commentary. There seems every reason to think that this brother of David Wedderburn was the minister of Forgan in Fife.[1] A person of the same name is styled by Dempster "vir literaturæ **Papers Col-** insignis," and under the same name there is a work in the Advocates' Library, Edinburgh, entitled **lected by** "Radii Augustiniani, sive Præcipuæ S. P. Augustini in S. Scripturæ locos annotationes." (Sylvæ **John Wedder-** Ducis, 1652 8°). David Wedderburne was eminent as a Latin Poet, a grammarian, and an instructor **burn 1819-89.** of youth. In the minute of Council, conferring him a high eulogium is passed upon his merits as a teacher. He appears to have enjoyed the friendship of the most distinguished people of the town. We find among the witnesses and godfathers at the baptisms of his children, Robert Johnston of Crimond, baillie (probably a relation of his first wife) ; David Rutherford, baillie ; Mr. William Forbes, afterwards first bishop of Edinburgh ; Dr. William Johnston, brother of Arthur Johnston and professor of Mathematics in Marischal College ; Dr. Patrick Dun, principal of Marischal College ; Sir Paul Menzies of Kinmundy, Provost of Aberdeen, and Dr. John Forbes of Corse, son to Bishop Patrick, and professor in King's College. On one occasion also, in 1629, at the baptism of a child of Dr. Robert Baron, professor of Divinity, Marischal College, Wedderburn was present along with Dr. John Forbes, Mr. Patrick Sibbald, one of the ministers of Aberdeen, and the Lord Bishop of Moray.

The mutual affection of Wedderburn and Arthur Johnston stood the test of fifty years. In his poem addressed to Wedderburn, Johnston gives a beautiful picture of their early pursuits. Their ages were equal and their dispositions of a kindred sort :

" Par, memini, cum noster amor æ prodidit, ætas :
Par genius nobis, ingeniumque fuit."

They wandered together by the banks of the Dee and the Don, and climbed the neighbouring hills:
" Sæpe petebamus vicinos collibus amnes,
Qui tibi uatali non procul urbe fluunt."

Johnston had begun to cultivate the muses—"Phœbi consceudere collem "—before his friend, whom he warmly incited both by example and precept to the same elegant pursuit. In his answer,Wedder- burn feelingly acknowledges his obligations in this respect, and while he states that Johnstou's fortune was equal to his genius, laments that his own adverse circumstances had damped his poetical aspirations :

" Nec mihi concessum pro spe juga visere Phœbi
Nec mihi fortunæ, qui fuit ante, tenor."

Besides addressing to him the above poem and celebrating his Reformed Grammar in a highly com- plimentary epigram, Johnston introduces Wedderburu lamenting with himself in alternate strains the death of John Johnston, the Latin poet, and Professor of Divinity at St. Andrew's, and the intimate friend of Andrew Melvil, and in another poem, when enumerating the famous men of Aberdeen, after mentioning the Menzies, the Rutherfords, the Collisons, the Cullens, and the two Cargill's,

" patriæ sidera fratres
Lumine qui replent orbis utrumque latus ; "

he adds
" Hic comes est meritis par Wedderburnus utrique,"
and, in proof even of his having a foreign reputation,
" Nec si de patria migret honore minor."

Dempster styles Wedderburn " utriusque linguæ doctissimus " and adds " vivit adhuc (1621) in Scotia, et laborioso bonarum artium experimento juventutem patriæ erudit, plura felicissimi iugenii monumenta relicturus et posteris profecturus."

The celebrated Vossius, with whom he corresponded, in the answer to one of his letters calls him " homo eruditissimus beneque promerens de studiis juventutis " and again " homo doctissimus et nostri etiam amans." In Benson's " Life of Arthur Johnston " he mentions " doctissimus ejus amicus Wedderburnus."

Authorities :—Aberdeen Council Registers, 1602-40. Aberdeen Registers of marriages, baptisms, and burials, 1578-1670. Dempsteri Historia Ecclesiastica Scotorum, Bannatyne Club Ed. 2 vols. 4to, 1829. Chalmer's " Life of Thomas Ruddiman," Lond., 1794, 8vo. " Lauderi Poetarum Scotorum Musæ Sacræ," Ed., 1739, 8vo. " Vossii Epistolæ," fol. Lond., 1690. " Delitiæ Poetarum Scotorum," 2 vols., 12mo., Amsterdam, 1637. Chamber's " Biographical Dictionary of Scotsmen," 4 vols., 8vo. Glasgow, 1835. Johnston's " Psalmi," (ed. Benson, Lond., 1741, 4to.)

Signed, A. TAYLOR, B.C.,

King's College, Aberdeen, 13 Sept., 1837.

98. Letter to J. W. from Mr. George Garioch, minister of Meldrum, dated from Meldrum Manse, 6 July 1837, as to Mr. William Wedderburn, formerly minister at Bethelnay. In it he says :—

" The date of the earliest parochial records in 1698, which is more than half a century later than the time at which Mr. Wedderburn lived. The parish Church was removed from Bethelnay to Meldrum at the above date, and there is an incidental remark in one of the Minutes of Sessiou of that year which shows that the last Minister of Bethelnay was Mr. Robert Urquhart. .... There is nothing to be gathered in regard to him from tradition in this quarter. .. .. There is just one family of Wedderburns in this parish, and I went to them after receiving your letter, but they had never even heard that such a man existed as Mr. Wedderburn. The site of his Manse can still be

---

[1] This is an error : Alexander Wedderburn of Forgan was the son of the Rev. James Wedderburn of Moonzie, and was born in about 1621, fifty years after the birth of this brother of David Wedderburn. See vol. I.

V

Papers Col-
lected by
John Wedder-
burn 1819-89.

shown at Bethelnay, and the foundation of the Church in which he preached can be seen, and the
Church-yard is still preserved as a burial ground.   I was told some years ago by a man who lived on
the spot where the Manse was, that he had found a stone (supposed to be the top stone of the door)
on which the words " William Wedderburn " were cut.   I was anxious to see it, and desired him to
look for it and send it to me, but he was never able to find it again."

99.   Letter to J. W. from Mr. Andrew Hamilton, minister of Kilmarnock, dated from
      Kilmarnock, July 31st 1837, as to Alexander Wedderburn, formerly minister there.
      In it he says :—
         "Mr. Alexander Wedderburn was Minister of Kilmarnock under King Charles II.'s indulgence.
      He came from Forgan in Fife to Kilmarnock, but the Records of Session do not inform us at what
      time.
         The Register does not shew whether he was married in Kilmarnock, to whom he was married, nor
      how many children he had, nor what were their names, nor what was his wife's name.
         The Highland Host visited Kilmarnock not in 1677 but in 1678.   Mr. Wedderburn was treated by
      one of them with great violence and was much injured in body, and probably this eventually
      occasioned his death. ' It may be worth while (saith Woodrow) to observe that before the Highlanders
      left Kilmarnock, they resolved upon the Sabbath to plunder the Town and did actually plunder
      several houses as we have heard, and had done the like to all if the matter had not been overruled
      with great intercession and considerable sums private persons advanced to their officers.   It was this
      day Mr. Wedderburn, Minister of the place, and well known by the books he had published, got the
      beginning of his sickness of which he died by the barbarity of a Highlandman's pushing him on the
      breast with the end of his musket when he was interceding to spare the place.'   (Woodrow, book II,
      chap. xiii, section 3.)   Accordingly the Minutes of Session that same year (1678) bear that in the
      Months of Oct[r] and November Mr. Wedderburn was absent from sickness.   And in December it is
      stated that the Minister being now removed by death the Magistrates and certain towns-people were
      appointed to manage the Poor during the vacancy.   Though I have no doubt that he was interred in
      Kilmarnock I find no person who can inform me in what corner of the Church-yard.   And there can
      be no grave stone else I must have seen or heard of it.
         Whether his widow survived him the Register of Session does not inform us.
         The Rev[d] Dr. Burns of Paisley, the Editor of the last Edition of Woodrow, makes the following
      remarks in a Note respecting the Works of Mr. Wedderburn.   " Besides what he gave to the Public
      during his life, after his death two volumes of his sermons were published partly from notes taken in
      shorthand by those who heard them and partly from his own MSS.   The subject of the first of these
      is the nature of the Covenant of Grace, or as he terms it ' David's Testament opened up in 40 Sermons,
      2 Sam. xxiii. 5.'   The subject of the second is the ' History of our Lord's Transfiguration evangelically
      and practically improved in twenty-two discourses.'   The Volumes were published after his death about
      the commencement of last Century and they are dedicated to the Countess of Rothes and the Countess
      of Wemyss, two of those " honourable women " who have adorned their high stations by the virtues and
      graces of personal godliness.   The discourses considered as posthumous remains are highly creditable
      to the talents of the author.   They abound in excellent expositions of Scripture, the style is simple
      and by no means vulgar, and they exhibit what we do not always find in the writings of the period,
      a paramount regard to the practical bearings of christian truth on the hearts and lives of christian
      professors.   No man who knows the sermons of Mr. Wedderburn will say that the Preachers of
      the olden times were exclusively polemical or that Calvinism is incapable of a most full and powerful
      application to ' the bosoms and business of human Beings.' "

100. Letter to J. W. on the same subject from Mr. William Anderson, session clerk of
      Kilmarnock, dated from Kilmarnock, 14 Aug. 1837.   In it he says :—
         " I have searched the parish records but find no register of Births, Marriages, or deaths so far back
      as Mr. Wedderburn's time.   I have enquired of the Church Officer whether any Monument to his
      memory remains in the Church or Church-yard but find none.   Alterations caused great havoc
      amongst the tombs and none remain but those of a very recent date.
         I am now seventy years of age and recollect my Grandsire conversing about Mr. Wedderburn,
      but being then very young I only recollect the name.
         The minutes of Session at the time of Mr. Wedderburn's death are still entire.   The following
      Extracts refer to Mr. Wedderburn at the time of his decease, viz. :—
         " Session, October Ult[o] 1678—No session since the preceding in August be reason of the Minister's
      illness.   Now they are holden in the Minister's chamber."
         (No date).   " No session further now kept by Mr. Wedderburn but occasionally by other Ministers
      as they come to preach."
         By Minute of 23 December Mr Wedderburn was still living and by a Minute previous to the 30th
      he was removed by death."

101. Further letter same to same, on the same subject, dated Kilmarnock, 1st September
      1837.   In it Mr. Anderson says :—
         " On searching among our Session Records for something else I found a small old looking Book and
      supposing there might be something in it referring to Mr. Wedderburn I immediately set to examine
      it.   I found the title of it " Register of Baptisms " and commencing in 1640.   A preamble by the
      Session Clerk in 1735 states that it was very incomplete, years and months being wanting.   He
      further adds " By this Register it would appear that Mr Michael Wallace was Min[r] in this place till
      An[o] 1640 or 1641 and that Mr Matthew Mowat succeeded him.   And Mr James Carnegie to him
      about An[o] 1663 and Mr Alexander Wedderburn to him about An[o] 1670.' "

I have carefully examined the Register from 1670 till the period of Mr W's decease, almost every page at the top is titled "Baptized by Mr Alexander Wedderburn Min' Kilmarnock" this commences in June 1671 and ends in June 1676. I have further examined the Baptisms and find only two of Mr Wedderburn's Childrens' names, recorded as being baptized in one day, from which I would infer they were twins : it is recorded thus—"May 4th 1671 William Wedderburn procreate betwix Mr Alexander Wedderburn Min', and Helen Turnbull, and Jean Wedderburn their Daughter, Both Baptized by Mr. Adair." As the Register appears to be very complete in Mr Wedderburn's time, I would conclude that these were the only children they had after coming to Kilmarnock." Papers Collected by John Wedderburn 1819-89.

(The Kilmarnock parish registers are now preserved in the Edinburgh Register House. They have been searched 1640-1750, but contain no other Wedderburn reference. There are some entries of Woodburns or Wodburns, which may be corruptions of the name, but there is nothing to prove this.)

102. Letter to J. W. from Mr. Charles Nairn, minister of Forgan, co. Fife, dated Forgan Manse, 15th August 1837. In it he says :—

"I regret that it was not in my power to return an earlier answer to your queries regarding Mr Wedderburn as the Minister of the Parish. From the Parochial Registers I could obtain no information, and I therefore made application to the Clerk of our Presby' who has made a search in the Records from which it appears that Mr W. was admitted as Minister of Forgan in Feb' 1647, and was deposed in 1655. He afterwards accepted the indulgence and preached at Kilmarnock."

103—119, *Miscellaneous Documents.*

103. Various rough notes by J.W. of papers in the Scrymgeour-Wedderburn charter chest, and, with few exceptions, included in the inventory of those papers already given in this volume. The exceptions are as follows :—

    1502. Entry illegible.
    1526.   "   "
    1528. Sasine in favour of James W., son and heir of Thomas W.
    1546. Sasine in favour of Thomas W., son and heir of James W.
    (These are similar to those noted in No. 669 of the Scrymgeour-Wedderburn papers, except that there the name Thomas in each case appears as Robert.)

104. Extracts from the "Compt Buik" of David Wedderburn, transcribed for J.W. by James Thomson, the historian of Dundee, 1827. See below No. 105 (f) and the full account of David Wedderburn's MS., post p. 163.

105. Copies of some old papers, made for J.W. by James Thomson, 1827.

This is a thin copybook, closely written. It contains :—

  (a) "The Book of the Lamentations of Charles the Prince, the son of James, written in 1747 by David Christian in Brechin." (From the original MS.).
  (b) Three inventories of the furniture, linen, &c., in the Castle of Finhaven, 1709—1712.
  (c) A blacksmith's account in 1704.
  (d) A Fence for the Tobacco Club, Edin., 1727.
  (e) Letter from Alexander Duncan, Edinburgh, to Alexander Duncan, Town Clerk of Dundee, respecting the Box in which the Freedom of Dundee was presented to the Duke of Cumberland in 1746.
  (f) An extract from David Wedderburn's MS. It is not stated where this is copied from, but from the style of the document there can be no doubt that it is written by the author of the "Compt Buik," and, singularly enough, there is clear evidence in the "Compt Buik" itself of a page having been cut out of it. I am inclined to think that this was done by James Thomson at the instance of my grandfather, whose pride could not brook anything which he thought the least discreditable to the family, and who would have accounted as such this record of complaints against Kingennie by his younger brother. The document is as follows [1] :—

"Ane remembrance to ye clerk my broyr off ye speciall Innaturall Iniuries and wrangis he and his wife hes done to me.

ffirst Immediatlie efter my fayris deceis he and scho pat me to ye gaet and sett out my kistis befoir me on ye calsay forñet ye gait.

Thairefter I past to calhne (?) wt petir claybillis beleifing they had no ill in yr hart to me : efter my hame cuming I cam first to Kyngany qr they dwelt becaus ye pest was in dundie and crafit ludgeing of yame, they vold not suffer me to lyt and causit qvoy me fra ye toun qr I was qstraint that nyt to ryd to Dunnoyn to Mr. Jon lovell to my bed.

[1] There are a good many abbreviated words in this document. Thus q stands for " con," and for "quhe" as in "qstraint," "qncat(communicat) and "qu"(when);and pstands for "pro" as in "pmittit," "pponit." Some old words also may not be clear to everyone, thus attr = attour (besides) ; blank satle = blank settlement; blokit = bargained ; bnis = bairns ; boist = boast, *i.e.*, threatening ; fornet = fornanent, in front of ; lyt = alight ; mt = Margaret ; prnas = premissis ; Reg', of course, stands for Register ; rot = Robert ; secret = secretary ; sma = summa (sum total) ; wald cu na speid = would cum no speed, *i.e.*, get no distance ; and zit = yet. With these notes the document can, I think, be fairly easily read.

Papers Col-
lected by
John Wedder-
burn 1819-89

Item. yrefter he causit me fynd out persones to by his wester closs and pmittit to gif me ye upmost hous for 9ᵈ merks. Efter .... (?) yrto he blokit wt Wm. Davidsone yoʳ for aue thousand mks fur yt hous and debarrit me fra ye samy. Sonayn I was qstraint to by a costly hous to my gryt hurt.

Item. Quhen I haid ryt to 4 bolls victuall out of Thoas maors gruuds cropt zeirlie be infeftment I pmit to have coft yis croft fra ye qstable and oyris haueand ryt to ye samy Qn I haid qncat my mind to him fur yis effeir he past and coft it himself and debarrit me yrfra.

Item. Qᵘ James bovare shrcfclerk deit I schew him I wes to deill for ye shrefisclerkschip, he schew me I wald qn na speid becaus he intendit to have it himself and wald na wayis suffer me to deill for it and so never got it his selfe.

Item. ye gudeman of Ardony causit ye secreᵗ and me agre for ye clerkschip of his regᵗ iu August. Efter I schew ye clerk ye samy he causit a geutillman ane freind of ye gudeman of pitkere caus ye secreᵗ dischairge me of itt beleifing to have gotten ye sam to himself.

Item. qᵘ I schew him I wes to get ye qstablis clerkschip he past to ye qstable and causit ye qstable subscryve a letter of it to Mr. James his sone aud defraudit me of it as ye Laird shew to me his selfe ye samy, and he never gat it him self.

Item. I wes prydit to be clerk to ye gild of yis burᵗ as my prvissione yrof zit extant will schew ; he debarrit me yrfra.

Item. qᵘ he past to England iu qmissioun he unnaturallie advaucit Johue Patton and substitutit him iu his place and office aud quittit na crydit to me and abhorrit me sa that I eschame to reherss.

Item. qᵘ ye bischop of S. Andross and oyris cam here to elect yᵉ baleis they pponit me ane. He wald not suffer me to be acceptit but offered James .... to be aue.

Item. to remember the clerk qᵘ he past to ye auld earle of Craufurd iu his Ludgeing iu Dundic. Mr. Alexʳ tuik me wt him. He crafit ye earle to be his freind aud qfessit he feillit to me in tymes past bot in tyme cuming faytfullie pmittit to mend to me agane qlk he never zit did.

Item. sen ye pturbmoue iu yis touu he never sufferit me to be acceptit in ony publict office nor zit to be on ye qsell agane. Qlk ye best sort of ye qsell will dcclair be disasentit ever I suld (be) ou yᵉ agane and said I wes not vorthy. I remit to God all his wrangis done to me to requyte.

Item. I causit Thoas Guthre gif him vᵉ merkes. Item. by my moyen he gat of auld rot's fayr's broyr the half of ye lugeing and sex acris of laud. I awuan ,, ... to ye twa meu ane hundret lib and inair he never debursit as he pmitit I suld be equall wt him in all benefitts and to satisfie me ye half my debursingis. I remit to his qscience gif he hes done ye sam or not And remittis to God to requyte his ingratitude.

I will not expreme how he craftely maid a decreit to have causit ye qstable of Duudie insert in ye blauk satle be yame & auld rot to ye qstable how to have reft me of all rot's lands as Mr Alexr's awu hand wryt extant will verefie qlk ye qstable gef me to keip. I will not expreme my honest liberaleteis & reddy service done to him seikiug his faur qlk (I) culd neuer geit bot hopis in God he will repent it agane.

Sma of all qlk he is justly awiu me. Aue hundret thre lib or yrby.

Item. The clerk deteint fra me the tyme of my fayers Deceiss aue number of wryttis maid be my fayr and left in his hands assiguit and left to me by my fayr as my ryt will schaw. Gif it were coptit it wald be bettir thau vᵉ merks.

Item. to lay to ye clerk's charge the supplies of guds aud geir suuntyme ptaining to my umqll fayr of gude memory and efter his deceis to ws all his bnis Qlk he receauit attr his airschip, my ryt exteuding to L. lib & bettir.

Item. my fayr directit ye said Mr Alexʳ to gif every aue of ws his bnis after his deceiss jᵘ merks ; my pt. jᵉ merks.

Item. my broyr the clerk aud his wyf in thaire aviu heiche chalmer bad me lat all secreute of rot's acris pas wt yame Aud as they suld ansʳ to God they suld ayr gif me Alexr's mekle land bak agaue or ye half of yame or ellis ye justly valedetie of yᵉ half yrof extending to thre acris qlk wald have been nyn huudret mks aud he only gef me thre hundret mks and is avaud me ye swmes befor wryttin aud qstraint me with boist to accept ye sau. This is of weretie. I remit to his qacieuce ye prmas as he wald God blissit him and his aud it wt yame to preserve his pnes to me for he knawis I wes ye lustrmt that movit rot and thoas Guthre to gif him ye benefitts he gat of yame.

Lastly at all occasiones how onwordely the clerk hes defamt me schawand to all men sic as I eschame to rehers a verry fals inveutione. I take God to be my avengr and his qacience to be witness to ye wraug.

Gif he amend not to me aud haue not my blissing and my bnis to his .... qlk I beleif in God that God sall move his hart to do the sam or ellis God will requyte his Iugratitude qlk my fayr that gef him all he had expectit oyʳ at his hands to his barnis. I ueid not to schaw to any psone bot its weill koawin mayr I nor my buis at yᵉ marriages wes neuer behaldu to him nor his, and all yᵉ dayis wes neuer Iutreatit sa mekle as anes to dyn wt yame Allbeit they wer liberalle euer to him of yᵉ giftis.

Item. ye clerk causit me be defraudit of mt mylaris legacie and vald not suffer me to get it qfirmit."

106. Letter in Swedish from Professor J. S. Wallenius to Alexander Therleff, adjutant to Governor-general of Finland, dated Abo, 22 July 1835, stating that there is in the Cathedral of St. Henry at Abo, a monument to a Samuel Cockburn, who served in the Swedish army, and died in 1623, but none to any officer of the name of Wedderburn. With a letter (in German) from A. Therleff to J.W., dated Helsingfors, 25 July 1835, enclosing the above and an English translation of it.

It would still seem, however, that a Scotch officer of the name of Wedderburn is buried in the Cathedral of Abo, although no monument to him is there. In the account of the Cathedral in Murray's *Handbook for Russia* (1893, col. p. 446) it is stated that there are buried in the Cathedral both Colonel Samuel Cockburn and "another Scot, distinguished in the service of Sweden (17th century), General Wedderburn." This General Wedderburn is, no doubt James Wedderburn (son of David Wedderburn of the MS.), who was on foreign service in 1644. See the account of him in vol. 1.

Papers Collected by John Wedderburn 1819-39.

107. Letter, dated Wallace Craigie, 30 Dec. 1782, from George Constable to Alexander Scrymgeour-Wedderburn of Wedderburn, enclosing an extract from Edward's "Description of Angus" (1678) as follows :—

"Deidoni Familiae patriciae ac spectatores sunt Wedderburni, Fletcheri, Halyburtoui, Kinlochi, Scrymgeri, Davidsoni. Ex perantiquo Wedderburnorum stemmate Mr Alexander Wedderburnus pullulavit, qui in prudentia politica saluberrima tautus evasit, ut illum Rex serenissimus Jacobus VI. ad intima maximique uomenti consilia saepius invitatum, nhuitus (ultimum?) amplecteretur, regalliterque remuneratum demitteret.

Cujus nepos ex filio maximo, hodie Alex^r Wedderburnus Baro: de Easter Powrie, est Gentis Wedderburniae Primus ; ex filio secuudo bini sunt uepotes equites aurati, D^s Alexander Wedderburnus, Baro: de Blackness, et D^s Petrus Wedderburnus, Baro: de Gosfurd, in Scotiae supremo senatu pluriunis jam annis judex purpuratus perspicacissimus et meritissimus ; ac commemorati M. Alexaudri tertius filius, Mr Johauues Wedderburuus, juvenilibus anuis Audreapoli iu collegio Leouardiuo Philosophiae professor eximius, post varias gentes, earumque eruditionis seminariis praesertim visitatis, medicinae animum applicaus, iu ea tautus evasit ut Loudiui Medici Regii equitisque aurati honoribus sit ampliatus ; taudemque iu patriam reversus, ejusque Aescupalius habitus, anno aetatis 81, virgo, satur annis, opibus, honoribus, Gosfordia', quam Christianissime reddens Deo auimam, bibliothecam Leonardinam quot selectiorum (?) voluminum millibus ornavit et auxit."

"Angusiac Barones liberi alphabeti serie sunt hi, Affleck de eodem, Blaire de Balgillo, ... Wedderburu de Easter Powrie, totius geutis Wedderburuiae stirps, Wedderburn de Blackness, Winton de Strathmartine, &c., &c.

(The Latiu "Description of Augus," by Robert Edward, miuister of Murroes, has never been reprinted. It was printed on a broad sheet to accompany a map, aud of this sheet ouly three copies (one of them imperfect) are knowu to exist. Of those that are perfect, oue belongs to the Earl of Dalhousie, aud the other to Mr. A. C. Lamb of Dundee. I have verified the extract given from the last mentioned copy in which there appear to be oue or two misprints. The grammar is also occasionally at fault, and some of the words are by no means classical. An English reuderiug of the " Descriptiou " was published iu the form of a pamphlet at Dundee in 1793, but this is also now rare.)

108. Extract from Richard Bannatyne's journal, 1570-73 (8vo, Edin. 1806) :—

This gives an account (pp. 120-127), of the siege of Dumbarton Castle aud mentions in the iuventory of arms in the castle, 2 April 1571, " Item. xviii cullaveris : of these at my Lord Lennox command ane giveu to Harie Wedderburne, aue uther to George Duudas " .. .. aud, 8-9 Nov. 1571, Captain Wedderburu is named again as at Dundee (p. 302-4), See " The Lennox " by William Fraser, 1874, vol. I, p. 106, where the above inventory is also quoted, and Holiushed's Chronicles (4to London, 1808), where it is stated that a soldier uamed Wedderburn followed Captain Crawford of Jordanhill, aud was the next after him to euter the castle (vol. v, p. 649).

109. Extracts from the diary of John Lamont of Newton, 1649-71 (Edin. 1830). All these are quoted or referred to in vol. I. of his work.

110. Extracts from History of Transactions in Scotland, 1715-16 and 1745-46, by George Charles, 2 vols, Stirling 1816, quoting :—
   (a) An account of the battle of Gladsmuir by au officer of the Elector's army, which says, " Brigadier Fowke must have falleu into their hands (*i.e.*, the troops of King James), if Captain Wedderburn, a foot officer of our's, had not called out aloud to him to apprize him of his danger " (II. 57.)
   (b) Cumberlaud's official report of the battle of Culloden, naming among the prisoners, " From the Life Guards, under the command of Lord Elcho, Sir John Wedderburn from Angus " (II, 302.)
   (c) " The Earls of Cromartie aud Kilmaruock, Lord Balmerino, Sir John Wedderburn, ... were sent aboard the ' Exeter ' man of war, at Iuverness, aud arrived iu Londou on the 20th May, 1746."

111. Five papers relating to James Wedderburn, Bishop of Duublane :—
   (a) Letter from M. Russell to J W., dated Leith, 21 Feb. 1836, to the effect that the Bishop, no doubt, published some works, but all anonymously. (b) Note as to the armorial bearings of the See of Duublane. (c) Extracts from Aikman. (d) Copy of iuscription on the Bishop's tomb iu Cauterbury Cathedral. (e) Another note as to the armorial bearings of the See of Duublane.

112. Copy of two letters from Charles II. :—(a) dated at Brussells, 6 July 1649, to Mr. Alexander W.; (b) dated at Perth, 17 Jan. 1651, to the provost and bailies of Dundee, in regard to Sir Alexander W.

See ante s. Blackness Papers, Nos. 6 and 7, and post s. Municipal Records, Dundee Charters, Nos. 67 and 69.

Papers Collected by
John Wedderburn 1819-89.

113. Memorandum by J.W. of historical articles in his possession. It includes—
(a) A parcel containing the hair of King James VIII, cut from his head at Rome, 29 Feb 1745.
(b) A bit of tartan of the clan of McDuff, cut from a dress worn in 1745-6, at Moyhall the seat of Mc'Intosh, co. Inverness, by H.R.H. Prince Charles Edward.

114. Two letters from Katharine Wedderburn (daughter to Thomas Wedderburn) to her nephew J.W., dated Edin: 4 April and 2 Oct. 1819. In the first of these she writes:
"Your aunt (Mary Wedderburn) was some time with Miss Read in London, and went with a friend of Miss Read's to Quebeck; when that family returned she remained there, and we could not hear any further particulars of her, but conclude that she died there.
"When I lived with Miss Read she drew my picture; at my mother's death it was sent me; pray will you accept it and place it with the family pictures; it was like me when it was done, tho' it is not so now."
(This portrait is now in the possession of the Rev. John Walter Wedderburn.)

115. Note on the Dunbars of Grangehill, correcting an erratum at pp. 89 and 90 of J.W.'s printed memoir, as follows:—
"Thomas Wedderburn married a daughter not of Robert Dunbar of Grangehill, but of Alexander, a younger brother of Robert, who died unmarried," and (p. 90) this Alexander married a daughter, not of Brodie of Brodie, but of Dr. James Fraser, who was a physician in London and first secretary to Chelsea Hospital for many years."

116. Letter, dated Keith House, Tranent, 31 July 1838, from John Wedderburn (afterwards second baronet of Balindean) to J.W. :—
In it he proposes to give J.W. particulars of the family portraits in Sir David's possession, and also says, "I am fully satisfied with what you now say of the occasion of the adoption of the 'Aquila non captat' by the Augus branch." Unfortunately, J.W.'s suggestion on this matter was does not appear.

117. Fly leaf, dated in MS. "1818," entitled "Execution of a mother and daughter."
An account of the trials and execution of Sarah Welderburn (æt. 19) and Francis (æt. 55), her mother, for the murder of a male child, son to the former, at Ditchburn, Yorks, in October last. Printed by ...... Catnach, printer, 2 Monmouth Court.

118. Two newspaper cuttings relating to Robert Wedderburn, the black preacher :—
(a) Dated in MS. 20 Dec. 1819, reporting his imprisonment in Newgate for a blasphemous libel.
(b) His trial at the London Sessions for "having kept a home so irregular as to become a nuisance," and sentence to twelve months' imprisonment with hard labour. The report states that he was then 69 years of age, and was "one of the persons who were tried for the Cato Street conspiracy."

119. Sketch of Wedderburn lineage sent by J.W. to Burke's *Peerage and Baronetage* in 1829.

This list has been compiled for me by Mr. T. Maitland Anderson, librarian to the St. Andrew's University. The Register begins in 1472, and is at first defective. It was made up every University March, and thus included students who had entered in the previous October. The age Register. of matriculation would seem to have been about fourteen or fifteen, though later on students did not matriculate so early. Up to about 1530 there were three steps to the Master's degree, Matriculation, Bachelor, and Licentiate, but after that date the degree of Master was given without the intermediate step. I have endeavoured in each case to identify the person mentioned, but, as, unfortunately, the Register hardly ever gives more than the name, it has not always been possible to do this with certainty.

1. William Wedderburn.   Bach. 1475 ; Lic. 1477 ; Dives.
    He is probably identical with the Sir William Wedderburn, monk in Aberbrothock or Arbroath, named 6 Oct. 1524, in vol. 235 of the Dundee Protocol Books. (See post s. Municipal Records). From that entry it is clear that he was son to Walter Wedderburn in Welgait. He must have been born about 1458.

2. John Wedderburn.   Matr. 1500-1504 ; Nac. Angusiæ.
    The words " Nac. Angusiæ," born in Angus, make it certain that he was of the Dundee family. The list in which his name occurs is undated, but is certainly not before 1500 and not after 1504. If aged about fifteen at the date of his matriculation, he would be born 1485-90. I am unable to make any suggestion as to his parentage. The earliest mentions of a John Wedderburn relate to the son of James Wedderburn and Janet Barry, one of the three brothers known for their author-ship of the " Gude and Godlie Ballates." (See vol. I) But the eldest of them, James, was admitted a burgess of Dundee in 1514, probably at the age of 20 or 21, and could not, therefore, have had a younger brother born in 1490. Possibly their father had a brother of the name of John ; but, if so, he must have either left Dundee, or died without issue, as the Dundee records contain no reference either to him or to descendants of his.

3. Robert Wedderburn.   Matr. 1500-1506 ; Nac. Angusiæ ; Bach. 1509, Pauper; Lic. 1511.
    Here again the date of the list is uncertain. He may be the Robert Wedderburn who married Janet Kyd, and was father to Alexander Wedderburn, the old clerk. Alexander Wedderburn, first of Kingennie, and eldest son to the clerk, was born in 1561, and as his father, when appointed clerk of Dundee in 1556-57, can hardly have been less than 27 or 30, we may assume that he was born about 1525-30 ; and if at that date his father was about 40, it would be consistent with the birth date (1490), indicated by this matriculation. If this is correct, Robert Wedderburn must have lived to a good old age, as he was certainly alive in 1573.

4. John Wedderburn.   Matr. 1507.
    Here the date is certain, but I am again at a loss to identify the person named with any one mentioned in vol. I, and can only repeat what I have said with reference to No. 2.

5. James Wedderburn.   Matr. 1507.   (See below s. No. 7.)

6. James Wedderburn.   Matr. 1509.   (See below s. No. 7.)

7. James Wedderburn.   Matr. 1514 ; Nac. Angusiæ.
    There are three persons of this name to each of whom any one of these entries may refer, viz. : James, elder brother to David Wedderburn in Murraygait ; James, son to Robert Wedderburn and Janet Froster ; and James, son of James Wedderburn and Janet Barry, and eldest of the three brothers of the " Gude and Godlie Ballates." If the 1514 entry refers to this last, it is odd that he should have been admitted burgess of Dundee in this very year, at so early an age. If it is to him that one of the two earlier entries refer, there must have been a considerable difference in age between him and his younger brothers. See below Nos. 8 and 9.

8. John Wedderburn.   Matr. 1525 ; Bach. 1526 ; Dives. Lic. 1528.
    This is with little doubt the second of the " Gude and Godlie Ballates " triumvirate, sons to James Wedderburn and Janet Barry.

9. Robert Wedderburn.   Matr. 1526 ; Bach. 1529 ; Lic. 1530.
    The third of the three brothers. He was instituted to the chaplainry of S. Katharine in Dundee in 1528, and afterwards (before 1551) became Vicar of Dundee.

St. Andrew's
University
Register.
10. Alexander Wedderburn. Matr. 1578.
      I have no doubt in identifying him with Alexander Wedderburn, first of Kingennie, born in 1561.

11. William Wedderburn. Matr. 1588 ; Grad. 1592.
      Probably the son of Alexander Wedderburn of Pittormie. He was minister of Pittenweem, and
      afterwards in Dundee.

12. Alexander Wedderburn. Matr. 1596.
      Probably Alexander Wedderburn, second of Kingennie, born in 1583 ; but, possibly, his namesake
      and contemporary, the son of Patrick Wedderburn and Elizabeth Low. I think, however, that the
      latter is the person mentioned below (No. 14), as in 1601 Kingennie's son was studying the law with
      his father. See the account of him in vol. I.

13. David Wedderburn. Matr. 1598 ; Grad. 1600.
      See below, No. 15, from which it appears that there were two David Wedderburns who
      matriculated within four years, and graduated within six years of each other. One of them is
      certainly the son of Robert Wedderburn, the merchant, and Elizabeth Coustonn, and the fact that he
      was a graduate of St. Andrew's, probably accounts for the constant prefix of " Mr. " to his name.
      The other may be David Wedderburn, afterwards the well-known grammarian and master of the
      Grammar School, Aberdeen, who was born at Aberdeen in 1580. There is no other David Wedderburn
      to whom I can suggest that the second of these entries refers. At the same time there is no record
      of the grammarian having been educated at S. Andrews, and one would expect him to have remained
      at Aberdeen.

14. Alexander Wedderburn. Matr. 1601 ; Grad. 1604.
      Son to Patrick Wedderburn and Elizabeth Low. See above s., No. 12.

15. David Wedderburn. Matr. 1602 ; Grad. 1606. (See above s. No. 13.)

16. George Wedderburn. Matr. 1602.
      The only person with whom I can connect this entry is George, son of Peter Wedderburn, of
      whom I find but one other mention, viz., in David Wedderburn's "Compt Buik" (post pp. 163 seqq.)
      where " Petir Wedderburn's twa sons Petir and George " are named. There is no reference to him
      in the Dundee records, and he probably died in youth.

17. James Wedderburn. Matr. 1604 ; Grad. 1608. (See below s. No. 19.)

18. James Wedderburn. Matr. 1604 ; Grad. 1608. (See below s. No. 19.)

19. James Wedderburn. Matr. 1605 ; Grad. 1608.
      One of these three persons is certainly James, second son to Alexander Wedderburn, first of
      Kingennie, who was born in 1589, and was afterwards town clerk of Dundee. He died in 1627.
      Another is James, Bishop of Dunblane, born in 1585. The third is probably James, son to Alexander
      Pittormie, and afterwards minister of Moonzie in Fife. He was born about 1588.

20. John Wedderburn. Matr. 1615 ; Grad. 1618.
      This is certainly Sir John Wedderburn of Gosford, the celebrated physician. He was youngest
      son to Alexander Wedderburn, first of Kingennie, and was born about 1595-1600. He died in 1679.

21. Alexander Wedderburn. Matr. 1625 ; Grad. 1628.
      This, no doubt, is Sir Alexander Wedderburn of Blackness, born in 1610.

22. Alexander Wedderburn. Matr. 1631.
      The only person named in vol. I, to whom this entry can well refer, is Alexander, third of
      Kingennie, born in 1615.

23. Peter Wedderburn. Matr. 1633 ; Grad. 1636.
      No doubt Sir Peter Wedderburn of Gosford, who was thus born probably about 1618.

24. Andrew Wedderburn. Matr. 1635.
      This is probably the son of David Wedderburn of Burntisland, and grandson of Robert Wedder-
      burn, merchant, and Eufame Coustoun. He was born about 1620 and died unm. in 1639. It might,
      however, be his contemporary, Andrew, the sole surviving son of Alexander Wedderburn and
      Barbara Auchinlek. He died 1683-84, but as he was a merchant, it is not likely that he went to
      the University.

25. Alexander Wedderburn. Matr. 1639 ; Grad. 1642.
      Son to James Wedderburn of Moonzie. He was afterwards minister at Forgan and Kilmarnock.

26. Andrew Wedderburn. Matr. 1642 ; Grad. 1645.
      Also son to James Wedderburn of Moonzie, and afterwards minister at Liff and Dysart.

St. Andrew's
University
Register.

27. James Wedderburn. Matr. 1650 ; Grad. 1653.
Also son to James Wedderburn of Moonzie, and later on himself minister there.

28. Alexander Wedderburn. Matr. 1655.
Alexander Wedderburn, fourth of Kingennie and second of Easter Powrie, who was born about 1640.

29. John Wedderburn. Matr. 1655.
This is the eldest surviving son of Sir Alexander Wedderburn, Knt. He was born in 1641 and was afterwards the first baronet of Blackness.

30. James Wedderburn. Matr. 1666.
This is probably the second surviving son of Sir Alexander. He was born in 1649 and was afterwards clerk of Dundee.

31. John Wedderburn. Matr. 1671.
John Wedderburn of Gosford, eldest son of Sir Peter Wedderburn, Lord Gosford. He was born in 1657.

32. Alexander Wedderburn. Matr. 1674.
Probably the youngest son of Sir Alexander Wedderburn of Blackness, Knt. He was born in 1658.

33. Peter Wedderburn. Matr. 1675.
Sir Peter Wedderburn, second but ultimately eldest surviving son of Sir Peter Wedderburn, Lord Gosford. He was born in 1660.

34. John Wedderburn. Matr. 1682.
Eldest son of Alexander Wedderburn, fourth of Kingennie, and Grissell Wedderburn. He was born in 1667, and died 1688 89.

35. Alexander Wedderburn. Matr. 1686.
Probably the second baronet of Blackness. Born 1672.

36. Alexander Wedderburn. Matr. 1690.
Probably the fourth baronet of Blackness. Born 1675.

37. David Wedderburn. Matr. 1693.
Perhaps the brother of the second baronet of Blackness. He was born in 1674.

38. John Wedderburn. Matr 1694.
Perhaps the second son of Peter Wedderburn and Catharine Man. He was born in 1681, and is said to have been at St. Andrews, and to have caused the death of a fellow student there. See the account of him in vol. I.

39. Alexander Wedderburn de eodem. 1697.
This is a curious entry. It can only refer to Alexander Wedderburn, fifth of Kingennie and first of Wedderburn or that ilk (de eodem). But, if so, he was at the university very late, as he was born in 1668 (see, as to this date, the account of him in vol. I.). Further, the barony of Wedderburn was not created by royal charter until 1708, so that in 1697 the expression would be inaccurate. It is clear, however, that some of the lands afterwards erected into that barony were called by the name of Wedderburn before the date of the charter, and the expression "de eodem" thus signifies "from" rather than "of" Wedderburn.

40. David Wedderburn a Wedderburn. 1728.
This is certainly the eldest surviving son of Alexander Wedderburn of Wedderburn. He was born in 1710.

41. John Wedderburn. 1738.
This is, I think, the son of Charles Wedderburn of Gosford. He was born in 1720, and afterwards succeeded to the Gosford baronetcy as Sir John Wedderburn-Halkett of Pitfirrane.

42. Charles Wedderburn. 1762.
This is Charles Wedderburn, afterwards of Pearsie, born in 1748.

43. David Wedderburn. 1790.
No doubt Sir David Wedderburn, afterwards first baronet of Ballindean, born in 1775.

X

ADMISSIONS OF ADVOCATES TO THE SCOTCH BAR.

Advocates' Admissions. This list is extracted from a MS. catalogue, compiled from the Minute Books of the Faculty of Advocates by Mr. Gray, the librarian of the Advocates' Library, and has been kindly sent to me by him for use in this book.

1. **1642.** Jan. 19.—Peter Wedderburne, son of the late Mr. James Wedderburne, town clerk of Dundee.
   (Afterwards Sir Peter Wedderburne, and a senator of the College of Justice under the title of Lord Gosford.)

2. **1662.** Nov. 13.—John Wedderburne, eldest son of Sir Alexander Wedderburne, of Blackness. Mylne MS.
   (Afterwards clerk to the Bills, and first Baronet of Blackness.)

3. **1687.** June 18.—Alexander Wedderburne, son to Lord Gosford. Mylne MS.
   (Afterwards a commissioner of excise. Father of Lord Chesterhall.)

4. **1715.** Jan. 29.—Peter Wedderburn, son to Mr. Alexander Wedderburn.
   (Afterwards a senator of the College of Justice under the title of Lord Chesterhall.)

5. **1754.** June 29.—Alexander Wedderburn, son to Lord Chesterhall.
   (Afterwards Lord Chancellor, Lord Loughborough, Earl of Rosslyn, &c., &c.)

6. **1766.(?)**—Alexander Scrymgeour.
   (Afterwards Alexander Scrymgeour-Wedderburn of Wedderburn.)

7. **1789.** Aug. 8.—John Halkett, third son of Sir John Wedderburn-Halkett of Pitfirrane, Baronet.
   (Afterwards Governor of the Bahama Islands, Island of Tobago, &c.)

8. **1803.** Dec. 17.—James Wedderburn, son of James Wedderburn-Colvile of Inveresk.
   (Afterwards Solicitor-General for Scotland.)

9. **1861.** Dec. 17.—David Wedderburn, son to Sir John Wedderburn, Baronet.
   (Afterwards third baronet of Ballindean and ninth of Blackness.)

DAVID WEDDERBURN'S MS.

This interesting volume has already been referred to in the account given of the
Papers collected by John Wedderburn of Auchterhouse.[1] It is a small quarto volume of
105 leaves, measuring about 8 by 6 in., and bound in thin vellum with a flap, similar to
that of an old pocket book. It is in perfect preservation, and complete, except that
one leaf appears to have been cut out of it. The book belonged in about 1827 to a
tobacconist in Dundee, of the name of Campbell, who is believed to have bought it as
waste for "snuff" paper. He is said to have been something of an antiquarian, and at
any rate he had lodging in his house an enthusiastic antiquary in the person of James
Thomson, the historian of Dundee. Thomson, no doubt, was quick to appreciate the
interest of the book, and since his time it has been treated with the care it merits. It
provides admirable material towards a knowledge of Scottish commerce at the end of the
sixteenth and beginning of the seventeenth centuries; it contains all that is known of
some of the Dundee churches and chaplainries; it is replete with references to persons
living in Dundee from 1587-1630, and it naturally affords valuable information in regard
to David Wedderburn himself and many members of his family. A large number of the
passages containing this information were transcribed in 1827, by James Thomson, into
a small pamphlet which he sent to my grandfather, among whose papers it is still
extant,[1] and when I was in Dundee in 1891 I was successful in tracing the old
volume. It had passed to Miss Campbell, the sister of its purchaser already named,
and by her had been given to Mr. William Ogilvie, bailie of Dundee, and manager of the
Northern Bank of Scotland at Lochee. Through the influence of his friend, Mr. Alexander
Lamb, F.S.A. (Scot.), whose reverence and enthusiasm for everything connected with
Dundee is only equalled by his knowledge of the burgh and its history, I obtained
permission to place the book in the hands of Mr. Macleod, in order that a complete
transcript of it might, for the first time, be made. This was done, and a copy of the
transcript sent to Mr. Lamb, who was then engaged on his monumental volume of
"Dundee—Its Quaint and Historic Buildings," since issued from the press. He, in
turn, handed his copy of the transcript to Mr. A. H. Millar, who, in an article on the
book, entitled, "A Scottish Merchant of the Sixteenth Century," which appeared in
The Scottish Review of October 1893, made the public acquainted with the existence of
this remarkable volume. Later on the Scottish History Society requested the loan of my
transcript, and, on their deciding to publish the book, Mr. A. H. Millar undertook to
edit it for them, and it is now (1896) passing through the press. As, however, the
Society's volumes are issued to subscribers only, and are thus not readily available to the
general public, I have asked Mr. Alexander Lamb, who now owns the MS., to allow me to
give some account of it here, and am enabled, by his kind permission, to print such
passages from it as throw light on the history of the family to which the writer of it
belonged. I have placed it here, after documents much later in date, because of its
connection with the burgh of Dundee, the records of which are dealt with in the next
division of this volume.

David Wedderburn, whom I have distinguished in vol. I. as "David of the MS."
or "Compt Buik," was the second son of Alexander Wedderburn, town clerk of Dundee,
and Janet Myln. A full account of him is given in vol. I. and there is no need to
recapitulate it here. This "Compt Buik," which has come down to us, is nothing more
than his account or memorandum book. The title page bears the inscription "David
Wedderburn's Compt Buik, 9 November, 1587," and the latest date to any entry in the
book is 12 December, 1630. I cannot do better than reprint the general account of the
volume[2] given by Mr. Millar in *The Scottish Review*. "The writer (he says) has used the
book during the forty-three years which it covers, as a memorandum book on business

---

[1] See ante, p. 155, Nos. 104, 105 (f).

[2] Mr. Millar prefaces his account with a sketch of his family, which, being largely founded on
Douglas' *Baronage*, is full of errors.

David Wedder-
burn's M.S. affairs, a record of notable events, an inventory of deeds relating to landed property, a register of the births of his numerous children, particulars as to his journeys to Flanders, Sweden and Norway, a list of the books which he lent at various times from his library, in short, everything which could well illustrate the private life of a well-to-do burgess during the long period from 1587 till 1630. The book seems to have lain constantly on the merchant's table, and was taken up by him whenever the circumstances of the day made it expedient to write some note as to family affairs or business matters. He was not particular as to which part of the volume he used, and there are thus two title pages at opposite ends of the book, the one side of each page having the writing in consecutive order up to page 127, and the other part forming a different book by merely reversing the volume and writing the notanda from the back page forward. The entries do not follow chronologically, for though the book has been begun with the intention of writing the notes consecutively, in course of time the pages were almost filled and then the writer looked through them for a blank space anywhere in which he might note down the subject of the day. It will be seen at once that such a volume as this is of great historical value, with reference alike to commercial and personal history."

The following extracts from this curious manuscript contain a good many old and quaintly spelt words. Of these the meaning is often clear from the context, but a considerable number require explanation. To give this in each case as the word occurs would involve an undue number of footnotes, and I, therefore, propose to add, at the end of this volume, just before the index, a glossary dealing with these and other words used in these volumes, the meaning of which may not be clear to every reader. Some notes on books and other things mentioned in these extracts will also be found in the glossary.

1.[1] Inside the cover of the book is written an epitaph on David's parents, but whether it was ever inscribed on their tomb, no doubt in the Howff of Dundee, or was only proposed by their son, does not appear. David gives it in Latin and then attempts an English version of it :—

Epitaphium Alexandri Wedderburne Archi-
graphi Deidonani et Jonete Myln eius
conjugis,

Hic vno quos vita thoro coniunxerat, vno
Mors vna tumulo condidit
Vna Ambos donec reddat Lux vnius olim
Beatitatis computes[2]

Qu. English thus:—

Tua quhome on lyve ane Bed did keip, ane dead[3]
In ane grave dois include
Quhill on ane day pairtaikeris they be maid
Of ane Beatitude.

2. Before, however, we deal with the many references to different members of his family, we may get some idea of David Wedderburn himself. An energetic merchant, as the entries relating to his commercial transactions show, he seems to have had some literary taste and to have possessed a library, out of which he constantly lent books to his friends. In his time, as in the present, to lend a book was one thing and to get it back again another, and David very sensibly made a careful note of the books borrowed from him.

(a) 28 August 1607.—Alexander Clayhillis hes borrit (my buik of walking sprittis and)[4] ane Inglis buik of Arithmetic (and fiftie[ss] of sylver). Arithmetic buik ordelyverit.
Upoun the 9 Junij 1608.—I lent Alexander Peirsone at Vardmyln my gude brother my Frensche Acadvmy[5] bundiu in red ourgilt. Item my sadil stirribbis and girdis. Item the parapris on the New Testament.
9 Juuij 1608.—Item. Alexander Peirsoue at Wardmyln hes boronit fra me my Freusche Academy and ane vthir buik aud my blew sadill the girdis and stirrowbis.
xxv September 1613.—Memorandum. Lent my buik callit Ortelius cost me vj lib to young Laird of Creche for 20 dayis.

---

[1] For convenience of reference in vol. i., I have numbered and lettered the extracts from the "Compt Buik," given in this volume.
[2] This word is curious. It is clearly written "computes," but I know of no such word, and think it must be a mistake for, or a corruption of, "compotes," which would have the meaning "partakers of" given it in the English rendering attempted by David.
[3] Dead, a corruption of "death," to suit the rhyme.
[4] The words in brackets are struck through in the original MS., the books having been returned.
[5] This book cannot relate to the famous institution of the name, which was not founded till 1637. It is probably some kind of grammar. A. Pierson and David had married sisters.

x November 1616.—The gudewyf of Pitlathy my Chaucer. The gudeman of Ardony boruit my David Wedder-
coronicles. Young Creiche my Ortelius. James my brother my 2 prophecies. Mr. David burn's MS.
Wedderburn 4 lib. 8ᵈ les.

Ultimo Martij 1618.—Robert Betoun and my sone James hes tane up with thame to Westhall to reid
on Plutarche in laten ourgilt ; Quintiliane Ante Signa lexicon to reid a quhyle thairin and to
bring thame with thame againe.

ix May 1620.—Send with James Symsoue my Hector Boethius[1] in laten weill bund and the Kyngis
Apologie to Stokholme to be sau'd, he has promosit to restore it or x lib. theirfor or the coper gnis
pan. Item, be hes my Llundewill buk cost me 6 lib.

(Undated). Lent James Symsone my Blundevill buik to reid on qubill he cum out of Stokholme.

26 Apryle 1621.—Lent James Ros my Inglis coruicles.

(Undated). Lent the Clerk the rottonfall.

(b) 7 November 1621.—Lent James Balfour sone to Michell Balfour of Mouquhany Metamorphosis
Ovidii in Laten with the pictouris bund in ane swynis skyn of verry braw binding sumtyme
apertening to Robert Wedderburn my uncle with ane uther buik of Inglis of Emblemis in meter
for the space of ane moneth.

Lent my coruieclis to (Mr. Robert Montgumry) John Ochterlony of Murrois.[2]

Lent Doctor Goldman 4 bukis Iliades Homerj ane uther Greik buik.

Mr John Mairis cornicle ane uther buik.

Lent James Symsone Blundevill Draekis Voyages and ane Sie buk.

Lent Mr. Josua Dury ane Hebrew Bybell.

Lent Michell Meill my gilt Ovid.

Lent Thomas Vichtan Smythis Sermones and ane uther buk.

Lent Mr John Dunnur tua buikis of Law.

Lent the gudeman of Crwnen ane buik and 2 bollis aitmeil awin.

Lent Creiche Ortelius.

Lent Mr John Wedderburn 4 buikis Socrates behyf Moral Philosophie Erasmus in Inglis.

Lout Mr William Ferguson Moreolphis.

Lent Ardouy the Roten fall and fynde buikis : to the Clerk the fall.

Lent Alexander Peirsone of Balmadois Frensche Academy and a sadill.

Lent Mr William Fergusone ane buik callit Morcolphis and ane Laten New Testament with the
pictour our gilt.

Lent young Petir Wedderburn Doctor Faustus.

The Bischop[3] Mr David Lyndsay 2 buikis.

Mr James Robertsone j buik.

Mr Colyn Campbell a buik the Laten Bybell.

3. He is equally careful in noting the loan of many other things :—

(Undated).
Lent Androw Thomsone my hinging lok.

Andro Kirkaldy awin me a lantern of quhyt iron and the hand of the myln.

To John Wedderburn vj cranca and a toddis heid and bur.

Peter Clayhillis a kist boruit.

Robert my father brother a compter and a lang sadill of aik.

Petir my father brother for glassis of my fatheris 3 lib.

Barbara for a broclet xvˢ vjᵈ.

Robert my brother 3 lib Item. a pair plet slevis a pair flasses.

James v lib xijᵈ.

Mr Alexander xvjˢ.

10 Feb. 1595.—Lent the young constable xxˢ and my ring.

7 Dec. 1596.—Patrick Wedderburn my dager and promesit me als gude thairfor.

3 Junij 161j.—Lout the litell saw to Mr James Wedderburn.

Nynt of August 1621.—Androw Boydis Wyf⁴ boruit fra my wyf 14 September 1622 a lynt quheill.
James Symsome content thame the foirsaid of the aikin lang sadill of the pres and the aikin cradel.

22 of December 1621.—Lent Patrik Newtoun a single pistolat 22 December.

Lent James Auchinlek the Lem dische and to get my baud of cautourie for Rychard Greif agane
becaus he wes payit, all payit (sic) except 7 merk a half in presens of Johne Forbes and young
Petir Wedderburn in Andro Schippertis heiche chalmer.

James Alansone the gluifis.

Andro Michel a bulgit.

Lent Helen 30ˢ. Item a merk for vnzonis. Item a iron crook.

Item payit Helen and James Ros jᶜ merkis.

William Wedderburn a coffer.[5]

v August 1622.—Lent Johne Wedderburne sone to Robert Wedderburn a lite camp bed of aik with
my father and motheris armes thairon with vj peces of a bodom, this for a moneth or thairby.

[1] Hector Bocce or Boethius, the Scottish historian. .was the son of a Dundee burgess. He died
in 1536.

[2] The letter R. is entered in the margin and stands for "returned," no doubt by Robert Montgomery,
whose name is struck out in the MS. The "coronicles" or "corniclis" had thus been often
borrowed, first by the "gudeman of Ardony," then by James Ros, and again by Robert Montgomery and John Ochterlony.

[3] Bishop of Brechin. cons. 16?9, d. 1640.

[4] See post p. 168, § 8 (d), note.[1]

[5] Son to David's brother the clerk. See post § 9 (b).

David Wedder-
burn's MS.

4. David's religious tendencies and his taste are indicated by a note of some mottoes with which he proposed to decorate his house in the Marketgait. Thus we read :—

1 January
1611 Thir
inscriptiones
to be ingravin
in the lyntis
above the
pilleris of
my galry.

Deum time. Gloria Deo De Creatione.
Gloria Deo De mortificatione.
Gloria Deo De Resurrectione et Redemptiour.
Gloria Deo in Æternum Lux nostra in Christo.

Victrix casta fides. Deus Abrahamj Isaacj
et Jacobj Is meus est Deus.

D. Wedderburn.

5. To his piety he added some superstition, and probably, in deciding when to start on a voyage, he had regard to the "evill" and "blissit dayis" which are noted as follows in his "Compt Buik" :—[1]

The zeir hes 33 evill dayis. This generalie forder contenit in the Schiphirdis calendar.	evill dayis alliowit be thame that wret this.	The blissit dayis of the zeir. The quhilk was revelit to the gude patriarche Joseph quhen he servit Kyng Pharow in Egypt be the angell of God.
8 Januar the first 2, 4, 5, 10, 15, 18, 19.	1, 2, 4, 6, 8, 5	Januar hes 2 to wit the 3 and 13.
3 Februar the 8, 10, 17.	6, 17, 18	Februar 2 viz. the 5 and 25.
3 Marche 15, 16, 19.	7, 15	Marche hes 3 viz. 2, 3, and 30.
2 Apryle 16, 21.	6, 16, 17, 18	Apryle hes 3 viz. 5, 22, 26.
3 May 7, 15, 20.	7, 15, 17	May hes 2 viz. 4, 27.
2 Junij 4, 7.		1 Junij hes 2 viz. 3, 8.
2 July 15, 20.	15, 18	July hes 3 viz. 12, 13, 7.
2 August 19, 20.	19, 20	August hes ane viz., 12.
2 September 6, 7.	16, 18	September hes 4 viz. 1, 7, 24, 27.
1 October 6.	6	October hes 2 viz. 13, 19.
2 November 15, 19.	15, 16	November has none.
3 December 6, 7, 9.	6, 7, 11	December hes 2 viz. 18, 27.

6. He seems to have believed in astrology, and was careful, as we shall see, to note the exact hour of the birth of each of his children, while on another page he records that of King James VI.

Robert my father
brother gef me this
quhilk he said was
giffin him in
Vittemberg.

1. 6. Rex noster natus fuerat in
carcere Edinburgense 19 Junij 1566,
inter horas 9 et 10 antemeridiem
in anno 1575.

R : erit versatus irrequietus Con-
siliorum Occultator. Ac fundet regui
sui amplicit.

7. One or two other historical notes are made by him, and are interesting as examples of his English style. He thus records the visit of the King to Dundee in 1617 :—

Vponn the xv Maij 1617.—James be the grace of God Kyng of Gryt Bretan France and Iyrland defender of the faith our native King being mowit of his awin gude inclenatione to wyssie Scotland and his avin people cam to Ediuburgh. Thairefter cam our the wattir of Kyngorne and cam to Falkland and on the xxj of May being Weddiusday cam our the wattir of Dundie and schippit at the South Ferry and landit at the rude And cam to Dudop lait and swippit thair. The morn tymous he red to Kynnard and remauit all that day Fryday, Settirday, Sonday, Mononday, Tysday, Weddinsday, Thursday aud iuterit in to Dundie on Fryday at (sic) houris quhar than the toun gef of his grace to thame his presence.

So again, the following is his account of an eclipse of the sun in 1597, the day of which was long after remembered as Black Saturday[2] :—

Upon the xxv day of Februar being Settirday 1597 the signe In pisces Quhilk wes accomptit the eeclips of the sone and cheynge of the mone Betuix ten aud ellevin houris befor nwn that day darknes overschaddowit the face of the haill earth that nane mycht knaw ane uther perfytly on the calsayis nor yit mycht one persone within thair houssis haif any lycht but candill Quhilk contenwit the space of half ane houre. And the peiple with gryt fair fled aff the calsayis to houssis mouruing and lameuting and the crawis corbeis and ravenois foullis fled to houssis to our steple and tolbuith and schip tappis maist merveulously affrnyit. Quhilk sycht wes maist terreble and fairfull to all peaple young and auld and nane persone levand culd declair they ever hard or saw the lyk thame selffis in ony tyme preceiding.

[1] A very similar list of evil days is given by David's uncle, Robert Wedderburn, the notary, at the end of one of his protocol books. See post s. Burgh Records—Dundee, Protocol Books, No. 245.
[2] See Calderwood's *Hist. of the Church*, fol. ed. 1678, p. 415.

8. His records of his commercial transactions were of course not less careful than those David Wedder-of the books and other articles which he lent to his friends. They occupy the greater burn's MS. portion of his " eompt buik," and provide a valuable picture of the trade of the time. I confine myself, however, to noticing such of them as mention members of the family, and are thus material to this work.

Many of his relations borrowed money from him, and we have repeated lists of " Debtis awin me," as well as separate entries of loans scattered all through the book.

(a) Thus in regard to his elder brother, almost always designed " Mr. Alexander " or " the elerk," we may instance the following[1] :—

21 March 1589.—Item. to Mr Alexander xl. xxxv⁸.
16 Feb. 1595.—Mr Alexander for the lend of a crown. Item. x⁸ for the swap : to be allovit in the the witsonday termes meill nixt.
7 Dec. 1596.—Mr Alexander x⁸ anent the scrap David Barclay restis of the clayth v lib. 2 merk.
4 May 1597.—Mr Alexander my brother xxj for the vrak of my salmond. Receauit 8 lib for my Merteines meill of his hous I occupy quyt in recompence thairfor xv lib.²
20 June 1597.—Lent Mr Alexander a x⁸ pece to pay the coll men.
(Undated).—Mⁱ Alexander 35⁸ xl⁴ receauit of that in Alexander Carnegy's hous.
  „   Mʳ Alexander 4xx lib.

(b) Of apparently later date is a longer memorandum of transactions between him and the elerk :—

My brother Mr Alexander Wedderburn the Clerk is justly restand awand me the swmes of money following and utheris efter mentionat in respect of the caussis efter expremit.
First the haill auld evidentis at the lest the transumpt thairof off the haill tenement of land sumtyme pertenand to auld Robert Wedderburn, our father brother, uow to the sald Mr Alexanderis sone Petir, and myn sone Alexander and thair airis.
Item he borouit and receauit fra me at his awin gait xj crounes of the sone of gold and efterwart a litell payit me agane only aucht of thame. Sua he detenis thre crounes as yit extending to 13 lib.
Item he sault to me twa barrele of salmond and receauit fra me fiftie merkis thairfor and quhen I wenturit thame to the mercat in France they wer found grissillis and I tynt on thame besyd the gaue I mycht have haid gif they haid Leue salmond as the testificat thairof will schaw extending to xvj lib.³
Item Mr Alexander receauit fra the Laird of Dynnoyn xl lib. for a yeiris meill of auld Robertis Inner boussis, my pairt is xx lib. thairof receauit 3 lib. thairof.
Item I debursat for reparing of the Bak boussis in the bak Clois laitly as the particular compt thairof will schow x merk my half thairof is v merk,   Summa Lij lib. ü⁸ 8⁴.
Item The said Mr Alexander is restand awand to me the equale half of all debursingis quhilk I avancit and debursit to auld Robert at his command and he faythfully promittit to me the just half thairof quhilk extendis in all to LI. lib. 4⁸. The half he is awin to his part extendis to xx lib. xij⁸.
Item debursit to Thomas Guthre and furnessit him at his command qubilk he promittit to pay the equale half thairof extending to fiftie lib.

(c) Similarly to his brother Robert,³ many entries refer, thus :—

(Undated).—Robert my brother 3 lib.
14 January 1590.—Robert my brother 5 lib. awin 7ˣˣ lib, j⁶ lib. 3 lib. awin.
23 January 1589.—Item Robert my brother awin me 4ˣˣ lib. to be payit at the said day (Witsonday).
21 March 1589.—Item. lent Robert my brother 4 lib. half a merk receauit xxxj⁸.
4 October 1589.—Item. Robert my brother xxv crwnes of the sone to be warit on wyn.
25 Dec. 1589.—Item. the said day lent Robert my brother 4 lib. and xlvj⁸ he was awin me befor.
26 Aug. 90.—Robert Wedderburn my brother. Delyuerit Robert my brother xxvj lib x⁸ for half a last hering to be send with him to Burdeaux and sauld to my proffit. Item he hes of myn xxj lib in his awin hand to be excheyngit for crwnes extendis to sewin crwnes a half. Item sex crwnes a half in awin hand of lent money this (sic).
8 September 90.—Nyn crwnes receauit heir to be delyuerit to me in Burdeaux. To delyuer thir to Robert my brother and to be warit as his awin conforme to my Bill and gif not to wair it als oft as his awin to my proffit before his hame cuming.
14 September 1590.—Robert my brother. Receauit fra yow to me be my brother Robert in ventour with him in the Nychtengail quhairof James Deis is Maister fourteue crwnes of the sone of gold and wecht. And half ane last of hering schippit with him in the said schip. The fre money of the haill to be imployit in all voagis that he sall happin to mak befor his hamecuming on sic profitable waring as he des to him self. And gif he cum hame the hie way to imploy it haill on the best

---

[1] Compare also some other entries. Thus in a list of " Debtis awin me of the Witsonday terme 1589 " we find " Mⁱ Alexander xxxvᵉ xvjˢ," " Robert my brother 3 lib," " Robertis tenementis in the Foirland ix lib," " Barbara Wedderburn xlijˢ, xvˢ," and again (undated) " Barbara xvˢ."

² Compare another entry later on § 12 (i).

³ Other entries relating to him will be found later on in §§ 11-13, 20-21. He was thrice married, first to Grissell Duncan, secondly to Elizabeth Lovell, and lastly to Elspet Hering, who survived him. See the last paragraph of § 12 (j), where both his widow and his " first twa wyffis " are named.

sort of waid to be schipit with him self and markit with this my mark. Item delyuerit him sex
crwnes of the sone of the same wecht quhilk makis in the haill tuentie crwnes of the sone to be
imployit to me in maner abone wryttin forby the half last hering foirsaid. Siclyk gifin him
commissioun to receaue nyn crwnes of the sone fra Thomas Heres. And tua crwnes fra Robert
Jaksone.   D. Wedderburn.
Mair delyuerit to him conforme to his directione sen the making of our last compt a crwn and a
half-summa xxj crwnes a half.

·16 Sept. 1591.—Lent Robertis wyf a xxxˢ peice : to himself 14ˢ.

16 Sept. 1591.—Delyuerit Robert my brother xv lib. for half hundreth lyning clayth extending to
lx ellis to be sould iu Spane and warit on . . . . (sic) restis awin me 3 lib.

xviij January 91.—He is awin for xj quarteris a half and thre quarteris a net les to be him a clok
and a pair of breekis at 3 lib. the eln. Henry Ogilny fifteen quarteris to be him a clok at v merkis
the eln.

1593. Apryle 17.—Schippit with Robert my brother ane pok vad of the ros and figour of 50, All my
vad is markit with this my mark besyd of blak Ink W Schippit in David Smythis schip.

(d) Robert died in November, 1593, but he left a son[1] Alexander, with whom in later
years his uncle David did business. Thus :—

5 May 1614.—Seud with Alexander Wedderburn my brother Robertis sone to France or Spane in
Waltir Reukynis schip callit the Diamont ane uther woffin bed standis 9 lib. to be sauld and warit
als aft as his awin befor his returning heir agane. 8 May.   David Blyth saellit.

(e) His brother James was for a long time a prominent merchant in Dundee, and to him
also there are occasional references—

xxj Sept. 95.—Seud with James my brother vj ellis a half small lyning cost xvˢ the eln to by me als
guddie fyn Inglis clayth to be my self awne cot of blak viz. ane yard that be not sa fyn as this
pece I send with him.   Receauit it.

4 May 1597.—James my brother v lib.

4 May 1609.—My brother James freud with him xl lib.

(f) So, again, we have similar references to his brother Peter, also a merchant in
Dundee—

15 March 1587.—Debtis awin me. Peter Wedderburn (sic).

14 Jan. 90.—Petir Wedderburn jᶜ x lib.[2]

11 September 1607.—Seud with Petir Wedderburn my brother sex ellis lange of blokit 2 ell bred to
be littet sad russet and I to pay a merk for ilk testan hes duble messour theron and to bring it
hame with himself.

14 Aug. 1608.—Lent Petir my brother v lib. Item 3 lib.

4 May 1609.—Petir my brother v. lib.

8 Sept. 1619.—I have giffin Petir my brother a pair of sylner spectacles and he has promesit to gif
me a propyn this woadge from Noraye.

(g) His sisters are also named ; thus as regards Katharine, who married William Duncan,
we read—

Eodem die (16 Aug. 1594) giffin my sister Katharen aue auld ros noble &c.

12 August 1597.—Robᵗ Wedderburn, notar, witnesses Alexʳ Kyd, elder, Alexʳ Johnson, aud Henry
Abercromby : David Wedderburn, procurator for Wᵐ Duncan my guid brother maid requisitione
to David Abircromby conforme to the contract to be delyvered him before Mertimis nixt his
thousand merkis aud byronis therof.

and of Margaret, wife of Peter Clayhills[3]—

16 Aug. 1590.—Delyuerit Meriory ten s. in compleit payment of three quarteris of the second yeir.

24 October 1590.—Gef her tua s.

24 Feb. 1596.—Item Peter Clayhillis lent him lxx lib. in v lib. peces.

Item lent him in Johne Follertouis xv lib. a merk to be payit quhen I requyr.
Item jᶜ lib.

Receauit agane the jᶜ lib. fra Margaret my sister.

Eodem die (16 Sept. 1596).—Delyverit young Petir Clayhillis my gud brother on his obligatione
ane hundreth aud fiftie lib. And he to delyver me fiftie crwnis of gold and wecht in Burdeaux at
his or the schipis first arryval to Burdeaux callit the Androw.

[1] He also left a daughter Helen, who is mentioued in the " Compt Buik," thus :—" The act quhair
Johne Lovell, son and air of Johne Lovell, elder, is oblist to Helen Wedderburn for 4ᵉ merkis
in the Court Buikis of Dundie the 21 July 1598." She married Audrew Boyd and has been
already named in another entry, ante 2 (b) under date 9 Augnst 1621. See also post 12 (j), p. 175.

[2] This and the preceding reference may be to David's uncle Peter. See post 12 (f).

[3] Peter Clayhills is also named in various other entries e.g. :—
Upoun the xvj day of Apryle 1597.—Memorandum. Thair is ane registrat Discharge of Alexander
Lyndsayis merchand burges of Edinburgh for him self and William Lynford in London of xlvij lib.
sterling money awin be my gud brother Petir Clayhillis, bailie to the said Alexander as actour
and factour for the said Lynford.

Item He to receave fra Michel Cokburn Alexander Cokburn cautioner for him aucht crounis a half **David Wedder-**
gold and wecht in Burdeaux. **burn's MS.**
Petir to war thir fiftie aucht crunes and a half of the sone of gold and wecht on gude wynis the ane
half on quhyt wynis the uther half on clarit wynis and gude treis gif he cunnis hame the
hieway ffailzeing to send hame the equale halfis waring with the first and the rest to retene and
war it als of and als proffitable as his awin and to mark myn with my awin mark.   D. W.

9. His dealings extended to more distant relations. Thus we find references to his
uncle Robert, his nephew William, his aunt Barbara, his distant cousins Robert,
the merchant, and Besse Wedderburn, daughter of James Wedderburn of Craigie,
and wife of James Kinnaird, and others.[1]

(a) Undated.   Robert my father brother 24ˢ 8ᵈ and xvˢ besyd.
    4 May 1609.—Auld Robert and the clerk.   34 lib. xˢ.
        The clerk of lent sylver xj lib, a scept xv lib. worth of treis.   Item. xvj lib. on
        the cobel of the salmon with uther thingis of auld.

(b) xxv August 1621.—Send a xijˢ pece with William Wedderburn my brother sone to Dansken
    to by me sum anneis (?) and a wax candill.

(c)[2] 4 May 1597.— Barbara Wedderburn x lib.
    12 September 1599.—Pro liberis Barbara Wedderburn.

(d)[3] 16 February 1595.—To Robert my gossip 5s.
    24 Februar 96.—Lent Robert Wedderburn merchennd first xx lb., and nixt uther xx lib. summa
    xl lib. to be payit quhen I pleis.
    7 Dec. 1596.—Robert the mercheand xxˢ.
    18 May 1598.—Robert Wedderburn mercheand hes coft fra me ane pyp of Spanes wyn sek for
    7xx lib. to be payit betuix this and Michaelmes nixt in presens of James Scrymgeour and his
    awin wyf Quhairupon I receauit 2ᵈ in arrels to the pwre quhilk I delyuerit.
    8 Sept. 1619.—Item.   Robert Wedderburn, zit xxˢ.
    Undated.   Roᵗ Wedderburn 24s. 8d.

(e) Memorandum.   6 January 1606.—Thomas Broun wrycht and Robert Wedderburn my father brother
    gef young Peter Wedderburn 28ˢ in pairt of payment of the Mertemes meill last in anno 1605
    of his zard and that for tymber awin be the said Thomas to me.

(f) 27 Junij 1615.—Lent Besse Wedderburn spous to James Kynnard ane treu flacon of a quarter to go
    with hir to Denmark and to be send hame immediatly price thairof xxˢ.
    8 July 1615.—Giffin Bessy Wedderburn a procuratorie and the obligatione and the Discharge on the
    bak thairof with my lettre to him hir husband to persew Johne Schoreswodis intromissious with
    his geir for ixˣˣ x lib all in a boyat.

(g) (Undated).—Patrik Wedderburn ffor xxiij pund a half pwlder at xˢ the pund.   xj lib. xvˢ.   payit.
     „   "The rentall of St Servis Chapleury," in which one item is "ffurth of Patrik Wedder-
         buruis tenement lyand at the eist end cf the tolbuith yeirly 7 merkis xxᵈ."
    7 Dec. 1596 }
    4 May 1597 } Patrick Wedderburn named in a list of debtors.

(h) xxiiij Apryle 1621.—Memorandum.   Patrik Guthre of Nethmuthie is restand awand me x lib. quhilk
    he boruit fra my wyf and dochter Helen.

10. David must have farmed some land, for he keeps a careful record of the persons to
whom he sold his rye and peas.   Thus :—
    (a) Nono Augusti 1596 My Ry.—To Elspet Hering a boll half boll v lib xs.
        My wyf 2 pekis xxiijˢ.

and again, on the same date, in an account of "My Pes," is entered—
    (b) To Mr Alexander a boll xx merk.
    To Elspet Hering a half boll x merk.

---

[1] There are numerous entries relating to dealings with his wife's family, the Betouns, such as—
14 Jan. 1590.   Lady our mother v lib. xvij merkis half.
21 Sept. 1596.—Lent my gudmother 6 lib. xlᵈ be hir g'dson Alexander Peirson 6 lib.   Item to hir 8ˢ.
But these are not material to the subject of this book and are not therefore included amoug these
extracts.
[2] See ante p 167, note [1].
[3] Robert Wedderburn, the merchant, is also named in a "Compt betuix the Constable of Dundie and
me," thus—"Item to Robert Wedderburn for wyld meit quhen the Earle of Mar was with him
(i.e., the Constable), lijˢ" ...... "Item to Robert Wedderburn I payit at the Lairdis command
thre pyntis wyn sek, extendis to .. ... xlˢ," and again "Robert Wedderburn, mercheand, a knag
of vinacre."

Y

(c) Of his lint he kept equally careful reckoning.[1]   Thus—

(i.) Nono Septembris 1596.

My lyut weyis 72 stanes. In fourtie tua boundis.[2]

vi lib. restis
vj lib. vˢpayit.

To Mr Alexauderis wyf fyve stane 1 pund in thre boundis quhairof thre staue aud a half wes hir awin the rest awin me a staue 9 pund is vj lib. vˢ.

To David Peirsone for Alexander Wedderburn younger in Cuper as his spruis atan xxxj pund in ane bound.

xv lib. xˢpayit.

22 September this Thursday.—To Margaret my sister tua bonndis weyis 3 staue 14 pund at 4 lib. the stane. Summa xv pund tuaˢ.

vj lib. vˢpayit.

To hir to gif Katharen my sister ane tound weyis ane stane 9 pund at 4 the stane. Summa sex lib. vˢ. Thir instantly to be payit.

To my wyf fyve boundis and sum lcus lynt weyis aucht stane 32 lib.

12 lib. 15ᵈ payit.

To Margaret my sister tua boundis agane weyis thrie stane aue pund to be payit the day forsaid 4 lib. the stane.

1 payit
6 lib. 18ˢ vᵈ.

To Mr Alexanderis wyf Helen Ramsay aue bound and sum brokin lynt weyis ane stane xj pund xij unce 4 lib. the stane to be payit the day forsaid.

6 lib. 2ˢ vjᵈ.

To my awin wyf ane bound weyis ane stane a half half a pund summa 6 lib. 2ˢ 6ᵈ. The number 3ˣˣ 9 stan 4 pund.

x lib. 7ˢ 7ᵈ
receavit 48ˢ
thairof for a
firlet salt.

13 September 97.—Sauld to Margaret Myln spous to Robert Wedderburn my father brother in presens of John Steill hir servand Elspit Idwye and the gud wyf of the weyhous and hir weman Tua boundis lynt weyis thre stanes tua pund four unce les at v merk the stane to be payit x dayis befor mertemes nixt.

xj lib. xᵈ
restis lvjˢ 8ᵈ
payit.

Sauld to Katharen my sister William Duncanis wyf 2 boundis weyis 3 stane fyve pund a half quhairof I discharge a pund and a half at v merk the stane summa quhairof 1 haif receavit 8 lib.

x lib. xvjˢ 8ᵈ.

Sauld to Margaret Wedderburn spous to C.[3] Waltir Haliburtoun Tua boundis lynt weyis thre stanes v pund wecht quhairof 1 haif dischargit a pund wecht at v merk the staue summa for 3 stane 4 pund is x lib. xvjˢ 8ᵈ to be payit 14 days befor mertemes nixt and I haif receavit a ring in pledge thairof.

x lib. xvjˢ 8ᵈ.

To my awin wyff tua boundis weyis thre stane four pund wecht.[4]

(ii.) Tertio Septembris 1600.

The Compt of my Lynt and the selling thairof.

Persons addebtit to me thairfor. All sauld to thame for v merk a half the stane to be payit 8 dayis before Mertemes next.

To Mr Alexander my brotheris wyf 7 bound weyis 1 stane xij pund.

To my wyf v boundis of 9 stane 3 pund les. Item ane brokin bound of x pund wecht a half.

To the Laird of Kyngany 2 bound 3 stane 7 punds.

To my wyf a brokin bound of x pund a half.[4]

11. A considerable part of the book is taken up with a long inventory of David's papers, which naturally contain a good many references to his various relatives. It is headed as follows :—

This is ane collection off the effectis and daittis of certain evidentis wryttis and tytellis apertenand to David Wedderburne sone lawfull to wmquhill Alexander Wedderburne commoue clerk off Dundie as followis. ffirst alis of certane his brether and sisteris tytellis and sum frendis:

Here are the entries which relate to members of his family[5] :—

(a) Ane chairtour of fewferme uaid be the provest and baileis of Dundie to wmquhill James Myln his gudschir off ane lache wolt with the bak chopis under the new tolbuith — uuder the commoue seill of Dundie — off the dait the   day of Marche 1546.

---

[1] So in another list he notes : " My Lynt xlii boundis. Mr. Alexander 3 boundis weyis v stane half a puud les."

[2] Only those items which name Wedderburns are given here, so that the greater part of the 72 stanes remains apparently unaccounted for. The full list occupies three pages and a half of the " Compt Buik " and names many other persous.

[3] C. i.e. Captain.

[4] He is always careful to bring into account things given to or used by his wife Matild Betoun, thus :—" 1590. Aug. 20.—Item for the peice that Matild bes of xx elnis at vj lib the scoir."

[5] A good many items in this inventory relate to small properties or annual rents acquired by David, and in the "evidents " or title deeds of which he is uamed. These aud some others naming Alexander Wedderburn, the clerk, and Robert Wedderburn, notary, as acting in their professional capacities, are omitted from the extracts given here.

Volt choipis of xls disponit away to George Stirling and he hes the auld evidentis I haif his discharge thairof.	My gudschir James Mylnis seasing heirof or extractit iu the buikis of John Duncasone notar fayther to William Duncasone in Parkland.

Ane chairtour of Alienatioune maid be Audrow Davidsone meassoun to wmquhill Alexander Wedderburne and Jonet Myln his spous in lyfrent and to David Wedderburne thair soue heretable of all and haill ane annuel rent of xl^s zeirly to be upliftit of ane lache wolt of the said Androis under his seill and subscriptioune off the dait the aucht day of July 1573.

Aue instrument of seasing off the said annuelrent of xl^s to be upliftit as said is conteauand thairin quhair the said Jonet is kend and interit air to the said wmquhill James hir fayther to the former wolt. And scho hir spous and Androw respective hes maid resignatioue of the said annuelrent and wolt in favouris of the said David heretable off the dait the xix of July 1573 under the signe and subscriptione of John Fwler notar publict.

* * * * *

(b) 40s. Disponit to Alexander Rychardson : Robert Wedder-burn Kyrkmaster hes the auld evidentis quhen he excambeit to Alexander Rychardsoue.	Item. Ane Transsumt instrument of seasing in the commone court buikis of Dundie upon the vj of Februarr 1584. And that of Harbert Gledstanes quhilk is of the dait the 22 of Februar 1565 Quhair wmquhill John Dog resignit ane few meill of xl^s zeirly to be upliftit furth of twa ruidis of his land lyand on the south syd of the seageit of Dundie in favouris of Alexander Wedderburn Jouet Myln his spous his airis and assignais,

Ane Chartour of Alienatioune thairof maid be the said Alexander to David Wedderburn his soue of the said xl^s under his seill and subscriptione of the dait the xiij of Apryle 1584.

Ane instrument of seasing thairof resiguit be the said Alexander in favouris of the said David his airis and assiguais heretable John Ferrear notar thairto of the dait the xx of Apryle 1584.

* * * * *

(c) Prothogole and Wryttis.	Item. Ane Dispositioue of the haill prothogole buikis of umquhill Alexander Wedderburn maid be him to his sone David and of uther wryttis under the subscriptioue of him Robert Kyd Alexander Wedderburn Petir Wedderburn Johne Lovell younger aud Robert Wedderburn of the dait the 8 of May 1583.

(d) Of the Sylver tass.	Item. Ane dispositioue of ane sylver tas ouer gilt of x unce of the said Alexanderis to the said David under his subscriptioue aud Petir Wedderburn and Petir Clayhillis of the dait the day of May 1585.

Ane obligatioue upon the delyverie thairof maid be the said Alexander to the said David of the dait forsaid and under thair subscriptioue.

* * * * *

(e) Towardis my titel to Katharenis iu-feftmentis. This redemit and renuncit be Katharen.	Item. Ane seasing Quhair the said umquhill Alexander hes iufeft Katharen his dochter faileing hir to be devydit equaly among David James and Petir his souis of that tenement of land perteuand to Robert Myln lyand on the north syd of Ergylis geit of Dundie and quhair scho and they faileand hir ar maid assignays to the hail byrenis under the subscriptioue of John Ferrear notar publict of the dait the xv of Apryle 1584.

(f) Off my brother Petiris buith.	My brother Petir Wedderburnis infeftment of the heiche foir buith in Johue Craellis land lyaud at the end of the Freir Wynd be eist the sam heretable Thomas Iyrlaud vicar of Dundie notar thairto Alexander Scryngeour bailie of the dait the 7 Marche 1575.

(g) My Gudames Testment. My sister Kath-aren hes recea-vit this.	Item. Ane Legacie of Elezabeth Guthre relict of umquhill George Wischert of Drymme of xl lib to my fatheris barnis efter his deceis under the signe and subscriptioue of Johne Ramsay iu Breichen notar publict of the dait the last of December 1581. Wituessis Alexander Bishop of Breichen George Barclay of Syde.

Item. Ane seasing quhair Robert Wedderburn elder my gudschir and Robert his soue resignit thair land bak and foir lyand on the north syd of Ergylis geit besyd St. Mathovis clois In favouris of Alexander Wedderburn my fayther in lyfreut and Robert his soue heretable Saiffaand the lyfrent of the foir hous to the said Robert soue to the said Robert of the dait the penult of Martij 1573 Thomas Iyrland uotar thairto.

Ane just copy heirof under the said Thomas subscriptioune.

(h) Of Robert my brotheris tytellis.	Ane copy of Seasing of excambioun maid be the said Robert with consent of the said Alexander his father of the Inner land with the yard of the said tenement for xvj merkis few ueill and ane tenement or lugeing lyan within the zaet of the wester clois of the said Alexanderis lyand on the uorth syd of Ergylis geit of the dait the penult of December 1577. Thomas Iyrland notar thairto.

* * * * *

David Wedderburn's MS.	(*i*) Of v merkis of James.	Item. Ane seasing of v merkis annuelrent zeirly to be upliftit furth of Thomas Monorgoundis land, lyaud ou the north syd of Ergylis geit aud specialy of James Jaksonis pairt disponit be Thomas Monorgouud in favouris of James my brother of the dait the xxij of September 1575 Thomas Iyrland notar thairto.
	(*j*) Of vj merkis of Petiris.	Ane seasing of vj merkis annuelrent annailet be the said Thomas to Petir my brother to be upliftit furth of James Nicollis pairt of the said tenement of the dait the xxj of Martij 1575. Thomas Iyrland uotar thairto.

* * * * *

	(*k*) Of Williamis annualrent of vij bollisrenuncit.	Item. Ane chartour of my brother Williamis under the seill and subscriptioue of my father of ane annuelrent of vij bollis victuall to be upliftit furth of the landis of Balrudry of the dait the xiij of Apryle 1584.
		Ane seasing thairof in John Ferrear notaris buikis of the same date or thairby,
	(*l*) Of Katharen my sisteris titellis of 46 merkis auuualrent.	Item. Ane copy of contract betuix Robert Low Patrik Wedderburn Alexander Traell and Katharen auent hir infeftmeut of 46 merkis auuuel to be upliftit furth of the landis of Breichen of the dait the 14 of Junij 1586 And registrat in the commone court buikis of Dundie about the sam dait. My brother Mr. Alexander hes all hir titellis.
	(*m*) My father and motheris Testmentis confirmit.	Item my fatheris testment confirmit be the commissaris of Edinburgh at Edinburgh the xiij of May 1587. The dait of the decreit quhair executouris dativis wer decernit the xxj of Apryle 1586.
		My motheris testmeut confirmit be the saidis commissaris off the sam daittis Johue Johnstoun subscryveris.

* * * * *

	(*n*) Off my 2 acris in lyfrent.	Upon the 24 of Februar 1569 hora 12. Henry Beatoun bailie to the coustable of Dundie be vertew of his lettir of tak and precept contenit thairin gef stait and seasing to David Wedderburn of 2 acris land lyaud in the West feild of Dundie for all the dayis of his lyftyme Robert Wedderburn notar thairto wituessis Robert Wedderburn younger Robert Jaksone George Lyndsay.

* * * * *

	(*o*) My evidentis of Lumlathiu aud annuelrent thair Redemit.	Ane contract betuix William Graham of Balluny aud his spous aud me and my spous Tuiching the alienatioue of the schade half quarter part landis of Lumlathin to us aud of ane annuelrent of xv bollis victuale to be upliftit furth of the auchten part laudis thairof now occupyit be Thomas Smyth and William Durham uuder reversion alway of ane thousand pundis to be redemit fra me the said David and my spous aud subscryvit be thame and the said tennentis as cautioneris and be James Bonar and Johne Patou notaris for the said Thomas becaus he culd uot wryt witnessis subscryviaris James Durham of Potkerro William Graham of Claverhous Mr Alexander Wedderburn Johne Durham Johne Graham Thomas Scot of the dait at Dundie aud Baldovy[1] respective the v and xxj dayis of Juulj 1595.
		Item. Tua Chartoris subscryvit be thame to us and be the saidis witnessis The ane to be haldin of the Kyng the uther of the said William upon the saidis landis and aunuelrent of the dait forsaid and sellit.
		Item. Ane seasiug gifin conforme thairto be William Duncan his bailie upouu the sam under the signe aud subscriptioue of Johne Patou notar of the dait the first of July 1595 wituessis thairin William Graham of Baldovy[1] Mr Alexander Wedderburn Thomas Smyth William Durham Johne Graham James Corbit Jeremy Lyn Johue Teylour.
	(*p*) My evidentis of Logy hauche aud fur bra aud ane acre iu the crukit hauche lyand be north the yat of Dudop.	Ane contract betuix the coustable of Duudie and me and my spous Tuiching the alienatioune of Logy hauche and fur bray abone the sam and ane acre in the crukit hauche at the end of all togidder with the medowis and pertineutis thairof To us under reversioun of fyve huudreth merkis under his subscriptioue and ouris Witnessis Gilbert Scryuigeour Johne Scrymgeour of Kyrktoun James Mylu and Johue Wobster notaris of the dait at Dudop the nyuteue day of May 1591 zeiris.
		Item aue speciall discharge subscryvit be the said constable to us on the recept of the said fyfe hundreth merkis witnessis forsaidis subscryvaris aud of the dait forsaid.
	Redemit.	Item Ane Chartour of Alienatioune with ane precept conteuit thairin to tak seasing under his seill aud subscriptioue of the saidis landis aud medow subscryvit be him and the saidis witnessis of the dait forsaid.
		Item. Ane seasing gifiu be Mr Alexander Wedderburn notar to us of the saidis laudis aud acris forsaidis under his signe and subscriptioue of the dait the xxj Maj 1591. Witnessis thairin James Forrester elder bailie of Duudie Robert Wedderburn younger aud James Fyf younger burges of Dundie.

* * * * *

---

[1] Baldovy, clerical error for Balluny.

(q) Robert my brotheris evident als befor wryttin | Ane seasing gifin be Robert Wedderburn elder my gudschir to Robert my brother **David Wedderburn's MS.** of ylie houss, bak aud foir, pertening to the said Robert and Mr Alexander my brether Johne Duucau bailie thairto under the signe and subscriptione of Thomas Iyrland notar thairto witnessis thairin Johne Coustoun Robert Kyd David Guthre of the dait the penult of Marche 1573.

* * * * *

(r) Robert my brotheris will to me. | Robert my brotheris legacie to me to be his only executour all of his hand wryt aud subscryvit by him. Witnessis thairin David Ramsay Thomas Heres of the dait at Dundie the x of July 1587.

(s) Ane obligatione maid by George Querrevour to Rechardus Wedderburn in Elisinor and ane compt be him and the said Rechardus of 4ˣˣ auld dolouris subscryvit be him and I maid assiguay thairto be the said Recardns My assignatione subscryvit befor Robert Fyf fu Campher Robert Wedderburn Bartil Brounhill Alexander Trumpit at Elisinor the 7 July 1589 yeiris.

Item. Ane obligatione maid and subscryvit be the said George to the said Robert Fyf for xxviij lib. Flemis mouey. And I maid on the tell thairof assignay thereto be the said Robert witnessis subscryvit Alexander Symmer Rechardus Wedderburn Johue Wedderburn Mr David Myrtoun the 24 July 89.

* * * * *

(t) To James my brother soue | Memorandum Upon the 28 July 1591 Gilbert Quhittet Robert Wedderburn couotaris Witnessis Waltir Key Andro Crystic Johue How Alexander Nicoll Maltman The clerk his wyf and with thair awin handis gef seasing to James thair sone of the west syd of the clos callit the greu landis haill yard and half for landis Robert Wedderburn notar thairto.

To James my brother sone | Memorandum of a seasing of William Davidsonis hous iu the heid of the clois quhairin James my brotheris sone is infeft under the sigue and subscriptione of Johne Patonu notar with special warrandice thairin contenit of the dait the last of September 1594.

Item of his | Memorandum his evident of the west syd of my brotheris clois is in Robert my fatheris brotheris protocole he uotar thairto the 28 July 1591.

12. At this point in the inventory the volume seems to have been already filled with other matters; so that David has to complete his catalogue in another part of his "compt buik," thus:—

ffollowis the iuventar of the rest of the wryttis pertenaud to me David Wedderburn burges of Dundie in maner as followis in the sam forme as the Inventar of the remancnt ar xl leavis befor wryttin

(a) Ane Declaratione of the just compt of onr father and mother-is gudis and geir and of the bairnis portionis.[1] | Ane declaratione and cleir compt maid in preseus of thir honest per·oues subscryvaris thairof the speciall freindis pertenand to me and the remaneut my brether and sisteris of the haill gudis and geir pertenand to our umquhill father and mother and destribute to ilk particular persone thair bairnis for thair bairnis portionu natnrall, discharging me the said David thairof Viz. to Robert compleit paymeut of thre hundredth merkis for his part as his speciall discharge heirefter minnttit will beir To James Tua hundreth merkis money payit be ane Act and ane hnndreth merkis on Anthon Haliburtonis tenement as his discharge particular heirefter minnttit will beir To Petir ane hundreth merkis on James

---

[1] David's executorship to his parents is also dealt with elsewhere in the volume as follows :—

The bairnis geir is payit in Mar as followis. James Lundy and James Fyndlasone actit to pay to James tua hundreth merk and xij merk of profit for ilk hundreth.

Anthone Halyburtoun maryner makis out his pairt quhilk is ane huudreth merkis and hes infeftment thairon.

Robert is payit and I haif his discherge.

Petiris portioun John Andersone and Cristell Traell actit for ane bundreth merkis.

William Allerdyse hes gifin him infeftment for ane uther hundreth merk He wantis yit ane hundreth. Quhilk mon be payit as followis The Lady Dudope xx lib Issobell Heres 14 lib C Halyburtoun 4 lib on his ring. The rest of my Mertemes terme to cum to mak it out of all my annuellis.

Katharenis pairt Robert Low hes 4 hundreth merkis and xx merk and threscoir x merkis of proffit I. merk of Dwry and xl lib of George Wischertis.

Williamis pairt 4ˣˣ lib Mr Alexander wilbe awin Robertis tennentis xx lib The Laird of Ballisuk xxij lib Anthone Halyburtoun xliij lib I my self the rest.

As for thair intromissioun with the restis Comptrell (?) my intromissionn of all that can be bayit to my charge I beleif ilk ane of thame salbe found awand me x lib. Quhilk will pay Williamis debt I am awin and Petiris bayth. As may be sene be the compt autentikly wryttin and put togidder. And quhen all is fonnd be computatione it wilbe found ilk ane of us to fall bot 3ᵒᵒ merk Chargis deducit and Katherene to ad to hir pairt L merk of Dwry and xl lib of George Wischertis with hir awin byrouis and John How to gett that of Henry Baxter and Margaret Barry quhilk wilbe nyn lib or thairby.

And again in another place :—

21 Sept. 1596.—"Everie ane of my brether and sisteria ar awin me In of thair barnis pairt geir that I have debnrsit mair nor I ancht conforme to the compt ..... 7 lib ...... summa 28 lib."

David Wedder-
burn's MS.

Haliburtonis land and ane hundreth merkis ou William Allerdyis land and the rest payit. To William three hundreth merkis in present money beand in James Forresteris handis and Mr Alexander Wedderburnis as the particular discharge heirefter minuttit beiris Siclyk declaring a satisfactioue of Katharen our sisteris portione and siclyk declaring a discharge to the said David subscryvit be Mr Alexander of his airschip etc. as the sam subscryvit be James Forrester Alexauder Scrymgeour James Auchinlek Robert Kyd James Durhame the said Mr Alexauder Petir Wedderburn Robert Wedderburn me the said David and Thomas Traell beiris of the dait at Duude the 27 of Marche 1591 yeiris.

(b) Robert my brotheris discharge of his portioun naturall.

Ane Discharge to David Wedderburn be Robert his brother of his bairnis part of geir etc. as the sam subscryvit be his hand be Mr Alexander David James Forrester John Auchinlek and Robert Wedderburn elder witnessis of the dait the xiij of March 1588 yeiris.

Ane Discharge of James my brotheris portioun naturall.

Ane Discharge maid be James to me of his portioun as the samin subscryvit be him James Forrester provest James Carmichnell James Durhame Mr Alexander and Robert my brether Witnessis of the dait at Dundie the xiij of May 1592 beiris.

Ane Discharge of William my brotheris portiouu naturall.

Ane Discharge maid be James Forrester provest iu uem of Thomas Traell confessing him to have receavit fra the said Thomas aue huudreth merkis in nem of the said David and als fra the said David xlix lib. xiijs iiijd and thairfor discharging the said David in nem of William Wedderburn his brother thairof as a part of his portioun naturall and oblissing him to warrand me thairof as the sam subscryvit be the said provest and James Forester his oy .... of the dait the 14 May 1592 and Johne Cudbert witnes.

Item iu the end of the sam peper ane speciall Discharge maid be Mr Alexander to me in uem of the said William of ane hundreth merkis for roupit geir in compleit payment of the said Williamis portioun with warrandice thairin etc. Witnessis thairin Walter Hay Alexander Ramsay bailie the said provest, Subscryvit be him the said provest aud James Durhame Qulairof the dait forsaid.

Of Petir my brother.[1]

Petir infeft ane hundreth merkis ou William Allerdyse and landis and in ane hundreth merkis James Halliburtouis land.

Mr Alexander is awin xx merk to Petiris part of the roupt geir.
Petir my brotheris discharge of x lib. Item. 8 lib. vs he receavit fra George Mudy. Item. xj lib. I payit at Mr Alexanderis command for his proceis fie to James Renkynis wyf.

Invetar etc.

Aue Iuvetar of my father and motheris gudis and geir conteuand the forme of the rouping thairof.

(c) Ane discharge of Robert my father brother.

Ane baud betuix Robert Wedderburn my father brother and me tuiching the discharge for repetione of xl lib. throw my double renunciatioue thairof anent the redemptione of 6 aud 7 merkis aunuell furth of Robert Mylnis landis as the samin subscryvit be him Johne Paton notar John Auchinlek James Ferguson witnessis of the dait the xiij of Ootober 1595 beiris.

---

[1] Peter Wedderburn's affairs, in counection with his patrimony, are the subject of other entries. Thus :—

(a) 26 Apryle 1587.—Is the dait of my Seasing of xj merkis out of James Haliburtonis hous in Ergylis geit. 17 Martij 1590.—Is the dait quhen I infeft Petir my brother thairiu as ane pairt of his bairnis pairt of geir of thre hundreth merkis he useit thro deceis of my father and mother. 25 Martij 1586.—Is the dait of my brother Petiris Seasing quhon he was infeft in 12 merk annuel under reversione of ane hundreth merkis upliftit furth of Eduard Chalmeris houssis in Ergylis geit in pairt of payment as said is. 2 January 1586.—Is the dait of my brother Petiris Seasing of x merkis annuel in compleit payment of his thre hundreth merkis upliftit furth of William Allerdyis land lyand in Ergylis geit. Thir all insert iu Mr Alexander Wedderburnis buikis my brotheris commoue Clerk of Dundie. (Undated). For Petiris pairt Wm Allerdys a hundreth merk.
       „   xj merkis Disponit to Petir my brother iu part of payment of his baruis part of geir with aue uther huudreth merkis on William Allerdyise land and the rest payit be vertew of his Discharge I haif thairof.

(b) Receauit fra Adame Balmanno in name of William Allerdyse for my brother Petiris annuelrent of x merkis furth of the said Williamis tenement lyand on the north syd of the kyrk yard and that for the Mertemes terme in anno 1590 and Witsuuday thairefter in anno 1591. The Swme was fourteue lib aud he is awine yit xls quhilk suld be payit to Petir Wedderburn elder togidder with a merk quhilk is in my handis that is mair nor xx merkis that belangis to my brother. And Petir Wedderburn elder was payit of all termes preceiding quheu he payit me a pairt of my obligatioue in Alexander Scrymgeouris presens in his awin hous. Destributit this xiiij lib as followis j merk I suld gif Petir Wedderburn. Payit to Rychard Clerk for 2 ellis Fleming gray to be litel Petir a stand of claythis 4 lib 4s.

(c) 4 Martij 1612.—A Discharge aud insert and registrat in the Court buikis of Dundie maid by Petir my brother to Eduard Chalmeris airis and me of ane hundreth merkis on their land, aud of samekle of his bairnis pairt of geir fra me.

(d) A dispositione of the xvj part of the Pelican.

Ane dispositioue of the xvj part of the schip callit the Pelican maid be James David Wedderburn to me subscryvit be him in presens of Mr. Alexander Wedderburn Robert burn's MS. Wedderburn mercheand and Robert my brother of the dait the 19 of November 1593 with a discharge of the bak thairof of the recept of the swmes promittit thairfor.

* * * * *

(e) A Memorandum of Robert my brotheris effectis.

Memorandum. Ane Invetar of my brother Robertis gudis and geir of Petiris hand wryt notit be Mr. Alexander and esteimit as the samin of the dait the xx of December 1594 beiris subscryvit be James Scryingeour James Carmichael and William Duncan.

Ane discharge of Elspet Heringis of certane rowpit geir and uther preseut sylver of my brother Robertis geir subscryvit be Johne l'atou and Johne Wobster notaris about 2ᶜ, tua hundreth, merkis In presens of David Coustoun, me, Robert Man, Johne Isak, of the dait the xx of September 1595 beiris.

My brother Mr. Alexander hes my brotheris Robertis obligatione to his dochter Helen and Johne Lovellis discharge of 3ᶜ merkis thairin.

* * * * *

(f) Petir my father brotheris Discharge.

Item a Discharge of Petir Wedderburnis my father brotheris of all he may acclame before the dait thairof of me as the samin of the dait the tent day of Apryle the yeir of God jmᵛᶜ four scoir twelf yeiris beiris subscryvit be his hand in presens of Mr. Alexander and Robert his brother aud subscryvit be Robert as witnes.

* * * * *

(g) My matrimoniall Contract.

My burgeschip.

My Contract Matrimouiall betuix me and the laird of Westhall and their cautioneris of the dait the 26 Februar 1589. Subscryvit be us all.

The extract of my burgeschip of the dait the xv May 1582 out of the lokit buik subscryvit be the Clerk.

* * * * *

(h) Toward my brother Robertis evidentis.

Robert Wedderburn mercheand burges of Dundie this day the xxvij Januar 1595 In presens of Archibald Hering, Mr. Alexander, me David Wedderburn, James Hering, and George Hay skletter hes receavit ane lokit blak boix quhairof the said Archibald hes the key and Invetar subscryvit be the said Robert and wituessis forsaidis of xiij peces of evidentis and wryttis perteniug to Alexander sone to Robert my uniquhill brother, and hes oblist him be the said band above wryttin iu the Invetar in the said Archibaldis handis to me be the samin furth cumaud to all parteis that sall pretend iutres thairto viz :—

Ane Sasiug quhair my brother was lufeft in my fatheris tenement eistmest uuder the signe and subscriptione of Thomas Iyrlaud notar the dait the peuult of Marche 1573.

Aue redemptione under his not of sex merkis upliftit be Effam Bell furth of the foirlaud the 3 of May 1578.

Ane excambion betuix my brether Mr. Alexander and Robert of the bak tenement with Robertis lugeiug and xvj merkis uuder Thomas Iyrland notary the penult of December 1577.

Toward Robert my brotheris evideutis.

Ane extract furth of the commone court buikis of Dundie quhair the sam is insert with aue aprobatione of bayth my Bretheris consent to the excambiou under the extract and subscriptioue of Robert Wedderburu and Gilbert Quhittet notaris of the dait the xvj of October 1588.

The rest ar thair.

(i) My Mertemes meill 1597 payit efter this form.

Upoun the xxj day of December 1597 I offerit to the gudeman my brother Mr. Alexander and his wyf in thair heiche chalmer 8 lib. all in ryellis and tenˢ. peces for the Mertemes meill of my hous of his quhilk I occupy and because of the insufficience of tua barrellis Salmond he sauld me and gat fra me 3ˣˣ lib. in gold thairfor and quhen thay wer sauld in Flanderis be James Fraser to me I tynt xxj lib. on thame they being all grissillis and he selling me thame for salmond sufficieut of Grange fisches he quhyttit me only the sauld 8 lib. for a recompance of my skayth. Sua in that respect my said Mertemes meill of his hous occupyit be me last by past iu this yeir of God 1597 is payit [1]

(j) Off Robert my brotheris barnis effairis.

Ane act contenit in the commone court buikis of Dundie William Man bailie quhair Johne lovell and James Forrester ar oblist that four hundreth merkis aperteniug to Helen my brother Robertis[2] dochter salbe furthcumand to hir and scho sustenit on the excresence thairof of the dait the 13 November 1596.

---

[1] See ante 8(a, b).   [2] See aute 8(d)n.

<table>
<tr><td>

David Wedder-
burn's MS..

</td><td>

Aue uther act quhair James Reyky and James Fraser his cautioner ar obliat in
the saidis buikis that aucht scoir merkis salbe furthcumand to Alexander Robertis
my brother sone and he to be susteuit on the excresence thairof of the dait the
xj Junj 1597.

</td></tr>
</table>

Aue compt of Johne Lorell recept of sum particularis of the last jᶜ merkis,

<table>
<tr><td>

Of my brother
Robertis effairs.

</td><td>

Ane speciall discharge of Elspet Heringis with consent of hir husbaud subscryvit
be him and takand the burding on him for hir of 3ᶜ merkis as hir portioun of my
brother Robertis guidis and geir. Witnessis Archibald Hering Mr Alexander and
Archibald Hering and my self.

</td></tr>
</table>

Ane particular recept of Elspat Heriugis.

The speciall Invetar of Robertis gudis Quhilkis gudis wes roupit and intrometti
with be Alexander Annand weyhous maister and the mouey distributit be him to
Johne Lovell and the baruis and to Elspet Hering.

Ane speciall Iuvetar of the restis quhilk belongis to Alexander my brother
Robertis sone extending about 3ᶜ merkis to mak out his 3ᶜ merkis quhairof James
Reyky has xl merkis with the 8 xx iu his haudis.

*   *   *   *   *

<table>
<tr><td>

Betuix James
Thomsome
litster and me.

</td><td>

Upon the xxvj Junj 1598 James Thomsone alias Reyky is actit in the commissaris
buikis of St, Andrus to releif me of the cautionry I became that day for him aneut
the furthcuming of sic gudis aud geir as he gef up pertenand to umquhill Robert
my brother and his first twa wyffis[1] to Alexauder his sone confirmit executor dative
thairto.

</td></tr>
</table>

13. In another part of the book is a list of three pages, enumerating twenty-eight
items, among which are the following :—

<table>
<tr><td>

Off Dischairgis
and uther richtis
and wryttis
maid to me.

</td><td>

(a) Aue discharge of xxxˢ quhilk I payit for my fatheris aunuelreut of his hous
efter his deceis quhilk my brother dwellis in the xvj of Marche 1585 to Schir
Johne barnis wituessis Andro Blyth Mr Alexauder and Patrik Wedderburnis.

</td></tr>
</table>

(b) Aue discharge of Williamis my brotheris burd to Johue Scottis wyf. Witnessis
Johne How Thomas Patersone James Scrymgeour Johne Auchinlek Robert
Wedderburu notar the 26 of October 1587.

(c) Ane discharge betuix me and Andro Blyth of all things he may acclame of
me befor this dat. Witnessis Mr Alexander Wedderburn George Mudy.

(d) Ane discharge of Andro Sibbaldis for 49 lib. for a twn of wyn. Witnessis Johne
Ogilvy Petir Wedderburn William Halyburtoun Maryner the xv of July 1585.

(e) Ane discharge of all thingis betuix Robert my brother and me that he may clame
of me befor the dait the xiij of Jun 1587.

Ane commissione of my brother Robertis to receave sum money of his creditoris
and to gif David Robesone a discharge subscryvit with his hand the x of July 1587.

Ane uther commissione of Robert my brotheris to receave sum debtis of his and
thairiu conteuit ane discharge of 6ˣˣ 11j ᵘᵇ or thairby of his barnis part of geir
with his hand subscryvit at Dunde the x of November 1587.

Ane commissione be missive of my brother Robertis to receave fra Andro Ray and
Johne Heudersoue in Perth sum of his debtis subscryvit with his haud at Deip-
the x of Februar 87.

Aue nominatione aud will of my brother Robertis maid to me subscryvit with his
hand befor David Ramsay and Thomas Heres maryueris of the dait the x of July
1587.

(f) Ane obligatioue maid be James Reiky to wmquhill Johne Wedderburn for vj
merkis xᶦᵈ before the 17 of July 1575.

(g) Ane obligatione maid be David Robesone to David Wedderburn of sum merche-
andyce of the dait the xj of Marche 1586. Befor George Ogilvy Johne Wallace
subscryvit with his hand.

(h) Ane dispositione of certane sylvir warkis to my brother William maid be Henry
Allane under reversionu of 44 lib. subscryvit with his hand the 5 of October 1587
befor Petir Imbrye Mr Alexander Wedderburn Johu How,

(i) Aue obligatione of Petir Wedderburnis of 22 lib. xˢ sul scryvit with his hand the
24 of August 1585 befor Murdo Makeynghe James Nichol

[1] See ante 8(c) n³.

14. It is to be regretted that it did not occur to David to insert in his notebook a regular account of his father's family. Of his own children he gives two very elaborate registers, of which the first covers the years 1590—1606, while the second goes down to 1621. The first of these is written in double columns, thus :— David Wedder-burn's MS.

(a) Upon the xxv of Marche 1590 att ancht houris at evin (beand weddinsday) Helen my eldest dochter wes born. Hir godfatheris James Durhame of Pitkerro Mr James Rutherfurd and Petir Clayhillis. Hir godmotheris Helene Ramsay Helen Cokburn Lady Westhall and Cristian Clayhillis.

(b) Upon the 28 December 1592 at 4 houris in the morning beand Weddinsday my second dochter Euffame wes born Hir godfatheris Mr Alexander Wedderburn John Ogilvy James Betoun of Westhall Hir godmotheris Euffame Wischert gudwyf of Persy Euffame Coustoun Margaret Carnegy spouse to John Peirsone.

(c) Upon the xxv day beand Weddinsday of Januar[1] 1595 at thre houris in the morning beand Weddinsday (sic) my thrid dochter Mettie wes born Hir godfatheris Alexander Peirsone Robert Wedderburn David Zeaman godmotheris Elspet Symmer Agnes Gibsoun Helen Beton gudewyf of Ardowuy.

(d) Upoun the 14 of May 1598 beand Fryday at sex houris at evin Jonet my fourth dochter wes born. Her godfatheris Henry Ramsay of Ardony Johne Scrymgeour Alexander Jak mercheand Her godmotheris Jonet Betoun Margaret Wedderburu and Katharen Wedderburn.

(e) Upoun fryday efter twelf in the nycht a litell the 7 of September 1599 David my sone wes born and wes baptisit on sonday thairefter the 9 of September be Mr James Robertson minister. His godfatheris William Man bailie William Duncane chirurgian David Coustoun Alexander Cokburn John Schevan David Ogilvy. Thir suld haif bene his godmotheris Helen Ramsay the clerkis wyf Margaret my sister and Euffame Scott.

(f) Upon the last of August 1600 being Mononday my fyfth dochter Katharen wes born and baptisit on Sunday thairefter Hir godfatheris Mr James Robertsone minister and Patrik Lyoun bailie Johue Betoun. Hir godmotheris my sister Kathereu and Katheren Erskyn Lady Westhall. at 9 houris in the day.

(g) The 6 of September 1601 James my sone born att 12 houris at evin and baptisit the xv of September being tyseday be Mr James Robertsone minister witness Sir James Scrymgeour of Dudop knycht James Halyburtoun of Peteur James Beton of Westhall and James Wedderburn my brother His godmotheris Margaret Moncur spous to William Spens and Margaret Scrymgeour Mr James Robertson's wyf.

(h) xxix August 1602 being Sonday at 4 houris in the morning my sone Alexander wes borne aud wes baptisit on Tysday thairefter in the eist Kyrk of Dundie be Mr. James Robertsone minister of Dundie. His godfatheris Mr Alexander Wedderburn commone clerk of Duude Mr. Johne Lovell Mr William Fergusone Alexander Broun. His godmotheris Jonet Wedderburn spous to William Davidsone Euffam Gray Jonet Blyth spous to Walter Rollok.

(i) xix Februar 1604 on Sonday at 8 houris at evin my dochter Issobel wes born and baptisit on Tuesday thairefter the 21 Februar be Mr James Robertsone minister of Dunde in the litil eist kyrk Her godfatheris Thomas Gardyn Walter Rollok William Davidsone elder Alex[r] Wedderburn younger Hir godmotheris Issobell Beton my gude sister Issobell Kyd spous to Alexander Smyth aud Issobell Aberdene spous to Audro Hill.

(j) 23 Februar 1606 being the last[2] sonday at xj houris at evin in Westhall my dochter Magdalen wes born and baptisit be Mr Henry Duncane quha mareit me. Hir godfatheris James Ogilvy of Dyntron Henry Ramsay of Ardony Mr. Henry Duncane and Wille Graham Hir godmotheris Dame Magdalen Leviugstoun Lady Dudop Magdalen Wedderburn my brotheris dochter.

15. The second of David's family registers is as follows :—

The Names of Barnis and Eild of thame procreat betuix Dauid Wedderburn and Matild Beton his spous with the names of thair godfatheris and godmotheris Baptisit and be quhat Ministeris is as follows :—

(a) Upoun the xxv day of Merche 1590 at aucht at evin beand Weddinsday Helen my eldest dochter wes born. Hir godfatheris James Durhame of Pitkerro Mr James Rutherfurd of Murrons Petir Clayhillis. Her godmotheris Helen Ramsay spous to Mr Alexander Wedderburn Commone Clerk of Dundie Helen Cokburn Lady Westhall and Christian Clayhillis spous to William Man and baptisit be William Crystesone Minister upon the last of Merche 1590.

(b) Upoun the twentie aucht day of December 1592 at 4 houris in the morning beand Weddinsday My Secound dochter Euffame wes born. Hir godfatheri Mr Alexander Wedderburn, John Ogiluy James Betoun of Westhall. Hir godmotheris Euffame Wischert gudewyf of Persy Euffame Coustoun spous to Robert Wedderburn mercheand and Margaret Carnegy spous to John Peirsone aud baptisit be William Crysteson upon the penult of December 1592.

(c) Upoun the xxv of Januar 1595 beand Weddinsday at 3 houris iu the morning my thrid dochter Matild wes born. Hir godfatheris Alexander Peirsone at Wardmylu Robert Wedderburn Dauid

[1] The word "langest" is here erased
[2] This is written over the word "December," which is struck out.

Z

David Wedder-
burn's MS.

Yeamen. Hir godmotheris Elspit Symmer spous to James Scrymgeour Agnes Gibsone spous to George Ramsay Heleu Betou gudewyfe of Ardowny. Baptisit be Mr James Robertsone Minister upoun the 26 Januar 1595.

(d) Upoun the 14 day of May 1598 beand Fryday at sex houris at ewin Jouet my fourt dochter wes boru. Hir godfatheris Henry Ramsay of Ardowny, John Scrymgeour Alexander Jak merchand. Hir godmotheris : Jonet Beton spous to John Ochterlony Margaret aud Kathtreen Wedderburnis my sisteris. Baptisit be Mr James Robertsone the said day. [In Gods mercie deceissit the 23 May 1616.]

(e) Upoun the sewint day of September 1599 beaud Fryday a litell efter twelf in the nycht Dauid my eldest son wes born aud baptisit on Sunday thairefter be Mr James Robertsone Minister the 9 of September. His godfatheris William Man bailie William Duncan Chirurgian Dauid Coustoun (Alexander Cokburn John Schewan). His godmotheris Helen Ramsay the Clerkis wyf Margaret my sister and Euffame Scot spous to James Fraser.

(f) Upoun the last day of August 1600 being Mouoday my fyft dochter Katharen wes born and baptisit on Sonday thairefter be Mr James Robertsone Minister. Hir godfatheris Mr James Robertsone Minister Patrik Lyoun bailie, John Beton. Hir godmotheris my sister Katharen Wedderburn and Katharen Erskyn Lady Westhall This is at 9 houris iu the day. The baptisme the 6 of September 1600.

(g) Upoun the sext day of September 1601 being Sonday at tuelf houris at evin James my secuund soue wes boru and baptisit be Mr James Robertsone Minister on the xv of September being Tysday. His godfatheris Sir James Scrymgeour of Dudope Knight Sir James Haliburton of Piteur Knight James Wedderburn my brother and James Beton of Westhall. His godmotheris Margaret Moncur spous to William Speus and Margaret Scrymgeour spous to Mr James Robertsone.

(h) Upoun the xxix day of August 1602 being Sunday at 4 houris in the morning my thrid son Alexʳ wes born and baptisit be Mr James Robertsone Minister on Tysday thairefter [and departit this lyf ix houris mornŭ the 22 day of Apryle 1616.] His godfatheris Mr Alexander Wedderburn commou Clerk of Dundie Mr John Louell Mr William Fergusone. His godmotheris Jonet Wedderburn spous to William Dauidsone Jouet Blyth spous to Waltir Rollok and Effie Gray spous to John Schurswod.

(i) Upoun the xix of February 1604, being Sonday at 8 houris at evin my sext dochter Issobell wes boru and baptisit on Tysday thairefter be Mr James Robertsone Minister. Hir godfatheris Waltir Rollok William Davidsone elder Thomas Gardyu Alexander Wedderburu younger. Hir godmotheris Issobell Beton spous to Alexander Peirsone at Wardmylu Issobel Kyd spous to Alexander Smyth and Issobell Aberden spouse to Andro Hill.

(j) Upon the 23 day of February 1606 being Soulay at xj houris at ewiu in Westhal my sewint dochter Magdalen wes born and baptisit be Mr. Heury Duncan iu the Kyrk of Murrois Miuister thairof quha mareit me and my wyf there. Hir godfatheris James Ogiluy of Dyutrouu Heury Ramsay of Ardowny the said Mr. Henry Duncau and Willie Grahame. Hir godmotheris Dame Magdaleu Lewingstouu Lady Dudop and Magdaleu Wedderburn dochter to the Clerk my brother.

(k) Upoun the auchtene day of Januar the yeir of God aue thousaud sex hundreth aud ten yeiris my fourt son Henry wes boru aud baptisit the 23 Januar instant be Mr. James Robertsone Miuister in the Kyrk of Dundie the eistmost of thame being Frijday at xij houris at eviu. The names of his godfatheris Heury Ramsay of Ardowuy George Auchiulek aud William Dauidsoue younger mercheand His godmotheris Margaret Wedderburu my sister Mariouu Jak spous to Alexander Cockburn Anna Thayu spous to James Fethe aud Besse Fethe his sister.

(l) Upoun the xxij day of May 1610 My dochter Helen wes mareit with George Auchiulek being Tysday at v houris at evin be Mr. James Robertsoue Miuister of Duudie iu the litel eist Kyrk of Dundie.

(m) Upon the xj of Nouember 1610 my dochter Effeme wes mareit with James Symsone mercheand in the Kyrk of the Mauys be Mr William Reat Minister thairof.

(n) 12 May 1613 wes Dauid Auchiulek born at 2 efter uone. Dauid Auchiulek soue to George Auchiulek is baptisit be Mr. Dauid Lyndsay Minister upoun the 13 May being Thursday at v houris at evin. His godfatheris Mr Dauid Lyudsay David Huuter David Wedderburn. His godmotheris Helen Ramsay the gudewyf, the clerkis wyf, Marion Jak spouse to Alexander Cockburu and Anna Thayn spouse to James Fethe.

(o) Upouu the xj day of Apryle 1621 Helen my dochter wes mareit with James Ros in the litel eist Kyrk of Duudie be Mr Colyn Campbell Miuister.

16. His sons-in-law are uamed elsewhere in the "Compt Buik," both in connection with their wives' tochers and in regard to business transactions between them and their father-in-law. Thus :—

(a) Penult July 1612 —Delyuerit George Auchinlek fiftie merkis in pairt of payment of jᶜ lib. quhilk rest awin him of his tocher gude. Quhilk huudreth lib with 8ᶜ merkis awiu me on James Haliburtonis Obligatione and his cautioueris compleittis George Auchinlekis tocher gude. Item gef George xl merkis I gat fra Audru Mores of my Wyn Syluer. Item gef George 36 lib I gat fra Robert Kyd of his burgeeship. Item gef his wyf 4 lib quhilk scho bocht beif with. Quhilk altogidder is compleit payment of aue huudreth lib. Quhilk altogidder is aue thousand merkis for his tocher gude.

(b) 2 Apryle 1626.—Comptit with Alexauder Smyth mercheand for all comptis of merchaudice that my dochter Heleu or James Ros wes awiu him conteuit iu his compt buik. He dischergit us thairof and that becaus I causit my brother the Clerk compleitly pay him of fyve or sex huudreth merkis he wes awiu him.

(c) Undated. Lent my cradill of alk to Effie my dochter.

(d) 2 Apryle 1611.—Giffin to James Symsone my gude soue John Yeamanis Discharge with the **David Wedder-**
Obligatioune on the bak quhair I payit for John Schoaswod sue hundreth and fiftie lib with a power a **burn's MS.**
commissioun to Cristeau Wedderburu aud hir husband C. Cuoenghame to persew him Als a
procuratorie to John Schorswod. Subscryve on xx merkis to get auswer at his hame cuming
of . . . (sic),

(e) Upon the xxiiij of May 1611.—Anent James Symsone. At command of James Symsone my gudesone
I payit to George Michell maltman in Murreget lxj lib 13ˢ 4ᵈ for his pairt of a crear coft be him fra
George as the first termes payment thairof.
Item gef at his command to John Fothringham xxiiij lib.
Item to John Fothringhame agane xxxv lib.
To Effie my dochter his wyf 6 lib.
To Effie agane 3 lib xijˢ.
To yourself to mak out 2° merkis 3 lib 1ˢ 4ᵈ.

(f) Upoun the 26 July 1611. Item gef yourself in my Chalmer tua hundreth merkis in Inglis mouey.
Summa in the haill four huudreth merkis. This in pairt of paymeut of the first vᵗ merkis I am
debtful to pay for the first terme of her tocher gude of a thousand merkis.

(g) 9 June 1612.—In preseus of Robert Trael, Mr. Johne Dunmnre. Delyuerit James Symsone in Petir
Balmanuois hous compleit payment of ane thousand merkes be vertew of his Discharge on the bak
of his Contract Matrimoniall Videlicet the some in money 14ˣˣ lib 4 lib.

Item xl lib xˢ to Robert Hamiltoun the rest off before in presens of Robert Trael gef him four
hundreth merkis as the forme insert in this buik will declair.

(h) 14 Apryle 1615. Send with James Symone to Stokholme twa wofflin beddis the price of the pece
vj lib. Item 24 ellis gryt hurdyn price of the eln 6s. Item delynerit Effie his wyf xx ellis
bleitschit lyning twidleu for xs the eln to war this to our proffit aud pay him self the Lynt he coft
to us fra James Walker aud Robert Clayhillis.
Item I leut him x lib I wes awin x merk thairof for the profittis—he restis awin me v merkis.

(i) Upoun the 10 of November 1615. Compted aud Reknit with my goodfather of all compt preceding
the dait herof that aither of us can lay till utheris charg he restis awaud till me thre scor ellevin
puodis and I have of his ane aikin kist in my booth in keping.

Memorandum. James Symsone hes relevit the xx ellis lyning   James Simsone.
tuidlan his wyf gat for x lb. to be deducit of the former swme.   D. Wedderburn.

Item. Upon the first of October 1616 Effe my dochter coft aud receavit fra my wyf Jonet hir
sisteris pled for ten puudis. The Kist estemat at eleviu puudis. restis only to James xl lib,

(j) 9 May 1620.—Item I have directit James Symsone to bring me hame a ratsche of a guo of fyve
quarter leuth,

(k) Last September 1621.—Send to Flanderis to James my sone thre hundreth merkis in gold xl ellis
pladding at xˢ the eln aud payit all his chargis to my unzeunis 8ˣˣ barrele or than benis in Alexander
Croyes bark.[1]

17. There are other references to David's immediate family in different parts of
the book. Thus :—

(a) I David Wedderburn burges of Dundie be thir preseutis nominattis my weilbelouit spous Matilde
Betoun [Helen and Euffame aud Matild Wedderburnis my dochteris][2] my ouly executouris aud
intromitteris with my gudis and geir ather Insicht planesiug debtis swmes of money or ony uther
way echo or thaj pleis dewyse to requyre quhilk belaugis to me And oblissis me be thir presentis be
vertew of our Contract Matrimoniall quhilk is in my brother Mr Alexauderis haudis to infeft hir in
all heretable tytellis I haif with power to my said spous and thame to use and dispoue heiron at thaer
pleassour Secludand aud dischargeand all former nominatiouis saif this only to thame be thir . . .
(sic) And willis this stand in effect perpetually heirefter Subscriuit with my hand at Dundie this
auchtene day of December the yeir of God jmvc and fourscoir teu yeiris befor thir wituessis Peter
Fyune William Kokburu Johu Onchterlony Henry Ogiluy Thomas Bruntfield.
                                                                Dauid Wedderburn, with my hand.

(b) I Dauid Wedderburn approuis my nominatioune abone wryttin to my spous and thre dochteris
forsaidis aud secludis all utheris and willis this saym stand perpetually heirefter Subscriuit with my
hand at Dundie the seavint of November 1595.   Dauid Wedderburne.

And Siclyk nominattis my said spous my Tutrix Testameutar to my saidis bairnis anno die
predicto.   D. Wedderburne.

[1] I think this must refer to his son-in-law James Symsone,' and not to his son James. then tweuty
years of age, who was not a merchant but a soldier, although he may have begun by being the
former.

[2] The words in brackets are written in the margin, and subsequently struck out. In December 1590
David had only one child, his daughter Helen, then a few mouths old. Five years later, when he
approves his nomination, he had three daughters, whose names he adds in the margin, but later
on, when he found himself with both sons and daughters, he strikes out their names to suit the
altered circumstances.

David Wedder-
burn's MS.

(c) xviij of August 93.—Delyuerit Issobell Barclay with my dochter Euffame for hir first quarteris buird xx^s Item. vj^s 8^d Item. xxiij^s 4^d.

24 November 93.—Deliuerit Issobell Barclay with my dochter Euffame for hir Secound termes quarter first xxj^s for a firlot mell nixt x^s for tua pekis Thirdly a xxj^s pece with her dochter. Item. v^s 40^d for flesche and xvitj^d restis of xj^s 4^d quhilk the Laird Westhall comandit me gif her 4^s 4^d.

(d) 26 December 1598.—The bailles and Clerk my brother gef Seasing to my wyf Matild Betonn induring hir lyftyme of St. Thomas Chaplenry and baill rentis thairof

(e) xix May 1608 hora sexta ante meridiem aut eo circa coram his testibus Jacobo Rollok chirurgo Johanne Gibsone chirurgo Roberto Drumond pinctore et Thoma Vichtan connotario cum Roberto Wedderburn seniore.

David Wedderburn suis propriis manibus contulit sasinam quinque acrarum terrarum arabilium jacentium in campo lie place schedde de Dudop per andream Thomsone et Alexandrum Nicoll occupatarum suos tenentes in favorem Thome Lyndsay auri fabri actornato et eo nomine Helene Wedderburn filie legititime dicti Davidis hereditarie salvis vitalibus redditibus ejusdem dicti Davidis et Matilde Betonn ejus conjugis durantibus eorum vite temporibus ac sub reversionibus infrascriptis vidclicet per constabularium de Dudop pro summa mille mercarum et in propria persona dicti Davidis persolvendo summam decem solidarum monete Scotie.   D. Wedderburn.

(f) John Patton notar hes this precept   23 May 1608 hora octava aute meridiem aut eo circa pre-
to forme the institutione to the   sentibus ibidem andrea Guthrie tinctore Johanne Watson
said Alexander thereon.   polentario Joanne Smyth calceario et Jacobo Blak mercatore
                                               Joanne Patton notario.

Dictus Andreas Guthre ballivus in precepto Davidis Wedderburn specialiter constitutus contulit sasinam sive institutionem capellauie S. Thome Martiris Patricio Gardyn pileario actornato Alexandri Wedderburn ejus filio durante spatie septem annorum secundum tenorem dicti precepti iu templo de Dundie Acta hec fuerunt per deliberationem libri psalmorum etc.   D. Wedderburn.

24 May 1608 hora nona aute meridiem presentibus Thoma Teyndel Andrea Crystie Patricio Lowsone et Alexander Wedderburn et patre suo Roberto Wedderburn notario.

David Wedderburne suis proprius manibus contulit sasinam Matilde Beton ejus conjugi predicti quinque acrarum terrarum arabilium sibi pertinentium in vitali redditu pro totu tempore vite sue tamen pro solvendo feudifirmam in veteris suis infeofamentis contentam.

(g) At x houris befor none upoun the xj of January 1624 Patrik Kyd bailie, witnessis Patrik Lyoun, Johne Renkyu, maryner, Mr. Robert Mongumry, Minister of Godis word at Kynnard, George Pikeu and Adame Crychton in Dundie, Mr. Alexander Wedderburn, Clerk, present. I, Dauid Wedderburn resignit in the said baileis handis my lugeing and tenement with yurd bak and foir lyand on the north pairt of the hie mercat gelt of Dundie iu fauoris of Mette Beton my spous present and the airis lawfully gottin or to be gottin betuix us quhilkis failzeand to me my airis and assignais heretable.
                                                                          D. Wedderburn with my hand.

18. The Compt Buik also contains a large number of miscellaneous memoranda. From some of these it appears that David was not content to be a merchant only, but desired also to follow the family profession of the law, and, with the aid of his father's protocol books, to do business in "transumpts" and documents of title. We have seen (ante 11 (c) p. 171) that in 1583 his father made a disposition to him of all his protocol books and that some of these certainly came into his possession is shown by the following entry :—

(a) Memorandum. I haif v auld subscryvit protogol buikis of my fatheris. Item 4 buikis of Harbert Gledstanes. Item of my uncle and uther litell buikis.

The mention of the books of his uncle (who is, of course, Robert, the notary) is not clearly worded, but it shows that this entry which must have been made after his death is later in date than 1611 as Robert died in the October of that year. Perhaps the "litell buikis" were some of the small minute books, several of which are now in the Dundee Charter room (post p. 206). Robert, however, left all his protocol books to his great-nephew James, afterwards clerk of Dundee. At this date (1611) David had got himself admitted notary. The record of his admission is not amongst those still extant in the Edinburgh Register House, but he has given a note of it in his MS.

(b) Upoun the xij of July 1603,—My creatione of notarie wes and insert in Mr. Alexander Hayis buik. My buik notit and merkit conteuit threscoir aucht leiffis James Hay of Fudie my cautioneer I payit ala to Mr. Hay a Bonet pece price 8 lib. Item a vj lib pece.

and he certainly made use both of his office and his father's books till very late in life.[1] Thus it was no doubt for work as a notary that he got, in kind, the fee mentioned in this entry :—

(c) The tent of September 1610.—In presens of Mr. James Wedderburn, Mr. John Dynmur and Dauid Mudy, telzeour in the hous of William Guthre. The said William promittit me a stik of fyu grewgren silk quhilk sald cost v lib gryt within 7 or 8 oukis heirefter aud awner eftir his hame cumiug from Flanderis for my consent to the aprobatione of his rychtis of his tenement.

---

[1] Thus 4 October 1630.—Memorandum. James Crystie in Adamestoun receauit fra me thre iufeftmentis extractit out of my Fatheris Protocol buik subscryuit be me and never hes payit me thairfor quhilk extends to xx lib. I have receauit only tua foullis fra him.

So again, one of the latest entries is as follows :—

(d) Memorandum on the 24 Junij 1615.—(4 *lines carefully obliterated in the original*). It is to be rememberit I have subscryuit him (? whom) ane Dispositione of the Nonûtre of v acris land formit be William Gray, Scheref Deput, quhairin I grant I have receauit syluer. Item quhair I deleit the uther wryttis maid betuix him and me in his conforme. Item quhair he promesit to gif me aue honest satisfactione in the agreing him and Mr. James Wedderburn in getting him a relief of his cautionrie anent Kynnard, etc.

Not long, however, before this date David had lost possession of these books. It seems that the provost sent two of the bailies to borrow them and that David thereupon lent them upon a guarantee that if the books were not returned to him within fourteen days, the provost should pay him a thousand merkis. Whether he ever got either the books or the merks does not appear. He makes the following note of the matter :—

(e) Memorandum to persew Thomas Halyburtoun, provost of Dundie, for the wrangis intromissione with my fatheris protocolis extending to sex gryt bukis futrouuettit with (be ?) him of myn in the counselhous on the 17 of March 1629 and promisit to restor me thame within 14 dayis thairefter or content me of a thousand merkis quhilk I askit fra Johne Ramsay and William Kyneres, baileis, sent be him to me in the Kyrkzaird thairfor.

The six books are now in the Dundee charter room though they do not appear to have been there in 1639, when Sir Alexander Wedderburn made an inventory of all books then in his possession as clerk (post p. 206).

19. Other memoranda record all sorts of matters. I have already dealt with David's grievances against his brother the clerk. He seems to have carried them beyond the grave. Thus there is an undated[1] memorandum made after Kingennie's death in 1626, as follows :—

(a) Memorandum to persew the clerk Mr. Alexander Wedderburn my brother sone as air and successour to Mr. Alexander Wedderburn his father and air and successour to Alexander Wedderburn, commone Clerk of Dundie, his gudschir my father for the soumes and cauasis specefeit in my clame.

Another note, also undated, gives one of the grounds of this claim.

(b) Memorandum to crave the clerkschip of the gild conforme to my provisione and Mr. Alexander Wedderburn for intromissione with the benefittis thairof my domage extending to 2000 merkis thairby.

20. The following references, scattered through the volume, all name a John Wedderburn, but cannot all refer to the same individual.[2]

(a) 2 Septembris 1589.—In presens of Alexander Duncan and John Wedderburn in Kyrkstyell delyuerit Robert Wedderburn my brother ane obligatione of William Kinlochs barbour of 2ᶜ merkis and actit in the buikis of Elgyn ane Lettre of Inhibitione to the quhilk Thomas Guthre maid him assignaj (to) This in Robertis awin hous and I am exonerit thairof.

(b) 20 Merche 93.—In presens of Thomas Stewart Hary Balfour and John Auchinlek, James Reyky litster is obliat to litt alsmekle clayth to be my tua dochteris ilk ane of thaine a cot of any hew I will requyre for the quhilk I delyuerit to him his obligatione of 4 lib 40ᵈ maid be him to my eme John Wedderburn, wryter, and rest the sam.

(c) Ane obligatione maid be George Vat to me of x merkis to be payit at Lambes 1597. Subscryvit be him and Andro Mathews and Johne Wedderburn witnessis.

(d) 21 July 1618,—Send to St. Andros with John Wedderburn and Mr. Danid Kid the Edik and Executioun to Mr. William Weyms.

[1] At the head of the page on which this memorandum occurs is written "Upoun the v of July 1620" but this relates to another entry only. It cannot be the date of this one, which must have been made 1627—33, the period during which David's nephew Alexander, here named as clerk, occupied that office. As the latest date written in the "Compt Buik" is 12 Dec. 1630, this entry was probably made 1627—30.

[2] John Wedderburn in Kirkstyell is, no doubt, the father of the Bishop of Dunblane. He died about 1606, and was the great great grandson of James Wedderburn and Janet Barry, who lived "at the West Kirk style." The second of the above entries cannot refer to him, as he was a mariner and not a "wryter." It refers, therefore, to John Wedderburn of Craigie, son of James Wedderburn and Margaret Dundas, who appears to have bred to the law. He died about 1600. The word "eme," as applied to him cannot, however, be taken in its usual sense of "uncle." David's father had no brother called John, and David always calls his uncles, Robert and Peter, his "fatheris brotheris" and not his "emes." The word, therefore, here signifies relative or cousin. The third entry (c) may refer to either of these persons, while the next three (d, e, f) cannot do so, as at the date of them both were dead. They probably refer to the son of Robert Wedderburn and Elizabeth Conatoun, the absence of the prefix "Mr." making it clear that they do not refer to John Wedderburn, afterwards Sir John of Gosford, the eminent physician, who has been mentioned ante 2(b).

(e) Memorandum to get the registrat discharge in the town of Dundeis buikis in June 1620 on Johne Wedderbnrne for 200 merkis to me.

(f) Ane registrat Discharge maid in the commone Court buikis of Dundie of the dait the 9 Marche 1621 maid be Johue Wedderburu to Alexander Inres, David Wedderburn, and Edward Cheislie of sex acoir 14 lib. x⁸.

21. Only a few passages remain. Several of them name Robert, the notary, while others mention David's brothers, Robert, James, and Peter, his son Alexander, his nephew of that name, "young Petir Wedderburn," his first cousin, and his more distant relatives Patrick Wedderburn and Robert, the merchant.

(a) Memorandum. Upoun the xix of Apryle 1597.—In presens of Robert Wedderburn, merchand, and Robert Guthre, fidler, I delyverit Robert Dumbar, servitour to Petir Wedderburn, my glnffis in satisfactione of a croun Robert. my brother. maid him assert to craif fra me be verten of my obligatione on my first land gottin and hes oblist him this sam wryt to rander me the said obligatione. This quhen Johue Byris, Petir Clayhillis, Robert aud I [were] in the bak chaltuer at the boreing of money be Petir fra the said Johne.

(b) 8 Nouember 1597.—Auld Robert Wedderburns infeftment of Robert and James Barreis laudis lyand in the west of the gren laudis is insert in my brother the Clerk of Dundeis Protocle.

(c) Memorandum. Upoun the ...... day of September 1599 yeiris.—Thair is ane apoyntment betuix auld Robert my father brother Robert the noter and James Ochterlony anent the grene laud, &c.

(d) 17 August 1601.—Auld Robert aud his wyf hes infeft Thomas Kyd in ane annuelrent of 24 merkis out of the grene land to get his renunciatione thairof or els to cause him register it on new in Mr. Alexanderis buikis.

(e) 7 Martij 1609.—Robert Clayhillis, William Goldman bailies, witnesses John Patton, Thomas Wichtan, notaris, Petir Wedderbnrn, younger, James Ochterlony, Gilbert Makduff.

Auld Robert Wedderburn noter hes resignit in the handis of the saidis Robert Clayhillis, baillie, his haill tenement westmest and eastmest aud baill yardis thairof in favouris of Alexander Wedderburn, sone to David Wedderburn senior, and to David his actornay, and to ...... as actornay for Petir, sone to Mr Alexander, their airis and assignais heretable but redemptione: Saiffing his awin lyfrent. The Clerk, Mr Alexander, Thomas Wichtan, and Johu Patton nottaris thairto.

Lykway in presens of the saidis witnesses he hes oblist him to infeft the said Alexander and Petir in his sex acris land lyand at the West Port of Dundie heretable as said is : Saiffing his awin lyfrent.

Efter the perfyting of the infeftment we, the said Mr Alexander and I, the said Dauid, [agree ?] yeirly and ilk yeir induring the said Robertis Lyftyme to pay him a chalder aitmeill equally betuix ns and to pay to Petir Wedderburnis tua sons, Petir and George, efter his deceis, six hundreth merkis equally betuix us.

(f) Tertio July 1610.—In presens of Mr. Alexander Wedderburn, William Rollok, Mr. John Dynmur, John Pattonn, Thomas Vichtau, James and Peter Wedderburnis. James Ouchterlony and Agnes Myln his sponse gef a Discharge subscryvit with their handis to auld Robert Wedderburn my father brother, of the compleit payment of sex⁰ merkis for the qnhilk Robert Wedderburn wes a cautioner and in compleit payment of all they may acclaim throw Robert Myln, James Myln or their deceiss. This in James haudis.

(g) 23 Junij 1612.—In presens of James and Petir, my brether, Andro Lichton, John Smyth, cordiner. I apoyntit with Thomas Guild cordoner for 12 lib. of instant sylver and 4 lib. worth of schone or Mullis to my wyf aud barnis in compleit payment of all byrouis of my annuel of 30⁸ upliftit out of his tenement in Skyrliugis Wynd aud gifin him ane acquittance thairon I raknit 16 yeir awin me at this present.

(h) 6 July 1612.—Memorandum. In presence of Petir and Dauid Mannis brether, I gef our Petir Manis ix lib he wes restand awand me of my registrat Band on him in the commone Court buikis of Dundie for wyn, etc. qnhilk wes on the xx of Apryle last wes to James Wedderburn my brother qnhilk Petir allowit to him in the first end of the fiftie merkis on Patrik Lowsonis Band. And this in pairt of payment of ten pundia 1 laitly borronit fra James. Sua rest I awin him xx⁸ and be is restand awand me xxvij⁸ I payit at his command in George Auchinlekis in presens of Thomas Juk, Patrik Wedderburn, Petir my brother. And James causit me deleit Petir Mannis registrat Band in the saidis buikis.

(i) Penult July, 1613.—Memorandum. Gef young Petir Wedderburnis woman callit Meriory Barry 33⁸ 4ᵈ for the Witsouday termes meill of the bak yard to gif Petir. Item x⁸ Sᵈ Summa 44⁸ for bairnis drink.

22. I have now given from David Wedderburn's "Compt Buik" every passage which throws light on the history of the family. The effect of each passage is dealt with in the first volume of this book, but I add here five tabular pedigrees, showing succinctly the different members of the family named by David, and enabling the reader to refer at once to the particular passages in which they are named.

TABULAR PEDIGREES OF THE FAMILY

SHOWING THE PERSONS NAMED IN THE "COMPT. BUIK."

Where the name is printed in italics the person is not mentioned in the foregoing extracts.

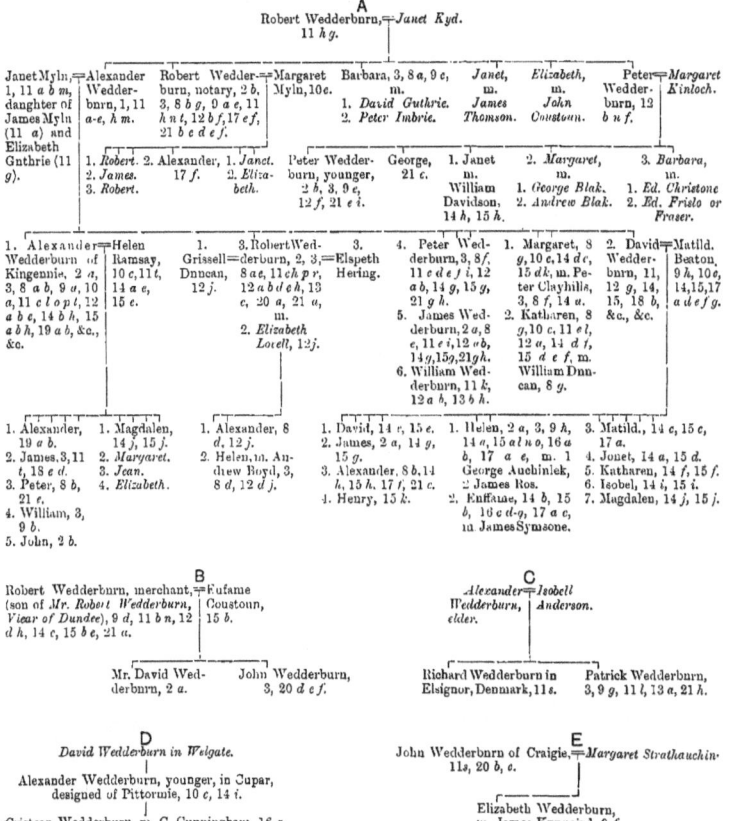

See also (1) John Wedderburn "in Kirkstyell," father of James, Bishop of Dunblane, 20 *a e*, and (2) Margaret Wedderburn, wife of Captain Walter Haliburton, 10 *c*.

BURGH RECORDS—DUNDEE.

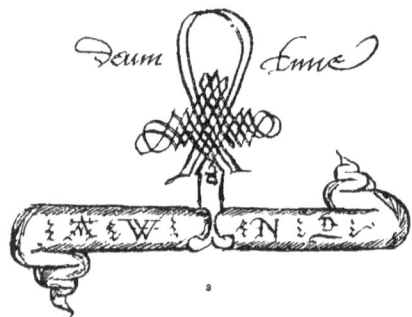

1. Symbol of Robert Wedderburn,
notary, 20 Sept. 1525. (From
the Dundee Charters, XLV. vi.
15).

3. Symbol of Alexander Wedderburn, town clerk of Dundee
(father of Alexander Wedderburn, first of Kingennie). 14 Oct.
1575. (From the Scrymgeour-
Wedderburn Papers, No. 30).

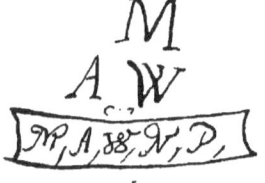

5. Symbol of Alexander Wedderburn, second of Kingennie,
clerk of Dundee, 3 July,
1626. (From the Scrymgeour-
Wedderburn Papers, No. 224).

2. Symbol of Robert Wedderburn,
notary, (uncle of Alexander
Wedderburn, first of Kingennie), 15 Dec. 1582. (From
the Scrymgeour - Wedderburn
Papers, No. 45.

4. Symbol of Alexander Wedderburn, first of Kingennie, clerk
of Dundee, 14 Sept. 1607.
(From the Scrymgeour-Wedderburn Papers, No. 164).

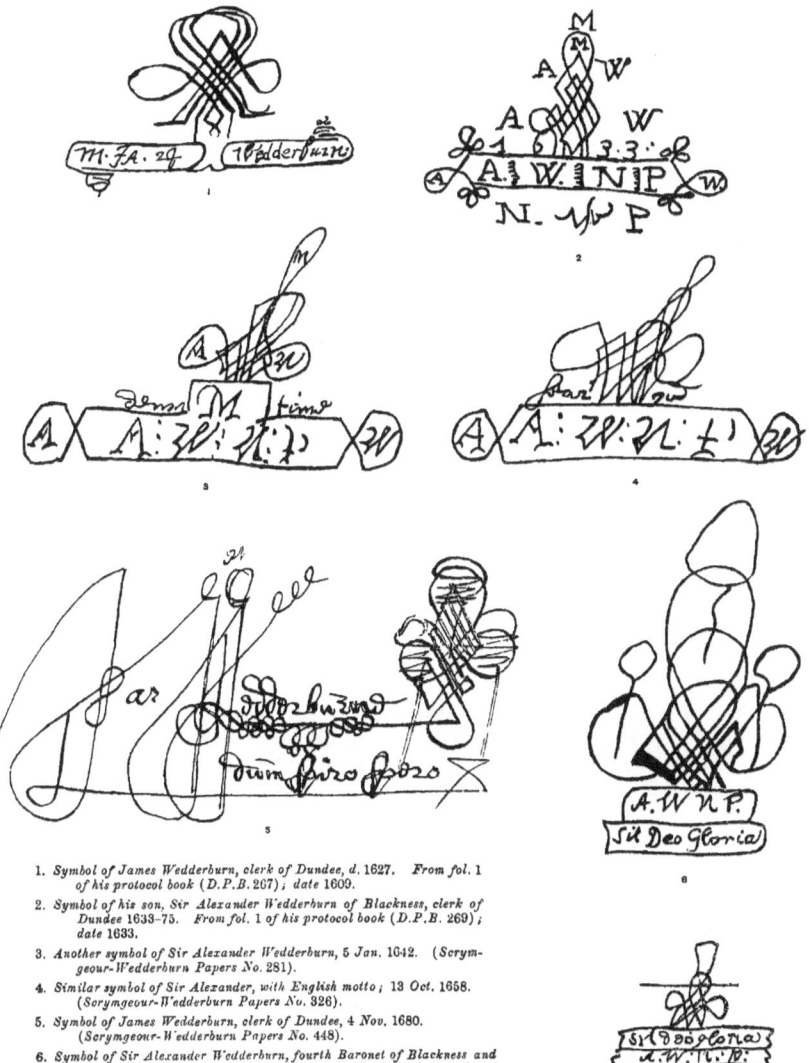

1. *Symbol of James Wedderburn, clerk of Dundee, d. 1627. From fol. 1 of his protocol book (D.P.B. 267); date 1609.*

2. *Symbol of his son, Sir Alexander Wedderburn of Blackness, clerk of Dundee 1633–75. From fol. 1 of his protocol book (D.P.B. 269); date 1633.*

3. *Another symbol of Sir Alexander Wedderburn, 5 Jan. 1642. (Scrymgeour-Wedderburn Papers No. 281).*

4. *Similar symbol of Sir Alexander, with English motto; 13 Oct. 1658. (Scrymgeour-Wedderburn Papers No. 326).*

5. *Symbol of James Wedderburn, clerk of Dundee, 4 Nov. 1680. (Scrymgeour-Wedderburn Papers No. 448).*

6. *Symbol of Sir Alexander Wedderburn, fourth Baronet of Blackness and clerk of Dundee. From a sasine among the Dundee Charters (III. ii. 14), dated 23 Jan. 1700.*

7. *Similar symbol of Sir Alexander, from fol. 1 of his protocol book (D.P.B. 279) date 1740.*

GENERAL NOTE ON THE DUNDEE RECORDS.

The Dundee Records are preserved in the Charter room of the Town House of Dundee. Dundee Records. It was not until 1890 that I came across the edition of "The Lockit Buik" of Dundee, edited in 1887 by Mr. A. H. Millar, and was made aware, through correspondence with him, of the existence of these records. I then visited Dundee, and with the assent of the authorities, made a personal examination of the contents of the Charter Room. The first ten items in the list on the preceding page, shew at a glance the different series of records that I found there ; the last two are in other custody. I shall give a detailed account of each of them in its turn, as I come to deal with extracts from it. Generally speaking, I found from the earliest times up to 1800 no less then 196 volumes, the majority of them thick folios, closely written in the small writing of the sixteenth and seventeenth centuries, and only legible by an expert in old scripts. In addition to these large volumes there were fifteen small books, containing minutes of sasines, and fifteen boxes of loose charters and writs. Personal examination of these was, of course, impossible to me, from want both of time and of skill in reading old handwriting. I, therefore, secured the excellent aid of the Rev. Walter Macleod and his staff, and had each volume carefully examined and every Wedderburn reference extracted from it. I had no difficulty in obtaining from the Town Council of Dundee the fullest facilities for this examination, and I desire to record my thanks not only to the Council, but to their officials, for the courtesy shown to Mr. Macleod and his assistants during the many months which they spent at the Town House, while conducting their search. To Mr. Macleod and his assistants my thanks are also due for the care which they brought to the work. I cannot give a better idea of its extent, than by stating that the extracts from these records cover over four thousand pages of foolscap, now bound up by me into eighteen volumes.

The records from which these extracts are made contain, largely in the handwriting of members of the family, materials for the history of the Wedderburns in Dundee. From 1557 to 1716 the office of clerk of Dundee was, as I have shown in the first volume of this book, almost uninterruptedly held by Wedderburns and their substitutes, and the records of the town over these years are chiefly written by them. Long before 1557, they were among the most prominent citizens of Dundee, and it may be that some of them held the office of clerk before that date. In 1716 when Alexander Wedderburn was deposed from office for his share in the rising of '15, the family ceased to be officially connected with the burgh, but they continued to reside in Dundee, and to own, as they still do, lands in the county, close to the town. Gradually, however, the occurrence of the name becomes less and less frequent in the records, which have not therefore been searched after 1800.

It has, of course, been impossible to print in extenso all the extracts from the records sent me by Mr. Macleod, and, even if space allowed it, there would be little object in doing so. There is of necessity a good deal of repetition in them. Persons holding office as clerk, bailie, councillor, or provost are again and again mentioned in their official capacities, but the entries add nothing to our knowledge of them or the family. So again, in many instances, the same person is repeatedly named as witnessing a transaction, but these entries do no more than show us that he was still alive at such and such a date, and only the first and last mention of him are thus of real value. Many of the entries, however, provide considerable information, and these I have given with more or less fulness, while I have dealt with others very shortly, and omitted a good many altogether. Those selected, taken as a whole, give, I think, a fair idea of the Wedderburn matter, contained in each series of the Dundee Records.

I have here inserted two pages of facsimiles of the notarial symbols of the Wedderburns, notaries and clerks of Dundee, 1525—1740. The actual examples, from which these are copied, are mostly from the Scrymgeour-Wedderburn papers, but as the Dundee Records are full of exactly similar symbols, used by the clerks and notaries in their public capacities, this seems the most fitting place at which to give them.

Dundee Charters, Writs, &c. These are contained in fifteen boxes, some account of the contents of which may be found in a volume entitled, "Charters, Writs, &c. of Dundee, 1292-1880, by William Hay (Dundee, 1880). The contents of Boxes I. and II., containing in all 289 Documents, of Box XIII. and part of Box XIV. are fully inventoried in this volume, and it is to be regretted that the same course has not been taken in regard to the other boxes, of which only a general account is given. Every document has, however, been gone over for the purposes of the present book, and all those naming members of the family have been noted. Out of these, all of any interest have been selected, and are given in the following inventory. The first of them, dated in 1497, is, with perhaps one exception, the earliest mention of the name in the archives of Dundee.[1] The contents of each box are done up in numbered bundles, and each document is also numbered. Thus, XIV, ix, 7, signifies Box XIV. Bundle ix, Document, 7.

INVENTORY.

1. **1497.** July 8.—Resignation by William Newman, burgess of Dundee, before Robert Seres, notary, of certain South Moraygate land in favour of Cristian And(erson) (re)l(ic)t and executrix of the late David Wedderburn, burgess. David Wedderburn, Robert Wedderburn, and James Wedderburn, burgesses, are all witnesses. XIV, ix, 7.
   The letters in brackets are illegible in the original through decay.

2. **1503.** Feb. 19.—Charter in favour of the parish Kirk of Dundee of an annual rent out of a North Flukergate land, bounded on the east by that of James of Wedderburn.
   XIV, vi, 34 (4).

3. **1508.** March 17.—Bond by James Rollok to the Town Council of Dundee, witnessed by Robert Wedderburn and others.
   This document is among some loose writs lying in Box VII. It is not numbered.

4. **1510.** Feb. 13.—Assignation by the magistrates of Dundee to James Rollok, burgess, of certain fishing rights in the Tay. Robert Wedderburn and James Wedderburn are among the witnesses. II, 288 (1).

5. **1513.** April 4.—Contract between William Barry and the town. Witnessed by James Wedderburn. XIV, viii, 4.

6. **1513.** April 4.—Indenture between the town of Dundee and William Barry, as procurator for John of Barry, his brother. Robert Wedderburn and James Wedderburn are among the witnesses. II, 270.

7. **1513.** June 30.—Minute of court held by Robert Wedderburn, one of the bailies of Dundee, at which Jonet Seres, spouse of James Lawsone, compears and consents to a resignation. XIV, viii, 3.

8. **1515.** Oct. 10.—Document endorsed "Copy of an ancient writing understood to be the original constitution of the Guildry incorporation in Dundee, 1515." It is headed "The just copy of Merchandis Letter of y[is] Burgh," and is signed by (among others) James Wedderburn. The burgh seal is appended,.10 Oct. 1515. II, 265.
   A full copy of the Royal Charter (17 July 1526) ratifying and approving this letter is given in Maclaren's *History of Dundee*, Appendix, Note G.

[1] Mr. A. H. Millar, in his edition of the "Lockit Buik," entitled the "Roll of the Eminent Burgesses of Dundee," cites the entry of the admission of James Wedderburn, junior, as burgess in September 1513, as the earliest mention of the Wedderburns in the existing burgh archives. That this is an error is shown by the first seven documents in this inventory; and possibly the mention of David Wedderburn in vol. ii, of the "Burgh and Head Court Records" (see below), is somewhat earlier even than these. There is also a still earlier document, dated 13 Sept. 1465 (x. i, 9), witnessed by "John Bell, common clerk of Dundee," which is of interest as shewing that the clerkship was not in the hands of the Wedderburn's at that date.

9. **1516.** April 1.—Sasine in favour of the Kirk of Dundee, witnessed by James **Dundee** Wedderburn. xiv, vi, 34 (8). **Charters, Writs, &c.**

10. **1517.** Dec. 22.—Resignation by Alex. Moneur into the hands of James Wedderburn, one of the bailies of Dundee, of a certain annual rent. vii, ii, 1.

11. **1520.** Sept. 25.—Charter by Robert Robesone in favour of the Kirk of Dundee of an annual rent out of a N. Marketgate land, bounded on the east by the land of the heirs of the deceased Robert Wedderburn. James Wedderburn is a witness. xiv, vi, 34 (11).

12. **1523.** March 25.—Charter by John Barry, canon of Dunkeld, for the sustentation of a perpetual chaplain to the altar of S. Peter, in the parish church of Dundee, witnessed by Robert Barry, Robert Wedderburn elder, notaries, James Wedderburn and others. xiv, x, 8.

13. **1525.** Sept. 20.—Sasine of an annual rent granted by David Coupar to the choristers of Dundee, to which Robert Wedderburn is notary and appends his mark. xiv, vi, 34 (15).
See No. 1 of the facsimiles of the Notarial Symbols of the Wedderburns 1525—1627, at p. 187.

14. **1531.** Aug. 20.—Charter by Sir Robert Gray in favour of James Scrymgeour, burgess of Dundee, witnessed by James Wedderburn, bailie, and James Wedderburn, councillor. xiv, viii, 8.

15. **1534.** Feb. 6.—Charter by James Scrymgeour, constable of Dundee, to William Bruce of Earlshall, witnessed by James Wedderburn. x, v, 1 (1).

16. **1534.** March 13.—Charter by William Bell, leper in the leper house on the east of Dundee, whereby for the benefit of the lepers there now and in the future he sets in perpetual feuferme to David Wedderburn, son of the late David Wedderburn, burgess of the burgh, certain land in the Welgate. xiv, x, 10.

17. **1537.** March 23.—Indenture between the town of Dundee and George Bois, to to which James Wedderburn, younger, is a witness. i, iv, 48.

18. **1537.** May 17.—Charter by Andrew Barry, witnessed by Henry Wedderburn, burgess, and others. xiv, viii, 13.

19. **1537.** Aug. 9.—Charter by James Scrymgeour in favour of James Esak, to which James Wedderburn, councillor, is a witness. xiv, viii, 12.

20. **1537.** Aug. 22.—Minutes of Court held by James Wedderburn, bailie.
xiv, viii, 9-10.

21. **1540.** Aug. 30.—Charter by Richard Jackson, of part of Craigie, bounded on one side by the lands now belonging to David Wedderburn.
This is among some loose writs in the safe of the charter room. It is not numbered.

22. **1546.** (no date).—Letter from Queen Mary. directing the council to "stent" the inhabitants of Dundee, in order to relieve David Wedderburn and others, of the sum paid by them for abiding from her Majesty's host, at Roslingmure, last July. i, v, 51.

23. **1551.** March 10.—Feu charter by Mr. Robert Wedderburn, perpetual Vicar of the parish church of Dundee, in favour of John Lovell, burgess, and Euphame Forrett, his spouse, of a South Marketgait tenement, reserving to the said Mr. Robert and his successors in office, one chamber measuring 18 feet long, 17 feet broad, and 10 high. Signed by the grantor, "Magister Robertus Wedderburn, Vicarius de Dundee," and with his seal attached, bearing the Wedderburn arms, a chevron between three cinquefoils or roses. (See the facsimile of the signature opp. p. 192.) iv, i, 1.

24. **1553.** March 8.—Decree acquitting various inhabitants of Dundee, including David Wedderburn, Alexander Wedderburn, and another David Wedderburn from charges of assisting the English from Lammas, 1548 to Feb. 1549, in the taking of Broughty Castle, destroying monasteries, &c. i, v, 54.

25. **1556-57.** Feb. 6.—Gift of the office of the clerkship of Dundee by the Council of the burgh to their "weilbelovitt Alexander Wedderburn zoungair, sone to Robert Wedderburne oure brodir and comburges... ...... with all feis, dewteis, and casualteis, usit and wount thairof and perteining thairto ffor all the dayis and space of the said Alexanderis lifetyme, now vacand in oure handis be the deceis of umquhile Robert Seres sumtyme oure clerk and scrybe and be the resignatioun and oure-geving of the richt of Henry Richardsone possessour for the tyme of the samin or be uthir quhatsumevir way, To be haldin," &c.   I, V, 57.

26. **1558.** March 16.—Minute recording the compearance of George Rollok, lawful son of George Rollok, burgess, who delivers to Sir Thomas Wedderburn, chaplain of S Michael's, a letter for presenting him to the benefice of S. Mary's in S. Clement's Church, Dundee. Alexander Wedderburn, clerk of Dundee, is notary and adds his symbol and motto, "Deum time."   XIV, X, 12.

27. **1559.** June 25.—Charter by Andrew Flesehcour in favour of James Murdo, among the witnesses to which are William Wedderburn and Alexander Wedderburn.   VII, i, 11.

28. **1561.** Aug. 21.—Charter by Sir William Bruce, of Earlshall, to Robert Bruce, his son, and Janet Dundas his spouse, of the lands of Wallace Craigie, witnessed by James Wedderburn, burgess of Dundee.   X, vi, 1.

29. **1565.** Sept. 26 —Charter by the Town Council in favour of Thomas Lamb, subscribed by John Wedderburn, magistrate of Dundee, and Alexander Wedderburn, notary.   II, xxi 288 (2).

30. **1566.** Oct. 2 —Charter by the town council in favour of Helen Wedderburn, relict of Thomas Duncan, burgess, of an @-rent of £20. John Wedderburn, one of the magistrates, and Alexander Wedderburn, notary, subscribe.   VII, i, 13.
      There is another document similarly subscribed by Alexander Wedderburn dated 2 Oct. 1565. II, 288 (3) See facsimiles opp. p. 192.

31. **1568.** March 25.—Precept of clare constat by Robert Wedderburn, chaplain of S. James Major, in favour of Herbert Stewart. The signature is that of Robert Wedderburn, the notary, and his seal (somewhat broken) is appended. It bears a chevron, charged with a fleur-de-lys, between three cinquefoils.   VII, i, 15.
      See facsimile of signature opp. p. 192.

32. **1573.** April 3 —Sasine to which Alexander Wedderburn is notary, and appends his notarial mark and motto, "Deum time."   IV, ii, 1 (2).

33. **1575.** Oct. 14.—Sasine to which Alexander Wedderburn, town clerk, is notary, with his mark and motto, "Deum time."   VI, ii, 1.

34. **1588.** May 21.—Infeftment of David Wedderburn, son lawful to the late Alex. Wedderburn, clerk of Dundee, in certain land in Dundee following on a charter (16 May) in his favour by David Baxter. Robert Wedderburn and Mr. Alex. Wedderburn, notaries, are witnesses, and the former acts as notary, and adds his motto "Patior ut potiar."   XIV, vii, 38 (a5).

35. **1592.** July 27.—Charter by James Walker in favour of George Stirling of four acres in the Westfield of Dundee, witnessed by Robert Wedderburn and David Wedderburn, burgesses.   XIV, vii, 38 (a7).
      This signature of Robert Wedderburn is not that of the notary or merchant, and must, therefore, be that of Robert Wedderburn, the brother of David, who died in 1593. See facsimile, opp p. 192.

36. **1595.** April 30.—Charter by James Scrymgeour of Dudhope, Dame Magdalen Livingstone, his spous, and John Monorgund, in favour of Mr. Alexander Wedderburn, clerk, and Helen Ramsay, of that croft called the Seres Hauch, for the sum of 1400 merks paid to the grantors by the said Mr. Alexander.   XIV, X, 17.
      There are other documents in the charter room referring to this matter. See XV, i, 6-11 ; ii, 1-5.

37. **1595.** May 23.—Sasine by Mr. Alexander Wedderburn, clerk, in favour of David Dundee Wedderburn, as procurator for James Wedderburn, son to Mr. Alexander, of the croft, called Seres Hauch, subject to the life-rent of Mr. Alexander and Helen Writs, &c. Ramsay, his wife. Peter Wedderburn is a witness. xv, ii, 6.

38. **1598.** Oct. 4.—Charter by George Stirling and Isobell Carmannow, his wife, witnessed by Mr. Alexander Wedderburn, clerk, and William Wedderburn, his brother german. xiv, vii, 38 (a9).

39. **1598.** Oct. 4.—Similar charter by George Stirling with Wedderburn seal attached. xiv, vii, 38 (a10).

40. **1600.** July 15.—Charter of confirmation by King James VI. in favour of David Wedderburn, burgess of Dundee, of a charter (18 June 1597), by Sir James Scrymgeour of Dudhope and William Guthrie of Kingennie, patrons of the chaplainry of S. Thomas the Martyr, of a annual rent out of lands in Dundee. xiv, v, (28) 3.

41. **1602.** Dec. 16.—Contract between the town of Dundee and Sir David Lindsay of Edzell, signed by Robert Wedderburn merchant, "of the counsell" and Robert Wedderburn (notary). See facsimiles, opp. p. 192. xiv, iii, 23.

42. **1605.** Jan. 1.—Precept of clare constat in favour of Thomas Ramsay, written and witnessed at London by Mr. Alexander Wedderburn, clerk of Dundee. viii, v, 10.

43. **1609.** June 9.—Sasine by the hand of Mr. Alexander Wedderburn, clerk, to Mr. James Wedderburn, his son, in implement of the contract of marriage between Margaret Jak, relict of James Goldman, merchant burgess of Dundee, William Goldman, bailie thereof, Robert Goldman, his brother german, taking burden on them for Margaret Goldman, lawful daughter of the said Margaret Jak, and sister german of the said William and Robert on the one part, and Mr. Alexander Wedderburn and Helen Ramsay, his wife, and Mr. James Wedderburn, their second son, of the other part, dated — 1608, of the croft called Monorgun's croft, and the land next it, called the "Green Orchard." James Wedderburn, burgess, is a witness. xv, i, 16.

44. **1609.** Oct. 26.—Sasine witnessed by Patrick Wedderburn and Alex. Wedderburn, his son, merchants, burgesses of Dundee. vii, v, 14.

45. **1610.** May 11.—Ratification by David Wedderburn, burgess of Dundee, patron of S. Thomas the Martyr's chaplainry, for himself and for Alexander Wedderburn his lawful son, chaplain thereof, in favour of James Myln, son of the late Thomas Myln. xiv, viii, 36.

46. **1611.** March 26.—Resignation to which Robert Wedderburn is notary, with his mark and mottoes, "Bona fide," "Nihil tam occulte q. non revelabitur." vi, ii, 2.

47. **1612.** June 18.—Disposition by George Ramsay to the town of Dundee, written by Mr. James Wedderburn, son of Mr. Alexander Wedderburn, clerk of Dundee. vii, v, 16.

48. **1615.** June 6.—Contract between George Stirling and certain bailies, councillors and ministers of the burgh, including Mr. William Wedderburne, minister, acting for the town of Dundee. James Wedderburn is named among of the councillors, and Mr. Alexander Wedde burn, notary, subscribes on behalf of the Deacons of Crafts. xiv. vii, 38 (a2-3.)

49. **1618.** June 24.—Document recording the entrance by Mr. Alexander Wedderburn, younger, bailie, of Patrick Thomson as heir to his father in a North Marketgate tenement. Mr. James Wedderburn is notary, and a fine example of his mark is appended. iii, i, 5.

See the facsimiles of the notarial symbols of the Wedderburn's, 1609-1740 (No. 1), at p. 187, where a similar, but somewhat modern example of his mark is given. He used no motto.

50. **1620.** March 13.—Sasine given by Mr. Alexander Wedderburn, younger, bailie ; the notary is Mr. Alexander Wedderburn, the clerk.   IV, xi, 1 (3).
    A fine Wedderburn seal (a chevron, charged with a fleur-de-lys, between three roses or cinquefoils) is attached.

51. **1620.** July 29.—Transumpt sasine of lands in favour of Andrew Ross. Witnessed by Peter Wedderburn, younger son of Mr. Alexander Wedderburn, clerk of Dundee.
    This is among some loose writs in the safe of the charter room. It is not numbered.

52. **1624.** May 13.—Sasine to which Mr. James Wedderburn, clerk of Dundee, is notary, and appends a fine example of his mark.   VII, v. 26.
    See note to No. 49. The mark here is of the same size and in every way similar to that given in the facsimile.

53. **1626.** Jan. 28.—Disposition by Alexander Wedderburn, merchant, burgess of Dundee, as brother german and heir retoured to the deceased Adam Wedderburn, lawful son to Patrick Wedderburn, merchant, burgess, in favour of David Smairt, of half a North Argylegate tenement, and other property apprised by Adam Wedderburn from William Davidson, son and heir of Wm. Davidson, younger, subject to the life rent of Jonnet Wedderburn, relict of the said Wm. Davidson younger. Signed "Alexr. Wedderburn with my hand." (See facsimile opp. p. 192.)   VII, i, 33.

54. **1626.** May 10.—Charter by Andrew Gairdyne in favour of William Gray, signed by Alexander and James Wedderburn as witnesses.   VII, v, 32.
    The signatures are fine specimens of those of Alexander Wedderburn, second of Kingennie, and James Wedderburn, the clerk. See facsimile opp. p. 192.

55. **1627.** July 9.—Disposition by Dr. Thomas Maule, D.D., and his spouse, for 1016 merks paid to them by various persons for the help of the poor of Dundee (including 500 merks so paid by Mr. Alexander Wedderburn of Kingennie, dean of guild, according as he was ordained by the late Mr. Alexander Wedderburn, common clerk, his father, at the time of his decease) of certain fen maills, including an annual rent out of a north Argylegate tenement, bounded by the lands of Patrick Wedderburn and others.
                                             XIV, vii, 38 (c1).

56. **1627.** Oct. 9.—Disposition by James Mudie to the magistrates and ministers of Dundee, on behalf of the poor, of an annual rent out of a tenement. bounded east by the lands of Peter Wedderburn, and west by those of Alexander Wedderburn.   XIV, vii, 38 (c2).

57. **1628.** March 21.—Renunciation by Helen Lovell, only lawful daughter and heir of Mr. John Lovell, burgess of Dundee, with consent of Peter Wedderburn, burgess thereof, now her spouse, in favour of Patrick Baxter, master of the Hospital of Dundee, of certain crofts sometime occupied by the said John Lovell. Signed by Helen Lovell and Peter Wedderburn, and by Alexander Wedderburn, "scriba," as witness. See facsimile of signatures opp. p. 192.   XIV, ii, 18.

58. **1629.** Jan. 12.—Sasine on chancery precept reciting that the late Peter Wedderburn, merchant, burgess of Dundee, was uncle of Mr. Alexander Wedderburn, son lawful of the late Mr. James Wedderburn, clerk thereof, immediate elder brother of the said Peter, and infefting the said Mr. Alexander as heir to Peter Wedderburn, his uncle, in a North Marketgate foreland and tenement, and in half of the burghal lands in North Argylegate, once belonging to Robert Wedderburn, elder.   VII, v, 39.

59. **1629.** Jan. 12.—Sasine on precept of clare constat, infefting Mr. Alexander Wedderburn as eldest son and heir to his father, the late Mr. James Wedderburn, clerk, in Scres Hauch.   XV, ii, 7.

60. **1632.** Sept. 13.—Sasine to which Alexander Wedderburn (second of Kingennie), clerk of Dundee, is notary and adds his notarial mark.   IV, i, 2 (7).

61. **1633.** July 31.—Notes of some acts of Council, from the Council Books 1613-1667, including a memorandum of this date "Mr. Alexander Wedderburn elected clerk."
                                                     II, 282.

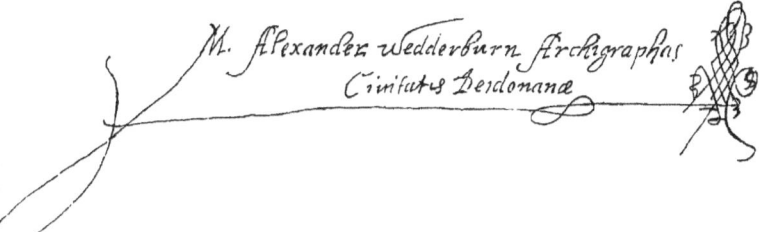

SIGNATURE ON THE TITLE PAGE OF THE LOCKIT BUIK OF DUNDEE.

62. **1633.** Informal minute or record of a bailie Court held on the — day of — 1633, Dundee Charters, Writs, &c. recording (*inter alia*) that Robert Clayhills compeared and claimed 500 merks of Catherine Wedderburn. Also that William and Peter Wedderburn compeared by Mr. Alexander Wedderburn and John Goldman, their curators, and claimed 5500 merks owing them by various persons (including 800 merks from Alexander Wedderburn, younger, mariner). Mr. Alex. Wedderburn, elder, of Kingany, James Wedderburn, merchant, Helen Lovell, relict of Peter Wedderburn, and Elizabeth Wedderburn, wife of Mr. Alex. Fotheringhame, also claim various sums from various persons.

Below the above is written : "I, Mr. Alexander Wedderburne, younger, commone clerk of Dundie, testifies by thir presents that thir [are ?] the just extracts of all sowmes of money given up to me, for the which extraordinary taxatione is so to be payed to his Majestie for the sext termes payment thairof, granted to his Majestie in July 1630, without eiking anything thairto or diminishing anything thairfrom, whilk I testifie to be trew upon my great oath, as I sall answer to God at the Latter day."

<small>This is among some loose papers lying on the shelves of the charter room. It is not numbered.</small>

63. **1633.** Oct. 14.—Charter indorsed with registration note by Mr. Alex. Wedderburn, keeper of the register of sasines for the shire of Forfar. X, v, 1-6.

64. **1643.** Feb. 28—Copy document in suit by the town of Dundee v. John, Viscount of Dudhope, and James, Master of Dudhope, his son. The town compear by Mr. Peter Wedderburn, their procurator. II, 267.

65. **1645.** Jan. 31.—Instrument to which Mr. Alexander Wedderburn, clerk of Dundee, is notary, with his mark and motto, "Deum time." VIII, iii, 4.

66. **1643.** May 18.—Charter in favour of Andrew Bathgaitt, witnessed by Mr. Peter Wedderburne, advocate in Edinburgh, and signed, "M. Pet. Wedderburn witnes." VI, ii, 9.
<small>This is an early example of the signature of Peter Wedderburn, afterwards Lord Gosford. See facsimile opp. p. 192.</small>

67. **1649.** July 6.—Letter from Charles II, "To our trusty and welbeloved Mr. Alexander Wedderburn, Clerke of the towne of Dundie." I xvii, 158.
<small>This and No. 69 were formerly in the charter chest of Mr. Scrymgeour-Wedderburn of Wedderburn, and were by him given to the town council of Dundee. See ante s. Blackness Papers, Nos. 6 and 7.</small>

68. **1650.** Sept. 9.—Sasine on Resignation by Sir Alexander Wedderburn of Blackness with consent of Dame Matilda Fletcher, his spouse, in favour of Robert Stratton of a North Argylegate tenement. VIII, iii, 11.

69. **1651.** Jan. 17.—Letter from Charles II, addressed " For our trusty and welbeloved the Provost, Baylies and Counsaill of Dundie. See ante s. No. 67. I, xvii, 159.

70. **1653.** March 9.—Disposition by Thomas Haliburton with consent of Margaret Wedderburn, his wife. IV, ii, 1 (14)

71. **1655.** Aug. 17.—Precept of Clare constat in favour of William Graham of Claverhouse, grandson of George Graham of Claverhouse, of (*a*) the lands called the Marmaiden Pot, bounded on the east by the lands of the chaplainry of S. James, once belonging to Robert Wedderburn, (*b*) the acres once pertaining to Robert Wedderburn, elder, merchant, and afterwards to Peter Wedderburn, deceased, merchant burgess, from whom they were acquired by the said George Graham. XIV, iii, 1.

72. **1664.** Feb. 13.—" Provision of L. Blackness[1] to his third sone Peter Wedderburne 1664." This document (so endorsed) is a settlement by Sir Alexander Wedderburn of Blackness on his said son of a South Flukergate tenement. It is signed by William Wedderburn, brother german to Sir Alexander, as witness, thus, " Villiam Verburne Vitnes " (IV, i, 2.) The sasine is given 17 Feb. (IV, i, 3.) Then follows 1675, 18 Dec. a renunciation by James Wedderburn, clerk of Dundee, second son of Sir Alexander, in

<hr>

[1] L. stands, of course, for Lord, or Laird of Blackness.

2 B

favour of his brother the said Peter, of a South Flukergate tenement, (IV, i, 4), and lastly come the cognition of Alexander Wedderburn as heir to his father the said Peter, 8-15 Oct. 1700, signed by James Wedderburn witness, servitor to Alexander Wedderburn, the clerk, and, 25 Sept. 1706, the disposition of this tenement, by Alexander Wedderburn, mariner, to Thomas Crichton.   IV, i, 2-8.

73. **1669.** Aug. 5.—Bond by John Stirling to produce to Margaret Lochmalony (a) a bond, 12 July, 1621, for 600 merks made by David Rollo in favour of Magdalen Wedderburn, relict of Mr. Wm. Wedderburn, minister at Dundee ; (b) an assignation thereof, 12 June, 1629, made by the said Magdalen Wedderburn and Mr. George Halyburton of Fotherance to —— (blank).   VI, ii, 14.

74. **1669.** Aug. 5.—Similar bond of forthcoming, same to same, includes a sasine 26 Nov., 1535, on resignation by George (son and heir of Walter) Rollo and Margaret Wedderburn, his spouse.   VI, ii, 15.

75. **1670.** Aug. 11.—Sasine by Sir Alexander Wedderburn of Blackness, as notary, with his symbol and motto, " Deum time," appended.   XV, i, 19.

76. **1672.** July 9.—Disposition by Sir Alexander Wedderburn of Blackness of the croft, called Seres Hauch, to the Hospital Master of Dundee.   XV, ii, 8.

77. **1672.** Oct. 5.—Certified copy of the will of Mr. Thomas Halyburton, indweller in Dundee, nominating his brother, Alexander, and his sister, Agnes (wife of Thomas Davidson), his executors, and leaving legacies to John Wedderburn, younger of Blackness, and Alexander Wedderburn, younger, of Kingennie, and naming his father, Thomas Halyburton, as deceased, and his mother, Margaret Wedderburn, as still alive. Dated at Dundee.   XV, iii, 3.

78. **1680.** (no date).—Opinion of Sir John Cunningham as to the titles of the lands of Logie and the Magdalen Yard, about 1680.   IX, i, 1.

79. **1685.** June 5.—Cognition of Alexander Wedderburn, of Easter Powrie, as heir to his late father, in a tenement in Dundee.   VI, i, 13.

80. **1685.** Oct. 11.—Sasine, to which James Wedderburn, clerk, is notary, and appends his notarial mark and motto " dum spiro spero."   III, ii, 9.

81. **1690.** June 13.—Discharge and assignation by Alexander Wedderburn of Easter Powrie, eldest lawful son and heir of the late Alexander Wedderburn of Easter Powrie, reciting a legacy by Janet Milne, daughter of the late Alexander Milne, merchant, burgess of Dundee, in favour of the poor of Dundee, left in trust to the said late Alexander Wedderburn, of Easter Powrie, and the late Alexander Milne, eldest son to her brother german, the late Mr. Alexander Milne, minister in Dundee ; and also reciting that Margaret Milne, her sister german, and sponse to the said late Alexander Wedderburn, was her executrix, and assigning all the rights, &c., of the assignor, under the said will, to Thomas Milne, of Milnefield, brother and heir of the said Alexander Milne, merchant.   VIII, iv, 16.

82. **1693.** May 4.—Sasine witnessed by Alexander Wedderburn, writer in Dundee.   IV, viii, 2.

See opp. p. 192 for a facsimile of his signature, which appears to be an early one of Alexander Wedderburn, afterwards fourth Baronet of Blackness.

83. **1696.** Jan. 1.—Two cognitions witnessed by Alexander Wedderburn, writer in Dundee.   V, i, 4.

His signature, clearly that of Alexander Wedderburn, afterwards fourth baronet of Blackness, is appended. See facsimile opp. p. 192.

84. **1700.** Jan. 23.—Sasine to which Alexander Wedderburn, clerk, is notary, and appends his notarial mark with the motto, " Sit deo Gloria."   III, ii, 14.

See the facsimiles of the Notarial Symbols of the Wedderburn's, 1609-1740, No. 6, at p. 187 of this volume.

85. **1701.** May 15.—Discharge witnessed by James Wedderburn, servitor to Alexander Wedderburn, clerk of Dundee. *See facsimile opp. p. 192.* xv, iv, 6

86. **1707.** Sept. 2.—Disposition by Andrew Ramsay in favour of Alexander Wedderburn, clerk of Dundee, of the croft called "Donald deall," or Donaldson's croft. x, viii, 1.

87. **1707.** Sept. 2.—Charter of novodamus by the town council in favour of the said clerk, of the said croft, subscribed by (*inter alios*), "A. Wedderburn shoremaster," with sasine thereon. *See facsimile opp. p. 192.* x, viii, 2, 3.

88. **1716.** Aug 9.—"Act of the town council depriving Alexander Wedderburn, town clerk, of his office for being concerned in the rebellion." The Act recites "the information (dated 14 July), given by William Gib maltman" . . . mentioning that on 6 Jan 1716, the clerk "came into the councill house accompanying the Earles of Marr and Marshall and several rebellious gentlemen when they were getting a treat and burges ticketts in the said councill house, and that the said W. Gib saw the said Alexander Wedderburn acting as clerk, and bring in the burges ticketts and called to Thomas Traill his servant to fetch more ticketts after the first quantity were done And that the saids noblemen and gentlemen had none when they went in to the councill house but had ticketts in their hatts when they came out, And that the said A. Wedderburn was clerk att the pettie customs rouping of the said Brough under those who exceed the Magistracy in the late rebellion, And that the said A. Wedderburn went to the cross of Dundie with the Rebells at one or other of their treasonable solemnities and also went and mett the pretender when coming to Dundie and came in with him and his sword drawn in his hand and also collected the Exeyse for the use of the rebells." The Act then relates that Wedderburn, although repeatedly cited, has refused to appear and answer the information, of which he had had a double, and that the council having also before them "burges ticketts for this Brough signed by the said A. Wedderburn as clerk the time of the Rebellion granted be those that then assumed the Magistracy and in favour of those in the Rebellion particularly two burges ticketts dated the twelveth of January last in favours of the therein designed James Earl of Tinmouth, and Collonell Francis Bulkley be the therein designed Sir Alexander Watson, provest, Mr William Ramsay, Dean of Gild &c And the Councill likeways considering that the said Alexander Wedderburn is both Shiriff Depute and Shiriff Clerk of fforfar which the Councill reckon inconsistent to be one and the same person with the clerkship of Dundie because of the difference betuixt the brough and the shire anent their jurisdictions and occasions incroachments on the town's priviledges And that the said Alexander Wedderburn had refused to come to the councill when cited and called as said is In respect of all which the councill finds the said Alexander Wedderburn culpable and after voting have deposed and hereby deprive him from being Clerk of Dundie and Barroney of Hiltoun thereof. Extracted be Robert Speid Clk Dept." i, xiv, 131.

89. **1716.** Nov. 17.—Assignation by Mr. Thomas Sanders, of Kettins, narrating (*inter alia*) a bond, 23 June 1675, assigned, 20 Feb. 1700, to Dame Agnes Wedderburn, relict of David Hallyburton, of Piteurr. This document deals mainly with the Hallyburton family. x, v, 4 (16).

90. **1717.** April 9, 15, 17, 22.—"Proof led against Alexander Wedderburn, Town Clerk, for his concern in the Rebellion."

From this document, it appears that, having passed the above act (No. 88), the Councill remitted the matter "to the provost and magistrates to hear and see probation lead of the articles in the said information."

The facts sworn to by different witnesses are then set out, the names of the witnesses being John Wast, James Gairlyn, William Hog, Thomas Watson, Lachlan Shippert, George Mawer, William Ogilvie, Thomas Marshall, Patrick Neilsone, William Maiden, David Crichton, Patrick Will, George Yeaman, James Ogilvy.

All these support the information of William Gib, and give evidence that the clerk rode out to meet the pretender and back with him into the town, on 6 Jan.

1716. William Maiden, a shoemaker in Dundee, depones that "about the middle of November j^mvij^e and fifteen he saw the Laird of Powry, then governour of the town, and several other gentlemen goe up to the cross to give demonstrations of their joy for Mar's victory at Shirriff Muir, and that he saw Alexander Wedderburn, then Town Clerk, upon the cross with the rest, with a glass in his hand ; saw him drink and throw the glass over the cross "
I, xiv, 132.

91. 1717. Dec. 28.—Decreet of declarator of the Court of Session in the process by the Town Council v. Alexander Wedderburn, late Town Clerk, finding that he was legally deprived of his office, and that George Duncan was lawfully appointed thereto in his place. It appears that Alexander Wedderburn was represented before the Court of Session (at Edinburgh) by Sir Walter Pringle and Mr. James Graham, advocates.
I, xiv, 133.

92. 1717. (no date).—Report of the provost and bailies to the councill of Dundee anent Alexander Wedderburn. This is a report against the clerk of what the provost and bailies find proven by the evidence (ante No. 90).
I, xiv, 132 ; VIII, x, I.

93. 1718. Feb. 25.—Decreet of the Court of Session ordaining Alexander Wedderburn, late town clerk, to deliver up the whole records of the burgh in his possession. The decreet states that A. Wedderburn compeared by Mr. John Ogilvie and Mr. Patrick Wedderburn, advocates.
I, xiv, 134.

94. 1722. August 18.—Disposition by John Watson of Turins, written and witnessed by John Wedderburn, son to Alex. Wedderburn, sheriff clerk of Forfar.
This is a loose and unnumbered writ.

95. 1727. June 22.—Proclamation at Dundee of the Accession of George II., signed by (among others) Sir Alexander Wedderburn of Blackness.
I, xvi, 136.

96. 1731. March 25.—Copy Act of Parliament 4 Geo. II., re the beer duties, naming David Wedderburn of Wedderburn and Sir Alex. Wedderburn of Blackness overseers.
I, xvi, 137.

97. 1733. Feb. 14.—Disposition by Grizell Watson, spouse to Alex. Wedderburn, shipmaster, who consents, to James Davidson of Cheapall, of half a North Murraygate land.
VII, ii, 3.

98. 1752. Aug. 17.—Sasine on precept of clare constat (29 Feb. 1744) at Edinburgh in favour of David Wedderburn of Wedderburn as heir of provision to his great uncle, Peter Wedderburn, second son of the late Alexander Wedderburn of Easter Powrie in a south Marketgate tenement. (This writ is lying loose and nnnumbered.)

99. 1752. Dec. 30.—Disposition witnessed by Alexander Wedderburn, servant to John Ballingall, writer in Dundee.
IV, vi, 5.

100. 1756. March 25.—Copy Act 29 Geo. II., re the beer duties, naming David Wedderburn of Wedderburn, overseer.
I, xvi, 138.

101. 1761. Jan. 27.—Extract disposition in favour of Margaret Ramsay, "wrote on stamped paper by Alexander Wedderburn, writer in Edinburgh," and witnessed by him 3 May 1758 (IV, xvi, 13). And 1783 Feb. 28, there is a decreet of absolntion in a suit by some Ramsays, referring to this deed as having been " wrote by Alexander Wedderburn, writer in Edinburgh, a man of unexceptionable character." IV. xviii, 18.

102. 1765. May 7.—Submission between the town and hospital of Dundee on the one part, and James Kyd, eldest son and heir of the late George Kyd, and grandson and heir of the also deceased James Kyd, both of Craigie, and James Guthrie, now of Craigie, purchaser thereof from the said late James and George, on the other part, of all claims respecting the moor of Craigie. The decreet is signed by Mr. David Scrymgeour at Birkhill, an arbiter for James Kyd, on 9 June 1766, before Mr. Alexander Scrymgeour, advocate, his eldest, and David Scrymgeour his third son. It is witnessed by Robert Wedderburn, of Pearsie. XIV, xiii, 2 (1).

103. **1767.** Dec. 10.—Extract disposition by members of the Webster family, including David Webster, druggist in London, whose signature is witnessed, 29 Sept. 1757 by John Wedderburn, his apprentice. **Dundee Charters, Writs, &c.** iv, xxv, 1.

104. **1781.** March 25. Copy Act of Parliament 16 Geo. III, *re* the boer duties, naming Sir John Wedderburn of Balindean, Bart., overseer. i, xvi, 141.

    This is interesting, because here we have Sir John called baronet in an Act of Parliament, despite the attainder of his father.

105. **1789.** Nov. 14.—Copy will of James Webster, of Clapham Common, co Surrey. The executors are his brother, John Webster, David Wedderburn, and John Wedderburn of Leadenhall Street. Legacies are left to the executors, to Catharine Webster, wife of John Webster; to the five daughters of George Webster, deceased, brother to the testator; to Doctor Thomas Webster, his brother; to James Webster Wedderburn (son of the said David Wedderburn) on his attaining 21; to Charles Wedderburn of Pearsie, and his wife Ann Read; to Elizabeth Wedderburn, wife of James Graham of Balmuir; to Catherine Wedderburn, wife of Robert Stewart of Dundee; to Isabella Wedderburn, wife of the Rev. James Stormonth of Airly. The testator bequeaths to David Wedderburn various sums of money, the leasehold houses in Leadenhall Street and at Clapham, and other property, on condition that he and his issue male shall immediately on the death of the said James Webster take the surname of Webster only, in lieu and stead of Wedderburn, and shall forthwith obtain a royal or legal license so to do. Further legacies are made to Sir John Wedderburn, Louisa Dorothea Wedderburn, his daughter, James Wedderburn of Inveresk, and James Wedderburn of Trelawny, Jamaica. A sum of £6,000 is also left (after all other legacies are paid) for founding an academy for 30 boys of twelve to sixteen and 35 girls in Dundee, where the testator was born. Proved in the Prerogative Court of Canterbury 13 Jan. 1790. xv, iii, 6.

    The clauses in the will relating to the academy are printed at length in Maclaren's *History of Dundee*, pp. 308-9, where an account of the charity is also given.

[The following is a complete list of references to all the Dundee Charters, Writs, &c., which refer to Wedderburns :—i, 15, 18, 48, 51, 54, 57, 61, 72, 72a, 76, 83, 85, 86, 94, 96, 100, 112, 114, 116, 124, 131-34, 136-38, 141, 145, 148, 158 59, 161a b. ii, 170, 265, 267, 270, 271 (5), 276 (3, 4), 278 (1, 2, 3), 280 (2-5), 282, 287, 288 (1, 2, 3, 6), 289. iii, i, 2-8, 10; ii, 1, 6, 7, 9, 11, 17-19; iv, 1; vi, 1, 3-4; vii, 2-4; viii, 1; ix, 3, 7. iv, i, 1-8, 11; ii, 1 (1-3, 5-7, 11, 12, 14-16, 23-25); iii, 1, 2, 35; iv, 3, 4; v, 1; vi, 1, 5; viii, 2 (1-4); ix, 2, 3; x, 1; xi, 1 (3, 6-8), 2; xii, 1 (1, 8-10, 12), 2 (1); xii, 2-4; xiv, 4; xvi, 1, 6, 8, 13, 18; xxv, 1. v, i, 2-4; ix, 1; x, 1, 2; xii, 1; xix, 1. vi, i, 1-2, 4-10, 12-14; ii, 1-6, 9, 14-15, 20; iii, 9-13, 15; iv, 3, 4, 7; v, 1; vi, 2; vii, 1-5; viii, 1-2; ix, 5; x, 1; xi, 1, 5, 8, 10; xii, 1-2; xiv, 4; xviii, 1; xx, 1 (2), 2 (1-3'. vii, i, 11-13, 15-16, 18-29, 31, 33; ii, 1-3, 6-10, 14; iii, 1, 4, 8, 11-12, 43, 50-52; iv, 1, 6-15, 22-23; v, 1-4, 6, 10-20, 22-24, 26, 30, 32, 34, 35, 38, 39, 43, 49-50. viii, vi, 2-3; vii, 1, 8-11, 30, 50; viii, 5; x, 1. ix, i, 1, 6. x, v, 1 (1, 2, 6, 7), 2 (21-22), 4 (4, 6, 16), 6 (3); vi, 1-3, 7, 10, 12, 16-20; viii, 1-4; xi, 1. xi, i, 1, 2, 3 (1). xii (ml). xiii, 1, 2, 3, 4, 16. xiv, ii, 15, 16; iii, 22 (1, 3), 23-25; iv, 26-27; v, 28 (3, 8, 9, 12, 13, 15, 17, 19); vi, 31 (4, 8, 11, 15); vii, 38 (a 3-10, b 1-3, c 1-2); viii, 3, 4, 8-10, 12, 13, 20, 22-29, 31-41; ix, 7; x, 5, 8, 10, 12, 13, 15, 17-18; xi, 1-6, 8; xii, 1, 2, 12, 13; xiii, 1 (6), 2 (1). xv, i, 2-19; ii, 1-9; iii, 2, 3, 6; iv, 4, 6. See also some loose and unnumbered writs, ut ante Nos. 3, 21, 51, 62, 94 and 98.]

The "Lockit Buik" of Dundee.
This book consists of the roll of the burgesses of Dundee, from 1513 down to the present time. The earlier part of it is not, however, contemporary with its entries, but was written in 1582 by Alexander Wedderburn, clerk of Dundee (afterwards first of Kingennie), and must have been copied or compiled by him from some earlier materials. The book has never been printed *in extenso*, but in 1887 Mr. A. H. Millar edited, for the Town Council of Dundee, a volume entitled "Roll of the Eminent Burgesses of Dundee," in which he printed a selection of some three hundred to three hundred and fifty entries, with elaborate notes on the persons named and their families. Among these are twelve recording the admissions of Wedderburns, chosen from the fifty-seven such entries which the "Lockit Buik" contains. Mr. Millar's notes, so far as the Wedderburns are concerned, are sometimes inaccurate or speculative. His time was limited and he had to deal with a large number of different families, and, as great research in the case of each of them was impossible to him, he was driven to rely on such published material as was readily available. An excellent general account of the original volume is given in an introduction to his book, to which anyone interested in it can refer.

The "Lockit Buik" is so called from its locked clasps, which indicate the jealous care with which enrolment in it was guarded. In the Town Council records (1 Oct. 1554) is an ordinance that it was "nocht to be openit, nor na burgess put in it, but in the tolbuith before the Provost, bailies and Council," and there are many other such ordinances extant in the Council and Burgh Records of Dundee. (See the "History of Old Dundee," by Alexander Maxwell Edin. 1884).

On the fly leaf of the book is written, in red ink, a Latin inscription by Alexander Wedderburn, the clerk—

Si tibi Propositum est Vrbem Donariis ornare Te ipsum Imprimis Illi dedicato, pulcherrimum Mansuetudinis, Justiciæ, Beneficentiæ monumentum.

Optime de Republica mereberis non si tecta ædium in altum eduxeris, sed si civium animos evexeris. Præstat enim in parvis Domibus magnos Habitare animos quam in magnis ædibus humilia delitescere mancipia.

Non Euboicis et Spartanis lapidibus structura Mænium interpolanda est, sed disciplina et bonarum Artium studiis, civium et Magistratum pectora adornare. Florentes enim et tranquillas faciuut Respublicas vivorum animi non bona et saxa. M.A.W.[1]

M. Alexander Wedderburn Archigraphus Civitatis Deidouanæ.

This inscription, the noble sentiments of which Kingennie carried in practice in his devoted service of the burgh, may be rendered thus :—

"Shouldst thou propose to adorn the city with gifts begin by dedicating to it in thyself, a splendid monument of courtesy, justice and beneficence.

"The debt of the commonwealth to thee will be greatest, not if thou has reared lofty buildings to the sky, but if thou hast raised the minds of thy fellow citizens. For it is better to see great minds living in little houses than great houses full of base-men and slaves.

"Not with masonry from Eubœa and Sparta should the walls of the city be strengthened, but with order and the pursuit of all that is fair and good, the true ornaments alike of every citizen and every magistrate. For her strength and her peace depend not on her possessions and palaces but on the minds of those who dwell within her gates."

After this inscription comes an ancient rent roll, occupying the first fifty-four pages of the book. An account of it is given in Maclaren's edition of Thomson's "History of Dundee" (1874). It contains several references to Wedderburns.[2] Then follows the Burgess Roll, headed thus :—

"Heir followis the Names of the Burgessis, friemen, and Brether of Gilde of the Burgh of Dundie, maid sen the moneth of September In the zeir of God ane thowsand fyve hundreth and threttene zeiris, and of sic persones as sall obtene the fredome and libertie Thairof in tyme cumming."

From this roll, I shall give all the entries recording the admission of persons of the name of Wedderburn, as well as one or two other mentions of them. It is to be regretted that the names of the fathers of those admitted are not given in the first three entries, but

---

[1] The addition of the initials seems to show that the inscription was composed as well as written by the clerk. The grammar of the word "adornare" towards the end seems questionable, and the exact meaning of it is not clear. Mr. Millar gives a version, which is not, I think, either adequate or correct. A facsimile of the beautiful signature is given opposite p. 192.

[2] See below p. 199, note.

the statement that they are admitted by reason of their fathers' freedom shows that already, at the beginning of the sixteenth century, the family had long been established in Dundee. The age for admission seems to have been about 20 or 21. Of course, many persons were admitted later in life, in recognition of their position, but they were seldom admitted earlier. Taking the persons whose birth dates are clear from other evidence, we find Alexander, first of Kingennie, admitted at the age of 21, and his brother David in the same year, probably at 20. James, the clerk (d. 1627), and his son, Sir Alexander, were both 21, and Sir John Wedderburn, first Baronet of Blackness, was 24. On the other hand, Alexander, third of Kingennie, was 17, and John Wedderburn of Gosford, who seems to have been wonderfully old for his years, was only 14. James, Bishop of Dunblane, was 38 ; Robert, the notary, 41 ; and David, Master of the Aberdeen Grammar School, 52. Not much, therefore, can be argued as to the age of a given individual from the mere date of his admission as burgess.

The "Lockit Buik" of Dundee.

EXTRACTS FROM THE "LOCKIT BUIK."[1]

1. **1514.** Jacobus Wedderburn, junior, frater gildæ ratione libertatis paternæ.

This James Wedderburn is either the eldest son of James Wedderburn and Janet Barry, or the son of Robert Wedderburn and Janet Froster. It is not clear which of the two were called "junior" at this date, as compared not with each other but with the father of the former. Mr. Millar makes no doubt that this is the son of James, but I incline to think it is the son of Robert, who was probably a little older than James' son, and would thus be admitted burgess before him. Later on, after the death of old James Wedderburn, the son of Robert was called elder, and the mentions of James Wedderburn, junior, then refer, no doubt to the son of James, who married Janet Forrester. See post No. 3.

Mr. Millar's error in calling this entry "the earliest appearance of the name of Wedderburn in the existing Burgh records" has already been noted. (Ante p. 188 n.) He is also in error in stating that John Wedderburn, the son of James Wedderburn and Janet Forrester was "the first of a succession

<hr>

[1] The ancient rent roll mentioned above is headed "The Book of ye comoun Rentallis of the Burgh of Dundie, Almishous and Kirkwark thairof ; This maid and dewys it in the tyme of Mr. James Haliburtoun, Provost ; Alexander Scrymgeoure, William forrester, James findlansoune, and Alexander Ramesay, Baillies of ye said Burgh."

It seems to have been made up in 1582 and is divided into three sections (i.) The Thesauraris Chairge. (ii.) The Kirkmaisteris Chairge. (iii.) The Chairge or Rentall of ye Maister of ye Hospitall. From each of these considerable extracts are given in Maclaren's *History of Dundee*, including the following references to Wedderburns :—

(ii.) Kirkmaisteris Chairge (Nos. 1, 21, 27) :
(a) In the first, furth of Robert Rollokis foirland lyand on the south syid of the Flukergaitt, betuix the land of Elizabeth Wedderburn on ye east, and ye land of the Abbott of Scone, now of the Laird of Banff, on ye west pairtis, zeirlie fyvetene ss.
(b) Item, furth of ye land, sumtyme of John Broune, now of Alexander Traill, lyand on ye north syid of Argyllis gait, betwix ye land of Alexander Wedderburn on ye east, and ye land of James Scrymgeoure on the west pairtis, zeirlie ane stane of wax.
(c) Item, furth of ye land of ye airis of vmqle William Clepen, lyand on ye south syid of ye Murraygaitt, betwix ye land of James Broun on ye east, and ye lands of the airis of vmqle David Wedderburn on ye west pairtis, zeirlie sex ss.

(iii.) Chairge or Rentall of the Maister of the Hospital (Nos. 15, 55, 74, 75, 102, 138, 150, 188) :
(a) Item, furth of ye land of James Forrester, lyand on the north syid of ye Flukergaitt, betwix ye land of the airis of Johne Wedderburn on ye east, and the land of the Laird of Ogilwie on the west pairtis, to ye Choristaris zeirlie fiftie ss.
(b) Item, furth of ye land foirsaid [in S. Argylegait] of ye airis of vmqle Alexander Alanesoun, havand on ye east the Kirkstyll and ye land of Peter Wedderburn, to ye greyfreiris zeirlie thrie lib. sex ss. viij d.
(c) Item, furth of ye said Alexander Traillis land foirsaid, haiffand on ye east the Land of Alexander Wedderburn, to the Choristaris zeirlie threttene ss. iiij d.
(d) Item, furth of ye said Alexander Wedderburnis land foirsaid, havand on ye east the land callit Mathewis land, pteniog to Johne Kynmounth to Sauct Katharinis Chaplainrie threttie ss.
(e) Item, furth of ye land of ye airis of vmqle Robert Clayhillis, lyand on ye north syid of ye Murraygaitt, betwix ye land of James Andersonnis airis on ye east, and ye land of Alexander Wedderburn on ye west pairtis, to ye Choristaris zeirlie Sex ss. vj d.
(f) Item, furth of ye land of Richardus Wedderburn, callit the Chaipell Zeard, lyand, on ye south syid of ye Kowgaitt, betwix oure Ladie Wynd on ye east, and ye zeardis of Walter Carmanow on ye west pairtis, to Oure Ladie Chaipell, Kowgaitt, zeirlie fourtie twa ss.
(g) Item, furth of ye land callit the Rwid Land, pertening to ye airis of vmqle James Rollok, betwix ye land of Petir Wedderburn on ye east, and Spaldingis Wynd on ye west pairtis, to ye Rwid Chaplainrie zeirlie sex lib.
(h) Item, the zeard callit the blakfrieris zeard sett to Petir Wedderburn for the zeirlie maill of sewine lib.

of Wedderburns who held the office of Town Clerk of Dundee for nearly a century and a half."
There is no evidence of any John Wedderburn ever having been clerk of Dundee. The first recorded
clerk of the name was Alexander, appointed in 1557, and he and his descendants held the office in
succession for just over a century and a half—till 1717.

2. **1516.** Oct. 10.—Robertus Wedderburn frater gildæ ratione paternæ libertatis.
This is with little doubt Robert Wedderburn who married Janet Kyd, and was probably second
son to Robert Wedderburn and Janet Foster. See post No. 30.

3. **1517.** Oct. 17.—Jacobus Wedderburn frater gildæ ratione libertatis patris sui.
See the note to No. 1. If No. 1 refers to James, the son of Robert (and the fact that No. 2
probably refers to his younger brother Robert, makes it more likely that it, rather than a later
admission, should do so) the present entry must refer to James, the son of James.

4. **1521.** June 20.—David Wedderburn named as dean of gild.
This David was, of course, admitted burgess before 1514, as he could not have been dean of Gild
unless already possessed of the freedom of the burgh. He is, no doubt, the same as the David
Wedderburn named below, No. 10-11, and is probably to be identified with David Wedderburn of
Craigie and the Murraygait, who m. Helen Lawson.

5. **1523.** Oct. 16.—David Wedderburn filius Walteri Wedderburn frater gildæ.
This is David Wedderburn in Welgait, the ancestor of the Cupar and Moonzie branches of the family.

6. **1523.** Oct. 16.—David Wedderburn filius Roberti Wedderburn frater gildæ.
Third son to Robert Wedderburn and Janet Froster.

7. **1523.** Oct. 16.—Henricus Wedderburn frater gildæ.
A son of James Wedderburn and Janet Barry.

8. **1527.** Jan. 15.—Alexander Wedderburn, filius quondam Roberti Wedderburn, frater
gildæ.
Alexander Wedderburn, the elder, fourth son of Robert Wedderburn and Janet Froster. As
Robert is here named as dead, and is not so named in No. 6, we may assume that he died 1523-27.
Alexander died in 1587.

9. **1527.** Jan. 15.—Georgius Wedderburn frater gildæ ratione paternæ libertatis.
Fifth and youngest son of Robert Wedderburn and Janet Froster.

10. **1529.** Nov. 12.—David Wedderburn, treasurer. See s. No. 4.

11. **1531.** June 20.—David Wedderburn, dean of gild. See s. Nos. 4 and 10.

12. **1535.** June 8.—Robertus Wedderburn frater gildæ quia filius est Jacobi Wedderburn
fratris gildæ.
This is probably the son of James Wedderburn and Janet Logan, though it may be Robert,
afterwards Vicar of Dundee, brother to James, son of James Wedderburn and Janet Barry (ante Nos.
1, 3, and post No. 22). Mr. Millar, while identifying it with the Vicar, also suggests that it is " Robert
Wedderburn, younger brother of the town clerk, and son of James Wedderburn, junior," an idea
based on much error. The James Wedderburn, junior, referred to by Mr. Millar had no son Robert,
nor any son who ever was clerk of Dundee. (See ante No. 1,) Alexander Wedderburn, clerk of
Dundee, had a brother Robert, the notary, who was admitted burgess in 1587 (post No. 30). Their
father's name, however, was Robert, not James.

13. **1535.** June 8.—Gulielmus Wedderburn, filius et hæres Davidis Wedderburn, frater
gildæ.
I cannot identify this individual. Mr. Millar after saying " The David Wedderburn here referred
to was the brother of James Wedderburn, junior, who was admitted burgess in 1514," adds, without
citing his authority, that "he appears as the proprietor of a property on the North side of the
Murraygait in 1488," and concludes that William was thus a cousin of John Wedderburn, whom he
supposes (ante No. 1) to have been clerk of Dundee. But there is no evidence that James Wedderburn, junior, had any brother of the name of David. David Wedderburn in Murraygait, father of
another David, who succeeded him there, was of an older generation than James Wedderburn,
junior. He may have been his uncle, but there is nothing to prove it.

14. **1537.** (no date).—Gilbertus Wedderburn, Jacobi Wedderburn filius, frater gildæ.
Youngest son of James Wedderburn and Janet Barry.

15. **1547.** (no date).—James Wedderburn, dean of Gild.

The "Lockit Buik" of Dundee.

This is, no doubt, the son of Robert Wedderburn and Janet Foster (ante No. 1), as his namesake the son of James Wedderburn and Jauet Barry (ante No. 3) had at this date fled from Scotland and was living in Dieppe.

16. **1552.**[1] (no date).—Joannes Wedderburn, filius Jacobi Wedderburn, junioris, frater gildæ.

This John Wedderburn, son of James Wedderburn, junior, and Janet Forrester, is the person supposed by Mr. Millar to have been clerk of Dundee. I doubt if the date here given for his admission is correct, as in the third volume of the "Burgh and Head Court Records" (see post. s. v.), there is an entry dated 26 Feb. 1554, recording that John, son of the late James Wedderburn, then took the oath of fidelity and was ordained to be entered in the "Lockit Buik."

17. **1554.** Nov. 15.—Gulielmus Wedderburn, filius Davidis Wedderburn, frater gildæ.

William, son of David Wedderburn in Murraygait and Helen Lawson. He was their second son and it is curious that he should have been admitted before his elder brother, James, who seems not to have got his freedom till 1560. (See post, No. 20).

18. **1555.** Nov. 15.—Alexander Wedderburn, Roberti Wedderburn filius, frater gildæ.

Alexander, son to Robert Wedderburn and Janet Kyd. He was appointed clerk in 1557, and died in 1585.

19. **1559.** Oct. 3.—Edwardus Wedderburn frater gildæ ratione paternæ libertatis.

He was second son to James Wedderburn (son of Robert) who m. Janet Logan. See ante, No. 1.

20. **1560.** Oct. 11.—Jacobus Wedderburn, frater gildæ ratione paternæ libertatis.

James Wedderburn of Craigie, eldest son of David Wedderburn and Helen Lawson. See ante, No. 17.

21. **1568.** Oct. 22.—Thomas Wedderburn, Gilberti Wedderburn filius, frater gildæ.

Son of Gilbert, whose admission is already given. See ante No. 14.

22. **1570.** Dec. 21.—David Wedderburn, magistri Roberti Wedderburn filius, frater gildæ.

The elder of the two natural, but legitimatized, sons of Robert Wedderburn, the Vicar, by Isobell Lovell. The fact that both he and his brother (post No. 25) are both admitted without reference to any liberty of their father, goes to show that the Vicar never was admitted a burgess and that the entry above given (No. 12) does not refer to him. This David d. uum. 1583-85.

23. **1570-71.** Feb. 7.—Patricius Wedderburn, Alexandri Wedderburn filius, frater gildæ.

Second son to Alexander Wedderburn, elder (ante No. 8), and Isobeil Anderson. His elder brother, Richard Wedderburn, burgess in Elsignor, never got himself admitted to the freedom of Dundee.

24. **1572.** July 16.—Robertus Wedderburn, Roberti Wedderburn junioris filius, frater gildæ.

Only son of Robert Wedderburn and Elspeth Scrymgeour, and grandson of James Wedderburn and Janet Logan. (See ante, Nos. 1, 3 and 12.)

25. **1580.** Dec. 14.—Robertus Wedderburn, frater gildæ.

This is Robert Wedderburn the merchant, natural but legitimatised son of Robert, the Vicar.

26. **1582.** May 8.—Eodem die Magister Alexander Wedderburn effectus est burgensis et frater gildæ ratione privilegii Alexandri Wedderburn, scribæ, dicti burgi sui patris.[2]

Alexander Wedderburn, afterwards first of Kingennie and clerk of Dundee, son of Alexander Wedderburn, then clerk, and Janet Myln. Born 1561. Died 1626.

Mr. Millar gets into considerable confusion over this entry, which he supposes to refer to Alexander Wedderburn, second of Kingennie, who was not born till after its date, instead of, as the fact is, to his father. He appends to it a long note, accepting with little correction, Douglas' account of Kingennie's predecessors, by which John Wedderburn, "of Tofts," said to have died in 1533, is made town clerk of Dundee, and father to David Wedderburn, who married Helen Lawson. This David, in his turn, is said to have died in 1590, and to have been the father of Kingennie, all mention being omitted (as Mr. Millar observes) of Alexander Wedderburn, the old clerk, who

[1] Mr. Millar also gives the admission in 1550 of Finlay Duncan, surgeon, and in a note speaks of William Duncan who married "Katharine Wedderburn, sister to the famous Sir (sic) Alexander Wedderburn, first Baron of Kingennie." This is an error, as Kingennie was never knighted.

[2] The admissions 1582-1637 are almost all in this form, which may be translated, "On the said day (the person named) was made burgess and brother of the gild by reason of the privilege of (such and such a person)." Sometimes the words "accidentibus gratis" or "solutis" are added, showing whether he got his freedom for nothing or by payment.

2 C

was in fact Kingennie's father. It would be difficult to crowd more errors into an equal space.
There is, as I have already said, no record of any John Wedderburn ever having been clerk of
Dundee ; there never was such a place as Tofts, the idea of which is due to the mistranslation of the
word "toftas" in certain great seal charters as a proper name, instead of as a noun meaning hillocks
or tufts of land. (See below s. Public Records, Great Seal Register, 8 Aug. 1542). David Wedderburn, who married Helen Lawson, was the son of David (not of John) Wedderburn, and died in
1559, not 1590, and had no son Alexander.
Mr. Millar goes on to state that Kingennie, for some time before he succeeded to the office of
town clerk, practised as a notary, but this, again, is an error, as he was appointed clerk 20 Sept. 1582,
and was not admitted notary till 1 June 1583. Finally, Mr. Millar, in further following of Douglas,
proceeds to give an account of James, Bishop of Dunblane, and Dr. John Wedderburn of Moravia,
as two brothers of Alexander Wedderburn, first of Kingennie. This is another error. The Bishop
and the Doctor were brothers to each other, but not to Kingennie, being the sons of John Wedderburn and Margaret Lindsay, not of Alexander Wedderburn and Janet Myln.

27.   **1582.** May 15.—Eodem die David Wedderburn, filius Alexandri Wedderburn, scribæ
civitatis dicti burgi, effectus est burgensis ac frater gildæ ratione privilegii dicti
Alexandri sui patris qui est frater gildæ, accidentibus gratis.
David Wedderburn of the MS. or " Compt. Bulk," and immediate younger brother to Kingennie.
Mr. Millar, already astray as to the person named in No. 26, is driven to make David the fourth
son of Kingennie !

28.   **1582.** Aug. 21.—Eodem die Alexander Wedderburn, mercator junior, effectus est
burgensis et frater gildæ ratione privilegii Davidis Wedderburn in Welgait sui patris
qui fuit burgensis et frater gildæ.
Alexander of Pittormie, burgess of Cupar. He is called " merchant, junior," as opposed to
Alexander Wedderburn, merchant, elder (the husband of Isobell Anderson), who did not die till 1589
(ante No 8.)

29.   **1584.** July 13.—Eodem die Joannes Wedderburn nauta effectus est burgensis et
frater gildæ ratione privilegii Joannis Wedderburn sui patris qui fuit burgensis et
frater gildæ, solutis accidentibus.
John Wedderburn, son to John Wedderburn and Agnes Hoppringill, and grandson to James
Wedderburn and Janet Forrester. He married Margaret Lindsay, and was father to Dr. John
Wedderburn of Moravia, and James, Bishop of Dunblane.

30.   **1587-88.** March 15.—Eodem die Robertus Wedderburn frater germanus quondam
Alexandri Wedderburn, scribæ civitatis dicti burgi, effectus est burgensis et frater
gildæ ratione privilegii quondam Roberti Wedderburn sui patris qui fuit burgensis et
frater gildæ, accidentibus gratis.
This is Robert Wedderburn, the notary, brother to Alexander, the old clerk, and son of the late
Robert Wedderburn, " who was a burgess and brother of the gild." This statement makes it
necessary to look for the admission of old Robert Wedderburn among the previous entries, and as he
can hardly have been admitted before 1514, his identification with the Robert named above (No. 2)
is almost certain.

31.   **1591.** May 7.—Eodem die Robertus Wedderburn junior, effectus est burgensis et
frater gildæ ratione privilegii quondam Alexandri Wedderburn, scribæ dicti burgi,
qui fuit frater gildæ, accidentibus gratis.
Robert Wedderburn, younger, third son of the old clerk. He died in 1593.

32.   **1591.** Oct. 20.—The accounts of the treasurer, John Pierson, are audited, and a
balance of £70 15s. 9d, due from him to the town, is paid over by him to Robert
Wedderburn, " for the reparation of the School wall."
This is Robert Wedderburn, the merchant.

33.   **1600.** July 22.—Eodem die Alexander Wedderburn, filius Patricii Wedderburn
mercatoris, effectus est burgensis et frater gildæ ratione privilegii dicti sui patris,
solutis accidentibus.
Alexander, son of Patrick, whose admission is already recorded, ante No. 23. He married Barbara
Auchinlek, and was the father of Andrew Wedderburn, admitted in 1634 (post No. 51).

34.   **1603.** Aug. 25.—Eodem die Jacobus Wedderburn mercator effectus est burgensis
et frater gildæ ratione privilegii quondam Alexandri Wedderburn scribæ curiæ dicti
burgi qui fuit frater gildæ, solutis accidentibus.
James, fourth son of Alexander Wedderburn and Janet Mylu. He was long a prominent merchant
in Dundee, and died in 1644.

35. **1605.** Sept. 17.—Eodem die Petrus Wedderburn mercator effectus est burgensis et
frater gildæ burgi de Dunde ratione privilegii Alexandri Wedderburn scribæ curiæ
dicti burgi qui fuit frater gildæ, accidentibus gratis.

The "Lockit Bulk" of Dundee.

Peter, fifth son of Alexander Wedderburn and Janet Myln.

36. **1609.** Sept. 22.—Eodem die magister Alexander Wedderburn filius magistri
Alexandri Wedderburn, scribæ curiæ dicti burgi, effectus est burgensis et frater gildæ
ratione privilegii dicti magistri Alexandri sui patris, accidentibus gratis.

Alexander, afterwards second of Kingennie, and for a few years, 1627-33, clerk of Dundee.

37. **1610.** July 10.—Eodem die magister Jacobus Wedderburn effectus est burgensis et
frater gildæ ratione privilegii magistri Alexandri Wedderburn scribæ curiæ dicti burgi,
acc. gratis.

James Wedderburn, second son to Alexander, first of Kingennie. He was born in 1589 ; succeeded
his father as clerk of Dundee in 1626, but died in the following year. He had married in 1608
Margaret Goldman,[1] by whom he left issue three sons—Sir Alexander, of Blackness ; William ; and
Sir Peter, Lord Gosford.

38. **1611.** March 26.—Eodem die Adamus Wedderburn mercator effectus est burgensis
et frater gildæ ratione privilegii Patricii Wedderburn mercatoris qui fuit frater gildæ.

Adam Wedderburn, second son of Patrick Wedderburn and Elizabeth Low. He died soon after
unmarried. The words " qui fuit " are peculiar, as Patrick was certainly alive at this date.

39. **1611.** July 9.—Eodem die magister Gulielmus Wedderburn pastor ecclesiæ deidonanæ
effectus est burgensis et frater gildæ ratione privilegii Alexandri Wedderburn olim
ballivi dicti burgi qui est frater gildæ.

The Rev. William Wedderburn, son of Alexander of Pittarmie (ante No. 28), was minister at
Pittenweem, and later at Dundee. He m. Magdalene Wedderburn, daughter to Kingennie.

40. **1620.**[2] Jan. 20.—Eodem die Petrus Wedderburn mercator effectus est burgensis et
frater gildæ ratione privilegii Magistri Alexandri Wedderburn scribæ curiæ dicti burgi.

Peter Wedderburn, third son to Kingennie.

41. **1621.** Oct. 16.—Eodem die Alexander Wedderburn nauta effectus est burgensis et
frater gildæ ratione privilegii quondam Roberti Wedderburn sui patris.

Alexander, son of Robert Wedderburn, younger (ante No. 31). He married and had issue two
daughters, Helen and Elizabeth.

---

[1] Mr. Millar gives the admission, 15 April 1562, of Margaret's father, James Goldman, and subjoins an
interesting note on him and his family. " He was married (he says) to Margaret Jack and had a
numerous family, all of whom were distinguished in the civic annals of Dundee. A very
interesting account of four of them is given in a long Latin poem, written by Peter Goldman, the
youngest son, and included in the ' Delitiae Poetarum Scotorum.' This curious work is entitled,
' Margaretae laccbae matris suae super tristi et immatura morte quatuor filiorum Lachrymae.'
(The tears of Margaret Jack, their mother, over the sad and immature death of her four sons.)
From the poem it appears that the first-named son, Patrick, was overtaken by a sudden squall and
and drowned in a harbour of Batavia (Holland). John, the second son, fell a victim to the plague
in Dundee, despite the efforts made by Dr. Kinloch to save him. The third son, Robert, was
thrown from his horse and instantly killed ; whilst the eldest son, William, ' the beloved of the
common people, and the guardian of the welfare of Dundee,' was carried off by death in the midst
of his labours. .... There are feeling allusions made in the poem to the comfort which the
sorrowing mother had derived from the ministrations of the three Pastors of Dundee, David
Lindsay, William Wedderburn, and James Robertson. .... Besides these sons, James Goldman
had two daughters, one of whom was married to James Wedderburn (son of the Town Clerk,
Alexander Wedderburn of Kingennie, and ancestor of Lord Chancellor the Earl of Rosslyn) and
the other to Sinclair of Ulbster. In several of the published genealogies of the Wedderburn
family, James Goldman's eldest daughter's name is given as Margaret, but from the monument in
the Howff, No. 812, this appears to be a mistake. .... She was married in 1608, and had two
sons, Sir Alexander Wedderburn of Blackness, and Sir Peter Wedderburn of Gosford, who became
a Lord of Session." The mistake is in the inscription on the monument, which is modern (see the
chapter on the Howff), and Margaret Goldman had, as stated above, not two sons only, but three.

[2] Between 1616 and 1644 there are various instances of Wedderburn signatures in the "Lockit
Buik." Alexander Wedderburn, afterwards second of Kingennie, audits the Treasurer's account 12 Dec.
1616, and is named as bailie and dean of Gild 12 Jan. 1617 ; 9 Jan. 1618 ; 20 Jan. 1629 ; 20 Sept.
1626, &c., &c. ; his brother Mr. James Wedderburn, notary, afterwards clerk, signs two discharges,
9 Jan. 1618 ; and their uncle, James Wedderburn the merchant, often acts as bailie, kirkmaster,
and dean of Gild, up to 8 March 1642.

42. **1622.** June 10.—Eodem die Joannes Wedderburn ratione privilegii Roberti Wedderburn sui patris.

John, eldest son of Robert Wedderburn, merchant (ante No. 25), and Eufame Coustoun.

43. **1623.** April 21.—Eodem die magister Jacobus Wedderburn doctor theologiæ effectus est burgensis et frater gildæ dicti burgi ratione privilegii quondam Johannis Wedderburn burgi ejusdem qui fuit burgensis et frater gildæ, acc. gratis.

James Wedderburne, Bishop of Dunblane, son to John Wedderburn (ante No. 29).

44. **1625.** March 1.—Eodem die Gulielmus Wedderburn filius legitimus magistri Alexandri Wedderburne scribæ curiæ dicti burgi effectus est burgensis et frater gildæ dicti burgi ratione privilegii dicti sui patris, acc. gratis.

William Wedderburn, fourth son of Kingennie.

45. **1629.** June 30.—Eodem die Joannes Wedderburne[1] nauta effectus est burgensis et frater gildæ dicti burgi ratione privilegii magistri Alexandri Wedderburñ scribæ curiæ dicti burgi sui patris, acc. gratis.

John Wedderburn, eldest son of Alexander Wedderburn, second of Kingennie, who was now (1627-33), clerk of Dundee. He died young.

46. **1631.** Sept. 13.—Quo die Magᵣ Alexander Wedderburn junior effectus est burgensis et frater gildæ burgi de Dunde ratione privilegii quondam magistri Jacobi Wedderburne scribæ curiæ dicti burgi sui patris.

Alexander Wedderburn, afterwards Sir Alexander of Blackness, and clerk of Dundee 1633-75.

47. **1632.** May 26.— Quo die magister David Wedderburn Ludi magister Aberdonensis ascriptus est numero civium deidonensium propter ipsius merita, eruditionem, et curam in erudiendo juventutem.

Mr. David Wedderburn, master of the Aberdeen Grammar School.

48. **1632.** July 26.—Magᵣ Alexander Wedderburne junior effectus est burgensis dicti burgi ac frater gildæ ratione privilegii magistri Alexandri Wedderburne scribæ curiæ ejusdem.

This is Alexander, eldest surviving son of Alexander Wedderburn, second of Kingennie. He was born in 1615, and was thus admitted at the early age of 17. He was afterwards twice provost of Dundee.

49. **1632.** Sept. 25.—Eodem die Gulielmus Wedderburne filius legitimus quondam magistri Jacobi Wedderburne scribæ curiæ deidonanæ effectus est burgensis et frater gildæ dicti burgi ratione privilegii dicti quondam sui patris.

William Wedderburn, second son of James, the clerk (d. 1627), and brother of Sir Alexander of Blackness. As he is admitted just one year after his elder brother, he was, no doubt, just a year his junior in point of age, and was thus born in 1611.

50. **1633.** Feb. 5.—Eodem die Gulielmus Wedderburn nauta effectus est burgensis et frater gildæ dicti burgi ratione privilegii Alexandri Wedderburn senioris mercatoris sui patris qui est burgensis et frater gildæ ; acc. solutis.

William Wedderburn, mariner, son of Alexander Wedderburn, merchant, and Barbara Auchinlek. This is the only mention of him either in the Dundee Records or elsewhere. Probably he died young.

51. **1634.** April 22.—Eodem die Andreas Wedderburne effectus est burgensis et frater gildæ de burgi de Dondei ratione privilegii Alexandri Wedderburne senioris mercatoris qui est burgensis et frater gildæ ejusdem ; acc. solutis.

Andrew Wedderburn, brother of the foregoing (No. 50), long a merchant in Dundee.

52. **1637.** Nov. 7.— Quo die Andreas Wedderburne filius quondam magistri David Wedderburne effectus est burgensis et frater gildæ burgi de Dundie ratione privilegii dicti sui patris qui erat burgensis et frater gildæ dicti burgi, accidentibus ordinariis iis quibus debentur solutis.

---

[1] This is the first clear use in the " Lockit Buik " of the final " e " in Wedderburne, although some earlier entries have, as in the second line of this very entry, a dash over the " n," or last syllable.

53. **1657.** Feb. 7.—The quhilk day Mr. Peter Wedderburne, advocate, was admitted The "Lockit
burges and broy^r of Gild of the burgh by reason of his father Mr. James Wedderburne Buik" of
who was common clerk of this burgh.

Sir Peter Wedderburu, Lord Gosford. He was again admitted, together with his two sons, Peter
and Alexander, in 1675 (post No. 59). Mr. Millar appends a fair account of his career, but says that
he was born about 1610 and took his degree at St. Andrews in 1630. This is inaccurate. He was
horn about 1618. and took his degree in 1636. There is no record of any graduate of the name of
St. Andrews in 1630 (see ante p. 160.)

54. **1662.** Aug. 14.—John Wedderburne, baxter, was admitted burgess by his father's
privilege.

This John Wedderburn was natural son to Alexander Wedderburu, third of Kingennie. He
married Helen Rodger, but had uo male issue.

55. **1665.** May 15.—The quhilk day Alexander Wedderburne, younger of Kyngany, was
admitted burgess and broy^r gild of the said burgh be his father's privilege.

Alexander, afterwards fourth of Kingennie. Mr. Millar in a note to his entry says, "His grandfather was town clerk of Dundee, and that office would have been bestowed on his father had he been
of sufficient age when his grandfather died, but it was then granted to James Wedderburn, his father's
cousin, from whom the Wedderburns of Blackness derive their descent." This statement is very
wide of the mark. The grandfather of this Alexander was clerk of Dundee, but at his death, in
1637, his son (born 1615), was old enough to take up his clerkship. It had, however, been already
bestowed, in 1633, on his cousin (Sir) Alexander, afterwards of Blackness. whose father, James,
formerly clerk, had died in 1627, at a time when his son was not of sufficient age to at once succeed him
and the clerkship was, therefore, held for a time (1627-33) by his uncle, Alexander, second of Kingennie.

56. **1665.** May 15.—John Wedderburne, appearand of Blackness, was admitted burgess
and broy^r gild be his father's privilege.   John Doull, servitor to the said John
Wedderburne, admitted gratis.[1]

Eldest son of Sir Alexander, and afterwards Sir John Wedderburn, first baronet of Blackness.

57. **1671.** June 13.— Joⁿ Wedderburne, sone to Sir Peter Wedderburne, of Gosfoord,
was admitted burges of the said burgh by reason of his father's privilege.

Mr. Andrew Anderson, pedagogue to the said Joⁿ Wedderburne, John Brown
and William Tait, servitors to the said Joⁿ Wedderburne, were all admitted burgesses.

John Wedderburn, eldest son of Lord Gosford. He died in a shipwreck off Calais, 26 May 1688.

58. **1671.** Dec. 26.—Peter Wedderburne, son to Sir Alexander Wedderburne, commone
clerk of the said burgh, was admitted burgess thereof be virtue of his said father's
privilege.

Peter Wedderburn, third surviving son of Sir Alexander, b. 1652, d. 1652, leaving two sons.

59. **1675.** July 20.—Sir Peter Wedderburne, of Gosfoord, ane of the servitors of the
Colledge of Justice, Peter Wedderburne, Alexander Wedderburne, his sones, was
admitted burgess and gild brother be thair father and goodsyre's priviledge.

Sir Peter, Lord Gosford, had already been admitted burgess fourteen years earlier (aute No. 53),
a fact which would seem to have been forgotten at this date. Of his two sons, now admitted with
him, Peter ultimately succeeded his father, through the death of his elder brother, John, and was
created a baronet of Nova Scotia in 1697. He married Janet Halkett, heiress of Pitfirrane, and was
thus the progenitor of the Wedderburn-Halketts, as well as of the Wedderburns of Gosford. Alexander,
the other brother, was a commisioner of excise. He married Mary Daes, and was father to Peter
Wedderburn, Lord Chesterhall, and grandfather to Lord Chancellor Loughborough.

60. **1689.** May 7.—Patrick Wedderburne, privilegio patris.

Peter (or Patrick) Wedderburn, only surviving son of Alexander Wedderburn, of Easter Powrie,
by Margaret Milne. He was a merchant in Dundee, and was twice married, but d. s.p. 1723-24.

61. **1700.** Nov. 5.—Alexander Wedderburne, clerk, was admitted burges and gild brother
by the privilege of his father.

Alexander Wedderburn, afterwards fourth baron of Blackness. There is no entry of the
admission of his father James Wedderburn, the clerk (d. 1696), but from 29 May, 1666 the Lockit
Buik is illegible or blank, and this is just the time at which James, born in 1649, would be admitted.

62. **1813.** Sept. 21.—Sir David Wedderburn, of Ballindean, Bart., and that for having
paid Ten pounds stg. to Patrick Whitson, Town's Chamberlain.

He is the last of his name admitted to the freedom of Dundee.

---

[1] There are occasional instances in the "Lockit Buik" from 1584 on, of the admission gratis of "servitors"
of the Wedderburns, a fact illustrative of the influence of the family in the burgh.

THE PROTOCOL BOOKS.

Dundee Protocol Books. This record begins in 1518 and continues, with but one important break, due to the loss of a volume, down to date. It has been searched through sixty-nine large volumes from 1518 to 1801. The volumes are numbered consecutively 235—303, and in addition to these there are three unnumbered volumes, and nineteen small minute books.

There is among some loose papers in the Dundee charter room an old Inventory (1659), of the then existing protocol books, made and written by Sir Alexander Wedderburn of Blackness, who was clerk from 1633 to 1675. It is as follows :—

" The Inventorie of the Prothogolles in the presse belonging to me,
which was taken up this 3rd of March, 1659.

Three ancient prothogolles of Thomas Ireland, which beginnes anno 1518 and ends in anno 1567.

Three ancient prothogolles of Halbert Glaidstanes, which beginnes anno 1552 and ends in anno 1567.

One of Alexander Maxwells, which he beginnes anno 1555 and ends in 1574.

Sex prothogoll bookes of Robert Wedderburne, which beginnes anno 1574 and ends anno 1606.

Thair ar 12 Minutt books of his.

Thair are 15 Prothogolles of Mr. Alexander Wedderburne, my goodschyr, which beginnes 1583 and ends in anno 1624.

Thair are 7 Minutt bookes.

Ane prothogoll of Mr. James Wedderburne, my father, which beginnes anno 1609 and ends anno 1622.

Ane prothogoll of Mr. Alexander Wedderburn, my uncle, which beginnes anno 1627 and ends anno 1632.

Ane prothogoll of Thomas Kessie, which beginnes anno 1616 and ends anno 1641.

Ane of Thomas Wightone, which beginnes anno 1648 and ends anno 1653.

Ane of my owne which beginnes anno 1633 and ends anno 1639.

Ane other of myne which lyes in my chamber, which beginnes anno 1639, and is not perfyted."

The above account includes most of the Dundee Protocol Books and Minutes of Sasines still extant and covering the period from 1518 to 1659. Then follow No. 274 (1659—1666), a volume of the time of Sir Alexander Wedderburn, but not his ; Nos. 275, 276, and 277 (1666—1690), the books of James Wedderburn, his son, who was admitted conjunct clerk with him in 1671, and was sole clerk 1675—96 ; No. 278 (1690—1699), the book partly of James Wedderburn and partly of his son Alexander, who was sole clerk 1696—1715, and No. 279, which covers the latter part of this period (1699—1715). In 1716 Alexander Wedderburn was demitted from the clerkship for his share in the rising of 1715, and thereafter the protocols of Dundee are in the hands of his successors, no longer of his name. They run without a break from 1717 to the present time. Of these volumes Nos. 280-289 have been searched throughout (1717—1767), and Nos. 290-303 have been examined by the indices only (1767—1801).

We can now sum up the position of this record ; marking with a * those volumes which are missing, with a † those which are extant but are not named in Sir Alexander's list, while those which have been left unnumbered in the arrangement of the Dundee Charter room, are indicated by a — instead of a number.

No.		Date.	Notary.	Notes.
235	...	1518—1534	Thomas Ireland.	
† 236	...	1526—1528	Robert Seres.	
*237		?	Thomas Ireland (?)	This may have been one of the three books of Thomas Ireland named in the above inventory.
—	...	1535—1572 ?	Thomas Ireland.	
* —	..	1552—1553	Herbert Gladstone.	
* —	...	? —1567	Herbert Gladstone.	
—	...	1555—1574	Alexander Maxwell.	
† —	...	1567—1575	Thomas Ireland.	
† 238	...	1554—1565	Alexander Wedderburn.	

No.	Date.	Notary.	Notes.
239 ...	1563—1567	Herbert Gladstone.	
† 240 .	1565—1570	Alexander Wedderburn.	
† 241 ...	1568—1577	Alexander Wedderburn.	
† 242 ...	1570—1577	Alexander Wedderburn.	
† 244 ...	1577—1581	Alexander Wedderburn.	
† 246 } † 248 } ... † 249 }	1577—1585	Alexander Wedderburn.	
243, 245 247, 251 } 261, 262 }	1574—1606	Robert Wedderburn.	
250 252 253 254—260 } 263—266	1583—1624	Alexander Wedderburn of Kingennie, clerk 1585—1626.	
268			{ Twelve of these are the books of
— ..	1571—1614	19 Minute Books.	Robert Wedderburn, notary, and seven, those either of Alexander the old clerk, or his son, Kingennie. (See below.) }
267 ...	1617—1622	James Wedderburn, clerk, (d. 1627.)	
• — ...	1627—1632	Alexander Wedderburn, second of Kingennie, clerk.	
269 ..	1633—1639	Sir Alexander Wedderburn, clerk (d. 1675).	
270 ...	1638—1641	Thomas Kessan.	
271-72 ...	1648—1653	Thomas Wichtane.	
273 ...	1639—1659	Sir A. Wedderburn of Blackness.	
† 274 ...	1659—1666	Sir A. Wedderburn of Blackness.	{ This is of the time of Sir Alexander, but is not his. }
† 275 } † 276 } ... † 277 }	1666—1690	James Wedderburn, clerk (d. 1696).	
† 278 ...	1690–1699	{ James Wedderburn and his son Alexander, clerk.	{ This book was begun by the father and continued by the son. }
† 279 ..	1699—1715	Alexander Wedderburn, clerk.	
† 280—289..	1717—1767	George Duncan and others, successors of Alexander Wedderburn, last clerk of his name.	
† 290—303...	1767—1801		{ Vols. 290-303 have been searched of the Index only. }

The minute books seem to contain drafts of sasines or notes of facts to be used in drawing up sasines. They do not add much to what is already clear from other and more formal records, and anything therefore in them worth recording here, has been introduced among the extracts from the protocol books. Some account of them must, however, be given. They are nineteen in number. Of these the first three, fifth, sixth and last, would seem to be those of Alexander Wedderburn of Kingennie, or his father the old clerk; while the rest are the books of Robert Wedderburn, the notary. Those of Robert are adorned with Latin mottoes, of which he seems to have been fond. "Lexibus pare," "Dii erepta secundant," "Verere deum, verere teipsum," "Patior ut potiar," "Cælum non solum," are amongst these; while other examples will be found in his protocol books.

In one of his minute books (No. 4, fol. 1), is the following family register :—

"Robert. The lad was borne the first day of June 1584 betwix vij and viij houris afoiruoune on ane Mononday under the signe of Pisces.

"James Wedderburn my second sone wes borne on ane Wednisday the 4 day of August 1585 under the signe of Aries between v & vj in the morning.

"Robert my thrid sone wes borne on ane Sonday the 29 of January 1586 betwix 7 & 8 houris eftirnoone under the signe of —."

Dundee
Protocol
Books. The following notes of entries in this record have been made with a view to brevity. The originals are almost all in Latin, and are often very lengthy, describing in detail the boundaries of premises in Dundee. From numerous entries, I have had to make a selection, and to abbreviate each note into a bare statement of facts, often little more than index-references to the original entries, the character of which resembles that of many of the Scrymgeour-Wedderburn or Blackness Papers, of which much fuller notes have been given. At the end of the extracts from each volume I have added a list of the folios or dates at which may be found in the original MSS. all the references to members of the family, including those which I have omitted as adding nothing to the selected entries.

VOL. 235.

Entitled (modern) " Town Clerk's Protocol, 3 Sept. 1518—July 1534." [1]

1. **1518.** (a) Nov. 3.—South Moraygate land, bounded on the south by that of the heirs of the late David Wedderburn mentioned. (b) Nov. 29.—Mr. Robert Wedderburn, witness.

2. **1519.** Jan. 11, Feb. 25.—James Wedderburn, bailic, present.

3. **1520.** Dec. 14.—At the town house at 10 a.m., before Hugo Fothringham and others, Henry Halis accepts from James Wedderburn a worsted doublet (dubloitum le worsit), and, therefore, binds himself that after the feast of the nativity he will never play " nd legas neque taxillas."

4. **1521.** April 8.—(On an inverted leaf), " James of Wedderburn, Robertis sone," named in a list of persons.

5. **1521.** Sept. 28.—James Wedderburn is entered as son and heir to his father, the late James Wedderburn, in an annual-rent out of the land of the late Andrew Wedderburn in Wellgate (bounded on the south by that of [*the late?*] Robert W.), and also in a piece of land in North Marketgate.

    The Wellgate land mentioned here is the same as that mentioned below in Nos. 8 and 10. In No. 8, Robert Wedderburn is named as deceased, although in this entry, as in No. 10, he is not. If, as I think, he is to be identified with Robert Wedderburn, who married Janet Foster, he was dead at this date. See the account of him in vol. 1.

6. **1521.** Nov. 12.—David Wedderburn rents part of the multures of the common mills from Alexr Kyd, and his brother, James Wedderburn, is security for the due payment of the rent. Dec. 14.—Land of James Wedderburn, elder, named as a boundary.

7. **1522.** (a) Jan. 13.—Mr. Robert Wedderburn, witness. (b) Feb. 14.—James Wedderburn, son of the late Robert Wedderburn, witness. (c) March 28.—James Wedderburn, son of Robert Wedderburn, witness. (d) Aug. 15.—Thomas Wedderburn, witness.

8. **1524.** Oct. 6.—At 8 a.m., before James Scrimgeour and others, James Dik, procurator of Sir (dompni) William Wedderburn, monk in Arbroth, heir of the late Andrew Wedderburn, with the assent of the monastery, resigns to the bailic the West Welgate land (bounded on the south by that of the late Robert Wedderburn), and thereupon the bailic gives sasine of it to Sir William's brother german, David, who again resigns it for sasine to himself and Elizabeth Dog, his wife, and the heirs to be gotten between them.

9. **1524.** (a) Oct. 28.—David Wedderburn, son of the late David Wedderburn, and brother and heir of the late James Wedderburn, resigns a South Ergadie Street property to John Low, who gets sasine thereof 26 Nov. James Wedderburn is bailic. (b) Nov. 7.—James Wedderburn, bailic, present.

---

[1] I have given almost all the Wedderburn references in this, the earliest of the Dundee Protocol Books. The book is written almost entirely in Latin, and the folios are not numbered.

10. **1524.** Nov. 24.—Before David Wedderburn, son of David Wedderburn, and others, Elizabeth Dog, spouse of David Wedderburn, son of Walter Wedderburn, consents in open court to the resignation of the West Wellgate land (bounded south by that of Robert Wedderburn) mentioned above, Nos. 5 and 8. Dundee Protocol Books.

11. **1524.** (*a*) Feb. 15.—David Wedderburn, witness. (*b*) Sept. 22.—James Wedderburn, mentioned.

12. **1525.** (*a*) Nov. 6, 22.—James Wedderburn, bailie. (*b*) Dec. 6.—David Wedderburn summoned by James Kinloch. (*c*) Dec. 12. —Robert Wedderburn, notary, in court.

13. **1526.** (*a*) Jan. 19.—David Wedderburn presides in court. (*b*) March 7, 13, April 20, July 16.—James Wedderburn in court. (*c*) March 15.—Robert Wedderburn acts as procurator for David Reid. (*d*) April 20.—David Wedderburn, burgess, acquires waste land in South Argylgate. (*e*) Sept. 7, Oct. 29.—David Wedderburn acts as curator to Henry Flescheour. (*f*) Nov. 26.—David Wedderburn resigns an annual-rent out of his land in South Murraygate, lying east of St. Paul's, and north of that of Andrew Fairny.

14. **1526.** Feb. 6. 28.—Sir Thomas Wedderburn, chaplain, is a witness. He also, on the same day, resigns to William Barry, two tenements in North Murraygate.

15. **1527.** May 15.—Before James Wedderburn, bailie, David Wedderburn, in South Murraygate, acquires from Andrew Fairny certain land in North Seagate, named ante No. 13(*f*), and two annual rents.

16. **1527.** (*a*) May 27.—John Tendall charges James Wedderburn with assault, "quod injuriose eum rapuit." (*b*) June 6.—James Wedderburn, dean of gild, present.

17. **1527.** June 8.—Before Mr. John Barry, vicar of Dundee and others, Janet Barry, relict of the late James Wedderburn, and Elizabeth Wedderburn, his daughter, relict of Robert Ferquhar, agree to confirm all contracts made between the said James Wedderburn and Andrew Ferquhar, burgess of Monros. . . . . . (This entry is incomplete).

18. **1527.** June 28.—Complaint by David Wedderburn *v.* James Scrymgeour, son of David Scrymgeour of Fordill.

19. **1527.** (*a*) July 10.—James Wedderburn, bailie. (*b*) July 11-12.—Mr. Robert Wedderburn and James Wedderburn, bailie, named as present at a transaction.

20. **1527.** July 15.—Alexander Blak, junior, sells to David Wedderburn his "maritagium," and agrees to accept in marriage any wife, however ugly, offered him by the said David.

This is a very peculiar entry as follows :—(1527) xv° die Julij hora decima nute meridiem coram pretorio de Dundee, coram Willelmo Lowson, Johanne Walcar, David Alexander et Willelmo Cathro duobus serjeandis—quod Alexander Blak, junior, scissor, vendidit David Wedderburn suum maritagium cum proficuo ejusdem pro xx^lib monete Scocie de qua summa fatetur se recipisse xiiij^s in solucione ejusdem et dictus David solvet residuum ad complementum maritagii et dictus Alexander accipiet in maritagio aliquam mulierem offertam per dictum David quamcumque sibi David placuerit, carentem istis egritudinibus videlicet le buck et cragyngour et abaque defaunecione non obstante quamvis sit ipsa lusca aut claudicata. Et si dictus Alexander recusat ipsam sic oblatam ut supra per dictum David accipere in maritagio quod solvet xl^lib dicto David pro dicta summa xx^lib etc pro coatis dampnis et expensis in lite fundis.

21. **1527.** (*a*) Aug. 20.—Lands in West Welgate are named as bounded on the South by those of James Wedderburn. (*b*) Aug. 30.—John Wedderburn present. (*c*) Oct. 23, 24, Nov. 26, Dec. 17.—James Wedderburn present.

22. **1527.** Nov. 6, 7.—Sasine of the lands of Croseo and Tullohill is given by Patrick Gray, "vice-comes" of Forfar to Henry Wedderburn, son of James Wedderburn, junior,

2 D

of Dundee, as attorney for Janet Forestar, daughter and heir of David Forestar, and wife of the said James Wedderburn. [Vol. 236, 20.]

23.   **1527.** Nov. 16.—Discharge in favour of Katherin Wedderburn, sometime spouse of George Rocht, late burgess of Dundee. [Vol. 236, 20.]

24.   **1528.** (*a*) Jan. 9.—Lands in North Flukergate are named as bounded on the East by those of the heirs of the late James Wedderburn. (*b*) Feb. 2.—Thomas Wedderburn a witness.
     In this entry (*b*) Thomas Wedderburn is not designed "Sir," as he is above in No. 14, and below in No. 30.

25.   **1528.** (*a*) March 2.—David Wedderburn, elder, present. (*b*) March 28.—Mr. Robert Wedderburn and James Wedderburn, present. (*c*) April 16.—Land of David Wedderburn in Murraygate, mentioned.

26.   **1528.** May 9.—In a court held by David Wedderburn, younger, bailie, appears Cristina Jameson, spouse of David Wedderburn, and consents to her husband's alienation of his inner land, etc., in North Moraygate, to Henry Wedderburn. (See below, No 49.)

27.   **1528.** May 10.—Robert Wedderburn binds himself quickly to receive iustitntion or collation to the chaplainry of S. Katherine the Virgin, vacant by the death of Sir Robert Lany, and as soon as possible to accept the order of presbyter, and to abide continually in the daily service of the parish church of Dundee. Henry Wedderburn is witness.

28.   **1528.** May 17.—David Wedderburn and others buy a ship.

29.   **1528.** (*a*) June 1, 7.—Henry Wedderburn present. (*b*) July 17.—Henry Wedderburn resigns to David Wedderburn, bailie, the lands acquired by him 9 May (see above, No. 26), for new infeftment to be given to him and his apparent spouse, Marion Lawson.

30.   **1528.** (*a*) Nov. 7.—Sir Thomas Wedderburn resigns an annual rent. (*b*) Nov. 24, 25. Henry Wedderburn witnesses a resignation by Andrew Barry of a South Murraygate land, bounded on the west by that of the heirs of the late Robert Wedderburn.

31.   **1529.** (*a*) Jan. 25 —Sasine to Henry Wedderburn and Matilda Carueros, his spouse, of two roods of the common land. David Wedderburn, younger, present. (*b*) March 5.—License by the bailies to Henry Wedderburn to build thereon with windows overlooking the parish church.

32.   **1529.** June 21.—James Dog resigns a North Flukergate land to James Wedderburn, son and heir of the late Robert Wedderburn. David Wedderburn, elder, is present.

33.   **1530.**—James, David, and Robert Wedderburn are often named as present on various occasions.

34.   **1530.** Dec. 25.—Thomas Carale resigns land in North Chakkeraw to Elizabeth Wedderburn, wife of Alexander Ogilvy. Robert Wedderburn is witness.

35.   **1531.** March 14.—Settlement by Henry Wedderburn (with consent of Matilda Carneros, his wife) of certain properties on their three sons, Henry, Robert and John.

36.   **1531.** (*a*) April 10.—David Wedderburn, son of Walter Wedderburn, present. (*b*) April 17.—James Wedderburn resigns an annual-rent. Sir Thomas Wedderburn is witness and James Wedderburn acts as bailie.

37.   **1531.** April 18.—James Wedderburn, elder, gets one-third of Drumgeth, from Janet Douglas, Lady of Glammys.

38. **1531.** June 22.—David Wedderburn, younger, son of the late Robert Wedderburn, gets from Agnes Farny, a North Seagate land. Sir Thomas Wedderburn, witness.

39. **1531.** July 8.—Elizabeth Olifer, wife of Robert Myll, consents to the resignation of an 8 merks annual rent, forth of David Wedderburn's South Murraygate land to William Myll, their son.

40. **1531.** Sept. 4.—David Wedderburn, younger, David Wedderburn, elder, Henry Wedderburn and James Wedderburn are all present.

41. **1531.** Oct. 13.—Elizabeth Wedderburn, relict of Alexander Ogilvy, named.

42. **1531.** Nov. 29.—Sasine to James Wedderburn, son and heir of the late James Wedderburn, of land in S. Margaret's close, North Marketgate, which he at once resigns to Robert Barry.

43. **1532.** Feb. 1.—Mr. John Wedderburn, chaplain of S. Matthew's chapel, resigns land to Alexander Fife.

44. **1532.** Feb. 23.—Before George Wedderburn. Robert Wedderburn and others, Elizabeth Wedderburn resigns her life-rent of land in North Marketgate, and gets sasine of it anew from James Lovell, son of the late Alexander Lovell.

45. **1532.** May 22.—Janet Wedderburn, wife of Nicholas Watson, agrees to a sale of land by her husband. She does so again on June 14.

46. **1532.** July 4.—David Wedderburn, son of Walter Wedderburn, present.

47. **1532.** Nov. 4.—James Wedderburn, younger, sheriff in that part by royal letters, requires the bailies to execute a decreet of limitation for Henry Wedderburn. James Wedderburn, bailie, protests that there is no precedent for such a requisition.

48. **1532.** Nov. 13.—Mr. Robert Wedderburn, present.

49. **1532.** Dec. 7.—Cristina Jameson, wife of David Wedderburn, agrees, in the absence of her husband, to the resignation of an annual-rent out of David's North Murraygate lands, bounded by those of Henry Wedderburn and James Dog. David Wedderburn then settles two North Wellgate lands on himself, his wife and their heirs.
   This resignation is registered in the Reg. Episcop. Brechin, and there David Wedderburn is designated "elder." See Bannatyne Club Ed., Aberdeen, 1856, pp. 184-85.

50. **1533.** May 17.—Henry Wedderburn and David Wedderburn, elder, his cousin (consanguineus), settle the boundaries of their adjacent Murraygate lands.

51. **1534.** (a) Feb. 27.—James Wedderburn, elder, and David Wedderburn present. (b) May 28.—David Wedderburn, elder, resigns an annual rent out of his North Murraygate lands. (c) June 3.—Sir Thomas Wedderburn and Robert Wedderburn witness a license by Alexander Fife to Elizabeth Wedderburn to build her mansion on her own land contiguous to his wall.

52. **1534.** July 30.—Helen Lawson, spouse of David Wedderburn, consents to the settlement of their South Seagate land on James Wedderburn, their son.
   [See also in this volume 8 dates :—1527, Jan. 17, 27 ; Feb. 7 ; April 3, 12 ; Aug. 13, 18 ; Sept. 7. 1528, July 6 ; Aug. 12. 1529, March 3, 25, 26 ; April 9 ; July 28 ; Aug. 6 ; Sept. 2. 1530, April, 1, 30 ; June 4 ; Oct. 11, 13, 26 ; Nov. 14, 17 ; Dec. 25. 1531, Jan. 30 ; March 8 ; June 27 ; July 4, 6 ; Sept. 27 ; Oct. 28 ; Nov. 21 ; Dec. 1. 1532, May 16 ; July, 1 ; Aug. 3, 7, 20 ; Sept. 20, 30 ; Oct. 29. 1533, Feb. 6 ; April 28 ; Aug. 5 ; Sept. 3. 1534, Feb. 10 ; April 10.]

Vol. 236.

Entitled (modern) Protocol Book (supposed of) Robert Seres, younger, town clerk, from 19 Nov. 1526 to 12 July 1528.

There are only one or two entries of interest relating to the Wedderburns in this volume, and these are placed in their order of date above. See ante Nos. 22 and 23. They both occur at fol. 20. Other Wedderburn references may be found at fol. 4, 7, 17 and 25, but they are unimportant.

VOL. 237.

This volume is, most unfortunately, missing from the Dundee Charter Room, and all efforts to find it have failed.

VOL. —

This is one of the unnumbered volumes. It is entitled (*modern*) " *Protocol Book of Thomas Ireland, Not. Pub.*, 1535—1572." Its folios are not all numbered, and have got loose and misplaced. The dates of the entries are thus not consecutive, though those given here are arranged in order of date.

53. **1534.** Nov. 7.—Patrick Blair of Bawmyll with consent of Thomas Blair of Balthyock, his tutor, resigns one fourth of Bawmyll, co. Perth, to Gilbert Blair and Elizabeth Wedderburn his wife.

54. **1563.** March 20.—Sasine of two roods of land on the Forfar road, given to William Man, burgess, and Janet Wedderburn his wife.

55. **1563.** March 20.—The lands of John Wedderburn on the Forfar Road mentioned.

56. **1563.** April 12.—Letter of tack (undated) by Lord Gray to Robert Rollok of Hiltoun of Wester Cragy reciting that " Forsamekle as Robert Rollok in Muirtoune hes payit to David Wathirburne, burgess of Dundy, and Helene Lasonne his spous," 1250 merkis to redeem one third of the lands of Cragy, sold by Lord Gray to the said David, therefore, etc.

57. **1565.** (*a*) Feb. 17.—Robert Wedderburn, a witness. (*b*) Feb. 18.—Sasine to Robert Man, son of William Man and Janet Wedderburn.

58. **1566.** April 20, June 29, Aug. 6.—Alexander Wedderburn, notary, acts as witness and procurator.

59. **1571.** Jan. 17.—James Wedderburn, burgess, witness.

60. **1571.** March 17.—An honourable man James Wedderburn, burgess, is named as occupying one acre of Cragy, and, with consent of Margaret Dundas, his wife, selling it to the Abbot of Kynlos. Alexander Wedderburn, elder, Patrick, his son, and Edward Wedderburn are witnesses.

61. **1571.** March 18.—James Wedderburn and Margaret Dundas, his wife, own 11 acres in Cragy.

62. **1571.** May 29.—Sasine to Christian Wischert, relict of John Wedderburn, burgess.

63. **1571.** Nov. 14.—Lands in the Eastfield of Dudope, sometime occupied by the late Henry Wedderburn, mentioned.

64. **1572.** May 5.—Land on the Forfar road, sometime occupied by John Wedderburn, mentioned.
[See also 5 dates :—1562, Aug. 16.   1565, Jan. 6 ; March 13, 24 ; Nov. 4.   1570, Sept. 16.   1571, Jan. 31 ; March 16, 30 ; May 20, 23 ; July 8, 17 ; Aug. 4, 15, 27 ; Nov. 22 ; Dec. 30.   1572, April 2 ; May 2, 6, 8, 12, 17 ; July 20.]

VOL. —.

Another of the unnumbered books.   It is that of Alexander Maxwell, notary, and covers
1555—1574.

65. **1555.** Nov. 5. –Thomas Wedderburn and David Wedderburn in Welgait, witnesses. (1.)

66. **1571.** May 28.—Sasine to Walter Haliburton, burgess, and Margaret Wedderburn, his wife, and George Haliburton, their eldest son, of lands in the barony of Auchtertyre, co. Forfar. Alexander Wedderburn is the notary. (41.)
[See also fol. 30 and 78]

VOL. —.

This is yet another unnumbered book, and is entitled, " Protocol book of Thomas Ireland, Not. Pub., 1567—1575.'

67. **1567.** May 5.—Sasine to Robert Wedderburn, younger, on resignation by Johnne Scrimgeoure of Dudhope, Constabill of Dundie, reciting that the constable has long since disponed to Robert Wedderburn the chaplainry of St. Johnne for his life, and now in warrandiee thereof dispones to him other lands, &c. Witnesses John Wedderburn, Alex^r Wedderburn, younger, and James Wedderburn. (6.)

68. **1567.** Nov. 4.—Discharge by Alexander Wedderburn, burgess of Dundee, with consent of Janet Myln, his spouse, to Henry Guthrie of Collestoun. (17.)

69. **1567.** (various dates).—Robert Wedderburn, younger, is often a witness. (22—23.)

70. **1568.** May 8.—Assignation by Gilbert Wedderburn, burgess of Dundie, "lauchfull sone and ——[2] of umquhill James Wedderburn, burges of the borough aforesaid," to Alexander Wedderburn, common clerk and burgess thereof, "of all maner of airschip guidis &c. pertaining to hym be ressone of the deceis of the said umquhill James his father " ...... until Gilbert repays Alexander a loan of £100 borrowed from him by Gilbert, who is now "to pas his wayage be schip furth of this realme to utheris pairtis and hes nocht presentlie in pois and in his hand of money to pay the said Alexander the sowme foirsaid." (31.)

71. **1568.** (? date.[2])—Between James Wedderburn and William, his brother. "James Wedderburn, burges of the burght " appears "in the renestrie of the paroche kirk " in the presence of his brother William, and, to satisfy a judgment pronounced against him, offers his said brother 200 merks, which William refuses to accept, whereon James protests, seeing that his brother "wes nather ydeot nor fooll," and William's wife, Margaret Rollok, also protests that William's said refusal shall not prejudice either her nor " hir bairnis lauchfullie gottin betwix the said William hir spous and hir." (32.)

72. **1568.** Aug. 7.—Robert Wedderburn, younger, chaplain of S. James' altar, gets from Janet Galloway two acres of land and a house. (44)   Aug. 10.--He is a witness. (45.)

73. **1569.** Jan. 18.—Letter of reversion in favour of James Wedderburn, burgess, and Margaret Dundas, his wife, upon the redemption of eleven acres in the Hiltoun of Cragy. Henry Wedderburn, burgess, witness. (45)

74. **1569.** Dec. 24.—Lands of Alexander Wedderburn and of the late John Wedderburn near the Forfar road mentioned. (46.)

75. **1569.** June 23.—Contract between Alexander Ouchterlowny and his wife, Cristiane Wedderburn, daughter of John Wedderburn, burgess, and the said John Wedderburn, whereby, on resignation of certain North Flukergait lands to him, John Wedderburn agrees to make the said spouses an annual payment. (48.)

76. **1568.** Oct. 30.—Robert Wedderburn, chaplain of St. James Major, resigns certain land to David Guthrie and Barbara Wedderburn, his wife (55) ; and Dec. 2, Janet Wedderburn, relict of William Man, renounces to them her interest therein. Edward and Robert Wedderburn, burgesses, witnesses. (60.)

---

[1] On two separate leaves, lying in this volume, but belonging clearly to some other record is the following:—Dundee, 2 Oct., 1690. Which day in the face of Counsell and in ane feuced court, the Magistratis and remanent members of Counsell of the said burgh, Deacon conviner and Deacones of crafts thereof after specified, electel for the year ensueing, subscryved the oath of alleidgance to ther Majesties King William and Queen Mary off the quhich oath the tenor follows Wee undersubscryvers do sincerelie promise and swer that we will be faithfull and bear true alleidgance to ther Majesties King William and Queen Mary. So help us God. Sic subscribitur Ja. Fletcher, provost, &c., &c., Alexander Wedderburne, Counsellor, &c. Then follows the oath of assurance, similarly signed.

[2] The word "heir" is erased in the record.

[3] It may be 14 Oct. 1569, some of the entries in the book being out of date.

77. **1570**. April 1.—Robert Wedderburn, younger, is witness to a sasine of land once that of the late David Wedderburn, in Skirlings Wynd. (72.)

78. **1569**. Aug. 6.—John Wedderburn, burgess, is bailie for Lord Torphichen. (81.)

79. **1570**. Nov. 14.—Robert Wedderburn, is witness to a charter by John Scrimgeour of Kirktoun of Erlistradichtie and Agnes Bruce. (102.)

80. **1571**. June 2.—Charter by Thomas Monorgund in favour of Alexander Wedderburn, clerk of Dundee, and Janet Myln, his wife, and David Wedderburn, their son, of an annual rent out of Monorgund's croft. (104.)

81. **1571**. Dec. 27.—Alexander Wedderburn, younger, named as being cautioner in a contract of 1565. (108.)

82. **1573**. March 30.—Robert Wedderburn, elder, and Robert Wedderburn, younger, resign their North Argylegait land (subject to the life-rent of Robert Wedderburn, elder) to Alexander Wedderburn, clerk of Dundee, for life, and to Robert Wedderburn, his son, heretably. This entry is headed, "Inter Alex. Wedderburn et Robertum eius fratrem germanum." (131—134.)

83. **1573**. May 4.—Discharge by Christian Wischart, relict of the late John Wedderburn, burgess, and her brother George Wischart, "armiger crucis Christianissimi regis Galliæ." (138.)
     [See in all fol. 3, 5-7, 17, 20, 22, 23, 26, 31-32, 35, 44-46, 48, 55, 60, 72-73, 80-81, 96-98, 102, 104, 108, 130-31, 138, 142, 146.]

Vol. 238.

This volume is entitled " Town Clerk's Protocol, 30 Nov. 1554—21 Aug. 1565."

On its first leaf is written "Liber Primus protocolorum Alexandri Wedderburn Scribæ civitatis burgi de Dunde." Below is the notarial symbol of Alexander Wedderburn, the old clerk, with his motto, "Deum time," and below this, the signatures "David Wedderburn," "Joannes Wedderburn."

84. **1556**. (a) Jan. 8.—The lands of Robert Wedderburn to the west of St. Matthew's close are mentioned. (6.) (b) Feb. 4.—David Wedderburn in Welgait, burgess, resigns an annual-rent. (7.)

85. **1558**. (a) July 6.—David Wedderburn, son and heir of the late Walter Wedderburn, resigns a South Welgnit tenement. (10.) (b) Robert Wedderburn, elder, burgess, is a witness. (11.)

86. **1558**. (a) Oct. 11.—John Wedderburn, burgess, is a witness. (15.) (b) Dec. 17.—Robert Wedderburn, elder, is a witness. (27.) (c) Dec. 18.—David Wedderburn, burgess, is tutor testamentar to the children of one William Merschell. (28.)

87. **1558**. Dec. 22.—Alexander Kid, burgess, settles certain lands in North Marketgate on himself and Isobell Wedderburn, his wife, and their issue. (31.)

88. **1558**. Dec. 24.—David Wedderburn in Murraygait, burgess, acknowledges that the marriage contract between his daughter Isobell Wedderburn and Alexander Kid has been implemented by A. Kid. William Wedderburn, burgess, is witness. (31.)

89. **1558**. (a) Jan. 4.—Sasine to David Wedderburn, son and heir of the late Walter Wedderburn, of premises in Tolbooth Wynd. (31.) (b) Jan. 9.—Lands of Robert Wedderburn, elder, in Murraygait mentioned. (34.)

90. **1558**. Jan. 18.—Elizabeth Carnegy, wife of Robert Fotheringham, is entered in a tenement in North Seagate as grand-daughter and heir of the late Margaret Wedderburn, wife of David Carnegy. (34.)

91. **1558**. Feb. 8.—Sasine to Alexander Wedderburn, elder, burgess, and Elizabeth Anderson, his wife, of three acres in the East-field of Dudope (of which two acres are south of those occupied by the heirs of the late Robert Wedderburn), sold to them by

Eufame Fowler, daughter and heiress of the late William Fowler, burgess, with consent of George Wedderburn her husband. Among the witnesses are David Wedderburn, burgess, and Alexander Wedderburn, notary. The signatures are as follows :—" Sie subscribitur George Wedderburn with my hand, Ewfame Fowlair with my hand at the pen led be the noter under-writtin beeaus I euld noeht wrytt my self." (37.)

92. **1558.** March 17.—The land of David Wedderburn in S. Murraygate mentioned. (41.)

93 **1558.** April 6.—David Wedderburn, son and heir of the late Walter Wedderburn, burgess, renounces an an annual rent out of the Tolbooth Wynd premises, described ante, No. 89a. (44.)

94. **1559.** May 13.—Sasine of one third of the lands of Lumlathin, given on preeept by David Betoun of Melgund and Margaret Lyndesay, his wife, to James Anderson and Grisell Wedderburn his wife. Alexander Wedderburn, notary, is a witness. (46.)

95. **1559.** June 4.—Compears personally, " ane honorable man David Wedderburn in Murraygaitt, burgess of Dundee, in his body hevelie weixit with infirmitie and yit as apperit havand perfyte knowledge and memorie, and now of eonseieuee and letter will declarit," that eertain sums are left to his seeond son William to eomplete his marriage contraet with Margaret Rollok, his wife; and on this James Wedderburn (his eldest son) asks instruments. (48.)

96. **1559.** Aug. 5.—Sasine on preeept by David Crawfurd, Earl Lyndesay, in favour of John Wedderburn, burgess of Dundee (son and heir of the late James Wedderburn, burgess of Dundee), and John Wedderburn, son of the said John and Agnes Hoppingrill, his wife, of one third of the lands of Curlungie, in the barony of Downy, eo. Forfar. (52.)

97. **1559.** Sept. 12.—David Wedderburn, son and heir of the late Walter Wedderburn, burgess, alienates to James Davidson a property in Skirlings Wynd. James and William Wedderburn are witnesses. (56.)

98. **1559.** Nov. 28.—John Wedderburn, bailie, apprentices to Thomas Ramsay, gold-smith, John, son of the late Gilbert Wedderburn, indweller in Leith. (60.)

99. **1560.** Jan. 10.—Sasine on resignation in favour of David Guthre and Barbara Wedderburn, his wife, of North Marketgate land. (65.)

100. **1560.** June 4.—Settlement by Mark Barrie, son and heir of the late Wm. Barrie, on himself aud Magdalen Wedderburn, his wife. John Wedderburn, bailie, is a witness. (74.)

101. **1560.** June 27.—Robert Wedderburn, elder, in North Argylegate, named. (79.)

102. **1560.** July 18.—Robert Lovell, elder, and his wife, Margaret Wedderburn, settle land on their son, Robert. (80).

103. **1560.** Aug. 18.—Mark Barrie and Magdalen Wedderburn, his wife, get sasine of au annual rent. (83.)

104. **1560.** Aug. 28. —Robert Wedderburn, elder, witness. (85-86.)

105. **1560.** Oct. 27.—Robert Wedderburn is entered in an annual-rent as son and heir of the late David Wedderburn, in Welgait. John Wedderburn, elder, is a witness. (95).

106. **1560.** Nov. 12.—Isobell Lovell, wife of David Cant, burgess, and her natural sons, Robert and David Wedderburn, get sasine from Alexander Maxwell of Tealing, of one-third of Balkello. (96.)

107. **1560.** Feb. 16.—The North Seagate land of the late David Wedderburn, burgess, and the North Murraygate land of the late Henry Wedderburn are mentioned. (103.)

108. **1560** March 3.—South Flukergate land, bounded by that of Alexander Wedderburn, is mentioned in a sasine, witnessed by Peter Wedderburn. (111.)

109. **1560.** March 3.—Sasine to John Anderson of a South Flukergait land, bounded on the east by that of Elizabeth Wedderburn. Patrick Wedderburn is a witness. (112.)

110. **1560.** March 17.—Sasine of certain premises is given to Grissell Wedderburn, wife of John Anderson, son and heir of James Anderson who resigns the same. John Anderson is described as "a prudent young man." (113.)

> This entry raises a difficulty. A Grisell Wedderburn married James Anderson (see ante No. 94), and they are both buried in the Howff of Dundee. According to the inscription on their tombstone James Anderson would at this date be forty-nine years of age, and hardly therefore a young man. They had a son James, named in a charter under the Great Seal, confirmed 12 Dec. 1539. There is no record of any Grissell Wedderburn having married a John Anderson, and there must, I think, be some error of names in this entry. See post No. 200, where another difficulty arises in regard to the same persons.

111. **1561.** March 26.—Margaret Wedderburn (daughter and one of the heirs of the late Henry Wedderburn), wife of Thomas Davidson, gets sasine of an annual rent. (113.)

112. **1562** Nov. 24.—(a) David Guthre and Barbara Wedderburn, his wife, resign an annual rent. (151.) (b) They get sasine of another annual rent from Mark Barre and Magdalen Wedderburn his wife. (ib.)

113. **1563.** Oct. 26.—John Coustoun settles some North Seagate property on himself and Elizabeth Wedderburn, his wife, and their son William (181.)

114. **1563-64.** (a) Dec. 11.—Lands in North Argylegate of Robert Wedderburn, elder. (187.) (b) Jan. 24.—The same lands are mentioned again. (189.)

115. **1564.** April 26.—Alexander Wedderburn, notary, and Robert Wedderburn, his brother, witness a charter, sasine on which is given before James and Archibald Wedderburn, witnesses. (202.)

116. **1564** April 28.—Thomas Nicholl (son and heir of the late Thomas Nicholl and Janet Wedderburn, his relict) resigns a North Murraygate property. (203.)

117. **1564.** May 29.—Mark Barrie makes a settlement on William Barrie, lawful son to himself and Magdalen Wedderburn, his wife. James Wedderburn, burgess, is witness. (209.)

118. **1564.** July 3.—Robert Wedderburn, younger, witnesses a resignation. (213.)

119. **1564.** Oct. 31.—Resignation by Thomas Nicoll, son and heir of the late Thomas Nicoll, with consent of Jonet Wedderburn, his mother, of a North Cowgate land. (224.)

120. **1564.** Nov. 13.—David Guthrie, burgess, and Barbara Wedderburn, his wife, give a receipt and discharge (224), and also settle land on David Guthrie, their son. (ib.)

121. **1565.** (a) May 23.—James Wedderburn, witness. (242.) (b) June 1.—Archibald Wedderburn, Edward Wedderburn, and others are witnesses. (243.) (c) July 20.—Elizabeth Wedderburn in North Argylegate named. (249.) (d) Aug. 19.—John Wedderburn in North Marketgate named. (251.)

122. **1565.** Aug. 21.—Mark Barrie and Magdalen Wedderburn, his wife, resign to John Coustoun and Elizabeth Wedderburn, his wife, their South Ergadie Street land. (252.)

[The following is a list of all the folios in this volume in which there are references to Wedderburns : Fol. 2, 5, 6-8, 10, 11, 15, 18, 27, 28, 31, 34, 37, 41, 42, 44, 46, 48, 52, 54, 56-60, 64-66, 69-70, 74, 76, 79-80, 83, 85-87, 92, 93, 95, 96, 99, 103, 111-14, 119-21, 125, 129, 135, 138, 140, 145, 148, 151, 153-55, 161, 163, 165, 167-68, 171-72, 181, 185-89, 191-92, 197, 199, 202-206, 209, 211-13, 224, 228, 230,. 234, 242-43, 246, 249, 251-52.]

Vol. 239.

Entitled " Protocol Book 20 Feb. 1562—26 Oct. 1567."

This is the book of " Harbertus Gledstanys, notarius," who signs the entries.

123. **1563.** July 19.—Sasine on assedation by Isobell Dykesoun, relict of Gilbert Wedderburn, and John Brown, her spouse, in favour of David Cockburn, of an acre known as the Vicar's croft. (14.)

124. **1565.** Oct. 3.—Helen Wedderburn, relict of Thomas Duncan, burgess, and John Duncan, their son, grant a discharge. (67.)

125. **1566.** Feb. 22.—Janet Mylne, wife of Alexander Wedderburn, younger, is entered heir to the late James Mylne, her father, in a South Seagate land (86), which she resigns to John Hog, who gives sasine thereof to the said A. Wedderburn, herself and their heirs. (87.)

126. **1566.** May 28.—John Hamiltoun, vicar of Dundee, gives sasine of the acre known as the Vicar's croft (see above No. 123), to Henry Wedderburn, son and heir of the late Gilbert Wedderburn, indweller in Leith. Alexander Wedderburn, younger, Robert Wedderburn, &c., are witnesses. (103.) The said Henry Wedderburn then confirms it to David Cockburn. (104.)

127. **1566.** June 6.—Robert Lovell, elder, obliges his eldest son, John Lovell, then a minor, within the years of curatory, to infeft Margaret Wedderburn, mother to the said John, in the life-rent of one-third, and Robert Lovell, brother of the said John, in the half of the fee of the lands of Ballyndoch. (106-7.)

[See, for all the Wedderburn references in this volume, fol. 3, 14, 15, 23, 66-67, 83, 86, 87, 89, 102, 104, 106, 107, 111-14, 116, 124, 126-32, 150, 152-59, 163, 169, 173-78.]

Vol. 240.

Entitled " Town Clerk's Protocol, 21 Aug. 1565—11 May 1570."

On front leaf is " Liber Secundus protocolorum Alexandri Wedderburn scribæ civitatis burgi de Dundie."

128. **1565.** Aug. 21.—Mark Barrie is entered as son and heir of William Barry in two annual rents, which he settles on Magdalen Wedderburn, his wife. (1.)

129. **1565.** Oct. 3.—Sasine by the Town Council in favour of Helen Wedderburn, relict of Thomas Duncan, of an annual rent. (2.)

130. **1566.** (a) Feb. 23.—Edward Wedderburn, burgess, witness. (13.) (b) June 17.—James Wedderburn, burgess, witness. (23.)

131. **1566.** Sept. 27.—Alexander Wedderburn, younger, is entered in a tenement in Skirlings Wynd, as brother and heir of the late Robert Wedderburn, son and heir of the late David Wedderburn in Welgait. (33.)

132. **1566.** Oct. 7.—James Wedderburn, bailie of Dundee, enters Robert Wedderburn, as son and heir of the late Robert Wedderburn, younger, and the late Elizabeth Scrymgeour, his wife, in a South Argylegate land. John Wedderburn is witness. (33.)

133. **1566.** Nov. 12.—Elizabeth Wedderburn, relict of Patrick Lyoun, resigns land in favour of James Lovell, her son. (36).

134. **1566.** Nov. 19.—Matthew Wedderburn, witness. James Wedderburn, bailie. (36-40.)

135. **1567.** Feb. 26.—Sasine on resignation by David Cant, son and heir of the late Thomas Cant, to his wife Isobell Lovell, and to David Wedderburn, her son by the late Mr. Robert Wedderburn, with consent of John Wedderburn, curator to the said David Wedderburn. (42.)

2 E

136. **1567.** July 11.—Isobell Lovell, with assent of David Cant, her spouse, gets the liferent, and her son, David Wedderburn, the fee of one third of Balkello from Alexander Maxwell of Tealing. (53.)

137. **1567.** Aug. 16.—The land of the heirs of the late John Wedderburn is named as the South boundary of some North Marketgate land. (55.)

138. **1567.** Aug. 20.—Edward Wedderburn is a witness. (55.)

139. **1567.** Nov. 23.—Sasine in favour of John Coustoun, burgess, and Elizabeth Wedderburn his wife. (62.)

140. **1568.** April 2—Robert Wedderburn, chaplain of St. James Minor, grants a precept of clare constat to Herbert Stewart as son and heir of the late James Stewart. (66.)

141. **1568.** (*a*) April 14.—David Wedderburn witnesses a sasine, mentioning the lands of John Wedderburn, south of South Argylegate. (66.) (*b*) Aug. 2. Sept. 14, Oct. 19.— David Wedderburn is again witne·s (70-71-74.) (*c*) July 10.—James Wedderburn, burgess, witness. (69.) (*d*) July 21.—Edward Wedderburn, witness. (70.) (*e*) Aug. 11.—Robert Wedderburn's land in North Argylegate mentioned. (70.) (*f*) Oct. 3.—John Wedderburn is one of the signatories to a town's charter in favour of George Spens. Alexander Wedderburn, notary. (73.)

142. **1569.** (*a*) April 29, May 21.—John Coustoun and Elizabeth Wedderburn, named. (82, 84.) (*b*) May 28.—James Wedderburn, deceased, in North Seagate, named. (85). (*c*) June 2.— Robert Wedderburn, in North Seagate, named. James Wedderburn, a witness. (85).

143. **1569.** June 8.—John Wedderburn, burgess, resigns his land on the West of the cemetery to Christian Wedderburn and Alexander Ouchterlony, her spouse. David Wedderburn, witness. (86.)

144. **1569.** June 30.—Resignation by Alexander Kyd and Isobell Wedderburn, his wife, to James Carmichael. (87.)

145. **1569.** Sept. 26.—Robert Wedderburn. elder, burgess of Dundee, resigns his N. Murraygate land to David Ogilvy, with a N. Argylegate tenement in warrandice. (91.)

146. **1569.** Dec. 9—James Wedderburn, a witness. (95.)

147. **1570.** March 17.—Janet Wedderburn, relict of Thomas Nichol, shipmaster, burgess, appoints tutors to her son. David Wedderburn, witness. (100.)

148. **1570.** April 29.—Patrick Wedderburn, burgess, witness. (105.)

[See, in all, for the above and other Wedderburn references, fol. 1·4, 7, 13, 14, 16, 18, 23, 28, 31, 33, 34, 36-40, 42-43, 45, 53, 55-56, 58, 62, 66-71, 73-74, 77-82, 84-88, 90-96, 99, 100, 104, 105.]

Vol. 241.

Entitled " Town Clerk's Protocol 1568—28 Feb. 1576-77.[1]

149. **1568.** April 20.—Heling Lawsone, relict of umquhill David Wedderburn, burgess, and Mark Barrie, her son-in-law, with Magdalene Wedderburn, his wife, compear, and the Barries discharge the said Helen of all sums due to Magdalene for tocher or bairnis pairt of guid, except a sum of 100 merks which Heling Lawsone ordains to be paid by James Wedderburn, her executor. (41.)

150. **1570.** June 10.—Mark Barrie and Magdalen Wedderburn, his wife, resign an annual rent to John Coustoun and Elizabeth Wedderburn, his wife. (77.)

[1] The entries in this book are not in order of date.

151. **1570.** Dec. 2.—Helen Wedderburn, relict of Thomas Duncane, makes her latter will in favour of her children, John Duncane, William Duncane, and Janet Duncane, wife of Olifer Lindsay. David Wedderburn is a witness. (83)

152. **1570.** April 26 —Richard Thane, burgess of Dundee, resigns an annual-rent in favour of Isobell Lovell, wife of David Trael (error for Cant), for life, and Robert Wedderburn, her natural son, heritably. (86.)

 See also Minute Book I., s.d. 1572, May 24, and 1573, Jan. 28, where Isobell Lovell and her sons, Robert and David Wedderburn, acknowledge the receipt of £100 from Richard Thane of Logy in redemption of this annual rent.

153. **1571.** (*a*) Nov. 7.—John Wedderburn, David Wedderburn, and Alexander Wedderburn, notary, are witnesses to a charter. (139.)[1] (*b*) June 26.—Sasine to Walter Haliburton, burgess, and Margaret Wedderburn, his wife, of a South Argylegate tenement. (155.) (*c*) July 6.—James Wedderburn, bailie, present. (156—66, 183.) (*d*) June 9.—David Wedderburn, elder, witness. (162.)

154. **1570.** Sept. 6.—Robert Wedderburn is acknowledged son and heir of the late David Wedderburn in Welgait. (201.)

155. **1572.** March 26.—John Duncan requires William Duncan, his brother, and Olifer Lyndsay, to produce, if they have it, the will made by Helen Wedderburne, mother of the said John and William, some year and half ago, but it is not forthcoming. (212.)

156. **1572.** May 7.—Alex. Oehterlony, burgess, acknowledges the receipt from James Forrester, one of the administrators of the bairnis of umquhill John Wedderburn, of 120 merks belonging to Grisild Wedderburn, daughter to the said John. (Min. Book I, s.d.)

157. **1572.** May 15, 23, 24.—John Wedderburn, witness. (*ib.* s.d.)

158. **1572.** June 2.—Alexander Oehterlony acknowledges the receipt from James Forrester of £65, money disponit to Grisild Wedderburn, dochter lauchfull of umquhill John Wedderburn, be Christian Wisehart, hir modir-in-law. (*ib.* s d.)

159. **1572.** Aug. 28.—Robert Wedderburn, son and heir of the late Robert Wedderburn, and grandson and heir of the late James Wedderburn, burgess, resigns to Edward Wedderburn, his South Murraygate land. (231.)

160. **1573.** Feb. 12.—Janet Logan, relict of James Wedderburn, elder, burgess, resigns to Edward Wedderburn her life rent in the said South Murraygate land. (219.)

161. **1573.** July 23.—Alexander Wedderburn elder, burgess, resigns to a "prudent youth," Patrick Wedderburn his son, a Skirling's Wynd land, subject to the life rent of himself and Isobell Anderson, his wife. (256.)

162. **1574.** March 17.—Edward Wedderburn settles the South Murraygate land (mentioned ante Nos. 159-60), on himself and Janet Inglis, his wife. (289.)

163. **1574.** Sept. 24.—John Turing, burgess, settles a tenement in the Cowgate on James Turing, his son and heir, and Elizabeth Wedderburn, his wife. Patrick Wedderburn is a witness. (290.)

164. **1574.** (undated.)—There are two Latin lines signed "ex chirographo Joannis Wedderburn" at the foot of fol. 292.

 [1] The figure 0 is now often inserted between the first and second figures of the pagination, but is omitted in the references given here.

Dundee Protocol Books. 165. **1574.** (a) July 20 —Alexander Kyd and Isobell Wedderburn, his wife, resign certain North Murmygate and (Aug. 11) North Marketgate property. (304-5.) (b) Aug. 28.— John Wedderburn is a witness, as often in this volume. (311.) Sometimes he is designed "John Wedderburn, younger." (351.) (c) Nov. 10.—Alexander Wedderburn, elder, and Isobell Anderson, his wife, acquire an annual rent. (357.)

166. **1573.** July 22.—Three acres in the Eastfield of Dudhope, bounded on the north by those occupied by the heirs of the late Robert Wedderburn, are settled by Eufame, daughter of the late William Fowlair, on Alexander Wedderburn, elder, and Isobell Anderson, his wife, for life, and on their son Richard, burgess of Elsinore in Denmark, in fee. Patrick Wedderburn is attorney for Richard. (359.)

167. **1573.** Nov 7.—John Lovell, second son of Robert Lovell, and Margaret Wedderburn, his wife, get sasine of a South Marketgate land. (367.)

168. **1573.** Dec. 17.—Janet Wedderburn, relict of umquhill James Retry or Thomson, and her two children, James and Margaret, with consent of Alexander Wedderburn, clerk, &c., their curators, grant a discharge to Alexander Boyter, their father's executor. (Min. Book II, s d)

169. **1574.** (a) Feb. 22, March 18, March 27.— Edward Wedderburn, with consent of Janet Inglis, his wife, resigns premises in Dundee. (Min. Book II, s.d.) (b) March 27.— Alexander Wedderburn, elder, guarantees that his son, Richard Wedderburn, burgess in Elsignoir, shall deliver 55 dollars to Robert Wedderburn, younger, on his arrival there. (ib. s.d.)

170. **1575.** Sept. 2.—Peter Wedderburn, counsellor and burgess, acquires a 38 years' lease of the Dominican friar's garden. (367.)

171. **1576.** July 2.—John Wedderburn is a witness. (377.)

172. **1576.** May 5.—Alexander Wedderburn is entered in an @ rent as brother and heir of the late Robert Wedderburn, younger, heir of the late David Wedderburn in Welgait. (378.)

173. **1576.** May 17.—Janet, daughter of John Duncan, and Patrick Wedderburn, her spouse future, renounce all goods she might claim at her father's death in consideration of a "tocher" now promised to Patrick. (Min. Book III, s d.)

174. **1575.** Aug. 2.—Alexander Wedderburn, younger, is entered in a Welgait tenement as brother and heir of Robert Wedderburn. (405)

175. **1573.** May 7.—Alexander Wedderburn, younger, is entered in Skirling's Wynd as brother and heir of Robert Wedderburn, son and heir of the late David Wedderburn in Welgait. (428.)

[See, in all, fol. 3, 31, 41. 48, 65, 78-83, 86, 124-32, 137, 139, 142, 144, 146, 150, 152, 155, 156, 160-62, 166, 173-78, 180-84, 188, 196, 200, 201, 205, 207, 211, 212, 214, 217, 222, 227 29, 231, 233-39, 249, 256-57, 269, 275-76, 289-90, 292, 269, 304-7, 311, 316-17, 328, 331, 339, 341-43, 346-47, 350-51, 353-54, 356-57, 359, 265, 367, 368, 372-73, 377-78, 380-81, 387, 392, 398-99, 400, 402, 405-6, 414, 415, 419, 422, 423, 428, 431, 437-39, 440, 449, 452]

VOL 242.

Entitled " Town Clerk's Protocol, 11 May. 1570—3 Nov. 1577."

On the first leaf is twice written in Latin, " Third Book of the Protocols of Alexander Wedderburn, clerk of Dundee."

176. **1570.** (a) May 18.—John Wedderburn, servitor to Alexander Wedderburn, notary, witness. (4.) (b) May 24.—David Wedderburn, servitor to Alexander Wedderburn, notary, witness. (4.)

177. **1570.** July 4.—James Wedderburn, younger, son and heir of the late John Wedderburn, is entered as such in the said John's burghal land in North Marketgate. (7.)

178. **1570.** July 11.—Alexander Wedderburn younger settles his Welgait land on him- Dundee self and Christian Ferny his wife and their heirs. (8.) Protocol Books.

179. **1571.** April 6.—Robert Wedderburn, son and heir of the late David Wedderburn in Welgait, is entered as such in one third of the said David's land in Welgait. (20.)

180. **1572.** Jan. 6.—Alexander Wedderburn, younger, burgess, resigns the tenement (mentioned ante No. 179) to Robert Wedderburn, his brother german. (64.)

181. **1573.** April 24.—Alexander Wedderburn, younger, "brodir and appearand air of umquhill Robert Wedderburn," acknowledges the receipt from John Watson in Innergourie of all the "evidentis" delivered to him be the said Robert. (Min. Book II, s.d.)

182. **1573.** June 9.—James Thomson makes a testamentary settlement of his property on his wife Janet Wedderburn and their children. (ib. II, s.d.)

183. **1573.** July 18.—The South Argylegate land once that of James Wedderburn, now that of his grandson Robert Wedderburn, is resigned by the latter to Peter Wedderburn, son lawful to Robert Wedderburn, elder, burgess. (89.)

184. **1573.** Dec. 17.—Comperit Janet Wedderburn, relict of umquhill James Retry alias Thomson, James Retry, his son, and Margaret Retry, his dochter, with consent of Alexander Wedderburn, clerk, and others, and grant a discharge. (Min. Book II, s.d.)

185. **1574.** (a) July 13.—Peter Wedderburn, witness. (141.) (b) Aug. 26.—John Wedderburn, scriba, witness; and again 27 May, 1577. (145, 235.) (c) Dec. 23.—John Wedderburn, son and heir of the late John Wedderburn, burgess, and James Forrester, his curator, give a discharge. (157.)

186. **1575.** July 27.—Patrick Wedderburn, brother german of Richard Wedderburn, burgess in Elsinore, Denmark, gives a discharge as attorney for his said brother. Matthew Wedderburn, witness.

187. **1576.** Feb. 25.—Edward Wedderburn and Janet Inglis, his wife, resign a tenement to John Ker. (223.)

188. **1577.** April 26.—John Wedderburn is a witness. (230.)

189. **1577.** Sept. 2.—Alexander Wedderburn, son and heir of the late David Wedderburn, with consent of Christian Ferny, his wife, and Elizabeth Strathouchin, relict of the said David, and William Lochmalony, now her spouse, resigns a Welgait land to Alexander Butchert (237-38.)

[See, in all, fol. 3, 4, 7-9, 13-18. 20, 23, 24, 26, 28, 32. 40, 41. 44, 45, 48, 51, 55, 57, 58, 62, 64, 67, 68, 70, 72, 82, 89, 91, 94, 99, 100, 102, 103, 105, 109, 111, 112, 121, 136, 141, 144, 145, 155, 157, 162, 170, 176, 178, 188, 193, 193, 207, 215, 216, 218, 223, 224, 230, 234, 235, 237, 238, 239. 241, 242.]

Vol. 243.

Entitled " First Protocol Book of Robert Wedderburn, N.P., from 30 March 1575—16 Nov. 1576."

Outside on the cover is "R. Wedderburn 1574," while inside it are various mottoes and quotations : such as " Temperantia prorogat annos," " Dies diem docet," " Vive ut Vivas :"—" Si bene quid facias, facias citò : uam citò factum Gratum erit, ingratum gratia tarda facit ; " and again, " Gratia quæ tarda est, ingrata est gratia namque Cum fieri properat, gratia grata magis." " Qui cito dat bis dat, qui tardat munera, nil dat." There is also a quotation from Lucan (LI, 1.) " Tolle mores, semper nocuit differre paratis," and a legal precept, " Nocte dieque leges si via addiscere leges." The favourite motto of the writer, and one which occurs in all his books, " patior ut potiar " ("through suffering, strength ") is twice written here.

190. **1574.** March 3.--At Edinburgh. Admission of Robert Wedderburn as notary. It recites that "comperit personale Robert Wedderburn, burgess of Dundee, quhair he was born within the diocie of Brechinen, of the age of twenty aucht yeiris or thairby unmaryit " . . . and that he "hes maid daylie serûice to Alex.

Guthre, commone clerk of Edinburgh, be the space of thre yeris and to Alexander
Wedderburne, commone clerk of Dundee, be the space of sevin yeres . . . and that
he is of sufficient qualification . . . to be ane notar public." Whereupon he is
examined by the Lords of Session and duly admitted. His notarial symbol with the
mottoes "Bona fide" and "Nihil tam occulte quod non revelabitur" is then
appended. (1.)

191. **1575.** (a) April 9.—A transaction takes place in the house of Cristina Wischart,
relict of the late John Wedderburn, burgess, before Alexander Wedderburn, the
clerk, Alexander Wedderburn, younger, and John Wedderburn. (6.)   (b) April 16.—
John Wedderburn is often witness with Alexander Wedderburn, younger, from this
date till 10 Aug. 1576. (7, 9, 10, 11, 67, 69.)   (c) July 3.—Peter Wedderburn,
burgess, witness. (18.)

192. **1576** (a) June 14.—Sasine in implement of the contract of marriage (1575)
between William Kynloch, surgeon, and Cristina Guthre, daughter of Barbara
Wedderburn. (57.)   (b) Sept. 22.—Patrick Wedderburn, witness (77.)

[See, in all, fol. 1, 2, 6, 7, 9, 10, 11, 12, 15, 18, 20, 31, 40, 43, 55, 57, 61, 67-69, 77.]

Vol. 244.

Entitled " Town Clerk's Protocol, 4 Oct. 1577—24 April 1579."

The first two leaves are imperfect.

193. **1578.** Nov. 4.—Agreement between Peter Wedderburn, burgess, and Robert
Kynloch, anent the Black Friar's yard. (63.)

194. **1579.** March 4.—Alexander Wedderburn, younger, merchant, burgess of Dundee,
joins in a protest. (65.)

195. **1580.** June 1.—The Council order preparation to be made for the King's visit and
"Petir Wedderburn, ane of thair counsel, to beir thair handseynzie." (100.)

196. **1580.** July 1.—Decree v. Alexander Mathow for "mispresoning and blaspheming
Robert Wedderburn alledgeand and sayand that he had maid and gewine ane
instrument to Robert Rollok quhilk wes fals." (100.)

197. **1581.** (a) Feb. 2.—Bond to Jonet Inglis, relict of Edward Wedderburn. (109.)
(b) Sept. 14.—Obligation by Robert Wedderburn, merchant. Alexander and David
Wedderburn, witnesses. (110.) (c) Nov. 10.—Bond by Elizabeth Low, relict of
James Reit, and Patrick Wedderburn, now her spouse. (148.)

198. **1581.** Feb. 24.—Complaint by John Coustoun and Elizabeth Wedderburn, his wife,
that Magdalene Wedderburn, relict of Mark Barrie, and life-rentrix of a North
Marketgate tenement, alienated by M. Barrie to the Coustouns, does not keep the
said tenement in repair. The provost and bailies decree in favour of the complainer,
and grant a mandatory injunction. (157.)

199. **1581.** April 6.—Bond in favour of Robert Wedderburn, merchant, burgess, and
Eufame Coustoun, his wife. (161.)

200. **1582.** March 11.—Margaret Anderson, as executrix, proves the will of the late
Grisild Wedderburn, relict of James Anderson, burgess of Dundee. (164.)
The word "relict" creates a difficulty, as according to the tomb in the Howff, James Anderson
survived her, dying in 1584, whereas she died 1572. See also ante No. 110 note.

201. **1578.** Aug. 27.—Discharge by John Cathro and Kathrene Lovell, his wife, to his
father-in-law, Robert Lovell, elder, and Margaret Wedderburn, his wife. (167.)

[See, in all, fol. 3, 5, 10, 28, 34, 39, 43, 50-52, 54, 56, 60, 63, 65, 70, 74, 77, 83, 95, 99, 100, 102,
109-10, 148, 155, 157, 161, 162, 167, 186, 189, 193, 194, 199.]

VOL. 245.

Entitled " Second Protocol Book of Robert Wedderburn N.P., brother of the first Alexander Wedderburn,
town clerk, from 20 Nov., 1576 to 18 June, 1580."

Various quotations and mottoes again, as in the case of Vol. 243, appear on the first leaves of the
book. They include the following :—

Da tua dum tua sunt, post mortem tunc tua uon sunt.

Quod fors fert fereudum est.

Doce me Domine viam tuam et ingrediar in veritate tua (Ps. 86).

Vine diu, sed vive Deo nam viuere mundo Mortis opus, vera est viuere vita Deo.

Bonum est habere bonum nomen.

The quotations include some from Ovid, Claudian, Cicero, Plato (in Latin, as quoted by Cicero),
Macrinus, Plutarch, and the Vulgate (Ps. 24 and 37 ; i. Thess ; 5 ; i. Tim., 4.)

On the fourth leaf is an English quotation as follows :—" Inwy is ane certane tre quha rute is
malice and illwill, quha branchis is ire and haitrent, quhais flowris is mocking and divysioun, quhais
fruit is detractioun and dissentioun, quha laiffis is pailnes and ...." (unfinished).

On the leaf facing the first sasine is " Adspirat coeptis Jesus."

202. (a) **1576.** Jan. 5, 12.—John Wedderburn and Patrick Wedderburn, witnesses. (6.)
(b) **1577.** May 25.—John Wedderburn and Alexander Wedderburn, witnesses. (13.)
(c) **1577.** Sept 9.—James Wedderburn, witness. (20.)

203. **1579.** Sept. 9.—Alexander Wedderburn, son and heir of the late David Wedderburn, burgess, resigns his Skirling's Wynd tenement to Robert Kynloch and his wife.
(83, 84.)

204. **1580.** April 20.—Sasine on charter by Alexander Maxwell of Tealing in favour of
Robert Wedderburn, merchant (son and heir of the late Mr. Robert Wedderburn) and
Eufame Coustoun, his wife, of an annual-rent of 105 merks out of the lands of Balkello,
&c. in consideration of 1000 merks paid to Maxwell by the grantees. Among the
witnesses are Alexander Wedderburn, son of the late David Wedderburn, John
Wedderburn, "mauta," and Robert Wedderburn, notary. (108.)

205. **1580.** May 19.—Will of Isobell Lovell, wife of David Cant, burgess, and mother of
Robert Wedderburn, merchant, given up by her, whereby "of her awin fre motyve
and for the lufe and fauour scho hes and beris to hir oy Elizabeth Wedderburn
doichter lauchfull of Robert Wedderburn hir sone," she appoints Elizabeth her
executrix, and leaves her all her " geir, plenishing, jowellis and gold," and further, at
the request of his mother, Robert binds himself to give Elizabeth v^o merkis " at her
perfitt aige," provided she marry with his consent. (113.)

At the end of this book a good deal has been written, much of which is now illegible, though
some is still decipherable as follows :—

(1.) " The maist peralus and dangerus dayis in the yeir, in the quhilk gif ony man or voman
be lett bluid of vound or of vair thai sall die within xxxj dayis following Or quha that fallis in
seikness in ony of the dayis following thai sall nocht excaip deid Or quha that takis ony grit
journay in ony of the said dayis to ga far fra hame he sall be in grit dangar or die ere he cum
hame agane Or quha that weddis aue wyfe in ony of thir dayis haistellie thai sall depart or sall leif
togidder with mekill sorrow Or quha that begynnis in any of thir dayis ony grit vark it sall nevir cum
to ane guid end. And thir be dayis following :—

In Januar ar 8 dayis that is to say the 1, 2, 4, 5, 10, 15, 17, 19.

In Februar ar 3 dayis the 8, 10, 17.

In Marche ar 3 dayis the 6, 15, 19.

In Apryle ar 2 dayis the 16. 21.

In Maii ar 3 dayis the 7, 15, 20.

In Junii ar 2 dayis the 4, 7.

In Julii ar 2 dayis the 15, 19.

In August ar 2 dayis the 19, 20.

In September ar 2 dayis the ..., 7.

In October is ane day 6.

In November ar 2 dayis the 15, 19.

In December ar 3 dayis the 6, 7, 17 et alii dicunt the 15, 16.

(2) The following lines:—

Is it nocht aue common cais,
Ane aip to haif ane austern face,
Ane owll to be noysum in the nycht,
Ane falcone to be fair of flicht,
Ane burgeas barne to be nedie,
Ane muirland man to be spedie, &c., &c.

[See, in all, fol. 6, 11, 18, 19-22, 27, 34, 35, 39, 64, 68-9, 83-84, 89, 91, 98, 104. 108, 113, 116.]

VOL. 246.

"*Fourth Protocol Book of Alexander Wedderburn, town clerk, from 8 Nov. 1577—30 Oct. 1581.*"
This is also written in Latin on the second leaf.

206.   **1577.** (*a*) Nov. 18.—Sasine of a tenement in favour of Peter Wedderburn and Margaret Kynloche, his wife. (3.)   (*b*) Nov. 26.—Peter Wedderburn, burgess, often a witness. (5-92.)

207.   **1578.** (*a*) March 10.—Sasine of an @-rent in favour of Alexander Wedderburn, younger, son and heir of the late David Wedderburn. in Welgate, burgess. (18.)   (*b*) March 14.—Patrick Wedderburn, burgess, witness. (19, 50, 53, 92.)   (*c*) May 19.—Isobell Wedderburn and Alexander Kyd, her husband, resign a North Marketgate tenement. (30.)

208.   **1578.** June 21.—Sasine of Patrick Wedderburn's eastle-hill lands in Skirling's Wynd, near those of Alexander Wedderburn, elder, is given to Elizabeth Low, relict of James Rait and spouse future of the said Patrick. (34.)

209.   **1578.** Aug. 11.—Sept. 25.—Sasines of @-rents in favour of Alexander Wedderburn, younger, son and heir of the late David Wedderburn, in Welgait, burgess (40-42), and Christine Fernye, wife of the said Alexander. (44-45.)

210.   **1579.** June 2.—Sasine of an @-rent in favour of Jonet Inglis, relict of Edward Wedderburn, burgess, in life-rent, and his daughters, Katrene, Eufame, and Elizabeth Wedderburn, in fee. (76.)

211.   **1579.** Oct. 17.—John Wedderburn's lands in South Argylegate, named. (97.)

212.   **1580.** (*a*) Feb. 3.—James Wedderburn deceased, in North Seagate, named. (114, 146.)   (*b*) Feb. 12.—Peter Wedderburn, burgess, and Margaret Kynloch, his wife, resign an @-rent. (116.)   (*c*) May 18.—John Wedderburn, burgess, witness. (131.)   (*d*) July 28.—Matthew Wedderburn, witness. (140.)

213.   **1581.** (*a*) Jan. 31.—Sasine in favour of Peter Wedderburn, burgess, and Margaret Kynloch, his spouse. (170.)   (*b*) Feb. 29.—Barbora Wedderburn and Peter Imbrie, her spouse, get a North Marketgate house. (174.)   (*c*) March 2.—The North Marketgate land of the heirs of the late John Wedderburn, burgess, named. (175).   (*d*) May 22.—Isobell Wedderburn, wife of Alexander Kyd, resigns her life-rent in certain lands in favour of her son, Alexander. (189).   (*e*) Aug. 31.—Alexander Wedderburn, David Wedderburn, and Robert Wedderburn, are often witnesses to charters, &c. (204, 208-210, 215.)   (*f*) Sept. 20.—Matthew Wedderburn, mariner, witness. (213-14.)

[See also fol.3.5, 8, 18, 19, 29-30, 34, 37, 38, 40, 42, 44, 45, 50, 53, 54, 62, 68, 76, 78, 80, 81, 84-87, 92, 95, 97, 108, 111, 114, 116, 118, 123, 127, 131, 137, 140, 143, 145-147, 153, 157, 160, 165, 167, 169, 171, 174, 175, 180, 183, 185, 188-89, 191, 194-95, 204, 207-216.

VOL. 247.

Entitled "Third Protocol Book of Robert Wedderburn notary public from 8 July 1580—24 April 1585."

On the first four leaves are written a great many Latin maxims and quotations, such as "Deterior animi morbus est quam corporis," "Accepta memineris, data obliuiscere," "Longior vita longior labor," "Id velis quod poesis," "Oculus index animi," "Nemo sibi nascitur."

214.   **1580-81.** (various dates.)—Alexander Wedderburn, clerk and notary, and Mr. Alexander Wedderburn, are named as witnesses, &c. (3, 24, 25, 26, 28, 53.)

215.   **1582.** (*a*) June 2.—Discharge by Robert Wedderburn, merchant, burgess, to James Scrymgeour of Dudope. (58.)   (*b*) Sept. 18.—Land in Skirling's Wynd, belonging to the heirs of the late David Wedderburn, mentioned. (68—9.)   (*c*) Nov. 10.—Alexander Wedderburn, elder, witness, (73.)

216. **1582.** Nov. 24.—Alexander Wedderburn, clerk of Dundee, settles five acres of land in Dundee, on Helen Ramsay, daughter of Alexander Ramsay, and spouse future to his son and heir apparent, Mr. Alexander Wedderburn, in implement of the contract of marriage between her and his said son, dated at Dundee 21st instant, subject to his own life-rent and that of his said son. (76.) Dundee Protocol Books.

217. **1582.** Dec. 15.—Sasine is given to the said Helen Ramsay of the said five acres. Robert Wedderburn, notary, and David Wedderburn, witnesses. (ib.)

218. **1582.** Dec. 15.—Sasine on resignation by the said Alexander Wedderburn to his said son, Mr. Alexander Wedderburn, of three tenements in Dundee (77), and sasine also to Helen Ramsay of another tenement near (78), and yet another such sasine to her of another tenement in North Argylegate. (78.)

219. **1583.** (a) Jan. 1.—Sasine of an @-rent in favour of Alexander Wedderburn, son and heir of the late David Wedderburn, burgess. Walter Wedderburn, witness. (79.) (b) Feb. 16.—Transaction in the house of Peter Wedderburn. (83, 117.)

220. **1583.** (a) April 11.—Bond by Thomas Guthrie to Margaret Rollok, spouse to William Wedderburn. (Min. Book v, s.d.) (b) Sept. 26.—John Wedderburn settles his Murraygate house on Margaret Strathauchin, his future wife, in implement of their marriage contract. (ib. v, s.d.)

221. **1584.** (a) Feb. 18.—David Wedderburn, adolescens, witness. (100.) (b) Dec. 30.—Patrick Wedderburn and Robert Wedderburn, notary, witnesses. (128.)

Inside the last leaf are various Latin and English mottoes, e.g.
" Virschip we suld, obey, and knaw
Ane God, ane King, ane fayth, ane law.

At meitt be glaid, sport honestlie,	Offend na man that is present
But sweiring or scurilitie,	Be word, deid or vain argument.
First thank the Lord that sends all fuid	Remembir the puir of veith deuude
Than frame your talk with modestie	Tharne to support be diligent
To pleis God & the companie	For although thai be indigent
And of the absentis speik bot guid.	Zit think thai ar your fleshe and bluid.

[See, in all, fol. 1, 3, 24-26, 28, 36, 53, 57-58, 68-69, 73, 76-79, 83, 86-87, 96-97, 100, 103, 107, 117, 128.]

VOL. 248.

222. **1581.** (no date.)—Mr. Alexander Wedderburn, David Wedderburn, Robert Wedderburn, notary, are often named in this volume. (1, 2, 3, 9, 13, 19, 29, 42.)

223. **1582.** (a) February 13.—Alexander Wedderburn, elder, witness. (14.) (b) Feb. 22.—Land of the heirs of the late John Wedderburn in North Flukergate, mentioned. (15.) (c) April 2, 23.—Lands, North Argylegate, of the late Elizabeth Wedderburn and, South Moraygate, of the late Edward Wedderburn. (18, 22.) (d) Aug. 13.—Robert Wedderburn, brother to Alexander Wedderburn, clerk, witness. (39.) (e) Sept. 21.—Peter Wedderburn and Margaret Kynloch, his wife, resign certain lands in Dundee. (41.) (f) Oct. 9.—Alexander Wedderburn, clerk, witness with his sons, Mr. Alexander and David Wedderburn. (43.)

[See, in all, fol. 1, 2, 3, 9, 10, 13, 14. 15, 17-19, 22, 25, 29-30, 39, 41-43, 47, 51, 53-55.]

VOL. 249.

On the first leaf is written " Gloria Deo in seculo seculorum."

224. **1583.** Feb. 4.—Sasine headed " For William Wedderburn and Margaret Rollok, his wife, and John Wedderburn." John Wedderburn is entered in the South Moraygate lands of his late father, James Wedderburn, son and heir of the late David Wedderburn, and thereupon he resigns a portion of them to James Wedderburn, mariner, son

2 F

and heir of William Wedderburn, father's brother to the said John, and to Margaret Rollok, wife of the said William, for whom James Wedderburn is attorney. Peter Wedderburn is witness. (2)

225. **1582.** Feb. 9 —John Wedderburn, "spectatus juvenis," is entered in a North Marketgate land as heir to John Wedderburn, his father, and also as heir to James Wedderburn, his brother german, and also in a North Flukergate land as heir to his father. He then resigns both properties in favour of himself and Margaret Lyndesay, his future wife. (4.)

226. **1582.** March 22.—Peter Wedderburn and Margaret Kynloch, his wife, resign in favour of William Allerdes that large tenement in South Argylegate, once that of Robert Wedderburn, grandson and heir of the late James Wedderburn. (10.)

227. **1583-4.** David Wedderburn is often a witness. (27-74.)

228. **1583.** May 25.—Richard Wedderburn, burgess in Elsignor, in Denmark, by his procurator, resigns certain South Cowgate lands in favour of Patrick Wedderburn, his brother german, who at once resigns them in favour of himself and Elizabeth Low, his wife. (28.)

229. **1583.** June 5.—" I, Margaret Wedderburne, bindis and oblissis me to delyver to my brother, David Wedderburn, thrie elnis of Frensche Fleming, sufficient or els alsmekle as salbe be him ane cloik the day of my marriage And I the said David oblissis me to pay to the said Margaret twa crownes of the sone in caise seho be noeht mareit or pule cum a yeir be thir presentis. Subscryvit with my hand at Dundee fyft day of Junii 1583. Margaret Wedderburne with my hand. David Wedderburne with my hand." (Min. Book v. s d.)

230. **1583.** June 22.—Resignation by John Coustoun, burgess, and Elizabeth Wedderburn, his wife, of various lands in favour of their sons David, John, Thomas, and George. (31.)

231. **1583.** July 3.—Sasine of a North Flukergate land in favour of Peter Imrie and Barbara Wedderburn, his wife. (32.)

232. **1583.** Aug. 6.—Peter Wedderburn, witness. (35.)

233. **1583.** Nov. 9.—Alexander Wedderburn, elder, burgess, acts on behalf of himself and his son, Richard Wedderburn, burgess of Elsiguore. (39.)

234. **1583.** Nov. 28.—Resignation for re-infeftment to themselves in conjunct fee of a North Argylegate tenement by Robert Wedderburn and his wife Margaret, daughter of Robert Myln, burgess. (39.)

235. **1584.** Jan. 24.—Alexander Wedderburn, younger, burgess of Dundee, and his wife Cristian Ferny resign a North Moraygate tenement in favour of Patrick Lyoun. (41.)

236. **1584.** Jan. 24.—John Wedderburn (son and heir of the late James Wedderburn, burgess) and Margaret Strathauchin his wife resign to Cristopher Traill their South Moraygate land. James Wedderburn, burgess, is witness. (42.)

237. **1584.** Jan. 28.—Margaret Myln, with consent of her husband Robert Wedderburn, her sister, Agnes Myln, and her father Robert Myln, resigns, as being with her said sister one of the two heirs of her late brother James Myln, a West Marketgate land in favour of her said father. (42.)

238. **1584.** March 20.—John Wedderburn, burgess, is a witness. (48.)

239. **1584.** Sept. 19.—Resignation of a land known as "Sympson's yard " by Alexander Dundee Kyd in favour of Alexander Kyd, younger, his son and heir by Isobell Welder- Protocol burn his wife. Also similar resignation of a reversion held by the said Alexander Books. Kyd, elder, of Peter Imry and Barbara Wedderburn. (56, 61.)

240. **1584.** Oct. 21.—Mr. Alexander Wedderburn and David Wedderburn, his brother, burgess, are witnesses. (59.)

241. **1585.** (a) Feb. 6, April. 8.—Peter Wedderburn's lands in South Moraygate near those of George Blak and William Lochmalony named (68, 70). (b) March 12. —John Wedderburn and David Wedderburn, burgesses, witnesses. (70.)

[See, in all, fol. 1, 2, 4-6, 10, 11, 14, 18, 19, 21, 23, 28, 31, 32, 35, 39, 41, 42, 46, 48, 54-57, 59, 61, 66, 68, 70, 72-74.]

VOL. 250.

Entitled " First Protocol Book of Alexander Wedderburn II., town clerk, from 8 June 1583 to 11 Sept. 1587."

This is the first book of Alexander Wedderburn, first of Kingennie.

242. **1583.** June 1.—At Edinburgh. · Admission of Mr. Alexander Wedderburn, " sone and appearand air of Alexander Wedderburn, common clerk of Dundie," as notary. It describes him as born in Dundee and now "off the aige of twentie twa yeirs or thairby, maried." His notarial symbol is appended to the document. (1.)

243. **1584.** Jan. 24.- -Discharge by Alexander Kyd in favour of John Wedderburn, son and heir of the late James Wedderburn, portioner of Craigy Hiltoun, of a charge on the said John's South Murraygate land. (11.)

244. **1584.** Jan. 24.—Similar discharge in favour of the said John, naming his mother, Margaret Dundas, and also resignation by the said John and Margaret Strathauchin, his wife, of their sixth part of the lands of Craigy Hiltoun. (12.)

245. **1584.** May 25.—Peter Wedderburn and his wife, Margaret Kynloch, resign a North Quaygate tenement in favour of their daughters, Margaret and Janet, equally. (24.)

246. **1584.** July 3.—Alexander Kyd, elder, and Isobel Wedderburn, his wife, resign a yard to Peter Imrie and Barbara Wedderburn, his wife. (29.)

247. **1585.** July 8.—Matthew Wedderburn, inhabitant of Dundee, is a witness. (62.)

248. **1585.** Dec. 28.—Discharge by Robert Wedderburn, as brother and nearest heir of David Wedderburn, merchant of Dundee, to John Pierson, as procurator of David Cant. (76.)

249. **1586.** March 25.—Sasine in favour of Peter Wedderburn, younger, son lawful of Alexander Wedderburn, clerk of Dundee, of the South Argylegate tenement of Edward Chalmers. (88.)

250. **1586.** June 2.—Peter Wedderburn, burgess, and Margaret Kinloch, his wife, resign an @-rent to Peter Wedderburn, younger, designed as in No. 249. (113.)

251. **1586.** June 13.—Elizabeth Wedderburn and John Coustoun, her spouse, resign a tenement in Dundee in favour of their sons David, John, Thomas and George, and their heirs male in successive substitution. Robert Wedderburn, James Wedderburn, and Matthew Wedderburn, burgesses, are witnesses. (115-116.)

252. **1586.** July 7.—Sasine given to David Wedderburn, " probo juveni," son lawful of the late Alexander Wedderburn, clerk of Dundee. (128.)

253. **1586.** Oct. 10.—Sasine of an @-rent in favour of Barbara Wedderburn, wife of Peter Imry, burgess of Dundee. (148.)

254. **1586.** Nov. 21.—Resignation by John Coustoun and Elizabeth Wedderburn, his wife, of a land South of St. Clements, in favour of Robert Wedderburn (son in law of the said John Coustoun), and Eufame Coustoun, his wife. (156.)

255. **1587.** March 3, April 20.—Resignation and sasine of two annual rents in favour of David Wedderburn, "spectato juveni," son of the late Alexander Wedderburn, clerk. (175, 194.)

256. **1587.** June 1, 7.—At Edinburgh and at Dundee, Alexander Wedderburn, bailie, and Mr. Alexander Wedderburn, clerk, are witnesses. (229.)

257. **1587.** July 18.—Thomas Nichol, shipmaster, burgess, is entered in an @-rent, as son and heir of the late Janet Wedderburn, his mother. (234.)

[See. in all, fol. 1, 2, 8, 11, 12, 14, 18, 20, 24, 22-31, 33, 38, 39, 45, 50, 53, 62, 65, 76, 77, 88, 97, 99, 113, 115-16, 118, 122, 125, 128, 142, 148, 152, 153, 156, 160, 167, 171, 174, 175, 194, 201, 212, 229, 231, 233, 234, 236, 239.]

VOL. 251.

Entitled " Fourth Protocol Book of Robert Wedderburn, Not. Pub., from 15 April 1585 to 25 Sept. 1588."

On the first three pages, as is usual with him, the writer has placed various Latin mottoes, *e.g.* "Utile est multa scire, et recta vivere," "Parsimonia et labore crescunt res." "Providentia omnia regnatur." "Plato—Facilius est movere quietum quam quietare motum. "Opem tibi Deus, justa si egeris, feret. Incede rectam, si vir es justus, visu." "Sit ultimum primumque in omnibus Deus," &c., &c., including some of those written in his earlier books. His notarial sign and docket, with his motto "patior ut potiar," is also given on the third leaf.

258. **1585.** May 20.—Alexander Wedderburn, younger, witness. (6.)

259. **1586.** Nov. 12, 19.—Resignation and sasine to Mr. Alexander Wedderburn, clerk, and Helen Ramsay, his wife, of an @-rent. (52.)

260. **1586.** Nov. 19.—Mr. Alexander Wedderburn, clerk, is seized in an @-rent of eight merks out of the land of the late David Wedderburn, in South Murraygate, as sister's son and heir to James Mylu, younger, burgess of Dundee. (53.)

261. **1587.** Oct. 12.—Mr. Alexander Wedderburn and Robert Wedderburn, his brother, witnesses. (85.)

262. **1587.** Nov. 11.—Discharge by Robert Wedderburn, merchant, of his claim to an @-rent out of the South Flukergate land of the late David Cant, and of all other things due to him, through the death of the said David Cant, and Isobell Lovell, his wife, mother of the said Robert, and David Wedderburn, his brother, also deceased. (91.)

263. **1588.** March 5.—Patrick Wedderburn, burgess, bailie to the constable. (95.)

264. **1588.** Feb 2.—William Kynloch, elder, now of great age, appoints Peter Wedderburn, his son in law, his assignee of all his goods and gear, Peter Wedderburn undertaking to maintain the said William Kynloch, who delivers to him as a sign and token of the bargain a ring of gold. (102.)

265. **1588.** May 29.—Peter Wedderburn twice acts as a witness. (132.)

266. **1588.** Sept. 6.—Sasine headed "pro Magistro Alexandro Wedderburn et Davide ac Roberto ejus fratribus." Thomas Guthrie, merchant, son of the late Thomas Guthrie of Kiublachmont, for the love he bears Mr. Alexander Wedderburn, clerk of Dundee and David Wedderburn, his brother, his second and third cousins (suos amicos ex secundo et tertio gradu consanguinitatis), resigns to them an @-rent, and also assigns to Robert Wedderburn, their brother, a claim he has on Wm. Kinloch, burgess in Elgin. (137.)

[See, in all, fol. 2, 4, 6, 16, 20, 25, 40, 52 53, 58, 62, 69, 77, 85, 91, 95, 101, 102, 104, 106, 109, 120, 124, 125, 132, 134, 137, 139.]

VOL. 252.

Entitled ' Town Clerk's Protocol (Book), 19 April 1587 —18 April 1589.''

On the first leaf is written in Latin, " Protocol Book of Mr. Alexander Wedderburn, clerk of the court of Dundee."

267. (*a*) **1587**. April 19, June 1.—Alexander Wedderburn, bailie, witness. (1, 16.) (*b*) April 26.—Sasine of a small @-rent in favour of David Wedderburn, "spectatus juvenis," son of the late Alexander Wedderburn, clerk. (1.) (*c*) May 5.—John Coustoun, burgess, settles a South Seagate tenement on his wife, Elizabeth Wedderburn, for life, and on his son, Thomas Coustoun, in fee. (3.) (*d*) May 24.—Robert Wedderburn, younger, burgess, witness. (6.) (*e*) June 3.—Robert Wedderburn, merchant, burgess, witness. (13.) (*f*) Sept, 22 —John Wedderburn, mariner, is entered in an @-rent as grandson and heir of the deceased James Wedderburn, burgess (27) ; and also in another @-rent, as son of the late John Wedderburn, burgess. (*ib.*)

268. **1587**. Oct. 13.—The North Flukergate land of Mr. John Lovell, grandson of the late Elizabeth Wedderburn, relict of Patrick Lyon, is mentioned. (31.)

269. **1587**. Oct. 30.—David Wedderburn, burgess, as procurator for Hercules Rollok, resigns a tenement to Alexander Wedderburn, merchant, burgess of Dundee, and Christina Fairny, his wife. (32.)

270. **1588**. Jan. 17.—Patrick Wedderburn, witness. (44.)

271. **1588**. April 25.—James Reat (son and heir of the late James Reat, burgess), entails a North Marketgate tenement on himself and his issue, whom failing, successively on Alexander Wedderburn and Robert Wedderburn, his uterine brothers. (54.)

272. **1588**. May 27.—David Wedderburn, burgess, gets sasine of an @-rent, as attorney for his brother, James, son of the late Alexander Wedderburn, clerk. (61.)

273. **1588**. Oct. 31.—The bai ie goes to the North Murraygate land of the late Henry Wedderburn, and enters in half of it Thomas Nicoll, as son and heir of the late Janet Wedderburn, pursuant to a letter of demission made between her and the late Margaret Wedderburn, her sister. (76.)

274. **1589**. March 28.—John Wedderburn (son and heir of the late John Wedderburn, burgess), with consent of Margaret Lindsay, his wife, resigns a North Marketgate tenement to Robert Smyth. (95.)

275. **1589**. May 31.—Resignation by Grissell Duncan (wife of William Duncan, bailie), with consent of Robert Wedderburn, her spouse, and discharge by them to William Duncan, of money payable under their marriage contract (date not given.) (108.)

[See, in all, fol. 1, 3, 6, 8, 13, 16, 20-23, 27, 31-32, 35, 38, 40-42, 44, 50, 52, 54, 57, 59, 61, 64, 65, 67, 70, 76, 79, 87-90, 95, 98, 101, 102, 108, 111.]

VOL. 253.

*Entitled " No. 13 Protocol Book of Mr. Alexander Wedderburn (II.), town clerk,
from 20 July 1589 to 16 October 1592.''*

On the first leaf is written in Latin "Book of Protocols of Mr. Alexander Wedderburn, clerk of the court of Dundee 20 July 1589 ; written by me, Thomas Fyiff, in the reign of our Sovereign Lord, King James VI. ; " after which is the following :—

Epitaphium Mariæ Reginæ Scotorum.

Regibus orta, auxi reges, reginaque vixi,
Nupta tribus, tribus orba viris, tria regna reliqui,
Gallus opes, Scotus cunas, habet Anglia sepulchrum.

Idem Scoticé

I cam of Kyngis, I Kyngis iucrest, my stait a crown did crave,
Thryis weddit, and als wedow thryis, thrie kingdomes heir I leave,
France hes my welth, Scotland my birth & Ingland hes my grave.

Inside the cover are some dozen lines in praise of Dundee, with a very curious figure of man, each of whose limbs is named, so as to form a map of the town. At the end of the volume is written several times " Finis coronat opus," and the statement that " This whole Protocoll bulk is written by the hand of Thomas Fyiff, servitour to Mr. Alexander Wedderburne, clerk of Dundie."

230   THE WEDDERBURN BOOK.

Dundee Protocol Books.

276.　**1589**. July 24.—The bailie goes to the South Argylegate tenement of Robert Wedderburn, son and heir of the late Robert Wedderburn, burgess, and grandson of the late James Wedderburn. burgess, and there as procurator for him, and by virtue of his mandate dated at Campheir 21 June last, gives sasine thereof to Robert Wedderburn, notary, brother german of the late Alexander Wedderburn, clerk. (1)

A puzzling entry, because in vol. xv. of the "Burgh and Head Court Records," s.d. 1580, Sept. 19, Margaret Wedderburn is cognosced " heir to umquhill Robert Wedderburn, younger, son and heir of umquhill Robert Wedderburn."

277.　**1589**. Aug. 21.—Sasine on charter (10 May), by Peter Clayhills, younger, and Margaret Wedderburn, his wife, in favour of George Lindesay, merchant burgess, and Grisild Wedderburn, his wife, of an @-rent furth of the mains of Ballisaik, &c., barony of Innerkeillour, co. Forfar. (5.)

278.　**1589**. Aug. 30.—John Wedderburn, portioner of Craigie Hilton, with consent of Margaret Strathanehin, his wife. settles an @-rent of £100 out of the said lands on his daughter, Elizabeth Wedderburn. (7.)

279.　**1589**. Sept. 25, 26.—The land of Peter Wedderburn, near that of William Loehmalony, and the windmill, South Marygate, referred to. (11-12.)

280.　**1590**. March 1.—Robert Wedderburn, younger, burgess, settles a North Argyle-gate tenement on himself and Elizabeth Lovell, his future wife. (36.)

281.　**1590** July 24.—Alexander Wedderburn and his wife, Christian Ferny, by James Durham, their procurator, resign various @-rents out of Dundee properties. (52.)

282.　**1590**. Aug. 5.—Patrick Wedderburn, Matthew Wedderburn. and John Wedderburn, son of Alexander Wedderburn, burgess, witnesses. (54-55)

283.　**1590** Aug 11.—Before Mr. Alexander Wedderburn, clerk, compear Patrick Wedderburn and Elizabeth Low, his wife, producing a charter of 28 July, signed at Dundee by Richard Wedderburn, burgess in Elsingoir in Denmark, son and heir of the late Alexander Wedderburn, burgess of Dundee, and Isobell Anderson, whereby Richard sold to Patrick and his wife various properties in Dundee. (56, cp. 59, 88.)

284.　**1590**. Aug. 16.—Peter Wedderburn, burgess, witness. (58, 90.)

285.　**1591**. March 10.—Sasine of a South Flukergate land to Robert Wedderburn, merchant, burgess of Dundee, and Eufame Coustoun, his wife, and to David Wedderburn, their attorney, his lawful son. (78.)

286.　**1591**. March 17.—Sasine of an @-rent to Robert Wedderburn, younger, brother and attorney of Peter Wedderburn, on resignation by their brother, David Wedderburn, son of the late Alexander Wedderburn, clerk. (79.)

287.　**1591**. May 21.—Sasine on charter by Sir James Scrymgeour of Dudope, constable and provost, in favour of David Wedderburn. (son of the late Alexander Wedderburn, clerk), and Matilda Beaton, his wife, of certain land in Dudope. known as Logyhauche, &c.　Robert Wedderburn, younger, witness. (91)

288.　**1591**. (a) July 7.—Robert and James Wedderburn, brothers of Mr. Alexander Wedderburn, clerk, witnesses. (98.)　(b) July 9.—The South Murraygate lands of (the late) Edward Wedderburn, mentioned. (98)　(c) Aug. 26.—Sasine on resignation in favour of George Lyndesay and Grissill Wedderburn, his wife, of a tenement in Skirling's Wynd.　Robert Wedderburn, younger, is attorney for Grissill, and David Wedderburn, burgess. is witness. (103.)

289.　**1592**. Jan. 6.—Robert Wedderburn, merchant, named as hospital master. (121.)

[See. in all. fol. 1, 2, 4, 5, 7, 8, 10-13, 16, 27, 29, 34-36, 42, 47, 48, 52, 54-56, 58-59, 62, 63, 67, 72, 75, 77-80, 84, 85, 88, 90-92, 94, 97-99, 103, 106-108, 120-22, 125, 134, 139, 144. 150, 151, 153, 159, 163, 166, 168-177.]

VOL. 254.

Entitled " Town Clerk's Protocol, 20 July 1589—25 November 1591.'

This volume appears to be a draft or copy of part of Volume 253. Its first leaf has on it, " Mr. A. Wedderburn, not. publ. ac scriba curiæ. Anno Domini 1614," and also the words, " Joannem Wedderburne with my hand." It seems therefore as if this leaf, though bound into this volume, does not belong to it. Some lines beginning, " In my defence God me defend, And bring my soul to ane guid end, &c. " are also written on this leaf.

VOL. 255.

Entitled " Protocol Book of Alexander Wedderburn (II.), town clerk, from 25 Nov. 1591 to 22 May 1593."

The first three leaves are blank: on the fourth is " Liber protocollorum M. Alexandri Wedderburn, scribæ curiæ Deidonamæ," and the epitaph of Mary Queen of Scots as at the beginning of Vol. 253. The folios of this book down to fol. 90 repeat folios 118—178 of Vol. 253.

290. **1592.** Oct. 17.—Catharine Wedderburn (wife of Thomas Blair), Eufame, and Elizabeth Wedderburn are entered in the South Murraygate land of the late Edward Wedderburn, burgess, as his daughters and heirs, and resign it for sasine to be given to the said Catherine Wedderburn, and her husband and their heirs, subject to charges in favour of Eufame and Elizabeth. (190.)

291. **1592.** (*a*) Oct. 26.—David Wedderburn, burgess, son to Alexander Wedderburn, deceased, clerk of Dundee, obtains the right of patronage of Saint Thomas' chaplainry from William Guthrie of Kingany. (94.) (*b*) Nov. 18.—Robert Wedderburn, younger, burgess, settles his land, mentioned ante No. 280, on himself and Elizabeth Hering, his wife. (106.)

292. **1593.** (*a*) Jan. 6.—John Wedderburn, burgess, resigns his North Seagate land to William Myln, burgess, and Magdalen Wedderburn, his wife, subject to the liferent of William Wedderburn and Margaret Rollok, his wife. (120.) (*b*) April 15.—Robert Wedderburn, elder, and Margaret Myln, his wife, resign two South Argylegate tenements in favour of George Thomson. (129.)

[See, for all the Wedderburn references from fol. 90 to the end of this volume, fol. **90, 94, 98, 106, 108, 111, 115, 120, 123, 125, 128-29.**]

VOL. 256.

Entitled " No. 15 Protocol Book of Alexander Wedderburn (II.), clerk, from 17 Oct. 1592 to 7 Sept. 1594."

The first twenty-eight leaves, 17 Oct. 1592—22 May 1593, are a duplicate of as much of Vol. 255, as is relative to those dates.

293. **1593.** (*a*) May 26.—Katharine, Euphame, and Elizabeth Wedderburn, daughters of umquhile Edward Wedderburn, burgess, give a discharge to Andrew Guthrie. (29) (*b*) July 20.—David Wedderburn, chaplain of S. James Major, and Matild Beaton, his wife, resign some land in the Westfield of Dundee to George Stirling. (39.) (*c*) Aug. 3.—Mr. James Coustoun resigns a North Seagate tenement, subject to a life-rent to be paid to his mother, Elizabeth Wedderburn. (41.) (*d*) Aug. 5.—Robert Wedderburn, elder, burgess, resigns a North Argylegate land to Robert Wedderburn, younger, burgess. (42.) (*e*) Sept. 7.—Patrick Wedderburn, burgess, mentioned. (61, 64, 89.)

294. **1594.** Jan. 8.—Sasine of an @-rent to Robert Wedderburn, merchant, burgess, and Eufame Coustoun, his wife, for whom Peter Wedderburn is attorney. Robert Wedderburn, younger, burgess, is witness. (66.)

295. **1594.** March 18.—Isobell Anderson, relict of Alexander Wedderburn, warrants a contract made between her and her son Patrick, touching her maintenance. (Min. Book xiii, s.d.)

Dundee
Protocol
Books.

296. **1594.** May 11.—William Duncan, son of the late Findlay Duncan, surgeon, burgess, is entered in a South Argylegate tenement as heir to his father, and settles it on Katharine Wedderburn "my sister german" and his future spouse. (79.)
> The words "my sister german" have reference to Alexander Wedderburn of Kingennie, the writer of the instrument.

297. **1594.** May 15.—Robert Wedderburn, notary, and Margaret Myln, his wife, resign a South Argylegate tenement to Ninian Copen. (80.)
[See, in all, fol. 28-30, 35, 39, 41-43, 55, 61, 64, 66, 68, 77, 79-80, 84. 87. 95-96.]

VOL. 257.

Entitled " No. 16 Protocol Book of Alexander Wedderburn (II.), town clerk, from 24 May 1593—7 Sept. 1594."
This volume is a duplicate of Vol. 256, from fol. 28, ad fin.

VOL. 258.

Entitled " Town Clerk's Protocol, 21 September 1594—4 December 1595.
On the first leaf is written in Latin twice over " Protocol Book of Mr. Alexander Wedderburn," and the words " Amen, per me, Wedderburne." It is, of course, one of the books of Alexander Wedderburn, first of Kingennie.

298. **1594.** Oct. 25.—Sasine of a North Marketgate tenement is given to Patrick Wedderburn, burgess, and Elizabeth Low, his wife. (5.)

299. **1594.** Nov. 21.—The South Murraygate lands once of David Wedderburn, and also the neighbouring lands of William Wedderburn, are named as boundaries. (7.)

300. **1595.** Jan. 28.—James Reat resigns a North Marketgate tenement, according to contract between him and Patrick Wedderburn, merchant, burgess, and Elizabeth Low, his wife, who thereupon resign the said tenement to the bailie for sasine thereof to their son Alexander. (26)

301. **1595.** Feb. 1.—James Turcing and Elizabeth Wedderburn, his wife, resign a South Cowgate tenement to John Scrymgeour and Agnes Lovell, his wife. David, James, and Patrick Wedderburn are present. (31.)

302. **1595.** (a) Feb. 6.—John Wedderburn, burgess, witness. (32). (b) March 24—Robert Wedderburn, elder, and Margaret Myln, his wife, resign a South Argylgate tenement to James Boytur. (40). (c) April 18,—Patrick Wedderburn, burgess, settles his N. Marketgate tenement on his sons Robert and Adam subject to the liferent of himself and Elizabeth Low his wife. (42) (d) May 19.—William Davidson, merchant, burgess, settles his North Argylegate tenement on himself and Janet Wedderburn his wife. Peter Wedderburn, elder, and Patrick Wedderburn, burgesses, are witnesses. (46). (e) May 31.—Peter Wedderburn, younger, a witness. (52). (f) June 6.—Robert Wedderburn (with consent of Margaret Myln his wife) and Robert Myln, his father-in-law, resigns an @-rent. (54-55). (g) Aug. 16.—James Reat (with consent of Violet Clerk, his wife) resigns a tenement to Patrick Wedderburn and Elizabeth Low, his wife. (75).

303. **1595.** (a) Sept. 3.—Robert Wedderburn, merchant. as procurator for David Wedderburn, chaplain of St. Stephen's chaplainry, resigns a piece of land to Robert Wedderburn, acting as attorney for Barbara Wedderburn, his sister german, relict of Peter Imbrie, burgess. (80.) (b) Sept. 13.—James Wedderburn, son of the late Alexander Wedderburn, clerk, is named as resigning an annual rent to James Durham of Pitkerro. (83).

304. **1595.** (a) Oct. 13.—Sir James Scrymgeour of Dudop resigns to his "weil belovit freind and servitour David Wedderburn, burgess" and his heirs, the patronage of the chaplainry of St. Thomas Martyr, once belonging to the Laird of Kingany. (90). (b) Oct. 20.—Peter Clayhills resigns a South Seagate tenement to his son Alexander, subject to the life-rent of himself and Margaret Wedderburn, his wife. (93.)

[See, in all. fol. 1-5, 7, 9, 16, 17, 21, 23, 26, 28-32, 35, 38, 40-42, 46, 52, 54, 55, 62-64, 66, 69-71, 74-77, 80, 83, 87-90, 93, 96-97, 102, 104.]

Vol. 259.

Entitled " Town Clerk's Protocol, 5 Dec. 1595—4 June 1597."

On the first leaf is written in Latin, " Protocol Book of Mr. Alexander Wedderburn, clerk of the community of the burgh of Dundee."

305. **1596.** (*a*) Jan. 17.—Walter Wedderburn, witness. (8.) (*b*) April 20.—Peter Wedderburn, elder, witness. (19.)

306. **1596.** April 28.—Peter Wedderburn, younger, son of the late Alexander Wedderburn, clerk, gives a discharge to William Davidson, merchant, son in law of Peter Wedderburn, elder, of a sum paid for redemption of an @-rent. (19.)

307. **1596.** May 18.—Sasine of an @-rent is given to David Wedderburn, burgess, son of the late Alexander Wedderburn, clerk. James Wedderburn, brother to David, is witness. (22.)

308. **1596.** May 22.—David Wedderburn, merchant, burgess, and Matild Beaton, his wife, acknowledge receipt of £1000 from William Graham of Baldowie, for redemption of one-fourth of Lunlathine, co. Forfar. (22.)

309. **1596.** May 31.—Similar discharge to the said William Graham for 1000 merks, by William Duncan, surgeon, and Katharine Wedderburn, his wife. (25.)

310. **1597.** March 28.—Resignation in favour of Peter Clayhills, bailie of Dundee, and Margaret Wedderburn, his wife, and Alexander Clayhills, their son. (91.)

311. **1597.** May 12.—Christina Lovell, daughter of the late William Lovell in Murroes (by his wife Margaret Roche), with consent of James Wedderburn, her husband, and in contemplation of their late marriage, resigns seven different @-rents for sasine to be given to herself and her husband, and any children of the marriage. (96.)

312. **1597.** June 18.—George Blak, burgess, in implement of a contract, dated . . . 159 . ., between him and George Blak, his son and heir, and Peter Wedderburn, burgess, and Margaret Wedderburn, his daughter, settles a tenement in Spaldings Wynd on the said George, his son, and the said Margaret Wedderburn, his said son's wife. (121-22.)

[See in all, fol. 5, 7-8, 13, 19, 22, 23, 25-27, 30, 32, 39, 41, 42, 46-48, 65, 90, 91, 94-99, 111, 116-17, 121-22, 125, 130.]

Vol. 261.[1]

Entitled " Fifth Protocol Book of Robert Wedderburn, Not. Pub. from 8 October 1588 to 25 January 1598—99."

The first leaves are, as is usual with Robert Wedderburn, covered with various Latin mottoes. (See ante s. Vols. 243, 245, 247 and 251.) Some fresh ones occur in this volume. "Acutus ad cernenda cuncta oculus Dei." " Ea fac quorum te non pœniteat." " Cœlum non solum." "Omnia in mundo immunda." " Quæ mea sors hodie est, cras fore vestra potest." " Adspirat cœptis Jesus." There are also some quaint verses. " Saif us guid Lord for thy Godheid, Fra sin, schame, and suddane deid." " Quheu hoip and helth, and welth is hieist, Then wo and wraik diseis and neid is neirest," and again :—

" Quha now a dayis wald all mennis favoris hafe,
Must gif mekill, tak lytill, and nathing ask nor crave.
Quha richtlie kepia thir twa estemit wyis may be,
Nocht for to be our haldane in nor zit to be our frie."

Robert Wedderburn's signature, symbol, and notarial docket are also given.

313. **1589.** March 7.—Discharge to John Small of Kinothrie, granted by Janet Lindesay, relict of William Kynloch, elder, Peter Wedderburn, their son in law, and Margaret Kinloch, his wife. (16.)

[1] This volume, ranging 1588—1599, is taken here before Vol. 260, the entries in which run 1597—1600.

2 G

314.   **1589**. April 5.—Andro Geddie, mariner, citizen in Sanct Androis, discharges Patrick Wedderburn, merchant burgess of Dundee, of the tocher due with Eufame Wedderburn, sister of the said Patrick. Done in the house of Alexander Wedderburn, elder. James Turcing, witness. (25.)

315.   **1589**. May 17.—Sasine on charter by John Wedderburn, portioner of Craigie, with consent of Margaret Strathauchin, his wife, in favour of his beloved cousin Mr. Alexander Wedderburn, clerk, of an annual rent out of Craigie. David and Robert Wedderburn, brothers of the clerk, witnesses. (39).

316.   **1590**. Aug. 27.—Sasine on charter by Rannald Brown of Wester Gourdie in favour of Robert Wedderburn, son and heir of the late Mr. Robert Wedderburn, of the lands called Kilmanis-tak, North of Wester Gourdie. John Wedderburn, shipmaster, is bailie, and Robert Wedderburn, notary, witness. (74).

317.   **1591**. (*a*) July 28.— Mr. Alexander Wedderburn, clerk of Dundee, and Helen Ramsay, his wife, give sasine of a North Argylegate malthouse to Alexander Nicoll. (94).
(*b*) Mr. Alexander Wedderburn and Helen Ramsay, his wife, settle land, being the West part of the Greneland close, North Argylegate, and an @-rent on James Wedderburn, their second son and his heirs. (95). (*c*) Aug. 11.—Mr. Alexander Wedderburn and Helen Ramsay, his wife, settle on themselves and their heirs the sixth part of Craigie acquired by them from John Wedderburn and Margaret Strathauchin, his wife. (95).

318.   **1591**. Oct. 7.—Sasine on Charter (6 June) by James Carmichael, portioner of Ethiebetoun, and Elizabeth Lovell, his wife, granting the sunny half of Wester Gourdie, Scone, co. Forfar, to Mr. Alexander Wedderburn and Helen Ramsay, his wife, and their heirs. (98).

319.   **1591**. [? date].— Robert Wedderburn, merchant (son and heir of the late Mr. Robert Wedderburn), and Eufame Coustoun, his wife, acquire part of Craigie from Richard Blyth. (101).

320.   **1592**. May 6.—Andrew Gourlaw in Dargo acknowledges the receipt of 800 merks for redemption of an @-rent out of Wester Gourdie, from Mr. Alexander Wedderburn, clerk, assignee of David Dunmuir. Peter Wedderburn is a witness. (109.)

321.   **1592**. May 13.—Sasine on charter by David Dunmuir, portioner of Wester Gourdie, in favour of Mr. Alexander Wedderburn, clerk of Dundee, of the shadow half of the town and lands of Wester Gourdie, once occupied by David's mother, Isobell Brown. (110.) The clerk at once settles these lands on his wife, Helen Ramsay. (111.)

322.   **1595**. Oct. 7.—Sasine on resignation by John Auchinlek, son and heir of Robert Auchinlek of Dundee, in favour of Alexander Wedderburn, clerk of Dundee, of an @-rent. Peter Wedderburn, younger, is a witness. (140.)

[See. in all, fol. 1-3, 16, 25, 32, 36-39, 44, 48, 58-59, 63, 74, 88, 91-92, 94-96, 98-101, 109-13, 115' 121, 134, 140, 147, 151, 165-66.]

VOL.   260.

Entitled " Town Clerk's Protocol, 26 Sept. 1597—5 July 1600."

This is another of the books of Alexander Wedderburn, first of Kingennie. On the first leaf is written in Latin, " The fear of the Lord is the beginning of wisdom."

323.   **1597**. Nov. 8.—Robert Wedderburn, elder, and Margaret Myln, his wife, get sasine of an inner tenement in North Argylegate. (10.)

324.   **1597**. Nov. 10.—Robert Wedderburn, merchant, burgess, and Eufame Coustoun, his wife, resign their South Flukergate foreland, in favour of James Fraser, merchant, and Eufame Scot, his wife, daughter of the late Robert Scot, first husband of the said Eufame Coustoun, her mother. (11.)

325. **1597.** Dec. 5.—Alexander Kyd, procurator for George Blak and Margaret Wedderburn, his wife, resigns an @-rent, furth of Spalding's Wynd. (19.)

Dundee
Protocol
Books.

326. **1597.** Dec. 12.—Robert Kyd, younger, resigns a North Marketgate property in
favour of William Davidson and Janet Wedderburn, his wife. (23.)

327. **1598.** Feb. 28.—Peter Clayhills, merchant, burgess, and Margaret Wedderburn,
his wife, get sasine of a North Seagate tenement. (52.)

328. **1598** Sept. 23.—Eufame Wedderburn, wife of Archibald Blyth, is entered in an
@-rent out of a South Murraygate land, as one of two sisters german, lawful heirs
of the late Edward Wedderburn, and acknowledges the redemption thereof from
her by Katharine Wedderburn and Thomas Blair, her husband. (100.)

329. **1598.** (a) Dec. 13.—William Wedderburn, burgess, witness (125.) (b) Dec. 16.—
Patrick Wedderburn, burgess, witness, (126.) (c) Dec. 26.—David Wedderburn
settles an @-rent and the liferent of the chaplainry of S. Thomas Martyr, on Matild
Beaton, his wife. (130.)

330. **1599.** Jan. 10.—Peter Wedderburn, son of Peter Wedderburn, elder, is entered in
a North Murraygate land, as heir to his mother, the late Margaret Kinloch. (149.)

331. **1599.** Jan. 19.—John Ogilvie gets sasine of part of Craigie Hiltoun, once
belonging to John Wedderburn, from Christopher Traill, together with (in warrandice)
a South Murraygate land bounded by that of the late David Clepen and William
Wedderburn, (151.)

332. **1599.** March 9.—Captain Walter Halyburton, Margaret Wedderburn, his wife, and
Mr. George Halyburton, their eldest son, resign a South Argylegate land to James
Halyburton, also son of Walter and Margaret, subject to the liferent of his parents,
and to certain charges in favour of Issobell and Jean Halyburton, his sisters. (166.)

333. **1599.** July 27.—William Wedderburn, burgess, witness. (224.)

334. **1599.** Sept. 12.—Barbara Wedderburn, relict of Peter Iurie, burgess, resigns an
annual rent to the bailie, who gives sasine as to part thereof to Katharine Guthrie,
daughter to the said Barbara, and as to the rest to William Wedderburn, attorney
for Christina and — (sic) Guthries, also her daughters, equally, subject to her own
liferent. She also resigns a land in South Kirkwynd in favour of Peter Iurie,
her son, and his issue, whom failing in favour of the said Katharine Guthrie, his
uterine sister. (234)

335. **1599.** Sept. 19.—James Fraser, merchant, grants a discharge to Robert Wedderburn, merchant, and Eufame Coustoun, his wife, of everything due to Eufame Scott,
wife of James Fraser, through the decease of Robert Scott, her father, first husband
of the said Eufame Coustoun. (238.)

336. **1600.** June 21.—The bailie passes to the land of Peter Wedderburn, burgess,
near that of William Kinloch and George Lochmalony, and there Janet Wedderburn,
wife of William Davidson, younger, resigns the same to the bailie, who gives sasine
thereof to her and her husband, subject to charges in favour of Peter Wedderburn,
elder, her father. Robert, David, and William Wedderburn, burgesses, witness the
sasine. (266.)

337. **1600.** June 18.—Captain Walter Halyburton, Margaret Wedderburn, his wife, and
Mr. George Halyburton, James, John, Margaret, Jean and Isobell Halyburton, their
children, resign a South Argylegate tenement to Andrew Thomson of Great Yarmouth,
in England, subject to the liferent of the said Captain and his wife. (313-315.)

[See, in all, fol. 3, 10, 11, 14, 16, 19-21, 23, 28, 30, 38, 45, 48, 52, 64, 68, 70, 80, 87, 91, 93, 100, 107,
110, 112, 125-26, 128-31, 144, 149, 151, 154, 166, 177, 182, 211-12, 224, 228, 230, 233-34, 237-38,
241-42, 254, 260, 264, 265-66, 271-73, 276, 282, 291, 296, 302, 304, 313, 315.]

Vol. 262.

Entitled " Sixth Protocol Book of Robert Wedderburn. Not. Pub., from 26 May 1599 to 16 July 1606."

This is the last of Robert Wedderburn's protocol books. On the first leaves are his notarial mark and symbol, with some of his usual Latin mottoes, including a fresh one "Summum nec timeas diem nec optes." A great many pages at the end are blank.

Inside the cover is written :—" Memorandum. The Pest come fra St Bartillis merket in Franchland to Dundie at the first fair thairof in anno 1605 and zit continenis to this present day the first of November 1608. In the quhilk thair depairtit 4000 persones.

Item upoun the 8 day of November 1608 thair wes ane grit earth quaik at 9 houris at evin in Dundie and in sum towuis of landwart quhilk wes testefeit be 200 persones."

338. **1602.** May 31.—Sasine on charter by Sir James Scrymgeour of Dudop to David Wedderburn, burgess and Matilda Beaton, his wife, and their heirs, of some acres of land near the road to Dudop. (7.)

339. **1601.** (*a*) April 25.—Robert Wedderburn and David Wedderburn, notaries, witnesses. (20.) (*b*) April 5.—Mr. Alexander Wedderburn of Kyngany. witness. (23.) (*c*) May 18.—Robert Wedderburn, notary, and Alexander Wedderburn, his son, and Alexander Wedderburn, younger, witnesses. (26, 30.)

[*See*, in all, fol. 1-5, 7, 11, 12, 14, **20, 23, 26, 30.**]

Vol. 263.

Entitled " Town Clerk's Protocol, from 9 July 1600 to 24 May 1607."

This is one of the books of Mr. Alexander Wedderburn, first of Kingennie, whose name is twice written on the first leaf.

340. **1600.** Dec. 13.—William Wedderburn, son of the late Mr. Alexander Wedderburn, clerk, witness. (30.)

341. **1601.** June 25.—Sasine of a South Argylegate tenement is given to William Duncan, chirurgeon, and Katharine Wedderburn, his wife, for whom Robert Wedderburn, elder, acts as attorney. (75.)

342. **1601.** June 27.—George Blak and Margaret Wedderburn, his wife, resign a Spalding's Wynd land. (76.)

343. **1601.** Aug. 17.—Robert Wedderburn, notary, burgess, and Margaret Myln, his wife, resign an annual rent. (85.)

344. **1601.** (*a*) Sept. 25.—Alexander Wedderburn, servitor to Mr. Alexander Wedderburn, notary, witness. (98.) (*b*) Oct. 2.—Alexander Wedderburn, son to Mr. Alexander Wedderburn, notary, witness. (100.)

345. **1601.** Nov. 17.—George Blak and Margaret Wedderburn, his wife, resign a tenement in Spalding's Wynd to William Davidson, younger, and Jonet Wedderburn, his wife and their heirs. Robert Wedderburn, notary, is attorney for Jonet, and David Wedderburn, burgess, is witness. (106.)

346. **1602.** Feb. 16.—Walter Wedderburn, son of the late James Wedderburn, portioner of Craigie, witness. (125.)

347. **1602.** May 18.—Sasine to David Wedderburn, burgess, son of the late Alexander Wedderburn, clerk, and settlement by him on his wife, Matilda Beaton, of a North Marketgate land, near that now of Patrick Wedderburn. (142.)

348. **1602.** (*a*) May 27.—Discharge by Peter Clayhills and Margaret Wedderburn, his wife. (147.) (*b*) Nov. 6.—Alexander Wedderburn, burgess, witness. (178.) (*c*) Nov. 13.—John Wedderburn, burgess, witness. (181.)

349. **1603.** Jan. 3.—Peter Wedderburn, younger, is entered in a North Marketgate **Dundee** foreland, as son and heir of the late Margaret Kynloch, according to the old infeft-**Protocol** ment of Peter Wedderburn, his father. Robert Wedderburn, younger, and Robert **Books.** Wedderburn, notary, witnesses. (186.)

350. **1603.** Jan. 27.—Peter Imrie is entered in an @-rent out of the North Marketgate land of the late David Guthrie, as son and heir of the late Peter Imrie, and thereupon with his mother, Barbara Wedderburn, resigns it to Eufame Jakson, reliet of Robert Guthrie, son of the said Barbara. (190.)

351. **1603.** March 18.—Patrick Wedderburn, merchant, and Alexander Wedderburn, his son, witnesses. (194.)

352. **1603.** June 15.—Sasine on resignation by James Halyburton (son of Capt. Walter Halyburton), of a South Argylegate land, in favour of Margaret Wedderburn, his mother, who again resigns it, subject to her own life-rent, to Jean and Isobell, her daughters. (210.)

353. **1603.** Oct. 3.—George Lindsay, merchant, burgess, and Grissell Wedderburn, his wife, resign a North Kirkwynd tenement to Thomas Blair. (227.)

354. **1603.** Dec. 16.—Sasine in favour of William Dunean, surgeon, and Katharine Wedderburn, his wife, of a South Argylegate tenement (235.)

355. **1604.** Feb. 9.—James Kinnaird, son and heir of the late Patrick Kinnaird, burgess, settles a cross-lodging near S. Clements, on himself and Elizabeth Wedderburn, his future spouse. (248.)

356. **1605.** March 2.—Alexander Wedderburn, son and heir apparent of Patrick Wedderburn, gets sasine of two annual rents. (269.)

357. **1605.** May 31.—George Blak, shipmaster, and Margaret Wedderburn, his wife, resign a Spalding's Wynd tenement to William Davidson, younger, and Jonet Wedderburn, his wife. (277.)

358. **1605.** July 3.—Peter Wedderburn, brother german of Mr. Alexander Wedderburn, notary, witness. (282.)

359. **1605.** July 6.—Memorandum, "Past to the dwellinghous of Robert Wedderburn, in Dundie, quhair David (Wedderburn), younger, remains quhen he is in the said brucht at bed and buirde . . . . (sic)." (Min. Book XVIII. s.d.)

This is a fragmentary note written in the margin at this date. If the reference is to David Wedderburn it must be to the son of Robert Wedderburn, the merchant, and he is called younger in distinction from David Wedderburn of the MS. or "Compt Buik."

360. **1605.** Oct. 10.—Sasine of a North Marketgate tenement in favour of Thomas Jak and Magdalen Wedderburn, his wife, for whom Alexander Wedderburn, is attorney. Patrick Wedderburn, burgess, witness. (293.)

361. **1605.** Dec. 24.—James Kynnaird and Elizabeth Wedderburn, his wife, resign a tenement near S. Clements, in favour of John Bursye and Barbara Kynnaird, his wife, under reversion of 600 merks. (302.)

362. **1606.** Aug. 2.—Helen Wedderburn, only daughter of the late Elizabeth Lovell (daughter of Mr John Lovell, now bailie), and the late Robert Wedderburn, her husband, is entered in a South Flukergate land, as one of the six heirs of the late James Lovell, her mother's brother. (317.)

363. **1606.** (a) Sept. 9.—Peter Wedderburn, younger, burgess, witness. (325.) (b) Sept. 17.—Peter Wedderburn, and James Wedderburn, son of the late John Wedderburn, witnesses. (325.)

Dundee
Protocol
Books.

364.   **1606.** Sept. 18.—Robert Wedderburn and Margaret Myln, his wife, resign a North Argylegate land to Elizabeth and Janet Wedderburn, their daughters, subject to their own liferent, and to a reversion on payment of 400 merks, in favour of Alexander Wedderburn, son and heir apparent of the said Robert. (327.)

365.   **1606.** Oct. 13.—Three sasines by Mr. Alexander Wedderburn of Kingenuie, in favour of James Wedderburn, his second son, and Magdalene and Margaret Wedderburn, his daughters. (Min. Book XVIII, s.d.)

366.   **1607.** Feb. 6.—Peter Wedderburn, burgess, in implement of a contract betwixt Peter Wedderburn, his late father, himself, Dr. David Kinloch, and others, resigns to Dr. Kinloch a North Flukergate tenement. (336.)

367.   **1607.** Feb. 7.—Thomas Blair, shipmaster, resigns a South Murraygate land in favour of Thomas Blair, his son by his late wife Katharine Wedderburn. (336.)

[See, in all, fol. 7, 9, 28-30, 32, 59, 66, 68, 75-76, 78, 85, 89, 92, 98, 100, 106, 124-26, 130, 140-42, 146-47, 152, 154, 155, 162, 170, 178, 181, 184, 186, 190, 194, 205, 207-11, 220, 222-29, 232, 235, 237-38, 240, 243, 244, 246-48, 252, 257, 261-263, 266, 268-69, 275, 277, 279-82, 292-94, 299, 302, 308, 316-17, 323-25, 327, 336, 340, 345-46, 349, 351, 353-54.]

Vol. 264.

Entitled " Town Clerk's Protocol, 29 May 1607—13 January 1613."

This, again, is one of the books of Kingennie. On the first leaf is written in Latin and Scotch the epitaph of Mary Queen of Scots as at the beginning of Vol. 253, and also the words " In my defence, God me defend." At the end of this volume is written " Finis coronat opus."

368.   **1607** June 14.—Robert Wedderburn, elder, and Alexander Wedderburn his son, witnesses. (8.)

369.   **1607.** Sept. 12.—" Barbara Wedderburn, relict of umquhill Peter Imrie, ratefies and approvis hir testament and latter will . . . . with this additioun that scho leavis and disponis to Johne Leslie her sone-in-law hir syluer cuip, her signet of gold, and the grit purs and ane furnist bed, and the rest of hir houshold geir to Margaret Guthre, her dochter." (Min. Book XVIII, s.d.)

370.   **1608.** (*a*) Jan. 27.—James Wedderburn, merchant, and Peter Wedderburn, witnesses. (24, &c.) (*b*) Feb. 28.—Alexander Wedderburn, merchant, witness. (28.) (*c*) April 28.—Alexander Wedderburn, son of Robert Wedderburn, notary, witnesses a resignation by John Craigtoun and Elizabeth Barrie. (Min. Book XVIII, s.d.)

371.   **1608.** Nov. 3.—Sasine on charter by Sir James Scrymgeour of Dudop in favour of his well-beloved David Wedderburn, burgess, and Matilda Betoun his wife, of certain land in the West-field of Dundee. (55.)

372.   **1608.** Dec. 18.—Peter Wedderburn and his wife Anna Walker, daughter of the late William Walker, burgess, acquire an @-rent. (57.)

373.   **1609.** Feb. 7.—James Wedderburn, son of Peter Wedderburn, burgess of Dundee, witness. (60.)

This is the only reference in the records to a James, son of Peter Wedderburn, and I question whether there is not here some error as regards the Christian names.

374.   **1609.** March 7.—Robert Wedderburn, elder, burgess, for the love he bears Peter Wedderburn, " my son " (*i.e.*, the son of Alex. Wedderburn of Kingenuie, the clerk, who is notary to the instrument), and Alexander Wedderburn, son of David Wedderburn, burgess, resigns to them, subject to his own life-rent, a North Argylegate land. (61.)

375.   **1609.** [Undated].—Patrick Wedderburn, burgess, resigns his North Marketgate land to Alexander Wedderburn, his son and heir apparent, and to Barbara Auchinleck, wife to the said Alexander, and their heirs, subject to the life-rent of the said Patrick and Elizabeth Low, his wife. (62.)

376. **1609.** June 29.—Mr. James Wedderburn, son of Mr. Alexander Wedderburn, notary, witness. (73.) Dundee Protocol Books.

377. **1610.** [Undated].—John Mitchell is entered in a North Seagate land, as grandson and one of the heirs of the late William Wedderburn, burgess, and thereupon resigns the same to William Henderson, son of Magdalen Wedderburn. (98.)
This entry is headed "Pro Joanne Mitchell, Magdalene Wedderburn, et filio." See post No. 480.

378. **1610.** Sept. 13.—Alexander and Adam Wedderburn, merchants, burgesses, witnesses. (114.)

379. **1611.** (a) Sept. 24.—James Wedderburn, burgess, and Mr. James Wedderburn, burgess, are witnesses. (139.) (b) Dec. 20.—Mr. William Wedderburn, minister of Dundee, witness. (144.)

380. **1612.** Jan. 5.—Sasine of various premises is given to Alexander Wedderburn, younger, burgess, as attorney for Adam Wedderburn, his brother, son of Patrick Wedderburn, burgess. (147.)

381. **1612.** Feb. 29.—Peter Wedderburn, younger, is entered as the heir of the late Robert Wedderburn, notary, his uncle, in various feu fermes and annual rents, which he at once resigns to James Wedderburn, merchant, burgess, and to Peter Wedderburn, James' brother, acting as attorney for Cristina Lovell, James' wife. (151.)
The two Peter Wedderburns here named are, first, the son of Peter Wedderburn and Margaret Kinloch, and, secondly, the son of Alexander Wedderburn, the old clerk, and Janet Mylu.

382. **1612.** May 16.—Peter Man resigns an @ rent to James Wedderburn, merchant, burgess, and David Wedderburn, attorney for Cristina Lovell, wife of the said James. (157.)

383. **1612.** Dec. 9.—Mr. Alexander Wedderburn, younger, David, James, and Peter Wedderburn, burgesses, all witness a sasine. (178.)

[See, in all, fol. 2-4, 8, 14-16, 19, 23-24, 27-29, 32, 34, 42, 55, 57-58, 60-67, 69-80, 82, 83, 86, 90-92, 94, 95, 97-103, 105-6, 110-11, 114-15, 119-21, 123, 126, 131-32, 135, 139, 144-47, 149, 151, 153-58, 161, 163, 166-67, 170, 174-75, 177-78, 180.]

VOL. 265.

Entitled "Town Clerk's Protocol, from 9 November 1614 to 31 December 1619."

On the first leaf is written in Latin, "Protocol Book of Mr. Alexander Wedderburn, clerk of the court of Dundee, in the year of man's salvation, 1614." Then follows the epitaph of Mary Queen of Scots, in Latin and Scotch, as in Vol. 253.

384. **1614-15.** Mr. James Wedderburn is often witness, etc. (2-46.)

385. **1615.** Feb. 27.—Peter Wedderburn is entered in a North Marketgate land as son and heir of the late Peter Wedderburn, his father, and the late Margaret Kynloch, his mother (25), and again, Sept. 20, in other lands in Dundee. (60.)

386. **1615.** May 22.—Mr. David Wedderburn and John Wedderburn, burgesses, brothers, are witnesses. (35.)

387. **1615.** Oct. 27.—James Wedderburn, merchant, burgess, as procurator for James Kynnaird and Elizabeth Wedderburn, his wife, resigns a tenement near S. Clements to Andrew Kynnaird. (64.)

388. **1615.** Nov 16.—Mr. Alexander Wedderburn, younger, bailie, gives sasine of a North Argylegate tenement to Alexander Halyburton, shipmaster, burgess, and Margaret Wedderburn, his wife. Mr. Andrew Halyburton, son of George Halyburton of Kyneaple, is a witness. (66.)
The Margaret Wedderburn mentioned here and post No. 397 is, no doubt, the daughter of John Wedderburn and Margaret Lindsay, and sister of James, Bishop of Dunblane. In other places, however, her husband's name is given as Robert. (See post Burgh and Head Court Records, vol. xxvi. s., 15 Feb. 1615 ; vol xxx. s., 23 Sept. 1643 ; vol. xxxi. s., 25 Aug. 1643, and the account of her given in vol. I.).

389. **1616.** Feb. 5.—William Halyburton, brother of James Halyburton of Piteur, Mr. Alexander Wedderburn, younger, bailie, and Mr. James Wedderburn, his brother " my sons," and Mr. John Dyumuir, notary, are witnesses. (75-76.)

The words " my sons " refer, of course, to the sons of the writer of the instrument, Alexander Wedderburn of Kingennie.

390. **1616.** April 17.—Sasine of an @-rent to James Wedderburn, merchant, burgess, and Christina Lovell, his wife. (88.)

391. **1616.** July 1.—Alexander Wedderburn, eldest son of Patrick Wedderburn, burgess, resigns certain feu fermes to Alexander Hering. (96.)

392. **1616.** Sept. 19.—John Lindsay is entered as son and heir of the late George Lindsay, shipmaster, his father, in a North Kirkwynd tenement, subject to the liferent of Grissell Wedderburn, his mother. Among the witnesses is " magistro Jacobo Wedderburn ministro." (108.)

393. **1617.** April 28.—Alexander Wedderburn, merchant, burgess, resigns premises in North Marketgate to Patrick Wedderburn, his eldest son, and to John Wedderburn, also his son, both by Barbara Auchinlek, his wife. (129.)

394. **1617.** Aug. 4.—Mr. James Wedderburn, burgess, acts as procurator, and Peter Wedderburn, elder, and Alexander Wedderburn, shipmaster, are witnesses. (139.)

395. **1617.** Oct. 31.—The bailie goes to the North Argylegate fore-tenement of the late Robert Wedderburn, younger, burgess of Dundee, bounded by those of Mr. Alexander Wedderburn and others, and there enters Alexander Wedderburn, mariner, burgess, as son and heir of the said Robert ; and thereupon the said Alexander Wedderburn settles the said premises on himself and Jonet Newton, his future wife and their heirs. Thereafter the bailie goes to a North Murraygate tenement, once that of William Newton, son and heir of the late William Newton, burgess, and there enters the said Jonet Newton as daughter of the last, and sister german of the first named William Newton, whereupon Jonet, in implement of her marriage contract (dated at Dundee, May 9 last), with the said Alexander Wedderburn, resigns the said premises in favour of Janet Clerk, relict of John Newton. (143.)

396. **1617.** Oct. 8.—Edward Frisło, merchant, and Barbara Wedderburn, his wife, acquire, by purchase from Thomas Halyburton, a South Flukergate tenement. (144.)

397. **1617.** Nov. 7.—In the presence of Alexander Wedderburn, younger, bailie, Alexander Halyburton, shipmaster, and Margaret Wedderburn, his wife, grant a discharge to William Bultie, for redemption by him of the premises in North Argylegate, mentioned ante, No. 388. (150.)

398. **1617.** Nov. 26.—Mr. David Wedderburn, burgess, gets sasine of a North Argylegate foreland. David Wedderburn, burgess, is a witness. (155.)

399. **1618.** Aug. 11.—James Wedderburn, merchant, burgess, and Christian Lovell, his wife, get sasine of an annual rent. (174.)

400. **1619.** Oct. 22.—Peter Wedderburn, merchant, burgess, is witness. (226.)

401. **1619.** Dec. 4.—James Kyd resigns certain premises to himself and his future wife, Margaret Duncan, daughter of the deceased William Duncan, chirurgeon, and Katharine Wedderburn, now wife of Mr. William Fergusone, bailie of Dundee. (232).

402. **1619.** (a) Dec. 22.—James Wedderburn and Mr. James Wedderburn, burgesses, are witnesses. (235.) (b) Dec 31.—Mr. Alexander Wedderburn, younger, bailie, and Mr. James Wedderburn, his brother, are witnesses. (236.)

On the last leaf are written the lines in praise of Dundee, as at the beginning of Vol. 253 ; also the words " Donum Dei," divided by a rough drawing of a pot of lilies, the emblem of the town. Then follows at the end, " Mr Al. Wedderburn, Aetatis suæ anno 1616, 55."

[See, in all, fol. 1, 2, 4, 5, 9, 13, 15, 23, 25, 29, 31-33, 35-36, 38-39, 44, 48, 50, 60, 61, 63, 64-66, 68, 73-76, 82, 86, 88, 90, 92-93, 95-96, 98, 103, 107-8, 112-13, 117-18, 120, 123, 129-30, 136, 139, 141, 143-46, 148-50, 152-53, 155, 159, 163, 165, 169-71, 173-74, 176, 178-81, 184, 188-89, 191-92, 196, 207-8, 216, 218, 226-32, 234-36.]

Vol. 266.

Entitled " Protocol Book, 25 February 1615—16 June 1619."

This protocol book also belongs to the period of the clerkship of Alexander Wedderburn of Kingennie, but the protocols in it are subscribed by Thomas Wichtane, notary. The first five leaves are missing, and folios 126, 239—40 are torn out.

403. **1615.** March 17.—Sasine on crown charter, dated at Edinburgh, 7 Feb., in favour of Mr. William Fergusone and Catharine, his wife, of the lands of Balbouchlie, in the barony of Dunkeld, co. Forfar. (8.)

See post s. Public Records, Great Seal Reg., Vol. 1609—20, § 1177.

404. **1615.** June 25.—" Pro Magistro Alexandro Wedderburne, Helenae Ramsay, ejus sponse et filiabus "—Sasine on charter by John Scrymgeour of Dudop, constable of Dundee, in favour of Mr. Alexander Wedderburn, clerk of Dundee, and Helen Ramsay, his wife, of the sunny half of Balruddrie ; whereupon Mr. Alexander Wedderburn for the love he bears " his youngest daughters Jean and Elizabeth Wedderburn " gives them sasine thereof, subject to the life-rent of himself and his wife. (46.)

405. **1616.** Jan. 5.—" Pro Petro Wedderburn, juniore." David Wedderburn, burgess, attorney for Peter Wedderburn, son and heir of the late Peter Wedderburn, burgess, and heir also of the late Robert Wedderburn, his uncle, produces a precept of clare constat reciting that the late Robert Wedderburn, younger, notary, son to Robert Wedderburn, elder, burgess, and uncle of the said Peter Wedderburn, younger, died possest of certain lands in the East-field of Dudop, and that the said Peter Wedderburn, younger, is nearest heir of the said Robert Wedderburn, notary, and is of lawful age ; and thereupon the said Peter Wedderburn, younger, gets sasine of the said lands. (67.) He resigns them the same day in favour of James Wedderburn, merchant, burgess (68), who, Feb. 9, resigns them to William Smyth. (73)

406. **1616.** April 6.—Alexander Wedderburn, merchant, burgess, brother german and heir of the late Robert Wedderburn, son of Patrick Wedderburn, burgess, is entered as such in one half of a North Marketgate land (83), and again on the same day in the other half thereof, as heir of Adam Wedderburn, also his brother german. (84.)

407. **1616.** April 6.—Patrick Wedderburn, merchant, burgess, and Alexander Wedderburn, his son and heir apparent, with consent of Elizabeth Low and Barbara Auchinleck, their wives, resign the said North Marketgate land (ante 406), to Mr. Alexander Wedderburn, clerk. (85.)

408. **1616.** Sept. 23.—Sasine in favour of Margaret Guthrie, only daughter and heiress of the late Robert Guthrie, mariner (son of the late David Guthrie and the late Barbara Wedderburn), of certain land in the West-field of Dundee. (109.)

409. **1617.** Oct. 27.—Mr. William Fergusone, bailie, fulfils a marriage contract made between William Fergusone, his son and heir apparent, and Helen Duncan, daughter of the late William Duncan, surgeon, and his wife, Catharine Wedderburn, now the wife of the said Mr. William Fergusone, by giving sasine to his said son and his future wife, of certain land on the road from Spalding's Wynd to Schoolhouse Wynd. (160.)

410. **1617.** Dec. 13.—Jonet Newton, only daughter and heir of the deceased William Newton, settles two annual rents on her husband, Alexander Wedderburn, mariner, burgess, and herself. (166-167.)

411. **1617.** Dec. 24.—Sasine by Mr. Alexander Ramsay, son and heir of the late George Ramsay and his wife Agnes Durie, in favour of Mr. James Wedderburn (son of Mr. Alexander Wedderburn, clerk), and his wife, Margaret Goldman, and their heirs, of a South Murraygate tenement. Among the witnesses are Peter Wedderburn, elder, and John Wedderburn, merchant, burgess of Dundee. (170.)

2 H

412. **1618.** April 24.—Sasine in favour of Thomas Halyburton, elder, bailie, and Agnes
Guthrie, his wife, and Thomas Haliburton, younger, their son, and Margaret Wedderburn, his wife, of the lands of Mylne-hill, in the barony of Lundie, eo. Perth. (181.)

413. **1618.** [? date.]—Mr. Alexander Wedderburn, clerk of Dundee, in implement of a
contract of marriage made between his son, Peter Wedderburn, and Helen Lovell,
only daughter and heiress of the late Mr. John Lovell, bailie, with consent of her
sureties, dated at Dundee 20 August last, resigns various lands, tenements and annual
rents to Mr. Alexander Wedderburn, younger, as bailie, for infeftment to be given to
the said Peter Wedderburn and Helen Lovell, his future wife. (190.)

[See, in all, fol. 5, 8, 19, 41, 46, 48, 51, 55, 58, 62, 67, 68, 73, 75, 81, 83-85, 105, 109-10, 127, 150,
154-55, 160, 166-67, 169-71, 179, 181, 183, 186, 189-90, 194, 204.]

VOL. 267.

Protocol book of Mr. James Wedderburn, notary, and afterwards town clerk of Dundee.

This book is inaccurately entitled "Town Clerk's Protocol, from 2 Dec. 1617 to 8 Feb. 1622."
It is that of Kingennie's second son James Wedderburn, and runs from 1609 to 1622. He was
admitted a notary in 1609 and later on (1617) became conjunct clerk with his father, at whose death
in 1626 he became sole clerk till his own early death in 1627.

On the first leaf is written, " This buike pertenis me, M. J. Wedderburn, July 1609." " Master
James Wedderburn with my hand," and in Latin, " The Book of the protocols of Mr. James Wedderburn,
son lawful of Mr. Alexander Wedderburn, clerk of Dundee, in the year of man's salvation 1609."
Then follows the epitaph of Mary Queen of Scots, in Latin and Scotch, as at the beginning of Vols.
253 and 264. It is repeated on the second leaf.

414. **1609.** June 20. —At Edinburgh. " The quhilk day in presens of Mr. Jhone Prestoun
of Pennceuik, &c., compeirit personallie Mr. James Wedderburn, lawfull sone to Mr
Alexʳ Wedderburn, common clerk of Dundie, being of the age of twenty yeires or
thairby and producit the Lettre under writtene subserivit be the Kingis Majesties
cashar quhair of the tenour followis &c." The letter is in the usual form, and recites
that Mr. James, "since his cunning from the scoles hes bene trainit up with his
father in exerceing of the said office, quhilk hes movit the provost baillies and counsall
of the said brught (burgh) to give thair consentis to admitt him to the said office, &c."
and finally, he is admitted notary, and appends his notarial docket, signature, and
symbol. (1.)

A facsimile of the symbol is given at p. 187.

415. **1610.** Nov. 6.—James Kynnaird, burgess, and Elizabeth Wedderburn, his wife,
resign lands near S. Clements to Andrew Kynnaird. (6.)

416. **1616.** May 18.—Alexander Wedderburn, merchant, burgess (son of Patrick Wedderburn, also merchant burgess), and Barbara Auchinlek, his wife, by her attorney,
produce a charter in their favour by the said Patrick and Elizabeth Low, his wife, of
certain acres in the East-field of Dudop. (34.)

417. **1617.** Oct. 27.—Mr. William Fergussone, in implement of a contract of marriage
between William Fergussone, his son and heir apparent, and Helen Duncan, eldest
daughter of the late William Duncan, surgeon, and Catharine Wedderburn, formerly
his wife, now the wife of the said Mr. William Fergussone. settles on the spouses the
lands of Balbenehlie, with tower, fortalice, manor-place, &c., subject to his own and
his wife's life-rent. Mr. Alexander Wedderburn, clerk, and his sons, Alexander,
Peter, and John Wedderburn, are witnesses. (35.)

418. **1617.** Oct. 27.—Mr. William Fergussone also charges Balbouchlie with an @-rent in
favour of Magdalen Fergussone, his daughter, by his wife, Catharine Wedderburn. (36.)

419. **1618.** July 21.—Sasine of a South Marygate tenement in favour of Edward Frislo,
burgess, and Barbara Wedderburn his wife. (44.)

420. **1619.** July 1.—Peter Wedderburn, younger, burgess, and Helen Lovell his wife
resign a tenement in Dundee. (47.)

This volume is blank from fol. 69 on. It consists of 184 leaves.

[See, in all, fol. 1-3, 5-6, 18-19, 29, 34-38, 43, 44, 45, 47, 48, 61, 63, 66-68.]

VOL. 268.

Entitled " Town Clerk's Protocol, from 31 Dec. 1619 to 18 March 1624."

On the first leaf is written in Latin " Protocol Book of Mr. Alexander Wedderburn, clerk of Dundee." It is his last book, and many of the leaves at the end are blank.

421. **1620.** April 22.—Thomas Jak, merchant, burgess, and Magdalene Wedderburn, his wife, grant a discharge to John Barry. (7.)

422. **1620.** June 20.—Mr. David Wedderburn, eldest son of Robert Wedderburn, burgess, in South Flukergate, settles a South Flukergate tenement on his wife Alison Watson for life. (15.)

423. **1620.** (a) June 23.—Peter Wedderburn, elder, is witness. (16.) (b) July 14, 29.—Peter Wedderburn, younger, son of Mr. Alexander Wedderburn, notary, is witness. (19, 20.)

424. **1621.** April 24.—Mr. Alexander Wedderburn, younger, Alexander Wedderburn, merchant, and Mr. James Wedderburn, son of Mr. Alexander Wedderburn, notary, are witnesses. (37.)

425. **1621.** Oct. 1.—Mr. David Wedderburn, burgess in South Flukergate, settles the said land (ante No. 422) on his beloved son Andrew Wedderburn, to whose attorney sasine is given. Mr. Alexander Wedderburn, younger, bailie, is witness. (50.)

426. **1621.** (a) Dec. 17.—James Wedderburn, elder, and James Wedderburn, son of David Wedderburn, burgess, are witnesses. (51) (b) Dec. 22.—Patrick Wedderburn, burgess, is a witness.

427. **1622.** Jan. 2.—Peter Blak is entered in a South Flukergate land, as heir to George Blak, his grandfather, and George Blak, mariner, his father, both deceased, and resigns it with consent of his mother, Margaret Wedderburn, and Andrew Blak, shipmaster, burgess, her spouse, in favour of Robert Forrester and Agnes Scott, his wife. (59.)

428. **1622.** July 3.—William Wedderburn, son of Mr. Alexander Wedderburn, notary, is witness. (77.)

429. **1623.** Nov. 11.—David Wedderburn and Matilda Beatone, his wife, and their son, James, resign a large tenement in the North end of St. Margaret's close, to Charles Goldman. (90.)

430. **1623.** Nov. 11.—James Wedderburn, eldest son of David Wedderburn, burgess, resigns half of a North Argylegate land, once that of the late Robert Wedderburn, elder, notary, to the bailie (Mr. Alexander Wedderburn, younger), who gives sasine thereof to the said David Wedderburn and Matilda Beaton, his wife. (91.)

431. **1623.** Nov. 17.—Mr. James Wedderburn, Alexander Wedderburn, younger, mariner, and William Wedderburn, son of Mr. Alexander Wedderburn, notary, are witnesses. (92.)

[See, in all, fol. 1, 2, 5, 7, 8, 10, 11, 13-17, 19-20, 22-24, 33-34, 36-38, 40, 45, 49-51, 56, 59, 61-65, 67-69, 74, 77-78, 81, 88, 90-93, 95.]

VOL. 269.

Entitled " Town Clerk's Protocol, from 11 April 1633 to 22 July 1639."

This is the first protocol book of Alexander Wedderburn, son of James Wedderburn, clerk, afterwards Sir Alexander, of Blackness. On the first leaf is written in Latin, "Book of Protocols of Mr. Alexander Wedderburn younger " and the letters M.A.W.N.P., with the date 1633. Then follows the epitaph of Mary Queen of Scots, as in Vol. 253, and below is a sort of notarial symbol, somewhat different, however, from the one the writer ultimately adopted. A facsimile of it is given at p. 187. The book begins with his admission as notary.

432. **1633.** March 16.—At Edinburgh :—" The quhilk day . . . . comperit personallie Mr. Alexander Wedderburn, laufull sone to umquhill Mr. James Wedderburn, sometime clerk of Dundie, at the age of xxiij yeires or thairby," who " hes beine traint np with Johne Lermont, writer to our signet in his airt and science of writing thir dyvers yeiris bygane," &c. Then follows his signature. (1.)

433. **1634.** (a) Jan. 20.—Alexander Wedderburn, elder, merchant, burgess, is witness. (10.) (b) Jan. 21—24.- John Wedderburn, merchant, burgess, is sheriff in a sasine, and Alexander Wedderburn, fiar of Kingany, and Alexander Wedderburn, younger, shipmaster, are witnesses. (19, 20.)

434. **1634.** Oct. 9.—James Wedderburn, son lawful of the late David Wedderburn, burgess, resigns, by his procurator, the lands in North Argylegate once belonging to Robert Wedderburn, elder, burgess. (36.)

435. **1635.** (a) June 3.—Alexander Wedderburn, elder, merchant, and Andrew Wedderburn, his son, are witnesses. (51.) (b) June 4.—Alexander Wedderburn, elder, and Andrew Wedderburn in St. Andrews, burgesses of Dundee, are witnesses. (51).

436. **1635.** Dec. 18.—The bailie goes to the South Marketgate land of the late Robert Murray, burgess, now occupied by Elizabeth Wedderburn, his relict, and gives sasine thereof to John Murray, his son and heir, subject to the liferent of the said Elizabeth Wedderburn. John Wedderburn, merchant, burgess, is named as curator to the said John Murray. Gideon Murray is also named as another son of the said Robert Murray. Alexander Wedderburn, elder, burgess, is a witness. (65.)

437. **1637.** Dec. 7.—The bailic goes to certain tenements of land in Dundee, formerly the properties of the late Mr. Alexander Wedderburn of Kingennie, clerk of Dundee, (and one of which belonged to the late Robert Wedderburn, his brother), and there enters Alexander Wedderburn, now of Kingennie, as only son and heir of his father, the said Mr. Alexander Wedderburn. (112.)
If this is rightly extracted, the word "brother" is an error for "uncle." The reference is to Robert Wedderburn, younger (d. 1593), brother of Alexander Wedderburn, first of Kingennie, the clerk. (See post, No. 463.) The person entered is Alexander Wedderburn, third of Kingennie, whose father had died in Sept. 1637.

438. **1637.** Dec. 8.—John Wedderburn, merchant, burgess, of Dundee, procurator. (113.)

439. **1638.** Jan. 4.—Alexander Wedderburn of Kingennie, is entered in an 8 merk annual rent out of South Murraygate, as heir both to his father, the late Mr. Alexander Wedderburn of Kingennie, and to his grandfather, the late Mr. Alexander Wedderburn of Kingennie. (115.)
See post No. 482.

440. **1638.** March 23.—Alexander Wedderburn, elder, merchant, burgess, procurator ; John Wedderburn, merchant, burgess, witness. (118-19.)

441. **1638** May 1.—A tenement in North Argylegate, described as bounded by the lands of the late Mr. Alexander Wedderburn, grandfather of Mr. Alexander Wedderburn, notary, on the north, and those of Alexander Wedderburn, his kinsman, on the west, is resigned by Mr. John Wedderburn, son of the said deceased Mr. Alexander Wedderburn. (125.)
Mr. Alexander Wedderburn, notary, named here, is the then clerk, afterwards Sir Alexander of Blackness.

442. **1638.** Dec. 26.—Sasine on charter (dated at Perth, 15 Nov.), by Alexander Wedderburn of Kingennie, in favour of his future spouse, Elizabeth, only daughter of John Ramsay, bailie, in liferent, and their heirs, in implement of his contract of marriage with her, of all and haill his lands of Kingennie, and Carnetoun of Kingennie, alias Trimbles, with manor place, yards, orchards, mill of Kingennie, &c., in the barony of Ethiebetoun, regality of Kirriemuir, and shire of Forfar ; and also of a North Marketgate tenement, formerly belonging to Patrick and Alexander Wedderburn, burgesses. (131.)

[See, in all, fol. 1, 6, 10, 20, 24-26, 29, 35, 37-38, 45, 47, 51, 52, 64, 66, 69, 74, 75, 77, 80, 109, 111-13, 115-16, 118-20, 122, 124-25, 131, 139-40.]

VOL. 270.

Entitled " Town Clerk's Protocol, 1 *June* 1638—25 *November* 1641).

Inside the cover is written, " Protocol book of Thomas Kessane, N.P., from 25 Nov. 1616 to 25 Nov. 1641, containing sasines passed by him as substitute town clerk, from 1 June 1638 to 25 Nov. 1641." A good many leaves at the end of this volume are blank.

443. **1616.** Nov. 24.—His admission as notary, æt. 24, at Edinburgh, is given. (1.)

444. **1621.** March 23.—Mr. Henric Danskine, master of the grammar school of S. Andrews, and Elizabeth Wedderburn, his wife, in implement of a contract between them and Thomas Haldine of Kellour, dated 9 Nov. 1620, are infefted in the lands of Ballungie, co. Forfar, under reversion of 4000 merks. (8.)

445. **1626.** Dec. 19.—William Wedderburn, burgess, witnesses the handing over by Thomas Halyburton, provost of Dundee, at Woodhavine on 19 Dec., of James Forbes, " lately apprehend in Dundee as a Jesuite" into the hands of . . . . . (*sic*), bailie of S. Andrews, conform to a warrant by the Archbishop of S. Andrews. (19.)

446. **1629.** July 9.—Helen Scharp assigns to Mr. James Read half of the lands of Craigie acquired by Sir John Scharp, her father, from John Wedderburn, son and heir of the late James Wedderburn, burgess. (27.)

447. **1631.** June 6.—At Kinganie. Mr. Alex. Wedderburn of Kinganie passes to " ane long deyk than biggit " be Mr. William Durhame of Umquhy as a boundary between the two estates, and protests against it as being built on the " common louing." Among the witnesses is Alexander Wedderburn, his son. (32.)

448. **1639.** April 8.—Mr. Alexander Wedderburn clerk of Dundee, resigns to the bailie the large North Marketgate tenement of the late Peter Wedderburn, merchant, his uncle, and now belonging to him as his said uncle's heir, for sasine thereof to be given to himself and Matilde Fletcher, his wife, and their heirs. James Fletcher, provost, is attorney for M. Fletcher. (70.)

449. **1640.** June 25.—James Boytar gets sasine of a North Argylegate malthouse once that of the late Mr. Alexander Wedderburn, clerk, and set by him to Alexander Nicoll. (76.)

450. **1640.** Nov. 5.—Alexander Wedderburn of Kingany, bailie, passes to two North Marketgate premises, once belonging to Alexander Wedderburn, merchant, and afterwards to John Wedderburn his son, and enters therein Andrew Wedderburn as heir to the said John, his brother german. (83.)
This and the next entry are repeated in Vol 273, fol. 33-34.

451. **1640.** Nov. 5.—Alexander Wedderburn of Kingany, bailie, passes to another North Marketgate tenement, once belonging to Alexander Wedderburn, merchant, and afterwards to Patrick Wedderburn, his son, and enters therein Andrew Wedderburn, as brother german and heir to the said Patrick. (83.)

452. **1641.** March 4.—Captain James Wedderburn, son of the late David Wedderburn, notary, burgess, as procurator for Andrew Hutcheone, resigns three roods of land. (89.)

453. **1641.** March 16 —The lands, once of Patrick Wedderburn, now alienated by Alexander Wedderburn, his son, to James Cochrane, in North Argylegate, are named. (90.)

454. **1641.** May 12.—Alexander Wedderburn, mariner, is witness on two occasions. (93.)

[See, in all, fol. 1, 8, 18, 19, 26, 27, 32, 33, 44, 67, 70, 76, 78, 83, 87, 89-91, 93.]

VOL. 271-72.

Entitled " Town Clerk's Protocol, from 23 Dec. 1648 to 20 May 1653."

The sasines in this book, which is numbered thus, 271-72, are all subscribed by Thomas Wichtune, notary public.

455. **1649.** Jan. 27.—Alexander Wedderburn, elder, shipmaster, is entered in an @ rent out of premises in North Marketgate, as heir to the late James Wedderburn, merchant, burgess, his uncle. (16.)

456. **1649.** (a) Feb. 1.—The lands of Peter Wedderburn, shipmaster, are named as bounding others in South Argylegate. (8.)   (b) March 21.—Andrew Wedderburn, merchant, burgess of Dundee, named. (15)   (c) May 29.—William Wedderburn, brother of Sir Alexander Wedderburn, of Blackness, witness. (23.)   (d) July 23.— Alexander Wedderburn, elder, merchant, witness. (26.)

457. **1650.** July 13.—A tenement in North Marketgate, now occupied by Andrew Wedderburn, merchant, is named. (48.)

458. **1650.** Sept. 9.—Sir Alexander Wedderburn of Blackness and Dame Matilda Fletcher, his spouse, resign some North Argylegate premises to Robert Straitone. (55.)

459. **1652.** Sept. 6.—Sir Alexander Wedderburn of Blackness resigns two acres in the West-field of Dundee to James Wedderburn, his second lawful son. (113.)

460. **1652.** July 16.—Alexander Wedderburn, skipper, is procurator for Sir Alexander Wedderburn of Blackness on the resignation of some East Welgate property to Elspet Bisset. (115.)

On the last leaf of this volume is written in somewhat youthful hand " James Wedderburne with my hand," probably by Sir Alexander's second son, the clerk. There are many blank leaves in the middle and at the end of this volume.

[See, in all, fol. 6, 8, 9, 15, 19, 23, 25-27, 31, 33, 34, 36, 48, 55, 113, 115, 124-25, 132-33, 136.]

VOL. 273.

Entitled " Sasines, from 22 July 1639 to 20 May 1659."

On the first leaf is written " The Sasine register of Dundie begining in anno 1639 and ending in anno 1659. Sir Alexander Wedderburn of Blackness, knight."

461. **1639.** Sept. 24.—James Kyde, merchant, resigns an annual-rent to Alexander Wedderburn, mariner, burgess. (3.)

462. **1640.** Feb. 27.— John Wedderburn, merchant, burgess, witness. (19.)

463. **1640.** Feb. 27.—The bailie goes to the three tenements of the late Mr. Alexander Wedderburn of Kingennie, clerk, now belonging to Alexander Wedderburn of Kingennie, his son and heir (of which tenements one belonged to the late Robert Wedderburn, uncle of the said Mr. Alexander, deceased) and there the said Alexander Wedderburn, now of Kingennie, settles the said premises on himself and Elizabeth Ramsay his wife. (19.)
      See ante No. 437.

464. **1641.** Oct. 25.—Sasine on charter of confirmation by William, Marquis of Douglas, in favour of Elizabeth Ramsay, wife of Alexander Wedderburn of Kingennie, confirming a charter granted to her by her said husband, and dated at Perth, 15 Nov. 1638, in implement of their contract of marriage of like date, disponing to her the life-rent of Kingennie. (59.)
      See ante No. 442.

465. **1642.** (a) Jan. 22.—Alexander Wedderburn, merchant, burgess, is a witness. (68.)
      (b) March 15.—Alexander Wedderburn of Kingennie, kirkmaster, is seised in various premises in Dundee. (72.)

466. **1642.** April 15.—James Wedderburn, bailie, goes to the South Flukergate land of the late Robert Murray, now of John Murray, his eldest son, who in implement of a marriage contract between him and Isobell, daughter of John Goldman, merchant, deceased, resigns the said land to "Mr. Peter Wedderburn, advocate, my brother german " (*i e*, brother of the writer, Sir Alexander) as attorney for the said Isobell, in life-rent, subject to the life rent of Elizabeth Wedderburn, mother of the said John Murray. Alexander Wedderburn, shipmaster, is witness. (74.)

467. **1642.** June 22.—Elspeth Ramsay, wife of Alexander Wedderburn of Kingennie, is entered in a North Marketgate tenement as only daughter and heiress of the late John Ramsay, merchant, and resigns it to her husband and herself for life, and then to John Wedderburn, their second son. (80.)

468. **1642.** July 6.—Alexander Wedderburn. bailie, gives sasine of a malthouse once belonging to Sir Alexander Wedderburn of Blackness, bounded by the 'grenchand' once belonging to the late Alexander Wedderburn. Alexander Wedderburn, younger, shipmaster, is witness. (83.)

469. **1643.** March 9.—Alexander Wedderburn of Kingennie, one of the bailies of Dundee, is entered in an annual rent as only son and heir of his late father, Mr. Alexander Wedderburn of Kingennie. (96.)

470. **1643.** June 10.—The bailie goes to the North Marketgate property once belonging to the late Alexander Wedderburn, merchant, burgess, then to the late Patrick Wedderburn, his son, and now to Andrew Wedderburn, merchant, burgess, brother of the said Patrick ; and there, on resignation by the said Andrew, gives sasine thereof in life-rent to Elspeth Fletcher, natural daughter of the late Sir George Fletcher of Restemoth, Knight, in implement of a marriage contract (dated 29 April), made between the said Andrew and Elspeth, with consent of James Fletcher, provost of Dundee. (101.)

471. **1643.** Sept. 6.—Mr. Peter Wedderburn, advocate, brother german of Sir Alexander Wedderburn of Blackness, notary, is a witness. (109.)

472. **1645.** Aug. 11.—William Petrie gets sasine of the malthouse once belonging to Mr. Alexander Wedderburn, grandfather of Sir Alexander Wedderburn of Blackness, and set by him in tack to Alexander Nicoll. (129.)

473. **1646.** (*a*) Jan. 14.—William Wedderburn, son of the late Mr. James Wedderburn, clerk, witness. (134.) (*b*) June 12.—Alexander Wedderburn, shipmaster, burgess, witness. (148.)

474. **1648.** Oct. 16.—The bailie goes to the North Marketgate property once that of Elspeth Ramsay, deceased, Alexander Wedderburn of Kingennie, her spouse, and John Wedderburn, their son, and enters therein Alexander Wedderburn, junior, also son to the said Alexander Wedderburn of Kingennie, as brother german and heir of the said John Wedderburn, deceased. Mr. Peter Wedderburn, brother of Sir Alexander Wedderburn of Blackness, is a witness. (220.)

475. **1651.** June 3.—The lands of the late Alexander Wedderburn, merchant, now of Andrew Wedderburn, his son, are named as a boundary. (231.)

476. **1652.** June 4.—Alexander Wedderburn, shipmaster, burgess, gets sasine of an annual rent. (248)

477. **1653.** Dec. 3.—Helen and Bessie Wedderburn, daughters of umquhill Alexander Wedderburn, skipper, are entered in various properties in Dundee as "aires portioneres of their granduncle, umquhill James Wedderburn." (257.) They are also entered "heirs portioneres " to their said father. (258.)

478. **1654.** Jan. 2.—John James Wedderburn of Drohanavitis in Moravia is entered "oy and air" of the late John Wedderburn in certain North Flukergait land. Alexander Halyburton acts as his attorney. (260.)

479. **1654.** Jan. 9.—Resignation in favour of Elizabeth Wedderburn, relict of Robert Murray, of various premises in Dundee. (262.)

480. **1654.** Sept. 20. —John Mitchell gets sasine of a North Seagate land once belonging to the deceased William Wedderburn, Magdalen Wedderburn, his daughter, and William Hendersone, her son, and then to Dr. Thomas Maull. (276.)
See ante No. 377.

481. **1655.** April 25.—Helen and Bessie Wedderburn with William Gasgiune and John Gayrdine, their respective spouses, resign a South Seagate land to Alexander Bower. (304.)

482. **1658.** Oct. 13.—Alexander Wedderburn of Kingennie is entered "air by progress to Robert Mylne, burgess, wha wes father to Janet Mylne, grand dame to the said Alexander Wedderburn of Kingennie on his father's side " in an eight merk annual rent out of the South Murraygate tenement, which pertained of old to David Wedderburn, burgess. (429-30.)

This entry is not quite correct.   Janet Mylne who m. Alexander Wedderburn, the old clerk, was great grand-dame to Alexander Wedderburne then (1658) of Kingennie ; and her father's name was James, not Robert.   The annual rent here mentioned was an old possession.   See ante No. 439 and Scrymgeour-Wedderburn Papers, No. 13.
At the end of this volume the words, "Jas : Wedderbnrne clerk of Dundie," are elaborately written four times in the hand of James Wedderburn, the clerk (son to Sir Alexander), d. 1696.)

[See, in all, fol. 2-5, 19, 33, 34, 59, 64, 68, 69, 72, 74, 78, 80, 83-85, 90, 92, 96, 101-3, 106, 109, 111, 115, 129-30, 134, 143, 146 152-53, 166-58, 161, 166, 171, 173, 178, 185, 198, 204, 212, 220-21, 224, 227, 231, 248, 257-58, 260, 262, 267, 274, 276, 281, 286, 303, 304, 311, 318-19, 321, 327, 331, 342, 369, 381, 404-5, 407-9, 414, 418, 429-30, 432, 436-37, 441.]

Vol. 274.

Entitled "Sisius from 25 May to 28 August, 1666."

483. **1659.** (*a*) May 25.—A South High-street tenement is named as now George Fletcher's, and once that of Andrew Wedderburn, merchant, burgess. (1.) (*b*) Nov. 30.—South Murraygate land, now that of the heirs of — Halyburton, once that of Andrew Wedderburn, named. (13.)

484. **1660.** Jan. 25.—Resignation of various subjects by John Goldman, as procurator for Helen Wedderburn, reciting the marriage contract, dated 15 Aug. 1657, between her "relict of the deceast William Goskine, Inglishman " and "Farten Bilsone, Inglishman, merchant in Dundie." The said subjects include (1) half a North Arrylegate tenement, once disponed by Sir Alexander Wedderburn of Blackness, to Alexander Wedderburn, deceased, father of the said Helen ; (2) half another North Argylegate tenement, bounded East by the lands of the heirs of the late David Dunbar, and North by those of Alexander Wedderburn of Kingennie ; and all are now settled on the said spouses and the "airs quhatsomevir to be lawfully gottin betwixt them." (19.)

485. **1660.** Oct. 30.—Sasine to T. Steill of a North Argylegate malthouse, bounded West by the lands of the heirs of Elizabeth Wedderburn and Mr. John Lovell. (33.)

486. **1661.** Feb. 23.—J. Copine and W. Rankine own a South Argylegate land, once that of Margaret Mylne and Robert Wedderburn, her husband. (42.)

487. **1662** June 9.—Sasine to J. Petrie of a malthouse in the old clerk's close, North Argylegate, set by the late Mr. Alexander Wedderburn to the late A. Nicoll, and bounded South by the lands of the heirs of the late Alexander Wedderburn. (81.)

488. **1662.** Sept. 16.—Sasine to Andrew Clerk, of a land of Alexander Symer in South Murraygate, bounded West by that of the late Robert Wedderburn. (91.)

489. **1663.** Jan. 17.—Sasine to Alexander Annand, of a South Argylegate land, bounded
South by that of Alexander Halyburton, once that of John Wedderburn. (113.)

490. **1668.** March 3.—Sasine of a great burghal tenement in North Schoolwynd, once
belonging to Peter Wedderburn, then to Thomas Gayrdine, now to Margaret Gayrdine.
(128.)

491. **1663.** Nov. 13.—Marriage settlement of Jean Wedderburn, second lawfull daughter
of Sir Alexander Wedderburn of Blackness, Knt., and William Kid, younger, her
spouse future (and brother's son to the late William Kid, son of the late Patrick
Kid of Grange of Barry.) The property settled is the life-rent of a South Seagate
tenement. (146.)

492. **1664.** (*a*) Feb. 17.—Sir Alexander Wedderburn of Blackness, dispones to his
second son, James Wedderburn, subject to the life rent of himself and his wife,
Matilda Fletcher, a South Flukergate tenement. William Wedderburn, brother
german of Sir Alexander Wedderburn, is a witness. (157.) (*b*) Similar settlement
by Sir Alexander Wedderburn, of another South Flukergate property on his third son,
Peter Wedderburn. (158.) (*c*) Similar settlement by Sir Alexander Wedderburn, of
other South Flukergate property on his fourth son, George Wedderburn. (159.) (*d*)
Similar settlement by Sir Alexander Wedderburn, of a North Argylegate and South
Seagate property on his youngest son, Alexander Wedderburn. (160.)

493. **1664.** March 24.—Lands once of Peter Imbrie and James Wedderburn, and a great
land in North Marketgate, once that of David Wedderburn, Charles Goldman, &c.,
bounded West by land once of James Rait and Patrick Wedderburn, mentioned. (164.)

494. **1665** March 20.—John Wedderburn, baxter, burgess, is a witness. (192.)

495. **1665.** Sept. 14.—Lands once of John Wedderburn, named as bounding those once
belonging to the late Robert Clayhills, elder and younger, and now to of David Clayhills. (208.)

496. **1666.** Jan. 26.—John Wedderburn, baxter, witness. (219.)

497. **1666.** March 13.—Alexander Wedderburn, provost, and Sir Alexander Wedderburn
of Blackness, clerk, sign a charter by the town to the orphan poor of Dundee. (221.)

498. **1666.** June 9.—Sir Alexander Wedderburn of Blackness, Knight, and John
Wedderburn, advocate, his son, witness a charter and sasine thereon. (229.)

On the last leaf is written "James Wedderburne."

[See, in all, fol. 1, 13, 19, 22, 33, 42, 49, 81, 91, 113, 128, 146, 153, 157-60, 164, 192-93, 200, 208-9,
213, 217, 219-21, 229.]

VOL. 275.

Entitled "Seisins from 28 August 1666 to 20 May 1676."

On the first leaf is written, "James Wedderburne totin clerk of Dundie. Robert Lauder, clerk
deput. James Wedderburn. Sir Alexander Wedderburn," and "Liber Protocolorum Jacobi Wedderburn Inchoatus Octavo die mensis Augusti anno Domini 1666 et finitus 20mo die mensis Maij in
anno 1676."

On the second page of this leaf : "Incipio libri sit laus et gloria Deo," and the signature
"Alexander Wedderburne, Anno Domini 1709."

499. **1666.** Aug. 28.—Alexander Wedderburn of Kingany, provost, gets sasine of a
North Argylegate fore-tenement, once that of Alexander Wedderburn, merchant,
then that of Barten Belsone, upon a resignation thereof to him by the said Barten
Belsone, dated 4 May 1660. (1.)

500. **1666.** Aug. 28.—Settlement by Sir Alexander Wedderburn of Blackness, of a
certain Dundee property (once belonging to Alexander Wedderburn, merchant), on
Alexander Wedderburn, his youngest son. (1.)

2 I

501.   **1666.** Sept. 18.—Lands of Andrew Wedderburn, North of North Marketgate. (5.)

502.   **1667.** Aug. 31.—Sasine given to Patrick Kyd, of Craigie, of the lands and toun of Grange of Barrie, by Alexander Wedderburn, younger, of Kingennie, as sheriff in that part. (22)

503.   **1668.** Feb. 10.—Andrew Wedderburn, merchant, acts as procurator, and (July 4), as witness. (30, 39.)

504.   **1668.** July 20.—Sasine in favour of Barten or Bartholomew Belson, Englishman, of certain @-rents, pursuant to his marriage contract with Helen Wedderburn. (41.)

505.   **1668.** July 28.—Settlement by Sir Alexander Wedderburn of Blackness, on Alexander Wedderburn, his youngest son, of certain annual rents, disponed to Sir Alexander by Barten Belsone. (41.)

506.   **1668.** Aug. 19.—Sasine to Barbara Kyd, on her marriage contract, dated Aug. 11, bypast, with Mr. Thomas Halyburton, son of Margaret Wedderburn, and grandson of the late Thomas Halyburton, provost of Dundee (44-45.)

507.   **1668.** Sept. 4.—Reference to a disposition, 1 April 1642, by William Stevensone, to the late Alexander Wedderburn, mariner. (45.,

508.   **1668.** Sept. 21.—Lands in North Argylegate of Alexander Wedderburn and of the heirs of Elizabeth Wedderburn, mentioned. (47.)

509.   **1668.** Sept. 21.—Sir Alexander Wedderburn gets sasine of an annual-rent out of the late Mr. James Wedderburn's North Argylegate land. (48.)

510.   **1668.** Oct. 6.—John Wedderburn, baxter, burgess, and Helen Rodger, his wife, get sasine of a North Nethergate property from Catharine and Grisell Tyrees. (49.)

511.   **1669.** Sept. 15.—South Nethergate lands, bounded East by those of the heirs of Robert Murray and Elizabeth Wedderburn, mentioned. (65.)

512.   **1669.** Sept. 16.—James Wedderburn, son of Sir Alexander Wedderburn of Blackness is a witness. (57.) And again at various dates. (77, 84, 87, 99.)

513.   **1670.** Jan. 22.—Andrew Wedderburn's land North Argylegate, mentioned. (72.)

514.   **1670.** Oct. 18.—James Wedderburn, writer in Dundee, witness. (84.) And again, Dec. 1, 17. (91-92.)

515.   **1671.** Jan. 16.—John Wedderburn, baxter, burgess, dispones his North Nethergate property (ante No. 510), to Alexander Wedderburn, younger, of Kingany. (91.)

516.   **1671.** Sept. 1.— Alexander Wedderburn of Kingany, sheriff, gives sasine of Wood-hill to William Kyd, brother to Patrick Kyd of Craigie. (103.)

517.   **1671.** Sept. 11.—Disposition by Sir Alexander Wedderburn of Blackness, to his eldest son, John Wedderburn, fiar thereof, of various lands in North Argylegate, North Murraygate, South Cowgate, &c. (104.)

518.   **1671.** Dec. 17.—Alexander Wedderburn of Easter Powrie, gets from Robert Stratone an annual rent out of a North Argylegate property, lying near the lands of the said Alexander Wedderburn, those of the late Alexander Wedderburn, merchant, and those of Andrew Wedderburn. (106.)

519.   **1671.** Dec. 29.—Sasine to John Wedderburn, fiar of Blackness, of a North Argyle-gate tenement. (107.)

520. **1673.** Sept 2.—".James Wedderburn, also clerk of the burgh, my son" is named by Sir Alexander Wedderburn as a witness. (132.) Dundee Protocol Books.

521. **1674.** Sept. 5.—Robert Davidson of Balgay, son and heir of the late Robert Davidson thereof, with consent of Elizabeth Davidson, his sister german, and James Wedderburn, common clerk of Dundee, her husband, dispone a North Seagate malthouse to John Cook. (150.)

522. **1675.** Aug. 21.—Sasine of various properties in Dundee to Patrick Leslie, late chamberlain of Sir Peter Wedderburn of Gosfoord, one of the senators of the College of Justice. (172.)

523. **1675.** Dec. 18.—James Wedderburn, second son of the late Sir Alexander Wedderburn of Blackness, dispones to Peter Wedderburn, third son of the said Sir Alexander, a South Nethergate tenement. (183.)

524. **1676.** (a) Feb. 21.—North Marketgate lands once those of Sir Alexander Wedderburn of Blackness, now of his son Peter, mentioned. (188.) (b) April 8.—North Argylegate lands of the heirs of the late Sir Alexander Wedderburn of Blackness, mentioned. (194-95.)

On last leaf is written " Ja : Wedderburne clericus in premissis. Jacobus Wedderburne "
The last time Sir Alexander Wedderburn subscribes a sasine is 29 July 1671 (fol. 100), after which they are subscribed by his son, James Wedderburne.

[See, in all, fol 1, 5, 8, 14, 22, 30, 34, 39, 41, 44-45, 47-49, 54, 57, 59-61, 65, 67, 72, 77, 84, 87, 91, 92, 94, 95, 99, 102-4, 106-7, 114, 118, 121, 126, 132, 142-44, 149-50, 159, 172, 183, 186, 188, 194-95.]

Vol. 276.

Entitled "Seisins 20 May, 1676—8 December, 1683."

On the first leaf is written, " This is the Regester of Seasins perteining to the Town of Dundie, the 27 day of July 1676."
" This book belongs to James Wedderburne, clerk of Dundie, for registrating the seasings within the said burgh."

On the same page occur the following mottoes :—

Soli Deo laus et gloria Christo.	Da tua dum tua sunt, post mortem tunc tua
Soli Deo gloria Christo (repeated)	non sunt.
Laus Deo semper.	Post mortem nulla voluptas.
Vivit post funera virtus.	Qui patitur vincit.

525. **1676.** Oct. 12.—Alexander Wedderburn of Easter Powrie, is entered as nearest heir in the North Argylegate fore-tenement of the late Alexander Wedderburn, merchant, and Elizabeth Wedderburn, his daughter. John Wedderburn of Blackness, and Patrick Kyd of Craigie, witnesses. (8.)

526. **1676.** Oct. 11.—Sasine to Alexander Wedderburn of Easter Powrie, as nearest agnate and heir of the late Alexander Wedderburn, "nauta," burgess, and Elizabeth Wedderburn, his daughter, in various tenements and annual rents, which he straightway settles on his youngest son, Peter. The witnesses are the same as in No. 525. (9.)

527. **1676.** Nov. 2.—Andrew Wedderburn in North Argylegate, named. (12.)

528. **1676.** Nov. 11.—Sasine to Alexander Wedderburn, younger, now of Kingennie, by virtue of his marriage contract, dated 18 Oct. 1665, with Grissell Wedderburn, fourth daughter of the late Sir Alexander Wedderburn of Blackness, of a great North Argylegate tenement, near the land once of Patrick Wedderburn, and also near that of the heirs of Alexander Wedderburn, shipmaster, and others, subject to the life-rent of Alexander Wedderburn, elder, of Easter Powrie, his father. (13.)

529. **1680.** Jan. 14.—Settlement by Peter Wedderburn, merchant in Dundee, on his wife, Catharine, daughter of John Man, of the life-rent of a South Nethergate property. (62.)

530. 1680. Nov. 4-5.—Alexander Wedderburn, youngest son of Sir Alexander Wedderburn of Blackness, deceased, sells to Alexander Wedderburn of Easter Powrie,
various properties and annual rents in Dundee. (78.) Thereupon Easter Powrie
settles them on Patrick (or Peter) Wedderburn, the only lawful son of himself and
Margaret Myln, his wife. (79.)

531. 1681. Sept. 2.—Lands of Peter Wedderburn, merchant, and Alexander Wedderburn of Easter Powrie, now provost, named. (107.)

532. 1682. Feb. 17.—Alexander Wedderburn, shipmaster in Leith, youngest lawful son
of the late Sir Alexander Wedderburn of Blackness, resigns his South Seagate
tenement to John Davidson. (111.)

533. 1682. May 3.—Sasine of a tenement once belonging to Andrew Wedderburn,
then to Robert Douglas, then to George Fletcher. (115-16.)
    At the end of this volume are several Latin mottoes, similar to those at the beginning.
    [See, in all, fol. 8-10, 12-13, 23, 62, 78-79, 88, 94, 101, 107, 111, 114-16, 119.]

VOL. 277.

Entitled "Seisins from 18 January, 1683 to 6 December, 1690."

On the first leaf is, "James Wedderburne Town Clerk of Dundie 1683." "Incepto libro sit laus
et gloria Christo." "Gloria perpetuo sit tribuenda Deo." Then follows the notarial symbol of
James Ramsay, clerk-depute at this date.

534. 1683. Sept. 18.—Alexander Bower of Kinealdrum, dispones to James Lyon a South
Seagate tenement, conquest by the late Alexander Bower of Kinealdrum, his father,
from Helen and Besse Wedderburn, daughters and heirs portioners of the late
Alexander Wedderburn, shipmaster of Dundee, and William Gaskein and John
Gardyne, their husbands. (9-11.)

535. 1684. May 12.—Alexander Wedderburn, merchant in Edinburgh, dispones a North
Argylegate tenement to George Wedderburn, merchant, burgess of Edinburgh. (22.)

536. 1685. June 5.—Alexander Wedderburn of Easter Powrie, is entered son and heir
to the late Alexander Wedderburn of Easter Powrie, in an annual rent out of
lands once those of the late Alexander Wedderburn, merchant, Andrew Wedderburn,
and others. James Wedderburn is notary. (28.) This rent he at once dispones to
George Grieve. (29.)

537. 1687. June 10.—The land in South Nethergate of the late Robert Murray and
Elizabeth Wedderburn, mentioned. (80.)

538. 1688. April 12.—The North Argylegate land, once that of Mr. Alexander Wedderburn of Easter Powrie, now of Peter Wedderburn, named. (110.)

539. 1688. May 31.—Alexander Wedderburn of Easter Powrie is entered in an annual
rent as son and heir of the late Alexander Wedderburn. (117.)

540. 1688. Aug. 5.—Alexander Wedderburn of Easter Powrie settles the North Argylegate tenement aequired by his late father, Alexander Wedderburn of Easter Powrie,
from Bartholomew Belson, on John Wedderburn, his eldest son. John Wedderburn
of Blackness, is attorney for the said John. (122.)

541. 1688. Oct. 30.—The above property of "John Wedderburn of Easter Powrie," is
named in a sasine to George Balfour, eldest son of Andrew Balfour, writer in
Edinburgh, and Elizabeth Bains. (133.)

542. 1690. July 21.—Peter Wedderburn, merchant, witness. (176.)

543. **1690.** Dec. 1.—Alexander Wedderburn, son of Alexander Wedderburn, now of Easter Powrie, is entered as heir of his late brother german, John Wedderburn, in the North Argylegate property settled on the said John by their father, ante No. 540. (177.) **Dundee Protocol Books.**

Ou the last leaf is written, "James Wedderburn Town Clerk of Dundee." "Finis coronat opus."

[See, in all, fol. 9, 11, 16, 22, 28-30, 33, 34, 80, 88, 102, 105, 110, 117, 119, 121-22, 128, 133, 143, 150, 152, 176-77.]

Vol. 278.

Entitled, "No. 23. Sasines from 9 June, 1691 to 21 October, 1699."

Inside the cover is written "James Wedderburn, toûu clerk of Dundie. James Ramsay his deput." The first eight leaves of this volume are wanting.

544. **1692.** Aug. 23, etc.—Alexander Wedderburn, writer in Dundee, is often named as witness and attorney. (36, 54, 57, 65, 67, 87, &c., &c.)

545. **1693.** Oct. 26.—William Garioch gets from George Crockatt an annual rent once disponed by Alexander Wedderburn of Easter Powrie, provost, to his son, Peter Wedderburn, merchant in Dundee, and by him to the said George Crockatt. (67.)

546. **1694.** Aug. 9.—Land in North Argylegate, once disponed by the late Peter Wedderburn, and his wife, Helen Lovell, to the late Sir Alexander Wedderburn of Blackness, passes to George Grieve. (94.)

547. **1694.** Aug. 10, 27.—At these dates occur the last signature and notary's docket of James Wedderburn, then clerk (fol. 96-99), after which the sasines are not subcribed at all until 16 Jan. 1696, when the signature of his son and successor in the clerkship, Alexander Wedderburn, first occurs, with his notarial docket and the motto, "Sit Deo Gloria." See facsimiles at p. 187.

548. **1696.** Nov. 24.—John Wedderburn, son of the late James Wedderburn, clerk, is procurator for John Scrymgeour of Kirkton. (153.)

549. **1698.** April 6.—Sasine of an annual rent made by A. Morison to Alexander Wedderburn, clerk of Dundee. (191.)

550. **1699.** Jan. 13, etc.—James Wedderburn, servitor to Alexander Wedderburn, clerk, witness (220, 229, 241.)

[See, in all, fol. 10, 12, 16, 36, 54, 55, 57, 60, 62, 67, 82, 87, 94, 104, 122, 124, 136, 137, 153, 158, 189, 191, 210, 220, 229, 241.]

Vol. 279.

Entitled, "No. 34. Sasines from 4 November, 1699 to 3 August, 1715."

On the first leaf is written : "Alexander Wedderburn of Blackness, clerk of the Borrow 1711 ;" and on the second page, "The Fourth Book of the Register of Sasins, Cognitious etc. for the Burgh of Dundee, begun the 4 day of November, 1699, and ended the 5 day of August, 1715 years—Fourth Book."

On the fourth leaf :—"Learning and grace are followed with honour and eternal peace." "If spending of thy time thou be, Remember time is spending thee." "Da tua dum tua sunt, post mortem tum tua uou sunt." Then follows the notarial symbol of Sir Alexander Wedderburn, fourth Baronet, with his motto, "Sit Deo Gloria." See facsimile at p. 187. A good many leaves at the end of this volume are blank. The rising of '15 interrupted the work of the clerk, and ultimately led to his loss of office.

551. **1699.** Nov. 4.—James Wedderburn, lawful son to George Wedderburn, merchant in Edinburgh, as procurator for Patrick Leslie, late factor to Sir Peter Wedderburn of Gosford, resigns certain premises in Dundee into the hands of the bailie, for new infeftment to be made to Alexander Wedderburn, clerk of Dundee. (1.)

552. **1700.** Feb. 14-15.—James Wedderburn, servitor to Alexander Wedderburn, clerk, is a witness. (21-22.)

553.   **1700.** Sept. 28.—Sasine on disposition by James Fletcher, late provost, in favour of Alexander Wedderburn, clerk, of a North Murraygate property. (43.)

554.   **1700.** Dec. 13.—Cognition of Alexander Wedderburn, as son and heir of the late Peter Wedderburn, third son of the late Sir Alexander Wedderburn of Blackness, and entry of him as such heir in a South Flukergate land. (50.)   Alexander Wedderburn, clerk, is present.

555.   **1703.** Feb. 2, March 2.—Sasines on disposition by Alexander Wedderburn, clerk, in favour of William Coppine and George Fotheringham of Bandean. (96, 100.)

556.   **1704.** Sept. 27.—Sasine in favour of Grisel Wedderburn, wife of Thomas Watsone, of various lands in Dundee. (128.)

557.   **1704.** Sept. 28.—Sasine in favour of Mr. Alexander Wedderburn, younger, of Blackness, of certain lands near the West Port of Dundee. (129.)

558.   **1706.** Sept. 26.—Sasine on disposition by Alexander Wedderburn, mariner, and grandson of the late Sir Alexander Wedderburn of Blackness, in favour of Thomas Crichton, of a South Flukergate land. (162.)

559.   **1708.** Sept. 18.—Sasine in favour of Sir Alexander Wedderburn of Blackness of two acres in the West-field of Dundee. Peter Wedderburn, merchant, is a witness. (184.) Another sasine in his favour of an annual rent is given on the same day. (186.)

560.   **1708.** Dec. 28.—Sasine on disposition by Sir Alexander Wedderburn of Blackness, Knight-Baronet, of two South Flukergate lands to Samuel Stewart, apothecary. (188.)

561.   **1709.** Nov. 10.—Alexander Wedderburn, "baylie," signs. (193.)

562.   **1710.** Feb. 15.—Alexander Wedderburn, bailie, gives sasine of certain lands in Dundee to Matilda Wedderburn, wife of Mr. James Brisbane, advocate, in pursuance of a decreet of adjudication obtained by her before the Lords of Session 21 July, 1709. (200.)

563.   **1710.** Aug. 25.—Peter Wedderburn, merchant, gets sasine of some North Seagate lands on disposition from John Melvill, son of the late John Melvill and Katharine, daughter of James Kyd, merchant, whose heir the disponer is. (205.)

564.   **1711.** June 30.—Alexander Wedderburn, skipper and late bailie, witness. (229.)

565.   **1713.** Aug. 1.—The North Argylegate lands of the heirs of Elizabeth Wedderburn and Mr. John Lovell are named. (258.)

566.   **1714.** April 10.—Sasine to David Ramsay of a tenement on the shore of Dundee, bounded on the north by the road passing between the lands of the heirs and successors of Peter Wedderburn and William Kinloch. (270.)

[See, in all, fol. 1, 6, 8, 10, 21, 22, 43, 50, 51, 59, 63, 75, 79, 91, 96, 100, 104, 111, 128-29, 133, 141, 158, 162, 166, 168, 169, 184, 186, 188, 193, 194, 196, 200, 203-6, 229-31, 242, 258, 263, 270-71, 277-78, 283, 297, 307.]

Vol. 280.

1717—27.

From this volume on, the ownership and character of the volumes is not noted, but only their contents, as they are no longer in the hand of members of the family.

567.   **1718.** Sept. 9.—Sasine on disposition (4 June 1700) by Patrick (*i.e.* Peter) Wedderburn, merchant, in favour of Thomas Paterson and James his son. (38.)

568.   **1719.** Nov. 21.—Sasine of land bounded by the large tenement once of William Watt, now of John Wedderburn, Doctor of Medicine. (69.)

569. **1722**. Dec. 31.—Land of the Grieves in North Argylegate, bounded by that once of Alexander Wedderburn of Kingennie and Donald Dunbar; and also land once disponed by Peter Wedderburn and Helen Lovell to Sir Alexander Wedderburn of Blackness, and by him to Thomas Butchart, is named. (132.) **Dundee Protocol Books.**

570. **1723**. Jan. 8.—Sasine to Margaret Watt of a great North Marketgate tenement once pertaining to Alexander Wedderburn of Kingennie and disponed by him to Thomas Scott. (135.)

571. **1723**. Nov. 13.—Sasine naming the North Overgate lands, once of Andrew Wedderburn, now of Alexander Watson of Wallace Craigie. (165.)

572. **1724**. July 29.—Isobel and Margaret Wedderburn, only daughters of the late Alexander Wedderburn, shipmaster in Dundee, and the late Christian Kinloch, his wife, are entered in a tenement of land on the South of S. Clement's Cemetery, as heirs portioners of their mother's brother, the late Robert Kinloch, eldest son of the late James Kinloch, merchant in Dundee. (193.)

573. **1724**. Sept. 20.—Sasine to John Brown of a North Flukergate tenement, bounded by that of the heirs of John Wedderburn, and now in possession of the heirs of Alexander Haliburton. (203.)

574. **1726**. June 29.—Sasine on disposition (1693), by the now deceased Peter Wedderburn, merchant in Dundee, to Alexander Wedderburn, sheriff clerk of Forfar, of certain annual rents. (253.)

575. **1727**. Feb. 24.—Sasine to Andrew Ouchterlony, of a North Overgate tenement, which belonged successively to Sir Alexander Wedderburn of Blackness, and his sons Alexander Wedderburn, merchant in Edinburgh, George Wedderburn, also merchant there, and thereafter to Andrew Wardroper, his son, Robert, and grandson, Andrew. (272.)

576. **1727**. May 22.—Sasine to Robert Fotheringham of Bandean, of a North Overgate house, built by David Hunter, and once that of William Hunter of Balgay, his son, John Hunter, his grandson, and Alexander Wedderburn, clerk of Dundee, who disponed it to George Fotheringham of Bandean. (274.)

[See, in all, fol. 2, 17, 38, 41, 42, 67, 69, 74, 88, 101, 128, 132, 135, 144, 161, 163-65, 167, 193-94, 203, 224, 245, 253, 255, 267, 270, 272, 274.]

Vol. 281.

1727–32.

577. **1727**. June 8.—Margaret Balfour, wife of Mr. John Wedderburn, doctor of medicine in Dundee, is entered in certain property as heir to her brother, the late George Balfour, son of the late Andrew Balfour, W. S. Edinburgh, and Elizabeth Bains, deceased, his wife (1); and also in an @-rent as the only lawful daughter and heir of her said father. (2.)

578. **1727**. June 8.—The South Seagate tenement conquest by Alexander Bower of Kincaldrum from Helen and Bessie Wedderburn, daughters and heirs portioners of the late Alexander Wedderburn, shipmaster, and William Gaskone and John Gairdyne, their husbands, is named. (3.)

579. **1730**. July 25.—Sasine to Margaret Davidsone of a South Seagate tenement once that of Sir Alexander Wedderburn of Blackness, and then that of Alexander Wedderburn, shipmaster in Leith.. (115.)

[See, in all, fol. 1-3, 5, 13, 23, 34, 71, 111, 115, 119, 124, 141, 146, 180, 182, 200, 208, 211, 213, 215, 220, 243.]

Vol. 282.

1733—39.

580. **1733.** Feb. 20.—Sasine on disposition by Thomas Watson, late of Grange of Barrie, to Alexander Wedderburn, shipmaster in Dundee, of a cross dwelling in North Marketgate, which Alexander Wedderburn now settles on his wife Grizell Watson for life. (10.)

This tenement is mentioned in Vol. 280, under date 1723 Nov. 11, as having once belonged to Alexander Tyrie, and being then acquired by Thomas Watson of Grange of Barrie, eldest son of Thomas Watson, also of Grange of Barrie.

581. **1734.** June 12.—Sasine on decreet obtained by Sir Alexander Wedderburn of Blackness, sheriff clerk of Forfar v. Sir John Wedderburn of Blackness, son and heir of Sir Alexander Wedderburn of Blackness, and grandson of Sir John Wedderburn of Blackness, and his tutors and curators, adjudging certain lands to belong to the said Sir Alexander Wedderburn for the sum of £62,905, 15s. 2d. scots paid by him. (77.)

The date of the decreet is not given. The clerk was not, of course, Sir Alexander at its date, as his cousin, Sir John, was then living, but died in 1723 before the date of this sasine.

582. **1737.** May 3.—Sasine on disposition (24 Feb. 1733) by the late Alexander Wedderburn, shipmaster, and late bailie of Dundee, of the N. Marketgate cross dwelling (ante No. 580), in favour of his children Alexander, John, Katharine, Elizabeth, Grissall, and Clementina, subject to the life-rent of Grissall Watson their mother. (296.)

583. **1737.** July 2.— Sasine, on decreet obtained (1678) by the late Alexander Wedderburn of Easter Powrie, provost, v William Morrison, in favour of David Wedderburn of Wedderburn, heir served and returned to the said Alexander Wedderburn, his grandfather. (304.)

[See, in all, fol. 10, 13, 43, 51, 57, 65, 71, 77, 80, 91, 126, 131, 136, 145, 155, 158, 181, 188, 202, 259, 262, 285, 296, 302, 304, 327, 341, 254, 361, 380.]

Vol. 282½.

This volume is all blank, except the first 17 leaves.

584. **1748** June 8.—Robert Wedderburn, sheriff clerk of Forfar, is witness. (13.)

Vol. 283.

1739—45.

585. **1739.** April 6.—The baxter trade guild in Dundee get sasine of various properties, including one disponed by James Lees to Margaret and Grizell Watson, daughters of the deceased Thomas Watson, merchant, of which half was disponed by the said Grizell, with consent of Alexander Wedderburn, shipmaster, her husband, to James Davidson. (7.)

586. **1741.** April 24.—The North Overgate land of Sir Alexander Wedderburn of Blackness, deceased, and then of his sons, Alexander and George, merchants in Edinburgh, is again mentioned. (142, 192.)

587. **1743.** Sept. 7.—A North Murraygate land, sold by David Wedderburn of that ilk to Alexander Brown, is named. (278.)

588. **1744.** March 12.—Sasine of land near the above, once that of Matilda Wedderburn, relict of Mr. James Brisbane, advocate. (311.)

[See, in all, fol. 7, 23, 24, 142, 192, 205, 259, 269, 278, 299, 311, 337, 348, 352.]

Vol. 284.

1745–50.

This volume contains references to members of the family at fols. 18, 32, 62, 112, 253, 294, 297, 312, 346, 349 and 409, but they merely repeat matter already given above.

Vol. 285.

1750-54.

589. **1715** Feb. 13.—Cognition in favour of David Wedderburn of that ilk, who is entered in that great tenement of land in North Overgate, once belonging to the late Alexander Wedderburn of Easter Powrie, who disponed it to his son, the late Alexander Wedderburn, younger, of Kingennie, whose grandson and heir is the said David Wedderburn. (25)

590. **1751.** Feb. 13.—Cognition in favour of David Wedderburn of that ilk, in that North Overgate land bought by the late Alexander Wedderburn of Easter Powrie from Barton Belson, and thereafter belonging to Alexander Wedderburn, his son, who disponed it to the late John Wedderburn, his son ; to whom his brother, the late Alexander Wedderburn of Easter Powrie, was heir, whose only lawful son and heir is the said David Wedderburn. (26.)

591. **1752.** June 14, March 4, June 4.—Cognition in favour of David Brisbane of Bullion, in a land in South Nethergate, once that of Mr. James Brisbane, advocate, and then of Matilda Wedderburn, his relict, as the only son and heir of the said James and Matilda. (141.) Margaret Brisbane is entered therein, in life rent, as heir to her brother, the said David (159); and David Wedderburn of Wedderburn, is entered therein, in fee, as heir to the said David Brisbane under his disposition, dated 14 Jan. 1752. (173, 175.)

[See, in all, fol. 18, 23, 25-26, 81, 96, 117, 133, 135, 141, 159, 173, 175, 195, 249, 258, 275, 296.]

Vol. 286.

1754—59.

592. **1758.** Dec. 12.—Sasine on decreet of adjudication (2 Aug. 1758), obtained by John Goodwillie *v.* Helen Wedderburn, only lawful child of the late Alexander Wedderburn, shipmaster in London, eldest son of Alexander Wedderburn, shipmaster and bailie of Dundee, and also *v.* Katharin Wedderburn, relict of John Higginson, merchant in Perth, and Elizabeth Wedderburn, both daughters of the said Alexander Wedderburn, late bailie, all of whom are charged to enter heirs in speciall to their predecessors in a North Marketgate cross dwelling, on which Goodwillie has a charge of £4,746 6s. Scots. (357.)

The other references to Wedderburns in this volume are merely references to properties already mentioned above.

[See, in all, fol. 39, 74, 77, 116, 120, 145, 226, 244. 262, 296, 346, 377, 395.]

Vol. 287.

1759- 62

The references to Wedderburns in this volume are again only to various properties already mentioned.

[See, in all, fol. 8, 10. 22, 27, 30, 32. 38, 41, 118, 129, 143, 154, 171, 176, 178, 183, 199, 202, 203, 215, 225, 247, 251, 306, 313]

Vol. 288.

1762—64.

593. **1763.** May 31.—Sasine of the cross dwelling in North Marketgate, mentioned ante No. 592, on disposition (11 April), by John Goodwillie, writer in Edinburgh, in favour of Katharine Wedderburn, relict of John Higginson, merchant in Perth, in

2 K

life rent, and as to the fee, one-third to the said Katharine Wedderburn, and two-thirds to her son, John Higginson, and Helen Wedderburn, lawful granddaughter of the late Alexander Wedderburn, shipmaster and late bailie in Dundee. (130.)

594. **1764.** July 10.—Proceedings in a decreet arbitral (1763), made by Mr. David Scrymgeour of Birkhill, advocate. (300.)
> Other references in this volume merely repeat previous ones.
>
> [See, in all, fol. 9, 64, 63, 72, 91, 118-20, 133, 167, 181, 222, 224, 227, 296.]

Vol. 289.

1764—67.

595. **1765.** March 5.—Sasine on disposition by various persons of the name of Preston, in favour of Dr. John Wedderburn, physician in Dundee, to which disposition, John Wedderburn, eldest son of the late Sir John Wedderburn, Baronet, has right (by a disposition in his favour from the said Dr. John Wedderburn, 1749), of a large tenement on the shore of Dundee. (50.)

596. **1766.** Sept. 18.—Sasine on disposition by the said John Wedderburn, now designed of Idvie, of the said tenement (ante No. 595), once belonging to Dr. John Wedderburn, physician in Dundee. (268.)
> Other references in this volume again merely repeat previous ones.
>
> [See, in all, fol. 17, 18, 91, 106, 107, 112, 193, 228, 241, 246, 255, 262, 270, 298, 316, 331, 341, 346, 349.]

Vols. 290—303.

1767—1801.

> These volumes have been searched only by their indices, which contain but few references to Wedderburns, all of which are noted below. It will be seen that these are contained in six of the volumes only (vols. 290, 295, 296, 298, 299, and 301), while the indices of the other eight volumes (291-94, 297, 300, 302, and 303), contain no Wedderburn references at all.

597. **1769.** June 2.—Sasine under the seal appointed by the Treaty of Union to be used in Scotland in place of the Great Seal, in favour of Catharine Wedderburn, relict of John Higginson, merchant in Perth, of half the cross dwelling in North Marketgate referred to ante Nos. 580, 592 and 593. (**290**, 263.)

598. **1785.** May 17.—Sasine on disposition by Mrs. Ann Fletcher, wife of Captain Alexander Read of Logie, in favour of Robert Wedderburn of Pearsie, and Mrs. Isobell Edward, his wife, of a flat in the Nethergate. (**295**, 346.)

599. **1786.** Dec. 19.—Sasine on disposition (29 Nov.), in favour of Alexander Wedderburn of Wedderburn, of a South Nethergate tenement. (**296**, 266.)

600. **1791.** April 8.— Cognition and infeftment of Charles Wedderburn of Pearsie, as eldest son and heir of the deceast Robert Wedderburn of Pearsie, and Mrs. Isobell Edward, also deceast, in the flat referred to, ante No. 598. (**298**, 369.)

601. **1791.** May 6.—Sasine on disposition by the said Charles Wedderburn of the said flat, in favour of David Wedderburn (now Webster), merchant in London, and Isobell Wedderburn, wife of the Rev. James Stormonth of Kinchane, minister at Airly. (**298**, 374.)

602. **1792.** Jan. 22.—Sasine on a disposition by the said David Webster, of all his interest in the said flat to the said Mrs. Isobell Wedderburn, wife of Rev. J. Stormonth. (**299**, 8.)

603. **1797.** Aug. 5.—License by Alexander Wedderburn of Wedderburn, to Captain David Laird of Strathmartine, to erect certain buildings or toofalls against a wall of the South Nethergate property of the said Alexander Wedderburn. (**301**, 363.)

This record consists, down to the year 1788, of forty-four large volumes. Of these Dundee the second is really the earliest in date, but it only deals, except for a few pages at the Burgh and end, with a very short and isolated period, 1520-24. The third volume begins in 1550, Head Court from which date the record continues with but few breaks, although one volume (No. 35, Records. 1676-86) is unfortunately lost, and there are also blanks from 1709 to 1717 and from 1749 to 1766. The forty-three existing volumes have been thoroughly searched and contain, of course, numerous references to members of the family. From these, as in the case of the "Protocol Books," I have selected all that are of value.

The following list of the different volumes readily shows in detail the periods covered by this record, and the occasional blanks in it.

Vol.							Vol.					
1	Oct.	6, 1594	—	30 Sept.,	1622		24	Nov.	8, 1609	—	13 Dec.,	1611
2	Nov.	28, 1520	—	30 Aug.,	1524		25	Jan.	13, 1612	—	19 March,	1614
3	Sept.	28, 1550	—	21 Jan.,	1555		26	May	2, 1614	—	4 Dec.,	1616
4	Oct.	—, 1555	—	13 June,	1558		27	Jan.	13, 1617	—	16 Nov.,	1618
5	June 13.	1558	—	14 April,	1561		28	Dec.	27, 1624	—	11 Jan.,	1633
6	Oct.	6, 1561	—	14 Sept.,	1562		29	Oct.	20, 1633	—	23 July,	1638
7	Oct.	6, 1562	—	28 July	1563		30	July	25, 1638	—	1 Feb.,	1647
8	Oct.	4, 1563	—	6 June	1565		31	July	31, 1633	—	2 Oct.,	1648
9	Oct.	31, 1565	—	4 April,	1568		32	Dec.	20, 1648	—	17 Sept ,	1656
10	May	12, 1568	—	28 Sept.,	1569		33	Oct.	3, 1656	—	1 Feb.,	1662
11	Oct.	3, 1569	—	2 Oct ,	1571		34	Oct.	7, 1662	—	17 April,	1676
12	Oct.	2, 1571	—	8 Feb.,	1573		35	This volume is missing.				
13	Feb.	17, 1573	—	2 Sept.,	1575		36	Jan.	2, 1688	—	7 June,	1690
14	Oct.	3, 1575	—	14 March,	1579		37	June	9, 1690	—	20 May,	1693
15	Mar.	25, 1580	—	3 Dec.,	1582		37A	Nov.	9, 1696	—	31 Aug.,	1698
16	Feb.	25, 1583	—	9 April,	1586		38	Feb.	11, 1695	—	19 Sept.,	1709
17	Feb.	—, 1589	—	3 April,	1594		39	Feb.	20, 1717	—	— March,	1735
18	April	8, 1594	—	4 Jan.,	1595		40	Mar.	17, 1737	—	18 Feb.,	1740
19	Jan.	12, 1595	—	21 June,	1597		41	April	5, 1740	—	6 March,	1749
20	June	20, 1597	—	28 Sept.,	1599		39A	Jan.	7, 1766	—	28 July,	1774
21	Oct.	26. 1599	—	26 July,	1602		40A	Aug.	4, 1774	—	30 Aug.,	1781
22	Jan.	11, 1602	—	8 Feb.,	1606		41A	Sept.	4, 1781	—	9 July,	1785
23	Dec.	4, 1606	—	24 Feb.,	1609							

N.B.—In four instances the same number is used for two different volumes. This may be due to the fact that four volumes (38, 39, 40 and 41) are each made up of four or five original small parts, which have been somewhat recently bound up into volumes. The dates covered by these parts are rather irregular and in the case of vol. 41 some leaves relating to Aug. 23, 1697—23 Aug., 1698, have been bound in at the end of the (1740-49) volume.

Vol. 1.

This volume has long been accounted lost, but Mr. Macleod has found in the charter room a volume which would seem to be it, entitled " Head Court Laws, 1550—1622." It begins on 6 Oct. 1550 and from fol. 5 to 72 appears to be a duplicate of Vol. 1 of the Council Books (see post s.v.). From fol. 73-112 it covers the period 6 Oct. 1594 to 30 Sept. 1622, and then, after a long blank, contains at the end "The Baillie Compts of the burgh of Dundee from 20 July 1627 to 1 July 1643." It contains but few references to Wedderburns (1560—1597) (fol. 14, 28, 36, 43, 52, 72, 77, 88, 93) which are not of importance and may be shortly summarized thus :—

(a) 1560. Oct. 4.—John Wedderburn is bailie on the bench (14) ; 1561. Feb. 27.—James Wedderburn is counsellor (28). (b) 1562. March 23.—John Wedderburn is on the bench (36). (c) 1564. May 8.—Robert Wedderburn, younger, is in court (43). (d) 1567. Jan. 22.—John Wedderburn is master of the almshouse (52); and (e) 1594. Oct. 6.— Mr. Alexander Wedderburn, clerk, signs, as also on some later occasions. (72, 77, 78, 93.)

At the beginning of this volume is an ordinance of the council respecting the registration of sasines, by which it is ordered that no sasines be given except by the clerk of the burgh. On a fly leaf, at the end of the book, is an order as follows :—

" I command and chairge in our Soveraine Lord the Kingis Majesties name and in name and behalff of the provost and bailies of this good burgh all and suudrie neighbours and inhabitantis of the sam that they and every one of tham for anent thair owine dwellings and head rowmes sett fourth thair bonfyres at four houres efter noone, in toakine of thair joy for the happie preservationn of his Majestie's persoune with the most pairt of the whole nobilitie and clergy of this Kingtome and our neighbour countrey of England from that fearfull powder treasoune attempted aganies thaim this instant fyift day of November and this vnder the paine of ten pundis to be vpliftit of ilk contraveiner heirof but favour."

Vol. 2.

This volume is described in Alexander Maxwell's " History of Old Dundee " (1888), p. 555, seqq. as " The Book of the Church," owing to its containing an inventory of the articles of value belonging to S. Mary's Church in 1454. It also contains various details about the church, but seems to have got into the hands of the town clerk, who used it for the Burgh and Head Court Records, 28 Nov., 1520, to 30 August, 1524.

1. **1490.** David Wedderburn is named as on the council. ("Book of the Church.")

2. **1520-21.** Dec. 5, 30 ; Jan. 14 ; Feb. 8.—James Wedderburn on assize. (8, 10, 14, 16.)

3. **1521** April 9.—James Wedderburn is named as present at a meeting of "al the merchandis of Dundee," held for the " chosing of certane personis to set the scot and lot of the gudis beand in skiperis Andres schip of Dundee." (22.)

4. **1521.** April 13.—David Wedderburn named as procurator to John Conquhar. (24.)

5. **1521.** March 15, May 8.—Two James Wedderburns, both named as on assize. (20, 27.)

6. **1521.** April 16.—(a) James Wedderburn, son and heir of James Wedderburn, is surety for William Nicholl. (b) James Wedderburn, younger, is surety for William Baweasky. (25.) (c) April 30.—James Wedderburn, elder, surety. (27.

7. **1521.** (a) May 26.—Two James Wedderburns on assize. (30.) (b) May 31, June 3, 7, 14.—James Wedderburn on assize. (30, 31, 33)

8. **1521.** June 17.—James Mallison is deeerned to restore to James Wedderburn's land a webloom, a chair, and a big mat, which he bought from John Cristeson, and which were arrested for James Wedderburn's maill. (35.)

9. **1521.** (a) June 18.—James Wedderburn chosen as an arbiter. (36.) (b) June 21.— James Wedderburn protests against the jurisdiction of the bailies in a certain process, and proceedings are stayed on his objection. (36.)

10. **1521.** (a) July 1.—James Wedderburn, elder, on assize, and James Wedderburn, James' son, are both on an inquest. (37.) (b) Sept. 30.—James Wedderburn and James Wedderburn, younger, are both elected on the council. (46.) (c) Oct 11.— Robert Wedderburn acts as bailie. (49.)

11. **1521.** Nov. 5.—Elizabeth Wedderburn, spous of Alexander Ogilvy, and mother of James Lovell, son and heir of the late Alexander Lovell, is named in connection with her son's "airschip." (54.)

12. **1521.** Dec. 30.—James Wedderburn, elder, James Wedderburn, younger, and James Wedderburn, son of James Wedderburn, are all on one assize. (67.)

13. **1522.** Jan. 2.—James Wedderburn is on an assize, when " Dave Wedderburn is maid quyt of the wrangous casting down of the laid of malt that Thom Fethy plenit on hym." (67.)

14. **1522.** (a) Jan. 14.—James, David, and James Wedderburn are on the same assize. (b) Same day.—William Chaip is fined for taking the anchor of his ship, which was arrested by the " custumaris " for their anchorage. James Wedderburn asks instruments. (69.)

15. **1522.** Jan. 16.—James Wedderburn, Robertis sone, is "lauborrowis" for David Wedderburn. James Wedderburn is on the assize. (70.)

16. **1522.** Feb. 5.—Elizabeth Wedderburn, wife of Alexander Ogilvy, and relict of Alexander Lovell, consents to the inventory of the goods of airschip of her son, James Lovell ; and James Wedderburn, her brother, becomes her surety for the delivery up of the goods to the heir " at his lauchfull agis." (75.)

This eutry contains some curious matter, and I, therefore, give it at length :—

1522. Feb^r. 5.—Alex^r Kyd, Johu Colstoun and Andro Dog, priŝaris at the commaud of the Proŭest of the said burgh, chosyn and sworn with consent of Alex^r Lovell, burges of the said burgh, on the tane part, aud of Alex^r Ogilvy and Besse Wedderburu his spous, the relict of umquhile Alex^r Lovell, the said Alexanderis sun, on the tother part, prisit the gudis of airschip pertenand to James Lovell the son and air of the said Alexander.

In the first his Dublet of Canny Dammes to fifty Schilliugis, a reid cap to xiij^s, a Hogtone of dowble worsat iiij^{lib}. Item a Gown of canny lynt with Buggis to vj^{lib} xiij^s iiij^d. Item a pair Hois of Flemy gray to x^s, a Hat ij^s, a Jak of Rane Deir to iiij merkis, a Sadill to vj^s viij^d, a Süerd, a Bulilar to iiij^s, a pair Spleuchis x^s, a Knapscall xl^{sl}. Item in the Chalmer a cuch Bed of aik v merkis. Item the Fedder Bed and Bowster to xl^s, ... a Verdour Bed with the Blankatis and a cod to ij merkis. The Mantill and Shetis to xx^s. The Pres to xx^s, a Silŭer Spune, a merk, a Burdclath, a Toweil, ij Serŭatoris of Lynniug to iiij^s. A Cumptour in the Hall to viij^s. A Rowndall to x^s. A Furm to ij^s. A Stuyll to xvj^d. A Langsadill Bed aud cupburd in the Hall to vij merkis and 3 merk. The Bassing and the Lawar to x^s. A Cusching iij^s; vij^{lib} of Pewter in Westhall to x^s vj^d. Item of tyu Stapis xij^{lib} to xij^s. Item a chandillar aud a Cranis v^s viij^d. A Westhall Byuk to v^s, a Riding Coit to xxiiij^s. A Chymua x^s. A cruk ij^s. A Tayngis viij^d. A Güys Pan, a Speit, Lantrone, Ladill to v^s vj^s. A pair Pepir Quernys xiij^s and Bolt to x^s. The Tabille and . . . to iiij^s. The Kamys and Kemmyng Stok, the Quheill, the Cardis xv^s vj^d. The Leding Stane to iiij^s. The Balk Breddis to iiij^s. The Lettroue x^s. The Schryne viij^s. The Ballaudia for Maddir v^s. Summa totalia xlv^{lib} xix^s vj^d.

The quhilk gudis ar deliŭerit to Alex^r Lovell the said barnis Grandschir and the said Elezebeth and Alexander dischargit of the sampn be the said Alexander Lovell.

The said day James Wedderburn modir brodir to the said barne is becum sourte for certane poyntis of the saidis arschip that thai sall be furthcumand to the said barne at his lauchfull agis, or than the sowme that thai ar prisit to, that is to say, a cuchbed of tre to v merkis, a cumptour in the Hall to viij merkis, a Rowndall to x^s, a Furm to ij^s, a Stule to xvj^d, a Laugsadill Bed aud a copburd to v^{lib}, a Westhall Byuk to v^s, ane Lettroue x^s, a pair grit Ballaudis to v^s. Summa totalia xv^{lib} vj^s viij^d.

And Alex^r Ogilvy aud Elezebeth his wife has bundyn and . . . . (sic) thar airis and executouris and assignais to releiff and keip skathles the said James of the sowme foresid submittaud thaune to the iŭriadiccioue of the Dioce of Brechyn be the faith of thar bodeis thar baudis vphaldyn, aud als the snidis gudia (sic) is bundyn to releif the said James of all skath heirof in tyme cum.

17. **1522.** Feb. 14.— James of Wedderburn, elder, has a judgment against him. (77.)

18. **1522.** (a) Feb. 18 —James Wedderburn and Esabell Serymgeour, his spouse, relict of William Barry, get a judgment v. Henry Widder. (77.) (b) Feb. 18, March 10. James Wedderburn, elder, and James Wedderburn on assize. (77. 80.) (c) March 20. James Wedderburn, son of James, is assessor to the Court. (83.) (d) March 26. James Wedderburn, son of Robert, is chosen oversman (i.e., umpire) in a dispute. (83.) (e) March 29.—Robert Wedderburn named. (85.)

19. **1522.** (a) March 31.—James Wedderburn is cautioner for David Wedderburn, son of Janet Nicholson (85). (b) April 25.—James Wedderburn, designed " son of Robert," appears for him. (87.)

20. **1522.** (a) April 11.—James of Wedderburn, is chosen arbiter. (87.) (b) July 15. James of Wedderburn, son of Robert, acts as surety. (97.) (c) Aug. 27.—James Wedderburn, son of Robert, chooses as his procurators, Robert Wedderburn, James Wedderburn, son of James Wedderburn, and others. (102.)

21. **1523.** (a) March 3.—James Wedderburn, son of Robert, has an action v. Henry Halis. (130.) (b) May 5.—James Wedderburn and Henry Wedderburn are on assize. (141.) (c) Oct. 3.—James Wedderburn, James' son, James Wedderburn, Robertis son, and James Wedderburn, elder, all elceted eouneillors. (158.)

[See, in all, fol. 8, 14, 16, 20, 24, 25, 27, 30, 31, 33, 35-39, 42, 43, 46, 48-50, 54, 57, 62, 67, 69-70, 72-73, 75-78, 80, 82-83, 85, 87-89, 91, 94-103, 105-6, 108, 110, 112, 118, 122, 124, 125, 127, 130, 136-38, 140-47, 151, 153, 158, 160-61.]

VOL. 3.[1]

1550—54-55.

22. **1550.** (a) Sept. 28.—David Wedderburn nominated on the eouncil for the year 1551. (b) Oct. 6.—David Wedderburn, elder, produces a bond to him by the town for £90, for his mansion bought by the town. It is paid Oct. 20, by a grant of six burgess-ships.

[1] The folios in this and the succeeding volumes of this record are not numbered, and the reference to the entries has thus to be by date alone.

23.   **1550.** Oct. 9.—Robert and Alexander Wedderburn are named arbitrators for Andrew and John Masone.

24.   **1550.** (*a*) Nov. 5—Decree in favour of Katrine Wedderburn for house maill. (*b*) Nov. 7.—Robert Wedderburn, younger, is named.

25.   **1550.** (*a*) Nov. 10 —Gilbert Logan and James Wedderburn in Deip are named as owing part of a cargo of wine from Deip. (*b*) Nov. 20.—Action by David Wedderburn and others *v.* John Bille for the price of 1,600 bowstrings. (*c*) Nov. 24.—Robert Wedderburn, elder, is named.

26.   **1551.** (*a*) March 3.—Alis Wedderburn is summoned by the Kirkmasters but does not appear. (*b*) Oct. 13.—Alis Wedderburn obtains a decree.

27   **1551.** March 3.—Friday next is assigned to Alexander Paterson and James Scrymgeour to produce certain rings, broken silver, and pearls, acclaimed from them by Robert Wedderburn, younger.   March 4.—Compeared Alexander Paterson, who consigned three rings of gold, one with a sapphire, one with a ruby, and one "garnat," with eight silver spoons and certain pearls upon one string with part of loose pearls in a pocket, acclaimed by Elspeth Scrymgeour and Robert Wedderburn, now her spouse, alleging the rings and pearls pertained to them.   The said James Scrymgeour also compeares and alleges that the said goods belong to his pupil James, son and heir of Jacques Richardson, and the late Katrine Paterson.

28.   **1551.** (*a*) March 16.—David Wedderburn, younger, and Robert Wedderburn, younger are made procurators for certain persons   (*b*) April 20.—Robert Wedderburn and Alexander Wedderburn are on an inquest for serving Peter Froster, heir to his father, John Froster. (*c*) June 5, 8.—David Wedderburn, elder, is named. (*d*) Aug. 3, 16.— David Wedderburn in Welgait, procurator for William Richardson. (*e*) Aug. 28.— Elizabeth Wedderburn's land in North Marketgait, named as a boundary.

29.   **1551.** (*a*) Sept. 23 —David Wedderburn, elder, nominated to the council. (*b*) Oct. 13. —Thomas Nichol and Janet Wedderburn, his wife, name as their procurators Mr. Robert Wedderburn, Gilbert Wedderburn, and others. (*c*) Oct. 21.—John Strathachine acclaims David Wedderburn, younger, for £7 for the "rest" of Martinmas term of the Weighouse, 1547.

30.   **1551.** Nov. 5.—Robert Anderson renounces his right to Henry Wedderburn's lands in the Murraygait and also his wife's right to the same, in favour of Jannet and Margaret Wedderburns, her daughters.

31   **1551.** Nov. 5.—Discharge of John Anderson, mariner, to Mr. Robert Wedderburn, vicar of Dundee.

32.   **1551.** Nov. 10.—David Wedderburn, elder, grants him fully paid for his mansion sold by him to the town.   See ante No. 22(*b*).

33.   **1552.** Feb. 22.—Decree in favour of Jonet Wedderburn, wife of Thomas Nichol, and her sister, Margaret Wedderburn, daughters of the late Henry Wedderburn, burgess of Dundee.

34.   **1552.** March 26.—A sum of money is arrested in the hands of Besse Wedderburn, spouse to Patrick Lyoun.

35.   **1552.** May 5.—William Wedderburn witnesses the receipt by John Black of £467 6s. 5d., from David Wedderburn, elder, for 420 barrels of beer.

36.   **1552.** May 25.—James Scrymgeour and David Wedderburn are named as owners of the ship "James."

37. **1552.** July 27.—Gilbert Wedderburn and many others are declared to have dis- Dundee obeyed the Queen's charge, and the acts of the commissioners, anent the duties of Burgh and Head Court freemen, and are decerned to have "tint" their freedoms, and to be unfreemen. Records.

38. **1552.** Aug. 23.—Decree in favour of Katrine Wedderburn.

39. **1552.** Oct. 24.—Elspeth Scrymgeour, relict of Robert Wedderburn, is amerciat for for not compearing at the instance of John Paterson and another.

40. **1552.** Nov. 9.—David Wedderburn, elder, of Cragy, becomes a cautioner to the provost and bailies for John, Abbot of Lindores, for £500.

41. **1553.** Feb. 6.—Alis Wedderburn, relict of Thomas Duncan, burgess, constitutes George Falconer her officer of her lands of Damfadine.

42. **1553.** Feb. 20.—David Wedderburn, in Welgate, is appointed arbitrator in a suit of Couston *v.* Forbes.

43. **1553.** (*a*) April 28, May 2.—David Wedderburn, elder, of Cragy, named as a curator to James Barry. (*b*) May 18.—Elizabeth Wedderburn, spouse to Patrick Lyone, named. (*c*) June 12.—George Wodbroane (*sic*) amerced. (*d*) Aug. 2.—Gilbert Wedderburn in Leith has constituted James Lovell and others, his procurators in Dundee.

44. **1553.** Oct. 2.—David Wedderburn, of Welgate, offers 40 merks a year for the common weighouse, but it is let (Oct. 6) to Alexander Annand at 46 merks.

45. **1553.** (*a*) Oct. 30.—Patrick Lyone enters David Wedderburn and James and William Wedderburn, his sons, in judgment, as having been surety for their entry this day. He and his sons are ordered to appear on the morrow. (*b*) Nov. 3.— David Wedderburn, and his two sons, are accused for the away-taking of one bag of wheat out of the market last Saturday, contrary to the burgh laws, and for troubling the good town that day and hurting Robert Merschell, all which David denied, and referred himself to God and a good assize. He is acquitted, but his two sons are ordained to ask forgiveness of the provost (James Haliburton of Piteur), and the good town, and to pay Robert Merschell £10. Patrick Lyone is surety.

46. **1553.** Nov. 3.—John Wedderburn is served heir to his late father, James Wedderburn, burgess of Dundee.

47. **1553.** Nov. 3.—David Wedderburn heads a list of maltsters in the Welgate.

48. **1554.** Jan. 12.—Sir Thomas Wedderburn asked at Elspet Scrymgeour and Robert Clerk, for his interest, two merks annual rent furth of the late Wat Scrymgeour's yard, occupied by the said Elspeth.

49. **1554.** Jan. 17.—Bond for £78 by Richard Corbe of Dundee to Gilbert Wedderburn and John Wedderburn ~~brother~~ (*sic*), indwellers in Leith.

50. **1554.** Feb. 19.—Robert Clerk undertakes to prove that John Walcar held a rood and a half of the chapel yard of Robert Wedderburn and Elspeth Scrymgeour, his spouse, in 1548.

51. **1554.** Feb. 20.—Robert Thomson admits the receipt of a key of a yard from Robert Wedderburn, younger.

52. **1554.** Feb. 26.—Gilbert and John Wedderburn apply to the court for Richard Corbe's body to be put in captivity for his debt of £78 (ante No 49). John Wedderburn appears personally.

53. **1554.** Feb. 26.—John Wedderburn, son of the late James Wedderburn, younger, takes the oath of liberty, and is ordained to be put in the "Lockit Book."

54.　**1554**. April 2.—Deduction by Sir James Wallace, chaplain of S. Serf's chapel, in the Dundee parish kirk, of the fourth penny of 9 merks, 6s. and 8d. to Alexander Wedderburn of his @ rent out of his South Marketgate lands betwixt S. Clement's Kirkyard and Skirling's Wynd.

55.　**1554**. (*a*) July 5.—John Wedderburn named as creditor of William Carnegy. (*b*) Aug. 2, 13.—He is named as arbiter, and on assize.

56.　**1554**. (*a*) Oct. 26.—David Wedderburn in Welgate named. (*b*) Nov. 5.—David Wedderburn, younger, chancellor of assize.

57.　**1554**. Nov. 16.—Decree in favour of Alexander Wedderburn and Issobell Anderson, his wife.

58.　**1554**. Nov. 16.—Decree *v*. William Wedderburn, as "outreddar" of his father's half of the ship "James."

59.　**1554**. Dec. 19.—The Flukergate lands of John Wedderburn, near those of John Forrester and the heirs of Andro Halis, named as a boundary.

60.　**1555**. Jan. 8 —The baillies inspect John Wedderburn's evidents and decern warrant of possession to be given to him conform thereto.

[See, in all, s. dates :—1550. Sept. 28 ; Oct. 6, 9, 17, 20, 27 ; Nov. 5, 7, 9, 10, 20, 24, 28 ; Dec. 5.—1551. Feb. 20, 25 ; March 3, 4, 16, 20 ; April 7, 8, 20 ; June 5, 8 ; July 6, 16 ; Aug. 3, 28 ; Sept. 23 ; Oct. 13, 21, 23, 27 ; Nov. 5, 10, 20.—1552. Feb. 16, 22; March 26 ; April 27 ; May 5, 18, 25, 27 ; June 20 ; July 27 ; Aug. 23 ; Sept. 6, 13, 25 ; Oct. 17, 24 ; Nov. 9, 18, 22.—1553. Feb. 6, 20 ; April 28 ; May 2, 18, 20 ; June 12 ; Aug. 2, 23 ; Sept. 25 ; Oct. 2, 10, 20, 30 ; Nov. 3 ; Dec. 19.—1554. Jan. 8, 12, 17, 29 ; Feb. 19, 20, 21, 26 ; April 2 ; June 1, 19, 26 ; July 3, 5 ; Aug. 2, 13 ; Sept. 10, 11 ; Oct. 26, 30 ; Nov. 5, 9, 16, 19, 21 ; Dec. 17, 19.—1555. Jan. 8.]

Vol. 4.

1555-58.

Several leaves at the beginning of this volume are imperfect from decay, and the dates are not always clear.

61.　**1555**. (*a*) Oct. (?).—David Wedderburn and Jhone Vedderburn are named, apparently in regard to Murraygait land. (*b*) Nov. 28.—Katrine Wedderburn, named. (*c*) Dec. 16.—Decree for David Wedderburn, owner of the ship "James."

62.　**1556**. Jan. 14.—Jhone Wedderburn, burgess, produces a title to a Flukergait land : and (12 April) is decerned to have possession.

63.　**1556**. Jan. 21.—Schir Thomas Vedderburn, chaplain, witnesses a discharge.

64.　**1556**. April 20.—Robert Salmont is cautioner for Robert Wedderburn for the fracht of three ton of wyne.

65　**1556**. May 21.—James Wedderburn pays Jhone Buttergas his dewtie for his part of the ship "James."

66.　**1556**. May 22.—"David Vedderburn has produeit ane gift lettre of our Soverane Ladyes under the testimoniale of his henes gryt seel makand hym tutor dative to Robert Vedderburn, sone and air to Robert Vedderburn last deceast."

67.　**1556**. (*a*) June 5, 12, 18, 22.—James Wedderburn mentioned *re* the ship "James," &c. (*b*) June 22.—David Wedderburn in the Welgait named.

68.　**1556**. (*a*) July 13.—Robert Wedderburn (with consent of David Wedderburn, younger, his tutor) is served general heir to the late James Wedderburn, his gudschir. (*b*) Oct. 14.—David Wedderburn, as tutor to Robert Wedderburn, younger, is charged to answer a claim anent the West Kirk style.

69. **1556.** Oct. 19.—Alexander Wedderburn, younger, is appointed common clerk for life, and consents that Henry Richardsone (formerly clerk) shall be his substitute.

70. **1556.** Dec. 18.—James Lovell, treasurer, produces an evident binding one John Anderson to maintain a kirkstyle at the North-west style towards the Argyl's gait, which style is to be provided by David Wedderburn, tutor to Robert Wedderburn, sone to Robert Wedderburn, heritor and feuar of the said lands.

71. **1557.** Jan. 12, 13, 19, 20.—William Wedderburn named as procurator and as obtaining a decree v. Thomas Strnquhin.

72. **1557.** Jan. 19.—Claim by John Fotheringhame, skipper, v. David Wedderburn, who compears by his son James.

73. **1557.** (a) Feb. 10.—Schir Thomas Wedderburn, chaplain of Our Lady's chapel in the Cowgait, named. (b) March 26.—David Wedderburn, younger, procurator for James Davidson. (c) July 9.—George Wedderburn and Effie Fowlar, his wife, apply to the council for William Elphinstone to be granted them as their officer.

74. **1557.** July 19.—Helen Lausone, wife of David Wedderburn, and Thomas Scot, burgess of Perth, are decerned to abide the decreet of Alexander Carnegy, David Wedderburn in Skirling's Wynd, and Patrick Lyon, as to a claim by the said Helen.

75. **1557.** Aug. 2.—Anent a brief purchest by James Davidson "to be scruit as narrest and lauchfull sire to vmquhile Andro Davidsone," his father, it is argued that "Henry Richardson, scribe of Dundee, suld be repellit be reason that he and David Wedderburn is sister's bayrns."

   This is the whole of this entry. Henry Richardson was now clerk substitute only, Alexander Wedderburn being principal clerk under his appointment of 6 Feb. 1557. (See ante No. 69 and Dundee Charters, &c. No. 25.) Unfortunately, the entry gives neither the names of the "sisters" nor the connection of David Wedderburn with the heir to be served.

76. **1557.** Sept. 26.—John Wedderburn named in a list of councillors.

77. **1557.** (a) Oct. 22.—The council grant to David Wedderburn, younger, the gutter stones which were on the south isle of the kirk he paying the kirkmasters for the same. (b) Nov. 9.—The petty customs are set to David Wedderburn in Wellgait for a year, on payment of 191 merks.

78. **1558.** March 18.—George Wedderburn and Effie Fowlair, his spouse, again apply for officers for their acres in the East-field of Dudop.

79. **1558.** May 6.—Bond by John Brown, mariner, to repay John Wedderburn a payment made to him by the said John Wedderburn.

   [See in all :—1555. Oct. (?) ; Nov. 8, 28 ; Dec. 16. 1556. Jan. 14, 21 ; March 13, 16 ; April 13, 20 ; May 21, 22 ; June 5, 12, 18, 22, 30 ; July 13 : Oct. 14, 19 ; Nov. 9, 24 ; Dec. 7, 9, 18. 1557. Jan. 12, 15, 19, 26, 27 ; Feb. 5, 10 ; March 18, 26 ; June 26 ; July 9, 19 ; Aug. 2 : Sept. 26 ; Oct. 22 ; Nov. 2, 9, 15 ; Dec. 10. 1558. Jan. 27 ; Feb. 4 ; March 4, 11, 18 ; May 6.]

VOL. 5.

1558–61.

80. **1558.** June 14.—Alexander Green decerned to deliver "ane double ducat" to Elizabeth Wedderburn, spouse to Patrick Lyon.

81. **1558.** (a) June 27.—William Wedderburn sits on an inquest. (b) July 1.—William Wedderburn assoilzied from the claim of James Rollok, younger, "concerning the custom of his salmon" and other matters. (c) July 5.—William Wedderburn decerned to pay a sum of money (£8 11s. 7d.) to Thomas Nicholson in Leith, skipper of the ship "James." (d) July 6.—William Wedderburn nominates David Wedderburn in Wellgait, an arbitrator for him in his action v. James Rollok.

   This action is again referred to Aug. 7, 8 and Sept. 1, 10.

82.   **1558.** Sept. 5.--Decree in favour of Peter Wedderburn.

83.   **1558.** Nov. 7 —The " boid " of David Wedderburn being " considerit to the maist and the maist profitable for the common weill," the " twa pairt" of the petty customs are " sett " to him for the space of 3 years from next Martinmas for the sum of nine score merks.   William Wedderburn is cautioner.

84.   **1558.** Nov. 16.—Registration of a tack (27 Aug. 1550), of a quarter of the lands of Grange of Kyntreith by Donald, Abbot of Cupar, to Patrick Lyon and Elizabeth Wedderburn, his wife.

85.   **1558.** Dec. 7.—Decree for David Wedderburn in Wellgait.

86.   **1559.** April 3.—" The quhilk . . . . day comperit Elene Lawson, spous of David Wedderburn in Murraygait, and actit hir self . . . to pay to Magdalane Wedderburn hir dochter 400 merks . . . in compleit satisfactione and payment of all maner of legaeies, bairnis pairt of guid &c. that may pertein to hir be the deceis of the said David hir fader, and this to be payit quhoe soune the said Magdalane's freinds thinks expedient that scho be mariet with ane partie aegrieball."

87.   **1559.** July 31.—James Wedderburn, part owner of the ship " Primrose," named.

88.   **1560.** April 22.—John Wedderburn, bailie, named.

89.   **1560.** May 30.—The baillies decern their " testimoniall under thair seall " that Richard Wedderburn is son lauchfull and begottin on matrimony of Alexander Wedderburn and Margaret Anderson.

  The name of the mother is wrongly given ; it was Isobel not Margaret.

90.   **1560.** May 31.—Alexander Wedderburn, younger, the clerk, having an action *re* the curatory of his wife's sister, Elizabeth Myln (one of the heirs of the late James Myln), the baillies allow that Mr. James Bonar, his substitute, occupy such clerkship pending such action. The said Elizabeth Myln chooses as her curators George Wischard, her father-in-law, and the said Alexander Wedderburn, younger, her brother-in-law.

  " Father-in law " in this entry, as often, signifies step-father, Elizabeth Guthrie, the widow of James Myln, having married, secondly, George Wischert of Drymme.

91.   **1560.** June 12.—Before the baillies (including John Wedderburn), compears Andro Sands, skipper, and protests that James Wedderburn withheld from him his " artail-zerie " to his damage, &c.

92.   **1560.** June 18.—Action by Peter Wedderburn v. Kyrtefer Andersoun for non-delivery of 400 bow-strings "sauld be him to the said Peter in Norruay," last May.

93.   **1560.** July 2.—Bond by John Wedderburn, baillie, to Robert Wedderburn, son of David Wedderburn in Wellgait, for three score pounds.

94.   **1560.** Aug. 2.—The baillies fix "Monunday next-to-cum" for the action of John Wedderburn v. John Fotheringham.

95.   **1560.** Aug. 23.—James Wedderburn, son and heir to umquhill David Wedderburn, produces for registration a discharge by Jacob Loheid, citiner of Dantzig.

96.   **1560.** Aug. 27.—James Wedderburn, coqueter for Dundee and procurater for William, Abbot of Kinloss, pursues David Gardyn *re* a cargo of salmon.

97.   **1560.** Oct. 4.—John Wedderburn and William Wedderburn, named as councillors.

98.   **1560.** Oct. 4.—The South Murraygait land of the heirs of umquhill Robert Wedderburn, bounded East by that of Archibald Burnett, is mentioned.

99.   **1560.** Oct. 9-10.—Action by William Wedderburn *v.* Helen Lawson his mother,
relict of umquhill David Wedderburn.

100.   **1560.** Oct. 10.—The provost and baillies set a piece of land called S. Clement's
Kirk and Kirkyard to Robert Wedderburn, elder, as the highest bidder.

101.   **1560.** Oct. 11.—James Wedderburn in Seagait, named as having five years ago
bought an @-rent for the cordiner's craft.

102.   **1560.** (*a*) Oct. 28.—Bond by Robert Blair to John Wedderburn.   (*b*) Nov. 5.—
William Wedderburn and Robert Wedderburn are on an inquest.   (*c*) Nov. 17.—
James Wedderburn bids for the weylions.

103.   **1560.** Nov. 18.—Helen Lawson, relict of David Wedderburn, and William Wedderburn, second son to the said David, actit themselves to abide by a decreet arbitral.

104.   **1560.** Nov. 23.—William Wedderburn is on an inquest for serving John
Wedderburn, burgess of Dundee, nearest agnate on the pairt of his father to David
Wedderburn, son of the late Mr. Robert Wedderburn, and also to Robert Wedderburn,
brother of the said David.

105.   **1561.** Jan. 13.—Action by John Wedderburn, part owner of the "Nightingale"
v. Adam and David Ramsay.

   [See, in all, s. dates:—**1558.** June 14, 27, 30 ; July 1, 5, 6 ; Aug. 7, 8 ; Sept. 1, 5, 10 ; Nov. 7, 16 ;
Dec. 7, 13.   **1559** Feb. 23 ; April, 3, 42 ; July 31.   **1560.** April 22 ; May 30, 31 ; June 12, 18, 21 ;
July 2 ; Aug. 2, 23, 27 ; Sept. 6 ; Oct. 4, 8, 9, 10, 11, 21, 26, 28 ; Nov. 5, 17-19, 23 ; Dec. 2, 12.
1561. Jan. 13.]

VOL. G.

1561—62.

   On the fly leaf is twice written : " Liber actorum curie burgi de Dundie tempore Alexandri
Wedderburne scribe eiusdem nunc inchoatus in mense Octobris anno nostre salutis 1561," and below
it : " This is the buik of the townis actis.   This is the buik of the town."   Also the words " David
Vedderburn is nocht guid."

106.   **1561.** Oct. 6, 11.—John Wedderburn and James Wedderburn, named as councillors
and baillies.

107.   **1561.** Nov. 3.—"Comperit Margaret Kyuloeh, relict of umquhill Robert Myln,
who was tutor lauchfull to umquhill James Myln, his brother's barnis," and agreed
to pay to Janet Myln, wife of Alexander Wedderburn, younger, and Elizabeth Myln,
her sister, daughters and heirs of the said James, 130 merks conform to a decreet
arbitral.   Robert Wedderburn acts as clerk *pro tempore.*

108.   **1561.** Nov. 5.—James Anderson, possessioner of the North Ferry and tacksman of
the town's salmon fishings in the Tay, assigns half the said tack to William Anderson,
his son by Grisild Wedderburn.

109.   **1561.** Nov. 21, 24, 26 ; Dec. 11.—Action by Robert Wedderburn, elder, *v.* Edward
Wedderburn and decreet on a decreet arbitral by James Lovell acting for Robert,
and John Wedderburn acting for Edward.

110.   **1562.** Feb. 16.—Decreet obtained by John Wedderburn *v.* John Patersoun.

111.   **1562.** Feb. 25.—Discharge to Alexander Monypenny of Perth by John Wedderburn
and James Wedderburn, owners of the ship "Nightingale," for moneys due by him
to them under a decreet.

112.   **1562.** (*a*) Feb. 27.—James Wedderburn protests that his late father, David
Wedderburn, and he were in possession of S. John's kirkyaird "divers zeirs bygane,"

and had not been lawfully warned to remove therefrom. (*b*) March 6.—The council set the said Kirkyard to James Wedderburn for three years, and he covenants by his tutor, John Wedderburn, to pay 11 shillings rent for the same.

113. **1562.** (*a*) April 8.—Decree in favour of "Thomas Wedderburn, sumtyme Sir Thomas Wedderburn," for an @-rent due in respect of his chaplainry. (*b*) April 30.—Decree *v.* Walter Carmannow in favour of Robert Wedderburn, younger. (*c*) June 19; July 3, 8, 24.—Action by James Straquhin *v.* Edward Wedderburn.

114. **1562.** Aug. 10.—Mathew Wedderburn and Patrick Walker, chirurgeons, submit themselves to the decision of Findlaw Duncan and Johnne Kinloch, chirurgeons, "anent the helinge of the said Mathewis thomie."

115. **1562.** Aug. 12.—(*a*) John Wedderburn and James Wedderburn, named *re* the ship "Nightingale." (*b*) Aug. 31.—John Wedderburn is assoilzied from the claim against him of James Wedderburn, James Barre, and Edward Wedderburn, owners of the ship "Nightingale."

116. **1562.** Aug. 28.—Alexander Bissett confesses the receipt from John Wedderburn's factors in Burdeaux of certain wine for which Edward Wedderburn and others were sureties.

[See, in all, s. dates :—1561. Oct. 6, 11 ; Nov. 3, 5, 19, 21, 24, 26 ; Dec. 11. 1562. Jan. 11, 21, 30 ; Feb. 2, 16, 18, 25, 26, 28 ; March 6. 18, 20 , April 8, 30 ; May 13, 16 ; June 19 ; July 3, 8, 16, 24 ; Aug. 10, 12, 26, 28, 31 ; Sept. 2, 4.]

VOL. 7.

1562—63.

117. **1562.** Oct. 6.—Decree on cognition by John Wedderburn and others that Isobell, Elizabeth, and Lucy Davidsoun are lawful daughters of Thomas Davidsoun, skipper, and umquhile Margaret Wedderburn, his spouse, and heiresses to their said mother.

118. **1562.** (*a*) Oct. 19.—James Wedderburn and John Wedderburn, named. (*b*) Oct. 23 —Bond by John Hoppringle to John Wedderburn.

119. **1562.** Nov. 16.—Decree *v.* Bessie Wedderburn, spous to Andrew Watson, to deliver a clonk to Thomas Philp.

120. **1562.** Nov. 20.—John Wedderburn levies an @-rent on the North Argylegate ground of John Ingraham, and South Flukergait ground of the heirs of George Lovell.

121. **1562.** Nov. 25.—Decree in favour of Helen Wedderburn, relict of Thomas Duncan.

122. **1562.** Nov. 27.—Decree for John Wedderburn and John Fotheringhame, co-owners of the "Elspeth."

123. **1562.** Dec. 11.—Discharge in favour of Robert Wedderburn, son and heir of umquhill David Wedderburn, and John Wedderburn, his curator, for an @-rent due out of his Skirling's Wynd land.

124. **1562.** (*a*) Dec. 16.—James Wedderburn refers a matter to arbitration. (*b*) Dec. 21.—John Wedderburn is on assize. (*c*) Decree in favour of Thomas Wedderburn for house maills.

125. **1562.** Dec. 25.—William Lochmalony acknowledges receipt of £80 pertaining to Alexander Wedderburn, son to umquhile David Wedderburn, as his bairnis pairt of gear.

126. **1563.** Jan. 11.—James Wedderburn, coqueter and searcher of this burgh, under Our Soverane Lady applies for the council's help in searching a ship.

127. **1563.** Jan. 13, 15, 18.—Action by Edward Wedderburn *v.* James Schiphird, in which reference is made to a deposition by Alexander Wedderburn, elder.

128. **1563.** Feb. 22.—James Serymgeour of Balbeuchlie is cautioner for Helen Wedderburn, ... (*sic*) for Thomas Wedderburn that he shall stand firm and stablo in the things she does in his name, whereupon the said Helen asks acts of Court.

Dundee
Burgh and
Head Court
Records.

129. **1563.** March 6.—Thomas Wedderburn, son to umquhill Gilbert Wedderburn, iudweller in Leith, compears with Patrick Cockburn, his curator, and revokes his minority acts, especially " the allegit compt he maid with Johnne Brown, his fader-in-law (*i.e.*, step-father) anent the biggin and reparation of his house in Leith."

130. **1563.** (*a*) March 8.—Decree for an @ rent in favour of Thomas Wedderburn, chaplain of Our Lady's chaplainry in the Cowgait. (*b*) March 10.—Action by James Gardin *v.* David Wedderburn. (*c*) July 9.—Decree for Janet Wedderburn, spous of William Man.

[See, in all, s. dates :—1562. Oct. 6. 19, 23 ; Nov. 16. 20, 25, 27 ; Dec. 2, 11, 16, 21, 26. 1563. Jan. 11, 13, 15, 18, 20, 22 ; March 6, 8, 10 ; April 30 ; July 9.]

VOL. 8.

1563—65.

This volume was originally intended by Alexander Wedderburn, town clerk (1557-85), as the second of his protocol books, but only four leaves of it were so used.

The following memoranda, &c., occur on the fly leaf :—" Secundus liber prothogollorum Alexandri Wedderburu scribe civitatis burgi de Dundie ac notarii Inchoatus in mense Januarij Anno Dui mill. quingentesimo sexagesimo primo.

Non vox sed votum, non musica cordula sed cor,
Non clamaus sed amans candet in aure Dei.

which we may render

" Worship not words, love not the lifted voice,
Hearts not sweet harmonies, God's ears rejoice."

Then follows :—" Liber actorum Curia burgi de Dundee inchoatus in mense Octobris Anno Domini millesimo quingentesimo sexagesimo tertio, regni illustrissime supreme donne regine Dei benignitate Marie Scotorum regine dotarieque regine Gallie anno vigesimo primo."

Below is Alexander Wedderburn's autograph and notarial symbol, with the motto " Deum Time."

131. **1563.** Oct. 4.—John Wedderburn, counneillor, and (Oct. 18) on assize.

132. **1563.** Oct. 13.—Decree *v.* Bessie Wedderburn, relict of Andrew Watsoun, ordering her to give security that the goods left by her husband in his will shall at her death be forthcoming to John Adam.

133. **1563.** Oct. 27 ; Nov. 10.—Action by Thomas Wedderburn, chaplain, and Mark Barrie, patron, of the Magdaleue altar, *v.* James Andersoun.

134. **1563.** (*a*) Nov. 15, 23, .26.—Cross actions between John Cathrow and Alexander Wedderburn, elder. Decree in favour of the latter. (*b*) Dec. 3, 6, 8.—Action by James Fotheringham *v.* James Lovell, Margaret Rollok (relict and executrix of George Lovell), John Wedderburn, and others. (*c*) Dec. 17.—Action by James Ferrier *v.* Edward Wedderburn.

135. **1564.** (*a*) Jan. 24 ; April 14.—Decree in favour of Mathew Wedderburn, mariner. (*b*) Feb. 21.—Edward Wedderburn and William Wedderburn named in a decree. (*c*) March 23.—John Wedderburn is on an inquest. (*d*) May 10, 19.—Decree *r.* William Wedderburn. (*e*) Aug. 29.—Robert Wedderburn, senior, is on an inquest. (*f*) Oct. 2.—John Wedderburn is on the list of bailies and councillors.

136. **1564.** Oct. 25.—Elizabeth Wedderburn claims fifty marks from John Matheson as occupier of the lands of Dunfin.

137. **1564.** Nov. 6.—John Caraill and Margaret Stewart, his spouse, discharge William Mann, elder, and Janet Wedderburn, his spouse, of the articles in the marriage contract of the grantors.

138. **1564.** Nov. 6.—Sir Thomas Wedderburn constitutes Edward Wedderburn, his factor and procurator, to pursue all claims re his benefices of S. Michael or Our Lady in Cowgait.

139. **1564.** (a) Nov. 13, 27.—John Wedderburn v. Walter Carmunnow continued. (b) Nov. 15. —Kathrene Wedderburn distrains on the land of John Cathrow.

140. **1564.** Nov. 27.—Simon Cloustoun, master of the "Fleaud Hart," a ship of Incusen in Holland, complains that James Wedderburn, coqueter of Dundee, seized part of his cargo. James Wedderburn replies that the cargo had been shipped unbeknown to him, but on Patrick Lyoun, customar, and John Wedderburn, his substitute, stating that the duty has been paid, James Wedderburn is ordered to return it.

141. **1565.** Jan. 8.—Edward Wedderburn protests that Mr. David Scrymgeour's process anent the back land of umquhile James Wedderburn is to be without prejudice to him.

142. **1565.** March 16.—Edward Wedderburn discharges Alexander Nairne "cietiner in S. Androis," of 50 merks due from him under his marriage contract, on behalf of Janet Inglis, spouse to Edward Wedderburn.

143. **1565.** March 20, 23.—James Wedderburn, coqueter and serchcor to the Queen's Majesty at the port of Dundee, reports various matters to the council.

144. **1565.** March 30.—Decree of poynding in favour of Thomas Wedderburn, chaplain of the chaplainry of S. John in Sklaitt Hewchis.

145. **1565.** (a) March 30 ; April 5 ; May 4.—Action by Archibald Wedderburn v. Margaret Rolland. (b) May 2.--Decree in favour of Richard Wedderburn and his factors

[See, in all, s. dates :—**1563.** Oct. 4, 13, 18, 27 ; Nov. 10, 15, 22, 26 ; Dec. 3, 6, 8, 17. **1564.** Jan. 24 ; Feb. 21 ; March 23 ; April 14 ; May 10, 19 ; July 19 ; Aug. 29 ; Oct. 2, 25 ; Nov. 6, 13, 15, 22, 27. **1565.** Jan. 8 ; March 16, 20, 23, 30 ; April 5 ; May 2, 4.]

VOL. 9.

1565-68.

146. **1565.** (a) Oct. 31.--Robert Wedderburn and Edward Wedderburn are members of two inquests. (b) Nov. 15.—Decree v. John Wedderburn. (c) Nov. 26.—Barbara Wedderburn, spous to David Guthrie, compears in an action.

147. **1565.** Dec. 4.—James Wedderburn and Helen Lawson, his mother, desire transumpt of a protocol from the book of the late Mr. Thomas Seres, "ane legall and famous notarey in his tyme."

148. **1566.** (a) Jan. 14.—Decreet of poynding v. the North Seagait back land of the late David Wedderburn. (b) Jan. 14.—Decreet of poynding in favour of James Wedderburn v. the lands of James Wilkeson. (c) Same day.—Bond by James Wedderburn.

149. **1566.** March 6.—James Lovell appears as procurator for his mother, Elizabeth Wedderburn, in an action v. Peter Newman, which is again referred to March 25 ; May 1, 15, 22 ; and Nov. 27.

150. **1566.** (a) May 31.—John Wedderburn is cautioner for Maister Walter Smettoun. (b) June 19.—Decree in favour of John Wedderburn.

151. **1566.** June 21.—"The quhilk day the said judges sittand in judgemcut be the Dundee
Burgh and
Head Court
Records. tenor theirof cognossis and acknowlagis Robert Wedderburn to be narest and lauchfull air to umquhill Robert Wedderburn, younger, his father."

152. **1566.** (a) June 26.—Decree v. John Wedderburn. (b) Same day.—Edward Wedderburn, named. (c) Aug. 6.—Alexander Wedderburn, notary public, witness. (d) Oct. 9.—James Wedderburn named as bailie; John Wedderburn as councillor. (e) Oct. 30.—Decree in favour of Mathew Wedderburn.

153. **1566.** Nov. 11.—James Wedderburn and James Thomson, bailics, hear an application by George Rollok v. Robert Wedderburn and James Scrymgeour of Balbeuchlie, his curator, and also v. Jonet Logan, as intrometter with the goods of umquhill James Wedderburn. This matter is again mentioned 1567, Jan. 31, Feb. 10, March 1, 7, 14, April 30, May 7.

154. **1566.** Dec. 11.—James Turing and Alexander Wedderburn, elder, compear and bind themselves to abide by the deliverance of the judges arbiters in all actions and specially "anent the rest of the said James' tocher guid."

155. **1567.** (a) March 7.—James Wedderburn, coquoter of Dundee, named. (b) Oct. 7.— John Wedderburn and James Wedderburn named in a list of magistrates. (c) Oct. 27.—Decree in favour of Edward Wedderburn. (d) Oct. 31.—Decree in favour of Jonet Wedderburn, spouse of William Man. (e) Nov 10.—Action by Edward Wedderburn v. Robert Wedderburn, younger, and James Scrymgeour of Balbeuchlie, his curator. (f) Nov. 17.—Decree in favour of James Wedderburn for possession of a boat.

156. **1568.** (a) Jan. 14.—Decree in favour of Thomas Wedderburn; Edward Wedderburn is surety. (b) Jan. 16.—Action by Alexander Valles v. Edward Wedderburn. (c) Jan. 20.—Decreet of poynding in favour of Alexander Wedderburn, elder, v. Thomas Gray and another.

157. **1568.** Jan. 23.—Robert Wedderburn, younger, compears in court and revokes his minority acts and renounces his curators, James Scrymgeour of Balbeuchlie and John Wedderburn, "becaus thai refusit to do the office to him" and obtains an edict for the election of new curators. (See, however, No. 169.)

158. **1568.** (a) Feb. 9.—Action by Elis Wedderburn v. Margaret Kinloch, relict of Robert Milne. (b) Feb. 17.—John Wedderburn is on assize. (c) March 12.— Decree in favour of Thomas Wedderburn v. George Michell. (d) March 15.—Decree v. Edward Wedderburn to produce his title to certain goods bought by him of Thomas Wedderburn.

159. **1568.** March 19.—Decree that James Wedderburn and Robert Wedderburn, younger, have no title to the annual rents of umquhile Sir Thomas Wedderburn on ground that Sir Thomas disponed them to Edward Wedderburn.

160. **1568.** March 22.—Action by Edward Wedderburn v. Elizabeth Wedderburn.

161. **1568.** March 29.—Decree discharging John Wedderburn of a claim made against him by Robert Barre for an annual rent due to Barre by the late James Wedderburn, father to the said John.

162. **1568.** March 31.—David Wedderburn and Alexander Wedderburn, notary public, witness a contract dated 9 March 1567 and now registered.

[See, in all, s. dates:—1565. Oct. 31 ; Nov. 15, 26 ; Dec 4, 20. **1566.** Jan. 14, 30 ; March 16, 25 ; May 1, 15, 22, 31 ; June 19, 21, 26 ; July 1 ; Aug. 6 ; Oct. 9, 30 ; Nov. 11, 27 ; Dec. 11, 16. **1567.** Jan. 31 ; Feb. 5, 10 ; March 1, 7 ; April 28, 30 ; May 7 ; Oct. 7, 27, 31 ; Nov. 3, 10, 17 ; Dec. 8. **1568.** Jan. 14, 16, 20, 23 ; Feb. 9, 17 ; March 12, 15, 19, 22, 31 ; April 2.]

VOL. 10.

1568—69.

163. **1568.** (*a*) May 12, 26.—Action by James Wedderburn *v.* Bonar of Rosse. (*b*) May 17.—Decree in favour of Elis Wedderburn.

164. **1568.** June 11.—Action by James Scrymgeour of Balbeuchlie, factor for Robert Wedderburn, son and heir of umquhile Robert Wedderburn, younger, *v.* Edward Wedderburn.

165. **1568.** June 21.—Decree for production of documents in the action between Elis Wedderburn, relict of Thomas Duncan, and Marione Matland, relict of John Spens.

166. **1568.** (a) July 7.—Claim by James Wedderburn *v.* his brother, William Wedderburn. (*b*) July 30.—Action by Robert Wedderburn, younger, *v.* Janet Gallway.

167. **1568.** Aug. 31 —Decree for Patrick Michell *v.* Alexander Wedderburn, younger, in respect of some goods of the pursuer in the hands of the defender, arrested by him at the instance of Charles Lovell and Patrick Walcar.

168. **1568.** Oct 4.—James Wedderburn and John Wedderburn are councillors.

169. **1568.** Oct. 8, 15.—Action between Jonet Logan, relict of Maister James Bonar, and Robert Wedderburn, younger, with consent of James Scrymgeour of Balbeuchlie and John Wedderburn, his curators.

170. **1569.** Jan. 5.—Edward Wedderburn, David Wedderburn, and Alexander Wedderburn, notary public, are all witnesses.

171. **1569.** Jan. 19, 21.—Action by Edmond Fermorer *v.* Alexander Wedderburn, elder.

172. **1569.** Jan. 19.—Action by David Scrymgeour in Mylnhoill *v.* Elizabeth Wedderburn, relict of Patrick Lyon. This action is again mentioned Jan. 24, 31, Feb. 7, 16, 23, March 30, April 20, 27, May 4, 11.

173. **1569.** Feb. 4.—Action by James Wedderburn, who takes to him James Scrymgeour and John Wedderburn, *v.* John Coustone, who takes to him Alexander Wedderburn and Alexander Scrymgeour. This action is again mentioned Feb. 11, 14, 23, 25, March 25, April 18, 20, 22.

174. **1569.** April 13.—Registered contract of marriage, dated at Dundee, between Andrew Auchterlownie in Barnyaird and Alexander Auchterlownie, his son and aperand heir, on the one part, and John Wedderburn, burgess of Dundee, and Christian Wedderburne, his daughter by umquhile Agnes Hoppringill, his spouse, on the other part. The tocher is 500 merks. The spouses, Alexander and Christian, sign with their own hands.

175. **1569.** (*a*) April 27.—Action by Elizabeth Wedderburn *v.* Margaret Kinloch. (*b*) April 29, May 13.—Action by Helen Wedderburn, relict of umquhile Thomas Duncan, *v.* Margaret Kinloch.

176. **1569.** (*a*) June 3 —Action by Robert Wedderburn, chaplain of S. James, *v.* Sir William Lind. (*b*) Decree in favour of Robert Wedderburn, younger, and James Scrymgeour, his tutor. (*c*) Decree in favour of James Wedderburn *v.* his brother, William Wedderburn.

177. **1569.** (*a*) June 15, 29.—Action by Christian Brown *v.* John Wedderburn. (*b* July 11.—Discharge in favour of Edward Wedderburn and others. (*c*) Sept. 2.—James Wedderburn is on assize. (*d*) Sept. 12.—Decree in favour of Alexander Wedderburn, elder.

[See, in all, s. dates :—1568. May 12, 17, 19, 26, 28 : June 1, 2, 11, 16, 21, 25, 30 ; July 2, 7, 14, 30; Aug. 4, 31 ; Oct. 4, 8, 15. 1569. Jan. 5, 19, 21, 24, 31 ; Feb. 4, 7, 11, 14, 16, 23, 25 ; March 25, 30 ; April 13, 18, 20, 22, 27, 29 ; May 4, 11, 13, 16 ; June 3, 15, 29 ; July 11, 15 ; Aug. 1 ; Sept. 2, 12]

Vol. 11.
—
1569–71.

178. **1569.** Oct. 3.—James Wedderburn and John Wedderburn are both named as councillors.

179. **1569.** Oct. 14.—James Wedderburn compears and "desyrit of the bailies to have access to his brother William, to the effect that he might delyver to him 200 merks" in pursuance of a decree by my Lord Regent's grace and the Lords of Secret Council.

180. **1569.** Nov. 4.—Decree in favour of Elizabeth Wedderburn, wife of James Turing.

181. **1569.** Nov. 16.—James Wedderburn is cognosced "sone and air of umquhill Johnne Wedderburn," and the bailies ordain that he have all the privileges of "ane burgess air," and that edicts be raised for giving him curators.

182. **1569.** Dec. 7.—Re the curatorship of James Wedderburn. Henry Wedderburn and Thomas Wedderburn are nominated as father's kin, and Janet Hoppringle and James Logan as mother's kin, whereupon he elects as his curators James Logan in Kinghorne, and James Lovell of Dundee.

183. **1570.** Feb. 20.—Registered decreet arbitral between James Wedderburn, sone and air of umquhile David Wedderburn, burgess, and William Wedderburn, his brother, and Margaret Rollok, wife of William, as to moneys due from James to William.

184. **1570.** Feb. 27, March 6.—Action by Peter Clayhills v. the executors of the late John Wedderburn.

185. **1570.** (a) March 15.—Breiff of Tutorie. Henry Wedderburn, son and air of umquhile Gilbert Wedderburn, burgess of Leith, and nearest agnat and cousin (consanguineus) of John Wedderburn, son of umquhile John Wedderburn, burgess of Dundee, refers himself to the deliverance of Alexander Wedderburn, James Wedderburn, and others, anent the tutorie of the said John. (b) March 17.—He dispones all his right to the said tutorie to James Forrester.

186. **1570.** (a) April 12.—Decree in favour of Patrick Wedderburn. (b) April 14, 19.— Alexander Wedderburn, younger, merchant, is named.

187. **1570.** May 1.—James Forrester, executor of umquhile John Wedderburn, is decerned to deliver to James Lovell and Alexander Wedderburn, clerk, all the evidents he has belonging to their pupils, Robert and David Wedderburn and (July 31) he is ordained to pay to them certain monies as "sons lauful of umquhile Maister Robert Wedderburn."

188. **1570.** June 9.—Action by Robert Wedderburn, younger, v. John Ferne.

189. **1570.** Aug. 31.—Robert Wedderburn is cognosced sone and air of umquhile David Wedderburn in Welgait, with all the privileges of a burgess air, and (Sept. 15) he sues James Forrester, executor of the late John Wedderburn for a debt. His affairs are again referred to Sept. 22; Oct. 23; Nov. 6, 8; Dec. 11, 13, 15. 1571, Jan. 19, 22, 24; Feb. 2; April 2; June 8.
  In some of the entries he is called "Robert Wedderburn, younger."

190. **1570.** (a) Sept. 20.—Decree in favour of Alexander Wedderburn, elder, and Richard Wedderburn, his son. (b) Nov. 13.—Decree in favour of Edward Wedderburn.

191. **1571.** Jan. 19.—Decree in favour of David Wedderburn, as cautioner for Isobell Lovell, his mother.

2 M

192.   **1571.** Feb. 5.—Registered contract (16 Sept.) by which George Wisehart, brother to Christian Wischart, relict of John Wedderburn, agrees to a certain division of the said John Wedderburn's property between his said sister and Gresscild Wedderburn.

> See ante No. 174 and post No. 195. Gresscild or Grissell Wedderburn was daughter to John Wedderburn by his first marriage.

193.   **1571.** Feb. 19.—Decree in favour of John Wedderburn and others.

194.   **1571.** (a) Feb. 21.—Robert and David Wedderburn, with consent of James Lovell, their tutor, discharge James Forrester, executor of umquhile John Wedderburn. (See ante 187.) (b) Feb. 23.—They grant a discharge to James Lovell.

195.   **1571.** (a) March 12.—Cristian Wischairt, relict of umquhile John Wedderburn, and the executors of the said John, compear and produce her marriage contract, dated at Logie Wischairt, 27 Jan. 1569, in which the said John is described as burgess of Dundee, and she, as daughter of umquhill John Wischairt of that ilk, contracting with the consent of John Wischairt now of that ilk, her brother german, and George Wischairt, &c. She now grants herself to have been paid all sums due to her under the said contract. (b) Same day.—James Forrester, executor of the said John Wedderburn, acknowledges the receipt from the said Christian Wischairt of £65 to be "furthcumand to the weill and utilitie of Gresseild Wedderburn, dochter lauchfull of the said umquhill Johnne."

196.   **1571.** June 1.—Decree in favour of Robert Wedderburn, elder.

197.   **1571.** June 8.—Alexander Wedderburn, elder, is named as father's kin to Robert Rollok, son of George Rollok, deceased, who needs curators.

198.   **1571.** Aug. 24—Registration of a contract made between John Cowstone, burgess of Dundee, and Elizabeth Wedderburn, his wife, on the one part, and Mark Barrie, with consent of Magdalene Wedderburn, his wife, on the other part, and witnessed by John Wedderburn and Alexander Wedderburn, notary.

199.   **1571.** Sept. 17.—James Wedderburn and William Forrester ordain James Forrester, only executor of umquhill John Wedderburn, to indemnify James Wedderburn, son and heir of the said John, and James Lovell, his curator, against certain claims.

> [See, in all, s. dates :—1569. Oct. 3, 14 ; Nov. 4, 16, 25 ; Dec. 7.—1570. Jan. 16 ; Feb. 13, 20, 27 ; March 6, 8, 15, 17 ; April 12, 14, 19, 21 ; May 1 ; June 9, 31 ; Aug. 2, 31 ; Sept. 15, 20, 22 ; Oct. 2, 23, 25 ; Nov. 6, 8, 13, 22 ; Dec. 1, 4, 6, 11, 13, 15, 18.—1571. Jan. 17, 19, 22, 24 ; Feb. 2, 5, 9, 14, 16, 19, 21, 23 ; March 2, 12 ; April 2 ; June 1, 2, 8 ; July 11, 13, 18 ; Aug. 7, 22, 23, 24, 31 ; Sept. 5, 10, 17, 22.]

VOL. 12.

1571—73.

On the second fly leaf of this volume is the notarial symbol and motto ("Deum time,") of Alexander Wedderburn, the old clerk. There are also several Latin and English verses, including the lines "Non vox sed votum," &c., already mentioned (ante Vol. 8) and some other verses, of which the last couplet is as follows :—

> "Stet liber hic douec fluctus formica mariuos
> Ebibet, et tostum testudo perambulat orbem."

and which he translated thus :—

> "This book shall last heir iu Dundee
> Quhill that the emmet driuk all ye see
> And quhill the snaill with speddie ferd
> Sall perambill throw all the eird.

On the first leaf are some irregular entries 1554—1556, referriu to the late Henry Wedderburn in Murraygait, James Wedderburn in Seagait, and Mr. David Scrymgeour.

200.   **1571.** Oct. 2, 6.—James Wedderburn of Cragy is named as on the council.

201.   **1571.** Nov. 20.—Decree v. James Forrester, executor of umquhile John Wedderburn in North Marketgait, in pursuance of another decree ordaining him to relieve

James Wedderburn (son of the said John Wedderburn) and James Lovell, his curator, Dundee
Burgh and
Head Court
Records. of certain matters.

202. **1572.** Jan. 14.—Decree *v.* John Fernie in favour of Robert Wedderburn, younger.

203. **1572.** Feb. 22.—James Forrester, executor of umquhile John Wedderburn, is decreed to pay Agnes, daughter of James Logane in Kingorne, a legacy left her by the late Agnes Hoppringill, spouse of the said John.

204. **1572.** Oct. 10.—Edward Wedderburn produces to the court evidence that he has not been able to recover an annual rent due to him from the land of the heirs of umquhile James Wedderburn.

205. **1572.** (a) Nov. 28.—Decreet of poynding in favour of Katharine Wedderburn *v.* Walter Cathrow and others. (b) Dec. 15.—Discharge in favour of Robert Wedderburn, son and heir of umquhile David Wedderburn, for an @-rent due out of Skirling's Wynd.

206. **1573.** Feb. 25.—The bailies assoilzie Andro May and Joneit Wedderburne from the claim of removing from Robert Wedderburne's yard, until Whitsunday.

207. **1573.** May 16.—Decree in favour of James Wedderburn.

208. **1573.** May 18.—Magdalen Wedderburn protests that she be not prejudiced if John Coustoun fail to poynd the Lady Warkis stairs for his @-rent.

209. **1573.** July 15.—Assize of the service and retour of Alexander Wedderburn as brother and heir to umquhile Robert Wedderburn.

The particulars are not given, though a blank space is left for them to be added.

[See, in all, s. dates :—1571. Oct. 2. 6 ; Nov. 20 ; Dec. 14.—1572. Jan. 7, 14 ; Feb. 22 ; March 3 ; May 19 ; June 9, 11, 16 ; July 14 ; Aug. 13 ; Oct. 10 ; Nov. 15.—1573. Jan. 16, 28 ; Feb. 25 ; March 4 ; April 20, 23 ; May 18, 18 ; July 8, 15, 16 ; Sept. 11 ; Oct. 15, 17, 30 ; Nov. 18, 20; Dec. 14.]

VOL. 13.

1573–75.

210. **1574.** (a) Feb. 24, 26.—Robert Wedderburn, younger, James Wedderburn, and Edward Wedderburn, named. (b) March 11.—Decree in favour of Barbara Wedderburn, wife of David Guthrie. (c) March 22.—Suit between Robert Wedderburn and Edward Wedderburn. (d) May 3.—James Wedderburn grants himself completely paid of all burgess-ships. (e) July 1.—Robert Wedderburn, younger, *v.* John Fernie. (f) July 21.—Patrick Wedderburn, brother to Richard Wedderburn, in Elsignoir, grants a discharge to Thomas Muir for 600 dollars, due from Muir to the said Richard.

211. **1574.** (a) Aug. 9.—Decree *v.* Elizabeth Wedderburn, wife of James Turing. (b) Sept. 20.—Discharge granted to Robert Wedderburn, younger, chaplain of S. James Major. (c) Oct. 15.—James Wedderburn, son and heir of umquhile John Wedderburn, acknowledges receipt from James Lovell of all his father's papers. (d) Nov. 2. John Wedderburn and Alexander Wedderburn, notary, are witnesses to a deed. (e) Nov. 26 —Decree for Peter Wedderburn.

212. **1574.** Dec. 21.—John Wedderburn requires curators, and, there appearing Alexander Wedderburn and Edward Wedderburn as father's kin, and James Hoppringill and James Logan as mother's kin, he nominates to act as such curators James Logan, Alexander Wedderburn, younger, and James Forrester.

213. **1575.** Jan. 19.—Mathew Wedderburn is cautioner for Patrick (Peter) Wedderburn, younger, who is sued by James Kinnaird.

214. **1575.** May 4.—Robert Wedderburn, younger, chaplain of S. James Major, produces his title thereto.

215. **1575.** May 6.—Robert Wedderburn, son and heir of umquhile Robert Wedderburn, burgess, revokes his minoritie acts.

216. **1575.** May 9.—Peter Wedderburn gets from the town a nineteen years' tack of the Blackfriars yard.

217. **1575.** May 17.—The bailies convict Robert Wedderburn, son and heir of umquhile Robert Wedderburn, burgess, of "invaiding and mispresonyng" Robert Wedderburn, younger.

218. **1575.** June 8.—The bailies discharge Robert Wedderburn, younger, of certain feumaill due from him to them in respect of our Lady Chappell's zaird in the Cowgait

219. **1575.** June 20.—The bailies assoilzie "Alexander Wedderburn, younger, Elizabeth Strathauchin his modir fra . . . ." (the rest is blank).

220. **1575.** July 4.—John Wedderburn, son of the late John Wedderburn, and his curators, Alexander Wedderburn, younger, and James Logan in Kinghorn, grant a discharge.

221. **1575.** July 25.—Margaret Strathauchin binds herself to pay to James Hopprlugill, guidshir of James Wedderburn, younger, certain house maills. James Wedderburn's "house in Leyth" is named.

[See, in all, s. dates :—1574. Feb. 24, 26 ; March 11. 22, 31 ; April 13, 21 ; May 3 ; June 14 ; July 1, 9, 21, 28, 30 ; Aug. 9, 20, 22 ; Sept. 6, 20 ; Oct. 4. 15, 20, 25 ; Nov. 2, 24, 26 ; Dec. 10, 15, 17, 21.—1575. Jan. 19, 21, 28 ; Feb. 16, 25 ; March 4, 11, 10 ; April 14, 20 ; May 4, 6, 9, 11, 13, 17, 24, 30 ; June 6, 8, 20 ; July 4, 13, 15, 25, 27.]

Vol. 14.

1575—79.

On the fly leaf is written, "Liber actorum Curie burgi de Dundie tempore Alexandri Wedderburn scribe ejusdem, nunc inchoatus in mense Octobris anno Domini millesimo quingentesimo septuagesimo quinto." Below are, in Latin and English, the lines beginning, "This buik shall last heir in Dundie," as at the opening of Vol. 12. At the foot is written, "Alexander Wedderburn, Peter Wedderburn, Joannes Wedderburn, David Wedderburn."

222. **1575.** (a) Oct. 14.—Bond by Thomas Kay to Peter Wedderburn, burgess. (b) Nov. 11.—Decree v. Margaret Dundas, relict and administratrix of the late James Wedderburn. (c) Nov. 11.—Decree in favour of Barbara Wedderburn, relict of David Guthrie.

223. **1576.** Jan. 23, Feb. 10.—Decree of an edict of curatory in favour of John, Helen, Elizabeth, Walter, and Euphame, children of umquhile James Wedderburn and Margaret Dundas.

224. **1576.** Jan. 23.—Decree in favour of Robert Wedderburn, younger.

225. **1576.** Feb. 2.—Resignation by Robert Lovell, son to Robert Lovell, elder, by his wife, Margaret Wedderburn.

226. **1576.** March 28.—Barbara Wedderburn, relict of David Guthrie, and her children, sue Thomas Dowie, who objects to Alexander Wedderburn, the clerk, acting as clerk in the cause, on the ground that he is brother german to the said Barbara, but the objection is disallowed.

227. **1576.** May 9.—Robert Wedderburn, younger, is sued by Robert Kynloch, and summoned to appear, but is absent and "furth of the cowntrie."

228. **1576.** June 25.—Janet Inglis, spous to Edward Wedderburn, is named.

229. **1576.** July 11.—John Wedderburn, son lawful to umquhile John Wedderburn, burgess, with consent of James Forrester, his curator, discharges James Logane of a debt.

230. **1576.** (a) Oct. 1.—Peter Wedderburn is a councillor. (b) Dec. 7.—Edward Wedderburn is on assize.

231. **1577.** Feb 6.—Judgment in favour of Margaret Kinloch, spouse to Peter Wedderburn.

232. **1577.** Feb. 22.—Robert Wedderburn, younger, son of the late Robert Wedderburn, binds himself to hand over to Peter Wedderburn one-sixteenth of a ship called "The Robert."

233. **1577.** March 22.—John Wedderburn is cognosced son and heir of umquhile James Wedderburn, burgess, and is entered as such in all his father's lands, &c., "with all privileges of a burgess heir."

234. **1577.** June 5, 19.—George Ramsay, laird of Banff, sues Alexander Oehterlony and Grisild Wedderburn, his spouse, for occupation of a house.
The name Grisild is an error for Christian. See ante No. 174, and post No. 250.

235. **1577.** Aug. 28.—William Fotheringhame and Margaret Dundas, his wife, are named re the affairs of umquhile James Wedderburn, to whom Margaret Dundas, his reliet, was executrix.

236. **1577.** Sept. 2.—Peter Wedderburn buys a ship called "The Swan."

237. **1577.** Nov. 25.—The lands of "umquhile David Wedderburn lying on the south part of the Murraygait" are named.

238. **1577.** Nov. 28.—Margaret Rollok, spouse of William Wedderburn, binds her son William Wedderburn to Robert Andersoun, mariner, for five years on certain terms.

239. **1578.** March 7.—Robert Wedderburn, chaplain of S. Thomas' chaplainry, named.

240. **1578.** June 13.—John Lovell, eldest son of Robert Lovell and Margaret Wedderburn, is constituted procurator for his said father and his brother Robert Lovell.

241. **1578.** (a) July 4.—Action of Edward Wedderburn v. Ramsay mentioned. (b) July 8, 9.—Inquest for the retour of John Wedderburn as brother german and heir of the late James Wedderburn. (c) Aug. 5.—Issobell Wedderburn is a witness. (d) Aug. 29.—The bailies decern Alexander Wedderburn to pay fifty-five shillings to Peter Wedderburn. (e) Sept. 5.—David Wedderburn, and Alexander Wedderburn, notary public, witness a charter. (f) Sept. 5.—Peter Wedderburn, John Wedderburn, and Alexander Wedderburn, notary public, witness a charter, dated 21 Aug. 1574.

242. **1578.** Sept. 10, 12, 16.—Patrick Wedderburn and Elizabeth Low, his spouse, get a discharge from George Reitt, brother german of the late James Reitt (first husband of the said Elizabeth Low), and tutor to his children, James and Gilbert Reitt.

243. **1578.** (a) Oct 8.—Decree in favour of Robert Wedderburn. (b) Oct. 20.—Decree in favour of Jonet Inglis, reliet of Edward Wedderburn.

244. **1578.** Dec. 17.—Discharge by James Lovell of Ballumbie in favour of Alexander Wedderburn, son and heir of umquhile David Wedderburn, burgess of Dundee.

245. **1579.** Jan. 12.—The lands of the heirs of umquhile James Wedderburn in Seagait are poynded.

Dundee
Burgh and
Head Court
Records.

246. **1579.** March 14.—Bond by Robert Wedderburn, spous of Eupham Coustoun, relict of Robert Scott, in favour of Eupham Scott, only child of the said Robert Scott and Eupham Coustoun. Peter Wedderburn and John Coustoun are named in the transaction.

247. **1579.** June 24.—Decree in favour of Alexander Wedderburn, merchant.

248. **1579.** Aug. 5.—John Lovell grants that he has received from Peter Wedderburn " ane lang springzie rapper quhilk appertenit to umquhile Edward Wedderburn."

249. **1579.** Sept. 9.—Alexander Wedderburn, elder, and Peter Wedderburn are named as mother's next of kin to William Barre.

250. **1579.** Sept. 23.—Christian Wedderburn, relict of Alexander Ochterlouey, is named in a judgment. She is named again Oct. 14, 19, Nov. 23, 30, Dec. 2 ; and 1580, March 4, 11.

251. **1579.** (a) Oct. 5.—The lands of the heirs of umquhile David Wedderburn in North Seagait are poynded. (b) Nov. 18.—Magdalen Wedderburn, relict of Mark Barre, is named.

[See in all, s. dates :—1575. Oct. 3, 14, 26 ; Nov. 11.—1576 Jan. 20, 23 27, 30 ; Feb. 2, 8, 10, 15, 27 ; March 7, 11, 28 ; May 7, 9, 28 ; June 4, 6, 15, 22, 25 ; July 11, 27 ; Sept. 17 ; Oct. 1, 3, 5 ; Nov. 19, 23 ; Dec. 7, 10, 12, 14, 19.—1577. Jan. 16, 18, 23 ; Feb. 6, 22, 27 ; March 22 ; April 22 ; May 31 ; June 5, 7, 19, 26 ; July 3 ; Aug. 12, 28 ; Sept. 2, 6, 13, 18, 25, 31 ; Oct. 4, 23 ; Nov. 1, 25, 27, 28 ; Dec. 2, 4, 6, 13.—1578. Jan. 21, 23 ; Feb. 17, 24, 26 ; March 7, 21 ; April 9, 14, 18, 21, 24 ; May 10, 12, 14, 16 ; June 13, 20 ; July 4, 8, 9 ; Aug. 5, 29 ; Sept. 5, 10, 12, 16, 26 ; Oct. 8, 17, 20, 22 ; Nov. 14, 28 ; Dec. 17, 19.—1579. Jan. 9, 12, 14. 20 ; March 14 ; April 27 ; May 15, 18, 25 ; June 12, 24 ; July 13, 17, 29 ; Aug. 5, 7, 10, 22, 28 ; Sept. 9, 16, 18, 21, 23 ; Oct. 5, 12, 14. 19 ; Nov. 18, 23, 25, 30 ; Dec. 2.—1580. Jan. 14, 25. 27 ; Feb. 9, 15, 28 ; March 4, 11.]

VOL. 15.

1580–82.

This is the book of Alexander Wedderburn of Kingenuie, begun on 25 March 1580. On the first page he writes :—

" To mak guid actis, it is actis done
To mak thame and to brack thame swne,
Better ondone I say for me
To mak and brak sa haistellie."
Alexander Wedderburne.

On the second page he writes :—
" O guid God be merciful unto me, Imprent Thy fear in my hairt
per me Alexandrum Wedderburne."
On the third page is written :—"Peter Wedderburne with my hand," " David Wedderburn," and " Liber Alexandri Wedderburn scribæ communitatis burgi de Dundie."

252. **1580.** May 27.—Decrees v Duncan Burne and another, to remove from Madlane Wedderburn's house.

253. **1580.** June 22, 27, 29 ; July 1.—Action by Robert Wedderburn v. Alexander Mathew, for that the defender "blasphemit him, calland him anesleistsluther vagabond." Peter Wedderburn is cautioner for Robert his brother, who (June 27) produces as witness Robert Rollok, to whom A. Mathew objects, on the ground that " he and the pursuer are second and third in consanguinitie."

254. **1580.** Sept. 3.—Robert Lovell, elder, burgess, only executor dative to his late wife, Margaret Wedderburn, produces and swears to the inventory of her goods.

255. **1580.** Sept. 19.—Margaret Wedderburn is cognosced nearest and lawful heir to umquhile Robert Wedderburn, younger, son and heir of umquhile Robert Wedderburn. See ante. s. Dundee Protocol Books, No. 276.

256. **1580.** Oct. 12.—Action by John Coustoun and Elizabeth Wedderburn, his wife, v. Magdalene Wedderburn, life-rentrix of " Ladiewark stairs."

257. **1580.** Nov. 11.—Discharge by Elizabeth Low, relict of umquhile James Reit, burgess, with consent of Patrick Wedderburn, her husband.

Dundee
Burgh and
Head Court
Records.

258. **1580.** Nov. 14.—Alexander Kyd, procurator for Magdalene Wedderburn in the action of John Coustoun against her, protests against Robert Kyd being a judge in such action on the ground that John Coustoun's spouse was Robert Kyd's sister's dochter.

John Coustoun had married Elizabeth Wedderburn, daughter of Robert Wedderburn and Janet Kyd, and sister of Alexander Wedderburn, the old clerk.

259. **1580.** Dec. 19.—Peter Wedderburn and Robert Wedderburn, his brother, are named as arbitrators.

260. **1581.** (a) May 19, 24.—The houses of Magdalene, Janet, and Isobell Wedderburn, are named on separate occasions. (b) Oct. 6.—Christian Wedderburn obtains a decree. (c) Nov. 22.—Jonat Inglis, relict of Edward Wedderburn, appears.

261. **1582.** (a) March 28—Decree in favour of Helen and Elizabeth Wedderburn. (b) Aug. 13.—Decree v. Marion Strathauchin, wife of James Wedderburn.

In the latter entry both Christian names are inaccurate. They should be Mariot or Margaret, and John. See post, No. 275 (c).

262. **1582.** Sept. 20.—"In the presence of the bailies, &c., compeared Alexander Wedderburn, common clerk of this burgh, and resigned and demittit his office of the common clerkship, with all fees, dewties, &c., into the hands of the said bailies in favour of Maister Alexander Wedderburn, his eldest lauful sone," whereupon the bailies, "according to the tenor of a letter subscribed by the provost, bailies, &c., anent the disposition of the said office, now elect and creatt the said Mr Alexander their common clerk for life, and received his oath for faythfull using thereof. And of new the bailies have, with consent of Mr. Alexander, maid and constitute the said Alexander Wedderburn, his father, substitute in the said office to be usit by him during his will and pleasure, and the said Mr. Alexander is actit to delyuer to the said Alexander, his father, all profettis that may result throw the said office during his said father's lyftyme, quhairupon ather of thame askit actis." Signed by A. Wedderburn, father and son, and by Hercules Rollok and Thomas Ireland, notaries.

[See, in all, s dates :—1580. April 20 ; May 2, 27 ; June 13, 15, 22, 27, 29 ; July 1, 4, 8 ; Aug. 8 ; Sept. 3, 19, 21, 27 ; Oct. 5, 12, 17, 26, 28 ; Nov. 2, 7, 9, 11, 14 ; Dec. 9, 16, 19.—1581. Jan. 11, 20, 25, 29 ; Feb. 3, 13, 17, 22, 24 ; March 6, 13, 17 ; April 7, 24, 26 ; May 8, 19, 24 ; June 21 ; July 12, 28 ; Sept. 15, 18 ; Oct. 2, 6 ; Nov. 22, 30 ; Dec. 1, 8, 16, 18, 20.—1582. Jan. 24, 29 ; Feb. 7, 23 ; March 5, 28 ; May 11, 14, 28 ; July 13 ; Aug. 13, 31 ; Sept. 20, 21 ; Oct. 1, 12 ; Dec. 7.]

VOL. 16.
1583–86.

263. **1583.** (a) March 8.—James Wedderburn and Margaret Rollok nominate arbiters in a dispute between them. (b) April 10.—Decree v. Margaret Wedderburn, spouse to John Rolf.

264. **1583.** May 21.—Mr. Alexander Wedderburn, on behalf of Alexander Ramsay, his father-in-law, pays to Mitchell Ramsay £100 scots for the catch of salmon in the said Mitchell Ramsay's waters in the Tay for 1583.

265. **1583.** (a) June 19.—Application by Peter Imry, spouse to Barbara Wedderburn, relict of David Guthrie, in respect of David Guthrie's estate. (b) July 10.—Decree v. Elizabeth Wedderburn and John Craigtoun, her husband.

John Coustoun is sometimes called Craigtoun. See post No. 279.

266. **1583.** July 18.—Patrick Wedderburn and Elizabeth Low, his wife, are made donators to a letter of tack to George Robertson, by Robert Wedderburn, son and heir of umquhile Robert Wedderburn, burgess, of a South Cowgait yard, for nineteen years from Candlemas, 1582.

The date of the letter of tack is not given, but see ante s. No. 255.

267. **1583.** Aug. 7.—Curatorie, Wedderburne.

    This entry is unfortunately blank. It may, perhaps, refer to the curatory of one or more of the three daughters of Edward Wedderburn (son of James Wedderburn and Janet Logan), who died, and the youngest of whose daughters, Elizabeth, is named with her curators, post No. 394.

268. **1583.** Oct. 19.—Margaret Wedderburn is named as spouse future to Peter C'ayhills, younger, son of Peter Clayhills, elder, burgess of Dundee.

269. **1583.** Nov. 18, Dec. 2.—Magdalene Wedderburn, relict of Mark Barrie, obtains a decreet of poynding.

270. **1584.** Jan. 15.—Registered contract (11 Sept. 1583) of marriage between Robert Wedderburn, brother german to Alexander Wedderburn, clerk, and Margaret, daughter to Robert Myln, burgess of Dundee.

271. **1584.** (a) Feb. 14, 26.—John Wedderburn, portioner of Cragy, and Richard Pent, choose arbiters. (b) March 9.—Bond by John Wedderburn, son and heir of umquhile John Wedderburn, burgess, and another. (c) March 14.—Alexander Wedderburn, merchant, and Robert Wedderburn, notary, witnesses. (d) March 27.—Alexander Wedderburn and Christian Ferny, his wife, named. (e) May 18.—Elizabeth Wedderburn and James Turing, her spouse, named.

272. **1584.** June 17.—John Adamson, skipper in S. Andrews, takes acts that Robert Wedderburn, notary, has said openly in judgment that he will pursue him "both be the law and by the law" for John Wedderburn's life, and the said skipper is ordained to remain in ward till he find sufficient caution to answer for John Wedderburn and his gear as law will.

273. **1585.** (a) Jan. 29.—An action by Robert Wedderburn v. his father-in-law, Robert Myln, is often referred to at this time. (b) Feb. 26.—Alexander Wedderburn, junior, and Janet Myln, his spouse, are named. (c) March 31.—Decree in favour of Bessie Wedderburn, relict of John Lawsone.

274. **1585.** April 30.—Margaret Lindsay, spouse to John Wedderburn, mariner, leases a North Flukergate tenement to W. Crystesone, minister of Dundee.

275. **1585.** (a) Sept. 26.—Bond in favour of Robert Wedderburn, merchant, burgess. (b) Oct. 8.—Bond by David Robesonn in favour of the executors and bairns of umquhile Alexander Wedderburn, clerk. (c) Nov. 14.—Bond by John Wedderburn, portioner of Craigie Hiltoun, and Margaret Strathauchin, his spouse.

276. **1585.** Dec. 28.—Discharge by Robert Wedderburn, merchant, only brother and heir of umquhile David Wedderburn, burgess of Dundee, to John Piersoun, assignee, &c., of David Cant.

277. **1586.** March 16.—Decree in favour of David Wedderburn, chaplain of S. Margaret's chaplainry.

278. **1586.** April 9.—Discharge by John Kyd to his father, Alexander Kyd, in respect of all due to the grantor through the death of his mother, Isobell Wedderburn.

    [See, in all, s. dates :—1583. Feb. 25 ; March 7, 8, 18, 23 ; April 8, 10 ; May 8, 10, 16, 21, 25 ; June 1, 19, 20 ; July 2, 4, 8, 10, 17, 18, 22, 26, 31 ; Aug. 7, 15 ; Sept. 9, 17, 19 ; Oct. 19, 28 ; Nov. 1, 18, 27 ; Dec. 2, 11.—1584. Jan. 15, 17, 20, 24, 25 ; Feb. 5, 10, 12, 14, 22, 26 ; March 9, 14, 27 ; April 10, 27 ; May 18 ; June 5, 12, 17, 24 ; July 20, 24, 27 ; Sept. 7, 8, 11, 25, 28, 29 ; Oct. 9, 23, 24, 26 ; Nov. 30 ; Dec. 8.—1585. Jan. 13, 15, 20, 27, 29 ; Feb. 3, 12, 17, 26 ; March 6, 8. 10, 14, 17, 19, 31 ; April 20, 21, 23, 30 ; May 7, 18, 25, 28 ; June 4, 9 ; July 7, 12 ; Aug. 19 ; Sept. 26 ; Oct. 8 ; Nov. 14 ; Dec. 15, 28.—1586. Jan. 10 : Feb. 11, 14 ; March 14, 16, 21, 23 ; April 9.]

Vol. 17.

1589–94

279. **1590.** (a) March 2.—Decree in favour of Elizabeth Wedderburn, relict of John Craigtoun. See ante No. 265. (b) March 30.—Robert Wedderburn, elder, and Robert Wedderburn, merchant, are both on assize.

280. **1590.** April 22.—James Rait, son and heir of the late James Rait, grants a
discharge to his mother, Elizabeth Low, and her now spouse, Patrick Wedderburn,
burgess.

281. **1590.** July 1.—Katharine Wedderburn, daughter of umquhill Alexander Wedderburn, clerk of Dundee, obtains curators.

282. **1590.** July 16.—Robert Wedderburn, elder, merchant burgess, and Patrick Wedderburn, his cautioner, acknowledge the receipt of certain money.

283. **1590.** Aug. 7.—Decree in favour of John Wedderburn, clerk of the " Rea."

284. **1590.** Sept. 12.—A protocol of the late Alexander Wedderburn, clerk, written by the hand of John Wedderburn, his servitor, is produced.

285. **1590.** (a) Sept. 24.—Royal licence to Richard Wedderburn, burgess of Elsignoir, to export from Scotland " seven haundy naigis." (b) Oct. 27.—Royal licence to Richard Wedderburn. burgess of Elsignoir, to export ten chalders of wheat yearly for ten years " for making of mayne flower thairof to the use and table of our dearest brother, the Kyng of Denmark, as he has bene accustomat thir divers yeiris by past."

286. **1591.** (a) March 3.—John Wedderburn, portioner of Craigie Hiltoun, agrees to an arbitration. (b) March 6.—Bond by David Wedderburn, merchant, to his brother James.

287. **1591.** March 15. (a) Discharge by Richard Wedderburn, of Elsignoir, to Patrick Wedderburn, his brother german, for 2000 merks paid to Richard for his lands in Dundee. (b) Isobell Anderson, relict of umquhile Alexander Wedderburn, elder, burgess of Dundee, sets her lands in South Marketgait, &c., in tack to her son Patrick.

288. **1591.** March 25.—Bond to Peter Wedderburn, son of the late Alexander Wedderburn, clerk.

289. **1591.** July 16.—Registered contract (3 Aug. 1590) between Archibald Kyd and Robert Jackson, son and heir of umquhile Robert Jackson, portioner of Craigie, with consent of Margaret Strathauchin, his mother, relict of the said Robert Jackson, his father, and John Wedderburn of Craigie, now her spouse.

290. **1591.** Sept., Oct.—In a list of magistrates occurs the name of " Robert Wedderburn, Major Hospitalis."

291. **1591.** Oct. 29.—Decree in favour of Barbara Wedderburn, wife of Peter Imbrie.

292. **1592.** May 8.—James Strathauchin, notary, clerk depute for that purpose, makes the act of renunciation by Marjorie Turnbull, wife of David Denmuir in Wester Gourdie, ratifying the heretable disposition by her and her husband on — Feb. last, in favour of Mr. Alexander Wedderburn, clerk, of their shadow half of Wester Gourdie.

See ante s. Scrymgeour-Wedderburn Papers, Nos 82-86.

293. **1592.** (a) June 12.—John Wedderburn, son to Alexander Wedderburn, merchant, obtains a decree. (b) Aug. 23.—Decree in favour of Elizabeth Wedderburn, relict of John Coustoun and conjunct fiar of the Lady Warkstairs.

294. **1592.** Oct. 20.—Elizabeth Wedderburn, " one of the three dochters and nearest and lawful heirs of umquhill Edward Wedderburn," with consent of her curators, ratifies certain infeftments in favour of Katharine Wedderburn and Thomas Blair, her spouse.

2 N

282   THE WEDDERBURN BOOK.

Dundee
Burgh and
Head Court
Records.

295. **1593.** (a) Jan. 19.—Decree in favour of Jonat Wedderburn, wife of Andrew
Auchinlek. (b) March 23.—James Chalmers removes from John Wedderburn's free
lands of Aberbothrie, co. Perth.

296. **1593.** July 20.—Discharge by Alexander Wedderburn, clerk of Dundee, as tutor
and administrator to Magdalene Wedderburn, his daughter, in favour of John Traill.

[See in all s. dates :—**1590**. Feb. (?) ; March 2, 5, 6, 13, 18, 20, 30 ; April 6, 22, 29 ; May 4, 27 ;
June, 8, 17, 19 ; July 1, 15, 16 ; Aug. 3, 7 ; Sept. 12, 18, 24 ; Oct. 27 ; Nov. 6, 16, 20, 25 ; Dec. 11,
19.—**1591** Jan. 20, 26 ; March 3, 6, 10, 15, 25 ; April 5, 12, 23 ; May 5, 24, 28 ; June 19 ; July 2,
14, 16 ; Aug. 7, 25 ; Sept. 1, 16, 20, 22, 24 ; Oct. 8, 19, 25, 27, 29 ; Nov. 19 ; Dec. 14.—**1592**. Jan.
17, 26 ; March 15 ; April, 7, 24 ; May 6, 8, 19, 31 ; June 12, 21, 25 ; July 24 ; Aug. 23 ; Oct. 4, 15,
20 ; Nov. 8.—**1593**. Jan. 15, 19 ; Feb. 10, 19 ; March 5, 19, 23, 24 ; May 25 ; June 29 ; July 20 ;
Aug. 18 ; Sept. 3, 24 ; Oct. 2, 5 ; Nov. 5 ; Dec. 3, 21.—**1594**. Jan. 28 ; Feb. 12.]

VOL. 18.
—
1594–95.

297. **1594.** (a) May 17.—Decree in favour of Barbara Wedderburn, spouse to Peter
Imrie. (b) May 27.—Decree in favour of Kathrene Wedderburn. (c) Sept. 6.—
Elizabeth Wedderburn is decreed to pay to Thomas Blair a sum of money.
(d) Sept. 11.—Robert Guthrie binds himself to pay an annuity to his mother,
Barbara Wedderburn. (e) Oct. 26.—Decree in favour of James Wedderburn as
assignee of Walter Wedderburn.

298. **1594.** Nov. 6.—Alexander Duncan is surety for the bond made by John Wedderburn of Cragy in favour of his wife Margaret Strathawquhane, relict of Robert
Juksone.

299. **1594.** Nov. 9.—Helen Ramsay, spouse to Mr. Alexander Wedderburn, son and heir
to the late Alexander Wedderburn, clerk, ratifies her husband's infeftment of William
Davidson in a North Argylegait tenement called the "Greneland," and, in warrandice
thereof, in another tenement, bounded on the South by that of the said Mr. Alexander's brother german, David Wedderburn.

300. **1595.** (a) Jan. 15.—Decrees in favour of Peter Wedderburn. (b) Jan. 20.—
Decrees in favour of David Wedderburn as chaplain of S. Tredwall's and Lytill
S. James' chaplainries. (c) Feb. 26.—Decree in favour of David Wedderburn as
chaplain of S. James Major and S. Margaret. (d) March 14.—Decree in favour of
Barbara Wedderburn, relict of Peter Imrie. (e) April 9.—Decree in favour of
Alexander Wedderburn, merchant, burgess of Dundee. (f) April 28.—Acknowledg-
ment and discharge by Peter Wedderburn, elder, and his son, Peter Wedderburn,
younger.

301. **1595.** (a) May 5, 21.—Two decrees in favour of Elizabeth Wedderburn. (b) June
13.—Decree in favour of John Wedderburn. (c) July 8.—Transumpt of a sasine
(17 Oct. 1563) in favour of John Coustoun and Elizabeth Wedderburn. (d) July
25.—Decreet arbitral between Robert Myln, burgess of Dundee, and Robert Wedderburn, his son-in-law. (e) Aug. 9.—Decree v. John Wedderburn, son of Alexander
Wedderburn, burgess of Cupar. (f) Aug. 27.—Decree in favour of Peter Wedderburn, elder, burgess of Dundee. (g) Oct. 15.—Discharge by David Wedderburn,
burgess of Dundee, of an annual rent owned by umquhile Alexander Wedderburn,
his father.

302. **1595.** (a) Oct. 24.—Decree v. Grissild Wedderburn, spouse to George Lindsay.
(b) Oct. 30.—Decree in favour of Walter Wedderburn. (c) Nov. 19.—Decree in
favour of John Wedderburn. (d) Dec. 4.—Decree in favour of Elizabeth Wedderburn. (e) Dec. 4.—Bond by John Wedderburn, some time portioner of Craigie
Hiltoun, to Walter Wedderburn, his brother german, for £350.

[See, in all, 's. dates :—**1594**. April 19 ; May 17, 20, 27 ; June 4, 12, 17 ; July 3, 15, 17, 24 ; Aug.
2, 9, 26, 30 ; Sept. 4, 6, 11, 13, 16, 21, 30 ; Oct. 1, 16, 21, 25, 26 ; Nov. 6, 9, 11 : Dec. 6, 11.—**1595**.
Jan. 13, 15, 17, 20, 28, 30 ; Feb. 10, 13, 26 ; March 14, 17, 21 ; April 4, 9, 28 ; May 5, 21, 30 ; June
4, 9, 13, 16, 17 ; July 8, 11, 16, 18, 25 ; Aug. 9, 11, 29 ; Sept. 1, 3, 5, 19, 28 ; Oct. 8, 15, 24, 30 ;
Nov. 14, 19 ; Dec. 4, 8, 22.]

VOL. 19.
—
1595—97.

303. **1596.** Jan. 15.—Peter Imrie, son and heir of umquhile Peter Imrie, burgess of Dundee, makes choice of his curators, viz., Peter Wedderburn, Robert Wedderburn, nearest of kin to him on his mother's side, together with Mr. Alexander Wedderburn, clerk.

304. **1596.** Jan. 27.—Elizabeth Hering, relict of umquhile Robert Wedderburn, brother german of Mr. Alexander Wedderburn, clerk, ratifies a renunciation made by the said Robert to his said brother of an annual rent.

305. **1596.** Feb. 25.—Barbara Wedderburn, relict of Peter Imrie, swears on behalf of her son Peter, then a minor, to the inventar of her late husband's goods.

306. **1596.** (a) March 12.—Bond in favour of John Wedderburn, now in Innerquiche. (b) April 7.—Decree in favour of Mathow Wedderburn.

307. **1596.** April 19.—Transumpt of a sasine, 18 Nov. 1577, naming Peter Wedderburn and Margaret Kinloch, his spouse.

308. **1596.** May 14.—Decree in favour of Christian Lovell and James Wedderburn, her spouse.

309. **1596.** May 17.—Mr. Alexander Wedderburn and Peter Wedderburn, his brother german, are named as witnesses.

310. **1596.** July 7.—Bessie Wedderburn, one of the three daughters of umquhile Edward Wedderburn, burgess, ratifies an infeftment already made to Thomas Blair and Katherine Wedderburn, his wife.

311. **1596.** (a) July 9.—Decree in favour of Peter Wedderburn, younger. (b) Aug. 25.—Decree in favour of John Wedderburn. (c) Sept 15.—Bond to John Wedderburn, merchant, burgess of Dundee. (d) Oct. 4.—Robert Wedderburn, merchant, and Patrick Wedderburn are named among the magistrates. (e) Nov. 5.—David Wedderburn is named as patron of S. Thomas' chaplainry.

312. **1596.** Nov. 13.—John Lovell, elder, burgess, grants him to have received from the intrometters with the goods &c. of umquhile Robert Wedderburn, younger, his son-in-law, the sum of four hundred merks and obliges him to sustain Helen Wedderburn, his "oye," lawful daughter to the said Robert, "honestlie at bed, burd and abulzeamentis upon the proffeit and excrescens thereof," and binds himself to hand over the said sum to the said Helen "at her removing from his company" and renounces "all ryeht to any pairt of the said umquhile Robert his guids, or to the guids of umquhile Elspit Lovell, his dochter."

313. **1596.** (a) Nov. 19.—Decree v. Grisild Wedderburne, spouse to George Lyndesay, merchant. (b) Dec. 18.—David Wedderburn, chaplain of S. Laurence's chaplainry, named.

314. **1597.** Jan. 8—John Auchinlek and James Durhame of Pitkerro are cautioners in regard to the payment over of a sum of money delivered by John Auchinlek to James Stewart at the command of umquhile Robert Wedderburn for fulfilling of a legacy made by umquhile Grisild Duncan, his spouse.

315. **1597.** Feb. 16.—"Tutorie Alexander et Helene Wedderburnis."
This is a mere heading left blank. It refers to the two children of Robert Wedderburn (a younger brother of Alexander, of Kingennie. See ante No. 304), by his second wife, Elizabeth Lovell. He died in 1593.

316. **1597.** (a) April 1.—Margaret Rollok, relict of umquhile William Wedderburn, is surety for William Mylne. (b) May 25.—Assignment by Walter Wedderburn. (c) May 27.—Decree v. Peter Wedderburn, elder. (d) June 2.—Discharge to John Scrymgeour on behalf of John Wedderburn, mariner.

317. **1597**. June 11.—James Thomson discharges Alexander Kyd of a debt due to Alexander Wedderburn, son and heir of umquhile Robert Wedderburn, younger, merchant, burgess.

[See, in all, s. dates :—**1596**. Jan. 15, 27 ; Feb. 4, 6, 25. 27 ; March 8, 10, 12, 15, 23, 26 ; April 7, 9, 12, 14. 19, 24 ; May 14, 17, 19, 29 ; June 4 ; July 7, 9 ; August 23, 25 ; Sept. 15 ; Oct. 4, 7, 11, 13, 22. 25 ; Nov. 5, 8, 13 19, 29 ; Dec. 7. 9, 18, 20.—**1597**. Jan. 8, 12, 17, 25 ; Feb. 9, 16, 21, 23 ; March 3, 14, 16, 21, 25, 31 ; April 1 ; May 23, 25, 27 ; June 2, 6, 11, 17.]

VOL. 20.

1597—99.

The names of " Maister Alexander Wedderburn," and " William Wedderburn " are several times written on the fly leaves of this book.

318. **1597**. (*a*) May 20.—Bond of Patrick Wedderburn, merchant, burgess. (*b*) Aug. 10.—Decree in favour of John Wedderburn, younger.

319. **1597**. Sept. 7.—Bond by Robert Wedderburn, merchant burgess, to Archibald Blyth, mariner, burgess, and Eufame Wedderburn, his wife, for £100 ; on payment of which Robert Wedderburn is to be discharged by Blyth and his wife, and by Robert Erskyne in Ardesty. on behalf of the executors of umquhill Bessie Wedderburn, sister of the said Eufame, of all claims by them on him, but this is to be without prejudice to the debts due by James Carmichael and others, to the " bairnis of umquhile Edward Wedderburn and Jonet Inglis, his spous."

320. **1597**. Oct. 21.—Decreet of poynding in favour of Eufame Coustoun, relict of umquhill Robert Scott, burgess, and Robert Wedderburn, now her spouse, *v.* the heirs of umquhile Edward Wedderburn.

321. **1597**. (*a*) Oct. 24.—Protest by John Wedderburn, master of the ship called the " Dragon." (*b*) Nov. 19.—Bond by George Lindsay, in favour of James Wedderburn. (*c*) Dec. 5, 9.—Two decrees in favour of Grisild Wedderburn.

322. **1598**. (*a*) April 17.—Decree in favour of Jonet Wedderburn, relict of Andro Auchinlek. (*b*) May 5.—Decree in favour of Magdalene Wedderburn. (*c*) June 11. —Peter Wedderburn, lawful son of umquhile Alexander Wedderburn, clerk, named with David Wedderburn, his brother. (*d*) June 19.—Decree *v.* Katharine Wedderburn.

323. **1598**. July 12.—Discharge by Eufame Wedderburn, spouse of Archibald Blyth, burgess (son of Richard Blyth), and by Robert Erskyne in Ardestie, for the heirs, &c., of umquhile Bessie Wedderburn, sister to Eufame, in favour of Robert Wedderburn, merchant, burgess, for £100, in full payment of all that Eufame, or the heirs of the said Bessie, may claim of the said Robert. through the decease of umquhile Edward Wedderburn and Jonet Inglis, parents of the said Eufame and Bessie Wedderburn. See ante No. 319. The matter is again referred to, July 24.

324. **1598**. July 21.—Disposition by John Lovell, elder, in favour of his son, John Lovell, younger, in consideration of the latter having agreed to pay to Helen Wedderburn, daughter of umquhile Robert Wedderburn, younger, on behalf of his father, the sum of four hundred merks.

325. **1598**. (*a*) Aug. 2.—Obligation (13 July, 1597) in favour of Walter Wedderburn, burgess. (*b*) Sept. 13, 20.—John Wedderburn, skipper of the " Dragon," is twice named.

326. **1598**. Oct. 9.—Bond (4 Oct., 1597) by John Wedderburn, merchant in Dundee, lawful son to Alexander Wedderburn, merchant, burgess of Dundee and of " Couper in Fyff," for £425, as " the price of 2½ tuns of French wine of Bordeaux."

327. **1598**. (*a*) Oct. 20.—Bond in favour of Barbara Wedderburn, relict of umquhile Peter Imrie, merchant, burgess. (*b*) Dec. 6.—Decree in favour of Peter Wedderburn, elder.

328. **1599.** (a) March 14.—Deeree in favour of David Wedderburn, chaplain of Little Dundee
S. James' chaplainry. (b) April 2.—Extract (1574) from the protocol book of late Burgh and Head Court
Alexander Wedderburn, written by the late John Wedderburn, his servant. Records.

This is no doubt Vol. 241 of the Dundee Protocol Books. See ante p. 219, No. 164.

329. **1599.** June 1, 15.—Decree for Robert Wedderburn, elder, burgess of Dundee,
anent the "lineation" or boundaries of his North Argylegait yard and tenement.

330. **1599.** July 30.—Contract (20 April 1598), between David Colvill, master of the
ship "Janet of Dundee," and John Wedderburn, burgess of Dundee, now indweller
in Coupar of Fife, for a voyage by Colvill to Sanda in Orkney.

331. **1599.** Sept. 4.—Agreement between Robert Smyth and Patrick Wedderburn,
merchant, by which Smyth gives license to Patriek to raise both the side walls of the
gallery of his house in North Marketgait, abutting on that of the said Smyth.

[See, in all, s. dates :—1597. May 20 ; July 8. 14. 27 ; Aug. 4, 10, 22, 26 ; Sept. 7, 26; Oct. 6. 7, 21,
24 ; Nov. 7, 18, 19 ; Dec. 5, 9, 19, 21.—1598. Jan. 13, 27, 30 ; Feb. 1 ; March 18 ; April 4, 11, 17, 21 ;
May 5, 8, 11, 22, 26, 27, 31 ; June 11, 19, 21 ; July 12, 21, 24, 26 ; Aug. 2, 4, 17, 31 ; Sept. 11, 13,
20 ; Oct. 9, 16, 20, 23, 30 ; Nov. 3 ; Dec. 4, 6, 18, 25.—1599. Jan. 12, 22, 24 ; Feb. 12, 16 ;
March 5, 14, 28 ; April 2 ; May 2, 25 ; June 1, 2, 11, 15 ; July 4, 13, 16, 30 ; Aug. 1 ; Sept. 3, 1 ;
Nov. 14.]

Vol. 21.

1599–1602.

332. **1599.** Dec. 14.—Bond (21 Aug.), in favour of Alexander Wedderburn, burgess in
Cupar.

333. **1600.** (a) April 14.—Decree in favour of Peter Wedderburn, elder. (b) April 16.
—Decree in favour of Katharine Wedderburn.

334. **1600** April 25.—Curatory of Elizabeth Wedderburn, daughter of umquhile John
Wedderburn, sometime portioner of Craigie. The father's kin named are Peter
Wedderburn, elder, and Walter Wedderburn ; the mother's kin, John Strathauquhane
of Claypottis, and his brother, James Strathauquhane. The curators chosen are
William Duncan, burgess, and Mr. Alexander Wedderburn, clerk.

335. **1600.** June 23.—James Halyburton, son of Captain Walter Halyburton and
Margaret Wedderburn is named (with George, John, and Margaret Halyburton, his
brothers and sister), in regard to a South Argylegait tenement.

336. **1600.** (a) July 16.—Decree in favour of Patrick Wedderburn, as master of the
Hospital in Dundee. (b) July 27.—Decree in favour of Matthew Wedderburn. (c)
Oct. 2.—Patrick Wedderburn and David Wedderburn are named in the list of the
councillors.

337. **1601.** (a) March 10.—Decree in favour of Agnes Wedderburn. (b) March 10.—
Registration of a contract (2 Nov. 1599) to which Mr. Alexander Wedderburn,
common clerk of Dundee, David Wedderburn, and William Wedderburn, his brother
german, are witnesses. (c) June 6.—Decree v. Jonet Wedderburn.

338. **1602.** (a) March 8, 12.—David Wedderburn is on assize. (b) March 22.—John
Wedderburn is on assize. (c) March 17.—Discharge by Walter Wedderburn.
(d) May 31.—Decree in favour of (Margaret) Wedderburn, relict of umquhile Captain
Walter Halyburton.

[See, in all, s. dates :—1599. Nov. 5, 9, 12, 14, 16, 30 ; Dec. 12, 14.—1600. Jan. 16 ; April 9, 14,
16, 25 ; May 6. 12, 16 ; June 4, 11, 16, 23 ; July 7. 9, 14, 16, 27 ; Aug. 27, 29 ; Sept. 1, 5 ; Oct. 2,
10, 27, 29 ; Nov. 24 ; Dec. 8.—1601. Feb. 5, 25 ; March 10, 30 ; May 18, 20 ; June 6, 8, 12 ;
July 13 ; Oct. 12, 21 ; Nov. 18: Dec. 7, 14, 21.—1602. Feb. 24 ; March 1, 5, 8, 12, 17, 18, 22, 23 ;
May 24, 31 ; June 7 ; July 19, 21.]

Dundee
Burgh and
Head Court
Records.

VOL. 22.

1602–6.

339. **1602.** Aug. 4.—Bond by John Wedderburn, mariner, as principal, and David Wedderburn, burgess, as cautioner, to William Goldman.

340. **1602.** Sept. 28.—Patrick Wedderburn, Robert Wedderburn, and David Wedderburn are all on the council.

341. **1603.** (a) Jan. 14.—Bond in favour of Barbara Wedderburn, relict of Peter Imrie. (b) Feb. 9, 23.—Decrees in favour of John Wedderburn. (c) March 4.—Decree in favour of David Wedderburn, chaplain of our Lady Chapel.

342. **1603.** March 25.—Registration of a bond betwixt John Wedderburn, mariner, burgess, and Walter Wedderburn, son to umquhile James Wedderburn, portioner of Craigie Hiltoun, by which the said Walter Wedderburn assigned to the said John Wedderburn, mariner, £350, due to the assignor by umquhile John Wedderburn, sometime portioner of Craigie Hiltoun, and by which the said John Wedderburn, mariner, binds himself on the receipt of the said £350 to infeft the said Walter Wedderburn in an annual rent of £35 out of his tenement west of the Kirkyard and out of his freelands of Abirbothric.

343. **1603.** (a) May 9.—William Wedderburn, son lawful to umquhile Alexander Wedderburn, clerk, witnesses a bond. Robert Wedderburn is notary. (b) Aug. 1.—Decree of poynding in favour of John Wedderburn, skipper, burgess. (c) Aug. 3, 29 — Decrees in favour of James Wedderburn.

344. **1604.** Jan. 30.—Margaret Myln, spouse to Robert Wedderburn, notary, burgess, ratifies the alienation by her and her husband to William Graham of Claverhouse, of one-sixth of the town and lands of Mylntown of Craigie, co. Forfar.

345. **1604.** (a) Jan. 30.—Decree v. Robert Wedderburn and Eupham Coustoun, his wife. (b) Feb. 3.—Decree in favour of Katherine Wedderburn, spouse to William Duncan, chirurgeon. (c) Feb. 27.—Decree v. Eupham Wedderburn.

346. **1604.** Feb. 27.—Decree in favour of Grissell Wedderburn for the delivering up to her by Margaret Sym of a signet of gold belonging to the said Grissell.

347. **1604.** June 15.—Euphame Kynnaird is decreed to restore to Bessie Wedderburn "ane goldein ring with ane turcas thairin," borrowed from Bessie by Euphame.

348. **1604.** June 27.—Decree for Alexander Wedderburn in Couper of Fyff (as assignee to umquhile John Wedderburn, burgess, and Margaret Lindsay, his spouse), for certain house maills due in respect of tenements in North Flukergait.

349. **1604.** Nov. 5.—James Wedderburn, son of John Wedderburn, skipper, burgess of Dundee, revokes his minority acts, especially his subscribing of the marriage contract of Agnes Wedderburn, his sister, with Mr. Gilbert Ramsay, reader, whereby he charged the lands of Freelands, and also his Dundee property, in favour of the said Ramsay.
It seems clear, in this entry, that James is an error for John, as of the two sons of John Wedderburn, skipper or mariner, John was the elder, and was now just twenty-one. James, the younger son, afterwards Bishop of Dunblane, was born in 1585, and thus was not of full age till 1606. See below No. 353.

350. **1604.** Nov. 5.—Edict of curatory of Peter Wedderburn, son of umquhile Peter Wedderburn, burgess. The father's kin named are Mr. Alexander Wedderburn, clerk, and Robert Wedderburn, elder, burgess; the mother's kin, Mr. David Kynloch, M.D., and William Kynloch, his brother german.

351. **1604.** Nov. 12.—Objection (4 Nov. 1603), by David Abercrombie of Pitalpie and others, to Robert Wedderburn, elder, burgess, and Margaret Myln, his spouse, whom failing to Jonet Wedderburn, their daughter.

352. **1604.** Nov. 16.—Bond (5 Jan.), to Margaret Wedderburn, relict of Walter Halyburton.

353. **1604.** Nov. 21.—Edict of curatory of James Wedderburn, son to John Wedderburn, skipper, burgess. Robert Wedderburn, younger, burgess, and Alexander Anderson, elder, are curators. David Lindsay of Aehnady, is named as one of the mother's kin.

354. **1605.** (a) April 15.—Inquest for serving Elizabeth Wedderburn, heir to the deceast Walter Wedderburn, her uncle. (b) April 17.—Decree for Barbara Wedderburn (not designed.) (c) June 5.—Decree for Barbara Wedderburn, relict of Peter Imrie. (d) June 17.—Decree for Patrick Wedderburn.

355. **1605.** Dec 6.—Decree v. Agnes Wedderburn and Mr. Gilbert Ramsay, her spouse, to deliver to Elizabeth Wedderburn, brother's doehter and heir to umquhile Walter Wedderburn, and to James Kinnaird, now her spouse, certain goods and pieces of heirship. These include "ane hagbit, ane pair of sword gairdis, ane frenche brydill, &c."

On the same day there is a similar decree v. Margaret Straquhan, mother of the said Elizabeth Wedderburn in respect of other such goods ; and again a similar decree v. M. Straquhan, 22 Jan. 1606.

[See, in all, s. dates :—1602. Jan. 11, 25 ; July 30 ; Aug. 4, 13, 25 ; Sept. 23, 28 ; Oct. 15, 25 ; Nov. 12 ; Dec. 13.—1603. Jan. 14, 17, 31 ; Feb. 9, 23 ; March 4, 16, 25 ; April 6, 8, 25 ; May 2, 9 ; June 13, 18, 27, 29 ; July 11, 13, 20, 25, 27 ; Aug. 1, 3, 6, 29 ; Sept. 14. 19, 26 ; Oct. 10, 17, 21 ; Nov. 4, 23 ; Dec. 5, 8, 14, 21.—1604. Jan. 25, 30 ; Feb. 3, 6, 22, 25, 27 ; March 2, 8, 12, 20 ; May 7 ; June 1, 8, 15, 25, 27, 29 ; July 23 ; Oct. 7, 8, 15 ; Nov. 5, 12, 16, 21 ; Dec. 14.—1605. Feb. 11 ; March 13 ; April 15, 17 ; May 17, 24, 30 ; June 5, 17, 28 ; Aug. 9 ; Sept. 13 ; Oct. 11 : Nov. 8 ; Dec. 2. 6, 20.—1606. Jan. 17, 22.]

VOL. 23.

1606—9.

This book is noted on the fly leaf as covering 6 Dec., 1606, to 24 Feb., 1609, but really runs down to November in that year.

356. **1606.** July 30.—Service of Helen Wedderburn and Elizabeth Lovell as heiresses of the deceased James Lovell, son of the deceased John Lovell, elder, burgess. Robert Wedderburn, senior and junior, are on the assize.

357. **1606.** Aug. 11, 25.—Patrick Wedderburn and James Wedderburn are on an assize.

358. **1607.** (a) March 11.—Robert Wedderburn, elder, and James Wedderburn are on an assize. (b) April 15.—Robert Wedderburn, elder, councillor, and Robert Wedderburn, younger, sit on an inquest.

359. **1608.** (a) Jan. 11.—Robert Wedderburn, younger, Peter Wedderburn, and Patrick Wedderburn are all named as officers for poynding. (b) Feb. 12.—David Wedderburn is chancellor of an assize.

360. **1608.** Feb. 15.—Decree v. Euphame Wedderburn, spouse to Archibald Blyth, in favour of James Wedderburn.

361. **1608.** June 27.—Decree for James Wedderburn, brother of John Wedderburn, son to Thomas Wedderburn, skipper.

The name Thomas is an error for John, the reference being to James Wedderburn, afterwards Bishop of Dunblane. Thomas Wedderburn (d. 1574) had only one child, a daughter, Agnes.

362. **1609.** May 24, 31.—Decree for Margaret Wedderburn, relict of umquhile George Black.

363. **1609.** July 17.—Decree v. Euphame Wedderburn, spouse to Archibald Blyth, and others, in favour of Peter Wedderburn, merchant, as executor of Grizzell Nicoll.

364.	**1609.** Aug. 12.—Registration of a charter (10 Sept. 1577) by Alexander Wedder-
burn, younger, son and heir of the deceased David Wedderburn, burgess of Dundee,
Christian Ferny, his spouse, Christian Strachan, relict of the said David, and Wm.
Lochmalony, now her spouse, in favour of James Black, of certain Welgnit lands.

> Christian Strachan is an error for Elizabeth Strachan. See ante No. 298, and s. Dundee Protocol
> Books, No. 189.

> [See in all s. dates :—1606, July 30 ; Aug 11, 25 ; Sept. 1.—1607, Feb. 6: March 11, 23, 25 ;
> April 15, 22.—1608, Jan. 11, 14, 22 ; Feb. 5, 12, 15, 17 ; March 2, 7, 16 ; April 7 ; May 9 ; June 6,
> 26, 27, 29 ; Nov. 28.—1609, Jan. 14, 16 ; March 8 ; April 28 ; May 24, 31 ; June 17, 28 ; Aug. 12 ;
> Oct. 9 ; Nov. 8.]

VOL. 24.

1609—11.

365.	**1610.** Feb. 2.—(a) Registered obligation (26 July 1605) in favour of Robert
Wedderburn, elder, burgess, notary, and Jonet Wedderburn, his daughter, and her
heirs. (b) Registered obligation (20 May 1605) in favour of Robert Wedderburn,
elder, Margaret Myln, his spouse, and Bessie Wedderburn, their daughter, and her heirs.

366.	**1610.** May 14.—David Wedderburn, burgess, patron of the chaplainry of S. Thomas
the Martyr, taking burden on himself for his son Alexander Wedderburn, chaplain
thereof, ratifies various charters made in connection therewith.

367.	**1611.** Jan. 18, 23.—Decree for the executors of William Davidson. Jouet
Wedderburn is named as mother and tutrix to Richard, Jonet, Margaret, and
Elspeth Davidson, his children.

> They are named again, March 8, 11 and April 5. See also post, No. 374.

368.	**1611.** May 12.—Patrick Wedderburn, merchant, Elizabeth Low, his wife, and
Alexander Wedderburn, their son, grant themselves to have disponed to Thomas
Young the right to put a window in the west wall of his North Marketgait tenement,
overlooking Patrick's property.

369.	**1611.** June 1.—Discharge (7 Aug. 1610) by Barbara Auchinlek (with consent of
Alexander Wedderburn, her husband) and her brothers and sisters. It is written by
Mr. James Wedderburn, son of Mr. Alexander Wedderburn, clerk of the burgh.

370.	**1611.** (a) July 19.—Alexander Wedderburn, burgess of Cupar, is chosen a curator
to William, son of the late William Lochmalony of Dundee. (b) July 19.—Mr.
James Wedderburn is procurator for the makers of three discharges.

371.	**1611.** Oct. 7.—Adam Wedderburn, burgess, is fined for an assault on James
Symson, burgess.

372.	**1611.** Dec. 13.—Registered obligation (19 Aug.), witnessed by Mr. James
Wedderburn, son of Mr. Alexander Wedderburn, clerk of Dundee, and Peter
Wedderburn.

373.	**1611.** Dec. 13.—At this date there is entered between the leaves of this book a
complaint and cross complaint between John Fotheringhame, mariner, and Robert
Wedderburn, servitor to John Boxer, maltman, in regard to various articles of
clothing. A decree, dated 13 Jan. 1613, is noted at the end of the complaint.

> [See in all s. dates :—1609, Nov. 10, 13, 22 —1610, Jan. 22 ; Feb. 2, 4, 9, 10, 23 ; April 16 ;
> May. 14, 18 ; June 1, 4 ; July 21, 30 ; Aug. 6 ; Oct. 8, 10 ; Nov. 30 ; Dec. 19.—1611, Jan. 14, 18,
> 23, 30 ; Feb. 6, 8, 11 ; March 1, 8, 11 ; April 5, 22 ; May 12, 13 ; June 1, 26 ; July 12, 19, 24, 26 ;
> Aug. 9, 30 ; Sept. 6 ; Oct. 7, 30 ; Nov. 1, 18 ; Dec. 6, 13.]

VOL. 25.

—

1612–14.

On the fly leaf is written in the clear and beautiful hand of Alexander Wedderburn of Kingennie : " Magister Alexander Wedderburn scriba curiæ Deidonanæ : M. Jacobus Wedderburn notarius publicus Ac filius legittimus M. Alex^{rt} Wedderburn communis clerici Burgi de Dundie Anno humanæ salutis 1612." Some of the leaves of this volume have been bound out of place, and consequently the dates are not consecutive in the original volume, although so arranged here.

374. **1612.** Jan. 17.—Jonet Wedderburn, relict of William Davidson, younger, burgess, declares that she has never acted as tutrix to Richard, Jonet, Elizabeth, and Margaret Davidson, his children, but only " in discharge of her natural duty."

375. **1612.** (*a*) Jan. 20.—Margaret Wedderburn obtains a decree for house-maills as factrix of John Wedderburn, her brother. (*b*) April 27.—Decree for Mr. David Wedderburn, merchant, partly on his own behalf, and partly on that of Elizabeth Wedderburn, his sister. (*c*) Dec. 1.—Decree in favour of Robert Wedderburn, merchant.

376. **1612.** Feb. 10.—Registered obligation (24 Oct. 1611) by Peter Wedderburn, younger, lawful son to umquhile Peter Wedderburn, elder, burgess.

377. **1612.** June 15.—Decree for Patrick Wedderburn *v.* William Pitillock, for the price of some hesp bought by Pitillock from Adam Wedderburn, son to Patrick, in his name, last March.

378. **1612.** June 15.—Decree *v.* Peter Wedderburn, to relieve Peter Man at the hands of Jonet Wedderburn, his sister, of a certain sum.

379. **1612.** Dec. 16.—David Wedderburn, proprietor of the great tenement of land lying in the head of S. Margaret's close,·North Marketgait, complains that the transe and passage through the close to the said tenement is so broken and standing in filth and water that he cannot pass through it to his house. The bailies decern its repair by the two other proprietors in the close.

380. **1613.** Jan. 21.—Discharge by Alexander Wedderburn, merchant, burgess, as assignee of Jonat Wedderburn, relict of umquhile Wm. Davidson.

381. **1613.** (*a*) Jan. 21.—Mr. James Wedderburn, notary, and Patrick Wedderburn, merchant, witnesses. (*b*) Feb. 1.—Peter Wedderburn, younger, burgess, witnesses an obligation (1612). (*c*) Feb. 19.—William Wedderburn, minister of Dundee, witness.

382. **1613.** Jan. 26 —Registration of several transumpted writs in which are named (*a*) Robert Wedderburn, notary, 31 March, 1530 ; (*b*) Henry Wedderburn, Sir Thomas Wedderburn, 2 Sept. 1539 ; (*c*) David Wedderburn, in Seagait, 10 March, 1544.

383. **1613.** March 14 —Mr. James Wedderburn is notary to a contract (3 Sept. 1611) between David Coustoune, merchant, burgess, with the consent of his spouse, and of Robert Wedderburn, his brother-in-law, and Euphame Coustoune, his spouse, in regard to the Lady Warkstair's tenement formerly belonging to his brother John Coustoune, and now to himself. Mr. Alexander Wedderburn is co-notary. Alexander Wedderburn, merchant, and Peter Wedderburn are witnesses.

384. **1613.** March 13.—Peter Wedderburn, merchant, burgess, son of umquhile Alexander Wedderburn, clerk of the burgh, grants a discharge.

385. **1613.** March 13.—Registered contract (30 March 1611) betwixt John Coustoune, burgess of Dundee, and Elizabeth Wedderburn, his spouse, and Mark Barrie and Magdalene Wedderburn, his spouse, in regard to the Lady Warkstairs tenement. Witnesses John Wedderburn and Alexander Wedderburn, notary public.

From this entry, it would appear that Mark Barrie was alive in 1611, whereas he had died before 18 Nov. 1579 (ante No. 251 *b*), when Magdalen Wedderburn is spoken of as his relict. See also s. Dundee Protocol Books, No. 198. I think the contract should have been described as between John Coustoune and his wife and Magdalen Wedderburn, relict of Mark Barrie.

386.   **1613.** May 18.—Registered obligation (17 June 1612) to Helen Wedderburn, daughter of umquhile Robert Wedderburn, younger, burgess, for 300 merks, payable to her before next Whitsuntide, or if she die to James Wedderburn, merchant, burgess.

387.   **1614.** (*a*) Jan. 17.—Decree *v.* Helen Wedderburn and George Auchinlek, her spouse. (*b*) Jan. 24.—Registered obligation (17 Nov. 1612) by Edward Christone, skipper, burgess, Barbara Wedderburn, his spouse, and Peter Wedderburn, merchant, burgess.

388.   **1614.** Feb. 7.—Mr. Alexander Wedderburn, David Wedderburn, James Wedderburn, Peter Wedderburn, and Alexander Wedderburn, are all on assize. Mr. James Wedderburn is procurator.

   See in all s. dates :—**1612,** Jan. 15, 17, 20, 22 ; Feb. 10, 22 ; March 21, 25 ; April 1, 12, 20, 27 ; May 8, 11, 15, 29 ; June 3, 15, 16, 18 : July 20. 23, 26 ; Aug 2. 6, 7, 9, 24, 28 ; Sept. 11, 22 ; Nov. 2, 6, 16, 18. 19, 26 ; Dec. 1, 13, 16.—**1613.** Jan. 17, 23, 24, 26, 29 ; Feb. 1, 3, 7, 11, 12, 15, 19, 28 ; March 1, 19, 24 ; April 14, 26, 28, 30 ; May 18, 21 ; June 7, 21.

Vol. 26.

1614—17.

   On the first fly leaf is written :—(*a*) in the hand of Kingennie "Magister Alexander Wedderburn Scriba Curiæ Deidonanie. Finis coronat opus" ; and (*b*) in that of his servitor, " Thomas Fyiff with my hand ye 23 Marche 1615." On the last is written, in the hand of Thomas Fyiff : " This court booke of the burghe of Dondee Beginuend in anno 1614 and ending in anno 1617. . . . Which Booke is whollie (almost) wrettene by the handis of Mr. James Wedderburne, Johne Pattone, and Thomas Fyiff. In Regno Jacobi sexti Scotiæ et primi Angliæ, franciæ et hiberniæ reg."

389.   **1614.** (*a*) May 11.—Decree for James and Peter Wedderburn, executors to Robert Wedderburn, elder. (*b*) June 17.—Decree *v.* Margaret Wedderburn, spouse to Andrew Black, and her husband. (*c*) Decree *v.* Grisel Wedderburn.

390.   **1615.** Jan. 25.—Discharge by Catharine Wedderburn, relict of umquhile William Duncan, surgeon, burgess of Dundee, and now spouse to Mr. William Ferguson, dean of gild, to Patrick Wedderburn, merchant, burgess, and Alexander Wedderburn, merchant, burgess, his son, for 600 merks.

391.   **1615.** Feb. 15.—Decree for Robert Halyburton and Margaret Wedderburn, his spouse, for house maill.

392.   **1615.** April 22.—Discharge written by Mr. James Wedderburn, notary, son to Mr. Alexander Wedderburn, clerk, and witnessed by James Wedderburn, brother to the said Mr. Alexander.

393.   **1615** (*a*) July 19.—The two North Argylegait tenements of Mr. James Wedderburn and David Wedderburn, are mentioned. (*b*) Decree for Peter Wedderburn for house maill. (*c*) Sept. 1.—Decree *v.* Peter Wedderburn, younger. (*d*) Oct. 11.—Mr. Alexander Wedderburn, younger, bailie on the bench.

394.   **1615.** Nov. 16 —Before Mr. Alexander Wedderburn, younger, bailie, compeared Mr. James Wedderburn, notary, procurator for John Mudy in Craigie, maker of an obligation in favour of Mr. David Wedderburn, merchant.

395.   **1616.** May 17.—Elizabeth Low, spouse to Patrick Wedderburn, and Barbara Auchinlek, spouse to Alexander Wedderburn, son and heir apparent of Patrick, with consent of their said husbands, ratify an alienation of a South Marketgait foreland made by Patrick and Alexander in favour of Mr. Alexander Wedderburn, the clerk.

396.   **1616.** Sept. 20 —John Lindsay, son and heir of umquhile George Lindsay, discharges his mother, Grisild Wedderburn, of all he may claim by decease of his father.

397.　**1616.** Nov. 8.—Elizabeth Wedderburn, daughter of umquhile John Wedderburn, sometime portioner of Craigie, is served heir to umquhile Walter Wedderburn, her father's brother, with consent of James Kynard, her spouse, burgess of Dundee, now indweller in Alsownuir (Elsinore).

[See, in all, s. dates :—1614. May 11, 23, 25 ; June 17, 20 ; July 13 : Nov. 2 ; Dec. 11.—1615. Jan. 9, 25 ; Feb. 15, 17 ; March 3, 22 ; April 15, 22, 28 ; May 1, 3, 31 ; June 2, 5, 7, 19 ; July 19, 28 ; Sept. 1 ; Oct. 4, 11, 13, 28, 30 : Nov. 1, 3, 8, 13, 16. 20. 22, 24, 27 ; Dec. 1, 8, 14, 23, 28.—1616. Jan. 8, 15, 17, 19, 22, 21, 26. 29, 31 : Feb. 2, 12, 16. 21, 26 ; March 1, 13 : April 6, 8, 12, 22, 24, 26 ; May 3, 6, 10, 15, 17, 27 ; June 3, 5, 7, 12, 14, 17, 19, 21, 24 ; July 1, 2, 3 ; Aug. 7, 9 : Sept. 20, 30 ; Oct. 29 ; Nov. 1, 8, 14, 19 ; Dec. 4.]

Vol. 27.

1617–18.

398.　**1617.** April 9.—Registered obligation (dated 11 Feb. 1615), witnessed by Peter Wedderburn, elder, merchant.

399.　**1617.** May 2.—Mr. Alexander Wedderburn, clerk of the burgh, is cognosced only nearest and lawful heir of James Mylne, his guidschyre, merchant burgess thereof, and is entered as such in all the said James Mylne's lands, &c , within the burgh,

400.　**1617.** (*a*) June 12, 23.—Mr. James Wedderburn is procurator. (*b*) July 26.— Decree in favour of Margaret Wedderburn, for the rent of a house, of which she has the life-interest. (*c*) Oct. 8, 13, 17, 20, 24, 27, &c.—Mr. Alexander Wedderburn, younger, is often bailie on the bench.

Similar mentions of Mr. Alexander Wedderburn, younger, and Mr. James Wedderburn, occur throughout this volume.

401.　**1617.** Nov. 3.—Procurators for Robert Wedderburn and Mr. David Wedderburn, his eldest son, both merchants, burgesses of Dundee, and for Robert Murray, and Elizabeth Wedderburn, his spouse, give in a contract between the said persons, dated 2 Sept. 1617, by which Robert Wedderburn and Mr. David Wedderburn let their large tenement in South Flukergait, for three years, to Robert Murray and his said wife, at 100 merks a year, which rent is to be satisfied by Robert Murray and his wife, entertaining and sustaining "the said Robert Wedderburn, their *(sic)* father, at bed and board honestly, and according to his estate," and in event of his death, by payment to Mr. David Wedderburn. Witnesses, Mr. James Wedderburn, professor of Divinity in the New College of S. Andrew's, John Wedderburn, merchant, &c.

402.　**1617.** Nov. 18.—Action by Helen Clayhills, executrix to umquhile Margaret Wedderburn, relict to umquhile Peter Clayhills, bailie, and William Spence.

403.　**1618.** Feb. 10.—Decree in favour of Jonet Wedderburn for house maill.

404.　**1618.** March 25.—Thomas Clayhills is absolved from the claim made v. him by David Wedderburn as assignee of the children of umquhile William Davidson, younger, and of Jonet Wedderburn, his relict, and their mother.

405.　**1618.** May 13.—Mr. Alexander Wedderburn, elder, of Kingany, and Mr. Alexander Wedderburn, notary, are named as curators to the children of umquhile Mr. James Nicolsone, parson of Megill.

406.　**1618.** June 17.—Registered bond, dated 6 July 1609, in favour of David Wedderburn, burgess, patron of the chaplainry of S. Thomas.

407.　**1618.** (*a*) July 22.—Decree v. John Wedderburn, son to Mr. Robert Wedderburn, merchant. (*b*) 7 Aug.—David Wedderburn and Patrick Wedderburn, merchants, are members of assize. (*c*) Oct. 14-31.—James Wedderburn, bailie, on the bench. (*d*) Oct. 15.—Decree in favour of David Wedderburn, burgess, for money paid by

Matilda Beatone, his spouse. (e) Nov. 16.—Mr. Alexander Wedderburn, clerk, and David Wedderburn, his brother, are named as mother's next-of-kin to John, son of umquhile Thomas Blair.

[See, in all, s. dates :—1617. March 7 ; April 5, 9, 25 ; May 2 ; June 12, 13, 23 ; July 7, 17, 26 ; Aug. 4, 8 ; Sept. 11, 12 ; Oct. 8, 13, 17, 20, 24, 27 ; Nov. 3, 7, 10, 18, 24, 26. 28 ; Dec. 1, 14, 17, 27. —1818. Jan. 1, 11, 17, 19, 27 ; Feb. 3, 6, 7. 10. 13. 17, 20, 23 ; March 11, 13, 15. 18, 22, 25, 27 ; April 1, 20, 24, 27 ; May 1, 4, 9, 11, 13, 18 23 ; June 1, 3, 5, 9, 17, 24 ; July 1, 2, 10, 22, 24, 27, 29 ; Aug. 7, 9, 11, 31 ; Sept. 29 ; Oct. 6, 12, 14, 15, 17, 21, 23, 31 ; Nov. 2, 4, 9, 16.]

Vol. 28.

1624—25.

More than three-fourths of this volume is blank.

408. **1624-25.**—James Wedderburn is constantly named as bailic.

409. **1625.** Jan. 12. – Patrick Wedderburn is on an assize.

410. **1625.** Jan. 28.—Decree in favour of Catharine Wedderburn and Mr. William Ferguson, her spouse, in respect of the maill of their South Argylisgait house.

411. **1633.** Jan. 11.—Alexander Wedderburn, younger, on an assize.

But for this one entry and a few in Vol. 31, the record is blank from 22 February, 1625 to 20 October, 1633.

[See, in all, s. dates :—1624. Dec. 27.—1625. Jan. 10, 12, 14. 17, 24, 26, 28, 31 ; Feb. 2 ; May 15; June 15, 26.—1633. Jan. 11.]

Vol. 29.

1633–38.

412. **1634.** (a) Aug. 6.—Alexander Wedderburn, merchant, on an assize. (b) Aug. 27. —Decree v. Robert Murray and Elizabeth Wedderburn, his spouse. (c) Nov. 24.— Decree v. Elizabeth Wedderburn, relict of umquhile Robert Murray. (d) Dec. 17.— Decree v. Grissell Wedderburn.

413. **1635.** Sept. 16.—Decree in favour of Robert Blyth, son of Euphame Wedderburn, relict of umquhile Archibald Blyth.

414. **1635.** (a) Feb. 8, 10.—Decree v. Andrew Boyd, mariner, and Helen Wedderburn, his spouse. (b) April 6.—Decree in favour of John Wedderburn.

415. **1637.** April 22.—Alexander Wedderburn, elder, on an assize.

416. **1638.** Feb. 14.—John Miller decerned to remove from the yard once belonging to umquhile Patrick Wedderburn, merchant.

417. **1638.** May 21.—James Wedderburn, merchant, Alexander Wedderburn of Kinganie, and Mr. Alexander Wedderburn are all on an assize.

[See, in all, s. dates :—1633. June 11 ; Oct. 20 ; Nov. 25 ; Dec 14.—1634. Jan. 24 ; May 12 ; Aug. 6, 27 ; Sept. 8 ; Nov. 12, 24 ; Dec 12, 17.—1635. April 15 ; Sept. 16 ; Nov. 23.—1636. Feb 8, 10 ; April 6 ; May 30; Aug 3, 22. - 1637. Feb. 15 ; April 3, 26 ; June 5, 9 ; Nov. 27.— 1638. Feb. 14 ; April 4, 9 ; May 21.]

Vol. 30.

1638–47.

418. **1639.** (a) June 10.—Alexander Wedderburn, merchant, witness. (b) July 22.— Decree for John Wedderburn.

Dundee
Burgh and
Head Court
Records.

419. **1640**. Jan. 1.—Decree in favour of James Wedderburn, merchant.

420. **1640**. Sept. 4.—Decree v. Margaret Wedderburn, relict of umquhile Robert Halyburton.

See ante, s. Dundee Protocol Books, No. 388, where the surname of Margaret Wedderburn's spouse is wrongly given as Alexander. On all other occasions it is given as Robert. See post, Nos. 431 and 446.

421. **1640**. Sept. 14.—Decree for Catharine Wedderburn.

422. **1640-41**. (a) (No date.)—Alexander Wedderburn of Kingany, bailie, is often named as on the bench. **1640**. (b) Dec. 12.—Decree for Alexander Wedderburn of Kingany, as son and heir of the late Mr. Alexander Wedderburn of Kingany.

423. **1641**. May 14.—Decree v. Euphame Wedderburn, as executrix of her son, umquhile David Blyth.

424. **1641**. June 23.—Decree for Bessie Wedderburn, relict of umquhile Robert Murray, burgess, and for Thomas Moncur of Seekiden, her spouse.

425. **1641**. July 28.—Memorandum as follows : " Nota, fra the tent of Junii 1640 till thir 28 Julij 1641. Thomas Kessane present at the baill Courts in the clerk's absence in Ingland for the tyme."

Alexander Wedderburn was absent at this time as one of the Scottish Commissioners for the treaty of Rippon.

426. **1641**. Aug. 23.—Robert Cheplen, servitor to Mr. Alexander Wedderburn, clerk, who is procurator for Mr. John Wedderburn, chief doctor of medicine in Moravia, produces a brief for serving the said John Wedderburn nearest heir to his brother, umquhile Mr. James Wedderburn, sometime bishop of Dunblane, and he is so served.

427. **1641**. Oct. 22, 25, etc.—James Wedderburn, bailie, is often on the bench.

428. **1642**. Oct. 12, 21, etc.—Alexander Wedderburn of Kingennie, bailie, on the bench.

429. **1643**. March 13.—Decree for Mr. Alexander Wedderburn of Blackness.

430. **1643**. April 19.—Alexander Wedderburn, skipper, is a witness.

431. **1643**. Sept. 4.—Decree v. Alexander Halyburton, son of umquhile Robert Halyburton and umquhile Margaret Wedderburn.

432. **1644**. Jan. 31.—Decree for Alexander Wedderburn, shoremaster.

[See, in all, s. dates :—1638. Dec. 4.—1639. Jan. 16; March 4; June 10; July 22; Sept. 6; Dec. 20.—1640. Jan. 1, May 17, 21; June 21, 23; Sept. 4, 14; Oct. 2, 26, 30; Nov. 2, 6, 16, 30; Dec. 9, 14, 18, 21.—1641. Jan. 27, 29; Feb. 1, 5; March 15; April 5, 12, 21; May 14; June 23; July 16, 21, 23, 28; Aug. 6, 11, 23; Sept. 17; Oct. 22, 25; Nov. 3, 8; Dec. 10, 22, 24.—1642. Jan. 10, 12, 19, 21. 26, 28, 31; Feb. 2, 16, 23; March 4, 7, 21, 23; April 4, 22; May 30; June 3, 13, 22, 29; July 13, 15, 20, 22, 27, 29; August 5, 26, 29; Sept. 19; Oct. 12, 21, 24, 26, 28; Nov. 2, 11, 16, 18, 28, 30; Dec. 21, 26, 20.--1643. Jan. 13, 16, 18. 27, 30; Feb. 3, 8, 10, 13; March 6, 8, 10, 13, 15, 17, 20, 22, 27. 29, 31; April 3, 19, 21; May 1, 3, 5, 29; July 28; Aug. 2, 7, 11, 21, 30; Sept. 4; Dec. 11.—1644. Jan. 31; Feb. 5; Aug. 5, 26.—1645. March 18.]

Vol. 31.
1633-48.

434. **1634**. Oct. 6.—Alexander Wedderburn, merchant, is collector to the guilds of the burgh of Dundee.

435. **1635**. Jan. 12.—Alexander Wedderburn, elder, is on the assize for the service of Elizabeth Bruce, daughter of umquhile Dr. Peter Bruce, principal of S. Leonard's

College, S Andrew's as heir to her father, with consent of Simon Mackenzie, her spouse.

436. **1635**. Feb. 10.—Mr. Alexander Wedderburn, younger, clerk of Dundee,` is in Court.

437. **1636**. July 8.—Elizabeth and Christian Bisset ratify a disposition made by them and their mother, Agnes Wedderburn, relict of umquhile Abacuk Bisset, writer to his majesty's signet, of her tenements in Aberdeen.

438. **1636**. Dec. 10.—John Wedderburn, merchant, and Alexander Wedderburn, mariner, are next of kin on the mother's side to John, Robert, and Gideon Murray, sons of umquhile Robert Murray, and of Elizabeth Wedderburn, his relict, who "acts herself cautioner" for the curators.

439. **1639**. March 8.—Alexander Wedderburn, elder, merchant, is a witness.

440. **1639**. Aug. 19.—Minute of bailie court in the house of Elizabeth Wedderburn.—Discharge by Magdalen Ferguson, relict of Alexander Lyne, and now wife of John Duncan, and daughter of Mr. William Fergusone of Balbeuchlie, whose relict was Catharine Wedderburn.

441. **1640**. (a) April 15.—Transumpt of a sasine (25 April 1632) from the protocol book of Mr. Alexander Wedderburn of Kingennie, clerk. (b) May 28.—Bond to Alexander Wedderburn, younger, skipper, burgess.

442. **1640**. Dec. 25.—(a) Transumpt of a sasine (23 April 1617) naming Alexander Wedderburn, merchant, Barbara (Auchinlek), his wife, and John Wedderburn, their son. (b) Also transumpt of a sasine (14 March 1609) in favour of Andrew Wedderburn, merchant, son of Alexander Wedderburn, merchant, burgess.

443. **1641**. Aug. 23.—Retour of John Wedderburn, protomedicus in Moravia, as heir to the late Mr. James Wedderburn, bishop of Dumblain, his brother.

444. **1642**. Feb. 2.—James Wedderburn, bailie, and Alexander Wedderburn, skipper, burgess, next of kin on the father's side to James, son of umquhile William Thomson, burgess.

445. **1643**. June 21.—Elizabeth Wedderburn, once spouse to Robert Murray, merchant, burgess, and now spouse to Thomas Moncur of Seggieden, ratifies, with Moncur's consent, in favour of her son Robert Murray, a disposition of a South Flukergait house, once that of her father, Robert Wedderburn, and afterwards that of her said husband, Robert Murray.

446. **1643**. Aug. 25.—Edict of curatory for Alexander Halyburton, son of the late Robert Halyburton and the late Margaret (Wedderburn) Dr. John Wedderburn, doctor of medicine in Moravia, is named as next of kin on the mother's side.

447. **1643**. Dec. 6.—Transumpt of a sasine (1612) to which Adam Wedderburn, son of Patrick Wedderburn, burgess, is a party, his brother Alexander Wedderburn, younger, burgess, being his attorney.

448. **1647**. Jan. 29.—Dame Matilda Fletcher, spouse to Sir Alexander Wedderburn, of Blackness, Knight, ratifies, with her husband's consent, a disposition (dated 8 Dec., 1646) of her life-interest in the Ketchpull close, in favour of James Wedderburn, their second son.

449. **1647**. Oct. 25.—Act of curatory of David and Andrew Bruce, minors, sons of umquhile Doctor Andrew Bruce, sometime principal of S. Leonard's College, S. Andrew's. Alexander Wedderburn, of Kingennie, and Mr. James Wedderburn,

minister at Moonsie, are named as mother's kin. The curators, who accept office, are the said Mr. James Wedderburn and Sir Alexander Wedderburn of Blackness.

Dundee Burgh and Head Court Records.

[See, in all, s. dates :—1633. July 31 ; Aug. 5, 14 —1634. May 14 ; Sept. 10 ; Oct. 6.—1635. Jan. 12, 26 ; Feb. 10 ; April 6, 25 ; May 13 ; Oct. 6.—1636. Feb. 15 ; April 27 ; July 8 ; Oct. 3 ; Nov. 8 ; Dec. 10.—1637. Jan. 6, 14 ; April 26 ; June 9.—1638. Jan. 5.—1639. March 8 ; Aug. 12, 19.—1640. Jan. 5 ; April 15 ; May 28 ; Dec. 25.—1641. Jan. 11 ; May 3 ; Aug. 23 ; Oct. 4 ; Nov. 15.—1642. Jan. 10, 24 ; Feb. 2 ; March 25 ; April 1, 18, 22 ; June 24 ; Aug. 5 ; Oct. 3, 10, 26 ; Dec. 14, 21.—1643. Jan. 9 ; Feb. 22 ; April 10, 28 ; May 1, 15, 17, 18, 22 ; June 21 ; Aug. 21, 25 ; Sept. 4, 28 ; Nov. 3 ; Dec. 6.—1644. Feb. 21.—1645. March 21.—1646. Feb. 20 ; Oct. 5.—1647. Jan. 29 ; Oct. 25.]

VOL. 32.

1648—56.

450. **1649.** Jan. 10.—Decree v. James Kyde, executor of Catharine Wedderburn, deceased, his mother-in-law.

451. **1649.** March 12.—Andrew Wedderburn and Alexander Wedderburn are on an inquest.

452. **1649.** May 12.—Sir Alexander Wedderburn, of Blackness, and his brother german, William Wedderburn, are named as mother's kin to the sons of David Weymis of Dundee.

453. **1651.** May 3.—Decrees for Alexander Wedderburn, elder, skipper, as executor of his uncle, umquhile James Wedderburn.

454. **1651.** Dec. 24.—Alexander Wedderburn, of Kingennie, is a curator to James Boytar, of Pilmor, whose sister, Helen Boytar, wife to George Hunter, son of William Hunter, provost of Forfar, discharges her curators of her tocher.

455. **1652.** July 21.—Decree v. Andrew Wedderburn, merchant, and Elspit Fletcher, his spouse.

456. **1652.** Oct. 4.—Helen and Bessie Wedderburn, daughters of umquhile Alexander Wedderburn, skipper, are served heirs portioners to their said father.

457. **1652.** Nov. 3.—Decree c. Magdalen Wedderburn and George Inglish, her spouse.

458. **1652.** Dec. 4.—Bond (23 Dec. 1646) by Andrew Boyd, skipper, and Helen Wedderburn, his spouse, in favour of Margaret Blyth.

459. **1653.** Jan. 19.—Decree v. Helen Wedderburn, relict of umquhile Andrew Boyd.

460. **1653.** Feb. 14.—Decree in favour of Helen and Bessie Wedderburn, spouses to William Gaskyne and John Gardyne, for the rent of their house in North Argylisgait.

461. **1653.** July 4.—Peter Wedderburn gives in for registration a revocation by Helen Wedderburn, relict of umquhile Andrew Boyd, merehant, burgess, of an assignation of her property, which she made in favour of Patrick Boyd of Kinkindie when " in her agony and grief, shortly after she was a little convalescit of ague fever."

462. **1653.** Oct. 29.—Decree v. the executors of umquhile Alexander Wedderburn, skipper, viz. : Sir Alexander Wedderburn of Blackness, Alexander Wedderburn of Kingennie, Helen and Bessie Wedderburn, daughters of the deceased, and William Gaskin and John Gairdin, their spouses.
    Another such decree is recorded 21 Jan. 1654.

463. **1654.** Jan. 2.—John James Wedderburn of Drohanavitis, in Moravia, is retoured oye and heir to umquhill John Wedderburn, his goodschir, and compears by Alexander Halyburtone, who has his factory, dated 4 July 1653.

Dundee
Burgh and
Head Court
Records.

On the same day he produces by a notary a document for registration, in which he is decribed as " John James Wedderburn, hereditary lord in Drohanavitis, lawful eldest son of the late lord (dominus) John Wedderburn, sometime chief doctor of the renowned states of the Marquisate of Moravia," and requires service as "truly nearest heir of his grandfather John Wedderburn, his uncle James Wedderburn, and his great grandfather John Wedderburn, and any or all of them," of houses in the Flukergait of Dundee, and of lands in Aberbothrie, &c.

464.   ·1654· (a) Jan. 7.—Decree for Helen Wedderburn and William Gaskine, her spouse, v. Elizabeth Wedderburn and John Gardin, her spouse.   (b) May 1.—Decreet of poynding in favour of Helen and Bessie Wedderburn and their spouses, William Gaskine and John Gairdine.

465.   1655. Jan. 9.—Decree v. Helen Wedderburn, relict of Andrew Kyde (Boyd), mariner.

466.   1655. June 25.—Edict of curatory for Margaret, daughter of the late Mr. Andrew Bruce, principal of S. Leonard's College. Amongst the father's kin named are William Bruce of Fingask and Mr. Andrew Bruce ; and among the mother's, Sir Alexander Wedderburn of Blackness and Alexander Wedderburn of Kingennie.

467.   1655. July 22.—Andrew Wedderburn, merchant, witness to a bond (13 March).
[See, in all, dates :—1649. Jan. 10 ; March 3, 12 ; May 12 ; June 23 ; Oct. 1, 21.—1650 March 6 ; April 3 ; July 8, 20.—1651. May 3 ; June 4, 7 ; Nov. 24 ; Dec. 24.—1652. July 10, 21 ; Aug. 12 ; Oct. 4, 5 ; Nov. 3 ; Dec. 4.—1653. Jan. 19 ; Feb. 14 ; July 4, 18 ; Oct. 29 ; Dec. 31.— 1654 Jan. 2, 7, 21 ; Feb. 22 ; March 13 ; May 1, 8 ; June 12 ; July 31 ; Nov. 13.—1655. Jan. 9 ; May 21 ; June 25 ; July 22 ; Aug. 14 ; Dec. 8.—1656. Feb. 23 ; April 5 ; May 31 ; July 25 ; Sept. 3.]

VOL. 33.
1656—62.
This volume contains little of importance as regards the family. There are a good many slight references to Sir Alexander Wedderburn of Blackness, who was clerk at the time.

468.   1657. (a) Feb. 18 —Discharge (23 June 1655) by Helen Wedderburn, relict of Andrew Boyd.   (b) May 18, Sept. 2.—Andrew Wedderburn named.

469.   1659. Feb. 26.—Decree v. Patrick Gourlay, writer in Dundee, to give up for registration the minute of a contract between James Gray, of Bullone, and Mr. Andrew Wedderburn.

470.   1659. May 28.— Decree for Helen Wedderburn, spouse to Barten Bilsone, for possession of a South Overgait house.

471.   1660. Oct. 1.—Alexander Wedderburn of Kingennie, provost, on the Head Court bench.

472.   1660. Dec. 1.—Bond in favour of Alexander Wedderburn, merchant, burgess. (1647)

473.   1661. Nov. 2.—Decree in favour of John Wedderburn, baxter.
[See, in all, s. dates :—1657. Jan. 24 ; Feb. 18 ; May 18 ; Sept. 2, 21, 29 ; Oct. 26 ; Dec. 19.— 1658. April 17 ; Nov. 17 ; Dec. 6.—1659. Jan. 12 ; Feb. 11, 25, 26 ; May 20, 28, 30 ; Aug. 12 ; Nov. 28 ; Dec. 10.—1660. Jan. 7 ; Feb. 6. 8 ; Aug. 3 ; Sept. 3 ; Oct. 1 ; Nov. 26 ; Dec. 1.—1661. Jan. 6, 16 ; Oct. 21, 31 ; Nov. 2 ; Dec. 11.]

VOL. 34.
1652—76.
Entitled : " Head Court of the Burgh of Dundee, holden within the Tolbooth thereof, 7 Oct. 1662, by Alexander Wedderburn of Kingany, provost, &c."

" James Wedderburue, clerk," is written on the first fly leaf of this volume, and on the last is "Ja : Wedderburn, Town Clerk of Dundee, James Ramsay his dep : 1675."

474.   1664. Dec. 21.—Bailie Court in the house in Dundee of Sir Alexander Wedderburn of Blackness.—Margaret Wedderburn, spouse to Patrick Kyd of Craigie,

renounces, in her said husband's favour, her interest, under her marriage contract, in **Dundee Burgh and Head Court Records.** the lands of Grange of Barric, Barrymure, called Nether Barry or Denhead, co. Forfar.

475. **1665.** Dec. 11.—Transumpt for Sir Alexander Wedderburn of Blackness of two sasines, of which one, dated 12 Jan. 1629, is in favour of Mr. Alexander Wedderburn, son of Mr. James Wedderburn, sometime clerk of Dundee, and heir to his uncle, Peter Wedderburn, merchant, immediate elder brother of the said James, of certain Marketgait property.

Elder is an error for younger. James Wedderburn, the clerk (d. 1627), was the second son of Alexander Wedderburn of Kingennie, and Peter, the third son.

476. **1667.** Nov. 12.—Janet Guthrie, spouse to Dougall Macphersone, once of Easter Powrie, now indweller in Dundee, ratifies the disposition, 12 Sept. 1662, made by her said husband, with her consent and that of her eldest son, to Alexander Wedderburn, elder of Kingany, and his heirs, &c., heritably and irredeemably, of the lands of Easter Powrie, and of the lands of Ogilvy, in warrandice.

477. **1669.** Feb. 6.—Alexander Wedderburn of Easter Powrie, Alexander Wedderburn of Kingany, and John Wedderburn, fiar of Blackness, are on an assize.

478. **1670.** March 28.—Decree c. Margaret Wedderburn, relict of Thomas Halyburton, and Mr. Thomas Halyburton, his eldest son and heir.

479. **1670.** July 28.—Euphame Weymes and Alexander Jacke, her husband, are decerned to give up to Robert Lauder certain writs, including :—(a) Charter to David Wedderburn, 15 April, 1558. (b) Sasine to Alexander Wedderburn as brother and heir to Robert Wedderburn, 27 Sept., 1566. (c) Sasine to Alexander Wedderburn, as son and heir of the said David Wedderburn, 25 April, 1571. (d) Contract of alienation by the said Alexander Wedderburn, in favour of Robert Kinloch, 19 Aug, 1579.

480. **1671.** Jan. 16.—Decree for John Wedderburn, baxter.

481. **1675.** April 7.—Sir Alexander Wedderburn, of Blackness, and John Wedderburn are on an assize.

482. **1676.** March 25.—Decree in favour of Peter Wedderburn, merchant, as assignee of James Wedderburn, his brother german.

[See, in all, s. dates :—1662. Oct. 20.—1663. April 27 ; June 27.—1664. Jan. 11, 20 ; May 2 ; July 2 ; Oct. 3 ; Nov. 14 ; Dec 21.—1665. Jan. 9 ; April 3 ; May 2 ; Aug. 2 ; Dec. 11.—1666. April 4 ; Oct 15.—1667. April 20 ; June 24 ; Nov. 12.—1668. Feb. 24 ; May 20 ; Oct. 17.—1669. Jan. 23, 27 ; Feb. 6 ; Sept. 4.—1670. Feb. 23 ; March 7, 28 ; July 23 ; Oct. 5.—1671. Jan. 16, 21, 28 ; Feb. 27 ; June 17 ; Dec. 29.—1672. Jan. 10 ; Nov. 30.—1673. Feb. 24 ; May 10 ; Nov. 3, 12. —1674. June 1 ; Oct. 12 ; Nov. 28.—1675. April 7 ; July 31.—1676. March 25.]

Vol. 35.

1676—88.

This volume is unfortunately lost, and the record is thus blank from April 17, 1676 to January 21, 1688.

Vol. 36.

1688—90.

Outside the cover is stamped I.W., and inside it is written :—"James Wedderburne, clerk. James Ramsay, dep¹, 1688. Testor Veritatem ('my witness is true ')," and the lines :—

Interpone tuis interdum gaudia curis,
Ut possis animo quemvis sufferre laborem.

Which we may render—

Mingle at times some pleasure with thy care,
So shall thy spirit every labour bear.

On the fly leaf is a list of certain tenants in the Nethergate and Overgate of Dundee, who bind themselves, 18 May, 1686, to "live peaceablie and regularly free of all fanaticall disorder vnder the respective paines and penalties contained in the Act of Parliament made thereannent, dated 2 June, 1685." Among the signatures is that of Alexander Wedderburn, second of Easter Powrie.

2 P

483. **1688.** Feb. 8.—Decree for Peter Wedderburn, merchant.

484. **1688.** July 30.—Transumpt, including a disposition (5 May) of land in North Kirkwynd, bounded by lands once Peter Imbrie's, then James Wedderburn's, and also of land in North Marketgait, once that of David Wedderburn.

485. **1688.** Dec. 10.—Decree for Alexander Wedderburn, son of the deceased Peter Wedderburn, merchant, for the price of a mirror bought at the rouping of Peter Wedderburn's goods.

486. **1689.** Nov. 18.—Decree for Alexander Wedderburn, son to umquhile Peter Wedderburn, merchant, and "Dame Matild Fletcher, Lady Blackness, his guyder, maintainer, and intertainer," for certain maills.

[See. in all, s. dates :—**1688.** Jan. 21: Feb. 8 ; April 14 ; May 5; July 30 ; Dec. 20.—**1689.** March 11 ; Nov. 6, 18, 23.—**1690.** March 10, 22 ; May 19.]

VOL. 37.[1]

1690–93.

On the second fly leaf is written, "Court Book of the Burgh of Dundee. Ja : Wedderburne, Clerk ; Ja : Ramsay, Deput.," and James Wedderburne, the clerk, is frequently named throughout the volume.

487. **1691.** Sept. 21.—Transumpt of sasines, &c., relating to a South Nethergait tenement disponed, 5 Dec. 1678, by George Wedderburn, merchant, burgess of Edinburgh, to Euphame Rollo, relict of Thomas Gray, and her daughter, in which the following documents are referred to :—(a) 1629. Sept. 30.—Precept of Clare constat of Mr. Alexander Wedderburn, as heir to his father, Mr. James Wedderburn (b) 1664. Feb. 13.—Bond of Provision by Sir Alexander Wedderburn of Blackness, Knt., to George Wedderburn, his fourth son, of the said tenement, to which William Wedderburn, brother german of Sir Alexander, is witness. (c) Disposition following thereon, dated 17 Feb. (d) Charter of confirmation by Charles Maitland of Hatton to George Wedderburn, dated at Edinburgh 9 Dec. 1679.

488. **1692.** Feb. 3.—Decree in favour of Peter Wedderburn, merchant.

489. **1692.** March 2.—Decree v. Alexander Wedderburn of Easter Powrie, and his tutors and curators, for payment of a sum of £100 due by his late father.

490. **1693.** Feb. 15.—James Wedderburn, town clerk of Dundee, witnesses a judicial renunciation.

See in all s. dates :—**1690** Nov. 1. 28.—**1691.** March 14 ; April 2; Sept. 21 ; Nov. 28.—**1692.** Feb. 3 ; March 2, 12 ; April 16, 25 ; Nov. 9.—**1693.** Feb. 11, 15.]

VOL. 38.

1695–1709.

This volume is in four divisions :—(a) Feb. 11, 1695 to Oct. 21, 1696. (b) Nov. 1696 to Aug. 4, 1697. (c) Nov. 1698 to July 18, 1702. (d) Aug. 25, 1705 to Sept. 19, 1709.

491. **1695.** March 30.—Action by Alexander Wedderburn, writer in Dundee, v. Alexander Cowan and William Milne.

492. **1696.** Oct. 19.—Robert and John Wedderburn, second and third sons of umquhile James Wedderburn, clerk, require curators, whose names, however, are not given.

493. **1697.** May 15 and 17.—Action by Margaret Wedderburn, relict of John Pearson, baxter, v. Euphame Smith.

[1] There is another volume also numbered 37 in this record, owing to some mistake, as it does not belong to this record at all, but to the Register of Decreets. See post. s. Dundee Decreets, Vol. 3.

494. **1699.** Jan. 14.—Action by George Balfour, son of umquhile Mr. Andrew Balfour, W.S., and his curators, including John Wedderburn of Blackness *v* Margaret Burgh.

495. **1699.** March 24.—Action by Margaret Wedderburn, Lady Craigie, elder, *v.* J. Davidson.

496. **1699.** June 28.—Action by Alexander Wedderburn, mariner, (by Alexander Wedderburn, the clerk, his factor), *v.* David Watson.

497. **1699.** Dec. 2.—Action by Janet and Margaret Grieve *v.* Isobel and Margaret Wedderburn, daughters of the deceased Alexander Wedderburn, skipper.

498. **1700.** May 13.—Action by Alexander Wedderburn of Easter Powrie, and his curators, *v.* Samuel Morisone.

499. **1701.** July 14.—Action by Elizabeth Davidson, relict of the deceased James Wedderburn, clerk, *v.* John Watt.

500. **1706.** May 6.—Action by Alexander Wedderburn of that ilk *v.* James Grieve.

501. **1706.** Sept. 2.—Action by Francis Craigie and another *v.* Robert Wedderburn, mariner, and Margaret Arnot, his spouse, and Alexander Wedderburn, clerk.

502. **1708.** May 15.—Action by Margaret Wedderburn, relict of John Pearson, baxter, *v.* Alexander Wedderburn of that ilk.

503. **1709.** April 23.—Action by Mathilda Wedderburn, relict of umquhile Mr. James Brisbane, advocate, *v.* David Brisbane, their son and heir, and his curators.

Vol. 39.

1717–35.

This volume is in five parts, stitched and put up in one bundle :—(1717-18. 1720-22, 1729-31, 1732-34, 1734-35.)

504. **1717.** June 1.—Action by Mathilda Wedderburn *v.* James Creighton.

505. **1717.** June 15.—Action by David Brisbane, writer in Dundee, factor for Sir John Wedderburn, of Blackness, and his tutors.

506. **1717.** Dec. 1.—Action by Alexander Wedderburn, shipmaster, and late bailie, *v.* J. Morgan.

507. **1718.** Feb. 5.—Action by Gilbert Stewart, merchant in Edinburgh, *v.* Alexander Wedderburn, sheriff clerk of Forfar, and indweller in Dundee, Alexander Wedderburn, shipmaster there, &c.

508. **1718.** Feb. 8.—Action by Peter Wedderburn, merchant in Dundee, *v.* Isobell Watson.

509. **1719.** March 8.—Marion (?) Wedderburn, and her husband (not named), *v.* R. Gilmore.

I find no other mention of a Marion Wedderburn, and think it must be an error for Mariot or Margaret. in which case it probably refers to Margaret Wedderburn, daughter of James Wedderburn, the clerk (d. 1696), and wife of John Paterson of Craigie.

510. **1734.** July 15, Aug. 19.—Actions *v.* bailie Wedderburn, shipmaster.

511. **1734.** Dec. 7.—Action by Mr. John Wedderburn, younger, of Blackness, *v.* Gilbert Thomson and others.

Vol. 40.

Five court books, unbound, 1735-36, 1736, 1736-37, 1737-38, and 1738-40.

512. **1735.** July 23.—Dr. John Wedderburn, physician, *v.* James Man.

513. **1736.** April 3.—David Wedderburn of that ilk, *v.* John Sellars.

514. **1736.** Nov. 1.—Katharine Wedderburn, mercatrix in Dundee, *v.* James Man.

515. **1737.** June 25.—Service of David Wedderburn, as heir to Alexander Wedderburn, his great grandfather.

516. **1738.** Dec. 16.—Robert Wedderburn, sheriff clerk of Forfar, *v.* David Haliburton.

517. **1739.** May 12.—John Wedderburn, factor for the Duke of Douglas, *v.* James Smith.

Vol. 41.

Four parts: 1740-41, 1742-43, 1745-49, and (altogether out of place) 1697-98.

518. **1740.** May 17.—John Guthrie, of that ilk, *v.* David Wedderburn, of that ilk, residenter in Dundee.

519. **1741.** June 13.—David Walker *v.* Sir Alexander Wedderburn of Blackness, residenter in Dundee.

520. **1743.** May 11.—Peter Kinnimond *v.* Bailie Wedderburn's relict, and others.

521. **1743.** Aug. 29.—Service in favour of the Laird of Wedderburn, as heir to Peter Wedderburn, his grand uncle.

522. **1748.** Aug. 8.—Decreet, Lady Wedderburn *v.* J. Brown.

Vols. 39a, 40a, 41a, 42.

These four volumes 1766-74, 1774-81, 1781-85, and 1785-88, contain nothing of importance concerning members of the family.

THE COUNCIL BOOKS.

This record begins in 1553 and continues, with two breaks one of five years (1582-87) and another of ten (1653-63) down to the present time. It has been searched through the first twelve, and part of the thirteenth volumes, down to the year 1800. These volumes are numbered 1-13 and also 85-97, in relation to the other volumes of other records, (protocols, deeds, decreets, etc.) in the Charter room.

VOL. 1.
—
1553-92.

On the first leaf is written in pencil, "Minutes of Head Courts and Laws for the burgh there enacted from 2 Oct. 1553 to ... Oct. 1588," but this is an error, as the volume ends 1 Oct. 1582. Some of the folios appear to be misplaced, as after going down to 1567 at fol. 68, 69, it goes back to 1562. There is also another volume in the Charter room entitled on the back, "Head Court Laws 1550-1622." This volume is largely (fol. 5-72) a duplicate of volume 1 of the Council books. See ante p. 259 s. Burgh and Head Court Records, Vol. I.

1. **1559.** (a) Oct. 3.—John Wedderburn, bailie (11). (b) **1560.** Oct. 4.—John Wedderburn, bailie (14). (c) **1561.** Feb. 27.—James Wedderburn, councillor (32). (d) **1562.** March 23.—John Wedderburn, councillor (45).

2. **1563.** May 17.—The Council having elected James Lovell, treasurer, Robert Kyd, dean of gild, and Alexander Wedderburn, the common clerk, "to pass to Edinburgh at this present parliament the 21 May as commissioners for the whole toun to treat of certain matters and especially of the liberty of burghs," the said commissioners require their commission to be sealed with the common seal of the burgh. (76.)

3. **1563.** Oct. 19.—James Lovell and John Wedderburn are elected piermasters.

4. **1564.** May 8.—Robert Wedderburn, younger, and other "inhabitaris" of the burgh, present. (52.)

5. **1566.** July 30.—Johne Wedderburn and Alexander Wedderburn "ressaes benevolence of Thomas Kynloch to repair the twfall of Alexander Wedderburn and David Wedderburn's land lying on Skirling's Wynd and to theik the samyn heall with the wyndois," reserving to the said T. Kynloch (their adjoining neighbour) all his rights "at the coming to perfect age of the bairnes foresaid." (96.)

6. **1566.** Sept. 25.—Alexander Wedderburn, elder, present in court. (99.)

7. **1567.** Jan. 22.—John Wedderburn, master of the almshouse. (63.)

8. **1568.** June 3.—Discharge by the council to John Wedderburn, master of the almshouse, for all his dealings during the time he used that office. (10.)

9. **1569.** June 4.—Alexander Wedderburn, common clerk, and others, are appointed to inspect the common malt mill of the burgh, also the common wheat mill of Pitkerrow. (108.)
[See, in all, fol. 11, 14, 32, 45, 52, 63, 70-71, 76, 78, 96, 99, 107-8.]

VOL. 2.
—
1587-1603.

On the first leaf is written :—"In this Buik is conteanit the Actis and conclusiounis of the counsall of the Burgh of Dundee. M. A. Wedderburn. Begun the sewint day of Marche the zeir of God MV^e and fourescoir zeiris." It will be noticed that this volume and the next overlap in date.

10. **1588.** (a) In a list of the "counsall" are named Alexander Wedderburn, piermaster, and Patrick Wedderburn. (1.) (b) March 12, April 25.—Patrick Wedderburn, present in council. (4, 6.)

11. **1588.** April 2.—John Wedderburn is convicted of hurting and wounding David Gardyne, officer, in the head, to the effusion of his blood in great quantity. He is fined. (5.)

12. **1588.** July 3.—Robert Wedderburn is elected a visitor for the Argyllis quarter (one of the four quarters into which the town was then divided) that it "might be substantiouslie attendit to and watchit so far as is possabill for the preservation of the sam" from the "plague of pest," lately in Leith. (10.)

13. **1588.** Sept. 23.—Alexander Wedderburn, "Mr. Hospitall," is named in a list of those elected as counsellors. (13)

14. **1589.** July 16.—Robert Wedderburn, elder, is elected procurator fiscal and "master of work" for the "bigging of the new school," and gave his oath for the faithful discharge of his office. (34.)

15. **1590.** Oct. 13.—Matthew Wedderburn, mariner, is elected by the bailies and council to be deacon of the coilmen. (30.)

16. **1590.** Oct. 27.—Commissioners are appointed to contract with Richardus Wedderburn, Patrick Kynaird, or others, for providing of timber for the Kirk roof. (52.) This was supplied by Richard Wedderburn, as in the following year there is a record of 22 great joists 44 feet long, and some 32 dozen trees of various lengths, from 8 to 32 feet, received from him. (66.)

17. **1591.** Sept. 19.—Robert Wedderburn is elected Mr. Hospitall. (64.)

18. **1591-95.**—Robert Wedderburn is often named as counsellor, &c. (71, 75, 82, 85, 86, 89.)

19. **1595.** Oct. 7.—Matthew Wedderburn is again elected deacon of the coalmen. (100.)

20. **1597.** Oct. 25.—Robert Wedderburn, elder, and others pursue Patrick Gardyne, deacon of the Skinner craft, for fouling the common burn with lime (108), and the Court (Nov. 8) order the craft to refrain from so doing. (ib.)

21. **1599.** (a) Oct. 2.—Patrick, Robert, and David Wedderburn are all named as counsellors. (114.) (b) 1601-2.—They are again so named. (116, 123.)
[See, in all, fol. 1, 4-11, 13-16, 18-19, 24-26, 34-35, 47, 50-53, 64-66, 71, 75, 82, 85-86, 95, 99-100, 107-8, 113-14, 116, 121, 123, 129, 135.]

VOL. 3.

1597–1618.

22. **1598.** Oct. 5.—Robert Wedderburn, merchant, is elected collector of the unlaws. (4.)

23. **1600.** Dec. 11.—Peter Wedderburn is fined for brewing 14 penny ale. (8.)

24. **1601.** Oct. 14.—David Wedderburn renders account of his intromissions with the unlaws. (9.)

25. **1603.** Sept. 24.—Patrick, Robert, and David Wedderburn are councillors. (16.)

26. **1603.** Dec. 11.—Henry Fyff, mariner, is convicted for troublance committed by him on the High street, after ten hours at even, against James Wedderburn, and is ordained to crave the said James' pardon. (17.)

27. **1604.** May 29.—Patrick and David Wedderburn are present on the council when it was resolved that, during the suspicion of pestilence, all the passage boats at the Ferry, except three, should be brought to the harbour. (22.)

28. **1604.** July 17.—Gift of the clerkship upon a decreet arbitral betwixt the **Dundee Council Books.** Magistrates and inhabitants of the burgh to make, seal, subscribe and deliver to James Wedderburn, second son to Mr. Alexander Wedderburn, present common clerk of the burgh, a letter of gift of the said clerkship after the death, or demission in case of his inability, of his father, which, of the date hereof, is subscribed by the council, including Robert and Patrick Wedderburn. (24.)

29. **1605.** May 25.—William Auchinlek, Dean of Gild, and Mr. Alexander Wedderburn are nominated commissioners, to pass to and keep the convention to be holden at Edinburgh on June 6. (18.)

30. **1605.** Oct. 7.—David Blyth is ordained to remain in ward for his offence in staying a reconciliation promoted by the elders of the Kirk betwixt James Wedderburn and Robert (son of William) Rollock, inhabitants of Dundee. (43.) On the same day James Thomson is cautioned for James Wedderburn, burgess, that he will not molest Robert Rollock, and "that he shall no way bear on his person within the burgh any sword, cutlass, or long dagger" without leave from the Privy Council, or the Dundee Council. James Wedderburn presently produces a warrant from the Privy Council allowing him to wear his sword. Robert Rollock gives similar security, but does not seem to have got a like license. (44.)

31. **1606.** June 10.—William Auchinlek, bailie, and Mr. Alexander Wedderburn, clerk, commissioners to the last parliament, are again nominated to convene with the estates in the next convention to be holden at Edinburgh on the 17th inst. (55.)

32. **1609.** May 8.—Robert Wedderburn, elder, David Wedderburn, and John Lovell declare that they know Patrick Auchinlek to be lawful son of the late James Auchinlek of Woodhill, provost, and Elizabeth Kynloch, as also Peter Imbrie to be lawful son of the late Peter Imbrie and Barbara Wedderburn. (84.)

33. **1609.** June 6.—Mr. Alexander Wedderburn, John Finlayson, and William Goldman are nominated commissioners to the coming parliament at Edinburgh on the 15th inst. (88.)

34. **1609-10.** (No date.)—Mr. Alexander Wedderburn, clerk, is often named as exercising that office. (189, 95 97, 100, 103, 104, 105, 109.)

35. **1611.** (a) Sept. 17, 22.—Patrick Wedderburn is present on the council. (b) **1612.** Sept. 22.—He is again present, when Alexander Wedderburn is elected for the merchants.

36. **1613.** Feb. 2.—The council understanding that they are bound by their contract to pay to Mr. William Wedderburn, one of the ministers of the burgh, as great a stipend as they pay to any of the remaining ministers, so soon as it should please God to give him the charge and burden of a family, and knowing perfectly that he is now burdened with the charge of his wife, bairn and family, ordain that he be paid 800 merks yearly. Mr. Alexander Wedderburn, clerk, and Mr. Alexander Wedderburn, merchant, sign. (129.)

[See, in all, fol. 1. 4, 7-9, 15, 15ᵃ, 16, 17, 19, 22, 24, 26-28, 30, 36, 40, 43, 44, 49, 52, 55, 58, 81, 84, 86, 88-89, 95, 97, 100, 103-4, 108-9, 113-15, 117, 123, 125-27, 129.]

VOL. 4.

1613–53.

On the fly leaf is written :—"Acts and Ordinances of the Counsell of the Burgh of Dundie, Anno Dom. 1613."

37. **1613.** June 29.—The council elect Mr. Alexander Wedderburn, their clerk, to be their only commissioner to compear for them before the Privy Council, on the 1st July, to answer the claim of Mr. Patrick Gordon, that certain expenses should be refunded to him ; as also to convene with the commissioners of the other burghs in their general convention at Dundee on July 6. (3.)

38. **1613.** Sept. 21.—Mr. Alexander Wedderburn, younger, is elected on the council. (5.)

39. **1614.** April 19.— Mr. Alexander Wedderburn, clerk, appoints Mr. John Dynmure, notary, his substitute. (15.)

40. **1614.** Sept. 21.—James Wedderburn is elected a counsellor.

41. **1615.** April 11.—Mr. James Wedderburn acts as notary to an assedation. (22.)

42. **1615.** Sept. 20.—Alexander Wedderburn, merchant, is elected on the council and put on the leet for bailie. (26.)

43. **1615.** Oct. 3.—Mr. Alexander Wedderburn, younger, elected Sept. 24, accepts the office of bailie, and gives his oath for faithful administration. (27.)

44. **1617.** Nov. 14.—Compeared Mr. Alexander Wedderburn, common clerk of the burgh of Dundee, and declared that he was employed to attend this winter season, in his Majesty's service, as one of the Commissioners, appointed by Act of Parliament for planting of the Kirks and modifying of the stipends of ministers serving the cure of the said Kirks, and that being careful that in his absence his office be served, he has, with consent of the Provost, bailies and council, nominated and elected Mr. James Wedderburn, his lawful son, to be his depute and substitute in his office, giving him power to use the same in all respects as any clerk depute within any burgh in the realm, untill it shall please Mr. Alexander Wedderburn to discharge him, without prejudice to the right of Mr. James Wedderburn to the office. The said Mr. James Wedderburn accepts of the same, and gives his oath for the faithful administration thereof. (43.)

45. **1618.** Sept. 27.—James Wedderburn is elected a bailie. (47.)

46. **1621.** Aug. 15.—James Gibsone, merchant, is convicted, on his own confession, of slandering Magdalene Wedderburn, wife of Thomas Jack, merchant, and Janet Clayhills, wife of Thomas Wichtane, in the market place of Perth, and is fined and bound over. (59.)

47. **1623.** Oct. 2.—James Wedderburn is elected kirk-master. (66.)

48. **1624.** Sept. 24.—Mr. Alexander Wedderburn, younger, is elected dean of gild. (73.)

49. **1627.** May 25.—Mr. James Wedderburne, present common clerk of the burgh of of Dundee, being sick and bedfast, and thereby not being able to exercise and use his office during that time, and being careful that no neighbour nor inhabitant thereof be harmed nor frustrated in their particular "adoes," appoints, with consent of the magistrates, Thomas Fyff, his servitor, his depute and substitute in the said office, during the time of his sickness. (83.)

50. **1627.** (*a*) Sept. 18.—Peter Wedderburn nominated for the new council. (84.)
     (*b*) Oct. 2.—Peter Wedderburn, younger, elected collector of the unlaws. (84.)
     (*c*) Oct. 14.—Alexander Wedderburn, elder, merchant, appointed a collector of taxations (88), and again 26 Nov., 1633, Alexander Wedderburn, merchant, so elected. (104.)

51. **1628.** Feb. 12.—Mr. Alexander Wedderburn, notary public, signs for various persons. (86).

52. **1628-29.** James Wedderburn is elected dean of gild. He also acts as bailie, &c. (89-93.)

53. **1630.** Jan. 6.—On a complaint by Mr. Alexander Wedderburn, eldest son of Mr. James Wedderburn, *v.* Matthew Thomson, pretended heritor and possessor of a tenement in North Argylegait, next to the land of the heirs of the said Mr. James

Wedderburn, to the effect that Thomson allowed the said tenement to become so Dundee Council Books. ruinous that on the 4th instant the east wall thereof fell down, "whereby (were not the providence of Almightie God) the whole peopill being in the said Mr. Alexander's tenement had been smothered dead," Thomson is ordered to remove or rebuild the said tenement. (93.)

54. **1633.** July 30.—Compeared Mr. Alexander Wedderburn, younger, lately elected common clerk of Dundee, and accepted the office and gave his oath for faithful administration. (102.)

55. **1633.** Oct. 1.—Mr. Alexander Wedderburn, elder, of Kingany, is elected town councillor for the coming year. (103.)

56. **1634-37.**—Mr. Alexander Wedderburn, elder, is often named as councillor and collector of the taxations. (108, 110, 113, 122, 126, &c.)

57. **1638.** May 22.—James Fletcher, provost, and Mr. Alexander Wedderburn, clerk, are elected to attend the general convention of burghs. (129.)

58. **1638.** Dec. 25.—James Fletcher, provost, commissioner to the last general assembly at Glasgow, together with Mr. Alexander Wedderburn, common clerk, and two others, assessors to him, make their report to the council, "whairwith the whole Counsill, collector, and deacons of crafts wer weill pleased." (132).

59. **1639.** June 28.—Mr. Alexander Wedderburn, clerk, of Dundee, with consent of the haill council, appoints Thomas Kessane, notary, his substitute clerk. (136.)

60. **1639.** (a) June 28.—James Fletcher, provost, and Mr. Alexander Wedderburn, clerk, are elected commissioners to attend the general assembly of the burghs, to be holden at Dunfermline, the 2nd July next. (136.) (b) There is granted a commission from the bailies and council of Dundee to James Fletcher, their provost, to attend the general convention of the burghs at Dunfermline, and "there to treat, reason, and conclude, in all common matters and affairs to be propounded, tending to the advancement of the glory of God and weill of the haill free burghs of this Kingdom, &c." The commission constitutes Mr. Alexander Wedderburn, the clerk, assessor for the commissioner, with full power to supply his place, in case of sickness, and the council declare that their commissioner and his assessor are men fearing God of the true religion then publicly professed, and expert in all the affairs of the burgh, bearing all portable charges with their neighbours within the same, and "such as may tyne and wine in all comone causis." (ib.)

61. **1639.** Sept. 17.—Alexander Wedderburn, of Kingany, and others, all said to be "faithful covenanters," are elected to the New Council.

62. **1640.** Sept. 22, 27.—Alexander Wedderburn, of Kingany, is elected a bailie. (139-40.)

63. **1641.** Sept. 21.—Alexander Wedderburn of Kingany, and Alexander Wedderburn, mariner, for the merchants, are elected to the new council. James Wedderburn is elected a bailie. (142.)

64. **1641.** (a) Dec. 21.—The council ordain to count with Major Wedderburn, and to see him completed during the time of his service. (144.) **1642.** (b) Jan. 24.—£100 is ordained to be given him in complete payment of all acclaimed by him for his service. (ib.)

65. **1642.** Feb. 17.—Compeared Mr. Alexander Wedderburn, clerk, and gave in a report anent the signature whereof he had been procurer and suitor to His Majesty, stating that he had obtained a charter under the Great Seal confirming all the town's ancient privileges with a gift "de novo damus," with power to the council to be sheriffs in themselves, &c., &c.; and also another charter under the Great Seal, whereby His

2 Q

Majesty gives to the burgh all and haill the parsonage and patronage of the kirk of
Longforgand, and lastly a gift by the Duke of Lennox of the Admiralty of the waters
of Tay. On which the whole council not only approve of the care and pains taken
by their clerk, but find themselves in a special manner thankful for the same and
bound to pay him all his expenses. (145.)

66. **1642.** Aug. 23.—Alexander Wedderburn, clerk, is appointed to attend a particular
convention appointed to be held at Edinburgh on Sept. 1st. (149.)

67. **1642.** Oct. 4, 11.—Alexander Wedderburn, mariner, is elected piermaster, and
accepts office. (119-50.)

68. **1643.** (a) Feb. 13.—Alexander Wedderburn (i.e., of Kingennie) and Alexander
Wedderburn, clerk, are appointed, with others, as commissioners to attend upon the
discussion of a suspension raised by the lawborrowes, wherewith Viscount Dudhope
has charged them. (158.) (b) March 7.—The said commissioners return from
Edinburgh, and report that the Lords of Privy Council find that the magistrates are
only liable for acts done by the inhabitants with their authority. (ib.) (c) May 30.—
The said commissioners are elected to defend the action of Viscount Dudhope before
the Privy Council. (162.) (d) Sept. 4.—They send in a report as to their mission. (16.)

69. **1643.** Sept. 26, Oct. 3.—Alexander Wedderburn, piermaster, is re-elected, and
accepts office. (165-66.)

70. **1643.** Oct. 3.—Election of officers for the weapon-schawing:—Alexander Wedderburn
of Kingennie, is elected captain of the Overgait, and Alexander Wedderburn,
lieutenant. (166.)

71. **1643.** Oct. 5.—Alexander Wedderburn of Kingennie, is ordained to go next day to
Fodderance, and the clerk to Panmure, the council having resolved that Lord
Fodderance and the Laird of Panmure should treat between Viscount Dudhope and
the town. (167.)

72. **1644.** July 14.—Compeared Thomas Halyburton and Mr. Alexander Wedderburn,
clerk, and made account of their proceedings during their last being in Edinburgh,
and particularly concerning the sum of 9,600 merks advanced by the town to the
late Northern expedition under the Marquis of Argyle, in order to complete which
sum they had given certain bonds, including one to Alexander Wedderburn of
Kingennie for £1,000. (180.)

73. **1644.** (a) Oct. 1.—Thomas Halyburton, dean of gild, and the clerk are elected
commissioners to the committee of estates to deal for the relief of the town from the
charges they will be put to in quartering the Earl of Crawford's regiment. (183.)
(b) Oct. 21.—They are ordered to go to Edinburgh "for fitting the accounts
disbursed in this time of trouble." (184.)

74. **1644.** Dec. 18.—Ordains that Monorgan's Croft be bought from the clerk, with
whom the provost, Kingennie, and others, are to treat. (105.)

75. **1645.** April 12.—The clerk and his colleague give in a report of their proceedings with
the committee of estates in regard to the army, but as they are a great way from
the town's desires, the Council determined to send another commission to Edinburgh,
including the clerk. (138.)

76. **1645.** July 1.—The council elect Mr. Alexander Wedderburn to be commissioner to
the ensuing Parliament, with Mr. Andrew Auchfleck as his assessor, and to supply
his place in case of sickness. (188.)

77. **1645.** Sept. 2.—A letter is produced from the committee of estates requiring the
clerk's presence at Berwick to treat with the English commissioners. To this the

council return a letter of excuse showing the necessity of his stay in Dundee on account of the great appearances of the infection. (190.)

78. **1645.** Nov. 4.—The council nominated Mr. Alexander Wedderburn, clerk, to be commissioner to the ensuing parliament to sit at S. Andrews, with Mr. George Halyburton as his assessor, and to supply his place in case of sickness or absence. (191.)

79. **1646.** Feb. 16.—Mr. Alexander Wedderburn, commissioner to the Session of parliament, which did lately sit at S. Andrews, made report of all proceedings there, and specially how he followed the particular employment intrusted to him concerning the losses to the town of Dundee, and produced the Act of Parliament for the silver work, quarterings, and losses sustained by the town when the rebels assaulted it, with which report the haill council were well satisfyed, and promised him his extraordinary pains should be taken into consideration. (192.)

80. **1646.** June 2.—Mr. Alexander Wedderburn delivered to the council his report anent his last employment in Edinburgh, as also £3,000 scots in complete payment of " Robert Johnstone, his legacie." which the council ordered to be used thus :—500 merks to be kept by the clerk for Monorgan's croft disponed by him for the use of the Hospital, and two thousand to be delivered to the Hospital master, William Duncan (194).

81. **1646.** July 14.—The clerk is nominated to attend the particular convention of Burghs appointed to sit at Edinburgh on the 23rd inst. (195.)

82. **1646.** Aug. 28.—The clerk compeared and made a report of the proceedings lately at Edinburgh, and the meeting of the council and committees of parliament, wherewith the council were pleased, and dispensed with the clerk's going to Newcastle with those chosen by the aforesaid meeting to go and supplicate his Majesty. (195.)

83. **1646.** Oct. 13.—The clerk is elected commissioner to the meeting of burghs on Nov. 2, as also commissioner (with Robert Davidson as his assessor) to the ensuing session of parliament. (197.)

84. **1646.** Dec. 15.—James Simsone is elected assessor to Sir Alexander Wedderburn, and to supply his place in his absence. (198.)

85. **1647.** April 6.—The clerk made his report of the proceedings of parliament since his employment, and delivered to the Council the Act in the town's favour for their quarterings and losses, and the Act for £20,000 for the poor, and an Act of this session, recommending their losses to the committee of estates, with the commission for trying the town's losses and the report thereof. The report is approved. (200.)

86. **1647.** June 1.—Sir Alexander Wedderburn, clerk, nominated to attend the coming convention of burghs, to be held at Edinburgh. (201.)

87. **1647.** June 29.—John Scrymgeour, younger, and Robert Davidson, younger, are nominated to act (with advice of Sir Alexander Wedderburn), for the farming of the burgh excise. (202.) They report 20 July. (203.)

88. **1648.** Feb. 2.—The clerk and Mr. George Halyburton are elected commissioners to the coming parliament. (208.)

89. **1648.** May 16.—The clerk reports the public Acts lately concluded in parliament, viz. : the Act for putting the kingdom in a state of defence, and the Acts of levie, of maintenance, and for excise. (209)

90. **1648.** June 20.—The clerk reported that the burghs had adjourned their convention till the last Tuesday of August, and that he had obtained the tack of the exciseable goods of the burgh for behoof of the town, from 1st May last, for a year, at 900 merks. (210.)

91.   **1648.** Dec. 19.—The council take into their consideration that Sir Alexander Wedderburn of Blackness, their clerk, in obedience to the Acts of the committee of estates, of Sept. 22 and Oct. 4 last, and for other reasons moving him, did forbear the exercise of his clerkship among them, and with one voice they elect Thomas Wichtane, notary, burgess of Dundee, to the office of the clerkship thereof. (215.)

92.   **1648.** Dec. 19.—The council elect Mr. Peter Wedderburn, advocate, before the Lords, agent for the town for life, in the room of John Ramsay, who had resigned, at £46 13s. 4d. yearly. (216.)

93.   **1649.** Jan. 5, 23, 26.—Alexander Wedderburn, skipper, late shoremaster, is ordered to produce his shore accounts, which he does, and they are approved. (216-18.)

94.   **1650.** Dec. 11.—Andrew Wedderburn is chosen a stentar to raise four month's maintenance from the inhabitants. (232.)

95.   **1651.** Jan. 14.—Sir Alexander Wedderburn, common clerk of Dundee, with consent of the haill Council, and in virtue of a power granted by them, of providing a substitute, appoints Thomas Wichtane, notary in Dundee, to the office of clerkship, and to do everything incumbent thereto, as freely as Sir Alexander himself may do, during his absence, by virtue of an Act of the council of the burgh. (233.)

96.   **1651.** Jan. 14.—Compeared in presence of the council, David Tendill, collector of the crafts of the burgh, assisted by the haill Deacons, and declaired that it was their earnest desire that Sir Alexander Wedderburn of Blackness, Knight, should be reponed to his place of the clerkship of the burgh, which the council did think reasonable ; and they unanimously, with consent of the collectors and deacons, and of Thomas Wichtane, notary, lately appointed clerk, reponed Sir Alexander in the office of clerk of the burgh of Dundee, and to all dues belonging to the office. (234.)

97.   **1651.** Jan. 21.—A missive letter sent from the King's Majesty, written with his own hand, dated at Perth 17th inst., was produced, wherein he desires the re-establishment of the clerk to his place. The council order the letter to be laid up and preserved. (235.)

      See ante s. "Dundee Charters and Writs," No. 69, and the account of Sir Alexander, in Vol. i.

98.   **1651.** Oct. 7-8.—Alexander Wedderburn, elected a member of the council, for the merchants, accepts office. (240.)

99.   **1651.** Oct. 8.—The Council ordain the clerk and John Scrymgeour to go to Leith and deal with the commissioners for the parliament of England for reserving the common mills for the use of the burgh. (240.)

100.   **1651.** Oct. 21.—Alexander Wedderburn, merchant, counsellor, signs an act of council in favour of the treasurer, that in respect of the troublesome times and the English having now possessed themselves of the common good, he shall be paid for all sums of money he shall deburse, by warrant of the magistrates. The minister's stipends are not to be paid till the town's rents are recovered. (241.)

101.   **1652.** (a) Jan. 20.—The clerk and others are elected commissioners to go to Edinburgh and treat for the recovery of the town's public revenues. (b) Feb. 3.—They make their report of the particulars entrusted to them to settle at Edinburgh, which the council approve. (242.)

102:   **1652.** Feb. 3.—The clerk and William Duncan are ordained to go to the presbytery and supplicate their aid in supplying the diets of preaching. (242.)

103.   **1652.** Feb. 14.—Before a full council and many burgesses, the clerk produces an order (21 Jan) from the English commissioners requiring them to elect persons to go to Dalkeith on the 23rd inst. and receive the declarations of the intentions of the

parliament of the commonwealth of England. The council unanimously elect Si^r **Dundee** Alexander Wedderburn, clerk, and Robert Davidson, treasurer, and draw up their **Council** commission, in which Sir Alexander is described as "on persone of integritie and good **Books.** affection to the weelfair and peace of this Island." (242.)

104. **1562.** May 8 —Mr. Peter Wedderburn, writer, is nominated to be employed to pursue for the teinds of Forgan. (245.)

      The word "writer" is an error for "advocate." See ante No. 92, and the next entry.

105. **1652.** Nov. 23.—Mr. John Fletcher, advocate, is nominated advocate for the town during the absence in London of Mr. Peter Wedderburn, their ordinary agent. (249.)

      [See. in all, fol. 3, 5, 9-11, 15, 17, 22, 26, 27, 31, 33, 35, 36, 38-48, 51-60, 63-64, 66, 68, 72, 73, 75-76, 80, 83-86, 89-93, 95, 96, 98, 100, 102, 103, 104, 107-10, 113, 115, 120, 122, 126, 128-29, 132-33, 136-40, 142-46, 149-50, 155, 158, 160, 162-67, 173, 180, 182-85, 187-88, 190-92, 194-95, 197-202, 205, 208-10, 215-18, 221, 232-35, 237, 239-47, 249, 253-55.]

VOL. 5.

1663—69.

106. **1663.** Nov. 12.—Alexander Wedderburn, provost, is often named. (3, 4, 5, 6, 7, 8, 9, 10, 11.)

107. **1664.** May 10.—Andrew Wedderburn is continued in the excise. See ante No. 94. (8.)

108. **1664.** Sep. 27, 29.—Alexander Wedderburn of Kingennie is nominated and re-elected provost, and takes the oaths of fidelity and allegiance. (11.) He is often named as present on the council 1664-65. (12, 13, 14, 15, 19-21, etc.)

109. **1664.** Dec. 26.—Andrew Wedderburn is ordained to surrender his accounts, which he does, and they are approved. (14-15.)

110. **1665.** May 10.—Sir Peter Wedderburn, Lord Nevay, and others, are proposed to arbitrate with the Laird of Bogie and the Duke of Hamilton, anent the differences between them and the town. The clerk (Sir Alexander Wedderburn) and George Brown, bailie, are, however, (May 30), elected to go to Edinburgh for this purpose. (18-19.)

111. **1665.** Sep 26, 28.—Alexander Wedderburn, of Kingennie, is again leeted and elected provost, and often named as such, 1665-66. (22-31.)

112. **1665.** Dec. 5.—Mr. George Mackenzie is elected to be the town's ordinary advocate in the place of John Wedderburn demitted. The yearly pension for life is £46 13s. 4d. Scots. (24).

113. **1667.** Oct. 29.—Ex-provost Wedderburne demands payment of 3000 merks principal due to him by the town and it is ordered to be paid out of the excise at Martinmas. (43.)

114. **1667.** Dec. 12.—A letter is produced from Sir Peter Wedderburn, desiring the council to send their subscriptions to a declaration to be recorded, and (1668 Jan. 7) there is a note of its being recorded and payment therefor to Sir Peter of six rex dollars. (44.)

      [See, in all, fol. 3-22, 24-25, 31, 43-44, s. dates :—1663. Nov. 12, 17, 24 ; Dec. 7, 8, 10, 22, 29.— 1664. Jan. 5, 11, 12 ; Feb. 1, 9, 23 ; April 19 ; May 3, 10, 17, 31 ; June 7, 14, 21 ; Aug. 2, 13, 23, 30 ; Sept. 20, 27, 29 ; Oct. 11, 25 ; Nov. 1. 29 ; Dec. 6, 26.—1665. Jan. 3, 10, 17, 24, 31 ; Feb. 28 ; March 16, 21, 28 ; April 3, 11, 18, 25 ; May 10, 17, 23, 30 ; June 6, 15, 20 ; Aug. 4, 17, 21, 22 ; Sept. 5, 21, 26, 23 ; Dec. 6.—1666. Jan. 9, 11, 16, 20 ; Feb. 6, 20, 27 ; March 6, 20, 27 ; April 10, 24 ; May 8, 15 ; June 5, 19, 26 ; July 31 ; Aug 9, 28 ; Sept. 1, 18, 25, 27 —1667. Oct. 29 ; Dec. 12.—1668. Jan. 7. Most of these references are merely to the presence on the council of Alexander Wedderburn of Easter Powrie, who was provost 1660-66, and an active member of the council, when ex-provost, in 1667.]

VOL. 6.

1669--1707.

A large folio volume of 540 closely written leaves.

115. **1669.** Sept. 21.—Andrew Wedderburn is named as stentar or collector of cess, vicarage, and burgh maills, and often thereafter till 13 Oct. 1670. (3, 5, 8, 9, 11, 12. 15.)

116. **1670.** Dec. 6.—A decision of Sir Peter Wedderburn of Gosfoord, senator of the College of Justice, is mentioned. (17.) **1671.** March 14.—Lord Gosfoord and others give an opinion. (20.)

117. **1671.** April 20.—The provost, bailies, council and deacons of crafts considering the earnest desire of Sir Alexander Wedderburn, their common clerk, on account of his frequent sicknesses, that James Wedderburn, his second son, who had formerly the gift of the clerkship, might be admitted conjunct clerk, and to succeed his father therein after his decease, unanimously consent thereto. The act of James Wedderburn's admission has twenty-six signatures, but these do not include anyone of his name. (22.)

118. **1675.** May 18.—The magistrates report that they found the tenants of Blackness pasturing on the "Magdalen Zaird," and lawfully expelled them. (70.)

    A dispute as to the respective rights of the town and the Wedderburn lairds of Blackness in the Magdalen Yard continued for some time. In 1678 (Feb. 7) it was reported to the Council by their officials that the soil belonged to the town, subject to Blackness' right of way over it and pasturage thereon. Three years later, 1681 (Dec. 27), however, Blackness "extracted a decreet" in Edinburgh declaring that the soil was his, subject to the right of the town to walk and rendezvous thereon, and on this the town seems to have taken out a summons of reduction. Eventually, 1683 (June 12), the differences were referred to Sir John Cunningham, with what result does not appear. (This matter is referred to at fol. 81, 82, 84, 90, 92, 95-99, 105, 152, 154, 171, 408.)

119. **1676.** March 7.—The council approve of James Pilmor as clerk depute to the burgh, presented to them by Sir Alexander Wedderburn and James Wedderburn, principal clerks, "ad vitam aut culpam," or during the council's pleasure. (80.)

120. **1676.** March 22 —Complaint to the council by Walter Ogilvy that a horse he had pasturing in the Magdalen Zaird was driven off by John Wedderburn of Blackness, upon which the council, considering that Blackness has no right to the yard, order it to be proclaimed by the drum through the town that no one is to pasture animals there, but that it is to remain as a recreation ground for the inhabitants and their children. (81.)

121. **1676.** Dec. 28.—Alexander Wedderburn of Easter Powrie, is unanimously elected provost. (91.)

122. **1677.** (a) March 1.—Andrew Wedderburn is admitted conjunct writer with John Watsone, and takes his oath of fidelitie. (92.) (b) James Wedderburn, clerk of the burgh, signs an act of council. (ib.)

123. **1677.** May 15.—James Wedderburn, common clerk, complains v. Thomas Anderson, merchant, for having at a court held last Monday used opprobrious speeches against the clerk and his predecessors, saying that they had made false instruments without ground or warrant, so taking away their good name, which rase, lase, and opprobrious speech Anderson, being charged, admits, whereupon he is amerciat in an unlaw of 100 merks scots, and decerned to remain in the tolbooth till payment, and then either to compear in a court of the magistrates and sit down upon his knees and acknowledge his transgression, and crave pardon for the same, and promise never to do the like hereafter, or else to stay in prison. (96.)

124. **1677.** Sept. 27.—Alexander Wedderburn of Easter Powrie, is leeted and elected provost. (100.)

125. **1678.** Jan. 28.—The council consider a petition of John Wedderburn of Blackness, for a convenient seat in the Church for himself and family, reciting that when the seats were erected in the East Church he was obliged to take one not very convenient, which was now altogether inadequate owing to the increase of his family and to his brother, the clerk, having half of it, wherefore he craves to be allowed, from his interest in the parish, to build a seat for himself in the West church and affix the same to a pillar there opposite the pulpit. The council order the Dean of Guild and Kirkmaster to view the ground and report. (104.)

  This petition was granted, as later on Blackness asked to be allowed to add to his seat. See post No. 145. He erected a seat in the southern portion of the church of S. Mary (destroyed by fire in 1841), where the words "Master John Wedderburne of Blackness, 1667" (the year of his marriage), together with his arms. were formerly legible on one of the pillars of the west wall. See James Thomson's "Ecclesiastical Antiquities of Dundee" (1830), p. 10, where the arms are given as "Argent a chevron between three eagles' heads, erased sable, crest, an eagle's head erased of the same. Motto obliterated." This is, of course, an error, due probably to the bearings not being clear. The arms must have been the chevron between three roses, possibly painted in black, and not attempting to show the true tinctures.

126. **1678.** Sept. 24, 28.—Alexander Wedderburn of Easter Powrie, is again leeted and elected provost. Peter Wedderburn, merchant, is chosen counsellor. (111-12.)

127. **1679.** June 9.—The council, in accordance with a former Act. settle their nightly guard from all invasion of enemies. intestine and foreign. Peter Wedderburn is named captain of the Overgait. (124.)

128. **1679.** June 28.—The council nominate Alexander Wedderburn of Easter Powrie, provost, to be commissioner at the next general convention of the burghs at Edinburgh, on the first Tuesday in July, and John Scrymgeour, bailie, to be his assessor. (125.)

129. **1679.** Sept. 23, 25.—Alexander Wedderburn of Easter Powrie, is again leeted and elected provost. (127-28.)

130. **1680.** Sept. 21, 23.—Alexander Wedderburn of Easter Powrie, is re-elected provost. (139-40.)

131. **1680.** Sept. 28.—Peter Wedderburn is elected councillor to the guild, and takes the oath of fidelity. (140.)

132. **1681.** Feb. 21.—Mr. George Gray is nominated clerk depute by Mr. James Wedderburn in virtue of the power granted him by his gift of clerkship, in case of absence or sickness, with the special consent of the council, who appoint Gray their procurator fiscal. (146.)

133. **1682.** Aug. 4.—The council appoint a committee to treat with Blackness for the purchase from him of Logie for the hospital, and (9 May) the committee report that they had agreed with him for 17,500 merks, but that the hospital master declined the agreement. The council (11 May) approve it. (158-60, 164.)

134. **1682.** Sept. 19.—Mr. James Wedderburn, with the approbation of the council, nominates Mr. Hugh Paipe to be his depute, and supply his place as clerk in his absence or sickness, in virtue of the power granted him in his gift of clerkship. (163.)

135. **1684.** Oct. 14.—Similar nomination of James Ramsay, as clerk depute. (183.)

136. **1685.** (a) Feb. 10.—The council adjourn the consideration of the admission of Alexander Wedderburn, eldest son of James Wedderburn, common clerk, to be conjunct clerk with his father during his lifetime and to the benefit thereof after his death, reserving power to the council to present someone to serve in his office during his minority, after his father's death, for whom they shall be answerable. (185.) (b) Feb. 17.—The matter is again adjourned. (185.) (c) March 5.—The council taking into consideration the earnest desire of James Wedderburn, their clerk, that

Alexander Wedderburn, his eldest son, should succeed him in the office of clerkship after his father's demission or death, think the same most reasonable and do receive him to be their clerk after such death and ordain a gift of the clerkship to be drawn out in his favour, subject to their right to choose their own depute during his minority, if the said James Wedderburn die during it.   In this event the depute is to have half the benefit of the office. (186.)

137.   **1689-90**. Alexander Wedderburn not designed, is often named as on the council, auditor of accounts, captain of the Seagate, &c. (243-48, 263-267.)

138.   **1693**. April 11.—Alexander Duncan, of Lundie, desiring the liberty of burying the deceist Anna Drummond, his lady, in the west side of the Howff betwixt the head rowme of umquhile James Wedderburn, sometime Dean of Gild, at the South, and the head rowme of umquhile James Malcome at the North, and the West Dyke of the Howff on the west, receives permission to bury her and others of his family in time coming there, and to erect a monument thereon, he noways incroatching on the head rownes and properties of others next adjacent thereto. (309.)

> The James Wedderburn here named was brother of Alexander Wedderburn, first of Kingennie, and died in 1644.   The elaborate monument erected by the Duncans of Lundie largely encroached on his "head rowme" in spite of the above condition.   See the chapter on the Howff of Dundee.

139.   **1695**. Jan. 28.—The council, considering the great trust reposed in the clerk's office, he having in his custody the whole registers of the burgh, and most important papers thereof, besides many papers belonging to the inhabitants, thought it expedient to order and regulate the clerk's chamber in the matter of servants, and of new nominate and appoint John Ramsay, clerk depute of the burgh. (329.)

140.   **1696**. (*a*) Jan. 14.—The council, considering that James Wedderburn, town clerk, was now deceased and that Alexander Wedderburn, his son, had a commission in his favour, but could not exercise it untill he was admitted and made faith "de fideli," ordained James Ramsay their clerk depute to serve till his admission. (344.) (*b*) The said Alexander Wedderburn compeared and accepted office and made faith "de fideli administration," took the the oath of allegiance, and subscribed the bond of assurance to his Majesty, and his admission was ordained to be further drawn up and also a "deputatione" to be drawn by him in favour of James Ramsay of the office of Clerk depute relative to the act of council of 28 Jan. 1695 (ante. No. 139), ratified in the head court on 1 April 1695. (344.)   The signing of the clerk's admission and James Ramsay's depute-ship is continued Jan. 25, Feb. 1, March 24, July 2. (344, 346, 349.)

141.   **1696**. Feb. 10.—The clerk intimated to the council that he had obtained a brief furth of the chancellary for serving him heir to his father, and seeing that James Ramsay, clerk depute, was now in Edinburgh, he, with consent of the council, appointed John Dick, writer in Dundee, to be clerk on the occasion of such service only. (344.)

142.   **1696**. Sept. 6.—The price of registering dispositions and other warrants of infeftment, inventories of rouping rolls, etc., is fixed at £1 10s. the first sheet, and 15s. each following sheet ; of which all shall pertain solely to the clerk, except one-third of the rouping rolls, which shall pertain to the depute. (353.)

> This entry does not name any members of the family, but is of interest as throwing light on the emoluments of the office of clerk, so long enjoyed by one or other of them.

143.   **1696-99**. The clerk (Alexander Wedderburn) is often named *re* the affairs of the burgh. (358, 361, 375, 376, 393, 401.)

144.   **1699**. Sept. 21.—The council consider a petition of Alexander Wedderburn, their clerk, showing that the office of the clerkship of the Barony of Hiltoun was vacant by the death of James Dick, clerk thereof, and desiring the office ; whereon they pass an act in his favour and appoint the trades to meet the next Tuesday to give their consent. (408.)

145. **1701.** Oct. 7.—Bailies Smith and Alison report that the ground which Blackness is craving for an addition to his seat in the West Church will prejudge no one, and the council sanction the addition at the sight of bailie Alison, kirkmaster. (455.) *Dundee Council Books.*

See ante No. 125. The original petition for a seat in the church had been granted, and Blackness was now seeking to add to his accommodation.

146. **1702.** Oct. 29.—The council propose to retire a bond given by the town to the Laird of Blackness, clerk to the bills. (475.)

147. **1703.** May 4.—The clerk presented his gift of clerkship, and desired that he might have freedom to make choice of his own depute, with consent of the council, conform to the tenor of his gift granted to him in 1685, and homolgate at his admission in 1696. (483.)

148. **1703.** May 11.—The council, considering the clerk's desire anent his clerkship, put it to the vote whether they should proceed to consider it or not, when it is carried to proceed, whereon seven bailies remove themselves furth of the council so that there was not a quorum, whereon the provost appoints the whole members of council and deacons of trades to assemble next Tuesday for that end. (483.)

See the account of Sir Alexander Wedderburn of Blackness, fourth baronet, in Vol. i. where I have dealt with his suit against James Ramsay, in which this very question of the right of the clerk to nominate his own depute was raised.

149. **1704.** Feb. 1.—The council grant two bonds, one to Alexander Wedderburn, younger, of Blackness, for 3,000 merks, and another to the clerk for 500 merks. (491.)

150. **1704.** Sept. 26.—The council appoint bailies Maxwell and Scott to speak to the Laird of Blackness as to his enclosing the march stones of the Magdalen yeard. (498.)

151. **1705.** March 6.—The council appoint the clerk to go over to Edinburgh to advise (i.e., look to) the town's affairs. (506.)

152. **1705.** Nov. 27.—Alexander Wedderburn, skipper, is lected and elected shoremaster, and accepts office. (517.)

153. **1706-7.** Alexander Wedderburn, mariner (or not designed), is often present in council. (518-27.)

154. **1706.** June 10.—In consideration of the good service done to the town by Alexander Wedderburn in getting "most part of the lands of Hilltown feued out and sold off, and for severall other good services done by him to the town this year, (the council) have quhyt and doe heirby quhyt and pass him from any composition for his entry to the lands of Clepington and discharge him for ever thereof." (531.)

155. **1706.** (a) Feb. 28.—The committee appointed to meet with James Kyd of Craigie, and Thomas Miln of Milnfield, about the sale of the lands of Logie, reported that the lairds of Craigie and Milnfield would give no more than the 17,500 merks formerly offered, which they now did in the name of Sir Alexander Wedderburn, of Blackness. . . . Whereon the council having considered Sir Alexander's offer for the said lands, unanimously approve it, and order a disposition by the town in his favour to be drawn up, with a clause of absolute warrandice. (b) March 21.—The council and deacons subscribe and deliver to Sir Alexander Wedderburn, of Blackness, a disposition of the lands of Logie, with the writs, except the town's charter under the Great Seal, to be delivered against the term of Whitsunday next, the price being 17,500 merks. (523-25.)

156. **1707.** April 9.—Alexander Wedderburn, skipper, is lected and elected shoremaster, and accepts the office. (539.)

[See, in all, fol. 3, 5, 8, 9, 11, 12, 14, 15, 17, 20, 22, 30, 38, 54, 58, 60, 70, 71, 73-75, 80-86, 89-93, 95-96, 99-101, 104-7, 111-12, 117-18, 120, 123-29, 139, 139-40, 144-50, 152, 154, 158-60, 163-66, 171, 183, 185-86, 240-41, 243, 248, 256, 260, 263, 267, 298, 305-6, 309, 329, 333, 344, 346, 349, 353, 358, 361, 375-76, 398, 401, 408, 415, 455, 464-65, 470, 475, 477, 480, 482-83, 485, 491, 497-98, 500, 502, 506, 514, 517-18, 520, 523-25, 527-33, 536-40.]

2 R

Vol. 7.

This is merely a duplicate of fol. 391-495 of Vol. vi (1699-1704).

Vol. 8.

The first sixty leaves of this volume merely repeat fol. 495 540 (1704-1707) of Vol. vi.

157.   **1707-8.**—Alexander Wedderburn, mariner, repeatedly present in council. (62-95.)

158.   **1707.** Sept. 16.—Alexander Wedderburn, shoremaster, has his accounts audited. (73.)

159.   **1708.** March 13.—The council having considered a method for the defence of the town in regard to an apparent invasion by the French being then on the coast, order all gunpowder and shot in the town to be brought into the town's magazine, and for that end appoint Alexander Wedderburn, skipper, and John Taylor to search the town. . . . They also, in case of necessity for arming the inhabitants, make choice of officers for the respective streets, including the said Alexander Wedderburn as captain for the Nethergate. (93.)

160.   **1708.** Sept. 28.—Alexander Wedderburn, skipper, elected shoremaster, compears (Oct. 23) and declares he cannot accept office, unless the council appoint a deputie to act when his health cannot allow him or his business calls him abroad. A week later (Oct. 30) he accepts office. (107-108.)

161.   **1709.** (a) Jan. 13.—A committee of four bailies is appointed to commune with Blackness anent the burial place craved by him in the Cross church. (112.) (b) The said committee report, whereon the council give and grant to Sir Alexander and his heirs the privilege of that part of the Cross church for the space of 14 feet from the west window, towards the Rollo's head room, and from the South to the North wall, for a burial place to him and his heirs, with power to the said Sir Alexander to lay the ground of the said burial place with pavement, and to sett up a lifting rail from the South to the North wall, which rail is to have a door for a communication to the rest of the Cross church, and is to be removed when the council or kirkmaster shall have occasion for the same; as also with power to the said Sir Alexander to sett up a monument on the wall of the said burial place: for which causes Sir Alexander binds himself and his heirs to pay to the kirkmaster 50 merks for each person buried at or above twelve years; and if at any time hereafter there be Divine service in the said Cross church, he binds himself and his heirs to erect and build a seat on the said burial place, by and attour the payments of the said sums for each person buried at the ages sett down. (114.)

162.   **1709.** (a) June 7.—Reported that Blackness will not subscribe the tack of the muck; therefore he is to be proceeded against according to law. (122.) (b) June 14.—The clerk reports that he has Blackness' order to subscribe the tack on his behalf, but the council will not accept the clerk's signature without Blackness' written order, and meanwhile adjourn extracting decreet. (123.) (c) June 18.—The clerk produces the necessary letter, which is approved, and the contract signed (June 21). (123, 125.)

For this letter, see post s. Dundee Deeds, No. 77.

163.   **1709.** June 14.—It being reported that Blackness' servants had removed a march stone in the Magdalen yaird, with the town's arms thereon, and that the servants confessed it was done at Blackness' special order, the council take instruments that it shall not prejudge their right, and consider whether Blackness shall be pursued therefor or not. (123, 125, 127.)

164.   **1709.** Sept. 27, 29.—Alexander Wedderburn, skipper, is leeted and elected bailie, and accepts office Oct. 4. (128-29.) He is often named thereafter as bailie. (129, 130, 136, 137, 142.)

165.   **1710.** July 6.—Alexander Wedderburn, clerk, produced his gift of clerkship, empowering him to nominate a depute with consent and approbation of the council,

which, being read, he, with such consent, makes choice of John Dick, writer, to be his depute during his absence or sickness. (147.)

Dundee Council Books.

166. **1710.** Dec. 19, 21.—Alexander Wedderburn, clerk, purchases from the town, certain barns, houses, and yards, once Duncan Muir's, for 850 merks, and obtains a disposition thereof to himself and his son John. (160.)

167. **1710-12.** Alexander Wedderburn, bailie, is often named. (151-54, 160-63, 170-186.)

168. **1712.** Sept. 30.—Bailie Wedderburn is elected Kirkmaster. (203.) He is noted as absent Oct. 30 (204), and does not compear and accept office and take the oaths till Jan. 6, 1713. (218.) He is again elected in 1714. (250.)

169. **1715.** July 29.—Bailie Robertson represents to the council that he was informed of a modern invasion to be made by the pretender with a foreign force from parts beyond sea. The council appoint officers (but none of the name of Wedderburn) for the different streets. (266.)

[See, in all, fol. 60-62, 65, 69-71, 73-76, 86, 92-95, 100, 106-14, 121-23, 125, 127-30, 135-37, 142, 147, 151-54, 160-63, 170, 173, 175-78, 180-84, 186, 190, 192, 200, 201, 203, 204, 218, 228-30, 235-40, 242, 244, 249-50, 263, 266.]

VOL. 8A.

1716—42.

There is a slight break in the register from Aug 1, 1715, the last date in vol 8, to April 26, the first date in this volume. This is no doubt due to the share of the clerk in the rising of 1715. The folios of this volume are not numbered.

170. **1716.** April 26.—The council appoint the new and old bailies or such of them as can, to meet and call the councillors they think fit, for a committee to enquire anent an information given in by some of the inhabitants of the burgh against Alexander Wedderburn, clerk, anent his carriage during the rebellion.

171. **1716.** May 1.—Bailies Maxwell and Wardroper report that they and some of the councillors met and enquired anent Alexander Wedderburn's affair, and that William Gibb, maltman in Dundee. informed and offered to prove that Mr. Wedderburn, on Jan. 6 last, accompanied the Earls of Mar and Marshall and several gentlemen who who were in the rebellion to the Council House of the burgh, where they were getting a treat, and burgess tickets, and acted as clerk as well then as at the rouping of the petty customs under those who acted as magistrates in the rebellion; and that he went to the cross with the rebels at some of their solemnities, went out and met the Pretender at his coming to the town, and collected the excise the time of the rebellion, for behoof of the rebels.

See ante s. Dundee Charters, Writs, etc. No. 88.

172. **1716.** May 8.—Two burgess tickets are produced in evidence against Alexander Wedderburn, clerk, both dated 12 Jan. last, the one in favour of the therein designed James, Earl of Tinmouth. the other in favour of Col. Francis Bulkeley, both granted by the therein designed Sir Alexander Watson, provost, Mr. William Ramsay, dean of guild, and signed by Alexander Wedderburn. as clerk. The council recommend the provost to write to the Lord Justice Clerk relative to these tickets and the information against Mr. Wedderburn.

173. **1716.** July 10.—The council having clerk Wedderburn's business under consideration, appoint any person who has anything to say against him, to put it in writing and give in the same to the council next council day.

174. **1716.** July 14.—Subscribed information given in by William Gibb, maltman, in Dundee, against Alexander Wedderburn, clerk, of which the council order a double to be given to him that he may use and answer the same next council day.

175. **1716.** July 21.—The council, considering Alexander Wedderburn's affair, appoint the provost, bailies and dean of guild, a committee to write to the Justice Clerk

relative to it, and Thomas Dowie to go to Edinburgh with the letter, and get a return.

176.   **1716.** July 28.—Thomas Dowie reported to the council that he had been at Edinburgh and delivered the letter he had from the committee of the council to the Lord Justice Clerk anent Mr. Wedderburn, who said it was not proper for him to give advice, but the town might do as they thought proper with their own servants. . . . The council appoints Alexander Wedderburn to be cited by the council officer to appear before them on Tuesday eight days to answer to the information given in against him by William Gibb.

177.   **1716.** Aug. 7.—The council having considered that Clerk Wedderburn was only cited at his house, appoints him to be cited anew against Thursday next the 9th inst.

178.   **1716.** Aug. 9.—The council having under consideration the information given in to them by William Gibb, maltman in Dundee, against Alexander Wedderburn, clerk of the burgh, and he having been warned to compear last council day, but compeared not, and was (sic) again warned for this day, and not compearing, the council ordered Thomas Marshall, officer, to go and call Mr. Wedderburn presently to the council, who stated on his return that he had met with Mr. Wedderburn, who asked him if all the nine deacons of crafts of the burgh were present in council and in respect they were not all present, he refused to come, which being considered, and the burgess tickets produced granted by the late magistrates and signed by Mr. Wedderburn as clerk, particularly those formerly mentioned, and the council considering that Mr. Wedderburn is both sheriff depute and sheriff clerk of Forfar, which the council reckoned to be inconsistent to be in one person with the clerkship of Dundee, because of the difference betwixt the burgh and the shire anent their jurisdictions occasioned (sic) encroachments upon the town's privileges, and that he had refused to come to the council when cited, in respect of which the council found him culpable, and deposed him from being clerk of Dundee and of the barony of Hilltoun.

179.   **1716.** Oct. 8.—The council ratify and confirm the act passed (9 Aug.) by the magistrates in depriving Alexander Wedderburn, lately town clerk, from being clerk of the burgh of Dundee and barony of Hilltown; and Oct. 23, Mr. George Duncan, W.S., is chosen town clerk in room of Mr. Alexander Wedderburn.
This act is given ante s. Dundee Charters, Writs, etc. No. 88.

180.   **1717.** April 9.—Bailie Zeaman represented to the Council the information upon which Alexander Wedderburn, their late town clerk, had been deposed, and although he had no doubt that the evidence of Mr. Wedderburn's behaviour, upon which the magistrates proceeded, was sufficient to support their sentence, he did not understand why the information was not laid upon other facts more heinous, and how they had not cognosced upon the whole, lest it might afterwards be pretended that Mr. Wedderburn had been removed upon too slender grounds, and upon that head he should attempt to call the proceedings in question. He therefore proposed that Mr. Wedderburn might be again cited to compear before the magistrates in order to hear trial taken of other facts beside those contained in the information upon which the magistrates had formerly proceeded, and likewise of his being clerk to the council during the time of the rebellion, upon which the council ordained Mr. Wedderburn to appear before the provost and bailies on the 15, 17, and 22 April instant, to answer the complaint, &c. They also appoint the treasurer and convener to require the keys of the town's press, and papers, and, on his refusal, to take instruments against him and report.

181.   **1717.** April 30.—The provost and bailies to whom the taking of the probation was remitted, report that in obedience to their interloquitor of April 9, Mr. Wedderburn was cited but failed to compear, and that they had taken the oaths and depositions of several famous witnesses on other points in the complaint besides those already found proven, which they desired might be advised by the whole council, in respect of which the provost, bailies, and council, found Mr. Wedderburn culpable, and deposed him from being clerk of Dundee, &c., and ordained a process of declarator

to be raised and pursued at their instance, and that of George Duncan, their clerk, against Mr. Wedderburn for having it found and declared by the Lords of Council and Session that he was justly and legally deposed and George Duncan duly elected.

182. **1718.** Feb. 4.—Bailie Yeaman represented that on the process of exhibition and delivery at the instance of the town and their clerk before the Lords of Council and Session *v.* Alexander Wedderburn, late clerk, for exhibition and delivery of the records, &c., in his hands belonging to the town, the Lords, by their interlocutor (14 Jan. last), ordained Mr. Wedderburn to exhibit and deliver to the magistrates, or their present clerk, the haill books, &c., upon inventary and receipt, against the 1st of February, and thereafter to compear before the said Lords and depone how far he had exhibited and delivered up the same, upon the 10th February, which he had not done, and the council empowers Bailie Yeaman to require Mr. Wedderburn to exhibit and deliver the records, &c., libelled, and to protest upon the non-delivery and upon delivery to grant receipt thereof and to require Mr. Wedderburn to depone.

183. **1718.** Feb. 11.—Bailie Yeaman reported that he went to Alexander Wedderburn's house on the 5th inst., and required him personally to deliver up the books and writs belonging to the town, which he promised to do in the afternoon, but failed to do so, and, therefore, the bailie went to his house next day with the same request, but he was not at home.

[Between this date and 6th May, 1736, there are no entries of importance relating to Wedderburns.]

184. **1736.** May 6.—On the occasion of the Prince of Wales' late marriage, Blackness and other gentlemen are invited to the town house to drink a "health," in addition to which four healths are to be drunk at the cross, to which Lord Colville is invited.

185. **1736.** July 20.—The council accept the offer of Mrs. Catharine Wedderburn to take one of the shops under the town house, and appoint to her that on the east side of the entry to the town house.

186. **1737.** (*a*) June 23.—Petition by John Wedderburn, younger, of Blackness, craving the council to allow him to build an office in any place they should think proper upon the wall which separates the churchyard from the School Wynd; which matter is referred to a committee. (*b*) Dec. 20.—The said petition and the committee's report being read, the council, instruct the clerk to prepare a disposition in the petitioner's favour of a piece of ground 14 ft. by 6 ft., immediately to the west of the steeple, he paying 3^d/4^d scots feu duty yearly to the kirk fabric, and covenanting to keep the office in good order. The disposition is signed 2 Jan. 1738.

187. **1738** Feb. 4, 16.—A process by David Wedderburn, of that ilk *v.* the tenants of South Clepington, &c., for abstracting the multures of Baldovan is mentioned, and Mr. David Scrymgeour of Birkhill, advocate, is briefed for the town, subject to his declining on the ground of his being "a near relation to Mr. Wedderburn."

188. **1739.** Sept. 17.—Robert Pitcairn, collector of the twopenny per pint, informs the council that Sir Alexander Wedderburn, collector of the excise, refused to give out any more extracts thereof, unless he got five guineas as formerly paid him. Subsequently, the town raise a process against Sir Alexander.

189. **1740.** July 16.—The provost informs the council that in regard to the town's claim *v.* Blackness for cess of his house in the town, he knew that Mr. John Wedderburn, his son, was his cautioner, and that his affairs not being in a good condition, it was needless to insist on it.

190. **1741.** Oct. 26.—The council considering that there is a decreet of exhibition obtained at the instance of the town against Blackness for delivery of papers in his hands belonging to the town, and that the same have never yet been delivered up, do authorize George Lyon, dean of Guild, and the clerk, to call for the papers from Sir Alexander Wedderburn, or any in his name, who may have the custody of them, and grant a receipt for them when delivered up.

191.   **1742.** Feb. 18.—The clerk reported to the council that he had now got from
Blackness the haill papers that were in his hands belonging to the town, and that
they were in readiness to be put up in the town's press, of which the council did
approve.

See, in all, s. dates:—1716. April 26 ; May 1, 8 ; July 10, 14, 21, 28 ; Aug. 7, 9 ; Oct. 8, 23, 30 ;
Dec. 25.—1717. April 9, 30 ; June 22 ; Nov. 5, 14 ; Dec. 17.—1718. Feb. 4, 11 ; May 1, 6 ; July 17.—
1724. June 2.—1727. June 23.—1735. June 5.—1736. May 6 ; June 15 ; July 20.—1737. June 28 ;
July 16 ; Dec. 20.—1738. Jan. 2 ; Feb. 4, 16 ; April 20 ; Aug. 2 ; Sep. 26 ; Oct. 9.—1739. Sep. 17 ;
Oct. 8, 24 ; Nov. 20 ; Dec 31.—1740. Feb. 9 ; March 3 ; May 26 ; June 28 ; July 14, 16 ; Sep. 6, 15.
—1741. Oct. 26.—1742. Feb. 18 ; Aug. 18 ; Nov 20.]

Vol. 9.

1743—55.

192.   **1750.** Aug. 21.—The council appoint David Jobson to pay to Mr. Wedderburn the
money in his hands received for quartering officers.

193.   **1753** May 28.—Petition by Elizabeth, Grizel, and Clementina Wedderburn, lawful
daughters of the late Alexander Wedderburn, shipmaster in Dundee, craving the
council would find that the property of a seat in the old church belonged to them, as
against William Guthrie of Clepington, who claimed it.   Referred to the Kirkmaster.

[See, in all, s. dates:—1748. Dec. 12.—1750. Aug. 21 ; Nov. 6—1753. May 28 ; Aug. 14 ; Sep. 17.]

Vol. 10.

1756—67.

194.   **1763.** Aug. 24.—Petition by Alexander Wedderburn craving that he might be
admitted into the hospital ; which is granted.

195.   **1764.** Feb. 27.—Petitions by Alexander Wedderburn and others to have their
pensions augmented, which is done.

[See, in all, s. dates : —1756. Dec 13.—1763. Aug. 24.—1764. Feb. 27.—1765. Oct. 7.]

Vol. 11.

1767-1779.

This volume contains no reference to Wedderburns.

Vol 12.

1779—93.

196.   **1779.** Nov. 29.—The council considering that by some late alteration in the
circumstances of Alexander Wedderburn, at present a pensioner on the Hospital
funds, he is no longer an object of charity, appoint him to be struck off the list of
pensioners.

Vol. 13.

1793-1805

This volume has been searched to 1800, but contains, so far, no references to Wedderburns.

THE REGISTER OF DEEDS.

This record runs from 1626-47 somewhat irregularly, and then from 1661 down to the present time. It has been searched from its commencement up to 1801. These years are contained in 43 volumes, numbered doubly, 1-43 and also 448-490, the former numbers referring to the particular register and the latter to all the volumes in the Dundee charter room. The original of many of the deeds registered in these books are preserved in some large drawers in the charter room, which also contain a few documents which are not registered. Six of these drawers have been searched.[1] Their contents are as follows :—

1. { 1634-45. 5 documents.
   { 1651-1710, 58 bundles.
2. 1711-42, 32 bundles.
3. 1743-63, 21 bundles.

4. 1764-83, 20 bundles.
5. 1784-96, 13 bundles.
6. 1796 on (searched to 1800).

Where the original of a document exists the reference is given to drawer and bundle, as well as to the volume and folio (or date) of the register. Thus, the addition of Orig. i, 51, signifies that the original document is in drawer i, bundle 51.

VOL. 1.

1626–47.

1. **1627.** July 3.[2] Discharge (28 May, 1626) by David Smairt to Patrick Wedderburn, elder, and Alexander Wedderburn, his eldest son and apparent heir, of a bond registered in Books of Council and Session, 5 June, 1616. James Wedderburn, bailie.

   The bond is registered in Gibson's office. See the extract given from that record, post, s. Public Records, Register of Deeds.

2. **1628.** July 28.—Sasine (3 March 1628) under the hand of Mr. Alexander Wedderburn, clerk, cited.

3. **1633** Dec. 5. – Before the provost and bailies, Mr. John Dunmuir, procurator fiscal, produces an act of the King's Council (7 Nov.), signed by Sir John Hay, Clk. Reg., as warrant to the provost, &c., to transume four protocol books of the late Mr. Alexander and Mr. James Wedderburn, clerks of Dundee, as also the sasines to which Mr. Alexander was notary, inserted in his book by his servant Thomas Fyiff (31 Dec., 1619—6 March, 1624) and those to which Mr. James was notary, and mostly written by him (29 June, 1610—9 May, 1622) or by his servant, 38 leaves in all ; as also another book (15 leaves, 15 May, 1626—30 March, 1627.) All the copies are to be signed by the then clerk, Mr. Alexander Wedderburn, younger.

   There are fifteen protocol books of Kingennie, or of his substitutes, still extant, but only one of his son James. (See ante p. 207.) It does not appear which are the four to be transumed. Of the three books named in the latter half of the extract, two are Nos. 267 (1610-22) and 268 (1619-24), while the third (1626-27) is not now extant.

4. **1634.** Nov. 19.—Bond (12 Dec, 1631) to Mr. Alexander Wedderburn, clerk, of Dundee, called, in the margin, "elder, of Kingeunie."

5. **1636.** June 22.—Bond by Margaret Couper and another to Euphame Wedderburn, relict of Archibald Blyth, sometime skipper, burgess of Dundee.

---

[1] The following is a list of such of the bundles preserved in the drawers of the Charter Room, as contain original documents relating to Wedderburns :—Drawer I.—Bundles 2, 7, 10, 12, 13, 17-28, 31. 32, 34, 35, 38-42. 44-58. II.—1, 2, 5, 8, 13. 16, 17, 19, 21, 23, 24, 27, 29, 32. III.—3, 4, 9, 10. 13. 14, 21. IV.—3, 6, 9, 13. V.—1, 2, 3, 4, 7. 9. 12, 13.

[2] These are the dates of registration ; where the actual date is of value it is given in the extract.

6. **1636.** Nov. 9.—Ratification (15 Sept. 1636) naming the lands of the late Patrick Wedderburn, now of Mr. Alexander Wedderburn, as a boundary in South Marketgate.

7. **1636.** May 31.—Disposition witnessed by Andrew Wedderburn in Burntisland.

8. **1636.** March 18.—Obligation to James Wedderburn, merchant, burgess.

9. **1648.** June 4.—Bond by Wm. Stevenson to Alexander Wedderburn, skipper. (Orig. i, 2. Not registered.)

> [See, in all, s. dates :—**1626.** June 7.—**1627.** July 3.—**1628.** June 12 ; July 14, 28.—**1633.** Aug. 31 ; Dec. 5.—**1634.** Jan. 26 ; Feb. 17 ; Nov. 19, 26.—**1635.** June 30.—**1636.** June 22 ; Nov. 9.— **1637.** Jan. 28 ; May 31 ; Oct. 28.—**1639.** Jan. 31 ; Feb. 17 ; March 18.—**1640.** April 1 ; Dec. 7, 12.— **1641.** July 29.—**1642.** Feb. 22 ; March 15 ; April 1, 25.—**1644.** Oct. 1.—**1646.** Nov. 17.]

Vol. 2.

1661—70.

10. **1662.** June 8.—Procuratory by Alexander Wedderburn of Kingennie, provost, to John Hastie, writer. Alexander Wedderburn, his eldest son, witness. (Orig. i, 10. Not registered.)

11. **1663.** March 11.—Bond to Sir Alexander Wedderburn of Blackness, Knight.

12. **1664.** June 10.—Factory by Patrick Kyd of Craigie with consent of Sir Alexander Wedderburn of Blackness and John Wedderburn, his eldest son and apparent heir.

13. **1665.** May 11.— Disposition (19 Aug. 1648) by Alexander Wedderburn of Kingennie to Thomas Scott of a large burghal tenement, in West Marketgait, once belonging to Charles Goldman and John Ramsay, reciting the death of John Wedderburn, second son to Alexander Wedderburn of Kingennie by Elizabeth Ramsay, and that Alexander Wedderburn, younger, is his only brother and heir. (Orig. i, 13.)

14. **1667.** Jan. 25.—Discharge (20 April 1665) witnessed by Andrew Wedderburn, merchant, burgess.

15. **1667.** Dec. 26.—Obligation (31 Dec. 1661) by James Kyd of Craigie to his younger sons, William and Thomas, reciting the marriage contract (15 Aug. 1655) of Patrick Kyd, his eldest son, and Margaret Wedderburn, eldest daughter of Sir Alexander Wedderburn, of Blackness, clerk of Dundee, by which the lands of Grange of Barrie, co. Forfar, were settled on Patrick and his heirs male. Agnes Clayhills, wife of James Kyd, is named in the document.

16. **1669.** March 22.—Bond to John Wedderburn, baxter, 11 May 1668. (Orig. i, 17.)

17. **1670.** Oct. 28.—Indenture (12 Nov. 1669) apprenticing James Aimer to John Wedderburn, baxter, for three years. (Orig. i, 18.)

> [See, in all, s. dates :—**1662.** May 6.—**1663.** March 11.—**1664** Feb. 1, 12 ; April 1 ; June 10, 30.— **1665.** May 11 ; Sept. 26.—**1667.** Jan. 25 ; Dec. 26.—**1668.** Feb. 12 ; March 20 ; June 3.—**1669.** March 22 ; Dec. 23.—**1670.** Jan. 21 ; July 22 ; Oct. 28.]

Vol. 3.

1671-77.

18. **1671.** Feb. 2.—Bond (11 Aug. 1669) of Margaret Bruce, relict of Mr. James Reid of Pitlethie, witnessed at Pitlethie by Mr. Alexander Wedderburn in Fordell.

19. **1671.** Aug. 10.—Tack. (1 Nov. 1667) of all and whole the lands of Kingennie, with the house and biggings, lying on the north side of the close of the town and lands of Kingennie, byres, stables, &c., lying in the parish of Moneyfeith and sheriffdom of

Forfar, granted by Alexander Wedderburn, younger, of Kingennie, to Alexander Maeliane in Kingennie, as the same was then possessed by him, for three years, for payment of three chalders victual, whereof twenty bolls to be bear and twenty-eight bolls oats, 300 merks money, a dozen capons and seven dozen poultry, at the terms stated, and relieving the landlord of the payment of vicarage duty and schoolmaster's stipend. (Orig. i, 19.)

20. **1672.** April 5.—Tack. (5 April 1665) by Sir Alexander Wedderburn of Blackness, Knt., proprietor of the lands, to Patrick Barryne of the town and lands of Dargo, parish of Endergavie, eo. Perth, for nine years, at £100 a year for the first six and £160 for the last three years, and a dozen of capons and hens at the terms of payment.

21. **1674.** July 19.—Obligation by John Graham of Craigie, to Doctor George Wedderburn for 400 merks. Dated at Craigie, 26 June, 1665. (Orig. i, 22, not registered, though noted as registered, 16 July 1674.)

   This document presents a difficulty. I find no other mention either of a Doctor George Wedderburn or of any George Wedderburn who could well be a party to this bond. George Wedderburn, son of Sir Alexander of Blackness, was born in 1654, and was, therefore, but eleven years old at this date; while Dr. John Wedderburn of Moravia died before 1654 (see ante D.B.R. 463), so that the document cannot be explained by supposing the name George to be an error for John. An error in the surname is possible, but not very likely.

22. **1675.** Dec. 2.—Two discharges witnessed by James Wedderburn, clerk of Dundee.

23. **1676.** Aug. 20.—Factory by Alexander Wedderburn of Easter Powrie, John Wedderburn of Blackness, Patrick Kyd of Craigie, Alexander Wedderburn of Kingennie, James Wedderburn, clerk of Dundee, curators to James Kyd, eldest son of the late William Kyd of Woodhill, to Andrew Young, to collect the Woodhill rents.

   [See, in all, s. dates :—1671. Jan. 6, 31 ; Feb. 2 ; Aug. 10.—1672 April 5.—1675. May 31 ; Aug. 2 ; Nov. 10 ; Dec. 2.—1676. May 6 ; Aug. 2, 20.—1677. March 22.—1678. Aug. 20 ; Nov. 22 ; Dec. 5.]

VOL. 4.

1677—80

The folios of this and the following volumes are numbered.

24. **1677.** May 12.—Discharge by Alexander Wedderburn of Easter Powrie, provost, and by John Wedderburn of Blackness, to Elizabeth Ogilvy and George Crokat, her spouse, of payment of an annual-rent, payable as to one half, to the said Alexander, as heir and representative of Alexander Wedderburn, deceased, merchant, burgess, and Elizabeth Wedderburn, his daughter, and as to the other half, to John Wedderburn, as assignee of Barten Belsone. (14.)

25. **1677.** Nov. 1.—Bond (1677, June 1), by Robert Lindsay, merchant, burgess, of Dundee, to Alexander Wedderburn of Kingennie, witnessed by John Wedderburn of Blackness and Peter Wedderburn, merchant, burgess, of Dundee. (36. Orig. i, 25.)

26. **1677.** Dec. 4.—Disposition (1676, Jan. 28), by Andrew Wedderburn, merchant, burgess, to himself and his wife, Christian Duncan, of an Overgate house. (41. Orig. i. 26.)

27. **1678.** Aug. 13.—Disposition (1660, July 18), by George Fletcher, bailie, of a tenement in favour of Andrew Wedderburn, merchant, burgess, and Christian Duncan, his spouse, in life-rent, and in case of their having a child, or children, then to the heir among such children. (58. Orig. i, 26.)

28. **1679.** July 17.—Discharge by James Wedderburn, clerk, and Elizabeth Davidson, his wife, to Alexander Duncan of Lundie, and Robert Davidson of Balgay, executors to Margaret Davidson, of a £100 left to the spouses by the testatrix. (79. Orig. i, 27.)

   The original has the signatures of the clerk and his wife.

2 s

29.   **1680.** April 8, 19.—Disposition (1675, Dec. 1) of one fourth of the ship " William "
to Peter Wedderburn, merchant burgess of Dundee (112. Orig. i, 28), and also
(1675, Dec. 4) of one eighth of the said ship to George Wedderburn, merchant in
Edinburgh. (116. Orig. i, 28.)

30.   **1680.** July 6.—Factory (1680, April 17) by Peter Wedderburn, merchant, burgess, to
his " very weell beloved spouse Katharine Man," to uplift his rents, &c. (124.)

     [See, in all, fol. 9, 12, 14, 15, 28, 36, 41, 58, 74, 79, 110, 112, 116, 124.]

VOL. 5.

1680—83.

31.   **1681.** July 16.—Discharge by Mr. Alexander Gibsone of Pentland, a clerk of Council
and Session, tutor to Thomas, son of the late Sir John Gibsone of Pentland, to
Alexander Wedderburn of Kingennie, of a bond (5 and 10 June 1676) granted by
him, as principal, and by his father, Alexander Wedderburn of Easter Powrie, and John
Wedderburn of Blackness, as cautioners, to the said Sir John Gibsone, his wife
Elizabeth Thomsone, and their son the said Thomas. (114.)

     This discharge is again registered in the same volume on 21 Dec. 1653. (585, Orig i, 31.)

32.   **1681.** Nov. 25.—Alexander Wedderburn of Easter Powrie is a commissioner of
excise for Forfar. (160.)

     [See, in all, fol. 6, 13, 41, 57, 114, 116, 160, 247, 258, 264, 272, 379, 400, 443, 460, 585.]

VOL. 6.

1684—87.

Inside the last leaf of this book is written, " This book belongs to James Wedderburne, tonue clerk
of Dundie, Ja: Wedderburne."

33.   **1684.** Feb. 21.—Bond (4 Feb. 1684) in which the land of the heirs of the late
Alexander Wedderburn of Easter Powrie is named. (12.)

34.   **1684.** July 14.—Factory (28 May 1684) by George Wedderburn, merchant burgess
in Edinburgh, to David Ross to sell the Overgate house lately belonging to Alexander
Wedderburn, his brother, made on account of the said George Wedderburn's abode in
Edinburgh and business there, which prevent his coming to Dundee. (63, Orig. i, 32.)

35.   **1686.** Jan. 27.—Charter (1 Aug. 1685) witnessed by Peter Wedderburn, merchant.
(239.)

36.   **1686.** Nov. 19.—Factory (1 June 1686) by Alexander Wedderburn, skipper, in
Dundee, to his wife Christian Kinloch, to uplift his rents. (416. Orig. i, 34.)

37.   **1687.** Dec. 17.—Factory (31 Aug. 1687) by George Wedderburn, bailie of Edinburgh,
tutor of law to Alexander and John Wedderburn, children of the deceased Peter
Wedderburn, merchant in Dundee, his brother german, given to John Hastic, writer
in Dundee, to collect the pupils' rents, &c. (559. Orig. i, 35.)

     [See, in all, fol. 12, 20, 32, 68, 339, 358, 416, 472, 491, 541, 552, 559.]

VOL. 7.

1688—91.

38.   **1690.** March 28.—James Wedderburn, the clerk, signs a factory (25 March 1690)
by the town to William Dunbar in Harlaw Sheills to despatch all packets and expresses
the length of Burntisland or elsewhere, as they shall be directed, with men and
horses, according to the Act of the Privy Council. Peter Wedderburn, merchant in
Dundee, is a witness. (172.)

     The Privy Council had ordained the magistrates to furnish men and horses for expresses to the
commanders of the King's forces benorth Tay, Montrose as well as Burntisland.

39. **1690.** June 23.—Factory (21 May 1690) by John Wedderburn of Blackness, clerk Dundee to the bills, to James Dick, writer in Dundee, to uplift from the Dundee maltmen, Register the price of his bear sold them 1689, and also to set his estate of Blackness, &c, in of Deeds. tack for three years. Dated at Edinburgh. (221. Orig. i, 38.)

[See, in all, fol. 10, 18, 28, 94, 172, 221, 284.]

VOL. 8.

1691—97.

40. **1692.** Feb. 26.—Discharge (10 Feb.) by Patrick Kyd (son of the late William Kyd of Woodhill), now aged 21, to his curators, including John Wedderburn of Blackness, James Wedderburn, clerk of Dundee, Margaret Wedderburn, relict of the deceased Patrick Kyd of Craigie, and Alexander Wedderburn of Easter Powrie, only son of the late Alexander Wedderburn of Easter Powrie, acknowledging complete payment of all things due to him by the death of his late father and the deceased Jean Wedderburn, his mother. (43.)

Alexander Wedderburn here referred to is the third proprietor of Easter Powrie, whose father had died in January 1692.

41. **1692.** March 29.—Assignation (24 March) by Mr. Andrew Wedderburn, minister of the united Kirks of Liff, Logie, and Innergourie (having right thereto by the second Act of the second session of William and Mary, giving free access to their churches and stipends to all the presbyterian ministers, then living, who were thrust from their charges since 1660 for not conforming to prelacy) to Johne Thomsone, of part of the said stipend. Dated at Dysart. (49. Orig i, 40.)

42. **1692.** May 28.—Factory (7 and 27 May) by the tutors testamentars to Alexander Wedderburn of Easter Powrie (being John Wedderburn of Blackness, James Wedderburn, clerk, Peter Wedderburn, merchant, burgess, Thomas Milne of Milnefield, Robert Hunter of Baldovie, and John Duncan) to William Gray, writer in Dundee, to uplift the rents of Easter Powrie, &c. (62. Orig. i, 40.)

43. **1693.** Feb. 7 ; May 25 ; Nov. 22, &c.—Documents witnessed by Alexander Wedderburn, writer in Dundee. (89, 105, 119, 135, 143.)

44. **1694.** Sept. 3.—Factory (of this date) by John Wedderburn of Blackness, clerk to the bills, to David Balvaird, writer, to uplift the rents, &c., of Blackness and Dargo for 1694. (170. Orig. i, 42.)

45. **1694.** Nov. 28.—Factory (20 and 23 Nov.) by John Wedderburn of Easter Powrie, with consent of his curators, to Thomas Milne of Milnefield his near kinsman, and one of his said curators, to uplift, &c., in place of William Gray (see ante No. 42), who did not manage the estate advantageously. (198. Orig. i, 42.)

46. **1696.** May 25.—Bond presented for registration by the servitor of Alexander Wedderburn, clerk of Dundee. (279.)

47. **1696.** Nov. 13.—Disposition (2 Jan. 1695) by Andrew Wardroper, merchant, to the town of Dundee, of a yard and a piece of waste ground called Corbie hill, once the property of the late Sir Alexander Wedderburn, of Blackness, then of his son, Alexander Wedderburn, skipper, who acquired it from his brother, George Wedderburn, and disponed it to the said Andrew Wardroper. (352.)

[See, in all, fol. 40, 43, 49, 62, 89, 105. 119, 129, 135, 143, 170, 174, 188, 196, 198, 235, 241, 249, 258, 279, 299. 305, 306, 314, 351, 352, 372, 376, 382, 384. 419, 432, 457, 465, 475, 496, 502, 507.]

VOL. 9.

1697—1700.

On the first leaf is written "The Register of Bonds, &c., of the burgh of Dundee, belonging to Alexander Wedderburn, clerk, of Dundee, was begun upon the seventh day of September, 1697 years."

48. **1697.** Oct. 26.—Bond (15 Feb. 1696) witnessed by Alexander Wedderburn, mariner. (29.)

Dundee 49. **1698.** Jan. 1.—Factory (3, 28 June 1697) by Robert and John Wedderburn, sons
Register of the deceased James Wedderburn, clerk of Dundee, who were going from home,
of Deeds. with consent of their curators, to their brother Alexander Wedderburn, clerk of
Dundee. (50.)

50. **1699.** Jan. 5.—Factory (30 Dec. 1698) by John Wedderburn of Blackness, clerk to
the bills, to Alexander Wedderburn, clerk of Dundee, to collect the Blackness rents.
Dated at Edinburgh. (219. Orig. i, 47.)

51. **1699.** Sept. 16, Oct. 31.—Documents witnessed by James Wedderburn, servitor to
Alexander Wedderburn, clerk. (355, 368.)

52. **1699.** Dec. 18.—Disposition (27 Sept.) by Peter Wedderburn, merchant, in Dundee,
to Thomas Paterson and James, his son, of a North Overgate house. (385. Orig. i, 47.)
[This volume contains a great many factories made, by different people, to Alexander Wedderburn, the clerk. See, in all, fol. 27, 29, 50, 57, 60, 66, 69, 80, 87, 100, 105, 122, 127, 168, 159, 185, 201,
219, 222, 247, 267, 347, 355, 368, 373, 385.]

Vol. 10.

On the first leaf is written "The third book of . . . Register of Bonds. &c., of the burgh of
Dundee, belonging to Alexander Wedderburne, town clerk of the said burgh, and began upon the
twentie day of Feby in anno 1700." His first two books are Vols. 8 and 9, although he only became
clerk during the currency (1691-97) of Vol. 8.

53. **1700.** March 27.—Factory (26 March) by John Wedderburn (son of the deceased
James Wedderburn, clerk, of Dundee). "whose intention was to go abroad out of the
Kingdom," to his brother Alexander Wedderburn, clerk. (16. Qrig. i, 48.)

54. **1700.** Sept. 9.—Discharge (27 May) by Matilda Wedderburn, relict of Mr. James
Brisbane, advocate, to John Wedderburn of Blackness, of a bond to herself in life
rent and to her children (David, Rachael, Margaret, and Barbara) in fee. (56. Orig. i, 48.)

55. **1701.** Aug. 14.—Disposition (15 Sept., 1699), by Duncan Ronald, writer to the
signet, to Alexander Wedderburn, clerk, of certain tenements in Dundee once Walter
Ranken's, and adjudged to Patrick Leslie, late chamberlain to Sir Peter Wedderburn
of Gosford, senator of the College of Justice. (122. Orig. i, 49.)

56. **1701.** Aug. 19—Tack (9 Feb., 1700), by Patrick (*sic*) Wedderburn, merchant in
Dundee, tacksman of the vicarage of Dundee, to James Strachan of the fish dues of
Dundee. (126. Orig. i, 49.)
In the original tack the grantor is correctly styled Peter, the two names being often used
indifferently.

57. **1703.** Aug. 16.—Protest by Alexander Wedderburn, mariner, of a bill endorsed
by him to Robert Wedderburn, mariner, and reindorsed by Robert Wedderburn to
Alexander Wedderburn. (274. Orig. i, 51.)

58. **1703.** Aug. 19.—Discharge (17 Aug.) by Robert Wedderburn, mariner in Dundee,
Dr. John Wedderburn, Doctor of Medicine there, Grissell Wedderburn, wife of
Thomas Watson of Grange of Barrie, with her husband's consent, Margaret Wedderburn and Matilda Wedderburn, children of the late James Wedderburn, clerk, and
umquhile Elizabeth Davidson his wife, of a bond (18 Nov., 1696), by John Wedderburn of Blackness, to the said Elizabeth Davidson in life rent, and to the said
children and Elizabeth Wedderburn their sister (since deceased) in fee. (276.
Orig. i, 51.)
The original is signed by all the dischargers.
[See in all fol. 16, 37, 49, 56, 58, 65, 71, 98, 122, 126, 133, 141, 161, 165, 174, 177, 199, 206, 207,
218, 219, 220, 222, 225, 228, 239, 256, 261, 274, 276.]

Vol. 11.
—
1703—7.

59. **1703.** Aug. 23.--Bond (22 Dec. 1701), by William Smith, mariner in Dundee, who
had fallen into the sin of fornication with Janet Creighton, and being bound to sail
furth of the nation aboard the ship called the "Neptune" of Dundee, whereof

Alexander Wedderburn is master, to Cadiz in Spain, he cannot stay to satisfy the church, but grants an obligation to Henry Auchinlek, merchant, being cautioner, that if spared to return back to Dundee with the said ship, he will pay to the kirk treasurer £100 for the offence and scandal. (1.)

60. **1703.** Sept. 13.—Factory (23 Aug.), by Alexander Wedderburn, skipper in Dundee, going furth of this kingdom, to Grissel Watson, his well-beloved spouse. (8. Orig. i, v. 51.)

The original is signed by Alexander Wedderburn.

61. **1703.** Nov. 27.—Factory (8 Feb.), by John Wedderburn (son of the deceased Peter Wedderburn and Catharine Mau, his spouse), to Alexander Wedderburn, mariner in Dundee, his brother german, to manage his affairs. Signed on board the ship "Sidney." (19. Orig. i, 51.)

The original is signed by John Wedderburn.

62. **1704.** March 22.—Factory to Alexander Wedderburn (15 March), by John Wedderburn of Blackness and Alexander Wedderburn, younger, fiar thereof, tutors testamentars to Margaret, only child in life of the late Andrew Balfour, W.S., and heir returned to George Balfour, deceased, her brother. (37. Orig. i, 52.)

63. **1704.** May 5.—Factory by Alexander Raitt, only son of the deceased Mr. Robert Raitt, minister of Dundee, with consent of his curators, including Peter Wedderburn, merchant in Dundee, to Thomas Milne of Milnefield. (48.)

There is another such factory, 1706, Jan. 10. (149.)

64. **1704.** Sept. 27.—Procuratory (26 Sept.), of resignation by Thomas Watson of Grange of Barrie, in favour of Grissell Wedderburn, his wife, by virtue of their marriage contract, dated 7 June 1700, of certain property in Dundee, once that of Alexander Tyrie. (65.)

65. **1705.** March 8.—Disposition by John Steill, maltman, to Sir John Wedderburn of Blackness, Knight Baronet, of certain moveable property, in security for debts due to Sir John. (36. Orig. i, 53.)

66. **1705.** June 5.—Contract (1690) to which James Wedderburn, clerk, and Mr. Alexander Wedderburn, councillor, are witnesses. (106.)

67. **1706.** Feb. 14.—Factory by Robert Wedderburn, mariner, "shortly of mind and intent to pass furth of Scotland for doing his lawful affairs," to John Paterson of Craigie and Alexander Wedderburn, clerk of Dundee. (156. Orig. i, 54.)

68. **1706.** April 25.—Factory (24 April) by Sir Alexander Wedderburn of Blackness, Knight Baronet, to Alexander Wedderburn, the clerk, to uplift the rents of Blackness and Logie. (160. Orig. i, 54.)

The original has the signature of Sir Alexander Wedderburn. There is another such factory 11 Nov. 1707. (214. Orig. i, 55.)

69. **1706.** June 13.—Discharge (21 July 1702) by Margaret Wedderburn, relict of Patrick Kyd of Craigie, to John Wedderburn of Blackness of certain bonds. (164. Orig. i, 54.)

70. **1706.** June 13.—Discharge (3 June) by Mr. John Paterson (or Pearsone) of Craigie, to Sir Alexander Wedderburn of Blackness, heir and executor of his late father, Sir John, of certain bonds assigned (1704) by the now deceased Margaret Wedderburn, relict of Patrick Kyd of Craigie, to Margaret Wedderburn, second daughter of the late James Wedderburn, clerk of Dundee, wife of the said John Paterson, and to Margaret, Jean, and Agnes Paterson, his daughters, and grandnieces to the said deceased Margaret Wedderburn. Mr. John Paterson grants the discharge on behalf of his said wife and daughters. (165. Orig. i, 54.)

71. **1706.** June 15.—Discharge by Alexander Wedderburn of that ilk (executor to his late father, Alexander Wedderburn of Easter Powrie), to Sir Alexander Wedderburn of Blackness, as son and heir of the late Sir John Wedderburn. (166. Orig. i, 54.)

72. **1707.** Sept. 25.—Disposition (1701) by Alexander Wedderburn, mariner, in Dundee, to Thomas Crichton, of a South Nethergate tenement, once belonging to Sir Alexander Wedderburn of Blackness, grandfather to the said disponer. (183. Orig. i, 54.)

The original has the signature of the disponer.

[See, in all, fol. 1, 2, 8. 14, 19, 26, 30, 32, 37, 43, 45, 46, 48, 57, 61, 62, 65, 74, 83, 86, 106, 108, 113, 118, 127, 134, 146, 149, 153, 155, 156, 157, 164, 165, 166, 180, 183, 185, 191, 193, 206, 214.]

Vol. 12.

1708—11.

On the fly leaf is written "Alexander Wedderburn of Blackness. Baronet, Constable Deput of Dundee." which must refer to the second baronet, unless, as is possible, this was written into the book after the succession of the fourth baronet, the clerk, in 1723. I do not find any record of the appointments of constables depute.

73. **1708.** July 15.—Factory (13 Oct. 1707) by Robert Wedderburn, mariner, intending to go abroad in his affairs, to his brother Alexander Wedderburn, clerk, of Dundee. (24. Orig. i, 56.)

74. **1708.** Oct. 23.—Disposition (16 May 1706) by Thomas Kessan and his wife, Margaret Small, of a charge on Baldovie, relative to a contract of alienation (1 May 1685) of part of Baldovie made to the late Robert Small by the late David Haliburton of Piteur, and Dame Agnes Wedderburn, his wife. (52.)

75. **1709.** Jan. 28.—Vendition (30 May 1702) by Peter Wedderburn, merchant, in Dundee, to John Graham, of a good ship the "Margaret of Dundee." (74. Orig. i, 57.)

76. **1709.** April 20.—Disposition (29 Feb. 1632) by Alexander Innes to James Preston of a tenement on the west of Spalding's Wynd, in which umquhile Adam Wedderburn (son lawful of umquhile Patrick Wedderburn) and David Smairt were once (16 Jan. 1612) infeft. (84.)

77. **1709.** June 11.—Registration of a letter from Sir Alexander Wedderburn of Blackness to Alexander Wedderburn, the clerk, as follows:—"Sir, I understand your magistrates will not allow of your subscription for me of that Contract betwixt the towne of Dundie and their neighbourhead gentlemen, (for eighty pounds yearly for the privileidge of the midding lairs and dung of the town for the space of nyn years, of which twentie four pound is reckoned my proportion) without my special mandat : therefor let these desyre you may subseryve the said Contract for me and I shall releive you thereof, and this shall be your warrand from, Sir, your Affectionate Cousen and very humble servant, sic subseribitur A. Wedderburn. Dated at Edinburgh, 16 June 1709." (96.)

See ante s. Dundee Council Books, No. 162.

78. **1710.** Jan. 19.—Nomination (3 Jan.) by Sir Alexander Wedderburn of Blackness, Baronet, of tutors and curators to John, Alexander, Margaret, Rachell, and Matilda Wedderburn, his children, if he should die during their minority. The tutors and curators are James Haliburton of Piteur, Mr. James Mairtyn of Grange, Mr. George Seaton, advocate, Peter Wedderburn, merchant in Dundee, and Alexander Wedderburn, clerk of Dundee. (133. Orig. i, 58)

79. **1710.** Feb. 7.—Obligation (2 Jan.) by Sir Alexander Wedderburn of Blackness, baronet, narrating that by his entail of his lands and barony of Blackness on his eldest son John, &c., whom failing on his second son Alexander, &c., whom failing on on the other heirs therein named, he has reserved power to himself to charge the entailed lands with his debts, whereby he now so charges them. (140. Orig. i, 58.)

[See, in all, fol. 2, 10, 24, 30, 35, 37, 52, 53, 59, 65, 74, 84, 96. 100, 116, 119, 133, 140, 164, 176, 183-84, 186, 189, 198, 202, 204, 217.]

VOL. 13.

1711–15.

*Entitled " Register of Deeds, &c., of the burgh of Dundee, belonging to Alexander Wedderburne, clerk of
Dundee, begun upon 1 March 1711, and ended upon 25th day of Februar 1715."*

80. **1711.** June 2.—Disposition (11 Nov. 1709), naming Alexander Wedderburn, mariner,
late bailie, as procurator for Alexander Duncan of Lundie. (18.)

81. **1711.** July 7.—Factory (21 June), by Robert Wedderburn, mariner, who is leaving the
kingdom on business, to his brother Alexander Wedderburn, clerk. (22. Orig. ii, 1.)

82. **1117.** July 13.—Disposition (3 Jan 1710), by Sir Alexander Wedderburn of
Blackness, Baronet, to John Wedderburn his eldest son, and the heirs of his body,
then to Alexander Wedderburn. his second son, &c., &c., of all his moveable goods,
houshold plenishing, and books, of which a catalogue in eight pages and a half was given
by him to Mr. Andrew Freebairn, minister, in order to sale. (23. Orig. ii, 1.)

83. **1711.** June 24.—Protest of a bill payable to Alexander Wedderburn, shipmaster in
Dundee, and master of the Dundee seamen. (70. Orig. ii, 2.)

84. **1712-14.** Alexander Wedderburn, bailie, is repeatedly mentioned as sitting on
the bench. (passim.)

[See, in all, fol. 5, 12, 18, 21-24. 26-27, 29, 41, 53, 58, 70, 72, 74, 80, 95-6, 127, 143, 158, 167-68, 214.]

VOL. 14.

1715.

On the first fly leaf is written : —

" Register of Bonds, &c., of the Burgh of Dundee belonging to Alexander Wedderburne, clerk of
the said burgh, begun upon the fourth day of March, 1715, and ended upon the ...... day ...... of
17 — years." — " 1715, 1725." — " This book belongs to Sir Alexander Wedderburne of Blackness,
town clerk of Dundee." — " Register of Bonds, &c., of the burgh of Dundee belonging to Alexander
Wedderburne, clerk of the said burgh, 1725."

These entries must be read with reference to the clerk's deposition from his office in 1716 for his
share in the rising of '15, which accounts for the blanks in the first entry. The second entry was
made after his succession to the title in 1723, when the book was no doubt still in his possession, as
for long after his deposition he claimed and kept all the books and papers of the burgh (see ante
s. Dundee Council Books Nos. 182, 190-91). The third entry would otherwise be misleading, as he
was not clerk in 1725. The volume is only partly filled, and only the first 17 leaves are numbered.

85. **1715.** May 19.—Discharge by Helen McGill to Thomas Wilson, sometime of Omachie,
of a bond (13 July 1705), for payment of which money due to Wilson had been
arrested in the hands of Sir John Wedderburn of Blackness and his tutors. (8.)

86. **1715.** June 4.—John Wedderburn, servitor to Alexander Wedderburn, clerk of
Dundee, witness. (s. d.)

[See, in all, fol. 8 and s. d. :—1715. April 22 ; May 13, 20 ; June 4 ; July 11.]

VOL. 15.

1716–21.

*Entitled " Register of Dispositions, &c., belonging to George Duncan, clerk of Dundee, begun 20 August 1716
and ended 15 April 1721."*

87. **1718.** July 11.—Disposition (25 Sept. 1711), signed by Alexander Wedderburn,
councillor. (106.)

88. **1720.** May 3.—Disposition (7 Dec. 1719), witnessed by Alexander Wedderburn,
sheriff clerk of Forfar. (256.)

89. **1720** Dec. 12.—Disposition by Mr. Thomas Sanders of Kettins, referring to a back
bond (20 Feb. 1700), made to Mr. James Haliburton of Waterbuts, by Dame
Agnes Wedderburn, relict of David Haliburton of Pitcur. (340.)

[See, in all, fol. 50, 59, 73, 87, 106, 117, 136, 166, 256, 261, 331, 340.]

VOL. 16.

1721—25.

90.	**1722.** March 22.—Discharge (8 Feb), written and witnessed by John Wedderburn, son of Alexander Wedderburn, sheriff clerk of Forfar. (52.)

91.	**1723.** Feb. 22.—Protested bill (5 Jan.), drawn by Alexander Wedderburn of Blackness, and payable 14 days after date at his dwelling-house of Blackness. Robert Wedderburn, his son, is witness. (87. Orig. ii, 13.)

92.	**1723.** June 3.—Disposition (27 May), to which Sir Alexander Wedderburn of Blackness, is a witness. (104.)

93.	**1723.** Nov. 2.—Disposition (17 May 1723), witnessed by Sir Alexander Wedderburn of Blackness, and John Wedderburn his son, by whom it is written. The lands once belonging to Andrew Wedderburn are named in it as a boundary. (136.)

94.	**1724.** Sep. 26.—Disposition (20 June 1717) witnessed by Mr. John Wedderburn, Doctor of Medicine in Dundee. (202.)

95.	**1725.** May 7, 17.—Dispositions written and witnessed by John Wedderburn, son to Alexander Wedderburn of Blackness, sheriff clerk of Forfar, 1722-23. (240-245.)

[See, in all, fol. 1, 42, 52, 87, 101, 104, 108, 116, 123, 127, 136, 167, 174, 185, 202, 203, 205, 207, 210, 212, 227, 240, 245, 258, 261.]

VOL. 17.

1725—32.

96.	**1726.** Aug. 10.—Disposition naming land once that of Andrew Wedderburn, and written by Robert Wedderburn, son of Sir Alexander Wedderburn of Blackness. (71.)

97.	**1726.** Nov. 12, Dec. 14.—Two bills drawn by John Wedderburn, younger, of Blackness. (89-92.)

98.	**1727.** Feb. 4.—Disposition by Andrew Wardroper to Andrew Ouchterlony of a tenement of land in North Overgate, once that of Sir Alexander Wedderburn of Blackness, then of Alexander Wedderburn, merchant in Edinburgh his son, and then of George Wedderburn, merchant. (107.)

99.	**1727.** June 20.—Disposition by Margaret Balfour, spouse of Dr. John Wedderburn, physician in Dundee, and only child in life and heir of the late Mr. Andrew Balfour W.S., and sister and heir of the late George Balfour (son to the said Mr. Andrew, by Elizabeth Bains, his first wife), with consent of her said husband and of Dr. James Eccles, heir of the late Henry Eccles (eldest son of William Eccles, M.D. in Edinburgh), who was her first husband. (145.)

100.	**1727.** Oct. 21.—Bill drawn by Matilda Wedderburn, relict of Mr. James Brisbane, advocate, and another, for the rent of a house on the shore of Dundee. (177. Orig. ii, 17.)

101.	**1727.** Dec. 5.—Back bond (20 Feb. 1700) to James Haliburton by Dame Agnes Wedderburn (referred to ante No. 89), again named, and it is stated that Dame Agnes owed the holder £162 (scots) at Whitsuntide, 1711. (194.)

102.	**1729.** Sept. 16.—Protested bill drawn by Sir Alexander Wedderburn of Blackness, whose son, Robert Wedderburn, is notary. (265. Orig. ii, 19.)

[See, in all, fol. 21, 31, 69, 71, 86, 89, 92, 93, 96, 100, 107, 145, 177, 187, 194, 197, 223, 314, 332, 347, 365, 381, 393, 419, 496, 510, 550, 553, 563, 609, 634, 637, 644, 654, 676, 686, 703, 764, 790]

Vol. 18.

1732–35.

103. **1733.** Feb. 14.—Disposition (15 Nov. 1723), by Thomas Watson of Grange of Barrie, to Alexander Wedderburn, shipmaster in Dundee, of a cross dwelling in North Marketgate. (33.)

104. **1734.** May 21.—Feu, dated at Blackness, 1 May 1730, by Sir Alexander Wedderburn of Blackness, Baronet, to Andrew Begg, of a piece of land in the Overgate of Dundee, in virtue of a decreet obtained (18 Feb. 1719) by Sir Alexander (therein designed sheriff clerk of Forfar), before the Lords of Council and Session, v. Sir John Wedderburn of Blackness, son and heir of Sir Alexander Wedderburn of Blackness, and grandchild of the deceased Sir John Wedderburn of Blackness, and his tutors and curators, adjudging to the pursuer (now Sir Alexander), the lands and barony of Blackness and other lands for the sum of £62,985 15s. 2d. (scots.) Recorded 20 March 1719. (197. Orig. ii, 24.)

See post s. Public Records. Register of Decreets (Dalrymple Office) s. 18 Feb. 1719.

[See, in all, fol. 33, 52, 73, 117, 141, 142, 177, 195, 197, 203, 300, 352, 359.]

Vol. 19.

1735–37.

105. **1733.** May 20.—Disposition (24 Feb. 1733), by Alexander Wedderburn, shipmaster and late bailie of Dundee, to Alexander, John, Katharine, Elizabeth, Grizall, and Clementina, his children, of the cross-dwelling referred to ante No. 103. (291. Orig. ii, 27.)

106 **1734.** July 12.—Disposition by David Wedderburn of that ilk, of a Murraygate tenement, once that of Alexander Wedderburn of Easter Powrie, provost, his great grandfather, to whom (25 May) David was duly returned heir. (308. Orig. ii, 27.)

[See, in fol. 160, 220, 223, 230, 284, 275, 291, 301, 308, 323, 357.]

Vol. 20.

1737–41.

107. **1737.** Dec. 15, 20, 23, 26.—Alexander Wedderburn, shoremaster, is named as witness, &c., 1697—1706. (22, 26, 29, 33.)

108. **1738.** Dec. 27.—Robert Wedderburn, sheriff clerk of Forfar, witness. (188.)

109. **1741.** March 6.—John Wedderburn, junior, of Blackness, arbitrator in a dispute. (591.)

[This volume also contains the record of various protested bills made by Sir Alexander Wedderburn of Blackness, and his son John. See, in all, fol. 22, 26, 29, 33, 47, 58, 101, 103, 106, 150, 180, 208, 259, 285, 301, 315, 334, 351, 357, 395, 441, 591.]

Vol. 21.

1741–45.

110. **1741.** Dec. 4.—Dr. John Wedderburn, physician in Dundee, named as part owner of the good ship " The Blessing of Dundee." (165.)

111. **1742.** Jan. 1.—Reference to the Overgate land, once belonging to Sir Alexander Wedderburn of Blackness, then to his sons Alexander and George. (168.)

112. **1743.** July 8.—Bond (5 Feb. 1741) to Dr. John Wedderburn of Idvies, as one of the tutors of Grizell, daughter of John Scott. (432.)

Dundee
Register
of Deeds.
113.   **1744.** Aug. 18.—Discharge (11 Aug.) by James Crawford of Scotstown, son of the late Henry Crawford of Monorgan, to Sir Alexander Wedderburn of Blackness, and Dr. John Wedderburn and his other curators. (570.)

> [See. in all. fol. 95, 99, 165, 168, 195, 252, 263, 290, 335, 355, 363, 403, 425, 432, 494, 539, 570, 590, 599, 611.]

VOL. 22.

1745-49.

114.   **1746.** June 20.—Disposition (20 Oct. 1707) to Sir Alexander Wedderburn of Blackness, of some acres, called the "Parson's Acres," in Dundee. (120.   Orig. iii. 4.)

> The docket of the original styles Sir Alexander " Clerk to the Bills."

115.   **1748.** Nov. 29.—Factory of Grizell Scott, with consent of David Brisbane of Bullion, writer in Dundee, Robert Wedderburn of Pearsie, sheriff clerk of Forfar, and William Scott, her curators, to obtain an account from Dr. John Wedderburn, physician in Dundee, and other the tutors and curators appointed her by her late father, John Scott, shipmaster in Dundee. (470.)

> [See, in all, fol. 22, 34, 71, 120, 135, 470, 535, 585, 590, 632, 646.]

VOL. 23. .

1750-52.

116.   **1750.** Dec. 24.—Assignation naming David Wedderburn of that ilk and Dr. John Wedderburn, physician in Dundee, as trustees for the creditors of David Campbell, elder and younger of Kethick. (373.)

117.   **1751.** April 26.—Disposition by David Wedderburn of Wedderburn, heir entered and infeft, &c., to his grandfather, Alexander Wedderburn of Kingennie, and to his father, Alexander Wedderburn of Easter Powrie, of a North Overgate tenement purchased by the late Alexander Wedderburn of Easter Powrie from Bartholomew Bilson, and thereafter belonging to his son, Alexander Wedderburn of Easter Powrie, and then to his son, John Wedderburn, from whom it passed to his brother german and heir, Alexander Wedderburn, father of the now disponer.   The price is £190 stg. (499.   Orig. iii, 9.)

118.   **1752.** May 22.—Disposition (1732) by David Brisbane of Bullion, writer in Dundee, to his sister, Margaret Brisbane, in life-rent, and to David Wedderburn of Wedderburn heritably, of a South Flukergate tenement, part of which once belonged to his mother, Matilda Wedderburn, relict of Mr. James Brisbane. (988.   Orig. iii, 10.)

119.   **1752.** May 28.—Ratification by Margaret Brisbane of the said disposition made by her said brother, now deceased. (1019.   Orig. iii, 10.)

120.   **1752.** Oct. 23.—Protested bill witnessed by Alexander Wedderburn, servitor to John Ballingall, notary public (1191.)

> [See. in all, fol. 24, 93, 113, 139, 276, 368, 373, 388, 393, 499, 672, 707, 715, 726, 732, 983, 988, 1019, 1122, 1191, 1249.]

VOL. 24.

1753-55.

121.   **1753.** Jan. 3.—Disposition witnessed by Alexander Wedderburn, servitor to John Ballingall, writer in Dundee. (2.)

> He is named again at fol. 96, 111, 317, 347, 368, 413, 519, 858.

122.   **1753.** Sep. 13.—Robert Wedderburn of Pearsie sheriff clerk of Forfar, witness. (387.)

123. **1755.** March 22.—Disposition (13 May 1743) by Robert Hill of an East Hiltown tenement, disponed to him by Alexander Wedderburn, sheriff clerk of Forfar.

Dundee Register of Deeds.

124. **1755.** July 8.—Disposition (1751) by Alexander, eldest son of David Graham, to Robert Mathew, of a South Seagate tenement, once that of Peter Wedderburn, merchant, then that of Sir Alexander Wedderburn, of Blackness, who (17 Sep. 1741) disponed it to trustees for his creditors, who disponed it to David Graham. (1313.)

125. **1755.** July 9.—Disposition (17 Sept. 1741) of the said tenement by Sir Alexander Wedderburn to the trustees for his creditors and those of John Wedderburn, his eldest son. The trustees are David Graham, James Graham of Duntroon, David Brisbane of Bullion, William Morison of Naughton, Thomas Arnot of Dunmay, Thomas Henderson and John Ballingall, writer in Dundee. (1334. Orig. iii, 13.)

[See, in all, fol. 2, 79, 96, 111, 205, 317, 347, 368, 387, 413, 468, 519, 783, 858, 945. 1008, 1105, 1813, 1328, 1834, 1886, 1425, 1471.]

Vol. 25.

1756—59.

The index of this volume shows no references to the name of Wedderburn, and any in the volume are therefore no doubt indirect and unimportant.

Vol. 26.

1763—64.

(Index only searched.)

126. **1763.** May 25.—Disposition (Edin. 11 April 1763) by John Goodwillie, writer in Edinburgh, to Katharine Wedderburn, relict of John Higginson, merchant in Perth, and daughter to the deceased Alexander Wedderburn, shipmaster and late bailie of Dundee, as also to Helen Wedderburn, only child of the late Alexander Wedderburn, shipmaster in London, eldest son of the said Alexander Wedderburn, bailie, of a cross dwelling in Dundee. It recites that in 1757, Goodwillie instituted a suit against the said Helen and her tutors, the said Katharine, relict of J. Higginson, and Elizabeth and Clementina, also daughters of the said Alexander Wedderburn, bailie, and that, 6 Dec. 1757, he obtained a decreet, which found that the said Alexander Wedderburn, bailie, died Oct. 1734, and his wife, Grizel Watson, Oct. 1756, and that Grizel Wedderburn, one of their daughters, died before her mother, and which decreed the defenders to pay him £4,746 (scots); that he then, 11 and 15 Feb. 1758, raised letters of special charge v. the said Helen, Katharine, and Elizabeth Wedderburn, the said Clementina Wedderburn being dead, and obtained a decreet, 2 Aug. 1758, charging them to enter as heirs in special to the said cross-dwelling, and decerning it to belong to him as security for his debt. It also narrates that Clementina Wedderburn, by her disposition, 5 Dec. 1757, left her property to her sisters, Katharine and Elizabeth Wedderburn, for life, and then to her nephew and niece John Higginson (son of Katharine Wedderburn) and the said Helen Wedderburn in fee; and finally it narrates a similar disposition by Elizabeth Wedderburn (5 May 1759) to her sister the said Katharine for life and to the said John and Helen in fee. (1335. Orig. iii, 21.)

See ante s. Dundee Protocol Books, No. 592

127. **1763.** Aug. 13.—Disposition (1 Oct. 1700) by James Wedderburn, son of George Wedderburn, merchant in Edinburgh. (1488.)

[See, in all, fol. 838, 1335, 1488.]

Vol. 27.

1764—66.

This and the remaining volumes have been searched by their indices only.

128. **1766.** Sept. 19.—Disposition (8 July 1765) by John Wedderburn of Idvie, Esq., now residing in Jamaica, to John Peatrie, of certain premises, being part of the great stone tenement once that of Dr. John Wedderburn, physician, in Dundee, and disponed by him to the now disponer. Dated at Lucia, Jamaica. (1324. Orig. iv, 3.)

[See also fol. 576.]

Vol. 28.

1767—69.

129. **1769.** Nov. 24.—Disposition (23 June 1767) by Katharine Wedderburn, relict of John Higginson, and Helen Wedderburn, her niece, to Andrew Wilkie, of the cross-dwelling referred to ante No. 126. (1529. Orig. iv, 6.)

130. **1769.** Dec. 16.—Disposition (4 Jan. 1769) by Mrs. Jean Fullarton, widow of the late Sir John Wedderburn of Blackness, baronet, to Katharine and Susanna Wedderburn, her unmarried daughters, jointly, of all her moveable goods and gear, including heirship moveables, pictures, jewels, &c., and appointing them her sole executors. (1599. Orig. iv, 6.)
The original is signed by the disponer thus, " Jean Wedderburn, alis (*sic*) Fullarton."

Vol. 29.

1770—72.

131. **1772.** Dec. 1.—Disposition by John Wedderburn of Idvie, then in Jamaica, similar to and of even date with that named ante No. 128, of another part of the same tenement. (1363. Orig. iv, 9.)

Vol. 30.

1773-75.

This volume contains no reference to Wedderburns.

Vol. 31.

1776-78.

132. **1776.** Sept. 23.—Contract (10 Aug 1774) between Katharine and Susanna Wedderburn, sisters german, daughters of the late Sir John Wedderburn of Blackness, Baronet, by which they agree that each will leave to the other all her property, and that if both die intestate it shall go to their brothers Sir John Wedderburn of Ballindean, and James Wedderburn, only surviving sons of the said deceased Sir John Wedderburn, equally. Dated at Balharry, and witnessed by James Smyth of Balharry, and another. (360. Orig. iv, 13.)
The original has the signatures of Katharine and Susanna Wedderburn.

Vols. 32-23.

1779—81 ; 1782—83.

The indices to these volumes contain no references to Wedderburns.

Vol. 34.

1784-86.

133. **1784.** Jan. 26.—Discharge (15 May, 1782) by Robert Wedderburn of Pearsie, to John Wedderburn of Ballendean, of a legacy of £500 stg. left to the said Robert by his uncle, the late Dr. John Wedderburn. (271. Orig. v, 1.)

134. **1785.** May 17.—Disposition by Mrs. Ann Fletcher, wife of Capt. Alexander Reid of Logie, and her husband, to Robert Wedderburn of Pearsie, and his wife, Isobell Edward, of a flat in Milu's buildings, Dundee. (885. Orig. v, 2.)

135. **1786.** Oct. 2.—Settlement or disposition by Miss Katharine Wedderburn.—" I, Katharine Wedderburn, sister german of Sir John Wedderburn of Ballandean, Baronett, Considering that it is the duty of every person while in health and strength to prepare for death and in so doing to settle their worldly affairs, And as my friends and near relatives are in such circumstances as do not require that I should make a distribution of what I have amongst them, And as David Wedderburn, my nephew, second son of the beforenamed Sir John Wedderburn was recommended particularly

to my care by his mother lately before her death, I hereby dispose and convey in event of my death to and in favour of the said David Wedderburn [all her estate] hereby nominating and appointing him my sole executor and universal legatee . . . under the following burthens and conditions viz : [in an event aforesaid] I leave and bequeath to the before named Sir John Wedderburn the whole household furniture I shall die possessed of, declaring that in consideration thereof he shall stand bound to pay my funeral expenses, which I request may be done on as moderate a scale as propriety will admitt : Item. to Margaret, my eldest niece, daughter of the said Sir John Wedderburn, one of the mourning rings which I have for her mother, together with my braclets and miniature picture of King James the Seventh ; to Jean Wedderburn, also my niece and daughter of the said Sir John Wedderburn, my gold watch and another mourning ring I have for her mother" . . . [then follows formal conclusion] Signed at Ballundean 22 Oct. 1779. (1883. Orig. v, 3.)

Dundee
Register
of Deeds.

The original has Katharine Wedderburn's signature.

136. **1786.** Dec. 19.—Disposition (29 Nov.) to Alexander Wedderburn of Wedderburn of a burghal tenement in South Nethergate. (1988.)

[See also fol. 1511, 1572.]

Vol. 35.

1787—88.

137. **1787.** Sept. 12.—Disposition and bond of provision (Edin. 15 Jan. 1779) by Robert Wedderburn of Pearsie to Isobel Edward. his wife, and his younger children, reciting that by a deed of even date he had, with consent of his wife and of Captain John Wedderburn, his eldest son, sold his landed estate to Lieutenant Charles Wedderburn, his second son, for £4,500 stg , to be paid at the first term after his death. and used first in paying his debts, and then in providing as therein mentioned for his eldest daughter Elizabeth, wife of James Graham of Meathie, and Katharine, Isobel, and David Wedderburn, his two youngest daughters and son ; after which the residue of his estate and effects is to go to his eldest son. (554. Orig. v, 3.)

The original has the signature of Robert Wedderburn and his eldest son, John Wedderburn.

138. **1788.** Jan. 9.—Last will (dated at Dundee, 2 Feb. 1787) of Isabel Edward, *alias* Wedderburn, relict of the deceased Robert Wedderburn of Pearsie. She directs that she be buried near to her husband, and bequeaths all her property equally among her three daughters, viz., Elizabeth Wedderburn, wife of James Graham of Meathie ; Katharine Wedderburn, wife of Dr. James Stewart, physician in Dundee, and Isobell Wedderburn, wife of the Rev. James Stormonth, minister of Airly. (747. Orig. v, 4.)

[See also fol. 603.]

Vol. 36.

1789—90.

139. **1790.** Nov. 15·—Discharge by Isobel Carnegie to Charles Wedderburn of Pearsie, sometime a captain in the service of the English East India Company, and executor of the late William Ronald, surgeon in the Bengal division of the Company's army. (1610. Orig v, 7.)

Vol. 37.

1791—92.

140. **1791.** April 4.—Decreet Arbitral on a submission (31 Dec. 1789) entered into by Charles Wedderburn of Pearsie, David Wedderburn (now Webster), merchant in London, Elizabeth Wedderburn, wife of James Graham of Meathie, Katharine Wedderburn, wife of Robert (*sic*) Stewart, surgeon in Dundee, and Isobel Wedderburn, wife of the Rev. James Stormonth of Kinelune, minister at Airly, as to their respective interests in the estate of the late Robert Wedderburn of Pearsie, their father. (The terms of this decreet stating the proportions in which the property was divisible are not important.) (222.)

Dundee
Register
of Deeds. 141. **1791.** May 16.—Disposition (9 May, 1791) in pursuance of the said decreet by
Charles Wedderburn of Pearsie, to the said David Wedderburn (now Webster) and
Isobel Wedderburn, of the South Nethergate flat, disponed by Mrs. Ann Fletcher to
the late Robert Wedderburn of Pearsie (see ante, No. 134.) (296.)

142. **1792.** Oct. 6.—Bond of provision by James Graham of Meathie, in favour of his
wife Elizabeth Wedderburn, and naming his son James and his "younger children."
(1396. Orig. v, 9.)

143. **1792.** Oct. 12.—Bond of annuity same to same, reciting their postnuptial contract
of marriage, dated 20 May, 1780. (1409. Orig. v, 9.)

144. **1792.** Oct. 6.—Nomination of tutors and curators by James Graham of Meathie,
to James, Robert, David, John, Isabel, and Katharine Graham, his children by his
wife Elizabeth Wedderburn. The curators are his wife, his brothers in law, Charles
Wedderburn of Pearsie, and David Webster, Charles Graham, his brother german,
David Laird of Strathmartine, Alexander Wedderburn of Wedderburn, and David
Ramsay, merchant in London. (1414.)

[See also fol. 821.]

Vol. 38.
—
1793—94.
The index to this volume contains no references to Wedderburns.

Vol. 39.
—
1795—96.

145. **1795.** June 3.—Contract of marriage (dated at Hawkhill, near Dundee, 10 Sept.
1787) between Charles Wedderburn of Pearsie and Ann, youngest daughter of the
late Captain John Reid of Cairnie, with consent of her mother Mrs. Ann Guthrie and
her curators, nominated to her by her father (28 Oct. 1768). By this contract
Charles Wedderburn charges Pearsie with provisions for his wife and younger
children (if any), and Ann Read dispones to him her third part of Cairnie, as one
of the three heirs portioners of her late father. (335. Orig. v, 12.)

146. **1795.** June 9.—Discharge by James Graham of Meathie, druggist in London,
son and heir of James Graham of Meathie, deceased, to his curators and factor. (368.)

147. **1795.** Dec. 15.—Disposition (7 Dec. 1786 with codicil 30 Aug. 1795) by Katharine
Wedderburn, relict of the late John Higginson, merchant in Perth, to Alexander,
Marion, Elizabeth, Hester, Catharine, Helen, and Margaret Finlay, daughters of
James Finlay of Bogside, and his wife, the late Helen Wedderburn, niece to the
testatrix. (728. Orig. v, 12.)

148. **1796.** Aug. 26.—Contract of marriage (Dundee, 28 Dec., 1785) between David
Wedderburn of London (son of Robert Wedderburn of Pearsie), and Elizabeth, only
daughter of Alexander Read of Logie, by his wife Ann Fletcher. It gives the
settlements made by the husband and the bride's parents on the marriage, and also
recites that Sir Robert Fletcher, brother of the said Ann Fletcher, by his will 10 Nov.
1776, left, in event of his dying without issue, £15,000 stg. to his sister and her
heirs, and that there are now only two of her children living, viz., the said Elizabeth
and another, &c. Her uncle Thomas Fletcher, and her aunt Katharine Read, as also
James and David Webster of Leadenhall Street (1781) are also named anent certain
lands. (1367. Orig. v, 13.)

The original has the signatures of the spouses and the wife's parents.

Vols. 40-43.
—
1797—1801.
The indices to these volumes contain no references to Wedderburns.

This record begins in 1676, and continues with only one break, 1689-92, down to the **Dundee Decreets Register.** present time. As usual, the volumes are doubly numbered both in relation to other volumes of different records in the charter room, and separately for the particular series. One volume of this record (1696-98), has been wrongly placed among the Burgh and Head Court Records, as Vol. 37 of that series ; but it should be counted as Vol. 3 of this record. (See ante p. 298 n and post p. 337.) The record has been searched through sixteen volumes down to the year 1757.

Vol. 1.

1676—87.

On the first leaf is written :—" This Register of Decreits pertains to James Wedderburne, town clerk of Dundie, beginning the 19 day of Apryle 1676 and ending the 24 day of December 1687."

1. **1677.** May 14.—William Murisone is decreed to pay to Alexander Wedderburn of Easter Powrie, provost, £392, being forty-nine years' annual rent at £8, out of a North Murraygate property. (25.)

2. **1678.** June 5.—Isobell Thomsone is decreed to pay James Wedderburn, clerk, £13. 6s. 8d. and £2. 8s. for certain transumpts and dues. (41.)

3. **1678.** Aug. 21.—Decree in favour of James Wedderburn, clerk, factor for his brother, George Wedderburn. (47.)

4. **1679.** May 15.—An action is referred to Peter Wedderburn and another as arbitrators. (60.)

5. **1679.** Dec. 13.—Decree in favour of Alexander Wedderburn, merchant in Ediuburgh. (67.)

6. **1680.** March 20.—John Wedderburn of Blackuess, and James Wedderburn, clerk, are named as mother's kin in au edict of curatory for James Kyd (son of the late William Kyd of Woodhill), who chooses as his curators, them and Alexander Wedderburn of Easter Powrie, Alexander Wedderburn of Kingennie, Patrick Kyd of Craigie, Peter Wedderburn, and George Wedderburn, merchant in Edinburgh, and others. (72).

7. **1680.** July 31.—Robert Gardyne is decerned to deliver up to Alexander Wedderburn of Easter Powrie all charters, writs, &c., which belonged to the deceast Alexander Wedderburn, mariner in Dundee, and now to the pursuer, as well as those of the said Alexander Wedderburn's authors, and his daughters Helen and Bessie Wedderburn. (89.)

8. **1681.** Jan. 13.—John Wedderburn of Blackness is named as mother's next of kin to Janet, daughter of the late Mr. Alexander Milne of Muirtoun, minister of Dundee. (93.)

9. **1682.** March 31.—Decree in favour of Alexander Wedderburn, younger. (101.)

10. **1683.** Jan. 2.—Officers are decerned to pass to that tenement of land of old belonging to David Wedderburu, burgess of Dundee, in South Murraygate to levy there au annual-rent of 5 merks, thirteen years in arrear, for Alexander Wedderburu of Easter Powrie, late provost. (136.)

    See ante s. Scrymgeour Wedderburn Paper, No. 13, where the annual rent is stated at 8 merks.

11. **1683.** June 13.—Dame Matilda Fletcher, relict of Sir Alexander Wedderburn of Blackness, sometime clerk of Dundee, assigns to John Hastie a debt due to her by David Hunter, maltman. (180.)

12. **1683.** June 13.—Andrew Wedderburn is named on an inquest. (180.)

13. **1683.** June 23.—Edict of curatory raised by Peter Wedderburn, son of the late Alexander Wedderburn of Easter Powrie, once provost of Dundee. Alexander Wedderburn, now of Easter Powrie, and John Wedderburn of Blackness are named as father's kin, and Thomas Miln of Muirtowne and David Lindsay as mother's kin. The minor chooses Easter Powrie, Thomas Miln, David Lindsay, Robert Kinloch, James Wedderburn, clerk, and Margaret Miln, Lady Dowager of Easter Powrie. (181.)

14. **1684.** July 16.—Alexander Wedderburn of Easter Powrie is served heir to Alexander Wedderburn, late of Easter Powrie, his father. (210.)

15. **1685.** March 2.—Decree v. Janet Hall, relict of William Crawford, sometime precentor of Dundee, to pay to Margaret Miln, relict of Alexander Wedderburn of Easter Powrie, the rent of a house belonging to Peter Wedderburn, her youngest son. (242)

    The expression "her youngest son" is strictly accurate, as, though Peter Wedderburn was her now only son by her second husband, she had had another son, John Wedderburn, and also male issue by her first marriage.

16. **1685.** Nov. 18.—Peter and Margaret Kid, children of the late William Kid of Woodhill, choose as their curators Margaret Wedderburn, relict of Patrick Kid of Craigie, Alexander Wedderburn of Easter Powrie, John Wedderburn of Blackness, and James Wedderburn, town clerk, &c. (270.)

17. **1687.** March 17.—Decree for Margaret Miln, relict of Alexander Wedderburn of Easter Powrie, in respect of annual rents and housemaills of Murraygate and Seagate lands belonging to her son Peter. (318.)

18. **1687.** June 18.—Decree for Peter Wedderburn, merchant. (341).

19. **1687.** Aug. 14.—Decree v. (Janet) Hall, relict of William Crawford, to pay to Peter Wedderburn, merchant, certain rent. See ante No. 15. (350.)

20. **1687.** Sept. 24.—Service of George Wedderburn, merchant burgess of Edinburgh, father's kin, as tutor to Alexander and John Wedderburn, sons of the late Peter Wedderburn, merchant in Dundee (355) and (26 Nov.) decree for a factor appointed by him in respect of the rents of the pupils' house in Dundee. In this entry George Wedderburn is called "bailie of Edinburgh." (363.)

    [See. in all, fol. 25, 41, 47, 46, 50, 60, 67, 72, 75, 89, 93, 97, 100, 101, 136, 154, 169-70, 178, 180-81, 210-11, 214, 223, 228, 231, 242, 248, 252, 260, 268, 270, 318, 341, 346, 350, 355, 363.]

VOL. 2.

1693—96.

On the first leaf is written, "This Register of Decreits belongs to James Wedderburne, Town clerk of Dundee, beginning on the 20 day of May 1693, and ending the (31st) day of (October 1696)." It must therefore have been finished by his son Alexander, as James d. Jan. 1696.

21. **1693.** July 3.—Decree for Margaret Wedderburn, relict of Patrick Kyd of Craigie. (82.)

22. **1693.** Oct. 9.—In an edict of curatory raised by Rachel Wedderburn, only daughter of the late Alexander Wedderburn of Easter Powrie, the father's kin named are Peter Wedderburn, merchant in Dundee, and John Duncan late bailie, and the mother's are John Wedderburn of Blackness and James Wedderburn, clerk. The pupil chooses them all, except John Duncan. (115.) .

23. **1693.** Oct. 19.—In an edict of curatory raised by Alexander Wedderburn, son of the late Peter Wedderburn, merchant in Dundee, the father's kin named are John Wedderburn of Blackness, and James Wedderburn, clerk, and the mother's are Mr. James Man, student, and James Man, late bailie. All except the last named are chosen. (117.)

24. **1694.** May 21.—Decree v. William Miln, baxter, to pay to Alexander Wedderburn, writer, £3 6s. balance due, conform to his ticket and payable May 16, under pain of doubling. (178.)

25. **1694.** Sept. 22.—Matilda Wedderburn, relict of the late Mr. James Brisbane, petitions the bailies for that some half-year since she gave to Jacob Dalhousie, goldsmith, eleven drop weight of silver to make a spoon, and Dalhousie without her knowledge added other three drops, for which she was content to pay, and a reasonable price for workmanship, which he refused in respect she had complained to the bailies for the recovery of the spoon, and that he had gone off leaving the spoon marked D.B., initials of her son's name. The bailies ordain Dalhousie's shop to be sighted for the spoon, and (the spoon to be) given to the petitioner upon her giving 10s. 6d. as the price of the three drops of silver added, and 12s. as the price of the workmanship. (225.)

26. **1694.** Oct. 20.—Margaret Wedderburn, relict of Patrick Kyd of Craigie, gets a decree in her favour. (245.)

27. **1694.** Oct. 20.—Alexander Wedderburn of Easter Powrie, and his tutors, get a decree. (246.)

28. **1695.** Nov. 9.—Curatorie (inserted here but noted as of 11 May) of Alexander Wedderburn of Easter Powrie. The persons named are Peter Wedderburn, merchant in Dundee, John Dunean, late bailie (father's kin), and John Wedderburn of Blackness, and James Wedderburn, clerk (mother's kin), and all are chosen to act, with Thomas Miln of Milnfield. (422.)

29. **1696** Feb. 10.—Alexander Wedderburn is served eldest son and heir to his father James Wedderburn deceased, the clerk. (464.)

30. **1696.** May 15.—Alexander Wedderburn, town clerk, is named. (485.)

31. **1696.** Oct. 19.—Curatory raised by Robert and John Wedderburn, second and third sons of the late James Wedderburn, clerk, against John Wedderburn of Blackness, Peter Wedderburn of Gosfoord (father's kin), and Robert Davidson of Balgay and George Brown of Horne (mother's kin). The curators chosen are James Fletcher, provost of Dundee, John Wedderburn of Blackness, James Man, Robert Davidson, and James Kyd of Craigie. (536.)

[See, in all, fol. 14, 15, 19, 54, 61, 67, 70, 79, 82. 90, 94, 96, 115, 117, 124, 130, 139, 145, 148, 164, 172. 178, 221, 225, 235, 237, 245, 246. 252, 291, 294. 302, 309, 404, 422, 456, 464. 469, 477, 482, 483, 485, 489, 493, 536.]

VOL. 3.

1696–98.

This volume has been wrongly placed as vol 37 of the Burgh and Head Court Records. On the first fly leaf is written, "Register of Decreits of the Burgh of Dundee belonging to Alexander Wedderburne towne clerk thereof, begun on the 9th day of November 1696." The folios are not numbered.

32 **1696.** March 29.—Barbara Brisbane, daughter of the late Mr. James Brisbane, advocate, chooses as her curators John Wedderburn of Blackness, and Mr. John Paterson of Craigie. Alexander Wedderburn, the clerk, is named as her mother's kin.

33. **1697.** April 17.—Decree v. Matilda Wedderburn, relict of Mr. James Brisbane, advocate.

34. **1697.** May 16.—William Gardner and Alexander Blair, masons, are decerned to finish building an outer gate at Blackness, pursuant to contract (2 Nov. 1696) with John Wedderburn of Blackness, who had already paid them in advance the agreed price, 200 merks.

2 U

35. **1698.** Aug. 22, 31.—Decree in favour of Alexander Wedderburn of Easter Powrie and John Wedderburn of Blackness, Thomas Miln of Milnefield, and Peter Wedderburn, merchant, his curators.

[See, in all, s. dates :—**1696.** Nov. 26, 28 ; Dec. 7, 9.—**1697.** March 22, 29 ; April 17 ; May 3, 22 ; June 19 ; Sept. 15 ; Oct. 9 ; Nov. 20, 22 ; Dec. 6.—**1698.** Jan. 5, 12 ; March 16, 26 ; May 16 ; June 11, 27 ; July 2 ; Aug. 6, 22, 31.]

Vol. 4.

1698—1703.

On first leaf :—" Register of Decreits of the burgh of Dundie belonging to Alexander Wedderburne, towne Clerke thereof, begune on the twelfth day September 1698 years."

36. **1698.** Sept. 12.—Decreet of transumpt obtained by Thomas Milne of Milnefield, v. John Wedderburn of Blackness and Alexander Wedderburn his son, upon their disposition (Sept. 2) to him of the lands of Dargo, co. Perth. The documents decerned to be transumed are (*a*) Resignation (1642) by Donald Thornetoun of Blackness and Thomas Gourlaw of Dargo ; (*b*) Great seal charter, 18 July 1642, of Blackness and Dargo, in favour of Sir Alexander Wedderburn ; (*c*) sasine thereon ; (*d*) Contract of marriage, dated at Dundee and Edinburgh, 27 Feb. and 8 March 1667, between John Wedderburn, younger, of Blackness, with consent of Sir Alexander Wedderburn, his father, and Rachel Dunmuir, with consent of Mr. David Dunmuir, advocate, her father, by which Sir Alexander charges the lands of Blackness and Dargo (united by Great Seal charter, 14 July 1662, into the barony of Blackness), Logie, part of Balgay, and parts of Dudhope, in favour of the spouses. The witnesses to the said contract are (1) at Dundee, 27 Feb., Alexander Wedderburn of Kingennie, George Fletcher, provost of Dundee, William Wedderburn, brother to Sir Alexander, &c. ; and (2) at Edinburgh, 8 March, Sir Peter Wedderburn of Gosford, advocate, Sir Mark Cass of Cockpen, Sir George Mackenzie, advocate, &c., &c. (*e* and *f*) Resignation by Sir Alexander to his said son, 27 July 1668, and Great Seal charter thereon, 21 Oct. 1668. (*g* and *h*) Great Seal precept and instrument of sasine 10 March 1669. (1.)

37. **1698** Nov. 23.—Decree in favour of Peter Wedderburn, merchant, for house maill due to him. (61.)

38. **1699.** Jan. 21.—John Wedderburn of Blackness is named as a curator to George Balfour, son and heir of the late Andrew Balfour, W.S. (76.)

39. **1699.** May 31.—Decree in favour of Margaret Wedderburn, Lady Craigie, elder. (119.)

40. **1699.** Sept. 26-28. — Report of the oath of alleadgance and assurance, taken by the magistrates, ends thus :—" At Dundee the twentie eight day of September 1699 years Alex^r Wedderburne, towne Clerk of Dundie, nominat Clerk of the barronie of the Hilltowne thereof, did, in face of counsell, swear and subscryve the oath of alleadgance to his Majestie Kinge William, whereof the tenor follows :—' I under subscriband doe sincerely promise and swear that I will be faithfull and bear trew alleadgance to his Majestie King William, so help me God : sic subscribitur, A. Wedderburne.' And sicklick the said twentie eight day of September 1699 years did in face of counsell subscryve the testificat and assurance under written mentioned in and subjoyned to the late Act of Parliament, whereof the tenor follows :—' I under subscryver doe in the sinceritie of my heart, &c.; sic subscribitur A. Wedderburne.'" (145-47.)

41. **1700.** Jan. 13.—David and John Mylls, hammermen, are decreed to pay £20 to Mr. Alexander Wedderburn of Blackness, as the price of a chimney and iron back for which the pursuer gave them a quantity of iron. (171.)

42. **1700.** March 20.—John Deuchars is decreed to pay to Alexander Wedderburn, clerk, as factor for Grissell Watson and her curators, and also on behalf of Patrick Balneavis, husband to Margaret Watson, her sister, the rent of a house belonging to the Watsons. (187.)

43. **1700.** April 3.—Decree for Matilda Wedderburn, relict of Mr. James Brisbane. (188.)

44. **1700.** April 15.—Margaret Stibles, relict of Alexander Williamson, is decerned to pay various sums for himself, and as factor for John Wedderburn of Blackness, including a balance of £5, the price of a table bought from Alexander Wedderburn's mother, Elizabeth Davidson. (191.)

45. **1700.** May 20.—Decree in favour of Alexander Wedderburn of Easter Powrie, and his curators, Thomas Milne of Milnefield, John Wedderburn of Blackness, and Peter Wedderburn, merchant. (199.)

46. **1700.** Sept. 24.—In the report of the oath of allegiance and assurance to King William, Alexander Wedderburne signs as notary for several persons. (215-16.)

47. **1700.** Dec. 13.—Decree for Margaret, heir of the late Andrew Balfour, W.S. (224.)

48. **1702.** March 21.—Suit by John Wedderburn of Blackness *v.* John Watt, son of the late Andrew Watt, *re* a bond of Andrew's, to which the late Sir Alexander Wedderburn was cautioner. (274.)

    See ante s. Scrymgeour-Wedderburn Papers, No. 424-26.

49. **1702.** Sept. 18.—John Scrymsour, provost of Dundee, as preses of the council, in obedience to the Act of her Majesty's Privy Council, dated 21 July last, and the Act of Parliament, swears the oath of allegiance to her Majesty Queen Ann, and subscribes the same, and immediately thereafter he administers to John Scott, younger, bailie, and to the clerk and his depute, the said oath, whereof the tenor follows :—
    " We under subscrivors doe sincerely promise and swear that we will be faithfull and bear true alleadgeance to her Majesty Queen Ann ; so help me God. *Sic* subscribitur John Scott baylie, A. Wedderburne, clerk of Dundee and barouncy of the Hiltoune, and notar publick. Ja : Ramsay, clerk deput, nottar and procurator before the towne court." Next day Alexander Wedderburne signs as notary for several of the Council who could not write. (289.) He also signs the testificat and assurance to Queen Ann, as only lawful sovereign of the realm. (292.)

50. **1703.** Jan. 27.—Decree *v.* Margaret Wedderburn, relict of John Pearson, younger, baxter. (339)

    [See, in all, fol. 1, 48, 61, 64, 66, 68, 70, 74, 75, 76, 99, 106, 107, 116, 117, 119, 128, 135, 139, 141, 144, 145-47, 160, 170, 171, 178, 187, 188, 191, 192,193, 199, 203, 205, 206, 207, 213-16, 221, 224, 246, 250, 252, 255, 258, 274, 276, 282, 284, 286, 289, 292, 301, 304, 306, 310, 338, 339.]

Vol. 5.

1703–9.

On the first leaf is written "Register of Decreets. Alexander Wedderburne, toune (clerk of) Dundie. Begunn on the first February 1703 years, ending on the — day of July 1709 years."

51. **1703.** Nov. 20.—Decree *v.* John Young to pay to Grizel Watson, wife and factrix of Alexander Wedderburn, skipper in Dundee, £23 2s. 6d. given by the said Alexander Wedderburn to the defender for buying two elbow and six other chairs. (20.)

52. **1704.** Feb. 21.—Petition by Alexander Wedderburn, skipper, and Patrick Balneaves, for a warrant to roup certain premises of which they were the heritors, for a year's rent. (39.)

53. **1704.** April 3.—Peter Wedderburn, merchant in Dundee, is named as one of the nearest of kin on mother's side to Alexander Raitt, only son of the late Rev. Robert Raitt and the late Elizabeth Wedderburn. (44.)

54. **1705.** July 2.—Robert Wedderburn, mariner, on an inquest. (88.)

55. **1705.** July 7.—John Wedderburn, doctor of medicine, and Peter Wedderburn, merchant, are on two inquests. (88.)

56. **1705.** July 9.—Decree for Alexander Watson of Wallace Craigie *v.* his mother, Katharine Clayhills, relict of the late Thomas Watson, for the delivery up of various writs, &c., including transumpt (1578) of a charter, &c., obtained by George Raitt, brother of the late James and Gilbert, sons of James Raitt, and Elizabeth Low, his relict, wife of Patrick Wedderburn; transumpt (28 Jan. 1594-95) of a disposition in favour of the said Patrick and his wife; and decreet of transumpt (1646) in favour of Andrew Wedderburn, brother of the said Patrick, and disposition (1653) by the said Andrew to Robert Douglas. (89.)

<small>Either this is wrongly extracted or there is an error in the record, as "brother of *the said* Patrick" should clearly be "grandson." Patrick Wedderburn, who married Elizabeth Low, had only one brother, Richard, and moreover no brother of his could have been living in 1646. His son Alexander had four sons Patrick, John (who both died before 1640), Andrew (their heir), and William. Thus Andrew Wedderburn had a brother Patrick, but was grandson to the Patrick Wedderburn of 1578 and 1594. See, for the transumed disposition, ante s. Dundee Protocol Books, No. 300.</small>

57. **1705.** Nov. 27.—Alexander Wedderburn, shoremaster, takes the oaths of allegiance and assurance to Queen Ann. (112.)

58. **1706.** May 11.—Decree in favour of Alexander Wedderburn of that ilk. (136.)

59. **1708.** Aug. 30.—Action by Margaret Wedderburn, relict and executrix of the late John Pearson, baxter in Dundee, *v.* Alexander Wedderburn of that ilk, as son and heir of Alexander Wedderburn of Easter Powrie, deceased, reciting that by the pursuer's marriage contract (26 Nov. 1690) the said Easter Powrie was bound to pay 400 merks tocher and, in event of children, 800 merks a year to the said Margaret; that John Pearson died just before Whitsunday 1695 and that there was now due to Margaret for the period from then till now £378 13s. 4d. Decree in her favour for her claim and for 800 merks yearly in future. (201.)

60. **1709.** May 25.—Action by Matilda Wedderburn, relict of Mr. James Brisbane, advocate, *v.* David Brisbane, her eldest son, reciting her marriage contract 15 Aug. 1676, by which the said James Brisbane was to put 11,000 merks to her tocher of 6,000 merks, and by which, if she survived him, she was to have 1,000 merks a year, and reciting also her appointment as his executrix 30 Aug. 1693, and now claiming £7,487 3s. 8d. arrears. David Brisbane renounces his heirship and is thereupon assoilzied. (262.)

[See, in all, fol. 5, 7, 15, 18, 20, 28, 29, 31, 32, 39, 41, 44, 46, 49, 52, 55, 56, 57, 67, 68, 71, 76, 79, 83, 88, 89, 91, 95, 112, 113, 115, 124, 136, 150, 151, 155, 158, 176, 180, 201, 203, 211-34, 246, 254, 262, 264.]

VOL. 6.

1709—13.

" Register of Decrees belonging to Alexander Wedderburne, clerk of Dundie, begun on the eighteen day of July 1709 years, ending on the fourteen day of December 1713 years."

61. **1709.** Oct. 3.—Alexander Wedderburn, chosen bailie, and Thomas Read, treasurer, in face of the council subscribe the following assurance to:—" We under subscryvers Doe in the sincerity of our hearts, assert, acknowledge and declare that her Majesty Queen Ann is the only lawful and undoubted soveraign of this realme, also weel de jure, that is of right, Queen, as de facto, that is in possession and exercise of the Government, and therefore wee do sincerely promise and engage that we will with heart and hand, life and goods, maintain and defend her Majestie's title and government, against the pretended Prince of Wales (now taking upon him the title of King of this realme) and his adherents and all other enemies who either be open or secret attempts shall disturb or disquiet her Majestie in the possessione and exercise thereof. Sic subscribitur, A. Wedderburn, Baillie; Tho. Read, Threasourer." (15.)

62. **1709.** Oct. 4.—The same parties take the oath of abjuration, "that their sovereign Lady Queen Ann was rightful Queen, and that the pretended Prince of Wales, taking the title of King of Great Britain, &c., hath no right to the crown of this realme, and they renounce all allegiance to him and after the decease of her Majesty and default of heirs of her body, being protestants, they acknowledge the Princess Sophia and Electress and Duchess Dowager of Hanover, and the heirs of her body, being protestants, as the heirs to the Crown." (16.)

63. **1709.** Nov. 23.—Decree for Alexander Wedderburn, bailie, and boxmaster to the fraternity of seamen in Dundee, for rents belonging to the fraternity. (28.)

64. **1710.** Jan. 16.—Alexander Wedderburn, clerk, sues the flesher trade of Dundee for non-delivery to him of a dozen nolt's tongues at Michaelmas, due to him as clerk of Dundee, by virtue of the magistrates gift of the clerkship to him with its whole dues and casualties, 5 March 1685. (48.)

65. **1710.** March 18.—Sir John Wedderburn of Blackness, eldest son and heir of the late Sir Alexander Wedderburn of Blackness, is ordered to pay a debt of his father to Robert Wedderburn, mariner. Alexander Wedderburn, the clerk, one of the tutors, and sole manager of Sir John's means and estate, acts in the matter, and admits the debt. (55.)

    There are many other similar entries. See fol. 56, 58, 60, 61, 62, 64, 66, 68, 82, 83, 106, 108, 109, 111, 125, 132, 144, 146, 154, 159, 161.

66. **1710.** August 19.—Sir John Wedderburn of Blackness, eldest son and heir of the late Sir Alexander Wedderburn, is decerned to pay to Patrick Christy, barber in Dundee, £32, resting of £36 libelled, owing by the deceased to the pursuer "for sheaving his head and beard thrice a week and pouthering his weig every day during his abond in Dundee in the year 1709. (82.)

67. **1712.** Aug. 11.—Sir John Wedderburn of Blackness is served heir to the deceased Sir Alexander Wedderburn of Blackness, his father, at an inquest held in the Tolbooth of Dundee. (194.)

68. **1713.** June 20.—Transumpt of writs obtained by James Paterson, merchant, against Peter Wedderburn, merchant in Dundee, re an Overgate tenement sold by the said Peter Wedderburn to Thomas Paterson, father of the said James. (227.)

    [See, in all, fol. 5, 8, 15, 16, 17, 21, 24, 28, 48, 55, 56, 58, 60, 61, 62, 64-66, 68, 73, 82-86, 88, 106, 108-11, 114, 123, 125, 132, 136, 144-46, 154, 159, 161, 177, 183, 194, 204, 206, 211, 220-21, 227, 245]

VOL. 7.

1714—15.

" Register of Decreets belonging to Alexander Wedderburne, Clerk of Dundee, begun on the fifth day of January 1714, and ending on the — day of — 171—,"

The clerk was no doubt interrupted in keeping this book by the rising of '15, in consequence of which he was deposed from his office.

69. **1714.** Feb. 3.—Decree in favour of David Brisbane, writer in Dundee, factor for the tutors of Peter Wedderburn of that ilk, for moneys due to the late Alexander Wedderburn of that ilk, father of the minor. (5.)

70. **1714.** Feb. 13.—Alexander Wedderburn, clerk, and Thomas Milne of Milnefield, are named as father's kin to Mrs. Elizabeth Fletcher, relict of David Nevoy of Nevoy, and daughter of Robert Fletcher of Ballinshoe. (6.)

71. **1714.** Aug. 4.—Peter Wedderburn, merchant, and Robert Wedderburn, mariner, are both on an inquest. (35.)

72. **1714.** Sept. 1.—Decree for David Brisbane, factor for the tutors of David Wedderburn of that ilk. (36.)

73. **1714.** Aug. 24.—Alexander Wedderburn, clerk, swears and subscribes the oaths of allegiance, assurance, and abjuration to King George. (38.)

74. **1715.** Jan. 17.—Edict of curatory raised by Sir John Wedderburn of Blackness v. Alexander Wedderburn, clerk, and Robert Wedderburn, mariner (father's kin), and William and George Seton (mother's kin). Sir John appears personally and chooses as his curators Alexander Wedderburn, clerk, Dr. John Wedderburn, Mr. George Seton, advocate, James Hallyburton of Pitcur, David Campbell, younger, of Kethick, &c. (59.)

    [See, in all, fol. 5, 6, 10, 19, 24, 30, 35, 36, 38, 39, 40, 46, 49, 51, 59.]

VOL. 8.

1716–20.

This and the succeeding books are those of George Duncan and others, successors of Alexander Wedderburn, last clerk of his name.

75.   **1718.** Jan. 25.—Decree v. Alexander Wedderburn, shipmaster, bailie, to pay £31 6s. to James Morgan, master of the " Hunter Gally of Dundee," as the damage to his boat when carrying down three heavy cannon from the Craig of Dundee to the place called the Hairs Craig, of which Alexander Wedderburn was commander under the rebels, about Dec.-Jan. 1715-16.   The witnesses' depositions state that Wedderburn "did in a most illegall and masterful way without consent of the pursuer ' press ' his vessel for this service and went on board and steered her down to the Hairs Craig, where, having unloaded the cannon, he left the craft exposed to the fury of the storm and the ice then upon the water, &c." (52.)

76.   **1718.** March 24.—Decree in favour of Peter Wedderburn, merchant. (61.)

77.   **1718.** April 30.—Decree v. Alexander Wedderburn, sheriff clerk of Forfar and indweller in Dundee, to pay to the Deacon of the Hammermen for work done for the late Sir Alexander Wedderburn, and for his son Sir John at the order of the defender, who takes objection to the jurisdiction, he not being sixty days a resident for six months past, to which it is replied that albeit he may sometimes have occasion to stay out of the town about his business it was nottour that his family always resided there and that was enough. (64.)

[See, in all, fol. 10, 24, 28, 40, 52, 64, 80, 96, 101, 103, 140, 152, 156, 169.]

VOL. 9.

1721–23.

78.   **1722.** Sept. 2.—Decree for Peter Wedderburn, merchant, for house rent. (67.)

79.   **1722.** Oct. 22.—Decree for David Brisbane, factor for David Wedderburn of that ilk and his tutors. (69.)

80.   **1722.** Oct. 29.—Robert Tailfor of the city guard of Edinburgh pursues a process against Matilda Wedderburn, relict of Mr. James Brisbane, advocate, and David Brisbane, writer in Dundee, her son, mentioning that Sir John Wedderburn, ensign in the Rt. Hon. Colonel Middleton's regiment of foot, by his order dated 11 June 1722, ordered the said David Brisbane to deliver to the pursuer or his order on sight thereof "his father's and mother's pictures in large and in little," and the said order without any further advice should be his warrand : as also the said Sir John Wedderburn by his other order subjoined to a letter, directed by him to David Brisbane, ordered him also to deliver to the pursuer his locket with his mother's hair and name ciphered for value received by him from the pursuer.   The bailie absolves and assoilzies David Brisbane from the process, and as for Matilda Wedderburn, there could be no process against her, in respect the orders were not directed to her, and David Brisbane deponed that he has not, nor never had in his custody the pictures in the libel, nor were they ever in his power, and deponed that he has a locket such as is libelled, but that he got it from Mrs. Rachel Wedderburn, Sir John's sister, to be kept for her use, and that he has not nor never had any locket from Sir John and this he declared to be a truth as he should answer to God. (12.)

[See, in all, fol. 3, 34, 67, 69, 72, 74.]

VOL. 10.

1723–28.

81.   **1723.** June 15.—Decree for house-rent in favour of Peter Wedderburn, merchant. (19.)

82.   **1726.** Nov 30.—Decree for the rent of a house in the Nethergate in favour of Sir Alexander Wedderburn of Blackness. (204.)

[See, in all, fol. 19, 99, 125, 143, 194, 199, 204, 216, 230, 257.]

Dundee
Decreets
Register

83. **1729.** June 23.—Decree in favour of Sir Alexander Wedderburn, (then designed Alexander Wedderburn, sheriff clerk of Forfar), for au @-rent disponed to him by the late Peter Wedderburn, merchant, 31 Oct. 1718. (105.)

84. **1732.** Sept. 6.—Decree in favour of Thomas Wedderburn, son of Sir Alexander Wedderburn of Blackness. (333.)

[See, in all, fol. 74, 105, 110, 200, 245, 333, 386.]

VOL. 12.

1732—34.

85. **1732.** Dec. 27.—Robert Fotheringham of Ballendean and David Wedderburn of that ilk, indwellers in Dundee, are on the inquest for serving George Kyd of Woodhill, heir to James Kyd of Craigie, his father. (77.)

86. **1733.** Oct. 22.—Petition by Grizell Watson, spouse of Alexander Wedderburn, ship-master and late bailie, and by the said Alexander Wedderburn himself, for a transumpt of a sasine 13 Aug. 1684, infefting her and her sister, Margaret Watson, as daughters of the late Thomas Watson, merchant, in a North Murraygate tenement. (177.)

87. **1733.** Nov. 26.—In an action by an assignee of George Dempster v. the children of the late Dr. John Kinloch of Clasbenie for goods supplied to the deceased, compeared (10 April) "Thomas Wedderburn, son to Sir Alexander Wedderburn of Blackness, unmarried, and aged twenty-three years or thereby, solemnly sworn, purged, and interrogate; Deponed that it consisted with his knowledge that George Dempster furnished the articles mentioned in the account lybelled on, and that the prices therein charged are the current and ordinary : *causa scientiæ*, that he was the said George Dempster's servant at the time of furnishing, and as such saw the said articles delivered and charged them in the said George Dempster his accompt book with his own hands, which is regularly kept." (182.)

88. **1734.** Sept. 4.—Robert Wedderburn, notary public, is notary to a sasine 1732. (260.)

89. **1734.** Oct. 19.—Robert Wedderburn, writer in Forfar, writes a disposition, dated 8 July 1729. (290.)

See, in all, fol. 15, 78, 163, 177, 182, 198, 202, 245, 255, 260, 264, 271, 276, 290, 295.]

VOL. 13.

1734—38.

90. **1734.** Dec. 11.—Decree for John Wedderburn, younger, of Blackness. (3.)

91. **1736.** Nov. 20.—Katharine Wedderburn, mercatrix in Dundee, is named in a decree. (220.)

92. **1737.** June 25.—David Wedderburn of Wedderburn is served heir to the deceased Alexander Wedderburn of Easter Powrie, his great-grandfather (proavus) at an inquest held in the Tolbooth. (323.)

93. **1737.** July 6.—Decree re the roup of the household plenishing of the late Margaret Wedderburn, relict of John Pearson.

94. **1738.** March 11.—David Wedderburn of that ilk, residenter in Dundee, is on an inquest. (431.)

[See, in all, fol. 3, 8, 9, 17, 19, 30, 86, 102, 103, 121, 136, 157, 162, 172, 176, 220, 283, 289 299, 323, 329, 338, 355, 393, 414, 431.]

VOL. 14.

1738—43.

95. 1740. Dec. 17.—Sir Alexander Wedderburn of Blackness, Baronet, residenter in Dundee, is decerned to pay £30 sterling to the collector of land tax, as the tax and king's mealls of a tenement in the Nethergate and another in the Seagate. (298.)

96. 1741. Oct. 12.—Decree in favour of Grizell Watson, relict of Alexander Wedderburn, shipmaster, in Dundee. (461.)

97. 1742. Nov. 2.—Decree v. Sir Alexander Wedderburn of Blackness, Baronet. residenter in Dundee, noting that Sir Alexander was warrand at his dwelling-house by intimating to his Lady, who was within. and to his servants. (588.)

　　[See, in all, fol. 35, 41, 84, 121, 133. 147. 212. 245. 260, 268, 298, 304, 332, 423, 461, 466, 487. 496. 536, 565, 588.]

VOL. 15.

1743—47.

98. 1743. May 23.—Decree v. Sir Alexander Wedderburn of Blackness, residenter in Dundee. (17.)

99. 1743. July 9.—Decree v. Margaret Wedderburn, Lady Craigy. (30.)

100. 1743. Aug. 29.—David Wedderburn of Wedderburn, is served heir of provision to the late Peter Wedderburn (second son of the late Alexander Wedderburn of Easter Powrie), his grand-uncle. (52.)

101. 1744. Sept. 24.—Decreet of transumpt of writs granted on petition by David Wedderburn of that ilk, who, 6 April 1743, disponed to Mr. Hugh and Mr. David Maxwell, the lands of Bridgend of Achray, Knowshade, Kirktown of Strathmartine, Waulkmiln of Baldovan, &c. Among the writs is a disposition, 18 Nov. 1727, of the haill lands of Baldovan, &c., by Thomas Nairn to David Wedderburn and his curators (Gilbert Stewart, Dr. Alexander Scrymgeour, Sir Alexander Wedderburn of Blackness, Dr. John Wedderburn, David Gardyne of Latoun, and David Graham) for 46,000 merks. (145-81.)

　　[See, in all, fol. 17, 30, 41, 52, 145-81, 259, 286, 306. 631, 632.]

VOL. 16.

1748—57.

102. 1749. June 21.—Action by Grizell Scott with consent of her curators, one of whom is Robert Wedderburn of Pearsie, sheriff clerk of Forfar, v. John Brown of Glasswell, Dr. John Wedderburn of Idvies, and others. Dr. John Wedderburn is assoilzied.

103. 1753. April 25.—Decree for Katharine Wedderburn, relict of John Higginson, . merchant in Perth. (531.)

　　[See, in all, fol. 5, 59, 168, 531, 590, 823]

ADMIRALTY COURT BOOK.

1622—51.

This book is more fully entitled, "Records of Burgh, Head, and Admiralty Court," and is inscribed on the title "Court Buik of Dundie, begun in October 1651." The book is blank 22 Jan. 1625—20 Sept. 1630. The folios are not numbered.

Dundee Admiralty Court Book.

1. **1622.** Oct. 11, 28 ; Nov. 18.—Three decrees in favour of Peter Wedderburn, twice designed " elder," and once not designed.

2. **1630.** Oct. 2.—Mr. Alexander Wedderburn, clerk of Dundee, extracts an instrument from the Court Books.

3. **1636.** (a) Jan. 9.—Mr. Alexander Wedderburn of Kingany, clerk of Dundee, holds a Court in his house. (b) June 28.—Mr. Alexander Wedderburn, elder, clerk of Dundee, extracts an act of court. (c) July 4.—Mr. Alexander Wedderburn, elder, holds a Court.
   Alexander Wedderburn of Kingennie can only have been acting as clerk at this date, his nephew Alexander (afterwards of Blackuess) having been clerk since 1633.

4. **1636.** June 28.—Transumpt of a sasine (1622 Sept. 28) to which Peter Wedderburn, elder, is a witness.

5. **1637.** June 29.—Mr. Alexander Wedderburn, clerk of Dundee, holds a Court.

6. **1638.** May 21.—Elizabeth Wedderburn, relict of Robert Murray, burgess, obtains a decreet ordering certain persons to remove from a South Flukergate house.

7. **1642.** March 14.—Admiralty Court appointing Mr. Alexander Wedderburn to be clerk of the courts and all else belonging to the admiralty of the waters of the Tay, granted by Duke of Lennox and Richmond, Great Admiral of Scotland, to the burgh of Dundee, by a grant, dated at Holyrood 20 Aug. 1641.

8. **1643.** Aug. 17.—Before Alexander Wedderburn, bailie, is heard a dispute between Alexander Wedderburn, mariner, and Elizabeth Wedderburn, spouse of umquhile Thomas Moneur, in regard to their claims as creditors of the estate of one Patrick Jack deceased. The result does not appear.

9. **1644.** May 10.—Officers are ordained to assist Alexander Wedderburn of Kingenny in poynding certain lands in Dundee. His infeftment in certain annual-rents out of these lands is dated 7 Dec. 1637.

[See, in all, s dates.—1622. Oct. 11, 28 ; Nov. 18.—1630. Oct. 2.—1636. Jan. 9 ; June 28 ; July 4.— 1637. June 29.—1638. May 31.—1643. Aug. 17.—1644. May 10. In addition, between 5 Oct, 1622 and 21 March 1642, James Wedderburn, bailie, is mentioned on 17 different occasions as sitting on the bench.]

Dundee
Register
of Ships This record consists of four volumes, 1580-89, 1612-1681, 1694-98, 1701-1713. There are, however. several blanks in the record, *e.g.*, 1631-33, 1673-75.

VOL. 1.

1580—89.

Entitled, " Ane buik conteanand the Intressis at Schippis dischairgeand at the port of Dundie beginning In the moneth of November in Anno Dom. 1580."

1. **1580.** Nov. 22.—Alexander Wedderburn (not designed) is named as purchasing part of a cargo of wine.

2. **1580.** Dec. 9.—Patrick Wedderburn and James Wedderburn are named as owning certain consignments from the Isles.

3. **1582.** July 28.—Peter Wedderburn is named as owning part of a cargo, just arrived from Norway.

4. **1584.** (*a*) Jan. 9, Feb. 20.—Robert Wedderburn and Alexander Wedderburn are named as owning certain consignments from Bordeaux. (*b*) March 27, 28.—Robert Wedderburn is again named in respect of consignments from there.

5. **1588.** Aug. 3.—John Wedderburn compears and enters the "Expedition" come from Dansken.

6. **1589.** Jan. 7.—Peter Wedderburn and John Wedderburn are named as owning goods just arrived from the North Isles.

7. **1589.** Jan. 10.—David Wedderburn and Robert Wedderburn are named as owning goods arrived from Bordeaux.

8. **1589.** Jan. 15.—Robert Wedderburn is named as owning goods arrived from the North Isles.

9. **1589.** March 17.—John Wedderburn is named as owning goods in the cargo of a crear of Anstruther, entered in port.

10. **1589.** March 17.—John Wedderburn enters the "James" from Dansken : among the cargo are goods for John Wedderburn.

[The above are all the Wedderburn references in this volume.]

VOL. 2.

1612—81.

" The Buik of the entresis of Schippis Arryvand at the Port and Heavin of Dundie. Begun in the moneth of March Anno Dom. 1612."

On the first page is written, " Sir Alexander Wedderburne, clerk of Dundie, his book of Schippie." " M. A. W.—Magister Alexander Wedderburne," and below an English version of the Latin epitaph of Mary Queen of Scots, as in Vol. 253 of the Protocol Books (ante p. 229), except that the first line runs : " I cam of Kingis, 1 Kingis mariet, my heart a crown did crave." This volume is blank from Nov. 9, 1618 to Oct. 14, 1619 ; Oct. 8, 1631 to Aug. 1, 1633 ; and Sept. 3, 1673 to Jan. 28, 1675.

11. **1612.** Dec. 17.—David Wedderburn is named as the owner of wine arriving from Bordeaux.

12. **1613.** May 9.—Mr. Alexander Wedderburn, notary, clerk, signs the piermaster's accounts. *Dundee Register of Ships*

13. **1615.** May 18.—John Wedderburn is named as the owner of wine arriving from Bordeaux.

14. **1616.** Feb. 19.—Alexander Wedderburn, bailie, audits the piermaster's accounts.

15. **1617.** Jan. 6, May 5, June 13.—Mr. David Wedderburn is named as the owner of various lots of wine arriving from Bordeaux.

16. **1617.** Jan. 25.—Alexander Wedderburn, bailie, and James Wedderburn, bailie, audit the piermaster's accounts. Mr. James Wedderburn, notary, signs for one of the auditors.

17. **1618.** Aug. 18.—Alexander Wedderburn, mariner, enters a ship from Norway, with a cargo of oak.

18. **1620.** Feb. 17.—Alexander Wedderburn and James Wedderburn, bailies, audit the piermaster's accounts.

19. **1620.** July 19.—Alexander Wedderburn is named as the owner of goods arriving from Flanders.

20. **1621.** April 16.—James Wedderburn, bailie, signs the shoremaster's account.

21. **1621.** Nov. 19.—James Wedderburn, younger, enters a ship called the "Gift of God," from Campheir, of which Alexander Boyes is master.

22. **1621.** Nov. 21.—Peter Wedderburn is named as the owner of goods arriving from Gothenburg.

23. **1622.** July 29.—Peter Wedderburn, elder, is named as the owner of goods arriving in the "Swift."

24. **1623.** Feb. 5.—James Wedderburn audits the piermaster's accounts.

25. **1623.** Oct. 15.—William Wedderburn, skipper, is named as the owner of goods arriving in the "James" from Supkie.

26. **1624.** Feb. 23.
   1625. Feb. 7. } Alexander Wedderburn, bailie, and James Wedderburn (kirkmaster 1624) audit the piermaster's accounts.
   1626. Feb. 2.

27. **1626.** Feb. 16.—Alexander Wedderburn is named as the owner of wine arriving from Bordeaux.

28. **1627.** Jan. 18.—James Wedderburn, bailie, and Alexander Wedderburn, dean of gild, audit the accounts.

29. **1628.** Feb. 6.—James Wedderburn, Kirkmaster, audits.

30. **1628.** Dec. 3.—Alexander Wedderburn is named as the owner of goods from Stockholm.

31. **1629.** Jan. 25.—James Wedderburn audits.

32. **1630.** Feb. 17 ; June 8. **1631.** Feb. (?)—James Wedderburn, bailie, dean of guild, audits.

Dundee 33. **1632.** July 18,— Mr. Alexander Wedderburn is named as the owner of timber arriving
Register from Norway.
of Ships.

34.　**1648.** Nov. 20.—Andrew Wedderburn is named as the owner of timber from Norway.

35.　**1649.** Feb. 25.—Alexander Wedderburn, piermaster, renders his accounts for audit.

[See. in all, s. dates :—**1612.** Dec. 17.—**1613.** May 9.—**1615.** May 18.—**1616.** Jan. 6 ; Feb. 19.—
1617. May 5 ; June 13, 25.—**1618.** Feb. 10 ; Aug. 10.—**1620.** Feb. 17 ; July 19.—**1621.** April 16 ;
Nov. 19, 21.—**1622.** July 29 ; Oct. 15.—**1623.** Feb. 5.—**1624.** Feb. 23.—**1625.** Feb. 7.—**1626.**
Feb. 2, 16.—**1627.** Jan. 18.—**1628.** Feb. 6 ; Dec. 3.—**1629.** Jan. 25.—**1630.** Feb. 17 ; June 8.—
1631. Feb. (?).—**1642.** July 18.—**1648.** Nov. 20.—**1649.** Feb. 25.

Vol. 3.

1697—1701.

' *The Book of the entrie of ships arriving at the port and haven of Dundie, pertaining to James Wedderburne,
town clerk of the said Burgh, and begun on the eighth day of May 1694 years.*''

On a fly leaf is added by his son, " Book for the entrie of ships, belonging to Alexander
Wedderburne, town clerk of Dundee 1697, 16 August."

This volume contains no references of interest.

Vol. 4.

1701—13.

36.　**1701.** Aug. 14.—Alexander Wedderburn is named as master of the " Neptune " from
Elphingstoun.

37.　**1702.** Sept. 15.—Alexander Wedderburn is named as master of the " Neptune " from
Clackmannan.

38.　**1706.** (*a*) Jan. 2.—Alexander Wedderburn is named as master of the " St. Peter "
from Newcastle. (*b*) July 4.—Alexander Wedderburn is named as master of the
" Thistle " from Lime Kills.

39.　**1707.** May 9.—Alexander Wedderburn, master of the " Thistle," compears and
enters the same from . . . . (left blank).

40.　**1708.** Oct. 13 —Robert Wedderburn, master of the " Thistle " from Dansick.

41.　**1713.** Jan. 29.—Alexander Wedderburn, master of the " Bea(u)ty " from Norway.

The above are all the Wedderburn references in this volume.

DUNDEE, HILTOUN CHARTULARY.

This record consists of several volumes, and runs from 1700 on. The first five volumes, 1700-99, have been searched.

VOL. 1.

1700—18.

" Record of entries of vassalls in the Baronie of the Hiltoun of Dundee pertaining to the town of Dundee and recorded by Alexander Wedderburn, clerk of Dundee, clerk to the said baronie."

1. **1706.** June 10.—Charter by the provost, &c., in favour of Alexander Wedderburn, clerk, of part of the lands of Clepington, &c. (103.)

2. **1706.** July 13.—Similar charter in his favour, of Easter Clepingtoun. (106.)

3. **1707.** Sept. 2.—Ditto, in favour of the same, of Donaldson's Croft. (144.)

4. **1710.** Dec. 21.—Charter of confirmation by the provost, &c., in favour of Alexander Wedderburn, whom failing, in favour of John Wedderburn, his eldest son, of certain lands in the Hiltoun. (184.)

5. **1710.** Dec. 21.—Similar charter, same to same, of other such lands. (187.)

VOLS. 2—5.

1718—99.

These four volumes of this record (1718-37), 1737-66, 1767-82 and 1782-99), have been searched only by their indices, which contain no references to members of the family.

THE LOCKIT BUIKS OF THE TRADE GUILDS OF DUNDEE.

These "Lockit Buiks" are not in the Dundee charter-room, but in the custody of the officers of the different guilds.

1. WEAVER'S CORPORATION.

This record consists of four volumes, beginning in 1557, but contains nothing of importance.

2. SKINNER'S OR GLOVER'S TRADE.[1]

This record also consists of four volumes, beginning in 1516, and contains a few entries worth noting.

(*a*) **1633.** Oct. 9.—"The quilk day Mr. Alexander Wedderburn, younger, common clerk of Dundee, is become ane of the masters of the skinner craft of the said burcht and hes given his oth of fidelitie for mantenence of the liberties of the said Craft in presence of William Rodger, deacon, &c. Signed Al. Wedderburne."

(*b*) **1676.** Oct. 5.—The which day James Wedderburn, son of Sir Alexander Wedderburn, clerk of Dundee and Laird of Blackness, is admitted frieman of the Glover Craft, being son of a frieman, and hath paid all deues thereto belonging and hath given oath of fidelity to defend the liberties thereof, &c. . . . God bless the Glover traid. Amen. Signed Ja: Wedderburne.

(*c*) **1677.** Sept. 27.—The quhilk daye John Wedderburne, present laird of Blackness, is admitted fremaster to the Glover Craft and hath pay'd all deucs belonging theirto and hath givine his oath of fidelitie, &c. . . . Signed J. Wedderburn.

(*d*) **1677.** Sept. 27.—The quhilk daye Patrick Wedderburne, sone to the Ry[tt] honored Sir Alexander Wedderburne, laird of Blaknes, is admitted free master to the Glover Craft and hath payed, &c. (*ut supra*). Signed Petter Wedderburne.

3. SHOEMAKERS' CRAFT.

The Lockit Buik of this craft is again in four volumes, beginning in 1560, but it contains nothing of value. There are, however, some old papers belonging to the guild, of which two may be noted.

(*a*) **1652.** July 18.—Sasine in favour of Andrew Barrie witnessed by John Wedderburn.

(*b*) **1677.** June 13.—Disposition naming a North Argylegate land as acquired by William Forbes from James Wedderburn, merchant, burgess of Dundee, and conquest by him from Peter Wedderburn, nephew and heir served and retoured to Robert Wedderburn, notary.

4. BAXTARS' CRAFT.

This record consists of two volumes, one covering 1554—1758, and the other running from 1758 down to date. The former is entitled

> "*The Comone buyk of the Craft of Baxtares of the burgh of Dunde maid and begowne the 23 day of Nouember the zeir of God 1554 zeirs.*"

It contains several material entries.

(*a*) **1555-58.** Schyr Thomas Wedderburn is often named as chaplain to the craft.

See s. :—1555. Nov. 20.—1556. Nov. 24.—1557. Nov. 23.—1558. Nov. 23.

---

[1] In an old quarto book, 1554-1653, belonging to the Glovers are named, 1620. Jan. 22.—Margaret Wedderburn. 1644-45. "To Andro Wedderburn for ribbins to our sojers 40s."

Lockit Bulks
of the Trade
Guilds of
Dundee.

(*b*) **1559-68.** Alexander Wedderburn, notary and clerk of Dundee, named.

See s.:—1559. May 19.—1565. June 29.—1568. Sept. 3.

(*c*) **1578.** Oct. 21.—Robert Wedderburn, notary, is named.

See also:—1593. Oct. 29.

(*d*) **1629-35.** Alexander Wedderburn (second) of Kingennie, clerk of Dundee (1627-33), is named as a member of the craft, and often signs.

See s.:—1629. July 13.—1630. March 9; April 22, 30.—1631. June 28.—1632. Oct. 31.—1635. July 20 ; Oct. 25.

(*e*) **1655.** Nov. 1.—John Wedderburn, natural son of Alexander Wedderburn of Kingennie, is apprenticed to William Petrie, deacon of the craft, for seven years. Signed by the said John Wedderburn, Alexander Wedderburn, and William Petrie.

(*f*) **1662.** Oct. 28.—The said John is admitted as free master.

He signs minutes 1663. Nov. 23.—1667. Oct. 9.—1668. Oct. 22.—1669. Sept. 22 ; Oct. 14.—1670. Nov. 3, 8.

(*g*) **1669.** Oct. 21.—Alexander Wedderburn, younger, of Kingennie, is admitted a free master.

(*h*) **1730.** Sept. 3.—David Wedderburn of that ilk is admitted.

He signs an admission 4 Jan. 1740.

5. Bonnetmakers' Craft.

This record begins in 1660, but contains nothing material.

6. Flesher Trade.

This record does not begin till 1713, and contains nothing of value.

7. Hammermen's Craft.

This record begins in 1587, but contains nothing of importance. Robert Wedderburn, notary, constantly signs admissions, &c., 1587—1611.

8. Maltmen's Craft.

This record begins in 1623. It contains nothing material except a single mention, 27 April 1670, of a payment by Andrew Moudie, printer, to John Wedderburn, no doubt the baxter, as baxters were often also maltmen.

9. Tailors' Craft.

This record begins in 1562. It contains only two material entries.

(*a*) **1600.** April 1.—Robert Wedderburn, merchant, is a witness.

(*b*) **1601.** July 8.—Andro Cok, cuik to Peter Wedderburn, is a witness.

10. Collectors of the Crafts of Dundee. (Nine Trades.)

This record begins properly in 1568, but the book contains some earlier leaves which seem to have been bound up with it about 150 years ago, all in the hand of "Alexander Wedderburn, younger, comoun clerk." It contains one or two material entries.

(*a*) **1556.** Oct. 5.—Minute of a meeting of the council of Dundee, when the gift (Feb. 6), of the clerkship of the burgh to Alexander Wedderburn, son of Robert Wedderburn, their brother and co-burgess, is recorded.

(*b*) **1568.** Sept. 27.—James Wedderburn and John Wedderburn are named as councillors, and Alexander Wedderburn, younger, as common clerk.

GILDRIE RECORD OF DUNDEE.

1570—1800.

Dundee Gildrie Record. This is a valuable record, as it contains the "mortcloth dues" from 1635 on, and thus supplies approximately the dates of many deaths. It is now bound up in five volumes, 1570—1696, 1698—1712, 1705—42, 1695—1751, 1751—1870. Of these, the last has been searched down to 1800 only.

Vol. 1.

On the fly leaf is written, "Gildrie Book of Dundee, Anno 1570. Vivat Rex 1729," which may be the expression of either Jacobite or Hanoverian loyalty, according to whom the writer meant by the word "rex."

1. **1578.** Feb. 6.—Alexander Wedderburn, clerk, extracts an act from the "Burgh Court Book," to the effect that no guild brother's son be received into the "Lockit Buik" under 21 years of age. (10.)

2. **1580-99.** (no dates.)—Alexander, Robert, and Patrick Wedderburn are all often named, but not designed. (10, 11, 17, 18, 19, 20, 24, 26.)

3. **1595.** Aug. 26.—David Kyd, is decreed to deliver certain merchandise to Barbara Wedderburn or her father. (30.)

4. **1600-24.**—Between these dates Patrick Wedderburn, Mr. Alexander Wedderburn, Alexander Wedderburn, collector of guild duties, David Wedderburn, Robert Wedderburn, and James Wedderburn are often named. (34-37, 39-42, 44-53.)

5. **1624.** Oct. 7.—Mr. Alexander Wedderburn, younger, is elected dean of gild, and nominates as his assessors Alexander Wedderburn, collector, Peter Wedderburn, and others. (53.)

6. **1630.** Oct. 5.—James Wedderburn, newly elected dean of gild, accepts office. (56.)

7. **1631.** Aug. 23.—John Wedderburn, son to Mr. Alexander Wedderburn, is admitted to the guild, 1628-29. (62.)

8. **1634.** April 15.—Alexander Wedderburn, elder, merchant, is still collector. (59.)

9. **1641.** Nov. 12.—William Wedderburn, son to Alexander Wedderburn, merchant, is named as having paid his "accidents," 1631-32. (61.)
   The dates of the entries are here irregular, perhaps owing to the shifting of leaves in binding.

10. **1671-72.** Peter and Alexander Wedderburn, sons to the clerk, pay their accidents. (126.)

11. **1685.** March 1.—In a dean of guild's court held in the tolbooth, the court ratify a gift of the clerkship granted by the Provost, bailies, &c., in favour of Alexander Wedderburn, eldest son of James Wedderburn, present common clerk of the same, after his father's death, and therein make mention of the true, ready, and faithful service done to them and the common wealth by their well-beloved James Wedderburn, their clerk, and the great care and solicitude he has in the education of his son at schools and otherwise, for making him ably qualified to be his successor.

12. **1685-89.** Peter Wedderburn pays his accidents.

[See, in all, fol. 1, 2, 4, 10, 11, 17, 18-24, 26-27, 29-37, 39-42, 44-59, 61-65, 68-70, 72, 74, 90, 102, 103, 105-7, 109-13, 115-27, 129-32, &c. The entries of Mortcloth Dues are given below.]

Vols. 2—5.

These contain no references of importance, except the entries of Mortcloth Dues in vols. 4 and 5, which are given below.

MORTCLOTH DUES.

1635—1800.

These are contained in Volumes 1, 4, and 5 of the Gildrie Record. Except where otherwise noted, they are made up from Michaelmas or Martinmas to the same period in the following year. There were two mortcloths, the great one for adults, and the small one for children. Where the letter " S " is added, or the reference is expressly to a child in the following list, the dues are for the small cloth, in other cases always for the large.

1. **1635-36.** Hellen Wedderburn.
   The date is Mart. 1635 to Whitsun 1636. She is either the daughter of James Wedderburn and Margaret Dundas, who seems to have died unmarried, or the daughter of David Wedderburn and M. Beaton, who would, however, probably have been described as her husband's wife.

2. **1636. Jan. 2.**—Alexander Wedderburn, his good sone ; the great cloth.
   It is not easy to identify either the person named or the person referred to as his " good sone " in this entry. The use of the great mortcloth shows that the latter was not a child. The Alexander Wedderburn named must be either (a) the second proprietor of Kingennie, in which case one would have expected him to be so designed, or (b) his first cousin Alexander Wedderburn, who married Janet Newton, or (c) his namesake who married Barbara Auchinlek. If " good sone " may be read to mean " son " only, and not, as it usually means, grandson, the person buried is, I think, John Wedderburn, eldest son (born 1612-14) of Alexander, second of Kingennie. He certainly predeceased his father, who died in 1637. The date of this entry makes this highly probable. It might refer, also, to either of two sons (Patrick and John) of Alexander Wedderburn and Barbara Auchinlek, both of whom died before 5 Nov. 1640, when their brother Andrew was retoured heir to them. They, however, probably died but shortly before he was so retoured. If " good sone " must be read to mean grandson, it is very difficult to identify anyone with the person buried in 1636. Alexander, second of Kingennie, married in 1612, and can thus hardly have had in 1636 any grandchildren for whom the great mortcloth would be used : his son did not marry till 1638, so that he certainly had no grandchildren of his name in 1636, and any children of his daughters would still be very young. His two namesakes, mentioned above, seem to have had no grandchildren at all.

3. **1658-59.** Mart. to Whit.—Alexander Wedderburn of Kingenie, his daughter.
   This is a daughter of Alexander Wedderburn, third of Kingennie, by his first or second marriage. Her name is not ascertained.

4. **1663-64.** Mart. to Whit.—Andrew Wedderburn's wife.
   Elspeth Fletcher, first wife of Andrew Wedderburn.

5. **1667-68.** Mart. to Whit.—William Wedderburn.
   Second son of James Wedderburn and Margaret Goldman.

6. **1667-68.** Mart. to Whit.—Kingennie's child.
   John Wedderburn, eldest son of Alexander Wedderburn and Margaret Milne, born 1665.

7. **1674-75.** Mart. to Whit.—James Wedderburn's child.
   Mathilda, daughter to James Wedderburn and Elizabeth Davidson, born Sept. 1674.

8. **1677-78.** Andrew Wedderburn's wife.
   Christian Duncan, second wife of Andrew Wedderburn.

9. **1679-80.** Kingennie's daughter.
   Great mortcloth. This may be either Janet Wedderburn, second daughter to Alexander Wedderburn of Easter Powrie by Margaret Milne, or it may be a daughter of his son, who, after the purchase of Easter Powrie, is often called " Kingennie " in his father's life. In the latter case, however, the the little mortcloth would be more likely to be used.

10. **1680-81.** John Wedderburn. (S.)
    The fact that it is the small mortcloth shows, I think, that John Wedderburn is not the person buried but the person who had the use of the cloth for one of his children and paid the dues for it, as in No. 17. The reference is to one of the younger sons of John Wedderburn of Blackness— Peter, James or George. See also Nos. 12 and 14.

11. **1681-82.** Pieter Wedderburn.
    Younger son of Sir Alexander Wedderburn of Blackness and Matilda Fletcher.

2 X

12.   **1681-82.** John Wedderburn of Blackness.   (S.)
One of his younger sons—Peter, James or George.

13.   **1682-83.** Provost Wedderburn.
Alexander Wedderburn of Easter Powrie, d. 9 April 1683.

14.   **1682-83.** The Laird of Blackness.   (S.)
One of John Wedderburn's of Blackness, younger sons, Peter, James or George.

15.   **1683-84.** Andrew Wedderburn.
Son to Alexander Wedderburn and Barbara Auchinlek.

16.   **1685-86.** Easter Powrie's leady.
Grissell Wedderburn, daughter of Sir Alexander Wedderburn of Blackness, and wife of Alexander
Wedderburn, fourth of Kingennie.

17.   **1685-86.** Blackness.   (S.)
Jean Wedderburn, fourth daughter of John Wedderburn of Blackness, born Feb. 1685.

18.   **1686-88.** Kingudie's daughter.
Kingudie, error for Kingennie?   If so, it refers to Elizabeth or Mathilda Wedderburn, daughters
of Alexander Wedderburn, fourth of Kingennie, both of whom died before 7 Oct. 1686.

19.   **1688-89.** John Wedderburn of Easter Powrie.
Eldest son of Alexander Wedderburn of Easter Powrie and Grizell Wedderburn.

20.   **1689.** April to Mich.—Peter Wedderburn.
Second son of Alexander Wedderburn, fourth of Kingennie.

21.   **1689.** April to Mich.—James Wedderburn's child.
Rachel, fifth daughter to James Wedderburn and Elizabeth Davidson.

22.   **1691-92.** Easter Powrie.
Alexander Wedderburn of Easter Powrie, fourth of Kingennie, d. Jan. 1692.

23.   **1692-93.** Margaret Wedderburn, daughter to Easter Powrie.
Margaret Wedderburn, third daughter of Alexander Wedderburn, fourth of Kingennie.

24.   **1695-96.** Provost Wedderburn's rellock (relict).
Margaret Miln, third wife of Alexander Wedderburn of Easter Powrie.

25.   **1695-96.** James Wedderburn, clerk.
He died Jan. 1696.

26.   **1695-96.** James Wedderburn's son.
James, fourth son of James Wedderburn, clerk, and Elizabeth Davidson.

27.   **1697-98.** Blackness' child.
No doubt his seventh son, Thomas.

28.   **1698-99.** Mrs. Wedderburn.
This is Rachel Dunmure, wife of John Wedderburn of Blackness, afterwards (1704), created a
Baronet.

29.   **1698-99.** The clark's child.
James, eldest son of Alexander Wedderburn and Katharine Scott, born 25 July 1698.

30.   **1701-2** Elizabeth Wedderburn.
Sixth daughter of James Wedderburn and Elizabeth Davidson, born 1686.   Had the reference
been to Elizabeth, daughter of Alexander Wedderburn of Easter Powrie, she would have been called
wife or relict of Mr. Robert Rait.

31.   **1701-2.** The clerk's child.
John, second son of Alexander Wedderburn and Katherine Scott.

32. **1703-4** Patrick Wedderburn's wife.
Helen Lyon, first wife of Peter (or Patrick) Wedderburn, son of Alexander Wedderburn of Easter Powrie and Margaret Miln.

33. **1703-4.** Lady Blackness, elder.
Matild Fletcher, relict of Sir Alexander Wedderburn, Knight. She was thus 83 years of age.

34. **1704-5.** Alexander Wedderburn's child.
Perhaps Alexander, eldest son of Alexander Wedderburn of Wedderburn.

35. **1707-8.** The clerk's daughter. (S.)
Christian, second daughter of Alexander Wedderburn and Katharine Scott.

36. **1707-8.** The clerk's child.
Alexander, third son of Alexander Wedderburn and Katharine Scott.

37. **1707-8.** Blackness's two children.
Elizabeth, third daughter of Sir Alexander Wedderburn, and another child, whose Christian name is not known.

38. **1708-9.** The Laird of Wedderburn's child.
Probably Robert, second son of Alexander Wedderburn of Wedderburn.

39. **1709-10.** Sir Alexander Wedderburn of Blackness.
Second baronet of Blackness.

40. **1709-10.** Sir John Wedderburn's sister.
Margaret, eldest daughter of Sir Alexander Wedderburn, second baronet, and Elizabeth Seaton.

41. **1712-13.** Blackness' son. (G.)
Alexander, third son of Sir Alexander Wedderburn, second baronet, and Elizabeth Seaton.

42. **1712-13.** The clerk's daughter. (S.)
Katherine, fourth daughter of Alexander Wedderburn and Katharine Scott.

43. **1713-14.** The Laird of Wedderburn.
Alexander Wedderburn of Wedderburn, died Dec. 1713.

44. **1713-14.** " Ougle and Wedderburn's children £1. 6. 8. Wedderburn's child £1. 6. 8."
This is a peculiar entry. The small mortcloth dues being 13/4 at this date, it looks as if Wedderburn lost three children. They are, perhaps, Rachel, Peter and Gilbert Wedderburn, children of Alexander Wedderburn of Wedderburn.

45. **1716-17.** Clerk Wedderburn's child.
Alexander, sixth son of Alexander Wedderburn and Katharine Scott.

46. **1717-18.** Blackness' daughter. (G.)
Mathilda, fourth daughter of Sir Alexander Wedderburn of Blackness, deceased, and Elizabeth Seaton.

47. **1720-21.** Mr. Wedderburn's child.
Perhaps refers to James Wedderburn, son of Robert Wedderburn and Margaret Arnot, born 1705. If not, it is Margaret, fifth daughter of Sir Alexander Wedderburn of Blackness (fourth Bart.), b. 1713.

48. **1721-22.** Patrick Wedderburn's wife.
Barbara Affleck, second wife of Peter or Patrick Wedderburn, son of Alexander Wedderburn of Easter Powrie and Margaret Miln.

49. **1722-23.** Laird of Blackness' child.
Mary, seventh and youngest daughter of Alexander Wedderburn (of Blackness) and Katharine Scott.

50. **1723-24.** Peter Wedderburn.
Son of Alexander Wedderburn of Easter Powrie and Margaret Miln (ante. Nos. 32 and 48).

Dundee Mortcloth Dues.

51. **1732-33.** Mr. Wedderburn, younger, of Blackness, a child.
Charles, fourth son of John Wedderburn (afterwards fifth baronet) and Jean Fullarton.

52. **1732-33.** The said Mr. Wedderburn, a child.
Alexander Wedderburn, eldest son of the above.

53. **1738-39.** Robert Wedderburn's child.
This must be a quite infant child of Robert Wedderburn of Pearsie.

54. **1744-45.** Sir Alexander Wedderburn.
Sir Alexander Wedderburn, fourth baronet of Blackness, died Sept.--Oct. 1744.

55. **1750-51.** Dr. John Wedderburn.
Dr. J. Wedderburn of Idvies.

56. **1757-58.** Clementina Wedderburn.
Fifth daughter to Alexander Wedderburn and Grissell Watson.

57. **1760-61.** Mr. Wedderburn of Wedderburn.
David Wedderburn of Wedderburn.

58. **1761-62.** Lady Blackness.
Katharine Scott, widow of Sir Alexander Wedderburn, fourth Bart. of Blackness.

59. **1764-65.** Mrs. Wedderburn.
Margaret Balfour, relict of Doctor John Wedderburn of Idvies.

60. **1774-75.** Lady Margaret Wedderburn.
Lady Margaret Ogilvy, first wife of Sir John Wedderburn, sixth baronet of Blackness.

61. **1775-76.** Miss Wedderburn.
Susanna Wedderburn, 18 Sept. 1776. (See also Dundee Reg. Burials.)

62. **1778-79.** Mrs. Grizel Wedderburn.
Grissell Wedderburn of Wedderburn, 12 Nov. 1778. (ib.)

63. **1785-86.** Mr. Wedderburn.
Robert Wedderburn of Pearsie, d. 19, buried 22 Feb. 1786. (ib.)

64. **1785-86.** Miss Wedderburn.
Katharine Wedderburn, 2 Oct. 1786. (ib.)

65. **1788.** Jan. 9.—Mrs. Wedderburn.
Isobell Edward, widow of Robert Wedderburn o Pearsie, d. 6 Jan. 1788. (ib.)

66. **1789-90.** Alexander Wedderburn.
Eighth and youngest son of Sir Alexander Wedderburn, fourth baronet of Blackness. He died 18 Jan. 1790. (ib.)

The Dundee Register of Burials (kept at Dundee from 1772, on) has been searched to the end of 1808, and contains, besides those noted above, the following :—

67. **1793.** Dec. 21.—Mrs. Catharine Wedderburn.
Second daughter to Robert Wedderburn of Pearsie, and wife of Dr. James Stewart in Dundee. Her maiden name is adhered to in this entry, according to an old custom, then ceasing to be prevalent.

68. **1795.** Dec 4.—Ann Wedderburn.
I have not been able to identify this individual. The name is not common in the family. John Wedderburn of Camuo (see Vol. i. s. the account of Peter Wedderburn, younger son of Sir Alexander Wedderburn of Blackness, and his descendants) had a daughter Ann, but she died there 18 May 1802, and, moreover, had she died in 1795 and in Dundee, she would have been but seven years old, and the small mortcloth would have been used.

69. **1803.** June 24.—Sir John Wedderburn.
Sixth baronet of Blackness.

PUBLIC RECORDS—SCOTLAND.

GREAT SEAL REGISTER.

PRIVY COUNCIL REGISTER.

EXCHEQUER ROLLS.

ACTS OF THE PARLIAMENTS OF SCOTLAND.

RETOURS OF THE SERVICES OF HEIRS.

PRIVY SEAL REGISTER.

GENERAL REGISTER OF SASINES.

PARTICULAR REGISTER OF SASINES (FORFAR.)

BOOKS OF COUNCIL AND SESSION.

    1. REGISTER OF BONDS, DEEDS, &c.

    2. REGISTER OF ACTS AND DECREETS.

RECORDS OF TESTAMENTS.
    (Edinburgh, Brechin, S. Andrew's, &c.)

PARISH REGISTERS.
    (Dundee, Edinburgh, Aberlady, &c.)

PROTOCOL BOOKS OF NOTARIES.

I now proceed to give the evidence which I have collected from the public records of Scotland, preserved in the General Register House at Edinburgh, and gradually becoming, either by publication or improved arrangement, more and more available to the public.

I do not, of course, propose to give any thing like an account either of the Scottish Records or of their chequered history. Carried to London by Cromwell in the time of the Commonwealth, they were returned to Edinburgh in 1657—1660. But a vessel in which many of them were embarked met with a storm, and, in order to lighten her, eighty-five of the barrels in which the records of Scotland were being sent home were transferred to another ship, which foundered, while the lightened vessel came safely north. Thus many of these historic documents were altogether lost, while others, again, otherwise scattered, have been only gradually recovered from private repositories.

Of the vast mass of material now contained in the Register House there is, at present, no official catalogue, and the only guides I have had to the records have been the advice of Mr. Macleod and a handbook[1] printed in 1885 by Messrs. Millar and Bryce, of which they very kindly sent me a copy. This book does not attempt more than a very general view, and there is great need of a detailed and well-arranged catalogue. Such a guide already exists for the Parochial Registers of Scotland, although the issue of this is, for some reason, confined to public libraries, and the book is not obtainable by private persons. It is to be hoped that before long the authorities may see fit to add to the now issuing series of Scottish Records a volume containing a guide to the whole collection, and embracing that to the parochial registers already in existence. In view, therefore, of the absence of any guide to which the reader can refer, I add, with the help of Messrs. Millar and Bryce's book, a tabular statement, which shows, I think, the principal ancient records now in the Register House. It will be at once evident that they are far too numerous to admit of exhaustive examination. Such an undertaking would be an affair of years, and may be rendered less difficult as time goes on, and either the public authorities or private societies, such as the *Scottish Record Society*, are enabled to enlarge their sphere of action. For the present I have had to confine myself to the examination of those of the records which are already published, or which seemed most likely to be productive of information. Calendars of the first five records named in the preceding list are in course of publication,[2] while the rest have been searched in the original MSS. A note on the character of each record will be given as the extracts from it come to be dealt with. Meanwhile, I append the tabular statement just mentioned.

---

[1] " Handbook of Records in H.M. General Register House, Edinburgh, by Millar and Bryce, Professional Searchers of Records, Edinburgh. 1885."

[2] The following is a list of the Scottish Record publications, which I have examined for the purposes of this work. 1. The Great Seal Register. 2. Privy Council Register. 3. Exchequer Rolls. 4. Acts of the Parliaments of Scotland. 5. Retours of the Services of Heirs. 6. Acts of the Lords Auditors, 1466-94, ed. (1839) Thomson. 7. Acts of the Lords of Council in Civil Causes, 1478-95, ed. (1839) Thomson. 8. Accounts of the Lord High Treasurer of Scotland, 1473-98, ed. Dickson. 9. Documents illustrative of the History of Scotland, 1286-1306, ed. Stevenson. 10. The Hamilton Papers, 1532-90. 11. Ledger of Andrew Halyburton, 1492-1503, ed. Innes. 12. Calendar of Documents relating to Scotland, 1100-1509, ed. (1884) Bain, 4 vols. 13. Calendar of State Papers relating to Scotland, ed. (1858) Thorpe. 14. Calendar of Border Papers, 1560-1603, ed. Bain. 15. Rotuli Scotiæ (2 vols., 1814). Of these, Nos. 1-5 are among the records in the Edinburgh Register House, and are dealt with at p. 362. seqq. Nos. 6 and 7 are also in the Register House and are dealt with later on in the extracts given from the Register of Acts and Decreets, while Nos. 8-11, contain nothing material. The remaining volumes (Nos. 12-15) are all from records in the Public Record Office in London and contain a few material entries all of which are noted in the extracts from the Public Records, London, given in the following section of this volume.

SYNOPSIS

OF THE

PUBLIC RECORDS OF SCOTLAND,

PRESERVED IN H.M. REGISTER HOUSE,

EDINBURGH,

(Compiled from Messrs. Millar and Bryce's handbook of the Records.)

NOTE.—The use of italics signifies that the record in question has been partly, if not completely, searched for this work. Where a reference to a page is added in brackets, thus (p. 35-36), the book referred to is Millar and Bryce's handbook; while in the absence of brackets, the reference is to the pages of this volume.

I. CROWN WRITS &c.

i. *Great Seal Record.* See below p. 362. . (pp. 35-36.)

ii. *Prince's Seal Record* (pp. 36-37.)
- (a) Charters, 1404-1624, 1620-1819.
- (b) Signatures, 1620-25.
- (c) Register, 1620-25.

iii. *Privy Seal Record* (p. 37.)
- (a) *Register,* 1491-1810.
- (b) *Responde Book,* 1752-74.
- (c) Warrants, 1627-1808.
- (d) Presentations,1567-1663
- (e) Remissions, 1611-22.
- (f) Charters (Nova Scotia Baronets), 1625-30.
- (g) Tacks of Teinds, 1782-92, 1795-1808.

II. SASINES, ENTAILS, &c.

i. *General Register of Sasines,* 1617-1868 (p. 29.)

ii. *Particular Register of Sasines,* for each shire, &c., *e.g.,* Forfar. Various dates. (p. 29, 33.)

iii. Interruptions of Prescriptions, 1697-1868. (p. 83.)

iv. Register of Entails, 1688 to date. (p. 34.)

v. Monastic Records. (p. 38.)
- (a) Holyrood 1545-67.
- (b) Lincluden, 1547-64.
- (c) Dunfermline, 1557-85.
- (d) Jedburgh, 1534-96.
- (e) *Coupar Angus,* 1543-1559.
- (f) *Coupar Angus,* 1543-62.
- (g) Various charters.

vi. Forfeitures, 1715, 1745-46. (pp. 45-52.)

vii. Diligences, (pp. 52-54.)
- (a) Adjudications, 1636 on.
- (b) Inhibitions, 1602 on.
- (c) Hornings, 1610 on.
- (d) Bill Chamber Records
  - Cautionaris, 1573-1694, 1705
  - Lawburrows, 1603-1706.
  - Loosings, 1617-1706.

Of these (e) and (f) have been published by the Grampian Club.

III. EXCHEQUER RECORDS.

i. General Records. (pp. 38-41.)
- (a) *Rolls,* 1262-1748.
- (b) *Accounts of Lord High Treasurer,* 1473-1635.
- (c) Acts of Lords Auditors of Exchequer, 1584-1659.
- (d) Rolls of Account.
- (e) Customs, &c.
- (f) Army Accounts, 1500-1700?
- (g) Crown lands.
- (h) Church lands.
- (i) Royal Household Books.

ii. Court of Exchequer (pp. 41-44.)
- (a) Crown Rents, &c., 1671-1773.
- (b) Customs, 1612-1765.
- (c) General Proceedings, 1654-1793.
- (d) Commissions,1667-1781.
- (e) Muster Rolls, 1667-91.
- (f) Miscellaneous Accounts, 1667-1745.
- (g) Bishop's Rents, 1691-1770.
- (h) Vacant Stipends, 1693-1706.
- (i) Royal Bounty, 1680, 1732-67.
- (j) Miscellaneous Papers, 1584-1783.
- (k) Marchmont Papers, 1697-1730.
- (l) Murray Papers, 1718-43.
- (m) Oaths of Allegiance.
- (n) Earl of Morton's Papers.
- (o) Whitehill (Fife) Writs.
- (p) Old Deeds, 1409-1723.
- (q) Clerk of the Pipe's Papers.
- (r) Taxation Records, 1500-1700.

IV. CHANCERY RECORDS.

i. *Retours of Services of Heirs,* 1545 to date. (pp. 58, 78-9.)

ii. Quarter Seal Record, 1750-61, 1831-47, 1847 on. (p. 78.)

iii. Responde Book, 1573-1847. (p. 79.)

V. Books of Council
and Session.
{ i. *Register of Bonds, Deeds, &c.*, 1554-1810, 1812 on. (p. 55.)
ii. *Register of Inventories*, 1696-1845. (p. 56.)
iii. *Register for the Earl of Findlater*, 1717-50. (p. 56.) }

VI. Records of the
Court of
Session.
{ (a) *Acta Dom. Aud.*, 1466-94.
(b) *Acta Dom. Conc.*, 1478-1532. (p. 56.)
(c) *Acta Dom. Conc. et Sessionis*, 1532-59.
    (p. 56.)
(d) *Acts and Decreets* { 1542-1659 }
                       { 1661-1810 } (p. 56.) }
{ (e) *Minute Book*, 1558-1659, 1661, &c.
    (p. 57.)
(f) *Outer House Rolls*, 1681 on. (p. 57.)
(g) *Books of Sederunt*, 1553-1852. (ib.)
(h) *Processes* (various dates.) (ib.)
(i) *Charters*, 1700-1800, with index. (ib.) }

Of these the Acta Dom. Aud (*Acts of the Lords Auditors of Causes and Complaints*, ed. by Thomson.)
are the record of the Court of Judges before the Court of Session was instituted.

VII. Parliamentary
Records.
{ These range from 1292
on and are of various
kinds. (pp. 70-71.) } { See the "*Acts of the Parliaments of Scotland*," edited by
Thomson. }

VIII. Privy Council
Records.
{ These, again, are various ; the principal being the *Register of the Acts of the Privy
Council* (1545-1707), now in course of publication. (pp. 71-72.) }

IX. Admiralty
Records.
{ These cover 1557-61, 1654-1830. (pp. 69-70.) }

X. Commissariots
(Testaments).
{ (a) *Books of the "Official" of S. Andrew's.* 1515-45. (pp. 58-59.)
(b) General Records for the different districts (Aberdeen, Argyle, *Brechin*, Caithness,
    Dumfries, Dunblane and Perth, *Dunkeld, Edinburgh, Glasgow*, Hamilton and
    Campsie, Inverness, the Isles, Kirkcudbright, Lanark, Lauder, Moray, Orkney
    and Shetland, Peebles, Ross, *S. Andrew's*, Stirling, Wigtown). They consist
    of testaments, inventories, minute books, &c. (pp. 59-68.) }

XI. Parochial
Registers
(p. 81.)
{ The Registers of all the parishes of Scotland from their earliest dates down to
Dec. 31, 1854, are now collected in the Register House. On Jan. 1, 1855, the
general register of births, deaths, and marriages begins, and continues down to
date. *See below for a note of those searched.* }

XII. Teind Office
(p. 87.)
{ These are in the custody of the clerk of teinds. They are scanty down to 1700,
after which date there are minute books, &c., down to the present time. }

XIII. Register of
Arms.
(p. 76, 86.)
{ (a) Book of Robert Forman, Lord Lyon,
    1557 on.
(b) Records of Grants, 1672 on.
(c) Lyon Register of Funerals, &c. 1681 ou.
(d) Birth Brief Register, 1728 on. }
{ (e) 14 Vols. of Proceedings, 1600 on,
(f) Admissions of Heralds, 1630 on,
(g) Register Book, 1770-75.
(h) Warrants, &c., for messengers. }

See the chapter on the armorial bearings of the family in Vol. I.

XIV. Miscellaneous
Records.
{ i. Burgh Records, *e.g.*, Fife, 1514-22 ; Forfar, 1568-69. (p. 73.)
ii. Sheriff Court Records, various dates. (p. 73-4.)
iii. Local Jurisdictions : Regalities, Baronies, Bailie Courts. (p. 74-75.)
iv. Teind Records. Various Papers ; tacks 1782-92. (p. 75.)
v. Johnstone of Johnstone Papers, 1567-1662. (p. 75.)
vi. (a) *Admissions of Notaries*, 1563-1873. with index 1680-1873, and warrants
        1736-1813. (p. 75-6.)
    (b) *Protocol Books of Notaries*, (p. 76.)
vii. *Register of Arms*, 1557 on. (p. 76.)
viii. Royal Commissions. Modern. (p. 76.)
ix. (a) *Ledger of Andrew Halyburton*, 1492-1503. (p. 76.) } Both these are
    (b) *Book of Customs, &c., in Scotland*, 1612. (p. 76.) } published. }

Great Seal Register. This important record begins in 1306 and runs down to the present time. It was at one time very voluminous, containing all charters and grants of land from the Crown, whether direct or by way of confirming the charters of private individuals, superior lords, &c. Down to the date of the union with England the great seal used was, of course, that of the Scottish Crown, but upon the union another great seal was specially appointed to be used in its place, while the use of the register remained unaltered. In 1874, however, charters of progress were abolished, and, at the present time, the only deeds recorded in this register are, Charters of Incorporation, Charters made with consent of the Board of Trade, Charters of Novodamus, and Gifts of Ultima Hæres to the Queen's Remembrancer in Trust.

The Great Seal Record consists of six divisions :—

i. *The Great Seal Register.*—(a) Rolls, 1306-1443. (b) Volumes, 1362 to date, with Index from 1582 on. (c) Warrants of the Great Seal 1663-1794, including some (1696-1702), presented to the Register House by Sir H. H. Campbell of Marchmont in 1848 ; and other warrants 1807 to date. (d) Inventories of the Great Seal 1663-1794.

ii. *Comptroller's Register of Signatures.*—27 Oct. 1561—3 Feb. 1642.

iii. *Register of Signatures (Signet of Office).*—Warrants 1607-1847 with index.
This contains resignations, confirmations, adjudications, infeftments of annual-rents, gifts of escheat, tutory, bastardy, ultima hæres, &c. It was discontinued by statute (10 & 11 Vic., c. 51), in 1847, when signatures and precepts as preliminary to Crown Charters were abolished.

iv. *Paper Register of the Great Seal.*—1608 to date. With warrants 1733 to date, &c., and an index referring back earlier than the existing record, 1596 to date. (There are also some special remissions for high treason 1611-22, and a brief register of comprysings, &c., 1656-58.)
This contains apprysings, life-rent charters, legitimations, remissions, &c. It now consists of pardons to criminals in Scotland, and commissions by the Crown to Scottish Public Departments.

v. *Register of Confirmations and Resignations,* 1858-1865 (21 & 22 Vic., c. 76.)

vi. *Register of Crown Writs,* 1809-1784 (31 & 32 Vic., 101).

The above record is now in course of publication. In 1814, a folio volume, containing the register of the Great Seal 1306-1424, was " printed by command of H.M. George III.," after which nothing further was done till 1882, when there was published the first of the series of quarto volumes, in which the Great Seal Register is now being edited. Of these volumes seven are now issued, 1424-1513, 1513-46, 1546-80, 1580-93, 1593-1608, 1608-20, 1620-32. They contain not only the register of the Great Seal itself, but also include the warrants and paper register, in fact, all the matter contained in the above mentioned §§ I. and IV. Each volume contains a complete index of both places and persons, and with the help of these, I have extracted every reference to members of the family, and, as the volumes are readily available, I have made the extracts as brief as possible.

From 1633, the Great Seal Register itself has been searched in the original down to 1800, and the Paper Register down to 1713. All grants to persons of the name of Wedderburn have been thus noted from the record, though not, of course, all the casual references to persons of the name, acting as witnesses, or otherwise mentioned in charters to members of other families.

1. **1426.** Jan. 20.—Royal charter of a holding in Blacater, co. Berwick, to William de Wedderburne and his heirs. (Vol. 1424—1513. § 79.)

2. **1431.** May 1.—Confirmation of a grant to Patrick Lyndesay of Angus, reciting a letter 12 May 1424, witnessed at Striveling (Stirling) by Haye of Yhester, Vylliamo of Wedyrburne, and others. (*ib.* 195.)

3. **1450.** May 16.—Grant of the lands of Wedderburn, co. Berwick, in favour of Sir David Hume of Wedderburne and Alice, his wife, and their heirs. (*ib.* § 349.)

4. **1452.** April 24.—Grant to Patrick of Dunbar, witnessed by William de Wethirburn.
(*ib.* § 547.)

5. **1482.** Feb. 18.—Confirmation of grant (9 March 1480-81) to John Graham of Fintre, witnessed at Abernethy by James Scrimgeour, constable of Dundee, David Wethirburn, and others. (*ib.* § 1558.)

6. **1484.** Feb. 18.—Confirmation of grant (7 Aug. 1476) to Robert Graham of lands near Kerymur, co. Forfar, witnessed at Abernethy by David Wedderburn, scutifer, and others. (*ib.* § 1560.)

7. **1486.** March 21.—Confirmed grant (7 Jan. 1484-85) to James Ramsay, witnessed at Dundee by James Ogilvy de Arly, miles, and David Wedderburn, scutifer, &c. (*ib.* § 1615.)

8. **1491.** Feb. 19.—Confirmed grant (3 Feb. 1489-90) by William Farquhar of Dundee to the parish church thereof, witnessed at Dundee by David Wedderburn and others. (*ib.* § 1935.)

9. **1490.** July 18.—Two confirmed grants (17 July 1490) witnessed at Dundee by David Wedderburn and others. (*ib.* § 1967-68.)

10. **1496.** March 31.—Confirmed grant (26 Oct. 1495) to Alexander Ogilvy, witnessed at Dundee by David Wedderburn and others. (*ib.* § 2305.)

11. **1502.** March 31.—Confirmed grant (8 March 1502) witnessed at Dundee by Robert Wedderburn and others. (*ib.* § 2637.)

12. **1524.** March 7.—Confirmed grant (26 Feb. 1524) to Andrew Barry of Dundee, witnessed at Tealing by Magister Robert Wedderburn, not. pub. (Vol. 1513-46. § 258.)

13. **1525.** Nov. 6.—Confirmed grant (21 Oct. 1525) to Thomas Hay witnessed at Dundee by Robert Wedderburn, Mr. John Barry, vicar of Dundee, and others. (*ib.* § 340)

14. **1527.** March 26.—Confirmed grant by the Walkaris craft of Dundee to the church and choir of Dundee, witnessed at Dundee 21 Dec. 1517, and again 29 May 1523 by James Wedderburn, bailie, who gives sasine. (*ib.* § 435)

15. **1528.** Jan. 20.—Confirmed grant (14 Jan. 1527-28) by Jonet Forestar, daughter and heiress of the late David Forester in Neva, with consent of James Wedderburn, younger, burgess of Dundee, her husband, in favour of John Wedderburn, their son, of the lands of Trosto, and part of Tullohill, in the barony of Ferne, co. Forfar. Witnessed at Dundee by D. Tho. Wedderburn, D. Rob. Wedderburn, and others, "chaplains and notaries," and signed by Jonet Forestar and James Wedderburn with their own hands. (*ib.* § 539.)

16. **1528.** April 1.—Confirmed charter (4 May 1521) by Andrew Abircromby to the parish church of Dundee, in which the lands of Andrew Wedderburn are named as a boundary. (*ib.* § 578 note.)

17. **1530.** June 1.—Confirmed grant (18 May 1530) by George Blair to his sister, witnessed at Dundee by Magister Rob. Wedderburn, not. pub. (*ib.* § 946.)

18. **1531.** May 8.—Confirmed charter (28 Feb. 1531) by James Scrymgeour, constable of Dundee, by which he sells to George Rollok, burgess of Dundee, and Margaret Wedderburn, his wife, some land in Dundee, occupied by Janet Froster, relict of Robert Wedderburn. (*ib.* § 1162)

19. **1533.** May 27.—Grant to Thomas Cullace of the lands of Trosto and one part of Tullohill (ut sup. No 15) on the resignation, as to the fee thereof, by John Wedderburn of Trosco, and, as to the free tenement (liberum tenementum) thereof, by Janet Forester. (*ib.* § 1286.)

20. **1533.** Oct. 14.—Confirmed charter (31 Aug. 1533) of sale by James Scrymgeour, constable of Dundee, to James Wedderburn, younger, burgess of Dundee, and Janet Forrester, his wife, in life-rent, and to their son, John Wedderburn, and his heirs heretably, of certain acres in Dundee. (*ib.* § 1311.)

21. **1534.** July 3.—Confirmed charter (21 July 1531) by James Scrymgeour to John Rolland, naming David Wedderburn and James Wedderburn among occupiers of lands in Dudop. (*ib.* § 1399.)

22. **1535.** March 15.—Confirmed charter (29 Mar. 1534) in favour of Thomas Duncan and Alice, *alias* Elyse, Weddirburn, his wife, of one third of Balrudery, Logie Wischairt, co. Forfar. (*ib.* § 1459.)

23. **1535.** Oct. 25.—Confirmed charter (22 Oct. 1535) of eight acres in Dudop to George Rollok and Margaret Wedderburn, his wife, and Richard Rollok, their son and heir. Thomas Wedderburn and others, chaplains and notaries, are witnesses. (*ib.* § 1517.)

24. **1535.** Dec. 16.—Charter (18 Jan. 1528) witnessed at Dundee by Dom. Thomas Wedderburn and others. (*ib.* § 1528.)

25. **1535.** Dec. 16.—Confirmed grant (20 Oct. 1534) to Adam Smyth and Matilda Andersoun of the "Hogfauld," lying between the Butterburn and the lands of David Wedderburn and others. (*ib.* § 1529.)

26. **1539.** Feb. 10.—Confirmed charter (9 Oct. 1535) by John, Abbot of Lindores, in favour of David Wedderburn, burgess of Dundee, and Helen Lausoun, his wife, and their heirs and assigns, of the shadow half of Hiltoun of Craigie, in the regality of Lindores, co. Forfar. (*ib.* § 1913.)

27. **1539.** June 8.—Confirmed grant (17 Jan. 1537) to Robert Lausoun of land near the Butterburn, including two acres occupied by David Wedderburn in Welgnit. (*ib.* § 1982.)

28. **1540.** Jan. 2.—Confirmed grant (2 Jan. 1539) by James Rynd of Carse to James Anderson and Grissell Wedderburn, his wife, and their son James, of two-sixths of Lumlethin, co. Forfar. Henry Wedderburn is a witness. (*ib.* § 2055.)

29. **1542.** March 9.—Confirmed grant (8 March 1541), to Elene Stewart, relict of William, Earl of Erroll, of lands called Inchenonan, some of which is mortgaged to James Wedderburn. (*ib.* § 2616.)

30. **1542.** Aug. 8.—Confirmed grant (13 June 1542), by Patrick Gray to David Wedderburn, burgess of Dundee, and Helen Lawson, his wife, of one half of the dominical lie mains of Huntlie (dimediatem terrarum dominicalium lie mains de Huntlie ac toftarum, croftarum, et domorum earundem), barony of Foulis, eo. Perth. (*ib.* § 2749.)
     See as to the word "toftarum," and consequent errors, ante s. Burgh Records, Dundee, "The Lockit Buik," No. 26 note.

31. **1552.** Aug. 8.—Confirmed charter (28 July 1552), dated at Blackness, by Patrick, Lord Gray, in favour of David Wedderburn, burgess of Dundee, and Helen Lawson, his wife, and their heirs and assigns, of one-third of Hiltoun of Wester Craigie, in the barony of Dundee, co. Forfar. (*ib.* Vol. 1546-1580, § 705.)

32. **1553.** Jan. 13.—Royal letters of legitimation in favour of Robert and David Wedderburn, sons natural to Mr. Robert Wedderburn, vicar of Dundee. (*ib.* § 742.)

33. **1555.** Nov. 4.—Grant (16 Oct. 1555), naming the lands of John Wedderburn, near the Butterburn, Dundee, and witnessed at Edinburgh, by Alexander Wedderburn, notary public. (*ib.* § 1010.

34. **1556.** Feb. 10.—Grant (8 Nov. 1555), to Robert Richardson. Alexander Wedder- Great Seai
burn, notary, is a witness at Edinburgh. (*ib.* § 1041.)   Register.

35. **1557.** (*a*) Feb. 18.—Grant (16 Feb. 1556), to James Kennedy. (*ib.* § 1153.)
(*b*) March 8.—Grant (11 March 1556), to Archibald Elliott. (*ib.* § 1156.)   Both
of these are witnessed at Edinburgh by Alexander Wedderburn, notary.

36. **1569.** Aug. 18.—Grant (5 Nov. 1569), to Alexander Lovell naming the lands of
John Wedderburn near the Butterburn, and those of Alexander Smyth. (*ib.* § 1876.)
See ante Nos. 25 and 33.

37. **1569.** Nov. 24.—Grant to Gilbert Ogilvy (8 Nov. 1569). Alexander Wedderburn,
notary, is a witness at Dundee. (*ib.* § 1896.)

38. **1574.** Feb. 3.—Grant to John Bonar (7 Feb. 1572); Alexander Wedderburn,
notary, is a witness at Dundee. (*ib.* § 2174.)

39. **1576.** Aug. 23.—Grant (10 Aug. 1576) to Patrick Maule. Alexander Wedderburn
and Robert Wedderburn, notaries, are among the witnesses at Dundee. (*ib.* § 2587.)

40. **1576.** Sept. 15.—Grant (5 July 1572) by the Abbot of Kinlos to William Abirnethie
and his wife, witnessed at Kinlos by John Wedderburne, and Alexander Wedderburn,
notary public. (*ib.* § 2588.)

41. **1577.** March 10.—Grant (11 June, 1576) to Robert, Earl of Buchan, witnessed at
Bonytown by Alexander Wedderburn, notary. (*ib.* 2660.)

42. **1580.** Dec. 31.—Charter (1 April, 1574) to Thomas Scott. Witnessed at Dundee
by Alexander Wedderburn, clerk of the burgh. (Vol. 1580-93, § 75.)

43. **1581.** April 9.—Charter (13 March, 1571) to Marjorie Campbell. Alexander
Wedderburn, notary public, is a witness at Dundee. (*ib.* § 162.)

44. **1581.** Nov. 19.--Charter (22 July, 1581) to Nicholas Wardlaw, witnessed at
Dundee by Mr. Alexander Wedderburn, and Alexander Wedderburn, notary public.
(*ib.* § 275.)

45. **1586.** Nov. 11.—Charter to George Anderson (29 Jan. 1581) of lands near Dundee,
bounded by those of S. James' chaplainry belonging to Robert Wedderburn. Witnessed at Dundee by Alexander Wedderburn, clerk, and Mr. Alexander Wedderburn,
his son. (*ib.* § 1055.)

46. **1588.** May 10.—Charter (24 April, 1588) to Alexander, Bishop of Brechin, and
Helen Clepan his wife, of lands in Perth. Witnessed at Findowrie by Mr. Alexander
Wedderburn, clerk of Dundee. (*ib.* § 1537.)

47. **1588.** Dec. 15.—Charter (16 June, 1587) to John Scharp. Witnessed at Dundee
by Mr. Alexander Wedderburn, notary. (*ib.* § 1604.)

48. **1592.** July 1.—Charter to John Carnegy of lands in Forfar. Witnessed at
Balnabreich by Mr. Alexander Wedderburn, clerk of Dundee. (*ib.* § 2118.)

49. **1594.** Jan. 24.—Confirmed grant (12 May 1592), to John Persoun and his wife,
witnessed at Newbigging and Dundee, by Robert Wedderburn, notary, Mr. Alexander
Wedderburn, clerk of Dundee, and others. (Vol. 1593-1608, § 50.)

50. **1594.** June 8.—Confirmed grant (18 and 23 May 1594), to Alexander Ramsay,
witnessed at Dundee and Kynnaird by Mr. Alexander Wedderburn, clerk of Dundee,
David Wedderburn, and others. (*ib.* § 103.)

51. **1595.** March 20.—Confirmation of charter (dated at Dundee, 6 Nov. 1594), by John Wedderburn, son and heir of the late James Wedderburn, burgess of Dundee, with consent of Margaret Strathauchin, his wife, (in implement of a contract made between them, Elizabeth Wedderburn, their only daughter, Mr. Alexander Wedderburn, clerk of Dundee, and John Scharp of Houstoun, advocate), of one-sixth of Hiltoun of Craigie, in favour of the said John Scharp. (*ib.* § 241.)

52. **1595.** March 24.—Grant (24 May 1592), to David Balfour, witnessed by Robert Wedderburn, notary. (*ib.* § 252.)

53. **1595.** July 22.—Grant (1 June 1593), to Michael Downy and Margaret Fairny, his wife, witnessed at Cupar by John Wedderburn, son of Alexander Wedderburn, burgess of Cupar, and others. (*ib.* § 321.)

54. **1595.** July 22.—Grant (12 Dec. 1593), to Patrick Glasford, witnessed by Alexander Wedderburn, burgess of Cupar. (*ib.* § 323.)

55. **1595.** Aug. 13.—Grant (Sept. 1594), to William Turnebill, naming Alexander Wedderburn, burgess of Cupar-Fyiff. (*ib.* § 328.)

56. **1596.** Feb. 18.—Confirmation of a charter (1 June 1593), to Peter Rolland, witnessed at Cupar by John Wedderburn, son of Alexander Wedderburn, burgess of Cupar. (*ib.* § 408.)
    See ante s, Private Records, Scrymgeour-Wedderburn Papers, No. 106 (1), where the year of the confirmation is wrongly noted as 1593, instead of 1595-96.

57. **1596.** June 6.—Charter (10 May 1594), to George Airth, witnessed at Cupar by Alexander Wedderburn, burgess of Cupar. (*ib.* § 437.)

58. **1598.** Nov. 24.—Charter (1 June 1598), to William Fullerton, witnessed by Alexander Wedderburn, clerk of Dundee. (*ib.* § 800.)

59. **1599.** Feb. 6.—Charter (5 June, 1595), to William Graham, written by David Wedderburn, and witnessed by him and Mr. Alexander Wedderburn, clerk. (*ib.* § 854.)

60. **1600.** July 15.—Confirmed charter (8 June, 1587) of sale by Sir James Scrymgeour of Dudope, constable and provost of Dundee, and William Guthrie of Kynganie, to David Wedderburn, burgess of Dundee, of an annual rent out of a tenement in the Cowgait. Witnessed by Mr. Alexander Wedderburn, clerk. (*ib.* § 1060.)

61. **1601.** March 3.—Charter (5 Dec. 1596) to David Crewkschank, witnessed by a servant of Peter Wedderburn, burgess of Dundee. (*ib.* § 1155.)

62. **1601.** June 15.—Charter (July and Oct. 1596) to Robert Flescher of Dundee, witnessed there by Patrick Wedderburn and others. (*ib.* § 1190.)

63. **1602.** Dec. 2.—Charter (13 Oct. 1601) to Patrick Gray, witnessed by Mr. Alexander Wedderburn, clerk of Dundee. (*ib.* § 1374.)

64. **1603.** Aug. 19.—Charter (23 Aug. 1596) by James Scharp to his son Alexander, of the lands of Hiltown of Craigie, acquired by him from the late John Wedderburn, son and heir of the late James Wedderburn, burgess of Dundee. (§ 1480.)

65. **1606.** April 21.—Charter (2 Dec. 1597) to Robert Guthrie, witnessed at Dundee by John Wedderburn, burgess, and Mr. Alexander Wedderburn, clerk. (*ib.* § 1731.)

66. **1606.** Sept. 16.—Royal grant in favour of William Goldman, reciting a resignation consented to by Mr. Alexander Wedderburn, clerk of Dundee. (*ib.* § 1795.)

67. **1607.** Oct. 27.—Royal grant (of this date) of Montquhany to Andrew Balfour, subject to a charge " per sasinam " of 29 Sept. 1599, in favour of Alexander Wedderburn and Christina Fairny, his wife. (*Ib.* § 1985.) Great Seal Register.

68. **1607.** Dec. 20.—Royal grant (of this date), to James Elphinstone, lord of Couper, of various lands and charges, including £3 6s. 8d. out of the lands of Alexander Wedderburn, situate in Dundee. (*ib.* § 2002.)

69. ¶ **1608.** Feb. 19.—Charter to David Lindsay (5 Aug. 1596), witnessed at Edzell by Mr. Alexander Wedderburn, clerk of Dundee. (*ib.* § 2033.)

70. **1608.** April 10.—Charter to John Steill (4 Dec. 1605), witnessed at Dundee by Mr. Alexander Wedderburn, clerk. (*ib.* § 2063.)

71. **1609.** June 22.—Charter (2 June 1609), witnessed at Kellie by Robert Wedderburn, notary. (Vol. 1609-20, § 88.)

72. **1609.** Aug. 10.—Charter (5 Aug. 1609), naming Mr. Alexander Wedderburn, clerk of Dundee. (*ib.* § 135.)

73. **1609.** Oct. 4.—Charter (of this date), naming lands of the late John Wedderburn, in North Marketgait, Dundee. (*ib.* § 148.)

74. **1609.** Oct. 21.—Charter (14 July 1609), naming Mr. Alexander Wedderburn, clerk of Dundee. (*ib.* § 158.)

75. **1610.** (*a*) July 9.—Charter (15 March 1610.) (*ib.* § 323.) (*b*) Aug. 3.—Charter of this date (*ib.* § 357). Both of these name Mr. Alexander Wedderburn, clerk of Dundee.

76. **1610.** July 17.—Charter to John Gordon of Lesmoir, of a third of the lands of Wedderburn, resigned by Gordon of Cluney, in the barony of Kinmundie, co. Aberdeen. (*ib.* § 337.)
    This does not refer to anyone of the name of Wedderburn, but it is of interest in regard to its use as the name of a place in Aberdeenshire at this date. See post s. Retours of the Services of Heirs, No. 1-7.

77. **1611.** July 18.—Letters of remission (of this date), to William Fergusson, Doctor of Medicine in Dundee, and Catharine Wedderburn, his wife, for taking over 10% annual rent. (*ib.* § 536.)
    There is some error here, as Mr. William Ferguson was not a doctor. Probably some words are omitted in the letters, which should describe Catharine Wedderburn as wife of Mr. William Ferguson and relict of Mr. William Duncan, doctor of medicine in Dundee.

78. **1612.** Jan. 14.—Charter (2 Nov. 1611), written by Mr. John Wedderburn, son to Mr. Alexander Wedderburn, clerk in Dundee. (*ib.* § 605.)

79. **1613.** Jan. 21.—Charter (17 June 1612), dated at Sandford, witnessed by Mr. James Wedderburn, son of Alexander Wedderburn, in Cupar. (*ib.* § 804.)

80. **1613.** July 12.—Reference (1609), to Mr. Alexander Wedderburn, clerk of Dundee. (*ib.* § 881, note.)

81. **1614.** March 8.—Mr. Alexander Wedderburn, clerk of Dundee, is named, 12-13 June, 1612. (*ib.* § 1018.)

82. **1614.** July 8.—Mr. Alexander Wedderburn, clerk of Dundee, named, 19 May, 1614, (*ib.* § 1071.)

83. **1615.** Jan. 26.—Mr. Alexander Wedderburn, clerk, and Mr. James Wedderburn, his son, named, Dec.-Jan. 1614-15. (*ib.* § 1164.)

1615. Feb. 7.—Charter of sale (25-28 June, 1614) to Mr. William Fergusson and Catharine Wedderburn, his wife, of Balbeuchlie, Dunkeld, co. Forfar, written by Mr. James Wedderburn, son of Mr. Alexander Wedderburn, clerk of Dundee. (*ib.* § 1177.)

85. **1615.** June 15. –Mr. Alexander Wedderburn, clerk, and Mr. James Wedderburn, his son, are witnesses 25 May, 1615. (*ib.* § 1251.)

86. **1616.** April 26 —Mr. Alexander Wedderburn, clerk of Dundee, named, 11-12 June, 1607. (*ib.* § 1427.)

87. **1617.** Dec. 4.—Mr. Alexander Wedderburn, clerk of Dundee, and Mr. Alexander Wedderburn, his son, are witnesses, 13 June, 10 July, 1617. (*ib.* § 1715.)

88. **1618.** May 13.—Mr. Alexander Wedderburn, clerk of Dundee, is a witness, 31 Dec. 1617. (*ib.* § 1827.)

89. **1618.** Dec. 24.—The lands in Dundee of Alexander Wedderburn, burgess of Cupar, are mentioned. (*ib.* § 1956.)

90. **1619.** April 20, July 2.—Mr. Alexander Wedderburn, clerk of Dundee, witness, 17-18 July, 1617, and 25 Nov. 1618. (*ib.* §§ 2021, 2051.)

91. **1620.** March 16.—Alexander Wedderburn, notary, is named as a witness at Dundee, 25 May, 1577. (*ib.* § 2155.[1])

92. **1620.** Aug. 23.—Mr. Alexander Wedderburn, younger, bailie of Dundee, and Thomas Fyiff, servant of Mr. Alexander Wedderburn, clerk, are witnesses at Dundee 29 June, and 15, 22 July 1620. (Vol. 1620-33, § 77.)[2]

93. **1620.** Dec. 14. ⎫
     1621. Jan. 23. ⎬—Mr. Alexander Wedderburn, clerk of Dundee, is a witness, 9 June
     1621. Feb. 8. ⎪ 1620, 12 Oct., 18 Nov 1619, and 4-5 Jan. 1620. (*ib.* § § 111, 117,
     1622 Feb. 5. ⎭ 125, 268.)
     See ante s. Private Records. Scrimgeour-Wedderburn Papers, No. 218 (*a*).

94. **1623.** Feb. 20.—Dr. James Wedderburn, one of the masters of the College of S. Mary in S. Andrew's, is a witness, 2 April, 27 July 1621. (*ib.* § § 424-25.)

95. **1625.** June 8.—Mr. Alexander Wedderburn, clerk of Dundee. and Mr. James Wedderburn, his son, are witnesses, Aug. 1620, and the former, designed Mr. Alexander Wedderburn, elder, of Kingany, is a witness, 17 Nov. 1621. (*ib.* § 799.)
     See ante s. Private Records. Scrimgeour-Wedderburn Papers, No. 218 (*b*).

96. **1625.** July 8.—Royal charter of the shadow-half of Leuchland to Marjorie Wedderburn, wife of Robert Carnegy of Leuchland, Brechin. (*ib.* § 824.)

97. **1625.** July 28.—James Wedderburn, bailie of Dundee, and Mr. James Wedderburn, son of Mr. Alexander Wedderburn, clerk of Dundee, are witnesses, 14 May 1623. (*ib.* § 847.)

98. **1626.** Feb 17.—Mr.AlexanderWedderburn,clerk, isa witness, 26 Jan. 1620. (*ib.* § 934.)

99. **1626.** Oct. 25.—Dr. James Wedderburn, professor of Divinity in the new college of S. Andrew's, is one of the persons to whom the king grants a commission · " pro exploratione papistarum." (*ib.* § 1007.)

[1] There are two other references to Wedderburns in the index of this (1609-20) Vol. of the Great Seal Register, viz., to ¶ 1940, 8 Dec. 1618. and ¶ 2124, 1 Feb. 1620, but these appear to be misprints. as the text does not contain any mention of the name at these dates.
[2] The index to this volume also contains a wrong reference to Mr. Alexander Wedderburn, clerk. (§ 644 s. 24 June 1624.)

100. **1627.** April 18.—A sasine (6 Feb. 1627) is named as registered in the register for Forfar by Mr. Alexander Wedderburn, clerk depute and keeper thereof. (*ib.* § 1068.) Great Seal Register.
The Particular Register of Sasines for Forfar is not extant for the year 1627. See post p. 413.

101. **1628.** March 7.—Thomas Fyiff, servant of Mr. Alexander Wedderburn, clerk of Dundee. is a witness, 14 Oct. 1617. (*ib.* § 1219.)

102. **1629.** June 26.—Mr. John Wedderburn, regent of S. Leonard's College, S. Andrew's, is named. (*ib.* § 1432.)

103. **1630.** Jan. 30.—Mr. Alexander Wedderburn of Kingennie is a witness 16, 23 Sept. 1628. (*ib.* § 1514.)

104. **1630.** March 13.—Mr. Alexander Wedderburn, clerk of Aberdeen (*sic*), is a witness July 1621. (*ib.* 1550.)
Aberdeen is, of course, an error for Dundee.

105. **1630.** July 10.—John Wedderburn, merchant, burgess, is named 3 May 1630. (*ib.* § 1596.)

106. **1632.** July 25.—Grant of half Strabrok, Linlithgow, to Mr. George Halyburton of Fodrans, senator of the College of Justice, and Magdalen Wedderburn, his wife. (*ib.* § 2043.)

107. **1632** Oct. 20.—Grant to Mr. John Seharp, junior, eldest son of Mr. John Seharp, of Houstoun, advocate, of one-sixth of Craigie, acquired from John Wedderburn, deceased, by James Seharp of Houstoun. (*ib.* § 2073.)

108.[1] **1635.** Oct. 14.—Diploma by King Charles I. to Doctor James Wedderburn, doctor of theology, of the deanery of the Chapel Royal of Stirling, together with an @-rent therein specified. Dated at the Palace of Roystoun. (Paper Register, IV, 71.)

109. **1636.** Feb. 11.—Diploma by the said King to the same, on petition of the dean and chapter of the cathedral of Dunblane, of the bishopric of Dunblane, with all its revenues. Dated at the Palace of Whythall. (Paper Register, IV, 112.)

110. **1642.** July 18.—Charter (dated at Edinburgh) by the King to Mr. Alexander Wedderburn, clerk of Dundee, his heirs and assignees, of one-fourth part of the lands and town of Blackness, and also one-sixth of an eighth of the said lands, and also of the manor place of Blackness, galleries, offices, tower-houses, dovecots, gardens, &c. ; and also of the teinds of the lands of Dargo, all once belonging to Donald Thornetoun of Blackness ; to hold of the crown in fee and heritage for the sum of £4. 11. 8 yearly, &c. (LVII, 70.)
See post s. Register of the Privy Seal. No. 34, and ante s. Dundee Decreets, No. 36.

111. . **1647.** June 14—Charter (dated at Edinburgh) by the King to Sir Alexander Wedderburn of Blackness, Knt, &c., of one eighth and one-sixth of another eighth of the lands of Blackness, on resignation of this date by James Boytar (son and heir of the late James Boytar, bailie of Dundee). They are now granted to Sir Alexander for his good and faithfull service, together with certain parts of the lands of Pitarrow, &c. Kincardine, in warrandice. (LVIII, 63.)
See post s Register of the Privy Seal, No. 36.

112. **1648.** Feb. 18.—Charter by the King to the said Sir Alexander, &c., of another eighth part and another sixth of an eighth part of Blackness, now occupied by Andrew Watt, &c., &c., together with other parts of the said lands of Pitarrow in warrandiee. (LVIII, 339.)[2]
See again s. Register of the Privy Seal, No. 38.

[1] The following extracts are from the original Register, and as, from this date, it is not yet printed, and the issue of the volumes is necessarily slow, I have given the entries with much more detail than I have those from the printed volumes.
[2] J. W. in his notes of Great Seal Charters (ante s. J. W.'s Papers, No. 2) gives a "Charter of confirmation to Sir Alexander Wedderburn of one yearly annual-rent out of Dudhope, granted after 22 July 1652 during the usurpation." The minute book, however, contains no such reference, and vol. 58 of the Register ends in 1639, while vol. 59 begins on 22 July 1652, but does not note any such charter on that date.

Great Seal
Register. 113.   **1658.** ·March 2.—Great Seal Charter by Richard, Lord Protector, to Sir Peter Wedderburn of the Barony of Gosford. (?)

In the "Genealogical Account of the Descent of Lord Loughborough' (*ante* Blackness Papers, No. 81) an account is given of his great grandfather, Sir Peter Wedderburn of Gosford, as having "acquired the Barony of Gosford in the county of Midlothian by disposition from Sir Alexander Auchmutie of Gosford, Knight, dated 3 Jan. 1658-59, which was resigned by the said Sir Alexander into the hands of Richard, Lord Protector, the then Superior. (by notarial instrument dated 28 Jan. 1658-59), who granted the same to Sir Peter by a Charter dated the 2nd of March following, to which is appended the Great Seal of his father Oliver, and he was vested and seized therein by an Instrument of Sasine of date the 11th of that month." In the margin it is stated that all the four documents mentioned are in the Pitfirran charter chest. As stated elsewhere in this book, I have not been allowed recourse to that repository, and on searching the record (for there is no minute book for the Cromwell charters) no such charter seems to have been registered, those of Richard Cromwell ending on 28 Jan. 1659. It would appear, therefore, that this charter, though granted, was never written to the Great Seal.

114.   **1660.** Aug. 28.—Letters (Whitehall) appointing Mr. Peter Wedderburn of Gosford, advocate, to the office of clerk to the Privy Council of Scotland, with all privileges, immunities, and salaries of the said office, for life. (Paper Register, VI, 159.)

See s. Private Records, Blackness Papers, No. 81, s.d., where this entry is described as the appointment of Sir Peter to the above office and that of Keeper of the Signet, though the latter office is not named in the record.

115.   **1662.** July 14.—Great Seal Charter (Edinburgh) to Sir Alexander Wedderburn of Blackness, Knt., clerk of Dundee, his heirs and assignees, of the town and lands of Blackness (with the barony of Pittarro in warrandice) and also of the lands of Dargo, which lands are resigned to the Lords of the Exchequer for new infeftment to the said Sir Alexander and are hereby erected into one free barony, to be called the Barony of Blackness. (LX, pt. i, 144.)

See s. Burgh Records, Dundee Decreets, No. 36. In some places this charter is referred to as dated 14 July 1666, but this is an error, which seems to have crept into some document, whence it was repeated into others. There is no Blackness Charter of 1666.

116.   **1663.** Jan. 19.—Great Seal Charter (Edinburgh) to Alexander Wedderburn of Kinganie, elder, provost of Dundee, his heirs, &c., of the lands of Easter Powrie, all erected into one free barony, to be called the Barony of Powrie (with the barony of Ogilvie in warrandice) which said lands were resigned by Dougal McPhersone of Easter Powrie, with consent of Janet Guthrie, his spouse, to the Lords of the Exchequer, for new infeftment to the said Alexander Wedderburn and his heirs. (LX, pt. ii, 233.)

See s. Private Records, Scrymgeour-Wedderburn Papers, Nos. 355-56. A Great Seal Precept to Alexander Wedderburn, elder of Kingany, of the lands of Easter Powrie, is referred to, post s. Forfar Sasines, No. 36, in a sasine registered 2 May 1663, but these precepts, though engrossed on the sasine, were not recorded in the Great Seal Register.

117.   **1663.** June 4.—Great Seal Charter of confirmation (Whitehall) to Sir Peter Wedderburn of Gosford, Knt., of a disposition to him (1 Aug. 1661) by Walter, Lord Torphichen, of that fourth part of the mains of Ballincrieffe, called Lochills, in the constabulary of Haddington and shire of Edinburgh, with a tenement and dwelling-house in Leith (sometime that of the late Robert, son of the late Bernard Lindsay of Lochills) in warrandice thereof. (LX, 254.)

See s. Private Records, Blackness Papers, No. 81 s.d. The date of this charter is curiously given in the register, thus :—" Anno domini millesimo sexcentesimo sexagesimo secundo et anno regni nostri decimo quinto—1663." The error is in the word " secundo," as the " fifteenth year " of the reign of Charles II. was certainly 1663.

118.   **1663.** Sept. 7.—Great Seal Charter (Edinburgh) to Sir Peter Wedderburn of Gosford, knight, advocate, clerk of the Privy Council, and Lady Agnes Dicksone, his wife, in conjunct fee, and the heirs gotten between them heritably, which failing, the heirs whatsoever of said Sir Peter, of the town and lands of West Mains of Ballincreiff, with mill, mill lands, &c., also of the fourth part of the Mains of Ballincreiff called Lochill, as for the principal ; and a tenement or dwelling house in the town of Leith, sometime belonging to Mr. Robert Lindsay, son of the late Bernard Lindsay of Lochill ; also of another dwelling house in Leith which belonged to the said late Mr. Robert Lindsay and Bernard Lindsay, his brother, with tower, fortalice, &c., and that in special warrandice of the lands of Lochill ; also of half

of the Mains of Ballincreiff called Standalane, which subjects belonged before to Great Seal
Thomas Hamilton of Redhous, and were resigned by him in favour of aud for Register.
new infeftment to Sir Peter Wedderburn. The charter also ratifies a disposition and
vendition granted by Sir Alexander Auchmoutie of Gosford, knight, with couseut of
Dame Helen Murray, his spouse, to the said Sir Peter Wedderburn of the barony
of Gosford, with mill, tower, &c., of date —— 165— with precept of sasine therein
and sasine following thereon ; and unites and erects all the said subjects into one
free barony to be called the Barony of Gosford. (LX, 297.)

119. **1664.** Dec. 20.—Great Seal Charter of confirmation (Edinburgh) to Mr. Andrew
Wedderburn, pastor at Disse (*sic* for Liffe) and Elizabeth Daw, his spouse, of
a disposition (28 Oct. 1663) in their favour by Sir Patrick Myretoun of Cambo,
Knt., and his spouse, of the lands of Grasmistoun, in the parish of Craill and shire
of Fife, with liberty of passage through the lands of Cambo. (LXI, 45.)

120. **1664.** July 22.—Great Seal Charter (Edinburgh) to Sir Alexander Wedderburn
of Blackness, Knt., confirming to him certain charters in his favour of parts of
Dudhope, called Berriebank, and parts of Balgay. (LXI, 354.)

    The charters specified are :—(1.) Charter (dated—1660) of alienation by John, Earl of Dundee,
therein designed Viscount of Dudhope, with consent of Lady Anna Ramsay, his spouse, of ten acres
of land lie shot, being part of the lands of Dudhope. called Berriebank, and other parts of the same,
extending to twenty-one acres in all, in the barony of Dundee, and shire of Forfar. (2.) Charter
(dated — 1660) of alienation by the said Earl and his spouse of other parts lie shode of the said lands
of Berriebank. (3.) Charter (14 and 19 Dec. 1663) by John Hunter in Balgay to the said Sir
Alexander of that part of Balgay called Langforbank of Balgay and Latch thereof. (4.) Charter
(6 June 1655) by the late William, Master of Gray, to the said Sir Alexander of ten acres and four butts
of arable laud in the Westfield of Dundee. (5.) Disposition (5 Feb. 1664) by the said Sir Alexander
(under reversion, in favour of himself) of the said ten acres and four butts, to James Wedderburn,
his second son.

121. **1667.** Aug. 2.—Great Seal Charter (Edinburgh) to Sir Peter Wedderburn,
Knt., advocate and clerk to the Privy Council, of the lands of Easter Spittoll,
or Redspittell, in the constabulary of Haddington and shire of Edinburgh. There
is also a confirmation of all charters, sasines, &c., of the said lands, which are
hereby united to the Barony of Gosford. (LXI, 254.)

    The Great Seal Charter of this date in favour of Sir Peter of the lands of Myretoun, referred to
s. Private Records. Blackness Papers, No 81 s.d., is identical with this charter, which includes
among its subjects a husband land in Ballincreiff, called Myretoun, resigued to Sir Peter by Mr.
John Eleis of Eleistoun.

122. **1668.** Oct. 21.—Great Seal Charter (Whitehall) to John Wedderburn, eldest
son and heir apparent of Sir Alexander Wedderburn of Blackness, Knt., and
his heirs, of (*a*) the town, manor-place, windmill, aud lands of Blackness (with the
barony of Pitarrow in warrandice) aud of the lauds of Dargo, erected into one
free barony by Great Seal Charter (14 July 1662) in favour of Sir Alexander;
(*b*) the lands of Logie, and the Langforebancke and Latch of Balgay; (*c*) that
shode of laud called the Brieriebank, with part of the lands of Dudhope ; (*d*) certain
acres of the mains of Dudhope and others in the Westfield of Dundee : all which
lands were resigned by the said Sir Alexander in favour of the said John Wedderburn and his heirs by letters of procuratory, dated at Edinburgh 23 July last, into
the hands of the Lords of the Exchequer, for new infeftment of the same, to
be holden of the King in free barony, &c., on payment of £16 15s. 10d. at
Whitsunday and Martinmas. (LXII, pt. i, 105.)

    See post s. Acts of Parliament of Scotland, No. 48. and ante s. Dun lee Decreets, No. 36, where
a Great Seal Precept and sasine (10 March 1669) on this charter are named, as to the absence of
which from the record, see above, No. 116 note.

123. **1670.** July 1.—Great Seal Charter (Edinburgh) to Sir Peter Wedderburn of
Gosford, Knt., one of the senators of the College of Justice, in liferent, and to his
eldest, second, and third sons, John, Peter and Alexander Wedderburn, and the
heirs male of their bodies, successively, whom all failing to the heirs and assignees
whomsoever of the said Sir Peter, heritably, of the rectory and vicarage teinds of
the parish kirk of Innerweeke, together with the advocation of the said kirk, and
two temple-lands of the lands in the town of Innerweeke with mansions, office of
Bailliary, etc., as contained in the infeftments of the late James, Earl of Dirleton ;
all which pertained to James, Earl of Salisbury, and were by him resigned to the

Lords of the Exchequer for new infeftment to the said Sir Peter and his sons, etc. (*ut supra*). LXII, pt. ii, 228,)

124. **1670.** July 11.—Sasine on Great Seal Charter (Whitehall) to the said Sir Peter and his said sons (as in No. 123) of the lands of Thornetoune, Whytehill, Crosshouse, Gaitsyde, Lawbatch, and Auldsheill, in the constabulary of Haddington, and shire of Edinburgh (and now by annexation in the shire of Renfrew), all which lands pertained to Sir William Ruthven of Dunglas, Knt., and others, by whom they were resigned to the Lords of the Exchequer for new infeftment to the said Sir Peter and his said sons, etc. By this charter the said lands are erected into the Barony of Thornetoune. (LXII, pt. ii, 245.)
See ante s. Private Records, Blackness Papers, No. 81, s.d. and post s. Acts of the Parliaments of Scotland, No. 49.

125. **1671.** Jan. 13.—Great Seal Charter (Edinburgh) to Sir Peter Wedderburn of Gosford, Knt., one of the Lords of Council and Session, in life-rent and to his three sons (*ut supra* No. 123), of the lands, lordship and barony of Innerweik, with towers, fortalices, &c., in the constabulary of Haddington and shire of Edinburgh, and now by annexation in the shire of Renfrew, following on resignation, after disposition, by Anne, Countess of Southesk, and Robert, Earl of Southesk, her husband, of date 27 July 1668, in favour of John Graham of Craigie, who now assigns the said disposition and resignation to Sir Peter. (LXII, pt. ii, 269.)
See ante s. Private Records, Blackness Papers, No. 81, s.d.

126. **1675.** May 15.—Charter to William Kyd of Woodhill of parts of Craigie reserving certain interests therein to Patrick Kyd of Craigie and Margaret Wedderburn, his wife.
See post s. Forfar Sasines No. 63. I have not looked up this Charter in the original register.

127. **1680** Feb. 20.—Charter of Confirmation (Edinburgh) ratifying an obligation (20 Jan. 1671) of real warrandice granted by Robert, Earl of Southesk, to Sir Patrick Wedderburn, Knt., one of the senators of the College of Justice, in life-rent, and his sons, etc. (as in Nos. 123—125), by which the said Earl bound himself, his heirs, etc., to infeft and sease the said Sir Patrick in life-rent and his said sons, etc., heritably in the lands and barony of Fairne, in the shire of Forfar, in warrandice of the lands of Innerweek in the shire of Renfrew. (LXVII, 82.)

128. **1682.** Feb. 10.—Charter of Confirmation (Edinburgh) to Mr. Andrew Wedderburn of Kingsleif, and Elizabeth Daw, his spouse, in conjunct fee, and to the heirs lawfully procreated or to be procreated betwixt them, whom failing to the heirs and assignees of the said Mr. Andrew Wedderburn whomsoever, of a right and disposition granted (3 August 1668) by Alexander Nairn of Sandfoord, eldest son and heir of the late Sir Thomas Nairn of Sandfoord, with consent of his curators, to the said Mr. Andrew Wedderburn, therein designed of Grasmistoune, and his said spouse, and disponing to the said Mr. Andrew Wedderburn and his said spouse the town and lands of Eister Kingsleif with teinds, in the barony of Cullernie, parish of Creich, and shire of Fife. (LXVIII, 58.)

129. **1683.** Dec. 20.—Charter of Confirmation (Edinburgh) of (1) a contract of marriage (18 Dec. 1665) between the late Alexander Wedderburn of Easter Powrie, therein designed of Kingennie, Provost of Dundee, heritable proprietor of the lands aftermentioned, and Alexander Wedderburn, now of Easter Powrie, only lawful son of the said Alexander Wedderburn, elder, procreated between him and Elizabeth Ramsay, his spouse, on the one part, and Sir Alexander Wedderburn of Blackness and Grizel Wedderburn, his fourth lawful daughter ; (2) a charter of alienation and disposition by the said late Alexander Wedderburn in implement of the said contract, in favour of the said Alexander Wedderburn, his son. (LXIX, 120.)
By the terms of the said charter the said late Alexander Wedderburn disponed to the said Alexander, his son, and the heirs male to be procreated between him and the said Grizel Wedderburn ; whom failing, to the heirs male whomsoever lawfully to be procreated of the said deceased Alexander his body ; whom failing to the heirs whomsoever lawfully to be procreated of the said Alexander, younger, his body ; whom also failing to the nearest and lawful heirs and assignees whomsoever of the said Alexander, younger, not excluding any daughters then procreated or to be procreated of the said late Alexander, his body, although they may not be sisters uterine of the said Alexander his son, the lands under-written, viz., the lands of Easter Powrie with the mill thereof, &c., which lands of Easter Powrie are called Wester

Maynes or Midletoune, the Easter Maynes and Burnesyde of Powrie, with houses, &c., all erected into one Great Seal free barony called the Barony of Powrie, in the shire of Forfar, as for the principal ; and the lands Register. and barony of Ogilvy, commonly called the Glen of Ogilvy, in warrandice thereof ; also the teinds of the said lands and barouy : To hold of the Crown in free barony, fee, and heritage, conform to a Charter granted by Charles the First, under the Great Seal, of date 15 Nov. 1641, in favour of the late Mr. James Durham of Pitkerow in life-rent, and of James Durham, his son, in fee, of the said lands and barony of Easter Powrie ; and to a Charter under the Great Seal, of date 19 January 1663, granted to the said late Alexander Wedderburn.

See ante No. 116 and s. Private Records, Scrymgeour-Wedderburn Papers, No. 461.

130. **1697. Dec. 31.**—Diploma or letters patent creating Peter Wedderburn of Gosford a baronet, with remainder to the heirs male of his body. (LXXIV. 145.)

Diploma Petri Wedderburn de Gosford de titulo et dignitate militis Baronetti ;—

Gulielmus Dei gratia Magne Britannic Francie et Hibernic Rex fideique defensor Omnibus probis hominibus ad quos presentes literæ nostræ pervenerint Quandoquidem nos serio perpendentes omnes honoris et dignitatis titulos in dominiis nostris a nobis tanquam fonte et scaturigine in subditos nostros de nobis bene meritos nunc promanare Et considerantes merita et fidelitatem Petri Wedderburn de Gosford durabilem ergo regalia nostri favoris in cum ejusque heredes subscriptos characterem conferre statuimus Noveritis itaque nos dedisse concessisse et contulisse sicuti per presentes has nostras literas damus concedimus et conferimus in predictum Petrum Wedderburn et heredes masculos de ejus corpore Titulum gradum dignitatem et honorem militis Baronetti ac ordinamus prefatum Petrum Wedderburn ejusque antedictos predictum titulum cum precedentia loco aliisque privilegiis et immunitatibus militibus Baronettis debitis virtute quorumcumque actorum statutorum seu consuetudinum predicti Regni nostri Scotie possidere et gaudere Et specialtim in omnibus sessionibus conventibus aliisque congressibus privatis seu publicis in dicto Regno Ordinamus pariter uxores et liberos dicti Petri Wedderburne ejusque heredum antedictorum locum precedentiam aliaque privilegia quecunque uxoribus et liberis militum Baronettorum debita habere eumque generalitate prosecutium omnibusque formalitatibus et ritibus similibus occasionibus usitatis dispensamus Leoni porro armorum Regi ejusque fratribus faciabilus talia insignia armorea vel prioribus additamenta quæ huic occasioni apta et congrua videbuntur predicto Petro Wedderburne dare et prescribere ordinamus. In cujus rei testimonium presentibus magnum sigillum nostrum appendi precepimus. Apud aulam nostram de Kensingtoune trigesimo die mensis Decembris anno domini millesimo sexcentesimo et nonagesimo septimo et anno Regni nostri nono.

Per signaturam manu S.D.N. Regis suprasignat.

131. **1699. Sep. 13.**—Charter of Resignation (Edinburgh) to Mr. Alexander Wedderburn, eldest son of John Wedderburn of Blackness, one of the principal clerks of petitions, and the heirs male procreated or to be procreated between him and Mrs. Elizabeth Seaton, his spouse (eldest daughter of Sir Alexander Seaton of Pitmedden, Knight, Baronet), whom failing to a succession of heirs therein specified, of the lands, windmill, manor-place, and barony in the lordship of Scone and shire of Forfar, erected into one free barony called the Barony of Blackness, conform to a Great Seal Charter to the late Sir Alexander Wedderburn of Blackness, father of the said John Wedderburn, now of Blackness, dated 14 July 1666[1] ; and of the lands and barony of Pittarro in warrandice of the same ; also of 18 acres and 4 butts of arable land in the Westfield of Dundee, reserving to the said John Wedderburn his life-rent of the said lands, baronies, &c., which lands of Blackness pertained heritably to the said John Wedderburn, and were by him, together with the said lands and barony of Pittarro, &c., resigned (28 July last) to the Lords of the Exchequer, in favour of and for new infeftment to the said Mr. Alexander Wedderburn and his said heirs male, whom failing to the said other heirs, to hold of the crown, under the reservations and conditions, &c., therein specified. By this charter also the foresaid lands are of new erected into one free barony called the Barony of Blackness. (LXXVI, 652, fol. 91.)

An annuity of 2,000 merks out of the said lands of Blackness, &c., is also confirmed to the said Mr. Alexander Wedderburn and his said spouse, and to the longest liver of them by this charter. The heirs called to the succession, failing heirs male of the said spouses, are the heirs male of the body of the said Mr. Alexander lawfully to be procreated in any other marriage, whom failing any other person whom the foresaid John Wedderburn shall be pleased to name at any time in his life or by writing under his hand (which shall be as valid and sufficient to the person so nominated and the heirs male of his body as though they had been named in these presents and in the Charter and infeftment to follow thereon) : and failing such nomination the heirs male of the foresaid John Wedderburn of his own body ; whom all failing the eldest daughter or heir female whomsoever (without division) of the body of the before-named Mr. Alexander Wedderburn, his son, whom failing the eldest daughter or heir female whomsoever (without division) of the before-named John Wedderburn his body ; whom failing the eldest daughter or heir female (without division) of the said person named by the said John Wedderburn as said is ; and, failing such nomination, the other eldest heir female whomsoever of the before-named John Wedderburn in the order foresaid, and his assignees whomsoever.

[1] See as to this error for 1662, ante No. 115, note.

**Great Seal
Register.**

The Charter also contains a declaration that all the heirs of tailzie and provision above written (male as well as female) shall be held bound by acceptance hereof, in all time coming to assume and take the surname of Wedderburn, and to use, bear, and carry the arms of the House and Family of Blackness, and no other surname, in the first place ; and the heirs female succeeding to the same shall be obliged to marry a person of the surname of Wedderburn, or who shall assume the surname of Wedderburn ; and he and their heirs shall bear and carry the surname and arms of the foresaid House and Family of Blackness, &c.

132.   **1703.** July 10,—Charter of resignation (Edinburgh) to Margaret Wedderburn, daughter of the late Mr. Andrew Wedderburn, Minister of the Gospel, and Mr. James Halson, one of the bailies of Anstruther Easter, her spouse, in conjunct fee and life-rent, of the town and lands of Easter Kingslieff, pertaining to the said late Mr. Alexander Wedderburn and Elizabeth Daw, his spouse (see ante No. 128), and now belonging to the said Margaret as heir served and returned to her said father, and by her resigned (20 March last) to the Lords of the Exchequer for new infeftment to herself and her said spouse. (LXXIX, 83, fol. 220.)

133.   **1704.** Aug. 9.—Diploma or letters patent creating John Wedderburn of Blackness a baronet, with remainder to his heirs male. (LXXXI, 61.)
The Latin text of this has already been given in full from the original patent.   See ante s. Private Records, Blackness Papers, 71 (3).

134.   **1707.** Feb. 24 —Charter of resignation (Edinburgh) to Sir Alexander Wedderburn of Blackness, Knight, Baronet, one of the principal clerks of petitions, in life-rent, and to John Wedderburn, his eldest son, procreated betwixt him and Elizabeth Setone, his spouse, eldest daughter of Sir Alexander Setone of Pitmedden, Knight, Baronet, and the heirs male of his body, in fee, whom failing to Alexander Wedderburn, his second son by his said spouse, and the heirs male of his body ; whom failing to the other heirs male of the body of the said Sir Alexander by his said spouse ; whom failing to the heirs male of the body of the said Sir Alexander, by any other marriage ; whom failing to the heirs female of the body of the said Sir Alexander ; whom failing to [Margaret] Wedderburn, his eldest sister, spouse of .... Eccles, doctor of medicine, and the heirs of her body ; whom failing to Matilda Wedderburn, his youngest sister, and the heirs male of her body ; whom all failing to his other lawful heirs whomsoever ; of all and whole the Barony of Blackness, as erected under Crown charter 14 July 1666, with all and sundry the lands of Pitarrow, &c., together with the lands of Logie and certain parts of Balgay, disponed to Sir Alexander by the provost and bailies of Dundee, by disposition dated 21 March 1706. This charter proceeds on a resignation by the said Sir Alexander (dated 21 October 1706), and of new erects the said Barony of Blackness. It contains a clause for the succession of heirs female without division, they and their husbands to bear the surname of Wedderburn and the arms of the house and family of Blackness.
Mr. A. C. Lamb of Dundee has an old extracted copy of this charter on sixteen pages of parchment, sewn bookwise.   On page 14 is written " Sealed at Edinburgh, 4 April 1707, and written to the Great Seal 8 April 1707."   As to the date 1666 referred to above, see again ante No. 115, note.

135.   **1708.** March 12.—Charter of resignation (Edinburgh) to Alexander Wedderburn of Easter Powrie and his heirs male lawfully procreated or to be procreated of his body, whom failing to the heirs female lawfully procreated or to be procreated of his body, whom all failing to his nearest heirs and assignees whomsoever, of the lands of Easter Powrie, with mill, &c., in the shire of Forfar, with the lands and barony of Ogilvy (called the Glen of Ogilvy) in warrandice thereof, which lands, barony, &c. were erected into one free barony called the Barony of Easter Powrie ; and were resigned (6 Nov. 1676) by the said Alexander Wedderburn to the Lords of the Exchequer in favour of and for new infeftment of the same to himself and his heirs above recited.   By this Charter the said lands, &c. are erected into one whole free barony, now and in all time coming to be called the Barony of Wedderburn, to be held of the crown in free barony, taxed ward, fee and heritage, the said Alexander Wedderburn rendering therefor conform to a resignation made in favour of the late Alexander Wedderburn, elder, of Kingennie, and a Charter under the Great seal dated 15 Nov. 1641. (LXXXIII, 137, fol. 149.)
See ante s. Private Records, Scrymgeour-Wedderburn Papers, No. 533-34, where the date of this charter is given as May, not March, though from an entry in the Forfar Sasines (post s.v. No. 123) the latter would seem to be correct.   The date of resignation, 6 Nov. 1676, is so given in the record,

but can hardly be correct, as Alexander Wedderburn of Wedderburn was then only eight years old, **Great Seal** and moreover was not at that time his father's heir, his eldest brothers, John and Peter, being both **Register.** living at that date. The Great Seal Charter (15 Nov. 1641) referred to at the end of the extract is a charter of the lands of Easter Powrie, erected into the barony of Powrie, granted in favour of the Durhams of Pitkerro, predecessors in title of the Wedderburns, who did not acquire Powrie till 1662.

136. **1722.** July 26.—Charter of resignation in favour of Alexander Wedderburn, sheriff clerk of Forfar, his heirs and assignees whomsoever, heritably and irredeemably, of the lands and barony of Blackness, previously pertaining to the late Sir Alexander Wedderburn of Blackness and to Sir John Wedderburn, his son, comprehending the town and lands of Blackness with windmill, &c., as for the principal, erected into a free barony called the Barony of Blackness, conform to a charter under the Great Seal granted to Alexander Wedderburn, grandfather to the said Alexander Wedderburn, and dated 14 July 1666 (together with the lands and barony of Pittarrow in warrandice of the same); and also of 18 acres and 4 butts of arable land in the Westfield of Dundee; which principal lands and barony of Blackness, &c., pertained to the said Sir John Wedderburn heritably and were by him, conform to procuratory of resignation, &c. (dated 17 Feb. 1722), made by him in favour of the said Alexander Wedderburn and his foresaids, resigned to the Lords of the Exchequer, in favour of and for new infeftment to be made to the said Alexander Wedderburn, his heirs male and assignees foresaid. (xc, 39, fol. 44.)

As to the date. 14 July 1666, see once more ante No. 115, note.

137. **1734.** July 26.—Charter of Resignation (Edinburgh) in favour of John Wedderburn, eldest lawful son of Sir Alexander Wedderburn of Blackness, whom failing to John Wedderburn, his eldest lawful son now in life, procreated between him and Jean Fullarton, his spouse, and the other heirs of taillie mentioned in the contract of marriage between the said John Wedderburn and Jean Fullarton, whom failing to the said Sir Alexander Wedderburn, his heirs and assignees whomsoever, of the lands and barony of Blackness, and lands of Pittarrow, &c., as specified in the foregoing Charter; resigned by the said Sir Alexander Wedderburn of Blackness on 9th July last into the hands of the Lords of His Majesty's Exchequer, in favour of and for new infeftment of the same to be made to the said John Wedderburn his son, and the heirs and substitutes foresaid, reserving to the said Sir Alexander Wedderburn his use of the fruits, manor-place, office-houses and yard, presently possessed by him, and his life-rent of the foresaid lands; excepting from the said reservation the lands occupied by John Bell and others, out of which is upliftable an @-rent of 157 bolls 1 firlot 1¼ peck of barley; reserving also to Lady Katharine Scot, wife of the said Sir Alexander Wedderburn, if she survive him. the dote provided to her, and also the dote provided to the said Jean Fullarton, conform to her contract of marriage. (xcv, 51, fol. 66.)

138. **1743.** June 22.—Charter of Resignation (Edinburgh) in favour of Sir Alexander Wedderburn of Blackness, Knight Baronet, his heirs and assignees whomsoever, of the town and lands of Blebohole, with houses, &c., and seats in the parish Kirk of Kembock, pertaining to said lands, in the parish of Kembock, regality of S. Andrew's, and shire of Fife; resigned by Isobell Traill, daughter of the late John Traill of Blebohole, to the Lords of His Majesty's Exchequer, in favour of and for new infeftment to the said Sir Alexander Wedderburn and his heirs, &c., conform to disposition (6 Nov. 1728) by the said Isobell Traill to Margaret Bonnar, spouse of Thomas Graham of Greigston; which lands with the said disposition were disponed by the said Margaret and her spouse to Thomas Traill, writer in Dundee, on 14 Oct, 1729, and were adjudged from George Traill, eldest son of the said Thomas Traill, at the instance of the said Sir Alexander Wedderburn, conform to decreet of date 4 December 1742. (xcviii, 43, fol. 31.)

139. **1751.** Feb. 12.—Charter of Resignation (Edinburgh) in favour of Alexander Wedderburn, now of S. Germain's, Esq., fourth lawful son of the late Sir Patrick Halcket of Pitfirren, Baronet, his heirs and assignees whomsoever, heritably and irredeemably, of the Easter third part of the lands of Aldingstoun called Greendyks, and of that husband land and fourth part of an husband land of Longnedry called Chesterhall, and of the lands of S. Germain's, with houses, &c., in the parish of Tranent and shire of Edinburgh, resigned by James Campbell of S. Germain's to

the Barons of Her Majesty's Exchequer, in favour of and for new infeftment to
the said Alexander Wedderburn conform to procuratory of resignation contained in a
disposition by the said James Campbell, dated 23 Nov., and registered in the Books
of Council and Session 24 Nov. 1750. (c, 108, fol. 67.)

140. **1754. Dec. 10.**—Charter of Resignation (Edinburgh) in favour of John Wedderburn of Gossford, Esq., eldest son of the late Charles Wedderburn of Gossford,
Esq. (second lawful son of the late Sir Peter Halket of Pitfirran, Baronet, *alias*
Wedderburn of Gossford, procreated between him and the late Lady Janet Halket,
his spouse) and the heirs male of his body ; whom failing to his daughters or heirs
female of his body successively without division ; whom failing to a succession of heirs
therein specified, of the barony of Gosford, and the lands, &c., forming the same,
&c., &c., as more particularly specified therein. (CIII, 1.)

The heirs called to the succession by this charter, failing sons and daughters of the said John
Wedderburn, are as follows :—" Any other son of the body of the said Charles Wedderburn and the
heirs male of his body; whom failing the daughters or heirs female of his body successive without
division ; whom failing any other son of the marriage between the said late Sir Peter Halket and
the said Janet Halket, his spouse, and the heirs male lawfully procreated or to be procreated of his
body ; whom failing the daughters or heirs female lawfully procreated or to be procreated of his
body successive without division ; whom also failing the heirs male of the body of the late Janet
Wedderburn, eldest daughter of the said Sir Peter Halket ; whom failing the daughters or heirs
female of the body of the said Janet Wedderburn successive without division ; whom failing Agnes
Wedderburn, second lawful daughter of the said Sir Peter Halket and the heirs male of her body
lawfully procreated ; whom failing her daughters or heirs female lawfully to be procreated successive
without division ; whom failing the heirs male of the body of the late Christian Wedderburn, third
lawful daughter of the said Sir Peter Halket ; whom failing the daughters or heirs female of the
body of the said Christian Wedderburn successive without division ; whom failing Sir Peter Halket,
now of Pitfirran, Baronet, eldest lawful son of the said deceased Sir Peter Halket, and the heirs
male lawfully procreated or to be procreated of his body ; whom failing the daughters or heirs
female procreated or to be procreated of his body successive without division ; whom failing the
heirs male procreated of the body of the late Mr. Alexander Wedderburn, advocate, brother german
of the said deceased Sir Peter Halket ; whom failing the daughters or heirs female procreated of
his body successive without division ; whom failing the heirs male procreated of the body of the
late Agnes Wedderburn, relict of David Haliburton of Pitcur, sister german of the said deceased Sir
Peter Halket ; whom failing the daughters or heirs female procreated of her body successive
without division ; whom failing the heirs male procreated of the body of the late Alexander
Wedderburn of Blackness ; whom failing the daughters or heirs female procreated of his body
successive without division ; whom also failing the nearest heirs male of the said deceased Sir
Peter Halket and the heirs male procreated or to be procreated of their bodies ; whom failing the
heirs female procreated or to be procreated of their bodies successive without division ; whom all
failing the heirs or assignees whomsoever of the said deceased Sir Peter Halket, heritably and
irredeemably with and under the provisions, conditions, &c."

The estates settled and the conditions of the settlement are set forth at length as follows :—
" The town and lands of Westmains of Ballincreif, with the mill, &c., in the constabulary of
Haddington and shire of Edinburgh and a fourth part of the mainlands of Ballincrief ; also
that tenement or dwelling house, sometime that of Mr. Robert Lindsay, lawful son of the late
Bernard Lindsay of Lochhill, in the town of Leith, within a building called the King's Wark ;
and another dwelling house in Leith, together with a part of the said King's Wark as therein
described ; likewise the half of the Mains lands of Ballincreiff called Stand-the-lane ; also the
lands and barony of Gossford in the Constabulary and Shire foresaid, sometime pertaining to Sir
Alexander Auchmutie of Gossford, all incorporated into one free barony called the Barony of
Gossford together with the tower, fortalice, and manor-place of Gossford, &c. Moreover the lands of
Easter Spitle called Easter Redspitle, lands of Wester Redspitle, held of the Earl of Winton, in
manner expressed in the infeftments of the same to the late Sir Andrew Hamilton, grandfather of
Thomas Hamilton of Redhouse ; and other husband lands possessed by Peter Haliburton and others,
called Myrton lying as aforesaid : All incorporated into the said Barony of Gossford, conform to
Charter by Charles the Second to the said Sir Peter Wedderburn of Gossford, and his foresaids,
under the Great Seal, of date 2 August 1667 : Further, the Rectory Teinds of the lands after
expressed, which teinds were excepted by express Reservation to the late John Wedderburn of
Gossford, brother of the late Sir Peter Halket, his heirs, &c., in Disposition by him to the late Sir
John Nisbet of Dirleton, of the lands and barony of Innerweek, and two Templelands in the town of
Innerweek : Also the Teinds of the lands and barony of Thornton specified in said Disposition, and in
Charter thereupon by Charles the Second to the said late John Nisbet : Which whole Teinds (excepting
as therein excepted), with advocation, Office of Baillary, &c., were contained in Charter under the
Great Seal, dated 11 July 1670, by the said King Charles to the late Sir Peter Wedderburn in
liferent and to the said deceased John Wedderburn his eldest lawful son in fee : Which lands, barony,
&c., pertained to the said late Sir Peter Halket, and were (in virtue of Letters of Procuratory,
contained in an Obligation or Deed of Tailzie, of date 9 September 1706, and registered in the
Books of Council and Session on 1st May 1753, made to himself in liferent, and to the now deceased
Charles Wedderburn, second son of the marriage between him the said Sir Peter and Lady Janet
Halket his spouse, in fee, and to the heirs lawfully to be procreated of his body ; whom failing to
James Wedderburn his third son, lately deceased without children, and other heirs of taillie and

provision therein mentioned and in the order above specified), resigned into the hands of the **Great Seal** Lords of His Majesty's Exchequer, in favour of and for new infeftment thereof to be made to the **Register** said John Wedderburn, eldest lawful son and heir of taillie and provision served and retoured to the said Charles Wedderburn his father, before the Bailies of Edinburgh on 20th July last, and to the heirs male of his body ; whom failing to the daughters or heirs female of his body ; whom failing to the other heirs of taillie in the order of substitution before written ; under the provisions, conditions, and irritancies, relative to heirs female succeeding without division and their husbands assuming the Surname of Wedderburn and bearing the arms, &c. of the Family of Wedderburn of Gossford. And because in virtue of an Obligation of Taillie of the lands and estate of Pitfirran made by the said late Lady Janet Halket with consent of her said husband, of date 9 September 1706, the lands and estate of Pitfirran (failing the said Sir Peter Halket now of Pitfirran and the heirs of his body) are provided to the heirs of the body of the said late Charles Wedderburn ; whom failing to the other heirs of taillie and provision therein expressed ; whence it may happen that the estates of Pitfirran and Gossford and the right of succession to them shall fall, devolve, and coincide in one and the same person, and whereas the proposal and intention of the said late Sir Peter Halket and Lady Janet Halket his spouse in the said Taillies of the said Estates was to conserve the said Family and Estate of Gossford separately and disjoined from the Estate and Family of Pitfirran should there happen to be more than one descendant of their bodies existing at the time of the said union, Therefore it is specially provided and declared, that if failing the said Sir Peter Halket now of Pitfirran and the heirs of his body, it should happen that the said Estates should coincide and unite in the person of the said John Wedderburn, then and in that case it shall be in his option to preserve, hold and retain his right and possession of the said Estate of Gossford : in which case he shall be held bound to denude himself, in the most convenient manner, of the said Estate of Pitfirran and of all other lands and heritages contained in the Taillie thereof in favour of the nearest son of the said Sir Peter Halket his grandfather, and the other heirs of taillie and provision substituted to him : with and under the conditions, provisions, &c., contained in the said Taillie of the lands of Pitfirran. On the other hand, if it should please the said John Wedderburn to enter to the right and possession of the said estate of Pitfirran and others contained in the foresaid Taillie thereof ; in that case he shall be held bound to denude himself of the estate of Gossford, from the date of his succession, in favour of the said nearest son of the said deceased Sir Peter Halket his grandfather, and of the other heirs substituted to him in the said Taillie of Gossford : which choice the said John Wedderburn is held bound to make within one year and day after his accession : otherwise the right of succession to the said estate of Pitfirran and all lands, etc. contained in the Taillie thereof shall devolve, accresce and pertain to the said nearest son of the said Sir Peter Halket and the heirs of the said estate of Pitfirran. In like manner if the said estates should happen to be united in the person of any other son procreated of the marriage between the said Sir Peter Halket and Lady Janet Halket his spouse, the said son shall be held bound to make choice of the one, and denude himself of the other estate, in favour of his immediate younger brother german, and failing such brother german, in favour of his eldest sister german and the other heirs of taillie and provision substituted in virtue of the Taillie of said estate : and failing of heirs male of the foresaid marriage the conditions foresaid to remain applicable to any daughter of the said Sir Peter succeeding as aforesaid ; moreover, in case of one only descendant having one son and one daughter or more the said son shall have choice and denude in favour of the eldest daughter : without prejudice to the said only descendant of the said late Sir Peter Halket, and his said spouse, enjoying both the said estates during his lifetime.

141. **1762.** Feb. 23.—Charter of resignation (Edinburgh) in favour of John Wedderburn of Gosford, Esq., his heirs and assignees whomsoever heritably and irredeemably, of the lands of Balmule, moor, manor-place, and mill of Balmulo ; town and lands of Lochend, Craigdukie, Wester Luscar, Eviot, &c. in the parish of Dunfermline and shire of Fife ; resigned by John McFarlane, W.S., to the Lords of the Exchequer, in favour of and for new infeftment of the same to the said John Wedderburn, conform to procuratory in disposition dated 15 Feb. 1762. (CVI, 60, fol. 94.)

142. **1766.** Aug. 6.—Charter of resignation (Edinburgh) in favour of John Wedderburn, Esq., residing in Hanover in the Island of Jamaica, eldest son of the late Sir John Wedderburn of Blackness, Baronet, procreated between him and Lady Jean Fullarton, his spouse, and the heirs male of his body, whom failing to James Wedderburn his brother german, second son of the said Sir John Wedderburn, and the heirs male of his body, whom failing to Robert Wedderburn of Persie, brother german of the said deceased John Wedderburn, and after his decease to John Wedderburn his eldest lawful son and the heirs male of his body, whom failing to Charles Wedderburn, second lawful son of the said Robert Wedderburn, and the heirs male of his body, whom failing to any other son procreated or to be procreated of the body of the said Robert Wedderburn, whom failing to Alexander Wedderburn, eldest son of Thomas Wedderburn, collector of excise at Inverness, also brother german of the said Sir John Wedderburn, and the heirs male of his body, whom failing to John Wedderburn, second son of the said Thomas Wedderburn and the heirs male of his body, whom failing to any other son procreated or to be procreated of the said Thomas Wedderburn and the heirs male of his body in fee, whom failing to the heirs and assignees whomsoever of the deceased John Wed-

3 A

derburn of Idvies, doctor of medicine in Dundee, heritably and irredeemably, of
the lands and estate of Easter, Wester, and Middle Idvies, Brackiullos, Auchinscurry, with mill thereof, lying within the parish of Idvie, now called Kirkdean,
barony of Kescobie and shire of Forfar, all of which, with the lands of Kinneres
(now incorporated into one free tenandry called the Tenandry of Auchinscurry)
pertained to the late Sir James Wood of Bonnington and to the late David,
Earl of Northesk, and were acquired at a public sale by the creditors of the
said Earl for the use and benefit of the said now deceased John Wedderburn,
doctor of medicine in Dundee, brother german of the late Sir Alexander Wedderburn of Blackness, and were afterwards disponed by Sir James Wood and the other
commissioners for the said Earl in favour of the said Doctor John Wedderburn by
disposition dated 20 April, 17 July, and 9 Aug. 1763 and recorded in the Books
of Session on 2 June 1766, and which lands, &c. the said Dr. John Wedderburn, by
disposition dated 22 March 1749 and registered in the said books on 25 July 1751,
disponed in favour of Margaret Balfour now deceased, then his spouse and afterwards his relict, in life-rent, and to the said John Wedderburn, his grand-
nephew and his heirs male in fee, whom failing to the other substitutes therein
and above mentioned, and which lands, conform to procuratory in the foresaid
disposition by the said Sir James Wood and Commissioners, were resigned into the
hands of the Lords of His Majesty's Exchequer, in favour of and for new infeftment of the same to the said Doctor John Wedderburn and the heirs male of his
body, whom failing to the other substitutes above mentioned, in the order of
succession above expressed, as authentic instruments taken under the hands of James
Smyth, under the order of a W.S. and notary, more fully proport. (CIX, 9, fol. 12.)

By this Charter are confirmed the said disposition by Sir James Wood, and an instrument of
sasine following thereon, dated 20th August, and recorded at Dundee 30th September 1736, made by
the said Sir James Wood and the Commissioners foresaid to the said Doctor John Wedderburn ; also
the disposition by the said Doctor in favour of the said John Wedderburn, dated 22 March 1749,
and sasine thereon dated 29th, and recorded at Dundee 31st. Aug. 1763. There are confirmed
also by this Charter, in favour of the said John Wedderburn, as heir in general served and
retoured to the said deceased Dr. John Wedderburn, of Idvies, his grand uncle, the writs aftermentioned, namely :—(1.) Contract of Wadset, of date 28 July 1660, between the late Sir John
Wood of Bonnington, Knight, Baronet, on the one part, and the late Thomas Fairweather in Kirkton of
Saint Vigean's, afterwards of Brayinston, and Thomas Fairweather, his eldest lawful son, on the other
part, by which, for the sum of 11,000 merks, the former disponed to the latter, under reversion, the
town and lands of Achscurry and Bractillo, in the regality of S. Andrew's and shire of Forfar : which
contract is recorded in the Books of Council and Session 3 Feb. 1688. (2.) Charter by the said Sir
John, in implement of the said contract dated 28 July 1660, with confirmation of the said contract by
Alexander, then Archbishop of S. Andrew's, of date 22 May 1682. (3.) Disposition of the said lands by
the said Thomas Fairweather, younger, then designed of Brayinston, in favour of George Dempster,
merchant in Dundee, of date 14 April 1732, and recorded in the Books of Council and Session on
2 June last. (4.) Disposition and assign. of the said contract of wadset by the said George Dempster,
in favour of Sir Alexander Wedderburn of Blackness, of date 23 Sept. 1732, and recorded in the
Books of Council and Session on 2 June last. (5.) Disposition and assign. of the said contract of
wadset of the said lands and others, and transmission of the same, by the said Sir Alexander
Wedderburn, in favour of the said Doctor John Wedderburn his brother german, of date 27 March
1735, also recorded in the Books of Council and Session on 2 June last. (6.) Oblig. of corrubation,
disposition, and assignation by the said Thomas Fairweather of Brayinston, in favour of James
Fairweather, merchant in Dundee, his brother, by which he disponed to him the lands of
Achscurry and Bractillo, and the sum for which they were wadset to the extent of 8,500 merks,
contained in an obligation therein narrated by the said Thomas Fairweather to him, of date 15 June
1709, with instrument of sasine following thereon dated 15 October 1709 and duly recorded ; with
disposition thereof by the said James Fairweather to the said Dr. John Wedderburn, of date 1 Feb.
1733, and recorded in the Books of Council and Session on 2 June last : with service of the said
John Wedderburn now of Idvies, as heir in general of the said Doctor John Wedderburn, his grand-
uncle, before the Bailies of Dundee, dated 1 May 1758, duly retoured to Chancery. (7.) Bond of
real warrandice by the said Sir James Wood of Bonnington, Brigadier-General, to the said Doctor
John Wedderburn, of date 2 April 1735, and recorded in the Books of Council and Session on
2 June last, whereby he obliged himself to infeft the said Doctor John Wedderburn, his heirs and
assignees, heritably and irredeemably in the lands of Lotham and Newbigging in the parish of
S. Vigean's and shire of Forfar, in warrandice of the said lands of Idvies and others
disponed as above, against an adjudication of date 28 July 1692, approved 26 Sept. 1682, led
at the instance of James Riddell, merchant in Edinburgh, against the late Sir John Wood of
Bonnington, his father, adjudging the lands of Idvies, among others, for the accumulated sum of
£2,500, and in warrandice of inhibition executed against the said Sir James Wood himself at the
instance of Marion Grieve, chirurgeon in Dundee, in 1724 or 1725, recorded in the General Register,
proceeding upon an obligation by him to Marion Wood, his sister, for the sum of 3,000 merks, of
date 6 July 1702, and transmitted by her and Alexander Forrester, chirurgeon in Dundee, her
spouse, to the said James Grieve, with procuratory of resignation and precept of sasine therein
contained, and instrument of sasine following thereon, in favour of the said Doctor John Wedder-

burn of date 7 January and recorded at Dundee 1 February 1749 ; declaring that it shall be in the option of the said John Wedderburn, now of Idvies, and his foresaids, to enjoy and possess the lands and others, above disponed, either in virtue of the foresaid disposition by the said Sir James Wood and commissioners of the said David, Earl of Northesk, to the said Dr. John Wedderburn, or in virtue of all or either of the rights abovementioned, the one without prejudice of the other.

143. **1769.** June 2.—Sasine under the Great Seal to Catharine Wedderburn, relict of John Higginson, of part of a cross dwelling in North Marketgate, Dundee.

This is mentioned above s. Burgh Records, Dundee Protocol Books, No. 597, but there is no mention of it in the Great Seal Register itself or in the Paper Register.

144. **1769.** Aug. 7.—Charter of resignation (Edinburgh) of the lands and barony of Wedderburn in favour of Mrs. Grizell Wedderburn and the heirs of her body, whom failing to a succession of heirs and the heirs of their bodies in the following order: (1) Mr. David Scrimgeour of Birkhill, advocate ; (2) Alexander Scrimgeour, his eldest son by Mrs. Catharine Wedderburn, his present spouse ; (3) John Scrimgeour, their second son ; (4) David Scrimgeour, their third son ; (5) Henry Scrimgeour, their fourth son ; (6) any other son procreated or to be procreated of the body of the said Mr. David Scrimgeour by his present or any subsequent marriage, successively in their order, and according to their seniority ; (7) Jauet Scrimgeour, eldest daughter of the said Mr. David Scrimgeour and his said wife ; (8) any other daughter procreated or to be procreated of the said Mr. David Scrimgeour by his present or any subsequent marriage ; (9) Marion, eldest daughter of the late Mr. Scrimgeour, Professor of Divinity in the College of S. Andrews ; (10) the heirs of the body of the late Joanna Scrimgeor r, second daughter of the said Mr. Alexander Scrimgeour ; (11) John Wedderburn of Idvies, eldest son of the late Sir John Wedderburn of Blackness ; (12) James Wedderburn, second son of the said deceased Sir John Wedderburn ; (13) Peter Wedderburn, third son of the said late Sir John Wedderburn ; (14) Margaret, eldest daughter of the said Sir John Wedderburn, and spouse of Richard Dundas of Blair, Esquire ; (15) Katharine, second daughter of the said Sir John Wedderburn ; (16) Susanna, third daughter of the said Sir John Wedderburn ; (17) Agatha Wedderburn, fourth daughter of the said Sir John Wedderburn, and spouse of Mr. John Smyth, writer in Edinburgh ; (18) the nearest and lawful heirs and assignees whomsoever of the said Mrs. Grizell Wedderburn ; the eldest heir female and the heirs of her body descending throughout the whole course of the succession before mentioned (excluding heirs portioners) succeeding without division, and the right of primogeniture having place between heirs female in the same manner as is established by law between heirs male, heritably and irredeemably. (ex, 109, fol. 210.)

The lands settled are described more fully as " the lands of Easter Powrie with mill, &c., called Wester Mains or Midletown, Easter Mains and Burnside of Powrie, and the lands and barony of Ogilvy, called the Glen of Ogilvy, in wartandice thereof, which principal lands, baronies and others were formerly called the Barony of Easter Powrie, and were erected and incorporated into one whole free barony, called the Barony of Wedderburn, conform to charter, of date 12 March 1708, granted by the late Queen Anne, in favour of the late Alexander Wedderburn, father of the said Grizell Wedderburn " ; likewise all and whole the sunny half of the lands of Wester Gourdie, as also the shadow half thereof, in the regality of Scone and shire of Forfar, conform to charter by the late David, Earl of Stormonth, to the late John, Lord Gray, and in which John, now Lord Gray, his son, stood infeft, and afterwards disponed the same to the said Mrs. Grizell Wedderburn ; also three-fourth parts of the lands of Bullion, as now divided, of old called Catterniline, in the lordship and barony of Dundee, afterwards in the barony of Auldbarr and shire of Forfar, and now by annexation in the barony of Longforgan and shire of Perth, together with the teinds of the lands of Cangainny and and Cairntoun of Cangainny, otherwise called Crymbles, with manor place, &c., in the parish of Monifieth and shire of Forfar, being part of the Lordship of Balmerino, with and under the conditions provisions, &c , particularly inserted in a procuratory of resignation and deed of taillie by the said Mrs. Grizell Wedderburn in favour of herself and the other heirs of taillie therein mentioned, including the usual clauses respecting the assuming, using, and retaining the surname and designation of Wedderburn of Wedderburn, which deed of taillie is dated 31 July 1766 and recorded in the Register of Taillies on 6 August following and in the Books of Session on the 19 of said month ; and which disposition by John, Lord Gray, to the said Mrs. Grizell Wedderburn of the lands of Gourdie is of date 13 April 1765. A disposition by John, Viscount of Dunlop, and Lady Ann, his spouse, to the late James Gray of Lauriestown, of the three-quarters of the lands of Bullion, dated 22 May 1660, and recorded in the Sheriff Books of Forfar on 8 May 1677, is mentioned, and it is recited that the lands of Bullion were disponed by Mr. James Gray, son and heir of the said James Gray, to the now deceased David Brisbane, writer in Dundee, by dispo. of date 3 July 1723, and by the said David Brisbane to Margaret Brisbane, his sister, in life-rent, and to the late David Wedderburn of Wedderburn in fee (who sold three-fourth parts of the said lands to Thomas Milne of Milnefield), conform to disposition by the said David Brisbane to his said sister and the said David Wedderburn, of date 13 January 1752, recorded in the Books of Session on 14 May 1767, with ratification and disposition thereof by the said Margaret

Brisbane to the said David Wedderburn of date 12 February 1752, and recorded in the Books of Council and Session on 14 May 1767. The charter then declares that to all the said dispositions and lands disponed by the same the said Mrs. Grizell Wedderburn has right as heir in general served to the said David Wedderburn, her brother german, before the Sheriff of Edinburgh on 23 September 1767, duly retoured to Chancery ; and that the teinds of the lands of Cangainy and Cairntoun thereof were disponed to the late Alexander Wedderburn of Cangainy, Clerk of the Burgh of Dundee, by John. Lord Balmerino, conform to contract of date 9 July 1618 ; to which contract, disposition, and teinds the said Mrs. Grizell Wedderburn has right as heir in general served before the bailies of Dundee to the late Alexander Wedderburn of Cangainy, her great great grandfather (abavus), on 13 April 1769. Finally, it declares that the lands of Powrie, now called Wedderburn, and the said lands of Wester Gourdie, &c., were, in virtue of proc. of resignation contained in the foresaid deed of entail, resigned to the Lords of the Exchequer in favour of and for new infeftment of the same to be made to the said Mrs. Grizell Wedderburn and the heirs of her body, whom failing to the other substitutes before named, and that all the above specified writs and rights are now by it confirmed.

See ante s. Private Records, Scrymgeour-Wedderburn Papers, No. 637.

145.   **1771.** Aug. 6.—Charter of resignation in favour of Henry Wedderburn, Esquire, second lawful son of the late Charles Wedderburn of Gosford (who was second son to the late Sir Peter Halket of Pitfirran, *alias* Wedderburn of Gosford, Baronet, procreated between him and Lady Janet Halket, his spouse), and the heirs whomsoever of his body, the eldest daughter or heir female having precedence of her sisters, and always succeeding without division ; whom failing in favour of the heirs of taillie, substitutes, and successors to the lands and estate of Gosford, according to a procuratory of resignation and letters of taillie of the same executed by the said Sir Peter Halket *alias* Wedderburn of Gosford, grandfather of the said Henry Wedderburn, on 9th September 1706, and registered in the Books of Session on 21 May 1753, heritably and irredeemably, of all and whole the lands and barony of Gosford. (cxii, 14, fol. 20.)

The barony of Gosford is described as comprehending the lands of Gosford, with mill and fortalice, etc., lands of Reid Spitle, lands of Coats, in the constabulary of Haddingtou and shire of Edinburgh, together with the teinds of the templelands and parish Kirk of Innerwick, and as being subject to the conditions, contained in a taillie of the foresaid lands, to be inserted in the resignations, charters, and sasines following thereon. It narrates the option granted to the foresaid Charles Wedderburn, in the event of his falling heir to the estates both of Gosford and Pitfirran (ut ante No. 140), and also states the barony to be subject to the burden of £15,500 sterling, which the said Henry Wedderburn stands obliged to pay to John Halket, Esq., of Pitfirran, his brother, with the annual-rent thereof from Whitsunday 1767 ; and to the payment to Mrs. Mary Wardlaw, relict of the said Charles Wedderburn of Gosford, of a life-rent annuity of £100 sterling, out of said lands ; which lands and others above written pertained to John Wedderburn of Gosford, now John Halket of Pitfirran, Esq., and were held by him immediately of the Crown, and resigned by him with consent of Mrs. Mary Hamilton *alias* Halket, his spouse, in virtue of a disposition of date 20 June 1771, recorded in the Books of Council and Session on 31 July following, in which he is called John Halket of Pitfirran, Esq., heretofore designed John Wedderburn of Gosford ; and which narrates the taillies foresaid of both the estates of Pitfirran and Gosford, and the devolving of the succession of both these estates on himself the said John Halket (in virtue of the taillies and destination, 14 October 1751, of the said estate of Pitfirran by the before mentioned Peter Wedderburn, afterwards Sir Peter Halket of Pitfirran ; and that he himself, in terms of the disposition and within the time prescribed in them, chose to hold the said estate of Pitfirran. It also narrates an obligation binding him to denude himself of the said estate of Gosford in favour of the said Henry Wedderburn, nearest heir of taillie to himself ; and a contract between him and his said brother, of date 18 January 1768, concerning the foresaid sum of £15,400 (*sic*) sterling, and the said life-rent of £100 sterling to the foresaid Mrs. Mary Wardlaw. Finally, the said John Halket dispones the said lands in favour of, and resigns the same to the Lords of the Exchequer for new infeftment of the same to be made to his brother, the said Henry Wedderburn.

146.   **1773.** Aug. 6.—Charter of resignation (Edinburgh) in favour of John Wedderburn of Idvies (eldest son of the late Sir John Wedderburn of Blackness, Baronet) and his heirs and assignees heritably and irredeemably, of those parts of the lands and barony of Ballidgarno, now called the Easter Half of the lands of Ballindean, and of the Wester Half of Ballindean, in the parish of Inchture and shire of Perth, together with those parts of the barony of Ballidgarno called the new mains or mansion-house of Ballidgarno, and now Ballindean, and bounded on the west by the said lands of Ballindean belonging to the said John Wedderburn, and part of the lands of Inchture belonging to the Lord Kinnaird, which lands were disponed by Thomas Carnegy of Craigo in favour of the said John Wedderburn by disposition of date 21 November 1769 and recorded in the Books of Session on 6 December thereafter, and were by him resigned into the hands of the Lords of His Majesty's

Exchequer, in favour of and for new infeftment of the same to be made to the said **Great Seal** John Wedderburn and his heirs foresaid. This charter confirms the disposition **Register.** foresaid, and sasine following thereon of date 30 Nov. and registered in the General Register of Sasines at Edinburgh 6 Dec. 1769 ; as also a contract of vendition between the said John Wedderburn and William Gray of Ballidgarno and John Gray, his son, of date 26 and 28 May and 6 June 1770, and decreet of adjudication in implement thereof. (CXIV, 6, fol. 232.)

117. **1794.** July 5.—Charter of resignation (Edinburgh) in favour of David Wedderburn, Esq., eldest son of Sir John Wedderburn of Balliudean, Baronet, and the heirs male of his body, whom failing to the said Sir John his heirs and assignees whomsoever in fee, heritably and irredeemably, of the Easter and Wester Half of of the lands of Ballindean *alias* Bandean, in the parish of Inchture and shire of Perth, which pertained to James Wedderburn, Esq., brother german of the said Sir John Wedderburn in life-rent, and to the said Sir John Wedderburn in fee ; to be held by them of the Crown, and which, by virtue of a procuratory of resignation by the said James Wedderburn and Sir John Wedderburn, of date 27 and 30 May last, were resigned to the Lords of the Exchequer, in favour of and for new infeftment of the same to be made to the said David Wedderburn and the heirs male of his body, whom failing to the said Sir John Wedderburn and his heirs and assignees whomsoever in fee heritably. (CXXVII, 163, fol. 150.)

148. **1799.** May 1.—Charter of Confirmation (Edinburgh) in favour of Mrs. Isabella Blackburn, now Colvill, spouse of James Wedderburn, Esq. of Inveresk, and the other heirs and substitutes aftermentioned, confirming a disposition, dated 26 March last, and granted by Mrs. Margaret Colvill of Ochiltree, in favour of the said Mrs. Isabella Blackburn *alias* Wedderburn, now Colvill, her eldest daughter and the heirs of her body, whom failing to the heirs of the body of the said Mrs. Margaret Colvill, whom failing to the heirs female of Andrew Aiton, merchant in Glasgow, her father, second son of the marriage between Sir John Aiton of that ilk and Lady Margaret Colvill, Lady Aiton, eldest sister of Robert Lord Colvill of Ochiltree, and the heirs of their bodies, whom failing to the nearest heirs and assignees whomsoever of the said Robert Lord Colvill, heritably and irredeemably, of all and whole the lands of Crombie, lying in the united parishes of Torryburn and Crombie, shire of Fife. with teinds, fishings, &c., conform to charter under the Great Seal, of date at Holyrood 3 Feb. 1605, in favour of the late Robert Lord Colville, therein designed Sir Robert Colville of Cleish, Knight ; as also of the lands of Craigflower, Meadowfurres, and Waulaws Bikers, in the barony and regality of Culross and shire of Fife ; with and under the provisions of an entail of the said lands (the date of which is not mentioned), including the usual clauses in regard to the assumption of the surname of Colvill and bearing the arms of Ochiltree without any addition or alteration whatever, &c. ; and reserving to the said Mrs. Margaret Colvill her life-rent use of the profits and duties of the said lands. Sasine is dated 30 March last, and registered at Cupar of Fife 13 April thereafter. (CXXX, 124, fol. 121.)

149. **1800.** Feb. 3.—Charter of confirmation (Edinburgh) in favour of John Wedderburn, Esq., of London, his heirs and assignees whatsoever, heritably, confirming a disposition (dated 13 Jan. and recorded in the Books of Council and Session 29 Feb. 1780) granted by Thomas Fletcher, Esq., of Lindertis, Lieutenant Colonel in the service of the East India Merchant Company, in favour of the late James Gardyne, Esq., of Midleton, the late Thomas Milne of Milnfield, James Guthrie (therein designed younger of Craigie), David Hunter of Blackuess, Mrs. Anna Hunter *alias* Fletcher, his spouse, and others, as trustees for the purposes therein mentioned, of the lands and barony of Reidie and Kinnalty, lying in the parish of Nether Airly and shire of Forfar ; and confirming also a disposition (dated 7 and 12 Oct. and 2 and 11 Nov. and recorded in the said books 9 Dec. 1799) granted by James Guthrie, now of Craigie, Robert Graham of Fintry, and David Hunter, then the only surviving trustees nominated by the foresaid late Thomas Fletcher, in favour of the said John Wedderburn and his foresaids, of the said lands of Reidie and Kinnalty, with manor place, &c., and certain parts of the barony of Baikie, viz., the lands of Newton of Airlie, Littletoun, Lindertis, &c., lying as aforesaid. (CXXXI, 64, fol. 102.)

Privy
Council
Register.

This is the register of the Acts of the Privy Council from 1545 to 1707. It is in course of publication (1877-96), in the same series as the Great Seal Register, and thirteen volumes are already issued, bringing the work down to 1625. From these volumes I have extracted every reference to Wedderburns, and, in addition to these, I am able to give, from notes sent me by Mr. Macleod, a few later references (Nos. 61-70) to some of the volumes of the MS. record (1631-32, 1632-34, 1667-73, 1673-78, 1682-85 and 1685) together with one or two extracts from the Privy Council papers.[1]

1. **1564.** Dec. 3.—Decreet in favour of Symon Clowson, master of a ship of Ineason in Holland, *c.* James Wedderburne, clerk of the cocquet of Dundee, in regard to a seizure of goods by the defender. (i, 295-96,)

The following is a full extract of this entry :—"Apud Edinburgh. Dec. 3, 1564.—The quhilk day, anent the complaint maid be Symon Clowson, maister of a schip of Incasen in Holand, callit the Fleand Hart, aganis James Wedderburne, Clerk of the Cocquet of Dunde, for the awaytaking fra the said Symon of four scoir elnis of quheit clayth. as at mair lenth is content in his supplicatioun, hayth the partiis being personalie present, and their allegationis hard and coussdderit, the Lordis of Secreit Counsall decernis the said James Wedderburne to restoir and deliver to the said Symon the saidis lxxx elnis of quheit clayth, ressavand fra him his dewitis thairfoir as use is, and that within xxiiij houris nixt eftir the said James be chargit thairto, under the pane of rebellioun ; and gif he failyeis, to put him to the horne and that lettres be direct heirupon, gif neid be, in forme as efferis." See ante s. Dundee Burgh and Head Court Records, No. 140.

2. **1567.** June 6.—Decreet in favour of Henric Nauchtie, burges of Kirkwall in Orkney, *v.* James Wedderburne, bailie of Dundee, for trespass, &c. (i. 517-18.)

The following is a fuller extract of the above :—At Edinburgh. June 6. 1567.—Anent oure Soverane Ladiis lettres rasit at the instance of Henrie Nauchtie. burges of Kirkwall in Orkney, upoun James Wedderburne. Baillie of the burgh of Dunde : makand mentioun that quhair he, with his complices, laithie upon twysday the xx day of maii last bipast, under silence of nycht, bodin in feir of weir, to the nowmer of xx personis or thairby, come on burd upoun the said Henrie's schip. callit the Sampsoun—quhair scho wes liand at ane anker befoir Bruchtie, cum fra Hull in Ingland upoun hir viage.—and take his haill kippage furth of the samyn, to the nowmer of sex men and ane boy, and put thame in captivitie in diverse houssis ; and swa be force and way of deid, he maner of plane piracie, hes reft, spulyeit, and takin fra the said Heurie his said haill schip of the birth of thre scoir tunnis or thairby, with hir laidnyng of clayth. and salt being thairin to the nowmer of twa hundrith bollis or thairby. togidder with hir ankeris, saillis, cabillis, towis, and all uther hir neces-saries ...... and as yit withhaldis the same and will mak the said compleaur na restitutioun thairof. nor of the dampnageis susteuit be him thairthrow. without the said James Wedderburne be com-pellit. Bot to cullour this his piracie, he now allegeis that the said complenaris schip is ane pirutt. quhilk git it be trew, he salbe fugitive fra na law. bot it is notour and weill kend that he is ane power young man laubourand and travelland sair for his leving and hes travellit in the same schip continewalie sen yule wes aue yeir ...... and now laithie is returnit without ony maner of artaillierie or any nther thing that may savour of piracie ...... Aud anent the charge gevin to the said James Wedderburne to compeir before his Hienis and Counsale foirsaid this day to answer ...... under the pane of rebellioun and putting of him to the horne with certificatioun to him and he failyeit, he sould be denunceit rebell and put to the horne ...... (and) the said Henrie Nauchtie comperand personalle, the said James Wedderburne being oftymes callit and nocht comperand be him nor na utheris in his name havand his power ...... the Lordis of Secreit Counsall decernis and ordanis lettres to be direct. to denunce the said James Wedderburne our Soverane Ladiis rebell, and put him to the horne. and to eschelt and inbring all his movabill gudis to oure Soveranis use for his con-temptioun, becaus he was chargeit in maner abone writtiu and dissobeyit ....

[1] The Register of the Privy Council, although the principal, is not the only record of that body. Messrs. Millar and Bryce, in their hand-book already mentioned, give a list of some twenty sets of records. State Papers, 1553-72 ; Warrauts, 1561-1708 ; Acta Obliv., 1564-69 ; Acta Caut., 1575-1664 ; Bishop's Estates, 1571-1607 : Acta Marcharum, &c., 1587-1623, with other Border Papers, 1603-43, and Border Court Book, 1622-23 ; Sederunts, 1598-1643 : Minute Book, 1604-31, 1666-1707 : Commissions, 1667-30 : Justices of the Peace, 1610-39 ; Decreets, 1612-1705 ; Fiues. 1611-31 : Grievances. 1623-26 ; Royal Proclamations. 1661-1706 ; Bonds of Caution, 1661-1707 ; Committees. 1675, 1684 ; Inventory of Royal Letters. Privy Council Proclamations. Fines for not Swearing Allegiance. 1689-1707. Mr. Macleod informs me that the whole of these may be regarded as embodied in the printed volumes, though not there arranged in separate divisions.

3. **1567.** Dec. 22.—James Wedderburn and others, burgesses of Dundee, claim relief from a fine imposed on the town of Dundee. (i. 597.)

4. **1568.** Jan. 9.—James Wedderburn, burgess of Dundee, and others, " who were in Edinburgh at the time of the late tumult " (between the inhabitants of Perth and Dundee) and were ordered not to leave the city, are decerned " fre and innocent of the samyn in all tymes cuming swa that thai may frelie depart hame." (i. 604-5.)

5. **1569.** July 25.—At Dundee. Comperit James Wedderburn, sone and air of umquhill David Wedderburn, burgess of Dundee, and William Wedderburn his brother (with his spouse Margaret Rollok) anent a decree for payment of certain moneys by James to William and his wife. In making the decree the Lords have " respect to the said James' faithfull service in his Grace's affairs and common weill of the realme." (i. 687-88.)

6. **1573.** Jan. 31.—Complaint of David Hendirsoun v. Ogilvy of Auchterleis, naming " the fre landis of Aberbrothie, perteuing in heretage to James Wedderburn, burgess of Dundee " (ii. 183.)

In the preface of this vol. (p. xxviii.), the editor notes this as the one signal instance in the register where a landed potentate, denounced at the horn for oppression, endeavoured in vain to clear himself of the shackles of "diligence."

7. **1574.** Jan. 27.—The same suit continued. James Wedderburn, sone and air of umquhile John Wedderburn in Dundee, appears by his curator, James Lovell, as the landlord of David Hendirsoun. (ii. 324.)

8. **1575.** Mar. 27.—James Wedderburn, clerk of the cocket in Dundee, named. (ii. 738.)

9. **1577.** Sept. 20.—Complaint c. James Scrymgeour, constabill of Dundee, Robert Wedderburne and others. (ii, 634-35.)

10. **1578.** Jan. 17.—Action by William Wedderburn, son of the late David Wedderburn, and by his spons, Margaret Rollok, v. Margaret Dundas, relict and executrix of the late James Wedderburn, son and air of the said David, and now spons of William Fotheringhame. This refers to the suit mentioned ante No. 5. (ii, 664.)

11. **1579.** Sept. 1.—Caution by David Lindsay of Edzell for the appearance of Thomas Wedderburn before the council on the 5th inst. (iii, 212.)

12. **1579.** Sept. 10.—Caution by David Lindsay of Pyottistown for the entry of John Wedderburn, servant to David, Earl of Crawfurd. (iii, 215.)

13. **1586** May 21.—Complaint by Boyd of Bonschaw v. John Dunlop of Halpland. The summons is named as being in the hands (for service) of Robert Weddirburne, officer and sheriff in that part. (iv, 73.)

Bonschaw is in Dumfries-shire, and Halpland in the district of Cunninghame, co. Ayr. " Sheriff in that part" signifies "in that matter," or "for that occasion," and does not refer to the places mentioned.

14. **1591.** May 26.—Complaint by William Milburne v. Robert Jaksoun, burgess of Dundee, for assault. It recites that Jaksoun asked him " giff he wes ane Englishman," and that on his saying that " swa he wes," Jaksoun struck him in the face ; and that thereafter Robert Wedderburn, younger, burgess of Dundee, came to him either from Jaksoun, or " of his awne heid," and took him to a house when Jaksoun again assaulted him, while Wedderburn took his " hors being quhyte in cullour, with twa hundreth merkis " out of the hands of his boy and "deliverit him in the landis of Jaksoun quha lapt on and raid away with him." (iv, 625.)

15. **1592.** April 5.—Alexander Wedderburn, notary, signs a caution dated at Dundaff, 4 April. (iv, 741.)
Dundaff is in the parish of St. Ninian's, co. Stirling.

16. **1594.** Jan. 19.—Mr. Alexander Wedderburn is a commissioner to the estates for Dundee. (v, 115.)

17. **1595.** Dec. 29.—Decree naming Mr. Alexander Wedderburn, clerk of Dundee. (v, 252.)

18. **1597.** March 3.—Mr. Alexander Wedderburn is a commissioner to the estates for Dundee. (v. 367.)

19. **1598.** Sept. 18.—Robert Wedderburn, notary, signs a bond dated at Dundee, 8 Sept. (v, 704.)

20. **1599.** May 18.—Mr. Alexander Wedderburn is named as witness to and writer of a bond by George Ramsay to David Bell. (v, 727.)

21. **1601.** June 11.—Summons by David Drummond c. various burgesses and inhabitants of Dundee, including Peter Wodderburne, taverner, Patrik Wodderburne and Patrick Wodderburne, his son, merchants, and Robert Wodderburne. (vi, 253) Decreet in favour of the defenders, July 1. (ib. 265.)

22. **1602.** Jan. 7.—In a list of commissioners for settling disputes between Perth and Dundee, "Mr. Robert (sic) Wedderburn, clerk," is named as one of those for Dundee. (vi, 331.)
      Robert is, of course, an error for Alexander.

23. **1602.** April 17, 19.—At Brechin, Robert Wedderburn, notary, is named as a witness to the settlement of a complaint, and as writer of a bond. (vi, 269, 723.)

24. **1602.** Sept. 19.—Caution for William Stewart of Setonn, and Robert Wedderburn, burgess of Dundee. Robert Wedderburn, notary, is the writer. (vi, 75.)

25. **1602.** Oct. 9.—Bond by Robert Wedderburn, elder, burgess of Dundee. Robert Wedderburn, notary, is the writer. (vi, 757.)

26. **1603.** May 9.—Robert Wedderburn, notary, writes and witnesses a bond ; also witnessed by Alexander Wedderburn, younger, and dated at Dundee, 7 May. (vi,788.)

27. **1603.** June 2.—Mr. Alexander Wedderburn, clerk of Dundee, is a witness. (vi, 790.)

28. **1604.** May 16.—At Dundee. Bond of caution for various burgesses and inhabitants of Dundee, including Mr. Alexander Wedderburn of Kingany, David Wedderburn, Robert Wedderburn, elder, Robert Wedderburn, younger, Patrick Wedderburn, merchant, and Alexander Wedderburn his son. (vii. 551-52.)

29. **1604.** Aug. 8.—Mr. Alexander Wedderburn, witnesses a bond at Dundee. (vii. 562.)

30. **1604.** Sept. 26.—Complaint by Sir James Scrymgeour and others anent disturbances in Dundee, naming Robert and David Wedderburn, councillors, as parties. (vii. 735-37.)

31. **1604** Dec. 6.—Treaty of union between England and Scotland signed by Alexander Wedderburn. In the act appointing him commissioner he is named among the "merchandis." (vii, xxxiv, 5 note.)

32. **1605.** Mar. 26.—Patrick Wedderburn, burgess of Dundee, witnesses a bond. (vii,590.)

33. **1605.** June 7.—"Mr. Alexander Wedderburn, Dundie," is a commissioner to the Estates for the burgh of Dundee. (vii, 55.)

34. **1607.** Jan. 20.—Report on municipal troubles in Dundee. Among those charged to appear is "Mr. Alexander Wedderburn, clerk to the burgh." (vii, 303.)

35. **1607.** Feb. 21.—Mr. Alexander Wedderburn, clerk of Dundee, writes and witnesses a bond. (vii, 667.)

36. **1609.** Jan. 27.—Mr. Alexander Wedderburn, commissioner to the estates for Dundee, is named on a commission. (viii, 232.)

37. **1609.** Aug. 3.—Order for admission of James Sheves as professor of philosophy in S. Andrew's, reciting that "Mr. William Wedderburn, who was regent for philosophy in the Auld College of Sanctandrois, has alreddy or at least is of purpois to leave that place and to be plantit minister at the kirk of Pittinweyne . . ." (viii, 339.) *Privy Council Register.*

38. **1609.** Nov. 16.—Complaint by the rector and masters of the said college to the effect that William Wedderburn has never resigned, so that his chair is not vacant. Decree in their favour. (viii, 375-76.)

39. **1609.** Dec. 21.—Action by Robert Wedderburn, younger, merchant in Dundee, v. David, Earl of Crawfurde, for £1,020 principal and £200 expenses, under a judgment. (viii, 392.)

40. **1610.** March 15.—Action by David Smart v. Alexander Wedderburn, younger, and another, merchants, burgesses of Dundee. (viii, 442.)

41. **1610.** Sept. 26.—Bond for 20,000 merks by various persons, sureties for the Earl of Crawfurd, debtor to Robert Wedderburn and others. (ix, 662.)

42. **1610.** Oct. 4.—Decree in the suit of Robert Wedderburn, burgess of Dundee, and others v. David, Earl of Crawfurd, reciting that the Earl "was apprehendit upoun warrandis" and "committit to ward in the Castle of Edinburgh." (ix, 68.)

43. **1611.** May 28.—David Wedderburn is witness to a bond by the Earl of Erroll. (ix, 180.)

44. **1612.** Feb. 13.—Complaint by Mr. William Fergusone, bailie of Dundee, and Katherine Wedderburn, his spouse, v. Crichton of Cluny and others, as unrelaxed from hornings, 30 April 1610 and 5 Oct. 1611, for not paying to the said Catherine 2,000 merks. (ix, 332.)

45. **1614.** July.—The minute book of processes has an entry "Rebellion, David Wedderburn v. David Ramsay." (x, 260.)

46. **1615.** Oct. 25.—Complaint Katherine Wedderburne, relict of William Duncane, surgeon, burgess of Dundie. v. David Spalding, burgess of Dundee, as unrelaxed from a horning (30 Sept. 1613) in respect of certain sums. Judgment for the pursuer. The suit is entered into the minute book of processes. (x, 400, 402.)

47. **1616.** March 28.- Complaint of Robert Murray, one of his majestie's guard, and Elizabeth Wedderburn, his spouse, assignees for Robert Wedderburn, burgess of Dundee, and the late Euphame Consland (sic for Constoun), his spouse, v. Hew Maxwell of Tealing and others, as unrelaxed from a horning (5 July 1614) for not paying various sums. (x, 486.)

48. **1616.** April 30.—Mr. Alexander Wedderburn is named as commissioner for Dundee in regard to a report to be made to the king re wool manufacture. The report is made 11 July. (x, 506, 572.)

49. **1616.** June 6.—Mr. Alexander Wedderburn is named re the roads between Perth and Dundee. (x, 530.)

50. **1617.** May 19.—David Wedderburn, master of the Aberdeen grammar school, presents a poem to the King at Falkland. (xl, xli, 138 n.)

51. **1617.** May 30.—Mr. Alexander Wedderburn, town clerk, receives the King with a speech in English on the occasion of his visiting Dundee. (xi, 143 n.)

52. **1617.** June 17.—Mr. Alexander Wedderburn, town clerk of Dundee, and commissioner for the burgh, is on a commission for unifying weights and measures. June 30.—He reports re the plantation of kirks. (xi, 156 n, cvii; 169.)

3 B

53.   **1617.** July 11.—The King visits S. Andrew's, and is addressed with speeches by Mr. Henry Danskine, schoolmaster, and Mr. Peter Bruce, while poems are presented by Mr. James Wedderburn, one of the professors, and by David Wedderburn of Aberdeen. (xi, 182n)

54.   **1618.** July 23.—Mr. Alexander Wedderburne is one of the commissioners for the burghs on a commission *re* disputes with foreign vessels. (xi, 413 ; cxvi.)

55.   **1618.** Dec. 8.—John Beaton, one of the gentlemen of the guard, sues Gilbert Rynd for assault, and Alexander Wedderburn, one of the bailies of Dundee, for not assisting him. The defender are both assoilzied. (xi, 482.)

56.   **1620.** Sept. 13.—Commission to Lindsay of Pitscandlie and Mr. Alexander Wedderburn of ———— (*sic.*), clerk of Dundee, to hold a court in Brechin to try Andrew Taylor for witchcraft. (xii, 362.)

57.   **1621.** July 10.—Acquittance by Margaret Davidson to the clerk of the council *re* property in Leith. The lands of umquhile John Wedderburn in Leith are named as a boundary. (xii, 527.)

58   **1621.** July 25.—Mr. Alexander Wedderburn, member for Dundee, is named as voting in favour of the ratification of the five articles of the General Assembly of the kirk at Perth in August, 1618. The articles were for (1) kneeling at communion ; (2) liberty of private communion ; (3) private baptism ; (4) confirmation of children by the bishops ; and (5) the observance of five holidays, Christmas, Good Friday, Easter, Ascension, and Whitsun-day. (xii, 558 n).

59.   **1623.** Jan. 15.—"Mr. Robert Hervie, principall of the New College of S. Andrew's, Dr. Wedderburn, and Dr. Melvine were directed by a letter from Dr. Young, in the King's name, to use the Englishe Liturgie, morning and evening, in the New Colledge, when all the students were present at morning and evening prayer, which was presentlie putt in execution." (xiii, 142 n.)

This is not from the Privy Council Register, but is a quotation from Calderwood (vii, 569), given in a note by the editor of this volume of the record.

60.   **1623.** July 31.—Mr. Alexander Home, master of the grammar school at Dunbar, having composed a Latin grammar for which he desires a monopoly, the Lords remit the consideration of it to certain of the judges, advocates, and ministers, who being unable to agree, summon various masters of the grammar schools, including Mr. David Wedderburn of Aberdeen, Mr. James Gleg of Dundee, Mr. John Rae of Edinburgh, Mr. Henry Danskene of S. Andrew's, and others, with two or three scholars each, to their assistance. (xiii, 318-19.)

61.   **1631-32.**—Ten entries relating to the grammar composed by Mr. David Wedderburn, master at the Grammar School, Aberdeen. (Vol. 1630-32, fol. 48, 50-51, 78, 84, 114, 118 ; Vol. 1632-34, fol. 132.)

These are as follows :—

(a) **1631.** March 10.—The Lords of Secret Council ordain the Bishops of Dunkeld and Dunblane, the Clerk of Register, advocate, and Sir John Scott to meet the morn after dissolving of the Commission, and to call before them " Mr. Alexander Home and Mr. David Wedderburne, and to deale and travell to sattle and agree thame anent impositioun aud satisfactioun to be made be the said Mr. David to the said Mr. Alexander for having the sole libertie of printing and selling of the grammar composed be the said Mr. David, and that the same grammar be solelie receaved and taught throughout all the Grammar Schooles of this Kingdom, with a prohibitioun to the Maisters of the Grammar Schooles of all teaching of anie other Grammar, without prejudice and with exceptioun alwayes of the grammar made be the said Mr. Alexander whome the Lords allowes to teache the same to his owne schollers allanerlie." (fol. 48.)

(b) **1631.** March 15.—" Forasmeekle as Mr. David Wedderburne, Maister of the Grammar Schoole at Aberdein, hes latelie, with the commoun advice of his brethrein, teachers of the Grammar Schooles within this Kingdom, framed and drawin up ane Grammar, as ane abridgement, for facilitating of Despauters Grammar for the weale of the youth and gayning of much tyme in the progresse of thair studeis and learning of good authors in the Latine tongue, and this his worke hes the approbatioun and allowance not onelie of the whole Maisteris of best marke, bot also of all the Colledges

and Universities iu this Kingdome ; and whereas his paines aud travellis iu so necessarie and good Privy
ane warke for the weale of the publict sould be in measoare acknowledged, quhairthrow he and others Council
in imitation of him may be encouraged to follow the like worthie and commendable enterprises Register.
heirefter, Thairfore the Lords of Secreit Conseil has thought it verie just aud equitable that the said
Mr. David sall have the sole and onelie libertie and privile lgs of printing of the said book for
certane yeires, to be taught allanerlie be suche who pleises to embrace the same voluntarilie, without
excluding of others to teache other Grammars at thair pleasure, and for this effect the saids Lords
hes given and grantit and be the teanour heirof gives and grants to the said Mr. David Wedderburn,
his aires and assigneyes for the space of twentie ane yeires next after the dait heirof the sole and
onelie libertie and priviledge of printing of the said Grammar, discharging heirby all others, &c." (fol.50.)

(c) **1631.** March 22.—" Forasmuch as the Lords of Secret Council passed a warrant to Mr. David
Wedderburn. schoolmaster at Aberdeen. for printing and publishing the Grammar composed by him
for the use of such as should please to embrace the same. and the said Lords also having appointed
certain of their number to have dealt with the said Mr. David anent some satisfaction to have been
given by him to Mr. Alexander Home. schoolmaster at Dunbar. who formerly had composed a
Grammar which was allowed and ordained to be only taught within this Kingdom. the said Mr.
David Wedderburn in the meantime as soon as he received his warrant for printing, departed home.
whereby the said Mr. Alexander Home is frustrated of his satisfaction. therefore the Lords ordain
letters charging the said Mr. Alexander Home and Mr. David Wedderburn to compear before them
on 14 June next, and discharge the said Mr. David Wedderburn from printing his Grammar." (51.)

(d) **1631.** July 19.—" Compeared Mr. David Wedderburn. schoolmaster at Aberdeen, and acted
and obliged himself that his Grammar being allowed and received, and all other Grammars discharged
to be printed, sold or taught, in any of the schools of this Kingdom, and the sole privilege of
printing and selling the same being granted to him and his heirs, to pay to the said Mr. Alexander
Home the sum of 1,000 merks : Reserving to the said Mr. Alexander Home and Mr. John Home, his
son, the liberty of teaching the Grammar composed by him in their own schools allanerlie." (73.)

(e) **1631.** Aug. 2.--" The Lords having heard the Report of the Burrows anent the course taken
by them touching Mr. David Wedderburne's Grammar, whereby they have ordained 200 copies
thereof to be printed, and the same to be given to learned men to make their observations thereon, the
said Lords allow the said course and ordain 200 copies to be printed and distributed as aforesaid." (84.)

(f) **1632.** Feb. 23.—" Which day Mr. Robert Williamson, Master of the Grammar School at
Cowper, gave in to the Lords of Privy Council some objections against Mr. David Wedderburne's
Grammar, which were delivered to the said Mr. David, and he ordained to answer thereto on Tuesday
next." (114.)

(g) **1632.** Feb. 29.—" The which day Mr. David Wedderburn gave in his answers to the above,
which were given to the said Mr. Robert Williamson to reply thereto on Thursday next." (114.)

(h) **1632.** March 1.—" Which day the said Mr. Robert Williamson gave in his replies to the
answers by Mr. David Wedderburn anent his Grammar ; which the Lords recommend to the Bishop
of Dunblane, Sir John Scot, Sir Thomas Henderson of Chesters, Mr. Andro Ramsay, Mr. John
Adamson, Mr. Patrick Nisbit, Doctor Sibbald, and Mr. Robert Barnet, elder and younger, or any
pair of them, to consider and report their judgment concerning the same on 22 March instant." (114.)

(i) **1632.** March 27.—" The which day compeared Adam, Bishop of Dunblane, and Sir John
Scot of Scotistarvet, two of the Commissioners nominated by the Lords of Privy Council for revising
of Mr. David Wedderburne's Grammar and gave in the Report following :—Apud Edr. 26 Martij 1632.
The Commissioners under subscryvand appointed be the Lords of His Majestie's most Honourable
Privy Counsell for revising and rectifeing of ane Grammar made be Mr. David Wedderburne, school-
maister at Aberdein. having sindrie tymes mett thereanent, and having heard the observationns and
animadversionns made against the same be Mr. James Glen, schoolemaister at Dundie, and having
atteudit to have heard the observationns of Mr. Robert Williamsone, sometime schoolmaster at
Cowper, who be the Lords of Counsell wes ordained to use the samine before the saids Commissioners,
and he not compearand anie of the saids dyets, except upon the nynetene day of this instant where
he produced no materiall objectioun worthie of consideration, and being ordained to compeir upon
this day the 26 of Marche, and not having compeired, deserted the said dyet ; the saids Commissioners finds according to the Lords of Secreit Counsell thair meaning that the said Mr. David
Wedderburne his Grammar sall onelie be recaived. rectified and amended in such particulars as the
said Commissioners hes thought or sall think expedient betwixt now) and the second Monday of June,
at quhilk tyme, God willing. the saids Commissioners sall report thair full judgement and determi-
nationns in the said mater concerning the said Grammar, that the Lords of Secreit Counsell may
interpone thair auctoritie and approve the same as they sall thinke most fitt, for weale of the youth
of the Kingdom, whilks they have willed my Lords of Dunblane and Scottistarvet to report to thair
Lordships. Sic subscribitur Ad. B. of Dunblane. J. Scottistarvet, T. Heurysou, A. Ramsay, Mr. Johne
Adamsone, Dr. George Sibbald, Mr. R. Barnet." (118.)

(j) **1632.** June 26.—Forasmuch as Mr. David Wedderburn, master of the Grammar School at
Aberdeen, having with great pains framed a Grammar as an abridgment for facilitating of Despauters
Grammar, &c....(here follows a narrative containing the substance of the foregoing extracts), the
Lords finding that equity craves that he should have the sole benefit of printing and selling of his
said Grammar, therefore the said Lords grant to the said Mr. David and his foresaids. for the
space of 21 years, the sole liberty and privilege of printing of the said Grammar, discharging all
others." (Vol. 1632-34, fol. 132.)

Privy
Council
Register.

62.[1] **1668**. June 18.—Discharge to Sir Peter Wedderburn of Gosford, as clerk to the Privy Council, on his appointment as a Lord of Session.

"Forasmuch as the King's Majesty upon the advancement of Sir Peter Wedderburn of Gosfoord to be one of the Senators of the College of Justice, hath appointed Mr. Alexander Gibson and Mr. Thomas Hay, two of the Clerks of Session, to be Clerks of the Council in his place, Hugh Stevenson in name of the said Sir Peter Wedderburn, his master, delivered to the Lord Chancellor in presence of the Lords of Council the Signett and Catchett of Council: Whereupon the Lords of Council exonered and Discharged the said Sir Peter Wedderburn of the said Signet and Catchet, and of the whole registers, warrants and letters from the King, etc." (Vol. 1667-73, fol. 85.)

63. **1670**. Jan. 27.—Appointment of Mr. Alexander Wedderburn as minister at Kilmarnock. (*ib.* fol. 319.)

"The Lords of His Majesty's Privy Council in pursuance of His Majesty's commands signified in his Letter dated the 7th June last, and in regard of the patron's consent do appoint Mr. Alexander Wedderburn, late minister at ——, to preach and exercise the other functions of the ministry at the Kirk of Kilmarnock, now vacant."

64. **1673**. Sept. 3.—Committal of Mr. Andrew Wedderburn for keeping a conventicle.

Whereas Mr. Andro Wedderburn having this day appeared before the Council to answer for keeping a Conventicle in his own house at Anstruther Wester conform to the Band given by him for that effect and having acknowledged that upon the —— day, being Sunday, he did preach and pray in his own house where diverse other persons were present besides those of his own family, the Lords of His Majesty's Privy Council do find that thereby he has contravened the Fift Act of the Second Session of this current Parliament and incurred the penalty therein contained and therefore they ordain the said Mr. Andro Wedderburn to be committed prisoner to the Tolbooth of Edinburgh, to remain therein until he find caution under the pain of 5,000 merks not to keep Conventicles hereafter, or else enact himself to remove out of this kingdom within one month after the date hereof and not return without His Majesty's License." (Vol. 1673-78, fol. 26.)

Mr. Andrew Wedderburn had been minister at Liff, but was deprived by the Acts of 1664, and retired to Anstruther Wester where he was now living. He had been summoned before the Privy Council on 31 July 1673, with the result here shown. The matter is referred to in the diary of James Brodie of Brodie, who writes, 18 Sept. 1673, "I heard from my brother the troubles honest people were in at Edinburgh: that Mr. Andro Wedderburn was imprisoned for having more than 5 at his famili exercis." (Diary of Alexander and James Brodie of Brodie 1625-85, Aberdeen, Spalding Club, 1863; p. 316.)

65. **1673**. Sept. 30.—Release of the said Mr. Andrew Wedderburn. (*ib.* fol. 30.)

'The Lords of Privy Council having considered a Petition by Mr. Andro Wedderburn, sometime minister at Liff, bearing that for a considerable time he hath been prisoner in the Tolbooth of Edinburgh for a Conventicle kept in his own house: and whereas the Petitioner was that same day at Sermon both forenoon and afternoon and had no intention by any private exercise in his own family to give any provocation, and as his carriage has been hitherto peaceable and he resolves so to continue, Humbly therefore supplicating that the Lords of Council might give order for his liberty, the said Lords do hereby ordain the said Mr. Andro Wedderburn against Saturday next to repair to the parish of Kilmarnock and to remain confined to that parish under the pain of a more severe restraint to be inflicted in case he do not give obedience, and grant warrant to the Magistrates of Edinburgh to set him at liberty to the effect foresaid."

66. **1674**. July 16.—Letters raised at the instance of Sir John Nisbet of Dirleton, Knight, His Majesty's advocate, against persons attending Conventicles, and especially against the ministers who preached at them, among whom are included Mr. Thomas Hog, sometime minister at Larber, Mr. Patrick Gillespy, Mr. John Gray, Mr. James Wedderburn in Couppar, Mr. Donald Cargill, and many others, all of whom are denounced as rebels for not compearing in answer to the said letters. (*ib.* fol. 131.)

67. **1676**. Aug. 3.—Act for Letters of Intercommuning against several ministers, narrating the foregoing Denunciation in July 1674, wherein the Lords of Privy Council ordain Letters charging messengers at arms to pass to the Market Cross of Edinburgh, Cupar, &c., &c., and charge the Lieges that they do not presume to reset, supply, or intercommune with any of the foresaid persons, including the foresaid Mr. James Wedderburn in Coupar. (*ib.* fol. 364.)

---

[1] I have also a note of one of the Bands of Caution among the Privy Council records, as follows :—
1667. Dec. 19.—Obligation of James Gordon of Carleton, Andrew Carsan of Sennik, and Robert McLellan of Bornessu, to Sir Peter Wedderburn of Gosfoord, Clerk to His Majesty's Privy Council for the sum of 1,000 merks. Dated at Edinburgh 15 August 1667; Hugh Stevenson, servitor to the said Sir Peter Wedderburn, is a witness. Registered in the Books of Privy Council on the 19 Dec. 1667, and extracted by 'Pet. Wedderburne.'" See also ante s. Private Records, Scrymgeour-Wedderburn Papers, No. 357, where a license of the Privy Council (12 Feb. 1663) to Alexander Wedderburn of Easter Powrie, permitting him and those at his table to eat flesh during Lent, is noted

There is among the Privy Council papers, a printed list of the "Persons Intercommuned and **Privy** declared Fugitives, since the year 1674, for not compearing before the Council, or Commissions of **Council** Council, to answer for Conventicles, &c., Whose names are to be affixt by Sheriffs and other Magis- **Register.** trates upon the publict places of Judicature, that they may not have the benefite of the Law in any Process ; and who are to be seized upon and secured until they submit themselves to the laws, and be relaxed from the Horn.

" Follows the names of such as are denounced and Intercommuned. Ministers Intercommuned are, (among many others) :--Mr James Wedderburn,

" The Persons underwritten, for the most part are residents in Fife, and are denounced, but not Intercommuned, viz., (among many others) :—Mr. James Wedderburn in Couper."

From this list it would seem that there were two ministers of the same name, both living in 1674. If so, they must be James Wedderburn, minister of Moonzie, and his son James, who was admitted his colleague in 1659. James Wedderburn, elder, however, is said (Fast. Eccl. Scot., II., 505) to have died in 1661, and, although no authority is quoted for this date, he would certainly have been of considerable age in 1674, as he took his degree at S. Andrew's in 1608. Possibly the compiler of the list overlooked the fact of his death, or erroneously placed his son (who died at Cupar 23 July 1687) in both its divisions ; or, perhaps, the Christian name of the first mentioned minister should be Alexander or Andrew, as Mr. James Wedderburn in Cupar had two such brothers, both ministers, of whom the latter was certainly in difficulties with the Government at about this time. (See ante Nos. 63-65, 68.) It may be well to explain that persons "denounced" were declared to be rebels, while, as appears from the above extract (No. 67), everyone was prohibited, under severe penalties, from holding any intercourse with those "intercommuned."

68. **1684.** Jan. 23.—Petition by Helen Turnbull, relict of Mr. Alexander Wedderburne, late minister at Kilmarnock. (Vol. 1682-85, fol. 221.)

The Petition shows that the Petitioner's husband died in November 1678, and left the Petitioner with the burden of "many young children with little or no provision," and that the Petitioner having applied to the Council in October 1680 for the stipend of that crop of the parish of Kilmarnock which was then vacant, the Lords declared they would allow the same to her for that year, or the equivalent thereof from the vacant stipends (the Archbishop of Glasgow being first satisfied of the sum of £300 sterling ordained to be paid to him out of the vacancies of his Diocese), and seeing the Petitioner did not receive the vacant stipend of Kilmarnock for that year, which the said Archbishop applied to other uses by virtue of the Council's Order ; therefore craves that the Council, from commiseration of her own and her fatherless children's condition, would allow them the vacant stipend of the parish of Dunlop for the year 1683 : which petition the Council grant, in place of the half year's stipend of Kilmarnock.

69. **1685.** Sept. 11.—The Lords of Privy Council, understanding that the troop of Horse under the command of Major John Wedderburne of Gosfoord are conveniently posted for His Majesty's service in the town and shire of Lanark, do allow the said Major John Wedderburne to continue them quartered there until further order. (Vol. 1685, fol. 160.)

70. **1686.** June 3.—At Edinburgh. His Majestie's High Commissioner and the Lords of His Privy Council in pursuance of His Majestie's Commands, dated at his Court at Whitehall the twentieth second day of May last by-past, hereby Recommend to General Lieutenant Drummond to remove from His Majestie's Service John Wedderburne of Gosfoord as Lievtennant Collonell of His Majestie's Regiment of Dragoones, commanded by Lord Charles Murrry as Collonell, and to signify His Majestie's pleasure therein, and to see the same punctually performed and that in pursuance of His Majestie's Letter aforesaid. Extr. by me Will. Paterson, Cler. See Concilij. (Privy Council Warrants, s.d.)

Rolls of the
Exchequer.
Calendars of these rolls, dating from 1264 on, have been in course of publication since 1880, under the editorship of the late Dr. George Burnett, Lyon King at Arms, and others. Fifteen volumes are now issued, coming down to the year 1529. These are among the most important of the Exchequer Records, a detailed note of which has been given in the tabular synopsis at p. 360.

1. **1407-8.** In the account of the customars of Edinburgh, for the period from 13 Mar. 1407-8 to 27 Mar. 1408-9, William of Wethirburn is named. (iv, 42.)

2. **1510.** April 19—Aug. 11—James Wedderburn is named with Thomas Dog, as a customar of Dundee. (xiii, 363.)

3. **1510** Aug. 2.—James Wedderburn, bailic of Dundee, is named as rendering an account of the bailies of the burgh for the period from 25 July 1508 to 1510. (*ib.* 375.)

4. **1510.** Aug. 11.}
   1511. July 10.} James Wedderburn, customar of Dundee, renders account. *ib.* 384.)
   The two dates placed together in Nos. 4—8 define the beginning and the end of the period in respect of which the account is given.

5. **1510.** Aug. 12.}
   1511. July 18.} James Wedderburn, bailic of Dundee, renders account. (*ib.* 398.)

6. **1511.** July 18 }
   1512. July 16.} James Wedderburn, customar of Dundee, renders account. (*ib.* 489.)

7. **1511.** July 18.}
   1512. July 26.} James Wedderburn, bailic of Dundee, renders account. (*ib.* 498.)

8. **1512.** July 26.} James Wedderburn, customar of Dundee, renders account.
   1513. July 30.} (*ib.* 578.)

9. **1514.** July 18.—Jonet Barry, relict of the late James Wedderburn, renders a Dundee account for 30 July—1 Nov. 1503. (xiv, 50.)

10. **1515** Aug. 4.—James Rollok, customar of Dundee, renders account from 1509 June 15 to 19 April 1510 " quo die Jacobus Wedderburn, quondam burgensis, intravit ad hoc officium." (*ib.* 97.)

11. **1527.** (*a*) July 15.—William Carmichael, customar of Dundee, and David Rollok and James Wedderburn, burgesses thereof, are ordered by the Lords Auditors to compear and produce the charter under which the burgh of Dundee claims to be custom-free in respect of certain merchandize (" futefelis, schorlingis, scaldingis, lantryn-ware and lambskynnis") (*b*) July 28.—William Carmichael compears and produces a charter, dated at Edinburgh 12 Jan. 1451, but the Lords declare it to be invalid as having been made during the " les-aige of umquhile King James II." (xv, 652.)

THE ACTS OF THE PARLIAMENTS OF SCOTLAND.

These records, which date from 1124 to 1707, are now published in twelve large (atlas folio) volumes, of which the first appeared in 1814 and the last in 1875. In addition to these "Acts of the Parliaments," there are various other parliamentary records, of which the following list is given in Messrs. Millar and Bryce's hand-book :—

1. Rotul. Placit. in Parl., R. Johannis 1292.— Rotul. Parl., R. David II et R. Roberti II 1368-89.
2. Antiq. Regist. Scoc. XIV, called "The Black Book."
3. Haddington MS, 1384-1400.
4. Records of Parliament 1124-1707.
5. Minutes 1661-74.
6. Acts of the Conventions of Estates 1598-1678.
7. Committee of Estates 1643-60.
8. Acts,&c. of the Committee of Estates 1660-89.
9. Committee for moneys, &c. 1646-48.
10. Committee for Common Burdings 1641-45.
11. Committee of both Kingdoms 1644-46.
12. Decreets of Forfeitures 1685-95.
13. Commission as to Trade, &c. 1699-1706.
14. Journal of the Commissioners for the Union, 1702-6.
15. Collection of Acts, &c. 1455-1707.
16. The Berne MS.
17. Various documents 1644, &c.
18. The Ayr MS.
19. The Drummond MS.
20. Records of the election of Peers, 1761 on.

Of these all, except Nos. 15, 17 and 20, are embodied in the twelve volumes of the printed "Acts."

1. **1540.** Dec. 10.—James Wedd'burn is commissioner for Dundee. (II, 356.)

2. **1585.** Dec. 1.—Alexander Wedderburne is commissioner for Dundee. (III, 374.)

3. **1593.** Jan. 18.--Mag^r Alexander Weddirburne is commissioner for Dundee. (IV, 50.)

4. **1596.** March 3.—Mr. Alexander Wedderburne is commissioner for Dundee. (IV, 110.)

5. **1604.** April 26.—Mr. Alexander Wedderburne is commissioner for Dundee. (IV, 261.)

6. **1604.** July 3.—Mr. Alexander Wedderburn is commissioner for Dundee. On the same day he is named among the "merchandis" as one of the commissioners for treating of an union between Scotland and England. (IV, 263-64.)

7. **1605.** June 7.—Mr. Alexander Wedderburne is commissioner for Dundee. (IV, 276.)

8. **1606.** July 3.—Mr. Alexander Wedderburne is commissioner for Dundee. (IV, 280)

9. **1607.** July 29.—Mr. Alexander Wedderburne is commissioner for Dundee. (IV, 365.)

10. **1609.** Jan. 27.—He is on a commission anent the ravishing of women. (IV, 409.)

11. **1609.** June 17.—He is again commissioner for Dundee, and June 24 is on a like commission. (IV, 417, 454.)

12. **1612.** Oct. 12.—He is again in parliament for Dundee and on two commissions, one for reliefs from penal statutes (IV, 466-67, 473), and the other anent taxation. (ib. 476.)

13. **1617.** May 27.—He is again in parliament for Dundee and on a commission for the plantation of kirks, and, 19 Feb. 1618, on another, appointed 23 June, 1617, for weights and measures. (IV, 525, 531, 585.)

14. **1621.** June 1.—He once more is member for Dundee, and is on commissions for the plantation of kirks and "anent moneyis." (IV, 593, 600, 629.)

15. **1633**. June 18.—Maister Alexander Wedderburne, commissioner for Dundie. (v, 9 a.)

> This may be the clerk, afterwards Sir Alexander Wedderburn of Blackness, but as he was then only twenty-three years old it is more probably his uncle, Kingennie.

16. **1633**. June 18.—Petition by Mr. David Wedderburne, "maister of the grammer skoole of Abirdeene, desyring, that the short and facile grammer drawn up by him and his paines" may be ordained to be the only grammar taught in the schools of Scotland. (v , 48.)
> See ante s. Privy Council Register, No. 61.

17. **1640**. June 8.—Mr. Alexander Wedderburn, clerk of Dundee, is on the committee of estates. (v., 282.)

18. **1641**. Aug. 6.—He is twice named re the act for ratifying the treaty of Ripon. (v, 336.)

19. **1641**. Sept. 16.—He is named on a commission for hearing certain accounts. (v., 355.)

20. **1641**. Sept. 22.—"Act of exoneratione and approbatione in favour of Mr. Alexander Wedderburne," towne clerk of Dundee, anent his conduct in the matter of the Ripon treaty. (v, 362.)

21. **1641**. Sept. 22 —He is again named as on the committee of estates. (v, 396.)

22. **1642**. Sept. 22.—Ratification to him of a contract, 11 Oct. 1641, by which the King set in tack to him "all and sindrie his hienes' customes of Dundie in payment of ane certane take duety," and gave him power to collect his majesties' impost of all wines within the burgh during the space mentioned in the contract, and also granted him " ane certane yeerlie pension " for the said space. (v, 521.) This is as follows :—

> " Ratificatione to Mr. Alexander Wedderburn. Our Soverane Lord with advyse and consent of the Estates of this present parliament For seene and weightie caus moveing his hienes Hes Ratified approvine and confirmed And be thir phtes Ratifies approves and confirmes That contract and appoyntment of the date the ellevint day of October jmvjc and fourtie ane yeires made betwixt his hienes one the ane pairt And maister Alexander Wedderburne towne clerke of Dundie one the wther pairt Be the qlke contract our said soverane Lord has set in take and assidatione to the said maister Alexander All and sindrie his hienes customes of Dundie In payment of ane certane take duetie, And als hes givine power to the said maister Alexr For collecting ingathering and receiveing of his Màtie's impost of all sortes of Wynes within the said burt Dureing the space mentioned in the said contract. As also hes givine and granted to the said Mr. Alexr ane certane yearlie pensione Dureing the space and for the caus specified in the samene contract. In all and sindrie the heedis clauss and conditiones therof with all that hes followed or may follow thairupon And declaires this present ratificatione To be alse valied and effectuall as if the said contract wer insert heirintill ad longum et de verbo in verbum."

23. **1645**. July 24 —Mr. Alexander Wedderburne is in parliament for Dundee, and on commissions for " prosecuting the present war r. the rebels," " treating with the English commissioners," and for excise. (vi , Pt. i, 441-42, 457, 460.)

24. **1645**. Nov. 26.— Mr. Alexander Wedderburne, member for Dundee. (vi., i, 475.)

25. **1646**. Feb. 2.—Mr Alexander Wedderburn and Alexander Wedderburn of Kingennie, are both named in the war commission, among the commissioners for Angus. (vi, i, 560.)

26. **1646**. Feb. 3.—Mr. Alexander Wedderburn, clerk of Dundee, is named on the committee of estates. (vi., i, 571.)

27. **1646**. Nov. 3.—Sir Alexander Wedderburn is commissioner for Dundee. (vi., i, 613.)

28. **1647**. Feb. 26.—He is one of the six commissioners for treating with the English. The others are Lords Lauderdale, Lanark, Lea, and Warrestowne, and Mr. Archibald Syidserfe. (vi., i, 711.)

29. **1647**. March 20.—Sir Alexander Wedderburn, clerk of Dundie, is on the committee of estates, (vi., i, 766.)

30. **1648.** March 2.—Sir Alexander Wedderburn is commissioner for Dundee. (vi, ii, 4a, 696, 1026.)

31. **1651.** March 31.—Sir Alexander Wedderburn is on the committee of estates. (vi,ii,663.)

32. **1651.** June 3.—Sir Alexander Wedderburn is on the committee of estates. (vi, ii, 679), and on a committee of excise. (*ib.* 685.)

33. **1651.** March 9.—He is ordained to lend certain sums to the Laird of Lawers. (vi., ii, 709.)

34. **1652-3.** Sir Alexander Wedderburn is a deputy for Scotland to attend the English parliament. (vi, ii, 794 and 805.)

35. **1654-56.**—He is summoned to Cromwell's parliaments in these years as member for Forfar, Dundee, Aberbrothock, Montrose, and Brechin. (vi., ii, 781-2.)

36. **1656.** March 17.—Warrant for the payment of his salary as deputy in England, anent the union, up to 3 June 1653. (vi., ii, 763a)

37. **1655.** Dec. 21.
    1656. Sep. 17. } Sir Alexander Wedderburn of Blackness, is a commissioner of supply
    1659. Jan. 26. } for both Forfar and Dundee. (vi, ii, 840a, 852a, 882a.)

38. **1661.** Jan. 1.—Sir Peter Wedderburn of Gosford is in parliament for Hadinton, and a commissioner of excise. (29 March.) He is also named (7 May) as clerk to the privy council. (vii, 4a, 90b, 197b. App. 66a)

39. **1661.** Jan. 1.—Alexander Wedderburn is in parliament for Dundee. (vii, 5a, 95a, 309.)

This is no doubt Sir Alexander, as in the same parliament "Sir Alexander Wedderburn of Blackness" is a commissioner of excise (29 March), and also on a commission of weights and measures.

40. **1662.** May 8. { Sir Peter Wedderburn of Gosford is in parliament for Hadinton,
    1663. June 18. { and Alexander Wedderburn of Easter Powrie for Dundee, at
    { both these dates . (vii, 369a-b, 447a-b.)

41. **1663.** July 10.—Sir Peter Wedderburn of Gosford, in consideration of " his constant and untainted loyaltie, sincere affection and fidelitie to his majestic and his royall father of ever blessed memorie during these late troubles, and his good and thankfull service done by him as clerk to the privy council," gets a ratification of a charter of the lands of Lochill. (vii, 456.)

42. **1663.** Sept. 11.—Sir Alexander Wedderburn is a commissioner for the plantation of kirks and valuation of teinds. (vii, 474.)

43. **1663.** (e. 88.)—Sir Peter Wedderburn and Sir Alexander Wedderburn are both made justices of the peace. (vii, 504, 508.)

44. **1665.** Aug. 2.—Sir Peter Wedderburn is member for Hadinton, and on a committee of taxation. (vii, 527.)

45. **1667.** Jan. 9.—Sir Peter Wedderburn, is again member for Hadinton, and on a committee of supply. (vii, 536, 539.)

46. **1669.** Oct. 19.—Sir Peter Wedderburn of Gosford, is again member for Hadinton, and on a commission anent trade. (vii, 549, 663.)

47. **1670.** July 22.—Sir Peter Wedderburn of Gosford is member for Hadinton. (viii, 4a.)

3 c

Parliaments.   Wedderburn of Blackness, of the charter (21 Oct. 1668) granting to him the barony
                     of Blackness. (VIII, 28.)

              49.   **1670.** Aug. 22.—Ratification to Sir Peter Wedderburn, senator of the College of
                    Justice, and to his sons John, Peter, and Alexander in succession, of the charter
                    (11 July, 1670) of the barony of Thornetown, co. Hadinton. (VIII, 32.)

              50.   **1672.** June 12.—Sir Peter Wedderburn is member for Hadinton, and (Aug. 28) on a
                    committee for the plantation of kirks. (VIII, 79.)

              51.   **1673.** Nov. 12.—Sir Peter Wedderburn, member for Hadinton. (VIII, 208b.)

              52.   **1678.** June 26.—Alexander Wedderburn, provost of Dundee, is member for that
                    burgh, and on a committee of supply.   John Wedderburn, younger, of Gosford, and
                    Wedderburn of Blackness, are on a like committee in this year. (VIII, 215, 224a, 228.)

              53.   **1681.** . . . .—Gosford's commission for Hadinton is rejected. (VIII, 239.)

              54.   **1685.** April 23, 29.—John Wedderburn of Gosford, is member for Hadinton, and on
                    a commission of supply. (VIII, 452, 464, 577.)

              55.   **1685.** June 11.—David Graham, tutor of Gorthy, is appointed conjunct clerk of the
                    bills for life with John Wedderburn of Blackness, who had been so appointed to half
                    the office 19 July, 1683, by Sir George Mackenzie of Tarbat. (VIII, 563.)

              56.   **1685.** June 15.—John Wedderburn of Blackness, is a commissioner of supply for
                    Forfar. (VIII, 610.)

              57.   **1690.** June 7.- -Patrick (sic) Wedderburn of Gosford, is a commissioner of supply.
                    (IX, 137.)

              58.   **1697.** June 7.—John Wedderburn of Blackness, and Wedderburn of Easter Powrie,
                    are both commissioners of supply for Forfar. (IX, 144.)

              59.   **1698.** Sept. 1.—Alexander Wedderburn is restored to his right to practise as an
                    advocate on qualifying himself. (X, 171a.)

              60.   **1703.** May 24.—Sir Peter Wedderburn is called as a witness re the Hadinton
                    election. (XI, 44a.)

              61.   **1704** Aug. 5.—Sir Peter Wedderburn of Gosford, Wedderburn of Blackness, and
                    Alexander Wedderburn of Easter Powrie, are all commissioners of supply ; the two
                    last for Forfar. (XI, 139, 149.)

RETOURS OF THE SERVICES OF HEIRS.

These are taken from "Retours of the Services of Heirs (Inquisitionum ad capellam Dom. Regis retornatarum Abbreviatio), A.D. 1546—1700," edited by Thomas Thomson, 1811-16 (3 vols., folio), and from the "Decennial Indices of the Services of Heirs in Scotland, 1700—1890" (Edinburgh, 1863 on.).

ABERDEEN.

These entries do not relate to the Forfarshire family, but are interesting as showing the existence of the name in another county, three centuries or more ago. See the Introduction to Vol. I.

1. **1600.** Oct. 31.—John Gordon is served heir to his father, Sir John Gordon of Petlwy, Knt., of various lands, including Kynmundie, Mylnehill, Durie, Brumchill, and one-third part of Wedderburn. (72.)

2. **1607.** July 11.—Alexander Gordon is served heir to his father, Sir Thomas Gordon of Cluny, Knt., in one-third of Wedderburn, &c. (110.)

3. **1642.** April 24.—Sir James Gordon of Lesmoir, Knt. Bart., is served heir to Sir James Gordon of Lesmoir, Knt. Bart , his great-grandfather, in one-third of the town and lands of Wedderburn. (260)

4. **1648.** Jan. 16.—Sir William Gordon of Lesmoir, Knt. Bart. is served heir to Sir James Gordon of Lesmoir, Knt. Bart., "nepotis fratris," in one-third of the town and lands of Wedderburn. (288.)

5. **1652.** Sept. 20.—Alexander Bisset of Lessendrum, is served heir to Robert Bisset, his father, in the third part of Wedderburn. (311.)

6. **1670.** July 15.—George Anderson, is served heir to Alexander Anderson of Camalegie, his father, in one-third of the town and lands of Wedderburn. (399)

7. **1693.** April 19.—Robert Bisset of Lessendrum, is served heir of Alexander Bisset, his father, in lands, as in No. 5. (492.)

BERWICK.

These, again, relate not to the family, but to the lands of Wedderburn, co. Berwick.

8. **1617.** April 10.—Various services of Homes, as heirs to the lands of Wedderburn in Berwickshire. (105, 286, 326, 379, 425, 445, 460, 464, 480.)

EDINBURGH.

9. **1680.** April 8.—John Wedderburn of Gosfoord is served heir of Sir Peter Wedderburn de Gosfoord, Knt., his father, lately senator of the College of Justice, in lands in the town of Leith. (1261.)

10. **1688.** Oct. 11 —Peter Wedderburn of Gosfoord is served heir of John Wedderburn of Gosfoord "fratris germani senioris" in lands in Leith. (1309.)

FORFAR.

11. **1628.** Oct. 22.— Mr. Alexander Wedderburn, son of James Wedderburn, clerk of Dundee, is served heir of Peter Wedderburn, merchant burgess of Dundee his uncle, in lands, &c., in Dundee. (177.)

12. **1637.** Dec. 15.—Alexander Wedderburn of Kinganny, heir of Mr. Alexander Wedderburn of Kinganny his father, in the sunny half of Wester Gourdie, &c. (239.)

Retours 13. **1686.** March 16.—Alexander Wedderburn of Easter Powrie, heir to his father,
of Heirs. Alexander Wedderburn of Easter Powrie, in Wester Gourdie. (500.)

14. **1692.** March 24.—Alexander Wedderburn of Easter Powrie, heir to his father
Alexander Wedderburn of Easter Powrie, in the lands of Easter Powrie (with the Glen
of Ogilvie in warrandice), and in the lands of Wester Gourdie. (521.)

HADDINGTON.

15. **1680.** April 8.—John Wedderburn of Gosfoord, heir to Sir Peter Wedderburn of
Gosfoord, his father, in various lands. (336.)

16. **1688.** Oct. 11.—Peter Wedderburn of Gosfoord, heir to his elder brother german,
John Wedderburn of Gosfoord, in various lands. (360.)

17. **1688.** Oct. 11.—Peter Wedderburn of Gosford, heir to his father, Sir Peter Wedderburn of Gosfoord, senator, &c., in Longniddry, Lochills, &c. (361.)

INQUISITIONES DE TUTELA.

18. **1687.** Sept. 24.—Georgius Wedderburn, mercator in Edinburgh, propinquior agnatus,
id est consanguineus, ex parte patris, Alexandro et Joanni Wedderburn, filiis Petri
Wedderburn, mercatoris in Dundee. (1105.)

INQUISITIONES GENERALES

19. **1616.** Dec, 8.—Elizabetha *alias* Bessie Wedderburn hæres Walteri Wedderburn
patrui. (666.)

20. **1641.** Aug. 23.—Mag\r Joannes Wedderburn, protomedicus in regione Moraviæ, hæres
Mag\ri Jacobi Wedderburn olim Episcopi Dunblanensis, fratris germani. (2594.)

21. **1642.** Dec. 31.—Elizabetha Wedderburn hæres Mag\ri Davidis Wedderburn burgensis
de Burntisland, fratris. (2777.)

22. **1646.** Nov. 27.—Alexander Wedderburn nauclerus burgensis de Dundie, hæres
Jacobi Wedderburn, mercatoris, burgensis de Dundie. (3208.)

23. **1654.** Jan. 2.—John James Wedderburn of Drohanavitis in Moravia, heir of Johne
Wedderburn, his gudsir. (3878.)

24. **1679.** Dec. 23.—Robertus Wedderburn, hæres Mag\ri Alexander Wedderburn, nuper
ministri verbi Dei apud Kilmarnock, patris. (6172.)

25. **1688.** Oct. 11.—Petrus Wedderburn de Gosfoord, hæres Domini Petri Wedderburn
de Gosfoord, unius Senatorum Collegie Justiciæ, patris. (6940.)

26. **1688.** Oct. 21.—Petrus Wedderburn de Gosfoord, hæres Joannis Wedderburn de
Gosfoord, fratris germani senioris. (6941.)

27. **1692.** March 24.—Alexander Wedderburn de Easter Powrie, hæres Alexandri
Wedderburn de Easter Powrie, patris. (7239.)

28. **1696.** Feb. 10.—Alexander Wedderburn, hæres Jacobi Wedderburn, clerici burgi de
Dundie, patris. (7665.)

DECENNIAL INDICES, 1700—1890.

29. **1703.** March 16.—Margaret Wedderburn or Halsone, wife of James Halsone, bailie
of Anstruther, heir general to her father, the Rev. Andrew Wedderburn. (She is
entered s. Halsone as having d. March 1708).

30. **1709.** April 9.—John Wedderburn, heir general to his mother Elizabeth Setone, wife
of Sir Alexander Wedderburn of Blackness.

31. **1709.** Aug. 25.—Rachael Wedderburn, daughter of George Wedderburn, merchant in Edinburgh, heir general to her grandfather James Sutherland there.

32. **1714.** Feb. 25.—Peter Wedderburn of Wedderburn, heir special in Powrie to his father, Alexander Wedderburn of Wedderburn, d. 7 Dec. 1713.

33. **1715.** Feb. 15.—David Wedderburn of Wedderburn, heir special in Powrie to his brother Peter Wedderburn of Wedderburn, d. 10 May, 1714.

34. **1718.** Feb. 27.—Peter Halket, heir of tailzie and provision general to his mother, Dame Janet Halket, wife of Sir Peter Halket of Pitfirrane.

35. **1732.** May 25.—Peter Wedderburn, advocate, heir general to his father, Alexander Wedderburn, advocate, a commissioner of excise for Scotland.

36. **1754.** June 20.—John Wedderburn of Gosford, heir male of line, tailzie, and provision general to his father, Charles Wedderburn of Gosford.

37. **1758.** May 1.—John Wedderburn, son to the late John Wedderburn, heir general to his granduncle, John Wedderburn, physician in Dundee.

38. **1759.** June 20.—Francis Halket, heir of provision general to his father Sir Peter Halket of Pitfirrane, Bart.

39. **1761.** Aug. 17. } Grizel Wedderburn of Wedderburn, heir general to her brother
    1762. Jan. 22. } David Wedderburn of Wedderburn, d. June 1761.

40. **1769.** (no date.) Grizel Wedderburn, heir to her great grandfather, Alexander Wedderburn of Cangenny (sic), town clerk of Dundee.

   This is an error. Grizel Wedderburn's great grandfather was Alexander Wedderburn, third of Kingennie and first of Easter Powrie, who was provost, but never clerk of Dundee. His father and grandfather were both of them clerks, 1585—1626 and 1627-33, when Grizel's maternal great grandfather (Sir) Alexander Wedderburn of Blackness (not of Kingennie) became clerk. Probably, however, the error is in the omission of a second " great " before grandfather in the printed index, see note s. Great Seal Register, No. 144, note (p. 380).

41. **1770.** Oct. 11.—John Halket (once Wedderburn), heir of tailzie and provision general to Francis Halket of Pitfirrane, d. Nov. 1760.

42. **1780.** March 29, April 21.—Alexander Wedderburn (once Scrymgeour) to Grizel Wedderburn of Wedderburn, who d. 7 Nov. 1778.

43. **1794.** Aug. 8.—Sir Charles Halket of Pitfirrane to his father Sir John Halkett, d. 7 Aug. 1793.

44. **1796.** March 29.} Mary, Lady Halkett, to her father, the Hon. John Hamilton, d.
    1801. April 9.} 11 Feb. 1772.

45. **1804.** April 23.—Sir Charles Halket to his mother, d. 3 Dec. 1803.

46. **1808.** April 5.—Andrew Wedderburn, merchant in London, to his father, James Wedderburn Colvile at Inviresk.

47. **1811.** Sept. 6.—Henry Wedderburn of Wedderburn to his brother, Alexander Wedderburn of Wedderburn, advocate.

48. **1815.** Jan. 6.—Sir David Wedderburn to his uncle, David Ogilvy of Airlie.

49. **1820.** May 31.—Sir David Wedderburn to his father, Sir John, d. 13 June 1803.

50. **1828.** Oct. 20.—John Wedderburn, shopman in Dalkeith, to his uncle, John Wedderburn, at Belhaven, near Dunbar, heir general.

Retours
of Heirs.

51.　**1829**. May 4.—David Wedderburn to his uncle, Charles Wedderburn of Pearsie.

52.　**1837**. July 26.—Sir Peter Halkett to his brother, Sir Charles Halkett. of Pitfirrane, d. 26 Jan. 1837.

53.　**1840**. Feb. 24.—Sir John Halkett to his father, Sir Peter Halkett, G.C.H., d. 7 Oct. 1839.

54.　**1842**. Nov. 18.—Frederic Ludovic Wedderburn to his father, Henry Wedderburn of Wedderburn.

55.　**1848**. Feb. 21.—Sir Peter Arthur Halkett to his father, Sir John Halkett, d. 4 Aug. 1847.

56.　**1864**. March 16-18.—Frederick Lewis Wedderburn of Wedderburn and Birkhill, to his great grand aunt Grizel Wedderburn of Kengennie (*sic*), d. Nov. 1778.
　　This is a curious entry. Grizel Wedderburn was not great-grand aunt to Frederick Lewis Scrymgeour-Wedderburn, or, indeed, to anyone else, as she never had either nephews or nieces. She was doubly his cousin, having been, as a descendant of Sir Alexander Wedderburn of Blackness, second cousin to his grandmother, Katharine Wedderburn (wife of David Scrymgeour of Birkhill), while, as a descendant of Alexander Wedderburn, second of Kingennie, whose daughter Maidelene married John Scrymgeour of Kirktown (grandfather to David Scrymgeour), she was third cousin to his father, Henry Scrymgeour-Wedderburn of Wedderburn.

57.　**1870**. Sept. 27-29.—Katherine Wedderburn (Maclagan or Stormonth) of Pearsie, to John Wedderburn of Pearsie, d. 20 July, 1870, heir of tailzie and provision general.

58.　**1871**. Feb. 6-8.—Sir Peter Arthur Halkett, heir to his father Sir John Halkett of Pitfirrane, Bart., d. 4 Aug. 1847.

59.　**1874**. Dec. 2-8.—Henry Scrymgeour-Wedderburn, heir to his father Frederick Lewis Scrymgeour-Wedderburn of Wedderburn and Birkhill, d. 16 Aug. 1874.

60.　**1880**. March 15-18.—Andrew Wedderburn Maxwell, heir of tailzie and provision general to his cousin J. Clerk Maxwell of Middlebie, and Glenlair, &c. (4 retours.)

61.　**1883**. Sept. 27, Oct. 2.—Sir William Wedderburn, heir general and special to his brother Sir David Wedderburn of Inveresk, d. 18 Sept. 1882.

This register dates from 1491 to 1873, and has never been published. I have had it searched in the original from its earliest date down to 1650, after which the record is blank till 1661, when it is renewed in two series, English and Latin. A brief note of the other records of the Privy Seal will be found in the tabular synopsis at p. 360.

1. **1512.** July 30.—At Edinburgh. Commission to James Wedderburn, burgess of Dundee, making him customer of the burgh and freedom of Dundee during the King's will, with power to use the said office, and to appoint deputies, with command to all concerned to loose and load at the port of Dundee, and at no other place, under pain of escheat of the goods. (IV, 196.)

2. **1528.** Dec 6.— At Edinburgh. Precept for remission to George Wedderburn, brother german to James Wedderburn, elder, burgess of Dundee, for assisting Archibald, sometime Earl of Angus, against the King, &c. (VIII, 27.)

3. **1529.** April 3.—At Edinburgh. Respite granted to John Wedderburn for slaughter of the deceased John Thomsoun, to last for the space of 19 years. (VIII, 35.)

4. **1538.** Jan. 6.—At Linlithgow. Respite to Robert Wedderburn, son of James Wedderburn, burgess of Dundee, for the slaughter of — Malisoun, and for all action or crime. (XI, 43.)

5. **1538.** Sept. 8.—At Linlithgow. Gift to Gilbert Wedderburn and John Paterson, burgesses of Dundee, of the escheat of the lands, goods, &c., formerly belonging to them, but which were in the King's hands through their being convicted of heresy. (XII, 23.)

6. **1539.** Feb. 10.—At Linlithgow. Precept for charter confirming to David Wedderburn, burgess of Dundee, and Helen Laswon, his spouse, their charter of fenferme, made by John, Abbot of Lindores, and convent of the same, of half the lands of Hiltoun of Cragy, now occupied by John Strathauchin, in the regality of Lindores and shire of Forfar. (XII, 70.)

7. **1542.** Aug. 8.—At Edinburgh. Precept for confirmation of charter by Patrick, Lord Gray, to David Wedderburn, burgess of Dundee, and Helen Lawson, his spouse, of the half of the mains commonly called the mains of Huntly, lying in the barony of Foulis and shire of Forfar. (XVI, 39.)

8. **1543.** April 6.—At Edinburgh. Gift to Robert Logan of Restalrig, knight, of the escheat goods, &c., which pertained to James Wedderburn, burgess of Dundee, and now in the Queen's hands, through the said James being at the horn for the slaughter of David Rollok, burgess of Dundee. (XVII, 44.)

9. **1543.** April 16.—At Edinburgh. Gift to Andro Barre, elder, burgess of Dundee, of the escheat of all goods, &c., which pertained to Gilbert Wedderburn, burgess of Dundee, and now in the Queen's hands through the said Gilbert being at the horn for the slaughter of David Rollok, burgess of the said burgh. (XVII, 47.)

10. **1543.** April 18.—At Edinburgh. Gift in favour of James Wedderburn and William Wedderburn, and the rest of the children of David Wedderburn, of the escheat of all goods, &c., which pertained to David Wedderburn, burgess of Dundee, and now pertaining or that shall happen to pertain to the Queen by reason of escheat, through the said David being fugitive from law and at the horn for the slaughter of David Rollok, burgess of the same burgh. (XVII, 48.)

11. **1543.** April 6.—At Edinburgh. Gift to Patrick, Lord Gray, his heirs and assignees of the escheat of all goods, &c., which pertained to David Wedderburn, burgess of Dundee, and now pertaining or that may pertain to the Queen by escheat, for the same reason as stated in preceding entry. (XVII, 53.)

12. **1543.** July 27.—At Edinburgh. Respite to James Wedderburn, Robert Wedderburn, John Smart, and Robert Child, for art and part of the slaughter of David Rollok, burgess of Dundee, committed in the said burgh in the month of March last. (XVII, 80.)

13. **1543.** Sept. 25.—At Edinburgh. Respite to David Wedderburn, burgess of Dundee, and four others, for art and part of the slaughter of David Rollok, burgess of the said burgh. (XVIII, 1.)

14. **1544.** June 6.—At Stirling. Remission to Gilbert Wedderburn, burgess of Dundee, for his remaining at home and absenting himself from the army, and for art and part of the murder of George Rollok, burgess of Dundee. (XVIII, 49.)

15. **1544.** Aug. 16.—At Linlithgow. Gift to Archibald Campbell of Murthlie, of the escheat of all goods, &c., which pertained to Robert Wedderburn, son of the deceased James Wedderburn, elder, burgess of Dundee, and now in the Queen's hands, through his breaking of the fence and arrestment made on the third part of the teind sheaves of the kirk of Dundee, by Alexander Blair, messenger. (XVIII, 77.)

16. **1545.** April 6.—At Linlithgow. Respite to Gilbert Wedderburn, burgess of Dundee, for art and part of the slaughter of David Rollok, burgess of Dundee, committed on old feud and forethought felony. (XIX, 2.)

17. **1547.** Jan. 30.—At Edinburgh. Gift to Patrick Lyoun, burgess of Dundee, and Elizabeth Wedderburn, his spouse, and the longer liver of them, of all the Queen's customs on all goods belonging to them imported into this country at the port of Dundee. (XX, 81.)

18. **1550.** Feb. 11.—At Edinburgh. Letter made to David Wedderburn, burgess of Dundee, of the gift of the office of Clerkship of Coket in the said burgh, and office of searcher of all goods, &c., shipped in the port and haven of the same, to be carried furth thereof uncustomed, for all the days of his life. (XXIV, 55.)

19. **1552.** Jan. 13.—At Linlithgow. Precept of legitimation to Robert and David Wedderburn, bastard sons of Mr. Robert Wedderburn, vicar of Dundee. (XXV, 43.)

20. **1552.** Aug. 8.—At Inverness. Precept for charter of confirmation of charter by Patrick, Lord Gray, to David Wedderburn, burgess of Dundee, and Helen Lawson, his spouse, and the longest liver of them in conjunct fee and the heirs lawfully procreate or to be procreate between them, whom failing to the lawful and nearest heirs of the said David, whomsoever of the third part of the lands of Hiltown of Wester Crage, with pertinents, &c., in the barony of Dundee and shire of Forfar, holden of the Queen. (XXV, 36.)

21. **1553.** Dec. 14.—At Edinburgh. Remission to David Wedderburn, senior, burgess of Dundee, James and William Wedderburn, his sons, Thomas Gardin and James Alison for their violent deforcement of Robert Marshall, officer of the burgh of Dundee, in the execution of his office, on the 21 of Oct. 1553, and for hurting and wounding of the said Robert on the same day in the time of the execution of his said office. Committed on forethought felony. (XXVII, 57.)

22. **1564.** Feb. 4.—At Edinburgh. Precept for confirmation of a charter granted by John Wedderburn, burgess of Dundee, to John Wedderburn, his son, lawfully procreated betwixt him and Agnes Hoppringle, his spouse, and to the heirs of the said John the younger, of the 13 acres of land bounded as under, six of which lie between the lands

of the chapel of the Virgin Mary in Welgate to the east, the lands of the heirs of John Rolland, elder and younger, to the north, the lands of the constable of Dundee of his lordship of Duddop to the west, and the street between the Welgate port and Duddop to the south ; occupied by the said John Wedderburn, elder, at the time of the making of the said charter ; also 2½ acres of the foresaid 13, lying between the proper lands of the constable on the north and west, the High street on the east, and the acres of the deceased John Rolland, younger, on the south ; and also 4½ acres of the same 13 called Cawdame, Grenedame and Dame acre, lying between the High street on the west, the lands of Clapentoun and John Crawfurd on the north, the High street on the east, the lands of the deceased Wm. Fowler, the lands of the College of S. Salvator of S. Andrew's, the lands of the deceased John Rolland younger, the lands of Andrew Barrie younger, and the acres of the late James Scrymgeour in Welgate on the south, occupied likewise by the said John Wedderburn and his subtenants at the time of the making up of the said charter, lying in the lordship of Duddop, in the shire of Forfar, to be holden of the Crown. (xxxii, 45.)

23. **1575.** March 25.—At Holyroodhouse. Letter made to James Wedderburne, burgess of Dundee, constituting him clerk of our sovereign lord's Coequet of the said burgh of Dundee and searcher of the same within all the bounds, &c., thereof, during his Highness pleasure, granting to the said James and his deputes (whom his Highness gives him power to substitute under him in the same office for the better exercising thereof) power to search for all "custumabile guidis passand furth of the realme fra the boundis foirsaidis uneustumat and sielike all victuall, flesche, talloŭn, gold, silŭer, and utheris," &c., and also to have the keeping of the said Cocquet seal. (xlii, 126.)

24. **1590.** Oct. 16.—At Holyroodhouse. Precept for confirmation of charter granted by David Baxter, *alias* Rannald, burgess of Dundee, with consent of Adam Malice, *alias* Melvile, chaplain of the chapel of S. James the Greater, situated in the parish church of the burgh of Dundee, also with consent of James Scrymgeour of Dudope, Provost of the Constabulary of Dundee, undoubted patron of the said chapel of S. James, to David Wedderburne, lawful son to the deceased Alexander Wedderburne, clerk of the court of Dundee, his heirs and assignees whomsoever heritably, without redemption, of all and whole one acre of arable land lying in Westfield of the town of Dundee, in the free shed thereof, between the lands of Blackness, on the west, and the acres once pertaining to George Blair and now to Thomas Man on the east, the sea tide on the south, and in the shire of Forfar: holding of the said Adam Malice, *alias* Melvile, chaplain foresaid, and his successors in fee and heritage for ever. (xi, 59.)

25. **1596.** Aug. 13.—At Falkland. Gift to John Lindsay, fourth lawful son to the late Robert Lindsay of Balhall, and to Katharine Lindsay, daughter of said Robert, equally betwixt them, and their heirs, of the escheat goods, &c., which pertained to John Wedderburn, burgess of Dundee, and which he shall happen to acquire during his rebellion, now in the King's hands, through the said John Wedderburn being put to the horne by virtue of letters raised, for not finding of caution to have compeired before the justices, &c., on a certain day by past to answer to the charge of the slaughter of the late Robert Lindsay of Balhall on the 19 July last by past, or as rebell denounced at the instance of —— Campbell, relict of James Leitch, Irelandman, his bairns, kin, and friends for non compeirance to answer for the slaughter of said James Leitch. (lxviii, 217.)

26. **1597.** July 18.—At Edinburgh. Gift to Mr. Alexander Wedderburn, common clerk of the burgh of Dundee, his heirs, &c., of the escheat goods, &c., which pertained before to James Scrymgeour, burgess of Dundee, and now in the King's hands through the said James being put to the horne, by virtue of letters raised at the instance of William Curving, Englishman, or at the instance of James Barroun, merchant, burgess of Edinburgh, or either of them, for non-payment of certain sums of money. (lxix, 130.)

27. **1600.** 26 May.—At Holyroodhouse. Gift to Alexander Wedderburn, his heirs, &c., of the escheat goods, &c., which pertained to David Jameson, lawful son to John Jamesou, burgess of Cupar in Fife, and now in the King's hands through said David

being put to the horne by virtue of letters raised at the instance of Jeremiah Strathauchin, mariner in Dundee, for non-payment to him of £46. (LXXI, 208.)

28. **1600.** July 15.—At Holyroodhouse. Precept for charter of confirmation upon a charter by Sir James Scrymgeour of Dudope, Knight, Constable and Provost of Dundee, and William Guthrie of Kinganic, two of the patrons of the chaplainry of S. Thomas the Martyr, in the parish kirk of Dundee, founded of old by William Strathauchin, to David Wedderburne, burgess of Dundee, his heirs and assiguees, of an annual rent of 18s. out of a tenement of land pertaining to David Robiesone, lying in the south side of the Cowgate of Dundee. (LXXIV, 21.)

29. **1601.** Dec. 1.—At Holyroodhouse. Gift of escheat to Robert Wedderburne, burgess of Dundee, his heirs and assignees, of the escheat of all goods, &c., which pertained to John Wedderburn, burgess of the burgh of Dundee, put to the horne (1 July, 1601) at the instance of William Goldman, merchant, burgess of Dundee, for not paying to him certain liquidat prices of certain bolls of victual. (LXXIII, 71.)

30. **1615.** Feb. 7.—At Edinburgh. Precept for charter of confirmation upon a charter by James Scrymgeour, fiar of Fardill, with consent of Margaret Grahame, his spouse, and of James Scrymgeour of Fardill, his father, and others, in favour of Mr. William Ferguson, bailie, burgess of Dundee, and Katharine Wedderburn, his spouse, in conjunct fee and their heirs, of the lands of Balbouchlie, with tower, fortalice, and manor place, &c., in the barony of Dunkeld and shire of Forfar. (LXXXIII, 290.)

31. **1616.** July 4.—At Edinburgh. Gift to Robert Murray, one of his Majesty's guard, of the escheat of all goods, &c., which pertained to Alexander Wedderburn, merchant, burgess of Dundee, at the horn for not paying Gilbert Williamsone, merchant, burgess of Edinburgh, the sum of 280 merks conform to his bond of date at Edinburgh, 11 Aug. 1614, and registered (——) in the Books of Council. (LXXXV, 214.)
      See post s. Register of Deeds, No. 48, where the details of the bond are differently given.

32. **1635.** 14 Oct.—At Royston. Grant of the Deanery of the Chapel Royal in Stirling, and of the lands and monastery and barony of Drumdrennane to James Wedderburn, Doctor of Theology, during all the days of his lifetime together with an annual rent of 10 chalders of victual. (CVI. 370.)

33. **1638.** 31 July.—At Edinburgh. Gift to Mr. Alexander Wedderburn, clerk of Dundee, of the escheat of all goods, &c., which pertained to Thomas Small of Kirkland of Caitness, and George Halyburton of the Mylne of Caitness, put to the horn at the instance of Mr. Alexander Wedderburn, younger, and Thomas Wichtane, notary in Dundee, as factors for Mr. John Wedderburn, son lawful of the late Mr. Alexander Wedderburn, sometime town clerk of Dundee, then designed one of the Regents of S. Leonard's College in S. Andrews, for not paying to them the sum of 630 merks, contained in a Bond dated 31 May, 1630, and registered iu the Books of Council and Session on the 15th October, 1634. (CVIII, 370.)
      See post s. Register of Deeds, No. 115.

34. **1642.** July 18.—At Edinburgh. Charter to Mr. Alexander Wedderburn, clerk of Dundee, his heirs and assignees, of the fourth part of the town and lands of Blackness, with windmill and mill lands ; and of the sixth part of the eighth part of the said town and lands, acquired by Donald Thornton, portioner of Blackness, from Sir John Wischart of Pittarro, Knight, and Lady Jean Douglas his spouse ; also of the manor place of Blackness, &c., in the lordship of Scone and shire of Perth. (CX, 186.)

35. **1643.** Sept. 9.—At Nottingham. Grant to Mr. Alexander Wedderburn, clerk of Dundee, reciting that his highness for the faithful service done to His Majesty by his trusty and well beloved Mr. Alexander Wedderburn, clerk of Dundee, and the more to encourage him, &c., to continue therein, was pleased to set to him a tack of the customs of Dundee for 5 years, and from 5 years to 5 years during his lifetime, and also to dispone to him furth thereof a yearly pension of £100 stg. (CXI, 14.)

36. **1647.** June 14.   At Edinburgh.   Charter in favour of Sir Alexander Wedderburn of **Privy Seal** Blackness, Knt., his heirs and assignees of the 8th part and 6th part of another 8th **Register.** part of the lands and town of Blackness, with tofts, crofts, &c., and in warrandice thereof, of all and whole the lands and barony of Pittarro in the shire of Kincardin. (cxiv, 172.)

37. **1648.** Jan. 10.—At Newcastle.   Grant to Dr. John Wedderburn, His Majesty's Physician in ordinary, in consideration of his thankful service already done, and to encourage him to continue therein, of a pension of £2,000, during the said Doctor John Wedderburn's life, out of His Majesty's revenues. (cxiv, 352.)

38. **1648.** Feb. 18.—At Edinburgh.   Charter to Sir Alexander Wedderburn of Blackness, Knt., his heirs and assignees of an 8th part, &c., as above, of the lands and town of Blackness with tofts, &c. (cxiv, 398.)

     [A gift under the Privy Seal, to Alexander Wedderburn of Kingennie, of the escheat of the goods of Patrick Guthrie of Auchmuthie, dated 22 Nov. 1653, is among the Scrymgeour-Wedderburn Papers. No. 308.]

GENERAL REGISTER OF SASINES.

General Register of Sasines.

1617—1800.

This register is a record (appointed to be kept by an Act of 1617) of writs affecting heritable property in every part of Scotland. It was, however, optional to record either in it or in the particular register for the county in which the property was situated. Sometimes a proprietor would record in both registers, but this was not necessary. It consists of three series :—

    I.   Aug. 19, 1617—2 Feb. 1652. (62 vols.)
    II. May 28, 1652.—26 Oct. 1660. (18 vols.)
    III. Oct. 27, 1660 down to the present time. (627 vols. 1660—1800.)

There are minute books for this register which provide a general index to the record, and these have been searched, 1617—1780. In some cases the record itself has also been examined and noted, but in most, the minute itself has been sufficient for my purpose. The following list gives all the entries in the minute book, and, occasionally, I have added, in smaller type, an abstract of the record itself. It is of interest to note that of the eighty-six entries relating to Wedderburns all, except seven, deal with members of the Forfarshire house, the few exceptions referring (Nos. 10, 13, 15, 19, 25 and 31) to members of a Berwickshire family of the name (1632-61), and one other (No. 27) to a family in Preston (1655) in regard to both of whom little is known.

FIRST SERIES.

1.   **1624.** June 8.—Perth. Renunciation by Mr. Alexander Wedderburne and his spouse to David, Viscount of Stormouth, of few meillis out of Wester Gourdie. (xv, 131.)

       The record is as follows :—" 1624. June 8.—Renunciation by Mr Alexr Wedderburn, Clerk of Dundee, and Helen Ramsay his spouse, in favour of David, Viscount of Stormont, of certain feu maills, feu ferms and feu duties out of the lands of Wester Gourdie inj the lordship of Scone and shire of Forfar ; disponed to the said spouses by the said Viscount, then styled David, Lord of Scone, with consent therein mentioned, conform to contract of date 23 June 1614. Dated at Dundee 15 May 1624.'

2.   **1627.** July 18 (?).—Forfar. Sasine[1] in favour of Mr. Alexander Wedderburne of the half lands of Wester Gourdie. (xxi, 378)

3.   **1627.** July 18.—Fyff. Sasine of Johne Wedderburne of the town and lands of Pittorny. (xxi, 407.)

       The record is as follows :—" Sasine on precept of clare contract by John, Bishop of S. Andrew's, in favour of John Wedderburne as heir of the late Alexander Wedderburne of Pittornye his father, of the shadow half of the town and land of Pittornye &c. in the regality of S. Andrew's and shire of Fife. Dated at Leith 21 June 1627. Sasine given on 4 July 1627.'

4.   **1630.** June.—Forfar. Sasine of Alexander Wedderburne of the lands of Kingany and others. (xxviii, 32.)

5.   **1630.** Aug.—Forfar. Sasine of Alexander Wedderburn of a land in Dundee. (xxix, 69.)

6.   **1630.** Aug. 2.—Forfar. Sasine of William Wedderburne and his spouse of a tenement in Dundee. (xxix, 71.)

       The record is as follows :—" 1630. Aug. 2—Sasine on Charter by Mr. Alexander Wedderburn of Kingennie, with consent of Sir John Scrymgeour of Dudop, Knight, Constable of Dundee, in favour of William Wedderburn, (lawful son of the late Mr. Alexander Wedderburn, sometime common clerk of Dundee), his brother german, and Jeane Peirson, his spouse, lawful daughter of Mr. Alexander Peirson, burgess of Aberbrothock, of a forland under and above, with privileges, etc., sometime pertaining to Patrick and Alexander Wedderburn, burgesses of Dundee, on the southside of the Marketgate, between the lands now of Thomas Gray on the east, the lands of Thomas Clayhills on the south, and the Cemetery of St. Clement and the Passage that goes from the east side of the Tolbooth to the Port of the said burgh on the west. Dated at Dundee and Dudop 23 and 30 Sept. 1629, and sasine on 15 June 1630. Alex. Watson merch kc, with Mr James Peirson, Clerk of the burgh of Aberbrothock, is attorney for the said Jeane Peirson.'

    [1] In the minute books the word sasine is variously spelt "sasine," "scisin," "saising," "saisine" "seasine," "seasin," or abbreviated into "sa" or "seas." I give it throughout as "sasine." The minutes differ from the record in almost always spelling Wedderburn with a final e.

7. **1630.** Sept. 21.—Forfar. Assignation by Jeane Peirsoue to Mr. Johne Wedderburn General of her conjunct fie right of a tenement in Dundee and others. (xxix, 149.) Register of Sasines.
The record is as follows :—1630. Sept. 21.—" Assignation by Jeane Peirson, relict of William Wedderburn above designed, with consent of her father foresaid and of Mr James Peirson Clerk of Aberbrothock his eldest son, in favour of Mr John Wedderburn, one of the Regents of St Leonard's College in St. Andrew's, of her liferent or conjunct right of the sum of 2000 merks, contained in a matrimoniall contract, of date at Aberbrothock 27 September 1627, between the said William Wedderburn on the one part, and the said Jeane Peirson with consent of her said father on the other part ; and also her right of the burghal tenement, etc. (as in the foregoing sasine). At Dundee and Aberbrothock 13 August 1630."

8. **1631.** August.—Forfar. Sasine of Mr. Alexander Wedderburne of ane land in Dundie. (xxxi, 348.)

9. **1632.** June 27.—Perth. Sasine of Mr. George Halyburton and Magdalen Wedderburne, his spouse, of the lands of Lawtoun. (xxxii, 385.)
The record is as follows :—1632. June 27.—Sasine on Charter by John Campbell of the Boat of Ilay, in favour of Mr. George Halyburton of Fodrans, Senator of the College of Justice, and Magdalen Wedderburn, his spouse, of the lands of Lawtoun, with manor place, &c., in the parish of Cargill and shire of Perth. Dated at Lawtoun 17 May 1632. Mr. Andrew Halyburton brother german of the said Mr. George Halyburton, George Halyburton, tailor, and Mr. James Halyburton, notary, are witnesses. The said Geo : Halyburton, tailor, is witness to the sasine given on 17 May 1632. Mr. Andrew Halyburton, burgess of Dundee, is bailie."

10. **1632.** Nov. 7.—Berwick. Sasine of James Wedderburne and Issobell Quhillow, his spouse, of a piece of land in Coldinghane. (xxxv, 20.)
The record is as follows :—"1632. November 7.—Sasine on Charter by Archibald Idington, portioner of Coldingham, with consent of Aleson Senton his spouse, in favour of James Wedderburn in Rickilsyd of Coldingham, weaver, and Isobel Quhillows his spouse, of an acre of arable land in the territory of Coldingham, in that feild called "ane How aiker," in the barony of Coldingham and shire of Berwick. Dated at Coldingham 3 Nov. 1632, and sasine on same day."

11. **1634.** August.—Fyff, Forfar. Sasine of Mr. Alexander Wedderburne of the lands of Wester Gourdie and others. (xl, 320.)

12. **1638.** April 2.—Forfar. Sasine of Alexander Wedderburne of the lands of Wester Gourdie. (xlvii, 130.)
The record is as follows :—"Sasine, on precept (dated Feb.) from Chancery, in favour of Alexander Wedderburn of Kingany, as lawful and nearest heir of the late Mr. Alexander Wedderburn of Kingany, his father, of the half of the lands of Wester Gourdie, called the sunny half &c. Sasine is given on March 27, 1638, before Mr. Alexander Wedderburn, clerk of Dundee, and Mr. Peter Wedderburn, his brother german.

13. **1638.** Dec. 29.—Berwick. Sasine of James Wedderburne and Issobell Quhillow, his spouse, of a half croft of land in the territorie of Coldinghane. (xlvii, 449.)
The record identifies the land as "a half croft of arable land in Cogangrein in the territory of the burgh of Coldingham." The sasine is given 24 Dec. on a contract (Dec. 21) between James Hopper in Coldingham and James Wedderburn, weaver, there.

14. **1639.** May 29.—Forfar. Sasine of Alexander Wedderburne and his spouse of ane tenement and others in Dundie. (xlix, 15.)
The record is as follows :—"1639, May 29.—Sasine on precept of Clare Constat by James Scrymgeour, apparent of Dudop, as commissioner of Sir John Scrymgeour of Dudop, Knight, Constable of Dundee, in favour of Alexander Wedderburn now of Kingynie as heir of the late Mr. Alexander Wedderburn of Kingynie his father, of a tenement formerly pertaining to Peter and Alexander Wedderburn, burgesses of Dundee, on the south side of the Marketgate ; and bounded as before described ; as also a Feuferme of £8 Scots out of a Tenement of the late James Ferrier, burgess of Dundee, on the North side of the Murraygate." At the same time Elspeth Ramsay, daughter of John Ramsay, bailie of Dundee, now spouse of the said Alexander Wedderburn, is infeft in liferent in the said subjects in implement of Contract of Marriage between them of date at Perth 14 Nov 1638. Precept is dated at Dundee 21 May 1639, and Sasine given on 24 May 1639. Alexander Wedderburn, elder, merchˢ in Dundee, is attorney for the said Alexander Wedderburn, and the said John Ramsay for his daughter."

15. **1640.** Feb. 13.—Berwick. Sasine of James Wedderburne and his spous of foure butts of land of Coldinghame. (xlviii, 477.)
The record is as follows :—"1640, Feb. 13.—Sasine on Disposition by James Hunter, e'der in Coldingham, in favour of James Wedderburn, weaver, in Coldingham, and Isobel Whilos, his spouse, of four butts of arable land in Coldingham, in that part called Crawbus. Dated 6 February 1640 and sasine given on the same day."

16. **1642.** August.—Forfar. Sasine of Mr. Alexander Wedderburne of ane croft of land callit the Temple croft. (LI, 281.)

17. **1642.** August.—Forfar. Sasine of Mr. Alexander Wedderburne of the lands of Blacknes and others. (LI, 287.)

18. **1642.** August.—Forfar. Sasine of Mr. Alexander Wedderburne of the lands of Blacknes and others. (LI, 295.)

19. **1644.** January.—Berwick. Sasine of Johne Wedderburne and his spouse of ane half tenement in Coldinghame. (LIII, 507.)

The record is as follows :—" Sasine on Charter by George Home, fiar of Wedderburn, in favour of James Wedderburn in Coldingham and Isabel Gresoue, his spouse, of a half cottage of land in Coldingham, lying in Begrengrene of Coldingham and shire of Berwick. Dated at Eyemouth 28 November 1643, and sasine on 12 December 1643 in presence of John Lumsden, George Wedderburn, and Daniell Laudells, indwellers in Coldingham."

20. **1646.** Dec 8.—Perth. Sasine of Alexander Wedderburne of the lands and milnes of Knap. (LV, 493.)

The record is as follows :—" 1646. Dec. 8.—Sasine on Letters Obligatour by Andrew Moneur of Knap, and James Moneur his son, in favour of Alexander Wedderburn of Kingany, of Knap, with Mill, &c., in the shire of Perth. Dated at Dundee 24 September and sasine on 20 October 1646."

21. **1646.** Dec.—Forfar. Sasine of Sir Alexander Wedderburne of certain parts of Blackness. (LV, 496.)

22. **1647.** Sept.—Forfar. Sasine of Sir Alexander Wedderburne of the lands and barony of Pitarro. (LVII, 136.)

23. **1648.** Aug.—Kincardin. Sasine of Sir Alexander Wedderburne of the land of Fettercairne and an @-rent furth therof. (LIX, 110.)

The record is as follows :—" 1648. August 16.—Sasine on Bond by Lieut General John Midleton of Fettercairn, in favour of Sir Alexander Wedderburn of Blackness, of an Annual rent of 1600 merks out of the lands of Fettercairn in the shire of Kincardin. Dated at Ediuburgh 24 June, and sasine on 10 August 1648."

24. **1649.** March.—Kincardin. Sasine of Sir Alexander Wedderburne of the lands of Pittarow. (LIX, 381.)

SECOND SERIES.

25. **1653.** July 22.—Berwick. Sasine, James Wedderburne and his spouse, of a husbandland in Coldinghame and others. (V, 123.)

The record is as follows :—" 1653. July 22.—Sasine on letter of Wodsett, by Patrick Home of Coldingham-law, in favour of James Wedderburn in Bickit-syde (sic) of Coldingham, and Isabel Griersone his spouse, of a husbandland possessed by James Idington, and two acres ' in the baronie off the Law,' and shire of Berwick. Sasine dated and given on 7 June 1653."

26. **1654.** Aug. 23.—Edinburgh. Sasine, Mr. Peter Wedderburne and his spouse of the lands of Inck and fore Spittalls. (Parl. Reg. II, 65.)

In this and the next entry, the particular register of sasines for the Lothians has been minuted in this minute book, either for convenience or because the same keepers had both under their charge. The record is as follows :—" 1654. August 23.—Sasine on Charter of Apprising granted by the Provost, Bailies, ministers, and Council of Edinburgh as Governors of Heriot's Hospital, in favour of Mr. Peter Wedderburn, advocate, and Agnes Dickson, lawful daughter of the late John Dickson of Hartrie, his spouse, of the lands of ' Bak and Foir Spittalls,' with houses, &c., in the regality of Broughton and Shire of Edinburgh. Dated at Edinburgh 18 and sasine on 21 August 1654."

27. **1655.** Jan. 8.—Hadingtoun. Sasine, John Wedderburne, of a tenement in Prestoun. (Parl. Reg. II, 276.)

The record is as follows :—" 1655. July 8.—Sasine on Precept of Clare Constat by Sir Alexander Morison of Prestongrange, Knight, in favour of John Wedderburn, weaver in Preston, oldest son and heir of the late George Wedderburn, also weaver, indweller there, of a tenement of land with yard, &c , in the town of Preston, northside of the High Street thereof, in the constabulary of Haddington and shire of Edinburgh. Dated at Prestongrange 21 Novr 1654 and sasine on 23 Oct 1654.

28. **1655.** Sept. 8.—Sasine, Sir Alexander Wedderburne, of aue @-rent furth of the lands
of Balthayok and others. (x, 56.)

29. **1658.** Dec. 16.—Forfar. Sasine, Alexander Wedderburne, of aue @ rent furth of
the toun and lands of Balgay and Logie. (xv, 306.)

30. **1659.** March 15.—Edinburgh. Sasine, Mr. Peter Wedderburne, of the landis and
barronie of Gossfurd and others. (xv, 485.)

TIIIRD SERIES.

31. **1661.** October 25.—Berwick. Sasine, James Wedderburne in Coldinghame and
Issobell Greirson, his spouse, of the lands called Whalrig. (I, 491.)

The record is as follows:—"1661. October 25.—Sasine on Charter by George Home of
Wedderburn, with consent of his curators, in favour of James Wedderburn, in Ricklesyde of
Coldingham, and Isobel Griersone his spouse, of that portion of land called the Whoill Rige, last
possessed by Alexander Watson, in the territory of Coldingham and shire of Berwick. Dated at
Wedderburn 18th and sasine given on 19th October 1661."

32. **1662.** Sept. 19.—Forfar. Sasine, Sir Alexander Wedderburne of Blacknes, of the
lands and barronie of Blacknes. (IV, 107.)

33. **1664.** Jan. 8.—Berwick. Renunciation, Robert Sandilands, merchant, burges of
Edinburgh, to the Lord Elibank and Sir Peter Wedderburne. (VIII, 38.)

34. **1665.** Aug.—Edinburgh. Sasine, Sir Peter Wedderburne of Gosefuird of an
@-rent furth of the baronie of Innerleith. (XII, 374.)

35. **1667.** May.—Forfar and Kincardine. Sasine, John Wedderburne (eldest son to Sir
Alexander Wedderburne of Blacknes) and Rachel Dunnur, his spouse, of the toun,
maner-place, and lands of Blacknes, and an @-rent out of the lands of Pittarro. (xvi, 398.)

36. **1669.** March.—Forfar. Sasine, John Wedderburne, eldest son of Sir Alexander
Wedderburne of Blacknes, of the lands and baronie of Blacknes. (xxi, 695.)

37. **1670.** Aug. 8.—Berwick, Hadington, and Edinburgh. Sasine, Sir Peter Wedderburne of Gosfurd and John Wedderburne, his son, of the lands and baronie of
Dunglas. xxv, 352.

The record is as follows:—"1670. August 8.—Sasine on Bond by Sir William Ruthven of
Dunglass, Knight, with consent of Dame Elizabeth Sinclair his spouse. in favour of sir Peter Wed-
derburn of Gosfoord, Knight, one of the Senators of the College of Justice in liferent, and John
Wedderburn, his eldest lawful son in fee, and the heirs male of his own body; whom failing, Peter
Wedderburn his second lawful son, and the heirs male of his own body; whom failing Alexander
Wedderburn his third lawful son and the heirs male of his own body; whom failing the said Sir Peter
Wedderburn his nearest lawful heirs or assignees, whatsoever, of the lands and barony of Dunglass,
with towers, fortalices. &c in the shire of Berwick; in security of the lands of Thornton disponed
by the said Sir William Ruthven, his said spouse, and Dame Barbara Leslie, Lady Waughton, his
mother, to the said Sir Peter Wedderburn and his foresaids by Disp" of date and in manner
expressed in the said Bond. Dated at Dunglass 15 July and sasine on 16 July 1670."

38. **1670.** Oct.—Hadington and Renfrew. Sasine, Sir Peter Wedderburne of Gosfurd, of
the lands and barronie of Thorntoun. (xxvi, 107.)

39. **1671.** Jan.—Edinburgh and Renfrew. Sasine, Sir Peter Wedderburne of Gossfurd
and John Wedderburne, his son, of the lands and baronie of Innerweik, &c. (xxvi, 423.)

40. **1673.** Feb.—Fyfe. Renunciation, Mr. Alexander Wedderburne, minister at Kilmarnock, and Helen Turnbull, his spous, to Robert, Earl of Southesk, of the half of the
toun and lands of Fordell. (xxxi, 101.)

The record is as follows:—"1673. February 6.—Resignation by Mr. Alexander Wedderburn,
minister at Kilmarnock, and Helen Turnbull his spouse, in favour of Robert Earl of Southesk, of
the Half of the town and lands of Fordell in the parish of Letlehers and shire of Fife. Dated
29 January juny° (sixty and) threttein yearis."
The bracketted words only are omitted in the record.

41. **1673**. Sept.—Forfar. Sasine, Alexander Wedderburne, younger of Kingennie, of ane @-rent of 480 mks., furth of the town and lands of Earlstradichtie. (xxxii, 274.)

42. **1673**. Sept. —Forfar. Sasine, Alexander Wedderburne, younger of Kingennie, of ane @-rent of 480 mks., furth of the town and lands of Burke. (xxxii, 276.)

43. **1674** Oct. 8.—Forfar. Sasine, Agnes Wedderburne, daughter to Sir Peter Wedderburne of Gosford, now Lady Piteurr, of the town and lands of Haltoun of Newtyle, manorplace, &c. (xxxiv, 186.)

> The record is as follows :—" 1674. October 8.—Sasine on Contract of Marriage between David Haliburton of Piteur, with consent of his Curators on the one part, and Agnes Wedderburn, with consent of Sir Peter Wedderburn, Knight, her father, on the other part ; under which the said Agnes Wedderburn is infeft in a lifereut annuity of 4000 merks out of the town and lands of Haltoun of Newtyle and Kilpunnie in the Shire of Forfar." The date of the Contract not given ; but there are mentioned as witnesses to the subscriptions of the said David Halyburton, Agnes, and Sir Peter Wedderburn the following persons, viz. : David Earl of Northesk, Sir George Kinnaird, Sir John Wedderburn, Physician to His Majesty, Alexander Wedderburn, elder and younger of Easter Powrie, John Wedderburn, younger of Blackness, Mr. John Dickson of Whitslade, John Pringle of Woodhead, Peter Wedderburn son of the said Sir Peter Wedderburn, Alexr Cheplane W.S., and Wm Carnegie. Sasine is given on Octr 2nd 1674. Sir John Wedderburn of Blackness, is attorney for the sd Agnes."

44. **1676**. Feb.—Lanerk. Sasine, Mrs. Cecilia Wedderburne, daughter to Sir Alexander Wedderburne of Blackness, of ane @-rent of 1,200 merks furth of the lands of Litlegill, &c. (xxxvi, 394.)

> The record is as follows :—" 1676. February 29.—Sasine on Contract of Marriage between William Baillie, younger of Littlegill, eldest lawful son of William Baillie of Littlegill, with consent of his said father, on the one part, and Mrs. Cecilia Wedderburn, with consent of Sir Alexander Wedderburn, Knight, her father, and of John Wedderburn, therein designed fiar of Blackness, her brother, on the other part ; in virtue of which the said Mrs. Cecilia, now spouse of the said William Baillie, younger, is seased in an annual rent of 1200 merks, out of the lands of Littlegill, in the parish of Hartsyde and Shire of Lanerk, and others. Subscribed at the Mott by the said William Baillie elder, 14 October 1675, in presence of Wm. Baillie of Hardington. William Baillie of Beglie, John Baillie of Whythill, Mathew Baillie younger, brother german to Littlegill. elder, and others. Alexander Wedderburn of Easter Powrie, Patrick Kyd of Craigie, Alexander Wedderburn younger of Kingainie, Mr. James Brisbane, advocate, James and Peter Wedderburn, sons of the said Sir Alexander, Thomas Mylne of Muirton, and others, are witnesses to the subscription of the remanent parties above mentioned, on the 18th October 1675. Sasine given on 16 Febry 1676· Thomas Baillie in Mott is one of the bailies in that part in the giving of the Sasine.'

45. **1680**. April.—Forfar. Sasine, Margaret Mylne, relict of the deceast Major Robert Lindsay, and now spouse to Alexander Wedderburne of East Powrie, and David Lindsay, her lawful son, of ane @-rent of ane 100 lib., furth of the lands and barronie of Auchterhouse, fortalice, &c. (xliii, 413.)

46. **1682**. July.—Forfar. Sasine, Mistress Agnes Wedderburne, spous to David Haliburtoun of Piteurr, of 35 chalders 6 bolls victuall furth of the touns, lands, manorplace of Ballgillo, several rounnes in Ketnes Baldanne Balgove, peattiehous yard and pertinents. (xlvii, 159.)

47. **1685**. Sept.—Peebles. Sasine, Archibald Law, servitor to John Wedderburne of Gosfoord, of the lands of Stevenstoune, and pertinents. (lii, 229.)

48. **1685**. Nov.—Hadingtoun and Renfrew. Renunciation, John Wedderburne of Gossfoord, to Sir John Nisbet of Dirletoune of ane @-rent effeirand to the principall sounne of 50,000 merks furth of the lands and barronies of Thornetonn and Innerweek. (lii, 352.)

49. **1686**. June.—Forfar. Sasine, John Wedderburne of Gosfoord of ane @-rent of four hundred pounds furth of the lands and baronie of Piteurr. (liii, 280.)

50. **1686**. July.—Hadington and Renfrew. Renunciation, John Wedderburne of Gosfoord, to Sir John Nisbet of Dirleton, of ane @-rent effeirand to the principall sounne of 12,000 merks furth of the lands and baronies of Thorntoune and Innerweik. (liii, 365.)

51. **1688.** March.—Hadingtoun and Renfrew. Renunciation, John Wedderburne of General Gosfoord to Sir John Nisbet of Dirleton of ane @-rent effeirand to the principall Register soume of 6,000 merks furth of the lands and baronies of Thornetoun and Innerweik. of Sasines. (LVII, 161.)

52. **1688.** Nov.—Peebles. Renunciation, John Law, only lawful sone to umquhile James Law of Netherurd, to Archibald Law, servitor to Peter Wedderburne of Gosfoord, of ane infeftment of releiffe furth of eight parts of the toun and lands of Netherurd with the eighth part of the milne and milne lands therof. (LVIIII, 412.)

53. **1690.** April.—Berwick. Sasine, Peter Wedderburne of Gosfuird, of ane @-rent of £480 furth of the lands and baronies of Langtoune. (LX, 249.)

54. **1693.** Feb. 22.—Berwick and Roxburgh. Sasine, Mr. Alexander Wedderburne, advocate, and Marie Daes, his spouse, of ane @-rent of £560 scots, furth of the lands of Dennesses, Craiksfurd, Kymersmylne, Hoysland, Whitlawsland and Coldingknows mains, and certain aikers and husband lands in Erlestowne. Dated 9 January last. (LXV, 173.)

The record is as follows :—"1693. February 22.—Sasine on Obligation by Mr James Daes of Coldingknowes, advocate, in favour of Mr Alexr Wedderburn, advocate, brother german of the Laird of Gosfoord, and Marie Daes his spouse, of an @-rent of £560, out of the Main Lands of Coldingknowes, with manor-place, etc, in the parish of Ersiltoune and shire of Berwick, and other lands therein specified. Dated at Edinburgh 16 July 1692, and sasine given on 9 January 1693 in presence of Mr Andrew Mein of East Moriestou and others."

55. **1696.** Oct. 23.—Lanark. Sasine, Cecilia Wedderburn, spouse to William Baillie of Littlegill, in liferent, of the lands of Mott and haill pertinents. Dated 29 Aug. last. (LXXI, 164.)

The record is as follows :—"1696. October 23.—Sasine on Disposition by William Baillie of Littlegill, in favour of Cecilia Wedderburn, his spouse, of the lands of Mott in liferent, with the manor place, &c., lying in the parish of Roberton and Shire of Lanerk. Dated at Mott 14 August 1696, James Stothart, servitor to John Wedderburn of Blackness, is a witness ; and also to the sasine given on 20 August 1696."

56. **1697.** March 12.—Forfar and Kineardine. Sasine, Mr. Alexander Wedderburne, younger, of Blackness, and Mrs. Elizabeth Seatton, his spouse, of the manor place of Blackness, and of an @-rent of two thousand merks scots, furth of the lands and baronic therof. Dated 1st inst. (LXXII, 77.)

57. **1699.** Dec. 23.—Forfar and Kineardin. Sasine, Mr. Alexander Wedderburne of Blackness, of the lands and barronie of Blackness, and lands and barronie of Pittarro, in warrandiee thereof, and of 18 acres and 4 butts of land, lying in the Westfield of Dundee, and Mrs. Elizabeth Seton, his spous, in liferent, of ane yearly annuity of 2,000 merks furth of the said lands and pertinents. Dated 28 Oct. last. (LXXVI, 404.)

58. **1705.** Oct. 27.—Fyff. Sasine, Dame Jannet Halket, spous to Sir Patrik Halket of Pitfirren, of the lands and barronie of Pitfirren and haill pertinents. Dated 24 Oct. inst. (LXXXVIII, 45.)

59. **1706.** June 6.—Berwiek. Sasine, Margaret Wedderburn, relict of Mr. Andrew Balfour, wryter to the signet, now spouse of Dr. William Eeeles, physician in Edinburgh, and Margaret Balfour, daughter of the said Mr. Andrew Balfour, of the lordship and barronie of Swintoun, Little and Meikle Cranshaws, and Kirklands of the same. Dated 23 April last. (LXXXVIII, 194.)

60. **1706.** Oct. 29.—Fyff. Sasine, Dame Janet Halket, daughter of the deceast Sir Charles Halket of Pitfirren, of two-third parts of the lands of Pitfirren. Dated 16 Sept. last. (XC, 151.)

3 E

61. **1707.** June 9.-- Forfar and Kincardine. Sasine, Sir Alexander Wedderburn of Blackness and John Wedderburn, his eldest son, of the lands and barrony of Blackness, and barrouy of Pittarrow, in warrandice, and lands of Logie and others. Dated 30 May last. (XCI, 373.)

62. **1708.** Nov. 11.—Forfar. Sasine, Alexander Wedderburn of that ilk, of the lands and barrony of Wedderburn. Dated 14 Sept. last. (XCV, 179.)

63. **1719.** Nov. 28.—Forfar. Sasine, David Wedderburn, son and air to the deceast Alexander Wedderburn of that ilk, of ane @-rent effeiring to £1,473 scotts, furth of the lands and barronie of Edziell and Glenesk. Dated 5 Oct. last. (CXV, 85.)

64. **1720.** June 27.—Perth. Sasine, David Campbell, younger, of Keithick, and Mrs. Mathilda Wedderburn, his spouse, of ane annuity of 1,800 merks scots, furth of the lands of Keithick, Craighead, and Kemphill. Dated 9 May last. (CXVI, 91.)

65. **1729.** May.—Sasine, Mrs. Janet Wedderburn, spouse to Robert Colvill of Ochiltree, in liferent, of some lands within the barronie of Crombie and parochine of Torrie for the principall, and lands within the barronie and parish of Cleish, in warrandice. Dated 23 April last. (CXXXIII, 73.)

66. **1735.** Dec. 20.--Forfar. Renunciation, Mr. John Walkinshaw of the parish of St. James's, Westminster, in the County of Middlesex, to Sir James Wood of Bonnytoun, and Dr. John Wedderburn in Dundee, of ane @-rent effeiring to 500 pounds sterling, furth of Lethem, Newbiggings, Gask, and Idvies. Dated 25 Nov. last. (CL, 415.)

67. **1736.** April 26.—Kinross. Sasine, Christian Wedderburn, spouse to James Carstairs, eldest son to John Carstairs, late of Kilconquhar, of an annuity of 720 pounds scots, furth of the lands and estate of Kinross. Dated 15 April inst. (CLII, 117.)

68. **1738.** July 6.—Perth. Renunciation, Mrs. Mathilda Wedderburn, spouse to David Campbell, younger, of Keithick, with consent of her said husband, to Sir James Mackenzie of Roschaugh, of her life rent right furth of the lands of Little Keithick, Craighead. Meikle Keithick, with corn and walkmilns thereof, Kemphill, and Boat of Coupar. Dated 15 May last. (CLXI, 329.)

69. **1738.** July 6.—Perth. Renunciation, the said Mrs. Mathilda Wedderburn and her husband to Mr. John Wedderburn, Doctor of Physick in Dundee, and John Guthrie, merchant there, trustees for the creditors of David Campbell of Keithick, of her life-rent right furth of the lands of Balbogie. Dated 15 May last. (CLXIV, 333.)

70. **1746.** March.--Fyfe and Edinburgh. Sasine, Lieutenent Collonell Peter Halket of Pitferran of an @-rent effeiring to £13,000 scots furth of the Lordship of Balmerino and Baronie of Restalrig. Dated 25 Feb. last. (CLXXXV, 254.)

71. **1748.** Nov. 19.—Fyfe. Renunciation, William Walker, clerk of Innerkeithing, to Mr. Charles Wedderburn of Gossfoord and John McFarlane, wryter to the Signet, of an @-rent effeiring to 3700 merks scots, furth of the lands of Craigdukie, Wester Balnule, and Bowershall. Dated 15 inst. (CXCI, 401.)

72. **1756.** April 16.—Alexander Wedderburn, apprentice to James Smith, W.S., is witness at Edinburgh on 3 March 1756, to a disposition by James Spalding of Bonytoun Mill to Thomas Rattray of Borland. (CCXX, 384.)

    This is in the record, but is not inserted, of course, under the name of Wedderburn.

73. **1756.** 26 April.—Lanark. Sasine. William Baillie, surgeon in Biggar, and Ann and Cecilia Baillies, heirs of provision of Cristian (*sic*) Wedderburn, reliet of the deceast William Baillie of Littlegill, of an @-rent effeiring to 2000 merks furth of the lands of Littlegill. Dated 19 April inst. (ccxx, 399.) General Register of Sasines.

"Cristian" is an error for "Cecilia." The record is as follows:—"1756, April 26.—Sasine on disposition (Edinburgh. 14 Nov. 1692) by the late Sir Patrick Nisbet of Dean in favour of the late Mr Andrew Balfour. W.S., disponing to the said Mr Andrew Balfour an @-rent of £80, corresponding to the principal sum of 2000 merks contained in bond of corroboration of date 5 March 1680, and registered at Hamilton 6 May 1680, granted by the late William Baillie of Littlegill to the said Sir Patrick Nisbet, out of the £4 land of Littlegill and others in the county of Lanark : which bond of corroboration, disposition etc., the said Mr Andrew Balfour, by his Assignation, of date the 7 October 1697, transferred in favour of Alexander Wedderburn, Town Clerk of Dundee, trustee for Cecilia Wedderburn, Lady Littlegill, who held the same under backbond to her ; and were by the said Cecilia and Alexander Wedderburn assigned in favour of Thomas, James, Ann and Matilda Baillie, lawful children of the said Cecilia Wedderburn, conform to Dispⁿ in their favour of date 2 and 17 February 1711, and registered in the Books of Session 29 July 1725." The present sasine also proceeds on the General Retour dated 17 April 1755, of Cecilia Baillie, resid-enter in Edinburgh, only lawful child on life of the deceased Thomas Baillie, who was second lawful son procreated of the marriage between the late William Baillie of Littlegill and the said Cecilia Wedderburn, as heir to her said father before the Sheriff of Edinburgh. It also names the said Ann Baillie, residenter in Edinburgh, as eldest lawful daughter procreate of the foresaid marriage, and William Baillie, surgeon in Biggar, as heir, served and retoured to the deceased James Baillie, stabler in Edinburgh, his father, who was third lawful son of the said deceased William Baillie of Littlegill, procreated of the marriage between him and the said Cecilia Wedderburn his wife, and states that the said Matilda Baillie died without issue. Alex^r Wedderburn, servitor to the said Mr Andrew Balfour, W.S., is witness and writer of the preeept of sasine, which is given on 9 April 1756.

74. **1757.** March 5.—Fyfe. Resig. ad rem. by the trustees for the creditors of the deecast Robert Wedderburn, merchant in Dumfermling, to Lieutenaut Collonell Arthur Forbes of Pittenereiff, off the lands of Baldridge. Dated 14 March inst. (ccxxiii, 279.)

" Ad rem." signifies " ad remanentiam," *i.e.*, that the subjects are henceforth to remain with the superior lord.

75. **1760.** April. 10.—Peebles. Sasine, Mr. Alexander Wedderburn, councellor at law in London, off the lands of Grange, ealled Romano Grange. Dated 10 April last. (ccxxxv, 381.)

The record is as follows:—" 1760. April 10.—Sasine on Charter under the Great Seal, in favour of Thomas Earl of Dundonald, of date at Edin^r 23 February 1760 ; and also on Disposition by the said Earl, in favour of Alexander Wedderburn, Councellor at Law, in London, of the Lands of Grange, called Romano Grange, in the parish of Newlands and shire of Peebles. Disposition dated 9 and sasine given on 10 April 1760."

76. **1762.** May 22.—Fyfe. Sasine, John Wedderburn of Gosfoord, off the tennendrie of Balmule. Dated 24 March last. (ccxli, 361.)

77. **1765.** June 3.—Forfar. Sasine, Mrs. Grizell Wedderburn of Wedderburn, sister and heir of the deceast David Wedderburn, off the lands of Kingany. Dated 23 May last. (cclii, 244.)

78. **1767.** May 6.—Perth and Stirling. Sasine, Mrs. Janet Wedderburn, reliet of Mr. John Erskine of Balgownie, advoeate, off an annuity of 200 pounds stg. furth of the lands of Balgownie and Thrask. Dated 10 April last. (cclxv, 118.)

79. **1768.** Feb. 25.—Forfar and Perth. Sasine, Mrs. Grizel Wedderburn of Wedderburn, of the lands of Bullion, ealled Cattermillie. Dated 2 Jan. last. (cclxviii, 197.)

80. **1769.** Nov. 13.—Perth and Forfar. Sasine, Mrs. Grizell Wedderburn of Wedderburn, of the lands of Wedderburn and others. Dated 2 Oct. last. (cclxxv, 102.)

81. **1769.** Dec. 6.—Perth. Sasine, John Wedderburn, Esq., of Idvies, of the town and lands of Ballendean and others. Dated 30 Nov. last. (cclxxv, 234.)

82. **1774.** March 8.—Banff. Sasine, James Wedderburn, late of the Island of Jamaica, in liferent, of the lands of Barnyards and others. Dated 4 March curr^t (cccxi, 204.)

> The record is as follows :—"1774. Mar. 8 —Sasine on Crown Charter of Resignation, of date at Edin^r 6 Augt 1773, in favour of James Ferguson, y^r. of Pitfour, Esq., Advocate ; and Disp^n by him in favour of James Wedderburn Esqr, late of the Island of Jamaica, in liferent, of certain parts of the Lordship and Barony of Inverugie in the Shire of Banff, vizt : the lands of Barnyards, Netherhill. Kirkton of St. Fergus, and others therin specfied. Disp^n is dated 3 Feb. and Sas. given on 4 March 1774 "

83. **1775.** July 13.—Perth. Resignation " ad remanentiam," George Oliphant Kinloch to John Wedderburn, Esq., of the Wester half of the town and lands of Baudean. Dated 17 May last. (cccxxx, 99.)
> See ante s. No. 74.

84. **1779.** Nov. 25.—Perth. Sasine, Alexander Wedderburn, Esq., of Wedderburn, of an @-rent etieiring to 1,000 pounds sterling, furth of the lands of Milnhill and others. Dated 13 Nov. current. (ccclxx, 267.)

85. **1779.** Dec. 1.—Perth. Renunciation, Alexander Scrymgeour, Esq., of Birkhill, now Alexander Wedderburn of Wedderburn, Esq., to Isabella Forrester, *alias* Crichton of Milnhill and Thomas Crichton, her husband, of an @-rent eſſeiring to 1,000 pounds stg. upliftable furth of the lands of Milnhill and others. Dated 30 Nov. last. (ccclxxi, 30.)

PARTICULAR REGISTER OF SASINES, FORFAR.

1620—1780.

This record has been searched from its earliest date, 1620, down to 1780. It is in Forfar three series, viz. :— Sasines.

1. A single volume from 6 Sept. 1620—16 Jan 1621, after which the record is blank till 13 Sept. 1637.
11. Five volumes 1637—22 March 1658, after which the record is again blank till 14 Nov. 1660.
111. A great many volumes (1660—1869) of which twenty-eight have been searched, from 1660—1780.

From the entries naming Wedderburns, contained in the thirty-four volumes examined, I have selected all that are of any importance. A good many others merely record the witnessing of documents by this or that individual of the name, and these I have often omitted. At the same time I have added after the last entry from each series a list of all the places in the record at which reference is made to Wedderburns, whether important or not, so that the number and places of the omitted entries may be easily ascertained.

Series 1.

1. **1620.** Sept. 4.[1]—Mr. Alexander Wedderburn, younger, bailie of Dundee, witnesses a renunciation written by Thomas Fyiff, servitor to Mr. Alexander Wedderburn, clerk of Dundee, and subscribed for one of the parties by David Wedderburn. (128.)

2. **1620.** Nov. 23.—Mr. Alexander Wedderburn, clerk of Dundee, and Mr. James Wedderburn, his son, are named as both acting for David, Lord Carnegy of Kinnaird. Mr. James Wedderburn, batchelor of theology, is named as one of the masters of the Mariseball College, S. Andrew's, granters of the barony of Ullishaven to Lord Carnegy. (147-149.)

3. **1621.** Jan. 2.—Mr. Alexander Wedderburn, clerk of Dundee, and Mr. Alexander Wedderburn, younger, fiar of Kingany, witness a charter. (175.)

[See, in all, fol. 128, 136, 137. 143, 146, 147-49, 152, 157, 159, 175, 177, 182.]

Series 11.

4. **1637.** Sept. 13.—Memorandum by Sir John Hay of Barro, Knight, clerk register, recording the delivery of this volume to his deputies, Thomas and James Wichtane, father and son, now appointed by him, "the place being vacant by decease of the late Mr. Alexander Wedderburn, last clerk thereof."
See post No. 34.

5. **1637.** Dec. 27.—Sasine on charter by Robert Carnegy of Leuchland, parish of Brechin, in favour of Peter Trumbill, of an annual-rent, made with consent of Marjorie Wedderburn, wife of the granter, David, Earl of Southesk, and James, Lord Carnegy. (i, 20.)

6. **1638.** Jan. 17.—Alexander Wedderburn, elder, merchant, burgess of Dundee, is witness, 2 Dec. 1637, and Mr. Alexander Wedderburn, clerk of Dundee, notary to a sasine. (i, 27.)

7. **1638.** May 2.—John Wedderburn, merchant, burgess of Dundee, witnesses a sasine. Alexander Wedderburn is procurator, and Mr. Alexander Wedderburn, clerk, notary. (i, 65.)

8. **1638.** Dec. 29.—Sasine on contract of marriage (dated at Perth, 15 Nov.) between Alexander Wedderburn of Kingenny and Elspet Ramsay, daughter of John Ramsay, bailie, burgess of Dundee, infefting the said Elspet in the liferent of Kingany, &c. Mr. Alexander Wedderburn, clerk of Dundee, is a witness. (i, 157.)

[1] The date in each case is that of the registration, generally soon after that of the sasine or instrument registered.

9. **1639.** May 29.—Retour of Alexander Wedderburn of Kingany as heir of the late Mr. Alexander Wedderburn of Kingany, his father, in a South Marketgate tenement, once that of Patrick and Alexander Wedderburn, burgesses of Dundee, and now settled by Kingany on Elspet Ramsay, his wife, in liferent.   Alexander Wedderburn, elder, merchant, burgess of Dundee, is attorney.   Dated at Dundee 21 May. (I, 222.)

10. **1639.** (*a*) June 13.—Sasine on disposition by Robert Carnegie of Leuchland and Marjorie Wedderburn, his wife, of an annual-rent in favour of Peter Turnbull. (I, 254.) (*b*) Dec. 19.—Sasine on charter by them of the lands of Leuchland to David, Earl of Southesk, for 28,000 merks. (*ib.* 287.)

11. **1642.** March 7.—James Wedderburn, son of the late David Wedderburn, witnesses a sasine in favour of Colonel John Beaton and Margaret Cockburn, his wife, of half the lands of Murrois (called Westhall), on disposition to them by James Beaton of Westhall, brother german of the said Colonel. (I, 508.)

12. **1643.** Feb. 9.—Robert Sympson is seised in five acres of land in the Westfield of Dundee, sometime those of James Wedderburn, son and heir of the late David Wedderburn, burgess of Dundee. (II, 60.)

13. **1644.** June 19.—There is a renunciation, recording the due registration of certain documents in the "register of the sheriffdome of Forfar, be umquhile Mr. Alexander Wedderburn, Keiper thairof, upon the twelff day June 1629 yeiris." (II, 270.)

14. **1646** (*a*) April 28.—Mr. James Kyd of Grange of Barrie, gets sasine of that sixth part of Craigie, which once pertained to John Wedderburn, and was by him alienated to Sir John Scharp of Houstoun. (II, 369.) (*b*) Oct. 21.—These lands are again named as once those of John Wedderburn, son and heir of the deceased James Wedderburn, burgess of Dundee. (*ib*, 412.)

15. **1646.** Oct. 26.—Sasine on precept from Chancery (14 June) in favour of Sir Alexander Wedderburn of Blackness, Knight, of certain parts of the lands of Blackness. William Wedderburn, burgess, is a witness. (II, 476.)

16. **1647.** Oct. 7.—Sir Alexander Wedderburn of Blackness, gets sasine of those 5 acres in the Eastfield (*sic*) sometimes pertaining to James Wedderburn, son and heir of the late David Wedderburn, burgess. (II, 488.)

17. **1648.** April 14.—Sasine of parts of Blackness, given to Sir Alexander Wedderburn by Alexander Wedderburn of Kingenny, sheriff of the shire of Forfar in that part. (II, 552.)

18. **1648** June 14.—Sasine to William Duncan of a tenement in West Skirling's Wynd, once that of the late Patrick Wedderburn. (III, 29.)

19. **1649.** May 20.—Sasine in favour of John Mortimer of Parkfoord, and his future spouse, Ann Boytter, eldest daughter of Thomas Boytter of Pilmour, and the late Jean Wedderburn, his first wife. (III, 122.)

20. **1649.** June 1.—Andrew Wedderburn, merchant, burgess of Dundee, is attorney for David Ogilvie of Kynaltic. (III, 124.)

21. **1649.** Sept. 20.—Mr. Peter Wedderburn, advocate, Edinburgh, witnesses a charter dated at Dundee. (III, 168.)

22. **1650.** March 6.—Sasine on charter by Robert Clayhills of Innergowrie, in favour of Sir Alexander Wedderburn of Blackness, Knight, of two eighth parts, and the third of another eighth part of Blackness. (III, 210.)

23. **1653.** June 28.—William Wedderburn, brother german of Sir Alexander Wedderburn of Blackness, witness. (IV, 80.)

24. **1654**. Jan. 25.—Sasine by John, Viscount Dudhope, to Sir Alexander Wedderburn, of an annual-rent of £584 out of the Viscount's lands. (IV, 169.) *Forfar Sasines.*

25. **1654**. Mr. David (*sic*) Wedderburne, minister at Liff, is a witness. (IV, 202.)
   " David " is an error for Andrew, which was the name of the minister at Liff.

26. **1654**. May 27.—Alexander Wedderburne of Kingennie, acts as attorney for Halyburton of Pitcur, and Fotheringham of Powrie. (IV, 239-40.)

27. **1654**. Sept. 18.—Sasine to Sir Alexander Wedderburn of Blackness, of certain parts of the lands of Blackness, on charter from Auchinlek of Balmanno. (IV, 297.)

28. **1655**. June 29.—Sasine on disposition by William, Master of Gray, in favour of Sir Alexander Wedderburn of Blackness of various acres of land in and about Dundee. William Wedderburn, brother german of Sir Alexander Wedderburn, is witness. (IV, 418-19, 421, 184.)

29. **1655**. Sept. 7.—Sasine on charter (15 Aug.) by Mr. James Kyd of Craigie in favour of Margaret, eldest daughter of Sir Alexander Wedderburn of Blackness, in implement of the marriage contract between her and Patrick Kyd, eldest son of Mr. James Kyd aforesaid, whereby Margaret is infeft in the lands of Grange of Barrie, Nether Barrie, and part of Craigie. Among the witnesses are Alexander Wedderburn of Kingenny, William Kyd, brother of the said Mr. James, &c. (IV, 495.) There is a further similar sasine of other lands registered Oct. 8. (*ib.* 500.)

30. **1655**. Oct. 8.—Sasine on charter by Mr. James Futhie to the kirk-treasurer of Dundee of six acres in the Westfield of Dundee, sometime those of the late Robert Wedderburn, elder, merchant, burgess of Dundee, and acquired by the late Mr. George Graham of Claverhouse, goodsire to John Graham, now of Claverhouse, son of the late Mr. George Graham of Claverhouse, from the late Peter Wedderburn, merchant burgess of Dundee. The lands of Sir Alexander Wedderburn of Blackness, are named as partly bounding these acres. (IV, 502, 505, 509, 511, 514, 516, 520.)

31. **1655**. Dec. 18.—Sasine on charter (28 Nov.) by the provost and bailies of Dundee to Margaret Wedderburn, daughter of Sir Alexander Wedderburn of Blackness, and to her spouse, Patrick Kyd of Craigie, and the heirs (if any) procreate between them, of one-third of the lands of Craigie, subject to the life-rent of Mr. James Kyd, father to the said Patrick. (V, 22, 26.)

32. **1657**. April 15.—Renunciation by the assignees of Jonet Auchinlek, daughter of the late Thomas Auchinlek, sometime provost of Dundee, and relict of Mr. Archibald Auchinlek, once portioner of Blackness, to Sir Alexander Wedderburn of Blackness, of an annual-rent out of certain parts of the lands of Blackness, disponed to Sir Alexander by the said provost. (V, 227.)

   See, in all, s. :—I (1637-42), 20, 27, 47, 65, 157, 222, 254, 287, 508, 541, 545, 558. II (1642-48), 60, 212, 270, 314, 318 369, 413, 476, 481, 488, 505, 552. III (1648-52), 29, 49, 122, 124, 150, 158, 168, 198, 210, 274, 279, 301, 316, 355-56, 366, 462. IV (1652-55), 42, 80, 169, 202, 232, 239, 240, 261, 297, 370, 407, 418, 419, 421, 484, 495, 500, 502, 509, 511, 514, 516, 520. V (1658-60), 22, 26, 132-37, 170, 227, 233.

SERIES III.

33. **1660**. Dec. 31.—Sasine in favour of Margaret Wedderburn, spouse to Alexander Forrester in Innerpeffer in liferent, and to Mr. David Bruce, M.D., her son, in fee, of an annual-rent. (I, 21.)

34. **1660**. Dec. 31.—Renunciation naming a sasine registered 1 Aug. 1637 by Mr. Alexander Wedderburn, keeper of the register of sasines for the shire of Forfar. (I, 23.)

35. **1663**. April 16.—Sasine to Patrick Kyd of Craigie, as heir to his father, the late Mr. James Kyd, of that third of Craigie, got by Sir John Sharpe of Houstoune, from the late John Wedderburn, son and heir of the late James Wedderburn, burgess of Dundee. (I, 245.)

Forfar Sasines.

36. **1663.** May 2.—Sasine on precept under the Great Seal in favour of Alexander Wedderburn, elder, of Kingenny, provost of Dundee, his heirs, &c., of the lands of Easter Powrie, also called Wester Maynes or Middletoune, lie Easter Maynes and Burnesyd of Powrie, all erected into one free barony of Powrie, formerly belonging to Dougall McPherson, and by him, with consent of his wife, Jonet Guthrie, and John McPherson, their son, resigned to the Lords of His Majesty's Exchequer for new infeftment to the said Alexander Wedderburn, and now granted by the King "for the good, faithful, and thankful service done to him and his predecessors by the said Alexander and his predecessors in times past." (I, 255.)

See ante s, Private Records, Scrymgeour-Wedderburn Papers, No. 358.

37. **1663.** May 7.—Alexander Wedderburn of Kingany, provost of Dundee, being bound by his contract of marriage (19 May 1660) with Margaret Mylne to "wair, imploy, and bestow" 9000 merks on himself and her for life and on their heirs, now charges his lands of Wester Gowrdie with an annual rent of £360 in her favour. Alexander Wedderburn, his eldest lawful son, is attorney for Margaret Mylne. (I, 257.)

38. **1663.** Nov. 8.—John Tarbitt renounces to Sir Alexander Wedderburn of Blackness, 24 acres wadset to him by the late Lord Gray and of which Sir Alexander is heritable proprietor, in the Westfield of Dundee. (I, 297.)

39. **1663.** Nov. 17.—Alexander Wedderburn of Kingenny, provost of Dundee, renounces to Sir Alexander Wedderburn of Blackness, heritable proprietor of Logie and the Bank of Balgay, an annual-rent of £60 out of the said lands. (I, 300.)

40. **1663.** Nov. 17-26.—Other renunciations of annual rents in favour of Sir Alexander Wedderburn of Blackness. (I, 301, 302, 316.)

41. **1664.** Feb. 17.—Grant by John Hunter of Balgay to Sir Alexander Wedderburn of Blackness, of an annual-rent of £100. William Wedderburn, brother german to Sir Alexander Wedderburn, is attorney. (I, 359.) Renounced 11 Nov. 1665. (post II, 360.)

42. **1664.** Feb. 23.—Sasine on disposition (15 Feb.) by Sir Alexander Wedderburn of Blackness, Knight, in favour of James Wedderburn, his second son, of (a) 5 acres in the Westfield of Dundee ; (b) 2 other such acres ; (c) 24 other such acres, being those named ante No. 38 ; (d) 18 other such acres, some of which are described as bounded by the lands sometime of Barbara Wedderburn. William Wedderburn, brother german of Sir Alexander, is witness and attorney. (I, 363.)

43. **1664** June 1.—Sir Alexander Wedderburn of Blackness, Sir Peter Wedderburn of Gosfoord, Knights, and John Wedderburn, apparent of Blackness, advocate, witness the marriage contract (29 April) of David Lindsay, eldest son of John Lindsay of Edzell, and Agnes Graham, daughter of James Graham of Monorgun. (II, 2.)

44. **1664.** June 1.—Mr. David Bruce and Margaret Wedderburn, his mother, with consent of Alexander Forrester in Innerpeffor, her spouse, renounce, in favour of Alexander Halyburton of Fodderance, the annual-rent named ante No. 33. Mr. David Bruce signs at London, 17 March ; and Margaret Wedderburn at Dundee, 17 May. Mr. Andrew Bruce, brother of Mr. David, is a witness. (II, 9.)

45. **1664** July 20.—Sasine on charter (14 and 19 Dec. 1663) by John Hunter of Balgay, in favour of Sir Alexander Wedderburn of Blackness, of the lands of Logie, Longforbank of Balgay, &c. (II, 66.

46. **1665.** Jan. 12.—Sasine on disposition by Patrick Kyd of Craigie, to Margaret Wedderburn, his wife, in life-rent, of 6 ploughs of the lands of Craigie. William Wedderburn, brother german of Sir Alexander Wedderburn of Blackness, is attorney for Margaret. (II, 234.)

47. **1665.** May 31.—Sasine on bond (12 Sept. 1662) by Alexander Wedderburn of Kingany, provost of Dundee, in favour of Douglas McPherson and Janet Guthrie, his third wife of an annual-rent of £220 out of Easter Powrie. (II, 298.)

48. **1666**. Jan. 1.—Sasine on charter by Alexander Wedderburn, elder, of Kingany, provost, in favour of Alexander Wedderburn, younger, his only son by the late Elizabeth Ramsay, of the lands of Easter Powrie, now one free Barony of Powrie, subject to the life-rent of the said Alexander Wedderburn, elder, and to the contract of marriage (18 Dec. 1665) made between the said Alexander Wedderburn, younger, and his future spouse. (III, 2.)

49. **1666**. Jan. 1.—Sasine on charter by Alexander Wedderburn, elder, of Kingenny, in favour of Alexander Wedderburn, younger, his only son by the late Elizabeth Ramsay, and Grissell Wedderburn. fourth daughter of Sir Alexander Wedderburn of Blackness, and future wife of the said Alexander Wedderburn, younger, of the lands of Kingenny. John Wedderburn, eldest son and heir of the said Sir Alexander, is attorney for his sister Grissell. (III, 45.)

50. **1666**. May 28.—Sasine of an @-rent in favour of Margaret Milne, relict of Major Robert Lindsay (and now wife of Alexander Wedderburn of Kingenny), provost, and Robert Lindsay, her son. (III, 76.)

51. **1666**. June 29.—Sir Alexander Wedderburn of Blackness and John Wedderburn, younger, of Blackness, advocate, witness a charter and sasine in favour of Patrick Kyd of Craigie. (III, 97.)

52. **1667**. Sept. 29.—Sasine on precept from Chancery in favour of Patrick Kyd of Craigie of the lands of Grange of Barrie, given by Alexander Wedderburn, younger, of Kingenny, sheriff in those parts. (III, 307.)

53. **1669**. Feb. 11.—Precept by the town of Dundee, signed by Alexander Wedderburn, provost, and witnessed by Sir Alexander Wedderburn of Blackness. (IV, 2.)

54. **1669**. June 18.—Sasine on charter by John Wedderburn, fiar of Blackness, in favour of his brother german, James Wedderburn, second son of Sir Alexander Wedderburn of Blackness, of certain acres of land pertaining to the house of Fowlls. (IV, 182.)

55. **1669**. Oct. 24.—Sasine on charter by James. Marquis of Douglas, to Alexander Wedderburn, younger, of Kingenny, and Grissell Wedderburn, his wife, and their heirs, of the lands of Kingenny. (IV, 209.)

56. **1671**. Nov. 8.⎱ James Wedderburne, clerk of Dundee, is witness and notary, and
  1672. Jan. 20.⎰   adds his motto, "dum spiro spero." (IV, 451, 462.)

57. **1672**. May 28.—Andro Wedderburn, burgess of Dundee, witnesses a sasine. (V, 50.)

58. **1672**. Oct. 8.—Sasine on bond of warrandice by Robert, Earl of Southesk, of the barony of Farn, in warrandice of the barony of Innerwick, in favour of Sir Peter Wedderburn of Gosford, senator of the College of Justice, for life, and, in fee, to his eldest, second, and third sons John, Peter, and Alexander, and the heirs male of their bodies in successive substitution. (V, 121.)

59. **1673**. Feb. 1.—James Wedderburn, clerk of Dundee, notary. (V, 179-181.)

60. **1673**. April 16.—James Wedderburn, clerk of Dundee, resigns to his brother, John Wedderburn, fiar of Blackness, the lands mentioned ante No. 54. (V, 198.)

61. **1673**. April 20.—Sasine on disposition by Sir Alexander Wedderburn of Blackness, with consent of James Wedderburn, his second son, clerk of Dundee, to John Wedderburn, fiar of Blackness, his eldest son, of various acres near Dundee. (V, 201.)

62. **1674**. Feb. 28.—Sasine in favour of Sir Alexander Wedderburn of Blackness, of a small @-rent. James Wedderburn, clerk, his son, is notary. (V, 276.)

63. **1675.** May 15.—Sasine on Great Seal charter in favour of William Kyd of Woodhill, upon resignation by Patrick Kyd of Grange of Barrie, of certain parts of the lands of Craigie, subject to certain life-interests of the said Patrick Kyd and Margaret Wedderburn, his wife, and providing that if the said Patrick ever have a son, part of the lands shall be redeemable by payment of one rosnoble of gold, and if he have daughters, they shall be chargeable with provision for them.   In event of his death without issue the lands are burdened with legacies, including 5,000 merks to John Wedderburn, fiar of Blackness, and £1,000 to Alexander Wedderburn of Kingenny. (v, 369.)

64. **1676.** July 25.—Andrew Wedderburn, merchant in Dundee, bailie. (vi, 160.)

65. **1677.** Dec. 28.—Sasine on disposition by Alexander Wedderburn of Easter Powrie in favour of Peter Wedderburn, his son, of the lands of Wester Gourdie, subject to the life rent of the said Alexander Wedderburn and his wife, Margaret Milne. (vi, 385.)

66. **1679.** June 18.—Sasine on disposition of the same date by Alexander Wedderburn of Easter Powrie, provost of Dundee, to Peter Wedderburn, his second lawful son, of a fore-tenement "of old belonging to Piter and Alexander Wedderburn and now to me (*sic*) air to the deceased Mr. Alexander Wedderburn of Kingenny, my father." (vii, 50)
The sasine follows the words of the disposition. The tenement was formerly that of Robert Wedderburn, notary, (d. 1611) by whom it was settled on Peter, son of Mr. Alexander Wedderburn, first of Kingennie, and on Alexander, third son of David Wedderburn "of the MS." See ante s. Private Records, David Wedderburn's MS., 56, 21c.

67. **1680,** May 17.—Sasine on bond of provision by James Wedderburn, clerk of Dundee, in favour of Elizabeth Davidson, his wife, of a South Flukergate house, next that of George Wedderburn, subject to the life-rent of Dame Matilda Fletcher, relict of the late Sir Alexander Wedderburn of Blackness. Peter Wedderburn, merchant, is witness. (vii, 178.)

68. **1682.** Feb. 6.—Sasine on disposition by George Wedderburn, merchant burgess in Edinburgh, to his brother James Wedderburn, clerk of Dundee, of a South Nethergate house, once belonging to their father, the late Sir Alexander Wedderburn. (vii, 344.)

69. **1682.** Sept. 26.—Sasine on disposition by John Wedderburn of Blackness, in favour of the provost and bailies of Dundee, of the lands of Logie, &c. (vii, 423)
See ante s. Burgh Records, Dundee Council Books, No. 133, and post No 95.

70. **1685.** Feb. 13.—Sasine on bond of possession by James Halyburton of Pitcur, in favour of Agnes Wedderburn, his wife, of an @-rent. (viii, 23.)

71. **1686.** July 5.—Sasine on Chancery precept in favour of Alexander Wedderburn of Easter Powrie, as heir to his late father in Wester Gourdie. (viii, 111.)

72. **1692.** July 1.—Sasine on chancery precept in favour of Alexander Wedderburn now of Easter Powrie, as heir of the late Alexander Wedderburn of Easter Powrie, his father, in the barony of Easter Powrie (and in the barony of Ogilvie in warrandice), and in the lands of Wester Gourdie. James Wedderburn, clerk of Dundee, witness. (ix, 26.)

73. **1692.** Sept. 8.—Sasine on precept of clare constat in favour of Peter Wedderburn of Gosford, as heir to John Wedderburn of Gosford, his brother german, in an @-rent of £400 out of the lands of Pitcur. (ix, 43.)
Peter (later Sir Peter) Wedderburn of Gosford, discharges Pitcur of this @-rent. 3 May 1704. Mr. Alexander Wedderburn, advocate, is witness. Registered 13 June 1704. (x, 648.)

74. **1697.** June 15.—Retour of Alexander Wedderburn now of Easter Powrie, as eldest son and heir of his father, the late Alexander Wedderburn of Easter Powrie and Kingenny, in the lands of Kingenny. (ix, 436.) See also sasine to him, Aug. 9. (*ib.* 461.)

75. **1699** Aug. 15.—Retour of Alexander Wedderburn, clerk of Dundee, as eldest son and heir of his father, the late James Wedderburn, clerk of Dundee, in a South **Forfar Sasines.** Nethergate tenement. (x, 164-65.) John Wedderburn, brother of the said Alexander Wedderburn, is witness.

76. **1703**. Nov. 3.—Sasine on contract of marriage (31 Dec. 1702) between Alexander Wedderburn of Easter Powrie, and Grizell, youngest daughter of Robert Gardyne, younger of Laton, infefting the said bride in an @-rent of 1,000 merks out of Easter Powrie and Kingennie. Peter Wedderburn, merchant, in Dundee, is a witness. (x, 552.)

77. **1704**. Nov. 29.—Sasine on contract of marriage (7 June 1700) between Thomas Watson of Grange of Barrie, and Grizell Wedderburn, infefting the said Grizell Wedderburn in an @-rent during the life of her mother, Elizabeth Davidson, and thereafter in a further sum. (xi, 13.)

78. **1706**. May 11.—Alexander Wedderburn, clerk, and Alexander Wedderburn, shoremaster, sign a charter. (xi, 118.)

79. **1706**. June 17.—Alexander Wedderburn, shipmaster, is attorney for James Man, and Alexander Wedderburn, sheriff clerk of Forfar, notary to a sasine. (xi, 129.)

80. **1706**. June 20.—Sasine on disposition by the town council of Dundee in favour of Sir Alexander Wedderburn of Blackness, Knight, Baronet, of the lands of Logie for 17,500 merks. Alexander Wedderburn, clerk, and Alexander Wedderburn, shoremaster, both subscribe. (xi, 134.)

81. **1707**. Jan. 30.—John Wedderburn, doctor of medicine, is witness. (xi, 247.)

82. **1707**. Oct. 10.—Sasine on charter by the town council of Dundee in favour of Alexander Wedderburn, clerk, of Donaldson's croft in the Wellgate of Dundee. Alexander Wedderburn, shoremaster, subscribes. (xi, 247.)

83. **1708**. May 8.—Sasine on bond in favour of Sir Alexander Wedderburn of Blackness, baronet, clerk to the bills, of an @-rent out of the lands of Kinnaird, Fearne, Carnegie, &c. (xi, 291.)

84. **1708**. Sept. 20.—Sasine of a South Nethergate land in favour of Sir Alexander Wedderburn of Blackness. Peter Wedderburn, merchant, witness. (xi, 304.)

85. **1709**. May 4.—Sasine of land in Dundee in favour of Alexander Wedderburn, clerk, and on his death in favour of John Wedderburn, his eldest son. (xi, 327.)

86. **1709**. Oct. 17.—Sasine on bond (9 Nov. 1695) by the Earl of Strathmore to infeft the late Margaret Milne, relict of Alexander Wedderburn of Easter Powrie, for life, and her son, Peter Wedderburn, merchant in Dundee, in fee, in an @-rent out of the lands of Glamis, &c. (xii, 22.)

87. **1711**. Feb. 9.—Sasine on charter by the town of Dundee of two plots of land in favour of Alexander Wedderburn, clerk, and John Wedderburn, his eldest son. (xii, 144.) These lands are disposed by them to Robert Hill, 1720. (xiii, 218.)

88. **1713**. July 20.—John Wedderburn, doctor of medicine in Dundee, witnesses a marriage contract between David Nevay of Nevay and Elizabeth, daughter of Richard Fletcher of Ballinshoe. (xii, 336.)

89. **1714**. June 25.—Sasine on chancery precept (April 1) returning Peter Wedderburn of that ilk as heir to his father, the late Alexander Wedderburn of Wedderburn, in Easter Powrie. (xii, 409.)

90.   **1715.** June 1.—Sasine on chancery precept (24 March) returning David Wedderburn, now of that ilk, as heir to his brother, the late Peter Wedderburn of Wedderburn, in Easter Powrie, &c. (XII, 487.)

91.   **1717.** Jan. 15.—Sasine on marriage contract (20 Aug. 1715) of Alexander Read of Turfbeg, and Elizabeth, daughter to Alexander Wedderburn, clerk of Dundee, infefting her in an annuity charged on Turfbeg. (XIII, 29.)

92.   **1717,** May 8.—Sasine on precept of clare constat by the commissioners of the Duke of Douglas, infefting David Wedderburn of that ilk, in the lands of Kingenny, as heir to his late father, Alexander Wedderburn of Easter Powrie. Thomas Scott, servitor of Alexander Wedderburn, sheriff clerk of Forfar, and Peter Kinmond in Cottoun of Wedderburn, witnesses. (XIII, 46, 49.)

93.   **1720.** Sept. 10.—Sasine on disposition (28 Feb. 1718) by Sir John Wedderburn of Blackness. Knight and Baronet, with consent of his curators, James Halyburton of Pitcur, James Kyd of Craigie, Mr. George Seaton, advocate, and Doctor John Wedderburn, doctor of medicine at Dundee, in favour of Alexander Wedderburn, sheriff clerk of Forfar, his heirs and assignees, heritably and irredeemably, of all and whole the lands and barony of Blackness, as erected into one barony, confirm to a Great Seal charter granted 14 July 1666 in favour of Sir Alexander Wedderburn of Blackness, great grandfather to the said Sir John, and also of the lands of Logie acquired by the late Sir Alexander Wedderburn, father of Sir John, from the town of Dundee. Signed at Edinburgh, 28 Feb. 1718, by the grantor and all his curators, except Doctor Wedderburn, who signs at Dundee, 29 April, and J. Kyd of Craigie, who does not sign. (XIII, 241.)
       As to the date 1666, see ante s. Great Seal Register, No. 115.

94.   **1723.** Oct. 14.—Sasine to Sir Alexander Wedderburn of Blackness, Knight Baronet, of the barony of Blackness, upon a great seal charter to him, (designed therein sheriff clerk of Forfar) and his son John, dated 26 July 1722. The sasine is given at Blackness by Alexander Read of Turfbeg, sheriff clerk of Forfar for that occasion. (XIII, 442.)

95.   **1723.** Oct. 14.—Sasine on Great Seal Charter (26 July 1722) to Alexander Read of Turfbeg, of the lands of Logie and Longforobank. (ib.)
       These lands of Logie changed hands more than once in a few years. In 1682 John Wedderburn of Blackness sold them to the town of Dundee (ante No 69), by whom in 1706 they were resold to his son Sir Alexander (ante No. 88). From his son they passed to the fourth baronet in 1718 (ante No. 93), who, in 1722, disponed them to his son-in-law, Alexander Read of Turfbeg.

96.   **1724.** July 6.—Sasine on disposition (10 and 11 Nov. 1712) by the tutors to Sir John Wedderburn, eldest lawful son to Sir Alexander Wedderburn of Blackness, who nominated them tutors 3 Jan. 1710, of a South Nethergate tenement (ante No. 84) in favour of Dr. John Blair. (XIII, 497.)

97.   **1726.** Jan. 25.—Sasine on bond of provision (25 Dec. 1725) by Sir Alexander Wedderburn of Blackness in implement of his marriage contract in favour of Dame Katharine Scott, his wife, of an @-rent of 800 merks charged on Blackness. Robert Wedderburn, servitor to John Mercer, writer in Perth, witnesses the sasine. (XIV, 18.)

98.   **1727.** May 30.—Robert Wedderburn, writer in Forfar, is attorney for Alexander Read of Turfbeg, as heir to his father, the late Alexander Read of Turfbeg. (XIV, 112.)

99.   **1727.** Sept. 5.—Sasine on disposition (5 June 1722) by Barbara Fleming, of land in Dundee which by the great tenement once that of Mr. Alexander Ramsay, then of Sir Alexander Wedderburn of Blackness, clerk, and now of (Sir) Alexander Wedderburn of Blackness, his grandchild. Thomas Wedderburn, merchant in Dundee, is bailie for Barbara Fleming. (XIV, 120, and cp. 192.)

100.   **1727.** Dec. 8.—Sasine on disposition by Thomas Nairn of Baldovan in favour of David Wedderburn of that ilk, of all the lands of Baldovan, with the Bank of Baldovan, &c. (XIV, 131.)

101. **1729.** May 20.—Sir Alexander Wedderburn of Blackness and Alexander Wedderburn, shipmaster, witnesses. (xiv, 232.)

102. **1729.** Sept. 26.—Robert Wedderburn is notary to a sasine, with the motto, "Libertas optima rerum." (xiv, 259.)

103. **1729.** Nov. 3.—Sir Alexander Wedderburn, sheriff clerk of Forfar, notary to a sasine to William Maule. His docket runs thus :—" Et ego vero Dominus Alexander Wedderburn, clericus Brechinensis Diocesis. scriba communis viceeomitatis de Forfar ac notarius publicus (manu Roberti Wedderburn mei filii fideliter scriptum, &c.) ...... Alexander Wedderburn, N.P., ' Sit Deo Gloria.' "

104. **1735.** April 3.—Sasine (29 March) on charter of resignation (Edinburgh, 26 July 1734) under the Great Seal, in favour of John Wedderburn, eldest son of Sir Alexander Wedderburn of Blackness, whom failing to John Wedderburn, eldest son of the said John by Jean Fullarton, his spouse, whom failing to the other heirs of taillie mentioned in their marriage contract, whom failing to the said Sir Alexander Wedderburn, his heirs and assignees, of all the lands and barony of Blackness (erected into one barony by a Great Seal charter to the late Sir Alexander Wedderburn of Blackness, 14 July 1666), subject to the life-rent of Sir Alexander and the dowry of Lady Catharine Scott, his wife, and the payment of provisions to their younger children. (xv, 104-106.)
Mr. A. C. Lamb of Dundee. has a contemporary extract of this sasine (eight pages of parchment) noted as registered at Dundee on the same day. though I have not found any such record. As to the year 1666 in the extract, see ante s Great Seal Register, No. 115.

105. **1736.** Sept. 30.—Sasine on disposition by Sir James Wood of Bonnington, with consent of the creditors of the late David, Earl of Northesk, in favour of Dr. John Wedderburn, physician in Dundee, &c., of the lands of Idvies in the parish of Kirkden, Forfar. Robert Wedderburn is notary, with the motto "Libertas optima rerum." (xv, 298.)

106. **1736.** Dec. 17.—Sasine on charter of adjudication in favour of Sir Alexander Wedderburn of Blackness, Knight Baronet, of the lands of Halkertoun, Eassie, co. Forfar, adjudged to belong to Alexander Alison, W.S., on decree v. Henry Crawfurd, merchant in Dundee, and also to belong to Sir Alexander Wedderburn on decree v. Henry Crawfurd for payment to Sir Alexander Wedderburn of £11,244 9s. 4d. (xv, 306.)

107. **1737.** July 1.—Sasine (27 June) on contract of marriage (22 April 1725) between John Wedderburn, eldest son of Sir Alexander Wedderburn of Blackness, and Mrs. Jean Fullarton, eldest lawful daughter of John Fullarton of Fullarton, whereby Sir Alexander Wedderburn settled on Jean Fullarton an annuity of 1,200 merks during the life of Dame Catharine Scott, his wife, and thereafter an annuity of £1,000 out. of the lands of Blackness, &c. (xv, 329.)

108. **1737.** Sept. 29.—John Wedderburn, constable depute and bailie in that part, gives sasine of a house in Dundee to the two surviving daughters of the late Sir John Guthrie of Westhall, son of the late Mr. John Guthrie, minister in Dundee. (xv, 347.)

109. **1738.** April 4.—Sasine on contract of marriage (30 Jan.) between Robert Wedderburn, writer in Forfar (second lawful son of Sir Alexander Wedderburn of Blackness, Baronet), and Isobel Edward, only daughter of the deceased David Edward, second son of the deceased John Edward of Persy, and heir retoured to her uncle the late Thomas Edward of Persy. By this contract, Robert Wedderburn settles an annuity of 1,000 merks (or 1,200 if he die s.p.) on his wife, and she settles on him and the heirs of the marriage the estate of Persy, in the parish of Kingoldrum and regality of Aberbrothock, co. Forfar. (xv, 394.)

110. **1740.** July 8.—Sasine on bond by Robert Wedderburn of Persie, sheriff clerk of of Forfar, to Dr. John Edward, physician in Dundee, of an @-rent of £325. 13. 8. out of the estate of Persie. (xv, 543.)

111. **1742.** Jan. 15.—Sasine on bond of provision (19 Nov. 1741) by Alexander Read of Turfbeg in favour of his wife, Elizabeth Wedderburn, of an annuity out of Logie. John Wedderburn, younger, of Blackness, is attorney for Elizabeth. (xvi, 32.)

112. **1743.** Aug. 25.—Renunciation (5 July) by Jean, eldest daughter of John Fullarton of that ilk, and wife of John Wedderburn, younger, of Blackness, of certain charges existing in her favour on the lands and barony of Blackness, reciting her post-nuptial marriage contract of 22 April 1725 (see ante No. 107), and also reciting that Sir Alexander Wedderburn and John, his son, had disponed the said lands and barony to trustees for their creditors for sale to pay their "great and insuperable" debts, and that Alexander Hunter of Balskellie had bought the same, 28 June 1743, and that it was necessary to free them of charges. (xvi, 151, 155.)

113. **1743.** Aug. 25.- Similar renunciation by Dame Kathrine Scott, wife to Sir Alexander Wedderburn of Blackness. (xvi, 155, 158)

114. **1744.** Jan. 27.—Sasine on disposition by David Wedderburn of that ilk to Mr. Hugh Maxwell of Strathmartine, of the lands of Bridgend, Achry, Pittengrin, part of Baldovan, &c. Mr. David Scrimgeour of Birkhill, advocate, witness. (xvi, 208.)

115. **1745.** Feb. 16.— Sasine on disposition (17 Nov, 1741) by Sir Alexander Wedderburn of Blackness in favour of the trustees for his creditors of a South Flukergate tenement. (xvi, 322.)

116. **1749.** Feb. 1.—Sasine on obligation of warrandice by Sir James Wood of Bonnington, in favour of Dr. John Wedderburn, physician in Dundee, of the lands of Letham and Newbigging, S. Vigean's, co. Forfar, in security of the lands of Idvies disponed by Sir James to Dr. John Wedderburn. (xvi, 554.)

117. **1752.** Aug. 28.—Sasine on precept of clare constat to David Wedderburn of Wedderburn as heir to his great uncle, the late Peter Wedderburn, second son of the late Alexander Wedderburn of Easter Powrie, of a South Marketgate land. (xvii, 285.)

118. **1753.** Feb. 9.—Alexander Wedderburn, writer in Dundee, presents a sasine for registration. (xvii, 299, 302.)

119. **1756.** Sept. 24.--Sasine on disposition to David Mullo by David Wedderburn as heir to his great uncle Peter Wedderburn aforesaid (No. 117) of the South Market-gate land inherited from him. Robert Wedderburn of Persie, witness. (xviii, 145.)

120. **1769.** June 11.—Sasine on disposition (31 Aug. 1718) by the late Peter Wedderburn, merchant in Dundee, to Alexander Wedderburn, sheriff clerk of Forfar, of the @-rent out of the barony of Glamis, registered ante No. 86. (xviii, 487, 517.)

121. **1760.** May 26.--Sasine on disposition by Alexander Blair to Captain John Ramsay of a Flukergate tenement with low gallery and study in the north end thereof, once belonging to the late Sir John Wedderburn of Blackness. (xix, 100.)

122. **1761.** Sept. 28.—Sasine on bond (20 May) by Henry Smith of Smithfield, to David Wedderburn of Wedderburn, now deceased, proceeding also on the chancery retour (17 Aug.) of Mrs. Grizell Wedderburn of Wedderburn, as heir general to the said David, her brother, of an @-rent of £75 stg. out of the lands of Smithfield. (xix, 321.)

123. **1762.** May 26.—Sasine on chancery precept in favour of Grizell Wedderburn now of that ilk, as heir to the late David Wedderburn of that ilk, her brother german, in the lands of Easter Powrie, &c., disponed to Alexander Wedderburn, great grandfather of the said Grizell, and erected into one free barony of Wedderburn by Great Seal charter, 12 March 1708, in favour of Alexander Wedderburn, father of the said Grizell, and also in the lands of Wester Gourdie, reciting that the said Grizell is the only sister german and nearest heir of the said David. (xix, 463.)

124. **1763.** Aug. 31.—Sasine on extract disposition (22 March 1749) by the late Doctor John Wedderburn, physician in Dundee, granting the estate of Idvies, parish of Kirkden, eo. Forfar, to his wife, Margaret Balfour for life, and then to John Wedderburn, Esq., eldest son of the late Sir John Wedderburn, baronet, and other substitutes of entail heritably, in favour of the said John Wedderburn. (xx, 184.)

125. **1766.** Dec. 27.—Sasine of the lands of Idvies on Great Seal charter (6 Aug.) in Forfar Sasines. favour of John Wedderburn, Esq., of Hanover, Jamaica (eldest son of the late Sir John Wedderburn of Blackness, Bart., and Dame Jean Fullarton, his wife), and the heirs male of his body, whom failing, to the following substitutes of entail, and the heirs male of their bodies in succession (1) James Wedderburn and Peter Wedderburn, brothers of the said John; (2) Robert Wedderburn of Pearsie, brother of the said Sir John, and John Wedderburn and Charles Wedderburn, his sons, and also any other son he may have; (3) Alexander Wedderburn, John Wedderburn, sons of Thomas Wedderburn, collector of excise at Inverness, and any other sons the said Thomas may have; (4) the heirs whomsoever of the late Dr. John Wedderburn of Idvies. (XXI, 333.)

126. **1770.** March 13.—Sasine on disposition (1741) by the late Sir Alexander Wedderburn of Blackness in favour of the trustees for the creditors of himself and his eldest son, John Wedderburn, of a South Flukergate tenement, and also on a disposition (1761) by the said trustees in favour of Mrs. Jean Fullarton, relict of the said John Wedderburn, now deceast, and Catharine, Susan, and Agatha Wedderburn, her daughters, of the said tenement. (XXII, 516.)

127. **1777.** June 27.—Renunciation by Thomas Carnegy of Craigy in favour of John Wedderburn of Ballindean, formerly of Idvies, of an @-rent of £200 stg. out of the lands of Idvies. (XXVI, 202.)

128. **1778.** May 19.—Discharge (14 May) by Mrs Grizell Wedderburn of Wedderburn of the bond granted by Henry Smith of Smithfield (ante No. 122) to David Wedderburn of Wedderburn, her brother.

129. **1780.** May 8.—Sasine on precept from chancery in favour of Alexander Scrymgeour, now Wedderburn (eldest son of the late Mr. David Scrymgeour of Birkhill, advocate, and Catharine Wedderburn, his wife) as nearest and lawful heir of taillie and provision to Mrs. Grizell Wedderburn of Wedderburn in the barony of Wedderburn, lands of Wester Gourdie, Bullion, and Kingenny, conform to a great seal charter in favour of the said Mrs. Grizell Wedderburn of Wedderburn and the heirs of her body whom failing to the following substitutes of entail and the heirs of their bodies successively. (1) David Scrymgeour of Birkhill and his four sons, Alexander, John, David, and Harry Scrymgeour, and any other sons he may have,·whom failing, Janet Scrymgeour, his eldest daughter, and any other daughter he may have. (2) Marion Scrymgeour, and the heirs of the late Janet Scrymgeour, daughters of the late Professor Alexander Scrymgeour in S. Andrew's (3) John Wedderburn of Idvies, eldest son of the late Sir John Wedderburn of Blackness. (4) James Wedderburn and Peter Wedderburn, younger brothers of the said John Wedderburn of Idvies. (5) Margaret Wedderburn (wife of Richard Dundas of Blair), Catharine Wedderburn, Susan Wedderburn, and Agatha Wedderburn (wife of John Smyth). sisters of the said John Wedderburn of Idvies, (4) the nearest and lawful heirs of the said Grizell Wedderburn of Wedderburn : the eldest heir female and the heirs of her body always succeeding without division. the right of primogeniture applying among the heirs female as among the heirs male, and under the provisions contained in a deed of entail made by Mrs. Grizell Wedderburn of Wedderburn (31 July 1766) and recorded in the Books of Session (19 Aug. 1766),[1] providing (*inter alia*) that all the heirs succeeding shall at once assume, use, and bear the surname and designation of Wedderburn of Wedderburn and no other, and use the arms used by the said Mrs Grizell and no other. (XXVIII, 41.)

[See, in all, s. :—I (1660-64. 21, 23, 72. 245, 255, 257, 297, 300, 301, 302, 316, 352, 359, 368. II (1664-65), 2, 9, 66, 234, 273. 298, 344. 360, 375-76. III (1666-68', 2, 4, 5, 24, 41, 48, 76. 81, 97, 307. IV (1668-72), 2, 182. 209. 413, 434, 451, 462. V (1672-75), 50, 121. 179, 181, 198, 201, 276, 369. VI (1676-78), 160, 216, 385. VII (1678-85), 50, 178, 344, 423. VIII (1685-92), 28, 111. IX (1692-98), 26, 43. 436, 461. X (1898-1704), 164, 165, 500 552, 625, 640, 652. XI (1704 9), 13, 118, 129, 134, 148, 163, 166, 171, 173, 205, 247. 291, 304-5, 322, 327. XII (1709-16), 22, 117. 118, 144, 318. 336, 409, 474, 487. XIII (1716-25), 29, 47, 132, 211. 218, 241, 306, 442, 456, 497, 557, 558. XIV (1725-33), 18, 112, 120, 131, 192, 223, 232, 259, 261. XV (1733-41', 81, 104-6, 298, 306, 329, 347, 394, 431, 543, and (1740-80)s, XVI, 32, 151, 155, 155, 208, 322, 554. XVII, 285, 299, 302. XVIII, 145, 487, 517. XIX, 100, 321, 468. XX, 184. XXI, 333. XXII, 516. XXV, 202, 506. XXVII, 41.]

[1] Register of Deeds, Durie's Office, Vol. 205, part 2.]

THE REGISTER OF DEEDS.

Register of Deeds. This is a register of bonds, contracts, &c., recorded in the Books of Council and Session. It is in two parts—(*a*) 1554—1659, (*b*) 1661—1811, of which the first is recorded by five different keepers, Scott (1554—1639), Hay (1605-34), Gibson (1611-48), Brown (1652-58), and Downie (1653-59), while the second is after the division of the record into three different offices, all co-temporaneous (1661—1811), and known, from the names of their first keepers, as the Mackenzie, Dalrymple, and Durie Offices. The whole of this record has been searched, first in the minute book or index and then in the record, and I give below notes of every Wedderburn entry found in it. This involves a good deal of repetition, but I prefer to give the complete result, partly because the labour of searching has been considerable, and partly because, as in the case of the General Register of Sasines, it is interesting to note that every entry, with only eight exceptions,[1] refers to members of the Forfarshire family alone.

I have arranged the entries in order of date, instead of dealing with each of the offices separately, which would have involved repeatedly going back to dates already passed.

The following abbreviations, Scott (Sc.), Hay (H.), Gibson (G.), Brown (Br.), Downie (Dow.), Mackenzie (Mac.), Dalrymple (Dal.), Durie (Dur.), are used to show to which of the several offices each of the extracts belongs, and at the end of these extracts from the "Register of Deeds" will be found a table classifying the entries according to the different offices.

1. **1586.** April 11.—Discharge (12 Feb. 1585) by Robert Wedderburn, son to umquhile Alexander Wedderburn, clerk of Dundee, with consent of Peter and Robert Wedderburn, his curators, in favour of Mr Alexander Wedderburn, now clerk of Dundee, his brother german, of a certain @-rent out of a North Argylegate tenement, now pertaining to the said Mr. Alexander, lying on the east of Mr. Alexander's close, called the Greneland. Dated at Dundee.[2] (Sc. 21.)

2. **1593.** June 5.—Bond (8 April 1593) by William Man, younger, to Robert Wedderburn, younger, burgess of Dundee, for £1 10s. stg. for each of 5 pocks of wade. Dated at Ritchmont. (Sc. 44.)

3. **1593.** June 5.—Contract (7 Dec. 1592) between William Man, younger, and Robert Wedderburn, younger, son, &c. (as in No. 1), whereby for £500 the said William Man binds himself to pay the said Robert Wedderburn £80 stg., bearing the hazard of conveying certain goods "that shall happen to be coft by the said William Man from Tees River in England to the Isle of Walker in Zetland." Mr. Alexander Wedderburn, clerk of Dundee, is a witness. (Sc. *ib.*)

4. **1593.** July 6.—Bond (31 March 1593) by James Wilson and Patrick Spens of Edinburgh to Robert Wedderburn, merchant, burgess of Dundee, for £1143 7s. 6d. (Sc. *ib.*)

5. **1594.** Aug. 6.—Bond (29 Jan. 1593) by James Wilson and Robert Tod of Edinburgh to the same, for £300. Dated at Edinburgh. (Sc. *ib.*)

---

[1] These exceptions are as follows : (*a*) No. 16 relating to John and Robert Wedderburn in Dirleton (co. Haddington) in 1616 ; (*b*) No. 23 to a Robert Wedderburn in S. Meddens (co. Ayr ?) and his wife Agnes Harper, 1607 ; (*c*) No. 54 to Thomas Wedderburn in Sorn (co. Ayr) and Robert Wedderburn "above the bray " ; (*d*) No. 182 to Peter Weatherburn in Edinburgh. 1683 (see note to No. 182) ; (*e*) No. 339 to James Wedderburn in Coldingham (co. Berwick) 1739 (son and grandson of his namesakes there in 1632-34, 1653, and 1661, see ante s. Gen. Reg. Sas., Nos. 10, 13, 15, 19, 25, and 31) ; (*f*) Nos. 338, 345 to John Wedderburn, merchant in Budal (co. Northumberland) 1741 ; and (*g*) No. 368 to John Wedderburn, formerly of Greenfield (co. Lanark ?) and then (1714) of Hankey, co. Northumberland.

[2] The first date given is the date of registration, while the date in brackets after the description of the document is that of the bond, discharge, &c., itself. Except where otherwise noted, it may be taken that all the documents throughout this register are dated at Dundee. There is an earlier reference in the Minute Book to the Scott record, viz. "1557. July 13.—Bond James Johnstoun of Elphingstoun to Wedderburne," which refers, however, to the Homes of Wedderburn.

6. **1600.** The Minute Book has two references to the record (Scott's office) which are not to be found in the record itself, viz. :—1600. Oct. 3.—Obligation Wedderburn to Goldman ; Dec. 17.—Duncan *v.* Wedderburne.[1] *Register of Deeds.*

7. **1603.** Feb. 28.—Contract (16 March 1597) between Mr. Alexander Wedderburn, clerk of Dundee, and Helen Ramsay, his spouse, on the one part, and William Davidson, younger, burgess of Dundee, and Janet Wedderburn, his spouse, on the other, whereby Mr. Alexander Wedderburn is bound to infeft the said William Davidson and Janet Wedderburn in a lodging on the east of the Greneland. Patrick Wedderburn and Robert Wedderburn, elder, witnesses. (Sc. 92.)

8. **1603.** April 5.—The following entry occurs in the Minute Book (Scott's office), but is not to be found in the record :—Obligation Wedderburne to Turnbull.

9. **1603.** Sept. 2.—Obligation (11 Nov. 1602) Patrick Spens and his wife to David Wedderburn, burgess of Dundee, for £200. (Se. 96.)

10. **1605.** Feb. 12.—Contract (1 Aug. 1604) between Dr. David Kinloch (son and heir of the late John Kinloch, merchant, burgess of Dundee, and oy and heir to the late William Kinloch, merchant, burgess there), and Peter Wedderburn, elder, burgess there, and Peter Wedderburn, his son and apparent heir, by Margaret Kinloch, his wife, daughter of the said William Kinloch, with consent of Robert Wedderburn, notary, Mr. Alexander Wedderburn, clerk of Dundee, &c., as cautioners for the said Peter Wedderburn, younger, whereby the said Peter Wedderburns, elder and younger, renounce a certain yard bounded south-east by the land of David Wedderburn, and west by that of Patrick Wedderburn, &c., &c. (Se. 106.)

11. **1605.** April 2.—Bond (dated at Edinburgh, 10 May 1600) by John Wedderburn, son to Alexander Wedderburn, burgess of Cupar in Fife, to John Arnot, tailor of Edinburgh, for 200 merks. (H. 104.)

12. **1605.** May 3.—Bond (25 May, 1602) by William Rollok and others, to David Wedderburn, merchant, burgess of Dundee, for £500. (Se. 107.)

13. **1605.** June 22.—Bond (8 Jan. 1605) by Robert Erskene in Logy, to Robert Wedderburn, younger, burgess of Dundee, for £30 scots. (H. 109.)

14. **1605.** July 22.—Bond (18 Aug. 1604) by David, master of Crawford, to Robert Wedderburn, younger, burgess of Dundee, for £270. (Se. 112.)

15. **1605.** Aug. 24.—Bond (12 Jan. 1605) by James Hay of Fithie, to the same for £195. (Se. 112.)[2]

16. **1606.** (*a*) Nov. 17.—Bond (dated at Gulane 28 May) by John Wedderburn in Dirltoun to George Livingstone, brother of Patrick Livingstone of Salteoats, for £165. (*b*) Nov. 21.—Bond (dated at Archerfield 31 Oct.) by Robert Wedderburn in Dirltoun, to Mr. Patrick Forrest of Archerfield, advocate, for £100. (H. 125.)[3]

17. **1608.** July 14.—Bond (23 Sept. 1607) by John, son to umquhill David Tyrie of Drumkilbo, and another, to Robert Wedderburn, younger, burgess of Dundee, for £24 12s. (Se. 150.)[4]

---

[1] Another entry (Scott's office), 1602, Dec. 15, contract, Innerwick to Wedderburne, relates to the Homes of Wedderburne.

[2] The Minute Book also gives two other references to the Hay register :—1606. June 23.—L. Mandersoue to Wedderburn. Nov. 12.—Obligation Arnot to L. Wedderburn. Both of these, however, refer to Home of Wedderburn.

[3] The Minute Book has the following references to Hay's register :—1609. June 3.—Obligation Laynge to Wedderburn. July 22.—Obligation Boig to Wedderburn. 1610. July 25.—Disposition Dundas to L. Wedderburn. All of these, again, refer to Home of Wedderburn.

[4] The minute book has a reference to Scott's office, 1607, May 28, Contract twixt Wedderburne and Polmout, which refers to the Homes of Wedderburne.

3 G

18. **1608.** July 14.—Bond (19 April, 1608) by George Seton of Parbroath, to the same for £46. (Sc. 150.)

19. **1609.** June 6.—Bond (July—Oct. 1608) by David Maull of Both, commissary of S. Andrew's, and David Lindsay, fiar of Kynnettels, and Alexander Lindsay of Pittarlie, as cautioners, to Alexander and David Wedderburn, burgesses of Dundee, his cautioners, in 500 merks due by bond granted by him to Peter, brother to William Blair of Balgillo, and another, 26 June 1608. Mr. Alexander Wedderburn, apparent of Kyngany, is witness. Dated at S. Andrew's and Moneky. (Sc. 161.)

20. **1609** June 26.—Bond (16 April 1609) by David, Earl of Crawford, and his spouse to Robert Wedderburn, younger, merchant, burgess of Dundee, for £1020. Written and witnessed by Mr. James Wedderburn, son to umquhill John Wedderburn, burgess of Dundee. (Sc. 161.)

21. **1609.** (*a*) Aug. 11.—Contract of marriage (—— 1608) between Margaret Goldman (daughter of Margaret Jak and the late James Goldman, burgess of Dundee), and Mr. James Wedderburn, second lawful son of Mr. Alexander Wedderburn, common clerk of Dundee, and Helen Ramsay, his spouse, whereby the said Mr. Alexander is bound to infeft his said son and the said Margaret Goldman, in a North Kirkwynd tenement, in Dundee. William Wedderburn, lawful son to the said Mr. Alexander is mentioned. (Sc. 164.) (*b*) Discharge (21 July 1609), by Mr. James Wedderburn. and his said wife, to the said Margaret Jak, of the tocher of 5,000 merks due under the said contract.. Peter Wedderburn is a witness. (*ib.*)

22. **1610.** Aug. 13.—Bond (16 Dec. 1609) by John New and Robert Wedderburn, younger, merchant, burgess of Dundee. (H. 176.)

23. **1610.** Sept 14.—Bond (Kilmarnock, 20 July 1607) by Robert Wedderburn in S. Meddens, and Agnes Harper, spouses, to Robert Harper in Unthank, for 50 merks. (H.176.)
     I have not identified " Saint Meddens," which may be the name of a small farm. Unthank is a common place-name in Scotland. There is one such place in the barony of Glengarnock, parish of Kilbirny, co. Ayr. See post No. 54 for other mentions of the name of Wedderburn in that county.

24. **1610.** Sept. 26.—Bond (1 June 1607) by James Forret, fiar of that ilk, to Alexander Wedderburn, merchant, burgess of Couper, for 800 merks. Dated at Couper. (Sc. 175.)

25. **1611.** April 18.—Discharge (14 Aug. 1609) by Janet Wedderburn, wife of William Davidson, younger, merchant, burgess of Dundee, to James Mudie and others, tutors to Robert and Margaret, children of umquhill George Bultie, for 200 merks, in part payment of 500 merks contained in the confirmed testament of the said George Bultie. (Sc. 183.)

26. **1611.** June 20.—Bond (27 May 1610) by William Davidson, younger, and another to James Wedderburn, merchant, burgess of Dundee, and Cristian Lowell, his wife. (G.184.)

27. **1611.** Aug. 29.—Bond (12 Jan. 1605) by William Blacadder to Alexander Wedderburn, burgess of Couper, for £80. Dated at Couper, (Sc. 187.)

28. **1611.** Oct. 10.—Bond (13 April 1611) by Patrick Wedderburn and Alexander Wedderburn, his eldest son, merchants, burgesses of Dundee, to Alexander Hering for 1,000 merks. Adam Wedderburn, son to the said Patrick, is a witness. (H. 189.)

29. **1611.** Nov. 8.—Bond (15 May 1611) by Patrick Wedderburn, merchant, burgess of Dundee, to Patrick Quhittit. Adam Wedderburn, son of the grantor, witness. (G.188.)

30. **1612.** Jan. 16.—Bond (12 Sept. 1611) by Alexander Wedderburn, merchant, burgess of Dundee, and another to Andrew Muresone. (G. 191.)

31. **1612.** June 22.—Bond (1 June 1607) by Andrew Moncur and others to William Duncan, chirurgian burgess of Dundee, and Catharine Wedderburne, his wife. Mr. Alexander Wedderburn, clerk of Dundee, and David Wedderburn are witnesses. (G. 193.)

32. **1612.** June 23.—Interdiction (14 April) *v.* Alexander, son and heir of the late Peter **Register** Clayhills, merchant, burgess of Dundee, restraining him from parting with his estates, **of Deeds.** &c., without the consent of Mr. Alexander Wedderburn, clerk of Dundee, and Mr. Alexander Wedderburn, his son, and others. (H. 197.)

33. **1612.** June 23.—Bond (3 June 1609) by Peter Hay of Kirkland and two others, his cautioners, to Margaret Wedderburn, relict of Peter Clayhills, bailie of Dundee, for 1,000 merks. (H. 197.)

34. **1612.** Oct. 1.—Bond (2 June 1612) by Patrick Wedderburn, merchant, burgess of Dundee, and Alexander Wedderburn, merchant, burgess thereof, to Alexander Hering. Adam Wedderburn, merchant. is a witness. (G. 198.) There is a similar bond registered 4 Nov. 1612. (G. 203.)

35. **1612.** Oct. 14.—Discharge (14 July, 1610), by Catharine Wedderburn, relict of William Duncan, chirurgian, burgess of Dundee. with consent of Mr. William Ferguson, bailie of Dundee, now her spouse, and others, tutors to the children of the said William Duncan, in favour of William Auchinlek of Woodhill. (G. 198.)

36. **1613.** March 5.—Bond (23 May, 1610) by Henry Philip to Alexander Wedderburn, burgess of Cowper, for 100 merks. Dated at Cowper. (Sc. 207.)

37. **1613.** June 10.—Bond (21 May, 1609) by Andrew Gray of Lowre and others to Catherine Wedderburn, relict of William Duncan, chirurgian, burgess of Dundee. Peter Wedderburn is a witness. (G. 210.)

38. **1613.** Aug. 24.—Bond (28 April) by Alexander Wedderburn, merchant burgess of Dundee, to James Walker there, for £180. (H. 213.)

39. **1613.** Sept. 24.—Bond (30 April. 1613) by Patrick Wedderburn, merchant burgess of Dundee, to James Fethie. Witnessed by David Wedderburn and Alexander Wedderburn. (G. 214.)

40. **1613.** Dec. 22.—Three bonds (31 Dec., 1612, 15 Jan., 26 July, 1613). two by Andrew Cowie, and one by Alexander Ranken, both burgesses of Dundee, to Mr. David Wedderburn, merchant, burgess there. (G. 217.) A similar bond (12 Feb. 1614) by Alexander Ranken to David Wedderburn is registered 23 June 1614. (G. 224.)

41. **1614.** Jan. 8.—Bond (21 July 1610) by Patrick Wedderburn, Alexander Wedderburn, his son, and Robert Baltic, merchants, burgesses of Dundee, to Katharine Wedderburn, relict of William Duncan, and Mr. William Ferguson, bailie of Dundee, her spouse, and failing her to James Duncan, her lawful son. (G. 217.)

42. **1614.** Jan. 18.—Bond (3 Aug. 1612) by Mr. Thomas Lyon and others to Mr. Alexander Wedderburn, clerk of Dundee, for 1,200 merks. (Sc. 220.)

43. **1614.** (*a*) Jan. 22.—Bond (6 July 1613) by Alexander Wedderburn, merchant, burgess of Dundee, to Alexander Hering there, for £200. (H. 219.) (*b*) Feb. 10.— Bond (dated at Campheir 24 July 1612) by the same to Neill Kae, factor in Campheir, for £96 16s. " great Fleming's money," &c. (*ib.*) (*c*) Bond (20 Aug. 1613) by the same to the said Alexander Hering for £319 12s. (*ib.*) (*d*.) March 2.—Bond (10 Sept. 1613) by the same to Thomas Chalmers of Edinburgh. (*ib.*)

44. **1614.** June 24.—Discharge (of this date) by Mr. James Home, minister at Dunbar, to Mr. Alexander Gibson, clerk of Session, and Mr. Alexander Wedderburn, clerk of Dundee, cautioners for George Ramsay of Dalindrynocht, for 700 merks. Dated at Edinburgh. (G. 224.)

45. **1614.** Sept. 2.—Bond (9 Feb.) by Patrick Wedderburn, merchant, burgess of Dundee, to Alexander Hering for £168. (H. 228.)

46. **1614.** Nov. 16.—Bond (25 May 1614) by John Walwood and John Myrtown, citizens of S. Andrew's, to Alexander Wedderburn of Pittormy. Dated at S. Andrew's. (G.227.)
This is wrongly entered in the Minute Book as " Obligation Wedderburn to Milwoodie."

47. **1615.** Jan. 4.—Bond (Perth, 17 Aug. 1614) by Marjorie Matthew, relict of Henry Mony-penny of Perth, to Mr. David Wedderburn, merchant, burgess of Dundee. (H. 231.)

48. **1615.** Jan. 9.—Bond (Edinburgh, 21 Aug. 1614) by Alexander Wedderburn, merchant, burgess of Dundee, to Gilbert Williamson of Edinburgh for 370 merks. (H. 231.)

49. **1615.** Feb. 20.—Bond (23 Aug. 1614) by David Ramsay, burgess of Forfar, and another, to Mr. David Wedderburn, merchant, burgess of Dundee, for £60. (G. 234.)

50. **1615.** May 12.—Bond (2 July, 10 Aug. 1612) by Patrick Wedderburn, merchant, and Alexander and Adam Wedderburn, merchants, and Alexander Halyburton, mariner, all burgesses of Dundee, as cautioners, to Mr. Alexander Wedderburn, clerk thereof. Mr. James Wedderburn, son to the clerk, is a witness. (G. 234.)

51. **1615.** May 12.—Bond (25 May 1607) by Patrick Wedderburn, merchant, burgess of Dundee, and Alexander Wedderburn, his son and apparent heir, to Mr. James Fotheringhame, person of Ballumbie, for himself, and in name of his " oye " Magdalene Serymgeour, daughter of John Serymgeour of Kirktoun, for 500 merks to be paid to the said Mr. James, or, in event of his death, to the said Magdalene " to help her to an honest marriage " to be concluded with the advice of her father, his brother Gilbert Serymgeour, Thomas Fotheringhame of Powrie, John Serymgeour, apparent of Dudope, and Sir William Grahame of Ballergous. Adam Wedderburn, son to the said Patrick, is a witness. (G. 234.)

52. **1615.** May 18.—Bond (8 July 1614) by Alexander Wedderburn and Robert Auchinleck, merchants, burgesses of Dundee, to William Godfrey, merchant tailor in London, for £28 14s. scots. (Sc. 235.)

53. **1615.** Oct. 15.—Mr. Alexander Wedderburn and Mr. James Wedderburn, lawful sons to Mr. Alexander Wedderburn, clerk of Dundee, are witnesses to a contract betwixt Fletcher and Drummond. (Sc. 237.)

54. **1615.** Nov. 22.—Contract (29 Oct. 1613) between Alexander Hamilton and others on the one part, and Thomas Wedderburn in Sorne and Robert Wedderburn " above the bray " on the other part, whereby the 20s land of Ladytoun, parish of Loudoun, and bailliary of Cuningham, is set in tack to the said Thomas and Robert. Dated at Kilmarnock (co. Ayr). George Wodburne in Auldtoun of Libertoun is a witness. (Sc. 241.)
Sorn is in co. Ayr, and Libertoun may be the parish of that name in co. Lanark.

55. **1616.** June 3.—Bond (30 May 1615) by George Straquhan and another, to James Wedderburn, merchant, burgess of Dundee, and Christian Luif (*sic*), his spouse, for 500 merks. (G. 250.)

56. **1616.** June 5.—Bond (15 May 1611) by Patrick Wedderburn and Alexander Wedder-burn, his son and apparent heir, merchants, and David Smairt, skipper, burgesses of Dundee, to James Rankene in Carnustie, for 1,000 merks (G. 250.)
The Minute Book gives the date of registration as June 25. This bond is referred to ante, s. Burgh Records, Dundee Deeds. No. 1.

57. **1616.** Nov. 19.—Contract (15 and 16 May 1610) between Patrick Dudingstone, portioner in Radernie (and others), with consent of James Balfour of Piteullo, and Alexander Wedderburn, burgess of Cupar, reciting a contract between them, dated 27 and 28 March 1610, whereby the lands of Pittormie were sold to the said Alexander Wedderburn, who is now newly infeft therein. Dated at Cupar and Radernie. (H. 255).
This is wrongly entered in the Minute Book as " Contract *Davidsone* to Wedderburn."

58. **1617.** Jan. 13.—Bond (28 May 1605) by Patrick Wedderburn, merchant, burgess
of Dundee, and Alexander Wedderburn his son, to Archibald Campbell, now of
Persie, for 400 merks. (Se. 257.)

59. **1617.** Jan. 15.—Renunciation (21 Dec. 1616) by Mr. Alexander Wedderburn,
common clerk of Dundee, to William Tyrie of Drumkilbo, of 500 merks, for the
redemption of the lands of Loggine-gill, &c., in the parish of Megill, eo Perth.
(Se. 257.)

60. **1617.** (a) Feb. 3.—Bond (dated at Perth, 26 June 1616) by Alexander Wedderburn,
merchant, burgess of Dundee, to Henry Douglas, burgess of Dunfermling, and
another. (G. 256.) (b) May 18.—Bond (10 May 1617) by Thomas Leutron, bailie
of S. Andrew's, to Alexander Wedderburn, merchant, burgess of Dundee, for
725 merks. (G. 260.)

61. **1618.** March 24.—Bond (21 Nov. 1611) by Patrick Wedderburn and his son
Alexander, both merchants, burgesses of Dundee, to James Halyburton of Piteur
for 300 merks. (H. 270.)

62. **1618.** (a) April 17.—Bond (3 July 1617) by Andrew Rollok, in Dundee, to Mr.
David Wedderburn, burgess thereof, for 100 merks. John Wedderburn, also burgess
thereof, is a witness. (H. 270.) (b) April 17.—Bond (dated at Perth, Nov. 1616) by
Common Schill, chirurgion, burgess of Perth, to the same. (ib.) (c) June 2.—Bond
(4 March 1618) by John Stevenson of Dundee to the same. David Wedderburn,
burgess of Dundee, is a witness. (H. 273.) (d) June 9.—Bond (2 Aug. 1617) by the
said Mr. David Wedderburn to William Halyburton. (ib.)

63. **1618.** Jan. 29.—Bond (15 Nov. 1615) by Hew Smith in New Milne and another to
Mr. Alexander Wedderburn, clerk of Dundee, for 200 merks, and also to Mr. William
Wedderburn, minister of Dundee, for certain victual for the ferms of the east half
of Over Logie Megill for the year 1616. (Se. 267.)
This is erroneously noted in the Minute Book as " *Tayt* to Wedderburn."

64. **1618.** June 9.—Ratification (28 May 1618) by Mr. Alexander Wedderburn, common
clerk of Dundee, of an alienation by David, Lord Scone, to Mr. Peter Hay of
Durdie, of the lands of Friertoun, in the barony of Drumduff, eo. Fife. Mr. James
Wedderburn, lawful son to the said Alexander Wedderburn, is a witness. (Se. 274.)

65. **1619.** (a) Jan. 26.—Bond (10 July 1616) by Alexander Wedderburn, merchant,
burgess in Dundee, to John Smith *alias* Melvill, at the mill of Pettie, shire of Forfar,
for £42. (H. 280.) (b) Similar bond (29 Oct. 1616) for 200 merks. (ib.)
Of these (a) is wrongly entered in the Minute Book, as " Obligation Meldrum to Wedderburn."

66. **1619.** Feb. 27.—Bond (dated at Dysart, 12 Jan. 1618) by Alexander Keith to
Janet Wedderburn, relict of William Davidson, burgess of Dundee. (H. 282.)

67. **1619.** July 31 —Bond (26 Feb.) by Alexander Innes, in the shire of Moray, and
Janet Wedderburn, his spouse, to John Wedderburn, merchant, burgess of Dundee,
for £134 10s. David Wedderburn and Edward Frissell are cautioners for the
grantors. (H. 285.)

68. **1620.** (a) Jan. 25 —Bond (dated at Bruntisland, 14 Sept. 1619) by Robert Skene to
Mr. David Wedderburn, indweller in Bruntisland, for 100 merks. (H. 292.) (b) Discharge (9 May 1618), by Robert Alison to Mr. David Wedderburn, burgess of Dundee,
in respect of a pair of pistols. (H. 296.) (c) Bond (1613-14), by Alexander Wedderburn, merchant, burgess of Dundee, and another, to Rodger Bowar. (H. 299.)

69. **1620.** Jan. 28.—Translation (21 March 1614), by Mr. James Wedderburn, lawful
son to Alexander Wedderburn, clerk of Dundee, to Charles Goldman, of certain sums
of money. The said clerk and Peter Wedderburn, his son, are witnesses. (G. 293.)

70.   **1621**. Feb. 27.—Bond (dated at Bruntisland, 13 Aug. 1619) by John Moydert of Electerune, captain of Clan Ronald, to Mr. David Wedderburn, merchant, burgess of Dundee, now indweller in Bruntisland, for 80 double ells of fine small plaiding or else £80 Scots. (II. 305.)

71.   **1621**. June 9.—Bond (16 May 1619) by James Forret to Alexander Wedderburn, mariner, burgess of Dundee, and Janet Newtoun, his spouse, to infeft them in an @-rent of 100 merks furth of his best lands. (H. 209.)

72.   **1622**. April 19.—Bond (dated at Edinburgh 23 Nov. 1620) by John Ker of Jedburgh to Alexander Wedderburn of Kinkeny (*sic*), clerk of Dundee, for 4,000 merks. (H. 321.)

73.   **1622**. May 22.—Bond (10 and 14 Dec. 1620) by John Ker in Inglistoun of Essie to Mr. James Wedderburn, son to Mr. Alexander Wedderburn, clerk of Dundee, for 100 merks. (H. 321.)

74.   **1622**. July 4.—Bond (3 June 1610) by John Stirling of Easter Brekie to Peter Wedderburn, younger, merchant, burgess of Dundee, and Helen Lovell, his spouse, for 1,000 merks. Written and witnessed by Mr. James Wedderburn, son of Mr. Alexander Wedderburn, clerk of Dundee. (H. 325.)

75.   **1622**. Oct. 28.—Bond (25 May 1618) by James Ramsay of Arilbekie, and others to Mr. James Wedderburn (son of Mr. Alexander Wedderburn, clerk of Dundee), and Margaret Goldman, his wife, for 500 merks. (Sc. 328.)

76.   **1623**. April 16.—Bond (29 May 1619) by Robert Kyd in Murrois to Mr. Alexander Wedderburn, younger, fiar of Kingany, for 600 merks. Written by Thomas Fyfe, servitor to Mr. Alexander Wedderburn, elder, clerk of Dundee. David Wedderburn, notary public, is notary. (H. 337.)

77.   **1623**. July 16.—Renunciation (31 Jan. 1615) by John Wedderburn to Alexander Wedderburn of Pittormie, his father, of the fee of the lands of Pittormie, in the regality of S. Andrew's and shire of Fife, in which he was infeft by his said father on 1 Sept. 1601. Dated at Coupar. (Sc. 342.)

78.   **1623**. July 28.—(a) Bond (dated at Bruntisland 1 Nov. 1621) by Martin Wallace, burgess of Kinghorne, to Mr. David Wedderburn in Bruntisland for £20. (H. 344.) (*b*) Bond (dated at Bruntisland 14 Sept. 1622) by John Scott and Andrew Scott, his only son and heir, both burgesses in Bruntisland, to the same for £20. (*ib.*)

79.   **1623**. Sept. 24.—Bond (8 June 1617) by David Skirling and others to James Wedderburn, merchant, burgess of Dundee, for 300 merks. (H. 347.)

80.   **1623**. Nov. 4.—Bond (14 Aug. 1619) by David Kyd in Kingeny (son of Robert Kyd in Murhous) to Mr. Alexander Wedderburn, clerk of Dundee, for 100 merks. (II. 349.)

81.   **1623**. Dec. 3.—Bond (dated at Leith 29 Sept.) by John Murray in Leith to Mr. David Wedderburn, burgess of Burntisland, for 600 merks. (H. 351.)

82.   **1624**. Jan. 1.—Bond (11 May 1623) by Mr. David Wedderburn, merchant, burgess of Dundee, now resident in Bruntisland, to John Richie. Dated at Edinburgh. (G. 352.)[1]

83.   **1624**. (a) June 5.—Bond (10 Nov. 1618) by Sir George Keith of Wodstone, Knt., and others, his cautioners, to Mr. Alexander Wedderburn, younger, fiar of Kingany, for 1,000 merks. (360.)—(*b*) Bond (20 and 24 July 1620), by the same to Magdalene Wedderburn, relict of Mr. William Wedderburn, one of the ministers of Dundee, for 300 merks. (II. 351.)

---

[1] The Minute Book has a Home of Wedderburn reference, "3 Nov. 1624. Obligation Edmaston to Wedderburne."

81. **1624.** July 14.—Discharge (1 July 1622) by Mr. Alexander Wedderburn of Kingany, clerk of Dundee, to Walter, Earl of Buccleuch, Sir John Preston of Pennycuik, and others, of 4,000 merks. Written by Mr. James Wedderburn, son to the grantor. (H. 362.)

85. **1625.** Sept. 14.—Bond (1 Nov. 1616) by John Lyon of Auldbar, and another, to Mr. David Wedderburn, merchant, burgess of Dundee, for £60. (H. 364.)

86. **1625.** June 26.—Bond (17 Nov. 1622) by Alexander Ramsay, fiar of Arberkie, and others, to Mr. James Wedderburn, son to Mr. Alexander Wedderburn, clerk of Dundee, for 525 merks. (H. 370.)

87. **1625.** May 4.—Bond (15 Sept. 1623) by Peter Wedderburn and Alexander Wedderburn, younger, merchants, burgesses of Dundee, as principals, with Mr. Alexander Wedderburn, younger, and Mr. James Wedderburn (sons to Mr. Alexander Wedderburn, clerk of Dundee), and Thomas Halyburton, younger, merchant, burgess thereof, as cautioners, to James Chrystie in Ademstoun, in name of his daughter, Margaret Chrystie, for £410. (H. 371.)

88. **1625.** June 30.—Two bonds (1620), one by David Lindsay of Balgarveis, the other by William Ochterlony of Cairny, in favour of Mr. Alexander Wedderburn of Kingany, clerk of Dundee. (G. 373.)

89. **1626.** July 28.—Two bonds (1624, 1626) in favour of Mr. David Wedderburn, burgess of Bruntisland. (G. 385.)

90. **1628.** Jan. 30.—Discharge (30 May 1626) by Alexander Guthrie, apparent of Kincaldrum, to Mr. Alexander Wedderburn, apparent of Kingany, one of the bailies and dean of guild of Dundee, for 4,200 merks, due by bond. (H. 404.)

91. **1628.** July 9.—Bond (dated at Airdrie 26 Sept. 1626) by Robert Turnbull of Bogmilne and Sir John Prestoun of Airdrie, his cautioner, to Elizabeth, daughter to the late Mr. Alexander Wedderburn of Kingany, clerk of Dundee, for 575 merks. (H. 407.)

92. **1629.** Feb. 18.—Bond (13 May 1619) by Andrew and James Moncur, brothers german, to Mr. Alexander Wedderburn, fiar of Kingany. (G. 414.)

93. **1629.** June 16.—Bond (22 Sept. 1628) by William Wedderburn, merchant, burgess of Dundee, and Jean Pierson, his wife, to Henry Guthrie for 600 merks. (Sc. 416.)

94. **1629.** July 3.—Bond (dated at Downymilne, Monckie, Forfar, and Dundee in March and April 1627) by Alexander Lindsay of Pitterlie and others, his cautioners, to Euphame Wedderburn, relict of Archibald Blyith, of Dundee, for 697 merks. (H. 418.)

95. **1629.** July 18.—Action by umquhile Andrew Wedderburn, only bairn and executor of umquhile Mr. David Wedderburn, burgess of Barntisland, and his tutors, against William Forbes, son and heir to umquhile William Forbes of Craigievar, for the registration of a bond (2 Sept. 1626) by Sir Donald McKye and the said deceased William Forbes of Craigievar, in favour of the said Mr. David Wedderburn. Registration is decreed. (G. 419.)

96. **1630.** Jan. 27.—Contract (21 Dec. 1626) by Mr. Alexander Wedderburn of Kingany, seting in tack the towns and lands of Kingany to Patrick Quhytheid in Drumgeieht for five years, at 88 bolls victual yearly. David Wedderburn, notary, burgess of Dundee, is a witness. (H. 426.)

97. **1630.** April 8.—Bond (dated at Cupar, 20 June 1626) by Thomas Small and another to Mr. John Wedderburn, one of the regents of S. Leonard's College, S. Andrew's. (H. 428.)

98.   **1630.** July 24.—Discharge (July 23) by William Gibson, merchant, burgess of Glasgow, to Alexander Wedderburn, merchant, burgess of Dundee. Dated at Edinburgh. (G. 433.)

99.   **1630** Nov. 4.—Bond (13 May 1626) by Mr. Alexander Wedderburn of Kingeny, bailie of Dundee, to Mr. John Wedderburn, his brother german, for 1,100 merks. Witnessed by Mr. James Wedderburn, clerk of Dundee, and Peter Wedderburn, brother of the grantor. (H. 436.)

100.   **1631.** June 7, 15.—The Minute Book at these dates contains two references to Gibson's office :—(a) "Factory, Mr. John Wedderburn to Wedderburn" and (b) "Obligation, Wedderburn to Campbell," as to both of which the record is blank.

101.   **1631.** Nov. 18.—Bond (16 Feb 1629) by Dr. James Blair, minister of Lundie, and his cautioners, to James Wedderburn, merchant, burgess of Dundee, and Mr. Alexander Wedderburn of Kynghinie (sic), tutors testamentar to William and Peter Wedderburns, lawful children to umquhile Mr. James Wedderburn, clerk of Dundee. (G. 444.)

102.   **1632** Feb 3.—Bond (5 Dec. 1627) by William Peirson of Dundee to James Wedderburn, merchant, burgess of Dundee, and Christian Lovell, his spouse, for 365 merks. (G. 419.)

103.   **1632.** April 26.—Bond (12 and 21 Jan. 1627) by Thomas Wishart in Bandarge and others to Euphame Wedderburn, relict, &c. (as in No. 94), for 664 merks 10s. (H. 452.) (b) Bond (12 May 1627) by same to same, for 660 merks. (H. 452)

104.   **1632.** May 14.—Bond (1631) by George Lammie of Dunkany, Gilbert Lammie, indweller in Balharrie, Thomas Lyon of Cossins, and others to Elizabeth Wedderburn, relict of Dr. Peter Bruce, principal in S. Leonard's College, S. Andrew's, for 1050 merks. Dated at Balharrie and Cossins 25 and 27 Jan. 1631. (Sc. 450.)

105.   **1632.** June 1.—Bond (31 March 1629) by George Lammie of Dunkany, and others, to James Wedderburn, merchant, burgess of Dundee, and Mr. Alexander Wedderburn of Kingennie (sic) tutors testamentar, &c, as in No. 101. (G. 451.)
       There are similar bonds (1627-29-30) in the same volume, registered 4 June 1632, and in Vol. 456 registered 19 Nov. 1632. In some of them James Wedderburn is designed "dean of gild of Dundee."

106.   **1632** July 25 —Bond (16—17 June 1631) by Sir John Ogilvy of Innerquharitie, as principal, and James, Lord Ogilvy of Airlie, and others, as cautioners, to Katharine Wedderburn, relict of William Duncan, chirurgian, burgess of Dundee, for herself, and in name of William and Mr. James Duncan, her lawful children. Dated at Kirriemuir, Cortaquhie, and Doune. (G. 453.)

107.   **1632.** Aug. 4.—Bond (26 May 1629) by Catharine Wedderburn, relict of Mr. William Ferguson, burgess of Dundee, to Robert Clayhills of Baldovie for 550 merks. (G. 456.)

108.   **1632.** Dec. 4.—Bond (21 and 26 Jan. 1632) by Thomas Blair and others to Bessie Wedderburn, spouse to Robert Murray, burgess of Dundee. (G. 459)

109.   **1632.** Dec. 6.—Bond (8 June 1627) by Agnes Rankene, relict of Thomas Bruntfield, as principal, and Mr. Alexander Wedderburn of Kingany, as cautioner, to James Wedderburn, bailie, of Dundee, for 100 merks. (G. 459.)

110.   **1633.** Nov. 15.—Bond (10 Dec. 1632) by Mr. Thomas Lyoune of Cossins, and others, his cautioners, to Elizabeth Wedderburn, relict of Peter Bruce, sometime principal of S. Leonard's College, S. Andrew's, for 600 merks. Dated at Glamis. (G. 467.)

111.   **1633** Dec. 3.—Bond (17 May, 18 June 1630) by Andrew Halyburton in Ballany, and others, his cautioners, to Elizabeth Wedderburn, youngest lawful daughter of umquhile Mr. Alexander Wedderburn of Kingany, for 550 merks. Dated at Dundee and Drumkilbo. (G. 469.)

112.   **1634.** Jan. 23.—Bond (21 and 22 Sept. 1629) by Andrew Halyburton in Ballany, and others, his cautioners, to Elspet Wedderburn, lawful daughter of Mr. Alexander Wedderburn, for 220 merks. (G. 472.)

113.   **1634.** April 30.—Bond (6 May 1633) by Mr. Alexander Wedderburn, younger, lawful son of umquhill Mr. James Wedderburn, sometime common elerk of Dundee, to Thomas Fyff, notary, for 125 merks. (G. 474.)

114.   **1634.** May 30.—Bond (dated at S. Andrew's, 8 Jan. 1629) by James Durie in S. Andrew's, to Bessie Wedderburn, relict of Mr. Henry Danskene, schoolmaster there for 110 merks. (H. 473.)

115.   **1634.** Oct. 15.—Bond (31 May 1630) by Thomas Small of the Kirkland of Kaitnes, and George Halyburton of the mill of Kaitnes and William Halyburton of Piteur, their cautioner. to Mr. John Wedderburn, one of the Regents of S. Leonard's College, S. Andrew's, for 630 merks. Dated at Piteur. (G. 478.)

116.   **1634.** Nov. 6.—Contract (3 Sept. 1631) between Thomas Aleson and Mr. Archibald Auchinlek, his son in law, for the infeftment of the latter in part of the town and lands of Blackness. Mr. Alexander Wedderburn, elerk of Dundee, is cautioner. (G. 478.)

117.   **1635.** May 25.—Bond (10 July 1630) by Alexander Wedderburn, elder, merehant, burgess of Dundee, to Robert Peterson of Cupar in Fife, for £100. (G. 486.)

118.   **1635** Oct. 24.—Bond (26 Nov., 8 Dec. 1632) by Alexander Guthrie of Kincaldrum, and his cautioners, to Elizabeth Wedderburn, relict of Dr. Peter Bruce, principal of S. Leonard's College, for 525 merks. (G. 489.)[1]

119.   **1636.** Dec. 17.—Action re the summonds raised by Mr. John Wedderburn, sometime regent in S. Andrew's, Mr. Alexander Wedderburn, younger, elerk of Dundee, and another, v. James Halyburton of Piteur, as son and heir to the late William Halyburton thereof, for registration of the bond, ante No. 115. (G. 499.)

120.   **1637.** Jan. 18.—Bond (20 Aug 1636) by James Young and another to John Wedderburn, as agent for Thomas Golladie in Danskein. Dated at Danskein. (G. 501.)

121.   **1637.** Jan. 20 —Discharge (13 June) 1636) by Simon McKenzie of Logstane and his spouse Elizabeth Bruce, daughter of umquhile Dr. Peter Bruce of S. Andrew's, to Elizabeth Wedderburn, relict of the said Dr. Peter Bruce, of half the heirship, goods, &c, belonging to the said Elizabeth Bruce as one of the two daughters and heirs retoured of her said father, and as one of the two sisters german and heirs of the late Helen Bruce. (G. 501.)

122.   **1637.** Jan. 20.—Bond (3 June 1635) by Thomas Halyburton to Alexander Wedderburn, elder, merehant, in Dundee. Witnessed by Andro Wedderburn (G. 501.)

123.   **1637.** Feb. 8.—Discharge (7 June 1636) by Mr. Alexander Wedderburn of Kingennie to James Halyburton of Buttergask and others for 550 merks. Peter Wedderburn, brother's son to the said Mr. Alexander, is a witness. (Se. 503.)

124.   **1637.** Nov. 21.—Bond (Feb. 1637) by Mr. Andrew Lermonth, minister of Libbertoun and his cautioner, to Mr. John Wedderburn, son lawful of umquhile Mr. Alexander Wedderburn, elerk of Dundee, for 1,040 merks. Dated at Edinburgh. (G. 508.)

125.   **1638.** April 20.—Bond (28 April 1630) by Gilbert Wentoun and another to Mr. John Wedderburn, one of the Regents at S. Leonard's College, for 210 merks. (Se. 511.)

[1] The Minute Book has a reference to Gibson's office. " 16 Nov. 1636. Obligation Porteous to Wedderburne," but on searching the record it appears that this is an error for " Porteous to Borrowman."

3 H

126. **1639.** Oct. 1.—Bond (2 July 1639) by Sir John Spottiswood of Dairsie to Mr. James Wedderburn, minister at Auchtermonsie, for £474 3. 4. Dated at Dairsie. (Sc. 523.)[1]

127. **1638.** June 5.—Bond (11 Nov. 1636) by Patrick Jak of Dundee, and his cautioner, to James Wedderburn, merchant, burgess, of Dundee, for £208. (G. 512.)

128. **1638.** June 27.—Discharge (17 April 1638) by Mr. John Wedderburn, son of Mr. Alexander Wedderburn of Kingeny, sometime clerk of Dundee, to Mr. Alexander Wedderburn, younger, his nephew, now clerk of Dundee, and Thomas Wichtan, notar there, factors for the said Mr. John, of their intromissions with his affairs during his absence from Scotland. (G. 512.)

129. **1638.** Oct. 19.—Bond (24 June 1636) by James Elphinstone of Innerdivot, to Mr. Alexander Wedderburn, clerk of Dundee. Dated at Harlasheills. (G. 515.)

130. **1639.** (a) Nov. 21.—Bond (Jan., Feb. 1639) by Patrick Monorgound in Polgavie, to Mr. Alexander Wedderburn, clerk of Dundee. (b) Bond (20 Jan. 1639), by Alexander Spens in Inchmichell, to the same. (c) Bond (June 1638) by Andrew Moncur of Moncur and Knape, to the same. Witnessed by William and Robert Scrymgeour. (d) Bond (13 Sept. 1638) by Patrick Stevenson, to the same. (G. 525.)

131. **1640.** Dec. 18.—Bond (21 May 1635) by John Tyrie in Dunkenye, as principal, and Alexander Tyrie in Nevay, and Patrick Murray in Dundee, as cautioners, to Bessie Wedderburn, relict of Robert Murray, merchant, burgess of Dundee, for 210 merks. (G. 528.)

132. **1641.** Dec. 13.—Discharge (7 Dec. 1641) by Margaret Wedderburn, relict of Robert Halyburton, skipper, burgess of Dundee, and sister german to umquhile James (Wedderburn), Bishop of Dunblane, to Mr. Alexander Wedderburn, clerk of Dundee, of 1,800 merks left her by her said brother. (G. 532.)

133. **1641.** Dec. 13.—Similar discharge (7 Dec. 1641) by Christian Halyburton, daughter of the said Robert and Margaret, to the said clerk, of a like legacy of 1,800 merks left her by her uncle, the said bishop. (G. 532.)

134. **1643-47.** The Minute Book has a reference to Gibson's office "24 Nov. 1643, Regist. Wedderburne to Monorgound," for which the record is blank, and another entry, "5 June 1646. Obligation Wedderburne to Simpson," for which the record is also blank, but adds a note, "Regist of new 17 June 1647," when it is again blank.

135. **1646.** Dec. 8.—Discharge (23 Nov. 1646) by Sir Alexander Wedderburn of Blackness, Knight, tacksman of H.M. Customs and great impost of wines lately within the River Tay, to Alexander Boytter of Dundee, of all dues on wines so imported by him up to 1 Nov. 1645. (G. 560.)

136. **1647-48.** The record of Gibson's office is blank, and there are thus no available particulars of the following references to it in the Minute Book :—**1647.** Jan. 13.—Obligation, Wedderburne to Kynnard. May 14.—Disposition, Thornetonne to Wedderburne. June 17.—Register, Wedderburne to Symsone. July 3.—Obligation, Wedderburne to L. Cowper. Dec. 28.—Discharge, Alison to Wedderburn. **1648.** Feb. 21.—Disposition, Wedderburn to Yeoman. May 5.—Disposition, Boyter to Wedderburne. July 28.—Obligation, Wedderburne to Crichtonne.

---

[1] The Minute Book also contains the following references to Scott's office, all of which relate to Home of Wedderburn :—**1621.** July 25.—Contract, Wedderburne and Home.—**1623.** Jan. 12.—Obligation. Wedderburne to Lady Spence.—**1625.** Dec. 10.—Obligation. Wedderburne to Bell.—**1626.** June 5.—Contract. Wedderburne and Quhyt.—**1627.** April 11.—Obligation, Wedderburne to Hamilton.—**1636.** Jan. 23.—Discharge, L. Wedderburne to L. President.—**1636.** June 6.—Obligation, Wedderburne to Whytelaw.—**1636.** June 6.—Contract, Wedderburne to Whytelaw.—**1639.** April 18.—Obligation L. Wedderburne to Smith.—**1639.** April 18.—Obligation, L. Wedderburne to Smith.

137. **1652.** June 29.—Bond (21 Sept. 1649) by William Bruce in Kaitt, to Alexander **Register of Deeds.**
Wedderburn for £187. (Br. 564.)

138. **1652.** July 30.—Bond (dated at Edinburgh, 8 June 1650) by Sir James Murray of
Skirling, to Mr. Peter Wedderburn, advocate, for 5,000 merks. (Br. 567.)

139. **1653.** May 27.—Bond (12 Nov. (1652) by Bessie Wedderburn, relict of James
Lovell of Kinoquhi, Elizabeth Murray, her daughter, and James Moneur, sometime
fiar of Knap, her husband, to David Campbell, fiar of Keathick, for 8,250 merks.
Alexander Wedderburn of Kingeny, is a witness. (Dow. 582.)

140. **1653.** June 8.—Bond (19 Feb. 1651) by Andrew Wedderburn, merchant, burgess
of Dundee, to James Liddell of Edinburgh for £661. (Br. 583.)

141. **1654.** Feb. 6.—Factory (1 Jan. 1646) by Mr. Alexander Wedderburn of Blackness
to Alexander Bower of Innerightie and his son to uplift the impost on all the
merchandise, &c., imported and transported at Dundee, Perth, Aberbrothock, and all
the ports of the river Tay. (Br. 594.)

142. **1654.** April 14.—Bond (dated at Dudope, 15 June 1650) by John, Viscount Dudope,
Lord Scrymgeour, to Sir Alexander Wedderburn of Blackness, Knt., undertaking to
infeft him in an @-rent of £584 furth of the grantor's best lands. (Dow. 599.)

143. **1654.** April 21.—Submission and decreet arbitral (dated at Edinburgh, 15 April
1654) between Sir William Dick of Braid, Knt., and his son Alexander, and Mr. Peter
Wedderburn, advocate, and Sir Alexander Wedderburn of Blackness, clerk of Dundee,
his brother. The arbiters (David Wilkie and John Jowsie of Edinburgh) decern Sir
Alexander to pay 8,000 merks to the said Alexander Dick. (Dow. 599.)

144. **1654.** (*a*) April 22.—Discharge (Edinburgh, 21 April 1654) by Alexander Bower
of Dundee to Sir Alexander Wedderburn of Blackness and another for 5,000
merks. (Dow. 599.) (*b*) May 27.—Bond (6 Sept. 1652) by John Campbell of Lundie
to the same for £584. (*ib.* 601.)

145. **1654** (*a*) July 5.—Discharge by Sir William Dick of Braid, Knt., to Sir Alexander
Wedderburn of Blackness, clerk of Dundee, of all debts standing between them.
Mr. Peter Wedderburn, advocate, is a witness. Dated at Edinburgh 20 April, and at
London 23 May 1654. (Br. 602.) (*b*) Discharge (dated at London, 23 May 1654) by
same to same of a tack duty of £3,600 for five years, conform to the decreet
arbitral of John Jowsie and David Wilkie, their chosen arbiters. (*ib.*) (*c*) Bond,
dated at London 23 May 1654, by same to same for £1,650. (*ib.*)

146. **1654.** Nov. 2.—Bond (12 Dec. 1635) by Francis Orme and another, to Euphame
Wedderburn, relict of Archibald Blyth, burgess of Dundee. (Dow. 607.)

147. **1654-55.** The Minute Book has two references to Downie's office, as to both of which
the record is blank :—(*a*) 1654. Dec. 18.—Obligation, Wedderburn to Houston.
(*b*) 1655. Feb. 22.—Obligation, Wedderburn to Browne.

148. **1655.** Nov. 23.—Bond (dated at Glamis, 22 Nov. 1647) by Dame Margaret Lambie
to Alexander Wedderburn of Kingeny, for 600 merks. (Dow. 615.)

149. **1655.** Nov. 23.—Bond (14 June 1651) by William Fullertoun of that ilk (and
George, Lord Spynie, as cautioner), to Sir Alexander Wedderburn of Blackness, Knt.,
for 500 merks. (Dow. 615.)

150. **1656.** June 21.—Disposition (1649) by David Lovell (eldest son of the late James
Lovell) of Kinnochey, to Sir Alexander Wedderburn of Blackness, of certain
tenements in Dundee. (Dow. 615.)

Register of Deeds. 151. **1655-58.** There is no record for Brown's office after 1654, and particulars of the following references to it in the Minute Book are not, therefore, available:— 1655. May 5.—Interdiction, Boyter to Wedderburne; Dec. 10.—Obligation, Brown to Wedderburn. 1656 Jan. 29.—Obligation, Lady Wedderburn to Brown; May 29.—Discharge, Rob. Wedderburn to Huison. 1657. April 7.—Obligation, Wedderburne to Boswall. 1658. May 13.—Discharge, Blair to Wedderburn; May 14.—Discharge, Wedderburn to Dougall; May 14.—Discharge, Wedderburn to Foven.

152. **1656-59** There is no record for Downie's office after 13 Feb. 1656, so that particulars of the following references to it in the Minute Book are, again, not available :— 1656. April 21.—Discharge, Erle Annandale to Wedderburn; May 8.—Obligation, Wedderburn to Halfour. 1657. Jan. 12.—Obligation, Wedderburn to Campbell : Feb. 5.—Obligation, Wedderburn to Lightbodie; May 14.—Obligation, Ladie Wedderburn to Browne; June 6.—Obligation, Wedderburn to Bruce; Sept. 30.—Obligation, Wedderburn to Auchterhouse. 1659 March 29.—Contract, Wedderburn and others to Ross; April 19.—Dispensation, Wedderburn to Auchmoutie.

153. **1661.** Nov. 25.—Contract of marriage (1655) between Mr. Andrew Wedderburn, minister at Leiph in Angus, with consent of Mr. James Wedderburn, minister at Moonzie, his father, and Elizabeth, daughter of Andrew Daw, portioner of Sachup, by the late Elizabeth Hamilton, his wife. The bride's tocher is 5,000 merks, and the husband settles a like sum. Dated at the burgh of Craill, 17 and—Jan. 1655. (Dur. 3.)

154. **1661.** Dec. 6.—Bond (6 June 1659) by William Kynnen of Hill to Sir Alexander Wedderburn of Blackness for 200 merks. Dated at Hill. (Mac. 3.)

155. **1662** July 22.—Contract (30 Jan. 1662) between Alexander Wedderburn of Kingany, provost of Dundee, and Henry Gib, for the sale to the latter of 200 bolls oats of the growth of the lands of Kingany. (Dur. 5.)

156. **1662.** Aug. 4.—(a) Disposition (13 Jan. 1650) by Robert Clayhills of Innergowrie to Sir Alexander Wedderburn of Blackness of two eighth parts and two sixths of another eight part of Blackness. (b) Disposition (8 Sept. 1654) by Sir William Auchinlek of Balmanno to the said Sir Alexander of another eighth and another sixth of an eighth part of Blackness. (Dur. 5.)

157. **1662.** Aug. 26.—Bond (12 April 1651) by Andrew Wedderburn, merchant, burgess of Dundee, to Thomas Beg, merchant, burgess of Edinburgh, for £350. (Mac. 6.)

158. **1663.** Jan 8.—Factory (1 Jan. 1646) by Mr. Alexander Wedderburn of Blackness, tacksman of H.M. Customs, to Alexander Bonar, elder and younger of Innerleith, to uplift the same at Dundee, Perth, Aberbrothock, and in the Tay, &c. (Dur. 5.)

159. **1663.** May 23.—Disposition (12 Sept. 1662) by Dougall McPherson to Alexander Wedderburn, elder, of Kingany, Provost of Dundee, of the lands of Easter Powrie. (Mne. 7.)
   See ante s Scrymgeour-Wedderburn Papers, No. 351, where this document is more fully noted.

160. **1663.** June 30.—Bond (Edinburgh, 12 Sept. 1662) by Alexander Wedderburn of Kingany, provost of Dundee, to Dougall McPherson of Easter Powrie, obliging himself to relieve the said Dougall of the payment of 4,400 merks, due by bond granted by the said Dougall to Mr. James Durham, sometime of Easter Powrie. Sir Alexander Wedderburn of Blackness, clerk of Dundee, is a witness. (Dal. 8.)

161. **1663.** July 3.—Bond (26 Nov. 1653) by Alexander Wedderburn of Kingany to Janet Guthrie, relict of Major William Scrymgeour, and Dougall McPherson of Balichroan, now her husband, to relieve the heirs of the said Major of a similar bond. (Dal. 9.)[1]

[1] The Minute Book has the following references to the Dalrymple Office, all of which relate to the Homes of Wedderburn :—**1663.** Sept. 5.—Obligation, Wedderburn to Sempill. **1665.** July 7.—Contract, L. Balfour to L. Wedderburne. **1667.** July 5.—Discharge, L. Wedderburne to Home.

162. **1663.** Sept. 17.—Assignation (7 Jan. 1657) by Dame Magdalene Wedderburn, relict of Sir George Halyburton of Fotherance, Knt., to Marjory Halyburton, and to John Ogilvy of Lowman, now her spouse, of certain annual-rents. Dated at Kathiek. (Mac. 8.)

163. **1664.** Sept. 27.—Bond (Cupar, 18 Jan. 1656) by the Town Council of Cupar to Mr. Alexander Wedderburn, minister of Forgan, for 550 merks. (Dur. 9.)

164. **1665.** March 4.—Agreement (11 Jan. 1664) between Sir Peter Wedderburn of Gosford, Knt., to sell to George Milne and Thomas Bookles the ferme bear due for Lochill and the West Mains of Bancreiff for 1663, and the whole bear of the mains of Gosford, at £7. 12. scots per boll. Dated at Gosford. (Mac. 12.)

165. **1665.** June 23.—Bond (Edinburgh, 12 Sept. 1662) by Alexander Wedderburn of Kingenny, provost of Dundee, to Dougall McPherson of Easter Powrie and Janet Guthrie, his spouse, for 8,000 merks. Sir Alexander Wedderburn of Blackness, clerk of Dundee, is a witness. (Dal. 13.)
  See see s. Private Records, Scrymgeour-Wedderburn Papers, No. 352.

166. **1666.** (*a*) Feb. 15.—Bond (Dudope, 4 June 1664) by John, Earl of Dundee, to Sir Alexander Wedderburn of Blackness for 4,932 merks. Robert Scrimgeour, brother german of the said Earl, is a witness. (Dur. 12.) (*b*) April 25.—Bond by George Gairdine in Logie and another to the said Sir Alexander for £300 scots. John Scrimgeour, merchant in Dundee, is a witness. (*ib.*)
  The name Gairdine is entered in the Minute Book as Gordon.

167. **1666.** July 9.—Discharge (6 July 1666) by Sir Peter Wedderburn of Gosford to James Halyburton of Innerleith and his curators for the annual rent of £80. Dated at Edinburgh (Mac. 16.)

168. **1666.** (*a*) Aug. 6.—Bond (London, 12 May 1663) by James Maxwell of Dirleton to Sir Peter Wedderburn of Gosford for £80 stg. (Dur. 13.) (*b*) Assignation (Edinburgh 14 Oct. 1663) by the said Sir Peter Wedderburn to Sir John Nisbet, now of Dirleton, of the said bond. (*ib.*)

169. **1666** Sept. 28.—Discharge (Edinburgh, 29 Nov. 1661) by Sir Peter Wedderburn of Gosford, Knt., advocate, one of the clerks of session, of 2,000 merks, contained in a bond by the said Sir John to the late John Dickson of Hairtree and by him assigned to Dame Agnes Dickson, spouse of the said Sir Peter, and by her to her said husband. (Dur. 13.)

170. **1666.** Dec. 27.—Assignation (13 June 1666) by George Gardyne in Logie to Sir Alexander Wedderburn of Blackness of the tack, &c. of the crops of Logie and bank of Balgay. (Dur. 14.)

171. **1667.** Nov. 20.—Discharge (Edinburgh, 19 Nov. 1667) by Dame Magdalen Stewart, Lady Reidhouse, with consent of Thomas Hamilton of Reidhouse, her spouse, to Sir Peter Wedderburn of Gosford, of 2,000 merks. (Dur. 17.)

172. **1668.** May 19.—Bond (Edinburgh, 21, 28 July 1668) by Alexander Carnegy of Pitarrow and David Carnegy, fiar thereof, his eldest son, to Alexander Wedderburn of Kingany, elder, for 1,000 merks. (Dal. 22.)

173. **1668.** June 27.—Bond (Edinburgh — July 1665) by David, Viscount Stormont to Sir Peter Wedderburn of Gosford for 19,000 merks. (Dal. 22.)

174. **1668.** Sept. 20.—Pond (Edinburgh, 27 Feb. 1652) by Andrew Wedderburn, merchant, burgess of Dundee, to Thomas Noble, merchant, burgess of Edinburgh. (Dal. 23.)

175. **1668.** (*a*) Nov. 24.—Discharge (1668) by Christian, daughter of the late John Liddell, with consent of Walter and James Stewart, her curators, to Sir Peter

Wedderburn of Gosford, one of the Lords of Session, of letters of inhibition (1657) raised by her *v.* Sir Alexander Auchmoutie sometime of Gosford, and of all actions of reduction in regard to the lands of Gosford acquired by the said Sir Peter from the said Sir Alexander. Dated at Allentoun and Edinburgh 12 and 13 Nov. 1668. (*b*) Discharge (Edinburgh, 19 Nov. 1668) by Mr. Alexander Auchmoutie of Powerhow to the said Sir Peter of an inhibition raised (1650) by him *v.* Patrick Lord Elibank, in regard to the lands of Lochill, disponed by Lord Elibank to Lord Torphichen, and by him to the said Sir Peter. (Dur. 19.)

176.   **1669.** June 11.—Bond (Edinburgh, 31 Dec. 1664 and 3 Feb. 1665) by Sir William Ruthven of Dunglass to Sir Peter Wedderburn of Gosford for 5,000 merks. (Dal. 25.)[1]

177.   **1669.** Aug. 14.—(*a*) Bond (13 Jan. 1669) by James, Earl of Findlater, to Alexander Wedderburn, elder, of Kingany, for himself, Margaret Milne, his spouse, and Peter and Elizabeth Wedderburn, their children, for 2,000 merks. (Mac. 31.) (*b*) Bond (14 Jan. 1669) by the said Earl to the said Alexander Wedderburn for £428 scots. (*ib.*)[2]

178.   **1669.** Nov. 9.—(*a*) Bond (Edinburgh, 21 Feb. 1668) by James Halyburton of Innerleith to Sir Peter Wedderburn of Gosford for 2,500 merks. (*b*) Bond (Edinburgh, 5 March 1669) by the same to the same for £100. (Dal. 26.)

179.   **1672.** July 11.—Bond (Gosford, 19 March 1668) by Janet Steill in Lochill to Sir Peter Wedderburn of Gosford for 960 merks. (Dur. 31.)

180.   **1673.** Jan. 31.—Discharge (Edinburgh, 17 Aug. 1672) by Sir Peter Wedderburn of Gosford to John, Earl of Rothes, High Chancellor of Scotland, and David, Earl of Weinyss, for £5,100. (Dal. 34.)

181.   **1673.** June 12.—Discharge (Edinburgh, 11 June 1673) by Charles Maitland of Hattoun, Lord Treasurer Depute, and a senator of the College of Justice, to Sir Alexander Wedderburn of Blackness, and John Wedderburn, fiar thereof, his son, of all debts, &c., acclaimable by the said Charles, as His Majesty's donator to the last heir, fallen in the King's hands by the late John, Earl of Dundee, his want of male heirs to succeed him. Mr. Peter Wedderburn of Gosford, is a witness. (Dur. 33.)
As to the suggestion of a "want of male heirs" see the account of the Scrymgeours in Vol. i.

182.   **1673.** July 4.—Bond (Kelso, 2 April 1673) by Charles Pott in Kelso, to Peter Weatherburn, merchant in Edinburgh, for £246 scots. (Dur. 33.)
The only member of the Forfarshire family with whom the grantee of this land can be identified is the third surviving son of Sir Alexander Wedderburn of Blackness. He was, however, a merchant in Dundee and not in Edinburgh, although he may have traded there. The spelling of the name, in a manner indicative of the North of England or South of Scotland, is also in favour of the reference being to a member of a distinct family. The parish registers of Kelso, the births of which have been searched, 1598—1800, contain only three Wedderburn entries, viz.: those of the three daughters of a John Wedderburn (perhaps the son of this Peter) and Agnes Turner, all born and baptised at Kelso,—Margaret, 14, 15 Oct. 1706, Grizle, 17, 21 Dec. 1707, and Elizabeth, 10, 11 Dec. 1709.

183.   **1674.** (*a*) Aug. 7.—Disposition (1 June, 2 July 1674) by Sir Peter Wedderburn of Gosford, one of the senators of the College of Justice, and formerly clerk to H.M. Privy Council, with consent of the Earls of Tweeddale, Kincardine, and Dumdonald, and others, commissioners of George, Earl of Wintoun, of part of an annual-rent, furth of the lands and barony of Tranent, in favour of Andrew Russell of Edinburgh. Dated at Edinburgh, Winton, and Barnes. (Mac. 35.) (*b*) Similar disposition (same date) by the same to James McLurg, of Edinburgh. (*ib.*)

---

[1] **1669.** Feb. 11.—There is a reference in the Minute Book to the Dalrymple Office under this date :—"Obligation, Home of Wedderburn to Bayne."

[2] The Minute Book has two other references to Mackenzie's Office :—**1668.** June 19.—"Discharge, Lo. Wedderburne to Lo. Balfour," which relates to Home of Wedderburn, and **1669.** Nov. 15.—"Obligation, Wedderburn to Smith," the record of which refers to Woodburn.

184. **1674.** Oct. 2.—Tack (1673) by Sir Peter Wedderburn of Gosford, Knt., and a **Register** Senator of the College of Justice, to Archibald Murray in Skaltraw, of five and a **of Deeds.** half acres there, for nineteen years. Dated at Edinburgh and Thornton-loch, 14, 19 July 1673. (Dur. 37.)

185. **1675.** June 2.—Tack (Sketraw, 13 Aug. 1671) by the said Sir Peter Wedderburn of Gosford, to Adam Hislop, miller, of Thorntoun-mill, for five years. (Dur. 39.)

186. **1675.** July 21.—Bond (Cupar, 11 Sept. 1663) by James Young of Kirtowne to Mr. James Wedderburn, minister at Monsie, and Jean Inglish, his spouse, for 1,000 merks. (Dal. 39.)

187. **1676.** Jan. 17.—Discharge (Edinburgh, 10 Jan. 1676) by John Wedderburn of Blackness, advocate, and son, heir, and executor of the late (Sir) Alexander Wedderburn of Blackness, for himself and Rachel Dunmure, his spouse, to Mr. David Dunmure, advocate, her father, of 5,000 merks. (Dur. 40.)

188. **1676.** May 1.—Bond (Edinburgh, 26 Oct. 1675) by James Brown, merchant in Edinburgh, to George Wedderburn, merchant there, for £291 5/. (Dur. 40.)

189. **1676.** (a) Nov. 15.—Bond (24 Oct. 1676) by James Crombie, burgess of Kirkcaldy, to George Wedderburn, merchant in Edinburgh, to deliver to the said George thirty-nine barrels of white herring. Dated at Edinburgh. (Mac. 40.) (b) Bond (same date) by the same to the same for £766 scots. (ib.)

190. **1678.** Jan. 4.—Bond (Edinburgh, 7 July 1677) by John Barclay, merchant in S. Andrew's, to the said George Wedderburn for £100. (Dur. 43.)

191. **1677.** Sept. 18.—Bond (Edinburgh 19 Dec. 1676) by James Graham in Mairns to the said George Wedderburn for £143. 4. 4. (Dur. 43.)

192. **1678.** (a) June 22.—Bond (25 Sept. 1677) by Walter Burne, merchant in Saltcraig, to the said George Wedderburn for £78. 18. 0 scots. Dated at Edinburgh. (Mac. 42.) (b) Nov. 22.—Bond (16 July 1678) by John Guthrie to the same for £636 scots. Dated at Edinburgh. (ib. 43.)

193. **1678.** Oct. 4.—Bond (Edinburgh, 23 March 1675) by Robert, Earl of Southesk, to Mr. Alexander Watherburn, minister at Kilmarnock, to infeft the latter in an @-rent of £300 furth of the Earl's lands conform to a bond of 27 Jan. 1673. (Mac. 43.)

194. **1679.** March 31.—Twelve dispositions of the lands of Ballincreiff, Dunglass, and Thorntoun, by the creditors of the Laird of Dunglass to Sir Peter Wedderburn, Lord Gosford, with a contract between Dunglass and him, are booked " per licet " under this date, having been all registered 26 Feb. 1679. (Dur. 45.)
These dispositions and contract (in order of date), are as follows :—
(a) 1661. Aug. 6.—Disp. by Walter, Lord Torphichen, to Sir Peter Wedderburn of one fourth of the mains of Ballincreiff, called the Lochill.
(b) 1662. Sept. 18. Dec. 2.—Disp. by Thomas Hamilton of Reidhouse, and Dame Magdalen Stewart, his wife, and Dame Helen Richardson, his mother, to the said Sir Peter of half the dominical lands of Ballincreiff, called the Standthelane.
(c) 1663. July 25-29.—Disp. by Patrick, Lord Elibank, to the said Sir Peter and Dame Agnes Dickson, his spouse, and their heirs, of the West Mains of Ballincreiff.
(d) 1667. July 6.—Disp. by Thomas Hamilton of Reblhouse and his said wife and mother, to the said Sir Peter of the lands of Easter Spittall, Easter Reidspittall, and part of Ballincreiff, called Wester Brietleyes.
(e) 1667. July 6.—Disp. by the said Dame Helen Richardson, relict of Sir John Hamilton of Reidhouse, to the said Sir Peter of half the dominical lands and mains of Ballincreiff, called the Standthelane, for 9,000 merks.
(f) 1667. July 30.—Disp. by Mr. John Elies of Eliestown to the said Sir Peter of part of Ballincreiff.
(g) 1670. April 7.—Disp. by Sir William Ruthven of Dunglass, Knt., to the said Sir Peter, and to his sons John, Peter, and Alexander, and the heirs male of their bodies in succession, of the lands of Thorntoun.
(h) 1671. July 1.—Disp. by Alexander Young to the said Sir Peter of the lands and barony of Dunglass and Thorntoun.

(*i*) 1672. Nov. 23.—Disp. by the said Lord Elibank to the said Sir Peter and his spouse and their heirs of the mains of Ballincreiff.

(*j*) 1678. Feb. 27.—Contract between the said Sir Peter and Sir William Ruthven of Dunglass in regard to payment by Sir Peter of the price of the baronies of Dunglass and Thorntoun.

(*k*) 1678. March 6.—Disp. by James Scot of Bristo, servitor to the Duke of Buccleugh, to the said Sir Peter of the lands and barony of Dunglass, with the salt pans, &c.

(*l*) 1678. Aug. 1.—Assignation by Patrick Brown of Colston to the said Sir Peter of 8,000 merks, balance of a bond for 10,000 given him (1668) by Sir William Ruthven of Dunglass.

(*m*) 1678. Aug. 2.—Disp. by Mr. Thomas Hay to the said Sir Peter of the lands, &c., of Dunglass.

195.   **1679.** April 5.—Bond (22 June 1678) by John Mitchelson, skipper, in Kirkcaldy, to Peter Wedderburn, merchant in Dundee, for 20 French crowns. (Dal. 48.)

196.   **1679.** July 25.—Bond (15 June 1678) by William Oliphant, master of the " William " of Dundee, to make just reckoning to George and Peter Wedderburn, and William Oliphant, merchants, owners of the said ship. (Mac. 45.)

197.   **1679.** Aug. 4.—Assignation (Edinburgh, 6 Dec. 1671) by Sir Peter Wedderburn of Gosford, a senator, &c., to Mr. Thomas Murray, advocate, of 10,000 merks, &c. (Dur. 46.)

198.   **1679.** Oct. 6.—Bond (Sketraw, 25 Sept. 1676) by George Symson in Gatesyde, to Sir Peter Wedderburn of Gosford for £65 9s. (Dal. 49.)

199.   **1679.** Oct. 16.—Contract (Edinburgh, 14 March 1679) between Sir John Nisbet of Dirletoun, Knt., and George Wedderburn and another, merchants in Edinburgh, for sale to them of certain of the crops of Dirletoun at £5 8s. scots per boll. (Dur. 46.)

200.   **1681.** Feb. 14.—Bond (Leith, 1 June 1680) by James Cockburn in Leith, to John Wedderburn of Gosford, for £1,265 12s. scots. (Dur. 49.)

201.   **1681.** Feb. 23.—Discharge (8 Dec. 1673) by Elizabeth Davidson, daughter to the late Robert Davidson of Balgay, with consent of James Wedderburn (second son of Sir Alexander Wedderburn of Blackness), now clerk of Dundee, her husband, to Robert Davidson, now of Balgay, her brother, for 6,500 merks, part of her tocher of 7,500 merks provided her by her father's bond of provision dated 8 July 1664. (Mac. 48.)

202.   **1681.** Aug. 24.—Bond (13 Sept. 1680) by John Guthrie, burgess of Perth, to Peter Wedderburn, merchant in Dundee, for £123. 10. 8. (Dal. 55.)
       Entered in the Minute Book as registered Aug. 25.

203.   **1682.** Oct. 13.—Bond (24 Aug. 1680) by Thomas Murray, tenant in Sketraw, to John Wedderburn of Gosford for £239 scots.   Dated at Thorntown-loch. (Mac. 51.)
       Then follow sixteen other bonds by various persons to the said John Wedderburn for various sums, all registered at this date. (*ib.*)

204.   **1683.** Jan. 12.—Commission (Edinburgh, 6 Jan. 1683) by John Wedderburn of Gosford to " Peter and Alexander Wedderburn, his weel beloved brethren," to be his factors to manage his affairs in this Kingdom. (Dur. 55.)

205.   **1683.** (*a*) Oct. 3. — Bond (Edinburgh, 11 Jan. 1682) by James Carnegy of Balnamoon to William Carnagie (*sic*), writer in Edinburgh, on behalf of John Wedderburn of Gosford, for relief of their equal shares of £178 16s. 9d. stg.   (*b*) Nov. 1.—Bond (Edinburgh, 11 Jan. 1682) by the said John Wedderburn and James Carnegy to Robert Falconer, merchant in London, for £178. 16. 9. stg. (Dur. 57.)

206.   **1683.** Dec. 5.—Factory (Edinburgh, 15 Aug. 1683) by Alexander Wedderburn, brother german of John Wedderburn of Gosford, to William Whyt, servitor to the Laird of Gosford, for managing his affairs during his absence from Scotland.   Peter Wedderburn, brother to the Laird of Gosford, is a witness. (Dur. 57.)

207. **1684.** Dec. 3.—Bond (1684) by David Keill, tenant in Wester Gourdy, to Alexander Wedderburn of Easter Powrie, for 1,000 merks. Dated at Easter Powrie, 1 March 1684. John Wedderburn of Blackness, is a witness. (Dur. 60.) *Register of Deeds.*

208. **1685.** Jan. 3.—Contract of Wadset (Edinburgh, 17 Nov. 1682) between Sir John Nisbet of Dirleton, and John Wedderburn of Gosford, by which for £100,000 scots resting due by him, the said Sir John dispones to the said John Wedderburn the lands and baronies of Thorntoun and Innerwick, which the said John Wedderburn sets in back tack during the non-redemption of the same by the said Sir John. (Dur. 61.)

209. **1685.** Jan. 5.—Bond (Edinburgh, 4 July 1684) by the said Sir John Nisbet to John Wedderburn of Blackness, one of the clerks of Council and Session, for 900 merks for behoof of John Wedderburn of Gosford. (Dur. 61.)

210. **1685.** May 27.—Commission (Edinburgh, 26 May 1685) by John Wedderburn of Gosford to John Wedderburn of Blackness, Mr. Colin McKenzie, a clerk of the Privy Council, and George Wedderburn, merchant in Edinburgh, to be factors for receiving from the said Sir John Nisbet the @-rent of 130,000 merks balance due of 150,000 merks, contained in a contract of wadset between Gosford and Sir John. (Dur. 61.)
See ante No. 208.

211. **1685.** (*a*) June 25.—Bond (Edinburgh, 7 Aug. 1682) by John Wedderburn of Gosford to the said Sir John Nisbet to deliver to him before 1 April 1683 the whole engines, &c., of the coal and salt-pans of Innerwick, which are sold to him by Gosford. (*b*) Bond (Edinburgh, 7 Aug. 1682) by the same to the same, to procure certain obligements, &c., therein narrated. (Dur. 62.)

212. **1685.** July 11.—Disposition (Edinburgh, 7 Aug. 1682) by John Wedderburn of Gosford for himself, and as heir served and retoured to the late Sir Peter Wedderburn, Knt, his father, to the said Sir John Nisbet, of the lands and baronies of Innerwick, Thornetoun, Fairn, Dunglass, &c. (Dur. 62.)

213. **1686.** March 1.—Bond (Edinburgh, 14 Feb. 1688) by David Carnegie of Pitarrow to John Wedderburn of Gosford and Alexander Wedderburn, advocate, his brother, with consent of Sir George McKenzie of Rosehaugh, advocate, Mr. Colin McKenzie, advocate, his brother, one of the clerks of Privy Council, and John Wedderburn of Blackness, one of the clerks of the bills, for proceeding in the communication of the rights and diligences upon the baronies of Thorntoun, &c., to be made between the said John Wedderburn of Gosford, Sir John Nisbet of Dirleton, and Sir John Hall of Dunglass, for disburdening the said lands. (Dur. 64.)

214. **1686.** May 6.—Bond (12 March 1686) by George Wedderburn, merchant, burgess of Edinburgh, to Alexander Henrysone, writer in Edinburgh, for £181. 15. 10 scots. Dated at Edinburgh. (Mac. 58.)

215. **1686.** June 15.—Bond (Edinburgh, 4 June 1684) by George Wedderburn, merchant in Edinburgh, to John Wilkie, merchant there, for £294. 16. (Dal. 66.)

216. **1687.** May 2.—Discharge (26 April 1687) by James Kyd of Craigie (son of the late William Kyd of Woodhill) to Alexander Wedderburn of Easter Powrie, John Wedderburn of Blackness, and James Wedderburn, clerk of Dundee, his tutors and curators, of all things done by them in his minority. (Mac. 60.)

217. **1687.** (*a*) June 23.—Bond (21 April 1687) by James Moffat of Edinburgh to John Wedderburn, Laird of Blackness, clerk of the bills, for £92 scots. Dated at Edinburgh. (Mac. 60.) (*b*) July 1.—Bond (29 Jan. 1687) by Thomas Elder in Ballegarno and another to the said John Wedderburn of Blackness for £138 and 1 merk. (*ib.* 61.)

218. **1688.** Feb. 29.—Factory (14 Feb. 1688) by John Wedderburn of Gosford to his brother Alexander Wedderburn, advocate, with consent (as in No. 213) to manage his affairs in his absence from Scotland. (Dur. 67.)

3 I

219. **1688.** March 10.—Factory (Edinburgh, 13 April 1687) by Peter Wedderburn, second brother german of John Wedderburn of Gosford. to Alexander Wedderburn, his younger brother, for managing his affairs in Scotland, during the said Peter's absence in England with the Earl of Dumbarton's regiment. (Dur. 68.)

220. **1688.** March 10.— Bond (Edinburgh, 20 Nov. 1684) by George Wedderburn, merchant in Edinburgh, and another to Mr. Stephen Ernault, merchant at Rouen, for £2,821. 13. scots. (Dur. 68.)

221. **1688** (*a*) April 5 —Bond (1 Aug. 1682) by the said George Wedderburn to Thomas Milne of Muirtown for 600 merks. Dated at Burntisland. (*b*) Bond (Edinburgh, 23 Nov. 1683) by the same to the same for 2,590 merks. (Mac. 62)

222. **1688.** April 27.—Bond (Edinburgh, 7 March 1682) by the said George Wedderburn to John Wedderburn of Gosford for 3,000 merks. Alexander Wedderburn of Easter Powrie is a witness. (Dur. 68.)

223. **1688.** (*a*) June 15.—Bond (Edinburgh, 12 Jan. 1685) by the said George Wedderburn to the tacksman of His Majesty's customs for £268. 16. 0. scots. (*b*) Bond (Leith, 2 Jan. 1685) by the same to Robert Mylne of Barntown for £268 16. 0. scots for the custom of four tons of wine. (Dal. 69.)

224. **1688.** Oct. 2.—Factory (Edinburgh, 28 Sept. 1688) by Peter Wedderburn, now of Gosford, to Alexander Wedderburn, advocate, his brother german, to manage his affairs in Scotland, with advice of Sir George McKenzie of Rosehaugh, Mr. Colin McKenzie advocate, his brother, and John Wedderburn of Blackness. (Dur. 69.)

225. **1688.** Oct. 5.—Factory (Edinburgh, 28 Sept. 1688) by the said Peter Wedderburn to William White, his servant, as his chamberlain, to uplift the rents of Gosford and Haystoun, in consideration of his many years faithful service to the late Sir Peter Wedderburn of Gosford, father of the said Peter. (Dur. 69.)

226. **1689.** Jan. 23.—Bond (12 May 1688) by Alexander Baillie in Brigend of Clyde, to John Wedderburn of Blackness, for £90 16s. Dated at Brigend. (Dur. 70.)

227. **1689.** March 12.—Bond (16 April 1688) by Mr. John Reid, writer in Edinburgh, to John Wedderburn of Blackness, for £60. Dated at Edinburgh. (Mac. 64.)

228. **1690.** Feb. 15.—Bond (18 March 1689) by Mr. James Arbuthnot, minister at Dysert, to the said John Wedderburn for £144 12s. Dated at Edinburgh. (Mac. 65.)

229. **1690.** July 28.—Charterparty (Rotterdam, 8 June 1690) between Alexander Wedderburn, skipper and master of the good ship "William" of Dundee, and various merchants, by which he agrees to convey their goods from Rotterdam to Aberdeen for 900 merks. (Dal. 71.)

230. **1690.** July 29.—Protested bill (Rotterdam, 12 June 1690) by Alexander Owen, merchant in Aberdeen, *v.* Mr. Peter Wedderburn, merchant in Dundee, and Alexander Wedderburn, his cousin. (Dal. 71.)

231. **1691.** Feb. 24.—Bond (7 Jan. 1691) by John Wedderburn, son of the late Mr. Alexander Wedderburn, minister at Kilmarnock, and Helen Turnbull, his relict, curatrix to the said John, to Patrick Hepburn, apothecary, burgess of Edinburgh, for 600 merks. Dated at Edinburgh. (Mac. 67.)

232. **1692.** Jan. 13.—(*a*) Assignation (Leith, 27 Dec. 1682) by Mr. Robert Wedderburn, son and heir served and retoured to the late Mr. Alexander Wedderburn, minister at Kilmarnock, in favour of Helen Turnbull, his mother, and John and Jean Wedderburn, his brother and sister, in and to their proportional part of the sum of 2,700 merks contained in a bond of provision by their said father to his children,

viz. : to John 1,000 merks, to Mary 2,000 merks, to Janet 2,000 merks to Susanna 1,500 merks, and to Jean 1,000 merks, by which "seeing that the said Janet was vallitudinary," he further appointed that, if she died, £1,000 of her portion should be equally divided between the said Mr. Robert and Mary and the surplus of 500 merks disposed of by herself. (Mac. 70.) (*b*) Assignation (Edinburgh, 19 April 1690) by the said Susanna Wedderburn to Helen Turnbull, her mother, and John, Mary, Janet, Margaret, and Jean Wedderburn, her brother and sisters, in and to certain sums. (*ib.*)

233. **1692.** Sept. 3.—Assignation, &c. (19 April 1688) by George Wedderburn, merchant in Edinburgh, to John Wedderburn of Blackness, his brother, of a decreet of adjudication (10 April 1688) obtained by him *v.* Robert Fyffe, as son and heir of the late Patrick Fyffe in Edinburgh. Dated at Edinburgh. (Mac. 71.)

234. **1693.** (*a*) Nov. 13.—Discharge, &c. (19 June 1692) by Sir Mark Carse of Cockpen to John Wedderburn of Blackness, clerk of the bills, of 1,000 merks, contained in a bond (30 Nov. 1686) granted to Sir Mark by George Wedderburn as principal, and the said John Wedderburn as cautioner. Dated at Edinburgh. (Mac. 73.) (*b*) Nov. 23.—Discharge (2 Nov. 1693) by Archibald Home, merchant in Edinburgh, to the said John Wedderburn for £800. Dated at Edinburgh. (*ib.*)

235. **1694.** Oct. 26.—Discharge (Edinburgh, 24 Oct. 1694) by John Wedderburn of Blackness, one of the principal clerks of the bills, to Mr. William Lauder of his part of a minute of a contract of marriage (dated at Edinburgh, 13 June 1693) between the said John Wedderburn taking burden on him for his eldest son Mr. Alexander Wedderburn, with consent of Mr. David Dunmuir of Curriehill, advocate, grandfather to the said Mr. Alexander, and the said Mr. William Lauder, taking burden on him for his grandchild, eldest daughter to Sir Alexander Seaton of Pitmedden, Knt., with consent of Dame Margaret Lauder, her mother, and Catharine Hunter, spouse to the said William Lauder. (Dal. 78.)

236. **1696.** Feb 4.—Bond (1 Feb. 1695) by William Gray, writer in Dundee, and another to Alexander Wedderburn of Easter Powrie, or to his curators (John Wedderburn of Blackness, James Wedderburn, clerk of Dundee, Peter Wedderburn, merchant, &c.) for 1,000 merks. (Mac. 78.)[1]

237. **1697.** March 22.—Bond (28 April 1680) by John Davidson, son of the late Robert Davidson of Balgay, narrating his intention "to goe abroad of this kingdom about my lawful affairs ;" and ordaining that "for the love, favour, and affection which I have towards John Wedderburn, my goodson, and Robert Wedderburn, lawful sone to James Wedderburn clerk of Dundee and Elizabeth Davidson his spouse, my sister german, . . . in case it shall please God to call me by death before my return home, without airs lawfully procreat of my body, Therfor I be thir presants bind and obleidge me and Robert Davidson now of Balgay or his airs, as my representatives to my means and estate, or their executors, to content, pay, and deliver to the said John Wedderburn my nephew the soume of one thousand merks, scots money, and to the said Robert Wedderburn the soume of fyve hundereth merks money forsaid, and failzeing of the said John Wedderburn by deceis, the said James Wedderburn and my said sister they having ane son thereafter named John, the said ane thousand merks to fall and belong to him, quhilks failzicing the same to fall and belong to the said Robert Wedderburn, and failzieing of him by decease before his said brother, the said fyve hundereth merks to fall and belong to my said goodson quhilks all failzieing to them their airs and assigneys whatsomever." (Mac. 80.)

238. **1697.** May 26.—Discharge (18 May 1697) by Peter Wedderburn of Gosford, heir served and retoured and executor decerned and confirmed to the late John Wedderburn of Gosford, his elder brother, who was heir and executor to the late Sir Peter Wedderburn of Gosford, their father, to David, now Viscount of Stormont, and Sir John Murray of Drumcairn, his tutors, of a bond (July 1665) granted by the said Viscount to the said Sir Peter for 19,000 merks. Dated at Edinburgh. (Mac. 80.)

---

[1] Two references in the Minute Book to the Dalrymple office :—**1696.** May 22.—"Obligation Wedderburn to Prestoun," and June 11.—"Disposition Wedderburn to Cant," refer to Home of Wedderburn.

239. **1697.** Dec. 31.—Bond (18 Oct. 1690) by Mr. Thomas Sanders, schoolmaster of Kettins, to Dame Agnes Wedderburn, lady of Pitcur, for 113 merks. Dated at Kettins. (Mac. 81.)[1]

240. **1699.** Feb. 10.—Interdiction (27 Jan. 1699) by David Wedderburn, eldest son on life of the late Mr. James Wedderburn, minister at Moonzie, to Alexander Inglis, merchant in Edinburgh, his uncle, Jean Inglis, his mother, and Robert Baillie of Balmedicside, binding himself not to become cautioner for any person whatsoever. (Mac.84.)

241. **1699.** June 21.—(*a*) Discharge (19 May 1692) by James Wedderburn, clerk of Dundee, and Elizabeth Davidson, his spouse, to Robert Davidson of Balgay, of 1,000 merks. (*b*) Discharge (4 Aug. 1680) by the said Elizabeth Davidson to the said Robert Davidson of 1,000 merks, and of a bond of provision relating to 3,000 merks at the disposal of Grissell Brown, relict of the late Robert Davidson of Balgay. John Wedderburn of Blackness is a witness. (Mac. 84.)

242. **1699.** July 22.—Discharge (14 Nov. 1698) by Matilda Wedderburn, relict of Mr. James Brisbane, advocate, to John Wedderburn, eldest son of the late Sir Alexander Wedderburn of Blackness, Knt., for 6,000 merks contained in a bond of provision (10 Sept. 1666) to her by the said Sir Alexander and John Wedderburn. Written by David Spalding, servitor to Alexander Wedderburn, clerk of Dundee. (Dal. 82.)

243. **1700.** Jan 3.—Disposition (Edinburgh, 13 March and 3 April 1685) by John Wedderburn of Gosford, son and heir retoured to the late Sir Patrick Wedderburn of Gosford, a senator of the College of Justice, to James Douglas, brother of William, Duke of Queensberry, of the lands of Skirline, &c., with consent of James Murray, their heritable proprietor. (Dal. 83.)

244. **1700.** Feb 14.—Discharge (of this date) by William Menzies, merchant in Edinburgh, to John Wedderburn of Blackness, clerk of the Bills, of £5,649. 15. 0. scots, contained in a decreet (24 Nov. 1696) of suspension obtained by the said William *v.* Robert Johnston of Dumfries. Dated at Edinburgh. (Mac. 86.)

245. **1700.** Aug. 10.—Discharge (16 May 1700) by Margaret Wedderburn, relict of Mr. Andrew Balfour, W.S , tutrix (sine quâ non) to Margaret Balfour, their only lawful child now on life, and factrix for Mr. John Dallas of Preston, another of her tutors, with consent of John Wedderburn of Blackness and others, to Mr. Colin McKenzie, brother of the Earl of Seaforth, and Mr. George McKenzie, nephew of the late Sir George McKenzie of Rosehaugh, and others, of £1,000 contained in their bond (25 Aug. 1697) to the said Mr. Andrew Balfour. Dated at Edinburgh. (Mac. 87.)

246. **1700.** Sept. 2.—Bond (18, 22 Aug. 1699) by James Ogilvy of Inschewan and Sir John Ogilvy of Innercharitie, Knt, to Alexander Wedderburn, clerk of Dundee, for £86 scots. Dated at Kirriemuir and Innercharitie. (Dur. 94.)

247. **1700.** Oct. 3.—Indentures (17 June 1696) between Alexander Wedderburn, clerk of Dundee, and David, eldest son of the late David Spalding of Corrydown, binding the latter as apprentice to the former in the calling of writer for three years. (Dur. 94.)

248. **170.1** Jan. 17.—Discharge, &c. (1699) by David Wedderburn, son of the late Mr. James Wedderburn, minister of Moonsie, narrating that the said minister by his will (28 Oct. 1683) left to his wife, Jean Inglis, mother of the said David, the life-rent of all he had, out of which she was to maintain, as in fact she did, her three surviving children, of whom David now alone survives (the other two, William and Mary, being dead), in favour of his said mother, of all her intromissions with his father's estate, and assigning to her in life-rent certain sums of his, including 1,150 merks, due by bond (15 Aug. 1687) of Mr. Andrew Wedderburn, minister of the Gospel. Dated at Edinburgh, 24 July, and at Lithrie. 6 Nov. 1699. (Dal. 84.)

[1] Three references in the Minute Book to Durie's Office refer to Home of Wedderburn, viz. :—1697. June 25.—Backbond, Wedderburn to Coldingknowes. (Dur. 87.) 1698. July 29.—Discharge, Wedderburn to Home. (*ib.* 89) 1699. Dec. 22.—Obligation, Wedderburn to Simpsone. (*ib.* 92,).

249. **1701.** Feb. 28.—(a) Bond (Edinburgh, 16 March 1700) by Sir John Swinton and **Register** others to John Wedderburn of Blackness for 1,000 merks. (b) Discharge (Edinburgh, **of Deeds.** 17 Feb. 1701) of the said bond by Blackness. (Dal. 85.)

250. **1701.** Dec. 2.—Factory (Edinburgh, 18 June 1701) by Alexander Wedderburn, advocate, with consent of Sir Peter Wedderburn of Gosford, to Mary Deas, his spouse, to uplift all debts, &c., due to him. (Dur. 98.)

251. **1702.** Feb. 20.—Obligation (Edinburgh, 17 June 1686) by Mr. John Wedderburn of Gosford to pay to —— (sic) Gray, Lady Balgillo, and others, various sums of money. (Mac. 90.)

252. **1702.** Aug. 1.—Discharge (14 July 1686) by Alexander Wedderburn of Easter Powrie to Sir David Carnegy of Pittarrow for 1,000 merks. (Mac. 91.)

253. **1702.** Aug. 6.—Discharge (Edinburgh, 20 Feb. and 23 July 1702) by John Wedderburn of Blackness and Mr. John Dallas of Preston, tutors testamentars to Margaret Balfour, only child on life of the late Andrew Balfour, W.S. conform to a "letter of tutory registered in the Burgh Court books of Edinburgh 7 Dec. 1697, with consent of Margaret Wedderburn, relict of the said Mr. Andrew, and now spouse of Dr. William Eccles in Edinburgh," to Mr. John Menzies and others, of certain bonds. (Dur. 99, pt. ii.)

254. **1703.** Feb. 22.—Back bond (15 May 1684) by Thomas Kennedy, merchant in Edinburgh, to George Wedderburn, merchant there, of certain sums and bonds specified. Dated at Edinburgh. (Mae. 92.)

255. **1703.** July 1.—Bond (8 Jan. 1702) by James Alisone, merchant in Dundee, to Peter Wedderburn, merchant there. Alexander Wedderburn, clerk of Dundee, is a witness. (Dal. 88.)

256. **1703.** (a) Oct. 16.—Protested bill (Edinburgh, 15 Oct. 1703) by Alexander Wedderburn, clerk of Dundee, v. Mr. James Robertson, merchant in Cupar of Angus, for £320 scots. (Dur. 101.) (b) Nov. 24.—Bond (18 May 1702) by Robert Turnbull of Bogmilne to the said clerk for £73. 13. scots. (ib.) (c) Nov. 24.—Bond (Cupar-Fife, 8 Jan. 1703) by Michael Balfour of Forrett and another to the said clerk for 500 merks. (ib.)

257. **1704.** April 6.—Indentures (17 Dec. 1702) of apprenticeship for 3 years in the mariner's art and calling between Alexander Wedderburn, skipper in Dundee, and Andrew, son of the late Mr. John Lyon, minister of Tealing. Peter Wedderburn, merchant in Dundee, is a witness. (Dur. 102.)

258. **1704.** May 18.—Bond (5 April 1704) by Alexander Preston to Alexander Wedderburn, younger, of Blackness, for £167. 18. 4. scots. (Mac. 94.)

259. **1704.** June 12.—Bond (Easter Powrie, 20 Sept. 1703) by George Kirkcaldie and another to Alexander Wedderburn of Easter Powrie for 300 merks. (Mac. 94.)

260. **1704.** July 6.—Obligation (29 June and 5 July 1704) by Margaret Wedderburn, relict of Mr. Andrew Balfour, W.S., and now spouse of Dr. William Eccles of Edinburgh, with consent of Mr. John Dallas, bailie of Dunse, cousin german to the said Mr. Andrew, to pay 2,000 merks to George McMaskell, son of the late Duncan McMaskell in Little Bannabar, by Margaret Balfour, sister german to the said Mr. Andrew, and thus nearest of kin and apparent heir to Margaret Balfour, only child on life of the said Mr. Andrew, and also (if she die) to unquhile George Balfour, her brother, and the said Mr. Andrew himself. Dated at Edinburgh and Dunse. (Mae. 95.)

261. **1704.** July 14.—Discharge (3 May 1704) by James Halyburton of Pitcur, son and heir of the said David Halyburton thereof, to Sir Peter Wedderburn of Gosford, as brother and heir of the late John Wedderburn of Gosford, of a bond (17 June 1686) granted by the said John to the said David. Dated at Edinburgh. (Mac. 95.)

262. **1704.** (*a*) Aug. 11.—Bond (18 Oct. 1703) by John Graham and Patrick Kyd in Dundee to Peter Wedderburn, merchant there, for £722. 9. 2. scots. (Dur, 103.) (*b*) Sept. 21.—Bond (31 May 1703) by Robert Christie and another to the said Peter for £240. 13. 7. scots. Alexander Wedderburn, skipper in Dundee, is a witness. (*ib.*)

263. **1704.** Nov. 22.—Bond (1699) by Robert Sinclair of Longformacus and Sir John Swinton to John Wedderburn of Blackness, conjunct clerk of the bills, for £800 scots. Dated at Swinton and Lochend 31 Aug.—1 Sept. 1699. (Dal. 89, pt. ii.)

264. **1705.** Feb. 26.—Bond (Edinburgh, 8 Nov. 1700) by John, Earl of Strathmore, to John Wedderburn of Blackness for 2,000 merks. (Dal. 90, pt. i.)

265. **1705.** April 27.—Bond (10 April 1704) by Cecilia Wedderburn, Lady Littlegill, to Arthur Brown of Edinburgh for £6 sterling, in corroboration of a bill accepted by her son, William Baillie of Littlegill, and protested 5 April 1703. Dated at the Mott. (Mac. 96.)

266. **1705.** Sept. 20.—Bond (5 Feb. 1704) by the provost and town council of Dundee to Mr. Alexander Wedderburn, younger, of Blackness for 3,000 merks. Alexander Wedderburn, clerk of Dundee, is a witness. (Mac. 97.)

267. **1705.** Oct. 11.—Bond (27 March 1702) by Peter Wedderburn, merchant in Dundee, and another to John Mann for £355. Alexander Wedderburn, clerk of Dundee, is a witness. (Dal. 90, pt. ii.)

268. **1705.** Nov. 19.—Bond (21 July 1705) by James Robertson, merchant in Cupar of Angus, to Alexander Wedderburn, clerk of Dundee, clerk to the roup of the goods of the late John Scott, younger, merchant in Dundee, for £223. 4. 6. (Dal. 90, pt. ii.)

269. **1705.** Dec. 20.—Bond (dated ?) by Robert Christie, younger, and another to Peter Wedderburn, merchant in Dundee, for £240. 13. 7. in corroboration of a bond dated 31 May 1703. (Dur. 107.)[1]
See ante No. 262 (*b*).

270. **1706.** (*a*) June 4.—Bond (4 Jan. 1706) by Alexander Abercromby to Alexander Wedderburn, clerk of Dundee. (Dal. 92.) (*b*) June 18.—Bond (23 March 1703) by Thomas Crichton of Ruthven to the same, as factor for Alexander Watson of Wallace Craigie. (*ib.*)

271. **1706.** (*a*) June 18.—Protested bill (28 Nov. 1705) by Alexander Wedderburn, skipper in Dundee, *v.* Mark Wood, merchant in Perth. (Dal. 92.) (*b*) Nov. 1.—Bond (8 Aug. 1702) by Patrick Kyd, merchant in Dundee, to the said Alexander Wedderburn. (*ib.*)

272. **1706.** Nov. 23.—Bond (11 Nov. 1706) by Sir Alexander Wedderburn of Blackness, Baronet, one of the principal clerks to the bills, to Alexander Gordon of Pitlurg and another for 4,000 merks. (Mac. 99.)

273. **1707.** July 8.—Contract (Gosford, 17 Jan. 1705) between Sir Peter Wedderburn of Gosford and Robert Seaton and another, for the sale to them by Sir Peter of certain victual grown on his lands of Gosford at £8. 3. 4. per boll. (Dal. 94.)

274. **1707.** Nov. 3.—Bond (8 Jan. 1700) by Cecilia Wedderburn, Lady Littlegill, and William Baillie her eldest son, to William Forrester, W.S., for 200 merks. Dated at Motte. Thomas Baillie, also her son, is a witness. (Dal. 94.)

---

[1] The minute book has two references to Durie's office, both of which refer to Home of Wedderburn:—1706. 11 Feb.—Bond, L. Wedderburn, y⁰ᵗ, to Thomas Calderwood. 20 March.—Obleigment, Wedderburn to Williamson.

275. **1709.** March 15.—Bond (Edinburgh, 14 Aug. 1706) for 1,000 merks by Sir Robert **Register** Forbes of Auchinhove, advocate, to Alexander Wedderburn, clerk of Dundee, on behalf **of Deeds.** of Grissell Brown, reliet, and Christian, Isobell, Margaret, and Elizabeth, daughters (by Isobell Guthrie, his first wife), and Grissell, John, and George, children (by the said Grissell Brown), of the late John Seot, younger, merchant there. (Dur. 119.)

276. **1709.** April 28 —Bond (10 April 1705) by James Tasker in Foid to Dame Agnes Wedderburn, Dowager Lady Piteur, for £116. 19. 6. Dated at Halyburton. (Mae.104.)

277. **1709.** Dee. 17.—Diseharge (Edinburgh, 25 Nov. 1709) by Mrs Matilda Wedderburn, daughter of the late John Wedderburn of Blaekness, to Sir Alexander Wedderburn, now of Blaekness, of £6,000 scots, due by a bond of provision (4 Mareh 1704) to her by the said John and Alexander. (Dur. 121.)

278. **1710.** Feb. 2.—Bond (27 May 1706) by Henry Crawford of Monorgan to Mrs. Rachael Wedderburn, sister german to Alexander Wedderburn of that ilk, for 400 merks. (Mae. 106.)

279. **1710.** Feb. 9.— Bond (14 July 1705) by Robert Wedderburn, mariner in Dundee, to Bessie, daughter of the late William Robertson, burgess of Perth, for 100 merks in eorroboration of a bond (3 Nov. 1702) to her by John Arnot, notary, burgess of Perth, father-in-law of the said Robert. (Mae. 106.)

280. **1710.** April 20.—Inventory (7 Dee. 1678) of materials delivered to Sir William Murray of Newtoun and another, eonform to a taek (30 Nov. 1678) of the eoal and saltpans of Innerwiek and Thorntown, set to them by Sir Peter Wedderburn of Gosford. Dated at Skaitraw. (Mae. 106.)

281. **1710.** July 4.—Bond (10 Sept. 1708) by Sir Alexander Wedderburn of Blaekness, Knight Baronet, to Mr.John Brown, minister at Dundee, for £2,200 seots. (Dal.96,pt.ii.)

282. **1710.** Aug. 14.—Taek (15 Feb. 1705) by Alexander Wedderburn of Easter Powrie to Thomas Scott of the lands of Serrioehhall, in the parish of Murroes and shire of Forfar for seven years. Dated at Easter Powrie. (Mae. 107.)

283. **1710.** (*a*) Dec. 13.—Bond (Edinburgh, 10 Dee. 1708) by Sir Alexander Wedderburn of Blaekness, baronet, clerk to the bills, to James Brown for £100 stg. (*b*) Bond (Edinburgh, 19 Feb. 1708) same to same for 2,500 merks. (Mae. 107.)

284. **1711.** June 21.—Bond (14 Nov. 1709) by Sir Alexander Wedderburn of Blaekness, baronet, to John Dick, writer in Dundee, for 5,000 merks. Alexander Wedderburn, elerk of Dundee, is a witness. (Mae. 108.)

285. **1711.** July 26.—Bond (16 Nov. 1705) by Alexander Wedderburn, elerk of Dundee, to James Mores of Clepingtoun and Barbara Lowrie, his spouse, for 1,000 merks. (Mae. 109.)

286. **1711.** Aug. 8.—Faetory (Edinburgh, 31 July 1711) by Mr. Alexander Wedderburn, advocate, to Alexander Laing of Edinburgh. (Dal. 100.)

287. **1712.** Jan. 17.—Bond (Edinburgh, 16 Feb. 1708) by Sir Alexander Wedderburn of Blaekness and Major David Wedderburn in Maj.-Gen MeCartney's Regiment of Foot, to Alexander Kirkwood for 2,000 merks. (Dal. 101.)

288. **1712.** Jan. 21.—Bond (Edinburgh, 12 Feb. 1703) by Alexander Wedderburn, younger, of Blaekness, and one of the prineipal elerks of the bills, to Mr. Robert Dallas, writer in Edinburgh, for 500 merks. (Dur. 130.)

289. **1712.** Feb. 9.—Disposition (3 June 1696) by Mr. Alexander Wedderburn, advoeate, seeond son now on life of the late Sir Peter Wedderburn of Gosford, senator of the College of Justice, to William Legat, writer in Edinburgh, of his great mansion house, formerly the said Sir Peter's, in Aikman's (now ealled Gosford's) elose, on the south side of the High Street, Edinburgh. Dated at Edinburgh. (Mae. 110.)

290. **1713.** Sept 16.—Bond (2 June 1711) by Mr. William Halkerstone of Rathillet and another to Alexander Wedderburn, clerk of Dundee, for 600 merks. Dated at Guardbridge. (Dur. 138.)

291. **1714.** Aug. 26.—Bond (Aberdeen, 11 Dec. 1712) by Robert Balvaird and another to Alexander Wedderburn, clerk of Dundee, for £86. 11. 6. scots. (Dur. 143.)

292. **1714.** Sept. 11.—Discharge (Edinburgh, 12 July 1714) by John Brown of Cleugh to Mr. Alexander Wedderburn, advocate, and others, of certain writs, &c. (Dal. 104.)

293. **1715.** Jan. 3.—Bond (25 April 1713) by Archibald Campbell of Rathen and another to Alexander Laing, factor for Mr. Alexander Wedderburn, advocate, and another, trustees for John Brown, portioner of Cleugh, for 1,000 merks. (Mac. 116.)

294. **1715.** July 1.—Assignation (16 May 1711) by Mr. Alexander Scott, minister at Liff, to Alexander Wedderburn, clerk of Dundee, of 3,000 merks. (Dur. 145.)

295. **1717.** (a) Feb. 4.—Bond (Montrose, 21 Aug. 1716) by John and James Ochterlony to Alexander Wedderburn, collector of excise, for £68. 15. 6. (Dal. 107.) (b) Bond (Montrose, 30 July 1716) by William Ross and John Adams to the same for £31.1.0. (ib.)

296. **1718.** Jan. 31.—Indentures (1714) between Alexander Wedderburn, shipmaster in Dundee, and David, son of the late James Balneaves of Carnbeadie, whereby the latter becomes apprentice to the former in the calling of navigation for three years. Dated at Dundee and Rothwell, 6 and 27 April 1714. (Dur. 152.)

297. **1718.** Aug. 18.—Heritable bond (3 April 1708) by James, Earl of Southesk, and his curators to Sir Alexander Wedderburn of Blackness, baronet, clerk to the bills, for 12,600 merks. Dated at Edinburgh. (Mac. 123, pt. ii.)

298. **1718.** (a) Aug. 19.—Bond (17 Nov. 1703) by Alexander Wedderburn of Easter Powrie to Robert Gardine, younger of Latown, for an @-rent £88. 7. 6. furth of David Lindsay's baronies of Edzell and Glenesk. (b) Heritable bond (Edzell, 1 March 1703) by David Lindsay of Edzell to the said Alexander Wedderburn for £1,473 scots. (Mac. 123, p. ii.)

299. **1718.** Aug. 19—Discharge.(Edinburgh, 26 May 1685) by Mr. James Elphingstone, W.S., to John Wedderburn of Gosford as cautioner for William Carnegy, writer in Edinburgh, for 2,000 merks, contained in their bond of 18 August 1682. (Mac. 123, pt. ii.)

300. **1722.** Jan. 3.—Revocation (Edinburgh, 3 Jan. 1722) by Sir John Wedderburn of Blackness of all deeds made by him during his minority. (Dal. 116, pt. i.)

301. **1722.** May 5.—Bond (Edinburgh, 6 Jan. 1712) by Sir John Wedderburn, ensign in Col. John Middleton's Regiment of Foot, to Rachel Wedderburn, his sister german, for 2,000 merks contained in a bond of provision granted by him to her. (Dur. 162.)

302. **1722.** Nov. 19.—Protested bill (Edinburgh, 27 April 1722) by Captain Robert Tailfer c. Sir John Wedderburn of Blackness for £11. 18. 5. (Dal. 116, pt. ii.)

303. **1722.** Dec. 8.—Commission (Edinburgh, 7 Dec. 1722) by Archibald, Duke of Douglas, to Alexander Wedderburn, sheriff clerk of Forfar, to be factor and chamberlain of Dudope, &c. (Dur. 163.)

304. **1723.** Jan. 18.—Protested bill (31 Dec. 1722) by Patrick Douglas in Edinburgh v. Sir John Wedderburn of Blackness for £24 stg. (Dal. 117, pt. i.)

305. **1723.** March 21.—Tack (1, 8 May 1704) by William Bodam, dancing master in Edinburgh, to Alexander Wedderburn, younger of Blackness, and others, of a lodging in Trotter's close, Edinburgh, at 200 merks a year. Dated at Edinburgh. (Mac. 133, pt. i.)

306. **1723.** March 26.—Disposition (Edinburgh, 22 July 1722) by Rachel Wedderburn, **Register** daughter to the late George Wedderburn, merchant in Edinburgh, and the late — (*sic*) **of Deeds.** Sutherland, his spouse, to John Davidson, writer there, whereby, for a certain sum of money she sells to the said John Davidson that great tenement, lately rebuilt, in the town of Leith on the south of the water thereof, in the barony of Restalrig. (Mac. 133, pt. i.)

307. **1723.** Dec. 21.—Contract of marriage (27 Aug. 1705) between Peter Wedderburn, merchant in Dundee, and Barbara Auchinlek (Mac. 134, pt. ii.)
    See s. Blackness Papers, Nos. 28 and 29. The date of the original contract is Aug. 25, not Aug. 27 as stated in the register.

308. **1724.** (*a*) July 22.—Bond (1710) by David, Earl of Northesk, and James Carnegy of Finhaven to Alexander Wedderburn, clerk of Dundee, for 1,000 merks. Dated at Edinburgh and Finhaven 18 and 29 Nov. 1710. (Dur. 169.) (*b*) Discharge thereof. Dated at Forfar 25 Jan. 1723. (*ib.*)

309. **1725.** Jan. 1.—Bond of relief (15 March 1723) by Mr. James Daes, writer in Edinburgh, to Peter Wedderburn, advocate, of 1,000 merks, contained in a bond by them to Sir Edward Eizet, M.D. Dated at Edinburgh. (Mac. 137, pt. i.)

310. **1725.** July 29.—Disposition (2, 17 Feb. 1711) by Alexander Wedderburn, clerk of Dundee, and Cecilia Wedderburn, relict of William Baillie of Littlegill, to Thomas, James, Anna, and Matilda Baillies, her children, of a bond granted by their said father to Sir Patrick Nisbet of Dean. Dated at Edinburgh. (Mac. 138, pt. i.)

311. **1726.** (*a*) Feb. 3.—Contract of marriage (1692) between Mr. Alexander Wedderburn, advocate, and Mary Daes, daughter of Mr. James Daes of Coldingknows, advocate, whereby the said Mr. Alexander settles 16,000 merks on his said spouse. Dated at Edinburgh and Temple 16, 21 July 1692. (Dal. 120, pt. i.) (*b*) Heritable bond (Edinburgh, 16 July 1692) by the said Mr. James Daes to Mr. Alexander Wedderburn, advocate, (brother german to the laird of Gosford), and Mary Daes, his spouse, to infeft the said spouses in an @-rent of £550, corresponding to the principal sum of 14,000 merks, furth of the mains of Coldingknows, in the parish of Earlston and shire of Berwick. (*ib.*)

312. **1726.** March 11.—Assignation (25 Feb. 1726) by Sir Alexander Wedderburn of Blackness to Andrew Barclay, writer in Edinburgh, of a bond (1711) granted to Sir Alexander by David, Earl of Northesk, and registered — Feb. 1723. (Mac. 139, pt. i.)

313. **1727.** (*a*) Aug. 3.—Submission (1727) by Sir Alexander Wedderburn of Blackness, as tutor of Margaret Strachan, and Mrs. Janet Lindsay to the arbitration of certain arbiters. Dated at Edinburgh 23 Jan., 12 Feb. 1727. Decreet arbitral dated at Leith 2 Aug. 1727. (Dur. 174.) (*b*) Aug 11.—Submission (1727) by the said Sir Alexander, as such tutor, and David Lindsay of Edzell, to the arbitration of the said arbiters. Dated at Dundee, Holyrood, and Edinburgh 5, 8 Aug. 1727. Decreet at Edinburgh 10 Aug. 1727. (*ib.*)

314. **1727.** Nov. 15.—Factory (Logie Almond, 7 Oct. 1727) by Charles, Lord Kinnaird, to Sir Alexander Wedderburn of Blackness to uplift his maills, &c (Dur. 175, pt. ii.)

315. **1729.** Feb. 27.—Bond (Edinburgh, 6 Oct. 1725) by Mrs. Rachaell Wedderburn, only child on life of the late Sir Alexander Wedderburn of Blackness, one of the clerks of the bills, to John Melvill of Cairney for £1,400 stg. (Dur. 178, pt. i.)

316. **1729.** July 30.—The Minute Book has another reference to Mackenzie's Office :— " Back bond, Alexander Wedderburn to Duncan," but in the record this is wanting, being marked " out on receipt." (Min. Book.)

317. **1730.** (*a*) March 4.—Discharge (9 Feb. 1705) by Sir John Wedderburn of Blackness to Sir John Swinton of that ilk for £800 scots. Dated at Edinburgh. (Mac. 147.) (*b*) April 7.—Bond (31 July 1703) by Mr. James Hamilton of Bangour, advocate, to Mr. Alexander Wedderburn of Blackness, conjunct clerk of the bills for £149. 7. 8. scots. Dated at Edinburgh. (*ib.*)

3 K

318.   **1730.** July 14.— Bond (8 July 1730) by Robert Wedderburn, writer in Forfar, son
of Sir Alexander Wedderburn of Blackness, to the creditors of Mr. William Gray of
Innerichtie, of which estate he is factor. (Mac. 148.)

319.   **1730.** Dec. 29.—Bond (29 Sept. 1720) by David Campbell, elder and younger of
Kethick, to David Brisbane, writer in Dundee, factor for the tutors of David Wedderburn of that ilk, for 100 merks.   Dated at Kethick. (Mac. 148.)
    The tutors named are those nominated by the will (1713) of David's father (see ante s. Scryn-
geour-Wedderburn Papers, No. 541). except Robert Gardyne of Latoun, who was now dead, Grissell
Gardyne (David's mother) who had married again, and Peter Wedderburn, merchant in Dundee.

320.   **1731.** Bond (10 Aug. 1720) by David Campbell, elder and younger of Kethick, to
Alexander Wedderburn, sheriff clerk of Forfar, for 2,000 merks.   Dated at Kethick
and Kemphill. (Dur. 184.)

321.   **1732.** April 25.—Protested bill (Langforgan, 13 Jan. 1732) by Sir Alexander Wedderburn of Blackness v. James Henderson for £53. 6. 8. scots. (Dur. 184.)

322.   **1733.** Feb. 28.—Submission (15, 26 June 1732) by Alexander Wedderburn, shipmaster and late baillie of Dundee, and Grizell Watson his wife, and James Davidson, of
all decreets anent the North Murraygate land of the said Alexander and his wife, to
the arbitration of certain arbiters.   Decreet 8 Jan. 1733. (Dur. 187.)

323.   **1734.** June 5.—Tack (Blackness, 23 Feb. 1726) by Sir William (*sic*) Wedderburn
of Blackness to Margaret, daughter of the late William Strachan, of the town and
lands of Eastlownie, in the parish of Dunnichen, Forfar.   John Wedderburn, son of
the said Sir Alexander, is a witness. (Dal. 133.)
    " Sir William " is an error for " Sir Alexander," which is the name given repeatedly in the body
of the document.

324.   **1734.** June 10.—Tack (3 Oct. 1734) by Sir Alexander Wedderburn of Blackness,
factor for the Duke of Douglas, to John Whittet, of the parks, &c. of Dudhop. (Dal. 133.)

325.   **1734.** Nov. 28.—Bond (9 Aug. 1716) by David Campbell of Kethick to Alexander
Wedderburn, shipmaster in Dundee, for 1,400 merks (Mac. 156.)

326.   **1735.** April 7.—Submission (Edinburgh and Gosford, 18 and 20 Jan. 1735) and
decreet arbitral (Edinburgh, 14 March 1735) between Mr. Peter Wedderburn, advocate,
secretary to the Commissioners of Excise, and his sisters and brother, Margaret, Agnes,
Janet, Jean, and James Wedderburn, children of the late Alexander Wedderburn, one
of the said commissioners, to the decision of Sir Gilbert Elliot of Minto, one of the
senators of the College of Justice, of all claggs, claims, &c., between them, especially
as to their shares in the estate of the late Alexander Wedderburn, late collector of
excise, their brother german.   The decreet arbitral declares that by the contract of
marriage between their said father and Mary Daes, their mother, dated 16 and 21 July
1692, the said Peter has, as eldest son and heir male, a preferable claim of
30,000 merks, &c. (Mac. 157.)

327.   **1736.** (*a*) Jan. 6.—Obligation (1 March 1732) by Mr. Peter Wedderburn, advocate,
secretary to the excise, to Mrs. Mary Daes, his mother, to pay her £100 yearly during
her widowity, and his tenure of his said office, in lieu of her life-rent provision under
her marriage contract.   Dated at Edinburgh. (Mac. 159, pt. 1.) (*b*) Jan. 21.—
Discharge (17 Jan. 1736) by the said Mary Daes or Wedderburn to the said Peter
Wedderburn, her son, of the said annuity.   Dated at Edinburgh. (*ib*.) (*c*) May 4.—
Contract of marriage between Alexander Wedderburn, advocate, and the said Mary
Daes. See ante No. 311. (*ib*, pt. ii.)

328.   **1736.** Dec. 29.—Disposition (23 Dec. 1736) by Sir Alexander Wedderburn of
Blackness, Bart., to Mr. Andrew Arrot of Dumbarro, minister of Dunnichen, and his
second son David, of the lands of Halkertoun, Forfar. (Dur. 195.)

329. **1737.** May 3.—Factory (Edinburgh, 17 Feb. 1737) by the Duke of Douglas to John Register of Deeds. Wedderburn, eldest son of Sir Alexander Wedderburn of Blackness, as factor of his lordships of Dudope, Abernethy, &c. (Dur. 196.)

330. **1737.** June 16.—Factory (Blackness, 29 Aug. 1729) by James, son of Mr. John Paterson of Craigie, to Robert Wedderburn, writer in Forfar, to manage his affairs during his absence abroad. John Wedderburn, younger of Blackness, is a witness. (Dur. 196.)

331. **1739.** June 29.—Bond (1 June 1711) by Alexander Wedderburn, clerk of Dundee, to Grizell Brown, relict of John Scott, younger, merchant there, and another, for 500 merks. (Mac. 163, pt. i.)

332. **1739.** (a) July 25.—Protested bill (Torryburn, March 1739) by Robert Wedderburn, merchant, in Dunfermline, v. Alexander Fraser in Torrie. (Dur. 199.) (b) Aug. 2.—Protested bill (Dunfermline, 31 Oct. 1738) by the said Robert Wedderburn v. John Grindlay in Kilsyth. (ib.)

333. **1739.** Dec. 12.—Disposition (13 July 1723) by Sir Alexander Wedderburn of Blackness, Baronet, and another, trustees for the creditors of William Lyon elder, of Easter Ogill, to Robert Fletcher of Easter Ballinschoe, of the lands of Wester and Nether Ballinschoe, in the regality of Kirriemuir. (Mac. 163, pt. ii.)

334. **1740.** May 15.—Submission (21-22 March 1740) by Grissell Watson, relict of Alexander Wedderburn, shipmaster and some time baillie of Dundee, and Alexander Wedderburn, shipmaster in London, to certain arbitrators. Decreet 27 March 1740. (Dur. 201.) "London" is written "Lathon" in the record, but the arbitration is clearly between Grissell Watson and her son in London.

335. **1740.** July 2.—Factory (4 March 1740) by Jane Cunninghame, spouse of Archibald Cunninghame, late resident at Gibraltar, to Janet Wedderburn, her sister german, daughter of the late Alexander Wedderburn, Esq., one of the commissioners of excise, for uplifting all monies due to the said Archibald Cunninghame in Great Britain or Ireland. (Mac. 164, pt. ii) Jane Wedderburn is here called by her husband's surname, though at this date it was more usual in Scotland to describe a married woman by her own patronymic.

336. **1740.** Oct. 27.—Translation (Slains, 1 Feb. 1731) by Dr. John Lamie to Katharine Leslie, relict of Charles Straehan of Balgavies, and to Sir Alexander Wedderburn of Blackness, tutor dative to Margaret, daughter of the late William Straehan of Balgavies, of a certain @-rent. (Dur. 201.)

337. **1740.** Nov. 6.—Factory (Canongate, 22 Sept. 1740) by Mrs. Mary Wedderburn, relict, and Agnes Wedderburn, daughter of the late Alexander Wedderburn, a commissioner of excise, to Thomas Boyes, writer in Edinburgh, to manage their affairs during their absence from Scotland. James Wedderburn, youngest son of the said Alexander, is a witness. (Dur. 201.)

338. **1741.** March 25.—Submission and decreet arbitral (Edinburgh, 24 March 1741) between John Wedderburn, merchant in Budal, eo. Northumberland, and Alexander Christie, merchant in Falkirk. (Mac. 165.)

339. **1741.** April 17.—Tack (1739) by Henry Morison of Hiltoun to James Wedderburn in Richlesyde of Coldinghame, of the husband laud and acres possessed by the said James, and by his father and grandfather, in the barony of Coldinghamlaw, co. Berwick, for 8 years. Dated at Mordingtown and Edinburgh, 7 and 26 July 1739. (Dur. 202, pt. i.)

340. **1741.** (a) May 11.—Protested bill (Perth, 23 May 1740) by John Gardner v. Sir Alexander Wedderburn of Blackness. (Dur. 202, pt. i.) (b) May 16.—Bond (Blackness, 24 July, 1729) by the said Sir Alexander and his son John Wedderburn to John Duncan. (ib.) (c) May 18.—Bond (8 Feb. 1740) by John Wedderburn, younger of Blackness, to Alexander Maxwell, bailie of Dundee, for 2,000 merks. (ib.) (d) May 18.—Bond (12 Nov. 1736) by the said Sir Alexander to Jean Preston. (ib.) (e) May 18.—Bond (25 March 1738) by the said Sir Alexander and John Wedderburn to Alexander Maxwell. (ib.)

Register of Deeds.

341. **1741.** May 19.—Bond (Blackness, 5 Oct. 1726) between Sir Alexander Wedderburn of Blackness, and John Wedderburn, fiar thereof, to Alexander Maxwell, bailie of Dundee, for 2000 merks. Written by Robert Wedderburn, writer in Forfar. (Mac. 165.)

342. . **1741.** (a) May 19.—Bond (10 Aug. 1736) by John Wedderburn, younger of Blackness, to William Duncan. (Dur. 202, pt. i.) (b) May 21.—Bond (Blackness, 9 June 1736) by Sir Alexander Wedderburn of Blackness and the said John Wedderburn to Mr. John Higginson, supervisor of excise at Perth, for £100 stg. (ib.) (c) May 22.—Bond (Blackness, 21 March 1728) by the same to Mr. John Barclay. (ib.) (d) May 22.—Bond (Blackness, 2 Nov. 1736) by the same to Janet Alison. Robert Wedderburn, writer in Forfar, is a witness. (ib.) (e) May 22.—Bond (15 Nov. 1736) by John Wedderburn, younger of Blackness, to Janet Alison. (ib.) (f) May 22.—Bond (13 Feb. 1739) by the same to Mr. Thomas Clapham. (ib.) (g) June 9.—Bond (19 March 1740) by Sir Alexander Wedderburn of Blackness and John Wedderburn, fiar thereof, to Alexander Kirkwood. (ib.) (h) June 9.—Bond (22 Nov. 1739) by the same to Mrs. Annie Dempster. (ib.) (i) July 8.—Bond (23, 25 Sept. 1733) by the same to Alexander Smith. (ib.)

343. **1742.** Feb. 25.—Discharge (1741-42) by James Halyburton, elder and younger of Pitcur, to Dr. John Wedderburn of Dundee and Thomas Ogilvy of Coull, of all their management of the lands of Pitcur under a commission dated 2 Nov. 1736. Dated at Halyburton 7 Sept. 1741 and at Whitchurch in Shropshire 6 Feb 1742. (Mac. 167.) A similar discharge (2 Nov. 1736) by the same to the same is recorded 2 March 1742. (Mac. 170.)

344. **1742.** March 5.—Protested bill (8 July 1741) by William Crawford, writer in Edinburgh, v. Thomas Wedderburn, Esq., collector of excise at Inverness. Dated at Burrowstowness. (Dur. 203, pt. i.)

345. **1742.** April 1.—Protested bill (11 Aug. 1741) at the instance of John Weatherburn, merchant in Budle, co. Northumberland, v. Mr. James Dundas, baxter, of Edinburgh, for £161 stg. Dated at Edinburgh. (Mac. 167.)

346. **1742.** June 8.—Consent (Edinburgh, 7 June 1742) by Thomas Kyd, merchant in Leith, for the relaxation of John Wedderburn, fiar of Blackness, from the horn where he lies for non-payment of the said bond, ante No. 342 (g). (Dur. 203, pt. i.)

347. **1742.** Oct. 5.—Protested bill (Falkirk, 2 June 1742) at the instance of Robert Wedderburn, merchant in Dunfermline, v. Mr. Gilbert Robinson, merchant in Elphingstoue, and Alexander Christie, merchant in Falkirk, for £31. 2. 0. stg. (Mac. 168.)

348. **1742.** Nov. 4.—Factory (16 July 1740) by Anna, daughter of the late Alexander Bruce in Dundee and spouse to Peter Lobrey of S. Petersburgh, to David Wedderburn of Wedderburn, Esq., to manage her affairs in Scotland. Dated at S. Petersburgh. (Mac. 168.)

349. **1743.** March 23.—Translation (1 Dec. 1741) by Sir Alexander Wedderburn of Blackness to John Pringle, W.S., of £3,000 scots contained in a bond (14 May 1694) by Patrick Lord Kinnaird to Mr. Robert Rait, minister in Dundee, and narrating a disposition thereof by the said minister to Peter Wedderburn, merchant in Dundee, his uncle. In the disposition Sir Alexander is designed sheriff clerk of Forfar. John Wedderburn, younger of Blackness, is a witness to the translation. (Mac. 169.)

350. **1743.** Aug. 15.—Bond (4 April 1743) by John Wedderburn, younger of Blackness, to Archibald Duke of Douglas for £513. 14 3¼. stg. David Wedderburn of Wedderburn is a witness. (Dur. 204, pt. ii.)

351. **1744.** Feb. 1.—Disposition (Kinross, 6 Jan. 1743) by John Hope (son of Sir John Hope of Kinross) to Robert Wedderburn (son of Sir Peter Halket, alias Wedderburn, of Pitfirrane) merchant at Dunfermline, of au @-rent furth of Kinross. (Dur. 205, pt. i.)

352. **1744.** May 23. —Discharge (1744) by Rachel Thomson, spouse to Robert Wedder- Register burn, merchant in Dunfermline (who consents thereto), to Alexander, second son of the of Deeds. late Mr. John Thomson of Charleton, W.S., her father, of 15,000 merks due by her said father's bond of provision (19 March 1733) to her. Dated at Edinburgh 22 May and there ratified 23 May 1744. (Mac. 170.)

353. **1745.** Feb. 27. —Submission (1744) by Alexander Duncan of Lundie and David Wedderburn of Wedderburn to the arbitration of Mr. David Scrimgeour of Birkhill and another of disputes as to the thirlage, &c. of Wester Gourdie and Denmilne, &c. Dated at Dundee 22 Feb, and at Edinburgh 6 March 1744. Decreet at Edinburgh 27 Feb. 1745. (Dur. 206, pt. i.)

354. **1745.** (a) March 20.—Disposition (23 June 1709) by John Duncan to Alexander Wedderburn, clerk of Dundee, of an @-rent furth of the Earl of Strathmore's lands. (b) Disposition (23 July 1715) thereof by the said clerk to John Mann. (Dur. 206, pt.i.)

355. **1745.** (a) May 7.—Contract of marriage (Edinburgh, 11 Feb. 1745) between Captain James St. Clair in Harrow of Stobo, and Mrs. Agnes Wedderburn, daughter of the late Alexander Wedderburn, Esq., one of the commissioners of excise in Scotland. The husband settles 7,000 merks over and above 3,000 merks to be provided by the wife, together with her share of the estate of her late brother Alexander, paid to her by her brother german Mr. Peter Wedderburn, conform to decreet arbitral (7 April 1735), and also the half of 3,000 merks due to the late James Wedderburn, her brother, and which was his share of his said brother Alexander's estate, and was left by him to his said sister Mrs. Agnes Wedderburn by his will dated 3 Dec. 1743. (Dal. 157.) (b) Factory (Edinburgh, 13 April 1745) by the said Mrs. Agnes Wedderburn, wife of the said Captain James St. Clair, to Henry Ker of Gradane to manage her affairs. (ib.)

356. **1745.** Nov. 15.—Protested bill (7 Feb. 1745) at the instance of Robert Dick, writer in Edinburgh, v. David Wedderburn of Wedderburn, Esq. for £26. 2. 11. stg. Dated at Edinburgh. (Mac. 171, pt. ii)

357. **1746.** March 22.—Protested bill (Berwick, 27 June 1735) by Robert Wedderburn, merchant in Dunfermline, v. Captain George Watson of Col. Lee's Regiment. (Dur. 206, pt. iii.)

358. **1746.** April 28.—Disposition, &c. (Pitfirrane, 27 Oct. 1725) by Sir Peter Halket of Pitfirrane, alias Wedderburn of Gosford, to Charles Wedderburn, his second son, of certain moneys, referring to Sir Peter's bond of tailzie (9 Sept. 1706) settling Gosford on his second son, in view of his eldest son Peter succeeding to Pitfirrane as heir of his now (1725) deceased mother, Dame Janet Halket. (Dur. 206, pt. iii.)

359. **1746.** Two protested bills, both dated at Edinburgh, 9 May, 1745, at the instance of (a) William Sibbald, tailor in Edinburgh; (b) John Brown, merchant there, v. Thomas Wedderburn, collector of excise at Forres, now of Fortrose. (Mac. 172) In the first of these bills Fortrose is written " Yorston," probably by miscopy from the original.

360. **1746.** May 20.—Factory (Edinburgh, 19 May 1746) by Alexander Wedderburn, fourth son of the late Sir Peter Halket of Pitfirrane, to Alexander Robertson, W.S., to uplift his @-rents, &c. (Dur. 206, pt. iii.)

361. **1746.** July 17.—Bond (1745) by James Drummond of Perth to Mrs. Grizell Wedderburn, only daughter of the late Alexander Wedderburn of Wedderburn, for £500 stg. Dated at Drummond Castle, 10 June 1745. (Dur. 206, pt. iii.)

362. **1746.** July 18.—Bond (Forfar, 13 Dec. 1742) by Robert Fletcher, younger, of Ballinshoe to Dr. John Wedderburn of Idvies. (Mac. 172, pt. ii.)

363. **1746.** (a) Co-factory and discharge (Charlestown in South Carolina, 1 May 1745) by James Wedderburn of Carolina, merchant (also designed merchant in Amsterdam) and son of Sir Peter Halket of Pitfirrane (alias Wedderburn of Gosford) to James Yeaman of Murie (also designed merchant in Amsterdam) of his intromissions with their co-partnery, under agreement dated at Amsterdam 6 Feb. 1728. (b) Factory (Edinburgh, 12 Dec. 1732) by the said James Wedderburn and James Yeaman, merchants, late in Amsterdam, in company under the name of " Wedderburn and Yeaman," to the said James Yeaman to manage the affairs of the said company during the absence furth of Scotland of the said James Wedderburn. Mr. Peter Wedderburn, advocate, is a witness. (Dur. 206, pt. iv.)

364. **1746.** Oct. 31.—Disposition (28 June 1743) by Sir Alexander Wedderburn of Blackness, and John Wedderburn, his eldest son, fiar thereof, to Alexander Hunter of Balskelly of the lands of Blackness. David Wedderburn of Wedderburn and Dr. John Wedderburn of Idvies are witnesses. (Mac. 172, pt. ii.)

365. **1746.** Dec 23.—Factory (4 Jan. 1746) by Captain James St. Clair in Harrow of Stobo to Mrs. Agnes Wedderburn, his spouse, to manage his affairs owing to his absence from home. Dated at Stobhead near Bannockburn. (Mac. 172, pt. ii.)

366. **1747.** March 7.—Protested bill (Edinburgh, 17 Feb. 1747) by Mr. Robert Wedderburn (not designed) v. the Countess of Kilmarnock. (Dur. 207, pt. i.)

367. **1747.** July 1.—Factory (Gosford, 12 Nov. 1746) by Charles Wedderburn of Gosford to Robert Wedderburn, merchant in Dunfermline, his brother german, to uplift the rents of Gosford and Balmule. (Dur. 207, pt. ii.)

368. **1747.** Oct. 14—Factory (Edinburgh, 24 Aug. 1747) by John Wedderburn, late merchant at Greenfield, now at Hankey, co. Northumberland, to John Watson, W.S., to manage his affairs in Scotland. (Mac. 173, pt. ii.)

369. **1748.** Protested bill (Clackmannan, 16 June 1744) by Mr. Robert Wedderburn, merchant in Dunfermline, v. William Young, in Hardiestown. (Mac. 174, pt. i.)

370. **1748.** Nov. 1.—Protested bill (Edinburgh, 3 March 1748) by Mr. David Scott v. David Wedderburn, Esq. and Mr. David Graham, advocate. (Dur. 208.)

371. **1748.** Nov. 3.—Factory (Gosford, 24 Oct. 1748) by Charles Wedderburn of Gosford to John Wedderburn, his eldest son, lieutenant in Sir John Bruce's regiment, to uplift the rents of Gosford. (Dur. 208.)

372. **1750.** Nov. 24.—Disposition (Edinburgh, 23 Nov. 1750) by James Campbell of S. Germain's to Alexander Wedderburn, fourth son of the late Sir Peter Halkett, of the lands of Aldingstone, Chesterhall, and S. Germain's for £6,688. 15. stg. (Dur. 210.)

373. **1753.** July 19.—Tack (21 Nov. 1735) by David Wedderburn of Wedderburn to Andrew Donaldson, of the lands of Hillhouses, co. Forfar. (Dur. 212.)

374. **1752.** June 26 —Declaration and opinion (Edinburgh, 13 Oct. 1750) by Mr. Peter Wedderburn, advocate, and others, as to the estate of Alexander Monteith of Todhall. This is in the nature of a decreet arbitral or award. (Mac. 178, pt. ii.)

375. **1752.** Aug. 14.—Consent (Duuse, 28 July 1752) by James Campbell to the trustees of the creditors of Mr. Thomas Menzies of Letham granting a firmance conveyance of all rights to the lands of S. Germain's, Chesterhall, and Greendyke to Alexander Wedderburn, fourth son of Sir Patrick Halket of Pitfirran. (Mac. 178, pt. ii.)

376. **1752.** Sept. 20.—Protested bill (Culross, 19 March 1752) by John Buntine, vintner in Dunfermline v. Captain Peter Wedderburn in General Halket's regiment. (Mac.178,pt.ii.)
      Peter is an error for John, the reference being to John, eldest son of Charles Wedderburn of Gosford (ante No. 371), who ultimately succeeded as Sir John Wedderburn-Halkett of Pitfirran.

377. **1756.** July 16.—Protested bill (Gallacantra, 21 July 1755) by John Smith, merchant in Aberdeen, *v.* Mr. Thomas Wedderburn, collector of excise. (Mac 182, pt. ii.) Register of Deeds.

378. **1756.** Dec. 24.—Factory (1756) by John Wedderburn, eldest son of the late Sir John Wedderburn late of Blackness, aud grand-nephew and heir apparent of the late Dr. John Wedderburn of Dundee, to David Wedderburn of Wedderburn and others to act in regard to the estate of the Campbells of Kethick, for whom the said Dr. John Wedderburn was trustee. Dated at the grantor's home Westmorland, Jamaica, 14 May 1756. (Dur. 215, pt. ii.)

379. **1757.** March 10.—Submission (1753-55) and decreet arbitral (1757) by Mrs. Rachael Thomson, relict and executrix of Robert Wedderburn, merchant of Dunfermline, and David Adic on behalf of the creditors of the said Robert, among whom are Sir Peter Halket of Pitfirrane, Baronet, and Charles Wedderburn of Gosford, in regard to the estate of the said Robert. The submission is dated at Dunfermline and Edinburgh 18 and 21 Jan. 1753 and is adjourned at Dunfermline 31 Dec. 1754 to 25 July 1755. The said Rachael Thomson produces a decreet of adjudication by Davie Adie *v.* Rachaell and Janet, only children and heirs of the said Mr. Robert Wedderburn, in regard to the land of Wester Balbridge, last possessed by their said father. The decreet is dated at Edinburgh 10 March 1757. (Mac. 183, pt. i.)

380. **1757.** March 18.—Discharge (Dunfermline, 3 Nov. 1744) by Rachael Thomson and Robert Wedderburn, merchant in Dunfermline, her husband, to her brother John Thomson of Charleton for 3,000 merks due by bond 26 Dec. 1738. (Dur. 216.)

381. **1757.** March 22.—The Minute Book has a reference to Mackenzie's office " Protest John Mair *v.* Robert Wedderburn," but on searching the record this refers to a Robert Woodburn, and is not material. (Min. Book.)

382. **1757.** (*a*) March 24.—Discharge (of this date at Edinburgh) by the creditors of Robert Wedderburn to his said relict, Rachell Thomson. (Mac. 183, pt. i.) (*b*) April 27.—Discharge dated at Cavil 6 April 1757, by the said Rachel to David Adie. (*ib.*) (*c*) April 28.—Discharge, dated at Edinburgh 26 March last, by John Wedderburn of Gosford, son and executor to the late Charles Wedderburn thereof, to the said Rachel Thomson and David Adic. (*ib.*)

383. **1757.** May 25.—Discharge (April—May 1757) by Lady Amelia Halket, relict of the late Sir Peter Halket of Pitfirrane, Bart., and factrix for Major Francis Halket, second son of the said Sir Peter, and other creditors of the late Mr. Robert Wedderburn, merchant in Dunfermline, to the said Mrs. Rachaell Thomson and David Adic. Dated at Dunfermline 5, 7, and 21 April, and at Pitfirrane 19 May 1757. (Mac. 183, pt. i.)

384. **1757.** June 11.—Commission (13 Sept. 1756) by Captain John Wedderburn of Gosford to Alexander Wedderburn of S. Germain's, Esq., and another to manage his affairs in his absence. Dated at Bowling-green. (Dal. 181.)

385. **1757.** Nov. 4.—Factory (Edinburgh, 26 Oct. 1757) by Mr. Alexander Wedderburn, advocate, being resolved to reside in London for some time, appointing John Flockhart, writer in Edinburgh, his clerk, to manage his affairs in Scotland during his absence. (Dal. 182.)

386. **1758.** Feb. 13.—Discharge (11 Feb. 1758) by Walter Ainslie to the said Rachel Thomson and David Adie. Dated at Edinburgh. (Mac. 184, pt. i.)

387. **1758.** March 21.—Protested bill (15 April 1757) by James Robertson *v.* Thomas Wedderburn, collector of excise, and another. Dated at Forres. (Mac. 184, pt. i.)

388. **1758.** (*a*) July 26.—Discharge (15 and 19 Dec. 1738) by the trustees of the creditors of David Campbell of Kethick and David, his son (including Dr. John Wedderburn, David Wedderburn of that ilk, and others), to Alexander Fraser of

Strichen, one of the senators of the College of Justice, of a bond (18 Dec. 1736) granted them by the said A. Fraser for £85,894. 12. 0 scots. Dated at Dundee and Edinburgh. (Mac. 184, pt. ii.) (*b*) July 27.—Discharge (9 June 1738) by the same to Stewart James Mackenzie of Rosehaugh, of £42,000 scots. (*ib.*)

389.   **1758.** Aug. 17.—Indentures (at Fortrose 3 Oct. 1752) between Thomas Wedderburn, Esq., collector of excise, and John Miller in Fortrose, binding the latter an apprentice to the former for 4 years. (Dal. 184.)

390.   **1758.** Sept. 11.—Protested bill (11 Sept. 1758) by Charles Gordon, writer in Edinburgh, *v.* Thomas Wedderburn, collector of excise, at Galleantry. Dated at Fochabers. (Mac. 184, pt. ii.)

391.   **1760.** Jan. 7.—Factory (Gosford, 12 Nov 1754) by Captain John Wedderburn of Gosford to Alexander Hart to uplift the rents of Gosford, and the @-rent of 62,000 merks contained in a wadset right by the late Sir John Nisbet of Dirleton to the late John Wedderburn of Gosford. (Dal. 187.)

392.   **1760.** Jan. 9.—Disposition (Edinburgh, 24 Nov. 1759) of the lands of Baldovan with the bank, manor-place, &c., thereof, by David Wedderburn of Wedderburn to Walter Tullideph of Balgay for £6,750 stg. (Dal. 187.)

393.   **1760.** Feb. 15.—Disposition (10 May 1755) by John Wedderburn of Gosford, Esq., to Patrick, Lord Elibank, of the lands and barony of Ballincreiff, narrating a prorogation of tacks obtained by the late Charles Wedderburn of Gosford, father of the dispouer, and others. Dated at Edinburgh. (Mac. 187.)

394.   **1760.** June 28.—Protested bill (Edinburgh, 26 Sept. 1759) by Thomas Barclay *v.* Thomas Wedderburn, collector of excise at Inverness. (Dur. 219.)

395.   **1760.** Nov. 11.—Submission (Edinburgh, 20 Sept. 1760) by David Wedderburn of Wedderburn for himself and Margaret Brisbane, and Thomas Mylu of Mylnefield, of differences as to the lands of Bullion. Decreet arbitral given at Dundee 7 Nov. 1760. (Dur. 219.)

396.   **1761.** Jan. 19.—Disposition (7 Nov. 1760) by the same to the same of three-fourths of the mill of Bullion. (Dur. 220.)

397.   **1762.** Feb. 15.—Disposition (Edinburgh, 15 Feb. 1762) of the lands of Balmule, in the parish of Dunfermline, by John McFarlane, W.S., to John Wedderburn of Gosford. (Dal. 191.)

398.   **1762.** March 8.—Submission (Jan. 1761) between David Wedderburn of Wedderburn, Esq., and Mrs. Marion Clayhills of Innergowrie, with consent of Dr. George Murray, her husband, as to the straightening of the burn of Innergowrie, &c., to the decreet arbitral of John, Lord Gray, and Alexander Hunter of Balskelly. The submission is dated at Edinburgh, 23 Jan., and Innergowrie, 27 Jan. ; the decreet at Gray and Blackness, 3 Feb. 1761. (Mac. 191, pt. i.)

399.   **1764.** March 1.—Protested bill (Alyth, 15 Nov. 1763) by Robert Wedderburn of Pearsie *v.* Laurence Brand. (Dur. 223.)

400.   **1765.** May 8.—Disposition (Dunfermline, 20 June 1746) by Robert Wedderburn, merchant in Dunfermline, to Dr. Charles Stewart, in London, of an @-rent, furth of Kinross. (Dur. 224, pt. i)

401.   **1766.** June 2.—Disposition (1733) by Sir James Wood of Bonytoun and others, trustees for the creditors of the late David, Earl of Northesk, to Dr. John Wedderburn in Dundee of the estate of Idvies, &c. Dated at Chelsea and Edinburgh 20 April, 17 July, and 9 Aug. 1733. (Dur. 225, pt. i.)

402. **1766.** (*a*) June 26.—Renunciation (London, 20 June 1766) by Alexander Wedder- **Register**
burn, Councillor at Law in London, to Thomas, Earl of Dundonald, of the lands of **of Deeds.**
Romanno Grange, in Newbattle, Newlands, eo. Peebles. (Dur. 225, pt. i.) (*b*) Nov. 11.
—Power of Attorney (London? 2 Oct. 1766) by the said Alexander Wedderburn, of
Lincoln's Inn, to Andrew Stewart, W.S., in Edinburgh, and another to sell twelve
shares in the Bank of Scotland standing in his name. (Dur. 225, pt. ii.)

403. **1767.** April 13.—Bond of provision (23 June 1759) by Mr. John Erskine of Bal-
gownie, advocate, to his wife, Janet, daughter of the late Charles Wedderburn of
Gosford, Esq., binding himself to infeft her in £200 stg. a year for life out of
Balgownie. Dated at Culross, co. Perth. (Mac. 201, pt. i.)

404. **1767.** May 14—Disposition (12 Feb. 1752) by Margaret Brisbane, sister german of
the late David Brisbane of Bullion, writer in Dundee, to David Wedderburn of
Wedderburn, of the lands of Bullion or Catermillie, in the barony of Auldbarr, Forfar,
and now by annexation in that of Longforgan, Perth. (Mac. 201, pt. ii.)
   The word "late" refers to the date of registration, as David Brisbane died 15 June 1752.

405. **1768.** Jan. 13.—Protested bill (Edinburgh 13 May 1767) by James Spencer *v.*
Captain Henry Wetherburn (*sic*), late of Bengall, and another. (Dur. 227.)

406. **1769.** Feb. 4.—Disposition (3 Feb. 1769) by Captain John Wedderburn of Gosford,
titular of the teinds of Innerwick, to Thomas Tod, W.S., of the lands and teinds of
Newbigging, &c. Dated at Edinburgh. (Mac. 205, pt. i.)

407. **1769.** Aug. 9.—Factory (March 6 1769) by Peter Wedderburn, now in Jamaica, to
John Wedderburn of Idvies, his brother german, James Paterson of Carpow, and
another, to manage his affairs in Scotland, England, and Ireland, and particularly those
as to his interest as one of the heirs of tailzie of the late James Carnegy of Boysack.
Dated at Savannah in Jamaica. (Dur. 228.)

408. **1769.** Aug. 25.—Contract of administration (Aug. 1769) between Charles, Earl of
Elgin, and John Wedderburn of Gosford, Esq., for himself and as tutor to Sir Peter
Halket of Pitfirrane, Bart., and Robert Welwood of Garvock, anent the making of a
road through Broomhall in the parish of Dunfermline. Dated at Broomhall 22 Aug.,
and executed at Edinburgh 24 Aug. 1769. (Mac. 206, pt. 1.)[1]

409. **1769.** (a) Aug. 12.—Obligation (London, 2 April 1735) by Sir James Wood of
Bonytoun and the creditors of David, Earl of Northesk, to Dr. John Wedderburn in
Dundee, to infeft him in the lands of Letham and Newbigging in St. Vigean's, eo.
Forfar, in warrandice of those of Idvies. (Dur. 228.) (*b*) Disposition (Edinburgh,
25 March 1736) by the trustees for the said creditors to the same of a heritable bond
for 5,500 merks, dated 9 Jan. 1683. (*ib.*)

410. **1769.** Dec. 6.—Disposition (21 Nov. 1769) by Thomas Carnegy of Craige to John
Wedderburn of Idvies of the lands of Kallindean and part of Balledgarno for
£6,500 stg. (Dur. 228.)

411. **1770.** June 11.—Heritable bond (21 Nov. 1769) by John Wedderburn, Esq., of
Idvies, to Thomas Carnegy of Craige for £4,000, charged on the land of Idvies, as
part of the price of the estate of Ballendean. (Mac. 207, pt. ii.)

412. **1770.** July 6.—Minute of sale (1770) between William Gray of Palledgarno to Sir
John Wedderburn of Idvies, with consent of Lady Margaret Ogilvy, his wife, of the new
mansion of Balledgarno, gardens, &c., in luchture, eo. Perth, for £5,500 stg. Dated at
Dundee 26 May 1770, and at Balledgarno 28 May, 6 June 1770. (Dur. 229, pt. ii.)

---

[1] The Minute Book has a reference to the Mackenzie office, 1769. Nov. 16.—"Protest Alexander Wedderburn *v.* John Paterson," but the record of this protest (dated at Kelso) refers to an Alexander Wether-
stone in Bellshill, and John Paterson in Douglas in Kilhead, and is not material. (Min. Book.)

413. **1771.** Feb 6.—A reference in the Minute Book to Durie's record (230) of this date is noted in the register, "Taken out on receipt."

414. **1771.** May 9.—Agreement (1763) between John Wedderburn of Gosford, as proprietor of Balmule, and as curator to Sir Peter Halket of Pitfirrane, his cousin, and George Chalmers of Luscar, &c., in regard to the working of their several coal works. Dated at Cavill 18 July, and at Edinburgh 19 July 1763. (Dal. 209.)
    See post No. 433.

415. **1772.** Feb. 13.—Tack (15 May 1767) by Mrs. Grizel Wedderburn of Wedderburn to Robert and Archibald Hears of the parks of Easter Wedderburn for five years. (Mac. 211, pt. i.)

416. **1772.** Dec. 2.—Disposition (13 July 1706) by the town council of Dundee to Alexander Wedderburn, their clerk, of those portions lately dissolved from the barony of Dundee and incorporated in a new barony, to be called the Hilltoun of Dundee, for payment of £9,727. 0. 2. scots. (Mac. 212, pt. i.)

417. **1772.** Dec. 2.—Disposition (28 Aug. 1717) by Alexander Wedderburn, sheriff clerk of Forfar, to Mr. Henry Guthrie, late provost of Dundee, of his lands of Clepingtoun and other acres on the east side of the Hilltoun of Dundee. (Mac. 212, pt. i.)

418. **1773.** Aug. 16.—Tack (1763) by Dame Agnes Murray Kinnymond of Melgund and Kinnymond. with consent of Sir Gilbert Elliot of Minto, Bart., her husband, to John Wedderburn of Gosford, of all the coals in the lands of Urquhart, &c., for 50 years at £1,000 stg. a year. Dated at London 2 Sept., and at Pitfirran 14 Sept. 1769. (Dal. 214, pt. i.)

419. **1773.** (a) Aug. 20.—Bond (Edinburgh, 23 June 1760) by Roderick Macleod, W.S., and William Ker, goldsmith in Edinburgh, to Katharine Wedderburn, relict of John Higginson in Perth, for £100 stg. (Dal. 214, pt i.) (b) Sept 14.—Discharge (11 Sept 1773) of the said bond by the said grantee to the said grantors. (ib.)

420. **1775.** March 6.—Factory (Calcutta, 25 March 1774) by Henry Wedderburn (second son of the late Charles Wedderburn of Gosford) to Alexander Wedderburn of S. Germain's, his uncle, and another, to deal with a bond for £1,000 stg. granted to the said Henry by John Belches of Innermay. (Dur. 234.)

421. **1775.** March 28.—Agreement (18-19 July 1763) between John Wedderburn of Gosford for himself and as tutor to Sir Peter Halket of Pitfirrane, Bart., his cousin. and George Chalmers as to the working of the coal of Balmule, &c. Dated at Cavill and Edinburgh. (Mac. 217.)
    The Minute erroneously refers to this as "Wedderburn *of that ilk* and Chalmers." It seems to be a re-registration of the document already recorded, ante No. 414.

422. **1775.** Aug. 10.—Bond (Edinburgh, 7 Oct. 1772) by Sir John Wedderburn of Ballendean, Bart., to John Davidson, Treasurer of the Society in Scotland for prorogating (sic) Christian Knowledge, for £5,500, in corroboration of a bond (Feb. 1758) by William Gray of Balledgarno to the said John Davidson and another on behalf of the said Society. (Dal 218.)

423. **1776.** March 18.—(a) Translation (Balharry, 25 June 1770) by Sir John Wedderburn of Idvies and others, for John Kinloch in Jamaica, to James Smyth of Balharry of certain lands. (b) Disposition (same place and date) by same to same of the lands of Kinloch. (Dur. 235.)

424. **1777.** Feb. 8.—Commission (Fort William, Calcutta, 19 Jan. 1776) by Henry Wedderburn to Alexander Wedderburn of S. Germain's, his uncle, and others, to sell his lands of Gosford. (Dur. 236.)

425. **1777.** Feb. 14.—Tack (19 Feb. 1772) by Mrs. Grizel Wedderburn of Wedderburn to James Speid, of the parks of Wedderburn for 5 years. (Mac. 221.)

426. **1777.** Dec. 15.—Disposition and settlement (28 Aug. 1771) by Mrs Rachel Wedderburn, daughter of the late Sir Alexander Wedderburn of Blackness, one of the principal clerks of the bills, to Lieutenant John Row of the 9th Regiment of Foot, her cousin, whom failing to Sir Andrew Lauder Dick of Fountainhall, her cousin, and his heirs, of the dwelling house in Bristo, near Edinburgh, presently possessed by her aunt, Mrs. Issobell Seaton and herself. Dated at the said dwelling house. (Mac. 222.) The cousins referred to were relatives on her mother's side.

427. **1778.** April 10.—Tack (3 and 5 March 1759) by Alexander Wedderburn of S. Germain's and another, commissioners for John Wedderburn of Gosford, to Peter Bairnsfather of the lands of Spital for nineteen years. Dated at S. Germain's and Edinburgh. (Dal. 223.)

428. **1778.** (a) June 18.—Two bonds (dated at —— 2 Jan. 1778) by Michael Anderson and John Colville, wine merchants of London, to Alexander Wedderburn of S. Germain's for £10,000 and 16,000 stg. (Dal. 237, pt. i.) (b) June 29.—Four letters of relief (18 Sept. 1773, 6 Jan. 1774, 18 and 24 Feb. 1775) by the same to the same for £3,000, £1,000, £500, and £2,000 stg. (ib.)

429. **1778.** Commission (30 Sept. 1778) by Mrs. Mary Wedderburn, eldest daughter and apparent heir of taillie and provision of the deceased Henry Wedderburn of Gosford, Esq., and wife of Lieutenant Colonel John Cummings in the service of the East India Company, with consent of her said husband, now absent from Scotland, to Andrew Mackenzie, W.S., for the sale of the lands and barony of Gosford, and ranking of his creditors. Dated at Edinburgh. (Mac. 224. pt. ii.)

430. **1779.** March 10.—Bond (4 and 8 March 1774) by Alexander Wedderburn of S. Germain's and others to James Spence, treasurer to the Bank of Scotland, for £1,200 stg. Dated at Torryburn and Glasgow, and witnessed by Alexander Davidson, servant of James Wedderburn, Esq., late of the island of Jamaica. (Mac. 225, pt. i.)

431. **1779.** April 20.—Discharge (Feb. 1773) by John Wedderburn of Bandine(sic), nephew and universal disponee of the late Dr. John Wedderburn, to Alexander Robertson, merchant in Dundee, and Thomas Kyd, merchant in Leith, and others, the trustees of the late David Campbells, elder and younger, of Kethick, of 2,800 merks due to the said Dr. John Wedderburn and Margaret Balfour his wife and their heirs by bond dated 4 March 1731. Dated at Edinburgh and Leith, 22 Feb. 1773, and at Dundee 25 Feb. 1773. (Mac. 225, pt. ii.)

432. **1779.** April 20.—Discharge (7 April 1773) by Katharine Wedderburn, relict of John Higginson, some time merchant in Perth, to the said trustees, of £201. 14. 0. contained in a bill (7 Dec. 1720) drawn by the late Alexander Wedderburn, shipmaster in Dundee, and accepted the said David Campbell, elder and younger. (Mac. 225, pt.ii.)

433. **1779.** May 4.—Bond (1778—79) by Alexander Wedderburn, Esq., His Majesty's Attorney General, Sir John Halket of Pitfirrane, and others, trustees for Alexander Wedderburn of S. Germain's, to his creditors, whereby the said Alexander Wedderburn of S. Germain's, with consent of his wife Elizabeth Haliburton, dispones his estate to his trustees to pay to his debts (amounting to £13,700 stg.) contracted by him on behalf of Messrs. Anderson and Colville in London, and Robert and Peter Colville of Ochiltree, who are bound to free the said Alexander Wedderburn of S. Germain's therefrom. Dated at London 23 Dec. 1778, at Cavers 11 Jan., Pitfirrane 14 Jan., Dysart 19 Jan., and Keir 25 Jan. 1779. (Dur. 238, pt. i.)

434. **1779.** June 10.—Factory (Bristol, 31 May 1779), by Alexander Wedderburn of Wedderburn to Samuel Mitchelson, W.S., to manage his affairs. (Dal. 225.)

435. **1780.** Jan. 14.—Contract (18 Jan. 1768) between John Wedderburn of Gosford, Esq., and Captain Henry Wedderburn his brother in regard to the suit pending between them and Sir Peter Halket of Pitfirrane, with reference to the entails of Pitfirrane and Gosford. Dated at Edinburgh. (Mac. 227.)

This contract narrates that "whereas the said Henry intends to bring and has given orders for bringing an appeal to the Lords spiritual and temporal of Great Britain in Parliament assembled from a decree and sentence of the Lords of Council and Session in Scotland, dated 27 November 1761, obtained at the instance of Sir Peter Halket of Pitfirran, baronet, only child in life, procreate of the marriage between Colonel Sir Peter Halket of Pitfirran deceased, and Lady Aemilia Stewart his wife, with concourse of Alexander Hart, writer in Edinburgh, curator *ad litem* appointed to the said Sir Peter, against the said John Wedderburn, eldest son of the late Charles Wedderburn of Glasfoord (*sic*) and the said Henry, second son of the said deceased Charles, and certain other defenders therein named, by which decreet the Lords sustained the reasons of reduction of the procuratory of resignation and tailzie made by the late Colonel Sir Peter Halket, dated 14 Oct. 1751, and reduced, decerned, and declared accordingly ; and that the said captain Henry is to prosecute the said appeal in common form of law for obtaining a reversal of that decree upon the appeal, in consequence of which the rights and settlements of the estates of Pitfirran and Gosford, and the succession to the estate of Gosford would devolve upon the said Captain with the burden of relieving the said John, his brother, of the debts and annuities affecting the same, and whereas questions might arise concerning the extent of the debts and burdens of which the said Captain would fall to relieve the said John, and that it might likewise be a question how far the sum of 62,000 merks scots only resting of the principal sum of £100,000 scots contained in a wadset right over the baronies of Innerwick and Thorntoun granted by the late Sir John Nisbet of Dirleton to the also deceased John Wedderburn of Gosford, dated 7 Aug. 1685 and registered in the Books of Session 3 Jan. 1685. to which the said John Wedderburn now of Gosford has right by progress. would fall to be imputed or applied towards payment of these debts or whether the said John Wedderburn might not retain his right thereto and at the same time make choice of and take up the right to the estate of Pitfirran, leaving the debts as a burden on the estate of Gosford ; To prevent all which disputes the parties agree (1) that the said Captain Henry is to enter and prosecute or cause to be entered and prosecuted the said appeal, the expense whereof is to be paid by the said John and Henry equally share and share alike (2) the said Captain (*sic*) John agrees to a reversal of the said decree and will make no opposition to the same, and if obtained so as the right and succession to the estate of Pitfirran should devolve or be found to have fallen to the said John, he binds and obliges him and his heirs to denude themselves not only of the lands and estates of Gosford which they presently hold, in favour of the said Captain Henry, his brother, and the heirs appointed to succeed him by the entail of Gosford and under the conditions thereof, and to assign and make over to him the rents of the said lands and estate for crop and year 1767, and in time coming, and to clear that estate of all incumbrances affecting the same, particularly any settlement made upon Mrs. Mary Hamilton, his present wife, and the bairns of the marriage, with the exception of the debts and annuities after mentioned which the said Captain Henry agrees to pay, but also to make over and assign to the said Captain Henry the foresaid sum of 62,000 merks. The said Captain Henry binds himself to pay to Mrs. Mary Wardlaw, his mother, the annuity of £100 stg. payable to her out of the estate of Gosford, and also an annuity of £23 stg. to Ensign James Wedderburn, his brother. in the terms of the bonds of provision granted to them by the late Charles Wedderburn and other articles of agreement therein narrated."

436 **1780.** Feb 17.—Trust disposition (S. Germain's, 16 Oct. 1778) by Alexander Wedderburn of S. Germain's to Alexander Wedderburn, Esq., His Majesty's Attorney General, Sir John Halket of Pitfirran and others, of his lands of S. Germain's, &c. in trust for him and Elizabeth Haliburton, his wife, subject to his debts. (Dur. 239, pt. i.)

437. **1780.** April 22.—Bond of provision (Edinburgh, 2 Feb. 1768) by Henry Wedderburn, Esq., second lawful son of the late Charles Wedderburn of Gosford, to Mary Wedderburn, his only lawful child, for £2,000 stg. to be paid to her at the first term after his death. Witnessed by Alexander Wedderburn of S. Germain's, Esq. (Mac. 227.)

438. **1780.** July 18.—Bond (Edinburgh, 10 Dec. 1779) by Sir John Wedderburn of Ballendean, Bart., to John Davidson, &c. (as in No. 422) for £5,500 stg. binding himself to infeft him in an @-rent of £275 out of the estate of Idvies and that part of Balledgarno purchased by Sir John from William Gray in 1770. (Dal. 228, pt. i.)

439. **1780.** Dec. 15.—Factory (1780) by Alexander Wedderburn, His Majesty's Attorney General, and others, trustees of Alexander Wedderburn of S. Germain's, to William Ramsay, W.S, to manage the said trust. Dated at Edinburgh, Dysart, London, and Cavers, March—May 1780. (Dur. 239.)

440. **1781.** Nov. 20.—Factory (Inveresk, 21 Dec. 1780) by Mrs. Elizabeth Halyburton or Wedderburn, relict of Alexander Wedderburn of S. Germain's, to William Ramsay, W.S., to uplift her annuity granted her by her said husband's trustees. James Wedderburn, residing at Inveresk, is a witness. (Dur. 240, pt. ii.)

441. **1781.** March 23.—Contract (Dunfermline, 6 Aug. 1770) between John Wedderburn of Gosford, otherwise John Halket of Pitfirrane, and Robert Welwood of Garvock in regard to the cornmills of Pitliver. (Dal. 231.)

442. **1782.** May 16.—Disposition (1782) by Alexander, Lord Loughborough, chief justice of His Majesty's Court of Common Pleas, Sir John Halket of Pitfirrane, James St. Clair of Sinclair, Esq., and Archibald Stirling of Keir, Esq., a quorum of the surviving trustees of the late Alexander Wedderburn of S. Germain's, Esq., and Mrs. Elizabeth Halyburton, or Wedderburn, his spouse, to Captain Gilbert Waugh of parts of the lands of Adingston and Chesterhall, and lands of S. Germain's. Dated at Edinburgh 6 and 15 May and at Keir 16 May 1782. (Dal. 232, pt. ii.)

443. **1782.** Oct. 28.—Disposition (Aug.—Sept. 1782) by Thomas Tod, W.S., assignee in trust for Dame Mary Wedderburn, alias Cuming, eldest daughter of the late Henry Wedderburn of Gosford, and now wife of Lieut.-Col. Sir John Cuming in the service of the H E.I. Company, with consent of the persons (including Sir John Halkett of Pitfirran) appointed by a commission (dated 7 Jan. 1780 and registered 3 May 1782) to manage the affairs of the said Sir John Cuming, while he is in India, in favour of the said Sir John Halkett, alias Wedderburn, of the lands and barony of Innerwick and Thornton, &c. Dated at Old Melrose, London, and Edinburgh, 20 and 29 Aug. and 9 Sept. 1782. (Mac. 232)

444. **1783.** Jan. 22.—Disposition (6 April 1743) by David Wedderburn of that ilk to Mr. Hugh Maxwell of Strathmartine, minister at Forfar, and his eldest son, of the lands of Bridgend of Aehray, part of Baldovan, &c. Mr. David Scrymgeour of Birkhill is a witness. (Dur. 242.)

445. **1789.** April 9.—Bond (20 Dec. 1788) by Alexander Wedderburn, Esq., of Wedderburn, formerly Scrymgeour of Birkhill, to John Brown of Coalstoun, his heirs and assignees for £1,000 stg. Dated at Edinburgh. (Mac. 245.)

This is a curious document reciting the descent of the granter from Sir John Scrymgeour of Dudope, progenitor of the Earls of Dundee, Viscounts Dudope. It was entered into and registered, I think, at a time when Mr. Scrymgeour-Wedderburn was proposing to claim those peerages, and it asserts him to be heir to them as great great grandson of a David Scrymgeour, son of Sir John Scrymgeour of Dudope and brother therefore to John Scrymgeour of Glastre, who was great grandfather's grandfather to James, second Viscount Dudope, father of the first Earl of Dundee. This is certainly inaccurate. Alexander Scrymgeour-Wedderburn, though, with little doubt, heir male to these peerages, through a son of Sir John Scrymgeour named David, was great great grandson of John Scrymgeour of Kirktoun who married Jean McGill, and who was himself the great grandson of James Scrymgeour of Kirktoun, whose father was probably the said David Scrymgeour. See the account of the Scrymgeour-Wedderburns in Vol. i.

446. **1790.** (a) Jan. 23.—Bond (Calcutta, 1 Oct. 1769) by Captain Henry Wedderburn of Calcutta to John Zephaniah Holwell, late of Bengall and now in England, for 15,738 rupees 2 annas and 6 pice. (b) March 13.—Probative statement by the same to the same for the said amount. (Dal. 248.)

447. **1790.** Feb. 3.—Two dispositions (Edinburgh, 2 Feb. 1790) by Sir John Wedderburn of Ballendean, Bart., to George Lord Kinnaird (a) of the lands of Idvies, (b) of the lands of Auchscurrie and Bractullo. (Dal. 248.)

The first of these is entered in the Minute Book as "Disposition John Wedderburn, Rotterdam, to L⁴ Kinnaird, &c.

448. **1794.** May 30.—Tack (1 May 1753) by Charles Wedderburn of Gosford to Alexander Milne, of the lands of Lochill for 80 years at £122 stg., 12 capons and 24 hens. Dated at Gosford and Galdraw. (Mac. 255.)

449. **1797.** May 10.—Disposition (Noram, near Balmerino, 7 July 1789) by Alexander Wedderburn of Wedderburn to James Morison of Naughton of certain houses and three acres of land in Balmerino, co. Fife. (Dur. 277.)

450. **1797.** May 26.—Will of Thomasina Wedderburn, "youngest daughter of the late Collector Thomas Wedderburn." Dated at Sciennes near Edinburgh 2 Jan., with a codicil dated 4 March 1797. She leaves small legacies of money chiefly for the purchase of memorials to various persons, including her sister Katharine, her cousins Mr. Hugh Fraser and his sister Jean (wife of Mr. Fraser, Glassfield), Mrs. Dunbar at Scrabeter, one of her "relations at Caithness," and Mrs. Moodie and Mrs. Nicolson also her cousins. She names with particular appreciation of his "interest in our concerns . . . . . . my cousin Mr. Wedderburn at Inveresk and his wife," and leaves

£10. 10. 0. to buy an ornament for their daughter Jean, to be engraved with the
words "To perpetuate family friendship." She entrusts the execution of some of
these small legacies to her sister-in-law Mrs. John Wedderburn. To one of her
brothers she leaves her watch, and to the other her seal. There is no residuary
bequest. (Mac. 261.)

Of the persons named in this will Mr. Hugh Fraser and his sister were, I believe, the children of
Mary Dunbar, maternal aunt to the testatrix, who m. Robert Fraser of Torbuch, though possibly
they were relatives of her grandmother, who was also a Fraser. Mrs. Dunbar of Scrabeter was the
second wife and now widow of Thomas Dunbar, maternal uncle to the testatrix, while Mrs. Moodie
and Mrs. Nicolson were his two daughters by his first marriage, viz. : Elizabeth who m. James Moodie
of Melsetter, and Mary Maxwell who m. the Rev. Patrick Nicolson of Shaerter. Mr. Wedderburn of
Inveresk is of course, James Wedderburn (or Colvile) whose daughter Jean. b. 1786, m. in 1807 Thomas,
fifth Earl of Selkirk. The two brothers referred to are John Wedderburn of Spring Garden (d. 1820)
and James who died, soon after this will, on 17 July 1797. Thomasina herself died 19 March 1797.

451. **1799.** Nov. 23.—Disposition (1799) by Sir John Wedderburn of Ballendean, Bart.,
and John Cockburn of Ronchester, as trustees of the late Dr. Martin Eccles in Edinburgh, to Mrs. Margaret Laing or Elliott, widow of John Elliott of Borthwick-brae, of
a house in George Square, Edinburgh. Dated at Ronchester 19 Aug. and at Ballendean 26 Aug. 1799. (Mac. 266.)

452. **1801.** Nov. 24.—Disposition (London, 9 Nov. 1801) by John Wedderburn, Esq. of
Lindertis to Gilbert Mason, Esq. of Moredun, of the lands and barony of Reidie and
Kemalty, with manor place, &c. in the parish of Nether Airly, Forfar, in consideration
of a minute of sale (13 and 15 Oct. 1801) between Sir John Wedderburn of Ballendean, Bart., for the said John Wedderburn, Esq., and the said Gilbert Mason, anent
the lands of Lindertis. David and Andrew Wedderburn, merchants in London, are
witnesses. (Dal. 273.)

453. **1802.** Dec. 3.—Probative contract (Edinburgh, 7 March 1774) in contemplation of
their marriage, between James Wedderburn, Esq., of Jamaica (second son of the late
Sir John Wedderburn of Blackness, Bart.) and Isabella, eldest daughter of Mr
Andrew Blackburn, merchant in Glasgow, settling on her at his death an annuity
and also his share of the estates of Glenisla and Bleweastle, par. Westmoreland, co.
Cornwall, Jamaica. Witnessed by Sir John Wedderburn of Ballendean and Alexander
Wedderburn of S. Germain's. (Dal. 286.)

454. **1804.** May 19.—Assignation (1804) by Sir David Wedderburn of Ballendean, Bart.,
Mrs. Margaret Wedderburn, wife of Philip Dundas, Esq., son of the Honorable Robert
Dundas of Arniston, late Lord President of the Court of Session, and Miss Jean Wedderburn, only surviving children of the late Sir John Wedderburn of Ballendean,
Bart., by the also deceased Lady Margaret Ogilvy, his first wife, eldest daughter of the
the now also deceased David Earl of Airley and the said Philip Dundas for his own right
and interest, to John Smith of Balharry, W.S., of the three principal sums of £1,333. 6. 8.
contained in three several bonds of provisions therein mentioned. Dated at London
28 April, at Ballendean 16 May, and at Drummore 14 May 1804. (Mac. 275.)

See s. Blackness Papers, No. 83 (11, 13, 14).

455. **1806.** Dec. 5.—Discharge (1734) by Charles Wedderburn, Esq., second lawful son
of Sir Peter Halket of Pitfirran, Baronet, and John McFarlane, W.S., to Adam
Rolland of the sum of 4 merks payable yearly out of the lands of Balmule in name of
dry multure. Dated at Dunfermline and Edinburgh, 4 and 6 Dec. 1734. (Mac. 280.)

456. **1809.** June 5.—Tack (1807) by Alexander Wedderburn of Wedderburn to Peter
Simpson of the lands of Wester Gourdie for 19 years at £594. 13. 4. yearly tack
duty. Dated at Birkhill and Dundee 10 and 12 May 1807. (Dal. 306.)

457. **1809.** Nov. 17.—Factory (31 Oct. 1809) by Sir David Wedderburn of Ballendean,
Bart., tutor to David Ogilvie of Airly, commonly called Earl of Airly, conform to gift
of factory in his favour dated 19 April and sealed 30 April 1804, to Robert Smyth,
W.S., to uplift the rents, &c. of the lands of the said Earl for the year 1809. Dated
at Balharry. (Mac. 287.)

458. 1811. July 5.—Disposition and tailzie (Birkhill, 25 May 1803) by Alexander Wed- Register derburn of Wedderburn, advocate, of the lands of Easter Powrie, with teinds, &c., also of Deeds. the lands of Birkhill, &c. for new infeftment thereof to himself and the heirs of his body, whom failing to the other heirs after mentioned, heritably and irredeemably, viz. : Henry, son of the late David Scrymgeour of Birkhill, Esq., advocate, (father of the disponer), and the heirs of his body ; Janet Scrymgeour or Gillespie, his sister german, relict of John Gillespie of Mountwhany, and the heirs of her body ; the heirs of the body of the late Marion Scrymgeour, eldest daughter of the late Mr. Alexander Scrymgeour, Professor of Divinity in S. Andrew's ; those of the late Jean Scrymgeour, second daughter of the said professor ; Sir John Wedderburn of Ballendean, Bart. (eldest son of Sir John Wedderburn of Blackness) ; James Wedderburn, brother to Sir John ; Margaret Wedderburn, eldest sister to Sir John, and wife of Richard Dundas of Blair ; Charles Wedderburn of Pearsie ; John Wedderburn, son of the late Thomas Wedderburn (who was brother of the said Sir John Wedderburn of Blackness), and the heirs of their bodies in order, whom all failing the disponer's own nearest heirs and assignees whatsoever, the eldest heir female and the descendants of her body, through the whole course and order of succession above set down, excluding all other heirs portioners and succeeding always alone without division, &c. And in regard John and David Scrymgeour, his brothers, both died unmarried, and the late David Scrymgeour of Birkhill, advocate, had no other children than those called by the entail of Mrs. Grizell Wedderburn of Wedderburn, and also in regard that Peter Wedderburn, the third son, and Katharine, Susan, and Agatha, the second, third, and fourth daughters of the said deceased Sir John Wedderburn of Blackness are all now dead without heirs of their bodies, it is stated that it becomes unnecessary to continue their names in the foregoing order of succession. (Dal. 312.)

459. 1811. (a) July 5.—Bond of provision (Edinburgh, 10 May 1803) by Alexander Wedderburn of Wedderburn to the children of Henry Scrymgeour, his brother german, viz. : Margaret, Katharine, Elizabeth, Janet, Mary, and Isabella Scrymgeour, and to any other lawful daughter of the said Henry who may be born of £300 stg. to be paid at the first term after marriage, and also the like sum to any younger son of the said Henry to be paid at the first term after majority. (Dal. 312.) (b) Bond of annuity (Edinburgh, 30 June 1811) by the said Alexander Wedderburn of Wedderburn to Gilbert Gardiner, his griev, of £15 stg., and to William Hindmarsh, his butler, of £10 stg. for their honest and faithful services. (ib.)

[The following is a list of the above extracts arranged according to the different offices in which they are recorded.

Scott's office, 1-10 12, 14, 15, 17-21, 24, 25, 27, 36, 42, 52-54, 58-59, 63-64, 75, 77, 93, 104, 123, 125-26.

Hay's office, 11, 13, 16, 22, 23, 28, 32, 33, 38, 43, 45, 47, 48, 57, 61, 62, 65-68, 70-74, 76, 78-81, 83-87, 90, 91, 96, 97, 99, 103, 114.

Gibson's office, 26, 29-31, 34, 35, 37, 39-41, 44, 46, 49-51, 55, 56, 60, 69, 82, 88, 89, 92, 95, 98, 100-102, 105-113, 115-22, 124, 127-36.

Brown's office, 137-38, 140-41, 145, 151.

Downie's office, 139, 142-44, 146-50, 152.

Mackenzie's office. 154, 157, 159, 162, 164, 167, 177, 183, 189, 192-93, 196, 201, 203, 214, 216-17, 221, 227-28, 231-34, 236-41, 244-45, 251-52, 254, 258-61, 265-66, 272, 276, 278-80, 282-85, 289, 293, 297-99, 305-7, 309-10, 312, 316-19, 325-27, 331, 333, 335, 338, 341, 343, 345, 347-49, 352, 356, 359, 362, 364-65, 368-69, 374-77, 379, 381-83, 388, 390, 393, 398, 403-4, 406, 408, 411, 415-17, 421, 425-26, 429-32, 435, 437, 443, 445, 448, 450-51, 454-55, 457.

Durie's office, 153, 155-56, 158, 163, 166, 168-71, 175, 179, 181-82, 184-85, 187-88, 190-91, 194, 197, 199-200, 204-13, 218-20, 222, 224-26, 246-47, 250, 253, 256-57, 262, 269, 275, 277, 288, 290-91, 294, 296, 301, 303, 308, 313-15, 320-22, 328-30, 332, 334, 336-37, 339-40, 342, 344-346, 350-51, 353-54, 357-58, 360-61, 363, 366-67, 370-73, 378, 380, 386-87, 394-96, 399-402, 405, 407, 409-10, 412-13, 420, . 423-24, 433, 436, 440, 444, 449.

Dalrymple's office, 160-61, 165, 172-74, 176, 178, 180, 186, 195, 198, 202, 215, 223, 229-30, 235, 242-43, 248-49, 255, 263-64, 267-68, 270-71, 273-74, 281, 286-87, 292, 295, 300, 302, 304, 311, 323-24, 355, 384-85, 389, 391-92, 397, 414, 418-19, 422, 427-28, 434, 438, 441-42, 446-47, 452-53, 456, 458, 459.]

Acts and Decreets Register. This is the record of the Judical proceedings of the Court of Session, and consists of three divisions.

1. The register of the Acts of the Lords of Council (*Acta Dominorum Concilii*) from 4 Oct. 1478 to 15 May 1532. This has been partly published in a folio volume, entitled "Acts of the Lords in Council in Civil Causes, 1478-95, printed by command of H.M. George III, 1839," which has been searched for the purposes of this book. The unpublished portion of this record has also been searched in the original MS. (1495—1532). Another series was also edited by Thomson in 1839, in a volume entitled "Acts of the Lords Auditors of Causes and Complaints, 1466-95," (*Acta Dominorum Auditorum*). This has also been searched and the few material extracts from it (Nos. 1-3) are given below.

II. The register of the Acts of the Lords of Council and Session (*Acta Dominorum Concilii et Sessionis*) from 27 May 1532 to 26 June 1559. This is a continuation of the former register. It runs without a break to 1549, after which there are two volumes (1549—1551) which are really not of Decreets, but of Deeds. The whole has been searched for this work.

III. The register of the Acts and Decreets of the Lords of Council and Session. This, again, is a continuation (though the earlier dates overlap) of the last register. It consists of two series. (*a*) Before the division of the record department of the Courts of Session into offices, 26 June 1542 to 26 February 1659. This has been searched down to 1616, and also from 1654-59. There is also a bundle of warrants (1527—1549) which has been searched but contains only one Wedderburn reference (see post No. 9). (*b*) After the division of the department in offices, designed the Mackenzie, Durie, and Dalrymple offices, and each running from 1661 to 1810. These have been searched down to 1780.

It will thus be seen that the only portions of this record remaining to be searched are III (*a*) 1616-54, not a long period, but one which it would take a considerable time to search as the record is voluminous; and (*b*) thirty years, 1780—1810.

The extracts have been arranged in order of date, while a table of those from 1661 on, showing the offices to which each belongs, is added at p. 477. As in the case of the General Register of Sasines and Register of Deeds, it is noteworthy that, with very few exceptions,[1] all the following entries refer exclusively to members of the Forfarshire family.

I.

(*a*) *Acta Dominorum Auditorum.* 1466-95.   (*b*) *Acta Dominorum Concilii.* 1478-1532.

1. **1476.** July 19.—Decreet in action by Jonet of Wedd'burne *v.* James of Oucht'lowny for 100 merks "aucht to hir ane obligation of Willia of Oucht'lowny grantsehir to ye said James." (Acts of the Lords Auditors, p. 53.)

2. **1491.** May 9.—Decree naming Patrick Lyell, James Wedd'burn, and others. They are apparently named as trading with Norway. (*ib.* p. 149.)

3. **1491.** May 17.—Decree naming Patrick Lyell, James of Wedd'burn, and others. (*ib.* p. 154-55.)
   See also the Acts of the Lords of Council (ed. Thomson, 1839) s. 22 March 1490, when the same matter is mentioned, and a day fixed for hearing it. (p. 189a.)

4. **1501.** July 30.—Action by Christian Farquhare, spouse to William Guthre of Dundee *v.* William Farquhare in regard to the mailis of a tenement in North Murraygate, Dundee, bounded west by that of Andrew Halis, and east by that of the late David Wedderburn. (**10,** 223.[2])

---

[1] These are six or seven in number, viz. : No. 15 referring to a John and Robert and yet another John Wedderburn in Jedburgh Forest, co. Roxburgh (1575) ; No. 56 to a John Wedderburn in the same county (1612) : No. 98 to James Wedderburn in Coldingham (1679) ; No. 119 to John Wedderburn in Pre-tonpans (1690) ; and No. 174 to John Wedderburn at Greenfield in co. Northumberland (1745). Walter Wedderburn in co. Clackmannan (No. 38) may be the son of James Wedderburn of Craigie. See vol. i.

[2] These references are to the volumes and folios of the original record.

5. **1503.** Nov. 23.—Action by Elspeth Mason, relict of Jak Scrymgeour, burgess of Dundee *v.* James Scrymgeour, provost, James Fotheringhame, and James Wedderburn, bailies, &c. for taking away from her house three pipes of wald (dyers' weed). Defenders are decreed to pay her £39. **(15,** 59.) **Acts and Decreets Register.**

6. **1515-16.** Jan. 26.—Testimonial of Dundee touching the goods taken in the prize of Hamburgh, naming James Wedderburn, bailie of Dundee. **(27,** 158.)[1]
   This record has been searched throughout, 1516-32, but contains no further Wedderburn entries.

II.

Acta Dominorum Concilii et Sessionis, 1532-59.

7. **1538.** July 12.—Letters purchased at instance of Mr. James Scrymgeour, chantor of Brechin, *v.* Gilbert Wedderburn, James Carnegy, and others, reciting that the defenders had been lately accused of heresy and that the pursuer had for his safety obtained letters of lawburrows of them under the pain of £200, yet they had by sinister and wrong information purchased letters against him. The Lords suspend the letters purchased by the defenders. **(10,** 134.)

8. **1541-42.** Feb. 3.—Action by Katharine Wedderburn, relict of Andrew Baldovy, *v.* David Baldovy, successor, &c. of the late Michael Baldovy, burgess of Montrose, his father's brother, for the life-rent of ten pounds worth of land in Montrose, pursuant to a contract made between Michael and Janet Barry, his mother. **(17,** 160.)

9. **1545.** April 10.—Summons in the action at the instance of John Campbell, as heir to the late Archibald Campbell of Murthlie, his brother, *v.* Elizabeth Wedderburn, indweller in the burgh of Dundee, as having certain writs relating to the lands of Murthlie and others, which belonged to the said Arehibald, and also *v.* Oliver Maxtoun, burgess of Perth, as having other writs relating to the lands of Strekkis. Execution is dated 11 May. (Warrants 1527-49. See ante p. 464).

10. **1546.** April 10.—Contract between Elizabeth Wedderburn, relict and executrix of the late Archibald Campbell, and now spouse of Patrick Lyoun, for himself and said Patrick for his interest, on the one part, and John Campbell, brother german and heir of the said deceased Arehibald Campbell of Murthlie, on the other part, for settlement of all matters between them. Dated at Dundee 15 March 1545. George Wedderburn is a witness. **(20,** 80.)

11. **1546.** July 3.—Action by David Logan, burgess of Edinburgh, as assignee of the escheat of the goods which pertained to the late James Wedderburn, burgess of of Dundee, *v.* the Abbot of Lindores, Jonet Logane, relict of the said James Wedderburn, Mr. James Bonar, now her spouse, and others, tenants of the lands of the said James Wedderburn and Robert Wedderburn, his son. (21, 13,)

12. **1546.** Dec. 17.—The Lords advocate the action brought by John Onsourik, burgess of Danskin, and others *v.* David Wedderburn and others, burgesses of Dundee, touchingthe spoliation by the defenders of certain "bowstringis and mastis furth of Michaell Arnold's schip" in 1545. **(22,** 59.)

13. **1546-47.** March 14.—Letters purchased at the instance of Elizabeth Wedderburn, relict of the deceased Arehibald Campbell of Murthlie, and Patrick Lyoun now her spouse *v.* John Campbell, brother and heir of the said Archibald, for suspension of letters purchased by the latter *v.* the said Elizabeth for non-implement of a contract betwixt him and John Campbell of Lundy, Knight, as his cautioner, and the said Elizabeth and her said spouse, and James Lovell, their cautioner. Dated at Dundee 15 March 1545. Decreet in favour of Elizabeth Wedderburn and her spouse. **(22,** 173.)

14. **1548-49.** March 22,—Letters of commission by James, Lord S. John's, preceptor of Torphichen, to Mr. Peter Sandelands, parson of Calder, and Mr. James Makgill of Edinburgh, as his commissioners, and Mr. Robert Wedderburn as his chamberlain. Dated at Torphichen 3 July 1548. **(25,** 174.)

---

[1] There is an entry 1504. July 17, where Alexander Welberne of Wodderay appears on an inquest as to the lands of Luckland, co. Forfar, but this does not appear to be relevant. (15, 193.)

3 M

III (*a*).

Acts and Decrees of the Lords of Council and Session, 1542-1810.

Acts and
Decreets
Register.

15. **1575.** June 25.—Action of removing by Archibald Earl of Angus, and his curators *v.* his tenants in the lordship and barony of Jedburgh Forest, Roxburgh, including Sir Andrew Ainslie in Cleithauch, John Wedderburn and Robert Wedderburn in Nunnislaw (Wanuislaw ?) and John Wedderburn also there. (**61,** 82.)

16. **1577.** June 15.—Process by Alexander Guthrie of that ilk *v.* Thomas Ireland, Alexander Wedderburn, notaries, Patrick Lord Gray, sheriff of Forfar, &c. in regard to an action pending between William Douglas of Glenbervie and the said Alexander Guthrie. (**69,** 330.)

17. **1581.** Nov. 5.—Alexander Wedderburn is named as procurator to register a deed between Wood of Bonytown and David Melvin of Baldovy. (**88,** 1.)

18. **1583.** April 10.—Decree at the instance of Alexander Guthrie of that ilk *v.* Alexander Wedderburn, clerk of Dundee, and Joan Fyiff and John Duncan, sheriff officers, for not compearing, although summoned, as witnesses in an action by Guthrie *v.* Patrick, Master of Gray. (**93,** 312.)

19. **1586.** April 29.—Peter Wedderburn, burgess of Dundee, is named in an action by Mr. Walter Lyndsay of Kemphill *v.* William Spalding of Newmyln. (**104,** 199.)

20. **1586.** Nov. 8.—Letters purchased at the instance of David Wedderburn, son to the late Alexander Wedderburn, clerk of Dundee, to enforce his rights as chaplain of S. James "the Mair," SS. Margaret, Ann, Tradwell, Laurence, Anthony, the Magdalen, Our Lady, &c. (**105,** 317.)

21. **1587.** Jan. 12.—Letters purchased by Mr. Stephen Wilsoun, parson of Moffat, *v.* David, Earl of Craufurd, ... Alexander Wedderburn, younger, and others, to make payment to him of a £40 pension granted him by the said Earl. (**105,** 492.)

22. **1586.** Nov. 10.—Letters purchased at the instance of Cristiane Wischart, relict of the late John Wedderburn, burgess of Dundee, *v.* John Wedderburn, burgess of Dundee, his son, as principal, and Alexander Wedderburn and James Forrester as cautioners, for a year's rent of a tenement of Temple land, pertaining to her in life-rent. (**109,** 27.)

23. **1587.** March 4.—Letters purchased at the instance of William Mudie *v.* various persons, &c. including Jonet Andersone, relict of the late Alexander Wedderburn, in regard to the chaplainry of S. Mathew, Dundee. (**110,** 100.)
    Jonet is an error for Isobell.

24. **1590.** Aug. 14.—Action by Robert Barrie of Dundee *v.* various persons, including Thomas, son and heir of the late David Fotheringhame, and Elspet Forrett, his mother. Alexander Wedderburn is named as notary. (**125,** 333.)

25. **1590.** Nov. 18.—Action by David McGill, King's Advocate, James Swan of Dundee and his wife, *v.* Edward Chalmers, reciting a resignation, 22 Feb. 1573, in favour of James Swan by the late Edward Wedderburn and Jonet Inglis, his wife, of a Murraygait tenement, of which Chalmers had wrongfully taken possession during the absence of the Swans in Zetland for some years. (**126,** 290.)

26. **1590.** Nov. 16.—Action by Robert Gray, brother to Andrew Gray of Ballnagerno, *v.* Robert Wedderburn, notary, for delivery up of a charter made in favour of the pursuer by James Scrymgeour of Dudop. (**127,** 276.)

27. **1591.** June 21.—Action by John Wedderburn, burgess of Dundee, *v.* Thomas Henrisone to flit and remove from the pursuer's free lands of Aberbothrie, lying in the sheriffdom of Perth. (**130,** 395.)
    This action is again referred to Vol. 133, fol. 6. See also a similar proceeding by the predecessors of the parties, Reg. Priv. Council i, p. 183.

28. **1591-92.** Jan. 15 —Letters purchased at instance of John Strauchin, merchant and burgess of Dundee, v. Peter Wedderburn, burgess thereof, James Forrester, provost, Patrick Lyoun, and others, reciting that Peter Wedderburn has sued the said John Strauchin for withholding from him one sixteenth part of the ship "The Lyoun of Dundee" and profits thereof for many years past. The Lords remit the action to the provost and bailies of Dundee. **(133,** 342.)

Acts and Decreets Register.

29. **1592.** Aug. 11.—Letters purchased by Andrew Gray v. David Wedderburn, burgess of Dundee, and others for delivery up of certain sasines, &c. of land in Dundee. **(139,** 30.)
The above action is continued 16 Nov. (*ib.* 104.)

30. **1593.** May 23.—Action by Robert Wedderburn, burgess of Dundee, and Margaret Milne, his spouse, v. Sir James Scrymgeour of Dudop, Knight, in respect of an annual-rent due to the pursuers out of the Mains of Dudop. **(140,** 392.)
The above action is continued 13 June. (**142,** 110.)

31. **1594.** March 6.—Letters purchased by James Pitbladow, baxter and burgess of Dundee, v. Alexander Wedderburn, common clerk of Dundee, for delivery up of a certain charter written by the clerk. **(146,** 187.)

32. **1594.** Dec. 30.—Letters purchased by James Weymis of Bogie, tacksman of the Earl of Gowrie, &c., v. Mr. Alexander Wedderburn of Wester Gowrie and others, tenants of the said Earldom, for payment of rents **(150,** 196.)

33. **1595.** June 9.—Action by John Wedderburn, son to Alexander Wedderburn, burgess of Cupar in Fife, v. Rolland Hammiltoun in Ross, William Carmichael, servitor to James Dalzeil, merchant burgess of Edinburgh, and others, as to the production of a contract between the parties. **(151,** 246.)

34. **1598.** Jan. 31.—Decree in action by David Wedderburn, brother german of Mr. Alexander Wedderburn, clerk of Dundee, v. John Muire, burgess thereof, *re* the pursuer's rights as chaplain of S. James. **(171,** 229.)

35. **1598.** May 26.—Action by Margaret Stewart, relict of John Caraill, and now wife of Andrew Bowar, v. Patrick, son to the late Alexander Wedderburn, clerk of Dundee, as to a tenement which belonged to the said Caraill. **(171,** 383.)
Patrick is here used as synonymous with Peter.

36. **1599.** March 3.—Anent the summons at the instance of John and Katharine Lyndsay, second son and daughter to the late Robert Lyndsay of Balhall, v. Elizabeth (*sic.*) Strachin relict of John Wedderburn, burgess of Dundee, and Elizabeth his daughter and heir, claiming the escheat of the goods of the said John Wedderburn, who, on 6 Aug. 1596, was put to the horn for not finding caution to underlie the law for the slaughter of Robert Lyndsay of Balhall on 11 July 1596, and also of James Leitch, Irishman. **(183,** 63.)
See ante s. Reg. Privy Seal, No. 25. *Elizabeth* Strachin is an error for Margaret.

37. **1599.** Nov. 24.—Anent the summons by John Forret of Dundee v. Mr. Alexander Wedderburn, clerk, and David Wedderburn, his brother, for delivery up of an act made in the Court Books of Dundee in favour of Katharine Forret, his sister. **(185,** 10.)

38. **1599.** Dec. 20.—Action by John, Earl of Mar, v Sir Robert Bruce of Clackmannan, Knight, Marjorie Bruce, relict of David Bruce of Lynmylne, Walter Wedderburne, now her spouse, Patrick Bruce in Greine, and others, *re* the teind sheaves (1598-99) of lands occupied by them in the parish of Clackmannan. **(185,** 51.)
This action is again referred to 8 and 12 January 1600. (**186,** 180, and 187, 165.)

39. **1600.** Dec. 17.—Action by Peter Wedderburn, burgess of Dundee, v. Sir Walter Ogilvy of Findlater for £82. 6. 8. for furnishing Pantoun of Pitmedden's brother with meat, drink, and other ordinaries at Sir Walter's order. **(185,** 355.)
This action is continued and decreet given for the pursuer 17 July 1601. (**196,** 186.)

40. **1600.** July 29.—Action by Mr. Henry Duncan, minister of Murroes, v. Mr. Alexander Wedderburn, clerk of Dundee, for production of a decreet arbitral made by the defender in a matter between the pursuer and James Durham of Pitarrow. **(191,** 242.)

Acts and
Decreets
Register.

41. **1601.** May 20.—Summons by Peter Wedderburn, burgess of Dundee, v. Robert, younger son of Lord Gray, as cautioner for John, Master of Orkney, in regard to money due from the said Master to the pursuer for meat, drink, &c. **(195, 37.)**
This action is again mentioned 31 July 1601. **(196, 254.)**

42. **1602.** June 1.—Summons by David Wedderburn, burgess of Dundee, chaplain of of S. Salvator, and Sir James Scrymgeour, patron thereof, v. Robert Wedderburn, elder, and others. **(195, 328.)**
Decree v. defenders is given 15 July 1602. **(201, 144.)**

43. **1602.** July 20.—Summons by Mr. Alexander Wedderburn, clerk of Dundee, v. David, Earl of Crawfurd, for payment of an annual-rent out of the lands in the barony of Downy, for 1585—1601, in which annual-rent the late Alexander Wedderburn, clerk of Dundee, and Janet Mylne, his wife (who d. June 1583) were infeft in life-rent, and the said Mr. Alexander their son, heritably, 29 Oct. 1579. **(195, 409.)**
Decree v. the Earl 4 Dec. 1602. **(201, 320.)**

44. **1602.** Nov. 9.—Summons by David Wedderburn, burgess of Dundee, v. Alexander Annand, for delivery up of a document re S. Margaret's chaplainry. **(195, 461.)**

45. **1602.** Jan. 5.—Decree in favour of Mr. Alexander Wedderburn, clerk of Dundee, and David Wedderburn his brother, v. Andrew Caraill. **(196, 371.)**

46. **1603.** March 15.—Action by Mr. John Ogilvy of that ilk v. Mr. Alexander Wedderburn and William Thomson, procurators fiscal in eo. Forfar, and others. **(208, 120.)**

47. **1606.** March 1.—Decree in favour of David Wedderburn, burgess of Dundee, v. John Forret, for the delivery of some Swedish iron. **(218, 398.)**

48. **1608.** Feb. 11.—Decree for a transumpt on summons by Sir James Scrymgeour v. David Wedderburn, notary, "haver" of the Protocol Book containing the sasine whereby (20 July 1605) the pursuer was infeft in the barony of Dudop, constabulary of Dundee, &c., conform to a precept dated at Dunkeld, 30 June 1565, on which instruments were taken by the late Alexander Wedderburn, notary. **(231, 286.)**
The first named notary is David Wedderburn of the MS. who had, for a time, possession of all the protocol books of his late father, the clerk. See ante s. Private Records, David Wedderburn's MS., § 18.

49. **1608.** Feb. 10.—Suspension of letters of horning raised by the provost and masters (including William Wedderburn) of S. Salvator's College, S. Andrew's, v. Beatrix West, their tenant. **(233, 229.)**

50. **1609.** Feb. 25.—Action by Henry Fethie, Mr. Alexander Wedderburn of Kinganie, and others, v. William Guthrie, sometime of Kinganie. **(244, 19.)**

51. **1609.** July 6.—Action by Agnes Wedderburn, oy and heir of the late Gilbert Wedderburn in Leith, and Abacuche Bisset, writer, her spouse, v. William, son and heir of the late John Brown, skipper in Leith. **(244, 152.)**

52. **1609.** Oct. 29.—Action by David Wedderburn, burgess of Dundee, v. William Guthrie. **(244, 276.)**

53. **1610.** Feb. 8.—Mr. William Wedderburn, minister of the kirk of Pittenweyne, compears personally before the Lords, and gives evidence of his appointment to the said kirk, which the Lords accept, although he ought to have compeared on 1 Nov., 1609, according to summons dated 15 Aug. 1609. **(250, 73).**

54. **1611.** Feb. 23.—Action against the said Mr. William Wedderburn, by Frederick, Lord Stewart of Pittenweyme, and Elizabeth Hepburn, Lady Pitfirrane, his mother, who were charged by the said Mr. William Wedderburn to flit from the Great House and Chapter Chalmer of the Abbey Place of Pittenweyme, designed by Mr. William for a manse. **(259, 273.)**
This action is again mentioned 9 July 1611. **(265, 73.)**

55. **1611.** Jan. 14.—Action by Robert and Margaret Bultie *v.* Janet Wedderburn, relict of William Davidson, burgess of Dundee. **(261, 322.)**

56. **1611.** July 4—Action by William, Earl of Angus *v.* John Wedderburn in Mervingslaw, David Wedderburn, there, William Olifer, also there, and many others, for removing of the defenders from certain lands in the shire of Roxburgh. Decree accordingly. **(264, 132.)**

57. **1612.** March 12.—Action by Robert Wedderburn, burgess of Dundee, and Euffame Cousland (*sic*), his spouse, *v,* Thomas Lyell of Murchill, and many others, for money due for maintenance, alleging that the pursuers are " ventineris and oistlaris keiping ane oppin oistlarie within the burgh of Dundee, as is notour to the Lordis of Counsell and the haill cuntrie." Decree for the pursuers. **(272, 175.)**

58. **1612.** June 12.—Decreet in action by David Wedderburn, burgess of Dundee, assignee of Margaret, Jonet, and Elspeth, bairns and executors of the late William Davidson, merchant, burgess of Dundee, and Janet Wedderburn, their mother, *v.* Robert Bultie. **(272, 296.)**

59 **1612.** Nov. 6.—Action of removal by Agnes Wedderburn, oy and heir served and seised to the late Gilbert Wedderburn, indweller in Leith, and Abacuck Bissett, W.S., her spouse, *v.* various defenders, in regard to a house in the town of Leith, on the south side of the water thereof, in the barony of Restalrig, and referring to the original charter (14 April 1553) thereof in favour of the said Gilbert and Isobel Dikson, his spouse, and the sasine (21 June 1581) thereof to the said Agnes as oy and heir to the said Gilbert. **(277, 1.)**
    This action is again referred to Vol. 284, 133. See also ante No. 51.

60. **1613.** July 16.—Action by David Wedderburn (son of Robert Wedderburn, burgess of Dundee) *v.* David Ramsay, burgess of Forfar, and others, for the price of some French wines bought by the defenders from the pursuer. **(279, 219.)**
    This action is mentioned again 29 July 1613 (*ib.* 274)

61. **1613.** July 21.—Compeared Mr. Robert Nairn, procurator for Mr. Alexander Wedderburn, clerk of Dundee, and David and James Wedderburn, his brothers german, and produced copy letters at the instance of James Monorgound of that ilk and Alexander Jackson of Wattriebutts, anent production of a contract between the said Mr. Alexander, David, and James Wedderburn, the late Mr. William Duncan, and Robert Wedderburn on one part, and the late James Kyle and George Traill (with the said J. Monorgound and A. Jackson as cautioners) on the other part, whereby the said J. Kyle and G. Traill were bound to abandon and never have ado with the late James Traill, alleged counmitter of the slaughter of William Wedderburn, brother german of the said Mr. Alexander Wedderburn, and themselves to depart out of this realm within 40 days, and, in case of breach, to pay to Mr. Alexander, "his brether aud sisteris," 10,000 merks. The Wedderburns having sued on this contract, and the defenders not having compeared, the said procurator protests that his clients be not holden to answer till summoned anew. **(279, 228.)**

62. **1613.** July 19.—Action by Mr. James Wischart of Glenfarquhar *v.* Mr. Alexander Wedderburn, clerk of Dundee, for production of the writs of Glenfarquhar. **(282, 44.)**

63. **1614.** Feb. 22.—Summons at the instance of William Sandilands of Sanct Monans *v.* Mr. William Wedderburn, minister at Dundee, for the return of certain books (here follows a list of them) lent to Wedderburn by Sandilands, and which the former bound himself, 9 Oct. 1611, to return in good condition before 2 Feb 1612. Decree *v.* the defender who did not compear. **(287, 299.)**
    These books, which are mostly in Latin, include a Virgil, Tibullus, Catullus, and Propertius, a Hebrew Bible, a Greek Testament, and a good many theological works.

64. **1615.** March 11.—Decree on summons by Mr. David Wedderburn, merchant, burgess of Dundee, *v.* Walter Angus in Burntisland, for payment of a bond dated 19 Dec. 1613. **(295, 273.)**

65. **1616.** Feb. 6.—Summons by John Gray in Dundee *v.* various defenders, including Mr. Alexander Wedderburn, clerk of Dundee, for production of a certain instrument. John Wedderburn, burgess of Dundee, is alleged to be a necessary witness. (**299,** 272.)

66. **1616.** March 27.—Action by James Cochrane, merchant in Edinburgh, factor for James Duncan, merchant in Campheir, *v.* Alexander Wedderburn, merchant, burgess of Dundee, who pleads payment, (**299,** 352.)

67. **1616.** March 22.—Summons at the instance of Jacob Keyne, merchant in Campheir, and John Scougall, writer in Edinburgh, his factor, against Alexander Wedderburn, merchant in Dundee, for the sum of £27. 11. 10., great Flemish money, contained in an obligation by the said Alexander Wedderburn to the pursuer, of date 25 July 1612. The Lords of Council and Session ordain the defender to pay as acclaimed. (**306,** 70.)

68. **1616.** Nov. 16.—Action at the instance of James Cochrane, merchant, as procurator for James Daman, merchant in Campheir, against Alexander Wedderburne, merchant burgess of Dundee, for implement of his obligation, of date 19 July 1612, granted in favour of the said James Daman for £10. 17. 2., " gret flemis money." The defender compears by Mr. James Lawtie, his procurator, and the lords ordain him to pay the sum mentioned. (**311.**)

[The register has not been searched from 1616-54. See ante p 464.]

69. **1654.** Jan. 17.—Decreet on summons by Sir Alexander Wedderburn of Blackness, *v.* — Blair of Bathayoch, for non-payment of 14,000 merks due by bond (1, 4 June 1646) to Sir Alexander, by the late Sir Patrick Ogilvy of Inchmartine, the late Sir Thomas Blair, and others. (565.)

70. **1656.** Feb. 29.—Act anent the supplication of Patrick Dundas of Breistmylne in regard to the affairs of the Master of Gray and Sir James Murray, one of the creditors of the latter of whom is Mr. Peter Wedderburn. (580.)

71. **1657.** Jan. 1.—Decreet on letters of suspension by John Ferrie and others *v.* Mr. James Wedderburn, minister of Moonsie, as to his stipend for 1654-55. (588.)

72. **1657.** Feb. 21.—Decreet on summons by Janet Guthrie, relict of Major William Scrymgeour, and Dougall McPherson, now her husband, *v.* Margaret Serymgeour, daughter and executrix of the said Major, and Alexander Wedderburn of Kingennie, her tutor, for non-payment of the 480 merks, being the @ rent of 8,000 merks, due to the said Janet under her marriage contract. The said Janet also claims £133. 6. 8 , debursed by her in bringing out of Dundee before the siege thereof her late husband's wrytes, houshold plenishing, &c. (588.)

73. **1658.** June 24.—Decreet on summons by Sir Alexander Wedderburn of Blackness, *v.* Hugh, son and heir of the late Colonel Hugh Fraser of Kinnaires, for the non-payment of a bond for 580 rex dollars. (598.)

74. **1658.** Dec. 30.—Decreet anent the summons by William Carrie, goldsmith of London, *v.* John Home of Renton, and Sir Alexander Wedderburn of Blackness, for non-payment of a bond for £30 sterling. (600.)

75. **1659.** Feb. 9.—Decreet on summons by Patrick Dundas (ante No. 70), *v.* Mr. Peter Wedderburn, advocate, who had arrested certain moneys as due to him as creditor of Sir James Murray, and obtained apprising of the lands of Innerleith. (607.)

III (*b*).

76. **1663.** July 28.—Ogilvie *v.* Wedderburn. (Min. Book only.)

77. **1663.** July 31.—Decreet in action by Alexander Wedderburn of Kingany, provost of Dundee. *v.* Janet Guthrie and Dougal McPhersone, in regard to the affairs of Margaret Serymgeour, daughter of the said Janet by the late Major William Serymgeour, her first husband. (Dur. 6.)

78. **1664.** Feb. 17.—Decreet in action by Margaret Serymgeour, daughter of the late **Acts and** Major William Serymgeour and her curators, *v.* Alexander Wedderburn of Kinganie, **Decreets** provost of Dundee, for production of an alleged decreet against her, 12 July, 1662. **Register.** The defender is assoilized. (Dal 11.)

    The litigation between Margaret Scrymgeour and Alexander Wedderburn, third of Kingennie, and first of Easter Powrie, has been often referred to see p. 3. note 2 and Scrymgeour-Wedderburn Papers, Nos. 370. 382-84 399-99*a*. 406-40, &c.) An action by Kingennie against Margaret Scrymgeour in regard to a legacy left him by her father, which the estate seems to have been inadequate to pay, is reported in Morison's Dictionary of Decisions under date 26 July 1666.

79. **1664.** July 22.—Decreet on letters of suspension raised by Dougal McPhersone, sometime of Powrie, *v.* Alexander Wedderburn, provost of Dundee, who had pursued the said Dougal for not removing from the lands of Easter Powrie, according to his disposition to the said provost, dated 12 Sept. 1662. (Dur. 10.)

    Further litigation in regard to the same matter is recorded 18 Dec. 1666 (Dur. 17), and 16 July 1667 (Dur. 19.) See also ante *s.* Private Records, Scrymgeour-Wedderburn Papers, No. 351, seq.)

80. **1667.** July 16.—Decreet in action by Sir Alexander Wedderburn of Blackness, and others, *v.* Mr. Henry Serymgeour, minister at Dundee, in regard to the stipend of the latter. (Dur. 19.)

81. **1668.** Jan. 14.—Decreet on letters of suspension by Alexander Wedderburn of Kinganie, *v.* Dougall McPhersone, sometime of Powrie, and Janet Guthrie, his spouse, for suspending letters of horning raised by the said Dougall and Janet *v.* the pursuer for non-payment of 8000 merks due by bond dated 12 Sept. 1662 and registered 5 June 1665. (Dal. 26.)

82. **1669.** (*a*) June 6.—Act, Wedderburn *v.* Fletcher. (Min. Book only.) (*b*) July 11.— Decreet, Wedderburn *v.* Fletcher. (*ib.*)

83. **1670.** Jan. 15.—Decreet in action by Sir Alexander Wedderburn of Blackness, *v.* Thomas Miller and others in the Hill of Dundee, for the few-maills of certain lands, which, with the customs of the first fair of Dundee, were (27 April 1666) adjudged to the pursuer as against the late John, Earl of Dundee and Lord Dudope. (Mac. 35.)

84. **1670.** (*a*) Feb. 4 —Act, Serymgeour *v.* Wedderburn. (Min. Book only.) (*b*) **1671.** July 8.—Act, Wedderburn *v.* Serymgeour. (*ib.*) (*c*) July 21.—Act, Wedderburn *v.* Serymgeour. (*ib.*)

85. **1671.** Dec, 12.—Protestation anent letters of suspension raised by George Brown in Chirnesyd, William Wedderburn in Chirnesyd Maynes and others, tenants in Chirnesyd, *v.* Charles Oliphant, writer in Edinburgh, anent payments alleged to be due from the said tenants. (Mac. 39.)

86. **1672.** Feb. 17.—Decreet anent summons by Sir Peter Wedderburn of Gosford, Knt., senator of the College of Justice, *v.* Thomas Hamilton of Reidhous, Sir James Richardsone of Smeatoun, and Sir John Wauchope of Niddrie, in regard to the purchase (12 Feb. 1668) by Sir Peter from the said Thomas Hamilton of the lands of Standelan, Easter and Wester Spittall, Easter Birithes, &c. (Mac. 40.)

87. **1673.** (*a*) June 28.—Act, Wedderburn *v.* Wedderburn. (Min. Book only.) (*b*) July 18.—Act, Serymgeour *v.* Wedderburn. (*ib.*)

88. **1673.** Nov. 6.—Decreet anent letters of suspension, &c,, by the children of the late David Gourley of Dundee *v.* Captain Edward Hodge and others (including Alexander Wedderburn, clerk of Dundee), in regard to payment of an annual rent. (Mac. 44.)

89. **1673.** (*a*) Nov. 28.—Act, Wedderburn *v.* Serymgeour. (Min. Book only.) (*b*) Dec. 13.— Act, Serymgeour *v.* Wedderburn. (*ib.*) (*c*) Dec. 16.—Act, Serymgeour *v.* Wedderburn.(*ib.*)

90. **1674.** Feb. 7.—Decreet in favour of Alexander Wedderburn of Kingenny, *v.* Patrick Ogilvy, now of Muirie, as son and heir of the late William Ogilvy thereof, for £792, balance due on a bond for £1,600, dated 14 Feb. 1661. (Dur. 45.)

Acts and
Decreets
Register.
91. **1674.** Feb. 12.—Decreet on summons by Agnes Campbell, relict of George Fletcher, provost in Dundee, *v.* James Fletcher, son and heir of the said George, and others, in regard to her marriage contract, dated 22 April 1664 (in which she is designed relict of John Pitcairn of Dundee), by which 20,000 merks was settled on her, to be invested at the sight of, among others, Sir Alexander Wedderburn of Blackness. (Mac. 45.)

92. **1674.** (*a*) Feb 19.—Decreet, Scrymgeour *v.* Wedderburn. (Min. Book only.) (*b*) Feb. 26.—Act, Wedderburn *v.* Scrymgeour. (*ib.*)

93. **1674.** Feb. 28.—Decreet in action by Sir Peter Wedderburn of Gosford, one of the Lords of Council and Session, on his own behalf and that of John Wedderburn, his eldest son (both of them being duly infeft in the barony of Innerwick), *v.* John Denholme, tenant of Branxholme, and others, in regard to the teinds of Branxholme. (Dur. 45.)

94. **1675.** (*a*) Feb. 2.—Act, Scrymgeour *v.* Wedderburn. (Min. Book only.) (*b*) Feb. 23.— Act, Wedderburn *v.* Scrymgeour. (*ib.*) (*c*) Feb. 13.—Decreet and Act, Wedderburn *v.* Scrymgeour. (*ib.*) (*d*) June 19.—Decreet, Scrymgeour *v.* Wedderburn. (*ib.*) (*e*) Dec. 15.—Act, Clayhills *v.* Wedderburn. (*ib.*) (*f*) **1676.** July 26.—Decreet and Act, Wedderburn *v.* Scrymgeour. (*ib.*) (*g*) July 29.—Decreet, Wedderburn *v.* Lord Ellieband. (*ib.*)

95. **1678.** July 26.—Decreet on summons by Alexander Wedderburn of Kingenny, *v.* John Scrymgeour of Kirktoun, in regard to a bond by the defender to the pursuer (7 Dec. 1672) for 8,000 merks. (Dur. 67.)

96. **1678.** Nov. 22.—Decreet on summons by Alexander Wedderburn of Easter Powrie, provost of Dundee, *v.* William Murisone, for adjudication to the pursuer of a North Murraygate land in satisfaction of £8 of few duty for ground annual, &c. (Dal. 75.)

97. **1679.** Feb, 8.—Decreet on letters of suspension by William Milne *v.* George Wedderburn, merchant in Edinburgh. (Mac. 56.)

98. **1679.** Feb. 17.—Decreet on summons by Jean, daughter of George Home of Heiringtoun, *v.* Sir James Cockburn of Plendergaist, James Wedderburn in Coldinghame, and others, as to an annual rent. (Mac. 56.)

99. **1679.** Feb. 18.—Decreet on summons by William Carnegy *v.* Robert Gray, in Montrose, and Sir Peter Wedderburn of Gosford, for moneys arrested in the hands of Sir Peter. (Mac. 56.)

100. **1679.** July 30.—Decreet on letters of suspension by Robert Thomson *v.* John Rennick, merchant-traveller, and George Wedderburn, merchant in Edinburgh, his assignee, who had letters of horning *v.* the pursuer in respect of 250 merks, the modified price of a saddle, spuilzied by him from them. (Dal. 78.)

101. **1680.** July 29.—Decreet in action by Alexander Chaplain *v.* John Wedderburn of Blackness and Robert Davidson of Balgay for certain sums. (Dal. 81.)

102. **1681.** June 8.—Decreet anent letters of suspension raised by John Dickson of Hairtrie, and John Wedderburn of Blackness, John Wedderburn of Gosford, Thomas Milne of Muirtoun, George Wedderburn, merchant in Edinburgh, his curators, and others, *v.* Mr. William Alesone, minister of Kilbucho, as to payment of his stipend out of the lands of Hairtrie. The decreet names — Wedderburn, mother of the said John Dickson, as life-rentrix of the said lands. (Mac. 61.)

103. **1681.** June 25.—Decreet on summons by George Wedderburn, merchant burgess of Edinburgh, and Mr. James Brisbane, advocate, *v.* William Baillie of Littlegill, Archibald, Earl of Forfar, and others, for the adjudication to them of the lands of Littlegill, &c., in satisfaction of £338, 9. (Dal. 83, Pt. ii.)

104. **1681.** July 13.—Decreet in action by George Wedderburn, merchant burgess of Edinburgh, *v.* George Tait in Littlehill, William Baillie in Littlegill, and others, for payment of a bond dated 5 Aug. 1679. (Dal. 84.)

105. **1681.** July 14.—Decreet on summons by Robert Lindsay in Dundee *v.* James Acts and Decreets Register. Wedderburn, clerk of Dundee, Alexander Wedderburn of Kingennie, and others, for payment of a sum of money. (Mac. 61.)

106. **1682.** March 7.—Decreet by David Lindsay of Edzell *v.* Margaret Mylne (spouse of Alexander Wedderburn of Easter Powrie in regard to the bond (2 June 1675) for 3,000 merks granted by the said David to Robert Lindsay, merchant, burgess of Dundee, of which the defenders claim the annual rent, and on which the pursuer claims a charge of £500. (Dal. 86.)

107. **1682.** March 10.—Decreet on summons by Robert Childers, saddler, burgess of Edinburgh, *v.* John Wedderburn of Gosford, for £237. 18. 4. price of a saddle covered with velvet and embroidered with gold and silver lace and with fringes to the value of £30 stg. The lords assoilzie the defender from from paying more than £10 stg. (Mac. 63.)

108. **1684.** Feb. 2.—Decreet in favour of John Coutts of Montrose *v.* Sir (*sic*) John Wedderburn of Gosford, for £100 due by the late Sir Peter Wedderburn, father to the defender. (Mac. 70.)
Sir John Wedderburn is an error ; he was never knighted.

109. **1684.** Feb. 12.—Decreet in action by John Wedderburn of Blackness, sole clerk to the bills, *v.* Harry Oliphant, writer in Edinburgh, for production of pretended gifts and writs anent the said office. The lords assoilzie the defender. (Dur. 94.)
See Lord Fountainhall's Decisions i, 217, 256-57, 269, where this suit is referred to under date 30 Nov. 1683, 8 Jan. and 12 Feb. 1684.

110. **1684.** March 22.—Decreet in action by John Wedderburn of Gosford *v.* Sir Charles Erskine of Alva and others, for non-payment of certain sums, reciting that the pursuer is executor nominated and confirmed to the late Sir Patrick Wedderburn of Gosford, one of the senators of the College of Justice, his father, by his will dated 5 Oct. 1574 and confirmed 22 June 1682. (Dur. 96.)

111. **1684.** March 29.—Decreet in action by John Wedderburn of Gosford *v.* Lord Bargenny in regard to the lands and barony of Innerwick, disponed (20 Dec. 1670) to the father of the pursuer in life-rent, and to the pursuer in fee. (Dur. 97.)

112. **1685.** Jan. 3.—Decreet on summons by James Dundas of Breistmilne *v.* Sir (*sic*) John Wedderburn of Gosford, as heir to the late Sir Peter Wedderburn, his father, for a certain sum. (Dal. 93.)

113. **1685.** Feb. 18.—Decreet on petition by John Graham of Montrose and Catharine Carnegy, relict of Robert Gray of Montrose, *v.* Sir (*sic*) John Wedderburn of Gosford in regard to a bond for £100 granted to the said Catharine by the the late Sir Patrick Wedderburn of Gosford, which bond she desires to be paid to the said John Graham. (Mac. 73.)

114. **1685.** March 21.—Decreet on summons by George Wedderburn, merchant, burgess of Edinburgh, *v.* Robert, son and heir of Patrick Fyff, for non-payment of £900. The defender is assoilzied. (Dal. 96.)

115. **1685.** March 25.—Decreet on summons by John Wedderburn of Gosford and others *v.* Charles, Earl of Lauderdale, and others, in regard to the lands and baronies of Innerwiek (with Fairne in warrandice) and Thornetoun (with Dunglas in warrandice) together with teinds, coals, coalheughs, &c. (Dur. 102.)

116. **1685.** Nov. 7.—Decreet on summons by George Wedderburn, merchant, burgess of Edinburgh, *v.* Robert Fyff, to have adjudged to him a house in the town of Leith and barony of Restalrig in satisfaction of the said sum of £900. See ante No. 114. (Dal. 97.)

117. **1686.** Nov. 9.—Decreet anent letters of suspension raised by George Wedderburn, merchant, burgess of Edinburgh, *v.* John Hall of Auldcambus in regard to £60 stg. said to be due by the said George to Mr. David Scrimgeour, fiar of Craigmore. Action adjourned. (Mac. 78.)
Later on, 3 Feb. 1687, the lords find the said letters in order and decern the same to take effect. (79.)

3 N

118. **1687.** Feb. 3.—Decreet, Hall v. Wedderburn. (Min. Book only.)

1687 ? (Undated.)—Decreet, Lyell v. Wedderburn, laird of Gosford. (ib)
This latter is undated, at the end of the volume.

119. **1690.** Nov. 26.—Decreet for the pursuers on summons by John Wedderburn, weaver in Prestonpans, and his wife Helen, daughter of John Corbie, sometime sailor there, v. Helen and Marion, daughters and heirs of the late John Nasmith, as to possession of a piece of land in the town of Prestonpans. (Mac. 88.)

120. **1691.** July 21.—Decreet of transumpt in favour of Sir John Hall of Dunglass, Bart., and James, his eldest son, v. William Nisbet of Dirletoun and Peter Wedderburn of Gosford for production of the old writs, &c. of Dunglass. (Mac. 88.)

121. **1695.** Nov. 22.—Decreet for the defenders in action by James Sutherland, late baillie of Edinburgh, v. Mr. John Wedderburn of Blackness, one of the clerks of the bills, and Alexander Wedderburn, eldest son of George Wedderburn, merchant in Edinburgh, as to the production by the defenders of a pretended disposition by the said George to the said John Wedderburn, his brother, of a bond for £100 sterling, and other deeds. (Dal. 124.)

122. **1696.** Jan. 31.—Decreet on bill of suspension, &c., by Peter Wedderburn of Gosford v. James Halyburton, now of Fotherance, as to a bond of the late John Wedderburn of Gosford for 1890 merks. The lords decree Gosford to pay 1450 merks. (Dal. 125, Pt. i.)

123. **1698.** June 18.—Decreet in favour of the pursuers on summons by Mathilda Wedderburn, relict of Mr. James Brisbane, advocate, Barbara Brisbane, their eldest daughter, and her curators (John Wedderburn of Blackness, Mr. John Paterson of Craigie, and John Duncan) v. Barbara Ferguson, heir of line, tailie, and provision to the late Mr. David Ferguson, minister of Strickmartine, her uncle, etc., in regard to a contract of marriage (20 Jan. 1658) between the said Mr. David and Barbara Pearson, whose rights thereunder were assigned (30 April 1696) to the pursuers. (Mac. 124, pt. ii.)

124. **1701.** Feb. 13.—Decreet for the pursuer on summons by Dame Agnes Wedderburn, Lady Piteur, v. George Halyburton of Edinburgh, eldest son and heir of the late Mr. James Halyburton of Watriebutts, for the eighth part of the west side of the town of Balbrogie, to satisfy certain sums of money due by the defender to the pursuer. (Mac. 134.)

125. **1701.** July 4.—Decreet on summons raised at the instance of Alexander Wedderburn, clerk of Dundee, v. Robert Rankine, skipper, and James Fletcher, late provost thereof, upon a decreet, obtained 27 Feb. 1674, by Patrick Leslie, late chamberlain to Sir Peter Wedderburn of Gosford, one of the senators of the College of Justice, v. Robert Rankine. (Dal. 137.)

126. **1703.** July 16.—Decreet in the complaint first raised before the magistrates and and Council of Dundee by Alexander Wedderburn, principal clerk of the said burgh, v. James Ramsay, depute clerk thereof, whereupon a bill of advocation was given in by the said Ramsay, the reasons whereof were appointed, with consent of both parties, to be discussed before the said lords. Which complaint showeth, that whereas by a gift of date, 5 March 1685, the said magistrates were pleased to confer upon the petitioner the principal clerk's office after the decease of James Wedderburn, his father, with the whole emoluments thereto belonging, and a power to remove the clerk depute in case he and the pursuer should not agree; and now, seeing the petitioner is desirous of having his said gift ratified and renewed, and that the said James Ramsay and he do not agree, he craved the magistrates to renew his former gift and ordain the said Ramsay to remove from his office, as clerk depute, and deliver up any books or records he may have relating thereto. The Lords assoilzie the said James Ramsay on all points and decern him quit and free therefrom in all time coming. (Dur. 218).

See also Lord Fountainhall's Decisions (ii, 186-87) where it is reported that James Ramsay, clerk depute of Dundee, sued Alexander Wedderburn. principal clerk thereof, for removing him from the said office, and contended that the office was his for life and that he was not removable without malversation or fault. Wedderburn, on the other hand, contended that the Wedderburns for fourteen generations had been clerks of Dundee and had always had the nomination of their own deputes, who precariously depended on them. Upon these issues the Lords (16 July 1703) sustained Ramsay's Acts and complaint. The allegation that the Wedderburns had for fourteen generations been clerks of Dundee Decreets is certainly an exaggeration. The defender in this complaint was the seventh consecutive (and last) Register. clerk of his name, the office having been exclusively held by members of his family since 1557, previous to which date it is clear that it was enjoyed by members of other families (See ante p. 188 u. and s. the "LockitBuik" of Dundee, No. 1 n. and Dundee Burgh and Head Court Records, Nos. 69 and 75). Although, however, there is no record of any Wedderburn having filled the office of clerk before 1557, it is, of course, possible that it was so held.

127. **1704.** Jan. 29.—Decreet on letters of suspension raised by Beatrix Linklatter, relict of James Whyt, shipper in Kirkcaldy, v. Alexander Wedderburn, clerk of Dundee, in regard to his claim against her for £43 15. sterling and £50 scots. The Lords decern in favour of the clerk. (Dur. 221.)

128. **1704.** July 5.—Decreet on summons, first raised before the sheriff of Lanarkshire, by Charles, Earl of Selkirk, v. Cecilia Wedderburn, relict of William Littlegill and others, for non-payment of an annual-rent of £126, furth of the lands of Littlegill, &c. (Dur. 225.)

129. **1705.** Nov. 21.—Decreet on summons, &c., by Margaret Wedderburn, relict of Mr. Andrew Balfour, W.S. (and now wife to Dr William Eccles of Edinburgh), and Margaret Balfour, only child now on life to the said Mr. Andrew, and her tutors testamentars (Sir John Wedderburn, elder of Blackness, Alexander Wedderburn, younger thereof, and Mr. John Dallas of Preston) r. — (sic) Campbell, eldest son and heir of the late Mr. Archibald Campbell, younger, of Calder, for payment of a bond given (3 July 1685) by Sir Hugh Campbell of Calder to the said Mr. Andrew Balfour. The Lords decern the lands of Calder to belong to the pursuers in satisfaction of their claims. (Mac. 153.)

Further litigation by the pursuers v. the Campbells of Calder is named, 4 Feb. 1708. (Mac. 165.)

130. **1706.** Feb. 1.—Decreet on summons by the said pursuers (as in No. 129) v. Samuel Aitchison and others, tenants of Swinton, and Sir John Swinton of that ilk, heritor thereof, for the non-payment of £10,000 yearly since 1704. (Mac. 155.)

131. **1707.** Feb. 12.—Decreet on summons, &c., by Janet Sutherland, relict of James McLackie, merchant in Edinburgh, v. —(sic) Wedderburn, only child on life of (George) Wedderburn, merchant in Edinburgh, and (Elizabeth) Sutherland, daughter of the late James Sutherland, and sister of the late — Sutherland, his eldest son, to whom, as her grandfather and uncle, the said — (sic) is retoured heir. The summons claims payment of 2,000 merks and the Lords decern accordingly. (Dur. 244.)

This proceeding is again dealt with 2 Jan. 1708, when the defender is described as Rachell Wedderburn, "only lawful daughter and chylde on lyfe" of her father, and "nearest and lawful heir of line, tailzie, conqueis and provisione served and retoured to the deceased, James Sutherland, her goodsir, and — Sutherland, her uncle." The 2,000 merks being unpaid, certain tenements in Edinburgh and Leith are adjudged to the pursuer. (Dur. 254.) See post No. 132 u.

132. **1707.** Nov. 6.—Decreet on summons in the action by John Mein, sclaiter, burgess of Edinburgh, v. Alexander and Rachel, children of the late George Wodderburn, merchant burgess of Edinburgh, and sister's children of the late Captain David Sutherland, Captain in Her Majesty's Foot Guards, for payment of £389 19. (Mac. 162.)

See for final decreet on this matter 22 Feb. 1709 when the said children of George Wedderburn are again named. (Mac. 171, pt. ii.) It will be noticed that in this entry both a son and a daughter of George Wedderburn are named as living, whereas in the preceding one the daughter is named as his only surviving child. Probably, though both children were alive at the date of the summons, the son died before this decreet, which disregards the fact and copies the parties named in the summons. Rachel's procurator, who compears for her, expressly mentions that Alexander was "furth of the country" at the time of its service. That the male issue of George Wedderburn failed soon after 1707 is clear from the retour of his daughter Rachel as heir general to her maternal grandfather James Sutherland, 25 Aug. 1709. See ante s. Retours of Heirs, No. 31, and post Nos. 147-48.

133. **1707.** Nov. 20.—Decreet on summons, &c., by the pursuers (as in Nos. 129 and 130) (except that only Sir Alexander Wedderburn of Blackness is now named as tutor to Margaret Balfour), v. Mr. John Dallas of Preston, for certain lands in satisfaction of sums unpaid. (Mac. 162.)

134. **1708.** Feb. 4.—Decreet, Wedderburn v. Campbell. (Min. Book only.)

135. **1709.** Jan. 6.—Decreet on summons, &c., by Sir James Kinloch of that ilk, Baronet, who stands infeft in the lands called "Wedderburn's aikers," or the Freland, in the

Acts and
Decreets
Register.

barony of Aleith and shire of Fife, now all erected by a Great Seal Charter (12
March 1686) into the barony of Kinloch, and by Sir James Stewart of Goodtrees, her
Majesty's advocate, v. William Charles Wedderburn, portioner of Aberbrotharie,
living in Moravia in Germany, for the production of all writs thereof, &c., said to have
been granted to him and others by the Crown. The Lords declare all such writs false
and forged, and repone Sir James the same as if they had never been made. (Mac. 170.)

136. **1709.** Feb. 22.—Decreet of adjudication of certain premises in Edinburgh, obtained
by John Mein v. Alexander and Rachel Wedderburn. (Mac. 171, pt. ii.)
See ante No. 132 n.

137. **1709.** June 15.—Decree for the pursuer on summons by Alexander Wedderburn,
clerk of Dundee, v. Henry Crauford, merchant there, for non-payment of certain sums,
and craving the adjudication to the pursuer of the lands of Halkertoun, &c. (Dur. 268.)
This matter is again dealt with 30 Nov. 1720. (ib. 340.) The suit is referred to in Fountainhall's
Decisions, ii, 550, s.d. 31 Dec. 1709.

138. **1709.** July 21.—Decreet on summons by Mathilda Wedderburn, relict of Mr. James
Brisbane, advocate, c. David Brisbane, eldest son and heir of the said Mr. James, for
non-payment of £7,487 3s. 8d. scots, arrears of annuity due to her down to last
Whitsunday, &c., conform to her marriage contract dated 15 Aug. 1676. The
Lords decern to her certain lands in Dundee in satisfaction. (Dur. 270.)

139. **1710.** Feb. 15.—Decreet in action by Janet Sutherland, eldest daughter of Alexander
Sutherland, sometime bailie of Dornoch, and executrix of the late James McLackie,
v. Alexander and Rachell Wedderburn. for the sum of 2,000 merks, which, by her
contract of marriage with the said James, dated 22 March 1692, James Sutherland,
her uncle, was bound to pay her in name of tocher. The defenders are sued as heirs
of the said James Sutherland, their grandfather. (Dal. 163, pt. ii.)
See ante Nos. 131, 132 note, 136.

140. **1710.** June 21.—Decreet on summons by Janet Sutherland, relict of James McLackie
in Edinburgh, v. Alexander and Rachell Wedderburn, grand-children and heirs of the
late James Sutherland, bailie of Edinburgh, for 2,000 merks, by which certain tenements are adjudged to her in satisfaction. (Mac. 178.)

141. **1711.** Feb. 17.—Decreet in action by Martha Stevenson, relict of Alexander Ogstoun,
bookseller in Edinburgh, v. Sir John Wedderburn, eldest son of the late Sir Alexander
Wedderburn of Blackness, for £264 12s. for books supplied. (Mac.166, Pt. ii.)
See post No. 144.

142. **1711.** July 6.—Decreet on summons by David Fyfe, chirurgeon of Edinburgh, v.
John Wedderburn of Blackness, his tutor and curators, for the production of certain
writs including an assignation (4 Dec. 1683) by Mr. John Inglis of Cramond to George
Wedderburn of Edinburgh and a disposition (10 April 1688) by the said George to
Sir John Wedderburn of Blackness, his brother. (Mac. 185, pt. I.)

143. **1711.** July 28.—Decreet for the pursuer on summons by Alexander Alison, W.S., v.
Sir John Wedderburn, now of Blackness, eldest son and heir retoured to the late Sir
Alexander Wedderburn of Blackness, for the return of two books lent by the pursuer
to Sir Alexander 5 Jan. 1703, and a large silver watch so lent him at Leith in
April 1708. (Dur. 288.)

144. **1712.** Feb. 1.—Decreet on summons by Martha Stevenson, relict of Alexander
Ogston, bookseller in Edinburgh, v. Sir John Wedderburn of Blackness, for £197 due
to the said Ogston by the late Sir Alexander Wedderburn of Blackness for books
supplied. (Dal. 170.)
See ante No. 141 and s. Private Records, Mounie Papers, Nos. 2 and 44. It would thus appear
that after discharging an account up to 8 April 1709, Sir Alexander made further additions to his
library before his death, early in the following year.

145. **1712.** Feb. 26.—The said decreet (No. 142) is again dealt with, and Sir John Wedderburn, now of Blackness, and his father, Sir Alexander, are found liable in £531 (scots)
and Sir John is ordained to cede to the pursuer two shops in Edinburgh and some
houses in Leith as from Whitsunday 1711. (Mac. 189, pt. ii.)
See in regard to this matter, ante s. Private Records, Mounie Papers, No. 55.

146. **1714.** Feb. 26.—Decree in the action by Henry Crawford, merchant in Dundee, *v.* the late Patrick Hay of Naughton and Robert Hay now of Naughton, his son, which action was transferred from the sheriff of Fife at the instance of Alexander Wedderburn, clerk of Dundee, who was assignee to the sum claimed under a writing dated 27 Aug. 1708. (Dur. 307.) **Acts and Decreets Register.**

147. **1714.** July 15.—Decreet on summons by Gilbert Stewart, merchant in Edinburgh, *v.* Rachell, daughter of George Wedderburn, merchant there, as lawfully charged to enter heir in special to the late James Sutherland, her grandfather, and Captain David Sutherland, her uncle, for payment of 5,000 merks. The loris decern to the pursuer a tenement of land near the college of Leith, on the south side of the water, in the barony of Restalrig, in satisfaction. (Mac. 201, Pt. i.)

148. **1716.** Dec. 20.—Decree for the pursuer on summons by William Main, merchant in Edinburgh, *v.* Rachel Wedderburn, daughter of the late (George) Wedderburn and Elizabeth Sutherland, and heir to James Sutherland, her grandfather, for non-payment of 1,000 merks, contained in a bond (15 Jan. 1700), by the said James Sutherland to Janet Sutherland, relict of David Robertson, vintner, burgess in Edinburgh, which bond was transferred to the pursuer. (Dur. 315.)

149. **1717.** Dec. 28.—Decreet on summons of declarator, raised by John Scrymgeour of Tealing, provost of Dundee, and the town council thereof, *v.* Alexander Wedderburn, clerk of Dundee, as to his citation to compear before the lords of council and session to answer to an interloquitor by the said town council, dated 9 Aug. 1716, whereby they found him culpable on the points raised in a certain complaint, and deposed him from being clerk of Dundee and of the barony of Hiltoun, and admitted George Duncan, W.S., to be clerk in his place. The lords find Wedderburn culpable, and warrantably deprived from office, 'and that George Duncan was legally appointed. (Dal. 188.)
See ante s. Burgh Records, Dundee Charters, Writs, &c., No. 88, and Dundee Council Books, Nos. 170-183, 190-91.

150. **1718.** Jan. 1.—Decreet on summons by Grissell Wedderburn, daughter and executrix dative of the late Alexander Wedderburn of that ilk, Grissell Gardine, her mother, Alexander Wedderburn, clerk of Dundee, John Wedderburn, doctor of medicine there, Mr. Alexander Scrymgeour, professor of divinity in S. Andrew's, Gilbert Stewart, merchant in Edinburgh, Patrick Barclay of Johnstoun, and David Gardine of Latoun, her tutors, *v.* William Graham late of Duntroon, John Scrymgeour of Tealing, provost, and John Scryngeour, younger of Tealing, bailie of Dundee, and others, for 500 merks and £18 scots. The Lords decern to the pursuer the lands of Duntroon in satisfaction. (Mac. 220, Pt. i.)

151. **1718.** Feb. 25.—Decreet on summons by John Scrymgeour of Tealing, provost, and the other members of the Town Council of Dundee, *v.* Alexander Wedderburn, late clerk thereof, for refusing to deliver to the pursuers the books and papers of the town, entrusted to him as clerk. (Dal. 190, pt. ii.)
See the references given ante No. 149 note.

152. **1718.** Nov. 1.—Decreet in action by John Lamb, provost of Aberbrothock, and others, the bailies and council thereof, *v.* Grissell Garden, Lady Wedderburn, relict of Alexander Wedderburn of that ilk, and executrix to the late Robert Garden of Laton, and others, for production of a bond (16 May 1715) for 4,000 merks, granted by the pursuers to the said Robert Garden. (Dal. 193, pt. i.)

153. **1719.** Feb. 18.—Decree on summons by Mr. John Crichton, minister of the Gospel, *v.* Rachell Wedderburn, daughter of the late (George) Wedderburn and (Elizabeth) Sutherland for payment of certain sums. The Lords decree as in No. 147. (Mac. 227, pt. i.)

154. **1719.** Feb. 18.—Decreet on summons of adjudication raised by Alexander Wedderburn, sheriff clerk of Forfar, *v.* Sir John Wedderburn now of Blackness (son and heir of the late Sir Alexander Wedderburn and grandson and heir of the late Sir John Wedderburn of Blackness) by which the lands and barony of Blackness (with the lands and barony of Pitarrow in warrandice) are adjudged to the pursuer in satisfaction of £60,110. 7. 5. scots, due to him from the defender or his father. (Dal. 193, pt. ii.)

In this decreet is recited another decreet obtained by the pursuer v. Sir John, before the sheriff of Forfar (2 Jan. 1718), apparently for the said sum of £60,110. 7. 5, and showing how it was made up. It recites the following bonds, &c. :—

(a) 1686. June 17.—Bond by the late Sir John Wedderburn to John Wedderburn, son to the late Peter Wedderburn, merchant in Dundee, for 500 merks, which bond John Alexander Wedderburn, shipmaster in Dundee, factor to the said John (under factory dated 8 Feb. 1703), assigned to the pursuer by assignation dated 6 Nov. last.

(b) 1704. Feb. 8, 14.—Bond by John Wedderburn of Blackness, and Alexander Wedderburn, fiar thereof, his son (afterwards Sir John and Sir Alexander Wedderburn), as principal and cautioner respectively, to Margaret Wedderburn, eldest daughter of the late James Wedderburn, clerk of Dundee, for 1,800 merks, which bond the said Margaret, with consent of Mr. James Paterson of Craigie, her husband, assigned, 2 Aug. 1711, to Sir David Threipland of Fingask.

(c) 1706. July 31.—Bond by the said Sir Alexander, James Halyburton of Pitcurr, and Alexander Wedderburn, clerk of Dundee, to the Bank of Scotland for £418 sterling.

(d) 1707. June 25.—Bond by the said Sir Alexander to Robert Wedderburn, mariner in Dundee, for 1,000 merks, &c., &c.

(e) 1708. Feb. 18.—Bond by the said Sir Alexander and David Wedderburn, major in Major-General MacCairtney's regiment, to John Scott of Malleny, for 4,000 merks.

(f) 1709. Jan. 28.—Bond by the said Sir Alexander to Peter Wedderburn, merchant in Dundee, for 500 merks.

(g) 1709. Oct. 20.—Bond by the said Sir Alexander to Alexander Wedderburn, bailie of Dundee, for 1,000 merks.

(h) 1715. April 12, 14.—Bond by Sir John Wedderburn, with consent of his tutors, James Halyburton of Pitcurr, Dr. John Wedderburn, doctor of medicine in Dundee, and others, to the pursuer for 2,000 merks, part balance of his account as tutor to Sir John, under Sir Alexander's nomination, dated 3 Jan. 1710.

155. **1719.** Nov. 18.—Decreet on summons by Alexander Read of Turfbeg v. Sir John Wedderburn of Blackness, eldest son and heir of the late Sir Alexander Wedderburn of Blackness and grandson and heir of the late Sir John Wedderburn thereof, narrating (a) a bond by the said late Sir John to Mr. Andrew Balfour and Margaret Wedderburn, then his wife, in liferent, and to Rachell, Margaret and Elizabeth Balfours, their daughters ; (b) a translation, 14 Feb. 1718, by Mr. William Eccles to Alexander Wedderburn, sheriff clerk of Forfar ; and (c) a bond, 6 Feb. 1708, by the said Sir Alexander of Blackness and Major David Wedderburn, in Major-General McKertnie's Regiment of Foot, to Alexander Kirkwood. The Lords decern the barony of Blackness to the pursuer in satisfaction. (Mac. 230.)

156. **1720.** Feb. 17.—Decreet on summons by John Sinclair of Duren (son and executor to Robert Sinclair of Duren) v. Sir John Wedderburn in Shannon's regiment, eldest son and heir of the late (Sir Alexander) Wedderburn, and others, for non-payment of £500 scots, in satisfaction of which the pursuer craves to have adjudged to him the barony of Blackness, created by Great Seal charter, 14 July 1666, and granted to Sir Alexander Wedderburn, great-grandfather of the said Sir John. Decree accordingly. (Mac. 233, pt. i.)

As to the date 1666, an error for 1662, see ante s. Great Seal Register, No. 115, note.

157. **1725.** Nov. 13.—Decree in favour of the pursuer on summons by Sir Alexander Wedderburn of Blackness, sometime clerk of Dundee, v. Mr. William Gray of Inverichtie, advocate, for payment of £1,000. (Mac. 266, pt. i.)

158. **1725.** Dec. 29.—Decreet on summons by Sir Alexander Wedderburn, now of Blackness. (sometime designed Alexander Wedderburn, clerk of Dundee), v. Mr. William Gray, younger of Innerichty, advocate, adjudging the lands of Innerichty, &c., to the pursuer in satisfaction of £1,000 unpaid (Dur. 356.)

Later on (9 Dec. 1742) the claim of Sir Alexander on the lands of Innerichty gave rise to litigation by his creditors v. one Mackenzie, another claimant against the same lands. See Elchies' Decisions s. Arrestment, 21.

159. **1726.** Dec. 7.—Decreet on summons by Sir Alexander Wedderburn of Blackness v. John Auchterlony, merchant in Dundee, for £250 scots, whereby a tenement in Dundee is decerned to him in satisfaction. (Dur. 359).

160. **1729.** July 19.—Decreet on summons by Mr. Thomas Donaldson, minister at Liff, v. David Wedderburn of that ilk, only son and heir served and retoured to the late Alexander Wedderburn of that ilk, for payment of 100 merks. (Dur. 369.)

" Only son " should accurately have been " only surviving son," or " only son now on life."

161. **1729.** July 24.—Decreet on summons by David Wedderburn of Wedderburn v. Thomas Nairn of Baldovan for non-payment of certain sums. The lands of Baldovan are decreed to the pursuer in satisfaction. (Mac. 298.) Acts and Decreets Register.

162. **1730.** July 4.—Act and factory on petition by Alexander, son of David Hunter, &c., creditors of Mr. William Gray of Inverichty (ante Nos. 157-58), to have Robert Wedderburn, writer in Forfar, son of Sir Alexander Wedderburn of Blackness, appointed their factor in place of the lately deceased Thomas Traill. (Mac. 305.)
    Robert Wedderburn is so named, 5 Jan. 1732 (Mac. 318), and 26 Feb. 1735. (Mac. 333.)

163. **1732.** Jan. 12.—Decreet on summons by Patrick Maxwell, merchant, bailie of Dundee, v. John Auchinlek, for non-payment of a certain sum, in satisfaction of which the pursuer craves to have adjudged to him a tenement in Dundee once belonging to Robert Stratoun and bounded by the lands of the late Alexander Wedderburn of Kingennie, and also another tenement there once belonging to the late Peter Wedderburn and Helen Lovit his spouse, and disponed by them to the late Sir Alexander Wedderburn of Blackness, Knt., from whom it was acquired by Thomas Butchart. Decree accordingly. (Mac. 318.)

164. **1732.** July 21.—Decreet on summons by Robert Carnegie in Newgate, v. Sir Alexander Wedderburn of Blackness, touching the production by him of a disposition (31 Oct. 1718), by Peter Wedderburn. son of Alexander Wedderburn of Easter Powrie, to the defender (therein designed sheriff clerk of Forfar) of an @-rent out of a property of the pursuer in Dundee. Among the writs produced is a cognition by the bailies of Dundee in favour of Alexander Wedderburn of Easter Powrie, as heir to Alexander Wedderburn, mariner, burgess of Dundee, and Elizabeth Wedderburn, his daughter, containing sasine of the said @-rent, dated 12 Oct. 1676. (Dur. 378.)

165. **1739.** Dec. 18.—Decreet on summons by David Wedderburn of that ilk, and others, v. William Guthric of Easter Clepington and others, charging the defenders with abstracting the multures of Baldovan. John Wedderburn of Blackness, and Thomas Kidd, merchant in Dundee, are named as commissioners to take evidence for the pursuers. Sir Alexander Wedderburn of Blackness, aged 60 years and upwards, appears as a witness. (Dur. 399.)

166. **1740.** July 15.—Decreet on summons by Sir Alexander Wedderburn of Blackness, Bart., v. George Traill, son and heir of Thomas Traill, writer in Dundee, whereby certain land called Outfield, near Kirriemuir, is adjudged to the pursuers in satisfaction of £372 3s. (Dal. 232, Pt. i.)

167. **1740.** Nov. 11.—Decreet on summons by Sir Alexander Wedderburn of Blackness, v. David Ramsay, baxter in Dundee, whereby certain tenements in Dundee are adjudged to the pursuer in satisfaction of £106 13s. 4d. due on a bill (11 May 1726), drawn by John Wedderburn, younger, of Blackness, and accepted by the defender. (Dal. 234.)

168. **1741.** Jan. 31.—Decreet on a bill for abstracted multures by David Wardlaw of Craighouse, tacksman, with concurrence of Charles Wedderburn, Esq., second lawful son of Sir Peter Halket of Pitfirran, and others, v. John Stobie and others, as to the mill of Balmule, and the lands of Wester Luscar, and Craig Luscar. (Dur. 410, Pt. ii.)

169. **1741.** July 29.—Decreet on summons by Thomas Kyd, merchant in Leith, v. John Wedderburn, fiar of Blackness, reciting a letter of gift under the Privy Seal (22 June 1741) to the pursuer of the goods gear, &c., of the defender, escheat from him, in regard to his non-payment of £100 stg. due to the said pursuer. (Dur. 405.)

170. **1743.** Nov. 9.—Decreet for the pursuer on summons by Mr. Peter Wedderburn, advocate, v. William Baine, miner, for £120 stg. (Mac. 402.)

171. **1742.** July 3.—Decree on summons by Charles Wedderburn, Esq., second lawful son of Sir Peter Halket of Pitfirran, Bart., and another, v. the late Mr. Hugh Murray

of Kinnimont, and others, in regard to a bond for £150 granted (11 April 1734) by the pursuers to the late Sir George Wardlaw in life-rent and his (also deceased) son (thereafter Sir) Henry, in fee. (Dur. 408.)

172. **1742.** Dec. 14.—Decreet on summons by Sir Alexander Wedderburn of Blackness, Bart., v. George, son and heir of the late Thomas Traill, writer in Dundee, in regard to the pursuer's cautionery for the said Thomas as factor for Innerichty, and craving to have the lands called Outfield near Kirriemuir adjudged to him for non-payment of £2,156 4s. 10d. scots. (Dur. 409.)

173. **1743.** Feb. 5 —Decreet on summons by Mr. Robert Wedderburn, merchant in Dunfermline, v. James Lundin of Lundin for a sum of money. (Dur. 412.)

174. **1745.** July 17 —Decreet on summons by John Wedderburn, merchant, in Greenfield, co. Northumberland v. James Dundas, baxter, in Edinburgh, for the adjudication to the pursuer of premises in Edinburgh for non-payment of certain sums. (Dur. 422.)
    See ante s. Register of Deeds, Nos. 345 and 368.   This entry shows that the Greenfield mentioned is in co. Northumberland and not in co. Lanark, as suggested at p. 424, note 1.

175. **1746.** Nov. 4.—Decreet on summons by Charles Wedderburn of Gosford, Mrs. Janet Wardlaw (oldest daughter of the late Sir Henry Wardlaw of Pitrevie, Bart.) and another, v. William Grieve, tenant in Wester Lochend and Patrick's Walls, in regard to the writs of the lands of Balmule.   Among the writs is a contract of marriage (13 June 1696) charging the said lands, between the said Sir Henry Wardlaw and Mrs. Elizabeth Halkett, second daughter of Sir Charles Halkett of Pitfirran. (Dur. 424.)

176. **1749.** Jan. 17.—Decreet on summons by Andrew Hunter and others v. Robert Wedderburn of Persie, sheriff clerk of Forfar, and others, in regard to the affairs of William Gray of of Innerichty. (Dur. 437.)

177. **1752.** Feb. 8.—Decree on summons by David Adie, writer in Dunfermline, trustee for the creditors of the late Robert Wedderburn, merchant there, v. Rachel and Janet Wedderburn, his only children, and their tutor, mentioning a receipt (29 Aug. 1747) by the said Robert to Sir Peter Halket of Pitfirran for £50 stg. and a letter by him to the factor of the said Sir Peter for £16 to buy horses for Lady Emilia Halkett, wife of Sir Peter, and a decreet obtained by Sir Peter (14 March 1750) v. Mrs. Rachell Thomson, his relict and executrix, for £66 stg.   The lords make a decree v. the estate of the said Robert Wedderburn. (Mac. 459.)

178. **1752.** June 24.—Decreet in favour of the David Adie, as such trustee, v. the said defenders, adjudging to him certain lands of Wester Baldrige and Blackburn of Pittencreiff, in the parish of Dunfermline, feu'd (21 Sept. 1745) to the said Robert Wedderburn by Captain Forbes of Pittencreiff. (Mac. 461.)

179. **1757.** Dec 6.—Decreet on summons by John Goodwillie, writer in Edinburgh, v. Helen Wedderburn, only child of the late Alexander Wedderburn, shipmaster in London (oldest son of the late Alexander Wedderburn, shipmaster and late bailie of Dundee), and her tutors (if any), Katharine Wedderburn, relict of John Higginson, merchant in Perth, and Elizabeth and Clementina Wedderburn, all three daughters of the said late shipmaster and bailie of Dundee, reciting the marriage contract (3 July 1702), of the said shipmaster and bailie with Grissell, daughter of Thomas Watson of Grange of Barry, whereby there was settled on her 9,000 merks, with half his household plenishing, and an annuity of £40 for her life ; and further reciting a disposition (10 April 1739) of all her rights under the said contract, made by the said Grissell Watson to her daughters, Katharine, Elizabeth, Grissell, and Clementina ; and a later disposition (13, 18 April 1757) of all their rights under the said first-mentioned disposition made by the said Katharine (then relict as aforesaid) and Clementina to the pursuer ; and making mention that the said Alexander Wedderburn late bailie in Dundee died in Oct. 1734, and the said Grissell Watson in Oct. 1756, and finally claiming a sum of £4,736. 6. scots as now due to him.   Decree accordingly.   (Dur. 486.)
    See ante s. Burgh Records, Dundee Protocol Books, Nos. 592-93.

180. **1760.** July 30.—Decreet on summons by David Wedderburn of Wedderburn, Esq., and Walter Tulledeph of Balgay, Esq., v. Lady Jean Ferguson, relict of Sir James Ferguson of Kilkerran, senator of the College of Justice, and only child of the late John, Lord Maitland, &c., and others, for the production of various documents in regard to the lands of Baldovan, disponed by Thomas Nairn to the said David Wedderburn, 18 Nov. 1727, and by him to the said Walter Tulledeph,—1759. (Dur. 499.) *Acts and Decreets Register.*

181. **1768.** Aug. 9.—Decreet on summons of *cessio bonorum* by Thomas Wedderburn, late collector of excise at Inverness, v. Mr. David Scrymgeour, advocate, and others, his creditors. It recites that the said pursuer, by different misfortunes and losses, the expenses of a family of eight children, and his falling fifteen years ago into a dropsy, rendering him ever since incapable of business, the attempted cure whereof at Edinburgh and elsewhere also involved him in much expense, became reduced in circumstances and was obliged to incur considerable debts to the said creditors. The summons then narrates " that in the night time of the 12 December 1767 the pursuer was most cruelly and in a barbarous manner, to the great danger of his life, dragged in a cart about five miles from his own home in Gallacantray to the burgh of Nairn, and there imprisoned at the instance of his said creditors." The pursuer craves that they may be ordered to accept a disposition *omnium bonorum* from him, and that he may be liberated from the tolbooth of Nairn. Decree accordingly. (Mac. 591.)

182. **1770.** July 12.—Decreet on summons by Mrs. Grizel Wedderburn, only sister and heiress of the late David Wedderburn of Wedderburn, her brother german, c. Thomas Milne of Milnefield in regard to the marches of Bullion and Balbunno. (Mac. 609.)

183. **1771.** Aug. 8.—Decreet on summons by John Wedderburn, Esq., of Ballendean and Idvies, v. William Gordon, now Gray, of Balledgarno and others, reciting a minute of sale (in which the pursuer is designed Sir John Wedderburn of Idvies, eldest son of the late Sir John Wedderburn of Blackness, Bart.), dated 26 and 28 May and 6 June and registered 6 July 1770, made between pursuer (with consent of his wife, Lady Margaret Ogilvy, eldest daughter of David, Lord Ogilvy) and the defenders, whereby the latter sold to the former the new mansion house of Balledgarno, and craving that, inasmuch as the defenders will not carry out the sale, the said mansion, &c. may be adjudged to the pursuer. Decreet accordingly. (Dur. 579.)

184. **1780.** March 9.—Decreet on summons by Gilbert Mason, merchant in Edinburgh, and another v. Rachell and Janet Wedderburn, only children of the late Robert Wedderburn, merchant in Dunfermline, for non-payment of £5,000 stg. contained in their bond of 24 Dec. 1779. The lords decern to the pursuers the lands of Wester Baldridge in satisfaction. See ante No. 178. (Mac. 708.)

185. **1780.** Aug. 4.—Decreet for the pursuer on summons by Sir John Halket of Pitferran, Baronet, v. Mrs. Mary Wedderburn, *alias* Cumming, eldest lawful daughter of the deceased Henry Wedderburn, late of Gosford, wife of Lieutenant-Colonel John Cumming in the Honorable East India Company's service, and Elizabeth Wedderburn, also daughter of the said Henry Wedderburn, heirs portioners of their said father, for non-payment of £15,000 stg. (Mac. 713.)

[The following is a list of the above extracts, 1661-1780, arranged according to the offices to which they belong:—
Mackenzie's office, 83, 85-6, 88, 91, 97-8-9, 102, 105, 107-8, 113, 117, 119-20, 123-24, 129-30, 132-33, 135-36, 140-42, 145, 147, 150, 153, 155-57, 161-63, 170, 177-78, 181-82, 184-85.
Durie's office, 77, 79, 80, 90, 93, 95, 109-11, 115, 126-28, 131, 137-38, 143, 146, 148, 158-60, 164-65, 168-69, 171-76, 179-80, 183.
Dalrymple's office, 78, 81, 96, 100, 101, 103-4, 106, 112, 114, 116, 121-22, 125, 139, 144, 149, 151-52, 154, 166-67.
Minute Books only (no record) 76, 82, 84, 87, 89, 92, 94, 118, 134.]

3 o

RECORDS OF TESTAMENTS.

Records of
Testaments. These are, first, four early books (1515-41, 1541-55, 1546-48, and 1551-53) known as the "Books of the Official of S. Andrew's," and, secondly, the records, from 1567 on, of the different commissariot courts of Scotland, of which a list is given in the tabular synopsis at p. 361 (No. X). These latter consist in each case of records of testaments, inventories, edicts of executory, decreets, warrants, &c For the purposes of this work the "Books of the Official of S. Andrew's" have been searched throughout,[1] together with the testaments of the commissariots of Edinburgh, Brechin, and S. Andrew's, selected as most likely to contain material entries, and productive of the results given below. The Dunkeld testaments (1687 on) have also been searched down to 1800, but contain nothing material, while one or two entries, casually found in the records of other commissariots, (such as the will of Mr. Alexander Wedderburn, minister of Kilmarnock, found among the Glasgow Testaments, the minute books of which have been searched, 1560—1780) are referred to in Vol. I. In the following notes the one word "will" is for brevity used in the place of "testament testamentary and inventory of goods, &c.," "testament dative," "grant of administration." Of these only the first are, in the modern sense, wills, the others being grants of administration by the authorities. To distinguish the first of these, they are marked with an asterisk. The reference number at the end of each extract is to the volume of the record.

EDINBURGH TESTAMENTS.
1514—1780.

The records of this Commissariot consists of the following divisions :—1. Testaments, 1567—1829; with an index, 1567—1800, referring to two fragments (1514-16, 1531-32) for which no record exists. 2. Inventories, 1804-30 (two series). 3. Edicts of executory, 1670—1831. 4. Decreets, 1564—1790 ; Decernitures, 1811-31 ; and copy decreets. 1741—1318. 5. Consistorial decreets, 1684—1832, and minute book, 1597—1790. 6. Deeds, 1624—1809 ; with minute book, 1564—1809. 7. Court Books, 1569—1788. 8. Acts of Caution, 1594—1834 ; and Bonds of Caution, 1684—1831. 9. Responde and Advising Books, &c., 1686—1650. 10. Processes, 1590—1835 : and Consistorial Processes, 1650—1832, with index. 11. Petitions, Edicts, &c., 1789--1816. Of these only the first has been searched, down to 1780.

1.* **1575**. March 29.—Will of the late Thomas Wedderburn (son of the late Gilbert Wedderburn, burgess of Dundee), who d. ... 1574, given up by his relict and executrix, Agnes Crawfurd. It is dated at Leith, 13 Aug. 1574, and appoints his said wife tutrix to Agnes Wedderburn, his only daughter, during her minority and "les-age," when the said Agnes Crawfurd is to deliver to her so much of the deceased's goods. &c., as Capt. Thomas Crawfurd of Jordanhill, James Wedderburn, burgess of Dundee, and Gilbert Thornetoun, writer, shall think expedient. (III.)

2.* **1577**. Nov. 13.—Will of the late James Wedderburn, burgess, who d. Sept. 1575, given up by Margaret Dundas, his relict and executrix. It is dated 25 October 1560, and made before Edward Wedderburn, burgess of Dundee, and others. He appoints his wife tutrix to his son John, and to his daughters Helene and Elizabeth. (V.)

---

[1] They contain only two material entries, both in the second volume :—
 (a) 1541. Oct. 15.—Sentence by Martin Balfour, canon and principal official of S. Andrew's, in an appeal by a prudent man, Robert Setoun, commissary general of Brechin, against prudent men, George Kollok and James Wedderburn, burgesses of Dundee, fermorars of three parts of the teind sheaves of the rectory of Dundee, in reference to payment of the victual dues of the said lands. (II, 4.)
 (b) 1542. April 20.—Sentence by the same in the appeal by Mr. John Jackson, burgess of Dundee, and Mr. Richard Jackson, chaplain of the altar of the blessed Virgin Mary, in the church of S. Clement in Dundee, to the commissary general of Brechin, against Henry Wedderburn in Dundee, in whose favour a decreet had been given by John, Bishop of Brechin, on 2 Sept. 1539. The official dismisses the appeal. (ib. 17.)

3. **1580.** Sept. 6.—Will of the late Margaret Wedderburn (wife of Robert Luvall, burgess of Dundee), who d. Dec. 1575, given up by her said husband. (VIII.)
   The date of her death is wrongly entered as 1575. She was certainly alive in June—Aug. 1578. See ante s. Burgh Records, D.P.B., 201 and D.B.R., 240. Probably she died in Dec. 1578.

Edinburgh Testaments.

4. **1582.** March 13.—Will of the late Grissell Wedderburn (wife of James Anderson, burgess of Dundee), who d. July 1572, given up by her only daughter Margaret Anderson, wife of Alexander Scrymgeour, burgess of Dundee. (XII.)
   See ante s. Burgh Records, Dundee Protocol Books. No. 200, where this will is mentioned, and Grissell Wedderburn wrongly described as relict (instead of wife), of James Anderson.

5. **1587.** May 13.—Will of Alexander Wedderburn, clerk of Dundee, who d. 28 June 1585, given up by David Wedderburn, his second son, for himself and Robert, James, Peter, William, and Katrene, his bairns and executors. A debt due by him to the estate of his late wife, Janet Myln, is named. (XIV.)

6. **1587.** May 13.—Will of the late Janet Myln (wife of the said Alexander Wedderburn), who d. 19 June 1582, given up by David Wedderburn, her second son, for himself and his said brothers and sisters. (XVII.)

7.* **1607.** Jan. 31.—Will of the late Katharine Wedderburn (wife of Thomas Blair, skipper, burgess of Dundee), who d. Aug. 1606, given up by him. It is dated at Dundee 28 Aug. 1606, and contains a legacy of £20 to the poor of Dundee. (XLII.)

   [It seems curious that from 1607-1725 the register contains no material entry, but it is probably due to the fact that from 1610 on the Forfarshire family registered in the Brechin Commissariot. It will be observed that all the later Edinburgh wills, with one exception, are those of members of the Gosford branch.]

8. **1725.** Oct. 27.—Will of the late Sir John Wedderburn (only son of the late Sir Alexander Wedderburn of Blackness, and ensign in Colonel John Midleton's regiment of Foot) who d. in Ireland ...... 1723, given up by John Melville of Cairny, his executor, and creditor for £1,400 stg. under bond dated 6 October 1725, of Mrs. Rachel Wedderburn, sister german and next of kin to Sir John, and "daughter and only child on life of the said Sir Alexander." The sum of the debts due to the deceased is named as £16,800. (XC.)

9. **1734.** Nov. 28.—Will of Alexander Wedderburn, collector of excise at Linlithgow, who d. 8 Feb. 1734, given up by Mr. Peter Wedderburn, advocate, his brother german, nearest of kin and executor. (XCVI.)

10. **1756.** Sept. 15.—Will of Charles Wedderburn of Gosford, who d. there ...... 1755, given up by his eldest son and executor, John Wedderburn, now of Gosford. (CXVI.) Also eik thereto of £50 stg., being one-third of a bond by the said Charles Wedderburn, Mr. Robert Wedderburn, merchant in Dunfermline, and another, to William Clifton, dated 14 Nov. 1747. (ib.)

11. **1756.** Nov. 16.—Will of Mr. Peter Wedderburn, senator of the College of Justice, who d. at Edinburgh 11 Aug. 1756, given up by Mr. Alexander Wedderburn, advocate, eldest son and only executor. (CXVI.)

12. **1761** April 29.—Will of Janet Wedderburn (daughter to the late Alexander Wedderburn, one of the commissioners of excise in Scotland), who d. Dec. 1759, given up by Henry Paton, wright in Edinburgh, creditor and executor. (CXVIII.)

13. **1780.** June 9.—Will of Alexander Wedderburn of S. Germain's, parish of Tranent, who d. there 11 Dec. 1779, given up by William Ramsay, W.S., only executor decerned as creditor (1 May 1780) for certain sums contained in a decreet obtained by him against Mrs. Elizabeth Hallyburton or Wedderburn, widow of the deceased, and Rachael and Janet Wedderburn, his nieces and next of kin. Sir James Ramsay of Banff is cautioner. (CXXV, pt. i.)

14. **1780.** Dec. 20.—Will of Elizabeth Fletcher (daughter of Andrew Fletcher of Saltoun, senator of the College of Justice, and wife of John Wedderburn of Gosford, now Sir John Halkett of Pitfirran, Baronet), who d. in Edinburgh ...... given up by Elizabeth Halkett, her only child and executrix. (CXXV, pt. i.)

Brechin   The records of this commissariot consist of the following :—1. Testaments, 1576—1823. 2. Inven-
Testaments. tories, 1806-23. 3. Minute Books, 1597—1823. 4. Edicts, 1661—1823. 5. Bonds of Caution, 1669—1823.
6. Deeds, 1636—1810. 7. Protested Bills, 1724—68. 8. Petitions, 1773—1823. 9. Processes, 1659—1823.
10. Miscellaneous Papers. Of these the first has been searched from 1576—1780.

1.* **1610.** Sept. 22.—Will (18 June) of William Davidsone, younger, merchant, burgess
of Dundee, who d. about June 1610, given up partly by his own mouth before Mr.
Alexander Wedderburn, burgess of Dundee, and partly by Janet Wedderburn, his
relict and tutrix to William, Richard, Jonet, Margaret, and Elspet, his children, and
to the bairn "in gremio." Among his debtors are named Robert Wedderburn, elder,
and James Wedderburn. There is also a legacy of £40 to Mr. Alexander Wedderburn of Kingennie. The cautioner is Peter Wedderburn, eldest son to the late Peter
Wedderburn, burgess of Dundee. (II.)

2.* **1612** June 7.—Will (12 Oct. 1611) of Robert Wedderburn, elder, burgess of Dundee,
who d. ... Oct. 1611, given up by him in his own house at Dundee, before Mr.
Alexander Wedderburn, clerk of Dundee, and others. Mr. Alexander Wedderburn
and David Wedderburn are named as debtors, and Janet Wedderburn as a creditor
of the deceased. The following legacies are left ; to Peter Wedderburn, son of
the late Peter Wedderburn, his brother, in satisfaction of all heirship claims,
200 merks ; to Margaret and Barbara Wedderburn, sisters of the said Peter, 100
merks ; to James Thomsone, his sister's son, and to Thomas Coustoun, his sister's
son, 100 merks each ; to Mr. James Wedderburn, son of Mr. Alexander Wedderburn,
clerk, all his protocol books. James Wedderburn and Peter Wedderburn, brothers
german of the said clerk, are nominated his executors. (II.)

3 * **1613.** Sept. 24.—Will of Euphame Coustoun, (wife of Robert Wedderburn, merchant,
burgess of Dundee), who d. ... Sept. 1612, given up by herself (17 Sept.), at their
house in Dundee, before Mr. William Wedderburn, minister there. She appoints her
husband sole executor, and leaves legacies (subject to his life-rent) to Jeane Fraser,
their oy, John Wedderburn, their son, and Elizabeth Wedderburn, their daughter.
She also acknowledges a debt of 300 merks to be due to Mr. David Wedderburn,
their eldest son. (III.)
The expression "their oy " is not strictly accurate. Jeane Fraser was the daughter (by James Fraser)
of Euphame Scott, who was daughter to Euphame Coustoun, by her first husband, Robert Scott.

4.   **1622.** May 9.—Will of Margaret Strathauchin, (relict of John Wedderburn, burgess
of Dundee), who d. . . . . given up by John Ogilvy, minister of Kerrimuir, executor
dative. (IV.)
See post s. Protocol Books (Edin.) No. 4.

5.* **1624.** Jan. 26.—Will of Magdalene Wedderburn, (wife of Thomas Jack, merchant,
burgess of Dundee), who died . . . . 1623, given up by her 22 Sept. 1623. She
nominates Patrick and Alexander Jack to be her executors, and leaves the following
legacies ; to Patrick Wedderburn, her father, £300 ; to John Wedderburn, merchant,
her brother, £100, as soon as he attains 15 years of age ; to Janet Wedderburn,
her father's sister, £10 ; and to Alexander Halliburton, skipper, burgess of Dundee,
a chain of gold with a tablet of gold hanging thereat. The will is signed by
Mr. James Wedderburn, notary, at the command of the testatrix, who is too weak
to write herself. (IV.)

6.* **1625.** June 14.—Will (19 Feb. 1625) of Archibald Blythe, skipper, burgess of
Dundee, who d. Feb. 1625, given up partly by him and partly by Euphame
Wedderburn, his relict and executrix. The will names his children Arthur, Robert,
David (then under 14), and Margaret. (IV.)

7.   **1626.** Jan. 16.—Will of Peter Wedderburn of Dundee, who d. July, 1623, given up
by Margaret Muddie, his relict and executrix dative. (IV.)

8.* **1629**. Nov. 4.—Will (26 March, 1628) of Peter Wedderburn, merchant, burgess of Brechin Dundee, who d. March, 1628, given up partly by himself and partly by Helen Loweill, **Testaments.** his reliet and executrix. He leaves all to his said reliet, except 500 merks to William Wedderburn, his brother german, and 500 merks to Alexander Wedderburn, younger, mariner, son of the late Robert Wedderburn, his father's brother. Mr. Alexander Wedderburn of Kingennie, is named as a debtor to the deceased, and James Wedderburn, uncle to the testator, is a witness. (IV.)

9. **1631**. June 23.—Will of Jeane Wedderburn, (wife of Thomas Boytter, burgess of Dundee), who d. Nov. 1630, given up by her husband in the name of James, Anna, and Helene Boytter, their bairns. (V.)

10.* **1631**. June 27.—Will of Mr. James Wedderburn, clerk of Dundee, who d. 1627, given up, 28 May 1627, by himself, and partly given up by James Wedderburn, dean of gild of Dundee, and Mr. Alexander Wedderburn of Kingennie, in the name of William and Peter Wedderburn, his youngest sons, executors, and sole legatees, after payment of 1000 merks to Alexander Wedderburn, his eldest son. The said Mr. Alexander Wedderburn of Kingennie, James Wedderburn, uncle to the deceased, and Peter Wedderburn, brother to the deceased, are nominated tutors to the said William and Peter. The will is signed by the testator at Dundee, and witnessed by Mr. John Wedderburn, the testator's brother, and Thomas Fyiff, notary. (V.)

11.* **1632**. April 30.—Will of Christiane Loweill, (wife of James Wedderburn, merchant, burgess of Dundee), who d. 26 May 1631, given up partly by herself, and partly by her husband and executor, to whom she leaves all her property, in acknowledgment of his kindness and tender love. David Wedderburn, burgess, is cautioner. She leaves 100 merks to the poor of the kirk of Dundee. (V.)

12. **1640**. Nov. 21.—Will of Mr. Alexander Wedderburn of Kingennie, who d. at Dundee, Sept. 1637, given up by Mr. Alexander Wedderburn, now of Kingennie, his only son and executor dative. (V.)

13.* **1648**. June 1.—Will of James Wedderburn, bailie and dean of gild of Dundee, who d. ...... 1644, given up by Alexander Wedderburn, skipper, burgess of Dundee, his nephew and executor. The will is dated at Dundee 4 April 1644, and leaves all to the said Alexander Wedderburn, subject to the following legacies :—to James Wedderburn, second son to Mr. Alexander Wedderburn of Blackness, 1,000 merks ; to Catharine Wedderburn, sister to the testator, 300 merks ; to Elspeth Wedderburn, relict of Mr. Alexander Fotheringhame of Parkzeat, 300 merks ; to Alexander Wedderburn of Kingenny "my emerode or otherwise as he shall think best my best purse-pennie of gold " ; to Lieut. Col. James Wedderburn " that great silver cup whereupon his father's and mother's arms are," but if Lieut.-Col. Wedderburn does not return to Scotland the said cup is to remain with James Sympsone as a pledge of the testator's love ; to Mr. Peter Wedderburn, 300 merks ; to William Wedderburn, brother german of the said Mr. Peter Wedderburn, 100 merks ; to Helen Fergusone, daughter to Captain William Fergusone, a scarlet vylieot with balgaryes of velvett; to Catharine Kyde, daughter to Lieut. James Kyde, a growgaine silver gown ; and finally 400 merks for a silver basin, for the use of the kirk of Dundee, which basin is to be engraved with the names and arms of the testator and his wife, and with such inscription as the said Mr. Alexander Wedderburn of Blackness shall think fit. (Unbooked testaments, s.d.)

Elspeth Wedderburn, relict of Fotheringhame of Parkzeat or Parkgate in the parish of Invera-ritie, was daughter to Alexander Wedderburn, first of Kingennie. Her sister, Marjory, married Robert Carnegy of Leuchland. Hence the reference in one of the Blackness Papers (No. 43) to " the daughters of Leuchland or Parkgate." as nieces of Sir John Wedderburn of Gosford. Lieut.-Col. James Wedderburn was nephew to the testator, being the eldest surviving son of his brother David.

14. **1662**. Jan. 2.—Will of Helen Wedderburn, (wife of Bertrame Willson in Dundee), who d. March 1660, given up by her said husband. (VI.)

15. **1676**. Nov. 7.—Will of Sir Alexander Wedderburn of Blackness, who d. Nov. 1675, given up by John Wedderburn, now of Blackness, his eldest son and executor. Alexander Wedderburn of Kingennie is cautioner, and Matilda Fletcher, spouse to the deceased, is named. (Unbooked testaments, s.d.)

16. **1683.** Feb. 14.—Will of Peter Wedderburn, merchant in Dundee, who d. June 1682, given up by Catharine Man, his relict, executrix, and creditrix for the life interest of 8,000 merks named in their marriage contract dated 17 Oct. 1677. (VII.)

17. **1695.** Dec. 4.—Will of John Pierson, baxter in Dundee, who d. . . . 1695, given up by Margaret Wedderburn, his relict and executrix, who retains one-third of the household plenishing under her contract of marriage, made 26 Nov. 1690, with consent of Alexander Wedderburn of Easter Powrie. Alexander Wedderburn, treasurer in Dundee, is cautioner. (VIII.)

18. **1700.** March 1.—Will of Catharin Man, (relict of Petter Wedderburn, mariner, in Dundee), who d. 168. . ., given up by Alexander Wedderburn, clerk of Dundee, in name of Alexander and John Wedderburn, sons of the said Catharine and Peter, and executors decerned to her 8 Nov. 1699. James Wedderburn, son to the late George Wedderburn, merchant in Edinburgh, is cautioner. (VIII.)

19. **1704.** April 5.—Will of James Wedderburn, clerk of Dundee, who d. Jan. 1696, given up by Alexander Wedderburn, now clerk of Dundee, his son and executor. A debt due to the deceased by Alexander Wedderburn, skipper in Dundee, in respect of the years 1691-95, is mentioned. (VIII.)

20. **1704.** Oct. 11.—Will of Alexander Wedderburn, skipper, in Dundee, who d. — 17— given up by Alexander Wedderburn, clerk of Dundee, executor decerned. (VIII.)
The suggested date of death is an error ; he died before the close of 1699.

21. **1709.** Nov. 18.—Will of Alexander Wedderburn of Easter Powrie, who d. January 1692, given up by Alexander Wedderburn of that ilk, his son and executor. (IX.)

22. **1716.** Aug. 22.—Will of Alexander Wedderburn of that ilk, who d Dec. 1713, given up by the authors of Grissell Wedderburn, his daughter and executrix dative, decerned as nearest of kin. (IX.)
" Authors " generally means the persons from whom a right is derived, but seems here to signify those who acted for Grissell Wedderburn.

23. **1716.** Aug. 22.—Will of Alexander Wedderburn of Easter Powrie, who d. January 1692, given up by the authors of Grissell Wedderburn, daughter of the late Alexander Wedderburn of that ilk, and granddaughter of the said Alexander Wedderburn of Easter Powrie. (IX.)

24. **1740.** May 6.—Will of Alexander Wedderburn, shipmaster in Dundee, who d. Oct. 1734, given up by Grissell Watson, his relict, executrix, and creditrix for the life-rent of 9000 merks named in her marriage contract, dated 3 July 1702. Eight-eleventh parts of the ship, "The Providence of Dundee," are named as part of his property, and valued at £660. (X.)

25.* **1757.** Feb. 17.—Will (dated at Dundee, 6 July, 1756) of the late Grizell Watson (relict of Alexander Wedderburn, shipmaster in Dundee) who died 175..., given up partly by herself and partly by her daughters and executrices, Katharine (relict of John Higginsone, merchant in Perth), Elizabeth, and Clementina Wedderburn. (XI.)

26. **1763.** Feb. 24.—Will of David Wedderburn of Wedderburn, who d. 17..., given up by Mrs. Grizell Wedderburn, sister german and executrix decerned. (XI.)

27. **1765.** April 10.—Will of Margaret Balfour (relict of Dr. John Wedderburn, physician in Dundee) who d. 176... given up by Robert Wedderburn of Pearsie, executor dative as creditor decerned. (XI.)

28.* **1777.** Feb. 8.—Will (10 Aug. 1774) of Susanna Wedderburn (daughter of the deceased Sir John Wedderburn of Blackness, Baronet) who d. 177..., given up by herself and by Katharine Wedderburn, her executrix. The will is in the form of a mutual contract registered at Dundee, 23 Sept. 1776, and made between the said Susanna and Katharine, sisters german, in favour of themselves, and Sir John Wedderburn of Bandean (*sic*) and James Wedderburn, their brothers german, now the only surviving sons of the late Sir John Wedderburn. (XII.)
See ante s. Burgh Records, Dundee Deeds, No. 132.

SAINT ANDREW'S WILLS.
1549—1800.

The records of this commissariot are as follows:—1. Testaments, 1549—1823 ; with Minute Books S. Andrew's 1718—1823. 2. Inventories, 1806-23. 3. Decreets, 1595—1823. 4. Deeds, 1564—1809; with Minute Testaments. Books, 1671—1745, 1780—1809. 5. Act Books, 1573—1791. Of these, only the Testaments have been searched, down to 1800.

1. **1598** June 26 —Will of Robert Wedderburn, younger, burgess of Dundee, who d. 30 Nov. 1593, given up by James Thomson on behalf of Alexander Wedderburn, son and executor to the said Robert. The testator's deceased spouse, Grissell Duncan, is mentioned. Alexander Wedderburn, clerk of Dundee, is a creditor, and David Wedderburn, burgess, is cautioner. (III.)

2. **1598.** June 26 —Will of Grissell Duncan (spouse of the said Robert Wedderburn, younger), who d. 20 Feb. 1591, given up by the said James Thomson, burgess of Dundee, father in law to Alexander Wedderburn, pupil. David Wedderburn is cautioner. (ib.)
   " Father-in-law " signifies " step father," though even so. the expression is not accurate, James Thomson being the second husband of Elspet Herring, third wife (and widow) of Robert Wedderburn, father to Alexander. " Step-mother's husband " would thus be correct.

3. **1598.** June 26.—Will of Elspet Lovell (reliet of the said Robert Wedderburn, younger), who d. 26 Aug. 1592, given up on behalf of Alexander Wedderburn, her son, by the said James Thomson. David Wedderburn is again cautioner. (ib.)
   " Reliet " is inaccurate, as Robert Wedderburn died in 1593 (see above No. 1), after having married again, as third wife, Elspet Herring. See the account of him in Vol. I. The word " relict " however, seems to be used equally to signify the person dying and the person left. See ante D.P.B.,200.

4. **1600.** April 15.—Will of Margaret Lindsay (wife of John Wedderburn, skipper, burgess of Dundee), who d. 12 August 1599, given up in the names of John, James, Agnes, Margaret, and Helen Wedderburn, her lawful bairns and executors dative. (ib.)

5. **1625.** Feb. 4.—Will of Cristean Wedderburn (wife of David Wedderburn, merchant, burgess of Cupar, eo. Fife), who d. Oct. 1624, given up by her said husband on behalf of David, Alexander, Margaret, and Cristean their children. Mr. James Wedderburn, minister at Moonsie, is named as a debtor to the deceased. (VIII.)

6. **1627.** Aug. 8.—Will of Alexander Wedderburn of Pittormie, who d. in Cupar, Fife, 15 Feb. 1627, given up by Christiane Fairny, his relict and executrix dative. Mr. James Wedderburn, minister at Moonsie, is cautioner. (ib.)

7.* **1628.** July 18.—Will of Mr. David Wedderburn, burgess of Burntisland, Fife, who d. ...... 162... given up partly by himself and partly by Allesone Watsone, his relict, in name of Andro and Alexander Wedderburn, their sons and his executors. The will is dated at Burntisland 22 Dec. 1627, and nominates Mr. John Russell, advocate, and others, tutors to his said sons. It also bequeaths a small legacy to Robert Wedderburn, son natural to the deceased. (VIII.)

8. **1639.** Will of Alexander Wedderburn (son of the late Mr. David Wedderburn of Burntisland), who d. ...... 1628, given up by Andro Wedderburn, his brother and executor dative. The deceased was, at the time of his death, owing to Robert Wedderburn, his late father's natural son, the legacy left him by his said father. (IX.)

9.* **1640.** April 1.—Will of Andrew Wedderburn, burgess of Burntisland, who d. July, 1639, given up by his mother and executrix, Aleysone Watsone, and dated 17 July, 1639. He leaves everything he has to his said mother, except a legacy of 500 merks to be paid to Francis Wedderburn, his son natural, on his reaching 14 years of age. (IX.)

10.* **1683.** Nov. 16.—Will of Alexander Wedderburn of Easter Powrie, parish of Murroes, Forfar, who d. April 1683, given up by Alexander Wedderburn, now of Easter Powrie, his eldest son and executor. It is dated at Dundee 17 Nov. 1682 and gives legacies to Margaret Myln his wife, Alexander Scrimseor his grandchild, Ma : Wedderburn, wife to John Wedderburn, Peter Wedderburn his son, and also appoints his said wife administratrix to his children, Peter Wedderburn aforesaid, and Elizabeth Wedderburn, till they choose their curators. John Wedderburn of Blackness is cautioner. (XIV.)

I find no mention elsewhere of any "Ma(rgaret ?) Wedderburn, wife of John Wedderburn," and make little doubt that the record is in error, and should read "daughter of John Wedderburn," in which case the reference is to Margaret, only surviving child of John Wedderburn, baxter, natural son to the testator. This is made almost certain by the terms of Margaret's marriage contract (ante s. Scrymgeour-Wedderburn Papers, No. 491), from which it appears that she was a legatee under this will.

11. **1699.** Aug. 1.—Will of Beatrice Wedderburn (relict of Patrick Crambie, merchant in Cupar, Fife), who d. . . . 1699, given up by John Burne of Midlemylne, curator to Patrick Crambie, her only son and executor. (XVI.)

12. **1717.** Nov. 6.—Eik of £330 to the confirmed testament of Alexander Wedderburn of that ilk, by Grissell Gardyne, his relict. (XVIII.)

13. **1722.** Nov. 7.—Will of Alexander Wedderburn of Easter Powrie, Murroes, co. Angus, who d. . . . 17 . . ., given up by David Wedderburn, of that ilk, his grandchild, executor dative and nearest of kin. (XVIII.)

14. **1748.** Oct. 19.—Will of Mr. Robert Wedderburn, merchant, in Dunfermline, Fife, who d. 21 Aug. 1748, given up by his relict, Mrs. Rachell Thomson. (XX.)

15. **1752.** June 30.—Will ad omissa of Mr. Robert Wedderburn, merchant, in Dunfermline, who d. . . . 17 . . ., given up by David Adie, executor dative quâ creditor decerned. The document refers to Mrs. Rachell Thomson, relict, and Rachell and Janet Wedderburn, daughters of the deceased ; to a bond (1737), by the late Sir Peter Halket of Pitfirran, and Charles Wedderburn of Glasfoord (sic), father and brother to the deceased, and in particular to a joint bond by them and the deceased "to Allan Ramsay, painter, in London," for 2,000 merks. It also mentions another bond (1748), by the said Charles Wedderburn and John Wedderburn, his son. Among the debtors to the deceased is Mr. Peter Wedderburn, advocate. (XXI.)

16. **1799.** May 10.—Will of Mrs. Rachell Thomson (relict of Robert Wedderburn, Esq., brother german of Sir Peter Halkett of Pitfirran, Bart.) who d. at Torryburn, Fife, . . . 177 . . ., given up 7 May 1779, by Rachell and Janet Wedderburn, her daughters. (XXIV.)

PARISH REGISTERS (SCOTLAND).

These registers have been already mentioned, in the general note on the Scottish Records at pp. 359-61 of this volume, as falling into two divisions, (*a*) the ancient records, from their earliest dates down to Dec. 31, 1854, and (*b*) the modern register for Births, Marriages, and Deaths throughout all Scotland, from 1855 on. I have myself searched this latter register from its earliest date, 1 Jan. 1855 down to 31 Dec. 1892, and have examined every Wedderburn entry during that period.[1] This, thanks to the printed indices, was no very great labour, and it enabled me to ascertain all the families of the name, living in Scotland during most of the latter half of this century.[2]

The ancient records, however, are the most interesting. Of these the principal one was, naturally, that of Dundee, while those of Edinburgh and (for the Gosford branch) of Aberlady have also proved of great value. In addition to these I have made several other searches, which may be called of minor importance, because the entries which they have produced are either few (though often serviceable) or relate to families of the name very distantly or indistinctly connected with the Forfarshire house. The result of these minor searches is not given below, but is noted under the accounts of the families or persons to whom they refer.

It is, I think, desirable to place on record a list of all the registers which have been searched, and which, in the absence of any reason to question the thoroughness at which I have aimed, need not be re-examined at any future time. I add, therefore, a list of all the ancient parochial registers searched for the purposes of these volumes, together with some other registers, which have been gone through with other primary objects, while this book has been in progress, and from which all Wedderburn entries have been extracted, or the absence of any such material as carefully noted. One or two isolated references to yet other parish registers will be found in vol. i, but are not included in this list.

PARISH.	EARLIEST DATE.	TO WHAT EXTENT SEARCHED.	REMARKS.
ABERDEENSHIRE :—			
Aberdeen (20 vols.)	B. 1563 ? M. 1568. D 1560.	B.1615-31,1788-97.	Of these the registers of
Crimond (1)	B.1743. M.1784. D.1784.	All 1743-1819.	Aberdeen, Fyvie, Old
Echt (2)	B. 1678. M. 1648.	B. all to 1819.	Meldrum, Tarves, and
Fraserburgh (1)	B. 1733. M. 1750. D. 1764.	All 1733-1819.	Turriff have yielded
Fyvie (2)	B. 1685. M. 1783. D.1783.	All to 1800.	substantial results as
Lonmay (2)	B. 1687. M. 1687. D 1716.	All 1687 to 1819.	regards persons of the
Monquhitter (2)	B. 1687. M. 1693.	All to 1800.	name in co. Aberdeen.
Newhills (1)	B. 1700. M. 1700. D. 1754.	B. 1751-1800.	I should like to have
Old Meldrum (2)	B. 1713. M. 1752. D. 1748.	B. to 1815. M to 1812. D. to 1800.	had the registers of
Pitsligo (2)	B. 1720. M. 1720. D.1798.	All 1741-1819	of Old and New Machar
Rathen (3)	B. 1704. M. 1704. D.1770.	All 1704-1819.	1641 on (10 vols.) and
Tarves (2)	B. 1695. M. 1736.	All to 1800.	1616 on (2 vols.), com-
Turriff (2)	B. 1696. M. 1724.	All to 1800.	pletely searched.
ARGYLLSHIRE :—			
Islands (9)	None before 1704.	All to 1819.	Nothing material.

---

[1] The results are dealt with in vol. i.

[2] A similar search in the General Register of births, marriages, and deaths in England and Wales (1837 to Sept. 1890), kept at Somerset House, has provided similar information for those countries during that period. I have also searched some minor registers kept at Somerset House, viz. : the Consulary Indices of births, marriages and deaths, 1849-55 ; the Miscellaneous Foreign Register, 1801 on (by the index to vols. 1-23) ; and the Indian Marriage Index, 1852-80. At the India Office I have examined the Indian registers kept there, for Madras down to 1884 for baptisms, and 1870 for marriages ; for Bengal down to 1867 for baptisms, and 1873 for marriages ; and for Bombay down to 1850 for baptisms, and 1890 for marriages. The burial registers of all three presidencies I have also searched down to 1870. The results of all these searches are embodied in vol. i.

Parish Registers (Scotland).	PARISH.	EARLIEST DATE.	TO WHAT EXTENT SEARCHED.	REMARKS.
	AYRSHIRE :—			
	Ayr (9)	B. 1664. M. 1687. D. 1766.	B. 1664-80.	Nothing material.
	Kilmarnock (6)	B. 1640. M. 1687.	All to 1750.	See s. Rev Alex. Wedderburn of Kilmarnock.
	BANFF :—			
	S. Fergus	B. 1688. M. 1783. D. 1784.	All 1688-1819.	Nothing material.
	BUTESHIRE :—			
	All Parishes (8)	None before 1691 .	All to 1819.	Nothing material.
	CAITHNESS :—			
	Wick (3)	B. 1701. M. 1703.	B. 1735-1800. M. 1735-1800.	Nothing material.
	CLACKMANNAN :—			
	Alloa (6)	B. 1609. M. 1609.	All to 1800.	
	DUMFRIES :—			
	Dumfries	B. 1605. M. 1616. D. 1617.	B. 1605-1780.	⎫
	Johnstone (1)	B. 1734. M. 1735-40.		Nothing material.
	Kirkpatrick-Juxta (2)	B. 1694. M. 1709. D. 1709.	All 1709-1810.	
	Moffat (4)	B. 1723. M.1709. D.1709-35	All 1709-1810.	⎭
	EDINBURGH :—			
	Canongate (19)	B. 1564. M. 1564.	All to 1800.	⎫ See below.
	City (54)	B. 1595. M. 1595.	All to 1800.	⎭
	St Cuthbert's (35)	B. 1573. M. 1655. D. 1740.		
	Dalkeith (9)	B. 1609. M. 1639. D. 1701.	B. 1690-1750.	Nothing material.
	Inveresk (15)	B. 1607. M. 1606. D. 1750.	B. 1730-80. D. 1800-3.	One or two entries only.
	Leith, North (7)	B. 1615. M. 1605. D. 1754.		Nothing material.
	„ South (17)	B. 1599. M. 1588. D. 1662.	B. 1599-1700. M. 1588-1700.	See account below.
	FIFE :—			
	Burntisland (3)	B. 1672. M. 1672. D. 1734.	B and M. 1672-1750.	Nothing material.
	Ceres (3)	B. 1620. M. 1620. D. 1620.	All to 1730.	One or two entries only.
	Cupar (3)	B. 1654. M. 1654. D. 1654.	All to 1740.	See s. David Wedderburn in Welgait and his descendants.
	Dunfermline (11)	B. 1561. M. 1561. D. 1617.	B. 1700-1800.	See s. Wedderburn of Gosford (Halkett of Pitfirrane).
	Forgan (1)	B. 1695. M. 1703.	B. 1695-1737.	Nothing material.
	S. Andrew's (18)	B. 1627. M. 1638. D. 1732.	B. 1627-75.	
	FORFARSHIRE :—			
	Dundee (14)	B. 1645. M. 1645.	All to 1800.	See below.
	Liff, Benvie, and Invergowrie (3)	B. 1651. M. 1633. D.1726.	All to 1750.	Nothing material.
	Monifieth (5)	B. 1562. M. 1562. D. 1659.	All to 1800.	Very few entries.
	Murroes (2)	B. 1698. M. 1699. D. 1705.	All to 1800.	Nothing material.
	HADDINGTONSHIRE :—			
	Aberlady (4)	B. 1632. M. 1634. D. 1632.	All to 1800.	See below.
	Dunbar (6)	B. 1672. M. 1637. D. 1642.	All 1651-1800.	⎫
	Ormiston (1)	B. 1637. M. 1637. D. 1642.	B. 1700-50. [D. 1668.	A few entries only.
	Pencaitland (2)	B. 1598. M. 1598. D. 1665.	R.1660-1790. M.1620-1790	
	Stenton (2)	B. 1679. M. D. 1668-1794.	B. 1707-90.	Nothing material.
	Whittinghame (2)	B. 1627. M. 1627.	B. 1700-50.	⎭
	KINCARDINESHIRE :—			
	Banchory Derwick (2)	B. 1713. M. 1716. D. 1716.	B. All to 1800.	⎫ Nothing material.
	Banchory Ternan (2)	B. 1670. M. 1670. D. 1670.	B. All to 1800.	⎭
	LANARKSHIRE :—			
	Glasgow (32)	B. 1609. M. 1612.	B. 1685-92, 1695-1735.	See s. Rev. Alex. Wedderburn of Kilmarnock.
	ROXBURGHSHIRE :—			
	Kelso (6)	B.1598. M.1597. D.1614-60.	B. 1598-1800.	See s. Reg. of Deeds, No. 182.

DUNDEE PARISH REGISTER.

There are fourteen volumes of this register, ten of births or baptisms, and four of marriages. The first eight volumes contain the baptisms 1645—1802, the next two, those 1803-19. Vols. 11-13 contain the marriages 1645—1803 (except 1676-82. which is blank) and Vol. 14 those 1804-19. Both marriages and baptisms have been searched down to 1800.

MARRIAGES.

1645—1800.

1. **1646.** Oct. 4.—John Gardyn, goldsmyth, and Elizabeth Wedderburn proclaimed the tent day of Oetober 1646 upon consignation of 2 eroee dolloris and a golden ring. *Dundee Marriages*

2. **1646.** Oct. 4.—James Lovell of Kinnewehie, in the paroch of Monymeall, and Elizabeth (Wedder)burn in this congregation, proclaimed upon consignation of twa ...... ble ringis, the 25 day of Oetober 1646.
   These two entries are from a number of proclamations contained in the first fifteen folios of the Register. The marriages proper begin on fol. 16.

3. **1646.** Nov. 24,—John Gardyn, goldsmyth, and Elizabeth Wedderburn solempnisit ther bandis of marriage the 24 day of November.

4. **1647.** Feb. 27.—James Lovell of Kinnewehie and Elizabeth Wedderburn solempnisit ther bandis of marriage.

5. **1655.** June 30.—Patrick Kid, younger of Craigie, and Margaret Wedderburn being eontracted, gave in their names to be proelaimed and married the 30 August.

6. **1657.** July 27.—Bertine Belson, Inglishman, merchant, and Helen Wedderburne being eontracted, gave up their names, &c. ...... married the 20 August.

7. **1660.** May 18.—Alexander Wedderburne of Kingennie and Margaret Mill being eontracted, gave up their names to be proelaimed.

8. **1663.** Nov. 26.—William Kid and Jean Wedderburne was maried, being Thursday, by Mr. Alexander Milne, one of the ministers of this burgh.

9. **1664.** Dec. 17.—Andrew Wedderburne, merchand, and Christian Duncan, being contracted, gave up their names to be proclaimed.

10. **1666.** May 16.—John Wedderburne, baxter, and Helene Rodger being eontracted, gave up their names, &e. ...... married June 27.

11. **1673.** January 10.—James Wedderburne, clerk of Dundie, and Elizabeth Davidsone to be proclaimed.

12. **1675.** Oct. 8.—James Bailie of Little Gill and Cieill Wedderburne eontracted and proclamed ; maried 28 October.

13. **1684.** Sept. 2.—Mr. Robert Rait, minister, and Elizabeth Wedderburne eontracted ; maried 8 Oetober.

14. **1685.** Apryl 14.—Alexander Wedderburn and Christian Kinloch were maried by lieense.

15. **1690.** Nov. 27.—John Person, baxter, and Margaret Wedderburne eontracted, and married 29 Jan. 1691.

16. **1697.** Oct. 15.—Alexander Wedderburn, clerk, and Katharen Scott contracted, and married 15 November.

17. **1700.** June 10.—Thomas Watson and Grisell Wedderburn contracted, and married 11 July.

18. **1701.** April 19.—Peter Wedderburn, merchand, and Hellen Lyon contracted, and married 23 April.

19. **1702.** July 3.—Alexander Wedderburn and Grisel Watson contracted, and married 22 July.

> This Alexander is often mentioned in the register of baptisms, being designed "mariner" in 1703-1706, "late bailie" in 1711, "bailie" 1712, and "present bailie" in 1714. He was (almost certainly) Alexander, eldest son of Peter Wedderburn and Catharine Mann, who .... was certainly a mariner, and had several children baptized in Dundee, among them Alexander (bapt. 19 May 1711), and Margaret (bapt. 14 Sept. 1714.) The Dundee register of baptisms, however, mentions another Alexander Wedderburn, also called bailie (1714), husband to Margaret Watson, and father by her of two children, Alexander and Margaret Ker, baptized, the one only a day, the other just a week, before their namesakes and contemporaries. (See below, Dundee baptisms, Nos. 62-3 and 67-8.) I have not been able to identify this other "bailie," whose existence is the only difficulty in identifying his namesake, as he may have been the son of Peter Wedderburn and Catharine Mann.

20. **1704.** May 27.—Robert Wedderburn and Margaret Arnot contracted, and married 14 June.

21. **1705.** Aug. 27.—Peter Wedderburn, merchand, and Barbara Affleck contracted, and married 27 August.

22. **1715.** Aug. .....—Alexander Reid of Terbeg and Elizabeth Wedderburne contracted, and married 1 September.

23. **1726.** March 18.—James Graham of Netherie (*sic*) and Grisel Wedderburn married 28 of March.

> Netherie is an error for Methie. James Graham's second marriage with Elizabeth Guthrie is registered Sept. 5-7, 1730.

24. **1738.** Jan. 27.—Robert Wedderburn, shiriff clerk in Forfar, and Mrs. Isobel Edward of Persie, being three times proclaimed in one sabbath; married 1 February.

25. **1739.** Aug. 10.—David Scrimsiour of Birkhill, advocate, Mrs. Katherine Wedderburn, being three times proclaimed in one sabbath; married 13 August.

26. **1766.** June 6.—John Smith junior of Balharrie, and Mrs. Agatha Wedderburn, youngest lawful daughter of the deceast John Wedderburn of Blackness; married June 8th.

27. **1769.** Nov. 25.—Sir John Wedderburn of Idvie in this parish and Lady Margaret Ogilvie, daughter of the Right Honourable the Earl of Airly in the parish of Cortachie.

28. **1785.** Dec. 24.—David Wedderburn of London, Esq., and Miss Elizabeth Read, daughter of Alexander Read of Loggie, Esq., both in this parish; December 26.

29. **1786.** May 27.—The Rev. Mr. James Stormonth, minister of the Gospel at Airly, and Elizabeth Wedderburn, daur. of the deceased Robert Wedderburn, Esquire, in this parish; June 2.

30. **1787.** Sept. 7.—Charles Wedderburn, Esq., of Pearsie, and Anne Read, daughter of the deceased John Read, Esq., of Carney; 11th Sept.

31. **1790.** (no date.)—John Wilson, sailor, and Jean Wedderburn, clandestinately married August 18th, 1790.

32. **1793.** June 24.—James Waddle, brewer, in this parish, and Catharine Wedderburn, daughter of John Wedderburn in parish of Meigle; 11th July.

BAPTISMS.

1645-1800.

In addition to the following extracts, the register contains many mentions of Wedderburns acting as witnesses or godfathers at the baptisms of the children of their friends. Of these, some note is occasionally given in Vol. I, in the accounts of the different members of the family to whom they refer.

1. **1645.** Dec. 22.—Alexander Wedderburn of Kingany, a man childe named David. David Graham of Fentrie, David Kinloch of Bandoch, David Fotheringham, Mr. David Abercrombie, witnesses.

2. **1646.** March 7.—Mr. Alexander Wedderburn of Blackness, clerk of Dundie, a woman childe named Helene. Sir George Haliburton, (Lord Fodderance, one of the Lords of Session,) Thomas Haliburton, Robert Davidson, bailies, and Mr. George Haliburton, witnesses.

3. **1647.** March 1.—Sir Alexander Wedderburn of Blackness, Knyght, a woman childe named Grissell. John Midleton of Kadow, General-Major of the Scotis forces, Thomas Mudie, bailie, Alexander Wedderburn of Kingany, Mr. Alexander Myln, minister at Longforgound, witnesses.

4. **1648.** April 13.—Sir Alexander Wedderburn of Blackness, Knyght, a man childe, Alexander. Sir Alexander Gibson of Durie, Knight and Clark Register, Alexander Wedderburn of Kingauie, Mr. Alexander Myln, person of Longforgound, Alexander Haliburton, Alexander Fletcher, Alexander Wedderburn, merchants, and Alexander Goldman, witnesses.

5. **1649.** Nov. 19.—Sir Alexander Wedderburn of Blackness, Knyght, a man child named James. Mr. James Kyd of Craigie, Doctor James Beaton, James Symson, Mr. James Glege, James Brisbane, James Ramsay, and James Glege, witnesses.

6. **1651.** Feb. 2.—Sir Alexander Wedderburn of Blacknes, Knyght, and clerk of Dundie, a woman childe named Cicilia : My Lord of Durie, George Preston of Craigmiller, Mr. John Nesbet and Mr. John Fletcher, advocates, witnesses.

7. **1652.** Sept. 28.—Peter Wedderburn, lawfull son to Sir Alexander Wedderburn of Blackness, Knight, and Dam Metall Fletcher, was baptized. Alexander Wedderburn of Kingennie, Mr. Peter Wedderburn, Mr. Peter Blair witnesses. He was borne upon the 18th of this instant betwixt four and five.

8. **1654.** Sept. 14.—Georg Wedderburn lawfull son to Sir Alexander Wedderburn of Blacknes and Dame Matilda Fletcher baptized. Witnesses, Georg Kinnaird of Rossie, Georg Fletcher, lawfull sone of unquhile James Fletchor, proveist, Georg Browne, Georg Fairnone, ... merchands.

9. **1656.** Aug. 18.—Mathilda Wedderburne, lawfull daughter to Sir Alexander Wedderburne of Blackness and Dame Mathilda Fletchour baptized. Witnesses, Thomas Gleg, Patrick Kyd, younger of Craigie, Thomas Bultie, Robert Straiton, apothecarie.

   This Robert Straiton seems to have been a person of some note as the register of the baptism at Dundee of his son Charles (by his wife Margaret Hunter), 1660 Dec. 6, records that " the godfather of this child is his sacred Majestie King Charles the Second, King of Great Britain, France, and Ireland."

10. **1658.** Jan. 26.—Alexander Wedderburn, lawfull sone to Sir Alexander Wedderburne of Blacknes and Dam Mathilda Fletchour baptised. Witnesses, Sir Alexander Gibson of Durie, Sir Alexander Blair of Bathayock, Alexander Halyburton younger, late baillie, Mr. Alexander Yeman, doctour of physick, Alexander Carmichaell, thesaurer, Alexander Duncan, merchant.

11. **1662.** May 1.—Elizabeth Wedderburne, lawfull daughter to Alexander Wedderburne, provost of this burgh, and Margaret Milne, baptised. Witnesses, David Fotheringhame of Powrie, Sir Alexander Wedderburne of Blackness, Mr. Alexander Milne, minister, John Serimseour of Kirktowne, Doctor Gleg, David Zeman and George Fletcher, bailies, John Hunter of Balgay.

12. **1663.** July 17.—Janet Wedderburne, lawfull daughter to Alexander Wedderburne of Kingennie, provest of Dundie, and Margaret Milne, baptised. Witnesses, David Fotheringhame of Powrie, Sir Alexander Wedderburne of Blackness, John Scrimscour of Kirktown, Mr. Alexander Milne, minister, Dr. Thomas Gleg, George Fletcher, dean of gild.

13. **1665.** Jan. 24.—John Wedderburn, lawfull sone to Alexander Wedderburn of Kingennie, provest of Dundie, baptised. The godfathers, Sir John Fletcher, Sir John Wedderburne, John Fotheringhame younger of Powrie, John Scrimscor of Kirktown, John Hunter of Balgay, John Wedderburn, fiar of Blackness, John Tarbit, John Kinloch, bailies, John Man, John Scrimseor, merchants.

14. **1667.** April 29.—Margaret Wedderburn, lawfull daughter to John Wedderburne and Helen Rodger, baptized. Witnesses, Alexander Wedderburne of Powrie, Alexander Wedderburne of Kingenie, Patrick Kyd of Craigie, and John Rodger, merchand.

15. **1667.** Oct. 10.—John Wedderburne, lawfull sone to Alexander Wedderburne, younger, of Kingenie, and Grissell Wedderburne, baptised. Sir John Wedderburne, Doctor of Medicine, John Scrimseor of Kirktowne, John Wedderburne (fiar) of Blackness, godfathers ; Sir Alexander Wedderburne of Blackness, Alexander Wedderburne of Kingennie, Doctor Thomas Gleg, Patrick Kyd of Craigie and William Kyde, witnesses.

16. **1668.** June 27.—Eupham Wederburne, lawfull daughter to John Wederburn, baxter, and Helen Rodger, baptised. Witnesses, Eupham Sanders, Bessie Davidson.

17. **1668.** Aug. 12.—Mathilda Wedderburne, lawfull daughter to John Wederburne, younger, of Blackness, and Rachell Dunmoore, baptised. Witnesses, Sir Alexander Wedderburne of Blackness, Mr. David Dunmoore, Patrick Kyd of Craigie.

18. **1668.** Aug. 25.—Alexander Wedderburne, lawfull sone to Alexander Wedderburne, younger of Kingenie, and Grissell Wedderburne, baptised. Witnesses, Sir Alexander Wedderburn of Blacknes, Alexander Wedderburne of Powrie, Alexander Duncan, late bailie, Mr. Alexander Milne.

19. **1669.** Aug. 23.—Elizabeth Wedderburne, lawfull daughter to Alexander Wedderburne, younger, of Kingennie, and Grissell Wedderburne, baptised. Witnesses, Alexander Wedderburne, elder of Kingennie, John Scrimzeor of Kirktoun, Patrick Kyd of Craigie, John Wedderburne, younger of Blackness, and William Kyd, brother german to Patrick Kyd of Craigie.

20. **1670.** Dec. 14.—Margaret Wedderburne, lawfull daughter to John Wedderburne of Blackness and Rachel Dunmoore, baptised. Witnesses, Sir Alexander Wedderburn, Alexander Wedderburne of Easter Powrie, Patrick Kyd of Craigie, Alexander Wedderburne of Kingenie, William Kyde, John Kinloch, Mr. David Dunmoore, Harie Crawfurd, merchand.

21. **1671.** Feb. 17.—Mathilda Wedderburn, lawfull daughter to Alexander Wedderburne, younger of Kingenie, and Grassall Wedderburne, baptised. Witnesses, Sir Alexander Wedderburne of Blackness, Patrick Kyd of Craigie, Alexander Wedderburn of Easter Powrie, Dr. Thomas Gleg, and William Kyd.

22. **1672.** Apprile 7.—Alexander Wedderburn, lawfull sone to John Wedderburne of Blackness, and Rachell Dunmure, baptised. Witnesses, Sir Alexander Wedderburne of Blackness, Alexander Wedderburne of Easter Powrie, Alexander Watson, provest of Dundie, Alexander Wedderburne of Kingennie, Alexander Duncan, late bailie, Alexander Foster, Alexander Goldman, Alexander Watson, merchant, Mr. David Dunmure, advocate, Patrick Kyd of Craigie, John Wedderburn, fiar of Gosford, William Kyd of Woodhill.

23. **1674.** Jan. 8.—David Wedderburne, laufull sone to John Wedderburne of Blackness,
and Rachell Dunmoore baptised. Witnesses, Sir Alexander Wedderburn of Blackness,
Mr. David Dunmoore, advocat, Alexander Wedderburne of Easter Powrie, Alexander
Wedderburne of Kingenie. Patrick Kyd of Craigie, William Kyd of Woodhill, Dr.
Thomas Gleg, James Wedderburn, clerk, Mr. David Ferguson, David Carnegie, David
Foster, maltman.

24. **1674.** Sept. 28.—Mathilda Wedderburn lawfull daughter to James Wedderburn,
clerk, and Elizabeth Davidson, baptised. Witnesses, Georg Browne, provest, Sir
Alexander Wedderburn of Blackness, Patrick Kyd of Craigie, John Wedderburn of
Blackness, William Kyde of Woodhill, Alexander Wedderburne of Kingenie, Robert
Davidsoun of Baigay.

25. **1675.** Sept. 2.—Peter Wedderburne, lawfull sone to John Wedderburne of Blackness
and Rachell Dunmore, baptised. Witnesses, Sir Peter Wedderburne of Gosfoord, one
of the senators of the colledge of Justice, Peter Wedderburne his sone, Peter Wedderburne, third sone to the laird of Blackness, Peter Wedderburne, sone to the laird of
Easter Powrie, Peter Wedderburne, sone to the laird of Kingenie ; Sir David Nevay,
one of the senators of the colledge of justice, Alexander Wedderburne of Easter
Powrie, Patrick Kyde of Craigie, William Kyde of Woodhill, Alexander Wedderburne
of Kingenie, Doctor George Midltoun, John Dicksoun of Hartrie, and David Dicksoune,
his brother. and Robert Straton, appothecarie.

26. **1675.** Nov. 13.—Alexander Wedderburne, lawfull son to James Wedderburne, clerk,
and Bessie Davidsone, baptised. Witnesses, Alexander Wedderburne of Kingenie,
Alexander Watsone, late provost, Alexander Duncan, late bailie, Alexander Forrester,
John Wedderburne of Blackness, Georg Brown, provost, Georg Brown, his son, Robert
Davidson of Balgay, James Man.

27. **1677.** Apprill 11.—Mathild Wedderburn, lawfull daughter to John Wedderburn of
Blacknesse and Rachel Dunmoore, baptised. Witnesses, Sir David Nevay, one of the
senators of the Colledge of Justice, Alexander Wedderburne of Easter Powrie, present
provost of Dundie, Patrick (Kyd) of Craigie, Alexander Wedderburne, younger of
Kingennie, Thomas Watson, present bailie, James Wedderburne, clerk of Dundie,
Mr. James Brisbane, advocate, Hendrie Crawfurd of Sitone, James Dunmore, John
Maitland, collector, Alexander Wedderburn, brother german.

28. **1677.** Apprill 18.—Robert Wedderburne, lawful sone to James Wedderburne,
present clerk of Dundie, and Elizabeth Davidsoun, baptised. Witnesses, Alexander
Wedderburne of Easter Powrie, present provost of Dundie, Thomas Watsoun,
Alexander Duncan, Thomas Bower, John Scrimseour, bailies ; John Wedderburn of
Blackness, Patrick Kyd of Craigie, Alexander Wedderburne of Kingenie, Robert
Davidsoun of Balgay, Robert Kinloch, merchand, Robert Lindsay, merchand, Robert
Straton, Mr. Robert Rate, Mr. William Rate, Mr. James Brisbane, advocate, James
Fletcher, merchand, John Maitland, James Man, George Davidson, merchands.

29. **1678.** Aug. 24.—John Wedderburn, lawfull sone to James Wedderburn, clerk of
Dundie. (No witnesses named).

30. **1678.** Nov. 30.—Alexander Wedderburne, lawfull sone to Peter Wedderburne,
merchant, and Cathren Man, baptised. Witnesses, Alexander Wedderburne of Easter
Powrie, Alexander Wedderburne of Kingenie, Alexander Wedderburne, sone to the
Lord Gosfoord, Alexander Wedderburne, sone to the laird of Blacknes, Alexander
Wedderburne, sone to the present clerk of Dundie. This childe was borne on the
24th of this instant betwixt nyne or ten in the morning.

31. **1679.** January 7.—James Wedderburne, lawfull sone to John Wedderburn of
Blacknes and Rachel Dunmoor, baptized. Witnesses, Alexander Wedderburne of
Powrie, present provost of Dundie, Patrick Kyde of Craigie, James Wedderburne,
clerk, John Man, bailie, John Scrimseour, bailie, James Fletcher, James Man, and
James Kyde.

32. **1679.** Oct. 29.—James Wedderburn, lawfull sone to James Wedderburne and Elizabeth Davidsone, baptised. Witnesses, Alexander Wedderburne, provost, Thomas Watson, John Scot, John Man, Hendric Crawfurd, bailies, John Scrymseour, dean of Gild, James Graham of Monorgone, Mr. James Brisbane, James Man, James Fletcher, James Kyd of Woodhill, James Pilmor, James Lawsone, Blackness, Craigie, Kingennie, Balgay, Peter Wedderburne, Mr. John Guthrie, Dr. Arbuthnet, John Maitland, Georg Davidsone.

33. **1680.** Dec. 29.—Grissill Wedderburne, lawfull daughter to James Wedderburn, clerk, and Bessie, *alias* Elizabeth Davidson. Witnesses (left blank.)

34. **1681.** Feb. 7.—John Wedderburne, lawfull sone to Peter Wedderburne and Cathren Man, baptised. Witnesses, John Man, lait baillie, John Wedderburne of Blackness, John Wedderburne of Gosfoord, John Wedderburne, younger of Kingennie, John Wedderburne. sone to James Wedderburne, present clerk, John Serymser, present bailie, John Colvile, merehant.

35. **1681.** March 27.—George Wedderburne, lawfull son to John Wedderburne of Blackness and Rachile Dinmoor, baptized. Witnesses (left blank).

36. **1682.** Oct. 11.—John Wedderburn of Blackness, Rachel Dinmure, John. Witnesses, John Wedderburne of Gosford, John Wedderburne of Kingennie.

37. **1683.** June 11.—Moonday. James Wedderburne, Elizabeth Davidson; Mathilda. Witnesses, John Wedderburne of Blackness, Robert Davidson of Balgay, Thomas Milne of Moorton (Muirtown), James Man, present bailie.

38. **1684.** Nov. 11.—Tuesday. James Wedderburne, clerk, Elizabeth Davidson; Rachell. Witnesses, John Wedderburne of Blackness, present clerk to the bills, Robert Davidson of Balgay.

39. **1685.** Feb. 16.—Moonday. John Wedderburne of Blacknes and Rachell Dunmore; Jean. Witnesses, John Fletcher, present balie, John Duncan, present balie, the Laird of Claverhouse, George Browne of Horne.

40. **1686.** Aug. 25.—Wednesday. Alexander Wedderburne, skipper, Christian Kinloch; Mathilda. Witnesses, John Wedderburne of Blackness, Mr. James Brisband, advocat, James Wedderburne, towne clerk, Patrick Kinloch, uncle.

41. **1686.** Sept. 21.—Tuesday. James Wedderburne, towne clerk, Elizabeth Davidson; Elizabeth. Witnesses, John Wedderburne of Blackness, Alexander Wedderburne of Easter Powrie, Alexander Wedderburn, skipper.

42. **1689.** July 4.—Thursday. Alexander Wedderburn, Christian Kinloch; Isobell. Witnesses, James Wedderburne, clerk, Robert Kinloch, merehand.

43. **1689.** Dec. 16.—Wednesday. James Wedderburn, clerk, Elizabeth Davidson; Jean. Witnesses, Alexander Wedderburne of Easter Powrie, Alexander Wedderburne, mariner, Peter Wedderburne, merchand.

44. **1690.** October 29.—Thursday. Alexander Wedderburne, Christian Kinloch; Margaret. Witnesses, Margaret Wedderburne, Lady Craigie, Margaret Wedderburne, spouse to Mr. Andrew Balfour, writer in Edinburgh, Margaret Kid, spouse to Mr. John Paterson of Cragie besyd Perth, James Wedderburne, clerk, Peter Wedderburne, merchand.

45. **1698.** July 31.—Thursday. Alexander Wedderburn, town clerk, Katharine Scott had a son, James. Witnesses, James Fletcher, present provost, James Man, late balic, James Guthrie, merehant.

46. **1699.** Oct. 30.—Moonday. Alexander Wedderburn, town clerk, and Katharine
Scott had a daughter baptised, Elizabeth. Her godmothers are Elizabeth Davidson,
relict of umquhill James Wedderburn, sometym town clerk, and Elizabeth Graham,
Lady to Robert Davidson of Balgay, Elizabeth Scott, spouse to Henry Cranford,
merchand.

47. **1700.** Dec. 19.—Sunday, Alexander Wedderburn, town clerk, and Katharine Scott
had a daughter baptised, Christian. Witnesses (or godmothers), Christian Watson,
spouse to John Scott. elder, merchand, grandmother; Christian Scott, spouse to
James Guthrie, merchand, aunt; Christrian Traill, daughter to George Traill,
merchand.

48. **1702.** Feb. 2.—Alexander Wedderburne, younger of Blackness, and Elizabeth
Seaton had a daughter baptised, called Elizabeth. Her godmothers are Elizabeth,
Countess of Hartfeild, principall godmother, Elizabeth Davidson, relict of James
Wedderburn, sometyme clerk of Dundie, and Elizabeth Graham, spouse to Robert
Davidson of Balgay.

49. **1702.** March 3.—Alexander Wedderburne, town clerk, and Katharine Scott had a
son baptised, called John. His godfathers are John Wedderburn of Blackness; John
Scott, elder, grandfather, John Scott, younger, present bailie, John Serymgeour,
present provost, John Serymgeour, younger. of Kirktoûne, John Duncan, dean of
gild, Mr. John Paterson of Craigie in Perthshyre, and John Wedderburne, M.D.[1]

50. **1703.** April 26.—Alexander Wedderburn, town clerk, and Katherine Scott, had a
son baptised Alexander. Witnesses, Alexander Wedderburn of Blackness, Mr.
Alexander Scott, probationer.

51. **1703.** June 2.—Alexander Wedderburne. mariner, and Grissell Watson, had a
daughter baptised caled (*sic*) Katharen. Her godmothers are Katharen Scott, spouse to
Alexander Wedderburn, clerk of Dundie, Katharen Serymsour, spouse to Samuel
Stewart, apothecarie.

52. **1703.** July 8.—Alexander Wedderburn of Blackness and Dame Elizabeth Seaton,
had a daughter baptised called Mathilda . . .

53. **1704.** Aug. 8.—Alexander Wedderburn, town clerk, and Katharine Scott had a son
baptised called John. His godfathers are Mr. John Wedderburn, D^r. of Medicin,
John Wedderburn of Blackness and clerk to the bills at Edinburgh, John Scott, elder
and younger, merchands. This chyld was born on the 4th instant.

54. **1705.** Feb. 10.—Alexander Wedderburne, mariner, and Grisell Watson had a
daughter baptised called Elizabeth. Her godmothers are Dame Elizabeth Seatone,
spouse to Sir Alexander Wedderburne of Blacknes, Elizabeth Watson, relict of
umquhile Patrick Balnaves sumtyme balie in Dundie.

55. **1705.** April 21.—Robert Wedderburn, mariner, and Margaret Arnot had a son
baptised caled James. Witnesses, James Man, merchand, Mr. James Goldman,
minister in the meeting house,[2] Mr. James Man, merchand, James Watson, son to
Thomas Watson of Grang in Barrie, James Griev, apothecarie.

56. **1705.** July 11 —Alexander Wedderburn of Blacknes and Dame Elizabeth Seatoun
had a son baptised called Alexander ......

57. **1706.** June 28.—Alexander Wedderburne, mariner, and Grisell Watson had a son
baptised caled Peter. His godfathers are Peter Wedderburne of Gosfoord, Peter
Wedderburne, merchand in Dundie.

---

[1] 1702. Sept. 7.—John Wedderburn, elder, and John Wedderburn, younger (not otherwise described),
are witnesses to the baptism of John son of John Croll. They are John, afterwards first baronet
of Blackness, and his sixth son, John.

[2] *i.e.*, Episcopal Church, as distinct from the kirk.

3 Q

58. **1706.** July 23.—Alexander Wedderburne, town clerk, and Katharen Scott had a daughter baptised caled Grisell. Her godfathers are Grisell Wedderburn, spouse to Thomas Watson of Grange in Barrie, Grisell Davidson, spouse to Alexander Watson off Vallis de Cragie.

59. **1708.** Feb. 16.—Alexander Wedderburn, town clerk, and Katharine Scott had a son caled Robert. His godfathers are Robert Davidson of Balgay, Robert Wedderburne, mariner, uncle, Robert Wedderburne, son to the Laird of Wedderburne of that ilk.

60. **1709.** Feb. 27.—Mr. Alexander Wedderburn, town clerk off Dundie, and Katharine Scott, his lawfull spouse, had a son baptised caled Alexander. His namefathers are Sir Alexander Wedderburn of Blacknes and Mr. Alexander Wedderburne of that ilk.

61. **1710.** April 5.—Mr. Alexander Wedderburn, town clerk of Dundee, and Katharen Scott had a son baptised caled Thomas ......

62. **1711.** May 18.—Alexander Wedderburn, balie, and Margaret Watson had a son baptized Alexander. His namefathers were Alexander Wedderburn off Wedderburn, and Alexander Wedderburn, town clerk.
     See ante s. Dundee Marriages, No. 19 note.

63. **1711.** May 19.—Alexander Wedderburne, late balie, and Grisoll Watson had a son baptised, called Alexander. His namefathers are Mr. Alexander Wedderburn, town clerk, Alexander Ballingall, balie.

64. **1711.** Nov. 29.—Mr. Alexander Wedderburn, clerk, and Katharen Scott had a daughter baptised named Katharen. Her namemothers are ......

65. **1712.** Aug 27.—Alexander Wedderburn, balief, and ...... (sic) Watson had a son baptised called John. His namefathers were Sir John Wedderburn of Blackness, and Mr. John Wedderburn, Dr. of Medicine.

66. **1713.** May 17.—Mr. Alexander Wedderburn, town clerk, and Katharen Scott had a daughter baptised Margaret. Her namemothers are Margaret Wedderburn, spouse to Mr. John Paterson of Cragie in Perth, &c.

67. **1714.** Sept. 6.—Alexander Wedderburn and ...... Watson had a daughter baptised called Margaret Ker.

68. **1714.** Sept. 14.—Alexander Wedderburn, present balic, and Grisel Watson had a daughter baptised in the meeting house[1] by Mr. Goldman, called Margaret.

69. **1715.** Jan 22.—Mr. Alexander Wedderburn, town clerk of Dundie, and Katharen Scott had a daughter baptised in the meeting house,[1] called Katharen.

70. **1716.** Aug. 30.—Alexander Wedderburn, clerk, Catharine Scott, Mary. Witnesses, Mary Drummond, Lady Pitcurr, Mary Deas, spouse to Mr. Wedderburn, advocate.[2]
     The register has been searched, as stated above, down to 1800 but contains no entries of Wedderburn baptisms after 30 Aug. 1716.

---

[1] See p. 497, note 2.

[2] 1725. 29 June. "Sir (sic) John Wedderburn of Blackness witness to baptism of John, son of William Garroch." The "Sir" is an error ; as the third Baronet was dead, and Sir Alexander the fourth Baronet had lately succeeded. John Wedderburn, fiar of Blackness, is meant.

This register consists of fifty-four vols. Of these, Nos. 1-39 contain the births or baptisms (1-25, 1595—1748 ; 26-39, 1748—1800 ; 40-42, 1800-19) ; while 43-54 contain the marriages (43-52, 1595—1800 ; 53-4, 1800-21). Of these, Vols. 1-25 and 43-54 have been searched throughout.

MARRIAGES.[1]

1595—1800.

1. **1641.** July 9.—Adam Wedderburn, weaver, and Agnes Borthwick.

Edinburgh Marriages.

2. **1643.** June 15.—Adam Wedderburn, weaver, and Margaret Walker.

3. **1649.** Feb. 1.—Mr. Peter Wedderburn, advocat, and Christian Gibson.

4. **1653.** Oct. 20.—Mr. Peter Wedderburn ; Agnes Dicksone.

5. **1667.** April 9.—John Wedderburn, fiar of Blackness ; Rachell Dunmuir.

6. **1676.** July 6.—Archibald Wedderburn, weaver ; Agnes Bruce.

7. **1677.** June 15.—Sir Peter Wedderburn of Gossfuird, one of the senators of the College of Justice, Elizabeth Goldman, relique of umquhile Robert Chaplane, married be Mr. John Robertson.

8. **1678.** March 7.—George Wedderburn, Elizabeth Sutherland ; be Mr. Andrew Cant.

9. **1679.** Feb. 20.—Thomas Milne of Muirtown, Helena Wedderburn ; married be Mr. William Annand, Dean.

10. **1679.** Dec. 11.—Robert Daniell, gairdner ; Jean Wedderburn.

11. **1681.** June 16.—Archibald Wedderburn, cordiner ; Eupham Symson.

12. **1690.** July 10.—Mr. Andrew Balfour, W.S., and Margaret Wedderburn, daughter to Mr. John Wedderburn of Blacknes, clerk to the Bills.

13. **1691.** Aug. 28.—James Donaldson, merchant, and Jean Wedderburn.

14. **1693.** (June 20).—Alexander Wedderburn, fiar of Blacknes, and Mrs. Elizabeth Seatoun, lawful daughter to Sir Alexander Seatoun of Pitmedden, married 1 June 1693, without proclamation.

15. **1700.** June 30.—Mr. Wm. Eccles, doctor of Medicine, and Margaret Wedderburn, daughter to John Wedderburn of Blacknes.
This marriage is noted on margin as on 19 July, but the note is erased. See also an entry 1714. March 28.—Dr. William Eccles married Dame Euphane Murray, relict of Sir Walter Setou, Bart.

16. **1708.** June 6.—Thomas Simpson, lawful son to Alexander Simpson, fermar in Newbotle parish, now in north-west parish, and Eupham Wedderburn, lawful daughter to the deceased Archibald Wedderburn, cordiner, burgess, now in south-east paroch, married 9th July.

[1] Of these entries, thirty in number, seventeen (3-5, 7-9, 12. 14, 15, 20, 21, 25-30) refer to members of the Forfarshire house, while the remaining thirteen (1, 2, 6, 10, 11, 13, 16-19, 22-24) refer to another and distinct family.

17. **1708.** Oct. 31.—James Ross, mason in Gilmertoun, in the parish of Libbertoun, and Helen Wedderburn, lawful daughter to Thomas Wedderburn, weaver in Pencaitland parish, now in north kirk parish, married 26 Nov.

18. **1709.** May 15.—James Mein (? Man), wright, indweller in north west paroch., and Grissell Wedderburn, daughter to umquhile Archibald Wedderburn, burgess in Canongate, also in north west paroch., married 3d June.

19. **1709.** Aug. 21.—William Wedderburn, burgess in Canongate, weaver, and Jean, daughter to deceased Abraham Pargillis, brewer in north-east parish, married 9 Sept.

20. **1711.** Feb. 4.—David Campbell, younger, of Keithick in Couper of Angus and Mathilda Wedderburn, daughter to the deceased Sir John Wedderburn of Blackness, married.[1]

21. **1716.** Jan. 1.—Mr. John Wedderburn, doctor of medicine, and Margaret Balfour, relict of Henry Eccles, merchant in Edinburgh, married 9 Jan. 1716.

22. **1719.** April 8.—Thomas Nimmo, barber, in south-east parish, and Bessie Wedderburn, daughter to the deceased Archibald Wedderburn, cordiner, also in the said parish, married 30 April.

23. **1721.** May 21.—James Man, wool-comber in north-east parish, and Mary, daughter to Alexander Wedderburn, cordiner in Glasgow, now in south-east parish, married 9 June.

24. **1739.** Jan. 7.—William Tait, merchant in Fetham in Traquair parish, and Elizabeth Wedderburn, relict of the deceased James Bunkle, saddler in south-west parish.

25. **1745.** Feb. 10.—James St. Clair, tenant in the parish of Stobo, and Mrs. Agnes Wedderburn, daughter of the deceased Alexander Wedderburn, Esq., in south-east parish.[2]

26. **1758.** Feb. 5.—Captain John Wedderburn of Gossford, Esq., in the New Kirk parish, and Miss Elizabeth Fletcher, daughter to Andrew Fletcher of Milton, Esq., and one of the senators of the College of Justice, now in the Iron Kirk parish.

27. **1762.** March 28.—John Wedderburn of Gosford, now in Iron Kirk parish, and Miss Mary Hamilton, daughter of the Hon. John Hamilton, Esq., advocate, now in College Kirk parish.

28. **1768.** Jan. 31.—Henry Wedderburn, second son of Charles Wedderburn of Gosford, Esq., and Miss Margaret Belsches, daughter to John Belsches of Invermay, Esq., now in Iron Kirk parish.

29. **1775.** June 11.—Joseph Elliot, painter, in Old Church parish, and Janet Wedderburn, Coledge Church parish, natural daughter to Sir John Halket Wedderburn, Baronet.

30. **1794.** June 20.—John McGlashan, writer, Old Kirk parish, and Mrs. Janet Wedderburn same parish, relict of Joseph Elliot, late painter in Edinburgh.[3]

---

[1] 1711. Oct. 21.—There is an entry of the marriage of a servant to Mr. Alexander Wedderburn, one of her Majesty's Commissioners of Excise, in south-east parish.

[2] 1756. May 28.—There is an entry of the marriage of a servant to Mr. Alexander Wedderburn, advocate, in south south-east parish.

[3] There is an entry 1798. June 11, as follows, " John Richardson, mason, Lady Yester's parish, and Wedderburn Laurie, same parish, daughter of the deceased William Laurie belonging to the excise, Edinburgh."

I have no record of a Laurie-Wedderburn marriage, and incline to think that the conjunction of the names in this entry is due to Alexander Wedderburn, the commissioner of excise, having stood godfather to the child of one of his subordinates.

BAPTISMS.[1]

1595–1747.

1. **1649.** Sept. 30 —Mr. Peter Wedderburne, advocate, and Christiane Gibsone, a son, named James. Witnesses, Sir William Nisbet of the Dean, Mr. Johne Nisbet, Commissar, Mr. James Primrose, Archibald Sinserff, James Gibsone, advocate, Hew Hamilton, merchant, south-east. *Edinburgh Baptisms.*

2. **1655.** Jan. 14.—Mr. Peter Wedderburn, advocat, Agnes Dicksone, a daughter named Margaret. Witnesses, Sir Alexander Gibsone of Durie, Sir John Gilmour, advocat, Mr. John Nisbet, Mr. John Pringle, Johne Ramsay, John Kello, writer.

3. **1656.** Jan. 27.—Mr. Peter Wedderburne, advocat, Agnes Dicksone, twaines—1, named Susanna ; 2, named Agnes. Witnesses, Sir Alexander Wedderburne of Blacknesse, Sir John Gilmour and Mr. John Nisbet, advocats, Sir Archibald Primrose of Chesters, Mr. John Pringle of Woodhead, and Mr. John Dicksone, sone to umquhill John Dicksone of Hartrie.

4. **1657.** Feb. 26.—Mr. Peter Wedderburn, advocat, Agnes Dickson, a son named Johne. Witnesses, John, Earle of Traquair, Doctour John Wedderburn, phisiciane, Sir John Gilmour, advocat, Mr. John Nisbet, advocat, Mr. John Pringle of Woodhead, Mr. John Dickson, second sone to my lord Heartrie.

5. **1658.** Nov. 21.—Mr. Peter Wedderburn, advocat, Agnes Dicksone, a daughter named Agnes. Witnesses, Sir John Gilmour, advocat, Mr. John Nisbet, advocat, Mr. John Fletcher, advocat.

6. **1678.** Dec. 31.—George Wedderburn, merchant, Elizabeth Sutherland, a son named James. Witnesses, James Currie, late Lord provost, James Sutherland, late town the-aurer, Gilbert Fyfe, late baillie, Mr. James Brisbane, advocat, William Cleland, younger, merchant.

7. **1679.** Nov. 28.—George Wedderburn, merchant, and Elizabeth Sutherland, a daughter named Jeane.

8. **1680.** Nov. 9.—George Wedderburn, merchant, and Elizabeth Sutherland, a son named Alexander.

9. **1681.** Dec. 25.— George Wedderburn, merchant, and Elizabeth Sutherland, a daughter named Mathilda.

10. **1682.** April 7.—Archibald Wedderburn, cordiner, Eupham Symson, a daughter named Margaret. Witnesses, Archibald Wedderburn and others.

11. **1683.** Nov. 11.—Archibald Wedderburn and Eupham Symson, a son named James.

12. **1683.** Nov. 25. —George Wedderburn, merchant, and Elizabeth Sutherland, a daughter named Elizabeth.

13. **1683.** Dec. 29.—George Wedderburn and Elizabeth Sutherland, a son named James, John Wedderburn of Blackness, &c., witnesses.

[1] In addition to the extracts given above there are some mentions in this register of Wedderburns acting as witnesses to baptisms. These are as follows :—(a) 1631. Nov. 28.—Mr. Alexander Wedderburn, wreater, witnesses an entry by James Ramsay. (b) 1638. March 3.—Mr. Alexander Wedderburn of Kinganie witnesses a similar entry. (c) 1658. Jan. 10.—Mr. Peter Wedderburn, advocate, is a witness. (d) 1662. June 22 ; 1664 April 15 ; 1665. Aug. 11 ; 1667. Jan. 17, Oct. 24 ; 1671. April 4 ; 1679. June 5.—Sir Peter Wedderburn is a witness on all these occasions, on the first of which he is designed " advocate," on the second " of Gossfuird," on the next " clerk of the Secret Council," on the two next " of Gossfuird," and on the last " senator of the College of Justice." On that of 24 Oct. 1667 John Wedderburn of Blackness is also a witness, the occasion being the baptism of a child of Sir George Mackenzie of Rosehaugh.

Of the extracts given twenty-three refer to members of the Forfarshire family, while of the others twelve (10, 11, 14, 16, 18, 19, 20, 22-26) deal with the children of an Archibald Wedderburn, four (29-33) with those of a William Wedderburn, and four others (35-37, 39) with other individuals, not connected with the Forfarshire house.

14. **1685.** May 5.—Archibald Wedderburn, cordiner, and Eupham Symson, a son named Archibald. Archibald Wedderburn, weaver, witness.

15. **1685.** Jan. 15.—George Wedderburn, merchant, and Elizabeth Sutherland, a daughter named Rachel. John Wedderburn of Blackness and Alexander Wedderburn, merchant, witnesses.

16. **1687.** Feb. 20.—Archibald Wedderburn, cordiner, and Eupham Sympson, a daughter named Barbara.

17. **1688.** April 16.—John Wedderburn of Blackness, and Rachel Dunmoor, a son named Thomas so named after the deceased Mr. Thomas Nicolson of Cockburnspath. Witnesses, Mr. David Dunmoor, advocate, and Bailly George Wedderburn, merchant. Child born yesterday being the Lord's Day, and baptised this day by Mr. Alexander Malcome.

18. **1688.** Nov. 11.—Archibald Wedderburn, cordiner, and Eupham Sympson, a daughter named Eupham.

19. **1689.** Dec. 20.—Archibald Wedderburn and Eupham Sympson—twins, 1, Thomas ; 2, Margaret. Archibald Wedderburn, weaver, witness.

20. **1691.** July 5.—Archibald Wedderburn, cordiner, and Euphame Simpson, a daughter Bessic. Witnesses, Rorie Pedison, Robert Crinzean, cordiners, and William Fulton, mason.

21. **1691.** Sept. 17.—John Wedderburn of Blackness, clerk to the bills, witness to baptism of John, son to Mr. Andrew Balfour, W.S , and Margaret Wedderburn.

22. **1692.** Aug. 14.—Archibald Wedderburn, cordiner, and Euphame Wedderburn— twins, 1, Grissell ; 2, Joannet. Witnesses, Rorie Paterson, cordiner, and William Baptie, baxter.

23. **1693.** Oct. 13.—Archibald Wedderburn and Eupham Simpson, a daughter Issobell. Witnesses, Rorie Pedison and Robert Crinzean, cordiners.

24. **1694.** Nov. 16.—Archibald Wedderburn and Eupham Simpson, a son Charles. Witnesses, as in No. 23.

25. **1697.** Oct. 3.—Archibald Wedderburn and Eupham Simpson—twins, 1, Elizabeth ; 2, Agnes. Witnesses, Alexander Turner, embroyderer, Peter King Gnaiden (sic), Herauld.

26. **1699.** May 26.—Archibald Wedderburn and Eupham Sympson, a daughter Elizabeth.

27. **1701.** June 9.—William Eccles, doctor of medicine, and Margaret Wedderburn, his spouse, a daughter Elizabeth. Witnesses, Sir John and Alexander Wedderburns, elder and younger of Blackness. The child was born the same day.

28. **1711.** Jan. 26.—Mr. Alexander Wedderburn, advocate, and Mary Daes, his lady, a daughter Jean. Witnesses, Mr. James Daes of Condownknows, and John Gordon, writer. Born Jan. 16.

29. **1712.** Aug. 3.—William Wedderburn, weaver, indweller, and Jean Pargillis his spouse, a son John. Witnesses, David Robertson, writer; John Johnston, candlemaker.

30. **1719.** Sept. 8.—George Cheap, chirurgeon, and Mary Wedderburn his spouse, a daughter Sarah. Witnesses, Mr. Andrew Massie, advocate, and Andrew Cheap, merchant. Born 7 Sept.

31.   **1724** Dec. 13.—William Wedderburn, indweller, and Jean Pargillas his spouse, a daughter Agnes.   Witnesses, Thomas Baveradge, indweller, and James Boyd, flesher.

32.   **1726**. Aug. 7.—William Wedderburn, weaver, and Jean Pargillas his spouse, a daughter Jean.   Witnesses, Thomas Baveradge, flesher, and John Black, taylor. Born the 2nd inst.

33.   **1728**. April 28.—William Wedderburn, weaver, and Jean Pargillis, a daughter Girzell.   Witnesses, James Rannie, merchant, and Adam Black, tailor. Born 22nd.

34.   **1728**. June 29.—Robert Colvill of Ochiltree, and Mrs. Janet Wedderburn, a son Robert.   Witnesses, John Learmont, Doctor of Medicine, and David Wilson, servant to Mr. Colvill. Born 29th.

35.   **1729**. March 16.—James Man, woolcombor, and Mary Wedderburn, a son Thomas.

36.   **1729**. Nov. 25.—James Bunkell, saddler, and Elizabeth Wedderburn, a son Edward

37.   **1731**. Nov. 12.—James Bunkell, saddler, and Elizabeth Wedderburn, a daughter Agnes.[1]

38.   **1733**. Feb. 15.—To Mr. Peter Wedderburn, advocate, and — Ogilvy, his Lady, a son, Alexander.   Witnesses, Mr. John Drummond, younger, of Blair, and George Cheap, Esq.   Born 13th.

39.   **1743**. Jan. 30.—Abigail Wedderburn, spouse to John Young, baxter, burgess. . . *(sic.)*

40.   **1744**. Jan. 1.—To Mr. Robert Wedderburn, merchant in Dumfermline, and Mrs. Rachel Thomson, his spouse. a daughter named Halket.   Witnesses, Dougal Gedd, jeweller and goldsmith in Edinburgh, and Richard Lothian, writer there. The child was born the same day and baptized by Mr. Thomas Carstairs, minister of the Gospel.

41.   **1745**. April 1.—To Mr. Robert Wedderburn, merchant, &c., and Mrs. Rachel Thomson, a daughter named Rachel.   Witnesses, as in No. 40.   Child born 31st March last and baptized by the said Mr. Carstairs.

42.   **1746**. Nov. 30.—To Mr. David Serymgeour of Birkhill, advocate, and Mrs. Catharine Wedderburn, his spouse, a son named John.   Witnesses, Mr. David Falconer, advocate, Henry Scrimgeour, W.S., and Mr. Charles Guthrie, writer in Edinburgh.   Child born 26th inst, and baptized this day by Mr George Wishart, one of the ministers of the city.

43.   **1747**. Feb. 14.—To Mr. Robert Wedderburn, merchant, and Mrs. Rachel Thomson, his spouse, a daughter named Janet.   Witnesses. Mr. Dougal Ged, jeweller in Edinburgh, and Mr. John Anderson, writer there.   The child was born 13th inst.

BURIALS.

In addition to the above register there are available those of the Greyfriars Burial Ground, 1658-1854, and of the Calton Burial Ground, 1719-1854.   Of these the former consists of about 40 volumes in the custody of the City Chamberlain, and the latter of 19 volumes in that of the City Recorder.   I have not been able to have either register searched.

---

[1] See also the three following entries :—(a) 1732. Sept. 1.—Mr. Peter Wedderburn, advocate, a witness to the baptism of child of Earl of Kello and Janet Pitcairn, his counters. (b) 1734. Oct. 7.—Mr. Peter Wedderburn, advocate, witness to baptism of child of the Right Hon. James, Lord Aberdour, and Agatha Hallburton. (c) 1739. Jan. 16 —Peter Wedderburn, secretary of excise. Esquire, witness to entry, Edward Wyvill, general surveyor of excise.

EDINBURGH. CANONGATE REGISTER.

This register is nineteen volumes :—(1) B and M, 1564-67 ; D, 1565-68. (2-10) B, 1600-1795. (11) B. 1795-1819. (12-16) M, 1600-1804. (16-19) M, 1804-19. Of these vols. 1-10 and partly 11, and vols. 12-16 have been searched. There are also thirteen volumes of Canongate Burials (1612-1854) in the custody of the Recorder of the Ground. These have not been searched.

MARRIAGES.

1564—1800

This register is blank from Nov. 1557 to May 1600, from 23 Aug. 1650 to 26 June 1651, and from 16 July 1675 to 17 Nov. 1685. Only the last two entries (6-7) relate to members of the Blackness family.

Edinburgh. Canongate Marriages.

1. **1646.** Oct. 27.—The same day Mathew Wedderburne, wobster, and Bessie Penman, both of this congregation, after thrie severall Sabbothis proclamatiounes without impediment took down their names and was married.

2. **1649.** Feb. 9.—Archibald Wedderburn and Mariune Moysey, both parochineris after 3 severall Sabbothis proclamatiounes without impediment was married.

3. **1662.** Nov. 14.—Robert Staveris and Margaret Wedderburne, both parochineris of Cannongate, eftir thrie Lordis davis proclamatioun of their purpose of marriage wer lawfullie married within the Kirk of Halyroodhous, be Mr. James Kid, minister for the time.

4. **1674.** July 21.—William Scott, in the parish of St. Cuthbert's, and Margaret Wedderburn, in this congregation, after three several Lords dayes proclamations were lawfullie married in the church of Holirudhouse.

5. **1709.** Aug. 19.—William Wedderburn, weaver in Canongate, and Jean Purgillis, daughter to the deceased Abraham Purgillis, brewer in Edinburgh.

6. **1774.** March 22.—James Finlay, Esq., of Jamaica, and Miss Helen Wedderburn, daughter to the late Captain Alexander Wedderburn, late of London, gave up their names, &c

7. **1780.** Dec. 26.—Sir John Wedderburn of Pallendean, baronet, and Miss Allicia Dundas, second daughter of James Dundas, Esq, of Dundas, deceased, gave up their names for marriage.

BAPTISMS.

1564—1803

This register is blank from March 1567 to 1660. None of the following extracts relate to members of the Forfarshire family.

Edinburgh. Canongate Baptisms.

1. **1627.** Dec. 25.—Baptised to Adam Wotherburne, vyvar, and Bessie Brown, tûynis, a son named Archibald, a daughter named Bessie, witnesses, Archibald Wrycht, James Wast. Robert Haistie, Adam Thomsoun.

2. **1644.** April 22.—To Adame Wedderburn, weaver, and Margaret Walker, a son, named James, witnesses, James Dasoun, James Fortoun, James Sheilds, George Cairncross and James Hayes.

3. **1646.** April 5.—To Adame Wedderburne, weiver, and Margaret Walker a son named John, witnesses, John Watsone, Johne Cook, and David Haistie, and James Crombie.

4. **1648.** Jan. 9.—To Adame Wedderburne, weiver, and Margaret Walker, a son, named David, witnesses, John Watsone, David Schira, David Haistic, and James Abercrombie. Edinburgh Canongate Baptisms.

5. **1649.** May 4.—Baptised to Adame Wedderburne, weiver, and Margaret Walker, a daughter named Margaret, witnesses, George Cairncrosse, John Watsone, James Abercrombie, David Haistic.

6. **1649.** Nov. 30.—Baptised to Archibald Wedderburn, weiver, and Marion Mosey, a son, named George, witnesses, George Turnour, James Crombie, David Haistic.

7. **1652.** Jan. 4.—The same, a son Alexander.

8. **1652.** July 23.—Adam Wedderburne, weiver, and Margaret Walker, a daughter Agnes. Witness, Mathew Wedderburn and Archibald Wedderburn.

9. **1654.** Dec. 17.—Adam Wedderburne, weiver, and Margaret Walker, a son named Mathew. Witness, Mathew Wedderburn.

10. **1656.** Jan. 13.—Baptised to Archibald Wedderburne, weiver, and Marion Mosey, a son named Archibald. Witnesses, Alexander Mathic, John Watsone, David Haistic, Mathew Wedderburne.

11. **1656.** Nov. 16.—To Adame Wedderburne, weiver, and Margaret Walker, a son named Adame. Witnesses, John Watsone, Mathew and Archibald Wedderburns.

12. **1657.** Dec. 27,—To Archibald Wedderburne, weiver, and Marion Mosey, a daughter named Grissell. Witnesses, Adam Duncan, David Haistie, John Nimok, Adame and Mathew Wedderburns.

13. **1678.** Feb. 24.—Baptised to Archibald Wedderburne, weaver, and Agnes Bruce, a son, named William. Witnesses, William Murray, writer in Edinburgh, William Scott, stabler, Andrew Rae, litster.

14. **1680.** Jan. 25.—To Mathew Wedderburne, weaver, and Marion Mitchell, a daughter, named Jeilles. Witnesses, John Turnbull, John Harroway, James Williamson.

15 **1680.** May 9.—To Archibald Wedderburn, weaver, and Agnes Bruce, a son, named Richard. Witnesses, William Murray, Hugh Cristell, Richard Hastic.

16. **1682.** Jan. 8.—To Mathew Wedderburn, weaver, and Marion Mitchell, a son, named James. Witnesses, James Mitchell, John Harrower and John Turnbull, William Paton.

17. **1682.** May 28.—To Archibald Wedderburne, weaver, and Agnes Bruce, a daughter, named Isobell. Witnesses, John Harroway and David Guij.

18. **1684.** Feb. 24.—Baptised to Mathew Wedderburne, weaver, and Marion Mitchell, a son, named William. Witnesses, Henry Mitchell, Andrew Sim and James Burne, John Harroway.

19. **1685.** Dec. 31.—Baptised to Archibald Wedderburn and Agnes Bruce, a son, named George. Witnesses, James Dick and William Carnegie, and James Bigger, mason.

20. **1690.** June 22.—To Christian Wedderburn, a son, named David, begotten in fornication, as she alleadges, with Alexander Reöch. Witnesses, James Dick, officer of the Canongate, and Archibald Wedderburn, indweller there.

21. **1710.** . . . . . .—William Wedderburn, weaver in Canongate, and Jean Purgillis, his spouse, had a daughter born July 25th, and baptised the 30th, her name Margaret. Witnesses, Robert Lindsay and David Robertson, indweller in Edinburgh.

3 R

EDINBURGH. ST. CUTHBERT'S REGISTER.

This register is in 35 volumes :—(1-15) B, 1573-1755 ; (16-17) B, 1755-72, M, 1744-72 ; (18-20) M, 1655-1800 ; (21-23) M. 1800-19 ; (24-29, 30-31) D, 1740-1801, 1801-21. St. Cuthbert's : (32-35) D, 1761-1819, Buccleuch Chapel. Of these vols. 1-20 have been searched with the result given below. Some search has also been made in vols. 32-35 for entries of particular deaths. See s. the account of Thomas Wedderburn of Cantra and his family in vol. i.

MARRIAGES.

1655—1800.

Edinburgh,
S. Cuthbert's
Marriages.

There are blanks in the Register from 24 April 1656 to Sept. 1683, Oct. 1686 to Oct. 1687 and April 1697 to Nov. 1699. There are some scroll entries, 1764-69, bound up with Vol. I. of this Register, and some Clandestine Marriages. 1775-95 which have also been searched, but contain no Wedderburn entries.

1. **1738.** Nov. 5.—John Young, son to the deceased William Young, baxter in Edinburgh, and Abigail Wedderburn, servant to John Cunninghame of Balbougie, Esq.

2. **1793.** March 2.—John Brand, baxter in Portsburgh, and Christian Wedderburn, residenter in Dalry, daughter of James Wedderburn, gardener in the parish of Newhills near Aberdeen, gave up their names for proclamation of banns matrimonial.

BAPTISMS.

1573—1800.

Edinburgh,
S. Cuthbert's
Baptisms.

This Register is blank, 26 Feb. 1576 to Feb. 1605, 1642, 1655, and June 1667. Sept. 1674.

1. **1636.** July 14.—Mr. James Wedderburne, bishop of Dunblain, is one of the witnesses to baptism of child of John Brown and Marjorie Tennent.

2. **1718.** Feb. 23.—William Wedderburn, weaver in Bristo, and Jane Pargilles, a daughter, named Margaret, born 22d instant, witnesses, Andrew Voy, weaver, Thomas McInvoir, cordiner there.
   This entry is under 2 March, but 23 Feb. is interlined.

3. **1739.** July 6.—Peter Wedderburne, advocate, witness to entry Edward Wyvill, general surveyor of excise.

SOUTH LEITH REGISTER.

This register is in 17 volumes :—(1-8) B, 1599-1819, except 1620-43, when it is blank ; (9-12) M, 1588-1819 ; (13-17) D, 1662-1819. It has been searched for marriages 1588-1700, and for baptisms 1599-1800.[1]

MARRIAGES.

1588—1700.

South Leith
Marriages.

1. **1594.** June 13.—Alysoun Wedderburn before the session for discipline.

2. **1595.** Sept. 4.—Thomas Deill and Bessie Wedderburn gave up their names to be proclaimed within a moneth according to the tennour of the act. Thomas Deill, cautioner.

3. **1606.** March 11.—Malcolme Bar (or Kar) and Bessie Wedderburn proclaimed.

4. **1622.** —— .—John Bishope in the parish of Tranent and Jonet Wedderburn their.

[1] The North Leith Register, which is in 7 volumes :—(1-4) B, 1615-1819 ; (5-6) M. 1605-1819 ; (7) D, 1754-1819, has also been searched.

BAPTISMS.

1599—1800.

1. **1610.** Nov. ....—Thomas and Janet Wedderburns had a maid child born the 21 day Nov. baptised the ...... called Elspeth.

2. **1654.** Feb. 2.—Jeane, daughter to Edward Dodger and Elizabeth Wedderburne. Witness, Thomas Wedderburne.

3. **1654.** Nov. 2.—James Wedderburne, son to Thomas Wedderburne and Isobell Oliphant.

4. **1770.** Dec. (?)—Captain Charles Stewart, at Bowling Green, and Mrs. Mary Wedderburn, his spouse, had a son Francis, born 7 Dec. and baptised soon after. Witnesses, Mr. Thomas Scott, minister, and William Drysdale, merchant, in Leith.

5. **1773.** Jan.—Captain Charles Stewart and Mary Wedderburn, his spouse, had a son named James, born 13 Jan. and baptized Jan. Witnesses as in No. 4.

ABERLADY PARISH REGISTER.

1634—1819.

There are four volumes of this register:—(1) B, 1632-79 ; M, 1634-81 ; D, 1632-87. (2) B and M, 1682-1747 ; D, 1697-1711. (3) B, M aud D, 1751-64. (4) B and M, 1764-1819. There are, however, a good many blanks in the record. All four volumes have been searched throughout with the result given below. There is only one marriage (No. 17) and one burial (No. 18) recorded.

1. **1663.** Sept. 25.—Baptized to Sir Peter Wedderburne a sone named James, Witnesses, Sir James Durhame, Sir Johne Wedderburn, &c.[1]

2. **1665.** Feb. 12.—Baptised to Sir Peter Wedderburn of Gosford, a son named George. Witnesses, Mr. George McKenzie, John Hay, &c.

3. **1679.** Jan. 22.—Baptized to John Wedderburn a son named David. Witnesses, William Nicholson and David Low.

4. **1695.** Born June 21, baptised 22. Baptised the said day to Peter Wedderburn of Gosfoord and Dame Jannet Hackit, his Ladie, a sone called Peter. Witnesses, James Durhame of Lufnes and John Hay of Atherstoun.

5. **1696.** Born May 29, baptised 30. Baptised to Peter Wedderburn of Gosford and Dame Jannet Hackit his Ladie, a son Charles. Witnesses, John Hay of Atherstoun, and Sir George Seaton of Garlingtoun.

6. **1699.** Born Feb. 20, and baptised the said day. Baptised the said day to Sir Peter Wedderburn of Gosfoord and Dame Jannet Hackit his Ladie, a son called James. Witnesses, Alexander Livingstoun of Saltcoats and Mr. Andrew Rule.

[1] In addition to these entries of baptisms, the register contains the following references to occasions when Sir John Wedderburn, Sir Peter, or his son Peter acted as witnesses :—
    (a) 1661. Dec. 23.—Sir Peter Wedderburn a witness to the baptism of a child of Sir John Durhame of Lufnes.
    (b) 1663. Feb. 25.—Sir John Wedderburn witness to baptism of a daughter of Sir James Durhame.
    (c) 1663. Feb. 6.—Sir Peter Wedderburn witness to baptism of the minister's son. (This entry, though a few days earlier in date, follows the preceding one.)
    (d) 1664. March 23.—Sir Peter Wedderburn witness to baptism of Sir James Durham's daughter, Jeaue.
    (e) 1664. May 30.—Sir Peter Wedderburn witness to baptism of minister's child.
    (f) 1665. Feb. 13. } Sir Peter Wedderburn witness to baptism of children of John Hay of
        1665. Apt. 20. } Aberlady, Sir Andrew Fletcher, and to au entry left blank.
        1667. Aug. 9. }
    (g) 1671. July 2.—My Lord Gosford, along with Lord Elibank, witness to baptism of Mr. Andrew McGhie's daughter, Isabel.
    (h) 1675. Sept. 26.—Lord Gosford and Peter Wedderburn are witnesses to baptism of James Warden's son Peter.
    (i) 1698. Sept. 22.—Sir Peter Wedderburn of Gosfoord, witness to baptism of child of Mr. Andrew Rule, advocate, and Agnes Bairnie, life-reutrix of Reidhouse, his spouse.
    (j) 1699. Dec. 4. and 14.—Sir Peter Wedderburn of Gosfoord, witness to baptism of child of Mr. Adam Glass, minister.
    (k) 1706. March (?)—Sir Peter Wedderburn is witness to the baptism of the minister's child.

7. **1700.** Born May 25, baptised 27. Baptised to Sir Peter Wedderburn of Gosfoord and Dame Jannet Hackit his Ladie, a daughter called Jannit. Witnesses, James Durrham of Lufnes, John Hay of Aderstoun and Mr. Louis Hay, son to the deceast Mr. John Hay of Aberlady.

8. **1701.** Born Sept. 25 and baptised the same day. Baptised the said day to Sir Peter Wedderburn of Gosfoord and Dame Jannit Hackit his Ladie, a daughter called Agnes. Witnesses, Alexander, Lord Elibank, and Louis Hay, son to the deceased Mr. John Hay of Aberladie.

9. **1703.** Born Jan. 20, baptized 21. Christian, daughter to the said Sir Peter Wedderburn and his wife. The witnesses are the same as in No. 8.

10. **1704.** Born March 26 and baptised the said day. Baptised to Peter Wedderburn of Gosfoord and Dame Jannit Hackit his Ladie, a daughter called Elizabeth. Witnesses, Alexander, Lord Elibank, and Adam Durrhame of Lufnes.

11. **1705.** Born July 26, baptised 27. Baptised to Sir Peter Wedderburn of Gosfoord, *alias* Hackit of Pitfirrin and Dame Jannit Hackett his Ladie, a son called James. Witnesses, Mr. Luis Hay and John Bruntoun.

12. **1706.** Born Dec. 12, baptized 13. Baptized to Sir Peter Hackitt of Pitfirne, *alias* Wedderburn of Gosfoord, and Dame Janet Hackit his spouse, a son called Alexander. Witnesses, Mr. Alexander Wedderburn, and James Haliburton of Pitcurr, and Mr. John Bruce of Kinross.

13. **1708.** Born April 9, baptized 9. Baptised to Sir Peter Halkit of Pitfirn, *alias* Wedderburn of Gosfoord, and Dame Janet Halkit his Ladie, a son called John. Witnesses, Mr. Alexander Wedderburn and David Ramadge.

14. **1709.** Born Dec. 10, baptised the same day. Baptised to Sir Peter Wedderburn of Gosfoord, *alias* Halket of Pitfirrin, and Dame Janet Halkit his Ladie, a son called Robert. Witnesses, Mr. Bruce of Kinross, Colonel Hop, Mr. Alexander Wedderburn, brother german to Gosfoord, Dr. Eccles and Mr. Alexander Dunbar, merchant in Edinburgh.

15. **1711.** Born Nov. 27, baptised 28. Baptised to Sir Peter Halket of Pitfirrine, *alias* Wedderburn of Gosfoord, and Dame Janet Halket his Ladie, a daughter called Mary. Witnesses, Mr. Alexander Wedderburn, advocat, John Erskine of Balgonie, Captain Charles Halkit, Alexander Dunbar, merchant in Edinburgh.
     This entry is out of its order and November should probably be December.

16. **1723.** Born and baptised Nov. 22. To George Cheep Esquire, and Mrs. Mary Wedderburn his lady, a son named Andrew. Witnesses, the Honourable my Lord Elibank and Adam Durham of Luffnes.

---

17. **1674.** Sept. 8.— . . . . . Haliburton of Pitcur, and Mrs. Agnes Wedderburn were married.

18. **1758.** Dec. 24.—To best mortcloth to Mrs. Wedderburn, junior, who died 16th and buried 21 Dec. . . . . . . £25 8s.[1]

---

[1] In addition to the above there are a few other entries, chiefly in reference to certain charitable bequests by the family of Gosford to the poor of Aberlady. These entries are as follows :—
(a) 1757. May 1.—Two poor persons in Gosfoord are not to receive payments as Mr. Wedderburn is giving out meall.
(b) 1758. Feb. 12.—To collection on Mr. Wedderburn's Infare Sabb £36 18s. 10d.
(c) 1760. March 2.—To cash received as part of the interest of Gosfoord mortify'd money £46 4s. 6d. Paid to the poor from the same 19/4.
(d) 1762. April 18.—To collection being Mr. Wedderburn's infare £36 17s. 3d.
(e) 1769. July 17.—To cash received of Gosfoord, mortified money, £75 6s. 6d.
(f) 1769. July 17.—By a discharge in writing for mortified money, £1 4s.
(g) 1782. Dec.—The session authorised the Rev. Mr. Neil Roy (Parish minister) to receive payment, and discharge a debt of 1,600 merks "due to them by the representatives of the family of Gosfoord."

PROTOCOL BOOKS OF NOTARIES.

There is in the Register House a considerable collection of the protocol books of notaries in all parts of Scotland. Of these, Mr. McLeod has made a general examination, and sends me the following list of the books likely, from the localities with which they deal, to contain material references. Of these, Nos. 16, 19, 66 and 145 have been searched, with the result given below. Nos. 16 and 19 each contained but one material entry, while No. 66 had twenty-five, and No. 145 none. I proceed to give the entries in Nos. 16, 19 and 66.[1]

Protocol Books of Notaries.

3.	1518-51.	Sir John Christison.	Aberdeen, Kincardine.
10.	1541-50.	Robert Rollok.	Perth. Stirling.
12.	1545-79.	James Nicholson.	Aberdeen, Edinburgh, Fife. &c.
14.	1547-85.	James Harland.	Edinburgh, Fife, Berwick, &c.
15.	1552-73.	Gilbert Grote.	Edinburgh, Fife, Aberdeen, &c.
16.	1554-72.	Duncan Gray.	Perth. Forfar.
18.	1555-59.	Sir Thomas Dalrymple.	Fife, Kinross.
19.	1555-73.	J. McNele, J. Robesone.	Edinburgh (Leith), Fife.
22.	1561-66.	John Foulis.	Edinburgh. Forfar, Berwick.
33.	1573-87.	George Fyff.	Aberdeen, Forfar.
36.	1576-1615.	John Auchiulek.	Forfar, Bauff, &c.
41.	1584-1607.	Ronald Brown.	Forfar, Perth.
49.	1587-1607.	James Justice.	Forfar. Fife, Edinburgh, &c.
56.	1597-1600.	William Chalmer.	Aberdeen, Banff, &c.
59.	1598-1624.	James Primrose.	Edinburgh, Fife, &c.
66.	1619-37.	Thomas Wichtau.	Forfar.
67.	1620-31.	Adam Keltie.	Forfar and Perth.
75.	1636-50.	Alexander Douglas.	Edinburgh, Fife.
77.	1637-64.	Patrick Gourlay.	Forfar, Perth.
82.	1649-63.	James Swan.	Forfar, &c.
145.	1671-84.	William Malcolm.	Cupar, Fife.
188.	1713-38.	William Seton.	Edinburgh, Fife, Forfar, &c.

(*No. 16.*)   *Protocol Book of Duncan Gray.*

1554—72.

1. **1554. Nov. 13.**—Discharge by David Wedderburn, burgess of Dundee, to John Gray, factor and servant of Patrick, Lord Gray, and Patrick, Master of Gray, his son, of 50 chalders of victual in meal, beir, and wheat market stuff and "mett" of the marquis of Huntly, in complete payment of all manner of victual that ever the said David ought or should have had or yet may claim of the said Mains of Huntly, or any other lands pertaining to the said Lord. (4.)
    The last part of this entry obliterated or torn away.

(*No. 19.*)   *Protocol Book of J. McNele and Robesone.*

1555—73.

2. **1570. June 16.**—Sasine on Precept of Clare Constat by William Kirkcaldie of Grange, Knight, provost, David Forrester, Mr. Michaell Chisholm, Symon Majoribanks and Henry Nisbet, bailies of the burgh of Edinburgh, council, and community thereof, lords superior of the town of Leith ; to James Wedderburn, as son and heir of the deceased John Wedderburn, burgess of Dundee, of the tenement of laud of the said deceased John, back and fore, with yard thereof and piece of waste ground on the south side of the said tenement, with the pertinents lying in the said town of Leith on the south side of the Water thereof in the barony of Restalrig and Sheriffdom of Edinburgh, between the lands of the late Henry Waus on the north part, and the common vennel which leads to the church of Restalrig from the said town of Leith on the south, lie Linx on the east, and the common way on the west. Precept dated at Edinburgh 15 June 1570. Sasine given on 17 June 1570. (78.)

---

[1] Mr. Macleod has also chanced to search, though not for me, some of the Register House protocol books not in the above list, viz. : Nos. 6, 21, 27, 29, 30, and reports that none of them contain any Wedderburn matter.

1619—37.

Protocol Books of Notaries.

3.   **1619.** Aug. 17.—Sasine to Alexander Watson, burgess of Dundee, of a tenement there, on the east side of the Castle hill, which once belonged to William Davidson, son and heir of the late William Davidson, younger, merchant burgess of Dundee, and Jonet Wedderburn, his relict. (6.)

4.   **1620.** May 1.—Testament of Margaret Strathauchin, relict of John Wedderburn, portioner of Craigie, declaring the amounts due to her by various persons (including John Duncan, for house maill, and James Peirson in Craigie, on a bond to her and — Kinnaird, her oye.) She leaves to Bessie Wedderburn, her daughter, "ane gros greane silk gowne ; " to her said oye, "ane frensche black goune ; and other legacies to Margaret Guthrie, wife of William Haliburton, and to Margaret Strathauchin, her niece. (15.)

5.   **1621.** March 21.—Precept, dated at Holyrood house, 21 Feb., for infefting Sir John Scrymgeour of Dudope, as heir to the late John Scrymgeour of Dudope, his grandfather, in the lands of Kirktoun of Strathichty, directed to Mr. Alexander Wedderburn, elder, of Kynganie, while Mr. Alexander Wedderburn, younger, fiar of Kynganie, acts as writer. (33.)

6.   **1621.** (*a*) June 4.—Sasine on charter dated at Dundee, 18 May 1621, and witnessed by Alexander Wedderburn, elder of Kingany, James Wedderburn, baillie of Dundee, and others. (39.) (*b*) Sasine, on charter, 14 May 1621, written and witnessed by Mr. Alexander Wedderburn, clerk of Dundee, of lands in South Marygate, bounded south by those of Mr. James Wedderburn. (42.)

7.   **1622.** Jan. 23.—Resignation of land in the King's gate of Dundee, once belonging to Gilbert, son and heir of James Scrymgeour, witnessed by Mr. Alexander Wedderburn, clerk of the burgh, and Mr. James Wedderburn, his son. (53)

8.   **1622.** Feb. 14.—Sasine on charter by James Kyd to his wife Margaret Duncan, daughter of the late William Duncan, surgeon, burgess of Dundee, and his wife, Catharine Wedderburn, now the wife of Mr. William Fergusone, bailie of Dundee, of an @-rent out of a tenement in Dundee, according to their marriage contract, dated at Dundee 26 Nov. 1619. Peter Wedderburn, merchant in Dundee, is attorney for Margaret. Mr. Alexander Wedderburn and Mr. James Wedderburn, his son, are witnesses. (55.)

9.   **1622.** March 26.—Sasine to William Davidson, younger, on a charter witnessed by Alexander Wedderburn, merchant, burgess of Dundee. (56.)

10. **1622.** April 15.—Sasine on charter (23 Jan. 1622) by Mr. William Fergusone, bailie, to Catharine Wedderburne, his wife, for life, and Magdalen Fergusone, their daughter, heritably, of a land in S Marygate. Witnessed by Mr. Alexander Wedderburn, clerk (and writer of the charter), and Mr. James Wedderburn, his son, &c. (59.)

11. **1622.** July 17.—Sasine on charter, dated at Dudop on the same day, by Sir John Scrymgeour to Mr. James Wedderburn, son of Mr. Alexander Wedderburn of Kynganie, clerk of Dundee, of the S. Flukergate or Ladygate tenement of the late George Ramsay. David Wedderburn, burgess of Dundee, is a witness. (68.)

12. **1622.** Oct. 14.—Possession is given, at a corn yard at the west part of Dundee, to Peter Wedderburn, merchant, burgess, on behalf of Mr. A. Wedderburn, clerk, his father, of two stacks of corn, some "aittis and uther beir, conforme to ane dispositione of this present dait by deliverie to the said Peter in his hands of ane soirt of ilk of the saidis twa stackis." Mr. James Wedderburn, son to the said Mr. Alexander, is a witness. (74.)

13. **1623.** Sept 4.—Sasine of the lands of Easter Densyd to Mr. George Graham, apparent of Claverhouse, on a charter witnessed by Mr. Alexander Wedderburu, clerk of Dundee, and Mr. James and Mr. John Wedderburn, his sons. (103.) Protocol Books of Notaries.

14. **1623.** Dec. 30.—Sasine to William Graham of Claverhouse and Mr. George Graham his son, of the lands of Mylntown of Craigie, &c., on a charter dated 29 Dec. 1623 and witnessed by Mr. Alexander Wedderburn, younger, bailie of Dundee, John Wedderburn, son of the late Robert Wedderburn, burgess of Dundee, and others. (114.)

The name of the second Wedderburn witness is written twice over in the record, but is much blurred. The signature, however, is clear " J. Wedderburn," and no doubt, therefore, the witness is John, son of Robert Wedderburn, the merchant, whose death is thus fixed as occuring before the close of 1623.

15. **1624.** (*n*) July 15.—Sasine to Sir William Grahame of Claverhouse, on charter (5 May), witnessed by Mr. Alexander Wedderburn, bailie of Dundee, and Mr. James Wedderburn, his brother german (136.) (*b*) Oct. 2.—Sasine on charter to David Guthrie, witnessed by Mr. Alexander Wedderburn, bailie, and Mr. James Wedderburn, clerk constitute of Dundee, who acted as bailie in the sasine. (140.)

16. **1626.** Feb. 20.—Sasine on charter of the same date by James Boyter, elder, of Nether Liff, merchant, burgess of Dundee, to Thomas Boyter, his second son, and Jean Wedderburn (daughter of Mr. Alexander Wedderburn, elder, clerk of Dundee), his future wife, in implement of their marriage contract, dated at Dundee 27 January last, granting to the said Jean and Thomas one-eighth part of Blackness, etc. The charter is witnessed by Alexander Wedderburn, fiar of Kingennie, Alexander Wedderburn, elder, merchant, burgess of Dundee, and others ; while the sasine is witnessed by David, James, Alexander (elder and younger), and John Wedderburn, all merchants, burgesses of Dundee, and by Mr. James Wedderburn, son of the said Mr. Alexander Wedderburn, elder. (163.)
    See Scrymgeour-Wedderburn papeis, No. 221.

17. **1626.** Nov. 4.—Sasine on charter to Robert Murray, burgess of Dundee, and Elizabeth Wedderburn, his wife (for whom Alexander Wedderburn, elder, burgess, is attorney), of the "boat passage of the ferry of Seamylnes" near Dundee. Alexander Wedderburn, younger, is bailie. (175.)

18. **1627.** June 4.—Sasine by Henry Ramsey of Ardownie, to John Ramsay of Dundee, on charter dated at Dundee, 12 May last, and witnessed by James, son of David Wedderburn, merchant burgess. (186.)

19. **1627.** Oct. 20.—Sasine on charter, dated at Dundee, 13 inst., by Peter Wedderburn, merchant burgess of Dundee, and Mr. John Wedderburn, sons of the late Mr. Alexander Wedderburn, clerk thereof, to Sir William Graham of Claverhouse, and Mr. George Graham, his son and heir apparent, of six acres of arable land in the Westfield of Dundee, formerly belonging to Robert Wedderburn. Witnessed by Mr. Alexander Wedderburn of Kingennie, dean of gild, William Wedderburn, his brother german, James Wedderburn, bailie, and others. (205.)

20. **1628.** April 15.—Sasine on the precept of clare constat, already noted ante s. Scrymgeour-Wedderburn Papers, No. 234. (216.)

21. **1630.** (*a*) April 30.—Sasine on charter witnessed by Alexander Wedderburn, elder, burgess of Dundee. (247.) (*b*) May 3.—Charter witnessed by John Wedderburn, merchant, burgess of Dundee. (249.)

22. **1630.** (*a*) June 3.—Sasine on precept of clare constat (dated 30 Sept. 1639), in favour of Mr. Alexander Wedderburn, now of Kinganie, as son and heir of the late Mr. Alexander Wedderburn, elder, clerk of Dundee, of a South Marketgate tenement. (*b*) Sasine on charter (30 Sept. 1629), by Mr. Alexander Wedderburn of Kynganie, as such son and heir, in favour of William Wedderburne, his brother german, and Jean Peirson, daughter of Mr. Alexander Peirson, burgess of Aberbrothick, his spouse, of the foreland of the said tenement. (*ib.*)
    See Scrymgeour-Wedderburn papers, No. 239.

23.   **1631.** June 1.—Sasine on precept of clare constat (31 May), in favour of Mr. John Wedderburn, son of the late Mr. Alexander Wedderburn, elder, of Kingeny, as heir to the late William Wedderburn, his brother german, in the said fore-tenement. Mr. Alexander Wedderburn (son of the late Mr. James Wedderburn, clerk of Dundee), is attorney for the said Mr. John Wedderburn. (261.)
See also Scrymgeour-Wedderburn papers, Nos. 249-50.

24.   **1631.** July 20.—Resignation ad rem. by Alexander Wedderburn, merchant, burgess of Dundee, into the hands of Sir John Scrymgeour of Dudop, Knight, as superior of three acres in the east field of Dudop. (263.)
See ante s. General Register of Sasines, No. 74, note.

25.   **1631.** July 28.—Sasine on charter by Mr. John Wedderburn. (264.)
This has been already given. See s. Scrymgeour-Wedderburn papers, Nos 249-50, with the latter of which it is identical.

26.   **1632.** Aug. 17.—Sasine on precept of clare constat by Sir John Scrymgeour of Dudop, Knt., as superior, in favour of Mr. Alexander Wedderburn, younger, son and heir of the late Mr. James Wedderburn, sometime clerk of Dundee, of part of a tenement in South Murraygate. Mr. Alexander Wedderburn of Kyngennie, is a witness. (271.)

27.   **1635.** March 25.—Sasine on precept of clare constat by the said Sir John Scrymgeour in favour of James Wedderburn, son and heir of the late David Wedderburn, burgess of Dundee, of five acres of land in Dundee. The sasine is witnessed by Mr. Alexander Wedderburn, younger, clerk in Dundee, Peter Wedderburn, his brother german, and others. (300.)

PUBLIC   RECORDS—LONDON.

———

STATE   PAPERS.
(Public Record Office, Tower of London, etc.)

WILLS   AND   ADMINISTRATIONS.
(Somerset House).

DOCUMENTS   AT   THE   HERALDS'   COLLEGE.

.

1296—1627.

I have already, in the second note to p. 359 of this volume, referred to certain State Papers, Record Office, &c., London. published volumes of Scottish records preserved in the Record Office in London. These are (a) *Calendar of Documents relating to Scotland*, 1100—1509, 4 vols., ed. (1884) Bain ; (b) *Calendar of State Papers relating to Scotland*, ed. (1858) Thorpe ; and (c) *Calendar of Border Papers*, 1560—1603, ed. Bain ; to which may be added the two volumes (1814) of *Rotuli Scotiæ* preserved in the Tower of London. Besides these, I have found one or two references in *Palgrave's Parliamentary Writs* (1827), the *Calendar of State Papers, Colonial Series, East Indies, &c.*, vol. 1625-29 ed. (1884) Sainsbury, and have also notes of some MS. documents in the Record Office, which are worth insertion here. The following notes from the above-named volumes and documents are arranged below in order of date.

1. **1296.** Aug. 28.—The Ragman Roll. This is the famous record of the fealty of the Scottish Barons (including Walter de Wedderburn) at Berwick-on-Tweed, to Edward I. of England. (*Calendar of Documents, &c.*, II. 201.)

    There is also an appendix of uncatalogued seals, among which is given, as attached to the 21st string of a fragment of homage, dated 28 Aug., a seal (tray. II., 272) bearing a seven-rayed star and the letters " s' WALTI DE WED'BVRN." (*ib.* 547.)[1]

    The full Latin text of this roll is given in Stevenson's "Documents Illustrative of the History of Scotland. H.M. Gen. Reg. House." Edin. 1870. Vol. II., 423.

2. **1296.** Sept. 2.—Berewyk. Among the abbots and other ecclesiastics to whom their lands are ordered to be restored is " Wills de Wodeburn p̄soua ecclesiae de Mynctowe vic' de Rokesb." (*Rotuli Scotiæ* I. 26 a.)

3. **1324-25.** John de L'Isle of Wodeburn (Johannes de Insula de Wodeburn) is returned to parliament for Northumberland for these years. (*Palgrave's Parliamentary Writs*.)

4. **1381.** March 7.—John de Wodeburn (apparently in London) and William Russell are named as attornies for Nicholas Wytty, then captive in the hands of the Scots. (*Rotuli Scotiæ* II. 35.)

5. **1433.** July 8.—Richardus Wodeborn is named in a safe conduct for Robert Vaus. (*ib.* II. 283.)

6. **1434.** Oct. 28.—Richardus Wodebourne de London, fyshemonger, is named in a similar document. (*ib.* II. 290.)

7. **1547.** The Jointe and Severall answerrs of Abraham de Deux-villes and David Otger, twoe of ye defts. to ye Bill of Complaint of John Wedderborne, Compl'. (*Record Office MS., Eliz.* W.W., 7. 17.)

    This is a plea to a bill in chancery, marked Riche, Chancellor, and dated, therefore, 1547-51, which was the period of his office. It relates to a suit in regard to various merchandise imported from Zealand into England, which John Wedderburne had prosecuted for the defts. for eight months, neglecting "his own affaires of trade of merchandise by travayle abroade to foraigne countryes." Wedderburne seems to have got imprisoned owing to this matter, and brought his action for his expenses and damage. The defendants denied all liability. The result of this suit does not appear.

8. **1550.** Sept. 23.—Letter from the Earl of Arran, at Edinburgh, to Edward VI., requesting letters of safe conduct for Gilbert Wedderburne of Leith and others to pass with a certain ship to England to buy merchandize. (*Cal. State Papers, &c.*, I. 99.)[2]

9. **1596.** Oct. 12.—Letter from Robert Bower, at Edinburgh, to Lord Burghley, mentioning " a murder committed by John Wedderburn." (*ib.* II. 722.)

    This was the murder of Robert Lindsay of Balhall, referred to ante. s. Register of the Privy Seal, No. 25 (13 Aug. 1596).

---

[1] All the other references to the name of Wedderburn in these volumes are to the vill, manor, or tower of Wedderburn, co. Berwick, 1300—1494. (Vol. II. 300 ; III. 277, 283, 325, 369-70 ; IV. 323, 324, 418.)

[2] These volumes also contain references to David Home of Wedderburn, 25 July 1518, and to the lauds of Wedderburn, co. Berwick, 1523 and 1545. (I. 7, 12, 57.)

State Papers, 10.
Record Office,
&c., London.

1597. July 17.—Letter from Ralph, Lord Eure, warden of the Middle Marches, to Lord Burghley. (*Calendar of Border Papers*, p. 359-60, No. 685.)

This Sonday being the xvj^th of July, Hugh Birde, bailife of Tynmothe and servaunte to the Earle of Northumberlande, . . . in searching of a Scottishe shipp nowe laitelie come into the river of Newcastle, hath found a Scottishe gentleman called Mr. John Wedderborne as he tearmethe him selfe, disguised in marineres apperell and that of the meaneste sorte. By his discourse he saith he is a follower of the Lord Bothwell, and came from thence some twentie dayes since, toke shipping with a Scott att Bullyn, lauded at Yarmonthe, where as he saith he sawe Mr. John Colvyn shipped for the Lowe Countries, and eschewing his companie leaste hee should be knowne, hee toke another Scottishe shipp, wherin Mr. Dent of Newcastle came. His errand which he seemethe to make knowne to me and Hughe Birde, is that the Lord Bothwell should send him into Scotland with purpose to use all the meanes possible to take away the life of Sir Robert Kerr—and hee hearing theese broyles betweene the wardens and us, dothe desire to make the same knowne unto me not craving myne ayde in the same, but relying upon his owne force and friendshipp. The manner howe he will doe the same is by traynes of powder in the castle at Halleden to blowe him up, or otherwise to intercept on the way or surprise him in some house. This Wedderborne hathe the Franche tongue reasonable well and hath served in Frannce on pleasure not under anie charge. He informethe that the King of Frannce is now before Amyenes, and that he was employed by the King to have brunt a madrill of the Spanyards wherein victall was, who with twoe Franche captaines undertaking that service, profered their service to the Governer of Amynes. and the secrete service being formerlie discovered, the twoe Franche captaines were hanged and this man perdoned for that he was a Scottisheman.

Theese vauntes, together with the wise carriage, his birthe and manner of disguising, yealding unto me apparaunte suspicion of more devilishe practises then he revealeth, I thought good to stay him in the safe keaping of the said Hugh Birde till your lordships further pleasure were known to me for him. The personne of the man is thus to be decerned—of reasouable stature, verie square bodyed, bigg legged, one or two scarres on the hight of his foreheade, faire complexioned, yellowe herded, the haire of his heade like unto white amber, a little rounde banld on the crowne of his heade, his left arme from the hight of his shoulder to the ende of his fingers on that syde, of eache side of his arme and hand, is spotted as reade as bloode. He conveyed letters from Yarmouthe as he saith to some of the Lord Bothwell's freindes, but I feare they were lettres of greater importaunce. He seemeth to be verie cuning in Staite causes, whose wisdome overreaching my small skill, I presume to make knowne this much to your lordship, craving knowledge of your honorable pleasure with speede, what shalbee done with the man. He is an ingyner, proferring to make for me petares and garnettes, ingynes of warr, in both which I am contented to bestowe some waiste money upon him till I heare your lordships pleasure, to the ende he without suspicion may remaine with pleasure.

This matter is also referred to in the "Border Correspondence, Historical Notes 1509—1714," compiled by F. S. Thomas, London, 1850, pp. 472, 1109.

11.   **1597.** July 21.—Letter, same to same. (*ib.* p. 364, No. 694.)

Robert Anderson, a Scotsman of "Dundee" in Angus, being at Newcastle, reported to Mr. John Wedderborne (the man of whom I lately wrote) that the King had secretly charged all the leaders of the country to have all persons between 16 and 60 in readiness on 20 days' warning, especially on the Border . . . and he intends nothing but war, and has sent Mr. John Colvyn to the Low Countries to press the States for their promisses.

12.   **1621.** Oct. 26.—Bill. John Wedderborne of the parish of S. Olave's, Southwark, co. Surrey, fustiane weaver, *v.* Thomas Wilkinson of Midellesex, vitcller. (*Record Office MS., James I.*)

13.   **1622.** June 4.—Answer of William Collyns, one of the defendants to the bill of John Wedderburn, complainant. (*Record Office MS., Chanc. Bills and Answers*, W. 106. 18.)

The answer alleges that Wedderburn never delivered any goods to this defendant in trust, as set forth in the complaint, but on the contrary sold to this defendant and John Dixon deceased, absolutely, certain goods for the sum of £10, by bill of sale dated 30 Oct. 1617. No particulars of the complainant's business or residence are given.

14.   **1625.** Jan. 12.—London. A commission under the privy signet presented, authorizing John Wedderborne to receive all estates of Scotchmen deceased in the Indies. (*Calendar of State Papers, Colonial Series, East Indies, &c.*, vol. 1625-29, p. 10.)

15.   **1627.** May 11.—Letter read from Sir Wm. Alexander to Mr. Governor on behalf of Wedderburne, to whom his late Majesty granted a patent to receive out of the estate of every Scottish man deceased in the Indies in their service 12d. in the £. Ordered to avoid clamour and Wedderburne's importunity that what was remaining collected by virtue of the said letters patent, a very small matter, be paid to him. (*ib.* p. 349.)

16.   **1627.** June 22.—The Hague. Ordered that the estate of John Boyd, deceased, be paid to John Ale, executor of Pat. Boyd. his brother, leaving for Wedderburne, depute (?) to Sir Wm. Alexander, 12d. in the £1 according to the grant from the King. (*ib.* p. 360.)

1697—1887.

The above heading is used, for the sake of brevity, to include the wills and administrations recorded at Somerset House, London. All the indices in the principal registry
there have been carefully searched, and every reference to any testator or intestate of the
name of Wedderburn noted.

The indices consist of nine different series, as follows :—

(1) Wills and Administrations, 1312-1888.
(2) Scotch Confirmations, 1876-1889.
3) Ireland, Wills and Administrations, 1858-89.
(4) Administrations, 1559-60.
(5) Commissary Court of London, 1604-1858.

(6) Consistory Court of London, 1362-1858.
(7) Commissary Court of Westminster, 1504-1808.
(8) Wills brought in. not proved, 1700-1896, 2 vols.
(9) Army Wills, 1 vol.

These have all been searched down to the dates stated above, and all the material extracts
are given below. Some possible corruptions of the name have been noted in the indices
but not looked up among the original documents with the exception of a few instances of
Weatherburn, of some of which notes are given at the end of the main extracts.
(See Note I.) A list of the possible corruptions is also given below. (See Note II.)

1. **1697.** March 18.—Administration of the goods of Robert Wedderburn, or Wetherburn, bachelor, of H.M.S. " Devonshire," granted to his mother, Elizabeth Daw,
widow, now resident in Fifeshire, Scotland. (*Pyne.*)
   This is entered in the calendar as Witherburn or Widderburn. The deceased is the son of the
   Rev. Andrew Wedderburn of Liff and Elizabeth Daw.

2. **1774.** Feb. 22.—(Parts). Administration of the goods of David Wedderburn, late
Brigadier-General and Commander-in-chief of the H.E.I. Company's forces at Bombay
and Major in H.M.'s 77th regiment of foot on half-pay at Bombay, bachelor, granted
to Alexander Wedderburn, Esq., brother and next of kin. (*Bargrave.*)

3. **1780.** May 29.—(Parts). Will, 13 May 1777 (proved 3 May 1780) of Henry
Wedderburn, Esq., of Calcutta and Fort William, Bengal. (*Collins.*)
   He leaves his property in equal shares to his wife Alice Wedderburn," at present in Calcutta,"
   and his daughter Elizabeth, then a minor, to whom Alexander Wedderburn of S. Germain's in
   Scotland, and Alexander Robertson, W.S., Edinburgh, are appointed guardians. If both wife and
   daughter predecease him, his property is left to Mary, wife of Colonel John Cummings, " now on
   their way home from India."

4. **1789.** June 9.—(Parts). Administration of the goods of John Wedderburn, late a
Lt.-Col. in the H.E.I. Company's service, granted to David Wedderburn, brother and
next of kin. (*Machan*).

5. **1795.** Oct. 7.—(Parts, North Britain.) Administration with the will annexed of the
goods of Katharine Wedderburn, wife of Robert Stewart, surgeon in Dundee, granted to
him as sole executor and residuary legatee under the said will, dated 4 Dec. 1793.
(*Newcastle*.)

6. **1799.** Feb.—(Parts.) Will (proved in Jamaica, Aug. 2 and 3, 1797) of James
Wedderburn of Westmorland, co. Cornwall, Jamaica. (*Howe*).
   He bequeaths legacies and annuities to his mother Katharine Dunbar, his sisters Catharine,
   Thomasina, and Robina Wedderburn, and a sum of £100 to his sister Elizabeth Blyth, to be laid out
   as his executors think fit. Other legacies are left to his sister-in-law, Mary Wisdom Wedderburn,
   his nieces, Elizabeth Susannah and Mary Wedderburn, his cousins Hugh Fraser of Jamaica, Henry
   Scrymageour of Hanover, Jamaica, James Wedderburn Dunbar and Peter Dunbar, and also to his
   dear brother John Wedderburn. His residuary legatee is James, only son of his brother John
   Wedderburn.
   This is the will of James Wedderburn, third son of Thomas Wedderburn and Katharine Dunbar,
   b. 23 Sept. 1751, d. unm. at Bluecastle, in Jamaica, 17 July 1797. At the date of his will and death
   his brother John had only one son, James ; the second son, John, not being born till 1798.

7. **1803.** November 29.—(North Britain.) Will, dated 20 May 1800, of Sir John Wedderburn, Bart., of Ballendean, co. Perth. (*Marriot.*)

By this will the testator's son David is appointed sole executor and the whole of the estate left to him subject to trusts to provide for the testator's widow (Alicia Dundas), and his younger sons and daughters, James, John, Alexander, Margaret, Jean, Maria, Susan, Louisa, and Ann. His estates are stated to consist of lands in Ballindean, bought of William and John Gray, late of Baledgarno, and lands in Baledgarno bought of Charles, Lord Kinnaird, and also of the estates called Blew Castle and Glenisla Castle, par. Westmoreland, co. Cornwall, Jamaica.

8. **1806.** Oct 24.—(Parts.) Will of Alice Wedderburn. (*Pitt.*)

See ante s. No. 3 and post No. 12.

9. **1808.** April.—(North Britain.) Will, dated 19 July 1802, and three codicils 4, 30 Sept. 1802 and 27 Nov. 1807, of James Wedderburn Colvile, "heretofore Wedderburn, second son of the marriage between the late Sir John Wedderburn of Blackness, Bart., and Dame Jean Fullarton, his wife, daughter of the late John Fullarton of Fullarton, Esq."

There are bequests to his wife Isabella Colvile, formerly Blackburn, his younger sons Peter and James Wedderburn, to Sir John Wedderburn of Balindean, and his son David, and to John Wedderburn.

10. **1810.** July.—(Parts.) Administration (Jan. 5) of the goods, &c, of John Wedderburn, otherwise Hunter, late boatswain's mate of H.M.S. "Penelope," bachelor, granted to John Wedderburn, lawful father of the deceased. (*Collingwood.*)

11. **1814.** July.—(Middlesex.) Administration of the goods of. David Wedderburn, late of King Street, Drury Lane, in the parish of St. Giles in the Fields, co. Middlesex, a seaman belonging to H.M.SS. "Volage" and "Resistance," granted to Sarah Wedderburn, the widow.

12. **1814.** Oct. 17.—(Parts.) Administration with will annexed of the goods unadministered by Elizabeth Wedderburn or Murray, the daughter, while living, of Alice Wedderburn, formerly of Hatton Garden, then of Windsor, then of Upper Seymour Street, Portman Square, late of Seclut Gunge, East Indies, granted to James Murray, husband, and administrator of the goods of the said Elizabeth Wedderburn or Murray.

The said will, dated 21 May 1799, is registered 1806. *Pitt.* 824 (see ante No. 8), and describes the testatrix as Alice Wedderburn, late of Upper Seymour Street, widow, now about to embark on board the ship "Asia" for Bengal. She bequeaths everything to her daughter Elizabeth, and in event of Elizabeth predeceasing her, leaves £500 to her brother James Tetley, Captain in the H.E.I.C.'s service, and the residue equally between him and her sister Elizabeth Carrick, widow, of Upper Seymour Street, aforesaid.

13. **1814.** April 17.—(Parts.) Administration of the goods, &c., of Elizabeth Murray, formerly Wedderburn, late of Harrow Weald, co. Middlesex, but thereafter at Havre in Grace in France, deceased, granted to James Murray, Esq., the husband.

This administration is registered October, 1814. The deceased is, of course, the daughter of Henry Wedderburn of Gosford by his third wife, Alice Tetley. See ante Nos. 3, 8, and 12.

14. **1815.** August.—(Surrey.) Will and two codicils of James Wedderburn, dated at Weymouth, 22 July 1812, Penge Place, 26 June 1814, and Toulouse, 30 May 1815. Proved 28 Aug 1815. Legacies are left to his mother Lady Wedderburn, his brothers Sir David, John, and Alexander, and his sisters, Maria and Susan. (*Pakenham.*)

15. **1821.** Feb.—(Middlesex and London.) Will, dated 16 Aug. 1819, of John Wedderburn of Devonshire Street, parish of St. Marylebone, Middlesex, and of Leadenhall Street, City of London. (*Mansfield.*)

The testator leaves legacies to his eldest son James and his son John Kellerman ; to his second son, when aged 25 ; to his sister Katharine ; to his daughters Mary, wife of John Wellings, and Catharine Georgina, widow of Patrick Stirling, also to Hugh Fraser of Honeyfield, near Inverness, and to John Wedderburn, a free mulatto planter in Jamaica. There are codicils dated 7 Oct. 1819 and 6 Dec. 1820.

16. **1823.** April.—(North Britain.) Will of James Wedderburn, advocate, dated at Edinburgh 27 Oct. 1813, proved in London 24 April 1823. His eldest brother Andrew Colvile and his brother Peter Wedderburn are both referred to. (*Richards.*)

This is the will of James Wedderburn, Solicitor General for Scotland, who d. 7 Nov. 1822.

17. **1829.** May.—(North Britain.) Will of Charles Wedderburn of Pearsie, referring to the tailzie of his lands, dated 8 Feb. 1821, and leaving an annuity of £50 to his nephew Sir James Webster Wedderburn, and legacies to his nieces and nephew Isabella, Catherine, and Robert Graham. A legacy is also left to Charles Wedderburn Walker, son of his gardener, John Walker. Peter Wedderburn, son of the late Peter Wedderburn-Ogilvy of Ruthven, is named. Proved 4 May 1829. (*Liverpool.*)

18. **1832.** Feb. 25.—(London.) Administration with will, dated 30 July 1830, of James Wedderburn. There are bequests to David Wedderburn of Pearsie and the testator's wife, Isabella, while the residue goes in trust for his only child, John Kellerman. (*Tenterden.*)
    Further administration of goods unadministered was granted to John Kellerman Wedderburn, 31 May 1856. (See post No. 29.)

19. **1835.** June.—(Surrey.) Will, dated at Brighton 19 May 1834, of Mary Wisdom Wedderburn, described as late of Queen Anne Street, Marylebone, now of Carshalton, Surrey, widow of John Wedderburn, late of Chigwell Row, Essex. (*Gloster.*)
    There are bequests to her second son John, his wife Lady Helen, and their son John Walter, then aged 9 ; also to her daughters Catherine Georgiana Stirling, and Mary Wellings, and the daughter of the latter, Catherine Mary Wellings, aged 14.

20. **1837.** Nov. 6.—(Middlesex.) Administration of the goods of Hope Wedderburn, late of 40 a, Rupert Street, Haymarket, spinster, granted to her sister and one of her next-of kin, Sarah, wife of John Lamb Dugdale.
    She d., æt 35, Oct. 22 1837, her sister, Lydia Duglas, being named in the certificate as giving information of her death. (*Reg. Deaths, Somerset House.*)

21. **1839.** Sept. 3.—(North Britain.) Will, dated 1 Sept. 1838, of Alexander Wedderburn, a colonel in Her Majesty's army. (*Vaughan.*)
    This is the will of the youngest son of Sir John Wedderburn of Ballindean and Alicia Dundas.

22. **1839.** June 20.—(Middlesex.) Administration of the goods of the Rt. Hon. Lady Frances Caroline Webster, Lady Wedderburn, late of Hertford Street, Mayfair, granted to Sir James Webster Wedderburn, baronet (*sic*), the husband.

23. **1840.** Nov. 6.—(Middlesex.) Administration of the goods of Sir James Webster Wedderburn, knight, granted to Lucy Sarah Ann Bishop, one of the natural and lawful children of the deceased.

24. **1840.** July 20.—(North Britain.) Administration of the goods of John Wedderburn, late of Auchterhouse, co. Forfar, N.B.
    This is a limited administration of the goods of the deceased granted to John Lyon, on behalf of David Lyon, who seems to have filed a bill in Chancery (1832) in regard to the estates of John Wedderburn of Spring Garden (father of the deceased), and his brother James, and now required this grant to enable him to proceed with his suit. Another such formal grant was made April 1841.

25. **1846.** Dec.—(Middlesex.) Will and codicil (Nov. 23, 24) of John Wedderburn of 1, Prince's Place, Duke Street, St. James, Westminster, by which he directs his burial in Old Brompton Cemetery, and leaves £10 each to Edward and Eliza Winsor of 1, Park Place, and Mary, their daughter, and bequeaths the residue of his property to his nephews, William and John Fowler, and his three sisters, Agnes Fowler, Henrietta Black, Mary Deans, and the children of his deceased sister, Christian Brand.

26. **1853.** March.—(Exeter.) Will, dated 21 Oct. 1852, of Alexander Wedderburn of Exeter, retired inspector of mail coaches. He leaves legacies to his wife Ruth, his daughter, Margaret Nesbitt Wedderburn, and her sisters. The executors are his son, William Thomas Wedderburn, and his son-in-law, James Taylor of London.
    Administration was granted 28 Feb. 1853.

27. **1854.** July 20.—(North Britain.) Administration of the goods of John Wedderburn, Esq.
    This is another formal grant (see ante No. 24) made to Charles Baylis, to enable the continuance of the Chancery suit brought (1831) by the Webster-Wedderburus against the deceased, in regard to the estate of David Wedderburn-Webster.

28. **1656.** May 30.—(Middlesex.) Administration of the goods of Margaret Nesbit Wedderburn, late of 1, Cleveland Road, in the parish of S. Mary, Islington, spinster, granted to William Thomas Wedderburn, her brother, Ruth Wedderburn, widow, the mother, renouncing administration. (See ante No. 26.)

29. **1856.** May 31.—(London.) Administration (with will) of the unadministered goods of James Wedderburn, granted to John Kellerman Wedderburn. (See ante No. 18.)

30. **1858.** Dec. 14.—Will of Sir David Wedderburn, late of Inveresk Lodge, Musselburgh, in North Britain, Baronet, who d. 7 April 1858 at Inveresk Lodge aforesaid, proved at the principal registry by the oath of Andrew Webster, of 3, Forth Street, Edinburgh, solicitor, the sole executor.

31. **1863.** April 2.—Will of Sir John Wedderburn, formerly of Inveresk Lodge and of Keith House, co. Haddington, both in North Britain, but late of Meredith, near Gloucester, co. Gloucester, Baronet, who died 2 July 1862 at Chichester Terrace, Brighton, co. Sussex, domiciled in England, proved at the principal registry by the oaths of Dame Henrietta Louisa Wedderburn of Meredith aforesaid, widow, the relict, John Stirling of Kippendavie, co. Perth, George Ashburner of Filgate, Crawley, co. Sussex, and Andrew Webster of 118, George Street, in the city of Edinburgh, solicitor, four of the executors.

32. **1863.** Oct. 27.—Scotch confirmation under seal of the Commissariot of Edinburgh, dated 13 Oct. 1863, of George Wedderburn, W.S., 25, Ainslie Place, Edinburgh, as brother and one of the next-of-kin of the late James Wedderburn (eldest son of the deceased James Wedderburn, advocate, sometime Solicitor-General for Scotland), lately residing at 39, Craven Street, Strand, London, who d. at London aforesaid on or about 17 July 1863.

33. **1871.** Feb. 4.—Administration of the goods, &c., of Robert Wedderburn, late of Robin Adair Cottages, Low Benwell, co. Northumberland, engine fitter, who d. there 16 Jan. 1871, granted at Newcastle to Catherine Wedderburn, the relict. Extracted by W. B. Elsdon, solicitor, Newcastle.

34. **1874.** Oct. 15.—Confirmation of the commissariot of Fife, dated 7 October 1874, of Henry Scrymgeour Wedderburn, Esquire, of Wedderburn and Birkhill, the son, as executor nominate of Frederick Lewis Scrymgeour Wedderburn, Esquire, of Wedderburn and Birkhill, who d. at Birkhill House, co. Fife, 16 Aug. 1874.

35. **1875.** Sept. 16.—Will (dated 30 Jan. 1873) of George Gordon Webster Wedderburne, late of Newcastle-under-Lyme, co. Stafford, staff officer of pensioners, who d. 20 Aug. 1875 at Abington, near Northampton, proved by Caroline Wedderburne of West Hill, Sydenham, co. Kent, the widow and sole executrix.

36. **1875.** Aug. 20.—(Ireland.) Administration of the goods of William Wedderburn, late of Stranocum, co. Antrim, shopkeeper, a bachelor, who d. there 11 July 1875, granted at Belfast to Margaret Wedderburn of Stranocum (Ballymony), spinster, the sister.

37. **1876.** Nov. 11 —Administration (with will) of the goods of Elizabeth Wedderburn, late of Meredith, co. Gloucester, spinster, who. d 26 Aug. 1876 at Harrogate, co. York, granted to Sir David Wedderburn, bart., the brother.
See Scotch confirmation of the same, 27 Feb. 1877.

38. **1887.** Dec. 4.—Scotch confirmation of the will of George Wedderburn, sometime Sergeant Major Royal Montgomeryshire Rifles, Welshpool, Wales, thereafter residing at 8, Mount Street, Aberdeen, intestate, granted at Aberdeen to George Leith Wedderburn, manager, Jericho Distillery, near Insch, executor *dative qui* next-of-kin.

39. **1879.** Jan. 25.—Will of John Wedderburn, formerly of 99, Earl's Court Road, Kensington, but late of 21, Park Road, Haverstock Hill, both in co. Middlesex, a Major-General in Her Majesty's army, who d. 4 Jan. 1879 at 21, Park Road, proved by Margaret Wedderburn of 21, Park Road, widow, the relict and sole executrix.

40. **1880.** Jan. 6.—The confirmation of the commissariot of Perthshire, dated 31 Dec. 1879, of Mrs. Margaret Anne Wedderburn, widow, the relict, John Ogilvy, Esq., younger, of Insbewan, residing at Hare Craig, near Dundee, and Donald Ogilvy, Esq., of Clova, as executors nominate of John Walter Wedderburn. Lt.-Col. (unattached) in Her Majesty's army, residing at Marfield, Blairgowrie, co. Perth, who died there 29 July 1879. London Wills, &c.

41. **1881.** March 22.—Will of Euphemia Scott (formerly Scrymgeour-Wedderburn, spinster), late of the Angles, East Sheen, co. Surrey, widow, who d. 3 Feb. 1881 at the Angles, domiciled in England, proved by Henry Scrymgeour-Wedderburn of Birkhill, co. Fife, in North Britain, Esq., the nephew, one of the executors.

42. **1881.** July 18.—Will of James Wedderburn, late of 34, Byron Terrace, Scotswood Road, Newcastle-on-Tyne, engine fitter, who d. 15 June 1881, at 34, Byron Terrace, proved at Newcastle by Thomas Lindsay of Benwell, co. Northumberland, machinist, and William Pickering of Newcastle, millwright, executors.

43. **1881.** (a) Oct. 17.—Will, with two codicils, of Dame Henrietta Louisa Wedderburn, late of Meredith, near Gloucester, widow, who died 7 April 1881, at 7, Ovington Gardens, South Kensington, co. Middlesex, domiciled in England, proved by Sir David Wedderburn of Meredith, baronet, the son and sole executor. (b) Oct. 22.—Scotch confirmation of Sir David Wedderburn as executor to his mother.

44. **1882.** Feb. 13.—Will of Jabez Wedderburn, late of 46, Blackheath Road, Greenwich, co. Kent, who d. 5 Jan. 1882, at 46, Blackheath Road, proved by Harriet Wedderburn, the relict and executrix.

45. **1882.** Sept. 6.—Scotch confirmation of Thomas Weatherburn, 8, Lothian Road, Edinburgh, who d. 1 Aug. 1882, at Edinburgh, testate, granted at Edinburgh to Alexander Mather, junior, executor nominate in the will (dated 27 July 1882 and recorded in the Edinburgh commissariot 5 Sept. 1882)
    In this entry Weatherburn would seem to be an error for Wedderburn, and the entry is therefore placed here and not in Note I.

46. **1883.** March 7.—Will of Christopher Wedderburn, late of 40, Freegrove Road, Hillmartin Road, Holloway, co. Middlesex, who d. 20 Oct. 1882, at 40, Freegrove Road, proved by Christopher William Wedderburn of the West Cliff Hotel, Folkestone, his son and executor.

47. **1883.** (a) March 10.—Will of Sir David Wedderburn, late of Meredith, near Gloucester, co. Gloucester, baronet, who d. 18 Sept. 1882, at Inveresk Lodge, Musselburgh, in North Britain, proved by Sir William Wedderburn of 14, S. James' Square, baronet, brother and sole executor. (b) March 14.—Scotch confirmation of above.

48. **1883.** March 27.—Confirmation of the will of Jannette Serymgeour Wedderburn, daughter of the late Henry Serymgeour Wedderburn of Wedderburn and Birkhill, who d. 4 Feb. 1883, at Birkhill House, testate, granted at Cupar to Henry Scrymgeour Wedderburn of Wedderburn and Birkhill, her nephew and executor nominate in her will dated 26 Aug. 1875 and registered in the Fife commissariot 17 March 1883.

49. **1884.** Feb. 14.—Administration of the estate of John Wedderburn of Starkie Street, Liverpool, co. Lancaster, tobacconist, batchelor, who d. there 11 Jan. 1884, granted to Thomas Cope of Liverpool, tobacco manufacturer, a creditor.

50. **1884.** March 5.—Will of Mary Ann Wedderburn, late of North Petherton, co. Somerset, spinster, who d. there 12 Dec. 1883, proved at Taunton by John Badcock, an executor. She leaves £25 to her brother William, "already well provided for," and other bequests to her first cousin, George Denman, and his two sons George and William.

3 T

London   51.   **1886.** May 5. --Administration (with the will) of the estate of Charles Francis Webster
Wills, &c   Wedderburn, late of 74, Warrior Square, St. Leonard's-on-Sea, co. Surrey, formerly
                    a Colonel in the 53rd Light Infantry Regiment, who died there 28 Feb. 1886, granted
                    to Edward Webster-Wedderburn of 129, Sackville Street, West Brighton, son and
                    one of the next-of-kin.

The will is dated 21 October 1885, and leaves legacies of trinkets, &c, to his sons Arthur
(miniatures and the Wedderburn pedigree book), Edward. Annesley, his daughter Violet, his wife
Emily, and his nephew Howard Bisshop. He directs that he be buried at Bournemouth, next to his
wife Emily, and that the following iuscription be engraved on copper and let into the obelisk there :—

> To the memory of Charles Francis Webster-Wedderburn, late of the 53rd Light
> Infantry, eldest son of the late Sir James and the Rt. Honble. the Lady Frances
> Webster-Wedderburn. and grandson of George, 1st Earl of Mountmorres, 8th
> Viscount Valentia. Died .. , aged ....

52.   **1886.** July 27.—Will of William Thomas Wedderburn, late of Dunkeld, Croydon
        Road, Anerley, co. Surrey, who died there 14 June 1886, proved by Mary Jane
        Wedderburn, his relict and sole executrix.

53.   **1887.** April 22.—Confirmation of the Edinburgh commissariot, 13 April 1887, of
        Henry Scrymgeour-Wedderburn of Wedderburn and Birkhill, co Fife, nephew, and
        William Duncan, solicitor, as executors nominate to Mary Turner Scrymgeour-Wedder-
        burn or Smith of West Grange (Edinburgh), widow, who d. there 25 March 1887.

NOTE 1.

The following are some of the references to the name of Weatherburn :—

(a) **1795.** March 3.—Administration of the goods of Creighton Wetherburn, otherwise Sanders, late
    a seaman, belonging to H.M.S. "Hind and Ardent," bachelor, deceased, granted to Alexander
    Wetherburn, the father.

(b) **1613.** August. —Administration of Ann Weatherburn or Weatherbourne of Berwick-on-Tweed.

(c) **1865.** July 18.—Letters of administration of the personal estate, &c., of Isabella Weatherburn,
    formerly of Berwick-on-Tweed, but late of Upper Holborn. co. Middlesex, spinster, deceased,
    who died at Upper Holborn 15 May 1864, granted to Robert Weatherburn, fishmonger, of
    Berwick-on-Tweed, the brother.

(d) **1865.** Oct. 2.—Administration of the goods of Francis Weatherburn, late of 14, Bower Street,
    Ratcliffe, co. Middlesex, engineer, bachelor, who d. there 16 Sept. last, granted to his brother
    John Weatherburn, engineer, of 14, Bower Street aforesaid.

(e) **1867.** June 22.—Will of Jane Weatherburn, late of South Shields, co. Durham, widow, who d.
    16 March 1867 at South Shields, proved at Durham by Margery Nicholson of South Shields,
    widow, sole executrix.

(f) **1868.** Aug 1.—Will of Martin Weatherburn, late of Leicester, engineer, deceased, who d. 22 July
    1868 at Leicester, proved there by J. B. Kilby of Leicester, executor.

(g) **1870.** Feb. 25.—Will of William Weatherburn, late of Castlegate, Berwick-on-Tweed, who d.
    there 3 Feb. 1870, proved by James Gray and H. L. Christison, executors.

(h) **1871.** Oct 31.—Will of Robert Weatherburn, of Castlegate and Tweed Street, co. Berwick, who
    d. 23 Jan. 1871, proved at Newcastle by his four grandsons and executors, Isaac Robson, Thomas
    Strother, Robert Weatherburn Watson of Liverpool, and Alexander Watson of Castlegate.

(i) **1873.** June 9.—Will of Jane Weatherburn of Campbell Street, South Shields, co. Durham, widow,
    who d. there 24 Jan. 1873, proved at Durham by the executors John Bowman and Ann Reah,
    widow.

(j) **1873** Sept. 12.—Will of Henry Weatherburn of Redhill, co. Surrey, engineer, who d. there
    25 Aug. 1873, proved by William Weatherburn of Redhill, son, and James Weatherburn of Birken-
    head, brother, engineers, the executors.

(k) **1884.** Aug. 28.—Administration of the estate of Margaret Weatherburn (wife of Thomas Weather-
    burn), late of Little Tosson, Rothbury, co. Northumberland, who d. 7 June 1882 at Little Tosson,
    granted at Newcastle to the said Thomas Weatherburn of Little Tosson, shepherd.

(l) **1887.** May 4.—Administration of the goods of Frederick J. Weatherburn, Redhill, Surrey,
    bachelor, granted to Robert Weatherburn, engineer, of Redhill, his brother.

NOTE II.

The following is the list of some of the possible corruptions of the name mentioned above (p. 517).

(p. 517).

London Wills, &c.

1522-24.	Wedderton, John. Bodfelde, 24.
1537-39.	Wetburby, Thomas. Dingelay, 5.
1540.	Wadeborne, Willelmus. Con. C't., London.
1559.	Wetherby, Robert. Mellercbe. 6.
1589.	Woodberu, William. Leicester, 53.
1606.	Woodburn, John. Admon. (34).
1607.	Winterburne, John. Com.Ct.,Westm.,529, 126.
1651.	Woodborne. Grey, 102.
1652.	Winterborne, Edward, York. Bowyer. 157.
1653.	Winterberne, Authony, Berks. Brent, 78.
„	Woodburne, Richard. Brent, 101.
1657.	Winterbourne, Hugh, Berks. Rutben, 21.
„	„ John, Berks. Rutben, 413.
1659.	Woodburne, Robert, York. Pell, 287.
„	Welburne, John, York. Pell, 411.
1659.	Winterborne. Joan, Berks. Pell, 285.
„	„ John, Dorset. Pell, 553.
1665.	„ Egidius. Hyde, 61.
1666.	Weatherby, Charles. London. Mico, 23.
1667.	Wadamond, Peter, London. Carr, 99.
1670.	Winterbanke, Maria, Middlesex. Penu, 30.
1674.	Witherby, Thomas. Bence.
1676.	Winterborne. Cuthbert, Middx. Bence,126.
1689.	Woodburn, Susanna. (March 29.) Admon.
1693.	Withinbrooke, John. London. Coker, 38.
„	Winterflood, John, Parts. Coker, 200.
1698.	Windebank, Christopher. Parts Lort.
1700.	Winterborne, Carolus. Noel, 109.
1704.	Westerborne, Sara, Middlesex. Admon.
„	Weatherby, Francis, Parts. Admon.
1709.	Weatherburne, James. Lanc. Admon.
„	Woodburne, William. „ „
„	Weatherby, Terry, Scotia. Lanc. Admon.
1710.	Woodborne, Edward, Parts. Smith. 235.
1711.	Weatherby, William, „ Young, Admon.
„	„ Thomas. „ (248.)
1713.	„ John. Leeds, Admon.
„	Woodburn, John. Leeds, 197.
1714.	Witherbrooke Dulcibella, Surrey,Aston,168
„	Weatherby, Benjamin. Aston, 251.
1715.	Woodbourn, Joseph. Fagg. Admon.
1718.	Weatherby, Edward, Middx. Tenison, 21.
1719.	Winterbourne.Marg., Berks. Browning, 58.
1722.	Wetherby, Robert, Bristol. Marlbro'. Ad-
1723.	„ William, Parts. Richmond Ad-
1726.	Winterborn, Geo., (Nov.) Com. Ct., Lond.
1732.	Weatherby, William, Parts. Bedford. Ad.
1735.	Winterbourne, James, „
1738.	Wetherby, William, „ Brodripp, 206.
1739.	„ „ Kent. Henchman, 143.
1748.	Wedyborow,John,Middlesex. Strahan,134.
1749.	Wetheron, George, Parts. Lisle, 202.
„	Wedderom, Thomas, Middlesex. Lisle, 30.
1750.	Winterburn, Will.,(Nov.) Com. Ct., Lond.
1751.	Weatherburn, Henry, Parts. Busby, Ad.
1758.	Weatherbourn, Ralph, „ Hutton, 317.
1759.	Woodburn, Will. (Aug.) Com. Ct., Lond.
1760.	Weatherby, Joseph, Middlesex. Lynch,345.
1761.	Weatberburn, Joseph, Parts. Cheslyn,113.

1761.	Weatherbury, John, Parts. Cheslyn, Ad.
1762.	Weatherby, Elijah, „ June. S. Eloy W.
1763.	Weatherbee, Joseph, „ Nov. Cæsar, W.
1765.	Weatherbey, John, Bucks, Rushworth, 37.
1775.	Woodburn, Christian, Northam. Alex. 35.
1782.	Winterborn, — (?), Middlesex, Jan.
1784.	Winterburn, Will., Pts. Rockingham.
1786.	Winterbourn, Mary, Oxford, Feb. Norfolk.
1788.	Whitbourn, Francis. Calvert.
1790.	„ David, Surrey. Bishop.
1792.	Winterborn, Phillis, Bucks. Fountain.
1794.	Weatherby, James. Cambridge. Holman.
1802.	„ Edward, Parts., July. Admon.
1806.	Winterbourne, Henry, Durham. Pitt.
1808.	Wetherby Thomas Moses, Parts. Admon.
1812.	Weatherby. John, Parts. Admon.
1823.	Winterburn, Will. Comm. Ct., London.
1825.	Weatherby, Joseph, Bucks., Jan. Admon.
1826.	Weatherburn, Jane (formerly Davis), Kent, Nov. Admou. Consist. Court, London.
1828.	Weatherby, Sophia, London, Dec.
1831.	„ William, Suffolk, April.
„	„ James, Middlesex, Sept.
1833.	Winterborne, John, Loudon, April. Con. Court, London
1840.	Weatherby, Sarah, Chester, Feb.
1841.	„ Martha. „ July.
1843.	„ Mary, Bath, May.
1845.	Winterburn, Thomas, Middlesex, Jan. Con. Court, London.
1846.	Winterburn. Elizabeth, Middlesex, April. Con. Court, London.
1852.	Winterborne. Hannah, London, April Con. Court, London.
1857.	Weatherby, Elizabeth, Berks, Dec.
1858.	„ Isaac, Durham, April 19.
1860.	„ Richard, Leek, co. Stafford, May 17.
1860.	„ Henry, Burslem, Sept. 1.
1863.	„ William, Chester, July 24.
„	„ Susannah, Durham, Oct. 19.
1866.	„ Thomas, Leek, co. Stafford, June 26.
1867.	„ Henrietta Hill, Cambridge, June 1.
1868.	„ Henrietta Hill, Ireland, Feb. 27.
1870.	„ William, Congleton, Chester, April 20,
„	„ John, Chester, July 11.
1871.	„ Thomas, „ April 24.
1872.	„ Harriett, Newmarket, Oct. 3.
1873.	„ Henry, Shrewsbury, April 4.
1875.	„ Joseph, Lancaster, May 11.
1876.	„ Maria, Chester, Dec. 9.
1879.	„ Joseph, Lancaster, March 24.
1880.	„ Charles, Middlesex, Sept. 14.
„	„ Mary, Shrewsbury, Nov. 17.
1882.	„ Mary Ann, Sydenham, Feb. 13.
1883.	„ John, Lancaster, April 3.
„	„ James, Aughton, Lancs., July 14.

Heralds' College Papers. In June 1891 I had a general search made at the Heralds' College in London for any Wedderburn material preserved there, and in response received the following list of references :—

Hawker's Index :—Peers, ii. 10 (Record) ; Peers (rough), i. 159, iii. 131 ; Baronets, ii. 521, 527-28 (Record), 8 D. 14. 58-59 (Record) ; L. xxxiii 280 ; xl. 121 ; xli. 194. H.-Z, xxvi. 278 ; xxvii. 177. B and P, K. iii. 138 ; D. ii. 403-12, vi. 134. W.C. Peers, i. 34-35. Barts., ii. 70. To these must now be added one later reference—"Norfolk, xvi. 94."

I was also informed that nothing material was to be found in the collections of Philipot, Vincent, Radcliffe, St. George Warburton, Francis Townshend, Sir Ralph Bigland, and Sir Charles G. Young.[1]

The material thus obtained is not very extensive. It consists of four pedigrees (1782—1893), which are termed "records," that is to say, that the facts stated in them have been accepted as proved by the Heralds' College, after a presumably strict examination. So far as these facts are obviously within the knowledge of the person signing the recorded pedigree, they may be said to be legally proved by these documents. In addition to these records there are three licenses for a change of surname and arms, a few casual notes, and one or two unrecorded "hearsay" pedigrees of little value.

The whole of the material may be classified thus :—

I. Pedigree of Alexander Wedderburn, Lord Loughborough, recorded on his elevation to the peerage, 1783, together with certain material relating thereto, and, later, an additional draft pedigree, which was never recorded.

II. Pedigree of Sir David Wedderburn, first baronet of Ballindean, recorded on his creation as a baronet, 1803, together with a note of the registration of his arms.

III. Pedigree of John Wedderburn of Spring Garden (son of Thomas Wedderburn of Cantra), recorded 1799.

IV. Pedigree of the descent from Thomas Wedderburn of Cantra, recorded 1892.

V. Licenses to assume and bear certain surnames and arms.

VI. Some casual notes.

I.

Pedigree of Alexander Wedderburn, Lord Loughborough, recorded (1782) soon after his elevation to the peerage.

(i.) The Recorded Pedigree (Peers ii. 10.)

ARMS.—The Wedderburn shield bearing a shield of preteuce (vert. a wavy bend charged with three martlets) being the arms of his first wife ; see pedigree. Above the shield is a baron's coronet, and above that an eagle's head and the motto, "Illæso lumine solem."

Peter Wedderburn of Chester Hall, in the shire of Haddington, one of the Lords of Session in Scotland. Son and heir of *Alexander Wedderburn*, a commissioner of the excise, youngest son of *Sir Peter Wedderburn* of Gosford in the said shire. Bart. D. 11 August 1756 ; buried in the Grey Friers New Church Yard, Edinburgh.	=*Janet*, daughter of *David Ogilvy*, Esq., Captain in the first Regiment of Dragoons ; died in June 1771, and was buried at Kensington in the county of Middlesex.			

Alexander Wedderburn, one of His Majesty's Privy Council and Lord Chief Justice of the Common Pleas. Created 14 June 1780 Lord Loughborough, Baron of Loughborough in the county of Leicester, to him and the heirs male of his body.	=*Betty Anne*, sole child and heir of *John Dawson* of Morley, in the county of York. Married at Battley in the said county 31 Dec. 1767. Died 15 Feb. 1781; buried at Morley.	*David Wedderburn*, a Brigadier General in the service of the East India Company and Colonel of His Majesty's forces;slain at the re-taking of Baroah in 1773. Unmarried.	*Janet*, only dau.	=*Sir Henry Erskine*, of Alva, Baronet, Lieutenant-Gen. Col. of the Royal Regiment. Died at York in July 1765.

Sir James Erskine, Baronet.	John Erskine.	Henrietta Maria Erskine.

This Pedigree proved before the Committee of Privileges in the House of Lords 27 May 1782.

Ralph Bigland, Garter.
Isaac Heard, Clarenceux.

[1] See as to these writers and heralds *Noble's History of the College of Arms.*

In compiling this pedigree recourse would seem to have been had to the Lyon Office in Edinburgh, from one of whose officials, James Cummyng, a letter and some enclosures was received by the Heralds' College in London, among whose papers they still remain. (Beltz and Pullman's Collection, B. ii. 403-12.) **Heralds' College Papers.**

(ii.) *Letter from James Cummyng, of the Lyon Office, Edinburgh, to the Heralds' College, London.*[1]

Sir,—Immediately on receipt of your letter of the 17th, I made an exact survey of the monumental inscriptions in Gray Friars church yard here (Edinburgh) and found but one relating to the family of Wedderburn, in the inclosed part of the burying ground on the south side where there is a long inscription in English cut in small letters on a white stone, but so much defaced on account of the badness of the stone as to be almost illegible[2] ; the first four lines are larger, and though much obscured appear to be as follows :—

> Here lies interred
> Alexander Wedderburn, Esquire,
> Younger son of Sir Peter Wedderburn
> of Gosford, one of the Senators of the
> Colledge of Justice ...

In the churchyard of Dundee there is the following monumental Inscription over the burial place of Alexander Wedderburn of Easter Powrie, the brother's son of James Wedderburn of Blackness, Esq., mentioned in the Birth-brief.

"Conditur hoc tumulo Alexander Wedderburn Dominus de Easter Powrie. Familiae suæ princeps, nuperrime huic urbi praefectus, ejusdem ad Parliamentum primum Supremi Domini nostri regia Caroli II delegatus; obiit 9 die Aprilis A.D. 1683, ætat 68. Hic etiam conquiescunt ossa Elizabethæ Ramsay illius primi amoris uxoris, filiæ unicæ Joannis Ramsay, Fratris Domini de Murie hujusque urbis olim prætoris, quæ obiit 2 Apr. 1643, ætat 22."

In the same burying ground is the following inscription over the burial place of Sir Alexander Wedderburn of Blackness, elder brother of Sir Peter Wedderburn of Gosford, Lord of Session, mentioned in the enclosed Birth-brief :—

"Hic jacet D. Alexander Wedderburn, Dominus de Blackness, Civitatis Taodunauac secretarius dignissimus, qui obiit 18 Nov. 1676, aetat suae 66."

Also the following :—"......Elizabetha Wedderburna ex antiqua Wedderburuorum familia oriunda Roberto Moravio marito sibique in memoriam ponebat quae post aliquos annos virum secuta obiit......

> Mors sola fatetur
> Quantula sunt hominum corpuscula."

There is in the churchyard at Coupar in Fife an inscription over the bodies of James Wedderburne, minister of Moonsie, and William his son.[3]

There is no record of any escutcheon used at the funerals of any of the persons mentioned in yours, but I have compiled from sundry evidents the enclosed birth-brief or proof of gentility of the two gentlemen you mention, from which the sixteen branches of the funeral escutcheons as exhibited in this country are taken. The Escutcheons of Sir Peter Wedderburn of Gosford and of Peter his grandson, who was a Lord of Session, if you think it necessary, shall likewise be made out but as you are desirous to have a return soon I send what is ready and shall wait your further orders. I am sir, your most ob[t] humble servant,
John Cummyng.

[1] With these papers is placed another pedigree, apparently a draft of the recorded one opposite, though it differs from it by reason of some additions, and one or two errors, viz., "Kennington" for "Kenshigtou," and "Henrietta, Maria" for "Henrietta Maria." Lord Loughborough's shield is inserted on an interleaf.

Alexander Wedderburn, youngest son=Mary Daes, daughter and	
of Sir Peter Wedderburn of Gosford in	heiress of John Daes of
the county of Haddington in Scotland,	Coldingknows in the
Commissioner of Excise.	county of Berwick.

Peter Wedderburn of Chester Hall, co.=Janet, daughter of David Ogilvy, Captain 11th	
Haddington aforesaid, one of the Lords	Regiment Dragoons. Ob June 1771. Buried
of Session in Scotland. Ob. 1756.	at Kennington, co. Middlesex.

Alexander Wed-=Betty Anne, only sur-	David Wedderburn, Colonel of	Janet,=Sir Henry Er-
derburn (same	viving child of John	Foot and Brigadier-General, in	born	skine, Bart., of
as the recorded	Dawson of Morley,	East Indian Company's service.	at —	Alva, d. at York
pedigree (a), but	Yorkshire, m. at Bat-	Slain at the taking of Baroach,		1765.
adds, "born at	ley in co. Yorkshire.	near Bombay 1774. Adminis-		
Ediuburgh ").	17—.	tration 22 Feb. 1774.		

Sir James Erskine,	John	Henrietta.	Maria.
Baronet.	Erskine.		

[2] It is now (1895) quite illegible.

[3] The last two epitaphs appear to be mentioned on the authority of Menteith's *Theater of Mortality*, and not on that of the original tombstones, which are now quite undiscoverable.

(a.) Birth-brief of the Wedderburns of Gosford, showing sixteen descents.

Heralds' College Papers.	David Wedderburn of Hilltown, Esq., mar. Helen, d. of Robert Lawson of Humbie.	John Ramsay of Jordinestown and Brachmont, mar. Isabella, d. of David Boswell of Balnuto.	Andrew Goldman of Sandford, mar. Jean, d. of Wm. Stewart of Grandtully.	Robert Jack of Woodhall, mar. Margaret, d. of Henry Foulis of Colinton.	Robert Dickson of Hartree mar. Anne, d. of John Eccles of Eccles.	Robert Boog of Staine m. Mary, d. of Wm. Duding ton of Sandford.	John Ramsay of Jordinestown and Brachmont mar. Isabella. d. of David Boswell of Balnuto.	George Gibson of Goldingstones, father of the President Sir Alexander, of Durie, mar. Mary, d. of Wm. Airth of Airth.
	Alexander Wedderburn of Kingennie. ═ Helen, d. of John Ramsay of Jordinestown and Brachmont.		James Goldman of Sandford. ═ Janet. d. of Robert Jack of Woodhall.		John Dickson of Hartree. ═ Agnes, d. of Robert Boog of Staine.		Robert Ramsay of Brachmont. ═ Mary, d. of George Gibson of Goldingstones.	
	James Wedderburn of Blackness, chief of that ancient surname. ═ Margaret, d. of James Goldman of Sandford.				John Dickson of Hartree, Lord of Session 1 Nov. 1649. ═ Jean, d. of Robert Ramsay of Brachmout.			

Sir Peter Wedderburn of Gosford, ═ Agnes, d. of John Dickson admitted a Lord of Session 17 | of Hartree.
July 1668.

John Wedderburn, Esq., apparent heir of Gosford.	Sir Peter Wedderburn of Gosford.	Alexander Wedderburn, one of the Commissioners of Excise in Scotland.

[This birth-brief is full of errors, due, no doubt, to Douglas. Alexander Wedderburn of Kingennie was not the son, nor a descendant even, of David Wedderburn and Helen Lawson; his wife's father was Alexander Ramsay of Dundee, and her mother a Spens not a Boswell; their son James was never "of Blackness" (though his son was) nor was he chief of his name as his eldest brother's line male line did not expire till 1761, and lastly his wife's mother's name was Margaret not Janet. These are some only of the errors, to which a close knowledge of the other families referred to would probably add a considerable number.—A. W.]

(b.) Notes relative to Lord Loughborough's family.[1]

1. 1714. Dec. 9. **1726.** Oct. 21. **1727.** Nov. 9.—Alexander Wedderburn constituted of the Commissioners of H.M. Revenues of Excise in Scotland.

2. 1730. Jan. 1.—Died at Edinburgh, Alexander Wedderburn, Commissioner of Excise.

3. 1733. May 8.—James Wedderburne to be Clerk of the Common Pleas in South Carolina.

4. Alexander Wedderburn ob. Jan. 1 1729-30. Peter Wedderburn ob. Aug. 1756. Janet Wedderburn ob. June 1771.

5. 1774. Feb. 22.—David Wedderburn, administrator to Alexander Wedderburn, brother of David Wedderburn, late Brigadier-General and Commander-in-Chief of the Hon. East India Company's forces at Bombay, and Major in 27th Regiment of Foot on half-pay at Bombay, Esq., Bachelor, deceased.

6. Escutcheon for funeral of John Wedderburn of Gosford in 1688, and for that of Peter Wedderburn of Gosford, his father, who d. between 1671 and 80.

7. 1771. April 12.—Administration, James Wedderburn. Administration to Keen Stables, attorney of John Halkett. Esquire, brother and next-of-kin of James Wedderburn, late of Heath, co. York, ensign belonging to Sir William Pepperel's regiment of Foot, a bachelor, deceased.

[1] In addition to the above there are also the following four further pedigrees :—

1. A rough draft of the above record, adding only the date of Lord Loughborough's birth, "Born 13 Feb. 1733," and a note that he "took his seat 19 June 1780." (Peers, Rough, i. 159.)

2. A draft of the above record. (H-Z, Vol. 26, p. 278.)

3. Another draft pedigree (Peers, Rough, iii. 131), which, being made later, gives certain additions :—
   (a.) Lord Loughborough's later honours, vizt., the second Loughborough patent (31 Oct. 1795) with remainder to Sir James Erskine, John Erskine, and their heirs male, and the Earldom of Rosslyn patent (21 April 1801) with similar remainders.
   (b.) Lord Loughborough's second marriage to "Charlotte, youngest daughter of William Courtenay, Viscount Courtenay, and aunt of the present Viscount Courtenay, born at Powderham. Baptized 28 Feb. 1750-51, married Sept. 12 1782."
   (c.) Under the name of Janet, Lady Erskine, it adds in pencil, "died June 1797."
   (d.) It describes Sir James Erskine as of Dysart, and his brother John as of Lincoln's Inn, Barrister-at-law.

4. Another copy of No. 3 which adds that Sir James Erskine took the name of St. Clair by Royal Sign Manual, June 9 1789. (Beltz and Pullman, vi. 134.)

II.

The pedigree of Sir David Wedderburn, Bart.. 1803, as recorded in the Heralds' College, London, with a note of the registration of his arms (Baronets ii. 526-7.)

Heralds' College Papers.

(a.) *The Recorded Pedigree.*[1]

The Wedderburn Arms aud Crest (but no motto or supporters).

Sir Alexander Wedderburn, Knight, Town Clerk of Dundee. Knighted by King $\mp$ Matilda, daughter of Charles I. A° 1642. Died 28 November 1676, aged 66. Buried at Dundee. Fletcher of Inner-pessor.

Sir John Wedderburn, eldest son and $\mp$ Rachel, daughter heir, had a charter of the lands of the of David Duns-Barony of Blackuess A° 1668. Created a moir, Esq. *Baronet* by patent dated August 9, 1704.

James Wedder- $\mp$ Elizabeth, daûr. of Ro-burn, 2nd son, bert Davidson of Balgay died A° 1696. in Angus, Esq.

Sir Alexander $\mp$ Elizabeth, eldest daûr. Wedderburne of Sir Alex Seton of of Blackness, Pitmeddeu, Baronet. Baronet, son One of the Senators of and heir, d. the College of Justice. 1713.

David Wedderburn, 2nd son, a Major in the army, killed at the siege of Douay. S.P.

Sir Alexander Wedderburn, $\mp$ Katherine, eldest sou and heir, purchas- daur. of ed Blackness of his cousin Sir John Scott John, aud assumed the title of Dundee, of *Baronet* on his cousin's merchant. decease in 1722.

Sir John Wedder-burne of Blackness, only sou and heir, died unmarried in 1722.

Sir John Wedderburn of $\mp$ Jean, eldest daur. Blackness aforesaid as- of John Fullerton sumed the title of *Baronet* of that Ilk. Died upou the decease of his about 1766. father. Forfeited aud died in 1746.

Robert Wedder-burn of Pearsie in the county of Angus, Esq..2nd son, married and had issue.

Thomas Wedder-burn of Inver-ness, &c., Esq., 3rd son, married and left issue.

1st wife. $\mp$ John Wedder- $\mp$ 2ud wife. Margaret burn of Black- Alicia. Ogilvy. eldest ness aforesaid, daur. of daur. of David, and of Baltin- Colonel commonly dean iu the James ealled Earl of county of Dundas Airley by Mar- Perth, b. at by Mar-garet, daur. of Blackness garet, James Johu- 1728 and as- daur. of stone of West- sumed the Lord erhall, died 23 title of Bar- Forbes. March 1775, onet, d. 13 Living aged27, buried June 1803 and 1803. at Dundee. was buried at Dundee.

James Wed-derburu of In-veresk, in the coy. of E. Lo-thian. Esq. mar. daur. of Andrew Black-burn of Glas-gow. $\mp$

John Wed-derburu, of Jamaica, merchant, died there unmarried iu May 1799.

Peter and Alexander Wedder-buru, both died un-married in Jamaica.

Andrew Wedder-buru of officer in the London, East merch- aut.

David Wedder-burn, sons d. in-fants. Loudou uumd.

Peter Wed-derburn, East India Coy.'s ser-vice.

Two other

James Wedder-buru.

Margaret, mar. Richard Dundas of Blair ; both dead; leaving is-sue.

Catherine and Susanna, both died unmarried.

Agatha, ra. John Smith of Ediu-burgh, writer, and d. s.p.

Jane,only surviving daur.

John Wed-derburn, eldest son, died about 1783, aged 13, and was buried at Clap-ham in Surrey.

David Wedder- $\mp$ Margaret, burn of Baltin- 2nd daur. dean aforesaid, of George Esq., ouly sur- Brown of viving son and Illisten, heir, born there eo. Rox. 10 March 1775 ; md. at Comrie, eo. Perth, Sept. 1800.

Margaret, md. May 1803 to PhilipDundas, Esq., M.P. for Gatton, ne-phew of Henry, Viscouut Mel-ville.

Jane, boru at Baltin-dean.

James, John, Al-exander, all boru at Baltin-dean a-foresaid.

Louisa Doro-thea, md. Feb. 1803 to Maj. General John Hope, brother of James, Earl of Hopetoun.

Mary, Auue, both born at Baltin-dean a-fore-said.

Living 1803 unmd.

John Wedderburn, only issue, b. 16 Oct. 1802, baptd. in the parish of St. George, Hauover Square.

The above Pedigree of my family is true to the best of my knowledge, information, and belief. Witness my hand this 11 Oct. 1803.
David Wedderburn.

Signed in the presence of Isaac Heard, Garter.

[1] The arrangement of this pedigree has been slightly altered from that of the original MS. to suit the printed page. It contains several errors. Sir Alexander Wedderburn, Kut., died 18 Nov, and more probably in 1675 than 1676. His wife was the daughter of James Fletcher, provost of Dundee ; his grandson, Sir Alexander, second baronet, died in 1710 not 1713, and his great grandson, Sir John, third baronet, in 1723 not 1722. The expression "assumed the title" used of the fourth and fifth baronets is misleading. as there was no question of their right of succession under the limitations of the (1704) patent. Baltindeau in the latter part is, of course, an error for Ballindean.

(b.) *Note of the registration of his Arms.*[1]

"To all and singular to whom these Presents shall come We, the King's Heralds and Pursuivants of the College of Arms, London, do hereby certify that the Family Arms and Pedigree of David Wedderburn of Ballindean, in the county of Perth, Esq., have been duly registered in this College pursuant to the Tenor of His Majesty's warrant under his royal signet and sign manual bearing date the third day of December 1783 for correcting and preventing abuses in the Order of Baronets. In witness, &c., 20 August, 43, G. III. (1803.)"

[Although this note exists, there is no such registration at the Heralds' College as it implies, and the authorities there are unable to explain the matter.—A.W.]

(c.) *An Account of the Expenses in Passing a Patent creating David Wedderburn, Esq. a Baronet, with one Remainder.*[2]

Secretary of State.	£	s.	d.
King's Warrant to the Att⁷ Gen[1]	35	1	0

The Attorney General.		£	s.	d.	£	s.	d.
Bill and Stamps	...	44	10	0			
Ingrossing Clerk	...	2	12	6			
Transcripts	...	11	7	0			
Gratuity ...	...	4	4	0			
					62	13	6

Privy Seal.		£	s.	d.	£	s.	d.
Fees and Stamps	...	19	5	0			
Office Keeper	...	1	1	0			
Gratuity ...	...	5	5	0			
Private Seal	...	2	0	0			
					27	11	0

Signet.		£	s.	d.	£	s.	d.
Fees	...	18	17	0			
Gratuity ...	...	5	5	0			
Office Keeper	...	1	1	0			
					25	3	0

College of Arms.		£	s.	d.	£	s.	d.
Register's Fee for Recording Pedigree	...	6	13	4			
Illuminating Armorial Ensigns		12	6				
Register for Recording Copy of Writ of Privy Seal dated 9th Aug⁵ 1704 advancing J. Wedderburn, Esq⁷ to the Dignity of a Baronet	...	2	6	8			
Fee for Certificate ...	...		13	4			
Corporation Seal ...	...	3	6	8			
Compilation Fee, and searching at the Offices for the Patent of Creation of John Wedderburne, Esq⁷ in 1704	...	11	11	0			
					25	3	6
Carried forward	...	£175	12	0			

	£	s.	d.	£	s.	d.
Brought forward	...			175	12	0
Crown Office.						
Receipt and Remainder	3	19	0			
Deputy Purse Bearer	1	1	0			
Lord Chancellor's Gentlemen	3	0	0			
Porter to the Great Seal		10	6			
Earl Marshall	3	13	6			
King's Household	62	11	6			
English Heralds	9	3	6			
Principal Usher of Scotland	5	0	0			
Scotch Heralds	9	3	6			
Crown Office, 1st Skin	6	0	0			
Dividend and Docquet	2	7	0			
Crown Office, 2nd skin	4	1	0			
Dividend ...	1	7	0			
Crown Office, 3rd Skin	4	1	0			
Dividend ..	1	7	0			
Remainder	5	7	0			
Stamps	48	1	0			
Boxes ...	1	6	0			
Deputy Clerk of the Crown	4	4	0			
Ingrossing Clerk	3	3	0			
Sealer and Chaff Wax and Deputys	1	10	6			
Hanaper ...	12	1	0			
Ditto, Remainder	2	10	0			
Deputy Hanaper	1	1	0			
Mess⁷ to Heralds' Office		2	6			
Heralds for Registering	2	10	0			
Private Seal	2	0	0			
				201	1	6
Sundries.						
Stamp Duty on King's Warr⁵	1	7	6			
Gazetting ...	1	1	0			
Under Marshalmen at St. James	2	2	0			
Under Porter ditto ..	1	1	0			
Yeoman of the Guard	1	1	0			
Queen's Porter ...	1	1	0			
Prince of Wales' Porter	1	1	0			
Messenger ...	1	11	6			
				10	6	0
				£386	19	6

[1] There is also at the Heralds' College a notarial copy of the patent of the Blackness baronetcy (1704), but this has been already given from the original, ante s. Blackness Papers No. 77 (3).

[2] I have added, from the original in the possession of Sir William Wedderburn, Bart., the above account of expenses, &c., which is not without interest.

Heralds' College Papers.

III.

Pedigree of John Wedderburn of Spring Garden (son of Thomas Wedderburn of Cantra) recorded 1799 (S D. 14, 58-59).[1]

ARMS :—The Wedderburn shield, bearing a shield of pretence (Vert, a chevron Argent, charged with three mullets azure, between two garbs of the second, banded gules, in chief and in base a cock rousant. or).[2] MOTTO :—Non Degener. CREST :—An Eagle's Head.

Sir Alexander Wedderburn of Blackness, in the county of Angus, in Scotland, Baronet of Nova Scotia. Died Anno 1741 ═ Katharine, daughter of John Scott of Dundee.

Sir John Wedderburn of Blackness aforesaid, ried and eldestson, had issue, died 1746.	Robert Wedderburn, 2nd son, married	Catherine, wife of David Schrymgeour of BurkHill, near Dundee in Scotland, Esq. Both dead leaving issue.	Thomas Wedderburn of Inverness and Cantra, 3rd son, born at Blackness April 1701, d. in Jan. 1771, buried at Cantra. ═	Katharine, 2nd da. ofRobertDunbar of Gruuge Hill, in the parish of Dyke, in the county of Moray. Born there 22 July1722and there married 20 Sept. 1740. Living 1799.	Elizabeth, married to Alexander Reid of Torbeg in Angus, Esq., and had issue.	Grisel, married to Jas. Graham of Methie, Esq., and died without issue.

Alexander Wedderburn of Westmoreland in the Island of Jamaica, Esq.,eldest son, born 28 Aug. 1741, died unm. 10 Feb. 1770. Buried at Westmoreland aforesaid.	John Wedderburn of Clapham, in the county of Surrey, Esq., 2nd son, born at Fortrose in Scotland, 19 August 1743. Living in 1799. ═	Mary Wisdom, dau. and heir of George Bedward ofWestmoreland aforesaid, Esq , borntherel June 1764, and married there27May 1782. Living 1799.	James Wedderburn of Westmoreland aforesaid, Esq., 3rd son,born 28Sept. 1751. Died unm. 17 July 1797, buried at Westmoreland aforesaid.	Katharine, b. 1 Oct. 1744. Living unm. 1799. Robina, b. 28 January 1749. Died unm. at Edinburgh. Thomasina, b. 7 March1750,died unmarried19May1797 buried at Edinburgh.	Elizabeth, b. 8 March 1747, married and has issue.

Elizabeth Susanna,born in the parish of Westmoreland aforesaid 1 January 1784.	Mary, born in the parish of Westmoreland aforesaid2 Aug. 1786.	James Wedderburn.born in the parish of Westmoreland aforesaid2 June1788.	KatharineGeorgina, born in the parish of St. Pancras, in the county of Middlesex 1 Feb. 1791.	Thomasine, born in the parish of St. Pancras aforesaid 19 Sept. 1793.	John Wedderburn, born at Clapham,in the county of Surrey 8 January 1798.

I do hereby certify the above pedigree of my family to be true to the best of my knowledge and belief. Witness my hand the 14th June 1799.

John Wedderburn.

---

[1] Here again the arrangement of the pedigree has been a little altered from that of the MS. record to suit the printed page. It contains several errors. Sir Alexander d. 1744 not 1741. Thomas Wedderburn was born 1710 not 1701 and, died, according to the date on his tomb, in 1769 not 1771.

[2] These arms are engraved of a seal and on several pieces of family plate formerly belonging to John Wedderburn. They are, presumably, the arms of his wife, but do not agree with the Bedward arms as given by J. W., who, in his printed volume, records them as "Argent, an orle gules, and in chief three martlets sable.

(8 D xiv, 58-59.)

Sir Alexander Wedderburn, of Blackn
baronet of Nova Scotia ; b. 4 Nov. 1675
Sept. 1744. M.I.

1. Sir John Wedder-burn, of Blackness af'sd, baronet, eldest surviving son ; d. in 1746.	2. Robert Wedderburn, second surviving son.	3. Thomas Wedderburn, of Inverness=Katharine, second dau. of Alex and of Cantra, co. Inverness, third surviving son ; b. at Blackness 2 and bap. 5 Apr. 1710 at Dundee ; d. in Dec. 1766 ; bur. at Cantra af'sd. M.I.	son of Robert Dunbar, of Gran parish of Dyke, co. Moray, b. 1722 ; mar. there 20 Sep. 1740 ; d 12 Feb. 1818, aged 95, bur. in Chapel Cemetery there. M.I.

1. Alexander Wedderburn, of Westmoreland, in the island of Jamaica, eldest son and heir ; b. at Grange Hill af'sd, 20 Aug. 1741 ; d. unmar. 10 Feb. 1770 ; bur. at Westmoreland af'sd.	2. John Wedderburn, of Clapham, co.=Mary Wisdom, dau. and heir of Surrey, second son ; b. at Forres, co. Elgin, 19 Aug. 1743 ; bap. there 22 of same month; d. at Chigwell, co. Essex, 29 Dec. 1820 ; bur. in St. James' Chapel, Hampstead road, co. Middlesex.	George Bedward, of Westmore-land af'sd ; b. there 1 June 1764 ; mar. there 27 May 1782 ; d. at Epsom, co. Surrey, 17 Mar. 1835; bur. in St. James' Chapel af'sd.	3. Ji burn, land a 1751s nish, c unma

1. James Wedderburn, of=Isabella, dau. of David Lyon, of Upper Seymour street, and afterwards of Clarges street, both co. Middlesex, eldest son and heir ; b. at Westmoreland af'sd 2 June 1788; bap. there; d. at Clarges street af'sd 23 Apr. 1831 ; bur. in St. James' Chapel af'sd ; first husband.	Portland Place, in the parish of St. Marylebone, co. Middlesex ; mar. at St. Marylebone Parish Church 5 July 1817; remar. at St. George's. Hanover Square, 8 Oct. 1836 to Sir Charles Howe Fremantle, G.C.B., Admiral R N., (who died s.p. 25 May 1869, aged 68, and was bur. at Brompton Cemetery); she d. 26 Dec. 1876 : bur. at Brompton Cemetery af'sd.	2. John Wedder-=Helen (commonly burn, of Bedding-ton, co. Surrey, and Auchterhouse, co. Forfar, second and youngest son; b. at Clapham, co. Surrey, 8 Jan. 1798 ; d. 2 Apr. 1839 ; bur. at Auchter-house af'sd.	called Lady Helen Wedderburn), young-est dau. of Walter Ogilvy, fifth Earl of Airlie ; b. 12 Feb. 1798 ; mar. privately at Airlie Castle, co. Forfar, 30 Apr. 1823; d. 29 Apr. 1868; bur. at Roslin Chapel, co. Midlothian.	1 a e l p n J 2 a b c

John Kellerman Wedderburn, of Upper=Charlotte, third dau. of Sir Tho-Seymour Street, and afterwards of Lowndes Square, and subsequently of Cadogan Place, all co. Middlesex, only child and heir ; b. in Upper Seymour Street af'sd 13 Feb. 1818 ; d. at Cadogan Place af'sd 4 June 1891 ; bur. at Kensal Green Cemetery, co. Middlesex.	mas McMahon, Baronet, G.C.B., Adjutant-General of Her Majesty's Forces in India, Lieutenant-Gover-nor of Portsmouth, Colonel of 10th Regiment of Foot ; b. 15 Feb. 1823 ; mar. 23 Feb. 1848 at Bombay ; living a widow 1892, she died . . .	1. John Walter Wedderburn,=Marga-Lieut.-Colonel Royal Perth-shire Militia and formerly Captain 42nd Highlanders ("Black Watch") Regiment; eldest son and heir ; b. 20 July 1824 at Beddington af'sd ; d. at Blairgowrie, co. Perth, 20 July 1879 ; bur. at Auchterhouse af'sd.	Thon Capta Regin Castl ham, living Marfi 1892.

Emily Frederica, eldest dau. and co-heir ; b. at Poona, Bombay Presi-dency, India, 21 Apr. 1844 ; mar. at St. Paul's, Knightsbridge, co. Mid-dlesex, 2 July 1863, to Carey John Knyvett, of Eccleston Square, co. Middlesex, C.B. Principal Clerk in the Home Office ; both living 1892.	Isabella Lottie, second and youngest dau. and coheir : b. in the parish of Marylebone 2 May 1854 ; mar. at St. Paul's, Knightsbridge af'sd, 30 Apr. 1874 to Henry Blackburne Hamilton, Lieut.-Colonel of the 14th Hussars ; she d. at Sialkote, Punjab, 6 Dec. 1881 ; bur. at Kensal Green Ceme-tery af'sd ; he living 1892.	John Walter Maurice Wedderburn, clerk, In-cumbent of St. Peter's Church, Stornoway, Isle of Lewis, eldest son and heir ; b. 17 Mar. 1855 ; bap. at Trinity Church, Stirling, 27 Apr. follow-ing; living unmar. 1892.	Charles Davi derburn, Ass Engineer, (Bhavnagar I thiawa, in the Bombay, see gest son ; b. bap. at Rosli 21 Mar. fol unmar. 1892

[Even in this recent record it has been impossible to avoid one or two errors and omissions. Thus the d
Scott's death has since been ascertained to be 1761-62 ; that of Thomas Wedderburn is wrongly given as 1766 ; w
born, it appears, in 1720 not 1722 and was aged 97 at her death, and the last words of the account of his sister G
"co. Angus. She d. s.p." as her husband married again and had issue.]

Thomas Wedderburn of Cantra.

Katharine, dau. of John Scott, of Dundee af'sd ; b. 16 Sep. 1680 ; mar. 17 Oct. 1697.

1. Alexander Wedderburn, ourth surviving and youngest on ; b. 13 Sep. 1718 ; d. inmar. in 1788 ; bur. at Dunlee af'sd.	1. Catherine, mar. in Aug. 1739 to David Scrymgeour, of Birkhill, near Dundee, co. Forfar.	2. Elizabeth, b. 25 Oct. 1699; mar. to Alexander Reid, of Torbeg, co. Angus.	3. Grisel, b. 26 July 1706; mar. to James Graham, of Methie, co. Aberdeen (who d. s.p.)	Four sons and four daughters, all of whom d. in infancy before 1717.

. Mary, b. at Forress, o. Elgin, 13 Sept. 1742; ap. there 18 same nonth ; d. unmar. at Quebec in the Dominion of Canada in 1772.	2. Katherine, b. at Rosemarkie, otherwise Fortrose af'sd, 1 Oct. 1744; bap. there same day ; d. unmar. at Edinburgh 22 Feb. 1825 ; bur. at Buccleugh Chapel Cemetery af'sd.	3. Elizabeth, b. and bap. at Rosemarkie af'sd, 8 Mar. 1747 ; mar. . . . Blyth ; she d. at Aberdeen 8 Feb. 1819 ; bur. in Old Aberdeen Cemetery.	4. Robina, b. and bap. at Rosemarkie af'sd, 28 Jau. 1749 ; d. unmar. 16 Dec. 1796 ; bur. in the Buccleugh Chapel Cemetery af'sd. M.I.	5. Thomasina, b. and bap. at Rosemarkie af'sd, 7 Mar. 1750 ; d. unmar. 19 May 1797 ; bur. in the Buccleugh Chapel Cemetery af'sd. M.I.

Andrew Colvile (formerly Andrew Wedderburn), of Crombie, o. Fife, and of Leadenhall street, u the City of London ; b. 6 Nov. 1779 ; by Royal Licence, dated 2 June 1814, he and his issue were uthorised to assume and bear the urname of Colvile only, and to ear the arms of Colvile, of Ochilree ; d. 3 Feb. 1856 ; bur. at he churchyard of Holy Trinity, Brompton, co. Middx. M.I.	= Mary Louisa, second wife (commonly called the Hou. Mary Louisa Colvile), fifth dau. of William Eden, first Lord 1788 ; mar. at the Chapel of Bromley Palace, co. Kent, 26 June 1806 ; d. 2 Dec. 1858 ; bur. at Churchyard of Holy Trinity, Brompton af'sd	2. Mary, second dau.; b. at Bluecastleaf'sd 2 Aug. 1786 ; mar. at St Marylebone Parish Church 7 June 1817 to John Wellings, clerk, chaplain to Lord Selkirk (who d. in Nov. 1840, and was bur. at Epsom af'sd) ; she d. 6 Apr. 1858 ; bur. at Mary's, Dunblane, co. Perth.	3. Katharine Georgiana, third dau. ; b. at St. Pancras, co. Middlesex, 1 Feb. 1791 ; mar. at St. Marylebone Parish Church 13 Feb, 1810 to Patrick Stirling, of Kippendavie, co. Perth (who d. at Hastings, co. Sussex, 30 Mar. 1816, and was bur. at Dunblane Cathedral) ; she d. 13 June 1863 ; bur. at St. Mary's, Dunblane af'sd.	4. Thomasina, fourth and youngest da. ; b. at St. Pancras af'sd 19 Mar. 1793; d. unmar. 21 Mar. 1806 ; bur. at St. James' Chapel, Hampstead af'sd.

. James Alexander Wedderburn, in the Hou. East India Company's Service (Madras Presidency) ; second sou ; b. t Beddington af'sd 1 ug. 1825 ; d. 19 May 854 ; bur. at Chingleut in the Presidency of Madras.	= Marion, fifth dau. of Sir James Cosmo Melvill, K.C.E., Under-Secretary of State for India; b. 23 Feb. 1826 ; bap. at St. James', Clerkenwell, co. Middlesex ; mar. at Hampstead, co. Middlesex, 28 Mar. 1848 ; living a widow at Cadogan Place af'sd 1892.	3. David Ogilvy Wedderburn, third and youngest son, Lieutenant in 37th Native Infantry ; b. at Beddington af'sd 18 July 1826 ; d. unmar. 2 Sep. 1853; bur. at Ootacamund in the Presidency of Madras.	Helen Georgiana Elizabeth, only dau. ; b. at Auchterhouse af'sd 9 Mar. 1830 ; mar. at Kippenross. Dunblane, co. Perth, 4 July 1871, to Andrew Webster, of Rutherford, co. Peebles (who d. s.p. 21 Sep. 1876, and was bur. at Ore, co Sussex) ; living a widow at Deaulieu, co. Southampton, 1892.	

ielen Margaret gilvy, only au. ; b. 12 ec. 1857; bap. ; St. John's hurch, Prince St., Edinurgh ; living nmar. 1892.	1. James Alexander Wedderburn, eldest son ; b. at Madras, India, 21 Jan. 1849 ; bap. there ; d. 20 Oct. 1852; bur. at Coimbatore, in the Presidency of Madras.	2. Alexander Dundas Ogilvy Wedderburn, of Cadogan Place af'sd, Barrister-at-Law of the Inner Temple, second but only surviving son and heir ; b. at Hampstead af'sd 7 Aug. 1854; privately bap. at Rosebank, Roslin af'sd ; living 1892.	= Mathilde, only child of Heury Segelcke, of Elfindale Lodge, Herne Hill, co. Surrey ; mar. at St. Stephen's Church, South Kensington, co. Middlesex, 13 Apr. 1887 ; living af'sd.	Mariou Hester, eldest dau.; b. at Ootacamund 28 Sep. 1850 ; bap. there; d. 29 Sep. 1851 ; bur. at Coimbatore af'sd.	Marion Hester, second and youngest dau. ; b. in India 29 Sep. 1852 ; bap. at Coimbatore af'sd; mar. at St. Peters', Eaton Square, co. Middlesex, 25 May 1881, to Stephen Blyth Moore, a Captain in the Royal Scots, second son of Richard Moore Killashee, co. Kildare.

Alexander Henry Melvill Wedderburn, b. at Cadogan Place af'sd 1 July 1892 ; bap. at Holy Trinity Church, Sloane Street, Chelsea, co. Middlesex, 7 Aug. following.	Margaret Griselda, b. at Sloane Street, Chelsea, co. Middlesex, 29 Apr. 1888 ; bap. at Holy Trinity Church, Sloane Street af'sd, 17 June following.

Certified (1892) &c.
Alexander Wedderburn.

Heralds'
College
Papers.

Licences to assume and bear certain surnames and arms :—

(a) To Andrew Wedderburn to assume and bear the surname and arms of Colvile, 22 June 1814. I, 40, 121.

(b) To David Wedderburn, to assume and bear the surname and arms of Webster, 13 Jan. 1790. I, 33, 280.

(c) To James Graham of Meathie to assume and bear the surname and arms of Webster, 22 July 1816. I, 41, 194.

(a)[1]

1. *License to Andrew Wedderburn Esqre. that He and his Issue may assume and bear the Surname of Colvile, and also use and bear the Arms of Colvile of Ochiltree.*

"In the Name, and on the Behalf of his Majesty, George P.R.

"George the third, by the Grace of God, of the United Kingdom of Great Britain, and Ireland, King, Defender of the Faith, &c. To our R^t trusty, and R^t entirely beloved Cousin, Charles D. of Norfolk, E.M. and H.M. of England, Greeting—

"Whereas, Andrew Wedderburn of Crombie in ye Co^y of Fife, and of Leadenhall S^t in ye City of London, Esquire, hath by his Petition, humbly represented unto Us, that we were graciously pleased in the Month of December, 1810, with the Advice and consent of the Lord Chief Baron, and the rest of the Barons of Our Exchequer of Scotland, to give and grant to the Petitioner, by the description of Andrew Colvile Esquire Merchant in London, eldest Son of Mrs Isabella Colvile of Ochiltree, by her Husband, James Wedderburn Colvile Esquire of Inveresk, and the Heirs of his body, with remainder to other heirs of the body of his said Mother ; remainder to heirs of the body of Mrs Margaret Colvile her Mother ; remainder to heirs female of the body of Andrew Ayton Merchant of Glasgow, father of the said Margaret Colvile, second son of Sir John Ayton of Codour, and Dame Margaret Colvile Lady Ayton, his Wife, eldest Sister of Robert Lord Colvile of Ochiltree, and the Heirs of their bodies ; remainder to the Right heirs of the said Robert Lord Colvile whatsoever, Subject to certain Provisions, Conditions, and Limitations, therein mentioned, certain Lands, Tenements, and Hereditaments, therein named ; which were heretofore the Lands, Tenements, and Hereditaments, of the said Robert Lord Colvile of Ochiltree, and which devolved upon the Mother of the Petitioner, by right of Inheritance, as the Lineal Descendant and Heir of the said Andrew Ayton, under and by Virtue of a certain Deed of Tailzie and Entail made by the said Robert Lord Colvile of Ochiltree, in which it is expressly conditioned, and enjoined, that if the said Andrew Ayton, or his descendants, succeed to the said Inheritance, he and they so succeeding, shall respectively be obliged, to assume, use, and bear, the surname and arms of Colvile of Ochiltree, without any addition, or alteration whatsoever : That the Petitioner being now in Possession of the Said Lands, is desirous of complying with the condition above recited ; and therefore most humbly prays, that We will be graciously pleased, to Grant him our Royal License and Authority that he and his Issue may assume, and bear, the said Surname of Colvile and no other, and also use and bear the Arms of Colvile of Ochiltree, without any addition or alteration whatsoever, according to the Condition of the said Entail and the Laws of Arms.

"Know Ye, that We of our Princely Grace and Special Favor, have given and granted, and by these presents do give and grant unto him, the said Andrew Wedderburn, our Royal License and Authority, that he and his Issue may assume and bear the said Surname of Colvile and no other, and also use and bear the arms of Colvile of Ochiltree, without any addition, or alteration whatsoever ; according to the condition of the said Entail, and the Laws of Arms ; Such arms being first duly exemplified according to the Laws of Arms ; and recorded in the Heralds' Office ; *Otherwise*, this our license and permission to be void and of none effect.

"Our Will and Pleasure, therefore is, that You, Charles, Duke of Norfolk, to whom the cognizance of matters of this nature doth properly belong, Do require and command that this our concession and declaration be recorded in Our College of Arms, to the end that our Officers of Arms, and all others upon occasion, may take full notice, and have knowledge thereof.

"And for so doing this shall be your Warrant.

"Given at our Court at Carlton House, the twenty second day of June 1814—In the Fifty fourth Year of our Reign.

> "By the Command of His Royal Highness The Prince Regent in the Name, and on the behalf of
> "His Majesty.
> "(Signed)   Sidmouth.

"Recorded in the College of Arms London, pursuant to a Warrant from The Most Noble Charles, Duke of Norfolk, Earl Marshall and Hereditary Marshall of England, and examined therewith, this 29th day of July 1814.

> (Signed)   "Ralph Bigland, Norroy-Register.
> "Francis Townsend, Windsor Herald."

---

[1] Copies of the order in Council relating to this license, the license itself, and the grant of arms thereon are among J. W.'s papers (No. 36-38, ante p. 145).

To All and Singular to whom these Presents shall come, Sir Isaac Heard, Knight, Garter, Principal King of Arms, George Harrison Esquire, Clarenceux King of Arms, and Ralph Bigland Esquire, Norroy King of Arms, send Greeting—

Whereas, His Royal Highness the Prince Regent, by Warrant under His Majesty's Royal Signet, and the Sign Manual of his Royal Highness in the Name and on the behalf of his Majesty, bearing date the twenty second day of June last signified unto the most Noble Charles, Duke of Norfolk, Earl Marshall and Hereditary Marshall of England, that He had been pleased to give and grant unto Andrew Wedderburn of Crombie in the County of Fife, and of Leadenhall Street in the City of London, Esquire, his Majesty's royal License and Permission, that He and His Issue, might, in compliance with an express condition contained in a Deed of Entail, made by Robert Lord Colvile of Ochiltree in favor of his Sister Lady Margaret Ayton, (Great Great Grand Mother of the said Andrew Wedderburn) and her Descendants, assume and bear the Surname of Colvile, and no other, and also use and bear the Arms of Colvile of Ochiltree, without any addition, or alteration, whatsoever, according to the Tenor of the said Deed of Entail, and the Laws of Arms ; Such Arms, being first duly exemplified according to the Laws of Arms, and recorded in the Heralds' Office ; otherwise the said royal Licence and Permission to be void and of none effect ;

And Forasmuch as the Said Earl Marshall did by Warrant, under his hand and Seal, bearing date the twentieth day of July last, authorize and direct Us to exemplify the Arms of Colvile of Ochiltree accordingly ;

Know ye therefore, that We the said Garter, Clarenceux, and Norroy, in Obedience to the Royal Command, in Pursuance of his Grace's Warrant, and by Virtue of the Letters Patent, of our Several Offices, to each of us respectively granted ; Do by these presents exemplify and confirm unto the said Andrew Wedderburn now Andrew Colvile, the Arms of Colvile of Ochiltree, that is to say " Argent, a Cross Moline, Sable ; and for the Crest on a wreath of the Colours, a Stag's Head, Couped at the Neck, Argent," as the same are in the margin hereof more plainly depicted, to be borne and used for ever hereafter by him, the said Andrew Colvile and his Issue, according to the Tenor of the said Royal Licence, and the Laws of Arms ; without the Let or Interruption of any Person or Persons whatsoever.

In Witness whereof We, the said Garter, Clarenceux, and Norroy, Kings of Arms, have to these presents subscribed our Names and affixed the Seals of our several Offices, this fifth day of August, in the Fifty fourth Year of the reign of our Sovereign Lord George the third, by the Grace of God, of the United Kingdom of Great Britain and Ireland King, Defender of the Faith, &c. &c.—and in the Year of our Lord, one thousand eight hundred and fourteen.

(Signed)

| Isaac Heard Garter | O | Principal King of Arms. | George Harrison Clarenceux | O | King of Arms. | Ralph Bigland Norroy | O | King of Arms. |

Recorded in the College of Arms, London, and examined therewith this 8th day of August 1814.

Ralph Bigland, Norroy, Register—Fras Townsend, Windsor Herald.

(b)
David Wedderburn, Esq.

This is similar in form to the foregoing license. The licensee is described as David Wedderburn of London, merchant, son of Robert Wedderburn of Piersie in North Britain, and the license is that he and his issue may, under the will of James Webster of Clapham, dated 14 Nov. 1789, take and bear the name of Webster only, and bear the arms of Webster.

(c)
James Graham, Esq.

Again, a similar document to that given above. The licensee is described as of Meathie and Balmuir, son of James Graham, Esq. and Elizabeth, daůr of Robert Wedderburn of Piersie, and the license is (under the will of Thomas Webster) to take the name of Webster.

VI.

Some Casual Notes.

Heralds'
College
Papers.

(a) Tabular Pedigree (Beltz and Pullman, K. iii, 138).

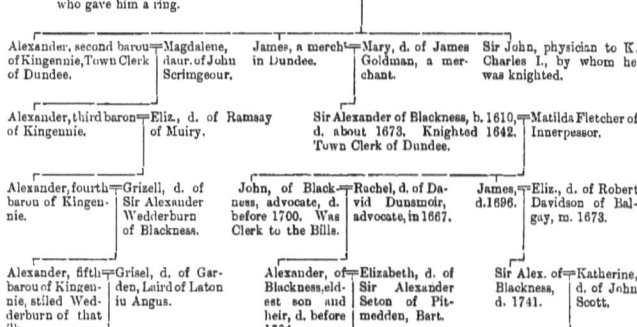

Alexander Wedderburn had the lands and barony═Helen, daur. of Ramsay of Brachmont,
of Kingennie, co. Angus, favourite of James VI., │ in Fifeshire.
who gave him a ring.

Alexander, second baron═Magdalene, of Kingennie, Town Clerk │ daur. of John of Dundee. │ Scrimgeour.	James, a merch[t]═Mary, d. of James in Dundee. │ Goldman, a mer- │ chant.	Sir John, physician to K. Charles I., by whom he was knighted.	

Alexander, third baron═Eliz., d. of Ramsay of Kingennie. │ of Muiry.	Sir Alexander of Blackness, b. 1610,═Matilda Fletcher of d. about 1673. Knighted 1642. │ Innerpessor. Town Clerk of Dundee.	

Alexander, fourth═Grizell, d. of baron of Kingen- │ Sir Alexander nie. │ Wedderburn │ of Blackness.	John, of Black-═Rachel, d. of Da- ness, advocate, d. │ vid Dunsmoir, before 1700. Was │ advocate, in 1667. Clerk to the Bills.	James,═Eliz., d. of Robert d.1696. │ Davidson of Bal- │ gay, m. 1673.

Alexander, fifth═Grisel, d. of Gar- barou of Kingen- │ den, Laird of Laton nie, stiled Wed- │ iu Angus. derburn of that │ ilk.	Alexander, of═Elizabeth, d. of Blackness, eld- │ Sir Alexander est son and │ Seton of Pit- heir, d. before │ medden, Bart. 1704.	Sir Alex. of═Katherine, Blackness, │ d. of John d. 1741. │ Scott.

David Wedderburn Grisel, heir to her of that ilk. d. unm. brother, living 17.... iu 1761.	Sir John Wedderburn of Blackness, created Bart. of Scotland to him &c., d. in Ireland 1722, unm.	Sir John of Black-═Jean, daur. of ness, executed on │ John Fuller- Kennington Com- │ ton, Esq. mon 1746.

[The above pedigree is not a "record," and contains several errors. For instance, Helen Ramsay's father was not (John) Ramsay of Brachmont, but Alexander Ramsay of Dundee, whose connection with the Brachmont family I have not ascertained. The christian name of his son James' wife was Margaret, not Mary. Sir John, the physician, was knighted by Charles II. Sir Alexander died iu 1675-76, and his wife, Matilda Fletcher, was not of Innerpessor. John of Blackness did not die before 1700, but in 1706, uor did his son Alexander die in 1704, but in 1710. His son John, agaiu, did not die in 1722 but in 1723, and it was not he, but his grandfather, who was created a baronet (in 1704). Fiually Sir Alexauder, the fourth baronet died iu 1744 not 1741.—A. W.]

(b) Genealogical Account. (H—Z, xxvii, 177.)
This is merely an MS. copy of the account of the family given iu Douglas' "Baronage of Scotland," with a tabular pedigree founded on Douglas. It is among a number of pedigrees collected by Robert Dale.

(c) A letter from Sir James Webster-Wedderburn to Debrett, containing nothing of value. (W.C., Peers, i, 34-35.)

(d) A letter from Sir James Chatterton, whose daughter Rebecca married Sir James Webster-Wedderburn's brother, Charles; also of no value. (W.C., Barts., ii, 70.)

GLOSSARY

AND

INDEX.

GLOSSARY.

I have included in this glossary most of the old and technical words used in this book. Words, however, which depend for their peculiarity merely on archaic or euphonic spelling, and which can thus be understood with but little trouble by the reader, are often omitted, as are repeated instances of words with the same termination, such as is for s, and for ing, it for ed, e.g., in actis (acts), beand (being), and askit (asked).

ABULZEAMENTIS (*abulziements, abilyementis*), clothes, but said to be distinct etymologically from "habiliments."

ACCIDENTS, the payment incidental to admission as a burgess.

ACTIS, acts, legal documents recording what has been done; thus "askit actis," *i.e.*, asked to have it recorded.

ADJUDICATION. CHARTER OF, charter granted by the crown to a creditor of the estate of his debtor in satisfaction of the debt.

ADOES (adois). business.

ADVISE, *e.g.*, advise affairs, look to, see after.

AGNATE, one related on the father's side.

AIK, oak.

AIR, heir ; *airis*, heirs ; *air by progress*, heir by virtue of the usual titles to the estate ; *airschip guidis*, moveable goods falling to the heir as such.

AIRTH, quarter from which the wind blows (*e.g.*, a room lighted to every airth) ; a particular quarter.

ALIMENT, process of legal process for the maintenance of children, wife, or parent.

AMAROLD, emerald.

AMRIE (aumrie), cupboard (Fr. armoire).

ANE, one.

ANENT, about, concerning ; *cp.* foranent.

ANIS, once.

ANNEXIS, appurtenances, things annexed to land.

ANNUAL RENT (annel-rent, @-rent, annnellis), interest on money, or mortgage ; literally, the yearly rent.

APPARENT (appeirand air), the heir apparent to a property.

APPRISING (apprysing), the same as adjudication, *q.v.*

ARBITER, arbitrator.

ARGYLEGAIT, a main street in Dundee, originally called the Ergaydillis-gat, or Ergeylis gat, probably from Ergadis, the early designation of the Argyle family. The street was also called the Overgait. See Maxwell's *Old Dundee,* p. 89 *n.*

ARRELS (or arles), earnest money given to servants to bind an engagement ; *cp.* arlis-pennie.

ARRESTMENTS, loosing, relaxing attachment for debt.

ARTAILZERIE, artillery.

ASLAMENT, easement, convenience, advantage.

ASSEDATION, a tack or letting (setting) of land for a term.

ASSIGNATION, deed assigning debts or rights to another.

ASSIZE, jury, or inquest.

ASSOILZIE, acquit.

ATTOUR, besides ; *by and attour*, over and above.

AUCHT. This sometimes means "eight," sometimes "owed."

AWAND (awin), owing.

AWARD (or awat), ground ploughed after the first crop from lea or ley ; see s. Ley.

BACKSEATS of land, backsets, subleases.

BAGINET (beginet), bayonet.

BAICK BREAD (balk breddis), kneading trough or baking board.

BAILIE (baillie, bailzie), magistrate in a burgh or in a barony, officer employed to give seisin or formal possession of land.

BAILIE-COURT, a court presided over by a bailie as magistrate.

BALLANDIS (for maddir), balances or scales for madder, a kind of dye stuff (or, quære, also a measure).

BALCLALOW, lullaby.

BAND, bond.

BARONY free, an estate holding of the crown, and erected by crown charter into a barony, with power to hold courts, inflict penalties, etc.; see s. Regality, Sheriffdom.

BASSING AND LAWAR, bason and laver (washing-jug).

BAXTER, baker.

BEAND, being.

BEE-SCAIPS (or bee-skeps), bee-hives.

BEIR, bear, *i.e.* barley.

BEITTING, building.

BENIS, beans.

BIGGING (biggin), building.

BLENCH FERME, mode of land-tenure, at a nominal or peppercorn rent ; *cp.* Blanch rent, or Free bleuch.

BLEW, blue.

BLOKIT, *sex ellis of lange*, bargained for ; *cp.* Blok, a bargain.

BOCHT, bought.

BODILY, personal (*e.g.*, bodily oath, great bodily oath), solemn oath personally given.

BODOM, bottum.

BOID, bid.

BOLL, the heaped measure of that name, *e.g.*, boll's oatmeal (measures of oatmeal), bear meal (barley meal), victual (grain generally).

BOND OF PROVISION, bond by a father, providing for his children.

BOND OF TAILLIE, entail.

BOREING, borrowing.

BOT (butt), without.

BOX MASTER, treasurer, keeper of the cashbox.

BREVE (brief), a writ from chancery authorizing an inquest or service.

BRIEVE BAUCK, a ridge of land left unploughed.

BRODER (brodir, broyr), brother, *cp.* Fayr, Moyr, Modir.

BRUCHT, burgh.

BUGGIS, lamb's wool.

BUIRDE, board.

BULGIT, a bag, budget. Fr. Boulgette.

BUR ("a toddis heid and bur "), brush (?).

BURD CLOTH, A, table cloth.

BURDING, burden.

BURGAGE, burgh law.

BURGESS AIR, the heir of a burgess.

Glossary. BURGESS TICKET, the document conferring the freedom of a burgh.

BY, apart from, e.g., "be aud by the law," according to and apart from the law.

BYRONIS, arrears.

CALSAY, causeway, street.

CANNY, cauvas ; e.g., cauny lynt, canny dammas.

CASTING UP THE HERETAOE, i.e., taking up peats on the estate (see vol. i., p. 148, n. 5).

CAUS WIN AND LEAD AWAY, cause to dry and cast away ; to "win peats" is to dry them.

CAUTIONER, surety ; coutioner, cawrie, suretyship.

CHAKKERAW, the Exchequer Row ; and also a chequered cloth or chess board.

CHALDER, a measure of sixteen bolls.

CHAMBER IRON CHIMNEY, au iron grate for a room.

CHAMLET, dyced, camlet in squares.

CHAPLAIN, chaplainry. See vol. i., p. 109, n. 1.

CHARTER, a document of title, grant from the crown or superior, the conveyance of an estate.

CHECK WHEEL, a wheel for spinning lint, with a check luserted to stop the wheel when so much is apun.

CHIMNEY CREWKES, hooks for hanging pots over the fire.

CHIMNEY GALLOWES, projecting beam ou which to hang cooking vessels.

CHIMNEY HAXES. See s. Raxes.

CHIMNEY SPEEL, a spit for roasting.

CHIRURGEON, surgeon. Gr., χειροῦργος, worker with with the hand.

CHOPIN (chappin), quart measure.

CHOPIS BAK, back shops.

CHYMNA, chimney.

CINQUEFOIL, a charge iu heraldry, consisting of five leaves.

CLARE CONSTAT, precept of, a writ granted by a subject superior for entering in a property an heir, whose right clearly appears (clare constat) from documents.

CLAYTH (claith, clath), cloth.

CLERK OF THE BILLS, the official who takes charge of the bills of complaint presented to the court.

COAD (cod), pillow or cushiou ; COADWAIR (codwair), pillow slip, cushion cover. Anglo-Saxon, codd, a bag ; waer, protection.

COBLE (cobel), e.g., of salmon, a small craft or fishing boat ; or of a kilu, a vessel for steepiug malt.

COCKET (cocquat, coket, coquet), a certificate under the seal of the proper officer that the customs have beeu paid ou goods exported from such aud such a post. Clerk of cocquet, or coqueter, the officer grantiug the certificates.

COFT, bought ; cp, German, kaüfen, and Eng., coffer.

COGNITION, the magisterial act of recognizing an heir, as entitled to be seized in property. Thus to be "cognosced heir" is to be formally re-cognised as such.

COMBURGES, co-burgess, fellow-burgess.

COMMISSARIOT, local registry for confirmation or probate of wills and for grants of administra-tion. Commissary, the officer making the con-firmatiou or grant.

COMITE OF STATES, committee of estates.

COMPEAR, to appear, generally in a legal proceeding before the Court.

COMPRYSING, lit. comprehending, but legally a process similar to apprysing, q.v.

COMPT (accompt), account.

CONDESCEND, to state the facts. Condescendance, a summary of the facts in a legal proceeding.

CONFIRMATION OF A GRANT, coufirmation of a charter by an overlord or subject superior.

CONFIRMATION OF A WILL ; see s. Commissariot.

CONJUNCT, joint ; e.g., conjunct fee, ownership of land by more than one person joiutly.

CONNEXIS, appurtenances, things connected with an estate ; cp. Annexis.

CONQUEISH, to conquer ; to acquire property by purchase, donation or exchauge, as opposed to by iuheritance.

CONQUEST, HEIR OF, an heir succeeding not by descent from the predecessor but by ascent, as representing an older line, e.g., when the second of three brothers or his heir dies, the youngest succeeded to the heretable but the eldest to the conquest property. The distinction between heritage and conquest was abolished in 1874.

CONTORAR, contrary.

CONTRACTED, betrothed, and in Scotland legally equivalent to marriage ; consent beiug legally euough, and the public ceremony of marriage being introduced in order to make so important a contract knowu, though not esseutial to it ; see Stair.

COPER GUIS PAN, copper pan for cooking geese.

CORDINER, cordwainer, shoemaker.

CORONICLES (cornicles, corniclis), chronicles.

COT, coat.

COUNCILLOR, connsellor, town councillor, or some-times advocate.

COURS (linen), coarse.

COURTEN-ROADS, curtain-rods.

CRANCA, quere cranoe, a garland ; also a stuff made of hair.

CRANIS, a crane of herrings is a barrelful of uusalted herrings.

CREEL, wicker basket for fish.

CREKP (a hood of), crape, crêpe.

CROFT, a small piece of land adjoining a house ; cp. Crofter.

CROSS DWELLING, or lodging.

CROWNES OF THE SUN (sone). French coins, so-called from the mint mark ; value about fourteen shillings.

CRUK, circle, hook.

CRUKIT HAUCHE, winding low grouud beside a river.

CUCH BED, a couch bed.

CUMPTOUR, A, couuter, accountant.

CUNZEHOUS, the mint ; cunzeour, master of the mint.

CURATOR, guardian of au iufant between fourteen and twenty-one years of age, as opposed to tutor, guardian of a child under fourteen.

CURATOR AD LITEM, guardian of a miuor in a suit, or of a wife in a process v. her husband.

CUSSING, cousin.

CUSTOMAR, collector of the customs.

DATIVE, testament or tutor, i.e., granted by the Court, as distinct from testamentar, made or appointed by the testator himself. Thus testa-ment dative is a graut of administration as opposed to probate of a will.

DEALL, a board of deal or pine wood.

DEAN OF GILD, president of the guildry. He is also judge of the dean of guild's court in re-ference to buildings, and has to see that they are erected accoruiug to law and do not en-croach on the rights of neighbours.

DECERNED, decreed.

DECREET, judgment of the Court ; cp. decreet arbitral, award of au arbitration ; decreet of removal, judgment ordering the defenders to remove from lauds.

DEFENDER, defendant in a law suit.

DEFORCEMENT, occupying property belonging to another ; *also* resisting the officers of the law in the execution of their duty.

DELATED, accused at law.

DELIVERANCE, judgment.

DEMITTIT, dismissed, resigned, handed over.

DENOUNCED. See vol. ii., p. 389, R.P.C. 67 n.

DEPONE, depose, give evidence.

DEPUTE, deputy. A sheriff depute is appointed by the crown ; a sheriff substitute by the sheriff himself.

DEWITIE, duty.

DIN MAIR, dun mare.

DISPONE, dispose of, alienate.

DOMINICAL LANDS, the mains or principal farm on an estate ; that of the lord or dominus.

DOMINUS, SIR, a title used by chaplains, as well as by knights, and later by baronets. It also means laird or lord.

DORNICK (dornyk), work or naperie, cloth wrought at Tournay in France.

DUTY ; see s. Dewitie, Feu.

DYTEMENTS, dyting ; poems, writing ; *cp.* Indite, indictment ; Ger., dichter.

EDICT OF CURATORY, edict summoning next of kin on both sides for election as curators to a minor.

EIK (eiking), addition, added to, adding.

EILD, children of, issue.

EME, uncle or near relative ; see p. 181, n. 2.

EMERODE, emerald.

EMMET, ant.

END, *e.g., out of the first end thereof,* out of the first available funds.

ENTRIE SILVER, dues paid on being entered in an estate as heir.

ESCHEAT (escheated, escheat goods), goods or estate forfeited by an outlaw.

EVIDENTS, documents evidencing ownership, title deeds.

EXCAMB (excambion), exchange, act of exchanging.

EXCRESCENS, interest.

FACTOR (factory), attorney (power of attorney) to manage affairs generally or in particular.

FAILLIE (failzieing), failure (failing).

FATHER-IN-LAW, step-father, and sometimes wife's father or "gude-father."

FAYR, father. The *y* is the *th* contracted, not a method of spelling.

FATVE, five.

FEE, full ownership as distinct from life-rent, or ownership for life only.

FENCE, breaking of, escaping from prison or arrest.

FENCED COURT, a court opened and held with due solemnity.

FEOFFMENT, legal giving of possession of land, or the fact of being so possessed, infeftment.

FERME, rent ; see s. Blench.

FEU (few), possession, holding of a superior for rent. *Feu-duty, feu-maills, feu-fermes,* the rent of a feu.

FEUAR, one who holds a feu (land or house) at a rent.

FIAR (fear), one who holds a property in fee ; the heir who has the fee, as distinct from the person in possession who has the life-rent ; *cp.* the use of "apparent," "younger."

FIRLES, metal rings uniting a fork or knife to the handle ; *cp.* ferrule.

FIRLOT MELL, an old measure of meal or other dry stuff ; in amount the fourth of a boll.

FLAGGAN (flacou), flagon ; *e.g., ane treu flacon of a quarter,* a flagon holding a true quarter.

FLEAND HART, flying heart (name of a ship).

FLIT, To, to remove from or leave lands or house; *cp.* the old proverb, "Three flittings make a burning," meaning that constant removal is fatal to the preservation of papers, etc.

FLUKERGAIT, a street in Dundee, also called the Nethergait.

FOIR, *e.g.,* bak and foir, back and front.

FOLD DYCKS, dykes or walls for enclosing sheep or cattle.

FORANENT, over against.

FORELAND (foirland), a front tenement or house.

FORTALICE, fortress, but often used of a tower to a house.

FURM, form or bench.

FURTH OF THE COUNTRY, or of land, abroad, removed elsewhere.

FRE LANDS, free lands ; see s. Barony.

FRETHING, freeing, disburdening.

GAIRN WAIRD BLEADS, PAIR OF, garden hedge blades or scissors.

GAIS SCARFE, gauze scarf.

GAIT (gaet), street leading to a gate of a town.

GALLOWES, swing beam ; see s. Chimney.

GARNETTE, an engine of war.

GEIR (gear), goods, tackle of a mill ; *e.g.,* household gear, or "lyeing and goeing geir" of a mill, some parts of which went to the tenant, while others remained the property of the landlord.

GERMAN, BROTHERS, children of the same father or parents, as opposed to brothers uterine, *i.e.,* of the same mother only.

GIRDS (girdis), girths of a horse.

GLUFIS (gluifis), gloves.

GODFATHER. This term, as opposed to witness to a baptism, was used by members of the Episcopal Church, chiefly about Dundee and Aberdeen. There was no fixed number of godparents.

GOODSONE (gudesone), grandson or son-in-law.

GOSSIP, cousin, friend.

GR'ALLITY, a contracted form of "generallity."

GRANTSCHIR, graudsire.

GREN, green.

GREWOREN SILK, "Gros-grain" silk.

GRIEVE, overseer of a farm or estate.

GRISSILLIS, grissels, grilse, salmon not fully grown.

GRIT, great.

GUDAME, gudsyr, gudesone ; graudmother grandfather, grandson ; or sometimes mother, father and son-in-law.

GUID, guidis, good, goods.

GUIDSCHYR, grandsire.

GUIS, goose.

GITHER, gutscher ; see s. Guidschyr.

GUYDER, guide, guardian.

GUYS PAN, goose-pan.

GYLE, guile.

HAGBUT, a kind of musket ; *hagbuttaris,* those who carried them.

HAIFFAND, having.

HAILL, whole.

HANDSELL, the first money received for goods, etc.

HANDSKYNZIE, banner, the hand-sign ; *cp.* Ensign.

HAUNDT, handy ; *e.g., haundy naigis,* handy nags.

HAVAND, having.

HAVER, the person who has custody of a document

HEICHE, high.

HEID, head.

HEILSOME, wholesome, heal-some.

HEIMS, quære short for *hemmynys,* shoes made of untanned leather.

Glossary. HEIR MALE, heir descending through sons.

HEIR OF TAILZIE OR PROVISION, heir by virtue of a deed of entail or provision.

HEIR PORTIONER one of several taking equally, e.g., in the case of daughters.

HEIR SPECIAL, heir to a particular subject (see as to Scotch heirship p. 96, n. 2).

HERITABLE PROPRIETOR, one who owns heritable property.

HERITABLY, by heritage ; pertaining in heritage, belonging to as heir.

HERITIER, heritor, inheritor, heir.

HESP, hasp, clasp, hinge.

HEUCH, a glen with steep sides, a crag, hence a pit ; e.g., coal-heuch.

HEW, hue.

HOOSTONE (OR HOGTONE) OF DOUBLE WORSAT, a jacket of worsted.

HOMOLOGATE, to indirectly approve of, or agree with.

HORN, AT THE, denounced as an outlaw.

HORNING, a writ under the signet obtained by a creditor ordering the debtor to pay or be " at the horn."

HORNING, LETTERS OF. the writ as above.

HORNING, RELAXED FROM, released from the effects of the letters.

HOUSE-MAILLS OR MEALS, house-rent; cp. black mail.

HOSPITAL-MASTER, keeper of the almshouse.

HOVISS, house.

HULSTER CAIRDS, holster cards.

HOWFF, hough, a burial ground, a place of resort.

HUSBAND-LAND, twenty-six acres of land ploughed by two oxen.

HYPOTHECATE, mortgage to secure a debt.

ILK, OF THAT, of that place or race. Lat., de eodem, i.e., the name of the family and estates are the same, e.g., Wedderburn of Wedderburn or Wedderburn of that ilk. The right to be so called was granted by royal charter, and survives to the head of the family even if the estate is lost. The mere identity of name with that of the place owned (e.g., by purchase) does not give the right.

IMPLEMENT, fulfilling, completion.

INCONTINENT AFTER OUR DECEISS, without delay after our death.

INFEFT, TO, to seize or give formal possession ; infeftment, the action or the deed drawn to record it.

INHIBITION, a writ under the signet prohibiting a debtor from parting with his heritage, or burdening it.

INQUEST, inquiry before a jury as to a person's right to succeed as heir to a parent or relative.

INSTRUMENT, legal document.

INTERCOMMUNED. See vol. ii., p. 389, R.P.C. 67 n.

INTERDICT (interdiction), inquisition.

INTERTAINER, entertainer, guardian with whom a child lives.

INTRES THAIRTO, interest in.

INTROMETTER, person mixing himself up with the affairs of another, e.g., an executor ; intromission, the act of so doing to.

INTRUSIT, intruded.

INVENTAR, invetar, inventory.

INVENTAR JUDICIAL, one made by order of the court.

IRON DAK, ash pau or basket of iron.

IRRITANCY, CLAUSE OF, a clause in a document attaching a condition to a right, e.g., the bearing of a specified name and arms as a condition of holding an estate, or the giving up of one estate as the condition of succeeding to another.

JAK OF RANE DEER, a bag made of reindeer skin.

JOCKTALEGS, large clasp knives.

JUSTI-COAT, a vest with sleeves.

KAIN rent paid in kind, as fowls, grain, etc. When joined with money it means the value of the other subjects.

KAMYS, combs ; applied to a place, it means ridgy ground.

KEMMYNG-STOK, the stock on which wool was set for combing.

KILL, kiln, stove or oven for drying malt, etc.

KIPPAGE, disorder.

KIRKMASTER, an official who had charge of the church buildings, and received the money exacted for the fabric.

KIST, kistis ; chest, chests.

KITHES, appears, shows.

KNAG OF VINACRE, cask of vinegar.

KNAPSCALL, headpiece in armour.

LACHE VOLT, low vault.

LADILL, ladle, large spoon for lifting broth, etc.

LANTRONE, lanthorn, lantern.

LAU'LL, a contraction of "lawful."

LAW-BURROWS (or borrowis), legal security which a man may be ordered to give that he will not injure the person or property of another ; being "bound over to keep the peace."

LEAT, late.

LEDING STANE,

LEET, list of candidates for election, e.g., as baillies, etc.

LEGATOUR, universall, sole legatee.

LENTH, length.

LETTERS, writ or warrant, e.g., of caption, a signet letter following on horning for the arrest of the debtor.

LETTRONE, lectron, reading desk.

LEY, lea, unploughed land, pasture land.

LIFE, on life, still alive ; e.g., only child on life, sole surviving child.

LIFE-RENT, life-interest, life-renter or life-rentrix, man or woman owning it.

LITSTER, dyer ; littet or littit, dyed.

LOCKIT BUIK, the locked book in which the admission of burgesses to the freedom of a burgh were entered.

LOGY HAUCHE AND FUR BRA, the hauch or heuch (i.e., glen) of Logie and the furrowed brae.

LOOSING ARRESTMENT, an arrestment (for debt) is loosed on security being found.

LOUS, loose.

LUDGKING, lodging.

LUGGS, A PAIR OF, ears, hinges, the two handles of a vessel,

LUIT-STRING HOOD, lute-string cover.

LYBEL, libel, indictment, etc. ; e.g., the lands lybelled, lands specified in the suit.

LYFRENT ; see s. Life.

MADDIR ; see s. Ballandis.

MAGISTER, Mr. This prefix signifies that the person so called is a graduate of some university.

MAILLS ; see s. House-maills.

MAINS (Mayns), the chief or home farm.

MALTHOUSE, brewery ; maltman, brewer.

MANOR PLACE, dwellinghouse, mansion of an estate.

MARABLE (marbole, marboll), marble.

MEASOUR, measure.

MEETING HOUSE, episcopal chapel, or other dissenting place of worship.

MEMELL (handles of forks), made of oak. Fr. Memell.
MERCATOR, mercatrix, merchant (of a man or woman).
MERCHANDIS LETTER, letter of the merchants.
MET AND MEASOUR, mete and measure.
MILN (milne), mill.
MISPRISON (mispreson, misperson), to slander ; also to conceal crime, *e.g.*, misprision of treason.
MODIR, mother.
MORTCLOTH DUES, dues payable for the use of the public pall (death cloth) at a funeral.
MORTIFYED MONEY, money left by dead persons in charity.
MOYR, mother. See s. Fayr.
MUCK, dung, manure.
MUIR, moor.
MUKED (of land), mucked, manured.
MULLER, moulded work, frame of a picture ; *cp.* Mullion.
MULTURE, multour, dewetie, payment in grain and money for having corn ground.
MUTCKIN, a pint (English).
MYLNE, mill.
MYRE, marsh.

NACKET. Fr., nacquet, the lad that marks at tennis. Hence lacquey, insignificant person. Nackety means "conceited." Another word "nacket" means a bit of stone used in the game of shinty, and also a small quantity of snuff or tobacco.
NAIGIS, nags, small horses.
NAPERY (naperie, naprie), table linen.
NOLTS' TONGUES, neats' tongues.
NONENTRY MAILLS, GIFT OF, the rents of lands in the hands of the superior till the heir is able to assume possession.
NOTARIAL DOCKET, the notary's certificate at the end of an instrument.
NOTARIAL INSTRUMENT, deed drawn by a notary.
NOTARIAL SYMBOL, the sign used by a notary for distinction.
NOVODAMUS, CHARTER OF, renewal of feudal grant by charter, with some alteration or addition.

OASTLAIR, master of an inn, host ; hence ostler.
OBLIGEMENT, bond, obligation.
ON-DELYVERIT, undelivered.
OST, host.
OUKIS, weeks.
OUR-GILT, overgilt, gilded over; of a book, gilt-edged.
OURE, our, over.
OUTREDDAR, to outred is to extricate or finish off ; the outreddar of a ship is thus the person who fits it out for a voyage, or disburdens it of its cargo.
OXENGATE OF LAND, an oxgate of land is thirteen acres : *cp.* husbandland.
OY, OYE, grandson, grand-daughter.

PAIRT, bairnis, of gear, a child's share in a parent's estate, patrimony.
PAND OR PANE, for a bed, the draperies for the frame of a bed, hence counterpane.
PARAPRIS, paraphrase.
PECES, pieces, title deeds ; or any article regarded singly.
PEKIS, pecks.
PENDICLE, appurtenance, thing hung on to, often a small portion of land.
PEPER, paper.
PETARES, petards.

PIER-MASTER, harbour-master.
PILGIT, a broil, a quarrel.
PINUT, pint.
PISTOLAT, a small pistol, also a coin of that name.
PLANTATION OF KIRKS, establishing and providing for churches in the various parishes.
PLENISHING (insight, outsight, *i.e.*, inside, outside), furniture of a house, stock on a farm or estate.
PLET SLEVIS, pleated sleeves.
PLEUGH, plough.
PLEY, plea, complaint at law.
PM'ES, promes, promise.
PNTLIE, contraction for "presently."
PNTS, contraction for "presents."
POCINO IRON, poker.
POK VAD OF THE ROS, A. *Pok*, pocket ; *vaid*, a dye ; *ros* or *rouse*, a kind of cloth.
PORTION NATURAL, the share of a child in the estate of an intestate father.
PORTIONER OF LAND, owner of a small bit of land.
PORTIONERS, heirs, daughters inheriting land jointly.
POT IRON, iron for setting the pot on.
POYNDING, attaching lands or goods for debt.
POYNDINO, DECREET OF, judicial order for poynding.
PRECEPT OF CLARE CONSTAT OR SASINE. See s. *Clare constat.*
PRESBYTERY (presbetrie), ecclesiastical court of the ministers and elders of a district of several parishes.
PRIMME, first, chief, prime.
PRINLL., contraction for "principal."
PRISARIS, apprisors.
PRISIT, apprised.
PROCURATOR, law agent or counsel.
PROFYN, gift or present.
PROSECUTION OF SIGNATURES. A signature is a warrant subscribed by the King for granting a charter. The prosecution may mean the following out or obtaining of such a warrant.
PROTOCOL, the first copy of an instrument, written by a notary in his protocol book.
PROTOMEDICUS, the chief doctor.
PRYDIT, provydit, provided.
PUNDIS, pounds.
PUPILLARITY, the state of being a pupil, *i.e.*, between birth and fourteen years of age.
PURRINO IRON, poker.
PURS, purse.
PURSUE, persew, to prosecute a suit.
PURSUER, plaintiff, complainer, in a law-suit.

Q. Often short for con ; *e.g.*, Qfess, confess.
QROF, whereof.
QUHAIR, where.
QUHAIRIN, wherein.
QUHATSOMEVIR, whatever, whatsoever.
QUHEILL, while, wheel.
QUHEIT, white.
QUHERIN, wherein.
QUHILK, whilk, which.
QUHYLE, while.
QUYT OF ENTRY, quit of entry, having paid fees due to the superior on succeeding to lands.

RACKEN, reckon.
RAISING LETTERS, taking out a legal summons.
RANKING, PROCESS OF, process by which creditors are arranged in order of preference.
RASE (base and opprobrious speeches), rash.
RATSCHE (of a gun), lock.

Glossary. RAXES, iron instrument consisting of various links, on which the spit is turned at the fire ; or perhaps tongs, *rax* meaning to stretch.

REFT, bereft.

REGALITY, a territorial jurisdiction conferred by the crown, the holder being termed lord of the regality, with power to hold courts.

REGENT, master of a school or college.

REMANENT, remaining.

RENUNCIATION, (1) by an heir charged to enter on possession ; (2) of redeemable rights when redeemed ; (3) of a lease. Also the deed by which these are carried out.

REPONIT, reponed, replaced.

RESIGNATION, the act whereby a vassal returns the feu into the hands of the superior, either to remain with the latter, or for the purpose of receiving it again by a new grant. The deed recording the act.

RESTING, remaining due, owing.

RETOUR, an extract from chancery of the service of an heir to his progenitor.

RETOUR OF INQUEST, the report of the jury summoned to find if an heir is duly entitled.

REVESTRIE, revestry, back vestry of a church.

REX DOLLAR, a silver coin (German) of varying value from 2s. 6d. to 4s. 6d.

RONDLE, A. This word has various meanings, *e.g.*, a tower, round shield, round table, and song (roudel).

ROTTONFALL. The context (ii., 165) seems to imply that this is a boat, but it might mean a rat-trap (rotton-faw).

ROUNDALL. rowndall ; see Rondle.

ROUND SHEETS, sheets put round the mattress to bind it.

ROUNDER BED PLAIDS, woollen coverlets.

ROUP, sale by auction.

SADILL OF AIK, seat (sedilium) of oak.

SAIDLES, saddles.

SAIFAND, saving.

SALBE, shall be.

SALMOND, salmon.

SALT BACKET, salt tub.

SALTFAT, OR SALTFOOT, of tun, a saltcellar of pewter.

SALTPANS, pits where salt is made.

SAMEKLE, so much.

SAMEN, same.

SANGIS, songs.

SASINE, act giving legal possession of property of land or house ; the deed recording the act.

SAULD, sold.

SCHADE, shadow.

SCHO, she.

SCHRYNE (*scrine*), shrine, desk, screen.

SCRUITTORE, escritoire, writing-table.

SCUTIFER, shield bearer.

SE'ALL, contraction for severall, several.

SELCH'S SKIN, seal's skin.

SELFFIS, selves.

SENSYNE, since that time.

SETT, let to.

SERVATOR (*servitor, servites*), agent, secretary, apprentice ; also napkin (ii., 120).

SERVICE, SPECIAL, as heir to a special subject, as property, etc.

SEVINE, sewin, seven.

SHADOW HALF, north side of land.

SHAO LYNING, cloth having a rough nap.

SHAMBO GLOVES, made of chamois leather.

SHEDS OF LAND, portions or fields of land.

SHERIFF CLERK, clerk to the sheriff court, and keeper of the records.

SHERIFF IN THAT PART (*i.e.*, in that behalf), one appointed by the crown to act in place of the sheriff in a particular instance.

SHERIFFDOM, the district under jurisdiction of a sheriff, a county ; see s. Barony, Regality.

SHUTTLES, small enclosed drawers of a cabinet.

SHOD, shode, shot, " lie shot," *i.e.*, lying separate from the rest.

SICKLIKE, siclyk, like as, likewise, in like manner.

SKAITHLESS, without hurt or damage.

SKAITH, hurt or damage.

SLEIST sluther vagabond ; lazy slothful slut.

SOAM (ii., 120), a rope or chain by which a plough is drawn.

SOMMANCE, summons.

SONEY, sunny.

SOUMES, sums.

SPEET (*speit*), spite ; also *spit*, for roasting.

SPLEUCHIS (A PAIR OF), splints.

SPRINOZIE RAPPER, springy rapier.

SPUILZIED, robbed or despoiled.

STAFF AND BATON, delivery by, symbols used on resignation of lands by a vassal into the hands of the superior.

STAIO, young horse.

STAITHLESS, skaithless, scaithless.

STAPIS, tyn, stoupa, large pitchers of tin.

STEALL, stale.

STENT, tax. Also as a verb, to tax ; *stentar*, one who collects the stent.

STOUP, a vessel for carrying water from the well.

STRIB, iron and girdis (stirroubis, stirribis), stirrups (iron) and girths.

STUIVER, a Dutch coin ; *cp.* " Stiver."

SUBMISSION ; see s. Decreet arbitral.

SUNNY HALF, south lying portion of lands.

SUPERIOR OF LANDS, the overlord from whom title is derived.

SURRENDER, DECREET OF, ordering the tithes or teinds to be yielded to the crown.

SUSPENSION, LETTERS OF, ordering the non-execution of charges proceeding on bills, bonds, or decrees until pleas be heard.

SYD, side.

STLEBOR GLASS, syllabub.

SWIPPIT, supped.

SWMES, sums.

SYMBOL; see s. Notarial.

TACK OF LANDS, customs, lease ; *tacksman*, lease holder.

TAILZIE, entail ; tailzier, entailer.

TAS, cup.

TAXT-WARD, the casualty of a superior for lands in non-entry.

TAYNGIS, tongs.

TEICK, tick, tick of a bed.

TEINDS, tithes ; teind sheaves, grain tithe.

TEMPLE LANDS, lands which belonged of old to the knight templars.

TENEMENT, a house, flat, holding or piece of land.

TESTAMENT, will. As to Scotch wills see p. 482.

TESTAMENTAR ; see s. Dative.

THEATS, horse traces in plough or carriage.

THESAURER, treasurer.

THIRLAGE, the obligation on owner or tenants of land within a certain district to have their grain ground at a particular mill.

THOMIE, thumb.

THRID, third.

THRONG OF BUSINESS, full of, " crowded with " business.

THROW, through.

TITELLIS, titles

TOCHER, dowry; *tocher guid,* the goods or money constituting the dowry.

TODDIS HEID AND BUR, fox's head and brush.

TOFT, land attached to a dwelling house, a messuage.

TOLBOOTH, the common prison of a burgh, the building in which the municipal courts are held.

TOLERANCE, deed granting some privilege.

TOWN, a steading, with the houses of cotters.

TOWN HOUSE, house occupied by the civic authorities for the public business.

TRANSUMPT, an official copy of a deed, usually an old one.

TRANSLATION OF A BOND, document transferring it from one holder to another.

TRED AND HANDLING, trade and business.

TROWBLANCE, molestation.

TUFFELL CLOATH, taffill cloth, table cloth.

TUTOR, one appointed to manage the estate of a pupil below twelve years of age if a female, and fourteen if a male.

TUTORY, the appointment of such tutor.

TUTELAGE, state of being under a tutor.

TWIDLEN (napery), tweeled, twilled cloth.

TYMOUS, betimes, timely.

TYNE AND WINE, lose and win.

UMQUHILE, umquhile, umquhile, umqle, deceased, erst-while, the late.

UNLAWS, COLLECTION OF THE, fines.

UTERINE, children, *i.e.,* of same mother, not same father.

UTHAIRIS, others.

VPHALDYN, upheld.

VENNEL, narrow street or passage.

VERDOUR BED, bed with tapestry representing woodland scenery.

VICARAGE TEINDS, the small tithes, as distinct from the rectorage teinds.

VICTUAL, grain of any kind.

VILL, village, buildings round a castle.

VINTNER, wine-merchant, keeper of an inn.

VOLT, vault, or sometimes the circular tread round a centre, *e.g.,* in grinding at a mill.

VRAK (WRECK) OF SALMON, salmon cast ashore.

WADSET, A, the deed by which a debtor gives his Glossary. lands, etc., to his creditor, who is to draw the rents in payment of the debt ; *wadsetter,* the creditor who holds the wadset.

WAIR AND BESTOW, spend.

WALED MEN, selected, chosen.

WALKARIS CRAFT, fuller's trade or guild.

WAND RUSKES. Quære wandrethes, misfortunes ; *wantrust,* mistrust.

WARRANDICE, assurance against any wrong to a right conveyed, arising from defect in the title or otherwise. Warrandice lands, lauds conveyed provisionally in case the purchaser should be evicted from the principal lands.

WEAPON-SCHAWING, muster for drill in arms.

WECHT, weight.

WENSCHOAT (wainscoat), oak furniture.

WESTHALL BYNK, a hive, or bench, from Westhall, a place belonging to the Beatons, near Dundee.

WEYING, weighing.

WEYHOUSE, house where the standard weights or measures were kept.

WHOIF, whip.

WILL ; see s. Testament.

WINESCOTT, wainscoat.

WOFFIN, woven ?

WRANGIS, wrongs, injuries.

WRITER, any clerk or scribe, attorney.

WRITER TO THE SIGNET, highest order of writers, having authority to prepare the writs which pass the royal signet.

WUIP, whip.

WYND, a narrow street or passage.

WYSSIE OR VISSIE, to inspect ; Fr., Visé.

YAT, THE, OF DUDOP, the gate of Dudop.

YOAK, yoke.

ZAIRD, zeard, yard.

ZEIRS, years.

ZIT, yet.

ZOUNGAIR, younger.

INDEX.

3 z

4 A

4 B

4 C

---

[1] In regard to these see a somewhat scarce book, *Fragmenta Scoto-Monastica*, " by a Delver in Antiquity," Edin. 1842, from which the following list is taken :—Aberdeen, *Arbroath*, *Balmerino* (A. 1841), Cambuskeneth, Coldingham, *Coldstream*, Cupar, Crail, *Dryburgh* (B. 1847), *Dunfermline* (B. 1842), Dunblane, Elgin, Fail, *Glasgow* (B. 1847, M. 1846), Holyrood, *Inchaffray* (B. 1847), Inchcolm, *Kelso* (B. 1846), Kilwinning, Kinloss, *Lindores* (A. 1841), May, *Melros* (B. 1837), *Moray* (B. 1837), *Newbattle* (B. 1849), *Paisley* (M. 1842), *S. Andrew's* (B. 1841), S. Anthony, S. Giles, *Scone* (B. 1843), Soltre, Stirling, Torphichen. Of these I have searched, by the indices, the editions of those italicized, published (as indicated above by the letters A., B., M.), by the Abbotsford, Bannatyne, and Maitland Clubs. That of Arbroath, *Liber S. Thome de Aberbrothoc*, 1178—1536, 2 vols., Edin. 1848, has also been searched. Of those so searched only those of Glasgow and Melrose contain anything material.

4 D

[1] The persons named in this article are, as a rule, given in the order in which their names occur in the text, so as to group together members of the same branches of the family. They are also numbered and their parentage given by reference to the number prefixed to the name of the father. Thus, " s. of 129," stands briefly for " son of No. 129 (David Wedderburn in Aberdeen)," etc. The dates in brackets, before the reference, are sometimes not those of births, marriages, or deaths, but of the first and latest mention of the individual.

[2] See also for families or persons of the name at different places (a) in Scotland, s. Aberdeen, Arbroath, Ayr, Banchory, Belhaven, Berwickshire, Bethelnay, Burntisland, Buss, Camno, Ceres, Coldingbame, Dirleton, Dumfries, Dunbar, Dysart, Echt, Edinburgh, Ellon, Fife, Forgan, Fyvie, Glasgow, Iuchmarlo, Kelso, Leith, Maryhill, Merse, Mervingslaw, Methlic, Newhills, Old Meldrum, Ormiston, Perth, Peterhead, Prestoupans, Roxburgh, S. Andrew's, Sorne, Tarves, Whittinghame ; (b) in England and abroad, Africa, America, Ashford, Australia, Canada, Chowringhee, England, Exeter, Horncliffe, Jamaica, Kent, Lancashire, Lindale, Longridge, Manchester, Newcastle, Northumberland, Scremerston, Seghill, Spittal, Tweedmouth, Tynemouth, Ulverstone, Weldon Bridge.
 And see also for various topics in connection with the family, s. Abo, Adie, Aquila, Arles, Armorial, Baliudean, Birkhill, Blackness, Boyue, Canterbury, Cantra, Colvile, Consilio, Craigie, Deum Time, Dundee, Easter Powrie, Gosford, Idvies, Kingennie, Lindertis, Loughborough, McLagan-Wedderburn, Moravia, Mottoes, Mounie, Music, Omachie, Pearsie, Pitfirrane, Pittormie, Portraits, Registers, Rings, Ruthven, Scrymgeour-Wedderburn, Seals, Trosto, Tullohill, Weatherburn, Webster-Wedderburn, Wetterburn, Wodbroane, Wodeburn, Woodburn.

[3] The Christian names of this and the four persons following are not recorded.

[1] See as to the difficulty of identifying some of the references to this name, i., 56 n.

[1] See as to the difficulty of identifying some of the references to this uame, i., 23.

[1] See as to the difficulty of identifying some of the references to this name, i., 19 n.

---

[1] Under this head are indexed the descendants of James Wedderburn, Solicitor-General for Scotland, and Isabella Clerk, although the name of Maxwell was not adopted in the family till 1879.

THE END.